RANKLEY GRANGE.

By the Author of

*"PAUL'S PERILS," "THE KNIGHTRIDERS," "THE MARQUIS OF
DALEWOOD,"* etc., etc.

WITH

THIRTY-FIVE ORIGINAL WOOD ENGRAVINGS.

LONDON:

E. & H. BENNETT, BEDFORD HOUSE, MAIDEN LANE, STRAND, W.C.

RANKLEY GRANGE.

THE THREAT OF VENGEANCE.

CHAPTER I.

BERNARD VARLEY.

THE season was autumn, and although the latter end of October was fast approaching, nature still looked beautiful in the maturity of her charms. The trees wore a thousand different magical tints, and the more rich and lovely of the summer flowers were yet lingering in their dazzling beauty, as if loth to leave the world to the chill and cheerless dominion of the coming winter. The keen northern blast was, however, rapidly stripping the trees of the hardy leaves which had outlived their fellows, and the sunshine, although bright and beautiful, was cold and pale, presenting but a faint mockery of the genial glow of the vernal season.

On a morning such as this, at the early hour of six, when but a dim and uncertain light gleamed from the awakening east, two figures stood in a shallow valley some half-a-mile from an irregular but picturesque building, situated about five miles from York, and called from time immemorial, "The Grange."

These two figures were those of men, but as dissimilar in personal appearance as any two human beings could be. One was a man apparently past the meridian of life, tall and fair, with that irresolute and undecided expression of countenance, denoted by the half-open mouth, ever-shifting eye, and general want of firm purpose in all his movements.

The other was shorter, and his dark, brilliant eyes were well contrasted with a deep olive complexion, and a firm, compressed mouth, which showed that for good or for evil he would hold his purpose.

At the first glance this man might have been thought handsome, but although a more minute investigation of his features might not entirely do away with the first impression, it would modify it in a remarkable manner, for there did not appear to be one kindly feeling in the expression of the physiognomy, and people would shrink from Bernard Varley instinctively, and they knew not why.

The air was loaded with a damp mist in the low ground where they stood, and its excessive coldness brought a shiver to the limbs of the taller and finer of the two men, as he remarked to his companion, in his usual irresolute tone and manner:

"Varley, the air is keen. You will look to my girl, should anything befall me. My poor, fond Miranda—you will miss your father. You solemnly promise me, Varley, to uphold her interests—to watch over her?"

"Could I," rejoined the other, "be so unhappy as to lose so good a friend as yourself, I should have but one consolation, and that would be, that the fair Miranda would allow me to take a father's place."

"You—you would marry her?"

"Even now—though twice rejected—I would."

As he said the words "twice rejected," an expression of a perfectly-demoniac character crossed his face, and the fire of smothered feeling flashed for a moment from his eyes.

"The affections are not our own," said the other, sadly. "We cannot make them dependent upon the will."

"No, Sir George; but——"

He paused, and silently pointed in the direction of the rising sun, as he laid his other hand lightly upon the shoulder of Sir George Rankley, who was his companion.

"They are coming," he said.

By the uncertain light that prevailed, two dim figures were seen slowly approaching, and, as they neared Sir George and Varley, some clock far off chimed the quarter-past six.

"Now, Varley," said Rankley, "as Heaven is my judge, let the issue of this contest be what it may, I have been forced into it."

"Forced?" cried Varley, his cheek reddening. "Yes, forced by insult past endurance. Yes—yes, most true—most true. You have

been hardly used. Think again of those injuries, and nerve yourself to expiate your wrongs upon the head of him who has inflicted them."

"The issue of such contests as these, Varley," said Sir George, "is in the hands of Heaven."

"Is it?" muttered Varley, to himself.

"It is for my—Miranda—my child, that I feel now pangs more exquisite than ever death can inflict upon me."

"Should your worst fears be accomplished," remarked Varley, with a scarcely-perceptible sneer, "you leave behind you Bernard Varley, a warm friend."

Sir George shuddered, and the other immediately added:

"You view the matter too seriously. The Squire of Larkswood may fall."

"Crime upon crime!" muttered, or rather groaned, Sir George Rankley. "Murder, for such it is, added to——"

"Hush!" cried Varley; "let not that word pass your lips! No more, now! The time has come for action!"

"It has, indeed. I feel it has," said Sir George Rankley. "I am prepared."

The approaching parties now paused, and at the moment there came from the distant horizon a straggling beam of sunlight, which, falling on the side of the gentle declivity, at the base of which the four men now stood, imparted to the scene a rich and varied beauty it had not hitherto possessed.

"You must remain where you are," said Varley to his principal, "while I settle the necessary preliminaries."

With these words, he advanced towards the new arrivals, and, bowing with much courtesy, although it seemed a little overstrained, he said:

"Does the Squire of Larkswood offer a humble apology?"

"No, sir, he does not," replied one of the new comers, a gentlemanly-looking man. "The Squire of Larkswood never yet did or said what he was ashamed of. It is for your principal to apologize, if he has so much grace left in him."

"Then, sir, we proceed," said Varley, "as we can accept nothing but the most humble and submissive apology."

There was about his tone a sneering air of insincerity as he spoke, which, coupled with the words themselves, evidently produced an effect that by his lurking smile he looked for and wished to see.

"This is really quite irregular," suggested he who had not yet spoken. "I believe I have the—the honour to address Mr. Bernard Varley?"

"My name is Varley, sir, and in this business I act as second to Sir George Rankley. You, I presume, perform the same friendly office for the Squire of Larkswood?"

The Squire himself fell back several paces, while the seconds advanced together. He was a fine specimen of an English gentleman, and he glanced towards Sir George Rankley with a look of painful regret, while the latter's eyes were fixed upon the gable-ends of the old Grange, which could just be seen above its shield of trees, glancing in the morning light, and its ancient rugged outlines made beautiful by the sunlight that was momentarily increasing now in brilliancy.

The thoughts were evidently of a painful nature that were passing through his mind, for tears slowly filled his eyes, and prevented him, after a few brief moments, from seeing anything clearly; so he turned away his head, and with one long-drawn sigh, appeared to take a last farewell of his home.

But what was that home to him, endeared as it was by a thousand associations, compared with the enthusiastic love he bore to one within its ancient walls, who slept the calm sleep of innocence and youth, while he, her father, was from home on such an unholy errand as his present one. Yes; his child, his dear, beautiful Miranda, the last of her race, slept on in peace, while such a storm was hovering over her young head as she, in the wildest moment of her fancy, could not have pictured to herself, or had she done so, would have smiled at the dreamy improbability of the imaginary circumstances.

"My child—my dear Miranda!" thought Sir George. "Am I never to see you more, my own beautiful child? Heaven knows that by some fell agency I have been hurried into this act, I know not how. May——"

"Twelve paces, and I have won for you the light," whispered, at this moment, Varley in the ear of Sir George. "Are you ready?"

"Quite—quite."

In a few more moments the combatants were placed in their proper stations, and then Bernard Varley, raising his voice, said:

"Gentlemen, your signal for firing will be my dropping this glove. Are you quite ready?"

"One moment yet, Squire of Larkswood," said Sir George Rankley. "As Heaven is my judge, I come to this extremity with you most reluctantly. We are both fathers—both love our children——"

His voice faltered, and he could not proceed, which his opponent perceiving, he in his turn spoke, saying mildly, but firmly:

"Sir George Rankley, time was when there was not a hand in all Yorkshire I could have grasped with more honest fervour than your's; but the insults you have heaped upon me—the contumely which you have so wantonly——"

"Gentlemen," interposed Bernard Varley, "shall I retire along with the friend of the Squire, while with mutual civil regrets you terminate this business between you? I am a peacemaker, as you both know, and have laboured to avert this meeting; even now it appears to me, that a very humble apology on each side may avert hostilities."

"Sir George, I fear you have been ill-advised," said the Squire; "why did you write to me in the terms you did?"

"I did but retort," said Sir George. "You know, Varley, how unwilling I was."

"Enough—enough," said the Squire, "we have gone now too far to retreat."

"Not so, gentlemen," said Varley, "you can each of you go comfortably to your houses, setting a peaceful example to the whole county. Some people may certainly smile at the Christian forbearance of Sir George Rankley and the great Squire of Larkswood, who, after defying each other to mortal conflict, made up matters on the battlefield; but what of that, gentlemen, you will have the approbation of all lovers of peace, all men of sound discretion."

The Squire of Larkswood turned his gaze full upon the eyes of Varley, as he said slowly and distinctly:

"I have received from Sir George Rankley insults which the usages of society compel me to resent; but, as for you, sir, I hold you as a villain."

A deadly paleness spread over the face of Varley as he replied:

"There may come a time, sir, when your too candid avowal of your opinions may cost you dear."

The second of the Squire of Larkswood was a mild, inoffensive-looking man, who seemed too timid to venture any opinion of his own, and during the whole of the foregoing dialogue, he had looked from one speaker to the other in a nervous state of mind, not knowing very well what to say or do. It was a relief to him when Varley now hastily added:

"Sir George, you are quite ready?" and at the same moment held his glove at arm's length.

Not a word now was spoken—the glove fell—one sharp ringing report awakened echoes far and near—and an execration burst from the lips of Varley as he saw that both the combatants were standing apparently quite uninjured.

It was but for a moment, though, that they thus stood, and then, with a shudder, Sir George Rankley placed his hand upon his breast, and turning round upon his heel, he made several desperate plunges to keep his feet, after which, with a gasp, he fell heavily upon the green sward.

CHAPTER II.

THE MEETING.

THE Squire of Larkswood was the first to fly towards the fallen man. Kneeling by his side, he said, feelingly:

"Rankley, Rankley, speak to me! Oh! what a madman I have been to do this deed. Rankley—my friend—my old companion—speak to me—speak to me!"

"He is not much hurt," said the Squire's second, as he tore open the coat and waistcoat of Sir George, and showed that the wound was high in the shoulder. He has only fainted from the shock the system has received. Can we have some water?"

"There is a spring not a hundred yards

along the valley," said the Squire; "take my hat—quick—quick."

Varley stood with his arms folded across his breast, gazing upon the prostrate man, but taking no part in the proceedings for his recovery. Such conduct, however, seemed rather the result of want of thought at the moment, than a determination to be a mere spectator of the scene, for he suddenly roused himself like one awakening from sleep, and affected a degree of officiousness about Sir George Rankley that was strongly at variance with his former indifference.

The water was soon brought in the Squire's hat, and upon dashing some of it in the face of Sir George, he gave a convulsive shudder and opened his eyes.

"Rankley, you are not much hurt," cried the Squire; "all will be well again."

"What has happened?" said the wounded man.

"A mere scratch," continued the Squire. "Come, come, think nothing of it."

"We had better," said Varley, "get Sir George home as quickly as possible. This may not turn out such a mere scratch as you suppose."

"I want none of your ill-omened croaking," cried the Squire. "Peace, sir—from my soul something strikes me that by some foul means you have produced all this unhappiness. There's a lurking devil in every line of your countenance. By Heavens, I was mad to be made your tool—a film appears now to have fallen from my eyes. Bernard Varley, you are a villain!"

There was a tempest of passion evidently labouring in the breast of Varley, but by a strong effort he repressed its exhibition, and merely replied:

"You do well, sir, after placing the life of him you call your old friend, in such great jeopardy, to turn upon me. I say you do well, sir. Should you find your way to the York Assizes for the murder of Sir George Rankley, I presume your line of defence will be in character with your present conduct. Perhaps, too, you can find some excuse for having provoked the quarrel you have brought to so successful a termination in your dislike of Bernard Varley?"

The Squire of Larkswood was about to make some angry reply, when a scream smote his ears with such terrible distinctness, that he involuntarily clasped his hands in horror, and was afraid to turn his eyes in the direction whence it came.

"Miranda is coming," said Varley; "she has recognized from the brow of yonder eminence who it is who lies so still at your feet. Squire of Larkswood, she is coming; shall I or you explain this little tragedy?"

"Father—father!" cried a young and beautiful girl, attired in a morning dress, her long, glossy, auburn ringlets serving as her only head-dress, as she threw herself on her knees by the side of the wounded baronet. "Father—oh, what has happened? There is blood upon you! Oh, Heaven help me! Why

do you look upon me, gentlemen, with such pitying eyes? Can none of you tell me what is the meaning of all this? Father—father, speak to me! It is your child—your Miranda, who calls you! Help—help! he does not speak! He does not move! Who killed my father? Who spilt his blood? Show me the man! Squire of Larkswood, you look pale and wan—speak, oh, speak!"

The Squire turned his face away and uttered no sound, but Varley stooped to the ear of the beautiful girl, and whispered:

"Miranda!"

She sprang immediately to her feet, and as she stood by the again insensible form of her father, she pointed with both hands at Varley, and in a voice of awful solemnity exclaimed:

"It—is all true—you are here to confirm the vision sent by Heaven to warn me of this deed of blood. Bernard Varley, since you by some mysterious means ensnared my poor father's soul, the shadow of some terrible catastrophe has been ever hanging like a funeral pall upon my mind—and—and now it is consummated. All is revealed—I know you—I know you."

For a moment, but no more, Varley stood the fixed gaze of that fair young creature, and then, as she continued speaking, he cowered before her, and shrank back, although he seemed unable to withdraw his eyes from hers. He trembled in every limb, and the big drops of perspiration stood upon his brow as he muttered:

"Miranda Rankley, what mean you? I am your father's friend. You are raving."

"What brought me here?" she said.

"I know not."

"I have had a dream, Bernard Varley—an awful dream. Shall I relate it to you? I—I——"

She cast her eyes upon her father at this moment, and her excitement gave way instantly. She sank upon his bleeding form, and wept with a bitterness of anguish that was terrible to hear.

Varley drew a long breath, and gave a sickly smile, as he said:

"Well, well—I suppose I am to be the butt of everybody's wild fancies. Look! here comes help."

There now approached the group a strange, grotesque figure. It was that of a young man, scarcely past the age of twenty, but habited in the most singular and opposite articles of costume that can be imagined. He wore a cast-off faded military coat, and dependent from a paper cap that was placed jauntily upon one side of his head was an immense bunch of various coloured ribbons. The rest of his attire was dotted here and there by bows and ends of ribbon.

He came forward with a wild bounding kind of step, that looked like an imitation of some wild animal, and as he neared the party, he shouted:

"Whoop, whoop—more sport. Where's the foremost dog? The hawk has had strange dreams."

" 'Tis the poor idiot boy, Martin," said the Squire; " but he can carry a message. Martin, come hither."

The idiot either did not hear, or did not heed the call of the Squire, for he paused opposite to Varley, and, with a loud laugh, cried :

" I dreamt of you last night. A famous dream."

" Indeed ?"

" Yes, all the night long. I've laughed ever since, and I've come on purpose to tell it to you. It's rather a secret, though, yet."

" Martin, run to the Grange," cried the Squire, " and bring some of the servants directly ; Sir George is wounded."

" Wait a bit—wait a bit," said the idiot. " I must tell Bernard Varley my dream first."

" Nay, you need not go at all," said the Squire, " for I see some of the household hurrying hither."

The idiot beckoned Varley, and, placing his mouth close to his ear, he shouted :

" I dreamt I saw you hanged at York !"

Varley changed colour, as he said :

" Fool ! How dare you ?"

" Ha ! ha ! ha !" screamed the idiot, " I saw the crowd round the scaffold, so I pushed in among them ; and some said : ' Let him see it—he knows the man.' Then I came quite close ; but I didn't know you then, for a cap was over your face, but the corner of it was lifted up by someone, and then I knew you. Ha ! ha ! ha ! Bernard Varley, I saw you hanged at York."

Varley sprang upon the idiot, and grasped him by the throat, as he cried :

" I will stop your villainous croaking, or know the reason why."

" Hands off," cried the Squire ; " leave him, whom God has afflicted, alone."

Varley released the poor creature, who said :

" Well done, Squire—well done. Bernard Varley will be hanged at York !'

Four of the male domestics from the Grange now arrived upon the spot, and, with an air of malicious gratification, Varley cried :

" Your master has been shot by his old friend, Mr. Percy, the Squire of Larkswood. Remove him gently home."

The men looked at each other perfectly bewildered for a moment, and nothing was said till the idiot shouted :

" That may be all true ; but Bernard Varley will be hanged at York !"

The Squire said not a word, but, with the care of a father, lifted the insensible form of Miranda—for she had fainted—from her father's breast, and, motioning to the servants to lift their master, he set off for the Grange, scarcely feeling the light weight of the lovely girl he carried.

The men carried their master among them, and followed the Squire with wonder, alarm, and grief depicted on their countenances. Varley tarried a few moments until they had got in advance of him. Then he raised his clenched hand and shook it menacingly, as he muttered :

" Sir George Rankley will never recover from that wound. An insurmountable barrier is raised between Miranda and the son of the Squire of Larkswood. I shall be master of the old Grange, Miranda will be dependent upon my bounty."

" And Bernard Varley will be hanged at York !" screamed the idiot, as he scoured off across the fields.

CHAPTER III.

THE MURDER.

AT the hour of twelve that night there sat in a small antique room in the Grange, two men, upon whose pale and ghastly features the flickering light of a small lamp shone with an unsteady lustre.

No one could have looked into the countenances of these men without the conviction that they had perpetrated, or were about to perpetrate, some crime at which humanity might shudder.

Even then they were suffering some of the pangs which would haunt them to their graves, and open for them a hereafter without hope. They were standing on the brink of that awful precipice of guilt, down which the murderer plunges, never—never to re-ascend to the height from which he had so madly dashed himself.

The minutes they were now passing were those horrible ones between the conception and the execution of the crime alike denounced by God and man—murder ! And now, that years had lapsed into months, months into weeks, weeks to days, until the actual hour had come for which they had plotted, longed, and toiled, they shrank from themselves and from each other aghast and trembling.

One of these men was Bernard Varley. The other, a person of mean dimensions, and crafty, sinister aspect, who, as he sat in his chair, trembled so excessively that he was fain to clutch the carved arms of it to give himself the least appearance of steadiness.

There was wine before them, and Varley now filled a brimming glass for each, and in silence pushed one over to his companion.

With cold and clammy fingers they clutched the glasses, and drained them off, but they might as well have drunk of the coldest spring, for all the reviving effect the generous liquid had upon them. They remained cold and trembling as before.

" What is the time ?" asked Bernard Varley.

" Some minutes after twelve," replied his companion. " That wine is—is very cold."

" And the fire," added Varley, " gives no heat."

They both shivered as they spoke, and glanced uneasily at each other, after which another long pause ensued, which was at length broken by Varley, who said :

"You heard what the surgeon said?"

"Yes—yes, I did. He said there was no danger whatever—none, none."

Varley turned his eyes upon the other, as he remarked, in a hollow voice:

"But we know better. There is great danger—sudden and immediate danger."

"Ye—yes, there is. Shall we persevere, Varley, or—or now draw back?"

"Draw back? Are you mad? What have I striven for, for two years, and you for one? No; we will not now draw back. Recollect your reward—the revenue of the Grange estates is about three thousand pounds per annum; you are to have one."

"Yes; that is understood."

"But Sir George must not recover. You have a great stake in this business, but I have a far greater. Rouse yourself, the time is near at hand."

"My strength will fail me, Varley; you had better depend upon yourself, and leave me here. I should, perhaps, mar everything. I am of weak nerves."

"Leave—you—here? And pray, of what earthly use would your testimony be if you are left here?"

"I—I will swear."

"I know you would; but your oath will want corroboration. Come, you must. Come, you shall. The nurse is prepared for our visit. Yes, I told her I would relieve her watch for an hour after midnight."

"Good. We have now no time to lose. Drink—drink."

"The wine goes through my veins like ice. I will drink no more. 'Tis very strange how the mind will thus conquer the body, and change its very nature, so that fire will not warm—wine will not intoxicate."

"Pshaw," said Varley, trembling, as he nervously rubbed his hands together. "These are the feelings that ever wait on great actions before their execution. Come, we must go."

Varley rose as he spoke, and stood holding by the back of his chair, while, with nervous haste, his companion left his seat.

"It will be all over soon," he added. "A moment's pang, and it is done. Then we begin indeed to reap a golden harvest."

Varley took up the lamp, and moved to the door, and the other tremblingly followed him; but, before they left the room, he laid both his hands upon Varley's arms, and, in a husky whisper, said:

"Shall—we—think—again?"

"No; we have now to act upon former thoughts."

"But—but, Varley. Consider."

The lamp shook in Varley's hand as his companion in guilt kept a trembling clutch upon his arm, and continued to mutter:

"But, Varley, if he should resist? You know, one cry, and we are lost—lost for ever."

"Fool!" said Varley; "do you see me tremble thus?"

"Your hand shakes, Varley."

"Let go my arm, and you will find it steady."

"A clammy moisture is upon your brow, and your lips are pale as ashes."

"The last meal, not well digested, will cause all these symptoms," said Varley, with so ghastly an imitation of a smile, that the other let go his arm, and recoiled from him in sudden fright.

"What now?" said Varley. "You are full of fancies."

"You looked dreadful, Varley. Do not try to smile again. It is too horrible."

Varley bent his brows upon the man with anger, as he said, slowly and sternly:

"Follow me at once. You have gone with me thus far, and I will not now allow you to pause. Come on. You are strangely frightened of a wounded and enfeebled man."

"Oh, if the pistol of the Squire had but been aimed at his heart, Varley, what would it not have spared us?"

"I would it had; but such regrets are useless. The wound, which is not mortal, must be made so. A safer, easier mode than this, of—of——"

"Murdering!" said his trembling comrade.

"Have it so, if the term please you," continued Varley. "I say a safer mode could not be devised. Suspicion cannot be awakened. We shall be quite secure."

As Varley spoke, a pang came across him, for the words of the idiot seemed to be ringing in his ears, and he could almost, such was the power of imagination, have sworn he heard a voice say: "Bernard Varley will be hanged at York."

He said no more, but, seizing the other by the arm, led him from the room on to a landing, whence a staircase led to the upper room of the house.

The lamp shed but a dim light as they in silence ascended the staircase, followed by their flickering shadows, which danced upon the walls and balustrades, assuming many forms and strange shapes, grotesquing humanity.

How awful is the state between the conception and the perpetration of some crime at which humanity shudders, and which even after its commission leaves upon the shrinking soul a "damned spot," which may not in this world, or that which is to come, ever cease to eat like molten lead into its inmost core.

But there are human passions which will turn men from humanity. There are dark feelings, lying like hideous coiled snakes at the bottom of some men's hearts, which have but to be aroused from their lethargic state, and they will rise, in all their glittering and hideous deformity, to carry death and destruction to all.

Revenge and avarice will stir some minds to awful deeds. Ambition will induce others to stoop from the high pinnacle of innocence on which Heaven has placed them, and grovel in crime and iniquity in order to seem great to those whose opinions they affect to despise and hold in utter contempt.

In these two men, who now crept shivering up the ancient staircase, might have been noted the two grand phases of action, which, however they might lead to a similar result, were widely different in themselves.

Bernard Varley's lips were compressed until all colour had forsaken them, and his features wore a livid paleness, that made him resemble one newly risen from the grave to complete some dreadful purpose that had been stayed by the hand of death.

He moved, breathed, and spoke not like a living man.

His companion, on the other hand, exhibited but one feeling, and that was cowardice. He had the will to have a crime committed by which he might reap advantage, but his courage failed him at the time of action. Now, as he crawled after Varley, his knees shook under him, his teeth chattered, and he grasped the banisters of the stairs with a nervous energy that made his fingers crack again, and forced the colour from their joints, leaving them cold and stark, like the hands of some galvanized corpse.

Varley, when they had reached the landing of the first flight of stairs, turned to his companion, and, in a low voice, which sounded hollow as if from a sepulchre, said:

"You tremble. It is too late now to shrink."

The other twined his arm in the banisters to support himself, as he replied, with a ghastly attempt at a smile:

"No—no—I am firm; my nerves may be weak, but the object is a great one. A—a very great one."

"It is; and, if possible, more advantageous to you than to me."

"I—I—don't see that. Miranda is very beautiful."

"Pshaw! what have you to do with beauty? Come on, each moment now is precious."

Varley now proceeded up the stairs, and the other cautiously followed him until they came to a door which was partially open, and through the crevice of which streamed a faint ray of light from a night-lamp that burned in the chamber of the wounded man.

Varley turned, and laid his finger on his lips, and then slowly pushed open the door wide enough to allow him to pass into the chamber.

His companion followed him, and, as they came fairly into the room, a low muttering voice reached their ears.

"No—no—a mad thought—a mad thought—Varley save me—save me!" murmured the wounded man, in the partial delirium occasioned by the shock his system had received.

The nurse, who was in the room, rose and curtseyed to Varley, who said, in a low tone, pointing to the bed, around which the curtains were very carefully drawn:

"Alas, he raves."

"Ah, poor soul," said the nurse in a whisper; "he has been going on about something that I can't make out a bit. He keeps talking about a cheque and some money."

"Indeed?"

"Yes, sir. Don't you think he'd better have the quieting draught?"

"Yes, I intend to give him a quieting draught. We will relieve you now in your watch, while you get an hour's repose."

"Thank you, sir—you are very good. Ah, poor gentleman, I'm afraid he's very bad."

"I'm afraid he is in great danger," said Varley, in a hollow voice.

"'Tis the next crime to murder!" muttered the wounded man.

Varley started, and his companion dropped into a seat with a heavy groan.

"Ah, poor soul," said the nurse; "that's the way he goes on."

"An hour's rest will refresh you," said Varley.

"Thank you, sir. If you should want me, I'm only upstairs. I'm very wakeful, dear heart. Ah, poor gentleman, he'll have a hard time of it, I know."

Shaking her head, and muttering to herself, the old woman left the room.

Then a sickness came over even Bernard Varley as he stood by the side of the bed, and listened to the heavy breathing of the man he had come deliberately to murder.

Neither spoke for some minutes. Then Varley beckoned to his comrade, and said:

"Come."

The other slid from the chair on his knees, and, in faltering accents, while he wrung his hands, he said:

"Oh, spare him—spare him! Have mercy upon me, and upon him. Oh, Mr. Varley—I cannot—cannot. Heaven help me, I cannot."

Varley ground his teeth together with passion, and, raising his clenched hand, struck the kneeling man in the face, which was in a moment covered with blood.

"Mercy—mercy," he groaned.

"Mercy!" echoed the wounded man from the bed.

Varley leaned his head down until his mouth was level with the ear of his companion, and then he said:

"If you dare to shrink now from performing what you have undertaken, I will do the deed myself, and, by all the powers of evil, I will seize you, and, alarming the house, accuse you of the crime to your face, declaring I was too late to save him whom you had murdered."

"Oh, no, no—mercy!"

"You will do your part?"

"I—must."

"True, you must. No power on earth can save you now. Remember, you are in my power, in consequence of the large quantity of plate you have from time to time stolen from this house. You are now on your road to independence."

"You have the will?"

"I have."

"I will consent to a reduction of my share if you will do all yourself; I am weak."

"Idiot! coward!" growled Varley, between his clenched teeth. "You shall do your part, or rue the consequences. Now! now!"

Varley approached the bed, followed by his trembling companion.

They both started, for when they drew the curtains partially on one side, it seemed as if he who lay wounded on that bed was glaring full at them. The eyes were wide open, although he slept; and, with a low, moaning noise, he continued to mutter disjointed sentences.

"He sleeps," said Varley.

"His look is horrible," said the other. "Oh, Heaven, save me from being haunted by that look."

"Miranda," muttered the wounded man; "Miranda, my beautiful child—my darling—my own dear child. Kiss me, dear, dear Miranda; so—so like your mother. Ah! ah! will they not pay the cheque? No, no, no. Who forged it, then; who, I say? Five thousand pounds—yes, yes, my child—God bless you. Bernard Varley is a villain. You are my own beautiful girl—my Miranda—joy of your poor father's heart. So, I—I nearly robbed you of all. Hence—he comes, he comes, he comes. The—the executioner. Mercy—mercy!"

"Lean off the bed," said Varley; "you shake it by your trembling."

"His words are very strange," remarked the other. "To what does he allude?"

"No matter; his allusions will soon cease," said Varley.

"My child—God bless you," murmured the still sleeping man. "May you and him you love be happy; bless you both—both."

"Curses!" muttered Varley, "on the wish. Now I am nerved. There wanted but this."

"The—the door," faltered his companion.

"Bolt it," said Varley, in a husky whisper; "bolt it, and then come here and hold him."

"No, no! I—I cannot."

"You must. Hold him, I say, while I stop his breath for ever."

"He will struggle. Mr. Varley, come away. I have heard of men having the strength of giants in their dying struggle. I am weak; oh, spare me, spare me!"

The light from the lamp fell across the demoniac features of Bernard Varley, as he turned his face to his supplicating comrade, and he might well have been taken for the spirit of all evil in his own proper person, so truly fiendish was the expression upon his face.

"Once for all, hear me," he said; "I love Miranda—the only human being I ever did love. She has scorned me for one whom this night's act will place for ever away from her. I love money, because with it comes power. I love power, because I can exercise it upon my fellow men, whom I hate—hate with a hatred so bitter, so intense, that I have no pleasure but in their pain—no pain but in their pleasure. You have your ample share of this night's deed: immunity for the past, and riches for the future. A rent-charge of five hundred pounds per annum is secured to you in the will."

The other made no reply, but he rubbed his cold, clammy hands together, and looked at Varley with an expression of terror that was perfectly frightful.

"Miranda, Miranda," murmured the victim; "Miranda, my darling, speak again to me."

He tossed his arms wildly about, and betrayed evident symptoms of increasing fever and delirium.

"We waste time," said Varley. Hold him, I say, hold him. Upon the next five moments hangs your fortune."

The scene that now ensued was a dreadful one. Varley drew the pillow from under the head of the sleeper, and, holding it for a moment in his hand, he then placed it across Sir George's face, pressing upon it with all his strength.

The wounded man awakened with a stifled cry, and drawing up his feet convulsively, nearly succeeded in freeing his mouth from the pillow. Varley then threw himself upon the bed, while his companion made futile efforts to grasp the arms of the struggling man.

The contest was brief but terrible. Once only did the wounded man succeed in getting his breath, and then he shrieked—a shriek so horrible that even Varley bit his nether lip through in the excitement of the moment.

"Hold him, hold him," he cried.

A few more plunges and struggles ensued, and then all was still. Varley still held the pillow tightly over the face of the now dead man; and his companion lay in a fainting fit at the foot of the bed.

At that moment a sharp knocking sounded on the door, and Varley, with a gasp of apprehension, removed the pillow from the face of the corpse.

CHAPTER IV.

THE BEAUTIFUL MIRANDA AND HER SOLITARY WATCH BY THE DEAD—THE MURDERED KEEPER.

THE knocking at the door of the chamber of death continued, and Varley, hastily arranging the disordered clothing of the bed, and composing the limbs of the murdered man, proceeded to open the door, while his whole frame was convulsed with fear.

When the bolt was removed, and Varley held the half-open door in his hand, his first exclamation was one of surprise, for before him stood Miranda, now an orphan, and little dreaming that she faced her father's murderer.

"Miranda!" exclaimed Varley; "this—this time of night, and you up?"

"I could not sleep," she said, with a shudder, rather as if addressing herself than Varley. "I could not sleep till I had seen my father."

She tried to pass into the room, but Varley stood in her way.

"He sleeps," he said; "his slumber is most critical, as you know."

"As I know?"

"Ay, have they not told you that if he die

not in the first sound sleep after his wound, that his hopes of recovery will be much greater."

"Hopes?" echoed Miranda, while the light tinge of colour that had still lingered on her cheeks deserted them. "Hopes? they told me no danger was to be apprehended, but I fancied I heard a cry for help, and I could not sleep till I had seen my father."

"Miranda retire—you must not——"

"Sir?" said the girl, fixing her eyes, with an inquiring look, upon the cold pale man who tried to stop her.

"I tell you he sleeps," said Varley, avoiding her gaze.

"Let me pass, sir; a daughter's footstep is far less likely to disturb a dear father's slumbers than that of any hired——"

"Hired, Miranda; I am your father's guest."

"Be anything, but let me pass."

"Consider, Miranda; because you have had a dream, are you to force yourself into a sick chamber?"

"Mr. Varley," said the beautiful girl, with a firmness that gave him a pang, because it augured future disturbance to his schemes and projects, "Mr. Varley, you call yourself a guest here. If you be such, do not assume the right of a master. Remember that one word."

"Ah, you threaten?"

"I do, Bernard Varley—I say to you, beware! Let me pass, sir, to my father."

"This is unmaidenly, at such an hour."

Indignation flashed from the eyes of Miranda as she said:

"Villain, I know that my father now lies upon a bed of sickness, you think that you can triumph in this house, but whatever be the horrible secret which you say gives you a hold upon my poor father's life, you shall not use it as an instrument of torture. I will pass this door, Bernard Varley, my mind misgives me that some monstrous villainy has been——"

"Hush, hush!" said Varley, trembling excessively; "you will wake him."

A loud crash at this moment from a distant part of the building, so alarmed Varley, that he involuntarily stepped back, and Miranda glided into the room.

She proceeded towards the bed, and, gently withdrawing the curtains, she looked, as well as the very dim light that burned in the chamber would permit her, upon her father's face, which was partially covered by the bed-clothes. He appeared to her to be soundly sleeping. The horrible truth did not for an instant glance across her mind, and, with a murmured prayer to Heaven for his recovery, she sat down in the nurse's chair by the bed-side, resolved to wait there until he should awaken.

"Alas! he slept the sleep that knows no waking."

Bernard Varley's companion had recovered from his partial swoon, during the discourse between Varley and Miranda, and with what he thought a felicitous idea, he crept under-neath the bed, supposing that she would take her departure in a moment.

His position, however, became rather an uncomfortable one, for he could now scarcely make his presence known without drawing down upon him much suspicion from Miranda.

Varley stood by the open door with his hands clenched, and his face working with diabolical passions. Alarmed, as he had been by the noise in another part of the mansion, he was still more alarmed, as each moment he expected the burst of grief from Miranda, which should proclaim her knowledge that her father was no more.

"She may faint," he thought, "and then all may—all must be well."

But moment after moment passed, and all was still, to the surprise of Varley, who now advanced towards the bed, and whispered:

"Miranda!"

She rose, and pointed to the still form on the bed, as she said:

"I will await his awakening."

"Be it so," said Varley, while a smile of ill-concealed triumph flitted across his features.

He walked to the door, and then, like a flash of lightning, it came across his mind that his comrade in guilt was still somewhere in the room.

With his clenched hands above his head, he cursed him in his heart, silently, as he foresaw that now the greatest danger consisted in Twitter having hidden somewhere in the room, and being discovered when Miranda should give an alarm that her father was dead, a fact which each moment increased the probability of her immediately discovering. Then, what could save him from a strong suspicion of being accessory to the death of the baronet, but his denunciation of him, Bernard Varley; which Varley knew sufficiently of the disposition of the other to feel certain he would do.

While these thoughts were rapidly passing through Varley's mind, Miranda was gently weeping by the bedside, for, being dispirited and weakened by her fears for her father, she could not stand with her usual firmness her altercation with Varley, and now, in silence, not allowing even one faint sob to escape her, she wept by her dead father, not knowing that he was so, and controlling every sigh, lest she should disturb him.

A half-suppressed cry suddenly burst from Varley's lips, as he saw something moving along close to his feet, and, although one moment's reflection convinced him it was his companion moving from the room, his heart beat so violently, that he could hardly speak to Miranda, who looked through the curtains in alarm.

"What means that cry?" she whispered.

"I know not," said Varley, stepping between her and the crawling form of his companion. "The house, to-night, seems full of strange cries."

"It does—it does," shuddered Miranda, as she again seated herself by her father.

The curtains of the bed fell around her once more, and the ghastly, trembling comrade of Bernard Varley stood in safety at the door.

Varley beckoned him from the room, and they both crossed the threshold. Then Varley turned, and shook his hand in the direction of the bed, as he muttered:

"Miranda, you are mine! Never in this world did the subtlest villain that inhabited it contrive so rare a plot. I have not a passion unavenged. I am master of the Old Grange."

"And—and—I—I——" suggested his companion.

"You?" sneered Varley. "Wretch! what share of my triumph do you deserve? But we will not quarrel. Your evidence will be wanted. Come now, we will sit up somewhere until we hear—— Ha! who comes?"

A gleam of light now flashed along the corridor in which they stood, and, presently, a man appeared, gliding along cautiously and noiselessly.

Varley, who wanted not for mere animal courage, but was deficient in moral attributes, would have rushed forward, but his companion grasped him by the arm, saying, in a whisper:

"Look—look. Do you see that dress?"

"Dress. Yes."

"It's the spectre of the murdered keeper!"

"The what?" said Varley, moving back a pace, as the word spectre came upon his ears.

As Twitter spoke, the figure appeared slowly to recede through a wall, and to disappear, as the light it carried became dimmer and dimmer.

"What mummery is this?" said Varley.

"The servants say," replied Twitter, "that, about fifty years ago, one Tom Renshaw was killed by accident in the preserves; he was shot, by mistake, at night—and ever after that, his spirit walks the Old Grange."

"Pshaw—absurd," said Varley, although his rapidly-shifting eye, and deathly paleness, betokened how ill at ease he was. "Come to the room we left," he continued. "There is a fire there. The night is very cold."

Trembling as they went, and starting at their own shadows, these men, with a weight of guilt upon their souls, which never—never—could be pushed off—repaired to the room they had so recently quitted, and on the table in which lay the wine they had left.

The fire upon the hearth was dim, and Varley threw on a log of wood to replenish it, as he said, without looking at his companion:

"Twitter, all has succeeded. You may remain here at the Grange, or go elsewhere, as it may suit your fancy."

"I—I—cannot speak—it is so cold."

"Well, as you please. I tell you, Twitter, that I would sell my soul for that girl. Did you see her pale—even as she was to-night? How beautiful she looked! She must be mine—dependent upon me entirely; she surely will give way at last. Twitter, I adore that girl."

"Hush—what was that?"

"Nothing. I heard nothing."

"We—we—shall hear something, Bernard Varley, soon. Do you not know that the moment must come when Miranda will find who and what she is keeping her solitary watch beside."

"What care I now? She might faint—she might scream; but I would rather the former, were I there to snatch a dozen kisses from her lips. By Heaven, I——"

Twitter buried his face in his hands, and Varley breathed with difficulty, as a scream, so loud, so shrill, so awful, that it seemed to linger an indefinite time upon the air, burst upon their bewildered senses.

"There—there," cried Twitter, "now she—she knows he's dead; oh, that horrible scream! It will haunt me till I die. Varley, you look like stone."

Varley snatched up the light, and strode to the door; then, turning, said, in a deep, hasty voice:

"She has discovered a corpse where she thought lay a sleeping man. Be careful of every word you now say. Upon your evidence and mine agreeing, everything now depends. Recollect when we left him he was breathing hard, and with difficulty."

"Ye—yes."

"But he was alive."

"I—I will swear, of course, all we agreed upon for my rent-charge."

"Now remain where you are, and leave me to manage the remainder of this business."

"Not in the dark; I—I cannot stay in the dark a moment," said Twitter.

"Fool—you have the firelight."

A trampling of feet now resounded through the house, and cries of help came plainly upon their ears.

Twitter had risen from his chair, and was trying to take the light from Varley, when the door of the room was flung open, and a crowd of servants appeared in the entrance.

CHAPTER V.

A DAUGHTER'S GRIEF—THE ROBBERY—A HOUSE OF WOE.

CONSTERNATION sat upon every countenance of the many that crowded the doorway of the room which Bernard Varley had been upon the point of leaving, and as the unanimity of feeling among the domestics was sufficient to induce them all to speak at once, the confusion of tongues was, when contrasted with the stillness that had reigned before throughout the mansion, perfectly confounding.

"The keeper's ghost!" cried some.

"Thieves!" shouted others.

"Sir George murdered!" was the cry of four or five at once.

"Peace!" cried Varley, "what is the cause of all this uproar? If you wish to be heard, certainly speak all at once. If understood, take it by turns. How dare you, when your master now is dangerously ill, make such an uproar in the dead hour of the night?"

"Hold! Bernard Varley," cried Miranda, suddenly bursting through the throng. "Be you the last to speak."

She held her finger pointed at him as she stood pale and still as a marble statue at the door, and Varley visibly writhed and shrank under her gaze.

The sudden appearance of Miranda struck everyone dumb for a few moments, and a more singular group could scarcely be conceived than was presented by the various persons assembled in and about the doorway of that small apartment.

By a great effort, Varley then spoke:

"Miranda," he said, "are you mad?"

"No. Heaven has yet spared my reason, that I may tell you all here—you who are all attached servants of my father—you who have known him so many years—that he is murdered."

"Murdered?" echoed every voice.

"Yes, murdered. You have no master; I—I have no father. I am not mad—'tis Heaven's mercy that I am not. For one whole year now—a year which has seemed an eternity of time—that man (pointing to Varley), he who now comes before my gaze—he who, you see, shrinks aghast from the daughter of his victim—that man has persecuted me; and I have loathed him more and more, as his black heart became known to me."

"Remove her to her chamber," cried Varley; "her wits wander."

"No—no—no," cried Miranda; "hear me all. Bernard Varley has murdered my father."

"Beware!" cried Varley; "I say, beware!"

"That word," cried Miranda; "that frown has no terror now. He is gone—gone. Fiend, monster, you have done your worst."

"You see she is mad; you hear her," said Varley, clasping his hands together, to endeavour to stop their agitated trembling.

Miranda wrung her hands bitterly.

"Follow me—follow me," she said, with a sudden dropping of her voice from passionate earnestness to the deepest pathos. "My poor fond father is dead. They have killed him—his blood is upon their heads. Bernard Varley must have this deed to answer for. I was watching by his bedside, thinking that he slept; then I tried to hear him breathe, but could not; and my own heart almost ceased to beat, as I placed my hand upon his. It was cold—cold. My father is dead. I shall never see him smile again—never hear his voice—never—never—nev——"

She was caught by some of the servants near to her, as her feelings overcame her, and she relapsed into a happy state of insensibility.

"Grief for her father's wounded state," said Varley, "has turned the girl's head, or she has had some dream."

The servants seemed perfectly bewildered, and looked in each other's faces like men suddenly aroused to some new state of existence.

Varley poured himself out a bumper of the wine that stood upon the table; and drinking it off at a draught, he held by the back of a chair, while he said:

"Go to your master's chamber, all of you, and see if it be really true that he is no more, or only the coinage of this girl's disturbed brain."

Miranda still continued insensible, and they placed her in an easy-chair which was in the room; he who had caught her, and saved her from falling, saying:

"I'll go and call up some of the women. Poor thing, she seems nearly dead."

"A little wine will restore her," said Varley. "Go—go, all of you, to your master's chamber. I will attend to Miranda until some of the female servants are up. Twitter, go you and see to your master."

A violent ringing of a bell now sounded in the house, and one immediately exclaimed:

"That is Sir George's chamber-bell."

"The—the nurse is ringing," stammered Twitter.

"For shame, men; are you afraid?" cried Varley. "Away with you."

The servants hurried now towards the staircase leading to their master's chamber; Twitter slowly following the last of all.

Varley listened for a moment; and when the last footsteps on the staircase began to be indistinct, he turned his eyes upon the pallid face of the young girl, who reclined in the large chair by the fireside.

"If I have lost Heaven," he muttered, "I have gained an angel. Oh, how I have panted for such an opportunity as this, to imprint unrebuked one burning kiss upon those lips, to clasp, for one maddening moment, to my heart she whom I love, but the more as she condemns me! Miranda—Miranda, you are mine. I have bartered my soul's salvation for you, and I will have my reward."

He trembled as he took her unresisting hand, and pressed it to his lips. He raised her drooping head. Once he pressed his mouth to hers—her long silken hair fell upon his breast—her brow, her cheeks, her lips, he kissed with maddening fervour.

"Miranda, Miranda," he cried; "who shall step between me and my prize? I triumph—I triumph. This, indeed, is joy; to hold her thus pillowed on my breast; to rain kisses of fire upon her lips."

A light flashed across Varley's eyes at this moment from the half-shut door. The same figure that he had seen disappear from the corridor stood before him; a stunning blow fell upon his head. It seemed to him for a moment as if he was surrounded by a million dazzling lights, and then all was a blank; the villain fell stunned to the floor.

* * * *

In confusion and dismay the servants reached the chamber of their master. The nurse was tugging frantically at the bell-rope as they entered, and with a "Thank Heaven! you're all come," she told them that Sir George was no more.

"He must have gone very sudden," she added. "I never knew the like; the first I heard of it was Miss Miranda screaming terrible-like. I was just waking and thinking to myself that it was time for me to go and let Mr. Varley and Mr. Twitter leave, when I heard her, poor dear thing, and when I came here she bolted past me like a shot, crying out that her father was dead, and there, sure enough, he was."

The nurse then drew aside the curtains, and there lay the corpse as if sleeping. The features were calm and serene, and the only sign of the least disturbance was a long scratch across the face, and a little blood which had oozed from the wound, some of the dressings of which had given way in the struggle between the victim and his murderers.

"Ah, poor soul," continued the nurse, "it's very sudden, a very sudden call indeed."

The servants looked on with blanched faces, and then one said:

"Who's gone for the doctor?"

"You—you see he's dead," said Twitter; "what's the use of a doctor now? My poor master is a murdered man, and the Squire of Larkswood must suffer for it."

"Henry Lee has gone for the doctor; I heard say he would," remarked one.

"And here he is, here he is," cried several who were nearest the door.

The medical man now made his appearance, having been much surprised at being called to Sir George in the night, for he really considered in his own mind the wound to be trifling, if proper care was taken. To hear, therefore, that his patient had slipped through his fingers so suddenly, very much amazed and surprised him indeed.

"How is Sir George?" he said. "I suppose he has fainted, or something of the sort."

"He is dead, sir," said four or five at once.

"Hush, hush," cried the surgeon. "I don't at all believe it."

He took the cold hand of the corpse in his —there was no pulsation at the wrist. He laid his ear flat against the heart—all was still.

"My good friends, it was very little use sending for me," he then said. "Sir George has been dead for some time. We must have an inquest, of course. My opinion is that a sudden shock to the nervous system, such as a shot wound, has occasioned the unexpected decease. It's very disagreeable—rather odd—and, I may add, provoking. Who was with him when he died?"

"His daughter, sir."

"Well, I'm sorry, very sorry—it can't be helped. I should like, above all things, to hear her account of it, if she is up and well enough to speak to me."

"Can nothing be done, sir?" said the nurse.

"Certainly not, my good woman. While a spark of life remains one can sometimes fan it up into a blaze, but when vitality has fairly ceased, why—a-hem."

"Ah, well, he was a kind soul, though a bit nervous and fidgety like. He's gone quite like a lamb."

"How did he get that scratch? I did not see it when I dressed his wound."

"Lor', sir, I don't know. Well I never, that is a long scratch, to be sure."

"Indeed it is. It's curious how he could have come by it—people may scratch themselves accidentally, but they never begin under the eye and go on to the chin."

The surgeon continued for some moments in deep thought, then he said:

"Has he had anybody to see him?"

"No, sir—not anybody."

"Well, the body must not be touched. There will be an inquest, I dare say, to-morrow, or the next day at furthest, and in the meantime, just leave everything as it is. In fact, the door had better be locked."

The servants now made a general rush from the door, as pale, tottering, and her hair dishevelled, Miranda came into the room. She had recovered without assistance from her servant, and, as quickly as she could, ascended to the chamber where lay her father. The first person she saw was the medical man, and to him she clung with frantic eagerness, crying:

"Oh, save him—save him—save my poor father, sir. He is not dead."

"My dear young lady, compose yourself," said the surgeon. "Come now, sit down, you must bear these things with fortitude."

"Alas—alas! What will become of me? Rowland, where are you now, dear Rowland."

"Whom does she mean?" said the surgeon.

"She means young Mr. Percy, sir."

"Oh, my dear young lady, he is not here."

"Not here? He should be here. Rowland —father. He was here. I dreamed he kissed me. My poor father is murdered—and—our last words were not so kind as they had been. Let me see him—let me see him!"

"No, no—indeed you must not—take her to her own room—take her away."

A simultaneous cry of surprise now burst from several of the servants, and one and all pointed towards the door, where, rapidly walking away, was the figure in the green hunting-dress, that Twitter had declared to be the spectre of the murdered keeper.

CHAPTER VI.

THE SPECTRE OF THE KEEPER—THE CHASE —THE CAPTURE—AN ACCUSATION.

FOR the space of a moment, everyone who looked on the strange figure seemed paralyzed, and it was only the voice of the medical man calling loudly:

"That's no ghost, lads—seize him. It's much more likely a thief!" That roused them from their lethargy, and then a simultaneous rush was made in the direction the figure had taken.

There were two staircases opening and descending from the corridor, and the supposed ghost chose the one furthest from the door of the chamber, descending with great rapidity. The foremost among the servants just saw which direction the figure turned in, when it reached the foot of the stairs, and then they pursued it with good speed; the excitement of the chase going far to dissipate the fear with which they had first beheld the phantom.

The Grange was one of those old, irregular buildings which contain so many intricacies and hiding-places, that anyone well acquainted with its topography might for a long time puzzle others not possessing so much knowledge; and, in the present case, it appeared that none of the servants were half so well informed with regard to all the ins and outs of the Grange as the spectre, for it found two or three doors in the old wainscoting, of which they were not at all aware, and darted up and down staircases, disappeared in various situations where there appeared no outlet, and altogether led its pursuers so troublesome a chase, that they finally all assembled in the great dining-room to consult, after quite losing all trace of the object of their active, but useless, pursuit.

Miranda, when first the pursuit had began, started from the arms of the surgeon, and would have flown after the servants, but he gently, though forcibly, detained her, saying:

"Now, be calm; you will make yourself ill. Let me persuade you to go to your chamber. This person is, most probably, either one of the servants playing off a prank—and, if so, he might have waited for a more seasonable time—or some thief, who, having heard of the legend concerning the ghost of the keeper haunting the house, has taken advantage of it to steal the plate."

"Or it may be real," said Miranda, with a shudder.

"Pho—pho—nonsense. Here, nurse, I will remain here while you see the young lady to her room. Pray, let me persuade you to go to bed, my dear young lady. Your grief, of course, is quite natural, but you should, nevertheless, control it as well as you can."

"I cannot sleep—let me remain here," sobbed Miranda.

"Well, if you will not go, just sit down by me here a little while and compose yourself."

"Oh, this frightful day! and now frightful night!" said Miranda. "If I could but awaken and find it all a dream. First, my father fighting a duel with his best and oldest friend. Then, being in his own house murdered."

"Murdered?"

"Yes—I know it."

"My good girl, how can you say so? Tell me all that happened while you kept watch by your father."

"Alas! I know not—my mind is all confusion; but my heart tells me he has been murdered—murdered!"

"Whom do you suspect?"

"Bernard Varley."

"Your father's intimate friend?"

"His worst—his most deadly foe."

"Indeed!"

"Yes—Bernard Varley is in possession of some terrible secret, which gave him a real or fancied power over my poor father."

"Oh, she's wandering in her mind," thought the surgeon; "she doesn't know what she's saying."

"All was happiness," continued Miranda. "till he came here. Then, as you may have seen some—some fair summer sky overclouded never to be bright again, all became dark, drear, and desolate."

She clasped her hands over her face, and wept bitterly.

"That will do her good," thought the surgeon; "she will be ten times more rational now."

"Yes," continued Miranda, "from the moment that Bernard Varley came to the Grange, all was changed. My father and the Squire have quarrelled about I know not what. Rowland, who I am sure my father loved, has been harshly forbidden to enter our doors, and the end of all is death—death!"

"Humph. Where is Mr. Varley, nurse?"

"Here!" said Varley, staggering into the room, his face covered with blood.

Miranda started to her feet, and the medical man regarded him with amazement.

"I am here," continued Varley; "I have been the victim of an attack from someone who is in this house, for no good purpose. I was struck down by a man in a green dress."

"Attired like a forester?"

"The same."

"Then," cried the surgeon, "it is quite clear that this supposed ghost is flesh and blood. My life on it, Miranda, if your father has come by his death unfairly, it is from the hand of the person now so closely pursued by your servants—this supposed spectre."

Varley was silent for a moment, then he suddenly exclaimed:

"Good Heavens! a new light breaks in upon me. Sir George has been murdered."

"You know it!" said Miranda.

"I?"

"Yes, Bernard Varley—I accuse you."

"This is midsummer madness," said Varley. "You see, sir, that I am badly wounded in endeavouring to secure a man, who, let him be who he may, we may all fairly suspect: and lo! I am myself accused by this young lady in consequence of some fancied offence I have given her. I am nearly fainting from loss of blood."

The surgeon now looked to Varley's wound, which, although merely a scalp one, was by no means slight.

"I think when you see that Mr. Varley is himself injured, young lady, you will be inclined to acquit him of any share in your suspicions of persons who may have injured your father."

"We've got him!—we've got him!" cried several voices from the staircase now.

The surgeon ran to the door.

"He's in the dining-room, sir, tied hand and foot."

Miranda, before they could prevent her, rushed down the staircase, and burst through the throng of persons in the dining-room, who were surrounding a tall young man, dressed in a green hunting-dress.

"Miranda!" he said.

"Rowland Percy!" shrieked Miranda.

"The same. Why do you look aghast, all of you? You know me now, though you have not seen me for some little time. Oh! I forgot my wig. Ah! Miranda, you have penetrated my disguise. Now, before you all here, I proclaim Bernard Varley a villain. I believe you will find him lying on the floor in his own room. I know I am in this house, unwelcome and unbidden. I assumed this disguise unknown to all, with the hope that I might encounter Miranda as she took her usual early morning's walk in the conservatory. Pardon me, if I have caused an alarm in the house. I suppose I—what—what makes you all so silent? Is your father up, Miranda?"

"My father?"

"Yes, I have not been two hours in this neighbourhood. What is the reason of your alarmed looks?"

"Rowland, Rowland," cried Miranda. "Tell me. Swear to me you know nothing of——"

"Of what, Miranda?"

"My father's death."

The young man started back as he exclaimed:

"His death? You—you jest."

"No, Rowland, my father is no more."

"Good Heavens!—I—I came here with the hope of healing the unhappy differences between him and my father. Absence was insupportable to me, and in this disguise I hoped——"

"Hold, young sir, hold," said Varley, walking through the throng of persons; "the less you now say the better."

"The less I say? Bernard Varley, you are a scoundrel. I bless my happy stars that I was here this night to rescue from your polluting touch innocence and virtue. Villain, I have not yet done with you."

"Nor I with you, unhappy young man."

"Unhappy?"

"Ay, be cautious, sir, in your speech. Sir George has been murdered!"

"Murdered?"

"You start, sir. 'Tis well acted. I expect Sir George is murdered."

"Then, if so," cried Rowland Percy, "he from whom I rescued the daughter, I suspect, has been the murderer of the father."

"Beware, misguided, unhappy young man! I forgive you freely your desperate attack upon my own life, for my soul is shocked at your situation."

"Explain yourself, villain, or I will pluck your meaning from your heart."

Varley turned to the assembled throng of persons, and, in an affected voice of deep grief and compassion, he said:

"Friends, all here assembled, I will make a long tale brief. Some time since, your poor master, now lying dead, discovered a clandestine correspondence between this young man—this Rowland Percy—and his daughter here. The consequence was a quarrel, and this young man was forbidden the house. His father took up his quarrel, and, after much aggravation, a duel was the result. Sir George was slightly wounded; but has been—I say it advisedly, for there are appearances upon the corpse to warrant me—murdered in his bed."

A thrill of excitement and horror ran through the assemblage.

"I repeat, murdered in his bed. Who did the deed? Who had a motive—who a quarrel? Who is found skulking about the house, and only secured after much toil and difficulty? Who made an attack upon me, and fancied he left me for dead? Who have we now a prisoner? Rowland Percy—Rowland Percy, who, upon circumstantial evidence, I here accuse of stealing into this house to-night, and taking some opportunity of murdering Sir George."

"Liar!" shouted Rowland.

"Hear me," cried Varley, as he fixed his eyes upon the trembling and utterly confounded Twitter. "Myself and Sir George's valet left him, as we considered, asleep for about five minutes; during that time the deed must have been done. My own opinion, by the look of the body, is that he has been smothered in his bed."

"Seize the murderer! seize him!" cried several voices.

"Hold!" said Miranda, rushing forward and clasping the hands of Rowland. "Hear me, all here present. I know not if I am mad or sane, for my brain whirls, and my temples throb with the awful events of this night, but if all this be not some horrible dream, I here proclaim my faith in the innocence of Rowland Percy to be equal to my faith in Heaven."

"My Miranda!" cried Percy.

"Hush—hush, Rowland; hear me out. You all knew and loved my father. Would I take the hand of his murderer? Look in this face and look in that."

She pointed from Rowland to Bernard Varley, and the difference was indeed most striking between the open, candid countenance of the young man, and the villainous physiognomy of Varley.

"See," continued Miranda, "he shrinks aghast from the words of truth—he has described the mode of my poor father's death, and he, and none but he, could describe it."

"Seize the murderer," cried Varley, pointing to Percy. "This girl raves, poor thing. The Percys are a ruined race, and Sir George alone stood in the way of patching up their broken fortune by a marriage with the heiress of the Grange. Secure him, and let the law, upon such evidence as can be produced, pronounce him innocent or guilty."

The servants made a rush towards the young man, for there was something so terrible in the charge made against him, that they forgot all their predilections in his favour in their horror at his supposed crime.

Rowland drew himself up proudly as he said:

"The man who attempts to lay a hand upon me had better look to his safety. I know not how far I may be entangled in the meshes of some plot woven by that villain," pointing to Varley; "but I have faith in my own innocence, and so far from avoiding, I claim investigation."

"Fetch me officers," said Varley.

"No, no," cried Miranda; "he is innocent —he is. I have no friend now in the wide world but him. I am the last of my race —an orphan. Rowland, let me cling to you."

"Miranda," said the young man, mournfully, "Heaven knows how dear you are to me! but a chasm so deep, that its far descent is lost in its own gloom, is now opened between us. Proof of my innocence must fill it up, and then we may meet again as we have met. Leap it, and all is lost!"

Miranda shuddered, but still clung to Percy. She spoke in a strange tone.

"Rowland," she said, "some fiends are at work about us—we are deserted of Heaven. Some terrible machinations against us have succeeded for a time—we are lost!"

"No, Miranda, innocence will, like an angel, burst its way through bars and bolts, through water, earth, and fire, and wing its flight to Heaven with not a pinion ruffled. Believe me, all will yet be well!"

"Well, well," she murmured, and with a shudder, fainted in her lover's arms.

CHAPTER VII.

THE EARLY DAWN—IS IT A DREAM?—
MIRANDA'S DESPAIR—THE REALITY OF
WOE.

LIKE a storm upon a fair smiling summer's day, had ruin and destruction fallen upon the house of Sir George Rankley, the once much-envied possessor of the Grange, one of the most magnificent estates in Yorkshire. But one short year previous to the melancholy occurrences it has been our duty to relate, everything wore a smiling aspect in and about the mansion which Sir George had purchased as a place of rest for himself and his child, the beautiful and accomplished Miranda.

Wearied with the bustle and excitement of a commercial life, for Sir George had accumulated his large fortune as a principal of a banking-house of great reputation, he had given a sum exceeding three hundred thousand pounds for the Grange, and thither retired to endeavour to forget one cankering care, that, like a plague-spot, ate into his heart.

What the mystery was, the thought of which would occasionally blanch the cheek of Sir George Rankley with terror, and produce a tremor of many minutes duration,

even in his hours of gayest converse, no one could for a moment divine.

All that was known of his history was, that he had entered the banking establishment, of which he ultimately became the head, as a junior partner, with but a very small share of the profits of the business.

From that day, however, his career of prosperity appeared to date itself, for he rapidly became a rich man; and finally, in an epoch of commercial pressure, he, to the surprise of his partners, offered to throw a very large sum into the concern, provided they would make him a partner on equal terms with themselves. His offer was gladly accepted, and he, in a very few years, by his energy and promptitude, became the head of the firm.

How all these things came about was a mystery to his partners, who were much older men than himself; but there was one circumstance which caused them the greatest uneasiness, and that consisted in a series of extensive forgeries on the bank, which nearly threatened the dissolution of the business.

Rankley, on these occasions, always came forward to the assistance of his partners, but invariably as he did so, had fresh articles of partnership entered into which gave him an increased interest in, and ascendancy over, the business.

This state of things continued for some years, when the senior partner dropped into the grave, leaving Rankley at the head of the concern, not nominally, but really.

An accommodation, then, to a noble duke of the blood royal to the tune of some forty thousand pounds, led to the baronetcy he retired with, and Sir George Rankley had arrived at the summit of his desires and ambition.

So far, the personal history of the baronet was well known, but behind the curtain there were fearful secrets which would, if divulged at any moment, have torn that man from his splendid home, and consigned him to a gallows.

It would seem in the history of human nature that there was ever a retributive justice going on, and that the higher bold villainy shall succeed in soaring, the more certain, rapid, and awful shall be its fall, and that the most subtle and high-working mind that ever gave impulse to human actions, was ever doomed in some manner to commit itself among its own intricacies, and fall a victim to its own wild ambitions.

The veriest wretch that ever solicited alms from door to door was happier than Sir George Rankley; and he would have given worlds, had he possessed them, to obliterate twenty-five years of his life, and to again commence his mercantile existence as the junior partner in the house he had so completely made his own.

But, alas! time may not be recalled, or how many who have been allured by the glittering *ignis fatuus* of life would bargain to be stripped of all the worldly dross they had collected about them, and sent into the public streets to beg their bread, provided they could obliterate some years of feverish vice, and blot out for ever the deep record of their hideous crimes!

The Larkswood estates joined to that of the Grange, and an intimacy had sprung up between the families—an intimacy which, in the case of Miranda and young Rowland Percy, had ripened into one of those soul-clinging affections which but few natures are capable of appreciating.

Theirs was a love inscrutable, unchangeable; full of the sweet confidence, the firmness, the enduring gentleness of a passion that knows no doubts, no fears, but glides in the deep consciousness of its own strength and purity, without a ripple.

But how true it is that—

"The course of true love never yet ran smooth!"

A cloud was hovering in the horizon of their joy; and, at a time when they fondly hoped that the sun of their happiness was climbing to the meridian of its glory, it was sinking, alas! in gloom and storm, leaving behind it but the traces of its God-like presence in their glowing hearts.

Alas! that it should be so; that ever the first dear feelings of the heart—that one inheritance from Heaven, which some pitying angel begged, might yet be left to man—love —oh, that love, in all its purity, in all its devotion, its self-sacrificing beauty and sublimity, should ever be wrecked on the sands of suspicion, or sacrificed on the altar of mammon!

But so it is ever. The first grand feeling of life is to love; the second, a fruitless effort to forget.

The sunshine, which had appeared in its intensity to be shining for ever upon the path of the lovers, was suddenly and awfully withdrawn, leaving behind a mass of horrors and darkness which no eye could pierce.

The early morning was dawning, and the birds were singing blithely among the tall trees that surrounded the Grange. The lowing of the cattle in the distance, the bark of dogs, the hum of many insect things, all bespoke and hailed the coming day; and there had been a time, and that, too, but a few short sunrises since, when Miranda had delighted in all these sounds of life, animation, and joy; a time when she had sprung from her dreamless couch to snatch the early rose, that to the first beam of sunshine had opened its odorous breast; a time when the wild notes of the forest birds were to her ear sweet melody; but now—now how was all changed!

It is the heart that makes or mars its own melody; and now, all that had been so fair and so beautiful—so lovely, so delightful—sounded harsh and discordant to the ears that were no longer attuned to listen to them with pleasure.

Miranda slept, indeed, but she had not retired to rest. She lay upon the outside of her couch, in an uneasy morning slumber, after a night of tears, agony, and watching.

Her sleep was now so light, that all the sounds of coming morning made themselves cognizant to her senses; but they brought no pleasure; no beaming smile enlivened the lark's sweet melody. Tears coursed each other down her pale cheeks, and, in her sleep, she muttered words of suffering and pain.

"Rowland, Rowland," she sobbed, "he is innocent, he is—unhand him! Think you I —I would screen the murderer of my own father? Oh, no, no, no—he is innocent."

Deep sobs now burst from her labouring breast, and she covered her face with one white, exquisitely-rounded arm, as a ray of sunlight came dancing, like a stream of molten gold, in at her window, and fell across her face, both borrowing and giving beauty.

The light slumber was broken. Miranda started, pressed her hands across her eyes for a moment, and then looked wildly about her. Each well-remembered object met her eyes— her vases, filled with flowers; the trailing crimson roses, that dappled her window with radiant beauty; her drawing implements; the gold-fish swimming, in their everlasting restlessness, around their glassy prison; her piano; all the little cherished remembrances of youthful friendships and affections which she set so much store by. Her eye wandered rapidly from one to the other, as if in bewildered surprise. Then she raised a cry of joy—of such ecstasy as the heart feels when some load of grief is, by one word, lifted from it.

Miranda clasped her hands, and a flush of colour rose to her cheeks, as she said:

"A dream—a dream! It was but a dream. Thank Heaven! I—I—— Oh, thank Heaven! it is not real. 'Tis all a dream—an awful dream!"

She sank into a chair, and burst into an hysterical passion of laughter, mingled with tears.

This convulsion of feeling gradually subsided, and she said, with more calmness:

"Foolish Miranda, to be so affected by a vision. Yet what an awful one. A dream so like reality, that even now I shudder. Yet, how is this—not undressed, the bed untouched. What could have possessed me? Oh, Heaven! am I mad? No, no; I must have come to my room wearied, and thrown myself on the bed, and then fallen into the uneasy sleep that brought me such torturing visions. What is to-day? I surely have slept long."

She flew to a small French timepiece, which had been a gift from Rowland Percy. It was silent, and the hands pointed to half-past four. She pressed her hands to her brow, as she said:

"What could have made me forget to wind up my pretty clock? A dream—a dream; yes, it—it must be all a dream. Can I put together its absurd creations? Let me consider; my father murdered by Rowland— Rowland, my Rowland, who will return and claim me for his own. Yes, it surely was a dream."

A knock at her chamber door now startled her, and she cried:

DICK PALMER REFUSES THE BAG OF PLATE.

"Who is there?"

"It's me, miss," said a female voice.

"Oh, it's you, Annie; come in and help me to dress. I declare—I—I—what, in tears?"

The girl's eyes were red with weeping, and she stood staring at her young mistress's smiling face in consternation, and as much surprise as if she had seen a spectre.

"Well, Annie," said Miranda, "what is the matter? Have you, too, had a dream?"

"A dream, Miss Miranda?"

"Yes; I—have had a terrible one."

"Lor! miss, I don't wonder at it, considering."

"Considering what, Annie?"

"All that's happened. I shall never, no, never, as long as I live, forget——"

Miranda staggered to her seat, as she said:

"Forget what, Annie?"

"Oh, miss, I haven't your fortitude, and I was so afraid that you would be quite ill."

"Fortitude! fortitude! I have had a dream—I dreamt my father was—dead."

"Dreamt, miss; why, goodness gracious, so he is!"

A scream burst from Miranda, and she clasped her hands together, crying:

"No, no, no—it cannot—cannot be."

"Oh, dear! oh, dear! miss, it is all true, and

young Mr. Rowland, sweet young man as he is——"

"Girl!" cried Miranda, clutching her tightly by the arm, "you—you are hatching some hideous tale to drive me mad!"

"Help! help!" cried the girl.

"Hush, hush, Annie! hush; I—will hear all. Oh, Heaven! is it real? is it real? You spoke of Rowland?"

"Ye—ye—yes, miss. They—they have taken him to York."

"For what?"

"The murder."

"Save me, Heaven!" cried Miranda.

She dropped on her knees, and, muttering, "It is real! it is real!" she prayed for strength, and that she might not go mad, but preserve her senses to proclaim the innocence of Rowland Percy. Tears rolled down her cheeks as she prayed, and then a passionate burst of weeping succeeded.

It was well that her highly-wrought feelings found such timely vent, or her fine brain might not have endured the awful shock it had sustained. She rose calmer and firmer—Heaven was, in its mercy, preserving her for other purposes. The storm of grief and horror was over, and Miranda was now prepared to take her part in the great drama of domestic life that was awaiting her.

CHAPTER VIII.

THE INTERVIEW—AN AWFUL DISCLOSURE—A VILLAIN'S PROPOSAL.

It was well for Miranda that the excess of her agonized feelings had subsided, for she had scarcely changed her apparel and refreshed herself by dashing cold spring-water over her eyes, than a message was brought to her with Mr. Varley's compliments, and a request for an interview.

"He request an interview with me?" said Miranda. "Go, Annie, and tell him I will not see him. What will become of me? Yet, stay! Send someone to Mr. Percy directly. Tell him to come to me."

"Lor', miss; Mr. Percy is gone away."

"Gone away?"

"Yes, miss; after the duel."

"I am distracted," said Miranda. "Even now all is confusion in my brain. Tell me, Annie, briefly, what occurred."

"Why, miss, as far as I know, your father fought a duel with old Mr. Percy, the Squire, and was shot somehow. Then they do say as young Mr. Percy came in the night, and murdered your father in his sleep."

"That is what you are told," said Miranda, forcing herself, by a great effort, to be calm. "I begin, now, to recollect all. There has been some fearful—some horrible machinations. Alas! where can I turn for succour? Have I a friend now in the wide world?"

"I'm sure, miss, there's one," sobbed Annie.

Miranda shuddered, and sat pale and motionless for some moments; then she rose, and throwing a shawl over her shoulders, she said:

"I will see this man—this Bernard Varley; yes, I will see him; my heart tells me he is the author of all this misery. From his hand has been launched the bolt which has fallen with such destructive vengeance upon our house. I will see him!"

"He is in the breakfast-room," sobbed Annie, "they say; shall I tell him, Miss Miranda, that you are coming?"

"No; I will go and meet my father's murderer alone."

"Lor', miss, you don't think——"

"I do, Annie; I care not who hears me say so; my firm impression is that Bernard Varley is my father's murderer; his very accusation of Rowland Percy is sufficient."

"Well, you knows best, miss, and you be now mistress of the Grange."

"Mistress of the Grange, Annie?"

"Yes, miss, as poor, dear master is dead and gone, why, in course, they says among all the servants that you be mistress now, and all belongs to you outright."

"I—I had not thought of that," said Miranda; "my poor father's remains shall no longer be insulted by the presence of his murderer; Bernard Varley shall leave this house."

"Well, miss, I am glad of that, because—because——"

"Because what, Annie?"

"Thomas says as he'll knock him down, and then Thomas might get into trouble; as you see, Miss Miranda, Mr. Varley is always teasing me so."

"He, or I, leave this house to-day," said Miranda; "by some means this man had acquired a power of ascendancy over my poor father—an ascendancy so great that even an insult to me dared not be resented; but that is over now—alas! how fearfully; and if I have the power to call this house my own, he shall now leave it."

Miranda paused a moment, then she said to the wondering girl:

"Annie, send one of the men-servants immediately to York, and tell him to bring back with him, if possible, one of the ablest lawyers he can find; I have duties now to perform which my private griefs must not interfere with. I—I must weep in secret, but be firm in the cause of innocence, and in punishing the really guilty. Another shawl, Annie; I am very cold."

"You are all of a shiver, miss."

"Yes, yes; I am cold."

"You had better breakfast, miss, afore you see Mr. Varley."

"No, no, I am better now; Heaven will grant me strength. If it were not, Annie, I should drop down at your feet; nay, don't look so much alarmed. You see I am calm, quite calm now. I will see this demon in human form—this Bernard Varley, who has made me an orphan; may Heaven forgive him. But I, now that my heart is bleeding with the fresh wounds he has inflicted upon it, I cannot—no, I—I cannot yet—yet I will see him."

There was a calmness about Miranda, but it was the calmness of overwrought feeling mingled with despair. It was well, too, that the gentle and affectionate girl was not thrown altogether upon her griefs, but that indignation and resentment claimed some portion of her attention, and contributed to keep her mind in a more healthy state than it otherwise would have been, had it been resigned to one set of feelings only.

Of Rowland Percy's innocence she was convinced, and the feeling that it probably lay with her, and her only, to save him from the dreadful suspicion which Bernard Varley strove to attach to him, nerved her to exertion.

"I have heard of young, feeble, tender-hearted women," she said to herself, as she descended from her chamber, "daring more than the mightiest and strongest men for a cause they threw their whole hearts into, and shall I shrink from saving Rowland from this most calumnious charge? Oh, spirit of my father! if from Heaven you can look down upon your child, and direct her in the right path to save the innocent, guide me now, and let the guilty alone tremble. Be still, my heart, now; I must go through this trying interview with nerve. Be still, my heart—be still."

Villain as he was, and unscrupulous in the ways by which he strove to accomplish his unholy purposes, Bernard Varley could not, with the confident air he would have wished, meet the daughter of his murdered victim.

The interview he had sought with Miranda, he knew was a necessary one, and he did not wish to avoid it; but still he shrank from it with an abject trembling fear, such as conscious guilt ever feels in the presence of purity and virtue.

He was pacing the breakfast-room with rapid strides, when the door opened, and Miranda, pale as any spectre, stood upon the threshold.

Varley started at the great change in her appearance, which the day and night of exquisite misery and suffering had inflicted upon her. She was not less beautiful; there was the same beautiful contour of face and form; there were the same lustrous beaming eyes; the same delicately modelled mouth; but it was the expression which was new.

But four-and-twenty hours since a look of cloudless joy had mantled on her cheeks, for although she had in her heart some cause for woe in the misunderstanding between her father and her lover, she believed it to be but slight, and that a very short time would make all friends again. In fact, some might have objected to the beauty of Miranda as being too infantine; for a lurking smile, like that upon a cherub's face, was ever ready to burst into a laugh of ringing melody—her fair countenance was ever ready:

"Like a sweet lake which the breeze is upon,
To break into dimples, and laugh in the sun."

But now, as she stood upon the threshold of that well-remembered room in which she had passed so many happy hours, it seemed as if the hand of time had gently touched the varied beauties of the young girl, but in all its stern reality swept across her mind, leaving behind it the trace of its presence in the expression of deep thought and contemplative sadness which sat upon her marble brow.

She held her hands tightly pressed upon her heart as she entered the room, and declining Varley's offer of a chair, she said in a tone of forced and painful calmness:

"I understand you have something to say to me. I am here, Bernard Varley."

"Lamenting, as I do," commenced Varley, "the most painful events——"

"Hush," said Miranda. "Leave me to lament. All sorrow must sink beside mine. The mockery of woe is—horrible."

"Mockery, Miranda!"

"Sir?"

Miranda drew her slight figure up proudly as she added:

"When you address me, sir, I am Miss Rankley!"

"So proud!" muttered Varley. "We shall see." Then he said aloud:

"With all due deference to Miss Rankley, I have something to communicate to her which may so far alter our respective situations as to make it not so stupendous an act of assurance for me to address her by her Christian name."

"Perhaps, sir, you still consider yourself a welcome guest here," said Miranda, "if ever you were really one."

"A welcome guest?"

"Ay, sir, a guest. I am waiting to know what Mr. Varley may have to say to me in my house before he leaves it, never again to cross its threshold."

Varley looked astonished at the tone and manner of the young girl, whom he had ever looked upon as a child in simplicity, and from whom he never could have expected, in his wildest dreams, any such exhibition of moral courage. The spectacle, however, added fuel to the unholy passion which was consuming him, and as he regarded her now in all her beauty—all her pride of virtue, loathing him and treating him with a bitterness of lofty contempt and horror, such as he might well quail before—his love for her became the master passion of his soul, and in the depths of his black heart he swore an oath terrible in its denunciations, that she should be his, or he would perish body and soul.

He spoke to her in a low tone of suppressed passion, and his words seemed to sink like liquid fire into her brain.

"'Tis well, Miranda," he said, "for those who have power to use it. 'Tis well for the haughty to make much of their pride—'tis well for the great and the rich to command; but 'tis better far before they assume so much, to be quite certain that their power rests on a more solid foundation than their own empty surmises."

"Surmises?"

"Yes. Do you understand me?"

"I am no reader of riddles," said Miranda. "I have, perhaps, foolishly and unadvisedly accorded you an interview. Say on, sir, and say explicitly, what you have to communicate."

"I will be most explicit. I am no guest here."

"No guest? True--true. I understand you. You are, indeed, no guest, Bernard Varley. He who, from some cause I know not of, was compelled to tolerate your presence, is now past your malice—he is now gone. Bernard Varley, leave this house."

"Indeed!"

"Ay, sir. Your presence is a contamination—an insult to the dead."

"What if I refuse?"

"You dare not."

"I dare."

"Then the servants shall force you from the door. Let the first act—oh, Heaven!—of my sad possession of this once happy home be to free it from the insidious monster who has banished peace from its fireside, and brought death and despair across its threshold."

"Hold!" cried Varley, as Miranda moved towards the door.

"Wherefore should I pause?"

"For his sake who lies above in the cold embrace of death."

Miranda shuddered.

"For his sake," continued Varley, "who now inhabits the cell of a felon."

Miranda clasped her hands and uttered the name of Rowland Percy.

"For your own sake," added Varley, "dependent as you are upon me."

"Upon you?"

"Yes."

"I? The daughter of as good and kind a father as ever drew the breath of life dependent upon you, Bernard Varley?"

"'Tis even so. You state the case most fairly."

Miranda for a moment felt as if her senses would desert her, and she sank into a chair.

CHAPTER IX.

THE INTERVIEW—THE PROPOSAL.

VARLEY gazed upon his victim with gloating eyes, and then in a low tone, which he adopted rather as an excuse for bending his head towards her, until his lips almost touched her cheek, than for any other reason, he said:

"Miranda, I am master here."

"No, no!" cried Miranda, starting to her feet; "this is some horrible delusion; such things cannot be. Bernard Varley, I was once a weak, irresolute girl, but that time has passed away, and now I have the courage and the strength to act."

"Act as far as you have power."

"I have power in my own house—my father's house, now mine. I have power, and

I will use it to drive you hence: you, who from the bottom of my heart I believe to be the cause of all the misery which has fallen, like a bolt from Heaven, upon so many persons. Once more I say, Bernard Varley, no longer pollute this once happy home with your presence."

"Pause yet a moment, beautiful Miranda; more beautiful to me in your wrath, when the fire of indignation is flashing from your eyes, than in your more melting moments. Hear me, and I swear, by whatever you may deem most sacred, that I have power, which you will do well to mollify and not defy."

"You, power?"

"Ay, power over you."

"Over me?"

"And Rowland Percy—ay, even the dead have I power over, for they leave behind them as their most imperishable legacy, their reputation. Miranda, one word from me would brand your father's memory with infamy."

"No, no, no—oh, Heaven! no."

"That one word shall never pass my lips while Miranda is willing to keep them sealed."

Miranda dropped her head upon the table and wept, while Varley proceeded.

"I can save Rowland Percy from an ignominious death, or I can, by evidence it is easy to produce, conduct him to the scaffold."

"You know he is innocent?"

"The admission costs me nothing," said Varley. "Agreed, he is innocent, and yet shall he suffer, if I, Bernard Varley, say he shall."

"Monster!"

"Nay, that is not all. By a will which your father has left behind him, properly signed and witnessed, all his wealth is left to me; the Grange, the estate, all."

"Impossible!"

"'Tis true; in trust—in trust, mark me, for you, always provided, you wed—me."

"You!" shrieked Miranda, springing from her seat, and holding her hands extended before her, as if to keep off some loathsome object. "You, Bernard Varley?"

"Even so; I love you."

"You love—love me? Impossible. It is not true. A more unfounded, base fabrication could not be. It is absurd. My father make such a will? No, no. He could not—he did not. Bernard Varley, still I defy you!"

"You do?"

"As I reverence Heaven, I abhor you."

"Beware, Miranda! I will paint you two pictures—pictures of the imagination, if you please. You shall examine both minutely, and then make your choice."

"I will not hear you."

"But you shall."

"Shall?"

"That was my word."

Miranda flew to the bell, but Varley caught her wrist, and, in a hissing whisper, said:

"To the first person who enters this room, in answer to your summons, I proclaim your father a felon, and brand his memory with a stigma of guilt which never can be effaced. Tempt me not, Miranda, for I can raise a cry against even the cold remains of your father that shall reach your heart, although it may pass over his."

Miranda released her hold of the bell-rope, as she gasped:

"What—what crime?"

"Forgery," said Varley. "Your father made his fortune by forging cheques on the bank he was himself a partner in, and others."

"No, no; he did not."

"I have proof."

"His sense of honour—his integrity."

"Ha! ha! ha! His sense of honour; I tell you I have proof, Miranda. You know now my power. Use or abuse your knowledge as you may."

"Still do I defy you."

"You do?"

"I do. The innocent will not fall, though the guilty be powerful."

"Look on this document," said Varley, drawing a small packet from his pocket. "Do you recognize that name?"

He turned down a corner of the paper, and Miranda saw her father's signature.

"This document," continued Varley, "invests me with full power over you, and all that belongs to you. If you wed not with me, or with my consent, you become a beggar; your inheritance becomes mine, and I turn you out into the world to starve."

"Then," said Miranda, clasping her hands, "if this be true, I commend myself to Heaven, and if it be its will that I should starve, that I should lie me down and die of famine in some lonely spot, let Heaven's will be done."

"Reflect, Miranda. In wedding me, you wed wealth. You remain mistress of your ancient home; your wildest caprices shall all be indulged. I swear, by Heaven!"

"Hold! hold! Take not the name of Heaven in vain for the most unholy purposes. You and your offers I alike despise and abhor. I will see closely to your right to exercise the power you talk of, and if it really be that my poor father was compelled to make you the depository of all that was his, and to attach to my very means of existence so terrible a condition, I shall lament the more for him, not love his memory less."

"You have no relations?"

"None."

"No friends?"

"Save Heaven."

"Pshaw! Bethink you what you lose—station, wealth, luxury!"

"Peace! peace! nor profane my ears with such base reasoning. I will leave you, if I must, to the quiet possession of what you have wrung from him who is now no more. Welcome poverty, welcome woe, want, death, in preference to breathing the same air with Bernard Varley, the murderer!'

"Murderer?"

"Yes, murderer! Bernard Varley, you know well that to accomplish your own dark and evil purposes you have contrived all the misery which now afflicts my throbbing brain."

"Miranda, you rave. From anyone but you such language would excite my warmest indignation. You rave, girl; you rave!"

"No, Bernard Varley, 'tis you who rave, when you fancy that the intricate path of guilt you have chosen will lead into aught but destruction. Heaven is not so unmindful of its creatures as to leave them at the mercy of the machinations of such men as you. Tremble, for a day will surely come when all your fine-drawn schemes will be overwhelmed in one common ruin. Oh, madman! madman! to fancy that treachery, deceit, and crime would bring you other results than despair and death! You rave, Bernard Varley —you rave!"

"Peace, I say," cried Varley. "Shall I be bearded here, where I alone have power? Girl, your wits desert you when you dare; but—but—no matter, let it pass; your wondrous beauty is excuse for much: your voice, even in anger, is sweet music. Miranda, I love you with a love as exceeding the cold passion, called by such a name, as do the mighty Alps a gentle bank of earth. I love you with a fierce, undying love that, in its intensity, absorbs all other feelings. Where, oh, where can you find one who will, as I do, prefer you even to Heaven?"

"Such love," said Miranda, shuddering, "is a wild and unholy passion. Bernard Varley, I almost doubt if you be human. You have, in this brief interview, revealed enough to make its mere recital on my part most dangerous to you."

"Indeed. Add to it, then, that Bernard Varley showed you this, which he picked up on the floor by the bedside of your father."

As he spoke, he produced a small set of ivory tablets, which Miranda had often seen in the possession of Rowland Percy.

"This conclusive evidence, coupled with other facts, will seal the fate of Rowland Percy," said Varley. "You alone can save him."

"Monster!"

"Call me what you will; but save your father's memory from shame, Rowland Percy from death on a public scaffold, yourself from a depth of poverty you cannot understand, and all those dependent upon you from deep woe, by giving me your hand."

"Never!"

"You have made your election?"

"I have. I swear——"

"Hold! you may repent your oath."

"There needs no oath," said Miranda.

"And yet I make one that you shall be my wife."

Miranda walked to the door.

"Bethink you well of how you act," said Varley, following her. "You stand upon a precipice, down which you may rashly precipitate yourself, or you may step back in time."

"You are far down the slippery descent," said Miranda; "there is no stepping back for you."

"I wish not. My blood dances through my veins like tongues of flame! My love for you is——"

"Peace! peace!"

"Nay, hear me!"

He rushed between her and the door.

"Beautiful being!" he cried; "beautiful in your pride, beautiful in your hate! I would barter kingdoms for one kind look, for one smile. I would give a hundred lives such as Rowland Percy's for one kiss!"

Miranda flew to the bell, and rang it violently.

Varley withdrew from the door, and, with a bitter smile, said:

"Pass out, heiress of the Grange, you are but as a bird held by a brace; you are in my power, go where you will. I am your good or evil genius, as you make me."

CHAPTER X.

THE RIDE TO YORK—A MEETING WITH THE SQUIRE OF LARKSWOOD—THE ATTEMPTED EXPLANATION—A DAUGHTER'S LOVE.

WHEN Miranda left Varley, she proceeded immediately to her own room, and, sinking into a chair, she burst into such a paroxysm of weeping, that the young girl who attended her was alarmed. She threw herself at the feet of her young mistress, crying:

"Oh, Miss Miranda, do pray leave off crying so. It's dreadful to hear you, it is, indeed. You will break my heart; you that was always so light-hearted, and so happy, that you made everybody happy around you——"

"Hush, hush!" said Miranda, dashing the tears from her eyes; "I am better now, and I hope this is the last time I shall give way to such weakness. I am much better now."

"Oh, miss, you don't know how much pleasure it gives me to hear you say so."

Miranda rose, and dashed cold water plentifully on her face to destroy the tears. Then, turning to the girl, said:

"I know not what may happen in the next few days; but believe nothing, heed nothing, that you hear from that dreadful man."

"Mr. Varley, miss?"

"Yes, Bernard Varley; he is a fiend in human shape. Let him say what he will—swear what he will, always do you, and all the servants in the house, remember that Rowland Percy is innocent. He would not have harmed a hair of my poor father's head; Heaven knows he is innocent."

"Yes, miss. I'm quite sure such a nice young man as Mr. Rowland Percy could not be guilty."

"He is innocent," repeated Miranda.

"Oh, miss! don't you take on so," said the girl. "If I could only see you a little calmer, and more patient-like."

"I am calm and patient," said Miranda.

"But your hands are so cold."

"My heart is cold, too, now; but I shall soon be much better. I am quite calm. Surely you and all will believe me to be calm when I can speak of—of my father, whom I loved next to Heaven."

"Oh! don't speak of poor, dear master, miss."

"Yes. I am calm enough, now. My father has been murdered. He who loved me—Rowland Percy—is accused of the awful crime. That is all I have to contend against now. My heart is nearly turned to stone, and I am very calm. Duty must henceforward take the place of feeling. I must see the innocent righted."

She sat down, and held her head with her hands for some moments, and then she said:

"I sent someone to York."

"For a lawyer, miss?"

"Yes, yes; I recollect now. Has he come?"

"No, miss."

"Then, let my horse be got ready. I must be in York within the hour. This is a time for personal action."

"What! your dear little 'Jessie,' miss, that——"

"Hush—hush! I mean 'Jessie,' of course. You know it was a gift from my father on—on my birthday. The patient, gentle creature will speed me on my journey. Give orders to have it ready as soon as possible. Quick—quick; and get together what things are mine by gift of my father in these rooms. Collect them all together; for, as Heaven is my judge, I know not but the very doors of my father's house may, by some machination of that man, be closed against me soon."

"Lor', miss! Why, old Matthew, the steward, was but half-an-hour ago a-telling of all the servants as you, and you only now, was missus and master of the old Grange."

"It may be so, or it may not," said Miranda, with a shudder. "But go—go at once, and do as I bid you. I must go to York."

"But, miss, don't you think as it won't look quite well for—for——"

"For what?"

"For you to be riding to York so very soon?"

"I understand you. You mean so soon after my father's death. No. It looks far from well. But there are duties that defy the world's opinion, and which, in their performance, must throw us for succour alone upon our consciences and the judgment of Heaven. All forms—all ceremonies—must give place to what I have to do."

"Lor', miss, you quite frighten me."

"Go—go. Delay no longer. Go!"

The girl left her, and Miranda stood by the table, pale as a marble statue.

"I have to rescue Rowland Percy," she said, in a faint tone. "Yes—I have to rescue Rowland Percy, and if the faith of a heart that knows but venial errors can nerve the mind to such exertions as may be necessary for that object, I will do it, and he shall be saved. Oh, what a tangled web of villainy has not Bernard Varley woven? How can I—how can Rowland escape its meshes? Yet, surely there may—there must be men accustomed to all kinds of guile, who will, with their clear judgments, see a clue to the plot which baffles my judgment. My trust is in Heaven—it will not desert the right. If my poor father be murdered, as I fear must prove too true, then Bernard Varley is the murderer, and seeks to screen himself by bringing the innocent Rowland to a scaffold."

A shudder passed over Miranda's frame as she pronounced the horrible word scaffold, and, in her mind's eye, she saw the throng crowding around to witness the awful preparations for the ignominious death of the noble, the gifted, and the innocent Rowland Percy.

"Oh, Heaven, preserve my senses," she exclaimed, as, with clasped hands, she dropped upon her knees, and tried to pray.

The door gently opened, and the tearful voice of the girl said:

"Please, miss, Mr. Varley says, as no horse shall leave the stables."

Miranda sprang to her feet, and a flash of resentment came from her eyes as she cried:

"Bernard Varley says so?"

"Yes, miss."

"How dare—but no, I will be calm. My riding-habit, girl—quick—my hat—my hat—there, that will do—now—now I am ready—we shall see if Bernard Varley can prevent me in my father's house from using that which is mine own. Oh! this is most surpassing insolence, and yet, I thank Heaven it is so, for, were I left to no feeling but grief—were all around me kind, and mild, and dutiful, I think I could lie down and die; but there is a slumbering spirit of resistance to insult and oppression in my heart, that a touch, a whisper, will awaken into life and energy. I will have my horse; I will ride to York within this hour."

The girl looked at Miranda terrified, for her small, beautiful figure seemed to dilate into dignity as she spoke, and the eloquent blood mantled in her cheeks, as it was wont to do in happier days.

"My horse, my horse," she added, and walked with a firm step from the room, followed by the trembling girl, who could not understand the feelings of her young mistress, and thought she must be going mad.

Without a tremor now that her gentle spirit was fairly roused, Miranda descended the marble staircase of the ancient mansion, and reached the hall without meeting with anyone. Then she entered a small room which was used as a waiting-room for strangers, and rang the bell therein.

The summons was answered by an old gray-headed domestic, who started with surprise when he saw Miranda attired for riding.

"Matthew," she said, calmly, "I want my little nag, 'Jessie,' directly."

"Ye—yes—yes—Miss Miranda; I'll go and see."

"Go and see, Matthew."

"Why, miss, there's Master Varley has been to the stables and locked 'em up."

"Indeed!"

"Yes, miss, and he swears you shan't have no horse nohow to-day, miss."

"We shall see, Matthew; it is time the servants should know who is to command here, and who is to obey—come with me."

Miranda walked from the room, followed by the old man, and, crossing the hall, she descended a flight of steps, which terminated near a door leading to the stables. Passing onwards, she paused not until she came to the stabling, when she turned to Matthew and said:

"Summon hither all the servants."

"All, miss?"

"Yes—without exception."

"This will do it, miss," said the old man, and he took hold of a rope which communicated with an alarm-bell, and gave it so lusty a pull, that the whole place echoed again with the deep sonorous sounds.

In a moment servants came running from all directions, and the old man, with a smile of self-complacency, said:

"That will do, I think, Miss Miranda."

When the throng of servants saw their young mistress, they fell back to a respectful distance, but Miranda beckoned to them to approach, and said, in her usual voice:

"I want my nag, 'Jessie.'"

There was a pause of a moment, and then a groom stepped forward, and said:

"Please, miss—that—that—I beg your pardon, miss, but Master Varley has locked the stable, and had the—the—hem—impudence to take away the key."

There was a dead silence for the space of nearly a minute, then Miranda spoke:

"My father," she said, "is now no more. I am his only child."

"And, in course, our young missus," said the groom, with a triumphant look at his fellow servants, who all nodded their approbation.

"How many of you are there?" said Miranda; "men, I mean."

"There's eleven of us, Miss Miranda," said Matthew.

"Eleven men-servants have I?"

"Yes, miss—yes," cried several voices.

"And one man keeps the key of my stable and detains my horse!"

The groom began slowly turning up his cuffs, and when he had accomplished that process, he turned to Miranda, and said:

"Please, missus, I'm going to get the key."

"Do so," said Miranda.

"What is the meaning of all this?" cried Varley, suddenly appearing from behind the throng. "How dare you all congregate here, you lazy hounds? Back to your several occupations this moment!"

"I want the key of my stable," said Miranda, to the groom, and not even looking at Varley.

"And you shall have it too, miss," said the sturdy fellow, as he stepped up to Varley, and shouted in far from a courteous tone:

"The key!"

"Scoundrel!" cried Varley.

"Vagabond!" said the groom; "I wants the key!"

Varley turned as white as a sheet, and, stepping back a pace, cried:

"Here, all you gaping there, turn this fellow off the premises."

No one moved, and the groom said:

"I ain't a-going. Give us the key!"

"You are drunk, sir," cried Varley. "I am master of this house, and I will be obeyed."

The groom looked at Miranda, who, still pursuing the same calmness of demeanour, said:

"I want the key of my stables."

He then seized Varley by the cravat, and held him in a grasp of iron, as he said:

"It'll save you trouble, and me, too, now, if you gives up the key."

Varley thrust his right arm into his breast, and drew a pistol; but the groom was too quick for him, and, with his disengaged hand, he snatched the weapon from him, and threw it singing through the air to a considerable distance over a wall.

"You cowardly vagabond!" he cried. "So you can't fight like a man, eh?"

Varley now put forth all his strength in an endeavour to shake off his antagonist; but the other stood the tussle as firmly as a rock, and, when Varley relaxed his exertions, the groom said:

"Now it's my turn," and immediately threw him on his back, with a heaviness that quite confused his faculties for a few moments, during which the key was taken from his coat-pocket.

CHAPTER XI.

THE PUMPING — THE RIDE TO YORK — MIRANDA'S REFLECTIONS — LOVE IN A COTTAGE.

A GENERAL hurrah from the assembled servants proclaimed their joy at the defeat of Varley, who was detested by the whole establishment; but Miranda held up her hand, and said:

"Peace! peace! Remember this is the house of mourning now. Saddle me my horse, I must ride to York. I will be back early. But, before I go, remember, all of you, that Rowland Percy is innocent."

By the time Miranda's little palfrey was ready, and she had been assisted to mount, Varley had risen to his feet. He was perfectly livid from passion, and, with clenched hands, he stamped on the earth, crying:

"You shall all repent of this. Miranda Rankley, as surely as the sun will rise to-morrow you shall most bitterly repent! I will have a vengeance against you more terrible than you are aware of. You have raised a spirit of evil you will in vain attempt to quell again! And you, you base hinds, I will have every one of you in York Castle for an assault."

"Friends!" said Miranda, as she turned her horse's head in the direction of the gate, which several of the servants had opened for her, "I leave you to accept of what insolence your English notions may enable you to put up with from this man."

"We won't put up with nothing," cried one.

The groom, who had gained such a victory over Varley, now appeared at the stable-door, leading a horse ready for mounting.

"How dare you bring that horse out?" shrieked Varley. "Take it back, sir."

"I'm a-going to ride arter my missus, if you please, sir, and has no objection," said the groom, with mock civility, as he sprang into the saddle.

"Will none of you side with me?" cried Varley. "Five pounds to the man who pulls yon scoundrel off his horse."

"It's dangerous work," said the groom; "for I bite, and the horse kicks. Perhaps you'd like to try to earn so much yourself."

The groom then commenced backing his steed towards Varley, who turned and ran towards the house, to the great amusement of all the domestics.

"Oh, you won't," said the groom. "Very good; and now, my boys, it's my opinion as our young missus don't, by any means, want Mr. Varley to stay to dinner. Good-bye to you."

He then galloped after Miranda, who, by this time, had got some distance from the house.

The servants looked at each other in some degree of doubt. They evidently wanted a leader now that the groom was gone, and it is doubtful whether Bernard Varley would have fallen into the mishap that soon befell him, had he not himself committed an act that at once aroused a spirit of indignation against him, among even the most irresolute of the servants.

It was this: the young girl who attended upon Miranda attempted to pass him in the doorway, whither he had flown for shelter from the heels of the groom's horse. She just touched his elbow accidentally, when he turned, and, boiling with rage against everybody, struck her a severe blow.

The girl screamed, and at once half-a-dozen of the men-servants rushed forward and secured Varley before he could take refuge in the house, which he attempted to do, for he saw at a glance his danger.

He was dragged into the stable-yard, and then there was a pause for an instant, to know what to do with him, when a stable-boy, who had received at different times several hard knocks from Varley's riding-whip, for not being quick enough in saddling a horse for him when he required one, called out:

"Pump on him."

The suggestion was adopted in a moment; and, amid a universal shout of "To the pump! to the pump!" Bernard Varley was dragged across the stable-yard towards an antique pump, that had stood there for a hundred years or more.

For a moment or two he seemed paralyzed

by the turn affairs had taken, and scarcely made any resistance. Then, however, he commenced kicking and fighting with desperation, but all was in vain: his enemies were too numerous, and four of the stoutest among them carried him along easily by his arms and legs, notwithstanding all his exertions.

"You'll all be hung!" he shouted. "You dare not—you cowards—villains! I'll ruin you all; you shall suffer for this the longest day you have to live."

They now reached the pump, and the malicious stable-boy planted himself at the handle, saying, in a voice of great exultation:

"I know how to work the old pump better than anybody. Pop him under, and shan't he have it—oh, no, not at all!"

"A hundred pounds among you to let me go!" screamed Varley, as they worked the pump. "You don't mean it—you can't mean it—I'll forgive you all up to now."

His assailants were inexorable, and he was held under the spout of the pump in such a position that the first deluge of the cold water came full upon his face, and well did the stable-boy redeem his pledge of making the ancient pump work well, for there came from the old-fashioned lion's head, that formed the spout, such a stream of cold water that, for a moment, Bernard Varley was nearly suffocated, and could neither speak nor move, being just turned about at the pleasure of his tormentors.

There was scarcely a servant in the establishment who had not some grudge to pay off against Bernard Varley, who had, since his residence at the Grange, been conspicuous for his petty tyranny: so that it was fully five minutes before he was removed from under the spout of the pump, and set upon his feet, completely saturated with water, and as cold and miserable as he could possibly be.

"Now, be off with you," cried one, "while you have a whole skin."

Varley looked around him, from one to the other, but he said not a word. His passion lay too deep for expression. Revenge engrossed all his faculties, and he had now but one immediate object, which was to reach York and procure warrants against the various servants who had treated him so roughly.

There was, however, one difficulty which came across his mind; and that was, he did not know some of their names. He turned round as he walked towards the gate; and in a voice thick with rage, he said:

"Who will come with me to York to earn fifty pounds, and be made steward of the Grange within a week?"

A general laugh was his only answer; and shaking his clenched hand in the air, he dashed out at the gate, in the direction of the city.

In the meantime, Miranda had gone on her journey at a smart canter, after waiting a moment to allow the groom to overtake her, whom she would not send back, although she had contemplated riding alone.

The road wound through a richly-cultivated country; but Miranda's thoughts were too much concentrated on the perils, and dangers, and treacheries that surrounded her, to know a smiling corn-field from the most desolate waste.

The course she meant to adopt, and it was certainly the most rational one she could think of, was to proceed at once to a solicitor in York, whom she knew had been employed occasionally by her father, and whose name she knew, although not his address.

Before him she meant to lay the whole circumstances, without reservation, and beseech him to take up her cause against the villain who was endeavouring not only to possess himself of all that she had been taught to consider her own, but to destroy the only being now in existence to whom her young heart yearned with affection.

As she rode along the beautifully-diversified road, she strove to recollect and arrange all that had passed within the eventful four-and-twenty hours, which had not only made her an orphan, but produced more extraordinary circumstances than would be crowded probably in the whole space of her future existence.

More particularly did Miranda strive to call to mind every word uttered by Bernard Varley in his interview with her of that morning, and she found, when she came to consider all that had passed, so much to engender suspicion against Varley, and so little against Rowland Percy, that her heart felt lighter, and she thought that the right would triumph.

But Miranda little knew the desperate subtlety of the man she had to deal with: nor was she so well aware as he was of the peculiar laws of legal evidence which made her conversation with him of but little avail without other corroborative evidence tending to prove the truth of his own partial admissions.

"Rowland must be free!" she cried; "and even if this man, this dreadful Varley, should succeed in retaining possession of the dear home to which I am so much attached, surely we can be happy elsewhere, however humbly. We need no wealth to make us happy. The humblest roof will shelter us as well as the stately Grange. He may wrest from us all but our innocence, our integrity, and our love. Those are dear possessions bestowed by Heaven, and no mortal power can tear them from fond, trusting hearts."

Comforted by these thoughts, Miranda urged her steed to quicker progress, and entered a narrow lane which ran along for some distance by the roadside, and then left it abruptly, cutting off a considerable part of the distance between the Grange and the city of York.

The lane was enveloped in deep shadow, for the tall trees on either side of it were amply sufficient to hide even a noontide sun from the narrow bridle-path which wound among them.

The delicious odours of a thousand wild

flowers here greeted Miranda, and when she reached the middle of the lane, she involuntarily allowed her steed to relapse into a gentle walk, and to nibble some of the soft, rich green herbage from the sloping banks.

It was a scene such as would have delighted the soul of any painter fond of shadow and deep masses of colouring. Miranda gazed round her with pleasure—the first pleasure that had dawned upon her mind since the calamitous events had occurred which had given rise to her present journey.

The groom was some distance in the rear, and Miranda was little dreaming that anyone was near her, when, from a gap in the hedge, there suddenly came forth a man who, at the first glance, Miranda knew to be Mr. Percy, the Squire of Larkswood.

She reined in her steed on the instant; and the Squire, shading his eyes with his hand, looked in her beautiful face before he spoke. Then, in a voice of deep emotion, he said:

"Miranda, friends we cannot be; but are we enemies?"

"Enemies, sir?" said Miranda. "Heaven knows I am no man's enemy; but——"

"But what? You hesitate."

"I do; for there is a circumstance too painful for me to refer to further, which must make us strangers, Mr. Percy."

"There is, Miranda," said the Squire, with a deep sigh. "A circumstance that will embitter the remainder of my existence. Oh, Miranda! to you I have to explain how and why it was I came to lift my hand against your father."

"Hold, sir," said Miranda. "I wish to hear no more. The deed was done. Let me know nothing of what led to it. It is done, and the cause is with Heaven."

"But you know your father was my friend."

"Did you know it when you met him in deadly strife? Oh, Mr. Percy, you have made hearts bleed with anguish by that one act, which would have resisted, with a stern command of feeling, misery from any other hand. Say no more, sir. There is an insuperable bar between even our acquaintance."

"But hear me, Miranda."

"What needs it that I should be told by you that the dread of the world's opinion made you risk your own and attempt my father's life? Mr. Percy, had an angel from Heaven come to tell me that from your hand would have come such a blow, I should have thought I dreamed."

"I have sought you, Miranda," said Mr. Percy, laying a trembling hand upon her bridle. "I have sought you to say some words which now stick in my throat."

"Say them briefly, sir."

"They are brief. But—but—you do not look at me, Miranda."

"I cannot, sir. The well-remembered face of a friend looks so different when estranged by the infliction of an act which I, as well as you, must ever dread to think of, that I cannot look upon you."

———

CHAPTER XII.

THE EXPLANATION—THE PROMISE—MIRANDA'S GRIEFS INCREASE—THE FATHER'S ANGUISH.

THERE was a pause of some moments, and Mr. Percy turned away his head. Miranda thought he was weeping, and her heart smote her for the apparent harshness of what she had said to him. Her gentle nature could not brook the idea of inflicting pain on anyone, and it was with a softened tone and manner that she said:

"Mr. Percy, I am bound to York upon an errand that concerns you as nearly as it does me. Time may be precious. Will you say now to me what you have to say, and let me go on my way?"

He turned his face towards her. It was deathly pale; and then, in a voice of deep emotion, he added:

"Miranda, you do not, you cannot know what forced this fatal quarrel on me. An insult past all bearing."

"Hold, Mr. Percy, I cannot listen to such a mode of justification. As Heaven is my judge, I do believe my father was incapable of wantonly insulting anyone, and much less you, of all living men. Oh, sir, you have stood before him with a weapon aimed at his life, and I have heard him speak of you in terms of brotherly love; he valued you next to the one being who now speaks to you, the only one who can claim his name, and yet——"

"Yet I fought a duel with him, Miranda."

"You did, and——"

"Hear me once more; and, oh! suspend your judgment for awhile, while I disclose to you the causes that led to this most fatal, awful encounter. Miranda, you see before you a ruined man. My fortune has long been tottering, and now it has fallen never again to rise."

"Ruined, Mr. Percy?"

"Yes; I am a beggar. I have scarcely a home now in which to lie my weary frame. The once wealthy Squire of Larkswood is, I repeat, a ruined man."

"Much, sir, as I grieve at misfortune," said Miranda, "I cannot see that that was cause to make you my father's enemy."

"It was remotely so, Miranda, as you shall hear. For more than twelve months now has ruin, most absolute and irretrievable, been hanging over me. The fact was known but to myself and one other, far, very far from hence, as I thought, but by some means it must have come to your father's knowledge."

"You are mistaken, Mr. Percy; on my life he knew it not."

"I have evidence, Miranda. My dear son, Rowland, was actually forbidden the Grange."

"But not on such grounds. Setting aside, sir, all false delicacy, and the natural dislike I have to converse on such a theme, I aver that the recommendation—for it was, at first, no more—of my father to Rowland not to visit at the Grange arose from a prudent doubt of the stability of the affection of one so young, and of such little knowledge of the great world."

Mr. Percy shook his head.

"Nay, on my soul's best hopes," said Miranda, "it was so. Rowland then reasoned intemperately; my father became angry, and they did part in one of those quarrels which compromise neither party, but which may, with mutual honour, be made up again."

"Miranda," said Mr. Percy, "will you read this letter?"

He handed her a note as he spoke, and, after a moment's hesitation, Miranda took it, and looking at the superscription, saw it was addressed to Mr. Percy.

"Read that," he said, "and then judge of my wounded feelings."

Miranda opened it, and then read as follows:

"Sir,—I am desired by Sir George Rankley to express to you his indignation at your presuming to allow your son to visit at the Grange, when you must know that both of you are on the verge of ruin. Your unsuccessful speculations are known to Sir George, and he desires me to say that he drops all communication with one who maintains, or endeavours to maintain, an appearance in the county so much at variance with his real means.

"I am, Sir, yours, etc.,
"Bernard Varley."

"Is not that proof?" said Mr. Percy, when he saw that Miranda had finished the epistle.

"No," cried Miranda, boldly.

The Squire looked astonished at her prompt negative, and then added:

"It is as strong proof as man can well conceive."

"This letter was never dictated by my father," said Miranda. "Oh, Mr. Percy! you have allowed yourself to be made the tool of a man so base, so crafty, that I sometimes doubt if he be really human."

Mr. Percy drew his breath hard, as he said:

"Have you proof of what you say?"

"I have belief."

"But you may be mistaken; you must be. Oh, Miranda, well I know that poverty perverts the understanding more than riches. It makes us see slights which, not otherwise suspecting, would pass us like the idle wind. It makes us fancy disrespect where none is meant; but here is surely proof that I have been led away by no absurd fancy. I was despised because I was poor, and my boy's trusting, honest heart was thought no longer worthy of meeting with the heiress of the Grange, because his father was unfortunate. Is not that the true reading?"

"No," said Miranda, "no; you are wrong, Mr. Percy, and, like myself, you are enveloped in a mist of circumstances most strangely contradictory, created by the villain, Bernard Varley. Time may explain what now to me is manifest as a whole, but obscure in its details. That letter never received the sanction of my father."

"You think it Varley's own act?"

"I do."

"No—no! It cannot be! Miranda, I answered this letter. Mildly and temperately I answered it, for I knew that my poor boy's happiness was at stake, and I suppressed my feelings. I admitted the distress of my circumstances; but I pleaded that, although I had lost all else, I had preserved my honour, and could leave my son an unsullied name."

"What followed then?" said Miranda, with much emotion.

"I received another note. It is here; and then a third. Read them."

Miranda, with a beating heart, and with eyes swimming with tears, took the two notes. The first one ran thus:

"Sir,—Your contemptible conduct, in endeavouring to bolster up your own fallen fortunes by a union between Miss Rankley and your son, has induced Sir George to command me to inform you that he will expose your conduct on every opportunity, and bring down upon you the well-merited disgrace which he will take care to see heaped upon your head. Sir George would, did he not deem it quite derogatory to his character to meet you, insist upon satisfaction in the field for your vile conduct; but he trusts you will spare him the necessity of adopting some means of chastizing your insolence, by instantly forwarding to me, for him, a humble apology.

"I am, Sir,
"By order of Sir George Rankley,
"Yours, etc.,
"Bernard Varley."

Miranda made no remark, but opened the other epistle. It contained only these words:

"Sir,—I am desired by Sir George Rankley to request you will name a friend for the purpose of arranging a hostile meeting.
"I am, Sir, yours, etc.,
"Bernard Varley."

The last epistle dropped from Miranda's hands, and she looked on the pale, suffering countenance of Mr. Percy with inexpressible anguish, as she said:

"And during all this correspondence you never saw my father?"

"Never!"

"Oh, Heaven!"

She resigned the bridle of her horse, and had not Mr. Percy supported her, she must have fallen to the earth.

"Speak, Miranda—speak!" he said. "For the love of mercy, speak! You hint at some frightful mystery; your words freeze my very heart. Tell me, though the news blast me, that I have been duped—deceived!"

"You have—you have!" gasped Miranda. "A light gleams through my brain. I begin to see the fiendish plot that has been laid for the destruction of us all. My father murdered —you deceived, and a store of remorse laid up that must last even unto the grave's brink. My poor, poor, devoted Rowland, innocent, yet accused of what may take his life, and I desolate—oh, Heaven! most desolate!"

Miranda burst into such a passion of hysterical weeping, that Mr. Percy was fain to help her from the horse, and seat her upon the verdant bank, where, for some moments, her deep grief knew no remission.

She felt that Bernard Varley had done all that she had enumerated, and while she sickened at the extent of his wickedness, she trembled for the future, when she thought of the success which had so far attended his frightful machinations.

CHAPTER XIII.

THE RECONCILIATION—THE ARREST—THE DESOLATION OF MIRANDA.

Mr. Percy himself was deeply affected by the inconsolable grief of Miranda, and he exclaimed :

"Oh, Heaven! what have we all done that we should be visited by such calamities?"

"Oh, how could you believe," sobbed Miranda, "that those letters came from my father? They are the fabrications of Varley. 'Tis he, and he only, who has caused all this dreadful suffering. Mr. Percy—you—you should have seen my father."

Mr. Percy clasped his hands, as he said :

"Reproach me, Miranda, as you will, I am a broken-hearted man."

"Forgive me," said Miranda ; "forgive me, sir, I knew not what I said. You have been, as doubtless was my poor father himself, the dupe of a villain's arts. I do not blame you. Forgive my heedless words."

She held out her hand to him, and he took it between his, as he replied :

"Miranda, you can never look upon me with friendly eyes. It is scarcely in human nature that you should, and I will not vex you by my presence or company. I have but one hope on earth now, and that is, that my poor innocent boy, Rowland, should be spared to me, and that you will forget his father, and still be happy with him, poor as he is, for he, at least, is in no way connected with these most melancholy occurrences. He was far away, and his return was as unexpected by me as by anyone else. Forget me, Miranda, and I will live the remainder of the life that Heaven spares me, in some solitude away from you."

"No, no," said Miranda, through her tears, "Heaven judges motives, not acts. Let me, with my weak human wisdom, do so likewise. The world may look strangely on me, and point the finger of scorn at me for clinging to you ; but as I have hopes of joy hereafter, I do believe that you have been the victim of the same plot that has made us all so unhappy. Together we will endeavour to effect the liberation of Rowland, and be you, Mr. Percy, my second father."

"Can you think and act thus generously?"

"Call it not by such a name. It is no more than simple justice."

"And yet, Miranda, dear to my heart as is your generous confidence, I should be base, indeed, to take advantage of it. You shall not hear one cold remark—be subjected to one cold look for companionship with me. Had I the means of offering you all that I could once have offered, I might hesitate ; but go, heiress of the Grange, and its wide possessions—shun the poor as you would shun mortal contagion. For your words of peace to me, accept the heartfelt thanks of one who not long will linger behind your father ; and should we meet in that blessed abode where sorrow never comes, and there be such feelings, grown purer with their Heavenly intercourse, as on this earth bind in the chains of dear love kindred hearts, I will tell him that his dear child—his much-loved Miranda, has forgiven me, and blotted out the word of my transgression with a tear, as pure as any shed by a bright angel for the sins of mortals. Farewell, Miranda! life is before you like a sunny landscape. Ah! that there may be no more shadow than will serve to make the light more beautiful. Save my boy—and then the old and sorrow-stricken man will lay him down in peace to die. Farewell— farewell."

"Stay—stay," cried Miranda.

Mr. Percy moved slowly away.

"Oh, stay with me," she cried. "Where have I another I can call a friend?"

He paused.

"You have that, Miranda, which will surround you with hosts," he cried—"you possess the glittering metal that will throng your halls with anxious men, each striving hard with the other to do you service."

"No—no—you mistake."

"Mistake?"

"Ay. Even that is denied me."

"You are heiress of the Grange."

"Bernard Varley claims all."

"Impossible!"

"He does. He taunts me with being dependent upon him. That I cannot be ; but he claims all. The—the old forest trees—all— all this arch-fiend claims as his own ; and I— I—Miranda, know not if I dare claim the meanest trifle that in fondness my poor father bestowed upon me."

"This passes all belief," said Mr. Percy. "Am I awake, or is this a dream of such frightful circumstantial reality that it appears all true?"

"It is no vision," said Miranda. "Shun me not that you are poor, for I know not but I am destitute."

"Then, Miranda, no power on earth shall tear me from you! I will beg for you, Miranda, but you shall know no want. May Heaven accept as some atonement for my sin in raising my arm in unholy strife against a fellow creature, this vow I now make—never to desert you, Miranda, if what you say should prove true. My fading strength shall all be expended in your service. I have done you grievous wrong—and my future life shall be one of atonement."

At this moment a crackling among the dry branches of the hedge, which was immediately opposite to where the Squire of Larkswood and Miranda were conversing, announced the approach of someone, and the next instant the singular face of Martin, the idiot boy, protruded itself from among the leaves.

"Aha!" he cried, "I'm here. Bold Hawk's my name, and I'm bold hawk by nature! They are coming! Do you hear me, Squire? They are coming! I have skimmed along the meadows like a bird—over hedge, ditch, and brier, I have come to tell you. Down by the old preserve I came with a whoop, and a hilloa, and a cry, and I heard the hares whispering together: 'Look at Bold Hawk! There he treads like the wind! See how he flies!' Ha! ha! ha! a southern blast tried to follow me, but it could not! No—no, Bold Hawk cannot be overtaken! They are coming, Squire! They are coming! Give the poor Hawk a silver piece; 'tis but to charm away pains and aches."

The poor fellow looked appealingly at Miranda, and held out his hand, in which she placed sixpence, as she said:

"Whom are coming, Martin?"

"Ah, you don't call me by my proper name. I was Martin once, but that was before my nature changed. I am Bold Hawk, and I tell you, Squire, they are coming."

"Who do you mean?"

"I have come from York—I heard them say they would have the Squire."

"What can he mean?" said Miranda.

The groom now rode up, and touching his hat, said:

"It's, may be, no business of mine, but there's two officers gone into the homestead by your house, Squire."

"Officers?"

"Yes—I have seen them in York."

"It is me they seek," said Mr. Percy. "I was told that a warrant was issued against me at the instance of someone for murder."

"Murder!" echoed Miranda.

"Yes—murder—the murder, they say, of your father. They will have it that my poor boy is guilty, and that I knew of his intention. Heaven above knows we are both innocent."

"And will you, too, be snatched from me?" cried Miranda. "It is decreed against me surely that I must be friendless."

"They are coming this way now," said the groom, as he raised himself in the saddle, and looked in the direction of the Larkswood grounds.

"I told you they were coming," cried Bold Hawk. "I came from York before them—like the wind came poor Bold Hawk."

"Fly, oh, fly!" cried Miranda, laying her hand upon Mr. Percy's arm.

"No—no," he said, "that were to encour-age a presumption of my guilt. Let them sacrifice me if they will—I am prepared."

"You are right—you are right," said Miranda; "'twas on impulse, not reflection, that I spoke; but I have learnt to dread the power of Bernard Varley."

"The triumph of the wicked shall be but for a season," said the Squire.

Even as he spoke, two men appeared in the lane, and the foremost one immediately pointed out to his companion the Squire, who stood by the side of Miranda, pale, but firm.

"Shoot them—shoot them, Squire!" said Bold Hawk. "They put me in prison once. That's strange, though, of them taking you. Have you been begging? Look! they are soon scared. Away—away with you."

As he spoke, the poor fellow took from his pocket a small piece of wood, and presented it at the officers, as if it had been a pistol, whereupon they immediately halted in great consternation, and one called out:

"Hilloa! hilloa! no violence. We come in the king's name."

"Aha!" cried Bold Hawk; "you are brave men—mighty brave men—you dare not face Bold Hawk though?"

"Keep off, fellow, keep off," cried one of the men, who was the parish constable of a little place about midway between the Grange and the ancient city of York. "I *discharges* you to *resist* me in the king's name."

Bold Hawk made a rush towards the men, and they immediately turned and sought safety in flight, till one of them happened to perceive the harmless nature of the weapon which the poor fellow presented at them, and then, with a degree of courage quite remarkable, they returned, and one of them, shaking his fist at Martin, cried:

"Very well—very well! You *mislisted* us in our duty. We'll make you smart for this."

"Nay—nay," said the Squire; "leave the poor fellow alone. He can scarcely be answerable for his harmless eccentricities."

"We've got a warrant agin you, Squire," cried the officer from York. "You are my prisoner."

"I shall not resist your warrant," said Mr. Percy. "On what charge am I arrested?"

"For murder."

"I am innocent."

"That may be, and it mayden't be," said the parish constable. "Don't be insolent, and it'll be all the better for you. Come quietly, and you may come as fast as you like, or more slowerer."

"Hold yet a moment," said Miranda. "I am the daughter of Sir George Rankley."

"Why, it's for his murder as we *reprehends* Mr. Percy!" cried the constable.

"Then, hear me declare my belief in the innocence of Mr. Percy. Surely, if I am satisfied, who shall call him guilty?"

"Why, you see, miss, he's considered as what we in the law calls *successory* afore the fact."

"'Tis useless, Miranda, to speak for me," said Mr. Percy. "These men must do their duty, they have no discretion whatever."

"Ellow—ellow!" cried the constable. "Do you hear that? He says we have no discretion. Why, he might as well call us fools at once. Isn't that abuse in the discharge of our duty?"

"If you don't hold your fool's tongue," said the officer from York, "I'll cram your staff down your throat. Be off with you."

"Be off with me?"

"Yes. I only brought you to identify the prisoner."

"Me! Do you mean me—parish constable, bell-ringer, sexton, and postmaster of the village of Beagles? Me—me?"

"Yes, you—you blockhead! Mr. Percy, you are my prisoner."

"Gracious! I'm topsy-turvy, or turvy-topsy. I'm all of an immense heap. Is we on our heads or our *eels?*"

"Who'll go to the hanging?" screamed Bold Hawk, in a startling voice.

"What hanging?" cried the officers.

"Bernard Varley's—Bernard Varley's."

Miranda sprang towards her horse, as she said:

"I will be at York within half-an-hour, Mr. Percy. Fear not; all may yet be well. Let us put our trust in Heaven."

"I do—I do, Miranda!" cried Mr. Percy, "Farewell for a time. As Heaven is my judge, let all here hear me declare my innocence."

"You hear that," cried Bold Hawk. "He's innocent—he says he is. I know it. My dreams all come true, and I'll tell you why. My name was Martin. I was a poor fellow then; but something changed me, and I am as you see me now. They say I'm mad, and so I am by daylight, for the sunshine makes me blink, and I don't quite understand all I see and hear; but God gives poor Bold Hawk dreams at night to make up to him for the scoffs and the gibes of those that ought to know better than he does, so I tell you Bernard Varley will be hanged at York. There will be a rare crowd. The like was never seen. Hurrah—hurrah—hurrah!"

He clapped his hands violently, and then bounded along the green lane like a hunted hare.

CHAPTER XIV.

TWITTER AT THE GRANGE—THE APPOINTMENT IN THE SHRUBBERY—A BOLD HIGHWAYMAN.

WHILE these occurrences were taking place in the green lane, between the Grange and York, the greatest confusion prevailed within the former abode.

The servants were in a state of excitement, from the scene which they had witnessed between her whom they considered their young mistress and Bernard Varley, which totally incapacitated them from following their ordinary occupations; and they retired to the hall, in which they usually sat in the evening, in a state of mind which could only be allayed by talking, and which admitted of no other exercise.

There was but one out of the whole household who, throughout the scene which had taken place, had never made his appearance, and that was Twitter, the valet of the murdered baronet.

He sat in his own small room, the same which has witnessed several memorable scenes in our history. His face was the colour of a corpse's; and he drew his breath short and thick, as he heard the various sounds of strife issuing from the part of the premises where Bernard Varley was undergoing so just a punishment for his brutality.

"They are murdering him," thought Twitter; "and then what shall I do? I—I need his support. I—I don't, at this moment, recollect one word of what I was to swear to. When I am examined at the inquest, I shall be lost, utterly lost without him. He is bold and resolute, fertile in schemes; while I am rather nervous. They shout dreadfully. It's all about that horse, too. He had better have let her have it, and go in peace. If I show myself, he will call on me for assistance, and—and I never like to assist anybody."

Twitter trembled, and rubbed his hands nervously together as he spoke, looking the most abject picture of terror.

In a few moments he crept to the door of the room, muttering to himself:

"I—I can peep into the stable-yard from the little window in the laundry. There I can see without being seen. If they kill Varley, I can be evidence against them all, and then rob the house."

Creeping along as if he feared his own shadow, Twitter made his way to the window he had mentioned, and which commanded a view of the whole of the proceedings in the stable-yard.

There was a low malignancy about Twitter which made him enjoy the punishment Varley was then receiving at the hands of the enraged servants; and something like a smile crossed his pallid face as he saw him dragged to the pump.

"Indeed!" he muttered; "they are going to pump upon him. Well, well, I cannot help it, and if I could I——"

Twitter glanced behind him before he ventured on saying, "I wouldn't"; and then he smiled again as he saw all Varley's frantic efforts to release himself entirely overcome, and his head placed under the pump.

"He—he often taunts me about many things," muttered Twitter, "and he has often struck me, too. I don't forget, although I'm not often in the humour to resent him; besides, he's stronger than I am. On my soul, I'm glad to see him so mauled; ha! ha! ha! Eh?—what was that?"

The echo of his own laugh had put him in a fright, which made his heart beat for several minutes.

"'Twas nothing — nothing. So, Master Varley, you are overcome. How your proud, revengeful soul must be maddened now. I

..m glad, very glad, and when next you taunt me, Master Varley, with stealing the plate, I'll mention the pump in the stable-yard, and make you fume again with passion. There, now they've left him—by Heaven, he's half dead already. Ha! he leaves the place—now he turns—he will come back—no—he is gone, and I am at liberty to keep my appointment, for doubtless Bernard Varley is off to York to concoct the means of vengeance. Well, well, I would fain see the Grange cleared of some of them. They already look with suspicious eyes upon me—I would that they were all gone."

He took his watch from his pocket as he spoke, and then exclaiming :

"So near my time?" he hurried from the room he was in, and making his way to a smaller apartment, in which were kept many valuable articles, he unlocked a plate-chest, and proceeded to fill a bag with numerous massive silver articles of great value.

"There is no one now," he muttered, " of whom I need be afraid. If Bernard Varley succeed in claiming the Grange, and all its possessions as his own, he dare not complain of me for taking the plate, as I have done for these six months past. If Miranda become mistress here by any accident, why, beyond a few articles she has seen in daily use, she knows not what plate her father possessed, and he is dead—yes, dead! Plate can be of no further use to him, so I will take it freely."

He nearly filled the bag with valuable articles, and then lifting it with some difficulty, for the weight was considerable, he passed out of the little room, and then taking his way by a private staircase towards the gardens, which were on the southern side of the mansion, he paused not until he reached a spot of considerable extent, nearly hemmed in by gigantic trees, and on one side of which was a low brick wall, fronting the road to London in one direction, and to York in the other.

"He is sure to come," muttered Twitter, as he placed the bag among the tangled roots of a tree which had stood for ages in the generous soil. "He is quite sure to come. Highwayman as he is, I know I can trust him to send me my fair share of the price the plate fetches in London. He boasts of being a man of his word, and pretends to keep a conscience—a highwayman's conscience! I may as well say as much—why I am no worse than he. I did not murder Sir George—no, no—not I. It was Bernard Varley's doing. I did not even see it done—no—I am glad it was not I."

He tremblingly approached the low wall, and, taking from his pocket a whistle, he blew one note upon it, which was immediately answered from the other side, and the hands of a man appeared on the top of the wall, who, in a few moments, drew himself up, and leaped down on the side nearest to the Grange.

"You are punctual, Dick Palmer," said Twitter; "you are a man of your word."

"I know it," said the stranger, who was a tall, wiry-looking man, past the prime of life, and slightly bald. "I know I'm punctual—Dick Palmer never breaks his word. But be quick, for I must be in London as soon as possible, and it's a long ride down here."

"But you do a little business on the road?"

"Certainly I do. Do you think I'd travel over a hundred miles, and stop nobody? Ha! ha! There was a fat grazier trotting on a Suffolk punch some fifty miles nearer London —I stopped him—your money or ears, said I. The fellow roared for mercy. He thought I meant to do it, so he gave up a leather bag, that was as greasy as his own mutton, with a hundred and sixty pounds in it."

"A famous booty," muttered Twitter.

"Yes—a windfall that seldom now comes in a professional gentleman's way, but for that very reason I must be off to London at once. There will be a hue and cry all over the country-side. I cannot take heavy plate with me this time, for I may have to ride for my neck."

"I have nothing but plate."

"Well, then, you must keep it till some other time—I must be off. You can write to me at the post-office as usual, and I will drop you a note to let you know when I can come down here again."

"Then you will take nothing?"

"Nothing. By-the-by, I heard from a countryman, as I came down the lane, some story about Sir George being killed."

"He—he is dead!"

"How?"

"He was shot in a duel, but some seem to think he was murdered afterwards."

"Then I'll be hanged if I don't suspect you did it! It's just a job in your line."

"I—I—upon my oath I did not.'

"Very well—very well. I suppose there will be some changes down here now."

"There may ; and should they occur before we meet again, I will be careful to send you word of the nature of them."

"Do so. We have been dealing on the square now for some months, and, of course, I knew it couldn't last for ever. You wrote to me to offer half the proceeds of the plate, if I would fetch it, and take the trouble to convert it into cash in London. There couldn't be a more straightforward businesslike transaction."

"Of course not. You take a right view of the case, Dick Palmer ; but I hope we may still do business together, for if I remain here my opportunities may be as great as ever."

"A young girl comes into the property, doesn't she?"

"Yes—a—yes."

"What do you mean by that? You say yes as if you meant no : but, as I suppose I am not left a legacy, I needn't trouble my head about it ; so good-day to you."

"Cannot you manage to take something with you?" said Twitter, who could not bear the idea of returning the plate to the place from which he had abstracted it.

"No; something tells me that I shall have a hard run for it. I may be wrong, but I think I shall be hard pressed between here and London. I have come the last fifty miles just to keep my word, not to encumber myself."

"You have your horse with you?"

"Yes, just over the wall."

"He would not feel the weight."

"Feel it or not feel it, I take nothing today. He is tired enough as it is. So now good-day to you, once more; I'm off."

The highwayman scrambled over the wall, and, mounting his steed, which was quietly cropping the short herbage that grew by the roadside, he set off at a smart trot towards London.

Twitter, with a bitter curse, took up the bag of plate, and, peering about him in great terror of being seen, re-entered the house, and deposited it in the closet from which he had brought it so short a time before.

"Lost! clearly lost!" he muttered. "Varley may make an inventory of these things. Yet, let him, let him. He is more in my power than I am in his: for he did the deed, and there can be no mercy shown to him! Why should I fear Bernard Varley, and allow him to make conditions, and have all things his own way, when 'tis I who should dictate to him? We shall see—we shall see, Master Varley!"

He was silent for a few moments, and then a new and agreeable thought seemed suddenly to strike him, and he said:

"Miranda has valuable trinkets, and in Sir George's bedroom are some articles of personal jewellery, of considerable price. Now is my time. Such an opportunity of secreting such things for my own purposes at a future time may never occur again. Miranda and Bernard Varley both away, and Sir George dead. Yes—yes—I will make a rare morning's work of this, although Palmer has disappointed me; and now for the trinkets of Miranda. Methinks I have seen her wear some costly gems."

The absence of Twitter from the servants' hall occasioned no remark, for, since his first coming to the Grange, he had never mingled with them, but, when not wanted by Sir George, had shut himself up so constantly and invariably in his private room, that the other servants would now have been much more surprised at his appearance than they could possibly be at his absence.

Hence he felt that there was every probability of his reaching Miranda's chamber without interruption, and, with a sickly smile upon his face, which was the very antipodes of all mirth, he crept up the principal staircase towards the corridor, from which the different bedchambers opened.

From his constant habit of peering and prying about, Twitter was well acquainted with the topography of the Grange, and there was not a corner in it that had escaped his inquisitive investigation.

He proceeded direct to the room in which the beautiful Miranda always slept, and adjoining which he knew was a smaller apartment, where she kept her wardrobe, and such books, jewels, and other matters as she most valued, either from their own intrinsic worth, or as being gifts at different times from her father.

The door of the bedchamber was open, and, with the stealthy step of a cat, Twitter entered.

"Humph!" he muttered; "all in confusion here; I must be quick, or some of the officious servants will be coming to put the room in order, and this is about the only one in the house that I should find it no easy task to account for being in."

As he spoke, he crossed to the small inner room, and then began hastily to put in his pockets various little valuable gems which lay upon a table. He next forced the lid of a small writing-desk, which was locked, and his gloating eyes fastened upon a set of brilliants which had been presented to Miranda by her father, on the occasion of her last birthday.

"Ha! here are, indeed, sparkling gems," he cried, as he eagerly tore them from their case, and crammed them into a pocket in his vest.

With a nervous eagerness, he tumbled over the papers in the desk in order to be sure that no other article of value had escaped his search; but he could see nothing that he thought worth the taking, saving a seal, which, although not of much value, he took, rather than miss anything.

As he was rummaging among the papers, one fell over the edge of the desk, on to the floor, and upon picking it up, he was struck by the name of Rowland Percy, written on it. Upon examination of it, his face assumed an expression of contempt. On the paper were some verses addressed by young Rowland to Miranda, and that she had placed them in the only locked depository she kept, showed the store she set upon them.

"Ah!" said Twitter; "love verses; I never loved anybody. Miranda is beautiful, and if ever I had felt such a sensation for anyone, I might for her; and then I should take some pains to place this Rowland Percy, perhaps, in a worse situation than he is; but I love money—I love the power that money gives to its possessor—I love the cringing lip-service that the rich always receive—I love, too, to play the tyrant over the poor—I love——"

He started, as a slight noise in a distant part of the mansion smote his ears, and so strong a fear of detection came over him, that he sank into a chair, unable to move hand or foot.

CHAPTER XV.

THE SERVANTS OF THE GRANGE—THE COPY OF VERSES—A FRIGHT.

TWITTER's alarm was greatly increased, as he heard a footstep in the outer room.

The necessity of adopting some immediate means of concealment came upon his mind with sufficient intensity, even to overcome the paralysis occasioned by his fears, and, rising, he softly crept to a corner of the room where there were several boxes, and other large articles, among which he crouched down, so as to be tolerably well concealed from anyone who might enter the room casually.

The step still sounded in the outer room, and as there was no mode of exit from the one he was in but through it, Twitter was fain to wait in an agony of impatience until whoever it was should have accomplished their errand and leave.

From the movement of the various articles in the room, he now became convinced that it was one of the female servants who had come to arrange the chamber, and, with a sigh, he calculated upon at least an hour more of durance.

"Curses on her," he muttered; "had she but come five minutes later, all would have been well; but now each moment teems with danger to me. What can I do? If I could alarm her in any way, so that she would fly from the room, and so give me an opportunity of escaping, all would be well. I must try."

It required the exertion of all Twitter's courage to enable him to make this resolution, and when he did, and was upon the point of carrying it into execution, he was as much startled by the sudden sound of the girl's voice, who was in the outer room, as he intended she should be by his.

"Ah! well," she said, "I wonder what will happen next? There's nothing but trouble now come over the old Grange. Master killed; poor, dear, young missus ever so unhappy; and young Mr. Rowland, who, I'm sure, is quite a nice young man, and never came here but he said, 'How do you do, Nancy? I see you are as pretty as ever,' is sent to prison. Ah, me! Now if they had hanged Mr. Varley, and that unsociable wretch, Twitter, there would have been nothing at all to grieve at."

"Indeed!" muttered Twitter.

"It's always the way," continued the girl; "misfortunes they never come single, they don't; and in the middle of all this, my sweetheart, Tom, he goes and has the banns put up atween him and the nursery-maid—a forward, disagreeable chit, that I'm sure only come here to stare at the men with her great eyes—oh, the wretch!"

Nancy having satisfactorily summed up the character of the nursery-maid, set to work making the bed, with all that vigour that is imparted to anyone's proceedings by considerable mental irritation.

"I could almost cry," muttered Nancy, as she threw the pillow into its place with a dash; "but I won't—no, I won't cry for nobody. There's Miss Miranda's watch-pocket has come undone—well, I must sew it on again I suppose, and there will be a trot downstairs for needle and thread."

"Thank Heaven!" said Twitter.

"No there won't though," hastily added Nancy; "Miss Miranda always leaves her work-box open, and there's some there in course."

So saying, the girl walked hastily into the small room in which Twitter was concealed.

A cold perspiration broke out upon the cowardly ruffian, as he heard the light foot-step of this young person cross the floor, and he calculated with fearful accuracy the consequences of discovery should he be arrested with Miranda's property in his possession, and consigned to a jail at the very time when he was looking forward to reaping the profits of his most unscrupulous villainy.

A thought flashed across his mind of murdering the girl; but then he had not nerve for such an act, and he knew it—moreover, who among all the household was more likely to be at once suspected of the deed than himself, in bad odour as he was with all the servants, and with a former character which he knew would not stand any very close examination.

In the midst of his reflections, Nancy cried:

"Well, I never did know Miss Miranda to leave her writing-desk open before; poor thing, she must have been flurried indeed. I dare-say now there's some sweet letters from Mr. Rowland Percy. Oh, dear me, nobody writes me sweet letters! Tom might have done so, but he can't write! to be sure I always send myself a valentine, just to show the servants in the hall, but that's nothing.—Oh, here's some verses, I declare."

Nancy picked up the verses addressed to Miranda by Rowland Percy, and then a fear came over her that she was not doing what was exactly right in thus prying into her young mistress's private affairs, and she hesitated a moment before she could muster courage to read any of the writing.

"Oh, dear!" she said, "I do wish Miss Miranda had not left her desk open. She never did before, and I never thought any-thing of it. It's quite a temptation now, I declare. Here's letters and verses, and oh, such loads of secrets, I daresay; and I am so fond of secrets. There's nobody upstairs at all. The house is quiet. It can't be much harm only to read a little. I won't take any-thing. I wouldn't for worlds do such a thing."

Nancy carefully unfolded the copy of verses, and then exclaimed:

"Ah! this is something like verses, and not like them as the gardener sent me in my last place, as begun:

"Oh, lovely, uncommonly pretty Nancy,
You strikes a great blow at my fancy,
And I hopes of my boldness you will be a pardoner
And without more ado marry the gardener."

"Them was very good, but these verses is lines I can see. I wonder if Miss Miranda would miss 'em if I was to take 'em away to read over afore I goes to bed of a night. I'm sure I should dream then, as some gentleman's gentleman offered me his hand and his heart, and vowed to make a lady of me, and open a house in the eating line. No, I mustn't take 'em. That would be very hard; for Miss Miranda, poor thing, might want to read 'em herself, so I'll just take a look at 'em here, and try to recollect 'em. Oh, dear: they is most lovely. What a good job it is I can read.

"TO MIRANDA.

"Listen! listen! dearest maiden
To thy lover's gentle vow,
And ever, dearest maiden,
He'll love as loves he now.

" Fond hearts are often broken,
By vows too rashly made,
But what thy love has spoken,
Can never be unsaid.

" Then listen, dearest maiden.
To thy lover's earnest vow,
And ever, dearest maiden,
He'll love as loves he now.

" Though years may leave their furrow
On thy brow so fair,
And wintry time may steal the hue
From out thy raven hair,

" Yet still thy own true lover,
Heeding not time's flight,
Will see thy cheek as fair,
Thy eye as sparkling bright.

" Then listen, dearest maiden,
To thy love's soul-felt vow,
And ever, dearest maiden,
He'll love as loves he now."

"Well, in all my life, I never. Oh, they is tender as a house-lamb, they is," exclaimed Nancy, when she had finished Rowland's verses. " He is a uncommon nice young man."

"I'll frighten her, if possible," thought Twitter, " or she will stay here another hour."

He then uttered a low groan.

For an instant Nancy was struck dumb and motionless with fright, and then she rushed from the room with a scream that made Twitter tremble in every limb, and put him in such a sudden tremor, that he could not immediately avail himself of the opportunity he had for flight.

With difficulty he rose from among the boxes, and rushed from the room. He crossed the bedchamber in a moment, and reaching the gallery, darted along it with the speed of lightning, nor paused until he reached his own chamber, where he scrambled into bed, and covered himself to the chin with the clothes, so that if any inquiry were made for him, he might be able to say that feeling unwell he had retired to rest.

Nancy continued her screams until she reached the servants' hall, where she was immediately surrounded by a crowd of anxious faces, and such a confusion of tongues ensued as would have quite astonished the builders of the Tower of Babel.

"What's the matter? What have you seen? Who was it?—a ghost?—a thief?—the keeper's spirit?—master's ghost?—where?—how?—when?"

Some even, in their impatience, went so far as to shake Nancy, to get sooner from her lips an account of her cause of alarm. One dashed a quantity of cold water in her face. Another poked a burnt feather to her nose, but Nancy was not going to faint, and her first intelligible words were the explanatory ones of——

"Oh, dear."

"Hush, hush, hush," cried everybody. "She's going to tell us."

"Oh, dear," said Nancy again.

"What have you seen?"

"I don't know."

"Then what did you scream for, you idle, slutterly thing?" cried the housekeeper, bustling through the throng.

"Because, Mrs. Morgan, I saw a groan."

"You *saw* a groan?"

"Yes. Oh, dear! oh, dear! I was a-making missus's bed—no, I wasn't. I was a-mending a watch-pocket—no, I wasn't."

"What do you mean?" said the indignant housekeeper, "and what is that you have in your hand?"

"My hand?" said Nancy, and looking down she saw that she still clutched the copy of verses.

"Oh, ma'am," cried the poor girl, "I brought this away by mistake. I did, indeed."

"And pray what is that?"

"Some verses."

"Verses! Some nonsense, I suppose."

"Yes—yes—yes. I was a-reading 'em when there came a groan, such as never was."

"Ah!" said the housekeeper, with a vibration of her head, implying superior wisdom. " ' The devil always finds some work for idle hands to do,' while, on the contrary, ' How does the little busy bee keep shining every hour.' Go to your work, you wretched girl. Go—go—and study the Reverend Elias Jones's pious work on the mortification of the flesh.—Is my luncheon ready?"

CHAPTER XVI.

MIRANDA AT YORK—THE HUMANE LAWYER —THE EVIDENCE AND THE WILL.

MIRANDA made great speed to York after her most distressing, but in some respects satisfactory, meeting with Mr. Percy. She entertained no doubt whatever in her own mind but that Varley had been the prime mover in, and suggester of, the quarrel between her father and the Squire. Nay, it was more than probable that the letters purporting to come from the Squire to her father, if such there were to be found, of a quarrelsome character, were written by Varley himself.

Miranda could easily imagine how two persons sufficiently estranged from each other as not to be on speaking terms, except in the phrases of ordinary civility, might, by the artifices of such a man as Bernard Varley, be made to inflict insults upon each other that nothing could efface.

Each moment of reflection seemed to make the whole affair clearer; and by the time she reached York, she had as good a notion of the conduct of Varley as it was possible to gather merely from conjecture and circumstantial evidence, and while in ignorance of the real facts in the order of their occurrence.

Miranda knew the names of her father's solicitors in York, but she knew not their exact place of abode. A very few moments' inquiry, however, enabled her to discover them, and, upon alighting, she was received by one of the partners with all the courtesy which distinguishes those lawyers, who are likewise, by a felicitous combination, gentlemen.

"You have heard——" said Miranda, when she was seated in the private room of Mr. Anderson.

"Spare yourself, my dear young lady, any painful explanations. I believe I am cognizant of all the unhappy circumstances of the last four-and-twenty hours. The unhappy criminal——"

"What criminal, sir?"

"Young Rowland Percy."

"Have you then, sir, adopted a belief in his guilt? Oh, Mr. Anderson! you may have heard much, and yet know but little of the circumstances which have made me an orphan; and first, let me at once declare to you, before Heaven, my entire belief in the innocence of Rowland Percy."

"His innocence?"

"Ay, sir, his innocence. I came to you to ask you not only to believe him innocent, but to use every energy with which you are gifted to save him from a most unjust persecution. If, sir, you are, however, so prepossessed with an opinion of his guilt that you cannot rid yourself of it, I will carry my griefs and my supplications elsewhere."

"God forbid, my dear young lady," said Mr. Anderson, earnestly, "that I should be prepossessed against anyone. It gives me much more pleasure to hear you express your confidence in the innocence of the accused than had you brought me undeniable proof of his suspected guilt."

"Then you will aid me, sir?"

"With all my heart will I."

Miranda could only look her thanks; and then she was silent for some moments, from excess of emotion. Hers was one of those pure spirits that a few kind words easily overcome, but which rise always in proportion to the pressure to which they are subjected, ever being most bold in most danger—most timid and tearful in confidence and peace.

"You will, Mr. Anderson," she said, "undertake to do all that is possible for Rowland?"

"I shall consider myself from this moment as not only his attorney, but his friend. Your opinion of his innocence, unless the evidence against him should be undeniable, will have great weight with everyone."

"Then there is hope?"

"Great hope. From all that I have hitherto heard, I expected to find in you an accuser of this young man, instead of a warm defender."

"I loved my father," said Miranda, "with a love that cannot be expressed. There is a grief now at my heart, which I sometimes think must break it; but the cause of the innocent is so sacred in the eyes of Heaven, that I must struggle to support my weight of private woe in order to avert the dreadful wrong that is sought to be perpetrated. Rowland Percy is innocent, but a subtle, dangerous villain is his foe, and his accuser."

"Do you mean Mr. Varley?"

"I do."

"It does not become me, in ignorance of facts, to give any opinion of Mr. Varley's conduct; but, believe me, all shall be done that can be done for the purpose of arriving at the truth."

"Save him, Mr. Anderson, and you will have the heartfelt gratitude of a bereaved heart. I am now an orphan—my poor father has been mercilessly snatched from me—but, oh! what an aggravation of my sorrow would it be to feel that the innocent had suffered for the guilty."

"Doubtless it would," said the lawyer, "but not by your conduct. It is very rare, indeed, that the laws, and particularly the criminal ones of England, are badly administered. There shall be the most searching examination instituted into this affair, and now let me request you to tax your memory to relate fully to me every little incident which you think can in any way, near or remote, bear upon this most painful subject."

Miranda then entered into a narrative of everything that had occurred, from the moment she was first alarmed by hearing that her father was fighting a duel in the immediate neighbourhood—when she rushed from the Grange, and was horrified at the sight of his bleeding form—to the last meeting with Mr. Percy.

Mr. Anderson listened to her with the profoundest attention, and her account of her interview with Bernard Varley, wherein he had more than hinted at the innocence of Rowland Percy, seemed to make a strong impression upon him, and to fill him with surprise.

"There is strong presumptive evidence," he said, "of an awful plot concocted by this man Varley; but there is very little legal evidence which can be brought to bear against him."

"Oh, sir, bring him to justice," said Miranda, "for, as I live, I do believe that he is the murderer of my father!"

"Control your feelings till after the inquest," said Mr. Anderson. "It will take place to-morrow, and, from the medical and other evidence there produced, you will be better able to judge of what grounds of accusation you may be able to discover against this man. There is, however, one matter which should be instantly seen to, and which very nearly, indeed, concerns yourself. That is, with regard to the will which Varley pretends your father has left."

"I had forgotten it."

"But it must be seen to immediately. I cannot believe it possible that such can be the case. Your father ever entertained not only the sincerest affection for you, but the justest possible notions with regard to his property. I have heard him frequently state that you and he were quite alone in the world; or, if you had any relations, they were in India, and very distant both as to family connection and geographical position, so that were I to die intestate—he has gone on to say—Miranda, as heir-at-law, must inherit all I possess. When he has spoken thus, I have ever tried to reason with him, and persuade him to leave behind him a will, which he has as often refused."

"Yet Bernard Varley says he has one."

"It may be forged."

"It must be."

"If it contains such provisions as he mentioned to you, I should say it surely was. But that is a subject which must be most fully investigated, and, if it be a forged will, Bernard Varley may have caught himself in his own snare; for the knowledge of that fact would invalidate as untrue any testimony he might give against Mr. Rowland Percy. For my present view of the case, as regards the accused young man, is, that he has far more to fear from the perjury of Bernard Varley than from the curious coincidence of circumstances that brought him to the Grange, on that most fatal evening."

"True—true," said Miranda, "and I dread the power of Varley. I do believe him, from my heart, to be so subtle and so crafty a villain, that, like the dreaded tiger of the wilderness, he will calculate well his chances ere he make a spring upon his hopeless victim."

"Do not despond. The craftiest, subtlest villain that ever lived will generally leave some point open through which he may be attacked, and the more deeply conceived and complicated the scheme he is engaged upon, the more probable is it that he will not be armed at all points. Be of good cheer, then, and hope for the best."

"I will not give way to sorrow while action is required of me," said Miranda. "But I must see Rowland."

"That will be difficult."

"Difficult to see an accused man? Surely it is misfortune sufficient to be wrongfully accused; and the needless cruelty of depriving him of all consolation in his unhappiness surely will not be added."

"Nothing but an order from a magistrate will enable you to see him, and no other magistrate but the one who has already seen and remanded Mr. Rowland Percy need be applied to, for from delicacy to him who heard an outline of the case others will not interfere, and with him I think you have small hopes. Indeed, under all the circumstances, I should advise you not to see him just at present. I, as his solicitor, shall have free access to him at all reasonable times, and be assured that whatever comfort he can experience from knowing your noble confidence in his innocence, shall not be denied him."

"Be it so, then, for the present," said Miranda, rising. "But concerning Mr. Percy, Rowland's father?"

"There can be nothing to implicate him. The inquest, and the evidence of the surgeon, will in all probability free him; for if it be sworn that the wound your father received from Mr. Percy was not mortal, or in any way dangerous to life, he cannot be detained on a charge of murder, and Bernard Varley can say nothing about the duel, because he himself was one of the actors in it, and equally criminal with all denounced. You may depend upon it that the arrest of Mr. Percy is of no consequence, and you need give yourself no uneasiness whatever about it."

"Thank Heaven, then, all is not so bad as I supposed," said Miranda.

"All may be well; but I will go with you to the Grange, for I am most anxious concerning this will."

Miranda shuddered at the mention of going back to the Grange, but what other home had she?

"I shall be thankful to you, sir," she said, "for, little as I value riches, I would not willingly allow such a man as Bernard Varley to wrest from me my birthright."

Miranda thought likewise of what Mr. Percy had told her of the sad condition of his fortunes, and she shuddered as the reflection came across her that, in addition to her other grievous trials, destitution might be staring her in the face.

CHAPTER XVII.

BERNARD VARLEY'S REVENGE—THE CHANCE MEETING—MORE MACHINATIONS.

WHAT tempest in its utmost intensity was equal to the rage which swelled in the bosom of Bernard Varley, as he took his way to York, after being so very summarily ejected from the Grange?

He flew, rather than ran, and taking a short cut across the fields, was soon even in advance of Miranda, mounted as she was; and her long interview with Mr. Percy in the green lane, enabled Varley to reach York considerably before her.

As he entered the suburbs of the city he felt not pain or fatigue, for the tumult in his mind had swallowed up every other consideration.

But one passion filled his mind, and that was an insatiable desire for revenge—bitter and wild revenge upon Miranda, and all at the Grange who had been in any way instrumental in his disgrace.

Once or twice he paused to debate with himself if he should really appeal to the law, or take some private means of achieving a much more exemplary revenge than it would allow him.

"What laws can satisfy a hate like mine?" he cried. "What cold proceeding, that they call justice, will satisfy me when I am burning to take lives? And she, Miranda, too, whom, in spite of all, I love—whom, the more she contemns me, the more I adore her. She knows that I have been mauled and disgraced by a common herd of lackeys and kitchen wenches. I, Bernard Varley, who, in my ambition, have defied Heaven itself! But I will have vengeance on them all! I must have my revenge!"

His hasty walking had done much to dry his saturated garments, and, by the time he arrived at York, he was getting into that most uncomfortable of all states after a wetting—namely, a half-feverish, half-moist kind of heat, which makes the skin dry and hard, while the steamy garments come against it with an unwholesome touch, mocking it with a semblance of moisture, only to leave it more feverish than before.

His lips were parched and dry, his hair hung about his face in wiry masses, and his whole appearance was so disordered and strange, that many a chance passenger stopped to look after him, and wonder where he could have been to get into so strange a state.

Varley, however, did not notice that he was an object of attention, for there was something about his compressed lips, dilated nostrils, and corrugated brow, which induced people to let him pass on before they indulged their curiosity by a long stare at him.

He proceeded directly to a house in a small, narrow street, leading from a handsome and commodious thoroughfare in the immediate vicinity of the Minster.

A brass plate, not more brazen than was the countenance of the man whose name it bore, was on the door, bearing the words, "Mr. Querral, Solicitor."

A dark smile came over Bernard Varley's face as he knocked at the door and muttered:

"Here is the man who, for a consideration, will do anything. A most useful member of your profession are you, Mr. Querral. I would not lose you for a thousand pounds."

The door was quickly opened, and the question if Mr. Querral was at home being answered in the affirmative, Varley was ushered into a little, mean room; the only furniture of which consisted of one stool, a desk with writings, and an old blue bag. In fact, Mr. Querral's waiting-room was coldly severe, and not at all calculated to induce people to wait long.

Bernard Varley's patience, however, was not much taxed; for in a few moments a big, burly man made his appearance, and, with an air of candour and sincerity quite astounding, said:

"My dear sir, how do you do? Ah! you are not looking well. You know me—the soul of sincerity and candour—I say what I think, and think what I say. Some people call me blunt, but I cannot temporize with my feelings, and, therefore, I unhesitatingly tell you to your face, Mr. Varley, that I never saw you look so strange in my life. Upon my word, of course, it's ridiculous, but do you know, Mr. Varley, I never saw anyone look like you but once"

"Indeed, sir?"

"No—upon my word; you know my sincerity and candour. There was a man who looked just as you do now—he had been pumped upon—he had, indeed."

Varley's face assumed the scowl of a demon as he said, in a voice of concentrated passion:

"Mr. Querral, I do not come here to listen to your absurd remarks, but to employ you professionally. You are aware, probably, that Sir George Rankley is dead?"

"Yes, and I beg to congratulate you, sir, upon the important trust left to you, for I cannot forget being so very recently honoured by drawing up the poor gentleman's will, in which he bequeaths to you everything he possesses in trust for his daughter, if she marries you, or with your consent, and absolutely to you, should she not do so."

"You are right, sir," said Varley; "most admirably have you stated the conditions of the will. By-the-by, did you procure the letter Sir George wrote to you containing his instructions?"

"I did."

"Then it may be useful; for this girl, Miranda, already shows symptoms of a wilful disposition, and may dispute the will."

"She cannot, my dear sir. I am the soul of candour, and I have no hesitation in saying, that when I draw up a will it cannot easily be disputed."

"Very well. You will be in readiness if sent for by me, and as you have had some trouble, Mr. Querral, and may have more, pray charge accordingly."

"I shall do myself that pleasure, Mr. Varley, always in moderation. Being the soul of candour and sincerity, I shall make my little bill most unobjectionable."

"Well, then, Mr. Querral, you must accompany me to a magistrate, for I am about to take out warrants against several parties for assault, and I shall place them in your hands for due execution."

"An assault, my dear sir? Then you have been pum—pum—pumped——"

"Sir?" said Varley.

"Eh? oh, nothing—I only thought——"

"Mr. Querral, if it is any satisfaction to you to know that, overpowered by numbers, I was pumped upon, you know it now."

"My dear sir, think nothing of it."

"I think a great deal of it, but you or anyone might have been subjected to the same thing under such circumstances."

"Certainly, certainly I have," added Mr. Querral, to himself; "I have been pumped upon twice."

"Come, sir," said Varley, rising. "We will go for these warrants."

The first object that presented itself to Varley when they reached the High Street, was Miranda leaning upon the arm of Mr. Anderson. He started, and would have avoided her, but he saw that Mr. Anderson's eye was upon him, and putting a bold face upon the matter, he confronted them, saying:

"It strikes me that Miss Rankley would look better in the eyes of the world were she to keep her home under present circumstances."

"When the hawk's abroad, sir," said Mr. Anderson, pointedly, "the bereaved dove may wander from its nest."

"Indeed, sir—you are metaphorical."

'And yet I would fain use plainer language. We are on our route to procure a conveyance to the Grange."

"And may I ask," said Varley, "what procures me the honour of Mr. Anderson's company at the Grange?"

"Mr. Anderson is my visitor," said Miranda.

"Oh, indeed. Then, as the guardian of this young lady, sir, I cannot at present approve of her seeing company."

"Then," said Mr. Anderson, "I believe this young lady declines the further honour of your stay at the Grange."

"And yet I shall stay," said Varley, with a perfectly unmoved countenance. "I have a will of Sir George Rankley's, which makes my stay there a matter of right."

"That will, I presume, you will have no objection to show me at once, as the professional adviser of Miss Rankley?"

"It shall be publicly read after the inquest," said Varley, as he walked away, with a smile of triumph on his face.

"Miranda," said Mr. Anderson, "you may depend this villain has taken his measures well, and has strong grounds to go upon, or he would never treat us thus superciliously."

"Alas! alas!" said Miranda, "my heart tells me that all is lost. Surely Varley must be some demon, permitted for a time to wear the human form, to bring ruin upon the innocent."

"Do not despair. My now going with you to the Grange would be useless; but to-morrow I will be with you on the melancholy occasion it will bring forth."

"Ah! the inquest," shuddered Miranda. "Well, I must nerve myself even for that. When—oh! when—will all these dreadful trials cease? I must see Rowland Percy. Ah! Mr. Anderson, take me to see him. If my agony be great, what must his be? I have heard it said that the consciousness of innocence is a support to the falsely accused; but it ever appeared to me that injustice was the hardest lot of all to bear. What can the felon feel, when accused of his guilt, in comparison with the honest heart, that knows no guile, and scorns deceit? The one may be angry at the discovery of his iniquity; but the other's heart must surely be near to breaking at the unjust charge. I must see him. I must, sir, see Rowland Percy."

"We will, at least, make the attempt," said Mr. Anderson.

CHAPTER XVIII.

THE INTERVIEW BETWEEN MIRANDA AND ROWLAND PERCY.

THE attempt to see Rowland Percy was made, and made successfully; for, within half-an-hour, Miranda was with Mr. Anderson at the gloomy door of the building in which the accused was confined.

Rowland Percy was sitting alone in a small cell, where, at his own earnest request, he had been placed, as he preferred solitude to the company of the vicious persons who inhabited that wretched home.

The coarse jest of the felon was to him a terrible infliction, and he infinitely preferred the company of his own thoughts, sad and mournful as they were, to such companionship.

The whole proceedings had been so strange, and his transition from liberty and hope to the gloom of a prison so rapid, that it was some hours after his incarceration before he could sufficiently arrange his ideas to come to a clear understanding of his situation.

The fatigue, both of mind and body, he had undergone, did not at all assist him in his endeavour to clear up the mysteries by which he was surrounded; and, more than once, so glaringly improbable did the whole circumstances appear, he was inclined to believe himself the victim of some mental delusion.

He paced the narrow confines of his room with rapid and unequal strides, repeating to himself, in a tone of surprise, which the familiarity of the idea by no means decreased:

"I am accused of the murder of Sir George Rankley, the father of Miranda; and to whom his death at all was a piece of news that came upon me like a thunderbolt. How can I unravel all this mystery—how connect the chain of circumstances, link by link, which has placed me in this awful situation? My brain is racked with thought, and I have but two ideas to ring the changes upon. First, I am accused of murder; and, secondly, Miranda believes me innocent. Oh, that is a thought that will, indeed, sustain my sinking spirits. Though the whole world should, with one voice, proclaim me guilty, let but that one pure and sinless heart believe me innocent, and I will find a consolation in my wrongs— a triumph in my sufferings. Oh, Miranda! Miranda!—my own much-loved Miranda— will you still resist the voice of calumny, and believe in my innocence? Will you believe that the heart which cherishes your image as its fondest, dearest treasure, would have risked its own annihilation rather than your father should have come to harm? Even in the face of condemnation—should it be my awful fate to suffer wrongfully—can you still cling to the holy belief in the innocence of him who loves you?"

Rowland Percy threw himself into the only chair which the apartment afforded, and, covering his face with his hands, gave himself

VARLEY'S INTERVIEW WITH MR. QUERRAL.

up for some moments to the saddest, gloomiest thoughts.

The unhappy young man heard not the opening of the door of the room, so absorbed was he in his own painful reflections. He heard not the footsteps of those who entered.

But a voice—a voice which even then he was dreaming of, though it spoke in low and gentle accents, such as scarcely reached his ear, aroused him from his lethargy, with more certainty than would the sound of a trumpet.

It was the voice of his Miranda. The voice of the one cherished idol of his heart, and he sprang to his feet with a cry of pleasure, and an animation of countenance that brought a flush of radiant colour to the pale cheeks of Miranda as she allowed him to clasp her hand in his.

For a moment thus, neither spoke, and Mr. Anderson beckoned the jailer from the door, and closed it upon the lovers.

"Miranda! Miranda!—my Miranda!" was all he could say for several moments, and the gentle girl herself—she who had carried so high a spirit to Bernard Varley, and haughtily repelled sorrow in the presence of those who sympathized not with her griefs, now burst into tears, and sobbed convulsively upon her lover's breast.

Not a sound disturbed the solemn stillness

of that small room, save the deep sobs of the beautiful being who had thus sought him who was accused of her father's murder.

Rowland could not speak; his heart was too full, and it was not until Miranda's passionate grief had somewhat subsided that he could master his feelings sufficiently to say:

"Miranda—you still believe me innocent?"

"As I believe in Heaven's mercy!" she replied.

Rowland Percy lifted up his eyes and exclaimed:

"Then I am prepared for all. Let evil fortune do her worst. Let them take my life. Let them brand me with a felon's name. Let them give me a felon's grave—I will still thank Heaven, for you believe me innocent."

"I do—I do, Rowland; you did not—you could not be my father's murderer. I will plead for you—pray for you. You are innocent, Rowland; you are innocent."

The young man's face kindled with enthusiasm as he exclaimed, in a voice of rapture:

"Bless you, Miranda, for those words. I am free, free in spirit—free in imagination; nor bolts, nor bars can now confine me. The mind—that pure, subtle essence which defies all oppression in its own integrity, will leap the prison walls, and coming through the rich domains of thought, will cheat the dungeon of its terrors. Oh! Miranda, you know not how happy you have made me by your words. I am innocent—Heaven knows I am; and the pure faith we both avow, teaches us to expect assistance from above. The time will come, my Miranda, when the guilty shall be confounded, and although your poor Rowland's ashes may be mingled with the dust, and the stigma of a false charge may be affixed to his name—Phœnix-like will he rise from his ashes, and the memory of his wrongs will live in the hearts of men, when he and all he loved are mingled with the elements of nature. The innocent may be sacrificed, villainy may triumph, but a day of retribution will as surely come as to-morrow's sun will shine upon the world."

"But Rowland—dear Rowland," sobbed Miranda, "you shall not fall a victim to that man. I will plead for you. They cannot say you did the deed."

"They will say so," he replied. "Hear me, Miranda, and I will tell you how I came so inopportunely to the Grange.

"When dissension commenced between your father and mine—from what cause I know not—I was compelled to absent myself, but still my heart lingered around the well-known home of all its affection. Though absent I was ever near to you. There was no joy for me but in the recollection of your voice, your latest words, and every fond word of our trusting, faithful hearts. Then memory from a blessing, became a curse, for it pictured to me scenes of happiness until I longed—with such a yearning, as we are told the Swiss exiles have for home—to look upon you once again. The wish grew into an impulse—I could think of nothing—dream of nothing but of the means of seeing you, and learning from your own lips that you still thought of your poor Rowland Percy, as one who with unshaken faith had loved you long, and as one who from no fault was banished from your side. I longed to hear your voice, to note if it were as kindly tuned as of yore. The impulse grew to a wild passion—I should have died, my Miranda, if I had not come to you."

"Oh, Rowland—Rowland," sobbed Miranda, "at what an unhappy hour did you come!"

"As it chanced, Miranda, I did come at a most unhappy hour. For many days I bethought me of some plan by which I could meet you, until, at length, the scheme I put in practice, wild as it was, grew into hope in my fevered brain.

"I knew that the servants of the Grange were all firm believers in the old legend of the murdered keeper haunting the estate. Upon this superstition I founded my plan, and attiring myself in the dress the apparition was supposed to wear, I thought to obtain, from my intimate knowledge of the localities of the house, easy access, when I trusted to good fortune to meet you, and enjoy the interview I so much panted for. As evil fortune would have it, I put my scheme in execution at an inauspicious time, and am accused of murder at the moment when I hoped to heal a difference which had arisen between our parents from causes which, to me, are still involved in mystery."

"You did, Rowland, come at an inauspicious time," said Miranda. "The villain Varley had sown the seeds of dissension between your father and mine, until they brought forth the bitter fruits of personal strife. They met in most unholy and deadly conflict."

"I have heard as much, but could not give credence to the tale."

"It is true. Some false sentiment of honour on both sides urged them on to a duel. My father fell."

Rowland clasped his hands with a deep sigh, and Miranda continued in a tearful voice, interrupted by frequent sobs:

"On the morning of that dreadful day my poor father met his death; how I know not, but something tells me it was by the hands of Bernard Varley, who seeks to throw his guilt on you."

"I see it now," cried Rowland. "My presence at that time, and in disguise, furnished him with an excuse for my arrest; but that will not suffice to condemn me of what I am innocent of. Fear not, my Miranda. They cannot call me a murderer on such scanty grounds of accusation."

Miranda shuddered as she replied:

"You know not Bernard Varley. I have learned to fear him. His machinations are awful. Heaven, which looks into all hearts, can only tell what means he has prepared for your destruction."

The door was now opened by the jailer, who uttered the one word :

"Time."

Miranda started, and then clung to the arm of Rowland.

"Must I leave you?" she sobbed.

"Yes," he sighed ; "but I am not alone. The memory of this visit will people my cell with images of the past. Oh, Miranda, you have made a palace of my prison."

Miranda could not speak, but she clung to Rowland, and sobbed aloud.

"Farewell," said the prisoner. "Be of good cheer. We have Heaven with us."

Mr. Anderson advanced, and gently put Miranda's arm within his.

She could but wave her hand, and the next moment the door closed upon him she loved.

CHAPTER XIX.

THE INQUEST—THE EVIDENCE—THE VERDICT, AND MIRANDA'S DESPAIR.

THE news of the extraordinary occurrences at the Grange had spread far and wide through the surrounding country, producing much excitement, in the city of York in particular, where all the parties connected with the melancholy transaction were well known.

Exaggerated as were the various rumours upon the subject, none came near the truth as regarded the real atrocity of the crime, or the magnitude of its results.

It was simply, in popular estimation, an extraordinary murder, for the medical man who had attended Sir George Rankley, had made but little secret of his opinion, that the baronet had come by his death from other causes than the wound received in the duel with Mr. Percy.

By order of the coroner, a post-mortem examination of the body was to be made a few hours before the inquest commenced, and, as twelve o'clock approached, all was bustle and expectation at the Grange.

Many professional gentlemen from York, both legal and medical, attended the proceedings, as well as a vast concourse of persons who could not get admittance to the mansion, but remained anxiously waiting the result in the vicinity.

But what were the feelings and the anxiety of all these in comparison with the mental agony endured by Miranda?

Accompanied by her father's attorney, she reached the Grange at an early hour, and sat in solitary anguish in her own room, looking like some beautifully-chiselled statue of purity and grief.

There was something inexpressibly terrible to Miranda in the very preparations for the judicial examination into her father's decease, and she clasped her hands with convulsive energy, as she exclaimed through her tears :

"Oh, would that this dreadful day were over. Who, a few days since, could have imagined this happy house to be in so short a time changed from its bright aspect of joy and sunshine, to one of desolation and gloom? There were but two spots upon the sunshine of my joy, the one was Bernard Varley, and the other, the unhappy difference between my father and Mr. Percy—now these spots have become one hideous mass of blackness, and Bernard Varley alone stands before my affrighted imagination, as the mighty Colossus-like fiend, who is predestined to be the shadow of my existence, and the evil genius of the innocent. Oh, Heaven, save Thy creatures who love and reverence Thee, from the machinations of that man."

A low knock at the chamber-door now startled Miranda from her reverie.

"Come in," she said, in so strange and altered a tone, that the young girl who entered could hardly believe that it was her mistress who answered her.

"Well, Annie," said Miranda, "am I wanted?"

"Oh, dear no, miss, not yet ; but Mr. Varley has just come, and I thought I would tell you—he has brought with him three such odd-looking men, Miss Miranda."

"It matters not—it matters not," said Miranda. "To-day must settle all."

"Yes, miss, so they do say. The coroner gentleman hasn't come though yet."

"What is the time?"

"It wants nearly twenty minutes of twelve, miss—James forgot to wind up your pretty French clock."

"I shall never touch it again," said Miranda ; "let it be, Annie—I—I have not the heart to do anything—a brighter sun must shine upon my heart than does at present ere I can attend to those things which formerly made up my days of happiness ; my heart is now absorbed in one object."

"Oh, miss, we must all die sometimes, you know, and you shouldn't grieve so much."

"You mistake me," said Miranda. "Even grief for my poor father is swallowed up in other feelings. He is free from the busy evils of mortal strife. He is with his God, but the living are still entangled in the meshes of the world's cares. The innocent may suffer because human judgment is fallible. My father will have justice at the bar of Heaven, but Rowland Percy may, though innocent, be sacrificed to the machinations of his enemies. It is for him I feel, because there is doubt and anxiety as to his fate ; of my father there can be none—all is over."

Miranda shuddered as she spoke, and then, as if human nature mocked the philosophy of the brain, she leant her head upon her breast, and sobbed bitterly.

The girl wept from sympathy, and, for a few moments, not a word was spoken.

Then the sound of carriage-wheels on the gravel drive which swept round the lawn, came upon Miranda's ears, and she started as she exclaimed :

"Who is that, Annie?"

The girl rose and left the room. As she did so the ancient clock of the Grange struck twelve.

"The time has come," muttered Miranda. "Rowland's fate must soon be decided. I am told that the evidence produced at the inquest to-day, will be decisive of his fate one way or the other. Ah, they cannot, dare not, sacrifice him."

"The coroner, miss, has come," said the girl, as she re-entered the room; "and there's quite a crowd of gentlemen in the dining-room."

"Yes, yes," gasped Miranda; "in a short time they will want me. Some cold water, Annie. Let me bathe away the traces of these tears. I should be firm, not weak and tearful. I must speak for him, for Rowland, the falsely-accused, or his enemies may overpower him. I must raise my voice for him. You know, Annie, he is innocent."

"Yes, miss; I'm sure such a nice young man couldn't do nothing wrong."

"He is innocent, quite innocent," continued Miranda. "Let me think. By an unfortunate coincidence he came here on the night of my father's death—but he is innocent—as innocent as I am. Why does Bernard Varley not accuse me? He might just as well—— Hark! what noise is that? Go, Annie, go and bring me word what noise is that. I hear the tramping of many feet. Why are they coming here? Hark, hark!"

The girl left the room, and then, in a moment, returned and said:

"It's the gentlemen, miss, going—going——"

"I know what you would say," interrupted Miranda, making a strong effort to speak. "They are going to view my poor father's remains. Yes, yes; it is proper — most proper."

So awful a paleness came over the face of Miranda, that the girl, in alarm, rang the bell before her mistress could prevent her.

"Hush, hush, Annie—I am better now," said Miranda. "Give me your Cologne water. There—I am better now—a sudden faintness. Hark, they are returning—how awful in the house of death sounds the tramp of those men. They have seen him."

The sound of the feet of the jury, as they returned from viewing the body, which lay in a chamber on the same floor as Miranda's room, died slowly away, and then all was still as the grave, for the dining-room was far distant.

For a moment or two Miranda stood as still as a statue; then, suddenly turning to the girl, she said:

"A scarf, Annie—give me a scarf. Quick, girl, quick."

"Oh, Miss Miranda, where are you going?" said the alarmed girl.

"The dining-room, you say," muttered Miranda, as she hastily arrayed herself in a large black scarf. "The dining-room?"

"The gentlemen are there, miss."

"And there I am going."

"Oh, dear, Miss Miranda, you had better stay away. Indeed you had."

"No," said Miranda, firmly. "Who knows what may be said of the innocent, and no one there to contradict? It is my duty—it is my duty."

"Then you must let me go with you, miss?"

"No, do you remain here. Should I want you I will send for you. Bernard Varley must not think me weak. See, I am firm and calm; my hand trembles not; I do not look or speak like one who has lost a dear father; but I will look, and I will speak, like one who would protect the innocent from the guilty. The dining-room—yes—the dining-room."

She glided from the room as she spoke, looking more like a spectre than the living, breathing, beautiful girl she really was. Her lips were firmly compressed, and there was a cold sternness upon her brow as if she had summoned every feeling of resistance in her nature to carry her through the scene which she felt was near at hand.

"I will raise my voice for him—for Rowland. They may call it unmaidenly, but what is justice in the eyes of Heaven, should be right on earth. He shall not perish undefended."

She rapidly descended the marble staircase, which was one of the finest ornaments of the house, and, crossing the hall, paused for a moment as the murmuring sound of voices from the large dining-room, in which the inquest was held, met her attentive ears.

For an instant the hall, and each well-known object it contained, swam before her eyes, and Miranda thought she should have fainted; but, by a strong mental effort, she sustained herself, and, whispering to her heart, courage! courage! turned the handle of the lock, and entered the spacious room.

Her sudden and unexpected appearance attracted universal attention, and there was a dead silence of a moment or more, then the coroner said:

"Gentlemen, we must proceed—will the lady be seated, or retire again?"

"Miss Rankley," said Varley, "is a heroine when she pleases—her nerves are strong—she will doubtless remain."

It was well for Miranda that Bernard Varley spoke, and better still that he spoke so mockingly, for all her sinking spirits revived at the insult, and in an instant she was calm, collected, and had better command of herself.

"Yes," she said, and her clear voice sounded through the room like the tinkle of a silver bell. "Yes, I will remain. Gentlemen, I am the daughter of him whose mortal remains you have but now looked upon. He loved me past the power of telling. My lightest wish found ever a ready echo in his heart—I am his only child. His heart was large enough to love many, but its concentrated tenderness all fell upon me; and with even his thoughts of Heaven he mingled his dear love for his darling child. Such was my father, nor was I insensible to such affection, Heaven knows, and many on earth can bear witness to how I returned that affection. I will not speak upon that head but you must judge that some motive strong enough to overwhelm by its power all traces of grief—that grief which I should feel for such a father—must have nerved me to this act of coming among you with a calm and steady mien—an eye in which no tear is visible. Oh, judge me not harshly—say not to your hearts that I am callous to a father's fate; rather look for some high feeling which has wrought upon me to whisper to my grief. 'Be still awhile, that I may do my duty.'"

Miranda raised her arm, and pointing at Varley, who shrank back immediately, continued:

"Look on that man. Mark him well! See even now how he shrinks before me—not from what I have said, but from dread of what I may say. Twelve months since this roof covered as happy and united hearts as ever beat in human breasts; but Bernard Varley came, and gloom and discord came with him. I denounce him as morally guilty, if I cannot prove him legally so. Mark him well, and when you see another like to him, proclaim him a murderer!"

All rose from their seats as Miranda spoke, and a general feeling of amazement pervaded every breast, and shone fully from every countenance.

Miranda still pointed at Varley, who, with his arms stretched before him as if he feared she would approach nearer, stood pale as ashes, and trembling in every limb.

CHAPTER XX.

THE EVIDENCE OF THE MURDERERS—THE IVORY TABLETS, AND THE FORGED MEMORANDUM.

It was, however, but for a minute that Bernard Varley lost the power of action, for rousing himself from the state of alarm into which the words of Miranda had thrown him, he cried, in a voice of harsh vehemence:

"Is this fair? Is this the mode of proceeding at a judicial inquiry? Am I to be insulted by a girl who is crack-brained, because there is good reason to believe her lover has committed a murder?"

"'Tis false," cried Miranda, "false as your own heart, and you know it."

"I claim protection from you, sir," cried Varley to the coroner. "Is this insane girl to remain here to the detriment of justice?"

"Remain here I will," cried Miranda. "If any human being has more right than another to remain here, it is I. If this awful inquiry concerns anyone more than another, surely—ah, surely, that one is myself. For the excitement of my feelings, which has led me to be rude of speech, I apologize to all but to that man. Too well he knows that no language can depict what he is."

"Let me recommend you to retire," said the coroner to Miranda; "your grief will but find fresh food in the details we must necessarily enter into."

"No, no; I am calm," said Miranda, in an altered tone; "but I have heard that at the trial of a murderer the very stones have risen up in judgment—I have heard that fresh blood has flowed from the stiffened corpse—I have heard that sighs have been breathed from breasts cold in death, and that Heaven has permitted strange things of preternatural import, when it has pleased it to visit upon the head of the murderer human vengeance for his crimes. Wonder not, then, that I, a timid maiden, should raise my voice when taunted by that dreadful, fearful man."

"This is midsummer madness," cried Varley, stamping violently, and flinging his arms about in wild passion. "The evidence—the evidence. I claim to be heard against these charges."

"Silence all," cried the coroner. "Miss Rankley, if you persist in staying here—a resolution which I hope you will change—you must let justice take its even course."

"I am still—I am still," said Miranda, as she sank into a chair, and leaned her face upon her hands.

"Bring in the prisoner," said the coroner.

Rowland Percy, who was brought from York Castle in custody, was led into the room.

His glance fell upon Miranda, and in a tone of sadness, he ejaculated her name.

She sprang from her seat, and dashing the hair from her face, which had fallen in wild disorder, she stretched out her hand, as she said:

"Here, Rowland Percy, before all these persons, as I would before the world, I take your hand, and proclaim it guiltless of shedding blood. You are innocent. God knows it, and one other."

"One other?" cried the coroner.

"Yes!" cried Miranda. "You may see him there."

She pointed at Varley, who gnashed his teeth in impotent rage.

"Let the witnesses be sworn," cried the coroner.

The first witness examined was the medical man. He gave his evidence clearly and distinctly. Sir George Rankley's wound was found upon dissection to be very slight, and could not have produced death.

"What was the cause of death?" said the coroner.

"From the appearance, both internal and external of the body, I should say that Sir George Rankley was suffocated."

A thrill of horror pervaded the assemblage, which was now increased by all the servants of the household.

"Of that you are sure?" said the coroner.

"My brother medical man and myself both agree on that point. It is our decided opinion."

"That is all you have to say?"

"It is."

"Bernard Varley," said the coroner; and the villain, with an assumption of confidence that sat but ill upon his ghastly countenance, stepped forward, crying:

"Here."

"State what you know of this transaction."

"Sir George Rankley," commenced Varley, "after some differences with Mr. Percy, fought a duel with him, in which, after much persuasion, I acted as second. He received a wound, a slight one, as I was led to believe, but it confined him to his bed. I felt the greatest anxiety concerning him, for he had been to me a kind patron, and I agreed with the nurse who was attending on him, that I and Twitter, his valet, should relieve her at night, and sit some time with the wounded man while she had repose.

"We kept our words, but on our passage to the chamber of the baronet, we thought we saw a figure glide past us on the stairs, and we pursued it, but in vain. Believing, then, that our imaginations must have deceived us, we went to the chamber."

"You found Sir George alive?"

"We did."

Miranda listened with painful interest to what would follow, and in a hollow voice Varley continued:

"We had not been many minutes by the bedside, when the light being nearly expiring, I left Twitter in the room while I went down to the apartment we had left to procure a fresh light. When I returned I found him lying in a swoon at the foot of the bed, and Sir George Rankley quite dead."

Here Varley paused, and reaching a glass of water which stood near him, he moistened his parched lips, while a silence as of the grave pervaded the deeply-interested assembly.

"Go on, sir," said the coroner.

"Before I could think what to do, for the occurrence confounded me, this young lady, Miss Rankley, came into the room. To my great surprise, she was dressed as if she expected someone. In vain I tried to keep her from the bedside, for I was afraid the shock would be terrible to her, of finding her father dead. She persisted, and I left her there while I hurried from the room to procure assistance. As I crossed from my own room, then, to the servants' hall, a figure rushed upon me, attired in a green hunting-dress. By the hall lamp I saw his face."

"Who was it?"

"Rowland Percy."

"You will swear that?"

"I will. He struck me on the head ere I was aware of his intention, and I lay for some time insensible. When I recovered, I cried for help, and immediately went to the chamber of the murdered Sir George, and on the floor I found these ivory tablets."

The tablets were handed to the coroner.

"You will find the name of Rowland Percy written in ink upon the first one," said Varley, "and you will likewise find a memorandum on another page I grieved to see."

"'Tis false," cried Rowland. "Those tablets were never written on by me."

"Silence," said the coroner; "you shall be heard. Gentlemen, I will read you the memorandum. It runs thus: 'An account of the Grange property, which would descend to M. R. in case of G. R.'s sudden death, without a will. Five farms, two tenements in York, seven hundred acres of cultivated land, the Deen Forest, the Grange—estimated value, twelve thousand per annum. Mem. To be at Grange by seven o'clock—after duel—if that not fatal.'

"That is the memorandum, gentlemen," said the coroner.

"I deny it before the God of Heaven," cried Rowland Percy; "as I hope for mercy hereafter—I never wrote one word of it."

"You hear," said Miranda. "He denies it. The villain Varley wrote it to destroy him. 'Tis forged—'tis forged. You hear, gentlemen, Rowland Percy did not write it."

"We are not trying the prisoner," said the coroner, "and all I can do is to seal up those tablets, and send them to the magistrate who committed the prisoner. What more have you to add, sir?"

"Nothing," said Varley, "with the exception that Sir George, before his death, expressed his firm conviction that Rowland Percy sought a marriage with his child to better his condition."

"Have you any questions to ask him?" said the coroner to Rowland.

"No," said Percy. "To ask him questions were, indeed, a vain task. He is a perjured villain. That I was in the house I will not deny, but——"

"You had better reserve your own statement," said the attorney, whom Miranda had retained for him, "until you have heard all the evidence."

"I bow to your decision," said Rowland.

"Although you all mark that he is innocent," cried Miranda.

Samuel Twitter was summoned next, and pale, trembling, and awful-looking, the guilty valet crept forward to the end of the large table at which the jury sat.

He licked his parched lips incessantly, and he clutched the edge of the table to endeavour to stop the nervous twitching of his hands.

His state of mind seemed a most pitiable one, and as he gazed around upon the many anxious and excited faces, all bent towards him, he could have sunk upon his knees from abject fear, and confessed all, but that his weak mind was enthralled by the dark spirit of Bernard Varley, whom he dreaded more than he dreaded the vengeance of Heaven, because the one was near at hand, and the other, in his ignorance, he considered remote—as if Heaven's mercy, and Heaven's justice were not ever present at all times and at all seasons.

He took the oath, and then stood breathing hard, as the coroner, with a firm, solemn voice, said:

"State now, Samuel Twitter, what you know of this melancholy affair."

"Yes, yes," he said; "I am—I was the valet of Sir George Rankley. On the morning of the duel, Mr. Varley came to my room, and asked me to sit up with him a few hours, while he kept watch in the sick-chamber of Sir George. On our route thither, we saw a figure glide by us dressed in green."

"Why did not you and Mr. Varley alarm the house, at sight of this figure?" said one of the jury.

"There is a superstition among the servants," said Twitter, "that the spirit of a murdered gamekeeper walks about the passages and staircases, and particularly when any inhabitant of the Grange is about to die."

"And did you suppose such to be the case?"

"The hour was midnight; and all men are, under certain circumstances, more or less superstitious. When we reached the chamber, Sir George was alive."

"You are certain of that?"

"I am."

"Pray go on."

"The truth," said Miranda.

Twitter's knees trembled, and he could not speak for some moments.

"Wherefore do you feel so much emotion?" said the coroner.

"I—I am a nervous man," he gasped, "and my master's death has quite unmanned me. He was very kind to me. We had not watched long, when Mr. Varley went for a light, leaving me alone with Sir George, who was moaning in his sleep. I was standing at the foot of the bed, and scarcely had Mr. Varley been gone two minutes, when, by the dim and nearly-expiring candle that was in the room, I saw a figure enter the apartment."

"Can you describe it?"

"I can. It was dressed in green—it approached the bed—I was paralyzed with fear. Then a sudden brightness from the candle, which will frequently occur when one is near expiring, showed me his face."

Every ear was now bent forward, and every heart beat with feverish excitement, as, after a slight pause, Twitter continued:

"It was Mr. Rowland Percy!"

A deep sigh seemed to come from the depths of every heart as Twitter gave this conclusive evidence against Rowland, and the young man himself clasped his hands, as he exclaimed:

"Is this a dream, or do I really hear these men perjure themselves before high Heaven? Oh, Miranda—Miranda! it is false—it is false!"

"I know it is false," said Miranda. "Heaven yet will right the innocent. Be patient, Rowland, be patient!"

"You will swear to what you say, distinctly and without reservation?" said the coroner.

"I will," replied Twitter, with a groan.

"What happened next?"

"He took the pillow from under the head of Sir George, and placed it over his face."

A thrill of horror pervaded the assembly, and several who were near to the unhappy Rowland shrank back from him as if he had been afflicted with the plague.

"I know not well what happened next," said Twitter. "My brain swam round—

whether he struck me down, or whether I fainted, I cannot tell; but it was long before I became sensible again, and then I was told that my master was dead."

"Villain!" cried Rowland Percy. "I pity you from my soul; for, as surely as you now stand there a false witness in the sight of Heaven, there will come a day of such dreadful—such fearful retribution, that your shrieking soul will howl in its despair, and ask in vain for that mercy you can never expect. On your death-bed this scene will rise before you in horror. Oh, man! man! repent you while yet you may."

CHAPTER XXI.

THE VERDICT—MIRANDA'S NOBLE CONDUCT—THE READING OF THE WILL.

TWITTER fainted and fell on the floor heavily.

The greatest sensation was produced in the room, and, while some raised the terror-stricken man, others opened the windows to let in air.

Such a scene of confusion as ensued for a few moments was hardly ever seen on such a solemn occasion.

"Gentlemen," said the coroner, "let me beg of you to keep your seats. The witness will be, no doubt, recovered sufficiently to resume his examination."

"We have heard enough," said one of the jury, "unless the prisoner wishes to ask him questions."

"No, I will ask none," cried Rowland. "I am innocent, so help me Heaven! and those two men are perjured. God forgive them this deep sin."

A whispered consultation now ensued between the jury and the coroner, and then the coroner said:

"Miss Rankley, the jury wish to put to you some questions."

"I am ready," said Miranda.

"Did you expect the accused to come to the Grange on the particular evening to which this inquiry refers?"

"I did not."

"Can you speak with certainty as regards your father being alive or dead when, as stated in evidence, you took your station by his bedside?"

"I cannot. I thought once I heard him breathe, but that might have been a delusion."

"The jury will not trouble you further."

"Then hear me," said Rowland.

"In courtesy," said the coroner, "we will hear you make what statement you please, but the evidence distinctly sworn to makes it quite impossible for us to return any other verdict than one of wilful murder."

"Then," said Mr. Anderson, "I strongly advise you, Mr. Percy, to say nothing beyond a declaration of your innocence. No statement from you can be of the least benefit here; for, under the circumstances, the jury have no sort of discretion. Nothing but a weight of contradictory evidence can have any effect."

"I thank you, sir," said Rowland, "for your kind advice; yet I feel strongly, at every stage of these unhappy proceedings, that I ought to speak. I cannot vary in my tale, because it is the truth. It is for them who hatch falsehoods to be careful what they say, and when they say it. I hear from you, sir, that you must return a verdict against me, upon the oath of these deeply-perjured men. Be it so; and yet am I innocent, and yet will I speak.

"Some time since, from what cause I know not, my father told me to forget Miranda Rankley, for that he, as well as I, had received deep insults by letter from Sir George; and, at the same time, he hinted to me that his circumstances were not flourishing.

"I entreated him to explain to me more fully what he meant; but he shrank from so doing, and, without taking leave of Miss Rankley, I was compelled to depart some distance from this place.

"What was then occurring in my absence I had no means of knowing. I wrote once to Sir George himself, begging for some explanation, but received no answer. Then, stung by the torments of absence from all I held dear, tortured by suspense, and unhappy beyond expression, I formed the perhaps foolishly-romantic notion of obtaining an interview with Miranda under cover of a disguise, which I knew would leave me unquestioned by the household.

"It was my cruel fortune, gentlemen, to arrive on that fatal night which has wrung so many tears from gentle hearts, and the issues of which are in the hands of Heaven.

"The Grange and its grounds have been familiar to me from earliest childhood. I believe, indeed, I know more of the intricacies of the building than any dweller now within its walls. Favoured, then, by such knowledge, I easily gained admission to the house, and, in crossing a corridor, I saw that man Varley and Twitter crawling, like men of guilt, towards the chamber-door of Sir George. They were trembling with fear, and their faces were ghastly.

"In my endeavours to avoid them, they saw me; but I escaped, and concealed myself for some time in the small oratory, which has been for years in disuse. From there, after a time, hearing much confusion in the house, and not knowing its purport, I advanced towards the suite of rooms on the ground-floor, one of which is an apartment usually occupied by that man Varley.

"Through the half-open doorway of that room, I saw a sight that made the hot blood rush through my veins like liquid fire. Miss Rankley had fainted, and yon villain, Varley, was about to take the opportunity to press his lips upon her cheek. I dashed into the room, and, with one blow, felled him to the ground.

"After that, all was confusion. My object was to leave the house, and ascertain from someone out of the establishment what had occurred; for even then I was quite ignorant of the death of Sir George. I was pursued, and allowed myself to be taken, believing that my utmost penalty would be the anger of Sir George Rankley; and, likewise, I longed to denounce the villain, Varley, whose base conduct I had witnessed. I never, for a moment, was in Sir George's chamber.

"The tablets are mine, but I never wrote one word on them—except my name. I am innocent—I swear it by my hopes hereafter—by the life to come! By the Majesty of Heaven—to which I now appeal—I declare to you my innocence."

For a few moments after Rowland Percy finished speaking, there was a dead silence, and Twitter, who had recovered partially from his insensibility, was seated, gazing at him, with a face as pale as that of some resuscitated corpse.

"Your declaration can do you no harm," said the coroner, "but our verdict must be in accordance with facts sworn before us. Gentlemen, how say you? What is your verdict?"

The jury whispered together for a moment or two, and then said:

"Wilful murder against Rowland Percy."

"No—no—no!" sobbed Miranda. "Oh, think again. Can you believe those men? Look at them! Perjury is written by the hand of Heaven upon their brows. See how they shrink—see—they have already received some of the wages of guilt. They are miserable men, for they have not the truth in them. Oh! spare him—he is innocent! He is innocent—innocent!"

"Our duty, Miss Rankley, is a painful one," said the coroner, "but we must do it. The verdict is recorded—gentlemen, you are relieved from your duties."

Miranda sank back in a chair, and covering her face with her hands, sobbed convulsively for a moment; then, suddenly rising, she walked up to Rowland, and while the tears still glistened in her eyes, she said:

"Rowland, when you were prosperous and happy, and life lay before you like a summer-garden, I could not say to you what I say now, and care not who hears me; you, and you only, have my heart's love, Rowland. My poor father is gone—a mother's care I never knew, for fate snatched her from me, ere I had breathed a few days in this world of sorrow. Relations, friends, I have none. You, and you only, are the link that binds me to a world which I never could have believed so bad as it seems now to be. In sickness or in sorrow, in grief or in joy, persecuted or acquitted, Rowland Percy, I am yours!"

"Then let fate do its worst," cried Rowland, "I defy it. Innocence, Miranda, ever comes brighter out of the fire of suspicion. My name may, for a time, be dimmed by the odium of the crime laid to my charge; but the day will come when it will survive its detractors, and I may be pitied, although not saved. If it be the will of Heaven that the wicked should triumph, I will not repine."

"You shall be saved, Rowland," said Miranda; "there are still warm-feeling hearts that will, for your own sake, as well as for mine, crowd round you. You will see no more tears from me—my mind is made up now to cast all weakness from me, and to be intent upon one object only—your freedom. My voice shall be heard loudly proclaiming your innocence, wherever the smallest whisper to your prejudice has reached. Rowland, be comforted."

"No angel's voice could bring such joy to my heart as yours," whispered Rowland.

"Come," said the officers, touching Percy on the arm, "we must go."

"Yet a moment," said Miranda. "Rowland, dear Rowland, I will visit you in your prison—you shall not be deserted."

"Nay, nay, Miranda, think of yourself more than of me. Though all the world should condemn me, I have a shield now over my heart which will resist all attacks—it is your dear love which will keep me from a wound."

"I cannot wait," said the officer.

"One moment more," said Miranda. "Rowland, I will send you books—letters—I will come often."

"Farewell!" said Percy, in choking accents, for the generous devotion of Miranda touched him deeply. "Farewell! hope for the best!"

"Now," said the officer.

"Farewell, Rowland! To-morrow I will see you! Do not despair. There is a Heaven above us, and all will yet be well. Treat him gently, sir," to the officer; "he is innocent—indeed he is!"

"I don't know anything about that," said the officer; "all I know is, I must take him to York."

"Once more farewell, Rowland, till to-morrow," said Miranda, as she slowly released her hold of Rowland's arm.

He could not speak, but taking her trembling hand, he pressed it to his lips.

Then a faintness came over Miranda, but she struggled against it, and overcame it.

"I—must be firm," she thought. "He shall not leave me, as he thinks, in sorrow; I—I will smile upon him even now!"

She slowly turned to the door—Rowland was passing through it, and his eyes were fixed upon Miranda. She waved her hand, and tried to smile, but the effort was too much for her. With difficulty she restrained her tears—Rowland was gone. The jury were leaving the room, and she sat down, unconscious for a few moments of anything.

She muttered to herself abstractedly the words:

"Wilful murder! wilful murder!"

Then, with a shudder, she said:

"No—no—I will not go mad! I will be calm, and save him yet!"

"Miranda," said Mr. Anderson.

She heard him not; her thoughts were with her lover, and she still muttered the awful words:

"Wilful murder!"

"Miranda," repeated Mr. Anderson, "calm yourself; there is still much to do. Your father's will."

She started, as she exclaimed:

"Bernard Varley claims all, but I can beg from door to door for Rowland Percy. Yes, Bernard Varley kills the father and robs the child."

"Hush, hush!" said Mr. Anderson; "come with me, and we will insist upon having this will read."

Miranda rose, and leaning heavily upon his arm, walked with him to the principal drawing-room of the mansion. It was empty, and when they reached it, Mr. Anderson said:

"Be seated now, Miranda, and endeavour to command your feelings, while I insist upon seeing the will which this man says he has."

"I will be calm," said Miranda, "and yet, oh, Heaven, what is to become of me? Wealth I never envied, but now the means of successfully defending Rowland may be wrested from me, and at the moment when I might do so much, I am about to be deprived of the means of doing anything but starve; starve—oh, horrible. Just Heaven, what have I done?"

"Hush, hush," said Mr. Anderson; "do not, I charge you, impugn the justice of Heaven's decrees."

"I know not what I say," gasped Miranda. "Heaven will forgive the few words of impatience wrung from a suffering heart."

"Do not abandon hope, Miranda. I will now summon this man here, and demand to know on what pretence he remains in this house?"

Mr. Anderson rang the bell, and when a servant appeared, said:

"Is Mr. Varley within?"

"Yes, sir," was the reply.

"Then tell him that Miss Rankley's solicitor wishes to see him immediately on business of importance—I will wait for him here."

"Now, Miranda," added Mr. Anderson, turning to her, "Varley must produce the will he speaks of, or leave the house; and if he should produce it, and I have any suspicions that it is not genuine, I will take upon myself, in your name, to have him turned out of the Grange."

"Alas!" said Miranda. "We have to deal with one who, I fear, is more than a match for honesty and determination. I dread the power of Varley. A man who is quite unscrupulous is to be feared."

"Hush—leave all to me. He comes—say not a word unless I ask you a question."

"I will be mute," said Miranda.

The door of the room was flung open, and Varley, with an insolent swagger, walked in.

———

CHAPTER XXII.

THE FATAL CLAUSE IN THE WILL—THE ATTEMPTED ASSASSINATION.

WELL did Bernard Varley seem to know that much depended upon the interview he was about to have with Mr. Anderson, for, although he strove to assume an air of perfect assurance and self-command, yet there was an evident anxious expression on his face, which did not escape the keen eyes of the attorney, who purposely remained silent for some moments, in order that Varley should not recover from his anxiety by immediately speaking.

"Well, sir?" said Varley, when he saw that Mr. Anderson did not at once open the conference. "I am here in obedience to your wishes."

"Very well, Mr. Varley; you will understand that I speak in the name of Sir George Rankley's daughter, now present, when I ask you when it will suit you to leave the Grange?"

"Suit me to leave the Grange, sir?" cried Varley, his face reddening with passion. "The Grange, sir, is mine—my own!"

"Yours, Mr. Varley?"

"Yes. It was devised to me by Sir George Rankley. I told you so. You shall see the will."

"It is very strange, Mr. Varley, that Sir George Rankley, loving his daughter, as all who were of his acquaintance knew he did, should disinherit her in favour of you."

"I said not disinherit," said Varley; "Miranda may still be mistress of the Grange. But I will read you the will, sir, from courtesy."

"I beg your pardon there, Mr. Varley," said the attorney; "you read it to me from necessity, for this young lady, as heir-at-law, claims the property, and it is for you to make out your title by proving the will you speak of."

"Very well, sir," said Varley, drawing from his pocket a folded paper; "here is the will. You shall hear it—whether from courtesy or necessity, I care not."

"You have no objection, I presume, to let me read it myself?"

"None whatever," said Varley, as he handed the document to the attorney, and, at the same time, kept a wary eye upon it.

Mr. Anderson opened the document, and, after a few moments careful examination, he said:

"Miranda, here is an enumeration, carefully made, of your father's property, after which the will consists of but one clause, which I will read to you."

Miranda said nothing, but fixed her eyes upon Mr. Anderson's face, while, in a clear audible tone, he read as follows:

"I hereby give and bequeath the whole of the above-mentioned property, together with whatever personal effects I may die possessed of, to Bernard Varley, my sincere friend, to have and to hold in trust, for my beloved daughter, Miranda; and it is my wish that she marry Bernard Varley. If she refuse to marry him, the whole of my property above-mentioned is to become his, absolutely and without reservation, excepting such allowance as he shall be pleased to grant to her, unless she marry someone with the said Bernard Varley's full consent, in which case she shall be entitled to the whole of my property, with the reservation of an annuity of one thousand pounds per annum, to be paid from my estate to Bernard Varley.

"This is my last will and testament.
          "GEORGE RANKLEY.

"Witnesses—
      "FRANCIS HEARN,
      "HENRY REEVES."

"This will is dated on the morning of the day which closed the mortal career of your father, Miranda," said Mr. Anderson, in a sad tone. "Will you look carefully at this signature, and say if it is your father's."

Mr. Anderson handed Miranda the document.

She took it in her trembling hands. For a moment a film seemed to come across her eyes, and then it cleared away, and the name, "George Rankley," stood before her in terrible distinctness.

Once or twice she essayed to speak, but the words died away ere they reached her lips.

"If, Miranda," said Mr. Anderson, "you were on your solemn oath in a court of justice, to say yes or no to the question of, 'Is that your father's signature?' what would be your answer?"

Miranda let go the will, and it fell, with a rustling sound, to the floor, as she said:

"Yes!"

Mr. Anderson clasped his hands, and Bernard Varley, advancing, pointed to the will, while a smile of triumph lit up his demoniac face.

"Miranda! Miranda!" cried Mr. Anderson. "Are you sure—have you no doubt?"

"None—none——" said Miranda. "All is over. There is no hope. Poor—poor Rowland! Who will help you now?"

"Ha! ha! ha!" laughed Varley, as he took up the will. "Poor Rowland needs help now, I think."

"Peace! scoffer of the pure feelings, you cannot understand!" cried Miranda. "Peace, I say! If you must exult in villainy, do so where none can hear you; but do not insult your victims."

"Harsh words, Miranda Rankley," said Varley. "Exceeding harsh words, considering who and what I am now."

"All the power which Heaven ever gave to mortal man—all the wealth which ever the depths of the earth yielded to the miner's toil—could not make you other than you are," said Miranda—"a most consummate villain!"

" Hush—hush, Miranda," said Mr. Anderson. " Remember your promise to me."

" I had forgotten," said Miranda. " I was bidded to speak. Pardon me, Mr. Anderson."

" You have ample excuse," said Mr. Anderson; " and now tell me, sir, what may be your intention, supposing, for a moment, we admit the genuineness of this document?"

" You shall—you must admit it," said Varley. " There is my evidence!"

He pointed to Miranda, exultingly, as he spoke.

" Enough of this," said the attorney. " Supposing, then, that this will is established, what do you intend to do?"

" Conform to the intentions of it," said Varley. " I hold the wishes of Sir George Rankley as commands. I here offer freely my hand and heart to Miranda Rankley, and every shilling of her father's estates shall be settled on herself."

" That is absurd," said Mr. Anderson. " You must feel that such a union can never take place."

" It was the wish of Sir George," sneered Varley; " and so pious and loving a daughter as this young lady will surely look upon the will as a command. It is as if her father spoke to her from the grave."

" Hold, impious man," cried Miranda. " Nay, Mr. Anderson, I must speak. Each moment I feel more and more convinced there is some juggle in this business. That signature, on my conscience, I could swear to be my father's; but, on my solemn oath likewise, I could swear he never dictated that will. I am placed most awfully. I know, in my own heart, two things I cannot prove—Rowland Percy's innocence, and the falsity of that will. You talk of a voice from the grave, Bernard Varley, and I say to you, beware, for one even now seems to ring in my ears, to tell me that the time will come when you, in your villainy, will be confounded; when you will cry—not as I do now for justice, and find none—but for mercy, and find none. You may well tremble, for your name shall become a byword and a reproach. Your memory shall be accursed. God has given me, for this minute, the gift of prophecy; and I proclaim that you, Bernard Varley, will suffer more pangs than ever you, in your height of iniquitous power, can inflict. You may turn me a beggar from my own home. You may bring to death him whom I love, but still do I, in my inmost heart, pity thee, for thy fate will be torment without end, while our tears shall be fleeting as an April shower, our misery short as a winter's day."

" Ha! ha! ha!" shrieked a voice, in wild laughter, at the window which opened upon a lawn. " There is Bernard Varley, who is to be hanged at York. Look at him now. The dead man's seal is upon his brow. Hanged at York!—hanged at York! And poor Bold Hawk there to see it. Ha! ha! ha!"

For a minute or more Varley seemed quite overwhelmed, and then, snatching a loaded pistol from his pocket, he fired at the window where the poor idiot was stationed.

Mr. Anderson rushed from his seat, and seized Varley's arm, but too late to prevent the discharge of the pistol.

Miranda screamed, and flew to the window.

" God bless you, Miss Miranda, and your bright eyes!" cried Bold Hawk. " He cannot shoot me. I am not what I was. Once swords would hack me, bullets pierce my skin, fire burn, and water drown me; but I am changed—changed, and Bernard Varley will be hanged at York."

With a wild cry, the poor creature bounded across the lawn, and was, in a moment or two, lost to sight in the thick plantations that bordered its northern side.

" Mr. Varley," cried the attorney, " you should take shame to yourself for this act."

" Why did he taunt me?" growled Varley, who had bitterly repented of the shot the moment he had fired it. " Why does he taunt me with his ill-omened croaking? Am I to be for ever the subject of such gibes? He has been taught by some enemy to say what he is continually shrieking in my ears."

" He is bereft of sense, and you should not heed him."

" There's no harm done—the pistol had no bullet in it. 'Twas only powder."

" Bernard Varley lies again," cried Miranda, as she pointed to a round hole in one of the large squares of glass.

" 'Tis false!" cried Varley.

" Swear it," cried Miranda, " and you will add another record to the book kept by the Eternal against the perjurer and the murderer."

" For Heaven's sake," said Mr. Anderson, " let us come to some better understanding. I again ask you, Mr. Varley, what are your intentions?"

" Will you read the will again?" said Varley.

" No; but what are your intentions upon it?"

" I love, as such a nature as mine only can love, this haughty girl. I will wed her, though she should rave at me morning, noon, and night, if she will go to church with me. I like her wild, untamed, haughty spirit—it jumps well with my own. As her legal, and, I presume, friendly adviser, you would do well, sir, to advise her to marry me."

" You jest, sir, most untimely," said Mr. Anderson.

" Nay, I adore her," said Varley. " If she will this moment pledge her word to be my wife, I will destroy this will before her face."

" Never—never—never!" cried Miranda. " Were on one side the most horrible death that man could devise to await me, and, on the other, life with you, I would embrace torments rather than——"

" Hush—enough," said Varley. " You are sealing your own fate. I shall act upon the will, unless you marry me. And if you do, I will save Rowland," he added, in a whisper, close to the ear of Miranda.

"Fiend !" cried Miranda, starting back. "Away ! Approach me not. Your touch is pollution."

"Mr. Varley, stand back !" cried Mr. Anderson. "I will not see this lady insulted by you."

"Then take her away !" cried Varley. "She is in my house. You are interlopers here. Away with you—you are no guests of mine !"

"Sir," said Mr. Anderson, "I will take the highest legal advice with regard to that most extraordinary will ; and if Miranda were other than a young and unprotected female, I should advise possession to be held of these estates until, by proper legal means, you succeeded in establishing your ownership. As it is, though, I advise her to take possession of what personal property she herself possesses, and to leave this place, although it would be far more decent for you to leave it until Sir George Rankley's remains are laid in the grave."

"You appeal to me for consideration ?" sneered Varley ; "to me, upon whose head this lady has heaped every epithet of scorn she could think of ? No ; she or I shall be in power here. She may remain ; but, if she does, she remains upon my kind clemency, and eats my bread at my table."

"Welcome death first !" said Miranda. "I will leave this place now, and, if it be the will of Heaven, for ever. On the day which sees my poor father's mortal remains hidden in the tomb, no power shall keep me from there ; but, until then, I will find a shelter where I may, for I will not sleep beneath the same roof with Bernard Varley, the perjured murderer."

"By Heaven, if you insult me by such names, I will take measures to make you repent it !" cried Varley.

"Perjured murderer !" shouted Miranda. "Can you really feel, perjured murderer, assassin, false witness ?"

Varley rushed forward as if about to strike her, so ungovernable was his rage ; but Mr. Anderson held his arm, crying :

"Help ! help here ! Servants, protect your mistress !"

CHAPTER XXIII.

THE REMOVAL FROM THE GRANGE—MIRANDA'S DESTITUTE STATE—THE PRISON.

SEVERAL servants, hearing Mr. Anderson's cries, at once hurried into the room ; but, before anyone could speak, or adopt any course of action, Miranda cried in a firm voice :

"I am prepared to go. Those who are my friends will respect the sanctity of this house now, for it contains the remains of one so dear to me in life, that even in death affection clings to the casket from which the bright jewel has fled. I will go now, Mr. Anderson. Let there be no strife—I am ready. Such few fond records of my poor father's love, as, of right, I can lay claim to, I will take with me. I ask for nothing more."

"Miranda," said Varley, "this is your home."

"I have no home," said Miranda, with shudder. "'Tis loving hearts that make home, and, were I free to choose now, I should call the prison-house of Rowland Percy the home to which I should go."

"You will repent this precipitancy," muttered Varley. "Miranda Rankley, I pledge you my word that by staying here you shall experience no annoyance from me."

"Peace, peace," cried Miranda. "You are master here. Enjoy, sir, your dominion. How acquired, ask your own conscience, and read the answer there in letters of blood ! I am going ; but first I will go to my chamber, and collect those trivial things which surely are my own."

"Mr. Varley," said Mr. Anderson, "surely you contemplate making some immediate and suitable provision for the daughter of Sir George Rankley ?"

"Here is the will," said Varley. "Does it say as much ? Can you torture one of its phrases into such an intention ? There are certain conditions named, and by them must I abide. If this young lady will remove herself from my protection, I cannot help it. The doors of this house shall ever be open to her, but I cannot force her to enter them."

"Nevertheless, you surely will not, cannot, allow her to go forth destitute, because she does not choose to reside in the same house with you, or permit herself to remain under your protection ?"

"Here is the will," said Varley, speaking with evident difficulty, and his very lips assuming an ashy paleness. "Let Miranda decide. I offer her wealth, a home, unbounded freedom."

"All of which I reject, coming from you," said Miranda. "Say no more, Mr. Anderson. Welcome poverty, welcome woe and distress, rather than one crumb of bread from Bernard Varley. If it be that the law will permit him thus to wrest from me my inheritance, I must suffer so much wrong ; and happier shall I be, perchance, in the humble state to which I am reduced, than Bernard Varley, with the never-ceasing small voice of conscience, whispering despair to his heart."

Miranda left the room, and, hastening to her own apartment, she, with a rigid calmness that had something more awful in its manifestation than the wildest grief, proceeded to pack into a small compass such few things as she prized, and would fain carry with her, even to the grave.

Then she lit a taper, and destroyed many letters and papers, which, under happier auspices, she would have kept ; but now all minor feelings were merged in the tremendous excitement which her mind had undergone, and was still undergoing.

Her own jewels—gifts from her father, she secured about her, and then with eyes, in which there were no tears—for her feelings lay too deep for such relief—she glanced around her on each well-remembered object in

THE DISCOMFITURE OF BERNARD VARLEY.

the room which perchance she was never more to see.

"Farewell!" she said, sadly; "farewell! I have been too happy, and Heaven is now pleased to reverse the picture, and show me the dark and gloomy side of human nature. I—must bear with it as I may. Farewell! farewell!"

She tottered to the door, and then she turned to look again.

Not an object in that room met her gaze but what was endeared to her by some fond remembrance. Either from love to the giver, or the occasion of the giving, each little cherished ornament of her chamber had an interest in the eyes of Miranda, and it was like parting with a troop of dear valued friends to tear herself away.

Once—twice—thrice she tried to leave the room, and as often turned back to glance again upon the roses as they trailed in at the open window, filling the air with a delicious perfume, and dappling the casement with rare beauty.

"If I could weep now," said Miranda—"if I could weep as many do on leaving much loved objects, I think my heart would not feel quite so heavy, but I think I have no more tears—I shall never weep again. The grief that finds a vent by the eyes, is weak and fleeting compared to mine. Oh! what a catalogue of miseries have I not to contend with! My father murdered—he who loves me, a prisoner—myself destitute—fortune has done her worst. What other arrow half so venomous can she have in her quiver to launch at poor Miranda Rankley?"

Miranda plucked one of the roses, and placed it in her breast.

"I will keep this," she said; "it will remind me of my once happy home, and when its leaves become withered, and its fragrance is gone, it will be a fit companion for me. We both shall have come from our home where we were happy, and we both are withered to the heart, but mine the most—mine the most."

She opened the door, and as she did so, someone turned the handle on the other side; Miranda started—a scream was upon her lips, but she repressed it, and summoning all her courage to support her, she confronted Bernard Varley.

For the space of several moments there was a dead silence, and Miranda had time to note the appearance of her enemy.

Varley trembled in every limb, and his face was the picture of agonized anxiety—the state of his mind was evidently awful. He spoke with choking accents, and his words were wild and fearful.

"Miranda, Miranda," he said, "have mercy upon me. You, in your well-schooled heart, cannot dream of the awful whirlwind of passion that sweeps through a breast like mine. Have mercy on me, and gaze not thus like a marble statue on one who, for your sake, has forfeited even the faintest hope of Heaven's mercy. Oh, think what must have been the love which has driven me to war, even with my God, to curse my soul—to foredoom myself to everlasting torment—mercy—mercy—Miranda Rankley, have mercy upon me!"

These words were rather shrieked than spoken, and Miranda shrank back, appalled at the awful vehemence of the wild confession.

"You shrink from me," he cried, "you loathe me—you abhor me—oh! girl—girl—drive me not quite mad—there is a raging fire in my brain—my blood no longer flows in healthful currents—I am a desperate man—I could now wage war with Heaven itself—and all—oh! Heaven, 'tis all for love of thee, Miranda."

"Love," said Miranda, "call you that love?"

"Yes, wild passionate love—the love that consumes the heart—that knows no bounds—that feeds upon the very soul—that begins in agony, and ends in madness. Hear me, Miranda—when first I came to the house, and saw you, I thought you some rare and wondrous work of nature, born but to be worshipped from afar. I had no thought of breathing my idolatry—I would as soon have dreamt of speaking vows of adoration to a statue—but there came one—a mortal breathing man like myself, and he approached the shrine, which, to me, was holy ground. He spoke to you of love, and you heard him with a smile. From that time my bursting heart knew but two passions—love and hate."

"I will hear no more," cried Miranda, as she passed him in the corridor. "Bernard Varley, I will hold no converse with you."

"Miranda—Miranda," he cried, "yet a moment, hear me, ere you leave me to despair. I will restore all—I will save him—ay, even him will I save who stands between me and hope."

"If," said Miranda, "it is true that you do repent of your great wickedness, Bernard Varley, and will save the innocent, I will pray for you."

"No—no—no prayers! I am past prayers. Heaven's gates are shut to me for ever. No—no—no prayers! but if you would save him yourself, and all who in your fall must fall too, in one common ruin, give me but the smallest room to hope—say but one word to turn the current of my dark despair."

"Never!" said Miranda.

"Think. Oh, think again!"

"I have thought, until reflection has dried up even the natural sources of grief. I have no tears even for my father's memory. Bernard Varley, you have been the evil spirit of me and mine. May Heaven have mercy upon you!"

"Miranda! Miranda!" he shrieked. "Are you an angel, or a demon in the shape of one, that you torment me thus? Why are you beautiful, but that men may love you?"

He sank on his knees at her feet, and when she strove to leave him he clutched her dress, and, in accents of wild despair, besought her to hear him.

"One word—one little word, to tell me that you will not always hate me—one word, to let me know that you pity the wild frenzy which could make me the wretch I am."

"Bernard Varley," said Miranda, "release me, or I will call for help. Kneel to offended Heaven—not to me."

"You are my heaven!" he cried. "I worship none else. I will be your slave. Love me but a day, an hour, and then kill me if you will."

"Detain me another moment, and I will alarm the house!" cried Miranda.

"See, I kneel—pray to you!" he shrieked. "Where will you find such love as this? You see I am abject. Miranda—Miranda—save me—save me!"

Miranda tried to leave him; but he still clung to her dress.

"I am going mad!" he cried. "Miranda, you will drive me mad!"

"Help! help!" cried Miranda, who began to be seriously alarmed at his vehemence.

A servant near at hand heard her cries, and suddenly appeared.

Varley sprang to his feet. He pressed his hands upon his head for a moment, then in a low voice he said:

"'Tis done—'tis done—the die is cast. Beware!"

He dashed down the corridor, and disappeared in his own sleeping chamber, leaving Miranda in a state of mind bordering upon despair; for now she knew there was the very worst to fear from the terrible passions of Varley, roused, as they seemed to be, to absolute frenzy.

"Just Heaven!" she thought, "protect me from this man. What an awful scene have I passed through! May reason yet conquer the storm within his breast, and make him penitent! Oh, Rowland, what an enemy you have!"

"Did you call, Miss Miranda?" said the servant.

"I did," said Miranda; "but it is no matter now. I am leaving here, it may be for ever. Do you, when I am gone, tell all in the house that I wish them happiness; and though doomed to leave this house——"

Miranda paused—she could say no more, and waving her hand to the astonished domestic, she walked quickly down the staircase to the room in which she had left Mr. Anderson.

She found him anxiously awaiting her return; and when she appeared, he said:

"Miranda, may I ask a favour of you?"

"Alas! sir, I have no power to confer one," she replied. "You forget who and what I am."

"It is," continued Mr. Anderson, "that you will become my guest as long as it shall be agreeable to yourself."

"Till to-morrow," said Miranda, "I will accept your kind offer, sir; but do not be offended with me when I tell you that I am resolved, since it has pleased Heaven to throw me on my own resources, to submit to the decree without more murmuring than human nature, in its weakness, cannot but give utterance to. I cannot eat the bread of dependence."

"Not when accompanied by as sincere a welcome, Miss Rankley, as man can give to it?"

"No, Mr. Anderson. Such accomplishments as my poor father's love has given me must now be turned to usefulness. I must work; but yet I have matured no plan. I scarcely know what I say. Forgive me till to-morrow."

"You grieve me much by your resolve," said Mr. Anderson; "but we will talk of this subject again to-morrow."

"Yes, to-morrow," said Miranda. "Let us leave this place now. I cannot breathe freely here. Come, Mr. Anderson, and as we go I will tell you of a scene I have just passed through, which I can never forget."

She took Mr. Anderson's arm, and they together passed out of the room into the hall.

Miranda started back, and a cry of grief escaped her as she saw there assembled all the servants of the household with sorrowing countenances.

"Friends," faltered Miranda, in vain endeavouring to command her voice, "why are you all assembled here?"

"God bless you, Miss Miranda," cried one, "we heard you were going away, and as we couldn't believe it, we all came here to ask you yourself."

"I am going," said Miranda.

The servants looked at each other in amazement, and then the spokesman said:

"We all understood you were our young mistress."

"It has turned out an error," said Miranda. "God bless you all—farewell."

She tried to move towards the door, but the domestics, not one of whom but had received some kindness at her hands, pressed around her, some tearfully, and some clamorously, beseeching her to stay.

"Dear Miss Miranda," cried one, "what are we all to do when you are gone? Do stay with us—we are all willing to work night and day for you. What have we done, Miss Miranda, to offend you?"

"Nothing—nothing," said Miranda. "Bernard Varley claims the Grange; so you see, my good friends, I am compelled to go. We shall meet once more at—at my father's funeral—farewell."

Miranda leaned heavily on Mr. Anderson's arm, and hid her face as she passed through the throng that opened to let her go. Some wept aloud, and then Miranda wrung her hands, saying:

"Tears are denied to me. Why cannot I weep?"

Many cried "God bless you!" as she crossed the threshold.

She could but wave her hand, and then, with one deep sigh, she left her once happy home.

CHAPTER XXIV.

THE VISIT TO THE CHAMBER OF DEATH—
THE DIAMOND RING—THE ROBBERY.

BERNARD VARLEY remained for more than an hour in his own room, and what were his thoughts, and what the mental agony he endured during that hour, was only known to Heaven and to himself.

When he emerged he looked some years older than when he had entered, but to all outward appearance he was perfectly calm.

He walked with a slow and steady step to the drawing-room, and then ringing the bell, he ordered Twitter to be sent to him, and in a few minutes the wretched terror-stricken valet made his appearance.

Even he, Twitter, absorbed as he was in his own hopes and fears, glared at Varley as if he had been an apparition, so remarkable was the change his countenance had undergone within the last hour.

"Wherefore do you fix your eyes on me with such surprise?" said Varley.

"You are much altered," said Twitter. "Good Heavens, Varley, I should scarce have known you!"

"Not known me!—what folly is this?"

"Your face is quite changed—I am sure

there are hollows and wrinkles in it that were not there before, and your eyes are much more deeply sunken."

Varley's lip quivered as he said:

"Pshaw, I did not send for you to criticize my personal appearance, but to consult upon our ulterior operations. I thought it safest to leave your name out of the will, Twitter."

"Leave my name out?" gasped Twitter. "Then—then am I to have nothing?"

"You shall have more than was promised you, and to set your mind at rest, I will give you now my note of hand for five hundred pounds, payable at the bankers, where I believe lies a large sum, whenever the necessary legal steps have been taken to prove the will."

"But I was to have so much each year," said Twitter.

"And so you shall have—ay, and twice as much if you please—provided I succeed in my purposes. I have solemnly sworn that Miranda Rankley shall be goaded to despair by poverty—want and distress shall assail her wherever she may fly, and Rowland Percy shall be hanged; if I part with all my wealth to obtain evidence against him."

"You are strangely passionate."

"No, I am calm, quite calm. Passion is all past now. My next intense feelings will be when I have had my revenge."

"Well, so long as in your revenge you do not lose the Grange estates, it matters not to me."

"Certainly not; but I have sent for you to know if you can identify any of the servants who assaulted me in the stable-yard?"

"I cannot."

"Very well. I must be content to have those apprehended whom I can name myself. I have brought the officers with me for the purpose. No one, high or low, shall escape my vengeance if once they give me cause. Now, Twitter, I think you had better remain here nominally in the same capacity you were formerly, but actually as my friend."

"Yes—yes," said Twitter, eagerly. "I will remain. Bernard Varley, who knows but you may die some day, and leave the Grange to me."

"When I do, I will," said Varley; "but something strikes me that I shall outlive you, Twitter. You are looking far from well."

"Who—I?" cried Twitter, much alarmed; "I am very well, and you are some years my elder."

"Well, well, we will not discuss that. I am now going to York upon several errands. I must appear against these servants for assaulting me, have the will forwarded to London, and give directions for Sir George's funeral. During my absence, do you always see anyone who may come to the Grange."

"I will; but tell me, Varley, does not the verdict of the jury virtually acquit the Squire of Larkswood?"

"It does, and he will, no doubt, be immediately set at liberty."

"Is he not to be feared?"

"No; he is a ruined man, and I am certain will scarcely know where to lay his head when he shall be released from prison. I have them all at my mercy. Miranda is entirely dependent upon me. Rowland Percy must suffer, for the means for defending him will not be found, and the Squire himself must skulk about in hourly fear of arrest for debt."

"You have managed well, Varley."

"No, Twitter; but for some fortunate accident, we should have been in great difficulties. Had not young Percy chanced to come here on that eventful night, I know not what might have occurred. I should, most probably, have had you to thank for a speedy transition to the gallows."

"Me, Varley?"

"Ay, even you. But this is idle talk now. Your very blunders through fear have, as chance has decreed, worked well for my purposes. I am now for York, and, remember, caution is the word should anyone call here during my absence."

To the consternation and anger of the whole household, Varley walked into the servants' hall, accompanied by the two constables he had well feed to come with him from York, and pointing out those he was able to name as being foremost in pumping on him, they were taken into custody, and hauled off without further ceremony.

Casting then a glance of contempt and defiance upon the remainder of the domestics, Varley turned upon his heel, and left the house, muttering to himself as he mounted his horse:

"There shall not so much as a scullion of Sir George's household remain on these premises three days; I will have servants who will more freely obey me as a master than these will ever be taught to do."

He then clapped spurs to his horse, and at a hard canter proceeded to York, whither he was followed by his prisoners in a cart.

When he was gone, Twitter glanced around him in his quiet, suspicious way, and then muttered:

"So I am left out of the will, and am dependent upon the generosity of Varley for my reward. Humph! By the assistance of Dick Palmer, my highwayman friend, I think I can manage to increase the five hundred per annum. Master Varley may graciously condescend to give me something more, and who knows but chance may place it in my power to play him yet as good a trick as he has played Sir George Rankley. If I had but nerve, which I have not, and a little courage, which I confess I have not, I might do something better than continually robbing the Grange of all its plate and valuable articles, which is all that I can see my way clearly to do at present. It's—it's very strange that none of them have said anything about the diamond ring Sir George had upon his finger when he died. I saw it glittering as his hand lay upon the bed. Bernard Varley has forgotten it. I may as well possess myself of it. It's worth a hundred pounds."

The struggle in Twitter's mind between avarice and fear was great. The dread he had of entering the chamber of the man he had passively helped to murder, brought such fear and trembling to his heart, that it was long before the tempting prize could induce him to seek the much-dreaded room.

What, however, will not the love of gold stimulate those men to do, in whose hearts the feeling has become a passion?

He lingered long, but at last consented to inflict upon himself an amount of suffering by which he was dearly purchasing the diamond he hoped to take from the dead man's finger.

Slowly, and afraid even of his own shadow, Twitter crept up the stairs, till he came to the corridor, from which the sleeping apartments opened. There was no sound to disturb him. Everything seemed as still as the grave. It would appear as if the corpse had spread around it the mysterious and awful silence of its own inanimation.

"'Tis nothing," whispered Twitter, to himself. "Why do I tremble? He is dead, and incapable of doing me any harm; he has no voice to speak; he is nothing but senseless clay. I must arouse myself from this state of nervousness, or it will surely kill me."

Striving hard to shake off the deadly fear that was at his craven heart, he paused for some moments at the door of the chamber containing the body, before he could find courage to turn the key, which was in the lock, and open it.

When he had done so, he paused again, and it was only by great efforts that he could induce himself to enter the chamber of death. The shutters were all closed, save one from which streamed a broad ray of light upon the corpse, which was entirely covered by a sheet, giving it a much more ghastly and dreadful appearance than even were the face exposed; for when we know that there is something of a fearful nature, the more of it that is left to the imagination's picturing, the more fearful it will ever become.

Twitter stood by the bedside for full five minutes, and neither spoke nor moved.

His clammy, cold face was fixed and rigid, and he drew even his breath with difficulty as he thought: "How am I to get his hand out, and see if he still has the ring?"

After much mental agony, he lifted one side of the sheet, and there was the cold hand of Sir George, with the ring, which, strange to say, had been forgotten by everyone, glittering in very mockery of the dead hand it adorned.

"Yes, yes—I am right, it is there," gasped Twitter; "it is there."

But to remove it was now the fearful task, and to him it was, indeed, a most fearful one. To take in his, the hand of a dead man, would be at any time a horrible idea to the cowardly valet; but when that man was one whom he had known in life, and from whom he had received many kindnesses—one, too, who, by the joint machinations of him and Varley, had been jostled, as it were, from existence, and made the fearful object he was—that was terrible.

The ring glittered, and appeared each moment to be sending forth brighter scintillations of light. Time was travelling fast, and the danger of interruption each moment increasing. Something must be done, and done quickly.

He touched the hand—the cold seemed to thrill to his very heart.

He, by a desperate effort, closed his fingers over the wrist, and then with the other hand strove to drag the ring from the finger, but the joints appeared to have swollen, and a moisture which had come upon the skin, made it difficult for him to succeed in his object of robbing the dead.

Scarcely less pallid than the corpse itself, Twitter tried hard to possess himself of the ring. He turned it round and round upon the finger, but off it would not come. His hands shook so much that he was nearly powerless; but, despite of all, his intense desire to possess the costly jewel increased each moment, although his dread of the corpse was far from decreasing in the same ratio.

Now he made one desperate effort, and the skin upon the finger broke as he dragged the ring over the joint which had hitherto impeded him.

It came off the finger then so suddenly that Twitter's hand jerked the sheet from the face of the corpse, a fact that he was unconscious of until he looked up and saw the pallid, ghastly countenance of the murdered man, with the long scratch—to which the surgeon had made allusion—painfully visible.

"I have it—I have it," muttered Twitter, as he nervously wiped the glittering bauble. Then his eyes fell upon Sir George's face, and, with a cry of terror, he started back to the door.

"Mercy! mercy!" he shrieked; for he thought, in his fright, that the corpse actually moved.

With his hands stretched out before him, and his eyes riveted upon the face, from which he had not the power to withdraw them, he stood for some moments immovable. Then, as he felt assured that all was still, he began to breathe a little more freely.

"Some accident uncovered the face, surely," he said. "It must be covered again—I must not leave it so. How horrible it looks! So pale—so ghastly! What expression is that which sits so painfully upon the countenance? I did not kill him. Heaven knows I did not do the deed. I know not but something might even have moved me to prevent it had I not fainted at the time. Yes! This is Bernard Varley's murder—not mine."

He crept slowly towards the bed, and taking the corner of the sheet in his trembling hands, he, with a shudder, placed it again over the face of the corpse; then, as he arranged the covering as it was before his robbery, and faint and sick at heart, turned to leave the room, the door was slowly opened from without, and, while terror rooted him to the spot, he saw Miranda enter the room.

After leaving the Grange, and seeing Varley pass by a bridle-road towards York, she had returned with Mr. Anderson, by a back entrance, to the house, in order to take one last look upon the face of her father ere she left the home of her love and happiness—perhaps for ever.

A cry of surprise came from Miranda's lips, and it was echoed by another from Twitter, who, thus caught in his guilt, was utterly confounded, and knew not what to say.

CHAPTER XXV.

THE LAST ADIEU—AN ADVENTURE ON THE ROAD TO YORK.

MIRANDA first spoke.

"What do you here," she said, "with my father? Perjured man—false witness! What awful errand brings you to invade the sanctity of this chamber?"

Twitter could do nothing but glare from her to the corpse, and from the corpse to her, in speechless terror for some time, and Miranda had repeated her question ere he found words to say:

"I—I—merely came to see that my poor dear master was not disturbed. I was his attendant in life, and I thought it my duty to visit even his remains."

"Base man," said Miranda, "are your nerves so hardened, is your conscience so callous, that, with the weight of sin you have upon your soul, you can venture into the presence of him who, from my heart, I believe you destroyed, or assisted to destroy?"

"No, no!" cried Twitter. "I am innocent—I am innocent!"

"Peace!" cried Miranda. "The pages of Heaven's word are blotted with your guilt. Protest not to me your innocence, or, if you must add new guilt to your already perjured soul, place even now your hand upon the heart of the dead, and swear——"

"No, no," interrupted Twitter, darting to the door. "I will not give way to such superstitions; I will leave you, Miss Miranda. I am innocent—I am innocent!"

He dashed out of the room as he spoke, and, encountering outside the door Mr. Anderson, he bowed humbly to him, hoping he was well; but the humane attorney shrank back from the wretch, and merely shook his head, to indicate his determination to hold no conversation with him.

Clutching the ring still in his hand, Twitter walked down the corridor, and when he had reached his own room, he sat down, and, drawing a long breath, smiled, after his disagreeable fashion, and muttered to himself:

"I have the ring—I have the ring. 'Twas worth the trouble; and yet how dreadful did that dead face look to me, and she came, too, when least expected. What evil fortune brought her back at such a juncture? But I have the ring—yes, yes, I have secured the ring, and, so far, have outwitted even Bernard Varley."

Miranda stood for some moments alone in the room, gazing on the lifeless remains of her father, and, as she did so, her heart swelled with grief, and a thousand memories of his kindness to her crowded to her recollection.

She slowly approached the bed, and removed the sheet from the face of the corpse.

A chill came over her heart as she gazed upon the immovable features, and she would have given the world then to have wept.

"Father—dear father," she whispered, "you are now, perhaps, from Heaven looking down upon your child, and if it be that mortal vow ever reach the fine sensibilities of immortal spirits, hear me now, in presence of your cold remains, swear to relax no energy—to spare no toil until justice has overtaken those who robbed you of life."

She paused, and, as she looked on the face of the dead, she fancied that a change came over it—it might have been her fancy, or it might have been some one of those sudden changes which occur during the rapid progress of decomposition; but, be it what it might, Miranda shuddered as she noted it, and, replacing the covering over the face, she said:

"Farewell—farewell, until we meet again in the world which is without end—farewell."

Her heart beat tumultuously as she turned from the sad spectacle, and she could not help telling herself how saddened with other thoughts and considerations her heart must be, to enable her to look upon such a sight so calmly as she had done, when the mere thought of a similar scene, but a few days before, would have brought tears to her eyes, and plunged her into exquisite grief.

Mr. Anderson gave her his arm when she left the room, and, without a remark, for he felt how sacred were a child's feelings towards a departed parent, he led her slowly down the corridor.

They descended a back staircase, which led them to the gardens behind the Grange, and were soon in the open air.

Then Miranda spoke, in a calm tone, but still one which had in it the cadence of deep melancholy:

"I will remain with you until to-morrow only, Mr. Anderson," she said; "and I have now a request to make to you, which I hope you will pardon. I have some jewels—gems that were much valued, and more for the giver than the gifts—will you take them, and as far as they will go in providing the necessary means, use them in the defence of Rowland Percy?"

"Miss Rankley," said Mr. Anderson, "you must grant me a favour, if you please. Now, although you have already refused me the one upon which I had set my mind—namely, your acceptance of the hospitality of my roof—let me, as a friend, request that you will allow me to undertake Mr. Percy's defence unaided by anyone. I have a solemn and firm conviction of his innocence, and let implore you to keep the jewels you mention, either for happier days, or for any contingency that may arise, which shall make them of importance."

Miranda was silent for a moment, then she said, in a tone of emotion:

"I ought not to refuse another's offer to befriend Rowland. Your kindness, Mr. Anderson, shall never be forgotten; and, if you save the innocent from an unjust persecution, your own conscience will bestow upon you a far higher reward than any which the applauding breath of thousands can bestow upon you."

"Say no more of it, Miranda. All that man can do shall be done to save Mr. Rowland Percy from the snare which is spread for his destruction; and you must recollect that what in anyone else would be seriously expensive, is not so to a professional man; so, if I am entitled to any praise for generosity, let me not be offered more than my due."

Mr. Anderson assisted Miranda into the chaise, and, in a few minutes, they were rapidly leaving the old Grange far behind them.

They had not, however, proceeded far, when they observed, coming rapidly in the opposite direction, a mounted horseman.

He was approaching at a smart trot, and, in appearance, bore a strong resemblance to a fox-hunting squire going to, or returning from, the chase; not that he was altogether attired in sporting costume, but still, the fashion of his garments, and the long boots he wore, showed a tendency that way. His horse was a splendid animal, and evidently of great value, although, from the foam that hung about his mouth, and his general appearance, he was evidently tired.

It is probable that the horseman would have passed Miranda and Mr. Anderson with merely such a passing glance at them as they cast upon him, had it not been that his horse, when within a dozen paces of the chaise, stumbled, and, after making several ineffectual efforts to rise, fell over on his side, entangling the rider so much in his stirrups that, without some assistance, it was more than probable he could not have disengaged himself.

In fact, he seemed to be injured, for he lay perfectly still, while the animal made some desperate efforts to recover its feet.

Mr. Anderson, with the promptitude of humanity, immediately drew up, and, saying to Miranda:

"Hold the reins, for Heaven's sake!" he leaped from the chaise, and flew to the assistance of the fallen horseman.

To disengage his foot from the stirrup was a work of some trouble, but, by great efforts, Mr. Anderson accomplished it, and then, taking him by the shoulders, drew him away from the horse, who now, after rolling over once or twice, rose trembling, and evidently much frightened, to his feet.

"Is he hurt?" said Miranda.

"I fear he is," said Mr. Anderson. "He must have struck his head against the ground, for he seems stunned."

"Will your horse stand quietly, Mr. Anderson?"

"Yes. He is used to waiting for me."

Miranda immediately sprang from the chaise, and, for the moment forgetting her own troubles and intense anxieties, approached the wounded man.

"Pray Heaven he be not killed," she exclaimed. "Place him in the chaise, Mr. Anderson, and I will walk."

"He is only stunned by the sudden fall. The ground is soft, and could not do much injury. If we had some water now to give him."

"Stay," said Miranda, to whom the neighbourhood was familiar, "there is a spring close by. I will fetch some in a moment."

"Then take his hat, Miranda," said Mr. Anderson. "You are a noble-hearted girl, oppressed, as you are, by troubles enough to appal the stoutest heart, to be able to still feel for the misfortunes of others."

Miranda did not stay to hear Mr. Anderson's praise, but hastened down a narrow turning to where she knew a clear, cold spring bubbled from its gravelly bed.

With some difficulty she got some water into the hat by lifting it up with her hand, and then, hastening back to where she had left the injured man, she knelt by his side, and dashed the cold refreshing fluid in his face and on his hands.

"See, he is recovering," said Mr. Anderson. "He will soon be all right again."

As Mr. Anderson spoke, the wounded stranger slowly opened his eyes and fixed them in unmingled surprise upon the lovely face of Miranda.

For several moments his whole returning powers of perception seemed absorbed in gazing upon her, while she, all unconscious that it was her rare beauty bursting so suddenly upon his sight, that gave rise to the surprised expression of his face, said anxiously, as she bent over him:

"Are you better now?"

"What—what has happened?" he murmured; "who did it?"

"You have had a fall from your horse," said Mr. Anderson, "and we fortunately were near you."

"A fall from my horse?" he muttered, "then I have fallen into Heaven, and this is an angel!"

Miranda drew back, and a faint tinge of colour came to her cheek, as she said:

"He raves, Mr. Anderson."

"Pardon me, lady," said the stranger, "I would not offend you for worlds! God bless you for feeling compassion for a poor fellow who might have died on the road-side. I recollect now, my horse stumbled, and I must have had an infernal rap on the head, for it is now beating like a hundred blacksmiths' hammers."

"Drink some water," said Mr. Anderson; "it will refresh you."

Miranda still held the hat, and she now advanced and handed it to the stranger, who, keeping his eyes still riveted upon her face, dashed the remainder of the cool spring water upon his head at once.

Then he drew a long breath as he said:

"I am better now—where is my horse?"

"He is quietly grazing there by the road-side," said Mr. Anderson.

"Poor Starlight," said the man, "it's not his fault. I had overridden him to-day.—Ho! Starlight, boy—ho! ho!"

The horse pricked up his ears and cantered up to his master, who narrowly examined him before he spoke again, and then with a satis-fied air he rose to his feet, saying, gaily:

"Well, I don't think there's much harm done this bout, at all events."

"I am glad you are not hurt," said Mr. Anderson.

"Thank you, sir, and your young lady. Now, tell me, did you really get me some water from the spring, or did I dream it?"

"She did," said the attorney, "and with the prompt humanity which ever distinguishes her."

"I can only thank you, miss," said the man as he mounted his horse, "and if you will tell me your name, I shall be proud always to re-member it with gratitude."

"This lady's name is Rankley—Miranda Rankley," said Mr. Anderson.

"Of the Old Grange?" cried the man.

"The same."

"God bless you then, miss. It may be in my power to do you more good than you know of, or myself either just now; but you shall never want a friend while Dick Palmer lives."

"Palmer—Palmer," repeated Mr. Anderson. "You don't reside about here, sir?"

"I reside nowhere," replied the highway-man; "all the world's my home, but when anyone wants me particularly, they put an advertisement in the *York Herald*, and say Dick's wanted at such a place, by such a one, naming the initials, and then I'm sure to come if I'm above ground. I've heard that there has been strange work at the Grange, Miss Rankley, but for your kindness to me to-day I will——but never mind. That's as much as I can say now, so good-day to you. Thank you, sir, and God bless you both."

So saying, he gave the rein to his horse, and without waiting for a reply to his singular address, he rode rapidly off in the direction of the Grange.

"Who can that be?" remarked Mr. Ander-son. "Amid the general coarseness of his manners, there peep out occasionally the traces of better breeding. His name I never heard of in York or its neighbourhood."

"It matters not," said Miranda, sadly; "we have but done our duty in succouring a fellow-creature in distress, Mr. Anderson."

"True; but, Miranda, may not this be one of the mysterious ways by which Providence works out its ends? This accidental en-counter may, trivial as it appears, be really fraught with great results. Something seems to whisper to me that this man will be in some manner woven up with your fate."

"'Tis strange," said Miranda; "but when I first saw him, before he fell from his horse, a similar feeling came over my own mind, although subsequent events quite obliterated it. It seemed to me as if I could have stopped him and said: 'tell me, how are you mixed up in the events which it is the will of Heaven I should go through?'"

"I have often," replied Mr. Anderson, "experienced such feelings, and it may be that Providence adapts the minds of its creatures to circumstances which are to sur-round them by permitting them such faint glimpses of the future."

CHAPTER XXVI.

THE VISIT OF MR. QUERRAL TO ROWLAND— NEW VEXATION.

POOR Rowland Percy left the Grange with a heavy heart.

He had, as we know, in the presence of Miranda, striven, and striven most success-fully, to put on an appearance of confidence, of hope, and of fortitude, which his heart was far from sharing in.

A noble spirit can struggle against mis-fortune in almost any shape. Pain, want, misery may we bear, and the pure spirit may rise triumphant over a combination of circum-stances of the most depressing character; but of all the hard trials for the mind, of all the maddening things to bear, false accusations are the very worst.

To find himself surrounded by men, ready with every circumstantial detail to perjure themselves before Heaven for the sake of in-suring his destruction, raised a tumult of passion in his breast, which only the presence and the sufferings of Miranda at all enabled him partially to subdue, and prevent from bursting forth in indignation, which would have known no restraint.

The thought of Miranda, however, was his strength—in the same manner that the fine sense of duty Miranda felt to rescue him, if possible, from his enemies, fortified her gentle nature to bear with misfortune under which, in ordinary circumstances, she must have sunk.

"She thinks me innocent," was the only solace Rowland could lay to his heart; and, when he was left alone in his dreary cell, he could only calm the effervescence of his mind by continually repeating to himself that as-surance, which, like a ray of light amid an unusual gloom, lit up his heart with hope, which would, otherwise, have sunk into the abyss of despair.

"I a murderer!" he cried, aloud. "Oh! could all this have been foretold me but a few days since, how I should have scouted the prophet! I accused of the murder of the father of Miranda! Oh! monstrous! What can these two men mean? What can they hope to gain which shall repay them for their perjury before high Heaven?"

While Rowland was busy with these reflections, his door was opened by one of the turnkeys of the prison, who, in a rough voice, said:

"Here's a lawyer come to see you."

In a moment, a man, who was an utter stranger to Rowland, entered his room, and, with an affectation of great politeness, bade him good morning.

Rowland eyed his visitor earnestly for a moment, and then, being quite sure that he did not know him, he said:

"Sir, you make some mistake, for I have not the honour of your acquaintance."

"No mistake, Mr. Percy," said the visitor, who was no other than Mr. Querral, the very questionable man of business of Bernard Varley, and who, with unblushing effrontery, had claimed and obtained admittance to Rowland by representing himself as sent for by him to arrange his defence. "No sort of mistake, sir, at all. I am a blunt man—plain and straightforward. In fact, I often injure myself by my unwelcome candour. You know, Mr. Percy, people don't like the truth to be spoken to them at all times."

"Will you oblige me, sir, by stating at once your business with me?" said Rowland, who by no means liked his visitor's manners.

"Why, then, sir, in one word, I came to serve you."

"I am obliged for any offer of service," said Rowland, "but you will excuse me when I state that my knowledge of human nature has been so different, within these few days, from what it was before, that I have grown suspicious."

"Ah!" said Mr. Querral, with a deep sigh, and moving his hands up and down like the fins of a turtle, "human nature does not improve upon acquaintance. Nevertheless, Mr. Percy, there are exceptions."

"To the point, sir."

"Well, then, my young friend, I am a solicitor, and, as such, I have no hesitation in saying that you stand in very perilous circumstances."

"That I know, sir," said Rowland. "The most perilous state a man can be in is to be falsely accused by villains, who scruple at no wickedness in carrying out their machinations."

"Ah, very true—very true, Mr. Percy; but safety, I take it, must be just now your principal object?"

"What do you mean, sir?"

"Why, sir, I have no objection on earth, to being very explicit indeed. I have seen Mr. Varley this morning."

"What!" exclaimed Rowland. "You dare to come to me when you have been in communication with that fiend in human shape?"

"Hush, hush! my dear sir, do not get into a passion now, but hear me out. I repeat, I have seen Mr. Varley, and, I can, in my blunt and candid way, assure you that no person feels greater regret at this prosecution than he does."

"Villain!" cried Rowland, "how dare you presume thus to insult me in my persecution?"

"Now, be calm—be calm," said Mr. Querral, "I have a proposition to make. Hear me out. What I mean to say is this: that, from consideration of your youth, Mr. Varley will, as he can, so temper the evidence on your trial, as to insure a verdict of acquittal."

Rowland's indignation was so great that he allowed Mr. Querral to go on for some time, merely because he could not decide in his own mind, what species of punishment he should inflict upon him.

"A verdict of acquittal!" repeated Querral, "always, provided, by-the-way, that you give up all claim to the hand of Miranda Rankley, and advise her to fulfil the wishes expressed in her father's will—you understand me, I hope, perfectly, Mr. Percy?"

"I do, sir," said Percy, "and your reward shall be an exposure of your villainy. You said you came to do me service, and unconsciously you have done so, for after this, who can believe a word that comes from the lips of such a man as Bernard Varley?"

"He—he—he!" laughed Mr. Querral, with a sort of disagreeable laugh; "we are one too many for you there, Mr. Percy. If you repeat any words that I have said, who will believe you? Where's your witnesses?—he—he—he!"

For a moment, Rowland was confounded at the cool impertinence of the scoundrel; and then, surmising that what he said was perfectly true, namely, that in his (Rowland's) situation, such a tale, coming from his lips, and contradicted by the attorney, would meet with no belief, he determined that his tormentor should not escape scot free for his unblushing assurance, and, suddenly clutching him by the collar, Rowland gave him such a shaking, that he had not breath to call for help, and it was not until the exasperated young man let him go that he could scream:

"Murder—murder!" at the top of his lungs.

Mr. Querral's cries soon brought several officers of the prison to his assistance.

"What's the matter now?" cried a man in a gruff voice, with a bunch of keys in his hand.

"He wanted to murder me," said Querral. "The scoundrel wanted to commit another murder, because I refused to go to Mr. Varley and persuade him to tamper with his conscience in giving evidence on the trial."

"Hilloa, my jail bird," said the turnkey to Rowland, "you are a nice article, surely."

"What that man says is false," cried Rowland. "He came here from his rascally employer to make such a proposition to me, because they know well my innocence of the crime laid to my charge."

"Oh," cried the turnkey, with a laugh, "everybody is innocent as comes here; Bill, did we ever have anyone who was guilty yet?"

"No," replied his companion, "I should think not."

Rowland turned in disgust from the men, and resolved to waste no more words in attempting to deny what he was accused of.

"He assaulted me," cried Querral, with malice—"he assaulted me like a ruffian as he is. Oh, my spark, this will mend your case nicely, I think—I am a blunt man—an uncommonly candid man; and I assure you, my fine young gentleman, that you will be hanged. Do you hear that? hanged like a dog."

"Come, come, none of this," said the turnkey. "If you can't agree, Mr. Lawyer, with your client, just come away, will you, at once."

"I his client?" cried Rowland, goaded to speak, despite his resolution to be silent. "I never saw this man's face before to-day, and knew not of his existence."

"Oh, oh, oh!" said Querral, lifting up his hands. "Gentlemen," appealing to the turnkeys, "I have a note from him at home, commencing with 'honoured sir,' and ending with 'your unfortunate, but humble servant, Rowland Percy.'"

"Liar!" said Rowland.

"There, that'll do," said the turnkeys, "we shall have the governor about our ears if we don't mind. Come on, I say."

They then hustled Mr. Querral out of the cell, leaving Rowland in a state of vexation and annoyance beyond description.

He paced his solitary place of confinement to and fro, like some melancholy caged denizen of the forest, and impatience getting the better of him, he exclaimed against the cruel fortune which had loaded him with such a weight of ills.

Not for long, however, was Rowland left to his own reflections. The door of his prison-house was opened, and a visitor of a much more welcome character than the former one was announced to him. It was his father.

Rowland was as surprised as he was delighted to see so very unexpected a visitor, for he had been informed that his father was in custody on account of the duel.

"Father, dear father!" he cried, "what merciful chance permits you to come and visit me?"

"Alas! my Rowland," said Mr. Percy, "call it not a merciful chance. The magistrates have only discharged me, because it is believed there is ample evidence to destroy you. Oh, my poor Rowland, what dreadful train of circumstances has brought you to this sad strait?"

"I can scarcely tell you," said Rowland; "but, on my conscience, I believe we are both in this most unhappy business the victims of some awful conspiracy, which Heaven may, in its mercy to us, some day bring to light, but which at present I can but guess at."

"I am myself," said the elder Percy, "quite bewildered by the rapid events of the last few days. I was goaded to fight with Sir George Rankley; but now that my judgment is calmer, I do most deeply regret that a false sense of honour and a too sensitive dread of the world's opinion drove me into the field. Oh, Rowland, the grave hides many failings, and when those we have once loved, and been on terms of dear companionship with, have left us for ever, and gone to that bourne from which no traveller returns, we sigh for the past, which we cannot recall, and passion sinks in its own ashes a prey to never-dying regret."

"But, father," said Rowland, as he saw how much oppressed was his parent's spirit with Sir George's death, "you did not kill Sir George."

"No, thank Heaven!" cried Mr. Percy; "but I gave myself too readily, Rowland, as an instrument in the hands of villains. From my heart I do mistrust that man, Varley. Something seems to whisper to me that he is the arch-fiend who has contrived all this load of misery, which has made so many weep tears of blood, and the issues of which are still in the hands of Heaven."

Rowland Percy was silent for some moments; then he said, in a tone of deep emotion.

"Father, Miranda is now an orphan. Do you be a father to her, and make up in loving-kindness to the child any want of discretion as regarded the father. I am confident she will see this most unhappy duel between you and her father in its proper light, and forgive you for being the victim of the same dark scheme, which in its horrible success has been the ruin of us all. Take her to your heart, father, as if she were a daughter of your own, and should it then be the will of Heaven that I suffer innocently, love and cherish her for my memory, and her virtues."

"Alas! alas!" cried Mr. Percy, "Rowland, you forget, or you know not that I have no longer a house—that all I had is swept away from me. I am a ruined man."

"All, father?"

"Yes, Rowland, all! With the exception of some trifles which may support me for a few days, I am destitute!"

Rowland was silent for a few moments, then, lifting up his hands, he cried:

"Oh, Heaven! why do these accumulated miseries occur when I am thus helpless? Give me liberty, and I would toil for those I love while nature would sustain me. But here—here, I must nurse my despair, and feed upon the bitter thoughts that rend my heart."

"Do not despair, my Rowland," said Mr. Percy, although his trembling voice belied the tenor of his words. "Do not despair—you are innocent—Miranda believes so; and after an explanation which I have given her, she exculpates even me from further blame than that which arises from the frailty of human nature in being misled too easily."

"Did I dream it?" said Rowland, "or is it true that the villain, Varley, claims all that Sir George possessed?"

"It is true, and even as we are ourselves nearly destitute, so is the once much-envied Miranda."

"When will all this have an end?" cried Rowland. "Have we already, father, felt the worst blows of fate, or, are we yet to expect some crowning misery to transcend all that have gone before?"

"We must be patient—patient," said Mr. Percy, as the tears slowly rolled down his cheeks, and he thought that the crowning misery of all might be the conviction of his innocent and noble-minded son. "We must be patient, my Rowland. Trust in Heaven—its mercy may come, even at the eleventh hour.—We will not despair."

The door of the cell was opened, and the turnkey, holding it in his hand, said:

"Time's up, sir. Besides, here's a gentleman with an order to see the prisoner."

"Must I leave?" said Mr. Percy.

"Yes, sir, time's up. You can come any time between eleven and two, but we can't let you stay long."

"Father, farewell," said Rowland, "and remember what I have said to you about Miranda. You can be near her, and protect her, though you cannot offer her a home."

"I will, Rowland, I will. Heaven bless her. In poverty or woe she shall never want one to stand between her and every ill while I live. Farewell, Rowland—we shall meet again to-morrow."

"Farewell."

Young Percy turned away his face to hide a tear, as his father wrung his hand, and then followed the turnkey from the gloomy room.

Misery, of however short duration, works strange changes in the physical structure; and in the midst of all his own engrossing distress, it was with an exquisite pang of grief that Rowland marked how much the last few days had altered his sorrowing father. His form was bent, and deep lines had appeared in his cheeks, while his voice had undergone as great a change as might have been expected in ten years.

Rowland, however, had scarcely time to breathe a sigh over these melancholy reflections, when Mr. Anderson was introduced to him, and, advancing towards the prisoner, he took his hand, saying:

"Well, Mr. Percy, I hope my visit is not an unwelcome one?"

"Unwelcome, sir, it cannot be," said Rowland. "The unfortunate may well feel gratitude for any kind attention."

"You will fully understand, Mr. Percy, that I come here as your legal adviser, with a full and complete assurance of your innocence."

The colour rose to the cheek of Rowland, as he said:

"Mr. Anderson, for your generous confidence in my innocence, I thank you from my heart; but with such poor eloquence as God has given me, must I plead my own cause, for at this juncture it so happens that I have no means of adequately repaying you for undertaking my defence."

"Oh, that is all settled," said Mr. Anderson; "Miranda has arranged all that with me; so you will give me leave, I hope, to consider myself as empowered by you to take whatever steps I consider necessary in my endeavours to unmask the villainy of which I feel confident you are a victim."

"Miranda?" exclaimed Rowland. "Am I indeed indebted to this suffering angel for so much? Oh, Mr. Anderson, could you believe that there does exist a villain bad enough to wrong her?"

"Gold, my dear sir," said Mr. Anderson, "is a bait which will lure thousands to the greatest iniquities. But my visit to you now must be a brief one. It was quite necessary that you should know that I am professionally engaged for you, but to-morrow we must have a long consultation, which I cannot now spare time for, as I wish to retain counsel this day, who, if I be not active, may fall into the hands of your enemies."

Mr. Anderson then shook hands warmly and cordially with Rowland, and hurried from the prison.

CHAPTER XXVII.

THE ROBBERY—THE ALARM OF GUILT.

THE sun had sunk upon the broad lands comprising the Grange estate, and the sighing wind was sweeping across field, orchard, and lake, closing the leaves of the wild flowers as it took its devious course, and gently rustling the corn, which, with an undulating motion like the sea, bowed before it, when Twitter crept from the Grange by the garden entrance, with an open note in his hand, which had been given to him about an hour previously by a servant, who had received it from a country lad.

He paused when he got a short distance from the house, and, holding the note so as to catch the faint light that still lingered in the west, as if loth to leave the world, he read it slowly and distinctly.

It was as follows:

"Meet me one hour after sunset at the old place.   "D. P."

"One hour after sunset," muttered Twitter. "'Tis that time now, and he will be there. Palmer is an important man—a most important man. I am glad he has come, for it might be dangerous to keep this ring about me, and he can take it to London, where it will fetch its price. 'Tis monstrous, though, to give him half—most monstrous. I must again represent that to him. He ought to be content with much less—very much less—and yet I scarcely think he will. One hour after sunset, at the old place. By Heavens, Master Varley, since you have left me out of the will, I will help myself, and likewise protect myself. I must ask Palmer to bring me some arms, for the thought keeps ever coming uppermost in my mind that Varley may, in order to make his safety doubly sure, destroy me some day. He would think nothing of taking my life. I must protect myself. Now, if I could trust Palmer, it would be a brave scheme to serve Varley even as he has served Sir George. Why should not I, as well as he, be master of the Grange? Heavens! how I would lord it over them all. They should feel my power, by its never-wearying exercise. I would make up for years of abject submission by showing my might. Oh, it would be glorious for me to be master of the Grange."

Pleasing himself with these thoughts, Twitter slunk onwards towards his place of rendezvous with Dick Palmer, the highwayman, which, upon reaching, he cautiously scrutinized before he gave the signal.

The moment he had done so, it was answered by the whistle of Palmer, who at once climbed over the paling.

"Well, Twitter," he said, "what news tonight?"

"No news, Palmer," replied Twitter; "at least, none in particular. I am glad you have come, very glad."

"Have you more plate?"

"No—not packed just now; although, if you could wait, I think I could get you some. But I have a diamond here set in a ring, which is valuable."

"Humph!" said Palmer, as he turned the sparkling gem about. "'Tis a rare one!"

"Yes, Palmer, it is; and I am thinking you ought to let me have more than half the proceeds of such an article. The trouble of conveying it is nothing, and, with your facilities of disposing of such things in London, I cannot but think you drive too hard a bargain with me."

"I tell you what, Master Twitter," said Dick, "I'll keep this ring altogether if you say any more in that strain, and that will be a needful lesson to you for the future."

"Gracious! no!" cried Twitter. "Give me the ring, Palmer, you surely would not rob me?"

"I don't know why I shouldn't," said the highwayman, with a laugh. "I rob everybody else, and why should you escape?"

"Honour among thieves," said Twitter, with a bitterness of tone that produced no further effect upon Palmer than a hearty laugh.

"Well said, well said, Twitter—most apt. Now, for that, you shall have your share of the ring, so that's settled; but don't talk to me about driving hard bargains. It's most ungentlemanly, that it is."

"Well, well," said Twitter, "I suppose I must submit. When can you come again, Palmer?"

"Why, I've some idea of staying in the neighbourhood a little while," replied the highwayman. "By-the-by, you have had a death here, and an inquest, and so on."

"Yes. Sir George Rankley is dead, and Bernard Varley, of whom I have spoken to you, is master of the Grange."

"Does that make any difference in your favour?"

"None, Palmer, none. What put that into your head?"

"Nothing. I only asked, because you always used to pay a great many compliments to this Mr. Varley's talents as a mighty great rogue, and as I knew you dabbled in the same sort of business, I thought you might have made something by the sudden change of proprietors."

"No. I merely continue in my situation."

"What's become of the daughter of Sir George?"

"The—the daughter? Miranda?"

"Ay, Miranda."

"Why, she has left the Grange; but she is nothing to us, Palmer. Sir George left all his property to Mr. Varley, on condition that he married Miranda; and he is quite willing, but she is not, so he keeps the property himself."

"Oh, indeed! Now, between you and me, Twitter, what an infernally unlikely will that was for a father to make."

"Unlikely? Oh, I—I don't know."

"Curse me, if I don't think it's a lie from beginning to end!"

"What do you mean, Palmer?"

"Why, I mean it's as likely as that twenty shillings make a pound, that there's some swindling in the whole affair."

It was too dark for Palmer to observe the colour in Twitter's countenance as he spoke, or his hinted suspicions would have been more than strengthened.

As it was, several minutes elapsed before the guilty man could reply; then, in a faint, low voice, he said:

"I have no opinion upon the subject. I have nothing to do with Mr. Varley's private affairs. I know nothing about the will or the estate."

"Oh, very well! I only asked out of curiosity. Then, I suppose the girl is not very well off?"

"Miranda, do you mean?"

"Yes, to be sure."

"No—that is, I daresay she is not. You must know she actually takes part with him who is, upon clear evidence, committed to prison for the murder of her father."

"That looks uncommonly queer again," said Palmer. "Why, no child would or could do that, Twitter. You may depend upon it he didn't do the murder, or else she never could take his part."

"It—it is supposed," faltered Twitter, "that he murdered Sir George with the hope then of becoming possessed of the Grange estates by marrying the daughter. He came here in disguise on the night of the murder, and everything points to him as the perpetrator of the deed."

"And yet she takes his part?"

"She does. Is it not strange? And—and very wicked?"

"I don't know; but, however, as you say, it's no business of ours. I'll see you again in this place, at the same hour, the evening after next."

"Do so, and I will have a packet of plate ready for you."

"Very well. You think you can carry on the old trade, do you? I saw this Varley once, and he seemed a keen hand."

"I will try," said Twitter. "Where did you see him?"

"At York once, and I shall never forget his confounded leer as long as I live. Why, he's just the sort of fellow to do a sneaking thing,

THE UNEXPECTED APPARITION.

but as for stopping anyone on the highway, why he wouldn't be equal to it on any account. Good-evening to you."

Palmer got over the wall, on the other side of which his horse stood patiently waiting for him, and, with some expressions of kindness, which the creature seemed fully to comprehend, he mounted him, and galloped down the lane which led, by luxuriant cornfields, rich orchards, and pasture land, into the bridle-road to York.

One of the most singular anomalies in human nature, and yet one far from rare, is the facility with which persons engaged in notoriously evil courses will separate their particular branch of iniquity from every other, and find some, as they think, redeeming features in it which do not belong to any other species of crime.

Our friend Palmer was a notable example of this obliquity of intellect, for, as he trotted along the bridle-path, he felt great indignation at the mere supposition that Bernard Varley had forged a will, and wondered, if he wanted money, why he didn't act like a gentleman, and take to the road at once.

"But," added Palmer to himself, "there is no accounting for tastes, and some people will go sneaking through the world when they might do quite different."

Dick went cantering on as these observations passed through his conscience, nor did he cease declaiming, now and then, against the supposed villainy of Varley, until he heard a horse coming towards him, in the direction from York.

"Hilloa," muttered Palmer, as he reduced his pace to a quiet walk. "Here may be a chance. There isn't a prettier spot than this in the whole country for stopping a greasy farmer, or lightening the pocket of a rich squire. There's not a public-house within a mile, or a private one within two. He's coming at a good rate, whoever he is. Well, that's not much matter—there isn't a great deal of room to spare in this bridle-path when two horsemen pass each other, and we must try to make that a little less."

The advancing horseman was within some hundred paces of him now, and Palmer, raising his voice, cried:

"Hilloa, friend, not so fast; there's an obstruction here that you may have an ugly fall over."

The horseman drew rein immediately, and answered roughly:

"What's the matter, curse you?"

"Thank you for nothing," said Palmer; "an oath breaks no bones; but there's a sink here."

"A sink?"

"Yes, nothing but gold runs into it, though, so my fine fellow, whoever you are, I'll trouble you to hand over your purse, or I'll pop a pair of leaden arguments in your brain that will sharpen its faculties a little."

As Palmer spoke, he dashed up to the horseman, and grasping the reins of his horse with one hand, he placed the cold muzzle of a pistol against his cheek with the other. Their eyes met, and then Palmer exclaimed:

"So it's you, Mr. Varley, is it? Well, this is a lucky chance—you've just come into some property, and I don't see why I shouldn't have a slice of it."

Varley's eyes flashed with rage, as he said:

"Who are you that wants to swing on the gallows?"

"I'm thinking you stand as good a chance as I do, Master Varley," said Palmer; "but we won't argue that point now. Your money—and your watch, if you have one."

A moment's reflection convinced Varley that submission was inevitable, unless he chose to throw away his life for the sake of retaining, for a few moments longer, a sum of upwards of a hundred pounds which he had in his pockets. Besides, he was completely unarmed, and any attempt at resistance would have been perfect madness.

"An unarmed man," he muttered, "is no match for one with firearms. There is my purse."

"You may look as hard at me, to know me again, as you like," said Palmer; "but if ever you venture to injure me, it will be the worst day's work you ever did in your life."

"What do you mean?"

"Remember the will," said Palmer, looking as closely as he could by the dim light, into the countenance of Varley, to note the impression his words made on him; nor was he disappointed, for Varley trembled, and turning ghastly pale, said:

"Come with me to the Grange, and tell me who you are, and I will treble the amount I have now handed to you."

"To the Grange?" said Dick.

"Yes—I will make it worth your while to explain to me how and where——"

Varley paused, for the thought struck him that after all he might be speaking too fast, and, blinded by his apprehension, saying something to do himself an irreparable injury.

"Oh, you can go on," said Palmer, "I know everything. So you may as well make a clean breast of it."

"Clean breast of what?" said Varley, who had now recovered from his first surprise, and became cautious.

"Just as you like—just as you like. I'll trouble you for your watch."

"I have none."

"You have," said Palmer, as he pressed the pistol closer to the cheek of Varley.

"Take it, then," said Varley, bitterly. "Now, I suppose, I can pass on?"

"Wait a moment, if you please. What put it into your head to suppose that Miranda Rankley would marry such a hang-dog as you look? Why, Varley, you are enough to frighten a horse, with your black brows and your cream cheese of a complexion. You must have been mad, man."

"In the name of all that's infernal, who are you?" said Varley.

"I'll tell you directly," replied Palmer. "But, between you and me, that will business is rather too bad."

Varley drew his breath heavily, as he gasped:

"Man or fiend, I implore you to tell me who you are. I will make it worth your while. Come home with me now, and you shall not repent it."

"Oh, yes, I should," said Palmer. "I only want to give you a little friendly caution, and, as I never give anything for nothing, you see I took the means to pay myself. Look out, Bernard Varley, you have done things that would place your neck in a disagreeable predicament, and I warn you now not to know me at any time unless I speak to you. You understand me?"

"I do," faintly replied Varley, "I do. But now tell me who you are."

"Incline your ear."

Varley leant forward, and Palmer, placing his mouth close to his ear, whispered solemnly:

"The devil!"

He then instantly set spurs to his horse, and galloped down the bridle-path, leaving Varley perfectly bewildered, and in a clammy perspiration from intense fear.

The wind howled past him, and now a

muttered roar of thunder afar off betokened a coming storm, while a vivid flash of lightning, preceding a louder clap, lighted up the landscape for one fleeting moment with its wild, awful brilliancy, and then left it in tenfold darkness.

Varley, with a cry of terror, plunged the spurs rowel deep into the horse's flanks. The animal reared for a moment, and then, with a terrific plunge, darted off at a headlong gallop.

CHAPTER XXVIII.

THE STORM—THE SPECTRE OF THE MURDERED KEEPER.

VARLEY'S steed continued its mad career, until he mechanically checked it, as he neared the Grange.

The storm was, each moment, increasing in violence—vivid flashes of lightning increased the terror of the horse almost to madness, and the rumbling thunder sounded to the guilty mind of Varley like the denunciations of Heaven upon his blood-stained conscience.

When he reached the stone steps of the hall, he, with difficulty, reined in the plunging steed, and calling loudly for someone to hold his horse, he flung himself from the saddle, and, with a face of unearthly paleness, stood upon the first step leading to the hall-door, holding the bridle in his hand.

With a wild laugh then, someone bounded from among the shrubbery of the lawn, and, coming close to Varley, screamed in his ear:

"Ha! ha!—hanged at York! Bernard Varley will be hanged at York—rare sport! There will be a frightful mob when Bernard Varley is hanged at York!"

"Fiend!" cried Varley, as the mocking face of the idiot, Bold Hawk, leered upon him. "Are you tired of life, that you thus mock a desperate man?"

"Ha! ha!" laughed the strange being, clapping his hands, "the fire won't burn, the water won't drown, the lightning won't scorch Bernard Varley, because how could he then be hanged at York?"

Varley let go the bridle of his horse, and strove to grapple with the demented creature; but Bold Hawk skipped away from him, and, with shrieks and yells, fled over the lawn, while the affrighted horse, with the stirrups goading him to fury, tore off at a tremendous gallop, and was quickly lost both to sight and hearing.

Varley lifted his clenched hand to Heaven, and was upon the point of uttering an awful imprecation, when the sky seemed to open, and a glance of electric light suddenly flashed across the whole extent of space.

Varley covered his eyes with his hands, and, trembling with fear, slowly ascended the hall steps.

He rang the ponderous bell, whose echoes seemed to fall upon his heart like a death knell; and, just as an awful peal of thunder appeared to shake the Grange to its foundations, the door was opened, and Varley, faint, weary, and alarmed, staggered into the hall.

He sank into the first seat that presented itself, and while the servant who had admitted him gazed with surprise and terror upon his ghastly face, he breathed heavily, and glared around him, as if he expected his eyes to be blasted by some fearful spectacle.

"Are you not well, sir?" the servant ventured at length to say.

"Why came you not to the door when I called?" gasped Varley. "Is this a night to keep me waiting?"

"Indeed, sir, we did not hear you ring but once. The storm must have drowned your voice. There's the thunder again. It's quite impossible to hear anything outside. The servants are all terrified, for they say there have been strange noises in the Grange."

"Noises? What—what noises?"

"I haven't heard anything myself, sir; but they say that, from the long corridor, there have been heard moans and groans, enough to frighten anyone."

"'Tis untrue!" cried Varley. "How dare they say such things? Am I to have my home made frightful by such superstitions? How dare they say so? Mark me, whoever sees or hears anything of such a character in the Grange, leaves it that hour. You understand me? I am free myself—quite free from superstition—but I will not have such tales circulated. You hear me?"

"Yes, sir."

"Let me have lights, then; and tell Twitter I would speak with him. The lights first—the lights first."

"In which room will you please to have the lights, sir?"

"In the small parlour. Quick—quick! Will the storm never abate? What an awful night is this! Who could that have been who seems to know so much? His dark hints were to me appalling! Could they be accidental, or are they really based upon a knowledge of things which I thought, at least, were confined to the breasts of three persons—myself, Twitter, and Querral? Surely I am not betrayed? No—no. What could they gain by my destruction?"

Varley would not leave the hall till the lights were brought him, and then he followed a servant, who carried them into the small room he had indicated.

In a few moments Twitter made his appearance, quite as glad of company on that night of storm as Varley could possibly be, and, closing the door, the two guilty men glared at each other with pale, ghastly faces, trembling at each peal of thunder, and shrinking as now and then a vivid flash of lightning would make itself be seen, despite the lights which were in the room.

"Twitter," said Varley, after a long pause, "this night, on my return from York, I met one who seemed to know too much for your safety and mine. He was an armed man, and I could not resist him, so he robbed me;

but that was little compared to the frightful hints he threw out concerning his knowledge of things which you and I thought could not possibly stray beyond the precincts of our own breasts."

Twitter felt sure in a moment that it must be Dick Palmer to whom Varley alluded, and he replied:

"Indeed. What manner of man was he?"

"A stout, tall man, mounted on a black horse. He spoke about the will, ay, as confidently as if he had been at our elbows when it was made."

"Your elbow," corrected Twitter, faintly. "You know I never saw the will. You and your friend, Querral, performed it. Your elbow, you mean, Varley."

"Pshaw! why quibble about words?" cried Varley. "There must be imminent danger somewhere. How on earth could yon stranger, if he be a mortal man, possibly come to the knowledge of that which he seemed to know so well?"

"I know not," said Twitter. "'Tis very strange! Would he not tell you who he was?"

"No; that question he turned to a jest, although, at the moment, it startled me."

"What jest?"

"He said he was——"

They both instinctively covered their eyes as a blazing flash of lightning seemed, for an instant, quite to extinguish the lights in the room, and to linger between earth and heaven an unusual time. Then succeeded such a peal of thunder, that, in its echoes, it seemed endless, and Twitter involuntarily grasped the chair on which he sat, as, with a voice of intense alarm, he said:

"Oh, Varley! Varley! what will become of us? Is this storm doomed to be our destruction? Heaven, have mercy! I did not do the deed! You know, Varley, it was you! You know it was—I could not prevent you! Have mercy, Heaven! Oh, have mercy!"

"Wretch!" cried Varley, as he rose and seized Twitter by the collar. "Make the night more hideous than it is by your vile croaking, and I will rid myself of you at once by taking your worthless life!"

Twitter could not speak, but he slid upon his knees, and looked beseechingly in the face of Varley, which was working with diabolical passion.

What might have been the result of the fury which was raging in Varley's heart at that moment it is impossible to say, for, ere another minute elapsed, the door of the room was flung open, and there stood in the entrance a figure, the exact counterpart of that which Rowland Percy had assumed in order to gain admittance to the Grange.

The form was dressed in the faded green dress of a gamekeeper, and, as it stood in the dim light cast by the candles through the doorway, it seemed of herculean size.

Varley's eyes were facing the door, but Twitter's were not, and the latter could only suppose that some sight of terror had met his companion's gaze, by seeing the cold perspiration break out upon his brow, and the fixed, horrible stare of his eyes.

"What do you see?" gasped Twitter. "Varley—Varley, why do you glare thus on vacancy? What is it?"

"Off—off—off," said Varley, in choking accents, as he let go his hold of Twitter, and retreated backwards to the further end of the room.

The valet then, as he still knelt, turned his head, and saw the object of Varley's alarm with a terror that at once deprived him of all power of speech or action.

The supernatural-looking figure then slowly stepped backwards, fading away in the darkness of the hall.

The door was slammed—shut violently—and Twitter, with a deep groan, fell on the floor, while Varley stood with his lips apart, and his arms stretched out before him, as if he feared the strange appearance would approach close to him and drive him to madness by its hideous contact.

It was many minutes before either of the affrighted men could speak, and then it was Varley who broke the silence, by pronouncing the name of Twitter.

He was answered only by a groan.

"Twitter—Twitter," he again said, and then the valet looked up in his face, and whispered:

"Is it gone?"

"Yes—yes," said Varley, "it is gone! Tell me, Twitter—good Twitter, tell me what think you of this visitation? Speak, Twitter, speak!"

"This was no idle superstition," said Twitter. "We have seen the spirit of the murdered keeper! Oh, Varley, this will be a terrible home! We dare not stay here. If the spirit of one murdered man, and that, too, one whose generation has passed away, be permitted to wander through this place, why may not another, the lifeless remains of which lie even now unburied?"

"Hush! hush!" said Varley. "Why utter so horrible a suggestion? Are you mad, Twitter, that you speak thus? Peace! peace!"

"What shall we do? What shall we do?"

Varley remained for some moments silent, then he said, in a low voice, as if he feared to be overheard by the beings of another world:

"Twitter, I cannot live here. The rents from the Grange estate will provide an ample revenue, and I will reside in York. I dare not sleep in this house now!"

"Nor I—nor I," said Twitter. "You will allow me money, Varley? Remember your promise. You will allow me money?"

"I will keep my word; to-morrow shall see me bid adieu to this place. I can reside at York in as much splendour as I wish. Constant fears would torment me in this house! We—we will sit up to-night, Twitter."

"Yes," faltered Twitter; "I would not be alone, Varley, for worlds."

"You are superstitious," said Varley, while

his teeth chattered with fear. " Yonder supposed figure that we saw could but be the coinage of our fancy. Do not be superstitious, Twitter. I will not think it real."

Twitter shook his head, as he said:

" No—no, Varley; it was no fancy. How could the door open and shut so mysteriously ?"

" That must have been the wind," said Varley, who would fain have reasoned himself out of his rooted belief that he had really seen a supernatural visitant. " I tell you that must have been the wind, Twitter; and yet I will not remain in the house, because the imagination would be ever active in playing the judgment such tricks."

" We will both live at York," remarked Twitter, " and we need never visit this place again. It will ever be frightful to us !"

" Ever—ever," said Varley.

" Let us have wine here, Varley, and then fasten the door. We will remain until the morning, and the light of day will then assure us that we may take some rest. I never heard of these frightful visitations when the sun was shining."

" Yes—wine—wine," said Varley, catching at the suggestion. " We will say nothing of what we have seen ; but to-morrow I will take measures to break up the establishment here."

As Varley spoke, loud cries, mingled with piercing and appalling screams, proceeded from the servants' hall, which was in the immediate vicinity of the small parlour in which he and Twitter were sitting.

They both immediately started to their feet, and glanced in terror towards the door, which in another moment was opened, and disclosed in the hall a crowd of the domestics, some of whom were bearing lights, and all pointing, with frantic gestures, in the direction of a conservatory, which led towards the gardens, the inner door of which was at the top of three steps from the end of the hall.

The door was open, and Varley could see the same figure which had alarmed him and Twitter slowly pacing down the centre of the conservatory.

" The keeper's ghost ! the keeper's ghost !" said a dozen in a breath ; and then the figure disappeared in the gloom towards which it was walking.

CHAPTER XXIX.

THE MORNING OF THE FUNERAL—VARLEY'S MISERIES INCREASE.

THE sun was shining, and the blithe birds were merrily singing from bough to bough of the tall chestnuts that graced the avenue to the Grange, ere Twitter and Bernard Varley ventured to steal to their respective chambers, to snatch some brief repose, before the business of the day should commence.

It was the day fixed for the funeral of Sir George Rankley, a ceremony which Varley had hurried on with almost indecent haste, because

his anxiety to get the corpse of his victim out of the house had been intense ; but now that the Grange had grown hateful to him, and he dreaded spending another night under its roof, such anxiety had ceased in a great measure, although he felt a sense of satisfaction that the grave would soon hide the mute evidence of his crime.

Sleep, however, would not visit the weary and terror-stricken man, and, after an hour's feverish tossing in bed, he again rose, and determined to proceed to York to consult with his prime counsellor, Querral, about the measures to be adopted for immediately giving up the establishment at the Grange ; though he by no means intended to let the lawyer know the reasons of his sudden resolve.

The funeral was not to take place until one o'clock, so that Varley had ample time to ride to York and be back again in time for the ceremony.

The churchyard of a humble village, within a mile of the Grange, was to receive the remains of Sir George, and as Varley, in his capacity of executor and trustee for the deceased, had given all the necessary directions, he left word at the Grange that he would be back in good time to join the melancholy procession, and that, if Miranda should make her appearance, she was to be allowed to assume whatever station she thought proper as regarded the funeral.

With his courage somewhat strengthened now that the dim and dusky shadow of night had given way to the clear sunshine of a glorious day, Bernard Varley then mounted his horse (which had been found in the early morning quietly grazing on the lawn), and cantered towards York.

He paused not until he reached the office of the man of law, and was soon closeted with the unscrupulous villain who for money would engage in any iniquitous enterprise, and without whose legal assistance Varley would have found some trouble in carrying out his wicked and nefarious designs.

It must not be imagined that Varley had wholly made a confidant of the lawyer, although the latter more than suspected all that Varley could have told him, had he sat down with an intention of concealing nothing from him. The only circumstance of which Querral was fully aware consisted in the preparation of a will which was to supersede one that was being likewise prepared by Mr. Anderson. Having thus the two documents in his possession, Varley had adroitly proved the signature of Sir George to the one prepared under his own instructions by Querral, and which that wily practitioner had taken care should be an unexceptionably legal document.

Mr. Querral looked curiously and scrutinizingly at the pale face of his client, and certain misgivings as to a sum of a thousand pounds, which he was to receive upon the will being proved, passed through his mind as he eagerly inquired if anything of an unfavourable character had occurred.

" Nothing, nothing," said Varley ; " but I

have a fancy to live in York instead of at the Grange, and I have merely come to you to consult you on the matter."

" Oh, you don't like the Grange?"

" No—it's too—too quiet for me—much too quiet. I shall see more life in York—I never was particularly fond of the country."

" That you unquestionably will, Mr. Varley; but may I ask what you intend to do with the Grange?"

" I would fain let the house and the immediate surrounding land," replied Varley, " although the income from the general estate is quite ample for my purposes."

" The recent facts connected with the death of Sir George," said Querral, " will deter many people from renting the house—but we can try."

" Certainly—that is all I wish; and now tell me what progress you are making in the prosecution of this young man, the murderer of Sir George."

" Read that," said Querral, handing him a note, which Varley took, and read as follows:

" SIR,

" Understanding you have the conducting of the prosecution against Mr. Rowland Percy for the murder of Sir George Rankley, I beg to inform you, in professional courtesy, that I have the honour to be retained for that innocent and falsely-accused gentleman's defence.

" I am, Sir, yours, &c.,
" STEPHEN ANDERSON."

" You see, Mr. Varley, the enemy is active," remarked Querral, with a smile. " And, what is more, I have had money refused by some of the principal men on the circuit on the plea that they had just been retained on the other side."

" Let them work their uttermost," cried Varley, " I can bring proofs of guilt that will confound them, and yet I would save that young man on one consideration."

" And that is——"

" Miranda's compliance with the provisions of the will. If she will become my wife, I would have Twitter removed, and so modify my own evidence as to ensure an acquittal."

" That might be done as regards Twitter, but your own evidence cannot now very well be altered."

" There will not be occasion to attempt it," said Varley, gloomily; " Miranda, with a haughty scorn, repels all my advances, and leaves me to the barren enjoyment of the estate, all of which I would barter for one smile from her."

" Well, Mr. Varley," said Querral, shrugging his shoulders, " give me leave to say that for a man of your very great enterprising spirit, your extraordinary feelings as regards this girl are to me most incomprehensible."

" I love her—I adore her," said Varley, with a groan.

Mr. Querral again shrugged his shoulders, and wondered what loving and adoring meant. Then he added:

" Well, Mr. Varley, that's your own private business, and as it is altogether out of my line, I can give you neither advice nor assistance in it."

" Poverty," said Varley, " may unbend the sternness of her nature; I must reduce her to abject want, and then make another effort to procure a welcome from her—but I must leave you now. The funeral takes place to-day, and I shall be for a brief time blessed with a sight of her, although she may treat me with scorn. Querral, you know not what it is to have a passion such as mine, filling your heart until you fancy it must burst. I have struggled with my infatuation for Miranda Rankley, until I have nearly destroyed my reason—but 'tis all in vain—a fierce passion for her fills my soul. To make her mine, I would forego all that used to make up the ambition of my life—I would even take the place of Rowland Percy in his dungeon, if Miranda would but come to me, and bless me with her smiles and words of consolation."

Mr. Querral took up a pen, and began very busily mending it in order to occupy his mind, while Varley was what he called raving.

The other then rose, and with a saddened air walked to the door, saying:

" You cannot understand these feelings—gold was once my idol, as it is now yours. The love of wealth held undisputed sway in my breast, until this new and more fearful passion took possession of me. I pray you search in York for a habitation that I may reside in. Let it be rich and gorgeous—I would fain still hope, that when Miranda has felt the chilling influence of poverty and want, she may listen to my suit."

" I shall do as you wish," said Querral, " and touching that trifle of a thousand pounds?"

" You shall have it," said Varley, " and more, for we shall have yet more business to do—I will never lose sight of this girl—I will haunt her like her evil genius, and there shall be no depth of poverty and woe but I will sink her to a lower, until either the grave closes over her, or she smiles upon my suit—I have sworn it by all the powers of Heaven, and I will keep my oath. Yes, I will keep my oath."

" That man must be a little mad," remarked Querral to himself, when Varley had left him. " However, it's nothing to me, so long as I get tolerably well paid. A thousand pounds to begin with is not so much amiss, and I do not exactly see how Mr. Varley can refuse to lend me a few hundreds now and then, when I may choose to want them, which shall be just as often as I think I can get them, without coming to an open rupture with him."

When Varley stepped into the street from Mr. Querral's house, he started back, and an exclamation of surprise escaped his lips, as the first object that presented itself to him was the highwayman of the preceding evening, standing, with all the cool indifference in the world, close to the doorway.

He turned his eyes full upon Varley, and with a familiar nod, said:

"Good-morning. You are early in York."

"Shall I denounce this man?" thought Varley, "and risk all, or shall I temporize with him in dread of his knowledge?"

It would seem as if Dick Palmer, by the glance which Varley cast around him, was conscious of what was passing in his mind, for he said:

"Beware, Bernard Varley—beware."

"Of what?" said Varley. "Tell me, man, in the open face of day, who you really are."

"I have told you once," said Palmer. "By-the-by, I suppose you were rather alarmed last night at the ghost of the murdered keeper?"

Varley looked astonished, as he said:

"How know you of that? Are you an inhabitant of this world, or a fiend sent to tempt me on until I sink for ever where there is no hope?"

"Hope!" laughed Palmer; "you don't mean to pretend that you have any hope? Good-evening; your soul would be a dear purchase at half a farthing."

"Stop!" cried Varley. "Tell me whence you got that ring. I know it well—it belongs to——"

"Sir George Rankley," said Palmer, calmly. "He gave it to me himself this morning just before cock-crow."

So saying the highwayman walked leisurely away, quite sure that Varley's superstitious fears would not allow him to denounce him as a robber.

For a few moments Varley stood looking after him with intense surprise, and a cold chill at his heart acknowledged the dreadful fear that he began to have of the stranger, who seemed, by some mysterious means, to be acquainted with every circumstance, as it seemed, in connection with him.

"Am I," he muttered, "the victim of some unearthly influence? Can it be possible that the agents of another world are environing me? Have I, indeed, gone so far in crime as to be obnoxious to the influence of beings not mortal? Who can this mysterious man be? If he be mortal, whence can he derive his strange information? That ring, too—I never thought of it till this day, when I saw it glittering on his finger—was the property of Sir George—nay, he wore it at the duel—it must have been on his finger when he died—how could this stranger become possessed of it? Bernard Varley, are you awake, or is all this some confused vision of slumber?"

The lad who was holding his horse looked at him with surprise as he glanced after Palmer, and muttered, in disjointed words, the reflections of his tortured soul.

"Shall I walk him up and down, sir?" said the boy, with a view of attracting the attention of Varley.

He started, and crying, harshly, "No, no," mounted his steed.

Then, throwing a small silver coin to the

boy, he said, as he pointed to the retreating form of Palmer:

"Boy, do you know yon man?"

The boy shook his head.

"No, sir; never seed him afore."

Varley put spurs to his horse, and galloped away with despair at his heart, and his teeth set close with passion, that he should be the victim of so much doubt and apprehension, at the very time when he had imagined that, by the removal of Sir George, all would be plain and easy before him, as regarded the amplitude of his means, and the contemplated possession of the Grange estates.

"The funeral—the funeral," he muttered. "I shall be easier when that is over."

CHAPTER XXX.

THE FUNERAL OF SIR GEORGE—MIRANDA'S GRIEF—THE WILD OFFERS OF BERNARD VARLEY.

MIRANDA rose with a heavy heart on the morning which was to see her father consigned to his last sad home.

Her rest had been disturbed by frightful images, which, had she been inclined to believe that in dreams was shadowed forth dimly the future fate of the vexed sleeper, would have exercised an additional depressing weight upon her mind, already burthened as it was with many sorrows.

She had resolved that she would no longer trespass upon the hospitality of Mr. Anderson, but that, by her own industry, if need should arise, she would not only endeavour to earn for herself an honourable subsistence, but assist the persecuted Rowland, whose destinies seemed yet darker than her own.

Mr. Anderson could not but mark the air of deep dejection that sat upon the countenance of Miranda, as she sparingly partook of the morning meal, and he strove, by such attentions and such topics of conversation as presented themselves to his mind, to wean her from the sad thoughts that occupied her sinking heart.

What human consolations, however, could withdraw Miranda from a contemplation of the solemn ceremony which was that day to take place.

To leave in the tomb the poor remains of her father, seemed like again losing him, for it was severing the last tie that still bound the senseless clay to the breasts of the living. It was passing that great barrier between life and death, where there is no return.

The funeral was to take place at mid-day, and Sir George was to be placed in a vault he had purchased beneath a humble, but picturesque, church, within one mile of the Grange.

He was the first of his race that would occupy that dreary abode, and, by the complexion of the present circumstances, it would seem as if he would be the last, for his dearly-beloved child—his Miranda—was doomed to wander from the home which, in the fondness of her father's heart, he believed he had provided for her, and become an alien from the scenes endeared to her by every blissful association—by every endearing tie that had previously made her life like a sweet walk in a sunny garden, where she had but to stretch forth her hand to pluck the fair flowers that bloomed in beauty around her.

But now how awfully was all changed—what a moral tempest had arisen to sweep before it all the traces of her happiness, and like our erring parents, when the gates of Eden closed on them, for ever shutting them from the glory, the sunshine, and the bliss in which Heaven had placed them, Miranda felt cold to the very heart's core, as her mental vision looked to her future life, and the long, weary pilgrimage she might have to endure.

It was hard for one so young to nerve her mind to meet so great a storm of sorrow. It was hard for one so nurtured in luxury, ever surrounded with loving hearts, ready to do her bidding, and anticipate the half-formed wishes of her heart, to meet the cold charities of a heartless world, and struggle against the waves of a destiny which might well have appalled the bravest.

These, and a thousand such gloomy thoughts, chased each other through the mind of Miranda, as, with a face as pale as death itself, she put on the dismal mourning apparel which Mr. Anderson had caused to be provided for her.

"'Tis well," she said, "I should mourn, but how weakly do these sad trappings portray the real grief of a wounded heart!—oh! what a mockery is this mourning apparel! when the heart really suffers, when the brain throbs, and all the faculties of the soul are absorbed in some great sorrow, this affected outward manifestation of the feelings is as futile as it is to the mourner an additional source of aggravation."

The hour of eleven was now at hand, and Mr. Anderson sent to Miranda to tell her that it was nearly time that they should go upon their melancholy errand.

Miranda was ready, and, obeying the summons, she glided down the staircase, looking more like one risen from the dead than a mourner at another's obsequies.

Her mental sufferings had robbed her cheek of all its healthful bloom, and the sombre garments she now wore gave a thinness to the form, and showed a striking contrast to the delicate whiteness of her complexion. In the words of the poet:

"She looked more beautiful than death,
    Though just as sad to gaze upon."

Mr. Anderson, when she entered the parlour in which he was awaiting her coming, strove to speak cheerfully to her, but he saw that her heart was too full to answer him, and he desisted from the fruitless attempt to win her from her sorrows.

In silence then he handed her into his chaise, and they were soon on the road to the Grange.

The birds were gaily singing from every bough as they passed along the tract of richly-cultivated country lying between York and the estate of Sir George. Thousands of busy insect things were humming songs of joy in the sunny air—all nature appeared rejoicing—and it was a painful and heart-striking contrast to glance from the face of nature to that of the beautiful young girl who sat by Mr. Anderson, looking as pale as monumental marble, and so deeply immersed in the sad feelings of her own wounded spirit, that sights and sounds of joy and gladness which, under happier auspices, would have inspired responsive feelings in her heart, passed by her quite unheeded, or were converted by the mind's subtle alchemy into wailing and sorrow.

"Miranda," said Mr. Anderson, as they came in sight of the old gable ends of the Grange, "let me hope that you will change your determination, and stay with us as our much-honoured guest."

"No—no," said Miranda, sorrowfully; "believe me, I am not unheedful of the kindness of the offer, but as Heaven has appointed me to feel the hand of woe heavily, I will abide my destiny. I am young, Mr. Anderson, and why should I be a burthen to anyone while I have strength or health to toil?"

"Toil, Miranda? Heaven forbid. I am not without a hope that I may wrest from Bernard Varley some portion of his ill-gotten wealth. Remain with me at least until the experiment is tried."

"I cannot, I cannot," said Miranda, "but I will ever look upon you as my best friend and counsellor. In poverty or in comfort I will make bold to consult you, but I cannot become a burthen upon you, although your generous heart would fain make me so."

Mr. Anderson saw that any attempt to shake Miranda's fixed determination would be futile, so he wisely abstained from pursuing the subject, consoling himself with the conviction that he should always be able to come forward to her assistance, and by keeping a strict watch upon her, prevent any very serious misery from assailing her.

As they now neared the Grange, all subjects, save the one mournful one that called her there, faded from the mind of Miranda, and her whole thoughts became concentrated on the approaching ceremony.

Over the principal entrance to the house was a hatchment, which struck a chill to the heart of Miranda as she saw it; but she made no remark, allowing Mr. Anderson in silence to hand her from his chaise, and place her arm within his own, as they ascended the hall steps.

The news of the arrival of Miranda, whom they still considered as their young mistress, soon spread among the few domestics of Sir George who still remained at the Grange, and she was greeted with affectionate sympathy by those humble hearts which felt for her the sincerest interest, and not one of whom but would have run any danger, or incurred any sacrifice, for her service.

Miranda strove to call a smile to her wan lips as she timidly thanked them, but the effort was too much for human nature, and, with a deep sigh, she passed onwards, clinging to Mr. Anderson's arm.

"Go, someone of you," said the attorney, "and tell Mr. Varley that I and Miranda are here."

"You will remain close to me," whispered Miranda, "for I wish not to have converse with that man."

"He shall not annoy you in any manner," said Mr. Anderson. "He will not attempt it, or, should he be so lost to every sense of common decency upon such an occasion as this, there are plenty of persons here, as well as myself, who will protect you."

In a few moments a servant came to tell Mr. Anderson that Varley desired to see him in his study.

"His study!" thought the attorney. "The insolence of this fellow grows daily. Miranda, will you permit me to leave you for a short time?"

"Go," said Miranda, "you had better see him, and tell him that the daughter of his victim only comes to see her poor father's remains laid in their last home, and then she will leave him to enjoy, if Heaven will permit it, the fruits of as deep villainy as ever mental brains conceived, or mortal hands executed."

Mr. Anderson followed the servant from the room in silence, and was ushered presently into a small, but richly-furnished apartment, where sat Bernard Varley and his man of business, the veracious Mr. Querral.

"Oh, Mr. Anderson," said Mr. Querral, "I hope I have the pleasure of seeing you perfectly well."

"Sir," said Mr. Anderson, "I have not your acquaintance."

"Oh, indeed! He! he! he!" answered Querral, with a short, disagreeable laugh. "You see, Mr. Varley, two of a trade never agree—the old maxim verified."

"You sent for me, sir," said Mr. Anderson, looking full at Varley, who wavered beneath his gaze.

"I did," said Varley; "but it was for your satisfaction, sir—not mine. Mr. Querral, my professional adviser, will prove to you that I have taken every necessary measure for substantiating the will of Sir George Rankley; and it remains for you—if you are so ill-advised—to do what you please in the way of attempting to resist that strictly legal document."

"What may be my intentions, or what advice I may give to Miss Rankley, remains with me alone," said Mr. Anderson. "My present visit here has sole reference to the funeral of Sir George; and his daughter, as a matter of course, claims the right of attending the ceremony."

"I wish," said Varley, his gaze shifting as he spoke, "to say a few words to — to Miranda."

"She positively refuses to hold any communication with you," said Mr. Anderson, coldly.

"Positively refuses?"

"Yes. Those were my words."

"And by your advice, I presume?"

"No, Mr. Varley; although, had she asked my advice, it would have been given in confirmation of her own expressed disinclination to hold any communication with you on any subject whatever."

"We understand each other," said Varley, setting his teeth, and looking with a savage scowl upon Mr. Anderson.

"I trust we do," was the other's reply.

"You might," added Varley, "have made me your friend, and, by a professional man, the friendship of the owner of the Grange estates is not to be despised; but you have chosen to make an enemy who never forgets an insult, nor forgives an injury."

"Your friendship I hold as lightly as your enmity," said Mr. Anderson. "Despising alike both, I leave you to your own choice."

"Dare you brave me in my own house?"

"Were it twenty times your own house I would," replied Mr. Anderson. "Robber of the orphan—despoiler of the virtuous and innocent, I do brave you here, on the spot where you have established yourself like a pestilence upon the ruins of all that is good, and great, and virtuous."

Varley would, in his passion, have rushed forward to strike Mr. Anderson, but he was restrained by Querral, who, holding him back forcibly, said:

"My dear sir, have patience. Bring an action against him. He called you a robber. That is clearly an actionable word. It will make a pretty suit—action for defamation—Varley v. Anderson."

Mr. Anderson slowly left the room, leaving Varley and his adviser to digest, as best they might, his frankness and his scorn.

CHAPTER XXXI.

THE FUNERAL—AN INTERRUPTION—AN UNEXPECTED GUEST—VARLEY'S DESPAIR.

WHEN Mr. Anderson reached again the room in which he had left Miranda, the time for the departure of the melancholy train was near at hand, and, saying nothing to her of the angry scene which had passed between him and Varley, he rang the bell, and desired the servant who answered the summons to let him know when the funeral *cortège* was ready to start.

The sound of many footsteps now came distinctly upon Miranda's ears, accompanied by a strange lumbering noise, which her heart too well told her was caused by the leaden coffin, in which the remains of her father had been early that morning encased, being carried down from the chamber in which he had died, into the hall.

Mr. Anderson, too, heard and understood the cause of the noise, but he said nothing to

Miranda, being greatly in hopes that she did not comprehend what was going forward.

The sounds then suddenly ceased, and all was as still as the grave for some moments, until the door of the room was gently opened, and, a servant appearing, said, in a low voice:

"All is ready, sir."

Mr. Anderson offered his arm to Miranda, who started to her feet, saying, in an abstracted manner:

"Yes—yes! Ready—quite ready for the grave. Oh, father! would that I was with you in your long, long sleep—that would be happiness!"

"Live for others," whispered Mr. Anderson. "What hope has Rowland Percy, but in you?"

"Thank you—thank you for that thought," said Miranda. "I have my duty to do—I have the innocent to rescue from death. Thank you—thank you."

She leaned heavily upon the arm of Mr. Anderson, as she walked by his side towards the hall. It was thronged with persons, who made a path for the pale, beautiful girl, and remained silent while she slowly moved on, in involuntary respect for her deep sorrow. Then the steps were descended, and there was the funeral coach, which was to follow first in the melancholy train.

Mr. Anderson assisted Miranda into the vehicle, and then followed after, and the door was closed.

Neither spoke, for at the moment the kind attorney felt that the ordinary topics of conversation would be impertinent, and he had none other to offer; while Miranda felt the greatest possible relief, by being spared the necessity of maintaining a conversation with anyone, which, to her, would have been a grievous effort just then.

A few moments then elapsed ere the funeral train got into motion, and when it did, the pace was so slow, and so solemn, that the movement was, to Miranda, scarcely perceptible.

It was a long and tedious journey, that one mile only, to Sir George Rankley's tomb, but it was at length accomplished; and as the clock of the little suburban church struck two, the *cortège* drew up at its entrance.

The deep tone of the solemn funeral bell struck upon Miranda's ear, as it seemed, in its melancholy tolling, to find a voice, and peal forth to the world that a human soul had gone to its account, and had passed away like a dream from among the living, to mingle with the spirits of the past, and form an item of that world which is eternal.

Mr. Anderson resolved within himself that should he see the spirits of Miranda much overcome, he would try again the potent spell of her lover's name, which had already had so happy an effect in weaning her from an indulgence in too great an abandonment of grief for the dead, by bringing to her recollection her self-imposed duties to the living.

How sad to the afflicted heart are the details of such a scene as that which Miranda was now going through; how "stale, flat, and unprofitable" appear all the various little formalities which the hirelings on such occasions take so much pains to surround death with.

Miranda, with a kind of stupor, arising from the intensity of her feelings, listened to the prayers within the church; and then, leaning still upon the arm of Mr. Anderson she approached the low door which led into the gloomy vault.

The attendants on the dead made way for her, and then the coffin was carried to the top of the steps. The necessity of sloping it, in order to carry it to its final resting-place, caused the pall to slip from it, and Miranda saw the plate on which the name of her father was engraved.

A convulsive spasm shook her frame for a moment, and then she was still again.

One of the bystanders whispered to another that the daughter of Sir George didn't seem much to care, for he had watched her, and she had not shed a tear yet! That was a happy man, for he had yet to experience the grief which lies too deep for tears.

As the coffin now slowly disappeared from before the eyes of Miranda, in its descent down the staircase, she became aware of the presence of a person directly opposite to her—one glance told her it was Bernard Varley. He was ghastly pale, his lips were quivering, and he seemed scarcely able to stand, as her eyes fell upon him.

"Miranda!" he said, in a deep, hollow tone.

Miranda clung closely to Mr. Anderson, who said:

"Beware, sir!—at such a moment as this, at least, be silent."

Miranda now made a movement to descend the narrow, dark staircase leading to the vault, but Mr. Anderson gently restrained her, saying:

"You will not surely descend, Miranda? Let me prevail on you to come away, now."

"No, no," she replied, faintly; "I will stay till the last—till the last."

Mr. Anderson made no further opposition, but accompanied her into the vault.

It was some moments before Miranda's eyes became accustomed to the dim light of that place of sepulchre, and, when they did, she looked round her with fearful interest, such as only that place could have awakened in her mind, associated, as she felt it would henceforward be, with her most dismal and distressing reminiscences.

The clergyman had now taken his place at the head of the corpse, and commenced in a low, solemn voice, reading the service of the dead.

His tones echoed in the gloomy vault, and the promise of the resurrection and eternal life which was to come, seemed to find a response in the moaning air that filled the abode of death.

All were hushed as so many statues, until the last words of that solemn and affecting ritual were spoken, and then with slow steps the clergyman left the vault, after pronouncing a benediction upon all present.

Miranda gazed upon her father's coffin, and at that moment it seemed to her as if her heart was breaking.

Mr. Anderson saw the terrible struggle of feeling which was going on in her breast, and, touching her gently on the arm, he whispered:

"Miranda—remember Rowland Percy."

She started, and said:

"Yes—yes—I do—Heaven knows I do. Father, father—farewell, farewell!"

These words were spoken with such exquisite agony that Mr. Anderson involuntarily trembled as he stood by her side, and his own voice was full of deep emotion, as he said:

"Come, come, Miranda. Let us now leave this place—all is over—oh! come away."

"Leave—me—here, alone," said, or rather gasped, Miranda, as she clasped her hands, and still kept her eyes fixed upon her father's coffin.

"No, Miranda, no," said the compassionate attorney, "I beg that you will leave with me. Do not injure your mental and bodily energies by indulging in such exquisite grief. I implore you to come away now."

"Command me," said Miranda, faintly, "in all else, but let the child remain for a brief space to breathe one prayer, with no ear but that of Heaven to listen to it, by her father's corpse."

This was unanswerable, and Mr. Anderson felt he had no resource but to comply.

He glanced round the vault, and saw that all had left it but Miranda and himself. Then, inclining his mouth to her ear, he said:

"For your own sake as well as for the sake of those who love you, Miranda, be brief. I will wait for you at the entrance of the vault. Call to me when you wish to ascend the stairs, and I will come to assist you."

He waited not for a reply, but hastily left the gloomy place, and Miranda fancied she was alone with the dead.

She lifted up her hands, and in a voice of thrilling emotion, she said:

"Oh, God! grant me tears of sorrow for my poor father! Let the gushing drops that, coming from the eyes, relieve the bursting heart, bedew my cheeks. It seems, oh! Heaven, that while I cannot weep, there must yet be in store for the unhappy Miranda some exquisite agony, some wild grief yet greater than that which now rends her heart for her father. Oh! Heaven! grant me tears—tears!"

She sank on her knees by the coffin, and a look came over her countenance expressive of the utmost despair. Her brain throbbed—the blood bounded through each artery of her frame like a bubbling torrent. She clasped her head with her hands, and cried:

"Save me, Heaven—save me from madness!"

Suddenly then she started. A human voice breathed her name.

Was it a delusion conjured up by her racked imagination? No—it was real. Someone, in a tone of agony as exquisite as her own, said:

"Miranda!"

"Who—who speaks?" she cried. "Who calls on the wretched Miranda?"

"I—I!" cried a voice; and, from a gloomy niche in the vault, Bernard Varley came slowly forward.

It was strange to see those two living persons in the presence of the dead, regarding each other with singular feelings.

Bernard Varley looked up in the face of Miranda like some evil spirit which had wandered from its allotted home, after warring with Heaven, and, having met some brighter, purer spirit, was employing its intercession with the offended majesty of Heaven, while Miranda, with lips slightly apart, her slender, delicate figure drawn back to evade his contaminating touch, and a look of abhorrence mingling with the painful feelings that were depicted on her countenance, looked, indeed, the pure seraph of Heaven recoiling from the touch of the being cast out from the realms of joy for its deep sinfulness.

"Once more—once more, Miranda," he said, as he knelt before her—"once more I pray to you—I, who never prayed before for mercy. Oh! you know me not! Miranda—Miranda—take the Grange—take all back again; but if you would save a mortal soul from the agony of despair—if you would light with joy the chambers of a brain which is nearly maddened, you will look with pity on me, Bernard Varley."

"Monster!" shuddered Miranda.

"I love you—I love you!" he cried, as he beat his breast in the bitterness of feeling. "I love you with such a love as man never yet felt for woman. You lie enshrined in my heart deeper than ever devotee enshrined the saint he looked to for salvation. Bid me deny Heaven, anything, so that you give me hope that in the fulness of time the day may come when you will not scorn me, Miranda, but, with a gentle voice, tell me that you pity me, that you will try to love——"

"God of Heaven!" cried Miranda, "has thy judgment fallen already upon this man, and made him what he is, filling his soul with this strange infatuation?"

"It is—it is an infatuation," said Varley. "There never, in the wildest, dreamiest pages of romance, was a love portrayed like mine. It is to me life, light, joy, breath, hope, the world that is, and that which is to come. Oh, Miranda, where can you hope to find a heart so bound to you as mine? I know that women are capricious, and are fond of slaves—make one of me. Smile upon me one moment, and frown the next. The memory of the smile shall charm away the perception of all harshness. Say that you will think kindly of me—do not loathe me—and then ask of me what you will, and it shall be granted. Am I not abject, Miranda? Miranda, I love—adore—I worship——"

"Appeal to Heaven," said Miranda, who

began to be alarmed by his wild, frantic distress. Appeal to Heaven, and not to one of Heaven's humblest creatures. What mercy can I show you, wretched man?"

"I am—I am," he cried, "wretched—most wretched. The world will envy me, because they will fancy me rich, and that to be rich is to be happy; but do you, Miranda, take all, so that you smile upon the wretched Bernard Varley, who will then be a prince in happiness, a Crœsus in the wealth which knows no diminishing—that wealth which is coined in the heart, and passes current in the teeming brain. Miranda—Miranda, say that you will be mine—feed me with hope—a word, a look will suffice to make me happy."

"Let me pass," said Miranda, "or I will call for help."

"Oh, leave me not to despair," he said. "Hear me, Miranda! I will save Rowland Percy—I, I will give him wealth which he can spend in some foreign land—I will—I will——"

"Peace—peace," cried Miranda. "Bernard Varley, I here swear by yon mute form, which lies so cold and still, and the pure spirit of which may even now be listening to my words, never to——"

"No—no, kill me not with such an oath."

"Never to relax in my endeavours to convict you of his murder, until justice has overtaken you. An invisible voice even now seems to assure me you did the deed!"

"Miranda," said Varley, in choking accents, "you—you are destroying two persons—one whom you love, and one whom you hate. Rowland Percy shall die, and I will die; but when, at the judgment seat of the Eternal, I am challenged for aught done in my mortal life, I will shriek your name, Miranda, and I will urge that you are less merciful than the wildest savage, who refused one word to save my soul."

"I will not hear this profanation," cried Miranda. "Help—help!"

Varley sprang to his feet; he darted towards Miranda, and, with a strength that her feeble efforts could not resist, clasped her in his arms, and pressed his lips to hers.

CHAPTER XXXII.

THE RESCUE FROM THE VAULT—THE DIAMOND RING.

MIRANDA uttered shriek after shriek as she found herself clasped in the embrace of the loathed Bernard Varley, until the vault reechoed with her frantic screams.

A wild, demoniac spirit seemed to possess the ruffian, and he laughed aloud as he struggled with the beautiful and horror-stricken girl, whose strength was decreasing each moment, when he was suddenly seized from behind by a powerful grasp, and hurled with such violence to the farther end of the vault, that he lay quite stunned with his fall.

"Save me! Save me!" cried Miranda, as she clung to the arm of her deliverer, without looking to see who it was that had rendered her so timely a service.

"You are a pretty scoundrel, I think," exclaimed he who had so unceremoniously worsted Varley, and who was no other than Dick Palmer. "So you are at your old tricks, are you, and didn't think I was so near at hand."

Varley sat on the floor of the vault, looking bewildered, first at Miranda, and then at Palmer, who he really began to believe must be his evil genius.

What with the wild excitement he had worked himself up to in his interview with Miranda, and the heavy concussion with which he had encountered the wall of the vault, he was in a state of mental confusion, which prevented him from speaking for some moments, and it was not until Palmer again addressed him that he recovered sufficiently to understand fully where he was, or what had happened to him.

"Mark me, Master Varley," said Palmer, "I will be always near you, and if you attempt any more of your villainies—I say, beware!"

"Fearful man," cried Varley, struggling to his feet; "tell me, now, though the information should kill me, tell me who and what you are? Why do you haunt me? Why dog me from place to place? In the name of Heaven, or by a more fearful adjuration, I charge you, tell me who you are?"

"I've told you once," said Palmer, who was much amused at the accidental train of circumstances which had enabled him to exercise so strange and so unexpected a control over the mind of Bernard Varley. "I've told you once; don't seek to know more till the time comes."

Varley groaned and struck his breast as he exclaimed:

"Am I to be haunted? Am I to be haunted?"

"Of course you are," said Palmer. "It serves you right, and you know it. Allow me, Miss Rankley, to see you safely to your friends. They are just above here, I believe."

"To whom am I indebted for this rescue?" said Miranda.

"Never mind me, or who I am," replied Palmer. "I am your friend. Let that suffice. In other respects, you might not like me half so well."

The dim light in the vault was not sufficient to enable Miranda to get a clear view of the face of her deliverer, or, it is probable, she might have recollected the circumstance of her first encounter with him, when proceeding from the Grange to York with Mr. Anderson; she, however, clung to his arm with confidence, and, without another glance at Bernard Varley, ascended the staircase leading from the vault.

The discomfited villain was, however, by no means inclined to be left alone in that receptacle of the dead, and he no sooner observed Miranda and Palmer half-way up the staircase, than, with a cry of terror, he rushed after them, for an impression had, on the

VARLEY THREATENS HIS ACCOMPLICE TWITTER.

moment, seized his mind that the strange man, who had thwarted him, might have both the will and the power to close up the entrance of the vault, and leave him, a living prisoner, in the tomb.

So firmly had this sudden thought taken possession of his mind, that, in a moment, it appeared to him as if he had actually been threatened with such a punishment, and, as he rushed up the staircase after Miranda and Palmer, he cried:

"No, no! Mercy—not that! Let me out. Air—air—fresh air! Oh, Heaven, leave me not with the dead! Mercy—have mercy upon me!"

"You deserve to be left where you are," said Palmer, "except that it would be a pity to cheat the gallows, which surely will some day come into its reversionary interest in you. Pass on, cowardly hound. Pass on—your time has not yet come."

Miranda and Palmer stood on one side, and allowed the trembling Varley to pass them on the narrow staircase, which he did with a frantic, trembling eagerness, that showed to what a height his apprehension had reached of being detained.

When he reached the mouth of the vault, and emerged into the daylight, he bounded across the churchyard with the speed of a hunted hare. His ghastly pale face, quivering limbs, and set teeth, gave him, to those who were standing near the entrance of the vault, more the appearance of some resuscitated corpse, embracing that opportunity to rush from the embraces of the grave, than a living man.

They fell back, and made way for him in silent horror, and when another glance at the narrow opening of the tomb showed them more forms advancing, one and all of the idle villagers, whom curiosity had brought to the spot, fled in wild dismay.

Then the guilty Varley fancied that they must be in pursuit of him, and he flew, rather than ran, in the direction of the Grange, where he hoped to find shelter. His agony of mind became excessive; he bit his lips through in his intense agitation, and although one glance behind him would have assured him he was not pursued, even in appearance, beyond the precincts of the churchyard, he paused not until faint, weary, and exhausted, he rushed up the marble staircase leading from the hall, nor paused in his frantic career until he had locked and double-locked himself in his own room, and snatched from a bureau some loaded firearms, with which he stood in an attitude of defence for a few moments, until exhausted nature would support him no longer, and he sank trembling into a chair.

While Varley was thus in terror and mental agony, in some measure expiating his crimes, Miranda reached, along with Palmer, the mouth of the vault, where she looked in vain for Mr. Anderson, who had promised to be within call, but who was now nowhere to be seen.

Miranda then turned to her companion, and by the light of day she at once recognized him, which he perceived by her glance.

"You know me now, Miss Rankley," he said; "that is, you know as much of me as I wish you to know, and as much as I hope you ever will. You have been kind to me, and as you are about the only person that ever was so, I ought to make much of it. Now, if you will recollect that you have a friend in me always, I shall be very much obliged to you, for though some folks think me no better than I should be, I am not ungrateful."

"I have cause to be grateful to you," said Miranda, "for you rescued me from yon ruffian when all my other friends seemed to have deserted me."

"Mine was the return of a favour," said Palmer. "Your kindness to me when my nag threw me was quite another thing; and now, Miss Rankley, I have a favour to ask of you."

"A favour?"

"Yes. Will you, without asking any questions about how I came by it, accept a present from me?"

Miranda paused a moment before she replied. Then she said:

"It is I who ought to make some return to you for your services; but I have not now the means."

"Never mind that. Will you accept my present?"

Miranda was perplexed extremely. She knew not what to say; but, when she thought of how she had been rescued from Varley by him who was now addressing her, she no longer hesitated, but replied:

"If it be such a present as I shall, upon knowing what it is, feel inclined to keep, I answer you 'Yes'; but I must reserve my right to return it to you should I think proper."

"As you please," said Palmer. "Take this ring."

As he spoke he took from his own finger the diamond ring which the avarice of Twitter had induced him to wrench from the dead hand of Sir George Rankley. The trinket was well known to Miranda, and, as she took it from Palmer, she exclaimed:

"Good Heavens! my father's ring! How could this come into your possession?"

"Remember your promise," said Palmer. "No questions as to how I came by it. Will you keep it, or return it to me?"

"I will keep it," said Miranda, "as a memento of him who is gone. You know not how I shall prize this glittering bauble. It will remind me of happier days, and when I see it glistening in all its beauty and brightness, it will make me think that, although the hand of misfortune may press heavily upon me, still the bright jewel of the soul—integrity, may never lose its lustre."

"Humph," said Palmer. "There are some people, Miss Rankley, who may have let that sort of lustre grow a little tarnished now and then, but who still possess a few good qualities that will peep out like bright spots among the rust; but that's neither here nor there, and, if I mistake not, here comes some friends of yours, so good-bye, and God bless you for a kind-hearted girl and a credit to your sex."

With this the highwayman walked briskly away, and, advancing from among the tombs, Miranda saw Mr. Anderson and the elder Mr. Percy.

"I have to apologize to you, Miranda, for leaving you," said Mr. Anderson; "but I was called away by Mr. Percy, here, and trust you suffered no inconvenience."

"It is no matter," said Miranda, who thought a recital of the insult she had been subjected to by Bernard Varley could not possibly do any good.

Mr. Percy advanced, and there was a tear in his eye as he took Miranda's hand, and said:

"Miranda, I have been trying to prevail upon Mr. Anderson to concur with me in a proposition which I wish you to consider kindly."

"What proposition?" said Miranda. "Name it, Mr. Percy, and, if it be within my poor ability, it shall be agreed to."

"It is," continued Mr. Percy, "that you would look upon me in some measure as a substitute for him who is gone. That as, if Heaven had so willed it, you would have been the wife of my dear boy—you will look upon me now, in your orphan state, as a second father. Together we can consult and contrive much for lightening the weary hours of Rowland's most unjust persecution. We can speak comfort to each other's hearts, and should my dear boy be returned to his father's arms—which, I trust, in the justice of Heaven, he will—we may once more, casting over the past the veil of resignation, be happy. Oh, Miranda! consent to an old man's prayer. The sufferings of the last seven days have added many years to those I had already numbered. I am alone now in the wide world, and with but one object next my heart, for which I would fain still preserve the embers of an existence that else I would most gladly render up to Him who gave it. That object is the liberation of my poor boy, Rowland."

The father paused. He would have said more, but tears choked his utterance, and, after a vain attempt to suppress his deep emotion, he sobbed audibly.

Miranda was deeply affected, as she replied:

"This is no time to fence the feelings of the heart round with cold formalities. I here declare it—and I would do so before the world—that let his fate be what it may, Rowland Percy is my affianced husband!"

"Bless you for those words! Bless you," said Mr. Percy.

"As such," continued Miranda, falteringly, "to you, his father, I, in my orphan state, will cling as a second parent, and oh! may it yet be in the designs of Providence that he, our joint hope and care, may be restored to us."

"Miranda — my dear child!" said Mr. Percy; "together we will talk of Rowland, and we shall never weary of the theme."

"Never," said Miranda. "I accept your offer, Mr. Percy, and such duty as a child should give a parent, will I give to you."

"I cannot," said Mr. Anderson, "object to such an arrangement as you are now making. My house and means, as Miranda knows, were freely offered to her, so long as she chose as a cherished friend, and honoured guest, to dwell beneath my roof. But let it be as you propose, and, although Miranda refuses my hospitality, I trust she does not decline my friendship?"

"Can you think me ungrateful to you, sir?" said Miranda; "you, who have sustained me through the weary week which has now passed. I were indeed ungrateful could I ever forget how much I owe to your disinterested friendship."

"Then let me add," said Mr. Anderson, "that I am not without a hope in the midst of all the gloom which has surrounded us, of finding one ray of light, however small. It consists in my belief that I shall be able to rescue some of Mr. Percy's property from the general ruin. It may be a very small portion, but when weighed against nothing, it becomes important."

"Heaven grant you success," said Mr. Percy. "My poor Rowland will require means."

"Put your mind at rest upon that point," said Mr. Anderson. "I believe I may say that I and Miranda have quite arranged all that. Nothing shall be spared in the conducting of his defence, which I have undertaken to prepare and see properly brought forward."

Miranda could only look her gratitude to Mr. Anderson, and the little party of attached friends declining to accompany the funeral *cortège* back to the Grange, walked on till they reached the stables, where was Mr. Anderson's chaise, after which they proceeded to York—Miranda being in a calmer and happier frame of mind than she had yet experienced since the full tide of troubles had set in upon the heaven of her joy.

CHAPTER XXXIII.

VARLEY'S HATRED TO THE GRANGE—THE DEPARTURE—TWITTER OUTWITTED.

IT was more than an hour before Bernard Varley recovered from the state of agitation into which he had been thrown by the proceedings in the vault, and, even then, when he became a little more composed, and could assure himself that his fears of being followed from the churchyard were groundless, he was lost in conjecture of the most painful nature, as to who and what the mysterious man could be who seemed ever at hand to thwart him, Varley, in his designs, and to know things which he had believed were locked up in the recesses of his own breast.

A more striking example of the terrors which beset a guilty conscience could scarcely be found than in the horror with which Varley had come to regard the highwayman, whose real knowledge of Varley and his proceedings was so very small, but whom Varley's fears converted into a being who had obtained a key to the most hidden secrets of his heart.

Thus is it ever with the overburthened conscience of the guilty—facts and circumstances, which, to the pure of purpose and innocent of heart, could produce no disquietude, are to them sources of dread and alarm, as the thief

"Doth fear each bush an officer."

Then Varley had another source of deep disquietude, and that consisted in his superstitious fears, which had been all awakened by the strange and mysterious appearance of the spirit of the murdered keeper to him—a visitation which he could not otherwise account for than by supposing it to be purely supernatural.

Thus he thought, and the drops of perspiration, engendered by fear, stood upon his brow, as he made the reflection—"why may not one disembodied spirit as well as another, re-visit in the likeness of its mortal form, the spots familiar to it? and if such be the latter case, how am I to know but the day may come, when, in the solitude of some chamber, remote from human aid, where my cries would be unheard, I may meet the spirit of Sir George Rankley, which might drive me to madness with horror."

Varley trembled with apprehension as these horrible reflections passed through his brain, and he became each moment more and more strengthened in his determination to remove from the Grange, every room of which was now, to him, replete with disagreeable associations, and residence in which could not but be exceedingly tormenting and agonizing to his guilty soul.

"Yes," he muttered, "I will remove from here. This is no longer a fit abode for me. I will dwell ever near Miranda, with the hope but of sometimes seeing her, and treading in her footsteps as she walks abroad. I think even now I could confess all, and suffer all the penalties of such confession, would she but smile upon me for one fleeting moment. Heaven help me! what can be the meaning of this world of passion that possesses my soul for this young maiden? Long since, 'tis true, I loved her, but it was with a feeling that my better judgment could control, and not with the wild fervour of my present feelings that know no bounds, but seem ever on the point of driving me to some act of madness, ending in destruction."

Bernard Varley groaned aloud as he made these remarks, and at one time he would pace his room with unequal steps, then throwing himself into a chair, he would assume a serious attitude, in the vain hope that by bodily ease and luxury, he should be able to calm the excitement of his mind.

A low, timid knock at his door suddenly aroused him, and before he could shape a reply to the summons, Twitter slowly entered the apartment.

Hating—detesting—despising Twitter as Varley did, even his presence was a relief at that moment of mental prostration, and it was almost in a tone of kindness and welcome that he said:

"Ah! Twitter, is that you? come in. I have something to say to you, and was wishing for your presence."

"Is—the funeral over?" said Twitter, glancing furtively round him, as if he each moment expected to see some sight which would unnerve him.

"The funeral is over," replied Varley, "but it is not of that I would speak to you. The time has come, as I always thought it would, when the Grange has become hateful to me."

"The Grange hateful?" said Twitter.

"Yes," added Varley, "and were you, which you may be, as full of—of—I will not call it apprehension, but of conviction, that this house was the abode of beings of another world, as I am, you would be equally anxious to quit it."

"You—you have no grounds," said Twitter, nervously, "for supposing that any being of another world is calculated to be a sight of terror to us?"

"Hush, hush!" said Varley. "Let it suffice that I have ample reason for quitting the Grange, and quit it I must and will."

Twitter's face assumed a sallow hue as he struck his hand feebly upon the table, in order to affect an energy he did not feel, and said:

"Then—then, how am I to be paid if you leave the Grange—where am I to find you? Recollect our bargain—I was to have an annuity."

"And so you shall," replied Varley. "I shall still require your assistance; for, know, Twitter, that what I have already succeeded in accomplishing is but as nothing compared to that I have still to do."

"Indeed!"

"Yes; think you it is as easy a task to bend the stubborn will of a girl, as it is to work upon the weak mind of a man, and so contrive that he shall go from mortal life as Sir George Rankley has done, so soon as all is accomplished that I wished; and that, instead of a great assistance and a source of ample means, he became an encumbrance in the steep path of my ambition?"

"You still, then," said Twitter, "intend to persevere in your hopeless pursuit of Miranda?"

"I do," said Varley, with vehemence; "but call it not hopeless—that it can never be. Until she or I have sunk to the grave I will hope on, in the face of scorn, contempt, derision, hate. Nothing but death shall turn me from my purpose. I love her with one of those wild, headlong passions rare in our northern clime, but which resemble a mountain torrent in fierce impetuosity and freedom. I love her with a love goaded to madness by opposition. Each glance of hatred, each word of scorn that I receive from her only adds fuel to the flame that already seems consuming my heart. I love her; I love her!"

"He's mad," thought Twitter; "he's mad. I never particularly loved anybody but myself."

"Listen to my plan of operations," resumed Varley. "You may, or may not, continue with me to assist as you please; my non-residence on the Grange estate can make no difference in its rental; nay, it may rather increase it, for this mansion may be let. I shall remove at once to York; and near to where Miranda lives, there will I take up my abode. Night and day I will watch her. She shall not stir abroad but I will be upon her path; she shall feel that I am as a shadow, ever closely following her for good or for evil, as she may herself make me. This lover of hers, if she will not save him by becoming mine, shall assuredly die on the scaffold the death of a murderer. She, herself, shall be plunged into poverty and destitution that she, the child of luxury, cannot even picture to herself."

"But—" interrupted Twitter, cautiously, for he was half afraid of contradicting Varley, his manner was so violent—"don't you think that it is possible there may be some who will step between you and your victim; and, by assisting Miranda, place her far above the state to which you would reduce her?"

"Yes," cried Varley, dashing his fist upon the table with a violence that made Twitter start and tremble. "Yes, there are such; but who shall dare to stand between me and my plans—my hopes and expectations? Let them beware who do! I have commenced a career, which, beginning in blood, may as well go on in the same ensanguined hue."

"You—you don't mean to say that you'd murder them?" faltered Twitter.

"Let them beware!—let them beware!" said Varley. "I am a desperate man! I have ample resources, and I am devoured by a passion which knows no bounds—has no scruples. I say, then, let those beware who cross me!"

Twitter groaned, for in perspective he could fancy he saw the absolute ruin which Varley must bring upon them both by his indulgence in a passion which set reason at defiance, and which, if he persevered in the course he was laying down, must end in his destruction.

"And then what is to become of me?" thought Twitter, with a groan.

"Surely—surely," continued Varley, in an undertone, as if rather reasoning with himself, than addressing Twitter, "hunger and wretchedness must have their effect even on such a mind as Miranda's. When she feels the acute pangs of absolute want, she may be glad of relief, even from my hands; when benumbed by the winter's cold, she may forget some of the stern pride of her heart, and give a smile to me for bringing her to warmth and comfort. One by one I will remove every prop she has in this world. I will follow her like the embodied spirit of an evil destiny, until she becomes mine—irrevocably mine!"

"You will bring trouble and destruction on us both!" groaned Twitter. "I see nothing but ruin in what you propose to do. Why can't you enjoy yourself now that you have ample means of doing so?"

"Peace—peace!" said Varley. "You cannot turn me from my purpose. Peace, I say! Let it suffice for you that I will fulfil my agreement with you. Remain with me or not, you shall have the sum I promised."

"If I remain with him," thought Twitter, "I shall be in a constant fright; but then I shall know when I am in danger, and when I am not, whereas, if I live away from him, I shall never know a moment's peace from constant apprehension that he is committing some wild extravagance for love of Miranda, that may place both his and my own neck in the halter."

"Have you decided?" said Varley.

"I tell you what I'll do," replied Twitter, a sudden thought breaking in upon him, which he imagined might extricate him from his difficulties. "Give me ten years' amount of the sum I am to receive yearly, and I will release you from all further charge."

"Five thousand pounds?"

"Yes—yes. Then you know, Varley, you

will be rid of me altogether, and might pursue this girl whenever you chose, you know."

"No," said Varley. "There are several reasons why I shall not do so; but one will suffice. I will not allow you to enjoy, without risk, the benefit in full of that which you lent so tardy and inefficient a hand in performing. You shall not escape, Twitter, if I fall! You understand me? While I hold the Grange estates, and escape all suspicion of the crime for which Rowland Percy is now in prison, you shall with me enjoy the proceeds."

"Then I implore you," said Twitter, who saw by the manner of Varley that he was inexorable on that point, "I implore you to give up this mad pursuit of Miranda, which can only end in our mutual ruin."

"'Tis in vain to talk to me," said Varley. "I have now but one object in life, and that is Miranda Rankley. Come death—come destruction—I will pursue her to the last."

"Lost—lost," said Twitter.

Varley rose, and paced the room for some minutes, then, turning to Twitter, he said:

"Once more I ask you, do you go with me or not?"

"I—I will go with you," said Twitter, "with the hope of in some measure protecting you from the consequences of your rashness."

"'Tis well—'tis well," said Varley. "Now for York. Leave here some trustworthy person in charge of the mansion and its contents. I will sleep in York to-night."

"There—there is one thing," said Twitter, "which I am sure is so very reasonable, you will consent to it at once, Varley."

"What is it?"

"Only, that in case of any accident to you, you see, you will make a will in my favour."

Twitter turned away his eyes from the face of Varley as he said these words, but Varley with two strides came close to him, and laying his hand heavily upon his shoulder, he said:

"Twitter, it may be, that in my wild passion for Miranda Rankley, I want the sober judgment which you know can usually guide my actions, but in all other things I am the same Bernard Varley as ever I was. Your shallow scheme is as evident to me as if you had proclaimed it openly."

"My—my scheme?" stammered Twitter.

"Yes—you would get me to make a will, leaving you my successor to the Grange estates."

"Only in case of—of accident, you know, Varley. Human life is—very uncertain."

"It is," said Varley. "Life is very uncertain. It is one of those things we cannot command; but, Twitter, death is very certain."

"Death?"

"Yes! Now, tell me, in sober sincerity, how long it would be after I had made the will you suggest, before the accident, which it is to provide you against, happened to me? Eh, Twitter?"

"You—you suspect me?" said Twitter.

"No," whispered Varley in his ear, with a hissing sound, like the noise of a snake. "I do not suspect you, Twitter, but I know you."

"You will not make the will?"

"I will not. But I will do this much for you, Twitter. Be assured, that as we are now living men, should anything arise to bring me to destruction, should there occur one of those trifling accidents, which will sometimes overturn the best-laid schemes, and like the abstraction of some supporting beam from a huge building, bring the whole fabric of our ambition upon our heads—you shall not escape. We have plotted, planned together, murdered together, taken the price of blood together, and be most amply assured, Twitter, that if there shall be a day of retribution, we will suffer together."

Twitter trembled as Varley spoke, and when he had ceased, he replied, in a faint voice:

"Enough, Varley, enough. We will speak no more upon this subject. Let us, as you propose, go to York."

"You understand me thoroughly?" said Varley.

"Too well—too well," shuddered Twitter.

"Then to York—to York."

CHAPTER XXXIV.

THE EVENING BEFORE ROWLAND'S TRIAL—A PRISON SCENE—MIRANDA'S ASSUMED SPIRITS.

IT wanted but an hour to sunset on the evening preceding the day on which the innocent Rowland Percy was to take his trial for the murder of Sir George Rankley, when two persons paused at the massive gates of the gloomy prison in which the unfortunate young man was confined. These persons were Miranda and Mr. Percy.

Although but a short time had elapsed since last we presented the once rich and happy Squire of Larkswood to the reader, anyone would have imagined from his bent form and trembling steps that years must have passed over his head, leaving behind them the traces of their onward march in the physical prostration of the prematurely-aged man.

Oh, how lightly time touches the happy; how gently it glides past them; how tenderly it marks the wrinkles of the once blooming face; by what imperceptible and gentle touches does it turn the raven locks to silver gray, until the mild autumn of life looks almost as healthful and as beautiful as the sweet spring-tide of existence.

But when misfortune—the heart's agony—the throbbing brain and the fevered pulse mark the progress of the fell destroyer—how quickly are the hale and strong prostrated to a state of trembling decrepitude; a single night will plant furrows in the cheek, and bend the stoutest form.

So was it with Mr. Percy. The time which had elapsed since his duel with Sir George Rankley, and the whirl of terrible events which had surrounded it so closely, could only be measured by weeks. But, oh! how changed was he in that brief time. Scarcely any who had feasted at his board, one little month before, would have imagined in the trembling, weak, infirm, old-looking man, who paused with the beautiful girl resting on his arm, they saw the hearty, jovial Squire of Larkswood, on whose cheek glowed the healthy tint of temperance, and whose clear eyes and open brow proclaimed a mind serene and quite at ease.

And Miranda, too—had no change marked the heart's painful throbbing on her gentle brow? Had suffering failed to rob her of the charms her beauty wore?

Yes, it had failed to do that; but it had converted her from the youthful Hebe she once was, to a living representation of melancholy.

The roses no longer bloomed upon her cheeks. Her charming eyes were no longer lit up with the radiance of the happy heart; but, pale and sad, although with a look of holy resignation on her face, that made her resemble more some sorrowing angel than a thing of earth, she looked up at the heavy gates which shut her lover from her sight.

"Miranda, my child," said Mr. Percy, for he loved to talk to her like a father, "you wrote to my dear boy that we should be here this night?"

"Yes," said Miranda—"Hark! The Minster clock strikes eight. That was the hour I mentioned."

As she spoke, the solemn-toned bell of the magnificent cathedral boomed forth the hour of eight. The two sorrowing friends paused involuntarily until the last stroke had died away, then the old man said, with a faltering voice:

"Let us now seek admittance, Miranda. He will expect us. Do you knock. Rowland will think we are late in coming."

Miranda timidly knocked at the small wicket, which was as a minor door let into the massive gate, and in a few moments a coarse, red face peered at her through a grating, while a not very harmonious voice cried:

"Well, what now?"

"We have an order to see Mr. Percy," said Miranda.

"Oh, have you?" said the turnkey. "Come in, then. I suppose you know," he added, as Miranda and Mr. Percy entered the stone vestibule, "that he is to be tried to-morrow?"

"Yes—yes!" said Mr. Percy. "Heaven protect him!"

"Oh! as to that, it'll all depend on the evidence, old gentleman," said the man. "To-morrow's Friday, that's why he's to be tried to-morrow. It gives him longer time, you see, miss, in case it goes hard with him."

Miranda shuddered, but made no answer. She knew too well to what the man alluded, and as she passed onwards through the narrow vaulted passages, she breathed silently a fervent prayer to Heaven to spare the innocent, even if the guilty should not be brought to judgment.

They were conducted into a small room, where the order of admission they had procured from a magistrate was duly inspected, and being pronounced genuine, they were given in charge of one of the under-turnkeys, with directions to conduct them to the prisoner.

In a few minutes Rowland was in his father's arms. Then he clasped Miranda to his breast, as he whispered to her with a forced smile, that sat but badly upon his wan, pale face:

"Courage, my Miranda—courage—all will be well—we shall be happy yet."

Miranda could not speak, but she looked earnestly in his face to see if indeed he felt the hope his tongue gave utterance to; then, turning away her eyes, she shook her head, saying:

"Heaven help you, Rowland. It alone can save you."

"And it will, Miranda," he said; "never doubt it. I am innocent—there is my strength. Indulge in no gloomy anticipations, dear Miranda. If I could see you smile, and look cheerful, and full of hope, I could almost be happy here."

"You smile, Rowland," said Miranda, "but——"

A rising sob choked her utterance, and Rowland said in a voice that slightly shook:

"You would say my smile is not one of joy, my Miranda; but it is one of hope over doubt. Ought I despair when I have such a heart as yours to feel for me? Here have I the two beings in the whole world who possess my warmest love—yourself and my father, to comfort me. There is such a heavenly majesty—such a glorious light from above around the truth, that it must triumph. I have great faith that to-morrow will be to us a day of great rejoicing—and then, Miranda, we shall be the happier for the trials we have gone through. The sunny joy of our remaining life will look the brighter that it has been preceded by such storms. Cheer up, dear Miranda, and let me, to-morrow, when I hold up my hand, and, in the face of Heaven declare my innocence—not feel weighed down by fancying you in grief. Oh, if I could see you now hopeful and serene, it would give me new life."

"Forgive me, Rowland," said Miranda. "I should come here to cheer you, not depress you. I will hope for the best. You are innocent, Rowland, and surely you will be protected by Heaven."

"Doubt it not, Miranda," he replied. "Moreover, the judges of the land are keen of discernment and knowledge of human nature. They look on things dispassionately, and the well-concocted tale of the villains, Varley and Twitter, may lack some connecting link, which, to the practised judgments of such, may invalidate the whole. It is the frequent fate of deep-laid plots to fail through some mere accidental omission, that the judgment of a child would have supplied, but which, through the interposition of Providence, escapes the acute perception of the most artful

and designing villains that ever conspired against the life of the innocent."

"I will hope all that, Rowland," said Miranda. "Do not, to-morrow, think of me as tearful and despairing, but as one calmly waiting for the consummation of a dear hope, that even now glows in my breast. Should you meet me to-morrow, Rowland, you shall see me smile, you shall, Rowland, I—I—promise."

Mr. Percy had sat down on a small bench near the iron-barred window of the room, and, leaning his head upon his hands, he seemed to have given himself up to the bitterest reflection.

"It is I—it is I," he said, "who am most guilty. I have caused all this misery. Can you, Miranda—can you, my own Rowland, forgive your erring father?"

"Talk not thus, father," said Rowland, "unless you would quite unnerve me for the morrow. You, as well as Miranda and myself, are the victims of the machinations of the villain Varley. I have no moral doubt whatever that he committed the crime of which I stand accused; and, be assured, the day will come, however distant, when the truth will be apparent, for never yet was 'man's blood by man shed' but, in Heaven's good time, the awful deed came to light."

"I believe it," said Mr. Percy. "And yet am I most guilty, for, by my weakness, I gave our enemies strength."

"Say no more, father, on that head. Let us look, now, to the future, and pray that it may be happier than has been the past. Mr. Anderson told me he would call you both as witnesses at the trial."

"And we will appear," said Miranda. "Surely those upon whose judgments you depend, Rowland, will listen to me. Who can doubt that I loved my father? Who can say I could commit, in the sight of Heaven, so heinous a sin as to perjure myself to screen his murderer? The truth must be apparent."

"It will, Miranda—it will," said Rowland, who was pleased to see her in so hopeful a frame of mind. "To-morrow will be a day of rejoicing to us."

"Oh, grant it may," said Miranda. "I will tell them how I have been persecuted by this Bernard Varley—how, with his fulsome addresses, he has knelt to me, ever saying that he would save your life if I would be his."

"And tell them, likewise, Miranda," said Rowland, "how you spurned the villain—how you scorned his cringing offers. Rather would I die ten thousand deaths than purchase a degraded life, for such it would be at such a sacrifice."

"Here's Mr. Anderson," said the turnkey, as he opened the door, and the humane lawyer entered.

"Welcome, my dear sir," said Rowland. "You have come in time to confirm the hopes I am giving to Miranda, that all will be well to-morrow."

As he spoke, Rowland looked significantly at the attorney, who understood him, and said:

"Yes; the innocent should be ever full of hope. All will be well, no doubt."

"You really do think so, Mr. Anderson?" said Miranda, fixing her eyes with such a painful interest upon his face, that he could scarcely say:

"Yes—yes! Certainly. Rowland and I must have another consultation to-night about some serious matters, and by this time to-morrow evening I hope to see him a free man."

Miranda breathed more freely, for she had a great reliance upon the judgment of Mr. Anderson, and to hear him speak such words of confidence gave her more comfort than she had felt from anything Rowland could say.

Mr. Percy rose to go, and again he embraced his son; his feelings would not allow him to speak, and, wringing his hands in silence, he tottered to the door.

Miranda tried to smile, as Rowland took both her hands in his, and said:

"Farewell, dear Miranda, till to-morrow."

"Farewell!" was all she could say, and then, placing her arm within Mr. Percy's, she went some steps from the door. She could not refrain then from turning again, and her eyes fell upon Rowland's face—it was sad-looking and depressed.

"Rowland—dear Rowland!" she cried, as she sprang to him, "you do not feel the hope you would fain light up in my heart."

"Yes, Miranda—yes, I do. I never can despair while I have your love to light up with joy the gloomiest chambers of my brain. Believe me, I am hopeful—most hopeful. Once more, farewell, dear Miranda—farewell!"

Miranda took a long, earnest look in his face, and then turned away, saying:

"To-morrow—to-morrow. We shall meet again to-morrow."

A shudder passed across her frame as the door closed between her and her lover, and she thought to herself, as she paced the gloomy passages to the outer gate:

"Heaven help me if I have more to suffer —preserve my reason—I—I think I shall go mad if Rowland be not saved."

CHAPTER XXXV.

DICK PALMER'S WARNING — VARLEY'S WILD PASSION FOR MIRANDA—THE FEARS OF TWITTER.

WHEN Miranda and his father had left him, Rowland Percy turned to Mr. Anderson, and, in a voice of deep emotion, said:

"Mr. Anderson, let the issue of to-morrow be what it may, you will ever carry with you the prayers and blessings of those you have been so kind to. I need not ask you when I am gone—if it should be my unhappy fate to fall beneath this persecution—to comfort my poor father, and her, who, in my happiest dreams of life, I have pictured to my fancy as the dear companion with whom I should pass through existence, serene and happy."

"Be assured," said Mr. Anderson, "that my own sympathies are too much enlisted for Miranda ever to permit me to lose sight of her; but I pray you not to contemplate so gloomy a prospect. Sufficient unto the day is the evil thereof. We might, by conversing on such themes now, be exhausting your energies and weakening your resolution for no purpose. Think of the bright side of your destiny, and let to-morrow speak for itself."

"I am content it should be so," said Rowland; "but there is one favour I would ask of you."

"Name it, and it shall be done."

"I have a young friend, by name Charles Trevor, to whom you have already forwarded one note. What I now beg of you is to forward to him this other one the moment the verdict to-morrow is pronounced, should it be an unfavourable one. If favourable, let me have the note back again."

"It shall be done," said Mr. Anderson, as he placed the note carefully in his pocket.

"Then I am easy," said Rowland.

There was something so peculiar in the manner in which this was said, that Mr. Anderson was half tempted to ask an explanation of it; but he forebore, as he thought that, perhaps, he had better not know, peculiarly situated as he was, than be made a confidant of in a matter that he might be forced to condemn.

In about an hour Mr. Anderson left the prison, promising to see Rowland very early on the following morning.

The night being miserably cold, he walked rapidly towards his own home, but he had not proceeded the length of three streets when he became conscious of someone following him with rapid steps, and, upon turning to see who it could be, he was accosted by a tall man with a hat very much slouched over his eyes, and a thick handkerchief concealing nearly all the lower part of his face.

"Your name is Anderson?" said the stranger.

"It is," said the attorney.

"You are the solicitor for Mr. Percy, who is to be tried to-morrow for the murder of Sir George Rankley?"

"I am—what then?"

"Why, then, if you won't be inquisitive to know who I am, I can suggest to you a question or two to ask Bernard Varley and his associate, Twitter, when they appear as witnesses against the prisoner."

"Indeed," said Mr. Anderson, "I am not much in the habit of trusting to friends without names."

"As you please," said the stranger; "you may, or may not, as it pleases you, accept of my proffered services. I do not pretend to say that what I have to suggest to you is of great importance, but it may have the effect of throwing Varley off his guard, which is no small matter with such a man as he."

Mr. Anderson had the interest of Rowland and Miranda so much at heart that he was loth to throw away the chance of obtaining any hint that might be serviceable in the approaching trial, let it come in whatever suspicious way it might, so he said:

"Whoever you are, you must be fully aware that any good you can do to the innocent Rowland Percy must be much more effectual if done openly and without concealment. I beg of you to make yourself known to me, and I pledge my word not to reveal to anyone who you are, if you do not wish it."

"I do not wish it," said the stranger, "so there can be no good in telling you."

"Then I must listen to you," said Mr. Anderson, "and use my own judgment with regard to what you may suggest."

"What I have to suggest, as I said before, is not much, but it may flurry Varley, and you may make good use of that flurry. Ask him, upon his oath, to detail what passed between him and the horseman he met at night in the bridle-path from York to the Grange."

"What did pass?" said Mr. Anderson.

"Nothing of any real importance, but the sudden question will confuse him, and the remainder of his examination may be more satisfactory to you as interested for the prisoner."

"This is very strange," said Mr. Anderson. "Won't you tell me what passed?"

"It would do you no service to know; but I have no more doubt that Bernard Varley, by some underhand means, procured that will to be made, upon which he claims the Grange estates, than that I am, at this present moment, talking to you."

"Have you any evidence?" said Mr. Anderson, eagerly.

"Not a tittle," replied the stranger, in whom our readers will readily recognize Dick Palmer; "but Varley thinks I have, which is sufficient to torment him. I will, however, promise you that, should I come by any positive information, you shall know it; and I am rather in the way of getting it than not."

"The question you propose, I will undertake, at all events, shall be put to Varley," said Mr. Anderson; "but I should certainly prefer your telling me, in strict confidence, who you are."

"No," said Dick; "it might be as awkward for you as for me. I have, by telling you what I have, done you and your client all the good I can; so, now, good-night, and good luck for young Rowland Percy to-morrow."

So saying, he turned from Mr. Anderson, and, walking very quickly away, was soon lost to sight.

For some moments the attorney stood in deep thought.

"Is this the commencement of some deep piece of villainy on the part of Varley?" he thought, "or has this man some knowledge, which the mere hint of will have an effect upon the nerves of Varley? Surely, it is worth the trying? The question is a very simple one, and can do the defence no possible harm. I will have it put, at all risks."

While this scene was passing between Mr. Anderson and Dick Palmer, two other personages, whose proceedings and actions are important to the course of our narrative, were slowly and cautiously following from the prison-gate the slow footsteps of Mr. Percy and Miranda.

Those persons were Bernard Varley and Twitter.

Varley was a pace or two in advance of his companion, and never, for one moment, took his eyes off the beautiful form of Miranda, who looked strikingly lovely by the side of the bent form of Mr. Percy.

"You don't mean to speak to them?" faltered Twitter, as he touched Varley on the arm. "Surely you don't mean to speak to them?"

"Hush, hush!" said Varley, in a hollow voice. "I must know what spot she blesses with her presence—I must follow her. Oh! is she not beautiful? And she scorns me—hates me!—while my love for her increases like a raging conflagration, until all objects, near or remote, are tinctured by its lurid glare. I must follow her—I must follow her, though she should lead me to death."

Twitter lifted up his eyes and hands, as, with a groan, he muttered:

"Who would have guessed this? He is infatuated! Each hour he becomes worse and worse. He has gone mad for love of this girl, and we shall both be ruined. Varley, Varley, think of your situation. Reflect upon your own danger, if you will not upon mine! Varley, Varley, oh! think of what you are about!"

"Hush, hush!" said Varley, "trouble me not. She is beautiful as an angel. I cannot choose but love her. The passion has grown upon me hourly, until now it has absorbed all other feelings. Miranda! Miranda! Miranda! Oh, if you would smile upon me I would give all back again to you, and you would surely be happy with one who would make you the idol of his fondest idolatry."

"Mad! mad! quite mad!" groaned Twitter.

"There! there!" said Varley, suddenly, as Miranda and Mr. Percy paused at the door of a small house, where she had taken a temporary lodging until the trial of Rowland should be over; "you see, Twitter, she pauses—saw you ever such wondrous grace? Is there not a sunshine around her—the halo of her beauty?"

"I wish she was dead!" replied Twitter, earnestly.

"Dead!" echoed Varley. "No, such beauty surely is immortal. She cannot die. There, she blesses that house with her presence. Now I shall know where to wander, and please myself with the idea that I am near her—that I am breathing the same air with her, and that, although she scorns me, I am watching over her. Now, now, she is gone! Twitter, we will see if we cannot live opposite."

"No, no!" cried Twitter. "You will not, surely, be so mad?"

"I must! I must!" said Varley. "An invisible hand seems to drag me onwards in my chase of her. My destiny commands me, Twitter, and resistance is useless. Henceforward I live but for her—I will haunt her footsteps—I will hang upon her path, and, for evil or for good, as she may frown or smile upon me, shall she ever find me hovering over her, constant as her shadow."

"We shall be lost, ruined, undone," moaned Twitter; "oh! that I should be so besotted as to league myself with a madman."

"Come, come," continued Varley, as he crossed to the opposite side of the way from that where he had seen Miranda enter her lodging. "We will inquire if we can have accommodation here."

"But we have one place already," urged Twitter; "what on earth can you want with another?"

Varley turned to him, and with flashing eyes, and an expression of countenance that made Twitter start back several paces in alarm, he said:

"Twitter, once for all, hear me, and mark well my words. What I determine upon, I will do. Shall I be turned aside, think you, by such a worm as thou art? Shall I forsake the fixed purpose of my soul, because you tremble and are afraid? No—'twere easier to stride onwards over your corpse. You understand me, Twitter. Do not tempt me."

Twitter trembled as he said in a whining, faltering tone:

"It was for your own good I presumed to advise you, Varley, you know."

"Then presume no more," said Varley; "you are in my power. Remember that, and do not tempt your fate."

Twitter wrung his hands as he silently followed Varley, with but too strong a conviction that he was, indeed, in his power.

"Oh! if I had but insisted upon my name being in the will," he thought, "all would have been well, and I could have made my escape to the Continent with a large sum. Then Bernard Varley might have brought his neck to the halter as soon as he liked, for mine would have been safe—but now——"

A disagreeable, sympathetic choking sensation came over Twitter, and he gasped again with terror as he muttered:

"We—we shall all be hanged some day! I feel sure we shall."

Varley strode up to the door of the house, which was immediately opposite to the one in which Miranda and Mr. Percy resided, and without hesitation knocked at the door. It was opened by a homely-looking woman.

"I want to hire some rooms in your house," said Varley.

"Rooms, sir!—Lor—we never lets none."

"But you can, and will, if you get a high price."

"Please to walk in, sir," said the woman, "and I'll ask my husband. To be sure we doesn't let lodgings; but then, as you please to say, as price ain't an object, sir, why it may be as we shouldn't mind."

"Exactly," said Varley. "Name your own price for one of your front rooms."

The woman looked surprised at Twitter, who uttered a groan as he followed Varley into the house.

"Please, sir, are you ill?" she said.

"No—no—quite hearty," replied Twitter, "only, nothing—nothing!"

"My friend," said Varley, "has just run the risk of his life, and is a little nervous—that's all."

"Yes—ye—yes," stammered Twitter.

"Oh, dear me!" said the woman, "I don't wonder at it, really. I should be all of a shake myself, I declare. Won't you take a seat, sir?"

"I thank you," said Twitter, in a despairing tone.

The woman then bustled from the room to report to her husband that any price would be given for one of their front rooms, which so worked upon the love of money inherent in human nature, that he at once consented to receive so rare and desirable a lodger.

While she was gone, Varley turned to Twitter, and said:

"These people will accept my offer, and I shall remain here to-night, while you can sleep at our other lodgings. We shall meet to-morrow, and remember well what has to be done before another sunset."

"You—you will not be persuaded?" said Twitter.

"Beware!" said Varley, and again his eyes assumed the strange demoniacal glare which so much terrified his weak companion in guilt.

The woman soon returned with the intelligence that a room on the first floor was quite at "the gentleman's service."

She only asked about three times its value, and when Varley said "Very well," an exquisite pang of self-reproach shot across her breast. At her own extortion? No; but because she had not "put on a few shillings more."

"Good night!" said Twitter, with something between a sigh and a groan. "Shall I call for you in the morning?"

"Yes—do," said Varley.

In a few moments Twitter was gone, and Bernard Varley was in the room which commanded a view of the opposite house, upon which he fixed his eyes, and never removed them for hours; while his brain became nearly maddened from intense thought, and the agony of his hopeless passion—a passion which Heaven had surely tortured him with as a punishment for his crimes.

———

CHAPTER XXXVI.

THE TRIAL — POPULAR EXCITEMENT — MI-
RANDA'S SPIRIT AND ENERGY—TWITTER'S
DESPAIR.

THE morning's dawn still found Varley at the window of the room he had hired.

The hope of catching a glimpse, however transient, of Miranda had fixed him to the spot, and in bitterness and anguish, such as the guilty alone can know—for even in the greatest misfortunes of the innocent there is a consoling power in the pure heart—he had scarcely moved from the position he had first occupied.

Sleep he felt that he could not, for if by chance slumber had closed his eyelids, how was he to ensure himself, upon that eve of Rowland Percy's trial, against some awful visitation to his disturbed fancy, that might drive his soul to madness, or, at all events, unnerve him for the ordeal which he was to go through on the morrow?

Gently and softly, like a smile upon the cheek of a babe, did the morning's light steal over the face of nature.

The first streak of glowing, beautiful sunlight fell upon the ancient Minster, gilding with rare beauty the fretted architecture, and making the worn edges of the old stones look like rich chasing, worked by a skilful hand.

The busy hum of life began to arise throughout the city. The artizan sought the place of labour for the day—the idler was unwontedly early, for the coming trial possessed an absorbing interest to all classes of society, and was amply sufficient to cause sloth to rise from its heavy slumber, and walk abroad in the first glory of the morning.

Soon as the sun climbed the eastern sky, floods of light streamed upon the house-tops. Each instant the sounds of animation became more and more distinct, until that unceasing war of sounds which the dwellers in cities, from long habit, do not notice, but which, to a chance visitor, from the silence of the woods, or the valleys, is so very apparent, filled the air.

But what to Bernard Varley were the hopes, the fears, the joys, the sorrows, the wishes, or the anticipations of the thousands of warm, beating hearts by which he was surrounded? What a lone man was he in this world, teeming with life and animation! What communion had he with his fellow-men? He felt like a wanderer on earth's surface, who had been cast out from the ranks of his species—one alike denounced by man, and accursed by Heaven.

But one all-engrossing subject filled his mind—but one anticipation—but one hope, if it could be called one, filled his heart—the love of Miranda, the passion that made now the whole sum of his existence.

How strangely had the heart of that man of crime become filled with a wild and unholy love for the daughter of his victim!—a love which seemed implanted in his heart by Heaven as a punishment, because it was so utterly hopeless a passion.

The sufferings of Rowland Percy in his prison—the anxiety he endured—the bitterness of his heart at the false accusation under which he was groaning, were as nothing compared to what was endured by his persecutor, Bernard Varley, who, had Rowland been upon the scaffold, would have changed places with him, provided by so doing he could tell himself that he possessed as much of the heart of Miranda as did the lonely prisoner in his cell.

Miranda had not slept that night, for her thoughts were too active for repose. She passed many of the weary hours, before the morning's light beamed in at her casement window, in prayers to Heaven for the innocent; and if ever prayers from a pure and unsullied heart ascended gratefully to Heaven's throne, surely those of the beautiful and good Miranda found a welcome where such spirits as her own dwell in bliss unspeakable.

But Providence works in its own way, and the complex issues of mortal life are worked out in mystery.

Twitter suffered as much during that night, if not indeed more, than his associate in crime, Bernard Varley; for he had a superadded terror of the result of Varley's infatuation for Miranda, which the other was free from.

When he reached the lodgings they jointly occupied, after leaving his companion in the house opposite to where Miranda dwelt, a feeling of such despair and terror came over him, that he could scarcely be said to possess the common use of his mental faculties for a time.

"What will become of me? what will become of me?" he moaned. "I am lost—I am lost. Bernard Varley is going mad, and soon he will commit himself in some manner that will bring destruction upon us both. What shall I do—oh, what shall I do?"

With clasped hands, and a face so ghastly pale, and so distorted by fear, that it would have alarmed anyone to look upon it, he now sat for more than an hour like a statue of grim despair.

Then, in a low, moaning voice, he spoke again, saying:

"He, too, Bernard Varley, of all men, to take so strange and wonderful a fancy—he who even affected to despise all human weaknesses, and to hold himself aloof from anything but the love of gold and power—he to fall a victim to a hopeless passion for a girl, and to drag me, as he will, into the abyss of destruction he is rapidly himself approaching! I cannot fly from him—I am quite dependent upon him for means. Beyond an inconsiderable sum I have realized by the robberies I have from time to time committed at the Grange, I am destitute. Oh, fool—fool—I have involved myself in this business for nothing, and every day I shall run the most frightful risk of detection. Then, to-morrow—ay, to-morrow—what a day will that be to me. How I shall be tortured—cross-examined—my every look watched—the tone in which

I speak commented upon—oh, how I dread to-morrow !"

He rose, and shuffled rather than walked up and down the room, occasionally wringing his hands, and groaning as his perilous and miserable situation presented itself to him in different shapes.

"I dare not denounce him," said Twitter; "I could turn evidence against him, and tell all. I could do so, and have the barren satisfaction of saving my life, while, with the execration of all, I retired to misery and want. If I had much money I would do it, but now I dare not—I dare not. I must run my risk; but should suspicion light upon me, and gather sufficient strength to be dangerous, I will tell all, and Bernard Varley shall ascend the scaffold alone—yes, I will denounce him. They may point at me the finger of scorn—they may hoot at me, but I will have my revenge upon Bernard Varley—yes, he shall be hanged while I escape; but what infernal miseries shall I not, in the meantime, endure? Then—then there is to-morrow—to-morrow—to-morrow !"

He again sank into a chair, and was seized with such an attack of nervous trepidation that he thought he was upon the point of death. He cried aloud for help, to the great alarm of the people of the house, who rushed into his room to know what was the matter with him.

The report of Rowland's trial coming on that day at the York assizes had brought many persons from all parts of the country to witness the proceedings, which had acquired great interest from the situation in life of all the parties concerned, as well as the very singular circumstances connected with the whole transaction; many strange statements and reports concerning which had been, from time to time, published in the metropolitan and country newspapers.

Altogether, so much popular excitement had seldom, if ever, been witnessed regarding a criminal prosecution; and never, perhaps, was popular opinion so much divided upon any subject.

Numbers of persons believed Percy to be innocent, for they could not conceive the possibility of his guilt under the circumstances of his attachment to Miranda, and her subsequent conduct towards him; while there were others who found in those very circumstances a deep aggravation of his presumed guilt, and openly expressed their great abhorrence of the unnatural daughter who could cling with such constancy of affection to the murderer of her father.

Before ten o'clock every avenue to the court was crowded to excess, and there was as much clamour and anxiety for admittance within its precincts as exists in a metropolitan theatre on the evening of some unprecedented attraction.

Each passing moment, too, added to the arrivals; and when, at about twenty minutes before ten, the judge who was to preside in the criminal court arrived near the scene, it was with the greatest difficulty, and only by the exertions of a powerful body of constables, that his carriage could get at all near to the entrance of the building.

The excitement of the multitude then became intense, and those in the rear made a rush forward with the hope of inducing so much temporary confusion as to give them a chance of getting more forward in the throng.

Cries, oaths, and shouts rent the air, and many persons were much hurt in endeavouring to escape from the dense pressure of the multitude.

The counsel, who were to take part in the trial, as well as many others who attended the court as spectators merely, became almost inextricably mingled with the crowd, and, by ten minutes to ten o'clock, a scene of confusion was proceeding, which presented but a slender chance of the business of the court commencing at the accustomed hour.

Someone now cried out:

"Open the doors—we are being crushed to death !"

And, immediately, a thousand voices echoed the cry of:

"Open the doors—open the doors !"

The judge became apprehensive of some serious disaster, and, collecting all the available constabulary force, directed the doors of the court-house to be opened, but for no more persons to be admitted than it would conveniently hold.

When this order for opening the doors was complied with, the rush was so tremendous that, in five minutes' time, the officers became completely mingled with the throng, being borne into the court, and totally unable to keep in a body, so as to act at all effectively. The consequence of this was, that the court became crammed to suffocation, while a large concourse of persons were still struggling and striving for an entrance.

Those who had been so fortunate as to get in, soon found that, if they expected to remain with the smallest notion of comfort, they must defend the vantage ground they had obtained, and, accordingly, a fierce struggle ensued between those within the court and those without: one party determining that no man should pass in, and the other as resolved to make good an entrance if possible.

This was a state of things which, of course, could not be permitted to last, and the judge determined upon having some of the foremost of those who were pressing at the doors for admittance taken into custody, as an example to the others.

The constables succeeded in struggling to the doors, and the crowd within, upon being informed by the crier of the court that a movement was about to be made to prevent the annoyance they were then suffering from the pressure without, assisted, as much as possible, the efforts of the constables to collect in force at the door.

The result of this was that, one by one, the foremost of the riotous crowd outside were

MIRANDA DENOUNCES BERNARD VARLEY.

seized upon, dragged into the court, and thence through a lane made by the spectators to a doorway at the back, communicating with a place of confinement.

By the time some dozen or more had been secured this way, the crowd began to see the propriety of making a backward movement, and, after much yelling and hooting, as great a rush was made from the doors as had been made to them, leaving the officers masters of the field of battle.

Comparative quiet was now restored, and by half-past ten o'clock the judge took his seat upon the bench, along with some of the authorities of the city.

Those of the counsel who had come in carriages had been fortunate enough to gain admittance to the building, and among them were the counsel for and against Rowland Percy; but their more unfortunate brethren, who had come on foot, were still absent, whereupon an application was made to the judge to swear in a body of special constables to assist the jurors, witnesses, and counsel into court.

The application was complied with, but it took some time to carry it into effect; and it was eleven o'clock before Miranda and old Mr. Percy, to whom all eyes were directed, entered the court.

What were Miranda's emotions upon the occasion, could not be gathered from her face, for that was covered by a veil of white lace, which effectually concealed her features from the prying eyes of the multitude, many of whom had travelled miles to catch a sight of her reported wonderful beauty.

There was a murmur of sympathy from many upon her appearance, and from some a subdued hiss, but the judge immediately said :

"Officers, seize anyone who gives expression to approbation, or disapprobation, in court, and I will commit him."

This threat had the effect of silencing both parties, and Miranda was suffered to take a seat in silence.

None saw the wan, pale face—none saw the look of deep emotion upon her face; but there was one heart that bled for her—one who could guess the feelings that agitated her gentle breast.

That heart was Mr. Anderson's.

With a deep sigh, he whispered something to the counsel he had engaged for Rowland, who shook his head, and looked distressed.

That something was, that Miranda would never be able to go through her evidence.

CHAPTER XXXVI.

THE PRISONER—STRANGE INTERRUPTIONS— THE TRIAL.

SCARCELY had Miranda and Mr. Percy taken their seats, and the excitement caused by their arrival somewhat subsided, when Bernard Varley, pale, haggard, and wearied-looking, was led into the court, closely followed by Twitter.

The villain had remained at the window, where we last left him, until he saw Miranda come forth with Mr. Percy. He had then followed her, but in the throng outside the court, he had lost sight of her; and now, his first glance around him was to discover if she was present.

The white veil caught his eye, and he said to the officers, in a suppressed tone :

"I—will sit there—there, by Miranda Rankley."

The officer conducted him to the same bench, but Mr. Percy saw him advancing, and said something to Miranda, who immediately rose, and throwing aside her veil, confronted her deadly foe.

Varley recoiled before the face of Miranda, which was as pale as monumental marble— a great sensation was produced in the court, and all eagerly pressed forward, to get as close a look as possible at that beautiful face, which, even when divested of all colour, was most lovely.

What a contrast was presented by these two persons as they stood for the space of nearly a minute opposite to each other in silence.

Varley's lips were white and dry, but his face was flushed with an unnatural colour, and his eyes were blood-shot, while he drew his breath with a hissing sound, as if to respire was a great labour to him, and so it was at that moment.

Miranda fixed her eyes upon him, and he could not advance. There was something in the mournfully beautiful gaze that deprived him of all power, and without a word being spoken, he felt that he dared not pursue his intention of sitting near Miranda.

He stepped back, slowly whispering :

"Somewhere else—somewhere else."

Miranda again covered her face with her veil, and sat down by Mr. Percy.

A deep sigh, that seemed to come from the very depths of her heart, was the only sound she uttered, and then all was still again.

Bernard Varley was, in the meantime, conducted to a seat on the other side of the court, closely followed by the trembling Twitter.

This incident, trifling as it was, caused a deep sensation in the minds of the spectators.

Varley's agitation, his look of horror as he shrank from the gaze of Miranda, and the expression of awful villainy that lurked in his knit brows, prepossessed all against him ; while the noble purity, the heavenly innocence depicted on the face of Miranda, looked perfectly incompatible with a bad cause.

The jury were rapidly sworn, and then a profound silence ensued. The very breathing of the spectators seemed to be suppressed.

The judge was conversing in a low whisper with the Mayor of York ; then he glanced to the dock, and slightly waved his hand.

All eyes were directed to the bar. There was a slight movement among the officials, and, in another instant, Rowland Percy stood forward.

He was pale, but perfectly calm.

Not a nerve shrank : his eyes quailed not, and the glance of calm integrity that he cast round the court astonished all who marked it, and many whispered to themselves :

"Can this man be a murderer ?"

The effect his appearance had was evidently highly favourable. His youth, the candour that was in his face, the gentle expression that pervaded every feature, and the intellect that was marked by the commanding brow, all pointed him out as of all men there assembled the least likely to commit a crime of the character he stood charged with.

Rowland's sudden appearance in the crowded court from the solitude of his confinement, prevented him for a moment or two from being able sufficiently to individualize the persons he saw around to name anyone in particular ; but, after a second glance, his eyes fell on his father, whose tearful gaze was settled on him.

The crowded auditory followed the direction of the prisoner's eyes with theirs, and, when Mr. Percy saw that he was seen by his son, he clasped his hands, and, while the tears coursed each other down his cheeks, he said :

"God bless you, my dear boy! God bless you!"

The "hush" of the crier was very faint, for he, as well as all present, was affected by the scene.

The judge pretended not to hear the father's blessing upon his son, and bent his head low over his notebook.

There was one who heard it, however, with an emotion that kindled every feeling of her mind. That one was Miranda; and by an impulse that she paused not to question or resist, she rose, and, throwing back her veil, said:

"The blessing let me echo. God bless you, my innocent, affianced husband!"

"Miranda!" cried Rowland Percy; and he stretched out his arms, while his face kindled with pleasure.

The scene overpowered almost all in court, and forgetting prudence or caution, many of the spectators clapped their hands, crying:

"He is innocent!—he is innocent!"

In the midst of this, Bernard Varley rose, and cried:

"Air! air! air!"

Some windows were broken then by those who were nearest to them, and a scene of confusion ensued for some moments, which completely baffled the attempts of the judge to quell it.

A rush of cold air from the broken windows was felt most gratefully by all, for the crowded state of the court rendered the ordinary ventilation ineffectual.

Then the judge's voice was heard, saying:

"I must have the court cleared if this sort of interruption continues. I am willing to believe that it has arisen from the suffering occasioned by the extreme heat of the atmosphere."

This was a kind construction for the judge to put upon the interruption which had occurred, and everyone felt it to be such, so that in a few moments the same breathless silence subsisted which had reigned throughout the densely-crowded court previous to Rowland Percy being placed at the bar.

The clerk of the arraigns now read the indictment, which charged Rowland Percy with the wilful murder of George Rankley, commonly called Sir George Rankley, by means of some deadly drug or weapon, or by suffocation. The indictment went on to a great length, in the usual verbose manner of such documents until it was finished, when the prisoner was asked to plead "Guilty or Not Guilty."

Upon this, Rowland lifted up his hand to Heaven, and in a voice that, although not loud, went with the force of conviction to almost every heart, said:

"Not Guilty, as I hope for Heaven's mercy!"

The names of the jury were then called over, after which there was a slight bustle, as everyone in the crowded court assumed the position he thought would best enable him to catch the speech of the counsel for the prosecution.

Before, however, any further progress could be made in the case, a loud voice cried from a distant part of the court:

"Bernard Varley will be hanged at York!"

The voice was something between a scream and a shout, and electrified the nerves of all who heard it, particularly as it was succeeded by such a wild, frantic scream of laughter, that every echo far and near was awakened.

"Good Heavens!" cried the judge, in the excitement of the moment, "what is that?"

The officers made a rush in the direction whence the sounds proceeded, and dragged to the front of the bench the poor idiot, Bold Hawk, who, then pointing the fore-fingers of each hand at Varley, shrieked:

"Hanged at York! Bernard Varley will be hanged at York! Ha—ha—ha! Ha—ha—ha!"

Varley immediately rose, and, while his eyes flashed with rage, and his whole countenance was distorted with passion, he cried:

"He is mad! Remove him! He is mad, I say! Am I to be insulted thus? Remove him! Imprison the madman!"

"See—see!" cried Bold Hawk, "he trembles—he turns pale. He knows the rope that is to hang him is already twisted, and he can't shoot me, though he has tried hard to do so."

"Remove him," said the judge. "He is surely mad."

Mr. Anderson whispered something to the counsel for Rowland, who nodded, and then immediately said to the judge:

"My lord, I am informed that this person is a poor lunatic, who is perfectly harmless; the only words of truth he has uttered being his assertion concerning Bernard Varley's attempt to shoot——"

"I really, my lord, submit that this is most irregular and monstrous," interrupted the counsel for the prosecution, in a loud voice.

"It is quite irregular," cried the judge. "Let that poor maniac be removed."

Bold Hawk was immediately dragged from the court by two officers, but for some minutes his wild, shrieking voice could still be heard shouting loudly:

"Bernard Varley will be hanged at York—ha!—ha!—ha! Bernard Varley is proof against steel and bullet. Water will not drown him, for he is a doomed man, and will be hanged at York!"

This event proved a disturbance of a more lasting character than any that had preceded it, and it was many minutes before the excitement into which the vast audience assembled in the court had been thrown, could be sufficiently allayed for the transaction of business.

When, however, comparative quiet was restored, the counsel for the prosecution rose, and, while every eye was fixed upon him, he commenced:

"My lord, and gentlemen of the jury——"

But before another word could pass his lips, the counsel for the prisoner rose, and said:

"My learned friend will pardon my interruption, but I have an application to make to the court on behalf of the defence, which I am quite sure my learned friend will pardon me for urging just now, before, with his usual perspicuity and eloquence, he proceeds to open the case."

The counsel for the prosecution looked very much vexed, as he replied:

"I apprehend my learned friend is extremely irregular in interrupting me at the present stage of the proceedings in this case."

"No," said the other, "certainly not. The case, after the pleading of the prisoner, is fairly in court."

"No doubt that is the fact," said the judge; "but there should be extreme delicacy in interrupting a learned counsel."

"My lord, we have too important interests at stake to be delicate," said Rowland's counsel. "When the happiness, the life, of an innocent man are in the issue, God forbid that I should be deterred by false delicacy from doing my duty."

These words were pronounced with such a fearless tone of confidence and candour, that they had a visible effect upon the jury, and some of the counsel, who were sitting under the judge, smiled at each other in a very meaning manner.

The counsel for the prosecution, however, was too vexed to admire the other's tact, and feeling a little partizanship, as all counsel do, more or less, in the cause they are retained in, he said to the judge, rather warmly:

"I beg to submit to your lordship that the time has not yet arrived for my learned friend to endeavour, with his usual tact, to interest the passions of the jury in favour of his client, if he cannot bias their judgments."

"The case," said the judge, calmly, "is certainly, after the prisoner has pleaded, before the court, and it is competent for the counsel on either side to make any application relevant to the subject in hand, or that may further the ends of justice in the opinion of the court."

The counsel for the prosecution sat down with a bounce, evidently very much put out, when he fully expected to be in the commencement of his speech against the unhappy Rowland.

"I have, then, to apply," said Rowland's counsel, "that two material witnesses for the prosecution, who, I am informed, will swear to similar facts, be separated."

"What witnesses?" said the judge.

"Bernard Varley and Samuel Twitter, my lord."

"You wish these witnesses to be examined separately and out of hearing of each other?"

"I do, my lord; and, likewise, I wish that Samuel Twitter should leave the court, in order that he may not hear the details which my learned friend is instructed to make on behalf of the prosecution."

"I daresay," said the judge, "the witness mentioned can have no objection."

"He has—he has," cried Varley, who all along was much afraid that Twitter would bungle in the evidence he had to give.

"Silence—silence!" said the crier.

"Let Samuel Twitter withdraw," said the judge.

Varley bit his lips, and Twitter, pale as a ghost, and scarcely able to support himself on his tottering limbs, rose from his seat, and moved towards the door.

When he was fairly gone, the counsel for the prosecution again rose, and said:

"Before I proceed to open the case, may I presume to ask my learned friend, through the court, if he contemplates any more of the little happy interruptions which I presume he is instructed to make?"

"None," said the other counsel.

"Then, my lord, if you please, I shall proceed."

CHAPTER XXXVIII.

THE PROGRESS OF THE TRIAL—THE FIRST DAY.

THERE was a breathless silence for some moments in the crowded court, and then the counsel for the prosecution of the innocent Rowland commenced:

"My lord and gentlemen of the jury,—

"The prisoner at the bar stands charged with one of the worst, if not the worst crime which can appertain to humanity; and if it should appear to you that the facts it will be my duty to lay before you are not sufficient to support that charge, no one in this court, whatever may be their affinity—whatever may be their feelings or their sympathies regarding the prisoner—will be more rejoiced than myself.

"The duty of a counsel for a prosecution is ever, my lord and gentlemen, a more painful one than that of a counsel rising to defend his fellow-man from an aspersion upon his character, which, if found to be true, must hunt him, as a proscribed being, from the ranks of his fellow-men, or bring him to a shameful and ignominious end; but which, if unsupported by that weight of evidence necessary to support a criminal charge, disappears, like a noxious vapour, before the pure light of his innocence, and leaves, or ought to leave, no stain behind.

"My lord and gentlemen,—It appears, by my instructions, that, about a year or more ago, the families of Sir George Rankley, deceased, whose death forms the subject of this solemn judicial inquiry, and Mr. Percy, became intimate. The estates of Sir George joined the apparently-thriving leasehold lands of Mr. Percy, and a friendship, sudden and great, sprang up between the families.

"Sir George Rankley had an only daughter —Mr. Percy an only son. Under the circumstances of intimacy and daily communication in which these young persons were placed, it is not a matter of surprise that feelings of the tenderest nature should spring up between them, and that in a short period Mr. Rowland Percy, who now stands charged with the awful crime of murder at the bar of this court, became the avowed suitor of the heiress of the large estates of the Grange, which, doubtless, are well known to the jury.

"You will, then, hear in evidence that Sir George Rankley, believing in the apparent respectability and prosperity of his neighbour, Mr. Percy, did not interfere to place any check upon the affections of these young persons, and this intimacy continued for some time uninterruptedly, until the prisoner at the bar, as will appear, acquired one of those extraordinary controls over the imagination of the daughter of Sir George Rankley, which we can only wonder at, but not attempt to explain or define.

"While things were proceeding in this quiet strain, it became known to Sir George that his apparently prosperous neighbour was engaged in reckless speculations, which had, in their failure, brought down upon him utter ruin.

"Then, as you will hear sworn to by some of the witnesses in this prosecution, Sir George became exceedingly indignant that the shattered fortunes of the Percy family should be attempted to be patched by a union with his only child and heiress.

"An angry correspondence which ensued will sufficiently prove that fact; and, finally, the prisoner at the bar was formally forbidden to visit at the house of Sir George Rankley, and to all appearance the intimacy, which would, had it resulted in a marriage, have proved probably so advantageous to the Percy family, was at an end.

"The quarrel, however, between the parents continued, and resulted in a duel, with which we have nothing to do, except to prove, by medical evidence, that the injury received by Sir George Rankley there and then, was not the cause of his death. Had it been so, my lord and gentlemen of the jury, the elder Percy, and not the younger, would have this day stood at the bar of this court.

"A duel, however, was fought—of that there is most abundant proof—between Mr. Percy and Sir George Rankley, in which Sir George was wounded, but far from dangerously.

"It was a slight flesh wound, which, certainly by inducing fever, might have proved fatal; but, my lord and gentlemen of the jury, it had not time to do so. Sir George Rankley was hurried into eternity by some other means, which it is our object to discover, in order to punish the perpetrator.

"For the purpose now of making more intelligible some portion of the evidence, which it will be my painful duty to lay before you, I must mention that among the servants residing at the Grange there has existed for a long period of time antecedent to the purchase of the property by its late lamented proprietor, a superstition of a strange and remarkable character.

"Many years ago one of the gamekeepers on the estate was found murdered on the lawn. By whose hand the deed was committed no one knew, except the perpetrator himself; but since then a superstitious belief has existed that the disembodied spirit of that murdered man has haunted the Grange.

"My lord, and gentlemen of the jury, I have no doubt you will find that every servant examined here to-day will be impressed with a full belief in the reality of what they call 'the spectre of the murdered keeper.'

"Having, then, premised thus much, I shall proceed to state as shortly as possible the facts, as I am instructed to state them, which occurred on the eventful night immediately succeeding the duel between Sir George Rankley and Mr. Percy.

"The wounded Sir George, my lord and gentlemen, was conducted to a chamber, opening from a long corridor, from which many bedchambers were approached. The medical gentleman who attended him, remained until a late hour with his patient; but, having satisfied himself that he was doing quite well, departed, leaving him in the care of an elderly female, whose evidence will be laid before the court.

"From that moment, my lord, a rapid succession of events took place, which terminated in the death of Sir George, and the apprehension of the prisoner at the bar, who, it will be proved in evidence, was a very long way from this country until the actual day on which the duel was fought, when, by design or accident, he unquestionably found his way to the scene of action, which was to him so very important—so very important, indeed."

The counsel made a slight pause at this part of his speech, and it was evident to everyone in court that he considered the arrival of Rowland at the Grange from a considerable distance off on that very day, as the first link in the chain of circumstantial evidence, which was to connect him with the fearful deed he stood charged with committing.

The attention paid to his words by everyone in the crowded court appeared intense; but it was curious to note the effect which the narrative had upon those who were most interested in the result.

Rowland Percy listened with calm attention. His eyes were fixed upon the face of the counsel, to whom he seemed to be attending rather with curiosity, to know what could possibly be said against him, than with the feverish excitement which might have been supposed to affect him.

The face of Bernard Varley presented a remarkable contrast to that of the prisoner. Anyone might well have believed that life or death to him hung upon the result of the trial.

The counsel proceeded:

"At the hour of midnight, my lord and gentlemen, Mr. Bernard Varley, an intimate and dear friend of the murdered baronet's, and Samuel Twitter, the valet, arranged, in their anxiety that Sir George should be well attended to, to relieve the nurse for an hour or so, in order that she might take some repose previous to resuming her duties.

"You will hear detailed in evidence, gentlemen, that at that most solemn hour, when men's imaginations are frequently more active than their reasoning powers, there appeared to Mr. Bernard Varley and Samuel Twitter on their route to the chamber of the wounded baronet, what at that moment they might be excused from really believing was the much-talked-of spirit of the murdered keeper.

"A figure dressed in green darted past them, and they ascended to the chamber with a firm conviction that some being not of flesh and blood was in the house along with the living.

"They then took their station in the room, relieving the nurse according to arrangement.

"To this point, my lord and gentlemen, I have thought it necessary to go in order that, without waste of time, what the various witnesses shall depose to should be clear and intelligible.

"What followed I shall now let you hear from the lips of those witnesses, and I can only say that it is my fervent hope that Heaven will enlighten us all sufficiently upon this painful inquiry to enable us to arrive at the truth."

The counsel for the prosecution now sat down, and a feeling of relief from intense excitement pervaded every breast—that mingled buzz of sounds arose, which always follows any great effort of silence and attention on the part of a multitude, and, by tacit consent, everyone seemed disposed to rest a few moments before proceeding with the investigation.

The first witness called was the medical man, who had attended Sir George immediately after his wound.

He merely recapitulated the evidence he had given at the inquest—namely, that the death of Sir George Rankley certainly was not attributable to the wound he had received, but must have arisen from some other cause, which, in his opinion, from the appearance of the body, was suffocation.

"Was there any wound—in addition to that inflicted by the pistol-shot in the duel—perceptible on the deceased when you saw him after death?" asked the counsel.

"There was a scratch upon the face."

"You will swear the scratch was not there previous to your departure from the Grange, when you, as you believed, left your patient out of all danger?"

"I will swear it was not there."

The counsel for the prosecution sat down, and the able and intelligent barrister, who had been retained by Mr. Anderson for the defence, immediately rose, and said:

"Have you had any opportunities of judging of the feelings of Miranda Rankley towards her father?"

"I have. Her conduct has always been marked by the greatest affection. I never saw deeper grief than she exhibited at her father's mischance in the duel."

"Did she make any remark concerning the supposed murder?"

"None further than declaring her belief in Mr. Rowland Percy's innocence."

"That will do, sir," said the counsel, sitting down at once.

The nurse was now called, and she merely deposed that Mr. Varley very kindly offered to sit up an hour or so with Sir George, in order that she might get a little rest, and that she had left the baronet asleep and moaning, as if in pain.

No questions whatever were asked of this witness by Rowland's counsel.

There was a pause for a few moments now, and all eyes were bent upon the counsel for the prosecution, who, at length, said:

"Bernard Varley!"

"Bernard Varley!" echoed the crier of the court.

Varley rose as if under the influence of a shock of electricity, and in a deep, hollow voice, said:

"I am here. Who calls Bernard Varley?"

His ghastly face, his livid lips, the clammy perspiration that stood upon his brow, and the wild demoniac expression of his eyes, conspired to make him an object of fearful interest to everyone in court.

The judge took a long look at him, and then whispered something to the mayor, who replied by a shrug of the shoulders; and many in the crowded court turned their eyes instinctively from Varley to Rowland.

It seemed to them something strange and unnatural that Varley, with his guilty looks and awful excitement, should be the accuser, and Rowland Percy, with his calm, unmoved glance, and general appearance of dignified innocence and candour, should be the accused.

The jury whispered together, and it was not until the counsel for the prosecution, who saw how the tide of feeling was going, said: "Mr. Varley, attend to me, if you please," that the eagerness to hear what Varley should say, overcame every other feeling in the breasts of the auditory.

While Varley was being sworn, he trembled so excessively, and looked so very ill, that the judge said to the counsel for the prosecution:

"Cannot you take some other witness's evidence before Mr. Varley's? He seems very much indisposed."

"No—no!" cried Varley. "I am ready—I am quite ready, and quite well. I never was better."

"Proceed then," cried the judge.

Varley made great efforts, by grasping the rail of the witness-box, to assume an air of composure.

He forced himself to look round the court, and his effort to appear calm and at ease sat so uneasily upon him, that it was evident to all it was an effort merely.

As his eyes, however, wandered over the crowd of eager faces in the court, he carefully avoided meeting Rowland's—that he could not stand.

Nor, at that moment of mental agony, would he have chosen to meet the gaze of Miranda, much as he would, at any other time, have given but to behold her face, and look into the depths of those beautiful eyes, which contained all of Heaven he had ever pictured to his mind.

CHAPTER XXXIX.

VARLEY'S EVIDENCE—THE PROGRESS OF THE TRIAL—THE CROSS-EXAMINATION.

"STATE what you know of this transaction, which engages the attention of the court," said the counsel.

"I will," gasped Varley, "I will. When Sir George Rankley, who was my dearest and best friend, came home wounded from the unhappy duel between him and Mr. Percy, I naturally felt the extreme of anxiety concerning his welfare and recovery. I could not think of retiring to rest on that night, and I accordingly sat up with Samuel Twitter, Sir George's valet. I had every reliance upon the nurse who was attending upon the wounded man, but I knew she was aged, and I believe it was I who proposed to Twitter that, as we were sitting up, at any rate, we might as well afford her an hour's rest, while we ourselves kept watch by the bedside of Sir George

"The hour was twelve, and we had told the nurse that she would be relieved at that time. Therefore, in accordance with our promise, when we heard the Grange clock strike the hour of midnight, we prepared to proceed to the chamber of Sir George.

"On our road thither, we were astonished to see a figure gliding away from the neighbourhood of the chamber. We pursued it, and, by the occasional glimpses we caught of it, we saw that the dress was green, and in all respects similar to what had been described to us as identifying the reputed apparition of the murdered keeper which was said to haunt the Grange.

"Fear took possession of our faculties for the moment. The hour, the exciting circumstances of the day, the danger, for aught we knew, which hovered over Sir George, all conspired to awaken in my mind those superstitious fears which all men feel more or less, and I am not ashamed to confess that I believed the appearance, at the moment, to be the supernatural being which popular belief had pointed out as gliding from chamber to chamber of the Grange."

As Bernard Varley spoke, he seemed to gather courage, and all the dark malignancy of his nature revived. He glanced around him with something of his usual expression of ferocity, and began to dwell upon that portion of his evidence which he thought would tell against Rowland Percy, and to put in with emphasis various words which gave a marked signification to some of his statements.

He proceeded in his evidence with a fuller and more assured voice, as he said :

"When we had overcome, in some measure, the shock our imaginations had sustained by the supposed supernatural visitation we had been subjected to, we proceeded at once to our destination, and, without saying anything to the nurse of what we had seen, for fear of alarming her, we allowed her to go to rest, determining to sit up with Sir George beyond

the time we had promised, for the nurse looked wearied, and we had no desire for bed after what we had seen, or thought we had seen.

"In a few moments, then, the light which we had, began to show symptoms of expiring, and, recollecting that there was a candle in the room below which we had recently left, I asked Twitter to fetch it.

"It appeared, however, that he had been much affected by the supposed supernatural appearance, and he trembled so—being a nervous, timid man—when I asked him to go, that I went myself, leaving him in care of Sir George, who was asleep.

"I was away rather longer than I intended, for in endeavouring to find the candle I struck it off the table, and it took me some time to find it again ; I could not, however, have been absent many minutes.

"When I returned, I was a little surprised to find the door of the chamber—which I had left shut—wide open. With a presentiment that there was something wrong, I walked into the room.

All was silent, and, to my surprise, I could not see Twitter anywhere.

"I lifted up my light as high as I could, and approached the bed.

"Sir George was, as I thought, still asleep ; but, upon a closer inspection, I found it was the sleep of death."

Varley now paused a moment, and not the smallest possible sound disturbed the solemn stillness of the court.

The counsel for the prosecution made him a sign to go on, and he resumed :

"I started back from the bed in horror, and then I saw Samuel Twitter lying in a state of insensibility on the floor.

"I tried to raise him, but in vain—he had fainted ; and, while I was so engaged, Miranda Rankley entered the room, inquiring, with apparent interest and eagerness, for her father.

"I tried to stop her, for I feared the shock she must receive upon finding he was no more. She, however, persisted in coming in, until I should have had to use actual force to prevent her. That I could not do ; and, accordingly, allowing her to pass into the room, I rushed downstairs to give an alarm, when again I was crossed by the figure in the hunting-dress. This time, however, I saw its face. I will swear it was the prisoner at the bar !

"The moment the seeming spectre found that he was detected and recognized he made an attempt to murder me by striking me on the head; and so hard was the blow, that I was rendered for a few moments quite insensible.

"I know not how long I was in recovering, but when I did so, I went to the chamber of Sir George Rankley on the instant.

"As I entered I trod upon something, and, upon picking it up, found it to be these tablets."

The ivory tablets were here produced, and the clerk of the court handed them to the judge, who, at the request of the jury, read what was written on them.

"Here is the prisoner's name upon the first

page, gentlemen," he said, "and a lengthened memorandum further on. I need not remark to you that there must, to connect this piece of evidence with the prisoner, be the fullest proof that not only the tablets are his, but the writing his also, as, without throwing aspersions upon anybody, we cannot imagine anything easier than to write a few words of very serious consequence to the prisoner on an ivory tablet. The words are:

"'An account of the Grange property, which would descend to M. R. in case of G. R.'s death without a will. Five farms, two tenements in York—seven hundred acres of cultivated land—the Deer Forest, the Grange—estimated value, twelve thousand per annum. Mem.—To be at Grange by seven o'clock—after duel, if that not fatal. A good exchange, by wedding simple M. R., from difficulties to splendour.'

"That is the whole of the memorandum," said the judge, "and it is for the prosecution to prove that it has any connection whatever with the prisoner now at the bar."

"That, of course," said the counsel for the prosecution, "it is for us to prove. Now, Mr. Varley, be so good as to answer my questions."

Varley bowed his head, and the first question was:

"Do you know the causes which led to the duel between Sir George Rankley and Mr. Percy?"

"I can guess them—or, rather, the principal one," said Varley. "Sir George told me that he had good reason to believe a marriage between Rowland Percy and his daughter was sought eagerly by the Percys on account of their distressed circumstances."

"Did he repeat that statement more than once?"

"He did. Such were, in fact, very nearly his last words to me before he composed himself to sleep early on the evening after the duel."

"Are you acquainted with the handwriting of the prisoner at the bar?"

"Only through casually seeing it."

"Could you swear that the memorandum on one of the ivory tablets is in his writing?"

"I believe it, but should not like to swear it."

Varley thought this piece of affected candour would do more against Rowland than were he unhesitatingly to swear to anything and everything which could advance the interests of the prosecution.

"I have no more questions to ask," said the counsel. "Call Samuel Twitter."

"Let Samuel Twitter wait a little," said Rowland's counsel, calmly. "I want to have some conversation with Mr. Bernard Varley first."

Varley turned a trifle paler as he said, with affected ease and calmness:

"I am willing to answer any questions to the best of my ability and belief."

"Then, Mr. Varley," said the counsel, raising his voice, "have you any objection to state to the jury what passed between you and a strange horseman in the bridle-path between the Grange and York?"

A cry of terror burst from Varley's lips as the counsel spoke, and clutching with frantic violence the rail of the witness-box, he gasped:

"What—what—prompted you to—to——"

"Answer me," cried the counsel, who saw in a moment what an effect the words had produced upon Bernard Varley's mind. "Answer me, I charge you."

"Water—water—water," shrieked Varley, and he would have sunk to the floor had he not been supported by those near him, for he thought that all was discovered, and he was a doomed man.

Judge, jury, and audience, all seemed alike astonished at the effect which the apparently simple and innocuous question of the counsel had had upon Bernard Varley—nor was Rowland Percy a whit less surprised than anyone else, for he had not the remotest idea as to the tendency of the question, or why it had so wonderful an effect upon the nerves of his great enemy.

Several officers supported Varley in their arms, while others eagerly brought water from the table, at which the counsel sat, while the spectators seemed to forget entirely where they were; and in the excitement of the moment, they pressed roughly forward, surrounding Varley and the officers so closely, that danger began to be apprehended of personal injury to the most forward.

Cries of all kinds arose—some females who had been driven into the court, amid the throng, which first made good an entrance, began to scream, imagining that something fearful must have occurred. There were loud cries of:

"Open the door—open the door—more air—air—down with Bernard Varley—Mr. Percy is innocent—down with Varley—he is a murderer!"

As this last expression caught the ears of Miranda, she rose from her seat, as if by an impulse she could not resist, and throwing back her veil, she cried in a voice which was clearly heard above all the surrounding tumult, on account of its musical beauty, and the clearness of her enunciation:

"Yes, Bernard Varley is a murderer—I am not mistaken. A voice, as it were, from Heaven tells me he is guilty—look in his face—can you doubt it—see—see—does he not in every feature look the murderer of my father?"

The judge having in vain several times tried to quell the tumult, now rose from his seat, and stretching out his hand, while he strove to raise his voice above the tumult in the court, said:

"I shall leave this court if my authority is to be held so lightly, that common decent behaviour cannot be obtained, when the life of a fellow-creature is at stake. Officers, take into custody all whom you can depose to as taking part in this outrage."

Several of the foremost now were seized, and a universal panic for the consequences of their conduct began to spread among the people.

A rush was made to the doors by those who knew themselves guilty, and the judge, observing that such was the case, prudently ordered the officers to let them go if they would, so that in a few minutes the court was half cleared of its motley contents, and the tumult was sensibly on the decrease.

"Keep the doors fast, now," said the judge, "allow no one to enter the court. Where is the witness whose extraordinary agitation has caused all this indecorum?"

"He is recovering," said the counsel for the prosecution, who was as much puzzled as anybody else to account for Varley's extraordinary and sudden breakdown when he was giving his evidence so triumphantly and so clearly.

"Let the examination then proceed," said the judge.

The counsel stooped, and whispered to Varley, in a tone of alarm:

"For Heaven's sake, Mr. Varley, what is the meaning of all this extraordinary scene?"

"The—the meaning?" gasped Varley, looking wildly about him. "What has happened?"

"Tell me who it was you met in the bridle-path, between the Grange and York."

"Th—the enemy of mankind," whispered Varley.

"The what?"

Varley shuddered.

"He is quite mad!" thought the counsel, as, with a vexed air, he resumed his seat, and began chewing his pen, believing that the prosecution was completely knocked on the head, and that some strange disclosures were about to take place.

CHAPTER XL.

THE CROSS-EXAMINATION CONTINUED—VARLEY'S CONFUSION—THE EVIDENCE OF TWITTER—MIRANDA'S FEARS.

WHAT would be the nature and issue of the cross-examination, which, in its commencement, had produced so startling an effect, no one could surmise; and yet all were in the greatest state of excitement to know what would follow, for they could not but expect some tremendous revelation to succeed so startling a beginning.

Little did judge, jury, and opposing counsel imagine that the question which had been asked of Varley would lead to nothing, but merely shatter his nervous system, depriving him of the self-confidence with which he had been giving his evidence.

But of all who were surprised at the effect of those few words upon Varley, and annoyed that they could lead to nothing, the counsel for Rowland was the most so. He was completely lost in conjecture as to the cause of the extraordinary emotion of the witness, and he could not help surmising that something of very great importance to the interests of his client, Rowland Percy, lay hidden in the breast of Varley.

In the course of five more minutes, Varley stood again in the witness-box, pale, trembling, and aghast, awaiting with terror what would next be said to him; and when the counsel again propounded the question:

"What passed between you and the strange horseman on the bridle-path between York and the Grange?" he could only reply by a deep groan.

The counsel for the prosecution then rose, and said:

"I must submit to the court that my learned friend has no right to put to the witness so very rude a question. His duty is to examine the witnesses on all matters touching and concerning the murder of Sir George Rankley; and who shall say that this question, which may relate to some of Mr. Varley's own private affairs, bears any relation to that calamitous and much regretted event?"

"The question is regular enough," replied Rowland's counsel.

"If," said the judge, "you can say that it is essential to the ends of justice that the witness should answer the question, there can be no impropriety in it."

"I require an answer," said the counsel.

"I advise, then," said the counsel for the prosecution, "that an answer be refused, provided the witness is in a position to declare on his oath that the matter concerns not this trial."

Here was a loop-hole for Varley to escape by.

A faint gleam of hope came across his mind that, after all, the counsel might know nothing, but had only been put in possession of the bare fact of his encounter with the mysterious person of whom he, Varley, had such a dread, by some accidental spectator of the meeting.

"I do declare," he said, "that the affair has nothing to do with the trial."

"On your solemn oath?" said Rowland's counsel.

"On my solemn oath," replied Varley.

"Then I admit," said the counsel, "that I am not in a position to press the question."

These words gave Varley new life.

The colour slowly revisited his cheeks—he breathed more freely, and altogether the remarkable change for the better that took place in his appearance surprised everyone, and made the curiosity to know what the question could possibly refer to ten times more intense than it had been.

A short, whispered consultation now took place between the counsel and Mr. Anderson, after which the former, turning to Varley, said:

"I shall still trouble you to answer some questions, which I hope will be less difficult than the one I have already put to you."

Varley merely inclined his head, and, by the curl of his lips, and the knitting of his brows, it was clear that he had recovered nearly all, if not quite all, his former confidence and tact.

"How long have you known the deceased, Sir George Rankley?" was the first question.

"Nearly twenty years," said Varley.

"What were you then?"

"I was a clerk in the banking-house in which he was a partner."

"What occupation have you followed since?"

"None. When Sir George retired from business he allowed me a sum per annum in consideration of my faithful services to him."

"Oh, indeed; and then you came to live at the Grange?"

"On Sir George's pressing invitation, I did do so."

"After which, occurred all this quarrelling between Sir George Rankley and Mr. Percy?"

"Yes. Through some commercial friends I ascertained the state of Mr. Percy's affairs, and I thought it my duty to communicate the same to Sir George. Since then I am aware I have incurred the hatred of the Percys, as well as the ill-will of other parties."

"What other parties?"

"Sir George's late solicitor, Mr. Anderson, and—and——"

"And who?"

"Miranda!" gasped Varley, glancing in the direction where she sat.

"On your oath, have you, or have you not, made proposals of marriage to that young lady?"

Varley paused for a moment, and then said, faintly:

"I have."

"Which were rejected with contempt?"

"Rejected," said Varley.

"In favour of the prisoner at the bar," said the counsel, raising his voice, "that more fortunate suitor being now accused by you of murder?"

"I—I don't accuse him," said Varley. "I only state that which I know."

"Now, sir, on your oath, have you not offered to Miranda Rankley to save Mr. Rowland Percy altogether from this prosecution, provided she would become your wife?"

This question produced a great sensation in the court, and the judge shook his head as he saw Varley move about uneasily, before he said:

"No."

"You swear that?"

"I do."

"Has Sir George Rankley left a will?"

"He has."

"Bequeathing all to you, Mr. Bernard Varley, I understand, and making his own child quite dependent upon your charity for her sustenance."

"He—he has left all to me."

"Did you not offer to destroy that will if Miranda Rankley would marry you? On your oath, sir, before Heaven, answer me."

"No," said Varley.

"Gentlemen of the jury," said the counsel, solemnly, "I shall be able to place a witness in this box, who, upon oath, will depose to these facts, and prove that this man would go through fire and water to obtain the hand of Miranda Rankley. Ay, gentlemen, that he would go from a faint lie to a charge of murder to accomplish his ends."

"'Tis false," cried Varley.

"Silence, sir," said the counsel. "Answer my questions, and make no remarks. Did Sir George Rankley's usual solicitor draw up his will?"

"No."

"Certainly not. He would have started at such a monstrous document—and which, I hope, will be successfully resisted by the deceased gentleman's daughter; but admitting for one moment that such a will would stand the test of legal proceedings, on your oath tell the jury, sir, what provision, out of twelve thousand pounds per annum, which I understand you claim under that will, you have been pleased to make to Miranda Rankley?"

"I have made her offers," said Varley.

"What offers?"

"Large ones. Offers which I am always willing to renew. She may be mistress of the Grange if she likes."

"But—uncoupled with the odious condition of wedding you—what offers have you made her? What offers will you now, in presence of this court, make her? On your oath, what income do you propose paying to her from her father's property?"

Varley was sorely puzzled what to say to this ingenious mode of either committing him to make an allowance to Miranda, or to leave the impression on the minds of the jury that he was actuated by the worst feelings in retaining the property. His grand hope, however, was to reduce Miranda to great poverty, and he would not forego it. After a pause, he said:

"I shall abide by the conditions of the will."

"And allow her nothing?"

Varley was silent.

"You may go," said the counsel, "and enjoy, as well as you can, your position as the robber of the orphan Miranda Rankley, and the prosecutor to death, if you can, of the only friend she has on earth. You may go, sir. You may go. I am sickened with this most hideous case."

A faint murmur of execration came from the people in the court as Varley stepped from the witness-box, and slunk among the crowd to endeavour to avoid the many eyes that were upon him.

The efforts of the counsel had been altogether directed to weakening the effect of his evidence by representing the motives which would induce him to give it, and he had thoroughly succeeded in loading him with infamy, as well as in resting a strong suspicion even upon the distinct story he had told concerning the events immediately preceding and succeeding Sir George's death—a story which Varley had too well arranged to enable it to be attacked directly.

Twitter's evidence, however, as the counsel well knew, was of much more importance than Varley's, and unless he could throw so much discredit upon his testimony, as well as upon Varley's, as to almost prove a conspiracy between them, he in his heart despaired of the acquittal of Rowland Percy, although he himself had a strong belief in his innocence, and no slight opinion concerning the real facts of the case.

The evidence, however, as far as it had gone, was but circumstantial, and upon that he had certainly succeeded in throwing as much suspicion as possible.

It was generally known that Twitter's evidence was very important, and when his name was loudly called at the doors of the court, every eye was eagerly bent upon catching the first glimpse of him as he entered the place.

He ascended the two steps leading to the witness-box with more the aspect of a prisoner going to execution than a witness coming to tell what he knew on his oath before a court of justice.

His mean, diminutive figure—his pale, unwholesome-looking complexion, and his evident dreadful nervousness, caused a painful sensation in all who saw him.

While the oath was being administered, his eyes wandered round the court in search of Varley, but in consequence of the position of the witness-box he could not see him, so he was left to his own conjectures as to how the case had hitherto proceeded, and these were, to such a man as Twitter, of the most painful and tormenting nature.

At length the oath was taken, and the counsel for the prosecution rose, and said:

"Samuel Twitter, state what you know concerning the death of Sir George Rankley."

"I will," said Twitter. "I was Sir George's valet. I knew nothing of the duel—I only saw my master brought home wounded, and was told by Mr. Varley that he had fought a duel with Mr. Percy because——"

"We don't want to hear anything of the duel," said Rowland's counsel, interposing. "I submit that that is not before the court, and, besides, what nonsense it is for a witness to come here and swear to the causes of events, which causes might be the sheer invention of someone who had his own bad ends only in view."

"Go on—go on," said the counsel for the prosecution.

"Mr. Varley," resumed Twitter, "spoke to me about the probability of the nurse falling asleep, if unrelieved all night in her attendance upon my master. He offered to sit up with me, and allow her to have an hour's rest, to which I, of course, assented.

"It was twelve o'clock when we thought of going. I carried the light, and as we were proceeding, I think it was I who first saw the figure we supposed to be the spectre of the murdered keeper.

"We attempted to follow it, but it eluded us, and we proceeded to the chamber of my master. He was sleeping, and when the nurse was gone I sat down by the foot of the bed, as I felt very much overcome by the, as I then thought, supernatural appearance I had seen on my passage to the chamber.

"The candle we then had was nearly burnt to the socket, and Mr. Varley asked me to go down to his room and get one which was there. Seeing, however, my agitation, for I am very nervous, he went himself—he—he went, I say, himself."

Here Twitter paused, and seemed unable to proceed for some moments, while he looked round in vain for an encouraging glance from Varley.

"Take your time," said the judge.

"He—he went himself," repeated Twitter, "leaving me alone with my master, who was moaning, as if in pain. But scarcely had he been gone a moment, when the same figure, dressed in green, which had so much alarmed me before, entered the room. I was paralyzed with terror—I could not move nor speak. The firelight fell upon the intruder's face, and I at once recognized Mr. Rowland Percy. I was nearly hidden by the bed-furniture, and I saw him glance round him a moment, as if to assure himself he was alone. Then he drew the pillow sharply from under Sir George's head, and laid it upon my master's face. I know no more—no more—no more."

CHAPTER XLI.

TWITTER'S EVIDENCE CONTINUED—THE DECLARATION OF MIRANDA—THE DEFENCE.

TWITTER repeated the words "no more" as if a tremendous weight had been suddenly taken off his breast.

He breathed more freely, and seemed to anticipate that the worst he had to go through was now over.

The counsel for the prosecution, however, rose and said:

"I have but a few questions to ask of you, Samuel Twitter, and the first is, how long have you been in Sir George Rankley's service?"

"Five years," said Twitter.

"He placed the greatest confidence in you?"

"He did."

"Are you left anything in the will?"

"Nothing beyond what every other servant has—a twelvemonth's wages."

"You are quite sure that Sir George Rankley was alive when you sat down at the foot of his bed?"

"Quite sure. He was moaning, and tossing his arms, now and then, about."

"And you have no doubt concerning the identity of the prisoner at the bar with the person you saw enter the chamber in a green dress?"

"None whatever."

"I have done."

The counsel then sat down, with quite a triumphant air, as much as to say:

"You can make nothing out of this witness, but what is favourable to the prosecution."

Rowland's counsel now rose, and said, abruptly:

"How did you get a living before you entered Sir George Rankley's service?"

"Get—a—living!"

"Yes. What did you do?"

"I was assisted by my friends."

"What do you mean to do now?"

"I shall remain in the service of Mr. Varley, in the same capacity as that in which I served the late Sir George."

"What happened when you recovered from your swoon in the bedroom?"

"Miss Rankley was there, and there was much confusion. I scarcely know what happened until I saw the prisoner in custody, and I felt much relieved in my mind when I found that he was the supposed ghost."

"Do you know a poor idiot, named Bold Hawk, or Mad Martin?"

"Yes."

"Does he not prophecy that Bernard Varley will be hanged at York?"

"He—he—does."

"I believe it, and so do you. Look at him, my lord and gentlemen of the jury—look at him!"

The counsel pointed his finger at Twitter, who was seized with such a fit of trembling that he could scarcely stand.

"Gentlemen of the jury," continued the counsel, "the fear and agitation of these two witnesses for the prosecution, who play into each other's hands so perfectly, is certainly the most extraordinary thing of the kind I ever saw in my life. I have done with you, Samuel Twitter, and Heaven have mercy upon you, if you are a perjured man."

"Call George Hessel," said the prosecuting counsel.

This George Hessel was an old servant of Mr. Percy, and when he appeared, and was sworn, the counsel said:

"Do you know the handwriting of young Mr. Percy?"

"I do," was the reply.

"Is that his writing?"

The ivory tablets were handed to the witness, opened at the page where was the memorandum. The man paused some moments, then he said:

"It is very like."

"You cannot swear it is not?"

"No."

"But you cannot swear it is," said Rowland's counsel. "And now, George Hessel, do you think, if you were going to commit a murder, you would make a memorandum of it on some tablet?"

"No. Oh, dear, no!"

"Do you think you are wiser than young Mr. Percy?"

"Oh, dear, no! I be but a poor man, and he has a mart o' larning."

"That will do. My lord, these tablets are nonsense. If the prisoner were convicted on such evidence, I would move an arrest of judgment on account of lunacy. Who but a madman would have made such a memorandum? It's a forgery."

Varley rose from a seat he had pushed himself into, and uttered an angry exclamation, but in an instant he seemed to be aware of the folly of what he was doing, and as rapidly sat down again, his sudden emotion being only perceptible by those immediately around him, and by Twitter.

Several witnesses were now examined to prove the chase for Rowland Percy through the house, and his ultimate capture in the identical green dress, concerning which so much had been said.

Here closed the case for the prosecution, and it was evident to every lawyer present that, unless Twitter's evidence could be materially shaken, it must suffice to convict the prisoner.

The dim shadows of evening were now beginning to steal over the face of nature, and objects in the still crowded court became more and more faint and confused. Judge, counsel, jury, witnesses, and spectators were alike exhausted, when, after a whispered word or two to the mayor, the judge said:

"If the counsel on each side are agreeable, I will bind over the jury to appear to-morrow, and we will adjourn the case at this point before the defence is entered into."

"I have no objection, my lord," said Rowland's counsel, "myself and the prisoner's solicitor being allowed free access to the accused."

"That may be," said the judge; "but he must see no other visitors."

"I consent to the postponement," said the counsel for the prosecution; "but the jury, I trust, will, by your lordship's direction, be prevented from holding communication with anyone."

At this, one of the jurors rose, and said:

"Please you, my lord, I've got a wife."

"The court cannot help that, sir," said the judge, "however it may sympathize with you."

A smile passed among the counsel, and the discomfited juryman sat down.

"The jury," added the judge, "will be accommodated within the precincts of the court. I think it quite impossible that either they, myself, or the counsel engaged on this case, can do their duty efficiently for perhaps six or eight hours longer, after the fatigue of both mind and body we have already undergone. The court stands adjourned until ten o'clock to-morrow morning, when it is understood the defence is to be entered upon."

The adjournment was most welcome to everyone, for, in truth, all were exhausted by so many hours' intense excitement.

A rush was made to the door of the court, and Miranda, rising, cast her eyes towards the bar just as a turnkey laid his hand upon Rowland Percy's arm to remove him.

"Rowland!" she cried, and in a moment she was as near to him as she could get.

verdict being favourable or unfavourable to the prisoner.

Never was there so much partizanship on behalf of an accused person before, and, at the very street corners, little knots of persons stood till a late hour, on the evening of the first day of the trial, anxiously and vehemently commenting on the evidence.

Varley retired to his new lodgings opposite to Miranda in a perfect agony of suspense and terror—suspense as regarded the verdict, and terror lest from the question which Rowland's counsel had asked him, concerning the mysterious horseman on the bridle-path, he had in reserve, some information which he would produce at the last moment, to his, Varley's, absolute confusion and ruin.

So strangely did this idea take possession of his guilty mind, that he was more than once during the night tempted to fly, and escape the possible impending storm of the morrow.

He knew well that he had communicated to no one the fact of his meeting with the stranger, and, therefore, it must be from that mysterious, and to Varley's heated imagination, terrible man himself, that the counsel for the defence had received his information; and so receiving it, what was to hinder a free communication of all, as well as of a part?

Thus reasoned Bernard Varley, and, as he did so, he passed such a night of horrors, that had Rowland Percy seen him, he must have pitied him.

Retire to rest he could not, but he continued to pace to and fro in the room he had hired, to the great consternation and wonder of his landlady; only varying that most monotonous proceeding by occasionally throwing himself into a seat, and fixing his eyes upon Miranda's window, while he muttered:

"Miranda—Miranda. What do I not endure for you? You will not give me one kind word—one gentle look, to save me from despair. Oh, Miranda—Miranda—beautiful being. You might even now save Rowland Percy, for at a word from you, couched in the tone I would fain hear, I would take measures even yet to save him."

Then a feeling of his own danger, as he considered it, on the morrow, would come over him, and he would slip down the staircase, and look anxiously up and down the street, to assure himself that no one was waiting to apprehend him.

Thus passed the wretched night of Bernard Varley, the much-envied possessor of one of the finest estates in the country, and a man, who, to all appearance, had reached the very summit of his ambition.

As the gray light of morning appeared, he sat down by the window, and stirred not, for he wished to see Miranda as she went forth —not knowing that she was at Mr. Anderson's.

Four o'clock pealed from the Minster clock, just as objects became faintly visible. Then five, and he was still there, with his eyes fixed as those of a corpse upon the opposite window.

Six o'clock still found him there, and then his wondering landlady knocked at his room door.

He started to his feet, and trembled in every limb, as he said, in a voice of terror:

"Who's there?"

"Please, sir, it's me," said the woman. "I thought you might want something, as you were up."

"Leave me," he cried. "Never think about me or my actions. I want nothing."

"Well, sir, I only thought——"

"Away, woman, away! am I to be pestered by you? Away, I say. Ha! who is that?"

A low, single knock sounded on the street-door, and it could not have had more effect upon Varley's excited nerves, had it been the sudden report of a cannon close to his ears.

The woman bustled down the staircase to open the door, and Varley stood, in an attitude of listening, with his own room-door open, for, to his imagination, every alarm sounded like a summons to him to come and take Rowland Percy's place in the dock, and be accused of the murder of Sir George Rankley.

With a feeling of relief he heard the voice of Twitter inquiring for him, and, in a few moments, the valet came sneaking up the stairs, slowly and cautiously, as was his custom.

Varley threw himself into a seat with his back to the light, and, when Twitter entered the room and closed the door, he said:

"Well, well, Twitter—have you any news?"

"None," said Twitter; "but I thought I had better come and see you. The whole town seems to be in an uproar. Yesterday was nothing to it."

"Let the rabble shout," said Varley: "let them, in their own minds, condemn whom they please, sympathize with whom they please. I care not—I care not, Twitter."

"No, certainly not," said Twitter. "Did I not," sinking his voice to a whisper, "did I not give my evidence well, eh?"

"You did—you did," said Varley. "What we two have sworn to should hang a better man than Rowland Percy."

"Yes—yes," said Twitter. "But I have come to you, Varley, to beg of you—to implore you to give up this insane love of Miranda. You must know how truly hopeless such a passion must be."

"It may be hopeless," said Varley, bitterly, "but if she will not have my love, she shall have my revenge, Twitter—my deep and ample revenge."

Twitter groaned, as he said:

"Varley, mark my words—upon that rock you will split. You will bring both me and yourself to ruin—to death!"

"Peace! peace! ill-omened croaker!" cried Varley. "As soon might you move a mountain from its base, as move me from my purposes. I am a desperate man, and I will run my course!"

"Varley, be advised."

"I will not. When you can move, by your entreaties, the stones that pave the streets of York, then expect to move me—but not before, Twitter, not before."

Twitter groaned, and turned to go; but Varley stepped up to him, and, laying his hand on his arm, said, in a nervous manner:

"Twitter, you came along the streets—you heard men carousing—are you sure we are not threatened with any danger?"

"Danger?" echoed Twitter.

"Yes—are you sure no being, perhaps of another world, has betrayed us to the—the counsel for the defence of Rowland Percy?"

"Oh! he is mad—he is mad!" exclaimed Twitter.

"Fool!" said Varley; "cease these exclamations, and answer me. Have you no hint of danger?"

"None—none!" said the alarmed Twitter. "Good Heavens! what danger do you apprehend?"

"No matter—no matter. Go now."

"I came for you, because the difficulty of getting into the court is so great if we delay later."

"I shall wait here," said Varley, resuming his seat by the window, "until she appears."

"Miranda has passed the night at Mr. Anderson's."

"Are you sure?"

"Quite sure."

"Then—then I will go with you, Twitter."

"Have you breakfasted?"

"No—no; but I cannot eat till all is over. On the road I will take some wine. Come—come!"

Varley was now quite in as much haste to leave his new lodgings as Twitter could be, and the two false witnesses left the house together, each in his own way, full of all sorts of painful apprehensions, and as thoroughly wretched as any two human beings could possibly be.

As they neared the court, they found a throng of people rapidly bearing towards it, with the same intention as themselves, namely, to be there early enough to secure admission on the first rush which should take place when the doors were opened.

Varley felt faint and exhausted from his long fasting, combined with the great anxiety of mind he had undergone; and, observing a small public-house a few doors down a narrow street, he turned towards it, saying to Twitter, who walked by his side:

"I will go here and get some wine. Eat, I cannot; but I shall find a stimulant that may enable me perchance to go through the day."

It was a little old-fashioned house, and Varley was glad to find that he was not recognized by anyone in it, although there were two persons in the bar, and a third talking to them.

"A pint of sherry," said Varley, trying to assume a tone of ease and confidence.

The wine was quickly placed before him, and, as he drank, he was compelled to be a listener to some little conversation, no way flattering to himself.

"You see," said the man, who was talking to the two persons within the bar, "I can't stand a crowd, but my son went, and he came home quite in a taking, he did."

"Indeed—what for?" said the landlady of the house.

"Why, I'll tell you. 'Father,' said he, when he came in, 'there's an innocent man being tried to-day for his life!' that's what my son said. Then I said to him, 'Ned,' says I, 'what puts that in your head?' 'I'm sure of it,' says he, 'and atween you and me, if Sir George Rankley has been murdered at all, someone else did it.'"

"Lor! bless us, who?" said the landlady.

"Hum—hum!"

"But you can tell me, sure, neighbour?"

"Well, I don't know; it ain't safe to speak one's mind always."

"But among friends," interposed Varley, "you know, sir, it is safe enough. Pray take a glass of wine, and let us know who your very clever son accuses of the murder?"

"You are very good, sir," said the man, whose intellects were not sharp enough to detect the tone of irony in which Varley spoke.

Varley poured him a glass of wine, and the man, as he raised it to his lips, said:

"Well, as we is among friends, I don't mind telling you my Ned's opinion, and though I say it as shouldn't, perhaps, Ned is no fool!"

"Children do not always take after their parents," said Varley, bitterly.

"That's true, sir," said the man, who took it as quite a compliment. "Well, then, my Ned thinks as Bernard Varley did it."

"The murder! Lor! bless us," ejaculated the landlady.

"Does he, indeed?" said Varley.

"He does. I assure you that's my Ned's opinion, sir."

"Then you may tell your Ned that Mr. Varley will prosecute him for his opinion."

"What?"

"Prosecute him."

"My Ned—eh? Mr. Varley prosecute my Ned?"

"Yes, sir. My name is Bernard Varley."

So saying Varley walked from the house, leaving everyone who heard him perfectly aghast, and as terrified as if they had just been visited by some awful spectre.

"Curses on them," said Varley, when he was once more in the high street leading to the court, "but what makes them suspect me?"

"I don't know," said Twitter; "I'm full of apprehension."

"Pshaw! you always were; but this is no place to converse in. Ah! who is that?"

"It is old Mr. Percy."

At the same moment that Twitter pronounced his name, Rowland's father saw Varley, and immediately stepping up to him, he said:

"Bernard Varley, you have borne false witness against my boy! May he be your accuser before that eternal Judge who cannot err!"

"Old man," said Varley, "your gray hairs protect you, or you should rue your insult to me."

"Did Sir George Rankley's gray hairs protect him from the hands of a murderer?" cried Mr. Percy.

"No, sir," replied Varley. "Your son had not so much kind consideration, it appears, in his nature."

"Villain," said Mr. Percy, "you are now at large, and can brave this matter out; but the time will come when you, without that aid from Heaven, which will surely be rendered to my innocent boy, will stand in the same position he now occupies."

"Old man," said Varley, as he passed on, for he saw that, in a few moments, they would be surrounded by a crowd, "your wits are wandering—you know not what you say."

"Vain subterfuge, Bernard Varley. Your own heart tells you what I mean better than I myself could explain. Oh, man—man! what a fearful account have you to settle when you shall be called upon by an immortal Judge to answer."

Varley walked hastily onwards, with a flushed brow and curses at his heart.

CHAPTER XLIII.

THE CONTINUED TRIAL—THE VERDICT—A SCENE OF STRANGE EXCITEMENT—THE DENUNCIATION—VARLEY'S TERROR.

WHEN Bernard Varley reached the entrance to the court, he found so dense a crowd there assembled, that it was next to impossible for him to make an entrance for some time.

In vain he attempted to press forward, and, receiving little or no assistance from the cowardly and trembling Twitter, his progress was but very slow indeed.

Determined, however, to hear the progress of the trial, he still pressed onwards, until he reached, after an hour's struggling, the door of the court.

There he was repulsed by some of the officials on duty, until he declared who he was, when he was admitted, together with Twitter, into the body of the court.

The doors, as yet, were not thrown open, and none had been allowed to enter, but such as were in some manner connected with the future progress of the important trial, which was about to be resumed.

Suddenly coming from the open daylight, it was some moments before Bernard Varley became acquainted with the presence of Miranda, who, with her extreme anxiety as regarded the fate of Rowland Percy, had even at an earlier hour than he, Varley, had thought proper, sought the scene of his acquittal or his condemnation.

When, however, his eyes fell upon the graceful form, to him more beautiful, if possible, in grief, than it had been in joy, he grasped the arm of Twitter so tightly as to cause a slight exclamation of pain from the valet, and said:

"She is here! She is here! The arbitress of my destiny—she is here, Twitter. Look upon her, and bewitch your mind with her rare beauty. She is here—and yet, oh, Heaven! she will not smile upon me!"

"Hush! for Heaven's sake, hush!" said Twitter. "This wild emotion may yet be our ruin."

"I must speak to her," murmured Varley. "Even in the height of her scornful beauty, I must speak to her—see, her eyes are wet with tears. She weeps for him who shall die."

"Are you distracted?" whispered Twitter, as he laid hold of Varley by the arm, and held him back for a moment from advancing towards Miranda. "For your own sake, as well as for mine, forego the mad exhibition of any emotion now. There are a hundred eyes upon you."

"Were a universe watching me," said Varley, "I must speak to her."

With these words, he tore himself from the detaining grasp of Twitter, and with a slow, unsteady step, walked up to where Miranda was sitting.

She did not observe him, for her thoughts were with Rowland Percy, in his lonely cell, and it was not until, in a frantic tone, he said:

"Miranda—Miranda!" that she became aware of his presence. Then turning, she faced the man who had worked her so much woe, and, with a tone of loathing horror, she cried:

"Away—away! Haunt me not, Bernard Varley—thou murderer of my father—false witness against the innocent! Away—away!"

"Hear me," said Varley, in a low tone of agony, as he leant forward towards her. "Hear me, Miranda! Even now I can save Rowland Percy."

Miranda rose on the instant, and cried:

"Listen to the perjurer—listen all to him who has taken in vain the name of Heaven. The false witness even now condemns himself."

There was a rush of the few persons in the court towards Miranda, and Varley, shrinking back, while a spasmodic change came over his face, cried:

"'Tis false—'tis false! The girl is mad because her lover is a murderer! The girl is mad!"

"Mr. Bernard Varley," said Mr. Anderson, who at that moment entered the court, he having been home on some important business, after escorting Miranda to her seat, "I will not allow you to insult this lady by addressing her, for such she considers an insult."

"Indeed, sir," said Varley, all the fiendishness in his nature showing itself in the diabolical expression of his face, "there may come a time when you—but no matter—no matter—I'm done now."

Smothering, then, as best he might, the expression of deep hatred that he felt towards Mr. Anderson, he slowly walked to the opposite side of the court, still followed by Twitter, who was in a state of the most pitiable agitation, for he feared each moment that Varley, in his wild passion for the beautiful Miranda, would say something that, while it committed himself, would likewise involve him, Twitter, in an inextricable dilemma.

The hour for resuming the business of the court was now rapidly approaching, but, from the precautions which had been taken in consequence of the proceedings of the day before, there was not a tithe of the confusion which then had reigned.

The court instantly became densely crowded, but all was comparatively still, and when the judge, accompanied by the Mayor of York, took his seat upon the bench, there was every appearance of the proceedings, deeply interesting as they were, proceeding tranquilly to a close.

Precisely at ten o'clock Rowland Percy was placed at the bar, and he appeared with the same unaltered mien as before, although Miranda, as she gazed at him, saw, or thought she saw, that he was much paler than he was yesterday, and that the smile with which he recognized her presence was fainter than it had been.

There was no demonstration of feeling on the part of the crowded auditory when he appeared, and, but for the low hum of voices, which suddenly broke out, and the loud sententious " Silence !" of the crier of the court, no one would have imagined that he whose life hung that day upon the opinion of twelve of his fellow men, had made his appearance.

The jury were sworn again, and as the bustle which was inevitably consequent upon this proceeding subsided, a look of care and gravity came over the features of Rowland's counsel, for it was now his turn to address the court in favour of the prisoner, and to produce what witnesses he could in support of his innocence.

There was a perfect silence for some moments, and then he rose.

He glanced at the prisoner, and around the court before he spoke, and then, in a clear, manly voice, but slightly tinctured with an emotion which gave it truthfulness, he commenced :

" My lord and gentlemen of the jury :

" I appear before you in one of the most onerous positions in which one man can appear before his fellows :—namely, to defend the fame and the life of a fellow creature, who, from my heart, I believe is innocent ; and who, before Heaven, I here, to the best of my judgment, proclaim the victim of as awful a conspiracy as ever was concocted against a human being.

" Gentlemen, I am not here to make

charges, but to refute them ; still, whatever the pains or the penalties of such a course of proceeding may be, I, as one man talking to my fellows, and with the ear of Heaven open to my words, declare my firm conviction that the principal witnesses for this prosecution are perjured men—ay, gentlemen of the jury, perjured men !"

There was a great sensation through the court at this bold declaration, and Varley was only prevented from some outburst of passion by the earnest and agonizing whispered remonstrances of Twitter.

" Perjured men," repeated the counsel, in a still louder tone, " and, gentlemen of the jury, having, in the face of this court, made to you so solemn a declaration, I owe it to them—I owe it to you, and lastly, I owe it to myself, to state to you the grounds upon which I found such a belief.

" My lord and gentlemen, I shall, in the first place, detail to you the real simple facts of this case as I have had them from the lips of the parties who now most anxiously await the issue of this judicial investigation, and, having stated these facts, I will proceed to bring before you what evidence I may in support of them.

" So far as my learned friend, who opened this case, went in his description of the contiguity of the estates of the Percy family and the Rankley family, as well as the reciprocal attachment which sprang up between the prisoner at the bar and Miranda, the only daughter of Sir George Rankley, I can agree with him ; but when he states that any scheme, plot, or contrivance entered the brain of the Percys, for the purpose of amending their shattered fortunes by a union with the Rankley family, I am compelled, by the exigencies of the present occasion, gentlemen, to contradict him in the most positive and unequivocal terms.

" No such plan—no such plot—no such contrivance was ever imagined, and, in evidence, I shall be able to prove to you that it was not many days before the duel took place, of which you have heard something, that Mr. Percy, the elder, was aware himself of the embarrassed state of his finances, and that Mr. Percy, the younger, the prisoner at the bar, was not at all aware of that fact until after the present charge had been made against him, for he, when in custody, begged of his father to extend to Miranda Rankley, who has been robbed of her patrimony—robbed is my word, gentlemen—the fostering care of a parent from his ample resources, and the news that those resources were dissipated fell like a thunderbolt upon the mind of my client.

" So much for the gratuitous assumption that any one action, any one thought of my much-injured and innocent client was engendered by a desire to rescue himself from monetary embarrassment, and so much, gentlemen, for the principal, if not the only alleged, motive, for the commission of this terrible crime with which he is charged.

"My lord and gentlemen of the jury,—My learned friend on the other side felt himself in a difficulty to get up an imaginable motive for a young gentleman, remarkable for humanity—remarkable for probity—remarkable for every manly virtue—committing so atrocious a crime as murder, and he has stumbled over the supposition that, by killing the father and marrying the daughter, he should better his condition; but, gentlemen, when I disprove the fact of his knowledge of any embarrassment, I humbly assume that the ingenious fabric my learned friend has based upon such a foundation must topple down likewise into the dust.

"That, then, gentlemen, is the first point I shall seek by evidence to establish in favour of my client.

"And now, my lord and gentlemen of the jury, if, taking up the admirable and ingenious line of argument of my learned friend, I admit with him that where we can produce a strong motive for crime there must be crime, and if I succeed in divesting my client of such strong motive, at the same time that I shift that great weight on to the shoulders of the prosecutor in this case, I apprehend it will wear a very different aspect. Ay, the prosecutor, gentlemen. Look at him."

Varley had risen to his feet in spite of Twitter's detaining grasp, and now the counsel for Rowland pointed full in his face, and kept repeating:

"Look at him, gentlemen! Look at him!"

Varley tried to speak, but his words died away in his throat, and he could but gaze, like one fascinated, into the face of the counsel, who, in so searching a manner, was diving, as it were, into the secrets of his inmost heart, and turning against his own breast the weapons he had used for the destruction of the innocent Rowland Percy.

"Silence!" cried the usher of the court.

"For Heaven's sake sit down!" said the counsel for the prosecution, addressing Varley.

"No; let him have his say," interposed Rowland's counsel. "People labouring under great agitation sometimes speak the truth, when, in their cooler moments, we cannot get it from them."

"We really cannot have these most irregular proceedings," said the judge. "If the witness, Bernard Varley, cannot preserve his equanimity, he must be removed from the court."

Varley sank into his seat, and, resting his head upon his hands, remained in that position during the continuance of the counsel's speech, which seemed to have lost none of its force or pungency by the interruption which had taken place.

CHAPTER XLIV.

THE SPEECH FOR THE DEFENCE—THE EVIDENCE OF MR. PERCY—THE WRITING ON THE TABLETS.

THE counsel continued:

"My lord and gentlemen,—Notwithstanding the interruption which has taken place, and which might, or might not, have been intended to intimidate me, I shall proceed to show you that the prosecutor in this case, and not the prisoner at the bar, was the person deeply interested in the death of Sir George Rankley.

"It appears that the late Sir George was in possession of very large property, and although what I am going to say is known well to you all, it nevertheless is an astonishing circumstance, taken in connection with this trial, that the whole of this property should be left in the hands of the prosecutor in this case; in trust, certainly, but on such revolting conditions only could the daughter of Sir George enjoy one penny of it, that the Grange and other property belonging to the late Sir George have become, subject to any questions that may arise in a civil court concerning it, wholly and solely Mr. Bernard Varley's, the prosecutor in this case, gentlemen, one of the principal witnesses against the prisoner, and a man who has, notwithstanding the circumstance, had the singular audacity to instruct counsel to talk of people benefiting by the death of Sir George Rankley as a suspicious circumstance against them.

"My lord and gentlemen, this is monstrous! My learned friend who addressed you for the prosecution, made a grand and particular point of this as a motive for a young gentleman, notorious for his humanity, his rectitude of conduct, and his good feelings, committing a most heartless, cold-blooded murder. And if such a proposition be correct, gentlemen, if we can stoop to the humiliation of believing such a libel upon human nature, what can my learned friend think of the prosecutor in this case, who has actually benefited so largely by the death of Sir George, and who you have not heard was ever notorious for humanity at all, and who, I here declare, to be a man destitute of the common feelings of human nature!"

"I must really object to that," said the counsel for the prosecution.

"Then I must justify it. Bernard Varley retains in his own hands the property that of right belongs, or should belong, to Miranda Rankley, with the hope that by poverty's severe sufferings he may induce her to submit to the loathsome alternative of becoming his wife. Gentlemen of the jury, wherever she goes he follows her with his hideous addresses; and you will recollect that the prisoner at the bar is the affianced husband of Miranda Rankley. So much for motives. If the prisoner had a motive the size of a grain of sand for murdering Sir George Rankley, the prosecutor himself seems to have possessed one as large as a mountain.

"Now, gentlemen, I admit that the prisoner at the bar was at the Grange on the night when, by some mysterious means, Sir George Rankley breathed his last; but his intention in that visit was as different from what has been unjustly imputed to him, as is the glorious light of day from the black, unwholesome vapour of a dungeon. Separated, he knew not why, from her he loved—condemned to reside at a distance from that spot, which was endeared to his heart by a thousand delightful associations—he took advantage of the popular superstition among the servants of the Grange—on which subject you have heard enough—in order to procure an uninterrupted interview with her he loved.

"This, and this only, was his motive in going to the Grange, and his arrival at so unfortunate a time was one of those accidents which are daily happening to every one of us.

"You will understand, my lord and gentlemen of the jury, that I am not attempting to explain, or to fritter away the evidence which has been given by the prosecutor and his creature, Samuel Twitter; but I boldly attack it as false—false, gentlemen, from beginning to end—as far as regards any material fact against the prisoner.

"Heaven knows that in saying so much I do not speak as a hired advocate, but from the real feelings of my heart upon this subject.

"The state of the case is simply this—Rowland Percy did go to the Grange in the disguise of the spectre of the murdered keeper; he found the house in some confusion he knew not why. He was chased from room to room, and naturally wished to escape, for fear of implicating Miranda Rankley in the reproaches which Sir George might have cast upon him for attempting a clandestine interview with her.

"He was, however, captured at length, and at the moment when he was preparing himself to make what excuses he might to Sir George Rankley, he was told, to his surprise, of the Baronet's death, and the next moment was accused by Bernard Varley of the murder; that murder of which he is as innocent as your lordship, or any of you, gentlemen of the jury.

"Now, it appears likewise that the prosecutor was the fortunate man to find those tablets upon which some stress has been laid by the prosecution. My lord and gentlemen, the prisoner at once owns the tablets as his, but he unhesitatingly calls Heaven to witness that beyond his name, he never wrote one word in them.

"Those words which have been read to you, gentlemen, from those tablets, were never written by the prisoner. Let him who did write them beware of that awful day when an immortal Judge shall read his heart!

"But, gentlemen, reasoning for one brief moment upon this question, how absurd is it—how monstrously ridiculous that the man who could conceive an exceedingly artful murder—the man who had such a nice perception of the results of his crime, should at the very time when he was placing himself in great personal danger—when as yet he could but calculate upon success—not know it—that he, I say, should purchase some tablets, write in them words of such fearful import to himself, and then deliberately place them in his pocket, with a strong chance of losing them, on the spot, of all others, where, if found, they would do him the most injury.

"Gentlemen, such a thing lies not within the compass of belief, and I repeat that if I thought the prisoner at the bar was a guilty man, and had written those words, I would apply for his acquittal on the ground of insanity.

"But, my lord and gentlemen of the jury, he stands before you an innocent man, craving at your hands the verdict which shall restore him to that society of which he is so eminently—from his education, his talents, and his warm, good feelings—calculated to become an ornament. He has been, as yet, the victim of some conspiracy, artfully contrived and carried out with singular boldness and rare effrontery; but he is innocent, gentlemen. He is innocent, and in support of the allegations I have made, I shall now proceed to call before you some witnesses in every way worthy of the highest credit from this court."

The counsel sat down, and it was clear that his address had created a strong feeling in favour of Rowland.

The jury whispered together, and cast some very suspicious glances at Bernard Varley and Twitter, as they both sat looking ghastly with rage at the insinuations of the counsel, which, to them, were most desperately annoying, because they were true.

After a slight pause, the first witness called was the elder Percy, and his appearance in the witness-box to speak for his son created a strong sensation in the court.

While he was being sworn, his eyes wandered to the face of Rowland, who answered his anxious look by a smile; but it was a sad smile, like a faint gleam of sunlight illumining the heavens for one moment on a day of gloom.

His examination was then immediately commenced by the question:

"You were on intimate terms with the late Sir George Rankley?"

"I was."

"Are you aware of an attachment on the part of your son to Miranda Rankley?"

"Perfectly so. He loved her well—loves her still with all his heart."

"Was that attachment sanctioned by Sir George?"

"It was virtually, although we never but once had any conversation upon the subject, and that was scarcely in a serious strain, although amply sufficient to convince me that Sir George would place no impediment in the way of their union. He said he had the happiness of his dear child too much at heart to control her affections, so long as they were directed to a worthy object."

"You swear to these words distinctly, Mr. Percy?"

"I do."

"My lord and gentlemen of the jury, how does that tally with the will which Sir George Rankley is said to have made in favour of the prosecutor in this case?"

All saw the force of this observation, and the judge was observed to take a note of it.

"State what circumstances broke up this desirable state of things, Mr. Percy."

"Since the residence of Bernard Varley with Sir George Rankley, there seemed a kind of waning of that hearty good feeling with which the deceased gentleman was in the habit of treating me and my son. Finally, I received a very insulting letter indeed, purporting to be from Sir George."

"How did it insult you?"

"The substance of it was, that I wished to repair my shattered fortunes by a union between my son and his daughter. I believe I wrote an angry reply."

"In what state, then, were your circumstances?"

"I thought myself for days and weeks after that letter a rich man; for I was not aware that an agent in London, in whom I had confided much, had absconded."

"But if Sir George wrote the letter you speak of, he must have been aware of it?"

"Certainly. I suspect strongly that he never wrote it, but that it was the production of some enemy of me and mine, who, by some means, had acquired the information earlier than I, and was desirous to use it in effecting a breach between Sir George and myself."

"Proceed, sir."

"An angry correspondence ensued, during which I sent my son a considerable distance from home; for I was so vexed at the insinuation contained in the first letter, that I would not allow him even to be on the spot. Sir George and I finally fought a duel, which was fomented and got up by Bernard Varley."

"Do you swear that solemnly?"

"I do. The quarrel would, in fact, have been made up, even on the ground, but for him."

The counsel paused to allow these words to have their full effect upon the minds of the jury, before he said:

"Now, Mr. Percy, on your oath, did, or did not, your son hear from you the state of your finances before the death of Sir George Rankley?"

"On my oath, he did not."

"Then he still thought you a rich man?"

"He did; and it was some days after the death of Sir George that he—hearing that Miranda was destitute, by the appropriation of all that should have been hers, by Bernard Varley—implored me to take her to my heart, and, treating her as a child of my own, not to let her know the want of those comforts and elegancies of life she had been accustomed to. Then—then——"

Here Mr. Percy became much affected, and the counsel said, kindly:

"Take your time, sir. Pray, take your time."

"Then I told my boy that I was as destitute as she was, but that I would beg for her from door to door, rather than she should ever want."

"Oh, my lord and gentlemen," said the counsel, elevating his hands, "what becomes, now, of the motives of this young man to murder Sir George Rankley? What becomes of the pretended writing in the tablets, now? I have nothing more to ask you, Mr. Percy, except if that is or is not your son's handwriting?"

The tablets were handed to Mr. Percy, open at the page containing the memorandum.

"It is a very good imitation," he said, "but I will swear that these words were never written by my son."

"That will do, sir. You can go down."

CHAPTER XLV.

MIRANDA'S ELOQUENT APPEAL—DOUBTS AND FEARS—THE COURSE OF THE TRIAL.

THE evidence of Mr. Percy had been so decidedly in favour of the prisoner, that Mr. Anderson whispered to Miranda:

"Hope and expect the best, Miranda. Things could not be going on more satisfactorily than they are."

"Thank Heaven!" said Miranda, in a low voice.

"Miranda Rankley," said the crier of the court; and Miranda started up, exclaiming:

"I am here."

"This way," said Mr. Anderson, as he handed her into the witness-box.

Every eye in the court was fixed upon her, and, when she slowly removed her veil, and her lovely countenance could be seen, there was a murmur of astonishment at her rare beauty, brightened, as it now was, by a slight flush of excitement.

She was sworn; and then there was a death-like silence for a moment or two before the counsel, in a kind, considerate tone, said:

"You are acquainted with the prisoner at the bar, Miss Rankley?"

Miranda turned her eyes upon Rowland, and, in a voice which reached every heart, she said:

"Rowland Percy is my affianced husband."

"You are aware of the crime of which he stands now charged. Pray relate to us what you know of the circumstances connected with this inquiry."

"We were very happy once," said Miranda, in a low tone, of such exquisite pathos and feeling that it brought tears into many eyes, "very, very happy. I was happy in my father's love, and in his approval of the one I had chosen for my companion through life. Then Bernard Varley came, and all was changed. Soon—too soon—I found that, from some most inexplicable cause, my father could not resent even insults from that man. He obtruded upon me his hideous attentions, and, when I complained, my father could do nothing.

"Then, for what reason I could not discover, Rowland was banished from the house, and there succeeded a period of uneasiness and restless conjecture, which the few words only which my father ever said to me upon the subject did not alleviate.

"That was all before the duel, with the exception that once I was compelled to implore my father to send me somewhere from home, to escape the importunities of Bernard Varley, and then he wept, and said he would do something soon to relieve me from him.

"Then, one morning, I was awakened by my maid, who, with cries and screams, told me Mr. Percy and my father were fighting a duel. In a few minutes I rushed from the house, and found my father lying bleeding on the ground. My feelings I will not attempt to describe—that would be impossible.

"The remainder of that awful scene seemed like a waking vision. I could not rest, and after taking leave of my father for the night, I sat for some hours in my own room deaf to all the solicitations of my maid to retire to rest. I heard the clock strike twelve, and a desire came strongly across my mind to see my father again before I attempted to procure any repose.

"Believing no person but the nurse to be in his chamber, I crept from my own room, and, crossing the corridor, opened the door of my father's chamber, when, to my surprise, I saw there Bernard Varley, who made every effort to stop me from entering the room; but I persisted, and finally sat down by the bedside of what I thought to be my sleeping father."

Miranda paused—but she shed no tears—and, after a deep sigh, continued:

"That sleep was the sleep of death. My father was no more, and I was watching a lifeless form."

Miranda again paused, and the counsel said:

"Did you see anyone in the room, or become conscious in any way of the presence of anyone but yourself while you thus watched?"

"No—no."

"What followed?"

"I can scarcely tell. My brain seemed on fire. I raised an instant alarm, and then I saw Rowland Percy surrounded by the servants."

"That is all you can tell the jury of the actual circumstances which occurred that night?"

"That is all."

"Have you since then had any conversation with the prosecutor in this case?"

"Yes, Bernard Varley has sought several interviews with me since that fearful night, and the purport of them all has been to promise Rowland Percy's acquittal if I would give him, Varley, my hand. But I knew that Rowland would rather suffer death, although innocent, than purchase life on such terms."

"A thousand times rather—a thousand times," cried Rowland.

"I knew it," said Miranda; "I knew it."

"You will swear," said the counsel, "that he said he could procure the prisoner's acquittal?"

"I will," replied Miranda. "He even tauntingly admitted his innocence to me, saying, at the same time, that I might state so much, if I pleased, but no one would believe me."

"You have a full and entire confidence in the innocence of the prisoner?"

"As full and entire as I have in the villainy of his accusers. Thinks anyone here that I, loving my father with an affection that knew no bounds, could thus step between justice and his murderer? Rowland Percy is innocent. Let Heaven, in its own good time, discover the guilty."

"I have no more questions to ask," said the counsel; "perhaps you have?" turning to the counsel for the prosecution.

"No," he said, "I shall not interfere with the witnesses for the defence at all."

"Very well—then we need detain you no longer, Miss Rankley."

Miranda was very doubtful in her own heart that the ordeal was passed, for she had never imagined she could have gone through it as she had done, although she felt immeasurably dissatisfied with herself, and thought she might have said more yet for Rowland.

This feeling she communicated to Mr. Anderson, who replied:

"No, Miranda, you said quite enough. Any stronger or more energetic advocacy of him would have been injudicious. You must see that the whole question at issue turns upon the credibility, or otherwise, of the evidence of Twitter."

"Yes—yes," said Miranda. "Oh! how deeply, terribly perjured is that man."

Mr. Anderson was now called, at his own request, for he wished to make one statement, which he did, to the following effect.

"Ever since Sir George Rankley took possession of the Grange estates, I have been his legal adviser, and had the preparation of every legal document, with the one exception of the monstrously unnatural will which is produced by Mr. Varley. I have with me now the rough draft of a will which Sir George gave me more than a year ago, wherein occurs this passage:

"'To my beloved child, Miranda Rankley, I give and bequeath the whole of my real estate, to have and to hold, at her will and pleasure, and may Heaven send her health, happiness, and long life to enjoy it with her father's blessing.'

"These, I will swear, were Sir George's own words, written after his dictation, and judge, therefore, of my surprise, when another legal gentleman produces so very contrary a document."

"I have no question to ask you, Mr. Anderson," said the counsel.

"You are the solicitor for the defence?" said the counsel for the prosecution.

"I am, sir," said Mr. Anderson; "and I trust in Heaven I may always be, as now, on the side of innocence."

"I thought my learned friend," said Rowland's counsel, sarcastically, "was not going to interfere in any way with the witnesses for the defence."

"Your learned friend," said the other, with some show of bitterness, "only thought it a little strange that the solicitor for the defence should be made a witness on the trial."

"We seek the truth," replied Rowland's counsel, "and come it from friend or foe, it is to us as welcome as the sunlight from heaven."

The next witness called was a man who answered to the name of Job Jackson, and who had all the appearance of a London ruffian of the lowest grade, so much so, indeed, that the counsel looked visibly chagrined at having him at all; but he soon became reconciled to Job's appearance, when he remarked the effect it had upon the nervous system of Twitter, who, at the mere announcement of the name, started up, and when he saw the witness enter the box he showed such signs of trepidation that all the counsel's fears about what Job Jackson should say, being believed by the jury, vanished before such confirmatory symptoms from Twitter himself.

"Now, Mr. Job Jackson," said the counsel, "do you know Samuel Twitter?"

"I should rather think I did," replied the witness.

"What do you know of him?"

"Him and me was on the dodge in London some years ago."

"On the what?" said the judge.

"The dodge, my lord," said the counsel.

"But I want to know what that is?"

There was a suppressed laugh in the court, and Mr. Jackson cried:

"Bless your innocence, old gentleman, being on the dodge means a-going on the grand cadge."

"Well, I'm no wiser now," said the judge, "I don't understand the witness a bit."

"My lord," said the counsel, "I rather think he means that he and Samuel Twitter, the principal witness in this case, were in London in a condition which induced them to seek the means of subsistence, without being particular as to the honesty of them."

"And that's being on the dodge, and the grand—what did he say?" remarked the judge, very carefully making a note of the same, to the great amusement of Job Jackson, who winked at the crowd, and in a variety of ways disturbed the gravity of almost every indifferent spectator of the trial.

"Now, tell me," said the counsel to Mr. Jackson, "was this same Samuel Twitter ever suspected of a theft?"

"In course."

"Can you see him in court?"

"I should think so. How do, Sammy—how do? How *air* you?"

Great laughter was excited at this, and Twitter, in a half-frantic voice, said:

"I don't know you. Never saw you. I thought you were transported years ago."

"So I was, Sammy, but I comed back in consikence o' my uncommon genteel behaviour."

"Can you specify, Mr. Jackson, any special act of criminality perpetrated by Samuel Twitter?"

"Can I *speechify* what?"

"I mean, what did he do in the robbery line?"

"Oh, why, he was always a-grabbing of whatever comed to hand, he was. He'd think no more o' boning your wig, or the old gentleman's specs up there, than I would—that is, I mean, than I'd think o' bringing of 'em back agin."

"Then you imagine Mr. Twitter to be rather a bad character, Mr. Jackson?"

"Rather—on the brink o' that ere.—You doesn't look well, Sammy."

"Curses on you!" muttered Twitter.

"You must tell us of some one particular thing that Samuel Twitter has done," said the counsel.

"Oh, why, he used to get places in families, and lay his hands on all sorts o' things, and, whenever there was a row, he used to put a spoon in one of the poor servants' boxes—he used."

"It's false—false!" cried Twitter.

"Sammy—Sammy, take it easy," said Mr. Jackson.

CHAPTER XLVI

A NEW WITNESS—THE CROSS-EXAMINATION OF A GENTLEMAN AT LARGE—TWITTER'S OLD FRIEND.

NOTWITHSTANDING Mr. Jackson's recommendation to Twitter to "take it easy," he was so exasperated at the revelations his old companion in guilt was making, that, had he possessed any means of inflicting a deadly injury upon him, he would have done so on the spot without scruple.

The counsel for Rowland was quite delighted with Twitter's rage, for it offered the very best confirmation of the truth of Mr. Job Jackson's statements that he could possibly wish for.

"Was he ever apprehended on any charge?"

"Yes—a thousand times. Sometimes he got off by crying and fainting away, and sometimes the beak wouldn't be gammoned no how, and guved him three blessed months of it."

"Was he ever committed for trial?"

"Once—yes; but the old bloaks as was on the grand jury did what they calls hignorin the bill."

"You are quite sure of his identity?"

"Don't I know Sammy's dentity? I should think so," was Mr. Jackson's pithy reply.

"That will do—you may go down now."

"Really, my lord," said the counsel for the prosecution, "this witness, I beg to remark, is a most extraordinary one, and although I certainly did say that I would not interfere with the witnesses for the defence, yet the unheard-of course my learned friend has pursued in bringing forward this man, absolves me from such a promise, and I insist upon asking him a question or two."

"As you please," said Rowland's counsel.

The counsel for the prosecution then assumed a very severe aspect, and, bending his brows upon Mr. Jackson, he said:

"Now, my fine fellow——"

"Thank you," said Job, promptly, "the same to you."

"Do not let us have any impertinence, sir," said the angry counsel, turning rather red, for he began to have a disagreeable suspicion that his cross-examination of Mr. Jackson might not result in anything very agreeable to himself.

"Very good," said Job Jackson, making a movement to leave the box.

"Stay where you are, sir," roared the counsel.

"Oh, I thought as you said as you'd done with your impudence," said Job.

This was almost too much for the gravity of the judge, and a slight smile forced itself into notice in spite of him.

"Who are you, Mr. Jackson?" was the next question.

"Job Jackson," was the brief reply.

"But I mean what are you?"

"I ain't a lawyer—I tries to earn a honest penny, I does."

"Then how comes it you are so very intimate with Samuel Twitter, of whom you have given us so entertaining an account?"

"Ah, that was long ago—I sposes as you've picked up with him since."

"Come, come, this won't do."

"I thought it wouldn't. You're a out-and-out oracle, you are."

"On your oath, sir, now tell me, have you ever been apprehended for felony?"

"Felony?"

"Yes, sir. Let us have no prevarication; felony I said, and felony I mean."

"Why, you know wirtuous people is always a getting suspected."

"Answer me, yes or no."

"Which would you like best? You look like a comfortable old pump, and I'll oblige you if I can."

"I appeal to the court," cried the counsel; "I really must appeal to the court."

"Do," said Job; "but don't over exert yourself. You'll be ill arter this, I know."

"You must answer the questions put to you," said the judge. "We cannot have the time of the court wasted in this way."

"Now, sir, were you ever in custody on a charge of felony or not?"

"Yes, I was. Sammy, there, is such a artful card he'd bring a sucking dove into trouble. He's been my ruin, he has. Oh, Sammy! Sammy! you *his* a wretch and no mistake!"

"I have done," said the counsel. "This witness has been brought from London, for no other purpose than to throw discredit upon the sworn testimony of Samuel Twitter, by stating that he has been accused of felony. Now, my lord and gentlemen of the jury, what face can my learned friend put on this matter when, from the mouth of his own witness I have proved a similar allegation as regards him. I submit that this man is quite unworthy of belief, and his evidence falls to the ground."

"Nay," said Rowland's counsel. "Two blacks don't make a white, and you may prove Mr. Jackson as bad as you like without cleansing Samuel Twitter from the spots on his character."

"I submit——"

"This is quite irregular," said the judge.

"Call Martha Monkton," said the counsel.

This was the nurse who had been with Sir George on the evening of the duel, and the first question put to her was:

"Are you a nurse by profession?"

"I am," was the answer.

"Are you accustomed to sitting up at night with invalids?"

"Of course."

"And you don't go to sleep, leaving your patients to take care of themselves?"

"I go to sleep, sir! I never did such a thing in all my life."

"You recollect nursing Sir George Rankley?"

"Certainly I do."

"Then you were not particularly anxious to be relieved from your duties by Mr. Varley and Mr. Twitter?"

"No, I wasn't; but it was very kind."

"And very extraordinary?"

"Yes."

"Call Mr. Querral. I have done with you, my good woman."

Querral, the attorney, entered the witness-box, with an air, as much as to say, you won't get anything to serve your turn out of me—oh, no!

Rowland's counsel, however, had been well instructed by Mr. Anderson in the man he had to deal with, and, as he only wanted to elicit one fact from him, he determined so to nail him to that, that he should not have the smallest opportunity of escaping from answering it.

"Your name is Querral?" he said.

"Yes."

"You are an attorney in this city?"

"I am."

"You made a will for Sir George Rankley?"

"I did."

"Who gave you the instructions?"

"Who—gave—me——"

"Who gave you the instructions, sir?" thundered the counsel. "Answer me at once, who gave you the instructions for the will?"

MR. JACKSON-JONES MAKES SOME DAMAGING DISCLOSURES.

"Mr. Varley."

Down sat the counsel, for he had got just the answer he wished, his object being to lead the minds of the jury to the supposition that Varley had all along had an eye to the property, and was a likely man to concoct plots and conspiracies to further his own ends.

"Is—is that all?" said Mr. Querral, who had prepared himself for a long examination, in which he had intended to show how very clever he was at doubling, turning, shifting, and equivocating.

"That is all," said the counsel.

With a disappointed air Querral stepped from the witness-box.

Several influential gentlemen of the county were now called, who, one and all, gave Rowland the very highest character for humanity, and the best feelings that could appertain to human nature.

Miranda felt her heart throb as she heard the kindly sentiments which were uttered concerning Rowland, and, clasping her hands, she silently breathed a prayer to Heaven to save the innocent.

There was a pause now of some minutes, during which the counsel for Rowland and Mr. Anderson earnestly consulted together.

The subject of this conference was the probability or non-probability of the mysterious man coming forward who had suggested the question which had had so great an effect upon Bernard Varley, an effect which could not be carried further for want of more information.

"Shall we attempt an appeal to him if he be in court?" said the counsel.

"It can do no harm," said Mr. Anderson. "Sometimes, on the spur of a moment, a man's good feelings may get the better even of all prudential motives, and he may come forward."

"As you say, it can do no harm. I will take upon myself to call him, and do you watch the effect it has upon Bernard Varley."

"I will."

The counsel then rose, and, in a loud, clear voice, which was distinctly heard by everyone, and produced no little surprise, said:

"I call solemnly and earnestly upon the man who met Mr. Varley on the bridle-path between the city of York and the Grange to come forward if he be here, and declare before God and man what he knows of this transaction."

Varley sprang to his feet, and his eyes looked like those of a maniac as he expected each moment to be confronted by the being who had taken such a strong hold of his imagination, and who, he verily believed, could reveal his most hidden actions.

There was a profound silence in the court, for all seemed to expect something strange as the result of the singular call made by the counsel on one whom he could not name.

Second after second passed slowly away, and there was no response to the call.

The counsel shook his head and sat down, while a look of disappointment came over the face of Mr. Anderson, who had entertained sanguine hopes that, at the last moment, the mysterious stranger might make his appearance.

Each moment that passed seemed to give Varley new life, and, when he saw the counsel sit down, as if giving up all hope of the appearance of the witness, he, Varley, likewise sank into his seat with a feeling of inexpressible relief.

Dick Palmer was in the court; but, as the reader is aware, he knew nothing which could be at all beneficial to Rowland, of whose guilt or innocence he might, like others, entertain an opinion, but could have no positive knowledge.

Accident alone had given him the power he held over the mind of Varley, and he felt that, should he come forward at his own personal risk, and do all he could—namely, blacken the character of Twitter—he should, without materially advancing the interests of the prisoner, lose all the power which might eventually be exerted much to the benefit of Miranda.

Everbody now felt that the case was concluded for the defence, leaving the direct sworn testimony of Bernard Varley and Twitter untouched, except very remotely, in the way of character.

The counsel for the prosecution had a right to reply, if he had chosen to exercise it; but he looked up to the judge, and shook his head, for he was, in his own mind, notwithstanding the numerous aggravations he had endured in the course of his cross-examination, quite satisfied that the case for the prosecution stood firm and unshaken, as not a tittle of the evidence had been shaken, except in the sworn opinion of Mr. Percy, that the words in the tablets were not in his son's handwriting; and, after all, that was but a collateral piece of evidence, which might have been altogether given up by the prosecution without injuring their case in the least.

CHAPTER XLVII.

THE JUDGE'S SUMMING UP—THE JURY AND THE VERDICT.

ALL eyes were now most anxiously turned towards the judge, whose duty it was to sum up the case and charge the jury.

A profound stillness reigned in the court, although the professional men present had no sort of difficulty in predicting to each other upon what points the judge must of necessity dwell, and what would be the verdict of the jury.

The judge commenced his address in a calm, low, dispassionate tone of voice, now and then only referring to his notes, when he wished to quote particular words which had been used by any of the numerous witnesses who had been under examination.

"Gentlemen of the jury," he said, "this important case, you must perceive, entirely rests upon the degree of credit you feel disposed to give to the evidence of Mr. Bernard Varley and Samuel Twitter.

"I cannot myself see anything in the depositions of the other witnesses but what may be considered as decidedly in favour of the prisoner at the bar; but, gentlemen, in a court of justice we must not forget that the sworn statement of one person—always provided that person be one worthy of belief—that he saw a crime committed, is of more importance than the statements of hundreds who may consider the commission of the crime by the man charged with it as improbable, and contrary to the usual tenor of his habits.

"I am far—very far—from wishing to prejudice the prisoner at the bar, but we have frequent instances of such anomalies in human nature as persons upon whose integrity we would have staked our fortunes, committing thefts, and persons upon whose humanity we have the fullest reliance becoming guilty of dreadful cruelties.

"In point of fact, gentlemen of the jury, the evidence for the prosecution in this case, I grieve to say, has gone to establish the fact that the prisoner committed a murder, and the evidence for the defence has only proved that, to the best of everybody's knowledge, nobody thought he was the sort of person to do such a thing.

"You are all, gentlemen, residents in this city, and familiar with the parties concerned in this most singular case, but I pray you to dismiss from your minds utterly and entirely any previous feelings or predilections which you may have in connection with the individuals affected by this investigation.

"It appears by the evidence which has been produced, that an intimacy sprang up between the families of the Percys and the Rankleys, which promised to result in a marriage that would unite their interests very closely; but that some pecuniary difficulties, which came upon Mr. Percy, caused a cessation of that friendly intercourse.

"One mysterious circumstance connected with this part of the business is that, from the evidence, it would appear that this pecuniary difficulty was known to Sir George Rankley before it was known to him, whom it more nearly concerned, namely, Mr. Percy himself. How Sir George arrived at that knowledge, and through whom he obtained it, I cannot pretend to say; but, at all events, the result seems to have been some very insulting insinuations with respect to the Percys' motives in wishing the marriage, which insulting insinuations terminated in a duel, in which Sir George Rankley received a wound, that we are assured, upon respectable medical evidence, could not have caused his demise, and hence we are compelled to look for other causes for that melancholy event.

"A series of circumstances now occurred on the evening of the same day on which it appears this duel was fought, that terminate in one point—that point being the apprehension of the prisoner at the bar, on the charge of murdering Sir George Rankley.

"Now, gentlemen, that the prisoner was at the Grange on the night in question—that he was there secretly, and in disguise, is admitted, and I must say that even all that is quite compatible with innocence; for it does not follow that a man has committed a murder, because he is placed in circumstances to do so if he feels inclined.

"We have the evidence of the nurse, who states that Sir George Rankley was alive at twelve o'clock, and that she wanted no assistance whatever in watching his sick chamber; but that Mr. Varley had proffered such assistance, and, thinking it very kind of him, she accepted it, and left her charge.

"You see, gentlemen, that after that the nurse has nothing to do with the affair, and the living Sir George Rankley is left in the hands of Bernard Varley and Samuel Twitter, they having to account for him, until he was found dead by his daughter Miranda some time afterwards.

"Now, gentlemen, you will see that the whole weight of this case rests upon the shoulders of these two men. They accepted the trust of tending a living man, and they are placed in a situation, consequently, which compels them to account for how he became a dead one.

"You will perceive, gentlemen, that the whole case narrows itself to this small compass, and comes to this, that either Bernard Varley and Samuel Twitter, or one of them, committed the murder, or they have accurately told you who really did so.

"These two witnesses, with great exactness, and tallying well together, describe to us first the supposed mysterious appearance of the spectre on the staircase, which it is admitted, on all hands, was the prisoner at the bar; then the incident of the light nearly expiring, and Bernard Varley's absence from the room to procure a fresh one, thus leaving Samuel Twitter with the still living Sir George, and throwing upon him the onus of accounting for his death. This he does most frightfully —circumstantially. He describes the prisoner at the bar—to whom he distinctly swears— entering the room, glancing around him as if to see that he was alone, and then, with awful deliberation, smothering the unhappy Sir George Rankley with a pillow.

"Now, gentlemen, if we choose to receive this account as it is given us, it throws an everlasting slur upon this man, Samuel Twitter, whose cowardice must have been great indeed, to allow him to become a passive spectator of such a scene. Moreover, it is to be wondered at, that his fear did not induce him to utter a cry or a scream, which would have frightened the murderer from his purpose; but, instead of that, Samuel Twitter, being at first hidden, in some strange manner, by the bed-furniture, comfortably faints away, leaving his master, mind you, gentlemen, quite at the mercy of this strange appearance, which, however, he had, previous to such fainting, ascertained *not* to be supernatural at all!

"But we have this testimony upon oath, and it is for you to believe the witness or not, according to the best of your judgments. If you have any doubt with regard to any portion of his evidence, it is your duty to give the prisoner the full benefit of such doubt, and acquit him; but, if you believe the witness Twitter, you can have no course open to you, but to bring in a verdict of guilty.

"I regret that the counsel for the prosecution in this case thought it necessary to search for some motives for the prisoner's commission of the crime with which he stands charged; for, gentlemen, if all the counsel in the world were to prove to you that no imaginable motive could have acted upon his mind, and yet you believed the evidence of Samuel Twitter, you could not help convicting him.

"I may likewise add that this attribution of motives to the prisoner has signally failed, and recoiled on the prosecution, for the witness, Bernard Varley, seems the only man who has benefited by the decease of Sir George Rankley.

"With regard to the credibility of the evidence of Samuel Twitter, you must bear in mind, gentlemen, that this could not be a concocted plan on the parts of Varley and Twitter to ruin the prisoner at the bar, for by the evidence on both sides, and by the instructions of the prisoner's counsel, his visit to the Grange is represented as a most secret one, he being thought to be a long way off from this part of the country.

"Evidence has been produced to show that Twitter was but an indifferent character, and if the allegations against him of the witness, Job Jackson, who describes himself and Twitter as being upon some expedition, or under some circumstances called the 'dodge,' be true, they tend to prove Samuel Twitter as despicable a character as ever came into a court of justice; but, gentlemen, if Samuel Twitter's evidence were to be rejected because he has committed felonies and misdemeanours, the very evidence of Job Jackson accusing him of such lapses of morality must fall to the ground from the same cause, leaving us without any allegation at all against Samuel Twitter. As thus, gentlemen:—If B is unworthy of belief because he has done something that A charges him with, A's charge is not to be believed against B, because he (A) admits himself to have done the same thing, and B's evidence upon a distinct matter stands untouched."

The jury looked very hard at each other as the judge put this case, and a doubtful, mystified expression sat upon their faces, for A and B had quite bewildered them.

"I repeat, therefore, gentlemen," continued the judge, "that you must judge this case entirely upon the evidence of Samuel Twitter, whom you must either disbelieve entirely, and acquit the prisoner; or believe wholly, and at once convict him.

"With respect to the tablets which have been produced in evidence, I do not lay much stress upon them. If, indeed, you can come to the conclusion that the words there set down, and which seem to hint at the murder, are in the handwriting of the prisoner, it would be a circumstance tending to strengthen the credibility of Samuel Twitter's evidence; but, on the contrary, if you think that those words were forged, in order to make another link in the chain of evidence against the prisoner, I should direct an acquittal, for such a circumstance would throw strong doubts upon the whole of the evidence for the prosecution, and induce a belief that Bernard Varley and Samuel Twitter were in a conspiracy together to destroy the prisoner at the bar.

"Some of the proceedings of the prisoner's counsel I must own myself completely at a loss to understand. I allude to the calling of a person with whose name even it appears the learned counsel is unacquainted, to depose to some facts with which he appears equally unacquainted. Some mystery seems to be lurking somewhere in this business, as was evident from the extraordinary agitation of the witness Varley, but what that mystery is, I cannot take upon myself to say, or even, in the most distant manner, conjecture.

"I pray, gentlemen of the jury, that Heaven may guide you in your deliberations, and that you may be enabled to come to a correct conclusion with regard to the credibility or noncredibility of the witness, Samuel Twitter."

The judge ceased, and the jury sat for a few moments looking at each other in silence.

The most intense excitement showed itself upon every countenance in the court.

"Would you like to retire, gentlemen?" said the judge.

The foreman whispered to his neighbour, and the whisper went round. That whisper was:

"I think he's done it. The idea of smothering a gentleman with his own pillow!"

"But what about that A and B?" remarked one; "I don't quite understand that."

"It means that if the prisoner didn't do the murder, who did?" said another.

"Oh!"

"Gentlemen of the jury, are you agreed?" said the clerk of the arraigns.

"Yes," said the foreman.

"Do you find the prisoner at the bar guilty or not guilty?"

"GUILTY!"

CHAPTER XLVIII.

THE SENTENCE—MIRANDA'S DECLARATION—VARLEY'S DANGER FROM THE CROWD—THE RIOT.

FOR a few moments after the verdict was pronounced by the foreman of the jury, the dense crowd in court looked in each other's faces, as if seeking from each other some confirmation of the dreadful verdict. The awful word guilty appeared as it were to hang in the very atmosphere of the place, exerting a stunning, deadening influence upon the hearts of all who heard it.

The foreman of the jury still stood facing the clerk of the arraigns, and it appeared as if he too felt almost doubtful if he had been heard aright, for in a low voice, but a very clear one, he again repeated the word:

"Guilty!"

The sound of his voice acted like the removal of a spell from the faculties of all present, and that confused murmur arose which is always produced from a multitude of persons, when they are released from any circumstances which have claimed their attention, and wrapped them in silence, either voluntary or compulsory, for a time.

Several voices cried "shame—shame—not guilty—not guilty!"

The officers looked confused, for these sounds arose from various parts of the court, and they knew not whom to pounce upon for the breach of decorum.

Then suddenly, like a flash of light, uprose Miranda, and casting aside her veil, she lifted up her hands to Heaven, in such an attitude of solemn adjuration, that every sound was in a moment hushed, and all waited in breathless expectation for the words which were about to issue from her lips.

Twice the judge opened his mouth as if he would have stopped her, but as often he produced no sound, and finally he sank back in his chair, as though resolved to hear her.

"I appeal to Heaven," she said, "against human error, and human iniquity—to the spirit of him whose death is the subject of this inquiry, I now appeal, and oh, God, let it not be in vain—save the innocent—he is not guilty—he is not guilty—he is not guilty!"

These words were pronounced with so much earnest solemnity, and in such a tone of soul-felt truth, that the feeling of the crowd, before much excited in Rowland's favour, became doubly so, and had not the judge then risen, doubtless a great outcry would have followed Miranda's words.

"Officers," said the judge, in a voice that rang loud and clear through the court, "remove that lady."

"No, no," cried Rowland, "she will now be still. If I am really standing on the brink of eternity, for a crime of which I am innocent, do not deprive me of the sight of those whom I love, and may not long look upon."

"We cannot be interrupted," said the judge. "God knows I have no desire to oppress the last hours of the prisoner, but we must not forget that this is a court of justice."

The officers, who had made a move towards Miranda, seemed now to take this as a permission for her to stay, and they fell back again to their former position, leaving her unmolested.

"Prisoner at the bar," said the judge, in a voice that slightly trembled, "have you anything to say why I should not pronounce the sentence of death upon you?"

All eyes were turned towards Rowland, who—drawing himself proudly up, while a slight flush of colour visited his cheek, and then as suddenly left it pale as before—said, in a mild, firm voice:

"I have something to say why I should not be unjustly condemned to death. It may be that the false witnesses against me will prevail—it may be that the most deep-laid awful plot that ever sprang up, like a rank weed in the brain of man, may fully succeed—for a time—for a time."

He cast his eyes upon Bernard Varley as he said these words, and the villain shrank back as if Rowland's gaze carried death with it.

"I say for a time," continued the unjustly-condemned; "for, as sure as that to-morrow's sun will light the world—as sure as that the bleak winds of winter will succeed the balmy gales of summer—as sure as there is a world beyond the grave, and a God in heaven, the blood of the murdered will rise up in judgment against the real murderer, and justice will be done. I shall be sleeping the long sleep of death. Those who love me will, perchance, have all gone to their last calm resting-place, where sorrow ceases, and the stilled heart knows no further anguish. Some there

may be of those who hear the tale of my accusation and my death, who will live to see the issue of this dark, mysterious story; but be it early, or be it late, the day of retribution will come at last. And long, long, perchance, before some human tribunal shall pronounce the doom of death upon the head of him who now hugs himself that an innocent man shall suffer for his crime, the torture, the exquisite agony, the hell of his own conscience shall begin, and, as a double murderer, shall he walk about accursed! accursed! accursed!"

The blood retreated from the heart of Bernard Varley, and then flew back with a frightful gush, as Rowland's words came upon his ears, like the voice of judgment from Heaven.

He rose from his seat, and staggered forward a pace or two. Then, as he found he could not get out of the court on account of the immense crowd which hemmed him in, he said:

"Air—air! Help! I suffocate! Save me! Air—air!"

The heat was, indeed, oppressive, and many voices joined in the same cry, but above them all rose the clear voice of Miranda, sweet as a silver bell, and making itself, in the excitement that gave it energy, heard to all above the din.

"A judgment!—a judgment!" she cried. "'Tis Bernard Varley who is my father's murderer!"

The crowd seemed to want but this as a watchword, and a hundred voices immediately shouted:

"Varley is the murderer! Varley is the murderer!"

A rush was made to where he was standing, and but for the timely intervention of the officers, who threw themselves in a body between him and his assailants, he would, no doubt, in the excitement of the moment, have met with some serious injury.

As it was, he was saved, and the judge said:

"This is too much. Officers, I must and will have the court cleared, and as many of the ringleaders in this tumult as you can secure, place in confinement."

There was something this time in the tone and manner of the judge which convinced the crowd that he was serious, and almost as frightful a rush ensued to get out of the court as before had taken place to get into it.

In obedience to a signal from the judge, the officers did not impede anyone in leaving, so that in a few moments more than two-thirds of those who had made the place so uncomfortably full were outside.

The doors were then closed immediately, and comparative comfort and quiet reigned in the court.

The judge then glanced to Rowland, as much as to say, have you finished? And the young man, understanding so, said:

"I have done. I can but assert my innocence, call upon Heaven to witness it, and implore that in its mercy it may yet save me from an unjust death."

"It is my duty," said the judge, "to pass the last dread sentence of the law upon you."

He then sat down a moment, and there was an awful period of suspense.

Miranda had buried her face in her hands, and appeared to be quite unnerved, while Mr. Percy looked at his son as well as he could through the blinding tears that rolled from his eyes—tears which he was unable to control.

Bernard Varley had shrunk back again into his seat, and, pale, ghastly, and trembling, was waiting the conclusion of this scene of woe and excitement.

There was a short, whispered conference then between the judge and the Mayor of York; after which the former placed something on the bench before him.

It was the black cap!

Most reluctant did he appear to put it on, but, at last, with a desperate determination, he placed it on his head.

A shudder passed through every heart, and then, in a voice of much emotion, the learned judge commenced:

"Prisoner at the bar,—You have had a long and, I think I am justified in saying, a most patient trial, and I do not see how, consistently with their oaths, the jury could return any other verdict than the one that they have pronounced.

"Certain facts have been distinctly sworn to, and either these witnesses are perjured, or you are, as you have been this day declared to be by the jury, a guilty man.

"My duty is now a simple, although, to me, a most grievous one. It is to pass upon you the last sentence of the law—it is my duty, and I must not shrink from it.

"There have certainly occurred, during the progress of this case, some extraordinary circumstances, and, upon the whole, I think I may call it one of the most singular cases that ever came under my notice. Nevertheless, I do not see how the evidence against you is to be got over, and we are bound to take facts, instead of and even in strong contradiction to all probabilities. I cannot help, therefore, concurring in the verdict of the jury, and I grieve to say, that I dare not hold out to you the slightest hopes of mercy on this side of the grave.

"The sentence of the court is, that you be taken now to the place from which you came, and that on Tuesday morning next you be removed to the place of common execution, and there be hanged by the neck until you be dead. May God have mercy upon your soul!"

The voice of the judge was scarcely audible as he pronounced the last few words, and, when he had done, he sank back in his chair, evidently deeply affected.

Miranda could stand this scene no longer, but springing from where she was towards the dock, she stretched out her arms to her lover, crying:

"Rowland!—Rowland! They shall not—they cannot kill you. You are innocent!"

"Miranda!" was all he could say, and reaching as far from the dock as he could, he just succeeded in clasping her hands.

One of the turnkeys advanced officiously to pull Rowland back, but the judge said suddenly:

"Officer, let the prisoner be. God help us all! we need not deprive him of one moment's joy."

"But he is innocent—he is innocent!" said Miranda. "He, Rowland Percy, murder my father? 'Tis too absurd—you cannot believe it!"

The judge rose, and, with tears in his eyes, turned to leave the bench.

"Stay, oh, stay!" cried Miranda—"but a moment—another word, and I am done. Let him live a month—a week—oh, God! be merciful."

The judge shook his head, and with a heavy heart passed out of the court.

"Come," said one of the jailers, "we can't wait here all night."

"Farewell, dear—dear Miranda!" said Rowland. "Hope still—hope still!"

"Hope, Rowland—oh, what hope have I yet to cling to?"

"Hush—hush! it may be I shall yet escape the scaffold, Miranda."

"Escape."

"Hush! we shall meet again. 'Tis a privilege not denied to the condemned to see those they love, and towards whom their hearts yearn, ere this mortal life closes on them for ever. We shall meet again, dearest one."

"I—I will be with you, Rowland. They shall not part us now. They shall kill me ere they part us, dear Rowland. I will cling to you, though the whole world should turn against you and call you guilty."

"I know you would, my Miranda—I know you would, and hence is it that death has no sting—the grave no victory. Farewell now, for a brief space."

"I cannot—cannot leave you."

"But you must," said the jailer, "this won't do. Come, young sir, we can't wait."

"One moment. Miranda, do not think too much of the mere passing pang that will take me somewhat earlier from a world that, after all, is but an abiding place for a brief season—we shall meet again, dearest, never—never to part."

"We shall, Rowland; but yet, my heart is breaking!"

"For—for my sake, Miranda, preserve more courage—I—I need support."

Miranda clung to him with a convulsive energy that he could not, without actual violence, free himself from, and, with a deep sob, he turned to his weeping father, and said:

"Father, take her—comfort her—love her, for your poor innocent Rowland's sake."

The jailer pushed slightly against Rowland's

arm, which nearly deprived Miranda of her hold of him, and she screamed loudly.

"Heaven help me!" cried Rowland; "I cannot bear this!" and disengaging himself from her frantic clutches, he added, "Father—father! to you I consign my heart's best treasure! 'Tis the only legacy your poor Rowland has to leave!"

He then resigned himself to the jailer and officers, who quickly hurried him away.

CHAPTER XLIX.

MIRANDA'S APPEAL TO THE CROWD—VARLEY'S DANGER—THE RIOT—THE PURSUIT—TWITTER'S AGONY AND ALARM.

THE Mayor of York only was on the bench during the brief and impassioned interview between Miranda and Rowland, and he had lingered with evident curiosity to watch the progress of the singular scene which was taking place—a scene singular as well on account of the relative situations of the parties concerned in it as on account of the circumstances under which it took place.

There was the daughter of the murdered man, whose death had been the subject of such solemn inquiry, clinging with all the frantic agony of despairing affection to him who, by the solemn verdict of a jury, had just been declared to be the murderer of her father, and who was condemned to suffer death for his supposed great crime.

Soon, however, the Mayor was awakened from his contemplations by a still greater source of inquietude, for when Miranda saw that Rowland was indeed taken from her, instead of, as many a commoner mind would have done, sinking into an agony of grief, a feeling of resentment rose up in her heart against him who had been the author of so much misery—against Bernard Varley.

She glanced in the direction where she had last seen the villain standing, pale and haggard, watching the face of the judge, as he pronounced the awful sentence of death upon Rowland, but she saw him not.

Then, with anxious eyes, she looked round the court, and just caught a sight of his retreating figure, followed by Twitter, as he was gliding towards the door.

In a moment she raised her voice, and pointing towards him and Twitter, she cried:

"See! see! there are the murderers! My father's blood cries for vengeance! I denounce those men as my father's murderers!"

Twitter, with a cry of terror, tried to get past Varley; but all the fury in his nature was aroused by the taunts of Miranda, coming so very near the truth, too, as they did, and he turned upon her with a face in which every demoniac passion was struggling for pre-eminence, crying:

"Miranda Rankley, you are mad! You make a bad cause worse by this affected show of violence. Rather plead for mercy, than defy and threaten."

"I do defy and threaten!" cried Miranda. "I defy villainy, and threaten guilt!"

"Indeed, I have heard that when a young maid falls so desperately in love as Miranda Rankley has done, she forgets all things but the object of her fond idolatry, clinging even to her father's murderer!"

"Do I cling to thee?" said Miranda, with a startling earnestness, that made Twitter push Varley on a pace or two, as he said:

"Oh, for Heaven's sake, come away, Varley! Do not, I pray you, stay to reason with her! Come away—oh, come away!"

"She is beautiful," muttered Varley. "She is most rare and beautiful in her passion and disdain."

"There again—there again," groaned Twitter. "He is beginning his madness!"

"Are you men?" said Miranda, turning to the throng of persons who were pressing around her. "Are you fathers? Have you warm, glowing hearts, in the inmost shrines of which you cherish holy feelings? And will you see this monstrous injustice done? Will you see the innocent condemned, while the foresworn, perjured villain walks to the home he has robbed from the destitute orphan with a smile, such as that—such as that?"

She pointed to the face of Bernard Varley, and then there was a cry from several persons of:

"Down with the villain! Down with Varley! The false witness and the murderer!"

"I tell you what it is, my good friends," said one man, "human nature is human nature, and I ask you if ever you, in all your lives, saw such a countenance as Bernard Varley's? Why, I wouldn't take his oath about the twisting the neck of a gosling."

Varley looked irresolute for a moment, whether to fly or not, but he thought to himself, "I am surely safe here, surrounded, almost, by constables, and within hail of high legal functionaries, who must protect me. I will, at least, make an effort to brave it out."

"Who dares say a word against me?" he said, aloud. "Let him beware who calls me any ill names; I have both the means, and the inclination, to punish him."

A general hoot followed this speech, and then the Mayor cried:

"Officers, clear the court."

"I am going," said Varley; "but let these hinds beware how they come within reach of my vengeance."

He turned as he spoke, and, doubtless, in the surprise of the moment, would have got clear off, had not one of the mob cried out:

"Let's show him out, at any rate, if it's only out of politeness;" and, coming forward, he was followed by a number of others, and Varley, as well as Twitter, although they were not struck, were projected into the open street with much greater speed than they had anticipated performing that transit with.

There now occurred a circumstance which had not at all entered into the calculations of Varley, namely, the appearance outside of not only all those who had left the court, from the alarming words of the judge, but a dense throng of idlers, who, in the early part of the day, had been occupied in various ways, but who now were free, and willing to take part in anything which promised diversion.

These received Varley and Twitter with open arms, and, without inquiring what offence against the majority of popular opinion they had committed, gave them so rough a reception that Varley called loudly for help.

Help, however, was far more easily called for than procured; for the constables, either from indifference or inability, in consequence of the density of the crowd, did not reach him, and he was compelled to make a desperate attempt to release himself from his persecutors.

"Gentlemen! gentlemen!" he cried, "what have I done? What have I said to any of you, that you should push me about in this way?"

"Oh! what—what—what have we done?" returned Twitter. "I'm sure we——"

What further Twitter was about to add was lost to the crowd and posterity by his hat being suddenly struck down to the very extremity of his nose, so that he was completely in the dark as regarded future proceedings, although he had a vivid perception, that directly afterwards some gentleman behind tore his coat open right up to the collar.

"Help—help—officers!" cried Varley.

He then made a desperate attempt to get back into the court, in which, however, he was completely foiled, and was at length, with a terror of death from the hands of the mob creeping over his heart, compelled to endeavour to fight and struggle his way towards the next street, which, being full of shops, he thought would afford him some sort of shelter.

The cries of the mob sounded terrible in his and Twitter's ears.

"Down with the murderers!" was shouted by hundreds of voices, and Twitter believed that his last hour was really come.

"Follow me—follow me," shouted Varley, as he struck right and left with the frantic strength lent him by despair.

It is true he overcame many, but then he was exhausting himself, while his foes sprang up each moment around him fresh and vigorous. Blows rained upon him on all sides. His coat was torn in ribbons from his back.

His voice now grew hoarse and discordant as he shrieked, rather than cried for help, while Twitter's screams as he plunged, kicked, and struggled to keep up with Varley, rose distinctly above every sound.

The tumult now had reached such a height that the magistracy felt compelled to make an effort to subdue it, and a strong body of constables were accordingly ordered to bring off Bernard Varley and Twitter, and lodge them in some place of safety, after which, in all likelihood, the crowd would, having lost the objects of its resentment, voluntarily disperse.

By this time, however, Varley and the mob had, together, got nearly to the bottom of the street in which he had first become surrounded, and he was making the most desperate efforts to turn a corner to his right, which led to a principal thoroughfare, where he hoped to find shelter, while the crowd seemed equally resolved that he should go to the left, which would conduct him to the outskirts of the city, where he would be more in their power in consequence of the more open spaces and deficient lighting.

It was at this juncture that the officers made a bold push, by forming themselves into a strong, compact body, to rescue Varley and Twitter.

The effort, however, was a vain one, for they only succeeded in getting firmly wedged among the crowd, and were carried along with it, without being able to do more than lay violent hands, if they were so minded, upon those persons who happened to be immediately next to them.

Faint, weary, bleeding, and exhausted, Varley now still pushed on, and, from the few dangerous blows he had received, it would seem as if the people were really more intent upon punishing him than taking his life, although it is rather rough work to be pushed about, hustled, struck, and half-trampled upon by a hooting, hissing crowd.

By a lucky chance for him, he was now swayed against some houses at the corner of the street, one of which was a small shop, with a glimmering light in the window of it.

There Varley cast his eyes, and, calling loudly to Twitter to follow, he tore down the few persons who were between him and the little haven of safety, and, dashing open the door, entered the humble shop.

Twitter had followed him with a degree of desperation which had enabled him to keep close to him, and he now fell on to the floor of the shop directly Varley had crossed the threshold.

There was no one but a woman in the place, and, strange to say, she did not seem in the least alarmed by the tumult, nor did she express any surprise till the entrance of Varley and Twitter caused her to utter a loud scream.

"Peace, woman—peace!" cried Varley, as he strove in vain to close the door against the mass of persons who were determined to push it open.

"Murder! fire! thieves!" cried the woman.

"Is there any backway from here?" said Twitter, in a low voice to her.

"Of course I back away for fear," replied the woman, who was one of that numerous class of deaf persons who always make a guess at what you say.

"Lost—lost!" said Varley, as he was compelled to give way at the door, and had only time to throw down a chair, over which the foremost three or four of the mob fell, which gave him a moment's time.

There was a small door at the further end of the shop, to which he now rushed, and opening it, he found that it led into a little back room, into which he dashed, still followed by Twitter, who, disfigured with blood and dust as he was, presented a most awful appearance.

The key of the door was on the inner side, and Varley's first act was to turn it in the lock.

"Help me, Twitter," he then cried, as he commenced throwing up against the door every article of furniture he could lay his hands on.

Twitter, with trembling hands, applied himself to the task, and in a few moments there was a barricade erected, which, at all events, would give the scared fugitives a few moments in which to endeavour to conceal themselves from their pursuers.

CHAPTER L.

VARLEY'S ESCAPE—THE EMPTY HOUSE—THE SOLDIERS AND THE MAYOR—THE SUPPRESSION OF THE RIOT.

A CRASH at the door, which had been barricaded, announced that his enemies were aware of where he had taken refuge, and were determined to continue the chase. It would, however, necessarily take some time to enable them to surmount the difficulties he had placed in their way, and, before that was done, there was a hope of escape.

Glancing eagerly round him in the small room, he observed another door that opened, apparently, into a narrow, dark passage.

All seemed quiet in that direction, and saying to Twitter, in a low voice, "Follow! follow!" he darted through this last doorway, and, taking the right-hand direction, pushed open another door, which conducted them into a very small garden, at the further end of which was a brick wall, the sides of the little slip of ground being only separated each way from those belonging to the neighbouring houses by slight, dilapidated palings, which were no obstacle whatever to anyone who might desire to pass them.

"This way—this way," muttered Varley, as there came upon his ears the shouts of the crowd, who were close upon his heels, and had now succeeded in removing all obstacles to entering the little back room.

"Haste! haste!" he added, as, seizing Twitter by the arm, he hurried him, half-dead as he was with terror, towards the palings on one side of the garden.

"Oh, save me! save me!" said Twitter. "What a death will this be, to be torn limb from limb by an enraged multitude—to feel oneself dying in the frightful crush! Oh, save me, Varley—save me!"

Varley replied not, but, climbing over the palings into the next garden, dragged Twitter after him, for he was most anxious to save his companion in guilt, who, he made sure, if taken in his present state of mind by the mob,

would volunteer a full confession in an attempt to save his life.

By the very dim light that shone from the evening sky, the garden in which they now were appeared in a state of utter neglect and uncultivation. What plants had been placed in it were completely choked up by rank weeds, and it was evident that the little spot of ground had not, for a long period of time, been tended by man.

"We shall be more secure here," gasped Varley. "Let us listen—let us listen!"

He grasped the arm of Twitter convulsively as he spoke, and the sounds of pursuit and shouts of anger at losing their victim came from the mob in loud denunciations upon his head.

Hundreds by this time joined the throng who were not at all aware of the slender grounds upon which Varley had first been merely hustled by the crowd, and these latter accessions to the multitude it was who were most violent, and who, in all probability, would have taken his life, hearing, as they did, that he was denounced as a murderer, and not having time to inquire how it had come about that he was known as such.

"Hunt the murderer! Hunt him! hunt him!" was the cry; and, full of terrors that he might yet fall a victim to the fury of his assailants, Varley made the best of his way to the house in the garden of which he now was.

Not a light was visible in the whole of it. It looked black and gloomy, not exhibiting the least sign of human inhabitants.

Varley tried the back door, and found it only on the latch. He then entered with a cautious step, and listened attentively; but no sound met his ears—all was still as the grave.

"Come, come," he said; "we will find refuge here."

Twitter, with a groan, followed him into the house, and Varley closed and bolted the door.

"It's—it's—very dark here," murmured Twitter.

"Darkness is better than danger," said Varley. "May my bitterest curse fall on all who have taken up the wild cry of Miranda, and followed me like bloodhounds seeking their prey!"

"We—we shall be murdered if we remain in York," said Twitter.

"Did you," asked Varley, "notice any of the faces of those who assailed us so as to be able to swear to their identity, Twitter?"

"No," groaned Twitter. "I noticed nothing—saw nothing—know nothing, but that I was upon the point of death."

"I will be revenged! I must be revenged!" growled Varley. "Am I to be hunted like a wild animal through York? By all the powers of evil I will be avenged!"

"Oh, Varley!" moaned Twitter, "be advised by me. For your own sake, as well as for mine—for your life's sake, leave York, and take up your abode somewhere far away from where you are known."

"Miranda," was Varley's brief reply.

"Can it be possible," urged Twitter, "that you can think of her with any feelings but those of deadly hate? Can you cling to a desperate passion for one who would doom you to death, if she had the power?"

"I—I cannot help it!" gasped Varley. "I love her—I love her still!"

"Oh, Varley, this is indeed infatuation!"

"It is—it is! I know it; but it is my fate, and I may not free myself from it. I love her still—I love her still!"

"But you surely must mark her deep loathing—her freely-expressed horror of you—a hatred which, on her part, is to the full as violent as her love for him who soon will be no more!"

"Name him not to me!" cried Varley, with vehemence. "Tell me not that Miranda loves him, for, although that fact is written on my brain in letters of undying flame, I cannot bear to hear it!"

"You will leave your mad pursuit, Varley?"

"With my life—with my life!"

Twitter groaned, and struck his own breast, as he said:

"Then we are lost—lost!"

"Peace, evil croaker!" said Varley. "I love her; she is my very breath of life. Oh! surely—surely some day, after, perhaps, years of privation, she may even smile upon Bernard Varley."

"Never!" cried Twitter. "Varley, upon all other matters you are clear and acute, but upon this you reason like a child. The end of all this will be destruction to us both."

"Hark—hark!"

As Varley spoke, the crowd had made their way into the garden of the next house, and their cries, shouts, and imprecations upon his head came to his ears with a painful distinctness.

Then a broad gleam of light flashed through a window of the house the fugitives were in, for the mob had procured links to aid them in their pursuit.

"They come—they come!" said Twitter. "What shall we do, Varley? What shall we do?"

"Hush—hush! They cannot know we are here. We are safe for the present. Be still."

Twitter sat down on the first of three steps which led to the front part of the house, and, rocking to and fro in an agony of terror, gave himself up to the death which he believed was really awaiting him.

Varley still stood by the door, and listened attentively to all that was passing without, and if, by one word, he could have taken the lives of everyone of the throng that had pursued him, how gladly, and with what fiendish malice, would he have spoken that word, and gloated over their destruction.

"Twitter," he said, as he heard the low moaning of his guilty comrade, "we will disguise ourselves, so that we shall not be known on Tuesday next."

"On Tuesday?"

"Ay, that will be a busy day in York."

"I dread it," said Twitter. "Something seems to tell me that, despite of all, Rowland Percy will yet triumph over us, and be saved."

Varley laughed—a short, unnatural, forced laugh—as he said:

"Then, Samuel Twitter, if Rowland Percy be saved, you will be hanged. Upon your evidence has he been committed, and nothing but your own confession that you have spoken falsely could save him now."

"You made me learn by heart the tale I was to tell," said Twitter. "I wonder I had strength to tell it."

"And so do I. But I give you great credit for your evidence, Twitter."

At this moment such a prolonged shout came from the mob, that it was evident something very particular had occurred, and such, indeed, was the fact, for the magistrates had become really alarmed at the numbers of the multitude, and the tumult that the whole city was in.

After a short consultation together, feeling the utter inefficiency of the constabulary force to subdue such a throng, the Mayor sent a message to the nearest military station, and the shout from the crowd arose from the sudden arrival of several mounted magistrates, with a troop of dragoons behind them.

Many of the crowd scampered away now that real danger presented itself, for, although they had no objection in life to hunting or persecuting anybody, they had the very strongest objection to encountering the soldiery.

The magistrates saw how quickly desertion was thinning the ranks of the mob, and purposely waited a few moments, until only the obstinate few were left to disperse, when more stringent measures would be required.

Then the Mayor, with the riot act in his hand, cried, in a loud voice:

"I call upon you all to disperse in the King's name."

"Down with Varley—down with Varley and Twitter, the murderers!" cried many voices.

"Down with the Mayor," roared a drunken cobbler, who, with his leathern apron and red nightcap, had joined the crowd. "Down with the King, and his crown, too. D—d—down with me. Down—down with everybody—down with everything!"

"Hurrah!" shouted the mob.

"Secure that fellow," said the Mayor; and several mounted police made a dash to get at the drunken cobbler, but they did not succeed, for the people near him hustled him out of the way, and finally pushed him through a parlour window, where he was perfectly safe, and accomplished one part of his wish, namely, that of being down himself.

"Once more do I call upon you to disperse," said the Mayor, "or, in pursuance of my duty, I must read the riot act, and then take violent measures to put an end to this unlawful and tumultuous proceeding."

He then commenced reading the riot act, and, as he did so, the mob slowly dispersed, so that by the time he came to the end, there were but some small knots of persons left, who exhibited the most peaceable demeanour that could well be imagined.

The Mayor laughed, as he turned to the officer in command of the dragoons, and said:

"We shall not have to trouble you, but I never saw our city in such a state of excitement; we have had a criminal trial, which has terminated contrary to the feelings and wishes of the populace. At the execution of the man who is convicted of murder, I fear we shall have some more rioting."

"You allude to the case of the murder of Sir George Rankley," said the officer.

"I do."

"It is a strange case, I am told."

"Very; but there was no getting over the evidence. It was quite clear."

Those of the rioters who had entered the house kept coming out now by twos and threes, and looking about them in very great surprise to find their companions—who, in some instances, had literally pushed them in —all gone.

The Mayor let some of them go; but he whispered to one of the police authorities to lay hold of some three or four, for the sake of example, in the morning, so that those who had emerged from the house into which they had pursued Varley and Twitter, were taken into custody, and marched off, escorted by the police and dragoons.

Where Varley had taken refuge, the magistrates did not trouble themselves to inquire, and, as he did not make his appearance, they supposed he had got housed somewhere much earlier than he really had.

The streets, so lately a scene of so much confusion, were now, for the time of the evening, much quieter than usual, for the shopkeepers had hastily closed their shutters, and decent people, who dreaded a street riot, had betaken themselves to their homes when first the tumult commenced and showed signs of being a formidable one.

It was some time, however, before Varley thought proper to venture from his hiding-place; but when he did so, he became perfectly sure that the mob had been dispersed, for perfect stillness reigned around, a stillness the more profound and remarkable, contrasted so immediately as it was with the recent scene of bustle and intense excitement.

"We are safe now, Twitter," he said. "We will now leave this friendly shelter."

"Are—are you sure?"

"Quite."

"But—but, Varley——"

"Pshaw! mobs cannot be quiet, if they would, and this was an affair in which no one or two individuals would act alone. All is still now, and we may proceed in safety. Come on—come on."

Twitter crept after Varley, who again crossed the palings into the garden of the in-habited house, and made his way to the parlour, against the door of which he had piled the woman's furniture.

The moment he made his appearance in the shop, the woman gave a loud scream, and it was in vain that Varley did all in his power to quiet her.

"Curse you," he cried, "do you want to bring a mob about your place again?"

"Murder!" cried the woman. "murder!"

Varley struck her a blow on the head, which half-stunned her for the moment, and then rushed from the shop into the now quiet and deserted street.

"Meet me to-morrow," he said to Twitter.

"At what time?"

"At two. Come to me at my lodging; and now, good-night. Such a day's work as this we shall never see again."

CHAPTER LI.

ROWLAND IN HIS CELL—THE PRISON CHAPLAIN—THE PROPHECY OF BOLD HAWK.

WHO can picture the feelings of poor Rowland Percy when he was removed from the court with the sentence of death hanging over his innocent head?

He began almost to think that the rapid events which had cast him down, as it were, from "a pleasant height of joy," could not be real, and that he must surely be suffering under some mental delusion which presented to him all the frightful images by which he had been and was surrounded.

He was placed in a cell of very small dimensions, and as it was not then the practice for anyone to torture the last moments of a condemned criminal, by sitting with him and watching his every look and gesture, Rowland had, at least, the comfort of being alone, if he could not have with him those he loved.

"God of Heaven," he cried, "when will all this end? Is this frightful tragedy really to terminate on a scaffold? Am I—innocent, even in thought of the crime laid to my charge—to suffer the most ignominious of deaths in a Christian country, where the meanest animal that crawls is believed to be protected from wanton cruelty, if it be not really so? Can it be possible that such a monstrous injustice can ensue? Surely, surely not; and yet I have heard and read of such things as the innocent suffering death, and then, years afterwards, when their remains have mouldered to corruption in the damp of the grave, their innocence has, by some strange accident, become apparent to the wonder of all men. Good Heaven! am I doomed to be one of these frightful examples of human fallibility? Oh, hard, cruel fate. Miranda—Miranda! What will become of thee? Unfriended, alone, and deprived of that wealth which should have placed you at least above the fear of that most sad aggravation of all other ills, poverty. What? Oh, what will become of thee, my own, my beautiful, my fond, trusting Miranda?"

These thoughts were sad and bitter ones for the prisoner in his lonely dungeon, and he sat himself down upon the solitary wooden seat, with which it was furnished, giving himself up for a time to grief, that was not for himself, but for her—the good and beautiful—whom he was denied by inexorable fate, the, to him, high and grateful privilege of guarding from the storms of fate, and protecting through the weary pilgrimage of life.

More than an hour passed thus, and then he was aroused by having the door of his cell opened, and immediately closed again.

He looked up, and saw before him a mild, gentlemanly-enough-looking man, dressed in black, who, when he saw that he was regarded by Rowland, said, in a voice that had a slight twang of the conventicle in it:

"My dear sir, I hope you will receive my visit with the same pure feelings and pious hopes that dictate it."

"Who are you, sir?" said Rowland.

"I am the chaplain of this place."

"I can have no objection, sir, to a visit from any gentleman who comes to me in courtesy," said Rowland. "But before you say another word, I tell you plainly and distinctly, that I am an innocent man, and, therefore, require no further spiritual consolation or hope than I have been accustomed to cherish in my heart as a consequence of my profound and deep appreciation of the goodness and justice of Heaven."

The clergyman shook his head, and with more of a whine than even he had used before, he said:

"Oh, young man, repent—repent."

"I am innocent," said Rowland, "if you allude to the crime for which I am so unjustly condemned. If you allude to the necessity of repentance for many other errors, venial perhaps, but still errors in the pure sight of Heaven, I do repent me, and have ever acknowledged them to God."

"But, young man, I fear your heart still yearns towards the world and its vain creatures."

"It does yearn to the world, and to some of God's creatures that inhabit it—creatures of His that He has made beautiful and good, that they might be loved with such love as I shall carry to my grave."

The chaplain gave a deep groan.

"Quite understand me, sir," added Rowland, "I will hold no sort of conversation or communication with anyone who comes here presuming me guilty."

"Harden not your heart, young man."

"I don't understand you, sir."

"You will find that you will be welcomed to another world by ten thousand angels to realms of bliss, if you will cast from you all earthly feelings, and live only for the life which is to come."

"Sir, sir," cried Rowland. "Here am I an innocent man—condemned to death for a crime I shudder at. Is it fair—is it just—is

it religious that I should be tormented in my last few hours by implied doubts of my solemn assertions of innocence and innuendos of my guilt?"

The chaplain looked rather confounded at this, and, muttering to himself something about a hardened sinner, he left Rowland to his own meditations, with a resolution of attacking him again when his mind should be more enervated from his confinement.

And what were the sad thoughts of Miranda on the morning of that eventful and terrible day which had begun in doubt, mingled with hope, but had ended in despair?

There was no comfort to offer her, for what could even the kind heart of Mr. Anderson invent that could give her one solitary ray of hope? He felt that nothing short of some special interposition of Providence could save from his most undeserved fate the innocent Rowland, for his (Mr. Anderson's) belief in his innocence was as firm as Miranda's.

The words of the judge had held out no hope of a mitigation of the sentence. Either some discovery of Twitter's and Varley's perjury must take place, or Rowland must fall a victim to the too-successful conspiracy against his existence.

Mr. Anderson could only clasp the hand of Miranda, and beg of her again to come to his house, but she clung to old Mr. Percy, saying, in a voice of deep dejection:

"No—no, I will not bring sorrow into your dwelling, Mr. Anderson. Such deep grief as mine should court solitude, and not obtrude itself upon others. Heaven reward you for all you have done for the innocent."

Mr. Anderson was deeply affected by her tone and manner, so much so, indeed, that he could not command his voice sufficiently to speak, and the counsel for Rowland, who had been unrobing, coming up at the moment, saw the agitated little group, which he immediately joined, saying:

"Do not yet despair. I advise a memorial to be got up to the Secretary of State, setting forth the strange conduct of Varley and Twitter at the trial; their previous bad character and motives for themselves committing the murder, and then accusing an innocent man."

"Oh, sir," cried Miranda, clinging to his arm, "is there still hope?"

"While there is life, certainly," replied the counsel. "I declare to you all that I have a most perfect conviction of the innocence of Mr. Rowland Percy."

"Heaven bless you for those words," said Miranda. "He is innocent, indeed he is."

"I firmly believe it, and, as there is guilt somewhere, between ourselves I think all our suspicions point to the right quarter."

"I know it, I know it," added Miranda. "From the first it seemed to me as if a voice from Heaven cried to me, 'Behold in Bernard Varley the murderer of your father.'"

"Let me advise you now to go home," said the counsel. "Leave to me the preparation of the memorial, which I will undertake to

THE ARREST OF THE RIOTERS.

have forwarded to London by an express within two hours, and should an answer not come by Tuesday morning, I have no doubt but the judge will himself grant a temporary respite till Wednesday."

Miranda looked in the face of the counsel as he spoke, and she saw a glistening tear in his eye, as he returned her gaze.

A convulsive sob burst from her heart, and she said :

"All can weep for my poor Rowland, but myself. Tears are denied to me, and yet, oh, Heaven! what sorrow sits brooding at my heart."

"Let your motto be Hope, Miss Rankley.

I will now hasten to prepare the memorial."

He shook hands kindly with the heart-stricken girl, and then hurried away to perform his self-imposed task, while Miranda, with a feeling of hope newly awakened in her breast, accompanied old Mr. Percy to his humble home, while Mr. Anderson walked with them to the door.

As Miranda turned upon the threshold to bid him adieu, she saw standing close to her the poor idiot Bold Hawk, who had so strangely interested himself in the fate of the unfortunate Rowland.

He laid one finger lightly upon her arm.

while he lifted his other hand above his head, and said:

"He will be saved. He will be saved!"

Miranda was interested by the manner of the poor creature, and in her distress and despair, even words of hope from such as he were sweet and welcome to her ears, even as the fond parent or lover, when the object of boundless affection lies stricken by disease, and expiring, will listen with eager confidence to the wildest empiric, who will promise restoration.

"Who—who will be saved?" she said.

"Rowland Percy. He who has a hand open as the day, and a heart as kind as summer's sunshine. He will be saved—he will be saved."

"All love him," faltered Miranda. "Even this poor creature, whose immortal part seems wrapped in strange mists, even he is sensible of Rowland's innocence."

"I know it," resumed the idiot. "Some call me Martin, but my real name is Bold Hawk, because I can look at the sun and the twinkling stars without winking. You understand me? Sometimes at night when all the tiny lamps of Heaven are lighted in the deep blue sky, I go out into the pleasant fields, and I lie me down upon the dewy grass. Held up am I then by a world to look to the Heaven above it. Then—ha! ha! ha! then Bold Hawk asks questions of the stars, and in their way they answer him.'

There was a wild and beautiful romance in his language that interested Miranda, despite her better reason; but the heart is never so ready to bend to superstitious impressions as when it is a prey to great grief, and is suffering much oppression.

"Go on," she said. "Tell me what they said of Rowland Percy?"

"Ah, they spoke of him. I'll tell you how. You have marked the broad starry belt that goes across the sky—they call it the milky way, because such floods of pale starlight are over and about it, that it glows with a faint beauty, outshining all the firmament beside?"

"I have. I have."

"Of those small stars I ask my questions, and when I do so, they dance before my eyes for awhile, like motes in the sunbeams, until they arrange themselves into some word, which give me an answer."

"And thus you saw——"

"That he would be saved. I did—I did, and I saw that Bernard Varley would be hanged at York. Hanged at York, surrounded by such a shouting, screaming crowd, as never yet awakened echoes in the ancient city."

"It may be in the mysterious ways of Providence," said Miranda, "that even such a one as this poor mindless man may be gifted with a prophetic knowledge of coming events. Heaven grant it may be so."

"Let there be peace here," said the idiot, indicating with his finger Miranda's breast. "Let there be peace here, for all shall be well. He shall be saved. The stars have said it, and who shall gainsay them?"

"I thank you for your kind wishes," said Miranda.

"Speak again—speak again, lady. Your voice is music to Bold Hawk."

"Good night," said Miranda.

"You neither hoot at me, nor pelt me with stones," he added. "You don't belong to this world. Ah, no, for real human creatures are cruel, revengeful, malicious, and always torment me when they can. They say I am mad, and if it be so, 'tis a sore affliction from God. Then why should I be hooted at and stoned at? Heaven help me, and save me from human beings. The dogs are kind to me. A horse will not kick me more readily than anyone else. No, no. 'Tis only human creatures, made in the image of God, and endowed with heavenly intellect, that persecute poor Bold Hawk!"

CHAPTER LII.

THE TEMPORARY RESPITE—MIRANDA AND THE JUDGE—THE PRISON ORDER—THE MEMORIAL.

THE counsel who had promised Miranda that he would prepare a memorial to the Secretary of State, praying for a postponement of Rowland's execution, was as good as his word. He lost no time in the preparation of the document. His object was to get to it, before dispatching it, the signatures of some of the leading members of the circuit, who had been present at the trial, and whose joining in such a request might have considerable effect upon the mind of the Secretary of State.

Such signatures he readily obtained, for, to say the least of it, almost every lawyer he spoke to considered the case a most serious one, and that there must surely be yet something behind hand which was strongly for or against the prisoner.

Varley's own counsel, now that the case was over, and he had, as he considered, done his duty, did not refuse his name to the memorial, remarking that he should be as happy as anyone at any new fact being elicited which should save the unhappy young man from the ignominious death to which he seemed absolutely doomed.

Lastly, then, the counsel repaired to the lodgings of the judge, whom he made no scruple of awakening, although the hour was most unseasonable.

That he, the judge, was humane and considerate the counsel well knew, and could he induce him to grant the delay prayed for, he felt how much anxiety would be spared to the prisoner and his friends; but even should the judge feel that his duty would not allow him to grant the temporary respite, still, there could be no doubt but, upon such a representation from the most respectable of the bar, he would consent to such a postponement of the sentence as should enable the answer of the Secretary of State to arrive, which it could scarcely do by the time appointed for the execution—seeing that it was then Sunday morning.

The judge heard the counsel with patience, and read attentively the memorial. Then turning to his visitor, he said, in a mild, compassionate voice:

"Believe me, my dear sir, talking to you now in a friendly way, which, now that the trial is over, I can do, I give you the greatest credit for your humanity and kind consideration in this case; but I am decidedly of opinion that you are awakening hopes in the mind of the prisoner, and his friends, which cannot be realized."

"While there is life there is hope," said the counsel, "and my opinion of his innocence is so strong, that I expect everything from delay. Some fortunate accident may save him."

The judge shook his head, as he said:

"You speak more like a friend than a lawyer. You must know there is no getting over the evidence."

"If these men, Twitter and Varley, are perjured."

"If they are," responded the judge. "How are we to know? Heaven only can see into men's hearts. The prisoner, you see, himself admits everything up to the very point where their evidence begins. They then circumstantially accuse him of a monstrous crime, and all he has to say is, 'I did not do it.'"

"The case is certainly strong, but I believe him to be the victim of as base a conspiracy as can be imagined."

"We cannot listen, in courts of justice, to anything but sworn evidence. I cannot, consistently with my duty, recommend the prisoner to mercy. I cannot—I cannot! I dare not."

"At least, then, my lord, let me hope that you will postpone the execution till Wednesday, in order to allow time for the answer of the Secretary of State to come?"

"Certainly I will do that, in deference to your own feelings, and those of the gentlemen who have signed this memorial. I will, notwithstanding the very few precedents we have for such a course, respite the prisoner until Thursday morning, which will give ample time."

"We are much beholden to you, my lord," said the counsel, "and I pray that Heaven, between this time and that, will in some manner interpose to save the innocent."

"If he be innocent, I echo your prayer with all my heart and soul," said the judge; "and now, before we part, can you give me any information as to who that mysterious person is, and what might be the nature of his connection with this case, the very mention of whom, without a name, caused such extraordinary emotion in the heart of the prosecutor?"

"That," replied the counsel, "is a mystery I would fain solve, and a most earnest and anxious search shall be instituted for him immediately. If found, he shall, by every means, be urged to come forward on oath with all he knows."

"Then your knowledge of him really extends no further than you were able to give at the trial?"

"No further, my lord. It appears this man, the very mention of whom excites such emotions of terror in the breast of Varley, accosted the attorney for the defence in the street, and desired that the question might be propounded as you heard me put it. Therefore, I asked the question, with a hope that he who suggested it would come forward, if its effect answered his expectations."

"Well, there is a mystery somewhere, and that it may be unravelled favourably to the prisoner is my earnest prayer. I need not say that upon any affidavit, altering the complexion of the case, being sworn before me, I will immediately extend the respite in order that a searching investigation of its truth may be made."

The counsel could not but be satisfied with the judge's conduct, and, thanking him warmly for his kindness, he bowed and left him, pleased that some time had been gained.

His next visit was to Mr. Anderson, who had arranged the means of sending the memorial immediately to London.

The moment the counsel entered the room, Mr. Anderson, with a pleasurable excitement of manner he could not conceal, handed to him an open note.

It was addressed to him, Mr. Anderson, and contained these words:

"Meet the solitary horseman to-night in the bridle-path leading from York to the Grange."

"Thank Heaven!" said the counsel. "This man will make himself visible at last. Meet him? I'd travel a thousand miles to find him. He must know something important, or Varley would never have exhibited the terror he did at his mention."

"I hope he does," said Mr. Anderson. "He gives no precise time in his note, so, I presume, I must go about sunset, and await his coming."

"I will accompany you," said the counsel.

"Do so. We mean him well, and, in fact, we could not take any advantage of his presence if we would, for an unwilling witness would be of no use. But what about the memorial?"

The counsel then detailed his proceedings, terminating with his interview with the judge, when he concluded by saying:

"It is important now that the prisoner and his friends should clearly understand the precise signification of this respite, and not be deluded into too much hope from it. I will myself proceed to the prison, if you will undertake to explain the matter fully to Mr. Percy and Miranda Rankley."

"That I will do," responded Mr. Anderson. "This note from the mysterious man has given me new hope. I will, however, say nothing of it to Miranda, as it would only cause her the most intense anxiety and surmise."

"Which, indeed, she may well be spared. I will trespass upon you, Mr. Anderson, for a breakfast, as I see the morning is close at hand."

* * * * *

The morning sun was shining in at the window of the room where sat Miranda, when Mr. Anderson was announced. She descended the staircase rapidly, and pausing for a moment ere she opened the door of the little parlour, into which, by the courtesy of the people of the house, he had been shown, she then, with as much composure as she could assume, entered the room.

He took her extended hand silently, and then led her to a seat, while she looked up in his face with such a sweet beseeching glance, to read therein if any new hope for Rowland had arisen, that the kind-hearted man had much ado to command his voice to any degree of firmness, as he said, in a low tone:

"The memorial has been sent to London, Miranda."

"Yes—yes," said Miranda, in a half-choked voice. "Surely it will save him."

"Hope without being too sanguine, Miranda. We must all bow to Heaven's decrees, and yet we should always hope."

"Always," gasped Miranda. "Always till death."

"The judge has kindly granted a delay."

A slight cry of joy escaped Miranda's lips, as she convulsively seized Mr. Anderson by the arm, saying:

"The—the judge—delay. They will not then murder him—I thought they were human, and could not."

"Hush—hush, Miranda. For Heaven's sake do not misconstrue my words—I said delay—delay only."

"Yes—yes—I heard—delay is life. Dear, precious life. What is a long existence, but a little delay ere the dawn of an eternity bursts upon the soul. They will not murder him. Oh, Mr. Anderson, you are not feeding my heart with false hopes. You said delay—you did."

"I did, Miranda, but I pray you do not give the word a wider signification."

"No—no—I will be calm—quite calm. How—long?"

"Till Thursday."

"Thursday—Thursday?"

"Yes, so as to give full time for the answer of the Secretary of State to come, which may grant yet further time."

"God help them all," said Miranda. "They are trifling with that gift of God's, which when once thrown back to Him may never—never be reclaimed—life—life. The life of the innocent—the good—the gentle. 'Tis very gracious of them not yet to dip their hands in his blood. God forgive them—God forgive them."

"Indeed, Miranda," said Mr. Anderson, who was sorry to find her in such a frame of mind, "there is nothing but sympathy and good wishes to Rowland among high and low."

"Sympathy—sympathy, and yet they will murder him while Heaven looks down upon the deed."

"Miranda! Miranda!"

A shudder came across her frame.

"Forgive me—forgive me," she said, in a low, plaintive tone. "I will bless thee for letting my Rowland live even another day. But he is innocent, and sometimes my heart will swell till it is nigh bursting, and you see, Mr. Anderson, I have no tears—I cannot weep, so the vexed spirit shows itself in bitterness. Thank Heaven he will live till Thursday. That is a boon—a great boon, for I shall be nearer death myself ere we part."

"Far be it from me, Miranda," said Mr. Anderson, with emotion, "to awaken too much hope in your breast; but, still, dark and gloomy as the prospect around you seems, I would not have you despair."

Miranda gave him her hand, as she said:

"I ought not, indeed, to despair, while I have such hearts as yours to feel for my distress. I am very ungrateful, Mr. Anderson, but you will forgive me?"

"It would be a poor heart, indeed, Miranda, that paused for words and expressions of gratitude from a wounded spirit such as yours. What I do, I do from a deep and sincere sympathy for one who, from my heart, I believe as innocent of the crime for which he now lies condemned as I am myself. Heaven help both him and you."

"In all affliction," said Miranda, "we may see the hand of Heaven in some ray of mercy—some gleam of light mingling with the otherwise universal desolation around us—a something which robs pain of its sting—a rest for the wounded heart. In my misery, in my heart's sadness and affliction, you have been to me that one bright spot which has saved me from utter annihilation and despair."

Mr. Anderson was very much affected, for Miranda pronounced these words with such exquisite pathos, such a majesty of feeling, and such a purity of candour, that it is impossible we can give any idea of her manner by description.

He turned aside for a moment to hide one tear that would, despite his efforts to control it, roll down his cheek, and then partially mastering his emotion, he said:

"I will leave you to tell Mr. Percy of this trifling change in the immediate aspect of affairs, Miranda, and again I reiterate my offer of my home for yourself and poor Mr. Percy."

"You have my heart's best thanks," said Miranda; "but let us be here, where we can cast no shadows upon the domestic joy of any house. Here we can talk to each other of Rowland, and when the old man weeps for his dear son, I can talk to him of hope, and chase away the tears. Let us be where we are, Mr. Anderson. It is better—believe me it is—far better."

"At all events, Miranda, it is a point upon which I have no right to press you, and I can only say that my offer still remains open whenever you please to accept of it, and, believe me, it is made with all sincerity."

"I know it—I know it," said Miranda. "Now tell me when—oh! when can I see Rowland?"

"There will be no difficulty now, Miranda. There are stated hours for visiting prisoners; but in the case of you, as well as in that of Mr. Percy, the judge will not scruple to give you an order to see Rowland when you please, during the hours that the prison is open for ingress or egress at all."

"The judge!—he who condemned my poor Rowland. Yet he wept, and none save I saw him weep."

"A more compassionate man never lived. The duty is a most painful one to him. I will get an order from him for you to visit Rowland."

A faint hope came across Miranda's heart, that if she had an interview with the judge, she might possibly move him to look upon the case somewhat differently—she might suggest something he had not thought of. Acting upon this impulse of the moment, she said:

"Would he see me?"

"Doubtless he would," replied Mr. Anderson. "However he might wish to avoid what to him and yourself might be a painful interview, he would not refuse."

"Time was," said Miranda, while a faint flush of colour visited her cheeks, "when I would have shrunk from inflicting an interview upon anyone in the least averse to it, but the most timid grow bold when those they love are in great peril, and it seems to me now as if the ordinary feelings which I possessed were all overcome by the one great object of my soul—the persecution of Rowland. I will see the judge, Mr. Anderson, even should he accord to me an unwelcome interview—still will I see him."

"You will receive nothing but courtesy from him, at all events; but if you do call upon him, let it be this evening when the court closes."

"Cannot I go now, for I would fain visit Rowland ere then?"

"Yes, certainly; any time within the next hour and a-half he will see you, I daresay, and now I bethink me, perhaps he would rather in the morning than in the evening. If you say you will be ready in half-an-hour, I will come again, and take you to where he is staying."

Miranda rose with more animation than she had for some time exhibited, as she said:

"Yes; let it be so. I will be ready."

Mr. Anderson, when he reached the street, felt rather pleased than otherwise that she had determined herself to solicit the order of the judge, for the effort appeared to arouse her from the state of deep despondency into which, when inactive, she seemed, from the pressure of her sorrows, inclined to fall.

—

CHAPTER LIII.

THE "YORK ARMS"—THE CONSULTATION—HONOUR AMONG THIEVES—DICK PALMER'S PROPOSAL.

WHILE this conversation was proceeding between Miranda and Mr. Anderson, there was scarcely a small public-house in York that had not its little knot of eager talkers on the all-engrossing subject of popular interest—namely, the preceding day's trial. The great man of every parlour—and there is a great man to every parlour—became tremendously oracular, and many were the opinions hazarded, pro and con, upon the subject.

With only one of these little throngs of persons, however, have we anything to do, and that was assembled in a dim, back parlour of a public-house, known as the "York Arms," and situated in an out-of-the-way, curious street, where it could not be supposed that any business would be done, and it was a wonder to every person how the "York Arms" continued to keep its doors open, and to maintain its thriving, bustling look.

The fact was, that the house had its regular customers—customers of a peculiar class—who, getting money lightly—somewhat in the style, and after the fashion, of our friend, Dick Palmer—spent it as lightly, to the great content of the landlady, who was one of those masculine females, who certainly do not depend upon the weakness of their sex for protection.

In this back parlour there was a collection of some twelve or fourteen persons, who, while they indulged themselves very freely with strong ale, argued and re-argued the trial and its result with noisy pertinacity.

"The jury be bothered!" said one. "He didn't do it. I'll lay my life on it he didn't."

"Oh, what a werry slippery sneak that 'ere Samivel Twitter is, to be sure—all on one end—kivey, kim up!" exclaimed the witness, Job Jackson, *alias* Jones, who, on the trial, had deposed to several little disagreeable particulars with respect to Twitter's early life and pursuits, and had afterwards so effectually got the better of the counsel for the prosecution.

What he meant by "kivey, kim up!" nobody ever knew; and it was only supposed that he used these euphonious words as a kind of garnish to his discourse, instead of an oath.

"You may say that," remarked another gentleman in a white top-coat, and an awful black eye. "Look at my *hi*."

"How comed you by that 'ere?"

"Guved it to me out o' a mistake."

"Gentlemen," said Dick Palmer, advancing from a dark corner, and taking a seat near the fire, "we all seem in one mind about this affair. That young man never did the murder, and it will be a murder to hang him for it."

"So it will," said several.

"Howsumdever, swing will he, and no mistake," remarked Jones: "kivey, kim up."

"Unless——"

Palmer paused, and a dead silence pervaded the room, for everyone was anxious to hear what he had to say.

"Unless," he continued, "we get somebody to confess who really did it, comrades."

"We?" said several.

"Yes," resumed Palmer; "I said we, when I ought, perhaps, not to have done so; but it does so happen that I have seen and heard perhaps more of this affair than most men in York, who really know so little of it. We all know what Twitter is. We all know what he would lend himself to. He didn't do the murder—he hasn't courage and nerve enough, but——"

"But what, Dick?" said Jones. "Yer goes on a speaking as if yer was a bolting hot peas, and some on 'em sticked in the vay."

"But I think he, Twitter, might be frightened into confessing the real truth."

"You may frighten Twitter into confessing a lie," remarked a man in a surly voice, who had not yet spoken. "That's the risk of meddling with such fellows."

"Granted," said Dick; "but such a man as Twitter——"

"A sneak, yer means," interposed Jones.

"Well, well, such as he, if frightened into confessing a lie, if he thought it was what was wanted of him, would not have cunning enough in his fright to make it tally with circumstances already known past dispute; whereas, if he told a tale that really did come in well, there would be every probability of its truth, do you see?"

"My eye," exclaimed Jones; "Dicky, yer can come it above a bit. A lawyer with a *hextra* wig is a fool to yer; kivey, kim up."

"You see my position," said Palmer.

"And we feels it, too," replied Jones, "for you're a kivering up all the fire."

"Jones," said Palmer, "none of your nonsense. You are not over particular in some matters, as we all know, but I never yet knew you to do a downright sneaking action. I am not joking, my friends. I wish you to agree with me—some of you to undertake this job of frightening Twitter. I can pounce upon him at any time."

"What's the good to us?" growled one.

"A thousand pounds divided among all who have any hand in the affair, provided it saves the life of Rowland Percy," said Dick Palmer, in a clear voice.

There was a silence of some moments among the gentlemen, and then Jones gave a long whistle, and exclaimed:

"Say it again, Dicky."

"A thousand pounds to be divided among us," repeated Dick Palmer, emphatically.

"How many will it take to do the job?"

"Two or three might manage it easily; but, as we are all here, why, let us act fairly towards each other, and divide it."

"Well said—well said," cried several.

"Stop a bit—stop a bit," said Jones. "Kivey, kim up! who's to pay the blunt?"

"I will undertake that it shall be paid. Listen to me, friends. What we say here among ourselves will go no further, I am quite confident. Now, I am convinced that the murder of Sir George Rankley has a good deal to do with the disposition of his large property, and that a discovery of who really did the deed will, in all probability, in one way or another, alter the disposition of that property very considerably."

"Go on—go on," said Jones, "go on, my oracle. It's as good as a sermon, it is."

"Well, then," resumed Dick Palmer, "I am quite certain that the reward I have named will be forthcoming, and rather increased than diminished."

"Very good," said Jones. "Now, how's it to be done, Dick?"

"Leave that to me. Agree among yourselves that some four or five are to meet me for the purpose of undertaking the job, and I will manage everything else. I wish that number of you to come, because we ought to have ample evidence, by a number of witnesses, of anything that Twitter, in his fright, may reveal."

"Agreed—agreed!" cried several.

"Then," said Dick, as he rose to leave the room, "let it be this evening. You know the green lane that leads out by the new cottages on the south side of the city?"

"Yes—yes."

"Meet me there, then, one hour after sunset this evening, and I will undertake to bring Twitter to you."

He then left the house, and, although his scheme for attempting to discover the truth, as regarded the murder, was something of the wildest, yet it was the only one that occurred to him by which he could hope to carry any information worth the hearing or bearing to Mr. Anderson, should he keep the appointment made for that same evening in the bridle-path leading to the Grange estates.

Palmer had taken a great and absorbing interest in the fate of Miranda and her lover; for, although his notions as to the rights of property were of a very loose description, he was like many other persons in this world, who feel particularly shocked at any species of iniquity but the one which long usage has made them familiar with.

The offer of the thousand pounds was a step ventured upon by Dick Palmer from a conviction that, should the result of the experiment be to implicate Varley in the murder and so release Rowland Percy, something would arise to restore to Miranda the property which had been wrested from her; for, at the worst, even if the will could not be attacked, even should there be no evidence to prove it a forgery, in the event of Varley's conviction for the murder, the property would revert from his hands to the Crown, when, without the shadow of a doubt, Miranda would be permitted, as the real heiress, to take quiet possession, and her ability and inclination to pay the thousand pounds would be as equal as undoubted.

Dick Palmer's object now was to make

sure of the presence of Twitter at the appointed spot, and that he thought he should have no difficulty in doing, as he held in his possession funds belonging to the valet, which were the result of sales of plate, etc., effected by him, Palmer, in London, for Twitter.

The highwayman knew that avarice was the reigning passion of the guilty wretch, and he wrote him the following note, which he knew, if anything, would bring him to the place of appointment:

"Samuel Twitter,—You know who has money for you, if you will meet him this evening, an hour and a-half after sunset, half-way up the green lane, where he met you once before, on the south of the city. Be punctual."

This note he sealed, and sent to the lodgings which had been jointly occupied by Twitter and Varley, but which, owing to the wild, maniacal manner in which Bernard Varley haunted Miranda's steps, had been now for some days in the sole possession of Twitter.

No invitation could be more welcome to him, Twitter, than one from which money was to result, for he had become so thoroughly and dreadfully alarmed at the infatuation of Bernard Varley, with regard to Miranda, that he had determined, in his own mind, to gather together, as quickly as possible, by every means in his power, as large a sum of money as he could, and leave England, to avoid the danger which, like the sword of Damocles, he believed to be hanging over his head from the indiscretion of his companion in guilt, whose very intellect seemed to suffer from the excess of his passion for her who was his victim.

CHAPTER LIV.

MIRANDA'S INTERVIEW WITH THE JUDGE—THE ORDER—THE VISIT TO THE PRISON.

Mr. Anderson returned to the humble abode of Miranda at the expiration of the appointed time, in order to conduct her to the judge's lodgings, in compliance with her wish.

He found her ready for the street, and after a few moments' conversation with old Mr. Percy, during which he seemed to be so much depressed as scarcely to be conscious of what he was saying, the benevolent attorney and his beautiful client departed arm-in-arm, on the errand which Miranda had a vague hope might possibly result in something beneficial to Rowland, and which Mr. Anderson was sure could do no harm, if it did no real good.

The distance was far from great, but there was one circumstance which made it wearisome and full of excitement of the most painful nature. That was the fact that she had not proceeded with Mr. Anderson a dozen paces from the door of the house in which she resided, ere Bernard Varley had left the window opposite, from which he had been

watching her movements, and hurrying to the street, followed her at a distance only of ten or twelve paces.

Mr. Anderson first saw Varley, and it was the sudden start of surprise that he gave which made Miranda cast her eyes in the direction of her arch enemy.

She shuddered and clung closer to Mr. Anderson, as she whispered to him:

"That dreadful man! my soul's enemy—my father's murderer—the prosecutor of my betrothed husband; he follows me like an evil genius. Oh, Mr. Anderson, think you he is really human?"

"I am sorry to say I do," replied Mr. Anderson; "but heed him not, Miranda. If I mistake not, that man, with all his villainy, has not the power to inflict upon his greatest victim one tithe of the misery that rends his own heart, and makes him the miserable, despicable wretch his appearance at once indicates."

"Heaven save me from him!" said Miranda.

"If ever," added Mr. Anderson, "a human being suffered in this world for his crimes, that man suffers: he carries the index of it in his face, he betrays it in every movement. I do verily believe that his wild attachment, if I may give it that name, to you is a retribution from Heaven against him, for it can bring him no feeling but despair."

"And yet—oh, yet," said Miranda, "I would it were not so. I fear him, while I loathe him."

"Fear him not, Miranda. He dare not even annoy you; but there is one piece of advice which I would give you in the present juncture of affairs, which, however unpalatable it may be to you, and I confess disagreeable to me, I ought to give you, for the sake of him in whose fate we are all so deeply and feelingly, but you most of all, Miranda, interested."

"You speak of Rowland?"

"I do."

"What advice, Mr. Anderson, would you give me? Coming from you, I am sure of its value and its sincerity."

"If my advice to you, Miranda, was as valuable as from my heart it is sincere, I should be rejoiced; but what I have to say concerns that man whose eyes are now glaring upon you, and whose whole guilty soul seems engrossed in watching your every movement."

"Concerns him?"

"Yes, Miranda. He is evidently labouring under an infatuation which may for a time overcome his caution. Should he, some of these times, speak to you, and make wild and strange proposals, I would advise, while you abate not one jot of your aversion—while you still show him by every word and every look what an abhorred thing he is to you—to listen to him."

"Listen to Bernard Varley?"

"Yes, Miranda. Some chance word—some wild chance assertion or promise of his may give us a clue which, if properly followed up, might possibly change the present sad aspect of affairs, and open Rowland's prison gates. You understand me, Miranda?"

"I do—I do! For Rowland's sake, I will even listen to Bernard Varley. Your advice is kindly offered, Mr. Anderson. I will strive to act upon it."

"We should neglect no chance of righting the innocent, and the justice of Heaven may make itself manifest in this transaction, by, after all, out of his own mouth, convicting him."

"It may—it may! I will not yet abandon hope."

They had now reached the judge's door, and Bernard Varley seemed in a moment to guess that Miranda's walk was ended there, for he crossed to the opposite side of the way, and, stepping into a doorway, he folded his hands upon his breast, and, with eyes from which shone a wild and unholy lustre, watched the beautiful form of her he loved, and yet had worked so much woe to, till it disappeared within the house.

"She is more beautiful than daylight," he muttered. "The sun that shines upon her has its beams reflected back with tenfold loveliness. Her voice is like the gentlest music. Oh, how blessed must be he who hears it in accents of tenderness? Who can help loving her? The very air around her is glowing as if with a divine halo, created by her pure breath, made glorious and beautiful by her rare loveliness. Miranda—Miranda! if I could win you, I would renounce all else. The world contains no other charms to bind me to it. Thou, and thou only, art the one blessing my heart covets. Can it be possible that such love as mine is in vain? Miranda, Miranda—beautiful being—beautiful in thy pride—beautiful in thy scorn—but most of all beautiful in thy sorrow! I would for thy dear sake consent to die, if that a smile from thy lips lit with beauty the last convulsive throb that parted me from life."

With clasped hands and upturned eyes he stood like one possessed, awaiting the re-appearance of her who was at once his only dream of joy, and his bitterest curse.

In the meanwhile Mr. Anderson had accompanied Miranda into a waiting-room, whence he sent up a card, on which he wrote Miranda's name, with a request for a brief interview.

An answer was speedily brought from the judge to the effect that he would see Miss Rankley in a few moments. Those few moments rapidly glided by, and then a servant came to conduct the beautiful girl to the presence of the man who, in pursuance of his sad duty, had been compelled to condemn her Rowland to a shameful and ignominious death.

Her heart palpitated painfully in her bosom as she entered the room, and every object for a moment seemed to swim before her. Then a kind, soft, musical voice said to her:

"Miss Rankley, pray be seated. I shall be most happy to comply with any request, consistent with my duty, which you may have come here to make to me."

She glanced at the face of the judge, and she saw that it was full of humanity and kindly feelings. Then, making an effort to recover herself, she said, in those low, sweet accents that reach the heart:

"Sir, my errand here is but to solicit your leave to visit him who now lies condemned——"

She paused, and the judge said, kindly:

"You want an unconditional order to see Rowland Percy?"

"Yes," said Miranda, "and—and——"

"Pray take your time, and tell me, without reservation, what you wish."

"I wish," said Miranda, "now that I am here, to tell you how truly, how firmly I am convinced of the innocence of him who is condemned for my father's murder. Oh, sir, can you believe for one moment that I, who loved my father so fondly, could think and speak as I do of his murderer? Nature would cry out against me—reason would shame me —imagination would terrify me. He is innocent—he is indeed innocent!"

The judge was silent for a moment, and then he said, in a tone of quiet consideration:

"That you are sincere in what you say Heaven forbid that I should doubt. Human judgment is fallible, and God help us if we err in judging each other. By the light which Heaven vouchsafes us alone can we be guided."

"He is innocent—he is innocent!" repeated Miranda, in a tone of such exquisite anguish that the judge was much moved, and a tear trembled in his eye, as he said:

"Under any other circumstances than the extraordinary ones of this trial, which is now concluded, I should have felt myself justified in refusing to hold a conversation with any-one concerning what came before me in my judicial capacity, and in which I have no sort of discretion. I sit but to administer the law. I am called a judge, and yet Heaven knows I judge not. He in whose fate you are so much interested has been pronounced guilty."

"And yet so innocent even in thought," said Miranda. "Oh, sir, think of the maddening regret—the frightful pang that must come across the hearts of all who have had to do with this great, this terrible error of judgment, when it shall come to pass in the fulness of time that his innocence shall be apparent to all men."

"If he be innocent," replied the judge, "I pray to Heaven as truly and as fervently as you can that it may be manifest in time; but what more can I do?"

Miranda was not so absorbed in her grief as to be unconscious how powerless the judge must be after the unqualified verdict which the jury had returned against Rowland, and she said:

"Pardon me, sir, for my importunity. I

know I cannot expect you to do more than you have—namely, to administer your office with the kind gentleness for which I feel so much your debtor; but I was anxious—very anxious—to tell you personally that I, the daughter of the alleged murdered man, believe in the innocence of the accused Rowland Percy as I believe in Heaven!"

"Your sincerity I cannot doubt," said the judge, in an undertone. "Do you doubt the fact of your father having been murdered on that night?"

"No, no."

"Then who, think you, did the deed, if not he who now lies waiting the sentence of the law?"

"Bernard Varley."

"Well," said the judge, "I expected from you that answer, and, having heard it, let me entreat you to be more discreet and guarded in what you say. That this Bernard Varley is a man of violent and bad passions it needs not much penetration to discover. I pray you, young lady, not to put it in his power to revenge himself upon you for the words you may believe true, but which he would find no difficulty in getting a jury to declare libellous."

"I take your caution, sir, in good part," said Miranda; "but no power on earth shall prevent me denouncing to God and man Bernard Varley as my father's murderer!"

The judge shook his head, as he wrote an order for Miranda to visit the prison at any hours between the time when the gates were opened in the morning and when they were closed for the night.

"Be prudent," he said, "and leave the issue of this matter in the hands of Heaven."

"I have to thank you, sir," said Miranda, "for as much kindness as it was possible for you to show to me and to the innocent prisoner, under the melancholy circumstances in which we are placed."

The judge inclined his head, and Miranda, who was now anxious to visit the prison, took her leave, and, in a few moments, was in the street again with Mr. Anderson, who listened attentively to her account of what the judge had said to her, from which, as he expected, he derived not the least shadow of hope.

Varley, the moment he saw Miranda emerge from the door of the judge's house, started from the listless attitude in which he had been standing, and, pulling his hat down upon his brow, followed her, at about the same distance he had before pursued, towards the place of Rowland's confinement.

"He follows me still," whispered Miranda to Mr. Anderson. "Am I ever to be haunted by this fearful man?"

"Endure it for a little time," said Mr. Anderson. "I will find means to free you from it eventually. Do you have your interview with Rowland, and I will wait for you in the vestibule of the prison. Then I would advise you to go on alone, although I will

keep you in sight, and be at your side any moment you wish. Let Bernard Varley speak to you, if he will."

"For Rowland's sake," said Miranda, with a shudder, "I will even do that; but do not leave me quite."

"Be assured that I will not."

They had now reached the wicket-gate of the prison, and upon Miranda presenting her order, she was at once admitted within the gloomy building.

CHAPTER LV.

THE POISON—THE APPEAL—ROWLAND'S DESPAIR AND RENEWED HOPE—THE UNEXPECTED MEETING.

ALTHOUGH Mr. Anderson, on account of being the solicitor of Rowland Percy, would have been admitted with Miranda to his cell, he would not avail himself on that occasion of his privilege, but remained in the vestibule, leaving the lovers to talk over their hopes and their fears—alas! how much the latter predominated over the former—by themselves.

The man who conducted Miranda through the gloomy passages to the still gloomier cell wherein was Rowland awaiting his doom, strode on with all the indifference of custom which will so habituate one human being to the distresses of others as to make him look upon their tears as things of course—their sighs as nothing to awaken any sympathy in his obdurate bosom.

He even whistled a few bars of a lively air as he neared the dungeon door, and when he turned to Miranda, he seemed surprised to see the look of suffering depicted on her face, and the deathlike paleness even of her very lips.

"Ain't you well, miss?" he said.

"Yes—yes," replied Miranda; "as well as, perhaps, I can ever hope to be."

"Oh!" was the brief reply of the official, as he selected one from among a bunch of keys, which admitted them into a little octagonal room, on each of the sides of which was a door opening into a small cell.

"These here," remarked the man, "are the condemned cells, miss, and uncommon snug they is."

Miranda made him no answer, but she dropped the thick black veil she wore over her face, and stood mutely waiting his pleasure to open Rowland's cell.

Upon this, seeing that the visitor was not disposed to enter into conversation, he began whistling again, and, having selected another key from his bunch, he approached one of the doors, and placed it in the lock.

Miranda's heart beat violently and painfully as she stepped hastily forward towards the door.

The turnkey, with great deliberation, for he was in no hurry, not he, turned the lock, and then, pushing the door open a little way, put his head into the cell, and, after completing the bar of the tune he was whistling, said :

"A visitor, Percy !"

"Rowland !" cried Miranda.

A cry of joy came from the lonely prisoner, and, in the next moment, she had rushed past the turnkey, and was hanging on her lover's arm.

"Miranda—Miranda—my own Miranda ! So you have come to cheer me ; to light with the glory of your presence this gloomy abode. Oh, how can I thank you, my own noble Miranda ?"

"I hopes as she ain't smuggled in no gin or 'baccy," was the remark of the turnkey to himself, as he locked the door upon the unhappy young persons, who, under brighter auspices, might have passed through life with scarce a shadow on the sunshine of their joy.

"Rowland, did you not expect me ?"

"I did, Miranda, with a fever of impatience that I could not moderate. I knew well, that though deserted by all the world, you would still be true to me."

"If I deserted you now, Rowland, I should indeed be most unworthy of your love. You have heard that some time has been granted ?"

"Yes, dear Miranda, that news was communicated to me most quickly."

"Has—has it, Rowland, awakened hopes ?"

He turned aside his face for a moment, and then, in a voice struggling with emotion, he said :

"It is indeed hard to be torn from love and from thee, Miranda ; and I am in the spring-tide of life—the season of existence, when hope, like the vine's tendrils, will cling around even a ruin."

Miranda silently pressed his hand, and for some moments their hearts were too full to speak.

It was Rowland who at length broke the silence, by saying, in a more composed and cheerful tone of voice :

"Life is a strange dream, Miranda. Let us look upon it but as a fitful vision ; the cares, the griefs, and anxieties of which are but like the phantasies of the imagination—here a moment, and then vanished in the dim records of the dreary past."

Miranda looked in his face, as she said :

"Rowland, your philosophy should have a higher, a nobler source—a source you overlook."

She pointed upwards as she spoke, and Rowland said, in a low tone, as if doubtful of his own words :

"I—I trusted to Heaven and my own conscience, but——"

"Rowland, Rowland," cried Miranda, "this is the sharpest pang of all. There should be one thought—one hope which should support you, and that belongs to Heaven."

"'Tis hard for the moment, Miranda. And to suffer in such a manner. To be made the spectacle of a gaping crowd ; to be brought out manacled, as if unfit to be trusted among my fellow men, with the faculties that God has given me ; to be held up to execration ; to

be the object at which the finger of scorn will point ; and then—then, innocent though I am, my Miranda, to be—be—strangled like a dog. Oh, God ! oh, God ! If there be a Providence which will not let the fall of a sparrow pass unheeded, why——"

"Forbear ! forbear !" cried Miranda, as she clung convulsively to Rowland's arm. "Oh, how little did I expect to hear such words as these !"

"They are forced from me."

"No—no—no, Rowland. Dear Rowland—for dear you are to me, and surely at such a time as this I may confess as much—let me beg, implore, on my knees beseech you to reconcile yourself to God, and doubt not His mercies. Oh, Rowland ! Rowland ! think again. Your better judgment will surely step in, and I shall yet hear you say, ' God's will be done !'"

"Miranda, would you have me submit ?"

"To all ! to all ! and, by so doing, triumph over all."

"A poor triumph."

"No, Rowland, a glorious one. One that will reach the skies, and there be chronicled when mortal victories are forgotten in the dust of their heroes."

There was something that seemed almost inspired in the tone and manner of the beautiful girl as she thus nobly pleaded with her lover's heart, and combated the gloomy philosophy with which he had in vain sought to cheat his situation of its terrors.

He passed his hand across his face, and then, in a humbled tone, said :

"You—you would not surely, Miranda, wish me to undergo the fate I have pictured to you ?"

"I would give my life for yours, Rowland."

"I want not that. I cannot—will not—make the show which shall bring about me the gaping crowd to gloat upon my dying agonies."

There was in his manner a hesitation which, for some moments, Miranda could not comprehend ; and then, all at once, there darted across her mind a dreadful supposition—a supposition which never for a moment previously had occurred to her, but which now came with a pang of anguish that made her brain reel, and seemed to threaten to overturn her reason.

Rowland saw the sudden change in her appearance. He saw the fixed look of terror with which she regarded him, and, in a voice of alarm, he cried :

"Miranda—Miranda ! For the love of Heaven speak to me, for your looks terrify me. Miranda ! speak—oh, speak !"

"For the love of Heaven," were Miranda's first words, " can aught be done for the love of Heaven ? Rowland, yourself have used these words. Search into your heart, and ask yourself the cause of my emotion."

"My—own—heart ?"

"Yes, Rowland. Is there not a frightful secret—a hideous spectre there which steps between you and your better self—casts a shadow between you and Heaven?"

Rowland trembled as he replied:

"What—what—spectre?"

"Its name is temptation, and it whispers—"

"What—what?"

"Suicide!"

As Miranda spoke she sank to the floor of the cell, and, covering her face with her hands, her bosom heaved with emotion, and a sharp cry of anguish escaped her lips.

"Miranda—Miranda," said the agonized Rowland, "you have conquered."

She rose up, and flung her arms around him, as she said:

"Dear Rowland, you will not make me the widow of a self-murderer? You will not take yourself that life which God has given you, and which, if it be His will to resume, you may be sure it is for some holy and wise purpose, unscanned by mortal eyes, but visible in that bright world which is to come, and without the hope of which, dear, dear Rowland, what could have supported your Miranda amid her sea of troubles?"

Rowland's eyes were humid with tears, as, pressing Miranda to his heart, he said:

"You are my good angel, Miranda. You have saved me from myself. Bless you, Miranda. They may murder me, but they shall not call me the coward I thought of becoming."

Miranda laid her head upon his breast, and then looked up in his face as she said:

"Heaven's will be done."

Rowland put his hand in his breast, and took therefrom an exceedingly minute phial.

"Miranda," he said, "I wrote to one who I knew would comply with my wish, and he sent me this."

"Poison!" shuddered Miranda.

"Yes, poison; one drop of this subtle essence would stretch me a corpse on the floor of my cell. I thought to have disappointed them when they came to fetch their victim; but you have conquered, Miranda. Take it—take it from me. I will submit."

Miranda eagerly took the bottle, and concealed it in her bosom.

"Rowland," she said, "this is, indeed, a triumph. Hope—hope, dear Rowland. It seems to me now as if a something whispered to me that the worst is over. My heart is lighter than it has been for many a day."

"And mine. And now, Miranda—my father—is he well?"

"Not ill, Rowland, and yet much shattered."

The key turned in the lock of the door at this moment, and the turnkey, putting in his head, said:

"Are you ready to go, miss?"

"To-morrow," whispered Miranda to Rowland; "to-morrow at this time I will be here."

"Heaven bless you, Miranda!"

There was a silent pressure of the hands, and Miranda turned from the cell.

CHAPTER LVI.

SAMUEL TWITTER AND THE GENTLEMEN OF THE ROAD—THE ATTEMPT TO EXTORT A CONFESSION—THE RESCUE.

DICK PALMER, by writing to Samuel Twitter the note which we have presented to the reader, certainly took the most effectual method of inducing the avaricious and cowardly valet to meet him.

As we have stated, Twitter had but one hope, and that was to escape from the great danger of an association with Varley, by entirely leaving England; but then, to do that, he required, or fancied he required, a much larger sum than he was already master of.

His attempts to procure a sufficient reward at once from Varley had, as we have seen, failed, and his only chance now of accomplishing his object was by degrees, and by such peculations as he could find an opportunity of committing upon Varley, with the assistance of Dick Palmer, who, he still believed, would be his ready agent in the disposal of whatever portable plunder he could lay his hands upon, either at the Grange or elsewhere.

Hence Twitter most readily determined to be punctual in meeting the highwayman at the place appointed, little suspecting the reception he was about to get from men who were unscrupulous by what means they fulfilled their purposes, and to whom the large reward mentioned by Palmer was, indeed, a most powerful incentive to action.

Varley had, during the day, insisted upon Twitter accompanying him to the proper authorities, in order to back him in a formal complaint of the ill-usage he had received during the riot, though Twitter would gladly have allowed the affair to pass over, for he dreaded nothing more than making himself well known by numerous appearances in public; but Varley was inexorable, and he was compelled to comply with his humour.

The magistrates, however, could only express their civil regret, and fine some of those who had been taken by the officers.

As the evening approached, Twitter became extremely anxious to know what Varley was going to do, or where he was going to remain. In fact, so extremely fidgety was he, and so very inquisitive—for he was in a perfect fever when absent from his companion in guilt, lest he should seek an interview with Miranda, and, in the excess of his wild adoration for her, sacrifice both himself and him, Twitter, by some incautious admission—that to see him, anyone would have thought Bernard Varley was some dangerous lunatic, and that he, Samuel Twitter, was under heavy responsibilities as regarded his safety.

The suspicious, crafty temper of Varley never deserted him, except in his intercourse with Miranda: then, indeed, the now master spirit of his soul drowned in its flush of power every other feeling, and his passion for her eclipsed even his love of self.

But widely different was he in his intercourse with others, and, most of all, with Twitter, who, he was aware, was smarting under the pang of disappointment at not reaping as suddenly as he expected—and, in fact, had been promised—a large pecuniary benefit from his share in the murder of Sir George Rankley.

This Varley would not permit him to do, for his knowledge of human nature had been derived from the very worst specimens, and he believed that he should not have a moment's safety if he permitted Twitter to be otherwise than entirely dependent upon him.

Hence he determined to keep him his slave, and to watch him with vigilance and activity.

Moreover, Varley had another reason—if reason it could be called, in which there was so little judgment. He was not without a wild and clinging hope that at the last, when hope was dead, and despair ran riot in her heart, Miranda, to save Rowland Percy from a scaffold, would make some agreement with him, either to become his wife then, or at some distant period, provided he saved the innocent Rowland from the awful fate that seemed so inevitably waiting for him.

This Varley intended to do, if it were to be done at all, by a concocted tale, which should denounce Twitter and sacrifice him to the law, or, if it did not from the lack of evidence do that, at least Rowland Percy could not be executed in the face of recantation on the part of a principal witness of the principal evidence against him.

This recantation he would have transmitted to the authorities on the eve of his own departure to another country, to which he would have repaired under such circumstance, provided he could carry with him any promise from Miranda, which would in some measure give him hopes of one day calling her his own.

So wild—so extravagant—so improbable a fabric of the imagination could never have entered, or—if it had entered—maintained a place for one moment in so politic a brain as Bernard Varley's, had his reason not been thoroughly besotted upon that one subject, and his love for Miranda not amounted to what it really was—a species of mania, that when once it began to act in his brain, disordered all reasoning, and presented him with the most absurd mental combinations.

Hence was it he looked upon Samuel Twitter as one to be sacrificed, and upon Miranda as the reward.

It was towards evening that Twitter, who felt his great danger until Rowland Percy should be no more—for, after that, what had Bernard Varley to offer Miranda?—endeavoured, in a cautious manner, to elicit how he, Varley, was going to spend the next few hours.

The very fact of his making such cautious inquiries let Varley know at once that he, Twitter, expected to be engaged in some scheme which would prevent him from watching his movements, and it came into his mind immediately to execute the very project of which Twitter was so much afraid—namely, of seeing Miranda, if possible, and tempting her, with her lover's life, to assume a smile towards him she abhorred, even as her pure, spotless soul abhorred evil and crime.

"We shall feel easier and more comfortable," whispered Twitter, as he took a side glance at Varley's face, "when Thursday next is over."

"Thursday?" replied Varley, with a start.

"Yes, Thursday—to that day the execution is, as you know, put off, Varley."

"The execution—yes, the execution," repeated Varley, in an abstracted tone. "Time is short—time is short."

"The better it should be so," said Twitter. "When that is over, we—we shall be much more safe."

"Are we not safe now?" said Varley.

"Yes; but——"

"But what?"

"Nothing—nothing; only, you know, the excitement of the affair will altogether subside after he is dead, and then, Varley, we can begin to enjoy a little the fruits of that which, as yet, at least to me, has yielded nothing but bitterness and terror."

"What has it yielded to me?" said Varley, in a tone that seemed as if it came from the depths of the grave.

"There is one thing," said Twitter, not noticing Varley's remark, for he wished then no contention with him, "which I think would be very, very desirable, Varley."

"What is that?"

"That you should visit the Grange as early as possible, and see that all is safe there. The servants owe you no good will, you know—at least, the few of the old ones that remain—and were I to go, they would, no doubt, dispute my authority completely."

"Think you so?"

"Yes: I am sure of it. Now, if you were to ride over to-night, I would come after you, which would be better than my going with you, I think, as, just now, it may be desirable that we should not appear too much together. You understand, Varley?"

"I hear you," said Varley. "At what time would you meet me at the Grange?"

"It wants now but a short time of sunset. Suppose I was to come over in about two hours from now."

"Agreed—let it be so, and I will proceed thither at once."

"Very well; I shall merely stroll gently on the road, so as to get there about the time mentioned. You will probably overtake and pass me, for I shall walk."

"No doubt."

Twitter, after making a few more remarks about different matters which he suggested required seeing to at the Grange, even before it could be advertised to be let to anyone, then left the room, quite felicitating himself that he had succeeded in getting Varley away from the immediate neighbourhood of

THE POISON PHIAL.

Miranda, while he should be engaged so as not to be able to interrupt any interview that Varley might otherwise have sought with her.

"Every hour," muttered Twitter, when he was alone, "is an hour gained. Let Rowland Percy once be dead, and I shall be rid of my chief dread. Miranda, then, will have nothing to hope. The very worst will have been realized, and Bernard Varley can have no possible motive to indiscretion, for, as it is, I verily believe he would place his neck, and mine, too, in the halter. if that girl chose, by a little of woman's duplicity, to give him any hopes of becoming her husband."

"What can Twitter be aiming at this morning?" thought Varley. "He has some secret enterprise on hand. He wants to get me away from York to-night. Did he think by such shallow excuses and mock reasons to persuade me to go alone to the Grange? No: I will this evening, being unencumbered by him, endeavour to procure an interview with Miranda. And yet, am I in danger from Twitter? What means the mystery of his conduct? He is disappointed, and yet—yet surely he would not, could not be so mad as turn against me now, after swearing to so much. He did not do the deed. There he has an advantage over me—a door of escape would be opened to him were he to confess all, which would for ever remain closed upon me as the actual perpetrator of the murder. His evidence would then destroy me—and yet who would believe the uncorroborated testimony of such as he? He could but swear to his new statement, and he has sworn to his old one. Yet I will endeavour to discover what he is doing this evening that makes him so anxious to get me out of the way. He will, no doubt, keep his word as to going to the Grange. I should overtake him on the road, he said. I will do so, and then, after getting some distance, I can return on foot, and keep an eye on him. After that I will visit thee, Miranda—beautiful being! Death even at thy hands were sweeter far than life without thee. If I could win but one smile—if I could be permitted to hold her hand in mine—if I could feel the soft, velvet pressure of her lips, I would sacrifice all—all!—yes, all!"

The shadows of evening were rapidly approaching, and Varley, after remaining for some moments silent, while his thoughts were with Miranda, suddenly rose, and, ordering his horse to be brought to the door with all convenient expedition, he, by many reasons, all of which were tinctured with the wildness of his mad passion, strove to convince himself that Miranda would some day be his.

It was strange that, on that evening, there should be so many persons, interested directly and indirectly in the fate of Rowland Percy, bound to the outskirts of York; but so it was.

There were Palmer, Twitter, Varley, Mr. Anderson, and the humane counsel, Mr. Lethwayte, as well as the questionable companions of Dick Palmer, who hoped to reap so golden a harvest from the, to them, common-place job of frightening a timid man nearly out of his wits.

Twitter fully intended to go to the Grange, for he had about the premises several secret places, in which, from time to time, he had deposited the proceeds of his various robberies, until they amounted to sums which, through a London agent, he could place at interest in the public securities.

These secret hoards he wished to visit, and empty of their treasures, since he resided no longer on the premises. For this purpose, as well as to keep faith with Varley, he intended to strike across the country to the Grange, after his meeting with the highwayman, which he judged would, as usual, be a very brief one.

While he was hurrying to the place mentioned by Palmer in his note, that personage had met six of his companions who were to form the expedition, and, collecting them round him, he said to them:

"Now, quite understand me in this matter. You must give it up on a signal from me, for I know how far to go with any chance of success. Twitter knows me, and were I to show myself in this business, it would spoil any future hope of thinking of another scheme to accomplish the object we have in view. So you six must waylay him, and do the job of frightening him without my assistance. I

will blow my whistle when you are to leave him alone; but, should he confess anything of importance, I will make my appearance directly."

"All right," said one.

"Remember the thousand pounds," said another.

"If we succeed, you will find it is not forgotten," replied Palmer.

The party now started by different routes to the scene of action, for some of them happened to be upon such intimate terms with the police of York, that, had they all gone in a body, some troublesome member of that force might have been smitten with a notion of following them, which, under the circumstances, would have been very awkward indeed.

Fortunately for the secrecy of the enterprise, the night set in uncommonly dark for the season of the year, and a cold, north-easterly wind was not likely to act as an inducement to anyone to take a rural walk in the suburbs, except upon pressing business.

The lane which had been named by Twitter was a wild, secluded place. It was very seldom visited by anyone except to admire the natural beauties by which it was surrounded, and which itself exhibited; and, as they could be only appreciated by daylight, it was, except when perhaps a full moon shone from a cloudless sky, rarely intruded upon after sunset. The fact was, that a discovery of extensive strata of gravel had been made years before about the spot, and hence the lane and its vicinity were cut up into pits and small excavations, which, in time becoming covered with vegetation, gave the place a wild and very picturesque aspect, at the same time that it ill adapted it for a thoroughfare.

CHAPTER LVII.

THE INTERVIEW WITH BERNARD VARLEY—THE PROPOSAL—THE ANSWER OF THE SECRETARY OF STATE—A FATHER'S REQUEST.

PALMER and his companions were on the appointed spot some time before Twitter could fairly be expected, and the highwayman posted his force in an advantageous position at a narrow part of the lane, where it would be impossible for any human being to pass without being observed.

Close, likewise, to that spot was one of the deepest, if not the deepest, of all the pits or excavations which had been made for the purpose of procuring the gravel. The bottom of this pit—long since neglected and exhausted—had become a reservoir for all the rain water which had flowed from the higher ground, and even in the driest weather there was commonly a black, stagnant-looking pool at the bottom of this pit, while at seasons when much rain had fallen, and there was considerable humidity in the air, the pool increased to a miniature lake, in which stood up, like fairy islands, the tops of masses of rubbish and huge stones, which had fallen to the lowest depths of the excavation.

"Conceal yourselves here," said Palmer, "and I will go the other side of the lane. I know the man well, and shall recognize him even in the dark. When you hear my whistle, one only of you step out and seize him; then let the remainder of you appear when he is much frightened, and the sudden additional shock may alarm him into a confession."

"I say, Dick," remarked Jones, who formed one of the party, "I supposes as you haven't no sort o' objections to us all being lords o' this here blessed manor? Kiver, kim up! Eh, Dick?"

"What do you mean?"

"I mean this here. Yer knows as them ere lords o' manors has some on 'em, as we all knows uncommon well, no manners at all. Lays their hands on what they calls waifs and strays."

"Well, what then?"

"Why, s'posing as some covey was to lose his way on this here dark night, and come down the lane, you know, Dick?"

"Well, Jones, what have we to do with that?"

"Wouldn't he be a waif and a blessed stray? Business is business, yer knows, Dicky, and as we is here, why, all's fish as comes to net."

"Nonsense, Jones," said Palmer. "You know as well as I how very dangerous it is to run after stray game when we are on any one particular expedition. Let all pass free to-night but the man we seek."

"What! not go for to rob nobody?"

"Certainly not. Besides, the danger is excessive so near York. Leave all that alone to-night."

"Well," said Jones, with a disappointed tone, "we has 'pinted you governor for to-night, and I s'poses as you must have your own way."

"Hush, now!" whispered Palmer. "I don't know a moment when our man may come, and the sound of voices would scare him off like a startled hare."

The Minster clock now sounded in the distance with gloomy grandeur, and Palmer counted eight.

"He will be here soon," he said. "Not another word."

The highwayman then stepped across the lane, and ensconced himself in a deep hollow on the other side, while his comrades kept a profound stillness, and not a vestige of them could be seen amid the mass of dark vegetation that concealed them so effectually.

At the same time that Dick Palmer was listening as the Minster clock struck eight, Twitter had arrived at the entrance of the lane, and paused, likewise, to listen to the sonorous announcement, as the wind bore it to his ears.

"I'm just in nice time," he muttered. "Dick is sure to be here. He is a man of his word; but, when I come to think of it, he can't have much money to give me, saving the

proceeds of the ring, which I never yet had of him."

He looked up at the dark, frowning sky a moment, and then he strove to pierce the impenetrable gloom in which the lane was shrouded, and to enter which resembled plunging into some deep hollow that went far from the light of day into the very bowels of the earth.

"This," muttered Twitter, "would be a fearful place to be attacked in. I never saw it so dark as this. When I came here last a harvest moon was shining, and I could see my way almost as if it had been broad daylight."

A step into one of the hollows of about a foot in depth, now suddenly warned Twitter that he must be exceedingly cautious how he proceeded, and, with a muttered execration, he cautiously felt his way with his feet before he trusted all his weight upon them.

"I will get Palmer," he thought, "to go part of the way home with me—that is to say, towards the Grange, for I might be robbed on my road of all that I have to receive from him. The lane gets surely darker and darker. I wish he would make his appearance."

Thus muttering to himself his fears, Twitter slowly proceeded up the lane, until he came to the narrow part, where those were posted who intended making so trying an experiment upon his nerves.

According to arrangement, Palmer blew his whistle when he saw the dusky form of Twitter slowly approaching.

"Is that you, Palmer?" said Twitter. "How dark this place is to-night."

"Stand!" cried Jones, coming forward, and grasping the terrified Twitter by the collar.

"Murder!" gasped the assailed man. "Murder—murder!"

"Jist say that agin," cried Jones, "and, if you'd as many lives as a cat, I'd take 'em all, one after the other."

"Spare me—oh, spare me! Palmer—Palmer, save me!"

Jones upon this gave Twitter so tremendous a shaking, that had he, at its termination, let go of him, he must have fallen to the ground, so confused and bewildered did he become.

"Take my money," he whined—"take it all—and—my watch, but spare my life. Oh, Palmer, Palmer, where are you?"

"I don't want your money," cried Jones, "nor your watch either. I wants a *atomy*."

"A—a what, sir?" said the trembling Twitter.

"A *atomy*, to be sure. Let's see."

Jones accompanied these latter words by divers pinches on Twitter's arms, who was perfectly in the dark as to what his assailant meant.

"For Heaven's sake, let me go," he said. "I will give you freely all the money I have with me. True, it is not much, but that I cannot help. You will let me go if I give you all?"

"You are more valuable nor money," said Jones, "and as you don't seem quite to understand what I means, in *consekence* o' your ignorance, I'll expiflicate to you. By a *atomy* I means a stiff 'un. There's four doctors in York as have subscribed a handsome sum apiece, you see, for a atomy, to divide among 'em. One on 'em wants a head, another on 'em wants two legs. You've got two, have you?"

This question was accompanied by several not very gentle kicks upon Twitter's shins, which made him jump again.

"Good Heavens!" he said, "you don't mean to say that you will murder me?"

"Murder's an uncommon ugly word, it is," said Jones. "We only means all for to make you sarviceable in a sort of *skientific* way."

"You—you are surely only jesting with me?"

"It's no joke."

"It must be. You have chosen this dark lane in which to carry on a mere joke, to frighten anyone who might come down it. I—I—could almost laugh myself. Tell me you are only joking; I was frightened, so you see you fully succeeded, and you will now let me go."

"Werry sorry," remarked Jones, "to find as you is a labouring under sich a delusion."

"Nay—nay, you are carrying it rather too far now. Oh, Palmer, Palmer, where are you?"

"Who do you mean?"

"One who I was to meet here; but I will go back now to York. I—will not say anything about this little bit of amusement."

"I'm werry glad as you considers it so dreadful funny," said Jones, "and I hopes as you'll keep it up. Back to York you sartinly will go; but it will be in four different bags, one of which belongs to each of the doctors, you see, so don't let's have any more gammon about it."

A cold perspiration broke out upon the brow of Twitter, for although the story of the four doctors was too improbable, yet he began really to think that he should be murdered for some purpose, in that lonely place, where no aid was likely to reach him, and where it was far from likely that even a chance passenger should come.

His only hope was that Palmer might arrive, and rescue him. Time, therefore, became to him the very breath of life, and he said, in a voice of abject entreaty:

"Set some fine upon my life, and you shall have it, I swear to you, to-morrow, if you will meet me in York. If you are going to murder me for the dreadful purpose you speak of, you can but receive money. Whatever sum, then, has tempted you to the deed I will double, if you will spare me."

"All werry fine," said Jones, "but we ar'n't sich unprincipled fellows as you seems to think. We have been paid aforehand, and we is pinks o' honour, we is."

"But why murder for such a purpose? Surely some graveyard would have supplied you, and saved you the great crime you contemplate?"

"Ah," said Jones, "there's the dodge. You don't understand these here matters. I'll expiflicate that ere, and then you'll be satisfied as all's right. I shouldn't like you to think as *everythink* wasn't proper."

Twitter groaned at the idea of any explanation reconciling him to being knocked on the head or having his throat cut for anatomical purposes.

"You must know," resumed Jones, "as these doctors wants a *corpus* as hasn't been ill —that's the dodge."

"Have mercy upon me!" cried Twitter.

"Hilloa!" said Jones, "come on, pals; bring them ere bags. The gemman is a getting impatient."

At this summons the five desperadoes, who were concealed, and who had half-stifled themselves with laughter at the conversation that had taken place between Jones and Twitter, made their appearance, and at once destroyed the faintest hope that the valet might have had of the affair terminating otherwise than with his destruction.

He dropped upon his knees, and, in a shrieking tone, said:

"Oh, spare me—spare me. I will pay you well, on my sacred honour, I will."

"But what are we to do for a body?" growled one.

"Someone else," suggested Twitter, "may come down the lane, and then you will make double profit; for I swear to pay you handsomely if you let me go."

"That's uncommon considerate o' you," said Jones, "as regards someone else; but we wait sometimes a week here and nobody comes."

"But, to-night," said Twitter, "I assure you someone will be here; a better subject than I—a tall, fine man in robust health—he will be here. You can let me go and take him."

"Who's he?"

"His name is Palmer. You will spare me?"

"The infernal scoundrel!" muttered Dick Palmer to himself, as he heard this kind suggestion of his friend Twitter.

"No," said Jones, in a tone of voice as if he had been considering the matter. "No, we will have you, so there's an end of it."

"No, no, no. Help — murder — mercy! mercy!"

"Hold your noise, will you? I tell you what'll be the best way, pals, let's tie a rope round him, and let him down into the pool close by; when he's dead, then we can pull him up again, and cut him up atween us without any bother."

"Ay, ay," said several, "that's the way."

Twitter now made a desperate effort to get away, and run for his life; but he was foiled by Jones, who held him with the strength of a vice, while another of the party slipped a rope round his neck, despite his struggles.

Shriek after shriek now came from the miserable wretch, as he was dragged to the very edge of the precipice, below which was the black pool into which he expected momentarily to be hurled.

Then when sensation had nearly deserted him, and he was half-dead with terror, Jones said:

"Your name is Samuel Twitter, and on that account you have one chance for your life."

"A chance!" he shrieked, "a chance! Oh, tell me what?"

"Disclose to us the real truth as regards the murder of Sir George Rankley, and you shall live."

CHAPTER LVIII.

THE RESCUE—RECRIMINATION—THE MEETING OF PALMER WITH MR. ANDERSON—DISAPPOINTMENT.

THE mental agony endured by Twitter was beyond description. The pain of a hundred deaths could not, in reality, have been equal to the awful sensations that beset his brain, as he believed himself now within a few moments of eternity; while the crimes that lay heavy on his soul, rose up before his mental vision with awful distinctness.

"My life—my life!" he howled. "I know nothing—I can tell nothing. My life! Spare me! Think of the horror you will one day feel, when my blood cries out for vengeance. I tell you, your feelings will be terrible. You will spare me—you will!"

"Who murdered Sir George Rankley?" said Jones.

"The man who did the deed is condemned. The law has him in its clutches. You may see him hanged at York on Thursday. Why ask me?"

"Because we have a fancy you know : but, as you don't, why such a ignorant *indiwidual* surely ain't fit to live. Come on, boys."

They dragged him to the brink of the chasm.

He gazed down with despairing eyes.

The next moment he firmly believed would be his last.

A thousand frightful images of horror gushed through him. A voice seemed to ring in his ears, saying:

"Save yourself, by denouncing Bernard Varley."

"Pitch him over when I say three," remarked Jones to his comrades.

"Shall I — shall I tell all?" thought Twitter.

"One," said Jones.

The man tightened his grasp on him, and placed him so near the edge of the precipice, that a few loose stones crumbled down beneath his feet, and fell dashing from rock to rock, till they reached the still waters of the black pool, which they then broke into a thousand eddies.

The sound was like a death-knell to Twitter, and he groaned aloud, as Jones said, in an assumed, hollow voice:

"Two."

"Now for it," said one of the men : "push him clean off, my pals."

"I—I will tell—I will tell!" cried Twitter. "Save me! Take me back to York. I will tell all."

The moment he uttered these words, a loud voice cried:

"Hold!"

It was the voice of Bernard Varley.

The men, with Jones at their head, shrank back from the edge of the gloomy chasm, and glanced at each other irresolutely for a few moments. Then Varley's voice again cried:

"Twitter, you are rescued. Officers, follow me."

"Oh, curse it!" said Jones. "We——"

"Silence!" cried Palmer, suddenly appearing among them. "Be off with you all. The game's up for this time. Off—off! Quick!"

Twitter was thrown down on his back, where he lay insensible, partly through fear, and partly from the blow that Jones had given him to put him there, so that he did not recognize Palmer, who—having given this advice to his wild, lawless comrades, who availed themselves of it by disappearing very quickly—advanced in the direction of Bernard Varley's voice, and stood directly in his way.

Varley had, in pursuance of his intention, ridden on for the purpose of overtaking Twitter, and ascertaining that he was really going to the Grange.

The road which he had taken was some distance from the old gravel-pits, but, in the stillness of the night, he had heard Twitter's first cry of alarm, and fastening his horse's bridle to a tree, he walked cautiously in the direction of the sound, when he saw quite enough to convince him that Twitter was in some danger.

He listened to the conversation that took place between him and his captors, incredulously. The whole affair seemed too improbable, but when he heard the condition upon which his life was offered him, he understood all in a moment.

He only waited now to see how far Twitter would go before he proffered a confession. When he, Varley, heard him do so, he called out in the manner we have described, affecting to have officers with him, and succeeded, as we have seen, in effecting a rescue.

He was always armed, and, with a pistol in each hand, he now advanced in the direction of where he had heard Twitter speaking, for by the sound of feet in different directions, he judged that his captors, whoever they were, had taken the alarm, and disappeared.

"Twitter—Twitter," he called, in a loud voice, "where are you now?"

"Stop, Bernard Varley," said Palmer, solemnly—"your evil genius is here."

A sharp cry of terror burst from Varley's lips as he heard the voice of him he so much dreaded, and who, in his own imagination, he had invested with a supernatural knowledge, and, perchance, power, he trembled to think of.

"Mysterious being," he said, "wherefore do

you haunt me? What have I done to you that you should fill my soul with such terror?"

"You are alone?"

"I am."

"Humph!" thought Palmer; "we have been too precipitate after all." Then he said aloud:

"Bernard Varley, beware! The blood of Sir George Rankley is on your hands, and you know it. Sooner or later the day of retribution will come. Beware—beware!"

"In the name of Heaven," said Varley, trembling, "tell me who you are, that I may give a name to the object of my fears."

"It matters not who I am," said Palmer: "for a time you are safe, but the day is coming."

Varley could scarcely stand; a mist seemed to spread itself before his eyes, and, when he recovered from his temporary stupor, his mysterious companion was gone.

"Speak again—speak—speak!" he gasped.

There was no reply.

A solemn and unnatural kind of stillness reigned around him.

Once more, then, in an agonized voice, he cried:

"Appear to me, thou being not of this world, or else whence comes your knowledge? I would know all. If you can see the past, which was hidden, I know well, from all mortal eyes, you can read, perchance, to me the future. I would know my destiny, and oh, most of all would I hear of Miranda!"

All was as still as the grave.

"He is gone," said Varley, with a shudder. "He is gone."

Even as he spoke a faint gleam of light came from the moon, which had been struggling through a mass of clouds in the southern sky.

It was not sufficient to make objects clearly visible, but it defined the grass from the bushes, the light, gravelly soil from the luxuriant vegetation that grew around, and Varley did not feel quite so lonely as he had done in the intense darkness that had before prevailed.

Being convinced now that the much-dreaded being whom he firmly believed knew all concerning the murder, was gone, his next effort was to find Twitter, who, he thought, would surely not leave the spot after hearing his voice.

He called him loudly by name, but received no answer; and then he cautiously walked forward in the direction whence the sound of his voice had first proceeded.

A few moments brought him nearly to the verge of the chasm, when he saw Twitter lying, to all appearance, dead, within a few paces of the edge.

With a feeling something between hope and fear—hope that he was dead, and fear to touch the ghastly remains of his companion in guilt, if such should be his fate—he stooped and lifted one of his hands.

Twitter uttered a hollow groan.

"He lives," muttered Varley; "but what is to hinder me from completing the work they have begun, and ridding myself of this trembling coward?"

A sudden thought then came across his mind that the mysterious man he had just parted with had his eye upon him from some secret nook close by, and the notion was one which gave Varley such a sudden fright that he sprang to his feet, and looked around him with an expression of terror truly pitiable.

"I dare not—I dare not," he muttered. "He is watching me. I feel, as it were, his eye upon me. No—I dare not kill Twitter."

He then stooped again over the prostrate man, and, shaking him roughly, cried:

"Twitter, Twitter—arouse yourself."

"Spare me, and I will tell all," murmured Twitter.

"Curses!"

"It was Bernard Varley did the deed. I—I will tell you all, but spare my life."

Varley gave him a savage kick, that made him utter a shriek of pain, and open his eyes, when he saw leaning over him, with a deep scowl upon his face, the very man whom he was betraying.

"Varley?" he said.

"Ay, Varley. Rise—rise, I say, and follow me. Samuel Twitter, we must have some conversation together of importance. Come on, or, by the fiends, I will blow your brains out, and throw your corpse down yonder chasm."

He presented a pistol at Twitter's head as he spoke, and the trembling valet could only gasp out:

"Varley—Bernard Varley—I have said nothing—on my soul I have said nothing. All is safe—quite safe."

"Did I not hear you proffer to tell all?"

"Yes, but I would not have done so. With some coined tale, that should have fixed guilt still more strongly upon Rowland Percy, I would have amused those who sought my life; but I would not have committed you, Varley."

"Indeed!"

"You may believe me. What hope have I but in you? Am I not quite dependent upon you, even for subsistence? Think you, then, that I would betray you? Oh, no! you may trust to me, Varley, as you would trust to yourself, indeed you may."

"You protest strongly," said Varley; "but how came you here? 'Tis out of your route to the Grange."

"How—how came I here? Why, I was dragged hither by those men. How could I resist so many?"

"Samuel Twitter," said Varley, peering into his companion's face, and speaking with intense bitterness, through his clenched teeth, "you have been this evening engaged in a piece of treachery and villainy, which has, in some strange manner, recoiled on your own head. I do believe from my heart that you would have denounced me: and if I was sure that, apart from the mortal peril you were in, you had harboured for a moment such an intention against me, this instant should be your last!"

"You much wrong me, Varley, by your suspicions," said Twitter; "indeed you do. I harbour any bad intention towards you? Impossible!"

"Recollect that this night I have saved your life," said Varley.

"You have—you have, and I am grateful."

"Be so, and beware of tampering with me. I am one standing on a precipice, down which I would rather hurl anyone who was too dangerously close to me—you understand—than risk a fall myself."

"I comprehend you."

"'Tis well. Go, then, on to the Grange. I have my horse close by here, and will follow you."

Twitter walked on, while Varley, slinking across a meadow, made towards the spot where he had left his horse.

It would have been difficult to have decided on that eventful evening which of the accomplices in crime was in the greatest state of terror; for circumstances had happened to awaken the most lively fears of them both.

CHAPTER LIX.

THE CONDEMNED CELL—THE CHAPLAIN—THE MEETING OF MIRANDA AND PALMER IN THE BRIDLE-PATH.

WITH a feeling of disappointment, that was very vexing to him, Dick Palmer hurried from the gravel pits to keep his appointment with Mr. Anderson.

"A dead failure," he muttered, "and all through the very scoundrel who would perhaps have been brought to the gallows if the affair had succeeded properly. Twitter's forced confession would not have been worth much, for he would have disputed it afterwards; nevertheless, if we could have got him to give a detailed account of the real particulars concerning Sir George Rankley's murder, it would have surely contained some circumstances that would have placed the case in a very different light, and saved Mr. Percy. However, that chance is over. Well, well, if the young man must die for what I am sure he is innocent of, I can't help him, and if poor Miranda breaks her heart, which she will surely do, and dies too, I can't help that."

With these melancholy reflections, Dick Palmer walked rapidly on till he came to the appointed place of meeting; he then lingered about for a few seconds till he saw advancing towards him two persons.

One of them he thought was Mr. Anderson, but the other was a stranger to him.

The moon had now acquired greater brilliancy from the dispersion of the vapours, which at an earlier hour of the evening had dimmed some of its lustre.

"It is Mr. Anderson," said Palmer: "but who on earth can he have brought with him—an officer? No, no: I will trust him."

Palmer then advanced slowly to meet the two persons, and, when Mr. Anderson was sufficiently near, he called to him, saying:

"Do you come to meet the solitary horseman, sir?"

"I do."

"But not alone?"

"This gentleman is the counsel who defended Mr. Percy at his trial, and who is as convinced of his innocence as I am. I have brought him with me, because I know you may rely upon his honour, and he is likely to be a better judge of the importance of what you have to tell than myself."

"Gentlemen," said Palmer, "you are both welcome; but it is with deep regret I inform you I have nothing to tell you."

"Nothing!" exclaimed Mr. Anderson.

"Nothing whatever; but do not believe that I brought you here upon so foolish an errand. I had a great and well-founded hope that I should by this time be able to communicate something to you that would have saved Mr. Rowland Percy. My scheme, however, has failed, and I know no more than youselves."

Mr. Anderson and the counsel looked at each other for a moment in doubt and surprise; then the latter said:

"Whoever you are, rest assured that in any communication you may make us you shall be personally protected, and, if you wish it, most liberally paid."

"I understand you, sir," said Palmer, with a mortified air. "You think I am trying to have a high price put upon my services, but I declare to you, before Heaven, that were you to offer me the wealth of this kingdom, I could tell you nothing which would be of any legal use as regards the condemned Mr. Percy."

"We cannot but believe so solemn an asseveration," said Mr. Anderson; "but, if such is the case, explain to us how it is that you have acquired so great a power over Bernard Varley. At a mere hint of your existence, he is quite unmanned and terrified beyond expression. Surely that must arise from his conviction of your power to harm him, from your knowledge of some very grave and criminal transaction."

"Ay," said the counsel, "that's the point. Pray, as we have come so far to see you, explain that to us."

"I will, gentlemen, as well as I can. Strange as it may appear, although I believe I have such a power as you mention, and can terrify Bernard Varley, I know nothing to criminate him. I met him accidentally one night, and, having my mind full of suspicions, both of him and Twitter, I dropped some hints, which, I presume, came so near the truth that he imagined I knew all. His mind was evidently in a state of great excitement, and I firmly believe that he looked upon me as a something scarcely human. He trembles when we meet; he believes I know all, when I really know nothing, although I suspect just what you do yourselves, namely, that he had far more to do with the death of Sir George Rankley than any other living soul."

"This is very strange," said the counsel.

"And yet I believe it," added Mr. Anderson. "There is an air of sincerity about the tale which convinces me of its truth."

"I see no reason to doubt it."

"It is true, so help me Heaven!" said Palmer; "and I have only to regret bringing you here for no good purpose."

"Never mind that," said Mr. Anderson. "We believe you intended to give us information of importance, and we have still to thank you for the intention, although some accident may have interfered with its completion."

"You do me but justice, gentlemen, when you call it an accident. If it should happen that I can yet accomplish anything for Rowland Percy, it shall be done."

"Will you tell us who and what you are?" said the counsel, as Dick Palmer turned away.

"Let me remain as I am—unknown but in person," said the highwayman.

Then, as a faint smile crossed his face, he added:

"We may some day be professionally acquainted."

He then walked rapidly away, and was soon lost to sight in the gloom of the deep shadows of the ancient trees.

"Well," said Mr. Anderson, "so this last hope seems to have crumbled away."

"It has," replied the counsel. "I have now scarcely a hope."

Discoursing thus, in a melancholy mood, they walked to the city, with a painful conviction on their minds that, after all, poor Rowland would suffer an ignominious death, for a crime of which he was as innocent as the babe unborn.

Bernard Varley, when he left Palmer, mounted his horse with all possible expedition, and galloped to York, for his mind was full of his project of seeing Miranda and succeeding in making some sort of compromise with her for Rowland Percy's safety.

The exciting scene he had been a listener to, and a spectator of, at the old gravel-pits, had by no means tended to lessen the fever of his brain, or enable him to judge more calmly and dispassionately of his hopes, in any interview he might be enabled to procure with the beautiful girl, who owed so much misery to him, and whose evil spirit he had certainly been.

All he kept muttering to himself was, "that for Rowland Percy's sake, she would surely sacrifice even herself."

But he knew not—he could not imagine the high and noble sentiments of the heart he projected attacking; he was not capable of comprehending that, loving Rowland Percy as she did, believing his innocence as she believed in Heaven, still Miranda could bear to see him sacrificed, with a conviction that they should meet again where there would be no sorrow, rather than secure a few fleeting

years of existence in this perishable world at the sacrifice of her integrity of heart.

Nor did Bernard Varley properly estimate the character of Rowland Percy, or he would never have reasoned regarding him as if his mere love of life was the ruling principle of his conduct.

But so it is, ill men reason upon all men from their experience of their own passions. Clever men fail in their plans and projects because they present motives of action to men of lower mental power to themselves. Villains, destitute of all the nobler feelings of humanity, reason upon human nature from their own despicable hearts, and they fail by encountering purer, abler natures than their own.

The difficulty of procuring his much-desired interview with Miranda was ever staring Bernard Varley in the face, ever intruding itself upon his thoughts; but still he rode on, and would not suffer it to interrupt his hasty progress to the city.

It was one of those difficulties which are of such great magnitude that they will not bear reflection, and he sped towards Miranda's temporary home without any fixed resolve, or arranged mode of action to be put in practice when he reached it.

He trusted, as hundreds and thousands of men do, to accident befriending him at the moment.

That he could receive no very serious interruption he was well aware, for the weak, enfeebled Mr. Percy was far from in a condition to offer any; and he alone who would have been dreaded and shrunk from, was occupying the condemned cell of a felon.

The night was considerably advanced when, with a recklessness that only the state of mental excitement Varley was in could ever have lent to him, he reached the door of Miranda's and Mr. Percy's humble abode, and knocked as if he thought himself a welcome visitor.

He had previously given his horse into the care of a boy, and, when the door was opened by the woman of the house, she started at the pale face and strange tone of the visitor, who asked for Miranda Rankley.

"Shall I take your name to her, sir?" she said.

"No, no," said Varley; "show me into some room, and then go and tell her that a person wishes to speak to her concerning Rowland Percy."

The woman hesitated some moments, for she really thought her extraordinary visitor was mad; but Varley himself finished her irresolution by stepping to an open door which led into a neat little parlour, into which he walked, and sat down, saying:

"Take my message. I will wait here."

The woman had now no other resource but to go to Miranda, to whom she communicated the strange message.

"A man?" asked Miranda.

"Yes, miss; and not the handsomest in the world, nor the best behaved," was the reply.

"You don't know him?"

"No, miss."

"Is—is he tall—and dark?"

"Yes, he is; and has peculiar, deep-set eyes, that look one through and through in such a way that it's quite disagreeable."

"I will go to him directly."

The woman left the room, and then Miranda clasped her hands, as she said:

"'Tis he, Bernard Varley, the murderer of my father—the false witness against Rowland—the despoiler of my patrimony—'tis he, 'tis he! Oh, Heaven, grant me strength to go through this interview, for Rowland's sake—for the sake of the innocent, grant me patience to suppress, for a time, my deep, unutterable loathing of this bad man."

She then slowly, and with trembling steps, descended the stairs, and stood a moment by the parlour door before she could gather strength to open it. When she did so, she saw Varley standing but a few paces from the entrance.

At her appearance, he shook fearfully, and, clasping his hands, cried:

"Miranda, Miranda, do not fly from me—do not curse me! By your hopes of Heaven, by your dearest affections, I conjure you to hear me!"

Miranda held the back of a chair for support, as she said, in low, agitated accents:

"Bernard Varley, what brings you here?"

The advice of Mr. Anderson was present to her mind, or with what scorn she would have repulsed the villain who dared to pollute with his presence the refuge he had driven her to seek.

"Hear me—hear me," he said. "Miranda, beautiful being, hear me!"

"I hear," she said, in a low, choking tone.

"Miranda, when first my eyes beheld thee, I felt a new existence dashing wildly through my veins. You were young then—a pure, beautiful spirit, at that sweet springtime of existence, when the world is all new, and life, like a budding rose, is but just expanding to the glory that surrounds it. Then I loved you, then I adored you, then I worshipped you. But another stepped between me and my choice. Rowland Percy came. Can you wonder that I hated him? Can you wonder that he became the shadow on my soul which dimmed the sunshine that the love of you had cast upon it? Love and hate—love and hate! The two master passions of humanity were struggling in my heart—love for you, hatred to him. Oh, Miranda, Miranda, turn not from me! Kill me, but smile upon the ruin you have made."

He covered his face with his hands, and hot, scalding tears flowed between his fingers as he there knelt—such a picture of moral debasement as human nature seldom exhibits.

Miranda was terrified. She fain would have called for help, or rushed from the room as from the cell of some maniac—for it was certain Varley was not accountable at these moments for his words or actions—but the image of Rowland in his cell came across her mind, and she paused, for his sake.

"In this man's wild passion," she thought, "in his ecstasy of despair, he may confess something that may save the innocent. I will hear him—I will hear him."

"You do not speak to me," continued Varley. "You do not look upon me. Oh! let me hear your voice. Miranda, where will you find such love as mine? Where such wild, fervent devotion?"

"Rowland Percy," said Miranda.

"He cannot love like I love. His blood flows temperately through his veins. Ah, no! He cannot love as I love."

"You are his murderer!"

"But I can save him. Miranda, I can save even Rowland Percy. Were the fatal noose round his neck, even then I could save him—I, and no one else. Think of that, Miranda. I have come to tell you I could save him yet!"

"He is innocent."

"Hush—hush, Miranda. Come nearer to me. I may not speak aloud. Nearer, nearer, beautiful Miranda, the air is more serene and balmy near you. I do not think you quite mortal. You should live among cloisters. Nearer, nearer, Miranda, nearer."

"Rowland is innocent," said Miranda, as, by a violent effort, she forced herself to stoop towards Varley, who replied, in a hissing whisper:

"He is!—he is!"

CHAPTER LX.

THE ANSWER FROM LONDON—THE SECOND VISIT OF MIRANDA TO THE CONDEMNED CELL — THE BALLAD SINGER — RENEWED HOPE—THE MYSTERIOUS EPISTLE.

PERHAPS of all the severe trials which Miranda had endured, this one was that in which she had most need of self-control, and felt most difficulty in exercising it.

Loathing Bernard Varley as she did—a stranger to guile and dissimulation as she was—how very difficult a task it was for her to listen with common patience to his words, loaded as they were with the fulsome adulations which, from anyone, would have been distasteful.

She absolutely shuddered as she looked upon Varley kneeling at her feet with uplifted hands, and a countenance of such imploring agony, that anyone would have supposed him some abject wretch, pleading to an offended Deity for that mercy he could scarcely expect.

In low, moaning accents he spoke again.

"Oh, bethink you, Miranda, how much hangs upon your answer to me this night—the life of him whom you would fain rescue from the death to which the law has doomed him. The mortal agony of your own mind—an agony which, in its climax, will almost tempt you to doubt Heaven's mercy — my destruction for ever and ever; for I vow, if you reject me, I will do some deed to shut out all hope of mercy hereafter. My soul's perdition shall be heavy on you, and in the agony of countless ages my writhing spirit shall shriek your name as the cause of its destruction. Think what an awful thing is death, and such a death as that which awaits Rowland Percy. Think of that, Miranda, and, in blessing me, spare him."

With great reluctance Miranda answered him.

"Spare Rowland Percy," she said. "What power can you, Bernard Varley, have to snatch him from death?"

"I have—I have power, Miranda. Believe me, improbable as it may appear, I have such power."

"You then admit that he is innocent?"

"I can save him," was Varley's reply.

"And for your reward, you ask me to sacrifice myself, and all the hopes of happiness this world can afford me."

"I ask you to be mine, Miranda. What greater happiness can you look for than in being the bright, particular star of the heart's worship of such as I? My love is not the cold, common feeling, which profanes the same name. Oh, no, Miranda, it is as a mountain torrent, wild, free, and irresistible, compared to a placid lake, whose stagnant waters show no signs of vitality. Say you will live the object of my idolatry, and Rowland Percy shall be saved."

"Tell me how he is to be saved," said Miranda.

Varley was silent for a moment, and then he said:

"Upon that may I build a hope?"

Miranda could not for worlds have said yes. She turned away with a loathing shudder; and, when she could command her voice, she said:

"Bernard Varley, if you yet can and will save him, whom you know to be innocent, from an ignominious death, I can offer you but one reward."

"Name it—name it," he said.

"Forgiveness," said Miranda; "forgiveness for the past, and my prayers to Heaven to have mercy upon you."

"Is—that—all?" gasped Varley.

"Surely," added Miranda, "it is much from me to you. Could you have ever hoped for so much from me, upon whose head you have brought so much misery? Oh, Bernard! if there still lingers in your heart one germ of human feeling—one lingering hope of a hereafter, save him who, upon your false testimony, has been condemned to death, and, at least, release your soul from the consequences of another murder."

"Another murder?"

"Yes, another—for, as Heaven is my judge, I do believe you the contriver, if not the executor, of my father's death."

"This—is—your—fixed purpose, Miranda? You will make no other terms with me?"

"No other."

"Then all is over. He—he shall die—die the death of a felon: and I shall exult in his

agonies, while you, Miranda, tell yourself that by a word you might have saved him."

He stood by the door and looked wildly at Miranda. He seemed to meditate some further appeal to her, but the words stuck in his throat, and he could not do other than utter from the bottom of his heart deep and heavy groans.

Miranda would fain have left the room, but he stood in her way; and she was afraid to pass him.

Each moment seemed an hour of suspense, and then the door was opened from without, and Mr. Anderson showed himself.

Miranda sprang forward, as she cried:

"Save me from the presence of this man!"

Varley waited not to say another word to Miranda, but, muttering some unintelligible words between his teeth, he strode past Mr. Anderson, and left the house.

"Has the villain confessed anything?" asked the attorney.

"No, no; 'tis all in vain," was Miranda's reply. "Rowland! Rowland! each moment seems to decrease even the fragile hope to which I would fain cling."

Mr. Anderson was silent for some minutes; and, when he did speak, it was with a painful effort that he said:

"Miranda, you ought to know all. It is not right that anything should be kept from you."

"Heaven, help me!" said Miranda; "what new calamity can reach my heart?"

"Nothing new, but a confirmation of present fears. The answer of the Secretary of State has arrived."

"And—and——"

"It is unfavourable!"

Miranda shook like an aspen leaf as she resumed:

"And this is Tuesday night! Oh, Heaven, must I count the existence of him who is so dear to me by hours?"

"If," said Mr. Anderson, with much emotion, "any new hope should arise, you may depend upon it being eagerly seized upon by myself and the counsel."

"I—know it," said Miranda; "we have much to thank you for—God knows we have, Mr. Anderson. And—and—this is Tuesday night. Oh, Rowland! Rowland!"

"Nay, do not give way thus to despair: put your trust even yet in Heaven."

"We never know," said Miranda, "how heavily we have leant upon some fragile hope, until it is suddenly drawn from us. Despair is thickening around me. I think my reason will fail, and perhaps I shall then be happier."

"Miranda, Miranda," urged Mr. Anderson, "consider you have still a high and holy office to perform. If it be the will of Providence that Rowland Percy shall be sacrificed, do you be the ministering angel which shall light his path to the tomb, and rob death of its sting."

"You are right," said Miranda, clasping her hands. "Rowland, you shall not be forsaken because I despair. I will cheer him in his dungeon, I will bless him with kind words softly spoken, and I will promise him, which Heaven knows I may, that I will meet him soon in that world where there are no false accusers, no weak, fallible judges; no sorrow, no tears. My heart will break, and then I shall die, and join him and my murdered father."

"Will you," said Mr. Anderson, "undertake the task of communicating to old Mr. Percy the result of the application to the Secretary of State?"

"Yes—yes. That shall be my duty. I will do so."

Mr. Anderson still lingered, although the hour was getting late. He would fain have found some words of consolation for Miranda, but what could he say? What new hope could he awaken? How, even, could he preach patience to that wounded heart?

After remaining silent for some minutes, he silently pressed Miranda's hand in his, and then walked to the door.

He turned, however, upon the threshold, and a faint "God bless you!" came from his lips.

In another moment Miranda was alone with her griefs and her despair.

Mr. Percy she knew was sleeping, and she would not have him awakened to listen to the extinction of a hope which he had clung to much more strenuously than she, Miranda, had.

"The morning—the morning will be time enough," she murmured, "to communicate such tidings."

She then sought her own chamber, but not to sleep. For the whole night she lay in a kind of stupor of despair, while her fancy over and over again depicted to her the fearful scene of an execution, in which Rowland Percy was the victim.

Wednesday morning dawned gloomily upon the ancient city of York, and with what different sensations was it received by many who watched its faint, increasing light. How many welcomed it with joy, and converted its gloom into beauty by the sunshine of their own hearts? How many saw its first streak of gray light in the eastern sky with shudders and aching hearts, that would have cast a shadow over the most glorious sunshine?

Some there were who had lingered long upon a death-bed, to whom that day was the least sad one of this mortal career. Some there were in the pure springtide of existence, who on that day were to make some move in life which was to tincture the future with its colours, be they bright or gloomy. But of all the varied hopes, the fears, and agonies that were the adjuncts of that Wednesday, there could be none equal to those which in different manners affected the *dramatis personæ* of our veritable narrative.

What awful images chased each other through the mind of Bernard Varley, peopling vacancy with terrors, and wringing his very soul with anguish—what sufferings Twitter, in his frightful state of mental anxiety and dread, endured, we will not pause to attempt to portray. Let those evil-minded men writhe under the still, small voice of conscience which will make itself heard in the most seeming callous breast, while we follow Miranda once again to the lonely prisoner, awaiting his dreadful doom.

Mr. Percy had not made his appearance when Miranda was ready to visit the prison, and, still without having told the heartstricken old man of the answer that had been received from the Secretary of State, she, with hasty steps, walked to the prison.

Her order from the judge gained her instant admission, and, with a trembling heart, she entered Rowland's cell, which was another one nearer to the outer walls of the prison than that which she had before visited him in.

Miranda was dreadfully shocked at the change in his appearance which one night had produced, and the faint smile with which he strove to welcome her, was far more harrowing to her feelings than would have been the greatest ecstasy of grief.

For some moments they held each other's hands without speaking, and then Miranda said faintly:

"Rowland, you know all?"

"Yes—they removed me here last night, immediately upon the unfavourable answer of the Secretary of State being known. My only other remove will be to my grave."

His lips quivered as he spoke, and his whole appearance betrayed that death, and such a death, was a subject of frightful contemplation to him, and one from which he found it impossible to turn.

"Rowland—my Rowland," said Miranda, "I cannot yet believe it. They will not murder you."

"What hope is there now, Miranda?"

She covered her face with her hands, and shook palpably, as something seemed almost to whisper in her ear:

"Be Bernard Varley's wife, and save him."

"Oh, God! no, no, no!" she said.

"What, Miranda?" said Rowland, alarmed at her extreme agitation.

"Rowland, hear me. I have had a visit from Bernard Varley."

A flush of colour crossed the pale cheek of Rowland Percy, as, lifting his hand, he cried:

"May Heaven punish——"

"Hush! hush! Curse no one," interrupted Miranda. "The vengeance of Heaven will reach the guilty, without being invoked by a human voice. Hear what I was about to say to you, Rowland. Bernard Varley came to tell me that he could save you, even now."

"Yes, Miranda, he could; but such men as Bernard Varley do not sacrifice themselves so easily."

"But he named a condition."

"What condition, Miranda?"

"One that, if you will consent to, Rowland, I will accede to; but, if you do not, I fear——"

"Tell me, Miranda, what condition is this you almost dread to tell me?"

"It is—that I consent to become the wife of Bernard Varley."

"The villain! Dared he? Oh, Miranda, you know well my answer. Were death ten times over to be my fate, unless averted by such means, I would smile upon the torments that awaited me, and defy the villain, who, to save a life, would break a heart."

"But, Rowland, bethink you."

"No, no, Miranda. I will not deny that life is dear to me. I will not deny that death is terrible, but you have now shown me that there is something yet more hideous."

Miranda looked in his pale face, and again she thought:

"I should soon die were I to consent to what Varley requires—but Rowland would be saved. I should die before probably my promise to become his could be ratified. I feel that my heart is breaking. Shall I not save him?"

"Miranda, you look strangely and fixedly upon me, as if some fearful thoughts were passing through your brain that you would not trust me with."

"No, no, Rowland. No—do not despair, I will come to you again soon—very—very soon. This is Wednesday—Wednesday."

"And to-morrow——"

"Hush, Rowland, hush. Speak not of to-morrow. You may, perchance, see many suns rise and set yet, and, even should I not be among the living, you will always think of your poor Miranda, and spare a sigh for her love, a tear for her memory."

"For Heaven's sake, explain yourself, Miranda," he cried.

"Yes—yes, I will be back soon," she answered, "very soon. Farewell, for a brief space."

She drew closely around her the cloak she wore, and hurried from the prison.

CHAPTER LXI.

THE WRECK OF A MIND—MIRANDA'S NEW GRIEF—THE FATHER AND SON.

THE new idea which had sprung up so rapidly in Miranda's mind was a self-sacrificing one, and in consonance with her nature.

It was to save Rowland at the price of her own life, for she felt that, if she gave her consent to become the wife of Bernard Varley, she must die, as the only source of relief she could find.

"Perhaps," she thought, "I can induce him to wait for a time for the fulfilment of my promise, and then I shall be wedded to the tomb long before he can claim me as his bride. That will be the only way of saving Rowland. He is young, and life is all before him. It may be that time will enable him to forget me, and be happy with some other, who may not love him as I do, but, still, may create for him a home of contentment."

With these self-denying thoughts crowding through her brain, the noble-hearted girl walked swiftly towards her own home, for she had not made up her mind quite how and in what manner she should signify to Bernard Varley that she was at length prepared to listen to his offers.

Suddenly she felt someone touch her arm, and, on turning, she saw a tall man, with his face muffled up, who said, in coarse, but not uncourteous tones:

"Is it you, Miss Rankley? Kim up."

"What?" said Miranda, who was far from knowing anything of Mr. Jones or his peculiarities, for it was no other person than that gentleman himself.

"I axes yer pardon, miss," he said. "I means, is you Miss Rankley, without the kim up? That's only a way as I've got, and don't mean no harm nohow."

"My name is Rankley."

"Then jist read that ere, kivey——"

As he spoke he placed in Miranda's hand a small piece of paper, and then made off as fast as he could.

Miranda opened the paper, which was folded, but not sealed, and on it she read the following words:

"A friend to Rowland Percy will suggest something to Miranda Rankley that may be serviceable, if she will receive him this day at twelve o'clock, at her own home."

Miranda read the little epistle twice before she could believe that she had read it right, and then, crumpling it up in her hand, she said:

"Oh, is it possible that, without the dreadful sacrifice I contemplated, there is still a hope? Has Heaven not quite deserted us? I will see this mysterious stranger, be he whom he may. At twelve? Yes, even then there will be time."

An itinerant ballad-singer at this moment commenced singing a strain, the words of which rooted Miranda to the spot:

"When the heart, full of anguish,
    Knows naught but despair,
And cast is its shadow
    O'er all that is fair;
When bright hope has vanished,
    And pale is the cheek;
When, so lost are the sad ones,
    No mercy they seek.
Even, then, straight from Heaven,
    A ray will be cast
On the dull, blighted heart,
    And 'twill *hope to the last !*
'Hope! hope to the last !'
    Some angel's voice whispers—
'Hope! hope to the last !'

"When guilt seems to triumph
    O'er all that is good,
And virtue is cast from
    The rock where it stood;
When the innocent suffer
    And might governs right,
When the heart's wild despair
    Is darkling as night—
Even then, straight from Heaven
    A ray will be cast
On the dull, blighted heart,
    And 'twill hope to the last.
'Hope! hope to the last !'
    Some angel's voice whispers—
'Hope! hope to the last !'"

DICK PALMER MAKES A STRANGE PROPOSITION TO MIRANDA.

"I thank thee, Heaven!" said Miranda. "I will hope to the last. There is boundless mercy yet."

Nervously then clutching the little epistle in her hand, she hurried with refreshed feelings to her home.

She found old Mr. Percy in anxious expectation of her return, and, the moment he saw her, he, with trembling eagerness, said:

"You have seen my boy. He will be saved—he will be saved, Miranda!"

"Saved!" echoed Miranda.

"Yes—yes! I have slept long, and had happy visions. My poor boy Rowland will yet be saved. The answer from the Secretary of State must and will be a favourable one. All will be well, and we shall be so happy."

There was a strange earnestness about the old man's manner, and an alteration in his voice, that much alarmed Miranda. Moreover, she saw, or fancied she saw, in his eyes a wild and unnatural lustre, which they had never worn before to her observation.

"Mr. Percy," she said, imploringly, "there is, I trust, still hope, but the answer of the Secretary of State is——"

"Well—well—Miranda—speak——"

"Against us."

Mr. Percy sank into a chair with a deep groan, and his face became deathly pale. He opened and shut his hands convulsively for some moments; then he heaved a deep sigh, and almost immediately placed one hand upon his head, as if some sudden pain had come across him. A look of anguish passed over his face, and then calmly died away. It was succeeded by a smile—a smile of insanity—then a loud, frightful laugh followed, and, in a screaming voice, he said:

"Saved—saved—saved! My boy is saved at last, and we are rich again. Ha—ha—ha! Let the bells take up the joyous sound! Saved—saved—saved! And my boy, too!"

Miranda clasped her hands in despair. There could be no mistaking that laugh. Reason was overturned; the unhappy father was a maniac.

"Mr. Percy," cried Miranda, clinging to his arm, "speak to me—Mr. Percy."

"God bless you!" he said, "for my poor boy's sake, God bless you! We will have a merry wedding — a very merry wedding. Rowland loves you, and I will love you, Miranda Rankley. Have you told your father yet?"

"My father?"

"Yes. He should know. We must not settle all without him. And, do you hear, Miranda, you need not repeat my words; but, from my inmost heart, I consider Bernard Varley to be a villain."

"Alas, alas!" cried Miranda, "what shall I do? How shall I encounter this new horror? Mr. Percy, think again; my father is no more."

"Ah, so they said," replied he, "but I know better. Where is my boy?"

Miranda was too overcome by her feelings to answer him; but answer he required not, for he went on talking with strange garrulity, mingling together the living and the dead, but showing no symptoms of anything like violence.

At the request of Miranda, the people of the house, who were as compassionate as they could be, procured the attendance of a medical man, who gave it as his opinion that the aberration of intellect under which Mr. Percy was labouring would subside in time, and even, while it continued, would be quite a harmless fatuity.

"You need be under no apprehension, young lady," he said to Miranda; "he will, in all probability, be perfectly docile."

"For so much comfort, I thank you," said Miranda. "I believe he has no one but myself in this world to look to for a kind word."

"Pardon my curiosity," said the medical man; "but may I ask if this gentleman is in any way connected with the unhappy young man now lying under sentence of death?"

"His father, sir."

"Oh, indeed."

"And I am Miranda Rankley."

The surgeon bowed, as he said:

"I have heard your story from many mouths, and, if it be any satisfaction to you to hear such an individual opinion, I beg to say that I have a strong conviction of Mr. Rowland Percy's innocence."

"I thank you, sir," said Miranda, with much emotion. "He is innocent. Heaven knows that he is innocent, and I even yet hope for some interposition in his favour."

"I fervently wish that such a hope may be realized," said the surgeon, as he took his leave.

"How strange is it," sighed Miranda, "that nearly all but those whose opinions would have saved poor Rowland believe in his innocence."

The hour of twelve at this instant sounded from the Minster clock, and Miranda listened, with breathless eagerness, to the sounds.

She looked again at the little note which had been handed to her in the street, to assure herself she had made no mistake, and that twelve was, indeed, the hour named.

While she was doing so, one heavy knock at the street-door aroused her to a hope that it might be her mysterious visitor.

She stepped to the room door, and heard a voice say:

"Is Miss Rankley within?"

"Yes," she herself cried, as she opened the door. "I am here—I am here."

In a moment she recognized in the visitor Dick Palmer, for she had never forgotten him since he had given her her father's ring.

"You know me?" he said.

"I do, and trust you," responded Miranda. "If you can tell me aught that will give me any hope for Rowland Percy, I will bless you."

Palmer spoke very seriously and diffidently, as he said:

"Miss Miranda, I have something to suggest; but it is a wild scheme, and will require upon your part, perhaps, more nerve than you, under your present circumstances, can be mistress of."

"Never!" said Miranda. "Show me, tell me how I can rescue Rowland, and you shall see that I can do anything."

Miranda then conducted him into the room which, by courtesy of the people of the house, she was permitted to use, in case of anyone calling.

"I almost regret," said Palmer, "that I have ventured to suggest to you a hope which may never be realized; but, under desperate circumstances, Miss Rankley, desperate measures are required, and this is a most desperate one."

"Name it, and let it involve what risk it may, it shall be tried. I will thank you, from the bottom of my heart, for the least shadow of a hope."

"We must be very cautious, then," said Palmer, lowering his voice, "for there is danger even in the supposition of the course I am about to recommend."

———

CHAPTER LXII.

THE PLAN OF ESCAPE—MIRANDA'S GRATI-
TUDE—THE FIRMNESS OF A LOVING HEART
—HOPE LIVES STILL.

DICK PALMER'S manner as he thus spoke to
Miranda, was such as to raise in her heart the
most conflicting and contrary emotions.

There was something of hope, something of
fear—a glimpse of sunshine amid the gloom
which surrounded her, and yet so small, so
very indistinct a glance of that celestial light,
that she could scarce separate it from the
darkness around.

That Palmer had some proposition, which
he, extensive as his knowledge of human
nature was, deemed possible, although perchance beset with danger, was evident, and
slender as that foothold for hope was to
Miranda, she clung to it with an eagerness
that afflicted Palmer, for he judged how great
would be her disappointment in the failure of
what he had to propose, and that failure was
far more probable than success, he could not
conceal from himself for one moment.

"Miranda," he added, in a voice which
sounded mournful rather than hopeful, " hope
little, but try all. Had I a better suggestion
to offer to you, I would bring it ; but circumstances grow desperate as time rolls on, and
then desperate, strange and unlikely remedies
suggest themselves to the mind."

"Speak—speak," said Miranda. " That you
are a friend to him who is innocent, yet condemned, my heart assures me. Oh, if you can
suggest a means of saving him—if you can
suggest a means from which I can extract the
faintest hope, I implore you to tell it to me,
and bless my ears with happier sounds than
have greeted them for many a weary day."

"From my soul," said Palmer, " I sympathize with you, and I believe Mr. Rowland
Percy to be innocent."

"He is—he is !"

"It is—it has ever been my most firm conviction. But what can we do now to impress
our belief upon those who alone have power
to snatch him from death ?"

"You surely know enough—nay, you have
shown that you do," said Miranda, " of the
strange tangled web of circumstances connected with my poor father's death, to assist
you with some power to stay, what in this
case is the hand of revenge, not justice ?"

"I would I did—I would I did."

"Does not Varley tremble at a mere hint
concerning you ?"

"He does."

"Then——"

"Nay, hear me. Bernard Varley's own
guilty fears make him tremble, not my knowledge. As there be many timid depredators
who fancy that they see in each bush an
officer, so Bernard Varley has, upon most in-
sufficient grounds, invested me in his imagination with a power that makes him suffer
much mortal agony, but is productive of no
other result."

"Then," said Miranda, faintly, " you cannot
save Rowland ?"

"Not by any knowledge I possess. I am
in the same situation as yourself. I suspect
much, know nothing."

"Alas—alas !"

"Nay, do not quite despair until the period
for action has passed away : I have not come
merely to tell you how powerless I am, but
to suggest a plan which, if successful, will
restore Rowland Percy to liberty, and which,
even should it fail——"

"Heed not the consequences of failure, if I
alone am to be the sufferer," said Miranda.

"You alone would be."

"Thank Heaven !"

"Have you, do you think, courage, personally to aid in a most perilous and uncertain
attempt to rescue Rowland from his prison ?"

"Rescue Rowland ? Have I courage ? Tell
me what to do : point out to me some path
bristling with danger ; show me some daring
act which men might well start appalled from
attempting, and you shall see that a weak
girl's fond and trusting heart will nerve her
to the task."

"I cannot, will not, doubt you. Listen,
then, to my plan for Rowland's escape."

"Escape !"

"Hush !—we must be cautious, beyond the
ordinary bounds of caution. Even walls have
ears."

"Yes, yes," said Miranda, in a low tone,
" I will speak with bated breath—I will be
very cautious. Oh! speak again—say on—
say on. Speak again of Rowland's rescue."

"I will, but calm your agitation, I pray
you. What you will have to do will require
nerves as strong as iron—a cool, collected
brain—a firm step."

"When the time shall come," said Miranda,
" that all these qualities are essential for
Rowland's safety, you shall find I will not
shrink. Oh! tell me how—when—where I
am to call to my aid all the firmness of
nature in the cause of him—the innocent, the
young, and the gifted."

"You are," said Palmer, with unfeigned
admiration, " the noblest specimen of gentle,
loving woman that ever I beheld. Heaven
help you and him who has won so great a
treasure as your fond heart. The plan I have
to propose is this."

Miranda came close to Palmer, and the expression of deep and earnest attention and
anxiety that beamed from her face, was
almost painful to look upon. Her very
breathing seemed nearly suspended, and it
was evident that each word which fell from
Palmer's lips, went direct to her very heart.

It was in a tone of some emotion that the
man of many crimes, but whose guilty heart
was still susceptible of some of the best and
noblest sentiments of human nature, continued :

"My plan for the escape of Mr. Rowland
Percy from prison is based upon two circumstances. The one is your possession of a
written order from the judge to visit the

prisoner when you please; the other, my acquaintance with one of the officials of the prison, who will do what he can to aid me in any enterprise so near my heart as this is, for I have set my mind upon rescuing Rowland Percy—if such a thing be possible—at any risk."

"How can I thank you?" murmured Miranda.

"If I succeed, one smile of joy upon your sweet face will amply repay me."

"And—and your plan?"

"I will tell you briefly. My plan is that to-morrow evening—that is, the evening before the——"

"Execution," said Miranda, with a shudder.

"I would have spared you the word, but it was what I meant. To-morrow evening, then, I would have you go to the prison in the same large cloak and long, black dress you have hitherto worn on your gloomy visits."

"Yes—yes."

"Persuade Rowland Percy to disguise himself in that cloak and dress. Then, the man I speak of, being on duty at the gate——"

"I see it all—I see it all!" cried Miranda, clasping her hands. "There is a hope—there is a hope!"

"A slender one."

"But still a hope!"

"Truly. He, then, being on duty at the gate, will, unquestioned and unscrutinized, permit Rowland to pass out."

"Yes—yes! Good friend! Oh, yes!"

"Should all this succeed, I will be there to receive him, and with my own life I will answer for his safety—if once he be clear of the prison walls."

"You are our deliverer!" cried Miranda, with animation.

"But, remember," added Palmer, "you cannot escape yourself. You will be left in the gloomy cell now occupied by Rowland."

"Gloomy cell! It will be to me a palace of light—radiant and beautiful. Gloomy—ah, no! The sunshine of my own joy will irradiate it, and make it glow with sunny lustre."

"By Heaven!" cried Palmer, "if ever human heart deserved the greatest happiness, it is yours."

"And Rowland will be free," said Miranda, evidently not hearing, or, if she did, not comprehending Palmer's words. "Once more he will breathe the pure air of Heaven—once more I shall see him smile as he has smiled of yore, before the blight of affliction fell upon us all."

"From my soul, I hope that such will be the case," said Palmer. "We can but try the enterprise; and would that its practical execution lay with myself! but the circumstances are such that none but you can afford the least glimpse of hope to the prisoner."

"That do I rejoice at," said Miranda; "for, save myself, who feels for him in his helplessness and persecution sufficiently to dare all for his preservation? I feel even now a conviction at my heart that Heaven is working

with us—that the full tide of our misfortune has reached its flood. The future contains hope—a hope that will be realized in joy. Rowland shall be saved!"

"You are enthusiastic, and sanguine of the success of the scheme," said Palmer; "and you have, by your confidence, made me think better of it than before. I would advise you to go at once to the prison, and prepare Mr. Percy for the effort that will be made to save him, and in that going be sure you wear as much over your face, as may be, the cloak that he is to conceal himself in. Indeed, as you come out of the prison, affect so much concealment of your face as to excite surprise—if not suspicion."

"I understand."

"Should you be stopped, even, it will be a step gained towards the success of our plan."

"It would—it would!"

"I would not desire a more favourable circumstance than that you should be stopped by some meddling officer, who should insist upon seeing your face. Affect, then, indignation at such want of courtesy, and threaten an appeal to the judge who gave you the written order of admission. Rowland, then, will be more likely, when so muffled up, to pass unquestioned."

"Thanks—thanks," said Miranda. "I will treasure up in my memory every word you say. I will forget nothing; all shall be as you direct."

"All that I can tell you, then, is, that he upon whose friendly offices I can depend will be on duty at the outer door of the prison at nine o'clock this evening."

"That is the hour the gates are closed against all visitors," said Miranda.

"It is; and here some management and caution will be necessary. You must effect the change in Rowland's dress as speedily as possible after your arrival, and take care to keep the door of the cell fast until you hear nine strike. Then he must not wait for the turnkey to come and warn you to be gone, but he must step out of the cell, closing the door behind him."

"Yes—yes. It shall be so done."

"When you are yourself left in the cell, place yourself at the table, with your back towards the door, and appear to be leaning your head upon your hands in deep affliction. You must have Rowland Percy's coat on, and you must conceal your hair as much as possible."

"Fear not," said Miranda; "all shall be well arranged."

"I have no doubt. Exactly as nine strikes, my friend will be at the outer gate. He will let Rowland Percy out as quickly as possible, and it may be hours before the affair is discovered."

"Perhaps not till morning."

"No. The cell will be visited every two hours during the night, but at the first visit you may not be discovered, if you affect to be sleeping."

"And in the meantime you will provide for Rowland's safety?"

"I will. At the second visit to the cell, which will be at one o'clock in the morning, I would advise you to declare yourself. They dare not then keep you in the cell, for that is only destined for condemned prisoners, and, although you will be detained, it will not be in a place so replete with unpleasant associations."

"But there would then be pursuit."

Palmer smiled, as he replied:

"There might; but I would consent to forfeit my head if it were successful. I have means of concealment which may defy all the police of York. When you hear one o'clock strike, you may tell yourself that Rowland Percy is quite safe."

"Oh, happy thought!"

"Farewell, now," said Palmer. "Heaven help you. If our enterprise should be successful, I will take care to find means by which Mr. Percy can communicate with you in writing."

"Before we part," said Miranda, earnestly, "tell me who and what you are."

Palmer shook his head.

"The knowledge would avail nothing. I am one who, too early thrown upon a bad world, took up bad weapons in self-defence."

"But your name?"

"Pardon me. There are reasons why you had better remain in ignorance of who I am. Pray take the good which I can offer you alone. My life has been a chequered one. I have done much wrong, and am in some things a proscribed man; but all natural feeling is not quenched within my breast."

"Let the world say of you—think of you—what it may," said Miranda, "my fervent gratitude is yours, and while I have a voice, it shall ever be raised in defence of you, my friend, and the friend of the innocent."

"God bless you!" said Palmer, with emotion. "When we meet again, may it be under far happier circumstances. Till then, farewell!"

CHAPTER LXIII.

THE PRISON—THE FATHER AND SON—MI-RANDA'S PROPOSAL—ROWLAND'S SUPPLICATION—THE ARRANGED PLAN OF ESCAPE.

In the meantime, little aware that such generous and self-sacrificing exertions were being made for his release, Rowland Percy was a prey to all the alternations of hope and despair.

As the time crept on, he began to think that his fate was, indeed, inevitable, and that he was doomed to form a cruel illustration in after years of the fallibility of human judgment.

A deep sigh escaped him, and for many minutes he remained in bitter contemplation.

"To die thus," he then muttered, "even in the morning of life. To linger for a few moments upon the verge of existence, and

that for an imputed crime, of which Heaven knows my innocence—to be held up to execration as a monster, as a shedder of human blood—one destitute of that great principle in the social code which forbids man to shed man's blood. Oh! 'tis sad—a sad—a fearful fate. And what is death? What sights and sounds are to greet us when once we have passed the dreadful portal which separates the mortal from the immortal part of God's creation?"

He paced his narrow cell with unequal steps, and strove, with what judgment Heaven had endowed him, to plunge among the mysteries of the world that was to come. How soon was he, then, in

"Wandering mazes lost."

How inadequate did he feel his mortal power to grapple with the great questions of immortality and eternity?

With a shudder he sat down again, and muttered:

"No—no. There human wisdom and human research avail nothing. We shrink before the rush of images that crowd upon the brain. We are lost—lost in an unfathomable depth of thought."

He started suddenly, for his prison door opened, and the turnkey made the usual abrupt exclamation when announcing anyone, of:

"Visitor!"

"To me?" exclaimed Rowland; "is it—is it——"

"Miranda," said she herself, as she entered the cell, and took both the hands of Rowland in hers. "It is Miranda, dear, dear Rowland."

The turnkey gave a grunt, as he left the door of the cell, and went away, muttering:

"Uncommon fine and loving, to be sure, but that won't hinder the hanging to-morrow. Ha! ha! ha!" And laughing loudly at what he considered his own great wit and cleverness, he proceeded to the outer gate to retail his joke.

"Once again—once again," said Rowland, as he gazed fondly on the face of Miranda, "once again you have, like a blessed messenger of holy peace and love from Heaven, sought the dreary dungeon of the solitary prisoner. My own Miranda, my beautiful and good! My latest breath shall be a blessing upon thee."

"Rowland," said Miranda, as she clutched his hands with convulsive earnestness, and glanced apprehensively about her. "Rowland, there is no one who can overhear what we say?"

"Certainly not, Miranda. We are, I believe, as much alone here as if we were in the wilderness of nature. But wherefore do you ask?"

"Because, Rowland, I wish to ask you if you really love your Miranda?"

"Love you—love you! Is this a time to doubt?"

"No, not to doubt, but to prove the dear

love that I believe glows brightly in your heart."

"How prove it?"

Miranda looked beseechingly in his face as she said:

"Hear me say all that now gushes from my heart to my tongue. The time is now come when I have that to ask you which will try your feelings, cause much false sense of honour, cause you to start, and possibly oppose yourself to your own and my happiness in this world while either of us are doomed to be sojourners in it. But you must promise me, Rowland. You must say you will consent. You must not doom me to the unspeakable misery of thinking I might have saved, and——"

"Miranda, Miranda," said Rowland, despairingly, "oh, urge no more that theme. You do, indeed, wring my heart. To see you another's—to purchase life—a life of wretchedness and remorse—by the sacrifice of you to such a monster——"

"You mistake me, Rowland," interrupted Miranda. "I came not to urge again that dreadful suggestion. No—no—Heaven be thanked, no! That has passed away."

"What hope would your words and glances instil into my heart? You look hopeful. You have something yet to tell me, which—which—Miranda—keep me not in suspense. If I am saved——"

His colour went and came like the flashing sunlight of an April morn, and he trembled more from the excitement of revived hope than ever he had done from the abandonment of despair.

The idea had got possession of him that some favourable turn must have taken place in his affairs, and that Miranda was fearful of communicating it to him, lest sudden joy should do him more harm than all his misery had accomplished.

Miranda saw in a moment that such was the idea of Rowland, and she hastened to undeceive him.

"Rowland," she exclaimed, hurriedly, "there is no secret—I know nothing—have no news. On my word, Rowland, I am keeping no intelligence from you."

He became very pale as he said:

"Then tell me, dear Miranda, what has given new colour to your cheeks, and fresher brilliancy to your eyes?"

"Hope—hope!"

"For me?"

"Yes, Rowland, for you—a hope founded on an act of energy, of enterprise and danger—that is, the danger of failure, for we have all to gain—fortune can place us no lower on her wheel."

"True. An ignominious death——"

"Hush, hush. I came not unadvisedly to breathe to you a hope of—of—escape."

"Escape from here? Alas, Miranda, you know not what you say—it is impossible."

"By force truly impossible, but stratagem may succeed where force were vain. I think I must make you promise me you will consent. For my sake, you will: you cannot say me nay, Rowland—I know you will not. They cannot harm me. You will consent to escape—to allow yourself this night to be enveloped in my cloak—to attempt a passage from the prison. All this you will do for my sake—for your poor suffering father's sake—you will, Rowland—oh, tell me you will?"

These words were uttered with a pathos that went to the very soul of Percy, for Miranda well knew that he would shrink long from exposing her to the consequences of aiding in his attempt to escape, and so strong did the feeling that he would not consent become in her mind, that it assumed to her imagination the shape of the greatest difficulty connected with the project.

Miranda was right, for if, indeed, there was any plan likely to aid him from which he would shrink more than from another, it would be such a one as Palmer had proposed, and Miranda, in her despair, adopted.

Rowland turned away his face for a moment to hide the sudden gush of feeling that came over his heart, and exhibited itself in his countenance, at this instance of pure, disinterested. and self-sacrificing affection on the part of Miranda.

"Oh, is there such another heart as this?" he asked himself. "Shall I—dare I accept so great a sacrifice?"

Miranda knew not for a moment, when he turned from her, how to construe the action; but when, in the next instant, he again looked in her face, and said, in tones of deep emotion—tones that gushed fresh and feelingly from the heart:

"Dearest—best——," she uttered a cry of joy, and throwing herself upon his breast, said:

"You consent, Rowland—you consent; my Rowland, you will save yourself?"

"Miranda," he said, "I were, indeed, the veriest wretch that ever crawled beneath the canopy of Heaven, if I felt not deeply, appreciated not fully, the generous, noble sacrifice you would make for me. It is, indeed, in misfortune and bitterness of heart that the purest, holiest feelings of human nature are summoned from the dreamy rest, which might for ever have hung upon them had the spangled veil of prosperity still hidden their proper sphere of action. My Miranda—my own beautiful Miranda, you would expose yourself to evils you dream not of by an attempt to take my place in this dreary abode. Think of my agony, even were this plan successful to escape myself, the dread of to-morrow, by entailing upon you a portion of the miseries I have undergone. Could I see you arraigned——"

"Rowland—Rowland—think of my greater agony."

"But, Miranda——"

"Nay, hear me. You yourself have called my love self-sacrificing; do you imitate it, and let yours likewise be self-sacrificing."

"My life, Miranda, were it freely mine, instead of holding it now, as I do, upon so frail a tenure, should be at any moment cast away to save you a passing pang."

"And so inflict a never-ceasing agony upon me. Rowland, your argument is false. Feeling blinds your judgment; you would die, to save me for a few days, perchance, from the tiresome *ennui* of a prison, and, by so dying, you would break the fond heart that clings to you—you see, Rowland, you are wrong. Upon my own account I came to you on this mission. Surely you will, of two evils, strive to ward the greater from your own Miranda. You see I am selfish, Rowland, and you will consent."

Rowland Percy was silent for a moment. His judgment could not but acquiesce in Miranda's reasoning, but his feeling revolted from purchasing liberty at the price of her freedom.

"Miranda," he said, "this plan might fail."

"It might—all human plans may fail. It is for Heaven above to say, let this be, and command the results of human action; but should it fail, I then shall know of the failure—were it untried, I should ever predict its success, and it would be a new source of woe and anguish. You see, Rowland, it must be done. To-night I will be here. Oh! I am full of hope. Heaven help us, Rowland."

"My—my noble Miranda."

A tear glistened in Percy's eye as he looked upon her beaming face, eloquent with the best feelings of humanity. Oh! what would the apparently triumphant Bernard Varley have not given to feel, for one fleeting instant, the pure sunshine of the heart that irradiated the breasts of those two innocent beings, as in silence—a silence more eloquent than words—they thus, for some minutes, gazed upon each other, making a very palace of that dungeon, by the light of love and truth that beamed upon its frigid walls.

Miranda first spoke, as she clung closer to her lover's heart. In soft, whispered accents, she murmured:

"You consent, Rowland—you consent?"

"Yes—yes."

"Joy—joy and hope," said Miranda. "Till eight this evening, farewell. I am happier now than I have been since last I saw my poor father in life. Heaven has not forgotten us. Farewell—till eight."

He clasped her to his heart. He could not speak, but he imprinted one kiss upon the marble brow, took one look at the beaming face, and then threw himself into the chair.

Miranda gathered her cloak about her, and stepped lightly from the cell.

"Now to awaken suspicion," she said. "Let me be questioned now, in order that Rowland may pass unquestioned to-night."

CHAPTER LXIV.

MIRANDA AND THE TURNKEY—VARLEY'S NEW HOPES—THE ARRANGEMENTS OF PALMER—THE HOUR OF EIGHT.

MIRANDA, when she left the cell, proceeded for some distance through the tortuous passages conducting to the outer gate of the prison, before she was met by anyone, and then she heard footsteps approaching her, which she guessed to be those of a turnkey, who had his post in a little nook in the passage, some short distance from where she was.

Pausing immediately, Miranda, in pursuance of the advice given her by Palmer, muffled up her face as much as possible with the ample cloak she wore, and purposely affected a wish to pass the officer without showing her face.

The man's suspicions were awakened in a moment, and, giving what he considered an amazingly knowing wink, he followed Miranda until she arrived at the vestibule of the prison, when he suddenly stepped forward, saying:

"Perhaps, before you go, miss, you will have the kindness just to let us see as it is you."

"Sir?" said Miranda, in an assumed tone.

"We just want one look at your face."

"Why this insult?"

"Just for the sake of satisfaction. It rather strikes me, too, that you've got a cold, for you don't speak just as I have heard you, miss—ahem!"

Miranda withdrew the cloak from her face, as she said, in a mournful tone:

"'Tis very hard that grief should not be permitted even to hide its face from rude curiosity. The thoughts of to-morrow may well weigh heavily upon my heart, and even impart to my voice an unnatural tone. You now see my face, and even have the poor satisfaction of having added an additional pang to sorrow already too—too—but I will not, for the few hours that I shall have cause to visit this place, be treated thus. I will see the governor, and surely he will give permission that I may keep my tears sacred from the observation of his menials."

The officer, who had thought himself so very cunning, and who really had suspected his prisoner was attempting an escape, looked confounded when he saw Miranda's pale face, and heard her talk of an appeal to the governor, for he knew perfectly well that he should be just as much abused for his mistaken zeal, as he would have been praised for his cleverness, had his suspicions turned out to be well founded.

"I—I," he stammered, "I beg pardon, but, you see, miss, I—I—really——"

"Enough, enough," said Miranda, "I ought not to complain. The wretched should suffer, perhaps, such things in silence. It will be time to appeal to a higher authority should the insult be repeated."

So saying, she passed out at the gate which the man who was on duty there was holding open for her. When she was gone, he turned to the discomfited officer, and said :

"Well, Joey, you've put your foot in it, I don't think."

"Well, I never !" said Joey. "Here is a kick up. Why did she look so blessed 'spicious ?"

"Feelings, Joey, feelings."

"Feelings be bothered, I never had none, and I don't see the use of 'em—not I."

"I can't say as I sees the use on 'em, Joey ; but you know people as comes to see other people as is a-going to be hung, always comes it strong in that ere line."

"They does—they does."

"Well, you ought to make lowances, Joey."

"So I does. When Dick Lee, the cracksman, was hung, and his wife comed with a bottle of gin the night afore, didn't I make lowances ?"

"Yes, you did, for you lowanced it out atween you and her, and never said to me so much as ' Bill, will you take a drain ?' "

" Feelins purwented me."

"You be bothered, and I tells you what, if that there young ooman complains to the guvnor, I wouldn't give tuppence for your place, Joey."

"Thank you for nothink," said Joey, as he walked away, and then muttered to himself, " Blessed if she mayden't come out and in, in a bag tied up tight at the top, afore I'll have anythink more to say to her. How do I hate feelins, to be sure. I ne'er had none—ain't got none, and don't want none. Feelins be blowed !"

Having thus vented his indignation, Joey sat down, with a conviction that he was a very greatly injured man.

In the meantime, strange as it may appear, Bernard Varley was in a more hopeful state than he had experienced since the trial. In the first place, he thought he saw symptoms of wavering resolution in Miranda's manner, and he nourished an expectation that, perhaps, at the last moment, she might save her lover at the sacrifice of herself, and, giving him a solemn promise which he could rely upon, enable him to take the necessary steps for saving Rowland Percy.

He arranged then, with singular clearness and perspicuity, what he meant to do. The only one point upon which his mind was evidently unable to think rationally concerned Miranda. His hopes of ever winning her to become his were based upon the most extraordinary improbabilities, and yet he clung to them with dogged perseverance, while his judgment would have at once detected their fallaciousness, had they presented themselves in any other shape.

After his interview with Miranda, he hurried homewards, not to his lodging opposite, but to where he expected to find Twitter, with whom he wished to have some more conversation concerning the adventure by the gravel-pits.

Neither of them had visited the Grange, and Varley found Twitter at home, seriously ill from the fright he had sustained, and in a state of mental and physical prostration, which was of the most alarming nature.

He was, however, Varley thought, more likely to return truthful answers to what he should ask of him than if he were in his usual state. The great fact which he wished to ascertain was, if Twitter had seen the mysterious man—from whose supposed knowledge he, Bernard Varley, shrank aghast—interfering in any way with the course of examination that he, Twitter, had undergone by the brink of the chasm, down which he had been threatened to be hurled.

That the mysterious horseman had a part in that transaction appeared to Varley more than probable, and what he wished to please his mind with as a consequence was, that the knowledge of the mysterious horseman concerning the murder of Sir George Rankley must be limited, or, perhaps, only conjecture ; for, if it were otherwise, if he really possessed ample information, why should he seek by threats to wring from Twitter a confession of that which, if known to him already, he could use to the destruction of them both ?

Hence it was that Varley, most anxious to rid his imagination from the bugbear that was ever present to it, in the shape of the solitary horseman, wished, if possible, to identify him with the attempt upon Twitter, which, if he could thoroughly succeed in doing, would calm his mind upon the subject.

These, then, were the two sources of Varley's consolation and easier state of mind. Hopes of Miranda at the last hour relenting, and becoming his to save Rowland, as well as a rescue from his dread of the unknown horseman.

His question to Twitter was :

"Were you aware of the presence of a tall man, wearing a riding-cloak, when you were assaulted by the ruffians, and threatened with death ?"

"No—no," said Twitter, "I saw no one distinctly but the man who held me and catechised me. You know, Varley, that I was staunch and faithful—telling nothing that could injure you—breathing no sort of suspicion upon your name."

"Peace !" said Varley. "I know better than perhaps you are aware of what you said, and well can I guess what you would have said had I not interfered to save you from what, after all, I believe firmly was but an empty threat that was never meant to be carried into execution."

"You think they would not have killed me ?"

"I am sure they would not. The thing was a mere trick on the part of Percy's friends to wring a confession from you, for well can I perceive they suspect the truth."

"Then we are in great danger ?"

"Wherefore ? Let the whole world suspect what it may, provided nothing can be proved, and Rowland Percy in the meantime will be hanged, unless——"

Varley paused, and Twitter said anxiously: "What can save him now?"

"Nothing, nothing, Twitter, but what would destroy us. The next hanging in York will be Rowland Percy's, or——"

"Oh, cease, cease," cried Twitter. "Can you command voice and nerve to indulge in such dreadful speculations?"

"Yes, when the result is certain. Now, Twitter, I have but one piece of advice to give you, and upon your own head be it if you neglect it."

"Advice, Varley; what is it?"

"This—until Rowland Percy is hanged, you must not stir from this house. Who knows what other plan would be adopted to scare you into a confession that would be our destruction?"

"I will not stir," said Twitter. "Believe me, Varley, I will not cross the threshold of this house until he is dead. I would not encounter such another attack for worlds."

"You are prudent—very prudent, Twitter."

"And you, too, Varley—you will be cautious. Oh, be warned, and abandon your mad chase after Miranda. It can end in nothing but ruin. Be warned in time. If there be any one circumstance fraught with danger to us both, it is that—it is that."

With a smile of contempt upon his lips, Varley left the room.

"He is gone—he is gone," muttered Twitter. "Shall I know more peace when Rowland Percy has met his doom? Will the horrible images that now persecute me through the long hours of the night then leave me? Surely, yes. They will—they will, and I shall be more calm—more composed—my blood will not then boil through my veins one moment, as if it would burst its bounds, and then suddenly pause, and seem to curdle round my heart, as if it never meant to flow again. Yes—yes, I shall feel a great relief when Rowland Percy is dead."

He lay, then, for some minutes silent, but his restlessness would not be appeased, and he spoke again.

"I must force myself from Varley," he muttered. "By robbery, and by what I can wring from him, I must get enough for comfort, and then leave him. If—if—my nerves and strength would let me, I would some day take his life. I would—I would! Oh, how I hate him! Curses—curses!"

He lifted up his hands, and his countenance assumed an awful expression, as he showered bitter maledictions on the head of the man who had tempted him to such iniquity, and then deceived him as to the promised wages of his crime.

Exhausted, then, by his own wild emotion, he remained passive for hours, only occasionally dropping off into an uneasy slumber, which was visited by crowds of frightful images, that gibed and mocked him, until, with cries of terror, he would awaken, and start half from his couch, gazing into vacancy, with eyes glazed with horror.

Varley, when he reached his room, opposite to where Miranda resided, sat himself down thoroughly to arrange his diabolical schemes.

The unprincipled attorney, who had assisted him so far as Sir George Rankley's will was concerned, had made him an offer for the Grange estates—of course, far below their value—and Varley's scheme was this:

Should Miranda consent, at the last moment, to become his, in order to save Rowland, he would at once proceed to the attorney, and accept his offer, with the deduction of a large percentage, provided that, there and then, he gave him the cash, which he knew he could do. Then, having extracted so solemn a promise from Miranda to be his, that she could not retract it, he would write to the judges, denying all his evidence upon the trial, and flatly accusing Samuel Twitter of the murder. At the same time, when he forwarded his letter, he himself would start for the Continent, in some obscure part of which he would wait the result of the affair.

CHAPTER LXV.

THE NIGHT BEFORE THE EXECUTION — MIRANDA'S COURAGE—THE CELL—THE DISGUISE—DICK PALMER'S ANXIETY.

WHEN Miranda reached her home, after the agitating interview she had had with Rowland Percy, her first inquiry was for the afflicted father, who exhibited such fearful evidence of what a wreck sorrow could make of the strongest mind.

Had her mind not been engrossed as it was, even to overflowing, with the condition of her lover, and the million of hopes, fears, and anxieties that waited on the enterprise of the coming evening, she might have felt more keenly and more deeply the state of Mr. Percy; but, as it was, she realized how true it is that great griefs, in their wild intensity and overwhelming power, swallow up all lesser ones, making the human mind look with comparative calmness upon events which, had they come alone, would have filled the heart with terror and the imagination with dismay.

Insanity, in any shape or form, is always terrible, and to a mind constituted as Miranda's was, it presented ever the most lamentable aspect; for the greater the degree of mental power, excellence, and beauty there may be in one mind, the more keenly and bitterly will such an intellect commiserate with those who, from temporary or permanent causes, have lost the God-like power which lifts humanity so near the pure throne of Heaven.

To her relief, she was told that Mr. Percy slept.

After talking much of his Rowland, and indulging in many visions of the happiness he should himself have, by witnessing the joy of Miranda and his son, who, as he supposed, were about to be married, with the consent of Sir George Rankley, whose death he would not believe, he had dropped into a peaceful slumber, from which the medical man anticipated the most beneficial results.

"If this sleep," he said, "should continue calm and unshaken for some hours, it may carry off his mental hallucination; but should he, during it, be tormented with dreams, the mind will scarcely be able to recover its equilibrium, and the temporary insanity may continue for some time longer. There is every appearance at present of the happiest result."

Such was the state of affairs when Miranda reached her home, where she resolved to wait, and see no one till the time should arrive for her to start upon her heroic expedition of love and devotion.

She sat down in silence by the bedside of Mr. Percy, and her thoughts wandered back again to Rowland's gloomy cell.

A bright smile played like sunshine upon her face, as she thought what a glorious habitation it would seem to her for the few hours succeeding the successful escape of Rowland, should Heaven in its mercy will that that escape should succeed, and save the innocent even in the hour of greatest peril.

Thus she pictured to herself what the future might still be, should Rowland escape destruction.

"Surely," she thought, "the day will come when his innocence will be apparent, and he will be able to walk abroad among his fellow men with an unclouded brow, an unshrinking heart—now all men's hands are raised against him, and he stands alone, with nothing but his consciousness of right to guide him through the tangled paths of mental disquietude, and save him from despair, or the worse fate which has befallen his poor, suffering father."

Miranda was silent now for a time, but her thoughts were very busy. They carried her far back, even to her happy childhood, when all around her was sunshine and joy. Not the dimmest shadow of the cloud which since had burst with such awful violence over her, and all that she loved, then showed itself in the sunny heaven of her heart.

"We were so happy," she murmured, "so very happy, so full of life, of joy, and love. Oh, who would have believed that of four human beings, upon whom the sun of prosperity was so brightly shining, there should be but one yet so far unscathed as to have even the liberty of action. My father murdered—Rowland condemned for a crime he never for one instant contemplated, and which the tenor of his life, and the constitution of his mind, should at once give a contradiction to—his father, the wreck of what he was, a maniac—and I—I, a poor, helpless girl, striving against such an accumulation of miseries, as formerly to read of would have tortured my brain, and given me hours of disquietude."

She clasped her hands upon her head, and, leaning down upon the bed, strove to weep, for she felt as if tears would be a world of relief to her.

A voice seemed, then, to whisper to her:

"Not yet, Miranda—not yet—no tears yet."

"I cannot weep," she said. "'Tis very strange. Time was when the death of a bird, the untimely fading of a flower, would have wrung my heart, and each fond pet had its tributary tear; but now, feelings that lie deeper than the source of tears are awakened, and I cannot weep."

She sank, then, upon her knees by the bedside, and offered up an artless, eloquent prayer to the Author of all good, to aid her in her enterprise to save the innocent. She asked not that the guilty should be punished, but with gentle, holy supplication, she wished the innocent to be saved, and virtue to be rescued from distress.

When does prayer ever fail to relieve the oppressed heart? Miranda, when she rose again, felt a holy calm stealing over her, her brain had ceased to throb, and her heart beat in more regular pulsations. Who will doubt that the supplications of that young, pure being had reached the throne of mercy, and been accepted by Him who has said: "Come to Me in your sorrow, and you shall be comforted."

Scarcely had she risen from her posture of prayer, when she heard a slight tap at the chamber-door.

Upon opening it she saw the woman of the house, who said:

"Mr. Anderson is below; he wishes to speak to you, and to know how Mr. Percy is now."

"Mr. Percy sleeps," said Miranda. "Tell him I——"

She paused, for she shrank from refusing to see the faithful friend, who throughout all her dire adversity had clung to her with so much disinterested devotion, and yet she felt the necessity of not seeing him, for she would not for worlds have him a party to the scheme for the liberation of Rowland, so far as to commit him professionally in the matter; for, should that scheme fail, what an additional source of anguish would it be to her to reflect that in its trial she had inflicted injury upon others as well as herself.

These thoughts flashed through Miranda's mind with great rapidity, as she said:

"Give my best regards to Mr. Anderson, and tell him to see me in the morning. Just now I am not equal to the task of seeing even my best and dearest friends."

This message was communicated to Mr. Anderson, who, of course, instantly departed, grieving sadly over the melancholy and despair which he felt sure were gnawing at the heart of the beautiful girl who must look forward to the morrow with such exquisite anguish.

"Yes, to-morrow," said Miranda; "to-morrow—Heaven send he may find me in Rowland's cell. Oh, with what joy he will see me looking upon those dingy walls. Methinks I could for ever take up my abode within them, were Rowland free."

An uneasy movement on the part of Mr. Percy now arrested her attention, and she looked earnestly in his face. He slowly opened his eyes. One glance of those orbs was enough for Miranda. They spoke not of mind—the wild, restless glare of insanity still shone from them. The sleep had not done its gentle office well, and the mind was still a chaos of disjointed images.

He knew Miranda, for, as a smile played upon his lips, he said:

"You are my dear son Rowland's beautiful bride. God bless you, Miranda. How happy we shall be for many, many years. Bless you and my boy—where is he? Surely he is not still tossing on those restless, white-crested waves?"

Miranda sighed deeply.

"Hush! hush!" said the old man. "Do not sigh—I think that was a dream. Have I slept?"

"You have."

He laughed a strange, wild laugh, as he added:

"I thought so—I thought so. Yet it was so very, very like reality. I will tell you. My boy Rowland, who lies so near my heart, I thought I saw him on a stormy ocean. Oh! how the wild winds howled, and how fearfully the waves dashed hither and thither the tiny barque which, like a shell, danced over the curling foam. My boy held bravely on—his eye flinched not—he looked like a spirit of the waters, watching them in their wild, boisterous play. Oh! it was beautiful to see how the one small boat, fashioned by the hands of man, thus sported with the wildest element of nature, and defied its utmost wrath."

Mr. Percy spoke in a tone of strange, wild enthusiasm, and Miranda was greatly interested by the romance of his singular dream.

"What more?" she said. "What more?"

"I will tell you. I watched the little shell-like barque, with its living freight, till my eyes ached again. It was my Rowland who was in it, and his face was very pale. He seemed wound up to some great pitch of mental endurance. I never saw him look so pale—except once—except once."

"When was that?"

"Hush!—don't speak of it. But it was once when I thought they accused him of murder."

Miranda shuddered, and cried:

"Alas! alas! how strangely reality mingles with fiction! How the fevered imagination trenches on the memory, making strange havoc and confusion in the brain."

"That was a worse dream than this," continued Mr. Percy, "and it very nearly drove me mad. They accused him of murder—my son—my own gentle, brave, tender, gallant Rowland!"

"But—but the dream?" said Miranda. "I pray you go on with the dream. What happened to the small boat in which was Rowland? Tell me all."

"I will—I will. The fierce wind from the south came rushing on, like a wild creature shrieking for prey. It curled round the misty waves, mingling them together in a wild confusion, till the sea looked like a seething caldron stirred by millions of evil spirits, and all for the destruction of that small, shell-like boat and its pale human occupant."

"And what did he?"

"Sometimes I saw him not. Sometimes, on the topmost pinnacle of a surging wave, I saw it balanced, for a moment, as if in mid-air; then down—down it flew, like a guilty thing, into the deep abyss below."

"But there was a Heaven above," said Miranda. "There was an eye, which never sleeps, gazing down upon that boat and the soul that was cradled by that wild waste of waters."

"Yes—yes; and then I lost it for a time, but a loud voice screamed in my ears one word, which seared my heart."

"What word was that?"

"Guilty!—guilty!"

"The trial again," murmured Miranda. "That ever mixes its dread realities up with his wildest ravings. I pray you say on, Mr. Percy. Was the boat then lost, or did it reach its wished-for haven?"

"When next I saw it, it had raised a snow-white sail, no thicker than a gossamer. I scarce could see it, save when it stood against the black waters that, like a wall, almost submerged it in their rage. It was so very frail—of such light texture—that I trembled for it; but it was of such pearl-like whiteness, that it looked most beautiful, and, as the mild reflection of its colour fell upon the face of him who was in that boat, it seemed to shed a halo of light upon it, and to bring that blest composure to his heart which innocence should impart."

"And the result?" said Miranda. "Oh, tell me, did the boat come safe to land?"

"Hush—hush! As the thin, white sail fluttered in the blast, and rose and fell with the tiny boat upon the world of waters, I saw the one word 'innocence' upon it, and, in another instant, it was rent to atoms by the howling wind."

"Lost—lost!" said Miranda. "Innocence would not suffice to save him."

"Tossed at the mercy of the lashing sea—now down as if seeking the depth of some hidden cavern of the earth, and then up, up, as if summoned by Heaven itself to mount to its radiant gates—I saw that boat. In the foremost part there sat a female form."

"A female form?"

"Yes. How very strange was the vision of my slumbers. That form resembled you, Miranda. You were pale, too—pale as my boy, Rowland; but I saw you take the tiller of the frail vessel, and point to the shore. I saw you smile, and my heart became glad, for there was hope, I felt, for my Rowland."

"Was he saved?"

"He was—he was! Saved—saved!"

"Heaven, I thank thee!" said Miranda. "Let me accept this vision as thy voice, telling me that he I would succour shall be free. Innocence has not saved him, but I shall. So says the dream. I will let it nerve me, even at the risk of superstition."

Eight o'clock sounded from a timepiece on the staircase, and Miranda sprang to her feet.

"Time—time!" she cried.

"Time for what? Where is Rowland?"

said Mr. Percy. "I want to speak to your father, Miranda. I did not like to tell you before, but, do you know, I have not been successful lately in what I fear your father will call rash speculations. I would fain speak with him."

Miranda could scarcely speak from the excitement of her feelings at this allusion to one who was in the cold grave, and alike indifferent to the world and all its concerns; but she managed, with difficulty, to say:

"Remain here till I return, Mr. Percy. Let me beg of you to try and sleep now."

"Where go you, Miranda? Send my son to me."

"You shall see him soon. Be patient till I return."

"I will try to sleep. I would fain have more dreams. They look so like the truth—only some are dreadful. Someone accused my son of a murder, and that was the most absurd of all. Good-night — good-night. Blessings on you, Miranda. Rowland is very happy."

"Good-night," said Miranda, in choking accents. "Good-night!"

With a quick step she left the room, and hastened down the staircase. She then called to the woman of the house, and when she came to her, said:

"Should I not return by to-morrow morning early, or by to-night even, please to send for Mr. Anderson. He will arrange all that should be done in my temporary absence."

"Yes, miss," said the woman. "I hope you will keep your heart up. We never know what good may come, even when we least expect it. My husband says as he is quite sure Mr. Rowland Percy didn't do the murder."

"Thank you—thank you!" said Miranda. "I am much beholden to you for your kind opinion. Thank you. Good evening."

"Good evening, miss."

In another moment, Miranda was at the door.

A gush of cool, fresh air, from the open street, was welcome to her fevered brow, and she drew her cloak more closely around her, as she hurried on in the direction of the prison.

A cold wind swept through the streets; but Miranda heeded it not. Her heart was glowing with hope.

"He will be saved—he will be saved!" she said; "and I shall know the exquisite joy of being the means of rescuing him. Oh, what an anxious time will be the next two hours! All seems now to me like a dream. Can the pages of fiction, adorned as they may be by the most brilliant imaginings, excel the romance of such truth as this? Oh, Rowland! Rowland! if you should be saved, I shall ever look upon you as some gift from Heaven—as one snatched by the hand of God himself from destruction."

"Miranda!" said a voice, close to her ear.

She started, and turning hastily, saw Dick Palmer gazing anxiously upon her animated face.

CHAPTER LXVI.

NINE O'CLOCK—THE DISGUISE—THE BAFFLED OFFICIAL — MOMENTS OF SUSPENSE — LIBERTY.

"My friend," said Miranda.

"Thank you for calling me such," said Dick. "I will not detain you a moment. My only object was to assure you I was here, and ready to do what in me lay to further the noble object you have in view."

"I thank you from my heart."

"The moment," added Dick, "that Mr. Percy leaves the prison-gate, I will meet him, and, in another quarter-of-an-hour, he shall be on his way to London, where, I have bethought me, I have much more ample and available means of concealing him than I have here, although I have friends in York who would do their best for him."

"To you we owe everything," said Miranda. "Your advice I have already followed with success, and the probabilities are all in favour of Rowland's escape."

"Tell him to stoop as he comes out, and impress upon him the necessity of walking slow. Should there even be a moment's hesitation at the gate I will have him out, for I shall not be alone there. Not a chance shall be thrown away."

Miranda held out her hand, which Dick took respectfully in his, and she said:

"Come what may—happen what may—you will ever hold a warm place in my heart. Do not needlessly run yourself into any danger. Farewell, until we meet again. And whether in joy or in sorrow, you will ever find a warm and grateful welcome from Miranda Rankley."

"God bless you! and success attend you," said Dick, in a tone of emotion, as he wrung her hand, and then turned away.

Miranda once more adjusted her cloak, and hastened towards the prison.

It was strange as Miranda neared the spot where she was to undergo so severe a trial of her nerves, that she should become more and more calm; but such was the case. Hers was one of those dispositions which suffer much during the idleness of expectation, but which become bold and firm when the period for action arrives.

As she neared the gloomy mansion in which so many unhappy persons were sighing for the pure and beautiful light of heaven, and the free air, which would invigorate their wasted energies, she felt a renewed hope, and a boldness which her heart had some hours before been a stranger to.

She repeated to herself a sentiment she had heard once attributed to Napoleon by an occasional guest at her father's hospitable table. It was this:

"The great element of success in all enterprises is to determine upon it—to believe we have the power, and confidently to anticipate the favourable result."

This she repeated to herself over and over

DICK PALMER DISPOSES OF THE SPY.

again, until she gave herself a confidence which much emboldened her to proceed and use every means for making success a certainty instead of a theoretical possibility.

She rang the bell at the wicket-gate of the prison without a tremor, and the moment she had done so, she gathered her cloak over the lower part of her face, and waited impatiently for the appearance of the turnkey.

In about a minute a small grating was opened, and a harsh inquiry of "Who's there?" saluted her.

"Miranda Rankley," she replied; "I come to visit Mr. Percy."

"Humph!" growled the man; "you know,

miss, we close to all visitors at nine o'clock. It's over five-and-twenty minutes past eight now."

"I have an order," said Miranda, "from the judge, as you well know, to admit me at all hours when the prison is considered open at all to strangers. Refuse me admittance, and I go directly to the judge's chambers."

"Oh! there's no occasion for that," said the man, opening the wicket, in some alarm. "You can come in, of course; I only meant to tell you what a short time you would have to remain."

"I know it," said Miranda, and then added to herself: "Heaven send I may remain here till to-morrow's dawn, and that Rowland be safe away."

A passing tremor came across her as she heard the wicket-gate closed and locked behind her.

In another moment she was calm again, and all was as before.

Her cloak she kept closely round her chin, and, as she waited to be conducted to the cell, she said, in a voice which she purposely made rough and strange:

"Has Mr. Percy had any visitors since last I was here?"

"Eh?" said the turnkey, looking at her.

"Has Mr. Percy had any visitors?"

As she the second time propounded her question, she purposely allowed the cloak to drop from her face, so that there could be no difficulty in seeing who she was.

"No, miss," said the turnkey, as he looked in her beautiful countenance with some surprise. "There ain't been nobody here. Hem," he added to himself, "what an out-of-the-way cold she has got, to be sure. I never heard her speak so afore."

Miranda followed him in silence, still keeping the cloak almost entirely over her face, until they reached the cell of Rowland, when the man knocked.

As he did so, he unlocked the door, and made the usual brief announcement of:

"A visitor!"

"Thank you," said Miranda, and she passed into the cell.

The turnkey stood a moment on the outside, and then, with what he considered an extraordinary clever shake of the head, he said, in an undertone:

"Well, cuss me! For a nice-looking and pretty girl, she has the most out-and-out extraordinary manners that ever I comed near. Hiding of her face, and then growling out 'thank you' like a young bear. Well, she is a rum 'un; there ain't much feeling there, I should say. She's like our Joey, she ain't got no feeling at all, nor don't want none."

With these remarks, the man went to the vestibule, and did what Miranda would have rejoiced to hear him do—namely, told all the officials, who were there assembled for a gossip, what an extraordinary, masculine, odd, gruff sort of young woman she (Miranda) was. Then Joey, whom Miranda had threatened to report to the governor, told circumstantially how he had very nearly got into a scrape, all through suspecting her, and terminated by saying:

"I won't have nothing more to do with her or say to her, not I, I can tell you. She'll go to make a complaint to the *guvnor*, and get a fellow the sack in half-a-minute. If she was to come in in a blessed hogshead, and only speak through the bung-hole, I'd jest roll her out and in, and I'm blessed if I'd say a word to her no how. She's an out-an-out rum 'un, she is, and it's my belief and *credit* as she wants to get us into some scrape 'cos we keeps her sweetheart, as is to be scragged to-morrow, too safe in quod."

"Werry right, werry right," cried another.

"Joey, you have hit the correct nail on the head this time, anyhow, my boy."

"I believe yer," said Joey. "Look at me—do I look like a ass?"

"Rather," said another; "only you hasn't so long ears as common. Howsumdever, I recommends when this here young *ooman* comes out as we gets the better on her by paying no sort o' attention to what she says, or what she does."

"That's the thing," said several. "We'll get the better on her, any way. We wasn't born yesterday."

How happy would this conversation have made Miranda; but still without a knowledge of it she was full of hope, and the moment she stepped into Rowland's cell she cast the cloak from her, and, holding out both her hands, cried out, in a voice full of joy:

"Dear Rowland, you will yet be saved."

"My Miranda," he cried, as he clasped her to his heart, "do you still intend to sacrifice yourself for me?"

"Sacrifice, Rowland! No; by saving you, I intend to save myself. You will escape, and I shall be happy. All has succeeded to the utmost of my wishes. There is no one circumstance which has gone awry. Rowland—dear, dear Rowland—you have, I believe, but to walk out of your prison, and you will be free. Trust implicitly a tall man who will speak to you outside—he is your friend, and has arranged everything to facilitate your escape and permanent concealment."

"But you—you, Miranda? Oh, what pangs should I not suffer with the thought that you were exposed to the insolence of the officials of this place, and——"

"Hush—hush, Rowland!" interrupted Miranda, "there are pangs of different degree. What frightful misery would be mine if I were to leave you here to perish, and know that to-morrow morning would find you a corpse!"

Rowland shuddered.

"I have your promise," continued Miranda, "and time presses. Envelop yourself in this cloak, and be firm, bold, and resolute. Stoop as you leave the prison, hide your face, heed not what you hear, but walk slowly—mind, slowly, Rowland—to the outer gate."

The prison-clock at this instant struck the three-quarters past eight, and Miranda took the cloak from the ground, saying:

"Quick, Rowland, quick, they will soon be here to warn you to go, and this will be your only chance."

Even as she spoke, and while she held her cloak in her hand towards Rowland, the door of the cell was opened, and to Miranda's, as well as to the prisoner's deep vexation, the chaplain stood in the entrance.

He looked as grave and solemn as he could, making a very slight bow to Miranda as he entered the cell, and then, before either of them could speak, he said:

"I have come once more in your presence, young woman—I beg your pardon, miss—to exhort this unhappy young man, who is so near to eternity, to repentance, and to a confession of his many sins and deep transgressions, in order, as I once before remarked to him, that he may be welcomed to another and a better world by ten thousand angels, who will sing anthems of joy over the brand which has been snatched by me, an unworthy labourer in the vineyard of the Lord, from the burning, and in order that grace everlasting, and——"

"Peace, sir!" cried Rowland. "If I am even now trembling upon the brink of eternity, at least I should be allowed the consolation of taking leave in peace of the one who is dearest to my heart, and for whom I would fain linger yet awhile in life."

"Ah," said the chaplain, casting up his eyes, "that is all vanity and vexation of spirit. Young lady, you should reason with this sinful man, and not uphold him in his obstinacy, which induces him to reject the means of everlasting grace, where ten thousand angels——"

"Cease, sir," said Miranda, "I have as pure, and, I hope, even purer notions of Heaven and its great Master, than you have. Rowland Percy is my affianced husband. I know his pure and spotless heart well. He is not sinful. Begone, sir; your avocation is thrown away here. He is innocent, and even yet I do not believe Heaven will permit him to die the death of a felon. Leave this cell, and make not the possibly last moments of an innocent man more bitter by your unwelcome presence."

"Do you, then, lost beings that you are, both utterly reject my ministrations?"

"We decline your services," said Rowland, "and request that you will leave this place."

"Hell flames will be your portion," said the chaplain; "and there will be gnashing of teeth and deep despair, and all sorts of wailing, and the wicked shall know no rest, for that they repent not."

"Begone, profane man! Doubter of the mercy of Heaven, begone!" said Rowland.

He advanced a step as he spoke, and the alarmed chaplain thought it prudent to make a hasty retreat.

Nine boomed forth by the Minster clock the moment his back was turned.

"The cloak, Rowland! the cloak!" cried Miranda. "Quick, quick, or we are lost!"

CHAPTER LXVII.

FROM NINE TILL A QUARTER-PAST — THE SCUFFLE — ROWLAND'S DANGER — DICK PALMER'S PROMPTITUDE AND COURAGE — THE ESCAPE COMPLETED.

Conscious that there was really not a moment now to lose, if he really intended to avail himself of Miranda's generous self-sacrifice in his favour, Rowland accepted the proffered cloak and long black skirt, in which he hastily enveloped himself.

His next step was rapidly to roll up the legs of his trousers, and then Miranda completed his disguise by placing her bonnet upon his head, and tying it securely under his chin.

"Wrap the cloak closely round you, Rowland," she said, in hurried accents, "and you will be safe. Speak not to anyone. Do not hurry through the passages. Rowland—dear, dear Rowland—Heaven aid and prosper you."

"My Miranda," was all he could say.

For one fleeting moment, then, he clasped her to his heart.

At that instant they heard the sound of a footstep leisurely approaching the cell. It was the turnkey.

Rowland well knew that step. Among the few incidents that relieve the tediousness of a prison life the peculiarity even of the jailer's tread becomes a subject of contemplation.

"We must part now, Miranda," he said. "I hear the turnkey even now coming."

"Hold the door a moment," said Miranda.

Rowland placed his back against it, while Miranda hurriedly put on his coat and hat. She then seated herself at the table in such a way that her head and shoulders only were in the light.

Scarcely had she completed her change of costume ere a knock came at the door of the cell, and the voice of the turnkey, in no very gentle accents, said:

"Hilloa! we don't allow doors to be fastened on the inside here."

"Are you ready?" whispered Rowland.

"Quite. Farewell. Heaven help you."

"God bless you, my Miranda. It will be a happy day when we meet again."

"Hush—hush! Let him in! Hush!"

Rowland moved away from the door, and, stooping so as to decrease his height as much as possible, he stood some few paces from it, in the direction where Miranda was sitting.

In a moment she dropped her head upon the table, as if too much affected to speak, and the truth was, that she could not at that moment have said anything for the world, for her anxiety almost prevented her breathing.

The turnkey stood on the threshold for a moment in surprise at the silence and singular relative positions of the parties. Then he said:

"Oh, there's been some feelings at work, has there? Well, there's a end o' everything, and, if you please, mum, we is a-going to put the kiver on the jug, and, in case you shouldn't understand what that ere means, why, I explains it to be shutting up the prison."

The man's tone and manner at once proclaimed him to be in the first stage of intoxication, and Miranda trembled for what might ensue during Rowland's passage from the cell to the outer gate.

All the light the turnkey had with him was a lantern, which he held swinging in one hand in such a manner as rather to confuse his vision than to afford it any essential assistance, and now he stood a little way outside the door, saying:

"Come on, we can't wait all night, if you please, mum. Don't be going and saying I wasn't civil, 'cos I am, but we can't wait for you."

Without a word Rowland passed from the cell, to the great surprise of the turnkey, who cast a glance at what he supposed to be his prisoner, and then muttered:

"Oh, I suppose as the feelings business has all been settled afore I comed. Well, it don't matter to me, but I did expect the usual skrimmage of crying and pocket-handkerchers to-night, considering as to-morrow morning there's to be the scragging."

It was not in human nature not to feel some terrors, situated as Rowland Percy now was, with his life hanging, as it were, upon a thread.

He did tremble, but he took care that it should not be perceptible as he walked after the turnkey, who now and then looked behind him to make some remark savouring more of insolence than courtesy; for, now that he was in a state of partial intoxication, his mistake in insisting upon seeing Miranda's face, and her threat of appealing to the Governor came fully across his mind, and made him think himself a very injured individual.

He accordingly made what he considered some of the most cutting remarks to Rowland, every now and then, such as:

"Perhaps you'd like to complain to the blessed Governor to-night about something—'cos, if you does, I'll ring his blessed bell for you, mum."

Of course, Rowland said nothing to this, which was ten times more aggravating to the turnkey than a regular wrangle would have been, and he got in such a rage, at last, as he came near the vestibule, that he swung the lantern about to its imminent danger, and when he fairly arrived there, he set it down with a bang and a curse that quite astonished the gate-keeper.

Here was the trying moment for Rowland.

Immediately above the wicket-gate was a lamp, within which there was a strong reflector, that cast a broad glare of light into the vestibule.

Had there been no person there but the friendly turnkey, who was, what he technically termed, on the lock that night, all would have been well; but there was also in the vestibule a keen, sharp-eyed under-turnkey, who, while Rowland waited the brief moment that was necessary to have the gate opened for him, eyed him with the closest scrutiny.

Now, had this gentleman not been so amazingly cunning and artful, as he believed himself to be, Rowland Percy would have been discovered, and conducted back to his cell, from which he would not again have departed, except to the place of execution on the morrow.

Such, however, did not occur, for although the under-turnkey suspected that something was amiss, he thought how very clever it would be for him to follow the supposed young lady in the cloak, and if she should prove to be the prisoner escaping in disguise, how amazingly to his credit and advantage it would be to bring him back himself, after he had passed out unsuspected by the other officials.

"I'm not quite sure," he thought to himself, "but I'm nearly sure that that's a man. If I was to say anything about it just now, I should have Joey and all the fellows in the place swearing they knew it, and only was waiting to see how far he'd go. I know a trick worth two of that. If they let him go without following him, why, they can't say as they had any suspicion. Very good. I will follow, and, if I'm wrong, why, they can't laugh at me, for they won't know it, and if I'm right, I shall come in for all the credit."

This reasoning looked so amazingly plausible in the eyes of the turnkey, that he adopted at once a course of action resulting from it.

No sooner had Rowland, with a thrill of delight such as in his whole life he had never before experienced, passed across the threshold of the prison, than the clever under-turnkey said to the man on the lock:

"Let me out—I shan't be long."

With a misgiving of the truth in his own mind, the friendly turnkey let him out, and saw him dart down the steps, and walk off in the direction Rowland had taken.

"Ha!" he said, "it's all up now. That prying fellow has his suspicions, I know. Well, I can do nothing. I promised Dick I would do my best, and I have."

He then threw himself into his chair, and calmly waited the result, which he expected would be the return of the prisoner in about a quarter-of-an-hour.

The quarter-of-an-hour, however, passed away, and another quarter at the back of it, without any such result ensuing, and surprise began to take the place of any other feeling in his mind.

How it was that the clever under-turnkey failed in his cleverness, we shall see.

The moment Rowland Percy gained the street, Dick Palmer, who was watching the prison door with the most intense eagerness, walked across the road, and, going up to him, whispered:

"Mr. Percy!"

Rowland started, his first impression being that it was an enemy who spoke.

"Who are you?" he said, at the same time that he prepared himself to dash the interrogator to the ground, if the answer should not be satisfactory.

"A friend," was Dick's reply. "My name is Palmer; I am your friend and hers, who is now there."

He pointed to the prison as he spoke.

"Enough, I will trust you freely," said Rowland; "but moments are now very precious."

"I know it. Take my arm, and walk slowly till we turn the next corner."

Rowland did so, and still muffling himself closely in the cloak, he walked at a very deliberate pace beside the highwayman, although his own impulse would have been to outstrip the wind in flight, if possible.

That walk from the prison-gate to the corner indicated by Palmer was one of the greatest agony to Rowland, for now that there appeared every chance of escape, the love of life came more strongly across him than it had done in his cell, and he would have died upon the spot, rather than again have visited, as a prisoner, the interior of the gloomy dwelling he had just left.

It took scarcely two minutes to reach the corner; but those two minutes were decidedly the most wretched Rowland Percy had ever passed during his existence.

To him they were lengthened into two hours, and when he reached the corner, the perspiration of intense excitement was pouring from his brow.

"Now — now," he whispered, " are we safe?"

"For Heaven's sake," replied Dick, " be not yet precipitate. A false step even now might ruin all!"

"How—how?"

"Hush, Mr. Percy—hush!"

Dick, without turning completely round, contrived to take a good look behind him.

A slight exclamation escaped him, for he knew well by sight the man who was dogging their footsteps.

"What's amiss?" said Rowland, anxiously.

"Hush—hush! walk slower."

"Why—why? we are round the corner."

"Yes; but——"

"But what?—speak!"

"We are followed."

A gush of agony came across Rowland's heart, and he pressed his hands to his breast, as he uttered a deep groan.

"Do not despair," whispered Dick; "there is still a chance. Walk slower still, and trust all to me."

"Oh, what chance can there be?"

"Hush—hush!"

"They shall not take me alive. If you are indeed my friend, I pray you—I implore you—for the love of Heaven, to give me some weapon with which I may defend my life."

"Hush—hush!"

"I will die fighting," continued Rowland. "I will not be dragged back to yonder dungeon. Lead me past some spot where they sell arms, if you have none about you, and I will rush in and help myself."

"Mr. Percy, this is madness," whispered Dick. "Leave all to me, I pray you. By any violence you sacrifice yourself, and jeopardize my safety seriously."

Rowland said no more, but it was agony to him when Dick said:

"Walk slower, still. Slower—slower; it is our only chance now, Mr. Percy."

A thought came across him, that after all, this man, in whom Miranda had put so much trust, was the dupe of a plot which was to show off the efficiency of the officials of the prison, and sacrifice her liberty in an abortive attempt to succour him.

Such a thought as this was terrible, and he said to Palmer, in a choking voice:

"Whoever you are, may the bitter curse of two broken hearts cling to you till your dying day, and follow you to another world, if you are betraying me and the pure, innocent heart of her who told me to trust you."

"Mr. Rowland Percy," said Dick; "I forgive you, for you are not master of yourself, and know not what you say."

"If I do you an injustice, it will be for me to implore your forgiveness."

"Hush—hush; no more of that at present. Slower—slower, still. All may yet be well."

The suspicions of the under-turnkey were each moment growing stronger.

There were numerous starts and unfeminine movements about Rowland's arms and head, that confirmed him in the supposition that it was indeed his prisoner attempting an escape.

Oh, how he congratulated himself, then, upon his own deep and amazing cunning that had kept it all to himself.

His object now was to capture both Rowland and his companion, and that he would either do in some populous street, or he would see them fairly housed, and then procure immediate assistance for their arrest.

By chance, Rowland and Palmer had to cross a drain, along which an ample stream of water was flowing, and on the opposite side of which several paving stones had been taken up for the purpose of repairs.

The manner in which Rowland Percy, at one bound, cleared the obstruction, at once settled the matter in the turnkey's mind. He had no more doubt, now, about the identity of the presumed young lady, and he almost chuckled aloud in his excessive self-congratulation, and the thought of the reward which would be his.

"Let me see," he muttered; "I shall be put into some snug situation safe, and, in course, the visiting magistrates will order me a reward. I shouldn't wonder if I netted a matter of fifty pounds by this job, besides the crow I shall have over Joey and Ted, and old Griskett, who think themselves so uncommonly clever, all of them. Ha! ha! ha! He! he! he! I rather think I have taken the shine out of them all just a bit—only a few. Ho! ho! ho!"

Thus chuckling to himself, and ever and anon rubbing his hands together like a fly who has just been gorging himself with treacle, did the under-turnkey closely follow in the footsteps of Rowland Percy and Dick Palmer.

Dick had now turned down a narrow street which was but very dimly lighted, and was promptly followed by the spy.

"Walk quicker now," he whispered to Rowland, who could see nothing for the sides of his bonnet.

"Shall we escape, think you, by speed?"

"No—no, we should have a hue and cry after us in a moment were we to attempt it. Follow my instructions as if you were a machine."

"I will."

"Walk fast, then."

They quickened their speed suddenly, and that at once put the clever turnkey upon his mettle.

"Ha!" he said, "they think they are all right now, and are putting on the steam a bit. Cut away. That's your sort. I can come out a little in that way myself."

So saying, he hastened on rather faster than Rowland and Dick, which had the effect of decreasing the distance between them considerably, and when, after proceeding thus for some time, Palmer suddenly turned a corner, leading into a very dull out-of-the-way street, where there were but two dim oil lamps, and not a single passenger, the turnkey made a run to get up to the corner, for fear they should pass into some house and elude him.

"Stop," said Dick, the moment they turned the corner, and he disengaged his arm from Rowland.

In the next moment the turnkey arrived quite breathless, when, instantly, on his turning the corner, he was met by Palmer, who, being a powerful man, and a practised boxer, gave him one blow between the eyes, which sent him down to the ground as if he had been struck by a cannon shot.

"There," said Dick, "our enemy is harmless now."

"Was it he," said Rowland, "who was dogging us?"

"Yes; and my object was to lead him on till I could rid ourselves of him as I have. If I mistake not, he will not recover that blow in time to do us much harm, for we shall be on the road to London now within ten minutes."

"How much I have wronged you by my unworthy suspicions of your good faith!" said Rowland, as he held out his hand. "Will you forgive me?"

"Freely," said Dick, as he took the proffered hand, "and all I can say is, that I dare say I should have been more suspicious than you were, for my acquaintance with human nature has been greater, and it doesn't improve on intimacy."

He then laid hold of the perfectly insensible turnkey, and laid him on the step of a door, after which, turning to Rowland, he said:

"Now, sir, make what speed you like, and follow me."

CHAPTER LXVIII.

VARLEY'S VISIT TO MIRANDA'S LODGINGS—HIS INTERVIEW WITH OLD PERCY—THREE O'CLOCK IN THE MORNING—HIS DESPAIR AND AGONY.

If the hours, as they slowly winged their leaden flight on that most eventful evening, were, to Miranda and to Rowland Percy, fraught with deep anxieties, how much more were they terrible and full of ghastly images of despair to the guilty soul of Bernard Varley, who, as each one passed away, found his hopes diminishing—his fears growing to a monstrous size.

Every moment his expectations of hearing from Miranda decreased, until he came to the despairing conclusion that, with all her love for Rowland Percy, she would allow the judicial murder of the morrow to proceed, rather than suffer him to call her his own.

By a strange perversion of intellect, then, Varley got angry with her, and he, of all people in the world—he, a murderer, and a false witness, began to accuse her of hardheartedness, not towards himself, but towards Rowland.

"So," he muttered, "this is her boasted love for the innocent Rowland Percy. She might save him, and she will not, because her silly girlish fancies stand in the way—and so much for the hearts of women. My curse light on her head. May she, some day, experience the pangs I feel; and she will—she will—and surely to-morrow's work will wring her proud heart, and cause it to weep tears of blood. He shall die! he shall die! and she shall have the bitter, sorrowful feeling of knowing she might have saved him, but would not—ay, would not, forsooth."

Till he commenced this tirade against Miranda, he had been sitting by his window, in gloomy meditation and in darkness, for he would have no light, lest he should be seen from the opposite house, or from the street, in which case he might have been foiled in his wish to see Miranda as often as possible.

When, however, this burst of hatred and rage overcame him for a moment, he rose from the sofa he had wheeled over to the window, and paced his room to and fro with hasty and perturbed strides.

Surely, Heaven was working for Miranda and her innocent lover, for it was precisely at that moment of Varley's absence from the window at which he had kept watch so long, that Miranda, enveloped in her cloak, walked from her humble house towards the prison.

When he returned again to resume his watch, it was without the least thought that she was gone; and while Miranda was conversing with Palmer, and afterwards in the cell with Rowland, Varley was watching the house to which it was improbable she should ever now return.

Ah! how little did the villain Varley—the author of so much misery—imagine, as he heard the Minster clock strike nine, with what different feelings it was listened to by Miranda and Rowland Percy, and what dear hopes to them hung upon the next ten minutes.

Could he have seen into that narrow cell, and watched his victim escape him, what torments would have been his—what agonies of baffled rage would have filled his bursting heart?

Still, and with the exterior appearance of calmness, he sat with his eyes riveted upon the house; but no Miranda came forth to bless his eyes for one fleeting moment, and give him new hope.

The quarter-past nine sounded from the

various clocks, and then the half hour, and all remained silent and still as before.

Then Varley's impatience rose again to a wild burst of excitement. The air of the room felt to him close and pestiferous; hot flames seemed to be scorching his heart and brain; he could no longer remain in that room: and, seizing his hat, he rushed down the staircase, and made his way to the cool, open air, which he let for some minutes play unrestrainedly upon his fevered brow.

"What shall I do—what shall I do?" he asked himself, as he uneasily paced to and fro in front of the house in which he believed Miranda to be waiting, with a heavy heart, the tragedy of the morrow.

A thousand wild plans and conjectures rushed through his brain, but he could fix none sufficiently long to give it the consistency of shape and outline. They were all vague, wild imaginings, dealing but little in the probable, but shadowing forth with just a faint hue of possibility, the wishes and aspirations of his guilty heart.

"She comes not forth," he muttered. "Why keeps she in on such a night as this? Surely she has not removed from here? No, no; I have watched too well for that. Perhaps a little more urging—a little more painting of the horrors of the execution, which will make a holiday show for the idle rabble to-morrow, might move her; but, come what may, I can no longer endure this suspense. It would soon drive me mad. I will call upon her again—at least, I may see her, although she taunt me with bitter reproaches—and to see her, is as if a condemned soul was allowed in its despair one radiant glimpse of Heaven in all its beauty."

This resolve gave him some calmness and relief, for it was a something to do, thus saving his mind from preying so hopelessly upon itself.

He approached the door, and knocked cautiously, for he was afraid that if Miranda suspected who it was demanding admission, she might order herself to be denied to him.

The door was opened by one of the children belonging to the woman of the house, who knew not whether Miranda was at home or not.

"That will do," said Varley, as he slipped a piece of silver into the child's hand. "I am a friend, and will go to her, if you will tell me which room she occupies."

The child directed him to Miranda's apartment, and before the woman herself, who heard some conversation going on in the passage, without knowing its purport, could get upstairs, Varley ascended to the room indicated to him.

With a firm expectation of seeing Miranda, he knocked gently at the door, but, receiving no answer, he turned the lock, and passed into the room.

It was empty. The mouldering remains of a fire were crackling and expiring in the grate, and the room presented every appearance of recent occupation, but she alone, whom he sought, was not there.

With a pang of disappointment, he glanced around him, and then he saw the door which led into Mr. Percy's chamber.

A hope sprang up in his mind that Miranda might be in that inner room.

He approached it, and listened for some few moments, but all was as still as the grave.

Then, just as he was on the point of opening that door, the woman of the house made her appearance in the front room.

"What may you please to want, sir?" she said.

"Is Miss Rankley at home?" he said, endeavouring to speak as calmly as he could, and hiding his face as much as possible from the light which the woman carried.

"No, sir, she has been out nearly an hour. Are you a doctor, sir, come to see the old gentleman? He is not much better, I'm sorry to say."

"Out one hour?—an hour and I—I not know it. Curses——"

These words were ground through Varley's teeth in a manner which prevented the exact signification of them from reaching the ears of the woman, and she again put her question of:

"Are you a doctor, sir, come to see Mr. Percy?"

The thought struck Varley that he might for some time, perhaps even till Miranda should return, assume such a character and wait; so he said:

"Yes, I am. Is he no better?"

"No, sir. He keeps on dozing; but when he wakes, he don't seem to know anybody."

"Indeed?"

"Yes, sir. Ah! poor man, he won't be long for this world, I'm sure. It's all grief about his son, who you know, sir, is to be hanged to-morrow morning for the murder of Sir George Rankley."

"Yes—yes," said Varley, "I know all that; and—and, Miranda, how is she?"

"Ah! poor thing, she is an angel if ever there was one; but she gets thinner and thinner every day, and paler—except to-night, and then she did look beautiful."

"To-night?"

"Yes, sir; when she went out she seemed to me as if something had quite set her up again, though she didn't tell me what it was. Perhaps, after all, sir, they won't hang the young man."

"Never doubt it," said Varley, with a bitter smile. "I will trouble you no further, madam. Is there a light in the next chamber? for I will remain here a short time."

"There is, sir; and should you want anything, just please to touch the bell, and I will come."

"Yes—yes—thank you—thank you."

Varley then opened the door, and in a moment stood by the bedside of the father whose mind had fallen beneath the pressure of woe he, Varley, had placed upon it.

Mr. Percy was in an uneasy slumber, and moaning occasionally, as if he were disturbed by frightful images. Now and then, too, he would speak, and it was ever on the one subject—that of his boy, Rowland.

"No—no," he muttered; "not guilty—not guilty. He is innocent. Heaven have mercy—mercy!"

"He raves," said Varley. "Can I act upon his disordered brain sufficiently to discover whither Miranda has gone? I will awaken him, and try."

He laid his hand upon Mr. Percy's shoulder, saying:

"Awake—awake—Mr. Percy, awake."

The sick man opened his eyes, and said, in a low voice:

"Who calls on me? Was that from the grave, or was it you, my dear boy—my Rowland? Yet no, it was not your voice, it is softer, sweeter far, and comes like music to your father's heart. Bless you, Rowland—bless you. You have made a worthy choice, for Miranda is beautiful and good."

"His brain is quite unsettled," said Varley. "I shall find but little to rely on in his conversation. Mr. Percy, do you know who I am?"

Mr. Percy started at the voice of Varley, and, raising himself up partially in the bed, gazed in his face long and earnestly ere he said:

"I did know you well—I do know you well; but latterly have thought you a fiend, which, having performed its hellish mission of destruction and despair among several hearts, had descended again to its hated home. Man or demon, what want you now with me?"

"Can you name me?"

"I can; but the name shall not pass my lips."

"Hear me, Mr. Percy, and if you have any love for your son—any pity for yourself—ponder upon my words. I can even now save Rowland. It is in my power, and mine only, to snatch him from death and restore him to your arms, provided you can induce Miranda to consent to my terms—those terms she knows; and her refusal makes her the virtual murderer of your son."

"How came you to know my dreams?" said Mr. Percy. "What have you to do with my Rowland?"

"Mad—mad," said Varley, with a bitter execration. "Where is Miranda?"

"Perhaps on a visit to some kindred soul in Heaven, where you may never, never be."

"Pshaw! Answer me at once, old man. She has left the house—where has she gone? When will she return? Answer me at once, I say."

"How long shall the fiend be allowed to mock me? Oh, save me from him, Heaven! Rowland, where are you now? They told me the shot was not fatal; then how could he kill Sir George Rankley? Another hand did that deed, and thrice have I dreamt that Bernard Varley was the man."

Varley rose, and stood for a moment with his hands clenched, and a feeling at his heart that he would like to still for ever the wild, yet truthful, ravings of the broken-hearted father.

His fears of the consequences in a house full of people restrained him, and, with a malediction too awful to record, he walked from the room, determining rather to wait in his own chamber opposite, and watch for the return of Miranda, than remain to have his conscience goaded by the remarks that fell from the lips of Mr. Percy.

He took his station once again at his window, and there, without a light, with nothing to commune with but his own dark and unholy thoughts, he remained until the Minster clock struck three.

CHAPTER LXIX.

MIRANDA IN THE CONDEMNED CELL—THE CHAPLAIN'S VISIT—THE EXHORTATION—MIRANDA'S JOY AND EXULTATION—THREE O'CLOCK—THE TURNKEY'S THREAT.

WHEN Miranda found herself alone in the condemned cell, she for some minutes could not have removed from the position she had assumed at the table, even if the whole success of the plan for Rowland's liberation had depended upon her so doing. Her feelings for the succeeding ten minutes were of the most powerful and agonizing description. A hundred times she asked herself:

"Is he clear of the prison? Has he passed the outer gate?"

The slightest sound that met her ears from any part of the building filled her with the most lively alarm; and, when she did rise from her seat, she stood in the centre of the floor so pale, so wan, and so tremblingly alive to the least alarm, that anyone who could, Asmodeus-like, have glanced into that gloomy cell, would indeed have thought her the criminal awaiting the coming day to be dragged to the place of execution.

But Miranda's thoughts never for an instant wandered to herself. It was of Rowland—of him upon whom her heart's best, holiest love was fixed, that she reflected with a painful intensity that made thought an actual agony.

"Has he passed the gate?—has he passed the gate?" she repeated, in a whisper, that made the question still more terrible to her imagination.

Then she strove to consider how many steps it would take to convey him from the door of the condemned cell to the open street. She could not tell, but she thought that by then he surely must be free.

"Yes—yes! He is saved—he is saved!" she cried. "By this time I should have heard some indication of his apprehension; they would have dragged him back here. Some noise would have reached my ears—he would not have yielded, perchance, without a struggle—and all is still. He is saved—he must be saved. I will believe it now. Why does my heart beat thus tumultuously? Why do I tremble. Can there be a doubt now? No—no. There has been ample time—I—think——I am sure now that he is safe. Rowland—Rowland, if I could see you now at liberty I should be happy."

She clasped her hands, and the colour which had retreated from her very lips during the awful period of doubt, which, although short as to actual duration of time, had concentrated such an age of anxiety within its brief space, slowly returned. Her heart ceased to palpitate with such fearful vehemence, and she no longer drew her breath with short, quick respirations. She turned her beautiful, beaming eyes upwards, as she said:

"The innocent are not deserted by Heaven! My Rowland is saved! He must be safe now. Thank Heaven! thank Heaven!"

With a deep sigh, which had in it much relief, for it appeared to carry with it a world of anxiety from her heart, she sat down again by the table. Then a holy and beautiful calm spread itself over her spirit, and a smile, such as she had not worn for many a weary day, broke like sunlight over her face. She repeated the same words that she had used before; but with how very different a tone did she now tell herself:

"He is saved!—he is saved!"

There was an awful doubt still lingering at the bottom of her heart when first she strove to convince herself that he had effected his escape, but now she was sure. There had been ample time to traverse the distance from the cell to the outer gate of the prison three times over. He must, therefore, be free.

By the light of the lamp which was in the cell, Miranda glanced round her, and oh, how different appeared the aspect of it, as she now viewed it with feelings of hope and joy, from when it had presented to her nothing but the dreary vestibule, as it were, in which her lover tarried ere he was ushered to the tomb.

It would have puzzled many a philosopher and deep speculator upon human nature to have accounted for the look of happiness that lit up the countenance of that beautiful girl in such a place. What a delicious contrast did her feelings then present to what they had been at the same hour on the preceding evening, when all was despair—when there appeared not one ray of hope to illumine the universal gloom in which her fortune and her lover's were shrouded.

Once free of the prison, she believed that Rowland would be safe, for her faith in Palmer was great, and she was now only anxious to give the fugitive as much time as possible before a discovery should take place, and a pursuit be commenced.

She paced the cell with firm steps—she could have sung for very gladness. It was more than as if she herself had been rescued from death; it was more than as if a pardon had reached the prison, and rescued from the scaffold him whom she loved; for a more fond, unselfish being than Miranda could not exist, and she felt much more acutely the sufferings of those to whom she was attached, than she would any amount of misery touching herself personally.

Moreover, how delightful a thought it was to her to know that she had been the direct means of rescuing Rowland from the fate that else had surely been his!

How exquisite was the gush of pleasurable thought with which she pronounced the words:

"I have saved him!"

Could Rowland Percy then have seen his Miranda in the prison to which he had so lately bidden adieu, he would have dismissed from his mind much of the anxious, painful thought that beset it while he was rapidly accompanying Palmer from York.

The time which had for the few minutes after Rowland's departure from the cell lagged so fearfully, now flew on more swift and joyous wings.

Ten o'clock struck by the Minster timepiece, and no one had disturbed Miranda in the cell. The sound, however, recalled her to a consciousness of the necessity, or, at all events, of the desirableness of getting over the next periodical visit of the turnkey without a discovery taking place

Again she arranged her long, silken hair so that it would show as little as possible, and placed Rowland's hat on her head. She then listened attentively at the door of the cell, but there was no sound of anyone approaching, and she sat down by the table, permitting her thoughts to wander sweetly to the time when she should again meet Rowland, and they should be able to talk over the events of that anxious yet joyful night.

What was to be her own fate, and what consequences were to arise from the position in which she had placed herself never for a moment crossed her mind. She had succeeded where success was life—where failure would have been death and despair. What then cared she for the results—how immeasurably short of the evil she had avoided must they be! What a solemn farce would appear to her the legal consequences of her act. How she could smile upon the detail of what would be called her crime, and with what joy, what exultation, she could say:

"I am satisfied. He is saved—he is saved."

Then they would meet, she and Rowland, in some other land, and calmly await the course of events which, from her inmost heart, she believed would some day proclaim his innocence, and welcome him back to his native land in contentment and honour. Then how gladly she would thank all those who had lent a willing ear to her assertions of his innocence, while those who had declared him guilty would shrink in terror from the judicial murder they had been near committing, and pause ere they again adventured to take the life they never could restore, and from usurping God's high and holy prerogative.

These thoughts, and hundreds like them, filled the lonely cell with crowds of speaking, moving images. No longer was Miranda alone, for fancy peopled vacancy, and in her mind's eye she sketched a future full of light, of joy, and love.

The sudden turning of the key in the lock of the door roused Miranda with a shock from her reverie, and she instantly moved the lamp so as to cast herself very much into the shade, and waited anxiously for the result of the visit of, as she supposed, the turnkey.

She heard the door open, and there was a silence for a few moments, as if someone was contemplating her from the threshold.

That silence, she thought, was ominous of detection, but she assured herself that Rowland had already had time enough, although she would gladly have given him more.

Her fears, however, were vain, for, in a moment more, she heard the voice of the chaplain.

"Young man, young man—are you so sinfully attached to the vain world that you have not spirit sufficient on this eve of your departure from it to look round even to see who enters your cell?"

Miranda made no answer, and he continued, after a pause:

"Sinner, sinner! repent ye. Time is but short—repent and confess."

Miranda made a gesture of impatience, and with a deep groan the evangelical man added:

"Satan is in your heart, and I believe that you think more of the sinful young woman—who is evidently a vessel of wrath and not one of the godly—than you do of your future state. Cast from you the evil spirit, and walk in the paths of righteousness; which, albeit they be not so flowery or pleasant to the eye at the commencement, yet do they abound with saving grace."

Here he paused again, and blew his nose with a true conventual blast, but as Miranda said nothing, the holy man waxed just a little wrathful, and added:

"Young man, young man, I would fain snatch you as a brand from the burning, but I fear the old man is strong within you, and that you are one of those who, rejecting the word of life, will descend to everlasting flame and torrents of burning brimstone, where you will wallow in liquid fire, and your soul, for ages to come, will, by the mercy of Providence, be tortured alway.—Amen!"

Miranda was so provoked at this atrocious speech, that she had an answer on the tip of her tongue, which would have been couched in the form of advice to the chaplain, to study and comprehend the pure and holy precepts of Christianity, ere he again adventured to use the name of Heaven as a sanction for his exhortations; but she controlled the impulse, for she considered even five minutes more time given to Rowland Percy as of infinitely more importance than a wrangle with a bigot.

"You will not speak?" continued the chaplain.

Miranda made a gesture, indicative of her determination to remain silent.

The chaplain then got up a series of extemporaneous groans, after which he commenced a prayer for the conversion, as he called it, of Rowland Percy, all which Miranda listened to with more patience than could be expected, or than she could have commanded under any other circumstances—but she was giving Rowland time.

Not for long, however, could she felicitate herself upon preserving her incognito, for, when the prayer was over, and no effect ensued therefrom, the chaplain got still more impatient, and said, in a tone of rather worldly asperity.

"Young man, I never had such a hardened sinner and obdurate rascal as you in this jail before. Eh? Oh! you won't speak; very well—it's dreadful. Come, come, young man, repent and confess."

As he spoke, he laid his hand upon Miranda's arm, and she, feeling that concealment for another moment would be impossible, calmly rose, and, taking off the hat, allowed her long hair to fall in dancing ringlets on to her neck and bosom, as she said:

"Thank Heaven—that Heaven of love and mercy, the name of which you use so profanely—Rowland Percy is not here! He is innocent, therefore he has nothing to confess. His and my reliance upon the goodness and mercy of God to His weak, erring creatures, is unbounded, therefore we have no fear."

The chaplain, in his amazement, actually staggered back, till he could get no further than the wall, and his little sleepy eyes opened to their utmost width, while he dropped on the floor of the cell a bundle of tracts, which he had brought with him, the first of which was entitled, "The Fast Coach to Hell, or Sinners put on the Drag," and gasped several times before he could say:

"Who—are—you?"

"Miranda Rankley," was the reply.

"Where—where—where is the murderer?"

"What murderer?"

"Young woman—young woman—I—I—where is Rowland Percy?"

"Escaped!" said Miranda, in a voice that made the pious man give a jump that brought him at once to the door of the cell.

"Escaped?"

"Yes, and, by this time, free as the air of Heaven. Make what alarm you like—use your utmost exertions. He is, I believe, under the protection of that Power which sees all hearts, and, in its own good time, saves the innocent."

"Help—help—Jones—Jenkins! Help—murder—fire! He has escaped!"

Shouting these words of alarm, the chaplain rushed from the cell, and, with his gown streaming behind him, sped along the passages towards the outer gate.

The word fire was the one which happened most of all to catch the ears of one of the turnkeys, who, catching up a pail of water, ran with it in the direction of the cry, shouting:

"Where?—where?—where?" till he met the chaplain, when they ran against each other with a violence that brought them both rolling to the floor, deluged with the water.

"Curse you!" said the turnkey. "Who are you?"

"Help!" shrieked the chaplain.

A mob of officials now, with lights, approached the prostrate pair, and the turnkey, when he saw who his opponent was, became very contrite indeed, but was cut short by the chaplain saying, in an angry tone:

"I'll have you discharged to-morrow, my man,—but, first of all, the murderer, Percy, has escaped."

"Escaped?" echoed everyone.

"Gone—gone—and left another vessel of wrath behind him."

"Gone off in a *vessel?*" said Joey. "Oh, my eye and Elizabeth Martin!"

"Call the Governor," said another. "Call the Governor."

"What's the matter now?" said the Governor himself, who, alarmed by the tumult, suddenly made his appearance in his dressing-gown.

"Oh, Captain Price," said the chaplain, "Rowland Percy has escaped."

A flush of surprise crossed the Governor's face, and he said in a tone of great annoyance:

"Pho—pho—it can't be. How could he—from the condemned cell? Impossible."

As he said so, however, he strode down the passage towards the cell with a very uncomfortable feeling that if it were true there would be something in the shape of a tremendous row made about his ears.

CHAPTER LXX.

ROWLAND AND HIS FRIEND PALMER—THE OLD "NAG'S HEAD" AT YORK—THE SECRET CHAMBER.

DICK PALMER and Rowland Percy proceeded at a very rapid pace through a great number of streets, after the quietus had been so unceremoniously given to the cunning turnkey, who, with all his cleverness, and all his bruises, lay doubled up in the doorway, as harmless as any very clever under-turnkey could possibly be.

"You have freed me from this danger," said Rowland, "most admirably. To your skill and courage I owe my life, and it shall go hard with me, indeed, if I find not some means of showing you that you have not thrown away your services upon an ungrateful heart."

"I am quite satisfied, Mr. Percy," said Palmer, "that you are an innocent man; that is enough for me, if I did not believe Miss Rankley to be, as I sincerely do, as brave and noble-hearted a girl as ever stepped."

"You do her no more than justice," said Rowland, with animation; "she is——But how can I find language adequate to a description of Miranda?"

"No how," said Palmer, "so don't try it. We are very near our first place of destination now. Yonder dim light, which is just on the outskirts of the town, is at an old public-house, called the "Nag's Head." You will find there a friendly shelter for an hour, within which time I will return to you with means for your conveyance to London, whither I will accompany you."

"I place myself solely under your guidance," said Rowland.

"Do so, and all will be well. Now, come on. Here we are at the door. Say nothing, but sit down among the company I shall introduce you to."

Without any hesitation Rowland entered the public-house, from which rose the sounds of jovial merriment, and rather boisterous enjoyment.

A few words of "A friend of mine, who doesn't want to be inquisitive himself, nor to be bothered," from Palmer to the landlord, seemed a sufficient introduction, for he nodded, and said:

"All's right—we have here none but good hands. Will the gentleman walk into the snuggery?"

"Yes," said Palmer; "come on."

Followed then by Rowland, he led the way through very intricate winding passages, until he came to a door covered with green baize, which he opened. Another door of the same outward material then appeared, at which he knocked. It was on the instant opened by a brawny fellow, who seemed fully capable of maintaining it against anyone.

The moment he saw Palmer his eyes danced with glee, and his mouth widened to a grin of pleasure.

"Come to stay, of course?" he said.

"No. I have important business, but here is a friend of mine who will remain half-an-hour. He doesn't want to see anyone, mind."

"All right."

"Remain here till I come," whispered Palmer. "I had hoped to have had a conveyance ready for you at once, but have been disappointed. You will be quite safe here, for even should any officer enter in pursuit of you, the people here will hide you."

"I trust you and them implicitly," said Rowland, "and I am sure I need not say come back to me as soon as you can."

"You need not, indeed. Expect me within the hour."

So saying, he made a signal to the man on guard, who, in obedience to it, opened the inner door.

The confused murmur of many voices came upon his ears, and, crossing the threshold, Rowland found himself in a long, low room, in which many people were assembled.

Curious and scrutinizing glances were cast upon him, but no further notice was taken, and Rowland, sinking upon the first vacant seat, prepared to wait with what patience he might for the return of his singular acquaintance.

CHAPTER LXXI.

MIRANDA AND THE GOVERNOR—A TROUBLE-
SOME AFFAIR—THE PURSUIT—UNWILLING
PRAISE—THE REMOVAL.

WHEN the Governor reached the cell, Miranda was awaiting his appearance with anxiety, certainly, but still with feelings of such an exultant nature, that they triumphed over any shade of disagreeable anticipation as regarded herself, and her own fate.

The object she proposed to herself, was to put off to the last moment anything in the shape of an active pursuit of Rowland—not that she doubted his safety, but she would, if she could, have made assurance doubly sure, and could she gain for him another five minutes by parleying with the Governor, she would.

The moment that official personage entered the cell, he saw that it was no false alarm that had been raised by the chaplain, and that, in lieu of the person who on the following morning would have been led to an ignominious death, he had in his custody a beautiful and heroic girl, whom he found it even difficult to speak harshly to.

The Governor had been an officer in the army, and all his preconceived habits and notions tended to make him in his own heart admire what Miranda had done, notwithstanding the disagreeable turn of circumstances which was likely to ensue, and the trouble and annoyance, not to say censure, he would in all likelihood receive from the enraged authorities.

"Young lady," he said, "for Heaven's sake, tell me where the prisoner is! How in the name of all that's da——I beg your pardon—wonderful—came you to project this scheme?"

"He has escaped!" said Miranda, with fervour. "He is safe! The innocent Rowland Percy is now far beyond the reach of his enemies. Sir, your appearance bespeaks you a gentleman. I know what I have done is a crime, but I glory in it, and all I have to ask of you is to let the consequences of my act fall upon myself alone, for I assure you old Mr. Percy, the father of the injured Rowland, knows nothing of my proceedings."

"But do you mean to say that you have had the—the audacity—I mean the courage—no, the criminality——"

"Sir—sir," said Miranda, "your heart is struggling against what you consider your duty. I do grieve that in rescuing one more dear to me than life itself from death, I have drawn you, probably, into some trouble. Accept my regrets—more I cannot say. I am, I presume, your prisoner, and thus I throw myself upon your humanity."

The Governor looked up at the ceiling, stroked his chin, and coughed several times—in fact, he had never felt himself so thoroughly puzzled before. What on earth to do, or what to say, he knew not.

Miranda, seeing the state of doubt and hesitation he was in, said:

"Sir, heed me not—but do your duty. God forbid that I should be a source of greater anxiety to you than necessary. You never injured my Rowland. He came here, and was detained by you in the due process of your duty—without, then, any hesitation, I beg of you to continue the exercise of that duty. I will not blame you, sir."

"For Heaven's sake, young lady," said the Governor, "save yourself, and let the law take its course."

"What?—surrender him again? Never! No, sir, sooner should the scaffold, which is preparing in expectation of him who, by the mercy of Heaven, is now far away, receive me as its victim, than I would breathe one word to place upon Rowland Percy's track the bloodhounds that would hunt him to death."

"I have already ordered a pursuit."

"'Twill be a vain one. Hear me, sir. I have set myself a task in this world, which, with Heaven's assistance, I will perform. When that awful word 'Guilty' fell upon my heart in the Court of Justice from the misguided lips of him who uttered it, I told myself that, from that moment, it should be the aim of my future life to blot it from the minds of men, and substitute for it the more glorious word 'Innocent.' Sir, I loved my father—a mother's tenderness I never knew. The concentrated affection of my young heart was all given to him. He was murdered! Think you I mourned not for him? Think you, because you see no tears now, that my heart feels no pang at that sad bereavement? Then, Rowland Percy was accused, and I knew him to be innocent. For him I have placed myself a prisoner here—yet, sir, I loved my father. Can human nature in its sanity become the slave of such contradictions, that the fond, doting heart of a bereaved child could risk all—dare all, in behalf of its father's murderer? No—no. He is innocent—he is innocent. If Rowland Percy be guilty, then he and I must both be mad."

The Governor listened to her with rapt attention, and then he said:

"Brave girl! I cannot blame you—your noble faith in him—your—hang it! I dare not, Miss Rankley, say what I think, but from my soul I admire——"

"Where's the hardened sinner?" said the chaplain, appearing at the door of the cell. "Oh! young woman—young woman!"

"Sir, you are the Governor of this place," said Miranda, appealing to him; "I request you to protect me from this man's impertinence—as you are a gentleman, I claim your protection."

"Impertinence!" cried the chaplain.

"Come, come, Mr. Salver," said the Governor, "I don't see that either you or I have any right to annoy this lady. She has certainly made herself amenable to the law, but we cannot call her morally guilty in any way."

"Not guilty! Is she not one of those vessels of wrath which look fair to the eye, in order to lead men from the proper path into the way of ungodliness?"

DICK PALMER FINDS A PLACE OF REFUGE FOR THE DISGUISED ROWLAND.

"Just as you please," said the Governor; "but she is not even my prisoner at present."

"What! Not a prisoner?"

"Charity—charity, sir."

"Oh, the time will come, when there will be howling and gnashing of teeth; when the everlasting flames——"

"I tell you what, Mr. Salver," said the Governor, "I think you and I will quarrel some of these days. My dear girl, don't mind what he says."

"I do not—I do not," said Miranda.

"I shall make a point," said the chaplain, with bitterness, "of representing your conduct to the magistracy."

"I hope you will; and very glad am I that you and I have, at last, come to a fair understanding. What is wanted in a person as a chaplain, is a man of education, talent, and liberality. One who knows human nature, and can make allowances for its weaknesses and great temptations. One who will kindly lead the unhappy person, with whom he may come in contact, to a better and happier mode of thinking. Such a one, I am sorry to say, sir, you are not; and I am resolved that either I will no longer be Governor here, or you shall no longer be chaplain, for I intend to explain what I mean, and what I complain of, to the magistracy."

The chaplain looked perfectly thunder-stricken at this calm and reasonable speech. He stared at the Governor with his fish-like eyes wide open, but could not say a word.

To Miranda the temperate rebuke of the Governor gave the greatest pleasure, and to find herself in the hands of one of such proper feelings and kindred sentiments to her own, joined to the conviction that Rowland was saved, gave her so much joy that, could she have commanded tears, she would have bid them flow to relieve her throbbing heart.

The Governor said to Miranda, in a kind tone:

"You shall not be long confined here; I will return soon."

"I shall not be lonely," said Miranda; "this once gloomy cell will be to me a palace full of rare thoughts. My now free and un-fettered fancy will people it with pleasant sights. I have not been so happy since I last saw my poor father in life."

The Governor stood by the door of the cell, and waited for the chaplain to come out; but the latter, with an assurance that was quite inexcusable, said:

"I shall remain here. My heavenly duties place me far above any human denuncia-tions."

"Remain here?"

"Yes; I shall reason with this sinful young woman."

"Indeed," said the Governor, "you shall do no such thing. If you are still chaplain here I will let you know that I am still Governor, and if you don't come out of this cell directly by fair means, you shall by foul."

"If you dare to assault me I will get you removed from your situation for a surety."

"I believe you wish me to assault you," said the Governor, "and, under the cir-cumstances, I shall gratify you. Are you coming?"

"No, I am not."

"Then you shall."

So saying, the Governor took him by the collar, and handed him out in a moment.

Miranda then heard the cell-door locked, and, for a time, all was silent around her.

The Governor said no more to the chaplain, but, leaving him just outside the cell-door, he walked to the lobby, and directed several of the officers connected with the prison to disperse themselves about the city in search of the escaped prisoner, while he himself re-paired to the nearest magistrate to know what was to be done with Miranda.

Without any clue to direct them where to look, the search of the officers for Rowland was not likely to be successful, and they could do nothing but wander up and down the city, visiting such houses as they thought by any possibility he might be concealed in; among which, to the great surprise of Miranda's land-lady, they searched her house, although they would not say what was their reason for so doing.

While this languid pursuit of Rowland was going on, the Governor had attired himself

for the streets, and started to the nearest magistrate, whom he knocked up, and insisted upon seeing on very urgent business.

When he explained the circumstance, the magistrate looked astonished, and remarked:

"Something must be done directly. I will go with you to another magistrate, and we two can take some step in the business, which is a very awkward one to act alone in. You have, I presume, taken all the steps in your power to recover the prisoner?"

"I have."

"Then, then—really I don't know what can be done."

"No," said the Governor, with a smile. "But what am I to do with the young lady who has played us this trick?"

"Why, to tell the truth, you have no right to lock her up, and she might bring an action against you for false imprisonment, as you have no warrant for her detention."

"I don't think she will," said the Governor; "but what do you advise me to do?"

"Why, you bring her before me and Mr. Angerstein, my brother magistrate, the first thing in the morning. We must commit her for the misdemeanour of aiding, comforting, and abetting a felon, you see."

"Very well; and, in the meantime, I must, of course, keep her in custody?"

"I suppose so. Dear me! it's an awkward affair altogether. Your turnkeys must cer-tainly lose their situations."

"Why, one would think," said the Governor, as he rose to go, "that the most ordinary cir-cumspection would have prevented such a thing from occurring."

"She must have had accomplices."

"So I think; but you will as easily make the sun shine at midnight, I am sure, as get her to name them."

"Indeed?"

"Yes. A more resolute, determined spirit, I never encountered in all my life."

"Well, well, we must make the best of the affair. Good-night, sir, or, rather, good-morning. We shall see you, I suppose, with your prisoner in the morning?"

"Certainly."

With this the Governor went back to the prison again, feeling more entertainment and pleasant excitement from the whole affair than annoyance.

When he reached the gloomy abode of crime and sorrow, he went at once to the cell in which Miranda was confined, and, unlock-ing the door, entered its narrow precincts.

"Miss Rankley," he said, "I am far from disposed to be unfriendly towards you; and now that we are alone, permit me to com-promise myself so far as to say, that, while in my official capacity, I am compelled to blame, and should certainly, had I had any suspicion of the trick, have thwarted your proceedings, yet I cannot, as a man, blame you. On the contrary, your courage and perseverance in the cause of one you believe to be innocent (for who can doubt you?) does you infinite credit."

"I thank you from my heart, sir," said Miranda. "I have much to be thankful for to many kind friends since my career of unhappiness commenced with the death of my father; but, least of all, did I expect to find within these walls the kind sympathy you have shown to me. Once more, sir, I thank you."

"You have half-convinced me of Rowland Percy's innocence," added the Governor: "and if such be really the case, and yourself be not deceived, I rejoice that I was not in the way to mar this night's work."

"Thank Heaven!" said Miranda.

"I have come now to tell you that it will be my duty to take you in the morning before the magistrates, when they will deal with you as the law directs."

"I shall not shrink from the consequences of my act," said Miranda. "I will not say that I reflected upon the consequences, and so prepared myself to meet them, for such was not the fact. I thought of nothing but the preservation of Rowland Percy, and, that accomplished, I knew would bring me strength to bear all else. I can remain here well enough till morning."

"Nay," said the Governor, "I have no authority to keep you here in a condemned cell. In the building you must remain; but I must confine you in a much less gloomy and dreadful place than this. Are you willing?"

"I will follow you wherever it is your duty to take me," said Miranda.

"Come, then, we must proceed at once."

Miranda followed the Governor through many devious turnings and long gloomy passages, where in nooks sat here and there a guard, who touched his hat to the Governor as he passed, and much wondered who it was that was with him.

Then he led the way up a long flight of stairs, and, taking a key from his pocket, unlocked a massive iron-door, which revolved on its enormous hinges slowly and with difficulty.

Immediately on the other side of this door was another, covered with green baize, and yielding to the slightest touch. Miranda felt the soft tread of carpeting beneath her feet, and the Governor, turning to her, and raising the lamp he held in his hand, said:

"We are near our destination, Miss Rankley. I wish you to make yourself as happy as you can while you are my prisoner, and if you bring an action against me for false imprisonment, do not say I aggravated its terrors."

He walked across the small room into which the door covered with green baize led, and opening another, discovered a large, handsome, well-lighted apartment, in which were a lady and a young child of about five years of age. The lady and child had evidently both newly risen from bed, and had merely thrown on some loose covering.

"My dear," said the Governor, "this is the heroic Miranda Rankley. Treat her kindly. Miss Rankley, my wife and child."

CHAPTER LXXII.

THE MORNING OF THE INTENDED EXECUTION —THE SCAFFOLD—THE EXPECTANT CROWD —THE STRANGE MESSAGE—THE PLACARD.

By six o'clock on that eventful morning, many hundreds of persons were up and stirring, who ordinarily never thought of showing themselves from their bedrooms for full two hours after that period.

The excitement which the approaching execution had created among all classes was unprecedented.

By the hour we have named a dense crowd had assembled at the place of execution, and each moment increased the pressure of the throng.

House-tops far and near, so that they commanded any view at all of the scaffold, were rapidly becoming covered with anxious spectators, and from the neighbouring counties many persons had come on horseback, having ridden for hours in order to be present at a scene which, from the peculiar condition in life of the parties concerned, and the singular train of evidence which had conspired to fix the guilt upon him who was to suffer death, had not its parallel in the history of the county of York.

So dense became the throng towards seven o'clock, that the workmen who were erecting the scaffold were compelled to desist from their labour until some constables could be brought to take the pressure of the throng off them.

By that hour, however, there was not an official person in the city who had not been made aware of the escape of the prisoner, but no orders were given to suspend the arrangements for the execution, as no one individual seemed inclined to act by himself in the matter.

A meeting of the magistracy and civic authorities was hastily called, and the judge, who was still remaining in the city, was pressed to attend, which, however, he would not, saying that he had nothing to do with the failure of the executive portion of the authorities in carrying the law into effect.

By a quarter past seven every magistrate who could be found, was with his colleagues in solemn conclave, considering what was to be done under the unexpected circumstances.

Where they sat they could hear the clank of the hammers used by the workmen in putting up the now useless scaffold, and it was not until one rose and said, "Gentlemen, as yet we know nothing but that we have no prisoner to execute," that they roused themselves to send for the Governor and Miranda.

The noise of the putting up of the scaffold still continued, as if in very mockery of the attempted jurisdiction of those assembled—men who, in their short-sighted human wisdom, would have solemnly put to death an innocent fellow-creature.

The chairman of the bench then proposed that, in order to disperse the mob, a placard should be placed upon the prison gate, offering a reward of a hundred pounds, to be paid by the county, to anyone who would apprehend, or give such information as should lead to the apprehension, of Rowland Percy, the convicted murderer.

This resolution was carried just as the Minster clock was sounding the half-hour past seven, and it was immediately written out (until some could be printed for general use) in a large, bold hand by the clerk.

Even while the document was being signed by some of the magistrates, the confused hum of the dense multitude assembled to witness the execution, came upon their ears like the sullen roaring of the sea upon a rocky beach.

A strong body of police was despatched with orders to bid the workmen take down the scaffold, while they were to post the placard, and then endeavour to induce the multitude to disperse, and quietly seek their homes.

A magistrate on horseback preceded the officers; and tremendous was the difficulty they had in forcing a passage through the dense throng of persons that were in their way.

Within about a hundred paces of the prison gates they were completely hemmed in, and the magistrate, waving his hand, said:

"Disperse—disperse! There will be no execution."

His words were only heard by those immediately about him, but they took up the cry, and a thousand voices shouted:

"No execution! no execution!"

Then one man, who had clambered up a lamp-post nearly in the middle of the crowd, and who had resisted, by heavy kicks, the many attempts that had been made to pull him down, drew a nightcap of red cotton from his head, and said:

"*Guv* him a cheer, my covies! They daren't hang him. My name's Jones. Hip—hip—hip—hurrah!"

The mob, more from diversion than any real sympathy with Rowland Percy, joined in the lusty cheer; and such a shout as was raised had not been heard in the ancient City of York for many a day.

The magistrate then called, in a loud voice, to the men who were at the scaffold:

"Remove it—remove it!"

"Let's help 'em," said Jones. "It will make beautiful firewood, and boil half the tea-kettles in York to-day."

A suggestion of a mischievous character thrown out to a mob, is like a lighted match in a powder magazine. The scaffold in five minutes was taken piece-meal, in spite of the efforts of the astonished workmen, who stood gazing on the scene of demolition with silent wonder.

"Run back to the magistrates," whispered he who was mounted to the constable nearest him. "Tell them we shall have a riot for a certainty unless they send more force."

The officer went on his errand as quickly as he could; and then the magistrate made a foolish attempt to take Jones prisoner, who, being the popular idol of the moment, was quite in a condition to defy him; and, accordingly, when the magistrate pointed to him, and said: "Seize that man!" Jones pointed back again at him, crying, in a loud, rough voice:

"Seize him!—seize him!—a handful of mouldy coppers reward. Seize him! He's a-getting wild—he is."

A roar of laughter followed this speech; and the magistrate was fain to content himself with a good look at Mr. Jones, in order that, on any future occasion, he might be able to swear to him as the cause of the riot; for, had he not spoken, the mob would in all likelihood have gone quietly away from the spot.

"Put up the placard," said the magistrate then, as he pressed forward to the prison-gate, in which direction, as it was away from Jones, he was now allowed a tolerably easy passage.

In a few moments the placard was fixed, and the last tack that held it to the gate was struck in at the moment that the Minster clock struck eight, and when, but for the heroism of Miranda, Rowland Percy would have been judicially murdered before the eyes of assembled thousands.

The foremost of the mob read the placard, and, turning to those behind, they shouted:

"He has escaped!—he has escaped!"

The impression had been that Rowland Percy was reprieved, and the news that he had escaped, came with all the freshness of a first announcement in the ears of the multitude.

"Well done he," said Jones. "Another cheer!"

Another shout then rose, which might have been heard for miles around.

At this moment the gate of the prison opened, and at the top of the steps, which were sufficiently high to be seen by every person that assembled, stood the compassionate Governor and Miranda Rankley.

Her face was beaming with pleasure; and she stood for some moments looking upon the vast throng before her, contrasting her present feelings at eight o'clock then, with what they might have been had she failed in her attempt to liberate Rowland.

CHAPTER LXXIII.

THE LONELY WATCH OF BERNARD VARLEY—
THE FRENZIED CRY AND INSENSIBILITY—
THE CROWD AND THE MAGISTRACY.

It must have been the rare and exquisite beauty of Miranda, as she stood in that commanding situation, accompanied by the Governor of the prison, that at once attracted all eyes and all hearts towards her.

Some there were who certainly knew her by sight, but the majority of the immense throng of human beings that assembled had not the slightest conception of who she was, beyond the fact that a more truly beautiful girl had never blessed their eyes.

There must be surely something in the old philosophy that beauty of mind is of necessity associated with exquisitely enchanting forms at least, let our reason do for us what it will. Let our modern systems of philosophy rise up in battle array as they may against the beautiful theory, still in all hearts will be found a place for it, and there never was yet a human cause pleaded by a human advocate that did not acquire one-half of its complexion from the peculiar physical appearance of the accused.

A more striking exemplification of our remark could not have been found than in the universal cheer from thousands of hearts which immediately greeted the beautiful and heroic Miranda.

Her beauty they all knew, and there was not a soul among them that did not feel its magic power, but her heroism none knew but he who stood by her side, and who felt full as proud of his lovely companion as if the circumstances which called forth such feelings in his heart had not been, as they were, inimical to himself, and greatly derogatory to his efficiency as a public officer.

Miranda clasped her hands, and, with a look of appealing emotion, she turned to the Governor, saying:

"You see, sir, Heaven is showing the innocence of Rowland to all men. Every heart here present appears to sympathize with him, and those who have come to see his execution are clamorous that he is saved."

The Governor shook his head, as he replied:

"My dear Miss Rankley, you don't know mobs so well as I do. I could give you a different interpretation of the clamorous shouts of this vast assemblage."

"A different interpretation!" echoed Miranda.

"Yes, Miranda, a far different one. There is one feeling common to humanity, and that is the admiration of such rare and unequalled beauty as yours."

"Nay, sir," said Miranda. "I would much prefer my own interpretation of those who thus cheer at the sight of me; or it may be that you are the special favourite, and I am assuming a character that I am not entitled to."

The Governor smiled, as he said, in a deprecating tone:

"No, Miranda, no. The choice of right belongs to you. Public officers seldom come in for any great share of popular favour or applause."

"But surely such as you," said Miranda, "must have won even the hearts of the most obdurate beings who have been confined within these walls. I might have smiled at every aggravation of the miseries of my situation, and laid to my heart, as an antidote to all other evils, the delightful recollection that I had saved the innocent Rowland Percy from an ignominious death; but, still, it would have been no small aggravation of the anxieties of the situation into which I had plunged myself, if I had met with harshness, instead of the kind sympathy which I have experienced at your hands."

"I am more than repaid," said the Governor, "by hearing you say so much. Heaven prosper you, Miranda Rankley; and my fervent wish is, that the noble confidence you have shown in him to whom you have plighted your faith, may be verified by the course of events."

"At least," said Miranda, smiling, "let me cherish the thought that I have made one convert. Tell me that you believe him innocent."

"Miranda, before I saw you," replied the Governor, "I had no opinion upon the subject, but received Rowland Percy as my prisoner in the ordinary course of my duty. It seems to me now, however, as if Heaven spoke from your mouth—from my soul, I believe him innocent."

"Thank Heaven!" cried Miranda, "I am fulfilling my mission; and that is, to proclaim to all men, heedless of censure or reproach, the innocence of Rowland Percy."

"You will have many converts," said the Governor.

The mounted magistrate, who was in the midst of the throng, now made various signs to the Governor to follow him with his fair prisoner, at the same time that he sent forward as many of the officers as he could spare from about his own person, to serve as an escort for them from the prison to the place where the magistrates were holding their extraordinary sitting.

Before, however, the Governor could descend the steps, in obedience to the summons, an extraordinary commotion in the outskirts of the mob attracted universal attention.

"Hold," said the Governor, "we may as well remain on the advantage ground until we can ascertain the cause of this tumult, for mobs are by no means particular whether friend or foe comes in for a share of their violence."

Miranda, as we have said, was considerably elevated above the level on which stood the enormous throng of persons, so that she could see the cause of this tumult more clearly than those who were mingled with it.

The mob was swaying to and fro like the vexed waves of the ocean, when many miles of water move with a restless impulse in enormous masses, the precursors of a coming hurricane.

Shouts, cries, and curses filled the air, and, at one particular spot, she could see as if the black, moving mass was being mowed down as by the irresistible hand of death.

Then, as she removed her sphere of vision to the particular spot from which diverged so much tumult and confusion, she perceived one tall, gaunt figure, from whom she found it impossible to withdraw her gaze.

Sweeping forward like something endowed with more than mortal strength, came that one frightful, pallid, human form. Bold and stout men shrank from before him. The crowd he tore down as with a giant's grasp;

the strongest he dashed aside as if they had been weeds upon his path.

But one word came from his lips as he thus proceeded through that dense crowd of human beings, and that was shrieked forth in a voice which betrayed such a tone and such an air of abandonment and despair, that had he striven not otherwise to force a passage through that living throng, one would have been accorded to him through pure horror of the preternatural tone in which he so spoke.

"Escaped—escaped—escaped!" was the one word which, as often as he could gather breath to scream, he shrieked out with a bewildered wildness of intonation.

Well might Miranda cling convulsively to the arm of the Governor. Well might her cheek grow pale, and her limbs tremble, as she gazed upon that frantic form, rapidly approaching the prison gate. Too vividly upon her memory were those features stamped. Too often, with shrinking horror, had she gazed upon that countenance to be doubtful of its identity, although distorted as it was now with demoniac passions. She might well have been excused for her want of knowledge even of him whom she believed had wrought her so much woe—her cruel enemy, Bernard Varley.

Yes, it was indeed he, who with such wild, demoniacal gestures—such an agony of heart, that it was nigh bursting in his bosom—was now rushing through that throng of persons intent upon but one thought, one object—namely, to satisfy himself if the, to him, dreadful report were true, that his victim—he, whom he thought was so securely entangled in the toils, that no chance or accident of human fortune could protract his existence to another sunrise—had escaped.

In his lonely room, opposite to the lodging of Miranda, he had waited the livelong night, with the expectation of seeing the gentle girl, in whose bosom he had planted such bitter thorns, emerge, with tottering steps, at early dawn, to take a last long farewell of him who was to be snatched from her encircling arms to the cold embrace of death.

As we are aware, he was grievously disappointed in his expectations; and, oh! what a night of horrors was that to Bernard Varley —what thronging phantom forms in the still watches of that night appeared to people the silent vacancy around him. The sinful thoughts, the wild aspirations, and the deep crimes of other years, rose up from memory's depths, and mingled strongly with the more stupendous circumstances in which he was now placed.

His former impulses had been those of avarice, or ambition, mingled with revenge against those who crossed his path in those unholy pursuits, and so might he have floated easily onwards in the present case with scarce a pang, had it not been that, with wild vehemence, that master passion of the human soul—the wild and ungovernable love of woman—engulfed in its worldly vortex all other thoughts.

The midnight hour tolled solemnly from the Minster bell, and by the dim, flickering oil-lamp that burned in the street he kept his painfully-strained eyes fixed upon the door of Miranda's temporary home.

Slowly the small hours of the coming morn waned, but she whose sight to him was light and life itself came not. He saw the first faint streaks of the approaching day struggling with the artificial lights still gleaming in the streets of the ancient city; but still she came not.

One by one the bright stars retired in the blue vault of Heaven—warmer and warmer grew the first gray tints of the coming dawn —he heard the hum of life slowly arising from the myriads of waking beings around him, and still she came not.

Despair seized upon his heart, the very silence around him became pregnant, to his imagination, with frightful sounds.

He leaned from the window, and scarcely knowing what he did, or what might be the consequence of his mad display of passion, cried:

"Miranda, Miranda—come forth, scornful but beautiful—bless my eyes again—although you blast my ears with words of hatred and detestation. Miranda—Miranda—time is flying—think, oh! think what a morn is this— come forth, and by one word light up a heaven of joy in my heart, and save yourself from everlasting regret, Miranda—Miranda—awake —awake—by Heaven, she hears not—she must be dead—dead—dead!"

With one gasping sob he reeled across the floor, and just as the first faint gleam of sunlight fell upon the topmost windows of the house, he dropped insensible in the lonely apartment, which had witnessed his melancholy vigils.

The people in the house, who in the early part of the evening had been alarmed at his ghastly countenance, and the singular expression of his eyes, were disturbed by the frantic manner in which he spoke, and they stood shuddering upon the staircase, afraid to venture into the room, where they might encounter one bereft of sense.

Nearly an hour thus passed away, and Bernard Varley remained insensible to the despair which, had he been in active existence, might, indeed, have driven him to distraction.

Then hearing that all was still, the master and mistress of the house gathered courage slowly to ascend to his door, which—after listening at it for a long time—they proposed to themselves cautiously to open sufficiently wide only to reconnoitre their strange, and, as they began to think, mad lodger.

The man himself was armed with an immense kitchen poker, which he protruded into the room some distance before himself, in order that Bernard Varley might be held *in terrorem*, and made cognizant of what desperate courage actuated the breast of his landlord.

At the suggestion of the good woman of the house, the poker was shaken menacingly for several moments before she would allow her worser half—as she most certainly considered him—to venture his life by entering the apartment. For, as she acutely reasoned, a very indifferent husband was better than none, and, in consequence of a court mourning, all the paraphernalia of outward grief was exceedingly dear in York at that moment.

Like most people, the man's courage was greatly increased as there became apparently less and less occasion for it, and he felt very much like the soldier who ran hard for five miles, till he placed a battery between him and the foe, and then cried :

" By Heaven ! if they had caught me, what a drubbing they would have had !"

" Speak to him, John," said the woman ; " then if he says anything, we can rush downstairs like a flash of lightning."

John then suggested, in a low tone : .

" What would be the use of speaking to him, if he said nothing in reply ?"

Upon which John was declared an idiot and a curse to any woman ; being finally told that he was no man, or he would have before that cried : " Hilloa, Mr. Varley !"

Thus urged, the no-man did cry : " Hilloa, Mr. Varley !" and receiving no answer, he ventured to open the door a little wider, when he discovered his strange and troublesome lodger lying insensible in the middle of the floor.

CHAPTER LXXIV.

THE AWFUL COMMUNICATION — THE WILD FEELINGS OF VARLEY — THE STRANGE INTERVIEW AT THE PRISON GATE.

THERE could not be much danger from a man in such a situation, " unless, indeed," as John's wife suggested, " that it might be only his artfulness, and he might spring up the moment he thought anyone was sufficiently near him to murder ;" but John was liberal in his estimate of human nature, and thought otherwise, so he entered the room on the instant, and approached the prostrate form of Bernard Varley, who it would have been a mercy to leave in the state of forgetfulness he was then in.

" He has fainted, wife," cried the man : " run for water. Perhaps he may be dead, and if so——"

" We should never let our lodgings again," cried his wife, filling up the sentence, as she hurried downstairs for some water.

By dint of various remedies Bernard Varley was restored to a state of consciousness, and then, looking wildly around him, he said, in a deep, sepulchral voice :

" Where am I ?—where am I ? Is this a place for condemned spirits ? and have I, indeed, passed through the portals of the tomb ?"

" No, sir, if you please," said the woman. " you are in our first-floor front, and your week's up to-morrow. We'll let you go without any notice whatsomdever, if so be as you'll go at once."

" Hush, wife !—hush !" said the man. " He is not in a condition now to talk of such matters. We ought, I think, to send for a doctor."

During this brief conversation between the landlord and landlady, Varley's memory was recovering from its state of stupor, and he was beginning to comprehend the situation in which he was placed.

" Tell me," he said, faintly, " what has happened. I now see where I am, but what has happened to me I know not."

" You must have fainted, sir," said the man.

Varley placed his hands over his eyes for a moment, as if, by shutting out the external world, he was endeavouring to call to mind the circumstances which had preceded his temporary oblivion from the many cares and deep anxieties which beset him.

" We heard you, sir," said the woman, " calling to somebody from the window, and then, as they wouldn't come, you were pleased to faint away with a great dab."

" Calling from the window ?"

" Yes, you called Miss Miranda, sir, who you know is——"

" Yes—yes," cried Varley, suddenly springing to his feet from the arm-chair in which the couple had placed him. " Miranda ! Miranda ! Has she not yet come forth ? Watch for her. Let me see her, if but for a moment, as she takes her melancholy way to the execution—ay, the execution."

" He's thinking of the hanging that's going to be, John," said the woman. " Poor man, he's quite a wandering, he is."

" The time—the time !" cried Varley— " what is the time ?"

He dragged his watch from his pocket with vehemence ; and when he saw it wanted but a short time to the fatal hour of eight, he dropped the watch upon the floor, and clasping his hands, cried :

" Time is flying. All will be soon over, and another spirit will be kneeling at the Throne of Heaven, to prefer its plaint against me. Where is she ? Miranda—Miranda, can you see him die ? Can there be such constancy in woman ?"

At this moment a loud, monotonous voice from the street immediately below the window was heard shouting with painful reiteration and distinctness what had been prepared the day before by a speculative printer, in the full expectation that Rowland Percy must be hanged. He had certainly suggested to the hawkers of the document the propriety of waiting till the Minster clock struck eight ere they commenced their avocation : but this one, ever with a laudable desire to be first in the field, had begun before that hour.

" Here you have," he cried, " the last dying speech *and* the confession *of* Rowland Percy, who *was* executed *for* the murder—the most atrocious and sanguine-*hairy* murder of Sir George Rankley ! Here you have it—here you have it, for the small charge of one half-penny—the dying speech and the confession, in which he says—here you have it for one halfpenny—with many curious and interesting and odd particulars never before heard of, and never to be heard of again—here, for the small charge of one halfpenny, the very last dying speech and the confession of Rowland Percy, who was hanged this morning, with a copy of verses, and all for the small charge of one halfpenny—here you have it—here you have it—sold again, and pocketed the browns. Now, young woman, for the small charge of a halfpenny!"

Bernard Varley listened to this singular harangue as if his very soul's salvation depended upon his hearing every word of it.

"'Tis done—'tis done!" he gasped, "and she came not—she came not! I—I thought that even at the last she would have saved him; but—but she came not—the tragedy is over—over—and what am I now—what am I now?"

"He forgets *hisself*," remarked the woman. "Please, sir, you are our lodger, you know, sir."

He sank back into the chair again, and, covering his face with his hands, cried aloud:

"Horror—horror—why do I live? Death—death, wrap me in the elysium of forgetfulness!"

Then, in strange discord to his feelings, rose the voice of the man in the street, as he commenced, with a stentorian voice, repeating the copy of verses which had been composed for the occasion, commencing with—and we presume the commencement will be quite enough for the reader:

> "Attend to me, ye mothers dear,
>   *Wot* hugs a precious babby,
> And while your blood turns curds and whey,
>   Let all your flesh feel flabby;
> By keeping of bad com—pa—ny,
>   And fostering of his malice,
> An *unfort'nate* young man, you see,
>   Has comed unto the gallows!"

"Lost—lost—lost!" groaned Varley, as he rocked himself to and fro in the chair on which he sat.

"John," said the woman, "just run down and buy one of *them* papers; I never heard anything so affecting in all my life."

On the instant, then, and before John could execute his mission, another voice rose with stentorian power in the street, and, but that the gentleman who owned it had a bad cold, it might have been clear and dulcet.

"Here you have," he cried, "the full and interesting particulars of the most wonderful and extra—ordinary and unkimmon *escape* of Rowland Percy, who was to be hanged, but wasn't—here you have it, just printed and published."

"Hilloa, spoony!" cried he, who was thus abruptly stopped in his recitation of the affecting copy of verses, "what do you mean by that?"

"What I says, my *werdant*," said the new comer. "Here you have it—here you have it! Don't attend to the humbug *oppersite*. Here, for the small charge of one halfpenny, you have the full particulars of the most wonderful, the most extra—ordinary escape of Rowland Percy, from the condemned cell, last night—just printed—leaving his sweetheart behind him—for a halfpenny."

The man with the last dying speech and confession, cast his eyes around him in despair.

"Here's a blessed do!" he gasped. "I feels *briled* brown. You out-and-out wagabond, will you be off?"

"The miraculous escape for a halfpenny," shouted the other.

"The last dying speech and confession," bawled the first comer.

"Be off with you—will you?"

"No, I sha'n't—for one halfpenny, and a copy of verses."

"The extra—ordinary escape, with the full and interesting particulars—and what he said, and what his sweetheart said—and what they nither of 'em said.—I'll just walk into you, if you don't cut."

"He was hung!" shouted the man with the dying speech.

"He wasn't," said the other.

"Then it's a shame of him not to be. That's the way people takes the bread out o' others' mouths. I'd a been hung twice, afore I'd a been so desperate shabby—for the small charge of one halfpenny."

"Take that," said he, who cried the escape, the particulars of which he had received from an acquaintance who was an under-turnkey, and giving his opponent what, in vulgar parlance, is called a bonneter, he effectually put a stop to his literary pursuits for some minutes.

Varley had listened to the words of the new comer with an interest that was fearfully manifest in his countenance.

"Escaped—escaped!" he cried. "No, no—that cannot be. I—never dreamt of such a thing as that. 'Tis false—false! He is dead—dead!"

"Please, sir, if you mean the murderer who is going to be hanged," said the woman, "it ain't struck eight yet."

"Hark!" cried Varley.

Solemnly and slowly the Minster clock went through the chimes, indicative of the lapse of four quarters of an hour, and then struck eight.

Varley counted the sounds with painful exactness, and when the air had ceased to reverberate to the last tone, he said:

"Now—now 'tis over—over. He is struggling—I think I see him writhing in his death agony. I see the contortions of the body, and fancy shows me, beneath that covering which hides them from all else, the frightful convulsions of the face. He—he is now dying—dying!"

"John," said the woman, "I am quite scared, and feel *sterical*."

"Don't be a fool," said John.

The man who cried the account of the escape of Rowland, having, by this time, overcome his antagonist, had all the field to himself, so that Bernard Varley heard him again proclaim the fact, which, while it would, if true, unburden his heart of one great weight, would load it with a thousand anxieties instead.

With a sudden impulse he rose from the chair, and, darting past the astonished couple, rushed down the staircase, and out into the street.

"Here, here," he cried to the man; "I—I want to know the truth. Tell me, on your soul, tell me if you speak the truth, and you shall have gold."

"He has escaped, sir," said the man, gazing at Bernard Varley's wild-looking face with wonder and astonishment.

"You are sure?"

"Quite, sir."

"How—how? Tell me how?"

"Why, sir, his sweetheart went to the prison last night, all for to see him, and they changed clothes, you see, and she stayed in the condemned cell while he walked out."

"She—she—Miranda. Mean you Miss Rankley?"

"That's the cretur, sir."

Varley threw the man a piece of gold, which he immediately pocketed, and then ran from the street, muttering:

"That ere mad gentleman's keeper will be coming out, and wanting this here *sucerin* back again if I ain't off quick."

Varley stood a moment irresolute, with his hands clasped, and his whole countenance distorted by a contrariety of emotions. Then he said, in choking accents:

"I must know the truth. To the scaffold—to the scaffold!"

Darting off, then, in the direction of the place of execution, he reached the outskirts of the immense mob which had assembled to witness the sickening sight of a fellow creature deprived of life.

Then, in the frantic manner we have recorded, he battled his way through the throng of persons, keeping his eyes fixed upon the one face which he saw by the prison gate—that was Miranda's, and, by an impulse he could not control, and sought not to question, he felt that he must ask her if the truth had been spoken by the man in the street, for from no other lips could he assure himself of the fact.

Nor was Miranda's gaze less fixed upon Bernard Varley's face, with scarce the power to withdraw it, than his upon her's, for she was full of dread that he might be rushing to her with some news of evil import.

CHAPTER LXXV.

THE CONFIRMATION OF VARLEY'S FEARS— THE AWAKENED SUSPICION—NEW DANGER FROM THE MOB.

PARTLY from fear of his wild vehemence, and partly from curiosity to know where he was making such desperate efforts to get to, the mob made way for Bernard Varley, as, with his glaring eyes fixed upon Miranda, he strove to reach the steps on which she stood.

"Who is that," said the Governor, "who fixes his eyes upon you, and you alone, in so strange and terrible a manner?"

"'Tis Bernard Varley," said Miranda. "'Tis he who, as I shall have to answer it before Heaven, I fully believe to be the author of all the misfortunes which have broken in upon my otherwise happy life; and although I cannot give a definite shape to my accusations, my heart tells me that in Bernard Varley I see my father's murderer, and the false, perjured witness who would have sacrificed Rowland Percy to his wild passions."

"His countenance is far from prepossessing," said the Governor. "I have heard much of the man, and was anxious to see him. My duties prevented me from attending the trial. With what a frantic perseverance he strives to reach this spot."

The magistrate now called with a loud voice:

"Bring your prisoner, sir, if you please. Hilloa there, constables, clear the way. Keep off the mob."

"Now, constables, do you hear his *washup?*" cried Jones, from his elevated position, in a tone which was one of such capital mimicry, that a roar of laughter arose from the multitude.

"Some other time, my man," said the magistrate, "when I am not so occupied as I am now, I shall have the pleasure of making your acquaintance."

"Oh, don't trouble yourself," said Jones. "My *wisiting* list's uncommon full, and I don't much like you."

"Scoundrel," muttered the magistrate. "If it would not, as I see too well it would, create a general riot, I would take him at all risks."

"Stay yet a moment," said Miranda, to the Governor; "I would fain hear what that ill-omened man has to say to me."

Varley by this time had arrived within about a dozen paces of the prison-steps, and then, with another desperate effort, he dashed those aside who were between him and Miranda, and stood at the foot of the small stone flight, unable to speak, and scarcely able to stand, from the violent exertion he had gone through to reach so far.

His apparel was torn, and his hands and face were disfigured by blood. He reeled from side to side like a drunken man, and when he in some measure found breath sufficient to utter an articulate sound, all he could say was:

"Miranda—Miranda."

"Bernard Varley, what have you to say to me?" cried Miranda, with a visible loathing of the man she addressed. "Monster, perjured villain, what have you to say to me?"

"Is—is—it true?" gasped Varley.

"What true?" cried the Governor. "Say what you wish at once, for we must be going."

"Tell me—tell me," almost shrieked Varley, "has he escaped—has he, the doomed one, escaped?"

"He has," said Miranda. "To your confusion—to your dismay, Rowland Percy is free, and hear me now, Bernard Varley, while I speak to you in the voice of prophecy, which for its own wise purposes is sometimes lent by Heaven to its weakest creatures. The escape of Rowland Percy, whom you know to be innocent, is, and shall be the first in a chain of events strikingly in contrast to those which have preceded it."

"What—what mean you?" said Varley.

"This," continued Miranda, "that, whereas every accident, every combination of events had conspired to fix guilt on the innocent Rowland Percy, and to make you fancy that Heaven was so unmindful of its creatures, as to abandon them to the mercy of such as thou, this escape shall be the first in a new train of events, each one of which shall do something for the innocence of Rowland, and the condemnation of the real murderer of my father."

"No—no—no," gasped Varley.

"Hear me, and tremble," added Miranda. "My words have sunk into your heart, and there shall they remain, a never-ceasing torment."

The effect of Miranda's words upon the guilty conscience of that miserable man was full as great as she could have anticipated.

He drew his breath short and thickly, a clammy moisture came upon his brow, and although he would fain have spoken, he could not, for his tongue seemed glued to the roof of his mouth, and his parched lips could not shape themselves to a human sound.

"I am ready," said Miranda, to the Governor. "Take me now where you will, I am ready. Let me not look longer on that hateful and fearful man."

"Clear the way," cried the Governor, to some officers who were at hand; and he commenced descending the steps, leading Miranda by the hand.

At this appearance of Miranda going, all Varley's fears seemed to unite to drive him to distraction. He recovered his power of speech, and, spreading out his arms, as if to detain her, he cried:

"Miranda—Miranda—form of more than earthly beauty—can you doom me to despair? Me, your worshipper—your adorer? Miranda—Miranda—I will be your slave! Trample on me; but, oh! do not, in my deep debasement, look with such killing scorn upon me. Mercy—mercy—as you are beautiful, have mercy!"

He clung to her dress, and, shrinking back, as from the touch of some loathsome thing, Miranda cried:

"Unhand me—unhand me, monster!—unhand me!"

"Take your hands from this lady's dress," cried the Governor, "or you shall repent your temerity. Away, sir, away!"

But for the words of the Governor, Bernard Varley would have disregarded the thousands of eyes that were gazing upon him, and further debased himself, in the vain hope of wringing from Miranda's pity or disgust that which she could not accord him from affection—namely, a smile.

At the sound, however, of the Governor's voice, he turned his eyes from the face of Miranda, and then, like one who had succeeded in wresting his gaze from some fascinating object, which held in control all his faculties, he seemed to become at once conscious of the situation in which he was placed, and the fearful risk he was running of committing himself past recovery by incautious expressions, which might be wrung from him in the extremity of his despair and anguish.

He drew himself up to his full, gaunt height, and, in a deep, guttural voice, said:

"Pass on, Miranda; you are the sun of my destiny, the star of my divinity; but the time may come, proud and scornful beauty, when you may yet feel the power of Bernard Varley, and tremble again at his testimony."

"Away—away with you!" said the Governor, "you are a madman; I would not take your testimony against the life of a dog."

A flushing accession of colour came across the pale and ghastly countenance of Varley, and his eyes seemed to kindle with fire as he turned them upon the Governor's face.

"Fool!" he said; "do you set so little value on your life that you taunt a man as desperate as I?"

"It matters but little to me," said the Governor, "whether you be desperate or calm; but if you prove any further annoyance, I shall give you into immediate custody."

For a moment, then, Bernard Varley seemed to measure with his eye the athletic proportions of the Governor; and, half-maddened as he was, a something seemed to whisper to him that he would stand but a poor chance in a personal encounter with the calm, determined-looking man before him. He, therefore, contented himself with muttering through his clenched teeth:

"There may come a time even for you—I never forget."

"Let us proceed," cried Miranda. "The air is oppressive while this man breathes it."

The Governor again placed her arm in his—he had momentarily let go of it during his brief colloquy with Bernard Varley—and, motioning to the officers to clear the way, he and Miranda proceeded rapidly from the prison gates.

As if then actuated by the infernal spirit of a fiend, Bernard Varley sprang up the steps which had been so lately occupied by the Governor and Miranda; and, turning his face to the astonished crowd, he, with the most frantic and violent gesticulations, cried:

"A thousand pounds for the apprehension of Rowland Percy! A thousand pounds for the murderer, dead or alive—dead or alive! A thousand pounds to him who will show me his face!"

The persons composing the immense assemblage one and all stood aghast and terrified at the wild tone and manner of him who offered so large a reward individually for the apprehension of one who was an escaped criminal.

Shouts of derision arose from some, loud

laughter from others, while Mr. Jones, who still occupied his elevated position, instantly seized the opportunity of raising a chorus of hoots and groans against Rowland Percy's relentless enemy.

Varley darted a glance of intense bitterness towards the lamp-post on which Mr. Jones held his enviable station, and, in a voice nearly inarticulate with rage, cried :

"Down with that man—down with him—throw him into the next horse-pond, and come to me for your reward."

"Uncommonly obliged to you," cried Mr. Jones, "but I come of a modest family, and I don't like to give trouble; perhaps you will come and do it yourself? Try if you can't borrow a stick long enough, you sack of bad-looking bones."

Varley, when he had done speaking, maintained the remarkable and striking attitude which he had assumed while uttering the words that had produced so great a sensation, and for the space of more than a minute so intent was every mortal soul there present in gazing at him, and listening if he should speak again, that not a sound came from among them, and they might aptly have been likened to a forest which had grown up in some wilderness of nature, and was there reposing in the unwonted placidity of an elemental calm.

Mr. Jones, however, who was not at all of a romantic turn, and who saw nothing in the whole proceeding but that Bernard Varley was in a great rage, and that he, Mr. Jones, would be happy to put him in a still greater one, suddenly cried :

"Will you give it us now, old Wire-wove, or let us wait till we get it?"

A straw will turn the tide of popular feeling, and Mr. Jones's remark seemed to unburden everyone's breast.

Not only was every heart, which had been filled with astonishment, and not a few with avaricious longings at the largeness of the offer, at once convinced of its unsound nature, but a feeling of indignation began to pervade them that they had been tampered with for a moment by such a golden dream.

Bernard Varley's tall, gaunt, misshapen form made Mr. Jones's simile far from inappropriate, and it tickled the mob so amazingly, that had Varley then possessed sufficient discretion to retire, he might have accomplished an escape before the loud roar had subsided.

But such was not the case; it is an old saying and a true one, that the last drop of water overruns the cup, and so it was with Bernard Varley; he had stood up against a world of disappointments, and battled with deep cares and anxieties, the effort to subdue which had driven him nearly distracted, but now he forgot all self-command, and rushed wildly into a throng of at least six thousand persons, to punish one who had added the last drop to his already full cup of wrath by a jeering remark.

The mob, as might be expected, was in a complete ecstasy when it saw that Bernard Varley was fairly intent upon placing himself in collision with its mighty power.

Shouts, oaths, groans, hisses, and every discordant noise the human voice was capable of, resounded on every side. Above all which arose the ironical voice of Mr. Jones, offering a thousand pounds down on the nail, and no gammon, to anyone who would catch Bernard Varley, and bring him to him.

Varley did succeed in getting about a dozen paces from the prison-door, and then the numerous bonneters, and the awful hustling he received, although no one struck him, so completely bewildered his faculties, that he knew not in which direction he was striving to proceed.

It was well for him that at that moment there arrived a strong body of police, headed by two mounted magistrates, who had been delegated by their body so specially assembled to attempt the dispersion of the crowd, and to read the Riot Act, if necessary.

At the same time, from a neighbouring barracks, a troop of horse was in readiness in case the civil authorities should not be sufficient to allay the tumult.

The magistrates and police had for one of their objects the apprehension of Mr. Jones, who had been such a source of deep aggravation to their brother official, and who had made himself so obnoxious to the law by being the suggester of the destruction of the scaffold, and appropriation of its fragments.

Who the man was that seemed to be tossed to and fro by the mob like a frail weed in a boiling torrent they had no means of knowing, for, although the Governor and Miranda had arrived at the police-office, they had made no mention of Bernard Varley, nor were they, indeed, at all aware of his danger.

The last Miranda had heard of him, and that when she had got some distance from the prison, was his wild offer of a thousand pounds for the apprehension of Rowland Percy.

His words fell upon her heart with a shudder, which was, however, changed in a moment to a feeling of hopefulness that the innocent Rowland was surely by that time far beyond the reach of his utmost malice.

"Who is that?" remarked one of the magistrates to the other, pointing to the struggling Varley.

"I really don't know," said the other, raising himself in his stirrups; "but something strikes me very forcibly that it must be —and yet I can't say for certain."

"Who—who?" said the other.

"Ned Wilks, the hangman."

"Bless me!" said the first speaker, with great indifference; "it is extremely likely. A mob may, very probably, fall on the hangman after tearing the gallows to pieces. How very imprudent of him to come out."

"I suppose we must bring him off, eh?" said the other.

"Well, I suppose so. Do you see to him, while I endeavour to take possession of yon knave on the lamp-post."

Union, in the case of the magistrates and the police, might have been strength, but they did not, when separated, possess much of that desirable quality, for, the more they diverged from each other, the more they began to discover how extremely innoxious they were to the mob, and that the extent of their possessions consisted of the small piece of ground on which they stood.

Mr. Jones waved his hand in an encouraging manner to the magistrate, who was endeavouring to approach him, crying:

"Come on—come on. It's all right—fair play, and no favour."

By a desperate effort the magistrate succeeded in getting within almost arm's length of Mr. Jones; but further he could not get, and, as each of the officers happened to be shut up in a sort of living sentry-box, composed of four men, the whole of the party became as harmless and inoffensive as anyone could desire.

"Disperse—disperse!" cried the magistrate, waving his arm authoritatively. "This assemblage is unlawful; disperse, in the King's name."

"Don't you hear his worship?" said Jones. "You'll put him in a passion, now, if you don't go. Why don't ye disperse, ye *warmint?*"

The magistrate shook his clenched hand menacingly at Mr. Jones, and said:

"Never mind—never mind, my fine fellow, I'll have you yet."

"Oh, thank you," said Jones, "I don't mind a bit. I am sorry I can't return that ere compliment, and, as for having me, I wouldn't give you that trouble, on no account."

"You scoundrel!"

"Listen to his worship—listen to his worship; where's your manners?" cried Jones.

The mob were delighted beyond anything, but when the magistrate, nearly wrenching the skirt off his coat, got out the Riot Act, and, waving it in the air, brought it so near to Mr. Jones, that the latter was enabled to lay hold of it, and, by one jerk, possessed himself of that mysterious document, the crowd could, as of one accord, have fallen flat down and roared with laughter.

Before, then, the magistrate could speak, Jones cried, as he affected to read the Riot Act:

"Oh, yes—oh, yes—oh, yes—here you have it. God save the King and hang the crier, his head in the ditch, and his feet in the fire. Mizzle—cut—notch your poles."

Mr. Jones had got thus far when the red coats and burnished helmets of a party of dragoons appeared flashing in the morning sun at the further end of the street.

"Game's up!" cried Jones; "drop the blessed curtain!"

Then, placing his fingers in his mouth, he produced a whistle of such astounding shrillness, that the unlucky magistrate involuntarily put his hands to his ears, and, before he removed them again, Mr. Jones had slid from the post, and disappeared among the now rapidly dispersing crowd.

A more popular man than Mr. Jones did not that night exist in York.

CHAPTER LXXVI.

ROWLAND PERCY'S JOURNEY TO LONDON WITH DICK PALMER.

IN order that our readers may keep pace with the circumstances of our varied and veritable narrative, we must leave for a brief space the beautiful and gifted Miranda, in order to return to the fortunes of her innocent and persecuted lover, Rowland Percy.

The hour, at the expiration of which Dick Palmer had promised to return, passed away to Rowland Percy, amid the strange motley group among which he was thrown, slowly and uneasily.

His tastes were far from sympathetic with the rude and boisterous throng around him, and but that he felt conscious that Dick Palmer had good reasons for placing him in such a situation, and had no doubt his safety was best assured by so doing, he could almost have blamed his generous friend for exposing him to the rough contact of such uncongenial spirits.

At length, when the hour had elapsed, with some ten minutes or quarter-of-an-hour added to it, the landlord of the house entered the room, and, walking up to Rowland Percy, whispered in his ear:

"Follow me."

Rowland said immediately:

"Has my friend come?"

"No," said the landlord, "but your enemies have. Hush, not a word; follow me, and you shall be placed in perfect safety."

Dick Palmer had told Rowland to trust this man implicitly, and, without another word, or the least hesitation in his manner, he arose, and followed him out of the room.

The landlord took a course directly opposite to that which led into the open street, and threading his way noiselessly and cautiously along a narrow passage, which seemed to Rowland to be interminable, he suddenly opened a door, when a gust of fresh air fell welcomely upon the young man's face.

"Come," said the landlord, and, in a moment, they stood in the open air, in what appeared to be a garden of considerable extent.

The clouds, which had hung heavily in the air during the early part of the evening, were now rapidly retreating before a brisk breeze from the north-west, and the moon's rays were alternately hidden by the black masses, and, then, partially illuminating the spot where they stood, but for such short periods that it scarcely sufficed to enable Rowland Percy to distinguish very minutely the objects around him.

"Are we safe in speaking now?" whispered Rowland.

"Quite," replied the landlord; "but we may as well keep it to ourselves as much as possible. There are three or four officers below who described you to a tittle. Now, barring that you are a friend of Dick Palmer's, you may be the man in the moon for aught I know,

VARLEY PURCHASES THE "LAST DYING SPEECH AND CONFESSION" OF ROWLAND PERCY.

for I'll be hanged if ever I clapped eyes on you before."

"My name is Rowland Percy."

"What! the fellow who was to be hung in the morning?"

"The same," said Rowland Percy; "but I solemnly assure you, on my soul's hope of salvation, that in aiding me, you aid an innocent man."

"I believe you," said the landlord, "or else Dick Palmer would not have been the man to take you by the hand. Now, come on, we have as pretty a hiding-place about these premises as anyone would wish to see."

Rowland followed the dusky form of the landlord for some minutes, and then the former, suddenly stopping, took from his pocket a very small dark lantern, the bull's-eye of which he turned upon a water-butt of most extraordinary dimensions.

It stood upon some brickwork about four feet from the ground, and from that elevation it rose at least twelve feet higher, seeming to be the depository of rain-water from a multitude of pipes and spouts that came from all parts of the house.

"What do you think of that?" said the landlord; "there's a hiding-place for you."

"You may be a very clever fellow," said Rowland, in a tone of disappointment, "but

I should consider it the height of folly to get into an empty water-butt with the view of hiding myself. Why, the merest child could ascend those steps, which are so handy, and at one peep discover me."

"Clever, uncommon clever," said the landlord, and then he laughed, as if he enjoyed some joke exceedingly, after which he added:

"You make a little mistake—just a slight mistake; it ain't an empty water-butt."

"Why, you don't expect me to get into a full one?" said Rowland, with a slight degree of impatience.

"Clever again—clever again," said the landlord, tapping his nose mysteriously with the edge of the lantern; "that's just what I do expect—the very thing—the cut and outer—the coper—the ticket."

Rowland knew not whether to be amused or angry, and, suspecting that there possibly might be some trick in the matter, he quickly ascended some steps that were placed against the wall very conveniently. He brought his head to a level with the top of the water-butt, when he saw at once that it was nearly running over.

"It is full," he said. "You are jesting with me, or betraying me. Moments may be precious to me now. I will seek my own safety in flight. Attempt to stop me at your own peril."

"Not so clever," said the landlord. "No hurry—no, I ain't—no, you won't."

"What, in the name of Heaven, do you mean?" said Rowland.

"Why, in the first place, there's lots of time, for the fellows are taking it easy in searching the front of the house, while there's a couple of them marching up and down just on the other side of that brick wall, so that they know quite well that you can't get out at the back. All's right, you see."

"Right!" said Rowland. "Upon my word, you have a strange notion of right and wrong; and is my only resource to drown myself in a water-butt!"

"That's it," said the landlord; "there never was such cleverness. Just take the lantern—fix your eyes on the top of that tree, and don't say anything till I call out 'oh!'"

"The man must be mad," thought Rowland, but he took the lantern mechanically, and looked up in the tree indicated, for which purpose he had to turn his back upon the burly landlord.

Scarcely had he remained in that position half-a-minute when he heard a strange, chuckling noise behind him, which sounded something like a cock attempting to crow with his head in a beer-pot, which was followed by a singularly smothered "Oh," in the voice of the landlord.

Rowland turned instantly, but no landlord was to be seen.

All was as still as the grave, and the young man looked around him for some moments in mute astonishment.

Then a curious sound came, apparently, from the inside of the water-butt, and Rowland said, in a low voice:

"Where are you?"

"In the blessed butt," was the answer; but the voice sounded so strange and unearthly, that Rowland involuntarily shrank back a pace or two.

"Cock-a-doodle-do," added the landlord. "Cockoroo—cockoroo—cockoroo—cockoroo!"

"Oh," thought Rowland, "he has got some means of letting the water off," and, ascending the steps, he again looked into the water-butt, which, to his surprise, was as full as ever, and not a bit ruffled.

He put his arm in up to the elbow, to convince himself that it was water.

"Cock-a-doodle-do—time's up," said the landlord; and before Rowland could descend from the steps, he saw, by the light of the moon, the two gaitered legs of his host projecting from under the brickwork, whence the body of that important individual presently emerged.

"Been in the water-butt," he said; "but we don't get in at the top. There's a false bottom, three foot from the brim, and there's some comfortable sticks laid across lower down, for a fellow to sit on. Just pop your head under, and you'll be able to draw yourself up in a moment."

Rowland took the lantern, and, peeping under, he saw there was space sufficient, actually, within the butt to hold three or four moderate-sized persons.

"That's ingenious," he said.

"Clever," said the landlord. "In with you. Quick! Don't move or speak, and you have a thousand chances to one of safety."

Rowland's slim figure accommodated itself in the water-butt in a moment, and scarcely had he done so when he heard the back door of the house open, and the trampling of several feet on the walks of the garden.

"Hilloa!" said a voice. "So you are here, landlord, are you? That don't look altogether the thing?"

"No, it don't," said the landlord; "but I was afraid you'd have asked me to treat you to half-a-pint of something, and I am so tender-hearted I should have done it. So I came out here to get a pail of water."

"Ah! we know you of old," said one of the officers. "You'll get into a mess some of these days; and if the fellow we seek is upon your premises, you won't come off so easy."

"Oh, what a way I'm in," said the landlord, affecting to tremble so, that he shook the pail in a most ludicrous manner.

"Keep an eye on the door," said one of the officers to another. "I'll soon ferret my gentleman out, if he is here."

While the landlord ascended the steps, and dipped for his pail of water, thus giving a convincing proof of what the butt contained, the officer stooped down and cast the full glare of the bull's-eye of his lantern between the brickwork on which the butt stood.

"Found him, my grand inquisitor?" said the landlord.

"No, cuss you!" said the officer to the landlord; "but, if he ain't under the butt, he may be in it."

"There's cleverness," said the landlord. "How uncommonly true. You'll be found a corpse some morning, smothered in your own wit."

The officer muttered an oath as he ascended the steps, adding:

"I did pull a fellow out of a water-butt once, who was up to his chin."

A glance, however, sufficed to let him see that such was not the case in this instance.

In another minute Rowland Percy was safe, for the search, although it continued actively in the neighbourhood of the immense water-butt, never again approached it.

Various and numerous were the jeers with which the landlord of the inn saluted the officers, who he knew would make so unsuccessful a search for Rowland Percy.

The low, common wit with which he assailed them was fully understood by them, and had all its due weight and effect upon men who entered upon their pursuit with a kind of partisanship in the capture of criminals, which made the pursuit more of a personal than a professional nature.

They, however, very soon satisfied themselves that a further search was quite useless, and one of them, turning to the landlord, said:

"Well, old Paunch, laugh away, it's your turn now, but ours may come; our man ain't here, that's clear, and all I have got to say is, that it is well for you he is not, for had he been, the magistrates were determined to put down your house once and for ever."

"How uncommonly kind," said the landlord; "I wouldn't give the magistrates so much trouble on any account whatever. Give my compliments to them, and tell 'em to take things easy, for if they put themselves out of the way so much they are safe to be ill."

So saying, Boniface escorted the officers from the garden, but it was far from his policy to allow them to leave the house in anything like an evil spirit towards him, so when they reached the bar he said, in a friendly tone:

"Now, my lads, a joke's a joke, and I know you can give one and take one as well as myself. It's dry work looking for something one can't find, so let's have a glass round for old acquaintance sake."

This was a proposition which no mortal constable could refuse, and accordingly declaring their entire concurrence in what he said, and their unanimous conviction that a joke was a joke, and that they always knew he was a good fellow, they fully acquiesced in the proposition of the glass by adding to their remarks that, in their opinion, no liquor was like brandy, and that the magistrates would put their foot in it rather, if they attempted to interfere with his licence.

"I believe you, my rummy pals," said the landlord; "you know very well I never harbours a sneak. Don't I give him up to you, if one of 'em comes into my place? And as for a murderer—oh! what an out-an'-out odd idea to suppose as I'd harbour one in such a house as this: no, I scorns it. Here's better luck to you next time—a highwayman is a gentleman, and an out-an'-out good cracksman, mind you, isn't small beer; but a sneak's a sneak, and a murderer is like touching a shovel full of hot ha'pence."

"That's true enough," said the officers, as they finished their glasses. "Good-night to you, and good luck to you—you know we never trouble you, except when we can't help it."

After all this politeness, the officers departed from the house, leaving the landlord with a broad grin upon his ruby countenance.

"There's fools!" he said. "Well, if ever I come near such a set of ninnies as officers is."

He then at once proceeded to the long room, where, for a brief space, Rowland Percy had found refuge, although among so strange and motley a group.

A glance from the landlord within the door, brought Dick Palmer, who had arrived during the search, from the room.

"They're off," said the landlord; "all safe."

"Are you sure?" said Palmer.

"Quite," was the reply.

"Thank Heaven!" said Dick. "I would not have had him taken for the best thousand pounds that ever mortal man set eyes on. I believe him innocent, as I believe I am in existence."

"So do I, Dick," replied the landlord. "I have seen a pretty goodish many chaps in my time who have done one thing or another, and I pretty well know by this time, by the cut of a fellow's face, what he is capable of, and what he isn't. Why, that young chap couldn't commit a murder if he wished it, and he wouldn't wish it if he could. I can see what he is—he's one of your out-an'-out humanity coves, and whosoever says he murdered Sir George Rankley has got the wrong sow by the ear."

"You are right," said Palmer; "he is as innocent as you or I."

"And we is more like sucking doves than *nothink* else."

"Pooh—pooh!" said Palmer. "I mean only with regard to the murder we were talking of—but where did you conceal him?"

"Oh, in the old place—in the old place."

"The water-butt?"

"Yes, to be sure; they looked into it and underneath it, but, unless he had hung out his foot and said, 'Here I am, my kiddies,' it wasn't very likely they should see him."

"It is a good hiding-place," said Palmer.

"I believe *yer*," said the landlord, "I should never be the man again as I am if that ere water-butt consarn was found out. I calls it the triumph of modern ingenuity, *I does*, and if I don't drown the fellow on the top of it as finds out the place at the bottom, if so be as ever that ere convulsion of nature ensues, I ain't me, that's all."

"But do you think," said Palmer, "the environs of the house are perfectly safe?"

"Think the what ?" said the landlord.

"I mean—do you think the door is not watched ?"

"Look at me," said the landlord, and, after a desperate struggle, which he was forced to assist with a stamp of his foot, he succeeded in winking with one eye.

"Well, I see you," said Dick.

"Did you ever catch a pig with a greased tail ?" said the landlord. "Did you think, now, Dicky, I was such a fool as to think of walking this ere young chap out of the door as if he was a wisitor come for a *kivarton*, or a blow out of *heavy* ?"

"No," said Dick, "I scarcely supposed so much."

"Just cut up them ere stairs, will yer, and I'll soon bring your man to yer. We've got two doors to this ere house, one of 'em opens to the street, and it's easy watching that ere —but the tother is rather in the attic-ceiling, and it ain't so easy by no means to watch that ere."

"I should think not," said Dick. "But do you mean him to escape by that means ?"

"Yes—to be sure. There's an empty house five doors off ; as it wasn't incommoding anybody, I just walked along the parapet, and took possession. You and your man can do the same, with the advantage of letting yourselves out three doors round the corner."

"That will be admirable," said Palmer. "I am most deeply indebted to you, Joe."

"Stow your gammon," said Joe. "I suppose you wants to pick my pocket now, and I never was *wery* much complimented but once, and then I'm blowed if the fellow didn't steal my watch. I was *green* afore that, and it did me *brown*, and I haven't been half so easy tookt in since."

With this practical remark, the landlord departed to release Rowland Percy from his somewhat disagreeable position.

In a very few moments he brought him into the house, saying as they entered :

"All's safe. Your friend, Dick Palmer, is here, but if it hadn't been for my water-butt, you'd have been in the condemned cell again before now, and, as it isn't many hours to eight o'clock, that wouldn't have been so pleasant—follow me, and don't say a word."

Rowland Percy obeyed him in silence, although he was about to utter some expressions of gratitude for the really kindly protection that had been extended towards him.

The landlord led him up the various staircases, until they reached the topmost story of the house, where Dick Palmer was already awaiting their coming.

It was a small attic, with a slanting roof, to which the landlord introduced the fugitives, and, setting the candle upon a table, he pointed to a trap-door in the roof, which was secured by three massive bolts.

"There," he said, "is a great deal better door than the front one. You'll find the steps in that corner, Dick, and I'll show you the way to the empty house, for it isn't quite safe, you know, to be crawling along the roofs of houses, at such a time of night as this."

The steps were placed, and the trap-door was speedily removed, leaving an orifice that was only just sufficiently large to allow the bulky landlord to pass through, which feat, however, he accomplished with greater ease and dexterity than could have been supposed, from his appearance.

Rowland Percy followed, and Dick Palmer ascended last of all, saying :

"You keep close in the landlord's track, Mr. Percy, and I will come after you, for, I daresay, you are not so much used to these adventures as either of us."

"I am greatly beholden to you both," said Rowland, "and I do hope and trust that the day will come when I can more adequately thank you than at present is in my power."

"There, there," said the landlord, "that'll do, lean towards the house as you creep after me, and if you do make a slip it can only be into the gutter."

It was a somewhat perilous journey, amid the darkness and obscurity of the night, to perambulate the housetops, secured only against falling into the deep abyss below by a narrow coping stone, which, as the houses were very old, was, in many cases, in a state of great decay, and, in some, wholly gone.

Their progress was slow and tedious, and to get across the roofs of those five houses consumed much time, for the landlord was himself extremely cautious, and crept along in a crouching posture, with his body much inclined towards the slanting roofs.

After a time, then, he paused, and in a low voice, said :

"Hist—hist, pull up here, all's right."

"Have we arrived ?" said Rowland.

"Yes ; here's the empty house. Confusion, what's that ?"

One of the crazy coping-stones had given way beneath a slight pressure from the foot of Dick Palmer, and it fell with a tremendous crash into the area of the next house to the empty one.

"Below there !" said the landlord, peering into the depth of darkness below.

In a moment a window was heard to open, and a female voice cried :

"Gracious ! what's that ?"

"Nothing, mum," said the landlord, in a deep, mysterious voice. "You had better pull in your head, for there's another coming."

"Gracious !" cried the woman again, and the window was immediately closed with a bang, sufficient to break every pane of glass in it.

"All's right," said the landlord, "just creep up this sloping roof after me, and we can drop through the trap-door of the empty house as pleasant as possible."

To Rowland it was a matter of great difficulty to ascend the roof, for the tiles, overlapping each other as they did, presented no sort of foothold, while the slope being considerable, he fancied that every moment he must inevitably roll back into the gutter.

Such, however, was not the case, and at last he succeeded in getting a firm hold of the edge of the orifice, which had been produced by the displacement of the trap-door.

"I have took the door," said the landlord, "to my place, and a fine, rousing kitchen fire it made. I thought if anybody ever happened to see me on the roofs, and got crawling about out of curiosity to find out where I was going, they might just as well drop into a hole as not; howsoever, this is the way to do it."

Letting himself down carefully by his hands, he disappeared through the trap-door.

There is always something fearful in darkness and undefined heights. To Rowland Percy it seemed like dropping down a well, to let go his hold of the edge of that narrow opening, and trust himself to the intense darkness below it. It required all his reason at the moment to induce him to do so, and when, at the solicitation of the landlord, he did leave go, he received a greater shock than if he had fallen through a large distance, by finding that he had not been six inches from the floor.

Palmer immediately followed, and the landlord then said:

"Lay hold of me, and I'll guide you downstairs safely. I daren't have a light here, because it's known as an empty house, and the neighbours opposite would, of course, take notice of it."

Rowland held by the coat of the landlord, and the party proceeded noiselessly and carefully down the attic staircase.

Just, however, as they arrived at the first landing, the loud sound of a watchman's rattle struck upon their ears.

"Who the deuce is that?" said Palmer.

"I'll lay any wager," said the landlord, "it's the woman who expected the other coping-stone on her head. If there's an old maid in the street, she's sure to keep a rattle."

A voice now sounded, clear and loud, crying:

"Watch! watch! thieves—thieves—murder—murder!"

"There," said the landlord, "that's the woman's voice. I knew it. Come, as quick as you can—we shall be out of the house before she can get anybody to her assistance."

All three rushed downstairs with great precipitancy—the landlord opened the door—and they were in the street in a moment.

CHAPTER LXXVII.

THE CHARGE AGAINST MIRANDA—THE INDECISION OF THE MAGISTRATE—THE PLEA OF GUILTY.

ESCORTED by more than one-half of the persons who had formed the outskirts of the mob, and who, as they had taken no part in the disturbances that had ensued, the police and magistrates did not interfere with, Miranda and the Governor proceeded to the meeting of the justices.

The proceedings of the authorities were, upon this occasion, as is too frequently the case, when anything like extraordinary energy and decision are required, characterized by a flurry and anxiety, and a want of fixedness of purpose that gave those persons against whom they fain would have acted, an ample opportunity of making the most of the lapse of time between the necessity for prompt measures and their actually being resorted to.

Thus the small party, which, by the command of one member of the magisterial body, was sent through York, in pursuit of the prisoner, comprised the only active step taken on the emergency, and even while Miranda was proceeding in the custody of the Governor, a violent altercation was taking place in the council chamber, as to whose fault it was that the prisoner had escaped.

Miranda had not proceeded half her distance, when, with a face beaming with satisfaction, and an excitement of manner, that showed the exhilarating feelings that were at his heart, Mr. Anderson made his way towards her.

The voice of popular report had informed him of what was taking place, and, from the deep melancholy he was experiencing at his own home, he at once started into life's energy and activity upon hearing that the prisoner had escaped, and that York and its authorities were spared the future reproach which would thereby have been theirs, had the judicial murder, which was contemplated, been really consummated.

He seized Miranda's hand, and, while his voice was almost inarticulate from emotion, he cried:

"Miranda, you have saved him. You have saved him. Heaven bless you, for a heroine as you are."

"He is saved," said Miranda, returning the smile of Mr. Anderson. "Heaven would not allow the innocent to perish, and has made me the humble instrument in the work of his preservation."

"I am sorry, sir," said the Governor, "that we cannot now delay a moment. You can follow me and this lady, if you please, to the magistrates."

"I am her professional adviser, sir," said Mr. Anderson, "and never did I in my life undertake a cause with the intense gratification I shall her's to-day."

"Very well, sir," said the Governor, with a smile. "I have my duty to perform, from which I cannot shrink, but, believe me, it is with no regret that I see this young lady so well surrounded by friends and able defenders."

"From my heart, I thank you, sir," said Mr. Anderson, "and, with pleasure, I perceive that the heroic Miranda Rankley has found a friend in you."

"I have, indeed," said Miranda, "and what might have been a night accompanied by some painful circumstances, has been stripped of everything of a disagreeable nature, and made replete with kindly sympathies. But I want no defence, Mr. Anderson; believe me, I am prouder of what they will call my guilt, than any one circumstance in my mortal career."

"I believe it," said Mr. Anderson, "and yet it shall be my duty to watch over your safety."

They had been walking on rapidly during this brief dialogue, and now reached the hall in which the magistrates were assembled, discoursing together in eager knots of two and three, concerning the unprecedented event which had called them together, and over and over again talking upon the peculiar line of evidence upon which Rowland Percy had been convicted, for his escape from the dreadful fate which had awaited him, seemed in every mind to have opened the whole case anew, and with many to have suggested grave doubts with regard to the nature of the evidence.

The assizes not being yet over, the court was densely crowded by barristers and attorneys of all grades and degrees, and, had Miranda required fifty defenders, she could instantly have procured them, so anxious was every professional man present to have something to do with the most extraordinary case they had met with on any of their circuits.

He who had been Rowland's counsel on the occasion of his trial was surrounded by some eight or ten of his brethren, to whom, with a flushed countenance and an eager voice, he was again running over all the principal points of defence, ever and anon earnestly declaring his conviction of Rowland's innocence, and that the day would come when some circumstances would arise to make it apparent, until when, he said, he hoped that Heaven would interpose between the persecuted young man and his enemies.

There was an earnestness of manner, and a devotion to the cause which he espoused, about the general tone and bearing of the young barrister, that were almost sufficient to bring conviction to every heart that the cause he espoused was one of truth, and the group around him was nearly presenting the singular anomaly of eight or ten lawyers being led away by feeling.

In a few moments, then, the attention of all was arrested by the senior member of the magistracy taking his seat.

Then immediately followed the loud "Hush —hush!" of the crier, and in a few moments every discordant sound was subdued to silence.

The chairman of the magistrates then rose, saying :

"Gentlemen, I understand that the sheriff has a communication of some importance to make to us, concerning the non-execution of a criminal, who was to have suffered this morning the last penalty of the law."

Immediately upon the magistrate taking his seat, the sheriff rose, and said :

"Having received due warrant for the execution of Rowland Percy, convicted at this present assizes of the capital felony of murder, he was by me, and under virtue of my warrant, confined in the jail, and in such place in that jail as is usually allotted to criminals.

"My duty this morning was to see that the sentence of the law was duly carried into effect, and all I can further state is that, upon arriving at the jail, I was told that the criminal had escaped. However, in what manner, you will hear from those who held him in actual custody; for myself, gentlemen, I can only deeply regret that the majesty of the law has not been fully vindicated as yet by the execution of this criminal."

A flash of indignation came from the eyes of Miranda as the sheriff thus spoke, but Mr. Anderson, who guessed her feelings, whispered to her :

"Pooh, pooh, Miranda, heed not what he says ; those are mere words, of course, which he is forced to use in the discharge of his official duties ; he is as kind-hearted and humane a man as ever lived, and I am quite sure would last night have given a hundred pounds out of his own pocket to have insured the escape of Rowland Percy, in order that he himself might be spared the pain of presiding at his execution."

"I am foolish," said Miranda, "to heed what anyone says. Rowland Percy is free, and I am satisfied."

The record of Rowland's conviction for murder was then put in and read by the clerk of the court. After which the sheriff produced the warrant for his execution, and the receipt he had received in the due form of official business from the Governor of the jail upon the occasion of Rowland being delivered into his custody.

This ended the preliminary proceedings, and it remained but for the Governor to explain his non-production of the prisoner upon the formal requisition which had been made at seven o'clock that morning.

Miranda saw with some pain the shade of anxiety that crossed the face of the Governor as he rose to speak, and if a feeling of uneasiness crossed her mind at all at the moment, it was that one whom she had so much reason to esteem, should be placed in so embarrassing a situation.

"I am aware, gentlemen," said the Governor, "that although the sheriff is presumed at law to be answerable for the safe custody of the prisoner who was committed to my charge, yet that I, and I alone, am virtually so answerable."

"Hear, hear," said the sheriff.

"Keep order, Mr. Crier," said the magistrate who was in the chair, and the "Hush, hush" of the crier resounded through the court.

The Governor continued :

"All I can take upon myself, gentlemen, distinctly to state, is, that as the various apartments of the jail were constructed for different purposes, which were pointed out to me upon my assumption of office, so I used them.

"Rowland Percy, having been cast for death this morning, was placed in the cell appropriated to condemned criminals, and, I rather think, that if any blame is ultimately to rest upon anyone in particular, it would be found to belong to the learned, upright, and humane judge, who presided at the recent trial, and who gave an unlimited order for the admission at all times to the jail and the cell of the prisoner, of one who, in her deep conviction of his innocence, would dare all for his liberation."

The magistrates looked at each other with some little degree of amazement, as the Governor thus adroitly shifted the principal blame of the transaction—for which he was called upon to account—to the shoulders of so much higher a personage than himself.

"Gentlemen," he continued, "you will readily perceive the peculiar position in which I am placed by this occurrence. True it is that I hold prisoners in my custody, but I am as one in whose custody might be placed a chest of plate, while some other person had the liberty of lending the key to whomsoever he chose. Thus, gentlemen, I humbly conceive it will be seen, that if the worthy and enlightened judge had not given the unlimited order, to visit my prison, to the person who aided the escape of Mr. Rowland Percy, such escape would not have taken place, and, therefore, I humbly throw myself upon the consideration and able advocacy of that learned personage to drag me out of the mire, into which, with the best and purest motives, he has unwittingly plunged me."

Some of the magistrates looked very grave at this, others laughed, and many looked extremely puzzled, as not knowing what to make of it.

The presiding magistrate then said:

"Perhaps, Mr. Governor, as we are, or, at all events, are presumed to be, very much in the dark with regard to the particulars of this transaction, you will have no objection to detail to us how it was that you came to permit your prisoner to escape?"

"I assure your worship, and this honourable assembly," said the Governor, drily, "that such a circumstance was completely without my permission, and that no man, not even Mr. Sheriff, could feel more shocked than I do at the untoward occurrence."

The Governor's looks betokened anything but a man whose mind was very much shocked, and was so strikingly at variance with his words, that a very irreverent laugh burst from some of the spectators.

"Keep order in the court," said the presiding magistrate. "Have the kindness to proceed, Mr. Governor, with your statement."

"Will you allow me to ask, Mr. Chairman," said a little, fat local magistrate, who had come to York in order to be present at the assizes, "if we are in order in conducting the business of this court in so desultory a manner?"

Then, before the chairman could reply, the under-sheriff, who prided himself much upon his facetiousness, said:

"After the grossly disorderly act which has

No. 16.—(RANKLEY GRANGE).

been committed by Rowland Percy, in not being quietly hung, according to law, it is not to be wondered at that the proceedings of this court, for a short time, should not be of so regular a character as might be wished; but, if he would have the kindness to surrender now, and undergo the sentence of the law, there could be no doubt but that the court would suffer a relapse into its usual state of regularity."

"I beg your pardon, sir," said Rowland's counsel, in a loud, clear voice, that was heard by everyone in court. "The warrant for my client's execution appoints the morning of this day, at eight o'clock, naming both the month and the year. Now, gentlemen, if my client were brought in this moment a prisoner, I defy you to hang him, for you have no authority so to do. What at eight o'clock this morning would have been a perfectly legal act, cannot be perpetrated at a quarter-past ten. Gentlemen, I humbly presume we cannot be too particular in cases of this nature."

"We should certainly hang your client," said the under-sheriff, "and leave him to bring his action."

A general laugh succeeded this sally, and it was with some difficulty that the President of the court made himself heard, and then he said:

"I shall certainly commit any person who interrupts the proceedings of the court, and I must, at the same time, express my great surprise that my brother magistrates, and the legal gentlemen connected with the circuit, now present, should treat this affair as the capital joke they seem to consider it."

"Really—really," said the Mayor, rising, "I—I don't see the joke; it don't appear to me to be funny at all. Upon my life, I don't see any joke."

The Mayor looked so uncommonly stolid as he uttered these words, and presented to the assembly a face about as full of intellectual fire as might be supposed to reside in a large turnip, that it upset the gravity of those who had suppressed their mirth, and a roar of laughter, which alike defied the crier and chairman, succeeded.

"This is frightfully irregular," said the presiding magistrate; "if such scenes as these are allowed to proceed, there will be an end of all order, law, and justice."

"Only think of that, my covies," said the voice of Jones, from the throng. "Penny polonies would ris, and you wouldn't get a ha'penny faggot for tuppence."

"Seize that man—seize that man!" cried the magistrate, from whom Jones had abstracted the Riot Act. "Officers, seize him—hold him fast—handcuff him—bring him before the bench! Whatever you do, secure that scoundrel!"

The officers made a great bustle in the direction from which Mr. Jones's voice proceeded, when the crowd pushed into their arms a mild, inoffensive man, who seemed struck dumb by the horror of his situation, and allowed himself to be conducted before the bench.

"That's not the man!" cried the indignant magistrate.

"I humbly thank your worship," said the man, trembling in every limb. "I know it isn't me; I assure your worship—upon my honour—my wife's here—and she——"

"Go along about your business," said the magistrate. "Gentlemen — gentlemen," he continued, "I shall leave this seat unless you assist me in the preservation of order. I wish Mr. Governor to proceed with his explanation, upon which we may found some substantial act that will restore us to regularity."

Comparative silence then being obtained, the Governor continued:

"From my own knowledge, I can vouch that up to half-past eight o'clock yesterday evening, the prisoner was in safe custody; about that period, however, as I have since ascertained from the officials under me, the prisoner was visited by Miss Miranda Rankley, the young lady who had procured from the learned judge the comprehensive order to enable her so to do.

"Of that visit—so long as it terminated, which, to all appearance, it did, at nine o'clock, the hour at which the prison is cleared of all strangers—I could know nothing. The first alarm that I received was a hasty message, in the dead of the night, to the effect that the prisoner had escaped; such escape, it appears, having been discovered by the Chaplain, concerning whom, at a fitting time and place, I have a presentment to make to the visiting justices.

"Upon then proceeding to the cell of the prisoner, gentlemen, I found, instead of the young man, Rowland Percy, who had been committed to my charge, this young lady, Miranda Rankley, who, at my own risk, I detained, although I had no means of charging her with anything beyond a trespass, and who, for all I know, may bring her action against me for such detention."

"Ridiculous!" cried the chairman.

"I humbly thank you, sir," said the Governor, "for your legal opinion, so luminously expressed."

The chairman looked very red, and the juniors among the barristers tittered amazingly.

"That is all you have to say then, sir?" said the magistrate.

"All," replied the Governor. "Here is the lady, she can now answer for herself if any charge is brought against her."

"She must be considered in custody, and Mr. Sheriff must prosecute," said the magistrate.

"I suppose I must," said the sheriff.

Miranda rose on the instant, and in a calm, clear voice, that sounded sweet as the tinkle of a silver bell, she said:

"I need trouble no one. I am guilty, but in that guilt is my triumph and fulfilment of my earnest prayers to Heaven."

CHAPTER LXXVIII.

THE LEGAL PROCEEDINGS AGAINST MIRANDA —A STRANGE SCENE, AND A STRANGE WITNESS.

In an instant, as if by magic, every angry and every mirthful feeling in that assemblage seemed hushed, and all bent their energies with one accord to admire the surpassing beauty, and listen to the lutelike sweetness of the voice of Miranda Rankley.

"Miranda," said Mr. Anderson, hastily, "you are not yet charged with any crime, and I can hardly suppose the magistrates are serious in intending to charge you with any."

"I certainly must disagree with you," said the presiding magistrate. "I consider Miranda Rankley as actually in custody, and brought before me as charged with aiding and abetting in the escape of a person convicted of a capital offence, and Mr. Sheriff, as I understand, will support that charge."

"Certainly," said the sheriff, "with whatever evidence I may. The act of Miranda Rankley is a misdemeanour of the highest class."

"Then so charged she comes before me, and now, gentlemen, we are, I believe, strictly regular. We can take whatever evidence may now be offered in its due course."

"I will spare all this," added Miranda, "by pleading guilty to the charge."

"I think," said the magistrate, "that the ends of public justice would best be answered by allowing the inquiry to proceed. Mr. Sheriff, call your witness to prove how the prisoner escaped from your custody."

The sheriff held a brief consultation with one of the barristers present, who then rose, and said:

"I appear on behalf of the prosecution, and have to request that the Governor of the prison may again relate his statement of facts upon oath, leaving out the extremely irrelevant matter with which he has thought fit to garnish his tale."

The counsel, true to the cause in which he had embarked, made this first hit at the Governor, because he plainly saw his bias in favour of the prisoner.

The statement was calmly and dispassionately made by the Governor, and when he had finished, the counsel said:

"Now, Mr. Governor, how often do you visit your prisoners?"

"Whenever I think proper," said the Governor.

"Were you a thief-taker before you were a thief-keeper, Mr. Governor?"

"No," said the Governor; "nor was I a hired thief-defender. I was in His Majesty's service, and the last puppy I kicked was for asking impertinent questions."

The Governor looked very hard at the barrister as he spoke, and the barrister looked very hard at the Governor. Then the counsel gave his wig a pull that brought it very near the bridge of his nose, and shook his head, as much as to say:

"This won't do at all: I must try another tack."

"Now, Mr. Governor, who was keeping watch at the outer door, last evening?"

"Samuel Twigg," said the Governor.

"Any relation of yours, Mr. Governor?"

"No," said the Governor; "but he is an impudent dog, and I believe has a connection that goes the York circuit."

"Oh!" said the counsel, with a jerk of his head.

"Exactly so," said the Governor, with a nod.

A titter ran through the court, and a cold perspiration broke out on the brow of the counsel, for he found himself in that most disagreeable of all predicaments—of a man who has been attempting to shine amazingly, and finds that his light is quietly put under a bushel by the sun of someone else's superior intellect.

He looked despairingly around the court; a broad grin sat upon the face of every professional man present; there was no sympathy to be found anywhere, and it was something in the shivering manner of a man who had been trying to show off in skates to a party of ladies, and found himself in the course of a few minutes indebted to the Humane Society, and dragged out of the water, like a half-drowned rat, that he said:

"Mr. Governor, this—this—affair may cost you your place, Mr. Governor. Do you hear that, Mr. Governor?"

"He ain't deaf, Mr. Minnikin," said Jones, from an obscure corner of the court.

The discomfited counsel sat down, while that disagreeable titter, which is really so frightful to the feelings of a nervous man, ran through the court.

The sheriff, however, came to his side, and, it is to be presumed, whispered some words of consolation in his ear, for, in a few moments, he rose, and said:

"Call Samuel Twigg."

"Samuel Twigg!" said the crier of the court, in a loud, sonorous voice, and the man who had really known Percy in his disguise, but connived at his escape, came forward.

"You kept the key of the outer gate of the prison?" said the counsel, "on the occasion of this escape?"

"I did," was the reply.

"Who passed out on that evening?"

"Miss Miranda Rankley, as I believe."

"Then, my man, you are unfit for your situation. You may go down."

"I wishes to be examined," said a voice, and there came through the throng an individual, the examination of whom, if conducted personally, would have taken up no inconsiderable time of the court.

In the first place, there was an amazing quantity of straps of sticking-plaster placed across his nose, until his face looked as if it were meant to represent the sun in some astronomical diagram. Across one eye was tied a bandage, and the other was ornamented with a green shade; his head was completely shaved, and sundry pieces of adhesive plaster, on sundry parts of it, betokened that some one must have been, with malice aforethought, punching the same.

This singular apparition had not before attracted any particular attention, for he had kept a large hat very much slouched down over his face; but now, when in a singular voice, the peculiarities of which arose from the recent violent extraction of his front teeth, he said:

"I wishes to be examined—I wishes to be examined," and, at the same time, took off his hat; the people shrank from him, right and left, and permitted him easily to approach the table.

"Who are you?" said the counsel for the prosecution, looking rather alarmed.

"They calls me Tommy Goggles, but my real name's Tommy Green. Ain't I a apparition?"

"Why—why—I must say, you—you rather are; and now, Mr. Tommy Green—*alias* Goggles—what have you to say, with regard to this business?"

"Why, I've been rather in the thick of it," said Mr. Goggles. "I wants *wengeance*, and I'll have it, or my name isn't Green—I mean Goggles."

"Well, Mr. Green Goggles," said the counsel, delighted at his own wit, "this, I must say, is the very place to come for *wengeance*."

"So I thought," said Mr. Goggles. "I am rather like you, old chap, in one particular."

"In what particular do you mean, Mr. Goggles?" said the counsel, with a laugh; "pray don't be shy."

"Why, I means I was trying to be remarkable clever, and put my foot in it."

"Come, come, sir," said the counsel, "let us have none of your low insolence here; remember, you are upon your oath."

"Oh, I knows it," said Goggles; "I ain't going to inwent nothink. The blessed truth's a stinger. I am under-turnkey at the prison, and, as I was standing in the westibule, I seed the chap as was to be hanged, come out with my own eyes, all for to make his escape in female toggery. Then I thinks to myself as I'd come it uncommon clever, so I doesn't so much as even wink at nobody, but walks out arter him—oh, dear, worse luck!

"I follers him down the street, and then another cove jines him; but I didn't think nothink of that, but went a-follering on; then, arter a while, they takes to running like mad, then I runs arter them like a streak of lightning; when, all on a sudden, they pulls up in an uncommon, deserted street like a clap of thunder, and, afore I could stop myself, or say so much as Jack, not to think of Robinson, one on 'em hits me this here blow, which conflummoxed my nose, sent three or four of my ivories into my stomach, doused my ogles, and did me up in a small heap—that's what's made me such a apparition as I is."

The roar of laughter that followed this speech transcends all description; nobody tried to stop it, for nobody could help joining in it, although the counsel for the prosecution nearly bit his lips through in the attempt.

Mr. Goggles alone, who dared not laugh, had he even felt so inclined, for fear of disarranging the adhesive plaster by which his face was covered, looked solemn and serious, and added largely to the shrieks of merriment, by the rage he seemed to be getting in.

In vain he tried to make himself heard, the only words that were audible being the occasional remonstrance of:

"It's all very fine, but——"

When, however, at length, from sheer exhaustion, the laughter subsided, the counsel for the prosecution merely said:

"That is my case—that is my case!" and sat down quite in a huff.

Then up rose the barrister who had defended Percy on his trial, and, in a tone of voice which at once changed the feelings of his audience from the ridiculous to the decorously attentive, he said:

"Gentlemen, my client, Miss Miranda Rankley, pleads, freely and unhesitatingly, guilty to the charge which is brought against her, of aiding and abetting in the escape of Rowland Percy, the alleged murderer of her father, from prison, and from an ignominious death. I mention the fact, gentlemen, of his being the alleged murderer of her father, to prove how deep, how sincere, how heartfelt, must be her conviction of his innocence.

"This young lady, then, possessed, as she truly is, of the higher and nobler feelings of human nature, while she still proposes to herself the task of crying aloud to Heaven for justice upon her father's murderer, through the agency of human tribunals, felt, when this innocent man was accused of the foul deed, that a purer, a higher, a far holier duty called upon her to rescue him from that terrible imputation.

"Oh, gentlemen, if it be consistent with human nature—if it be praiseworthy—if it be great—if it be just—to seek for the vengeance of the law against an evil-doer—and to cry aloud in the emphatic words of scripture—'he who sheddeth man's blood, by man also shall his blood be shed'—how much more praiseworthy—how much more just—how much greater—how much nobler—how much holier—in the sight of the great God that sees us all, must be that effort which, heedless of all human consequences, has urged this young and shrinking girl to rescue an innocent man, and step between the erring ministers of the law and the perpetration of a judicial murder, for which, in after years, when gray-headed old men, and trembling on the grave's brink, they will be shrunk from with horror?

"Yes, gentlemen, guilty is the plea—but glorious, great, noble, and God-like is the guilt!"

So rapt was the stillness of the throng in that densely-crowded court, during the delivery of these fervent and eloquent words, that the very echo of them seemed to remain, for some moments, in every heart, preserving the stillness of deep attention, even after the young and enthusiastic counsel had ceased to speak.

Then ensued that buzzing noise, which is heard in every assembly, when the minds of all are suddenly released from something which has enchained every sense—there was a loud and very general clapping of hands, and a most striking illustration of the power which one human mind may acquire over a multitude, by the utterance of sentiments at once recognized as just, in appropriate and graceful language.

The under-sheriff leaned over to the counsel for the prosecution, and said:

"What do you think of that?—and what do you think a jury would say to it?"

"There would be only one chance?" whispered the counsel for the prosecution: "but that would be a good one."

"Indeed!"

"It's rather too good, and I don't think they quite understand it."

"I presume, then," said the presiding magistrate, "that the affair is now fairly in our own hands. The case is quite an unprecedented one, and I am of opinion it can be dealt with both by fine and imprisonment."

"I beg to suggest," said an elderly magistrate, rising, "that the prisoner be called upon to enter into her own recognizances, to the amount of five hundred pounds, and produce two sureties of two hundred and fifty pounds each, to appear and receive judgment when called upon."

A majority of the magistrates immediately cried, "Hear, hear."

Mr. Anderson and the counsel for the defence at once proposed themselves as the required sureties, and, in five minutes more, Miranda was at liberty.

CHAPTER LXXIX.

THE ROUTE TO LONDON—DICK PALMER'S AVOWAL—THE ALARM AT THE ROAD-SIDE INN.

For a moment or two, Rowland Percy and his two friends stood on the doorsteps of the empty house, while the springing of the rattle continued violently from the neighbouring habitation.

"We shall have a glorious row in a few moments," said the landlord. "I daresay the old lady thought the coping-stone that fell with such a bang was some out-and-out cracksman who had dropped from the parapet, with an idea of getting in at the window as he came down."

"She is making noise enough," said Dick Palmer.

"Ah," continued the landlord; "the worst of women is, they never know when to leave off anything—but here you have the watchman."

"Had we better not leave this place?" said Rowland,

"Not at all," said the landlord. "there's nothing to fear." Then, stopping the first watchman who made his appearance, he said:

"It's a chimney on fire, and an old gal in hysterics—there, don't you see her up at the window? You hold on by the street-door, while somebody else runs for an engine."

While the watchman was stupidly staring up at the window, Rowland and his friends walked gently away, the landlord quietly remarking:

"If there had been any time now for a bit of fun, I'd have had it with that old woman; I'd have called out fire till an engine came, and wouldn't I have drenched her then a little; but, however, there's a time for all things, and she and I are too near neighbours not to provoke each other a little occasionally."

"You had better leave us now," said Dick Palmer. "I believe that the worst danger is over, and that my young friend here has nothing more to fear. I have a chaise-cart waiting out in the London road with a good horse that will go fifty miles in little better than six hours; we shall be in London in all probability much earlier than anyone could follow us, even were the route we had taken suspected."

"Good night, then," said the landlord, "and good luck attend you."

"Stay yet a moment," said Rowland Percy; "how am I, proceeding to so great a distance, to obtain information concerning the fate of her who has so nobly saved me from destruction?"

"Fear not," said Palmer, "I have arranged all that. We shall receive full intelligence of everything that occurs to her from a friend of mine, who will find out everything, and write to me daily, and whose letters I will communicate to you."

"I am much—very much beholden to you," said Rowland; "I never was a disbeliever in the existence of warm hearts and generous dispositions, but I certainly never expected to meet with the disinterested friendship you have shown me."

"I hope," said Dick, "all may turn out fortunately as it has begun. In London you will, without doubt, be safe enough, for there is no hiding-place equal to it, and you must just wait with what patience you may for better news."

The deep, solemn tones of the Minster bell struck at the moment upon Rowland's ears.

"It may be the last time," he thought, "that I shall hear those sounds. It seems like parting from a dear friend to leave this ancient city, in which so many of my happiest hours have been passed. Ah! what a world of unhappiness and deep anxieties have been crowded into the last few months of my existence! Already do I seem aged, if I count my years by the multitude of the events that have oppressed my life. Farewell, Miranda!—for a brief space only, I hope—farewell! Thou best, noblest, dearest one—farewell!"

A deep sigh arose from his heart, and Dick Palmer said, in a kindly tone:

"Come, come, Mr. Percy, cheer up; sorrow is the worst enemy to succumb to; for when you own yourself beaten, it gives you no quarter."

"You are right," said Rowland, "viewing my situation now, as compared to what it was, it is, indeed, a blessed one, and I, of all men, should not repine."

"Besides," said Palmer, "there are happier days in store, and a merry peal from the old Minster bells may some day welcome you in triumph back to York."

"True—true; I will not despair."

"Besides," added Dick, "you have a treasure which an Emperor on his throne might envy."

"I know it—I know it!" cried Rowland; "you mean the love of Miranda Rankley?"

"I do," said Dick Palmer.

"Oh! that is, indeed, a treasure," said Rowland; "could I, for one moment, forget that no human malice, or human weakness, could rob me of that Divine possession. My good friend, you have properly corrected me; I ought, indeed, to find ample materials in my own mind for joyful felicitation."

"Here we are!" said Dick, as, suddenly turning a corner, he pointed to a chaise-cart a few paces down the street.

"We must make ourselves as comfortable in this conveyance as we can," he added, "although it will be rather a cold ride, and some of the road between here and London not so pleasant as might be."

"I ought to be, and am thankful for any conveyance that will assist me in leaving York," remarked Rowland.

In a few moments they were seated in the chaise-cart, which had been in charge of a boy, to whom Palmer spoke some words in an undertone, among which Rowland thought he heard the name of Miranda.

"Did you not mention *her* name?" said Rowland.

"I did," replied Palmer. "It was to tell the boy by no means to forget his father's promise to write to me concerning her, every day."

"Who is his father?" said Rowland.

"The man named Jones, who gave evidence against Samuel Twitter at your trial."

"He is a strange, rough man, but seems an honest one," said Rowland.

"Why, as for his honesty," said Palmer, with a laugh, "that's neither here nor there—he has his peculiar notions upon that subject, as well as the rest of us—but he is a good fellow in the main, and, I believe, never did a deliberately sneaking action in his life. You must understand, Mr. Percy, that there are grades even in what is called dishonesty."

"So I believe," said Rowland, "although dishonesty is so positive a thing as to be governed by one great principle."

"Ay, that may be very true," said Palmer, as he spoke cheeringly to the horse; "I have had so many ups and downs in my life, that I scarcely know what is honesty and what isn't."

"Now that we are doomed to so long a journey together," said Rowland, "will you not confide in me, by telling me really who and what you are?"

"Oh, certainly—certainly. My name is Dick Palmer, although they call me in the profession the 'Slashing 'Squire,' and sometimes other names."

"But that profession?" said Rowland.

"I am a highwayman," said Dick, as coolly as possible. "Kim up," he added, addressing his horse, "so you'll shy at the first mile-post out of York, will you?"

"A highwayman!" repeated Rowland Percy, in some surprise.

"Yes," replied Dick; "there must be people of all professions in the world, and what would become of the lawyers and judges if there were no gentlemen of my way of thinking?"

"I ought, certainly," said Rowland, "to be the very last person who should think about being captious as to who or what you are; the great assistance you have rendered me demands the warmest sentiments of gratitude that one man can feel towards another. I regret that I asked you the question of what you are, for there could be no occasion for my doing so."

"I am glad you've asked it," said Dick Palmer; "and, if you had not, I should have taken the first opportunity of telling you, for I thought it would be no bad thing to convince you, that a man who sets at defiance one of the great principles of social life might not necessarily be a great scoundrel. I have a peculiar way of thinking with regard to my professional pursuits. In early life I commenced in what they called the honest line. I went into business; but I failed signally, because I was not rogue enough. I found out then, by degrees, in my intercourse with society, that the greatest breaches of good order, morality, and honour, were those of which the law took no cognizance. It is only the great staring crimes, about which there can be no mistake, that society seems inclined to arm itself against."

"There is some truth in that," said Rowland Percy.

"I know there is," resumed Dick. "I think there is a great deal of truth in it. The deep vices, that are the most pernicious of all, and strike at the very foundation of happiness and contentment, remain untouched, because it is quite impossible to define them. So, you see, I found myself a touch too honest for society at large; and, as I was not an independent gentleman, I was compelled, in order to earn my living with as little self-reproach as possible, to turn a highwayman."

"I certainly," said Rowland, "never heard such an excuse before for a very criminal line of conduct; at the same time, however, my reason cannot but at once admit that a highwayman may be an angel of light in comparison to many a man who might sit as one of his judges."

"That's the thing," said Dick Palmer; "I think we now understand each other, Mr. Percy. I am very far from defending myself from the charge of taking other people's goods and money; but what I do mean to assert is that, when I say I am a highwayman, I do not admit that I am wholly bad."

There was now a silence of some moments' duration. It was broken by Rowland, who, turning to his singular companion, asked, with natural anxiety:

"When do you think we shall reach London?"

"If our nag holds out well to its work, and meets with no particular accident on the way, I think we may venture to say that we shall hear the next midnight chimes at St. Paul's."

"Thank Heaven," said Rowland, "that I shall at least be removed so far from the scene of the greatest danger that in all likelihood I shall ever endure."

The road they were now on was a hard and level one, and they proceeded at a capital pace for a number of miles, when the country became more hilly; and, in a hollow, after passing the first eminence, Dick Palmer drew up at the door of a small roadside public-house, from one window of which proceeded a long stream of light, indicating that at least some one was up in the establishment to receive any chance guest who might arrive.

"We shall bait here for a short time," said Dick; "you must be in need of some refreshment: and, as for myself, such has been my hurry and anxiety for the last four-and-twenty hours, that I have scarcely tasted food."

"How far are we from York?" said Rowland, as he got out of the chaise-cart.

"A trifle over thirty miles," was Dick's reply; "and if your enemies were only to start after you now, we have as fair a chance of beating them as we could desire."

"I do not see," said Rowland, "how they are to guess at our progress in this direction."

"Leave them alone for that," said Palmer; "let us rather hope to baffle them than that they will not attempt to find you. Come into the house, for it appears to me that we shall have rain to-night, and that shortly, too."

Rowland, on hearing this, looked up towards the sky, and could see that the clouds were chasing each other across the moon's disc, and ever and anon throwing the earth in deep shade, while a dampness pervaded the air, that rendered him chilly.

The wind, too, came moaning across the country, and whistled past the gable ends of the solitary house, but, having spent its force, again sank into sullen silence.

But though the gusts were short, yet they rose and fell, and, as they did so, gained

ROWLAND PERCY ESCAPES WITH DICK PALMER.

gradually, though slowly, in strength and duration, while the clouds came heavier, and a freshness pervaded the air, that surely indicated a storm so soon as the wind should entirely lull.

"We shall have a stormy night," said Rowland Percy.

"That I am sure of," rejoined Dick, "for there is every indication of it. Hush! hark!"

Even as he spoke the sound of horses' feet came plainly upon their ears.

CHAPTER LXXX.

MIRANDA AT LIBERTY—THE REITERATED PROPOSAL OF MR. ANDERSON—MIRANDA'S NOBLE SENSE OF HER DUTIES—THE MAGISTRATES' PLAN FOR ROWLAND'S CAPTURE.

THE news that the high-spirited Miranda Rankley had escaped so easily from the consequences of her devoted act in favour of her lover, spread like wildfire throughout the city.

It was carried from mouth to mouth that the magistrates dared not harm her, and Mr. Jones remarked to a number of his popular admirers, that he thought he had rather scared them, and "they'd be afeared to do nothing."

"Sides," he added, "I have boned the blessed Riot Act, and you may kick up the jolliest rows you like in York afore I'll read it."

This reasoning did remarkably well, both for Mr. Jones and his admirers, for they seemed to fancy the Riot Act was a something which, when once they had got possession of, fully exonerated them from pains and penalties on account of future disturbances.

As for Miranda, her feelings were certainly joyful and enviable.

True it was that Rowland Percy was a fugitive, but the mere fact that he was so, implied his rescue from a fate that she shuddered to reflect upon. True that she herself was in a state of comparative destitution; that in the course, perhaps, of a few short weeks, she might not know where to turn for sustenance; but then, was not Rowland free, and, as a consequence, was there not hope—dear hope, which, had he fallen a victim to his enemies, must have been extinguished for ever; for could all the lament—could all the sympathy of a nation, or a world, restore to her arms him who, but for her own intrepidity and exalted courage, would ere then have been a murdered man?

Oh, how sweetly delightful to her seemed the sunny sky that smiled upon the ancient city as she once more emerged into its crowded streets, free to go whither she listed—free to search for him whose danger had caused her such exquisite pangs—whose safety, such exquisite delight.

She was immediately recognized by the crowd which had waited outside the court during the legal proceedings against her; but now that all excitement was over—now that she had achieved everything—now that that night, which had been so full of deep anxieties, had passed away, and she told herself she had little to fear, while what she had to hope—namely, the complete establishment of Rowland's innocence to all men, might be very far distant, although she looked upon it as a circumstance which in Heaven's own time must happen—she shrank from the popularity with which the events of the last eight-and-forty hours had invested her.

Besides, she could not but recollect that the very mob whose cheerings and vociferations now sounded in her ears was the same mob that had assembled to gloat over the dying agonies of Rowland Percy, and find an hour's amusement in his execution.

With these feelings, was it to be wondered at that she shrank from the shouts of those persons who, with the same cries, would not have hesitated to herald into eternity him who was her heart's best, fondest treasure.

Turning to Mr. Anderson, she said:

"How shall I escape these people? My self-imposed duty now calls me to visit the unhappy father of Rowland Percy; before his present mental blight fell upon him, he declared that my fortunes should be his, and

that he would cling to me, protecting and comforting me, while he should live, through that stormy season of my life that had begun with such accumulated horrors; but now that his mind has become a wreck, and he is the shadow of his former self, it is my duty to cling to him, which I will do as well for Rowland's sake as for his own."

"You are right, Miranda," said Mr. Anderson, "as you always are when real feeling has to be consulted."

"And, moreover," said the barrister who had conducted her defence, "Miss Rankley is quite right in the estimate she sets upon popular applause."

"Where can I go," said Miranda, "for a brief space, to free myself from what amounts to a persecution from these people? I am fearful they should follow me to my home, and there commit some indiscretion that might much aggravate Mr. Percy's malady."

"You shall come to my house, Miranda," said Mr. Anderson; "and, although they may certainly follow you there, they will soon be tired of looking at my uninteresting street-door."

"I don't know that," said the Governor, with a laugh; "since the fork, which was the companion to the knife with which Margaret Nicholson tried to stab the King, became a popular exhibition, and attracted a crowd of people, I can believe anything of popular credulity; however, Mr. Anderson's plan may answer for an hour or two, if he adds to it a little cold water from one of the windows, and the intimation that he is a lawyer."

Miranda turned to the Governor as he spoke, and, with a grateful expression of countenance, said:

"I have much kindness and courtesy to thank you for, sir, and I have only sincerely to hope that your advocacy of the cause of the unfortunate Miranda Rankley may not expose you to any evil consequences from those who are really, and those who are officially, compelled to become her enemies."

"Far from it," said the Governor. "I am quite sure, from another reason, that I should not have held my situation long."

"And what reason may that be?" said Mr. Anderson.

"Why, I have quarrelled with the hypocritical chaplain, and, as the mass of mankind are fools—not even excepting visiting justices—he is sure to get the better of me, for, of course, they would rather offend me than one who seems on such intimate terms with the infernal regions, that he can send anybody there at pleasure; so, Miranda, I beg you will have no uneasiness on my account, for I have no doubt, for the reason I have mentioned to you, I shall lose the situation I never was particularly well fitted for. Farewell, and may health and happiness attend you, and, believe me, it would give me as sincere pleasure as any I have experienced in my life, to hear, some happy day, that you have succeeded in clearing your lover's character, when, after which, I wish you all the happiness, as a wife, to which, I am sure, you are so eminently entitled."

With a graceful bow, the Governor then walked away, before Miranda could reply to him.

"That man," said Mr. Anderson, "is a gentleman in the truest acceptation of the term; he is no more fit to be the Governor of a prison than for the situation of a slave driver. But here we are at my door; come in, Miranda Rankley, and I can truly say that a more honoured or more welcome guest never crossed my threshold."

When Miranda had entered the house, Mr. Anderson turned to the throng that followed her to his door, and said:

"Now, my good people, you won't see any more of her. She is going to stay here for a month, and never stir out of doors; besides, I won't have a crowd round my door, and when I say I won't, I won't. So you had better walk away, all of you, recollecting that I am a lawyer, and can get, consequently, more law and justice for a penny than you can get for a shilling."

"Well," said Mr. Jones, "I never did hear a more sensible speech than that 'ere in all my life. It beats nothing into unkimmon small bits. One cheer, and let's mizzle. Hurray—hip, hip, hip, hurrah!"

The mob seconded the cheer with right good will, as all mobs are always willing to do upon any and every occasion or excuse.

Then Mr. Jones, who guessed that Miranda was anxious to be clear of the assemblage, and be left free to act as her feelings might dictate, drew off the throng more quickly and easily than such a feat could have been accomplished by threats or remonstrances.

When Miranda and her friends had left the court, the chairman of the bench, after a short consultation with some of his colleagues, ordered the court to be cleared of all persons but themselves and the parties holding official situations connected with the administration of the law.

When this was accomplished, he said:

"Gentlemen, in consenting to the easy, and somewhat triumphant, manner in which the prisoner, Miranda Rankley, has left this court, I daresay we each had the same natural motive.

"If any one circumstance more than another was likely to lead to the recapture of Rowland Percy, that circumstance is the leaving Miranda Rankley apparently at perfect liberty, but, at the same time, keeping upon all her movements and her correspondence, such a watchful eye as may speedily lead to a discovery of the hiding-place of the prisoner."

"Hear! hear!" cried several of the magistrates.

"Gentlemen," continued the presiding magistrate, "there has not been a capital conviction in York for some years, and let it not gain currency that, when we are so unhappy as to have among us a notorious criminal, we cannot execute the sentence of the law upon him."

"Hear! hear!" was the response again to this remark; and one of the magistrates, rising, said:

"I would propose, then, in accordance with the very accurate view taken of this subject by our chairman, that two of our most active and intelligent officers be specially appointed to watch Miranda Rankley, and follow her from house to house, wherever she may go."

This resolution was agreed to, and after informing his brother magistrates that he, the chairman, had already taken care that Miranda's immediate steps should be made known to him, two officers, with full instructions and a *carte blanche* as to expense, were deputed as spies upon the movements of Miranda.

That the magistracy of York, considering their peculiar position, were sufficiently justified in taking this course, we are not prepared flatly to deny, for although we and our readers are aware of the innocence of Rowland Percy, and the villainous machinations by which his name had been blackened, and he had been made to appear the ruthless murderer that many believed him, they were not; and as administrators of the law, they were compelled to take every legitimate means of again securing the escaped criminal.

Leaving, then, the magistracy to adopt what measures they might think proper, in pursuance of their duty, we shall again follow the fortunes of the heroic girl, who, we hope, has placed herself so near the affections of our readers.

When Mr. Anderson saw that the mob was fairly drawn away from his door by the interposition of Mr. Jones, he insisted that Miranda should partake of some refreshment, before he would speak to her concerning her ulterior views or future objects.

This, at his earnest solicitation, she was compelled to do, and then, with great earnestness of manner, he said to her:

"Now, Miranda, you must be extremely cautious in your future acts, for although, as circumstances are at present, you will never be called upon to answer the charge preferred against you, yet were it to be discovered—as no doubt it will be attentively watched for—that you hold any communication with Rowland Percy, it may lead not only to his recapture, but your own lengthened imprisonment."

"I will be cautious," said Miranda, "both for his sake, and for the sake of those dear friends who have so kindly assisted me in this exigency. I must strive, Mr. Anderson, to meet him. I must strive again to look into his face with calmer feelings than those which necessarily agitated us when last we parted. It may be wrong, and I may be foolish, but I do wish again to see him smile, and hear him tell me that I have saved him."

"You run the greatest risk, Miranda," said Mr. Anderson; "besides, how can you tell the direction in which Mr. Percy has proceeded?"

"He will go to London," said Miranda, "of that I am aware, and thither must I go to follow him. Believe me, Mr. Anderson, I will be most cautious, and doubly so, when I consider that indiscretion upon my part may commit, in some manner, you, and the kind friend who, with you, has become a surety for me."

"Nay," said Mr. Anderson, "understand that clearly, Miranda. All that we are committed to is upon pain of forfeiting a certain sum of money to produce you, should you be called upon, so that we are safe enough. Your commission of any new act obnoxious to the law, cannot affect us, so long as you surrender yourself to its consequences; but it is for your own sake, Miranda, that I implore you to be careful, as well as for the sake of Rowland."

"I will—I will," said Miranda.

"Do not," continued Mr. Anderson, "be lulled into any fancied security; do not imagine that you will be unwatched, or that your minutest actions will be unnoticed. Our greatest, dearest hope must still be rather in circumstances arising to clear Mr. Percy of his alleged guilt, than from a continued success in secreting him from the ministers of the law."

"You are right," said Miranda, "it is, indeed, on the establishment of his innocence that I build my dearest and fondest hopes."

"Do so ever," rejoined Mr. Anderson; "and now, Miranda, I am sorry to say, that the expectation I once entertained of rescuing from the general wreck some private portion of old Mr. Percy's property, has proved fallacious—he is utterly and totally destitute."

"And so am I," sighed Miranda. "Our trust must be in Heaven, for it alone can step between us and the miseries of want."

Mr. Anderson for some moments looked as if a little confused, and then he said in a low tone:

"Miranda, you will, I am sure, pardon me for repeating to you the offer I have before made to you, which is, that you shall honour my humble abode by becoming its permanent guest. You can remain with me in peace and tranquility, awaiting calmly that happy time which I hope will soon dawn upon your fortunes."

"I cannot," sighed Miranda.

"Nay, think again," urged Mr. Anderson, kindly.

"I have thought," she said, mournfully, "thought deeply of this, the kindest offer I shall ever meet with; but I have duties, Mr. Anderson, which prevent me accepting it. You wish me to sit down here in peace, waiting with serenity for a happier day. Think you I could know peace or serenity, while my mind is tortured with uncertainty concerning the fate of those with whom, now that my own parents are in the cold grave, I must henceforward remain? We may suffer greatly, but we must suffer together."

"I am answered, Miranda," said Mr. Anderson; "but it is with grief that I say so. At least, let me have the consolation of knowing beforehand of any step you may take for the furtherance of those views so near and so dear to your heart."

"You shall know," said Miranda, "and, let my fate be what it may, there is no name that will mingle itself more purely with my better and happier feelings than yours."

Miranda then rose to depart, and Mr. Anderson strove to conceal his emotion, by affecting to search for his hat, in order to escort her to her lodgings.

CHAPTER LXXXI.

THE CONVERSATION BETWEEN VARLEY AND TWITTER—THE DISCOMFITED VILLAINS— THE CRAFTINESS OF VARLEY, AND THE DEFEAT OF THE AVARICE OF TWITTER.

It was some time after Miranda's liberation upon bail, that, in the lodging first occupied by Bernard Varley, sat Samuel Twitter, confronted by the dark instigator of his more recent crimes, and trembling in every limb as he listened to Varley's account of the escape of Rowland Percy from prison, and the manner in which Miranda Rankley had succeeded, after all, in foiling their villainous schemes.

Bleeding and disfigured as he was from the violence of the crowd, and with his clothing rent in many places, Bernard Varley's exciting narrative carried with it to the shrinking soul of Twitter a terrible truthfulness, and filled him with an alarm that seemed almost sufficient to stop the even current of his existence.

He wrung his hands despairingly when Varley finished.

"What is to be done?" he cried. "We are lost! All will be discovered. I think I see the scaffold even now being prepared for us; I see the fatal noose—I hear the infuriated populace. Oh! Bernard Varley, what a pit of horrors have you led me into, and how can I escape?"

Varley looked upon Twitter for some moments in silence; but, during those moments, such an expression of ferocity crossed his countenance, that Twitter shrank as far from him as possible, as if anticipating some sudden act of violence from his hands.

Nor were his fears diminished when Varley took from his pocket a large knife, which he opened deliberately. The blade was secured by a spring, so that the weapon became as formidable a dagger as could be constructed.

"No—no—no!" cried Twitter. "Have mercy, Bernard Varley! Do not murder me. I cannot—dare not die; and, at least, not from your hands should the blow come."

"Listen to me," said Varley, in a tone of such concentrated rage, that it sounded more like the voice of a wild beast, than the utterance of a human being. "Listen to me, Samuel Twitter. If you favour me with any more of your reproaches about what you say I have led you into, I will cut your throat, and so be rid at once of the dastardly coward who shrank not from the wages of murder, but avoided, in abject fear, the deed itself."

"Mercy—mercy!" said Twitter. "I did not mean, Varley, to accuse you. You have been a great friend—an excellent friend to me; but I was so sadly grieved at the escape of Rowland Percy, that, you may believe me, I knew not what I said."

"Beware for the future," said Varley. "Upon any, even the slightest motion of treachery from you—you shall die."

"You do not suspect me?" said Twitter.

"Of what?" said Varley.

"Treachery."

"I shall, if you protest too much; and, if my suspicions be once aroused, I will wash away the uncomfortable thought in your blood. Now, beware of what you say or do."

"Yes, I will," said Twitter. "You may depend upon me, Varley; but, you know, I have not your bold, daring spirit; and, after all—I—I—but no matter—excuse me."

"Speak," cried Varley. "What were you about to say?"

"Oh, it was nothing—I'd rather not say it. You would be angry—and—besides—I forget it, Varley."

"This moment let me hear it," said Varley, or——"

He opened the knife again, and pointed it significantly at Twitter's throat, who, under such compulsion, really said what he had so prudently stopped himself in, for he was in too great a state of mental perturbation to invent anything less true and less offensive.

"It—it was merely a casual remark, Bernard Varley," he stammered, "and what it meant, was that I am not in any hurry. Oh! far from it; but as yet I have not pocketed any of the profits of the murder, although you know I have had several of the disagreeables. That was all, Bernard Varley. Don't be offended; it doesn't mean anything. A mere passing remark—that's all."

"Indeed," said Varley, "I shall give you some of what you call the profits when I please, and not before. In the meantime, I permit you to exist, for which you ought to be sufficiently thankful."

"But—but you know," gasped Twitter, "I was to have had six hundred a year, Varley."

"And shall have, unless I cut your throat before the first twelvemonth comes round. You did not expect it in advance, did you?"

"No—no! not exactly; but it would have been a little pleasanter."

"Once for all, Samuel Twitter," said Varley, "understand your position. When all these affairs in which I have so great an interest are satisfactorily concluded, I will reward you handsomely; but till then, I tell you candidly, I will not trust you. Eat what you like, drink what you like, and sleep where you like, at my cost, and then, if you provoke me not in the interim to cut your throat, or blow out your brains, the time may come when I shall place money in your hands, and

such a sum, too, as shall gratify your avarice. At the same time I shall bid you adieu for ever."

"Oh! thank you—thank you," said Twitter; "it's a very pleasant arrangement, but I have scarcely eaten anything for two days, my appetite isn't near so good as it was, and, as for drinking, I am positively afraid to begin upon it."

"In those matters you may please yourself," said Varley; "you see, I have been quite confidential, and told you of my plans and intentions."

"I can't sleep, either," whined Twitter; "could you be so good as to name when you think you can quite conveniently give me some money, provided the little contingencies you mentioned do not occur in the meantime. I should rather like to know, too, how much you intend to make it?"

"These are considerations which will keep," said Bernard Varley; "for the present, one sole consideration must be, in what manner, so as to present us with the greatest chance of success, we can commence an active search for Rowland Percy, for until he is surrendered to the law and executed, we shall be kept in continual apprehension on the score of the murder, all questions concerning which will be set at rest by his execution."

"Yes," said Twitter, abstractedly, "who would have thought of him getting away?"

"Besides," added Varley, as much to himself as to Twitter, "his death would have at once crushed all Miranda Rankley's energies, for she is not one who would fight up against sadness, for the mere ultimate prospect of revenge."

"Certainly," groaned Twitter; "if he had but been hanged it would have been much more agreeable. But what is to be done, Bernard Varley—what is to be done?"

"The proper authorities," said Varley, "will, of course, as they are bound to do, use their best endeavours for the prisoner's recapture; but, as we are much more largely interested than they, so will our exertions be more earnest, and more likely to be effectual. We must ourselves seek him, and, if possible, deliver him again to the hands of justice."

* * * * *

Although Miranda spoke trustingly of her hopes of the future to Mr. Anderson, each moment, as her mind became more and more relieved from immediate anxiety concerning Rowland, the melancholy destitution of both his and her own situation would obtrude itself upon her mind, filling her with uneasy thoughts, and suggesting much prospective misery.

There was, likewise, one circumstance which rendered both her and Rowland's situation considerably worse than it might have been under circumstances of ordinary poverty. That circumstance was, that Rowland Percy, from the peculiarity of his position, could not have the free use and action of those powers with which Heaven had gifted him; nor could she, from the necessity for extreme caution in all her movements, as associated with him, be said to be quite free to turn those accomplishments to account, upon which she shuddered to think she must rely as a provision for the future.

These were thoughts which she would not communicate to Mr. Anderson, because she feared that his generous spirit would outrun his means in some attempt to better the condition of those for whom he felt such true sympathy.

As for inhabiting his house on the footing of a guest, whose period of stay should be unlimited, and entering into, or attempting to enjoy, a life of comparative luxury, while Rowland Percy might be wanting the common necessaries of existence, it was a thing she could not think or dream of for a moment, without such an exquisite pang of agony, that she at once discarded the thought from her bosom.

Nor could she make up her mind to tell Mr. Anderson of her immediate intention of following Rowland to London, which, from her previous communication with Dick Palmer, she was aware would be his place of destination.

It will look, she thought, so like begging of him the means wherewith to accomplish the journey; and that idea she so much shrank from, that she could not bring her lips to utter the words:

"I am going to travel nearly penniless from York to London, having, too, in my care one whom the heavy hand of misfortune has made prematurely old, and shattered the god-like power of reason to its base."

"And yet," she asked herself, "how are we to travel the many weary miles between here and London upon a sum something less than twenty shillings, which is all that I have in my possession?"

This was a question she could not answer, but the painful thoughts it gave rise to brought her to the street in which she lived, when, taking a kind leave of Mr. Anderson—a farewell which he thought temporary, but which really lasted for a long and weary time, she approached the step of her own door.

Before, however, she could make any application for admission, a singular-looking creature stepped up to her. It appeared to be a woman by the apparel—although the size of the lady was prodigious, and Miranda was not a little surprised to hear the voice of Mr. Jones say:

"Don't be arter being skeared, mum—miss, I mean—the people takes me for an interesting female—that is, excuse me mum—miss, I doesn't know what I was going to say exactly."

CHAPTER LXXXII.

MR. JONES'S SYMPATHY—THE LETTER TO ROWLAND PERCY—THE FIVE-POUND NOTE.

MIRANDA looked with the most intense astonishment at Mr. Jones in his singular disguise, the purport and object of which she could not for a moment imagine.

"I do not know you," she said, "but I recognize your voice as one which has uttered friendly sentiments to me and mine."

"That ere is the blessed ticket, mum," said Mr. Jones, "though more politerer than I could have said it, notwithstanding, mum, my edication. The slashing 'squire, that is to say, mum, Dicky, the Night Owl, and me is elderly pals, we knows what's o'clock, mum—and we's up to a whole blessed jar of snuff, and ever such a pile of pinches above it. I thinks it's right and proper to be explanatory, mum, as you mightn't know what a slashing toby was, and, not belonging to the family, mightn't understand crummy patter."

Miranda looked, as well she might, rather amazed at this explanatory speech, and a slight suspicion crossed her mind that Mr. Jones must have been sacrificing largely to the rosy god.

"I daresay," she said, "your intention is either to congratulate me upon my success, or to sympathize with me in my sorrows. In either case, I thank you, and as I am now at my own home, I will bid you farewell."

"Niver so fast—niver so fast," said Mr. Jones. "Is that ere the way you treats a lady, mum? I tells you what it is. It won't be safe for you to be-awriting walentines and love-letters to young Mr. Percy. Dickey and I knows that; so I am to be what he calls the blessed medium of correspondence. You are to tell me as you isn't particular down on your luck, and I'm to write to Dicky, when, you see, he'll show your sweetheart the hepistles."

Miranda now began to have a glimmering of what Mr. Jones meant, and she said:

"By Dicky, you mean the unknown friend who so kindly assisted me in effecting the escape of Mr. Percy?"

"Right again," said Mr. Jones. "I'm going to send off my blessed letter to-day, and I only wants to know what I shall say in the tender line on your account."

"Say that I am well, very well," said Miranda: "say that I have met with kindness, sympathy, and protection: and say that I am happy in the hope of soon meeting him who is dearer to me in his misfortunes than he ever was in his prosperity."

Mr. Jones listened to this speech with the most ludicrous air of attention, which showed that he was, indeed, making a violent mental effort to understand it.

"I'll try and say it, mum," he remarked, when Miranda had done speaking; "but I'd ha' preferred it being in English, mum, as I ain't larned in furrin languages."

"What I have said, I have endeavoured to

say simply," said Miranda; "but shall I write it?"

"No, mum, that wouldn't answer, said Jones; "Dicky and I has a perticlar way of speaking about people, that you'd be never so long in larning, so that if our letters should come across the hands of the beaks, they wouldn't know what to make on 'em."

"But why are you in this singular disguise?" said Miranda.

"'Cos of the blessed Riot Act," said Jones. "They is making wiolent exertions to nab me on account of that ere, so I thought I'd come it in the delicate young female line. I'm rather afeard of the fellows, to be sure, but only let one on 'em follow me too close, and if I don't fetch him a rum 'un on the right ogle, my name isn't Jones; and now, mum, just look down the street at them ere two gentlemen as is pretending to converse about nothing."

"There are certainly two persons conversing," said Miranda.

"It's gammon—it's gammon, mum," said Jones. "You've been to a theatre, I suppose?"

"Yes," said Miranda, "I certainly have."

"Then you've seen fellers purtend to drink goblets of rosy wine, but that's gammon—broad-wheeled gammon; they don't drink nothing. So it is with these ere fellows. They ain't a-talking nothing, but they've got such a eye on you as never was."

"An eye on me?" said Miranda.

"Yes, mum. Them's officers, they're 'pinted to watch you, and you'll see if they doesn't; so just put the kibosh on them, if you please, mum."

Miranda quite despaired of asking Mr. Jones what the kibosh was, so she merely said:

"I thank you for your caution, and doubly thank you for the kind feeling you have manifested towards me and mine."

Miranda then knocked at the door of her humble dwelling, while Mr. Jones proceeded down the street, with the most ridiculous affectation of a female walk and manner that can be imagined.

He was quite right when he pointed out the two individuals—apparently conversing, at the corner of the street—as officers, for they were those who had been deputed by the magistracy to watch Miranda's minutest proceedings, and, immediately that they saw her fairly within the house, they walked up to the door. One then said to the other:

"We must take this job, now, by turns. You stay here, and, if she should come out again, you must follow her closely, and see where she goes, and, in the course of two or three hours, if you fairly get her housed anywhere, you can get some boy to come to me at my house, and I will relieve your watch."

"That will do," said the other. "There's no occasion for two of us at once; but my own opinion is, that we may watch her about York to no purpose, for Percy is off long before this, and a great fool he is if he don't get out of the country."

"Do you really think he did the murder?" said the other.

"What's that to us?" was the reply. "We're officers, and it's our duty to get him hanged if we can, while, certainly, he's a great flat if he lets us."

The one officer was then left as a sentinel at Miranda's door; a proceeding, however, which, now that she had been warned both by Mr. Anderson and Jones that she was watched, was not likely to be half so effective as it otherwise might have been.

Her first inquiry of the people of the house was concerning Mr. Percy, and she was told that he had slept nearly the whole of the time she had been absent, only waking now and then at long intervals, to utter some incoherent words respecting her and his son, and then again to relapse into a deep and quiet slumber.

With many thanks for their attention to him during her absence, she repaired to her own room, on the table of which was a letter, with the simple address of:

"Miss Rankley."

Miranda timidly opened it, in some suspicion as to whom it could come from.

The inside was a complete blank, but from the inclosure fell a Bank of England note for five pounds.

Small as this sum was, it was indeed a treasure to Miranda Rankley, for the harassing, and, to her, dreadful thought had arisen, that her small amount of cash could not possibly suffice, even to discharge the rent due at the temporary lodging, a matter which, in the hurry and excitement of the last deeply anxious week, she had not thought of previously.

"From whom," she said, "can this kind donation come? From Mr. Anderson, doubtless, or from Rowland's counsel. Either of them would be capable of this generous and delicate act. Heaven reward and bless them both for their kindness to me in my deep affliction, and the best present thanks I can give them is, without scruple, to make use of their kind bounty."

Miranda was wrong, for the five pounds had come from Dick Palmer, whose resources, being rather of a variable nature, would not, at that present moment, permit him to bestow more upon Miranda, or he would have lacked the means of reaching London with Rowland Percy.

The letter had been left by Mr. Jones, who had received a strict injunction from Dick Palmer not to mention it to Miranda.

As Mr. Percy still slept, Miranda sat down in the silence of her own little chamber, fully and carefully to consider what should be her next step.

Her thoughts all tended towards London, where alone there could be a hope of meeting with Rowland, and the more she considered her situation in York, and the many disagreeables it would give rise to, the more did her plan present itself to her in attractive colours.

Besides, the idea of being under police surveillance at York, was to her painful and harassing. Such, she thought, would not be the case in London, so very far as it was from the scene of the events which had placed her in so remarkable a position.

While she was immersed in these reflections, all of which were tending towards her resolution to leave York as speedily as possible, a circumstance occurred which materially strengthened her resolution. This was the entrance into the room of the woman of the house, who, with a hesitation of manner that showed she rather shrank from her task, said:

"If you please, Miss Rankley, I am very sorry, but my husband thinks we shall want the apartments. There's been so much noise and disturbance in York about you, you know, miss, that my husband thinks, you see——"

"Enough—enough," said Miranda; "I quite understand—I will leave here to-morrow."

"Thank you, miss," said the woman. "There's no particular hurry; but my husband is such a quiet man, that he can't bear notorious characters."

"I will go to-morrow evening," said Miranda.

There was nothing in Miranda's tone to encourage further conversation, so the woman left the room without another word.

"Now I am decided," said Miranda; "I am become a proscribed being in York—a person to be shunned, and shut out from the ordinary feelings of humanity, because I have been so unhappy as to have my father murdered, and my betrothed husband wrongfully accused of the crime. Well—well, be it so. I am decided. To-morrow night I will leave York. Far from here, I shall, at least, have the satisfaction of sinking into obscurity, and avoiding that terrible notoriety which I perceive, in York, would become so harassing and full of evils. To-morrow night—to-morrow night. Shall I, or shall I not, communicate my intention to Mr. Anderson? What would be his course of conduct? He will try to combat my intention by every means; he will try to dissuade me from this step, and I should then have the pain of acting in opposition to the urgent remonstrance of my best friend. Then, when he found me obstinately fixed upon my purpose, he would think himself called upon to make some effort to assist me, that might prejudice himself and his family. I will tell no one—trusting only in that Providence which has already saved Rowland Percy from the death which seemed inevitable. I will, with no other company than his afflicted father, proceed to London."

Miranda had been so brought up as the child of luxury, with not a wish ungratified, and so little care, knowledge, or concern about money, or its value, that when she had formed this resolution she had not the slightest idea of how far her limited pecuniary resources would second her inclination.

Nay, how far she should be safe in making inquiries on that subject she knew not. That there were frequent conveyances from York to London she was well aware; but what a frightful risk of detection in her flight, and what a risk of being followed she would run by proceeding in a public conveyance.

From these considerations Miranda certainly correctly enough concluded that her best and safest plan would be to proceed on foot on her journey, however long and toilsome it might become.

By such a course of proceeding, too, there would be the greatest possible facility in discovering if she were really followed; while, among the passengers in a stage-coach, how could she pick out anyone in particular on whom to fix the suspicion of following her to the metropolis.

The constant recurrence, however, of the same face halting where she should halt, and keeping pace with her and old Mr. Percy to London, would be conclusive evidence that a spy was watching her movements, and she could accordingly make what deviations in her direct route that such a circumstance might render politic.

Now she wished repeatedly that she had asked of Jones, during her recent interview with him, some direct clue by which she could find Palmer and Rowland Percy in London; for she had heard sufficient talk of the vast metropolis to be aware of the extreme difficulty of finding any stranger within its populous precincts, particularly when that stranger was using his utmost endeavours to render his name and abode a secret.

But where was she to seek Jones in order to procure this information?

That was a question which Miranda could not answer, and, after much more anxious and painful reflection, she felt herself compelled to trust to chance, and what good fortune might occur to her in the prosecution of her arduous undertaking; but, having once made that resolution, she swerved not from it, and looked upon her approaching journey to London as a thing determined upon, and not to be set aside.

She then rose, and gently approached the bedside of the slumbering Mr. Percy.

He opened his eyes at the moment, and fixed them upon hers, with a mournful expression, as he said:

"Is it indeed you, Miranda Rankley, or some pure spirit that is borrowing new grace and beauty by assuming your face and form?"

"It is I—it is I," said Miranda.

CHAPTER LXXXIII.

THE PURSUIT FROM YORK—JOE AND HIS TURNIPS—A TOO ACTIVE OFFICER—DICK PALMER'S SCHEME OF ESCAPE.

WE left Rowland Percy and his friend, Dick Palmer, at the roadside inn, precisely as the sound of horses' feet, proceeding from York, caused a pang of alarm to pervade Rowland's bosom, and to proclaim to Palmer the necessity of extreme caution and circumspection in their proceedings.

"Hush—hush!" he said; "do not betray the slightest flurry or alarm. If those who are approaching be enemies, you may depend they will at least receive no assistance from the people who keep this house. Get into the cart again, and trust to me."

Rowland did as he was desired, and sprang with celerity into the chaise-cart, while Palmer was busy opening a gate by the side of the house, which led to some stabling and a wilderness of a garden at the back of the premises.

Meantime the clattering sound of the hoofs of the approaching horses came more and more distinctly to their ears, now and then intermingled with the sound of voices, as if those approaching were conversing in loud and eager tones.

Dick Palmer, without another word, took the horse by the head, and then leading him through the gate, closed it, saying, in a low tone, to Percy:

"We must give them the double, if possible—always provided they are our pursuers, which we shall have but little difficulty in discovering."

At this moment a side-door of the house opened, and a man appeared, with a lantern in his hand.

"Hilloa!" he cried. "Make yourself at home, do, whoever you are, there's nothing like it. Open people's gates at any hour of the night, and tramp in. Curse you, who are you?"

"Find out," said Dick.

The man laughed, as he immediately added:

"I suppose I'm getting a fool in my old age, for I ought to have known that voice, and I ought to have known, too, that nobody but you would have had such infernal impudence. Well, well, squire, the road from London to York, I believe, is all your own, and is likely to remain so for many a year to come."

"Silence," cried Dick. "You hear the sounds of those horses' feet?"

"Rather," said the man. "They seem in a hurry; but they have got the hill to come up, and won't be here for five minutes yet, though you'd fancy by the sound of their hoofs that they were almost at our door."

"When they do come up," said Dick, "mind, there's nobody here; and I'll trouble you to ask them what they want, and repeat their answer in as loud a voice as you like, and leave me, then, to take care of myself."

The man seemed to think this was very funny, for he chuckled enormously under his breath, and then said:

"Leave you to take care of yourself; I rather think I may. Going to London—eh?"

"Yes," said Dick.

"Ah, well," added the man, "you must have began business soon out of York, if so be as these horsemen are after you."

"You're right," said Dick. "Good-night to you."

He then led the horse in the dark for some four or five hundred yards over an uneven piece of waste ground at the back of the house, when he took down another gate, whispering to Rowland:

"If these are our pursuers, and I must say it looks a little like it, they had better be before us than behind us, for we don't want to catch them, and they do want to catch us."

"But think you they will go on," said Rowland, "without the news that we are before them?"

"Yes," replied Palmer, "no doubt they will. At least, for some considerable distance. My principal object, however, is to find if we are pursued so closely or not. If this should turn out to be a false alarm, we have amply sufficient start of them to pursue our journey without further trouble; but, if the officers are really upon our heels, why, we must even make the best of it, and outwit them if we can't outrun them."

By this time the horsemen had reached the door of the little old-fashioned inn, but not a light was visible, and the man who kept it was too determined to seem profoundly asleep to pay the slightest attention to the bawling and shouting of the four well-mounted and well-armed men, for there was that number who drew up at his door.

"Hilloa!" cried the foremost. "Curse him. he sleeps too sound for it to be real."

He flung himself off his horse, and applied the butt-end of his whip with violence against the door of the house.

Scarcely, however, had he done so, when, with a loud oath, he rushed into the road again, for, from one of the upper windows, the landlord had poured a bucket of water over him, at the same time that he cried out:

"So I've nabbed you at last, have I? You won't try that again, anyhow."

"Why, what do you mean, you fool?" said the horseman.

"Why, this is the third night you've been hammering at my door," said the landlord: "but I'm even with you at last."

"Come, come," cried one of the horsemen. "none of that. My name is Viggers; I daresay you've heard of me before."

"Oh, dear, yes," said the landlord; "how's Mrs. Viggers and the little Viggerses? Are you any relation to Viggers, the officer?"

"You know well I am Viggers, the officer," was the reply.

"Oh!" said the landlord, raising his voice to a stentorian pitch, "you are Viggers, the officer, from York, are you?"

"What the deuce makes you holler that way?" said the officer.

"Because I've got a stiff neck," was the reply.

"Curse you and your neck, too," muttered the officer to himself, and, then, in a loud tone, he cried:

"Has there been a chaise-cart past here, with two men in it?"

"Yes," said the landlord.

"Ay, indeed," said Viggers, the officer. "When?"

"Why, let me see——" said the landlord, in a deliberate tone of voice.

"Tell me the exact time, and here's a guinea for you," cried Viggers.

"Throw up the guinea, and I'll tell you, honour bright."

"Thank you, for nothing," cried the officer; "you shall have the guinea when I come back. I've got a stiff neck, too."

"Oh! indeed," said the landlord, "you'll never get rid of that till a good strong rope is put round it, I'm thinking."

"Come—come, nonsense—earn your guinea, Joe. When did the chaise-cart go past?"

"Last Monday was a week, my fancy pippin," said Joe, as he shut the window with a bang.

The officer stood for a moment uttering some diabolical curses, for he was sadly provoked at being outwitted in the little dialogue before his three companions. He then said:

"Here, Ned Wilkins, dismount and come with me, we shall soon find if any chaise-cart is on old Joe's premises. You, Evans and Smith, keep a good eye on the road."

The voice of the landlord had been quite sufficiently high to reach the ears of Palmer and Rowland Percy, so that they became well possessed of the danger which awaited them.

"It is as I suspected," said Dick, "we have been seen by someone, and are now pursued hotly from York, but it will go hard with us if we do not get the better of them. It is a great object to know where the foe is situated, and those fellows will now go galloping a considerable distance on the road with the notion of overtaking us, little suspecting that we are behind them."

"But still we must meet them," said Percy, "for if they precede us the whole of the way, I do not see how we are to prevent ourselves encountering them on their return."

"We shall certainly encounter them," said Palmer, "unless, by some rare piece of good fortune, we are housed somewhere and passed by them on their return; but our object, now that we know our danger, must be to render a meeting with them as harmless as possible, which, if you will leave it to me, I think I can accomplish."

"I am but too thankful," said Rowland, "to be in such good hands."

While this conversation was proceeding in a low and cautious voice, Palmer had led the horse through the second gate he had opened, which brought them into a meadow, over the long grass of which the wheels rolled noiselessly, and which seemed of immense length.

"This meadow," said Palmer, "is nearly seven acres in extent, and takes us a considerable distance parallel to the road back again towards York. From another gate, at its extremity, we can emerge into the high-road, allowing our pursuers to proceed at as hard a pace as they please ahead of us."

"We are succeeding in avoiding them," said Percy, "and one great uneasiness off our minds consists in what I think we may fairly presume to be a fact—namely, that we shall have no other pursuers from York."

"True," said Palmer; "and, in consequence, we need not be listening with apprehension to the sound of every horse's foot that is behind us. Hark! now. Our pursuers are off again."

As he spoke, the whole party of officers were heard leaving the door of the public-house at a hard trot, in the direction of London, fully believing that those they sought must be still in advance of them, and that they must speedily overtake one horse encumbered with a chaise-cart, and the weight of two men.

Dick Palmer then took down the gate which terminated the long meadow, on the other side of which was the road, and got into the cart, saying:

"Now, Mr. Percy, I have better hopes of your escape than ever I had. This man, Viggers, is an active and daring officer, and it is something to know what he is about, and that he is not behind us."

"Who could have given notice," said Percy, "of the direction of our flight?"

"Oh," said Palmer, "that may have been quite accidental. Very diligent inquiry would be almost certain to obtain a description of every kind of vehicle that passed from York on the London road, combined, too, most probably with some sort of notion of the persons within it. But here we are again at Joe's door."

The landlord seemed to be well aware that Dick Palmer would make his appearance, and was waiting for him at his door-porch, accompanied by the lantern, with which he had not condescended to lighten the darkness of Mr. Viggers and his companions.

At Dick's suggestion Rowland alighted from the chaise-cart, and they entered the low doorway of the ancient roadside inn.

"Come in," cried the landlord, as he held the lantern up to Dick's face. "I thought you would come back, and it does my eyes good to see you." Then, as his glance suddenly fell upon the pale, pensive face of Rowland Percy, he cried, "Hilloa, Dick! who the deuce is that? I have heard you say you would never have a pal in your line of business."

"Nor is this gentleman one," said Dick. "He is merely a friend of mine in a little difficulty."

"Then it was arter him that Master Viggers come?"

"It was; but, when I tell you he is a friend of mine, that is sufficient for you, Joe."

"In course—in course," said Joe. "Walk in, sir."

"Joe," said Dick Palmer, in an earnest voice, "you must pull up a lot of your turnips, for I mean to take them to London with me."

"Do yer?" said Joe. "That's a rum start, anyhow."

"I want a smock-frock, too," said Dick, "and a carter's hat: so, bustle, Joe, bustle."

"How many turnips do you want?" said Joe.

"Enough to fill the chaise-cart," was the reply.

"Then it will take me and Bob a full hour to get 'em, purvided we works like niggers."

So saying, the landlord departed to do Palmer's bidding.

The landlord was better than his word, for, in less than an hour, the chaise-cart was tolerably filled with good bunches of turnips, and the necessary materials of dress for changing Dick's appearance were produced.

"Now, Mr. Percy," he said, "we can get on a little. I think I shall make a cavity down among these turnips, upon which I will spread my cloak, where you may lie comfortably, and, should it become necessary, you must not mind me covering you up, face and all, with some of the bunches. You will find plenty of crevices through which to breathe, and every petty village and farmers name between York and London, is so well known to me, that you may trust to me for making good a story, should we be questioned. Moreover, you must hide yourself as we go through every turnpike, so that there shall be no report current of a chaise-cart, with two men in it, being upon the road. Good-night, Joe."

"Good-night," said Joe. "You is a rum 'un, you is, and no mistake. Muster Viggers don't stand no chance agin you."

With this sage remark, Joe closed his door, just as the sound of Dick Palmer's chaise-cart was dying away in the distance.

CHAPTER LXXXIV.

TWITTER AT HOME—THE LETTER TO VARLEY —THE SCHEME OF SAFETY—THE SILVER SPOON AND A LITTLE MISUNDERSTANDING.

IF to Miranda the city of York had become a peculiarly uncomfortable place of abode, in consequence of the notoriety which had attended the spirited action she had committed, how much more disagreeable was Varley's position in that theatre of action, where he had been so singularly worsted.

He was certainly in full and undisturbed possession of the Grange estates, the ample revenue of which had excited his cupidity before his wild adoration of Miranda had grown to its maddening height, but so replete was the superb mansion in which the death of Sir George Rankley had taken place, with the most frightful reminiscences, that he, Varley, shrank from even a visit to the spot, and had been, for some days past, possessed with a notion of getting rid of it for a large sum in cash.

The sudden and unexpected escape of Rowland Percy had sadly deranged all his thoughts and plans. He felt towards that unhappy victim of his malice and his hatred all that revengeful feeling which actuates such minds towards those whom they have deeply injured.

Nothing but Rowland Percy's death could possibly satisfy him that he had nothing to fear from the fearful retribution which he felt that Rowland Percy had a right to exact from him.

Then, his passion for Miranda was far, very far, from being weakened by the crowd of unsurmountable obstacles that seemed to surround it. Indeed, it seemed to gather strength and fresh fire, as it lost hope, and when he spoke of following Rowland Percy to the metropolis, he had a full conviction that he should be likewise following Miranda, for he felt that with her spirited determination and devotion she would not be long absent from the side of him for whom she had already sacrificed so much.

His fears of Twitter were decidedly on the increase, for he saw that the valet deeply regretted his involvement in the whole transaction, which had called upon him for so much more personal exertion and deep anxiety than he had ever calculated upon.

To regret his connection with him, must surely be but the precursor to the adoption of some means of severing it, and Varley was resolved to keep him destitute of finances, in the manner he had openly avowed, for the purpose of having a hold upon him from hour to hour, which he could not otherwise obtain.

The proposed journey to London, in search of Rowland Percy and Miranda, provided it were to be found that she had left York, presented itself to Samuel Twitter in far from alluring colours, and yet what could he do.

"I might turn king's evidence," he groaned, "and Bernard Varley would be hanged, which certainly, would be a great satisfaction to me, and exceedingly pleasant to my feelings; but what should I get by it? Nothing—just nothing. I could expect nothing from Miranda, for she would hardly reward me for telling the truth, because I was disappointed of being paid for keeping it a secret. I daresay they wouldn't hang me—that is, I don't think they would; but they would be sure to put me in prison for a good while, or transport me, and what is called in all the newspapers the learned and humane judge, would tell me to think myself well off that a merciful view was taken of my case by his Majesty's advisers, and that I was not to be hanged upon my own confession, but transported beyond the seas for my natural life, or put in prison for a long while to hard labour."

Twitter uttered a deep groan as he summed up these reflections, by saying, "I should like very much to turn king's evidence, but I dare not. Fool that I have been. I was a great deal better off before this transaction than I am now, for then I had my salary as valet to Sir George, and, besides, he was very unsuspicious, and I kept on robbing the house wholesale. Now what a wretch I am. I've no salary from anybody, and since I have been in this house I have only got possession of one silver tablespoon, and that I'm afraid to sell, although I've rubbed out the man's initials, by working it to and fro on the window-sill."

Tremblingly alive likewise as he was to the perils of his situation, or to what he supposed the perils of it, from the violence of the York mob, he feared to venture into the streets, although Varley's prohibition extended not after the morning appointed for Rowland's execution, and, perhaps, had he been not so tortured and afflicted by Varley's want of faith with him, and the manner in which he found himself so completely in that villain's power, he might have looked upon his journey to London with no very disagreeable sensations, but, as it was, he shrank from it as entailing upon him additional trouble and inconvenience, literally for nothing.

He was thus reflecting, and in this most unenviable state of mind, when a letter was brought into the room addressed to Bernard Varley.

Twitter, upon an examination of the postmark, found that the letter came from Liverpool, and concerned as he was with Bernard Varley, he became seized with an earnest curiosity to know what it could contain, since, during the whole period of Varley's residence at the Grange, not one communication had arrived for him.

"Varley has but recently left me," he said. "He cannot know of this letter coming. If I could but obtain a glimpse of its contents, it might possibly give some hint as to my future action, that would force him to draw his purse-strings in my favour. If I could possibly convict him of any other transaction, which would make him amenable to the laws, than this one in which I myself am so deeply involved, it would give me more hold upon him. If I dared now open his letter, my wish might be gratified; and yet I tremble—I tremble—lest he should discover it."

As he spoke, Twitter turned the letter over and over, and carefully examined the large black seal with which it was fastened.

"I will try," he muttered. "I have before opened letters and resealed them without detection, and why should I not this one? I will try—yes—I will try."

He then rang for a light, and when one was brought to him, he heated the blade of his penknife, and carefully slipped it under the wax seal, so as to release it whole, and unblemished, from its hold.

There was scarcely a mean act of this description which Samuel Twitter had not, at one time or other during his life, practised; he, therefore, got through the present manoeuvre with tolerable cleverness, and there lay Bernard Varley's letter open before him.

It was short, and to the following effect:

"SIR,—Agreeably to your written instructions, I have purchased for you a small yacht, which, with her complement of five men, will cruise off the mouth of the Mersey, awaiting your good pleasure to come on board of her, for the trip you mention to the Mediterranean, but which I would not advise you to undertake at this season of the year, as you will scarcely derive the pleasure from it that you anticipate.

"The name of the yacht is the *Argus*, and I have given full instructions to the intelligent men on board to attend particularly to your signal words of 'New Owner B. V.,' which you say you will use should you feel inclined to board her in an open boat.

"The price of the vessel, with her stores and fittings for three months, has rather exceeded sixteen hundred pounds, so that I have placed to your account the fifteen hundred pounds, transmitted to me, per cheque upon the Liverpool bankers, and shall feel happy to attend to your further commands.—I am, sir, your very obedient, and most humble servant,

"THOMAS SINGLETON, Shipping Agent."

Twitter read this epistle thrice over before he uttered a word concerning its contents; then he drew a long breath, as he said:

"So Bernard Varley contemplates escaping. I see it all—I see it all. He will convert, some day, all his ill-gotten property into money, and leave me to destitution and despair. That is his plan, or why should he keep me in this state of abject dependence upon him. I am lost—lost—lost! what will become of me? what will become of me? This letter is conclusive. It is as clear as the sun at noonday. Why should he buy a yacht at such a large expense but for such a purpose? What shall I—what can I—do to thwart him? I must adopt some instant action, and——"

A loud knock at the street-door at this moment made Twitter's heart, to use common, but expressive words, leap into his mouth; for the dreadful supposition came across him that it might be Varley, and what time had he to re-seal the letter with that nicety and exactness which should defy the scrutinizing eyes of his companion in guilt.

To attempt it were madness, and in his agony of apprehension he blew out the candle, thrusting it, candlestick and all, into his pocket together with the letter and his open penknife, after which he stood in the middle of the floor in such an agony of apprehension that no one could have avoided suspecting he had been guilty of something which he was frightfully anxious to conceal.

In another moment the door opened, and Bernard Varley entered the room.

The first glance he bent upon Twitter showed him that something extraordinary must have occurred, and, in a voice hovering between alarm and anger, he said:

"How now, Twitter? Your countenance betrays that you have some unusual cause of uneasiness, or——"

"Or what?" gasped Twitter.

"Or of concocting some villainy against me," said Varley.

"No—no," said Twitter, whose lips were perfectly livid with fear, "indeed you are mistaken." Then he added, quite unconsciously adopting the concluding words of the letter: "I am, sir, your very obedient, humble servant. I am, sir, upon my soul—I am, Bernard Varley. Don't look at me so; I—I—don't feel certainly very well just at this moment. It's a kind of dizziness, and I can only just

VARLEY ENDEAVOURS TO EXTORT THE TRUTH FROM HIS CONFEDERATE TWITTER.

at this moment repeat that—sir, I am your very obedient and most humble servant."

So saying, Twitter sank into a chair with a deep groan, for he had a glimmering perception that he was saying a little more than he ought, and that the more he kicked and floundered, the more he should get into the mire.

Bernard Varley bent a keen, scrutinizing glance into his face, as he muttered, between his clenched teeth :

"Cowardly scoundrel, what have you been about ? Your looks betray you ; with all the will to become a villain, you lack the nerve, Samuel Twitter, to carry you through any

one act. Speak, or this moment shall be your last."

"Your most humble servant," groaned Twitter, in a perfect agony of fright, "I didn't do it—I'd scorn the action."

"What action ?" said Varley, seizing him by the throat.

"N—n—n—nothing ; I'm like a babe unborn, and, sir, your very obedient servant."

"Are you mad ?" said Varley ; "or has temporary fear of my discovery of something you have done deprived you of your reason for a time ? Tell me all this moment, or, by the infernal powers, I'll stop your breath——"

"Have mercy upon me !" said Twitter.

"Give us our daily bread, as we forgive them that trespass against us!"

Varley shook him to and fro so violently, that the candlestick in his pocket swung about, and rattled against his knife with an ominous sound.

"What have you in your pocket?" he cried—"what have you in your pocket?"

"Nothing," said Twitter, gasping for breath; "I never had anything in my pocket in all my life—it's all a joke—amen! Don't you see me smile?—what will you take to drink?—I am, sir, your obedient and very humble servant."

Bernard Varley remained for some moments silent, for he really knew not what to say next, nor could he imagine what on earth could occasion Twitter's extreme emotion.

Then suddenly a thought came across Twitter's mind that was as welcome as a ray of light from heaven to some benighted wretch sinking from fatigue and hunger—as welcome as the word forgiveness to a shrieking soul which feels itself condemned by Heaven.

He really laughed, and his face changed from a ghastly hue to its usual tallowy, but not so horrible complexion.

He plunged his hand into his pocket, and, in a tone between a scream and a laugh, cried:

"Bernard Varley, I have stolen a silver spoon, and I was afraid they had found it out. Don't be angry; there was 'W. M. B.' on the handle, but I've nearly scrubbed it out. Here's the spoon, and I am, sir, your very obedient servant."

"Curse you for a fool, as you are," said Varley, as, snatching the spoon from Twitter's hand, he threw it in his face, and then, in great anger, left the apartment.

CHAPTER LXXXV.

THE WANDERINGS OF A BLIGHTED BRAIN—
MR. JONES'S SECOND VISIT, AND IMITATION
OF A DELICATE YOUNG LADY.

MR. ANDERSON, although far from being a rich man, still felt that he could do something for Miranda, even out of his limited resources, and with him to feel such a conviction was to act upon it immediately to its utmost extent.

After Miranda had left him, he proceeded to the young barrister who had taken so warm an interest in her cause, and with him held a consultation as to what could be done for Miranda's permanent benefit.

It was then arranged, and fully agreed upon, between them that, without saying anything to her upon the subject, they should go among the friends of the late Sir George Rankley, and those influential and wealthy persons in and about York, who might be induced to believe in Rowland Percy's innocence, and admire the heroism of Miranda, in order to raise quietly, and without any public éclat, a subscription which should enable her to turn the abilities and accomplishments she possessed to some permanent advantage.

The delicacy which Mr. Anderson felt of communicating any such proceeding to Miranda, prevented him from visiting her that day, and thus it was that a want of free and unreserved confidence arose between Miranda and the kind-hearted attorney, from the highest and purest motives in both cases.

Had Miranda communicated to him her intention of leaving York, he would have prayed her to delay until what he was about had been accomplished, and she would have been spared much misery, and many fearful scenes through which she had to pass.

But such was not to be; and these two persons, with the best feelings, were acting at cross purposes, for, while Mr. Anderson was pleasing himself with the idea that he was doing all that mortal man could do for Miranda, she was, with a sad and lonely heart, making her quiet preparations for her departure to London.

Mr. Percy, at whose bedside we left her, seemed refreshed by the sleep he had obtained; but too soon did the saddened Miranda find that his mind was still lost, for his words presented nothing but a mass of chaotic images.

"You are better, Mr. Percy," she said, as she bent over him.

"Much better," he said; "but it is strange we should change our nature in sleep, and fancy such horrors—such frightful horrors, that it requires, dear Miranda, many moments of waking reality ere the soul can shake itself free from the mysticism of dreams. Who would suppose I was a king?"

Miranda heaved a deep sigh, as she said:

"Mr. Percy—Mr. Percy, think again—think of your son Rowland, and, by reflecting upon him, you will know yourself."

"Ay, that was a dream again," he said. "I thought, Miranda, that I saw your father. He was in his shroud, and dabbled in his heart's blood."

Miranda shuddered, and he added, instantly:

"You weep, Miranda—weep at a dream."

"No," she said, "I do not weep. 'Tis strange and unnatural; but, from the first moment that I heard the frightful words accusing Rowland Percy of murder, my feelings seemed to rise above tears, and, although there have been many times when they would have been a merciful relief to my overcharged heart, I could not command them. I know not when I shall weep again, for common sorrows cannot touch me, and those I have lie too deep for ordinary expression."

"Ay, 'tis well," said the old man. "There should be no tears from such eyes. I have heard my Rowland talk of their brightness until I have thought the boy distracted. But you shall be a princess yet, Miranda; nay, your beauty shall make you one of nature's queens, and who shall dare dispute your sovereignty? But for my dream—my dream—I have not told you all."

"Hear me first," said Miranda, imploringly. "Hear me first. Do you think, Mr. Percy, that with me you could undertake a journey?"

"A journey?" he muttered.

"Yes," said Miranda, in a low tone, for she was fearful that anyone might be within hearing, and arrive at a knowledge of her intention of seeking Rowland in his place of concealment. "I wish you to proceed with me to London to see your son, Mr. Percy—your son, who is so dear to both of us."

"Ay, but my dream, my dream!" said the old man, abstractedly.

"I must hear it," thought Miranda, "however much it may harrow my feelings. And yet, what does it matter. He cannot tell me aught but what I know already, and no words from anyone can paint more vividly to my mind the circumstances of distress and terror I never can forget."

"Yes, I knew it was your father," continued Mr. Percy, "for there was on his finger the bright diamond he so much loved to wear."

These words, for the first time since her father's ring had been given to her by Dick Palmer, brought the circumstance to Miranda's mind, and it was with mixed feelings of pain and pleasure, that she thought, after all, should she be driven to greater extremity, the ring would present a valuable resource, although to part with this last sad memento of her father, would inflict upon her the greatest misery.

"You remember the ring, Miranda?" said Mr. Percy.

"I do," said Miranda, sadly.

"Then by that I knew him. The bright gem shot forth its long rays of sunny light, as if in mockery of the cold hand it adorned. Then, as dreams will strangely shift from place to place, I thought you and I sat in a crowded court—there was the sound of many voices, but, above them all, I heard my Rowland's, declaring he was innocent. Ere I could ask of what he was accused, the dreadful words 'murder,' and 'guilty,' rang in my ears. Miranda, how could my boy Rowland be guilty? how could he have done murder? What could they mean by accusing him?"

"Do you not know," said Miranda, "that the dream is true, and but the echo of events which preceded it? He was accused of murder. They did call him guilty, but how wrongfully, Heaven knows. He is innocent, and the day will come when his innocence will be apparent as the light of heaven. Till then, however, there must be gloom and darkness over us all, and we must endure with what patience we may the afflictions with which a gracious and benign Providence chooses, in its great mercy and great love for its creatures, to visit us."

"No, it was a dream," said the old man.

"I would it were," sighed Miranda: "but answer me, Mr. Percy, are you willing to accompany me to London?"

A sudden change seemed to come over his feelings, and, from the rather exalted tone in which he had been speaking, his voice turned to one of deep grief and despondency.

"Miranda," he exclaimed, "where is my boy Rowland?—where is he? What have they done with him? Oh, can it be true, Miranda, that they have taken his life?"

"No," said Miranda, in a tone of grief. "It is not, but they would have done so, Mr. Percy; they fain would have done so. He is saved! And it is to seek him in his place of concealment from his enemies that I wish you to come with me."

"Yes—yes! I will come, Miranda," he said. "to the world's end I will come, in search of my poor boy Rowland. So they would have taken his life, but Heaven would not let them, and he is saved—he is saved! Let us go at once. Are we not now in York, Miranda?"

"We are," she said, eagerly, for her heart hailed the question as some proof of returning reason. "Do you not remember, Mr. Percy, misfortune has come upon us both? But it is not so bad as it might have been, since Rowland still lives. Oh, try to think!"

He passed his hand across his brow, as if making a mental effort of clear reflection, and then he said, sadly:

"There have been so many events, Miranda, that I know not which preceded which. You must tell me all as we go to meet Rowland. Let the carriage be ordered, and we will proceed at once."

"Alas—alas!" thought Miranda, "my hope is a vain one. His reason is completely shattered. Time alone may ameliorate his sad condition, and to that must I trust."

At this moment a low knock at the chamber door attracted Miranda's attention, and, upon hastening to it to ascertain who demanded admission, she found her landlady there, who said:

"If you please, miss, there's a most singular female, of the name of Mrs. Jones, who wants to see you."

Miranda in a moment surmised who the Mrs. Jones was, and, as she was, in reality, most anxious to see Jones before her departure, she said:

"Will you oblige me by allowing me to see her in your parlour below?"

"Oh, yes, miss, certainly," said the woman, "and, if you please, as I was a-coming up at any rate, I have just brought my little bill."

"Very well," said Miranda, "it shall be discharged after I have seen this person."

Upon this assurance, the woman's respect seemed greatly to increase towards Miranda, for she had had her own suspicions—which, when duly given utterance to, and, of course, greatly increased at a tea-drinking with some five of her neighbours on the preceding evening—that the little bill would have been found a little inconvenience when presented, and, just possibly, a very great one.

She was, therefore, agreeably surprised upon finding that such was not the case, and that it was to be settled so promptly and easily.

She preceded Miranda to the passage, in

which stood Mr. Jones, who, in his female garments, nearly filled it up, and who was standing most unfemininely, with his arms akimbo, whistling, with great power, one of the popular tunes of the day.

When he saw Miranda, accompanied by the woman of the house, he thought it necessary to keep up his female character, and he, accordingly, executed a curtsey, from which he recovered with such a sudden jerk upwards, that he brought his head in violent contact with something hanging in the passage, bearing a remote resemblance to a lamp, which, as nobody was ever insane enough to attempt to light, answered its purpose very well, and kept up a popular delusion that there was a passage—we beg pardon, a hall-lamp—at number seven.

Upon this untoward circumstance occurring, Mr. Jones, rather for the moment forgetting the delicacy of his assumed character, exclaimed:

"Cuss it, what's this? Is a delicate female's knowledge-box to be pummelled in this ere way, mum?"

"Gracious! you've broken the hall-lamp," said the landlady.

"Have I?" said Mr. Jones; "then I'd advise you, mum, to save the blessed pieces. I never was so insulted in all my life. A female, a female, I hope, mum, and delicate, quite natural. Oh, my blessed narves! I'm a good mind to faint, and if I does, I shall come down with a whop that would break the passage in. Beware of love, mum—beware of love!"

The landlady looked perfectly aghast at the specimen of female delicacy before her, and it was with difficulty that she stammered out:

"Will you walk into the parlour?"

"Suttenly, mum," said Mr. Jones, as with one kick he sent a chair that was in the way quite down the kitchen staircase, where its sudden arrival set the maid-of-all-work screaming. "It's all the same to me, mum, whether I goes into the parlour or the tap-room. I means the drawing-room, mum, excuse my wulgarity. I was brought up in a band-box, and fed upon carraway-seeds, but somehow or other I have fallen into the company of rum ones, and evil association, mum, corrupts good manners, so I ain't so delicate as I once was. Here's a beastly lock, and be cursed to it."

This latter exclamation arose from a little difficulty in opening the parlour-door, which Mr. Jones solved by the immediate production of a skeleton-key, with which he opened it, and then walking into the room, sat down upon the flimsy sofa with a crash that made it groan again.

"Well, miss, I must say," remarked the landlady, "that of all the extraordinary females that ever I came near, this one beats them."

"In course," shouted Mr. Jones, from the parlour, "my father was a whopper, and my mother a stunner—and as I was the only young lady as they produced, I takes arter them, in course. I should like to see the blessed female as I can't beat."

Miranda knew not what to say, but she thought her best plan would be to proceed at once to the parlour, and get Mr. Jones out of the house as speedily as possible.

She accordingly, without making any remark to the woman concerning the peculiarities of the supposed female, walked into the parlour, and closing the door, said:

"For Heaven's sake, Mr. Jones, be more careful and circumspect. You will bring down, both upon me and yourself, the greatest suspicion and danger, if you proceed as you have done. What on earth could induce you to think that violence and disorder would enable you to pass for the character you assume?"

"I begs yer pardon, miss," said Jones, "but I really thought I was a-coming it rather. People shouldn't hang things in the passages to nob other people's heads. I'm sure, miss, you'd a sworn like one o'clock if you had had such a crack."

The parlour-door was at this moment opened again, and the landlady made her appearance with the exclamation of:

"Four and sixpence! four and sixpence! as I'm a sinner."

"Guv us hold of it," cried Jones. "'Never despise trifles,' says the blessed proverb."

"I mean you are to pay it, you wretch," said the landlady. "A likely thing, indeed, that I am to have my hall-lamp broken by such as you. It will take four and sixpence at the very least to repair it, and that I'll have, or I'll know the reason why."

"Don't make a noise, and disgrace your sex, mum," said Jones. "Can't you take pattern by me, and behave with delicate propriety? I'm always ready to faint away at the least provocation, and I'd go into *histrikes* at a minute's notice for nothing. There's breeding for you."

"The wretch," said the landlady, turning her nose up.

"There's the money," said Jones, throwing down two half-crowns, "and there's sixpence change, you know, mum."

The landlady, who had evidently expected a row, took up the two half-crowns with rather a quiet look of astonishment, and after a moment's hesitation, during which she deeply regretted she had not asked more for the lamp, she said:

"I will send up the sixpence."

"The change yer means," said Mr. Jones.

"Yes, four and sixpence is considerably under the walley of the lamp, but I consents to take it."

"You're very good," said Mr. Jones, "and as for the change——"

"Yes," said the landlady, eagerly expecting to be told she might retain it.

"Why," said Mr. Jones, "you may send it up in gin."

———

CHAPTER LXXXVI.

MR. JONES'S PROPOSAL—A NEW PHILOSOPHY
—THE PROMISE OF ASSISTANCE.

WHEN the indignant landlady had retired, Mr. Jones carefully closed the door, and then, turning to Miranda, said:

"If you please, mum—miss, I have made so bold as to kim and pay you this here visit, with the wery best of motives, as the prig said when he picked the gentleman's pocket in the fair. It ain't for me, oh, no, kim up, for to pretend as my manners is so genteel as they might be. The blessed school as I was brought up in, mum, didn't teach them ere, leastways, they was something extra, and the man as walloped me by wirtue of being my paternal relative, wouldn't pay it, so you see, the other man as walloped me by wirtue of being the schoolmaster, wouldn't teach 'em. What's the consequence, then, Miss Miranda—why all my perliteness is nateral talent."

"Let sympathy or kindness be clothed in what rough guise it may, it is ever welcome."

"Wery good," said Mr. Jones, "what I comes all for to say to-day is, that we have put up a crack, and you shall have your share of the swag."

"You've what?" said Miranda.

"Ignorant people as ain't wersed in the dead languages," said Mr. Jones, "calls a crack a robbery, and the swag, what we gets by it."

"Good Heavens!" said Miranda, "you can never mean to proffer me a share in the proceeds of a dishonourable action?"

"Bravo—kim up," said Mr. Jones. "Me and some friends of mine goes on the good old plan of catch who can, keep who may, it saves a world o' trouble, and makes people blessed sharp. All I means then to say is, that as the people have sarved you as they sarved me, why we must lay hold of the same rope to save ourselves from being drowned."

"I really cannot comprehend your meaning," said Miranda, "further than I am sure you mean to do me a kindness."

"Why, you see, there was a blessed conspiracy against me, and the folks wouldn't let me be honest, though I tried hard and fast. 'No,' says society, 'you sha'n't be honest, Jones, for if so be as you tries it, it sha'n't be a go; we'll starve you out. Prigs is wanted, and you shall be one.' So then I say to society: 'Blow yer,' says I, 'if so be as that's the caper, why there's no perwenting it, so I suppose I must do it.' Now, that ere reminds me unkimmon of you. If people would let you have your own, you'd have been as right as nothink; but they wouldn't, and what is you to do but sarve 'em out the best way you can. We are going to be down upon somebody, as I needn't mention, who can spare a few silver spoons, and you shall have your share, never fear."

Miranda was fairly puzzled with Mr. Jones's notions of morality, and what answer to make him which should convince him of his very erroneous logic she knew not: moreover, she felt his proposal was not a deliberate attempt to draw her into guilt.

She was certain such was not the motive, and she, therefore, hesitated to speak to him with the harshness she would have used if resisting a similar proposal from anyone else.

After a few moments' thought, she said:

"Mr. Jones, you and I differ most materially upon the subject upon which you are speaking, and I doubt if ever we should understand each other concerning it. You see no crime in retaliating upon society for the difficulties it has imposed upon you. To me, your proposition carries with it a feeling of absolute terror, and I beg you will not mention it again, and I am sure you will not when I tell you that, to my mind, absolute starvation would not be worse than the frightful resource you have pointed out."

"That beats me hollow," said Mr. Jones. "I can't come over that at all, Miss Miranda. Howsomdever, you may be right and I wrong—I don't deny that ere. You is a cretur with a hedication; I isn't. Whether it's betterer or worserer to be able to read writing, and think, and speak, like a printed book, I leaves to wiser heads nor mine; but what I wants to know is—where's the prog to come from? And what are you to do when yer feels yer inside tantalized for want of grub? Where's wirtue then, miss—mum, I mean? And what's to become of that ere rum dodger as people calls morality? When I'm all of a heap, Miss Miranda—and some people in just such a fix would take to crying, and some to religion—I takes to gin. That's what I calls philosophy. A *kivorton* and three outs I calls a home argayment, and it beats the tother things all to fits. I repeats my humble *kivestion*, as the parson says to the sinners: 'What is ye going to do, my werdant tulip?'"

"I can comprehend what you mean," said Miranda, rising, "although not all the words in which you express it, and in unhesitatingly rejecting your offer, and repudiating the false reasoning by which you endeavour to support it, let me assure you that it detracts in no way from my grateful feeling towards you for what you have done for me."

Mr. Jones likewise rose, as he said:

"Wery well, mum. I hope there ain't no offence; what I said wasn't intended to give none. Is there anybody in York as you'd like me to give a blessed nobbler to? If there is, only say the word, and I'll do it."

"No," said Miranda; "I have no enmities. All I wish is, that you would give me a piece of information that may be of the greatest service to me."

"In course, mum. What is it?"

"Tell me where, in case I should go to London, I should find your friend Palmer."

"What, Dicky?" said Jones.

"Yes," said Miranda.

"If I tells yer, will yer tell me one thing? And that is, do yer mean to go?"

"I scarcely need keep such a secret from you," said Miranda. "I therefore say, unhesitatingly, I do mean to go."

"When?" said Jones.

"This very night, if possible."

"You've made up your mind, and no flinching?"

"I am thoroughly resolved."

"Then I'll tell yer. You must go to the 'Star and Tinder-box,' in Steeple Court, Drury Lane, and ask for the Slashing Squire. Then the landlord will say to yer: 'What's the dodge?' And you shall say: 'The old caper.' When he'll tell yer where Dicky is to be found."

"I thank you," said Miranda. "It would, indeed, be a great object with me, when I reach London, if I should be so fortunate as to be able at once to find your friend Palmer and Rowland Percy."

"They are together, no doubt," said Jones, "and you need never fear for Mr. Percy's safety, as long as he's with Dicky."

"I thank you for the assurance," said Miranda, "and that is all I require of your kind services."

"Then I'll go, mum. But, first of all, tell me when yer means to go?"

"At midnight," said Miranda.

"Precisely?" inquired Mr. Jones.

"That I can scarcely say," replied Miranda, "as I must be much guided by circumstances. My greatest uneasiness now arises from the fact, which you have informed me of, namely, that my proceedings are watched by the police."

"Don't be troubled about that, Miss Miranda," said Jones, cheerfully. "I'll make that all right, you may depend."

"If you could do that," said Miranda, "you will be conferring a great benefit upon me, and I shall be much your debtor."

"All's right," said Mr. Jones. "You will see me to-night."

So saying, he left the parlour; but, when he reached the passage, he walked to the head of the kitchen stairs, and called out, loudly:

"I say, mother thingamy, where's that ere gin as was to come out of my change? Don't make a bilk of it, old lady."

"You horrid wretch," said the landlady, as she flung some halfpence up the staircase; "there's your beastly change, you low feller, for a feller you are, I know, though you pretend to be a delicate female. Oh, you Grogon!"

It may be presumed that the landlady meant Gorgon; but Mr. Jones, hearing the word grog, cried:

"Well, make it grog, if you like, old 'un."

Then, making a noise with his feet, as if he were about to run down the kitchen stairs, to the great alarm of the landlady, who screamed violently, he walked out of the house.

Then the landlady, after deep consideration, had what she considered the greatest revenge that was in her power, which was to proceed at once upstairs with her bill.

Miranda had ascended to her own apartments, but the vindictive landlady followed her, and, in a voice trembling between passion and anger, said:

"Now, miss, that your highly respectable visitor is gone, perhaps you will look at my little account."

"I will pay it," said Miranda. "What is its amount?"

"Four pound seven," said the landlady, as she placed the uninviting document in her lodger's hands.

"So much?" said Miranda.

"Oh, dispute it—do, by all means," said the landlady, in a sarcastic tone. "Certainly dispute it."

"I have no intention to dispute it," said Miranda, sadly. "I was only for the moment surprised at its amount. Take it from that, and give me the change. I shall leave your house to-night."

As she spoke, she handed to the landlady the five-pound note which had been anonymously sent to her, and it is doubtful whether that lady was not more indignant at being paid so promptly, than she would have been if she had been refused, for she flounced out of the room as if some deep insult had been put upon her, and then returned in a few minutes with the thirteen shillings change, and receipt, both of which she banged on the table, as if Miranda was far from entitled to them.

To this gratuitous insolence the persecuted girl made no reply, but was glad when once more left alone to her thoughts.

She gazed upon the small sum which made up all her possessions, and, with a shudder, she asked herself:

"How far would this carry me on my long and weary journey to London? What would become of me when this small fund is exhausted? Shall I, indeed, so early have to rely upon the proceeds of my father's ring, which I would fain reserve for the wants of Rowland, when I shall meet him in that great metropolis, of which I have heard so much, and where he must have but a fugitive and uncertain existence—an existence which would be ever trammelled with alarm, until it shall please Heaven to make manifest his innocence? Alas, if direful circumstances should indeed compel me to make use of that resource, it must go. Heaven help me, Heaven help me. Ah! that we, Rowland and myself, whose fortunes are so strangely mingled, were together."

CHAPTER LXXXVII.

TWITTER'S PECUNIARY DESTITUTION—THE APPEAL TO VARLEY—THE PLAN OF ESCAPE.

WHEN Bernard Varley came to consider alone the interview he recently had with Twitter, he found more and more reason to feel suspicious of the conduct of that individual, and, as is ever the case with such persons, he extracted the greatest food for alarm from the most trivial circumstances.

The, to him, unnecessary confusion of Samuel Twitter, had in it a something fearfully mysterious, and to account for it merely as Twitter himself had done, by his possession of the silver spoon, was far from sufficient to satisfy the suspicious mind of Bernard Varley.

"What can he mean?" he thought: "he must be plotting something, he must be contriving something against my peace, or he would never have shown so much confusion and uneasiness while in my presence; and yet, what has he power to do? Destitute of pecuniary resources, as he is, I am surely safe from the utmost reach of his malevolence? What could he do to me, that would not fall doubly upon himself? and yet, although my reason tells me I need not fear him, my imagination tinctures every word he has said with suspicion, and I am full of dread when I reflect upon his slightest actions."

Varley had taken up his quarters at an hotel, in a magnificent room of which he now was, and, by the splendours that were around him, he had hoped, in some measure, to mitigate those pangs of conscience from which he was never free.

He had deputed, since the escape of Rowland Percy, a person to watch the lodging of Miranda, to give him notice of wheresoever she should go, for he thought himself safe now in adopting such a course, inasmuch as he could lay it to his anxiety that the ends of justice should not be frustrated; and, as the magistrates had taken up the notion, that by watching Miranda there would be a chance of discovering the retreat of Rowland Percy, he felt himself at liberty to do the same, and to act accordingly.

It was some hours after Miranda's interview with Mr. Jones that Varley again sought an interview with Twitter; but this time the valet was not in such an abject state of fright as he had been upon the former occasion, for during Varley's absence he had contrived to restore the letter to its original, or nearly original state, and it was lying on the table as if newly arrived, and waiting but the coming of him alone who had a right to it.

Varley purposely entered the room abruptly, and, fixing his keen, scrutinizing eyes upon the trembling Twitter, saw, at a glance, that he was far from being in the agitated state he had exhibited so short a time before.

Twitter certainly did start at the sudden appearance of his fell tempter—the man who had urged him to deeds from the commission of which his own poor spirit would have shrunk in dismay, although he wanted not, at the bottom of his soul, the inclination to be as desperate and bloodthirsty a villain as ever trod the earth, or libelled humanity.

"So, Twitter," said Varley, "you have recovered from your extreme fright at the commission of a petty larceny, which one would have thought so incidental to your existence as scarcely to have disturbed your equanimity."

"Yes, Varley—certainly, Varley," said Twitter, "I was alarmed, and surely there are circumstances enough in our present situation to make us both nervous."

"Yes," said Varley; "but not so suddenly

and strangely nervous as you were, even now; besides, Twitter, why are you better? Circumstances still remain the same, and, while Time is so young, Twitter, each moment is rather against us than for us. It seems to me, from my knowledge of human nature, and particularly of your nature, Twitter, that something unusual has occurred to disturb you, which now no longer exists. Learn this, Samuel Twitter, that your slightest secret movement, inimical to me or my interests, or my wishes, shall be your death. You had better be confidential, Samuel Twitter."

"I—I am very confidential," said Twitter, "upon my life I am. Indeed, you mistrust me without reason, Bernard Varley; you know I would do anything in the world for you—anything. I will risk my life for you; for what hope have I in this world but through you."

Varley laughed bitterly, as he said:

"Protest not to me, Samuel Twitter; such words, to my mind, go for nothing, and you may spare your breath. I doubt you, and, once let that doubt be ripened into certainty, and I will kill you. My words are plain, and I would have you reflect upon them deeply."

"There is a letter for you," said Twitter, who was most anxious to change the conversation.

Varley immediately took it from the table, and, to Twitter's great relief, opened it so hastily, that, had it been resealed much more clumsily than it was, the cheat would not have been discovered.

"'Tis well," he muttered, as he read the epistle; "'tis well. Money, indeed, does wonders. My orders have been promptly enough obeyed. I shall remember; yes, I shall remember."

"So shall I," thought Twitter; "and, perhaps, my memory may be effective earlier than yours, Master Varley. I have but two hopes in this world—the one is to make money, and the other to see you hanged."

"Safer, much safer," continued Varley to himself; "by post-horses, the journey could be performed quickly—very quickly—and then away."

"What did you say?" asked Twitter.

"What matters it to you what I say?" replied Varley. "Nevertheless, I will tell you, for I know your suspicious character. I was remarking that, with the aid of post-horses, to employ which someone must have supplied him with means, Rowland Percy could have escaped with great speed from York, and been away before the officers of justice were thoroughly alive to the fact of his escape. Are you satisfied now, Samuel Twitter?"

"Oh, quite," said Samuel Twitter, "I was before. As you say, post-horses will carry people away quickly that have got the money—that are not like me, so dreadfully poor."

Here Twitter gave a deep groan, as the consciousness that he had no money came disagreeably across him.

"I have none—I have none," he muttered.

"Nor want any, most admirable Twitter. You are like a king or queen, whose wants are so abundantly supplied that it is of no consequence if you never see a coin."

"But I should like to see a few," groaned Twitter.

"Oh, I understand," continued Varley, in the same bantering tone. "From motives of curiosity, you would like occasionally to see a few. You shall be gratified now and then, Twitter, when I have a leisure hour; but, in the meantime, my post-horses will suffice to carry you to London, saving you a world of trouble. You see how mindful I am of your happiness, Twitter, and, likewise, to show that I am not unheedful of what is of vast importance to us both, look at that bill."

As he spoke he took from his pocket a printed handbill, and laid it before the eyes of Twitter.

Its head-line contained the words, "One thousand pounds reward," and it went on to state that "Charles Rowland Percy, condemned to death for wilful murder, at the York Assizes, had broken prison and escaped." Then followed a description of his person, and the whole concluded by stating that one thousand pounds reward would be paid one hour after his, the said Rowland Percy's, execution, to any person who would be directly instrumental in apprehending him, and safely lodging him in any jail.

"What think you of that?" said Varley. "Will it reproduce the prisoner, destitute of means as he must be, and surrounded by those to whom such a sum would appear an exhaustless treasure?"

"It may," said Twitter; "it may, Bernard Varley. I should like to earn it myself, for, as you are perfectly well aware, I have no money, and it's of no use stealing silver spoons here, for I've nowhere to sell them. I took another to-day, and I've got it in my coat-pocket; but it is only an aggravation."

"Ever—ever harping about money," said Varley. "Once for all, Samuel Twitter, I tell you, you shall have none until the circumstances by which we are surrounded have assumed a pleasanter complexion."

"Do you think they can ever be very pleasant?" suggested Twitter.

"Peace," cried Varley, "I will hear no more of this. It seems to be now well ascertained by the authorities at York, that Rowland Percy has proceeded to London, for they have sent officers in pursuit of him. I should follow to-night—ay, this very hour—were it not that the air of York is hallowed to me while breathed by Miranda Rankley. When she leaves I leave, but not before."

"Varley—Varley," said Twitter, "let me once more, if it be for the last time, warn you against the terrible insanity that has come over you as regards Miranda. This infatuation of yours concerning her is the only one thing I dread as likely to produce our ruin. Oh, be warned, Bernard Varley, be warned of that fatal passion which has sprung up so strongly in your soul, and which seems to deprive you at times of your reason. I implore you—not for my sake, but for your own —to relinquish the mad pursuit of one who evidently looks upon you with terror and hate."

"Speak to me no more on that head," said Bernard Varley. "If I am mad in my exceeding love for Miranda Rankley, mad I shall remain until my dying hour. It is in vain you argue with me, Twitter; my adoration of the angelic beauty of Miranda will overcome all your reasonings. Say no more; it is in vain."

Samuel Twitter groaned aloud as he thought to himself, "It is, indeed, in vain."

Varley then left the room, and the trembling Twitter was again alone.

"What will become of me?" he said. "How shall I carry into effect my intentions? Escape I must from the fearful meshes around me. To tarry were certain destruction, for Bernard Varley will be warned by no one, and soon, too soon, will he commit himself in some manner which will bring destruction to us both. It may be then, at the last moment, he will begin to see his own danger, and adopt those means of escape which his wily nature has pointed out to him, leaving me to perish as the victim at once of his indiscretion, and his crimes. There is no other resource. I must rob him, and that quickly, too, to as great an extent as possible, and then make my escape with the proceeds. Yes, that yacht at Liverpool shall serve my turn instead of his. That were a deep trick to serve Bernard Varley, and it shall be played."

CHAPTER LXXXVIII.

THE PREPARATIONS FOR DEPARTURE—THE MANIAC—AN UNEXPECTED INTERRUPTION.

As the midnight hour drew near, Miranda made her hasty preparations for leaving York.

The few articles of apparel she had to take with her, were easily confined within the compass of a small bundle; and, before the hour of eleven had struck, she had everything in readiness for her long journey.

Of the road to London she knew nothing. All her information extended merely to which direction out of York she intended to go, and now her greatest anxiety arose,—namely, to get Mr. Percy, in his present state of mind, to comprehend the object of the journey, and to set about it cheerfully.

An hour or so previously she had persuaded him to rise, and he had been seated some time in the front room, gazing with meaningless eyes upon the preparations she was making.

Then the Minster clock chimed the quarter past eleven, and a solemn stillness seemed to reign about the ancient city.

From eleven to nearly twelve, in all large towns, is generally a quiet period, for many persons then are at home for the night, while those who are accustomed to later hours, are either making merry at the houses of their friends, or shut up in the various places of public amusement, which, not until a much later hour, would disgorge their multitudes.

Occasionally a footfall sounded down the narrow street in which Miranda resided; for as we know, there were persons in that street, whose attention was wholly and solely fixed upon the one house then inhabited by that persecuted and noble-hearted girl.

Of them we shall speak anon; but let us, for the present, listen to the gentle Miranda, as with quiet earnestness she urged Mr. Percy to be up and stirring.

Approaching him, clasping her hand affectionately upon his arm, she said, in a low, soft voice:

"Shall we seek Rowland? He is sighing for us, and shall we not seek him?"

"You were speaking of my dear boy," said the bereaved father, with a faint smile. "Say on, my darling Miranda—what of him?"

"I said that we should go to seek him," said Miranda. "He is far, very far from us, and shall we not go to him? He is very lonely without us, and who else can love him as we love him?—who anticipate his slightest wishes as we shall?—who watch over him as we should watch? Let us go to him, Mr. Percy—let us go to seek Rowland."

"Yes, yes," replied Mr. Percy, "you say well, Miranda. We will seek him. Come, let us hasten. It seems long since I have seen him."

"It is long," said Miranda. "Time counted by sighs is ever long."

"And then, besides," said Mr. Percy, "I have had some dreams of him that have vexed me sorely. I thought they wished to hang my boy; and, although I know they have not, for you have told me so, I would fain see him with my own eyes, and assure myself that he is well."

"Hark!" said Miranda, "do you know that sound?"

"It is the Minster clock," said the old man; "I have heard it often. What is the hour, Miranda?"

"It is half an hour to midnight," she said; "see here, Mr. Percy, is your hat and cloak. Will you come with me?"

"To the world's end," said the prematurely aged man, as he rose from his seat. "To the world's end, beautiful Miranda, I will come with thee."

With anxious eyes Miranda watched his steps as he crossed the room. His gait was infirm and faltering, and she asked herself, with a deep sigh, "can he bear the fatigue of the journey I contemplate? Can he, in his debilitated state, ever reach London? Alas! —alas!—Heaven must speedily assist us, or we perish!"

"Come, Miranda," he said. "Come, are we not going to my boy Rowland? Is it very far?"

"It is," said Miranda; "but we have time, and can take the journey at our leisure."

"Why not order the carriage?" said the old man. "Where are my servants? The idle knaves fatten on one's bounty, and then refuse their service when most needed. Where are they now? Call them, Miranda— call them! My voice is, perhaps, too weak and old."

Miranda uttered a deep sigh ere she replied, and then she said:

"Oh, bethink you, Mr. Percy, there has been a sad reverse of fortune. Do you not recollect, we are not as we were? Our hopes are blighted, our fortune is not merely decayed, but gone. What is to become of us Heaven only knows, but we are fighting against great and deep calamities."

"Calamities—calamities?" he said.

"Yes," added Miranda, "you will surely recollect."

"Dreams, dreams," said the old man. "Why will you let dreams disturb you? Banish these idle fancies, Miranda, and order the carriage."

Miranda felt for a few moments utterly hopeless, for if such feelings were to continue in the breast of Mr. Percy, how was she to hope that he would calmly accompany her the long and weary distance from York to London.

Then a thought struck her, that by perhaps gently humouring his malady, she might succeed better than by attempting to awaken memory, or by reasoning with a shattered intellect.

"Listen to me, Mr. Percy," she said, "Rowland is in very great danger."

"Danger!" echoed Mr. Percy, "my son in great danger?"

"Yes, he has many and bitter enemies."

"Gracious Heaven!" said the old man.

"But be not too much afflicted," hastily added Miranda, "he has already gained one great victory over them, and, by caution, he may escape their machinations altogether."

"Ay, caution," said the old man, while his face assumed that peculiar expression so characteristic of the insane, when they think themselves peculiarly cunning. "Caution is the word—we must be very cautious. We must use much art, and, as you say, with care and caution, he may be saved."

"For that object," said Miranda, "we will dispense with the carriage."

"Of course," said Mr. Percy, "they would laugh at us for being foolish were we to take it. We will send it another way, Miranda, and they will follow it. So shall we save Rowland. They will know the gray horses in a moment. Yes, we will be very cautious— and we shall save him."

"Come, then," said Miranda, as she assisted the old man on with an ample cloak, which he had often worn in happier days.

"I will follow you," he said. "You are my guardian angel, for you will save Rowland, and in so doing, you will save me; but, Miranda, yet a moment tarry."

"What would you say?" said Miranda.

"Will not your father miss you?" said the old man; "he is apt to be hasty of temper, and of late I do not think we have been such good friends as we used to be. Tell me, Miranda, think you he will not miss you?"

"I am sure he will not," said Miranda. "Come, Mr. Percy, come."

"That is well," he muttered, as he followed her down the staircase.

There was no obstruction to their passing to the street-door, but when that was opened, Miranda saw by the dim light of a neighbouring lamp, that someone was sitting upon the steps.

She instinctively shrank back, saying to Mr. Percy:

"Hush, not a word! Wait here a moment."

"Is that an enemy of Rowland's?" whispered Mr. Percy.

"I know not," said Miranda, "but will quickly ascertain. For Heaven's sake, be still."

These few words passed in much less time than it has taken to record them, and while they were being spoken, the person who was seated on the step, appeared to be aware, from the sudden opening of the door, of the necessity of rising.

In another moment the huge form of Jones, in his female apparel, presented itself to the eyes of Miranda, and she instantly pronounced his name.

"Yes, mum," said Jones, "it's me. Is yer serious?"

"What mean you?"

"I means, does yer really mean to notch yer blessed mahogany, and mizzle from York?"

"I am even now about to start on my weary journey," said Miranda.

"Then just wait till I comes to yer again, or else you'll be watched like one o'clock, and never lost sight of by those who wouldn't do you a good turn on any account."

"Do the officers, then, keep so watchful an eye on my movements?" said Miranda.

"Rayther," said Mr. Jones. "Mum's the word, and keep the door shut."

"I will wait," said Miranda; "but think you it will be long?"

"Ten minutes ought to settle the hash," said Mr. Jones; "but I thinks as it'll be out an' out cooked before that ere time. Shut the door, and if anybody comes, give 'em an ewasive answer."

"An evasive answer?" said Miranda.

"Yes; tell 'em you wasn't born yesterday, and to take it out o' nothink."

Mr. Jones then walked away from the door, and as Miranda could not see what was passing outside, we will, with the privilege accorded to faithful historians, place before the reader what there occurred.

As we are well aware that Miranda had not stirred from home the whole of the day, the active watch of the two constables set on by the magistracy had been signally unproductive of any results.

They had continued to relieve each other at stated intervals, and those intervals happened to be at the even hours; that is to say, there was a change of guard at ten o'clock, and there would be another at twelve, so that while Miranda was making preparations for her departure from York, one of the constables was pacing to and fro in the street, now and then dodging round the corner, and taking sly looks to see if he were observed: then getting up into a doorway for a time, and occasionally skulking behind a pump that was in the street, all of which proceedings, it so happened, excited a great deal of anxiety and suspicion in the minds of every person but those most intimately connected with his proceedings: for although Miranda never saw the active officer dodging and fretting about the street, there were others of its inhabitants who did.

Many and alarming, then, were the speculations which the phenomenon gave rise to, and on that eventful evening many shutters were fastened that were never fastened before, and divers intricate and ingenious fastenings were resorted to for dilapidated doors.

The bottom bolts of street-doors were shot with suspicious energy, though usually left undone, because people do so hate stooping, and the bottom bolt, moreover, always screams for want of use, and awakens the children.

It seemed as if society in that street was seized with a mania of apprehension as regarded that solitary man, and were determined to lock him out, and bar him out, and bolt him out in every possible way.

In the meanwhile the officer fumed and fretted exceedingly, for it is very provoking to be extremely cunning, and careful, and watchful, and nothing come of it.

So much aggravated, indeed, was he at the apparent calmness of Miranda, and the absolute no notice she took of him, that at a quarter past eleven o'clock he came up to the door and gave utterance to a great volley of oaths, which seemed to have a sedative effect upon his system, for he sat down upon the next step, and only came out with a hearty curse occasionally.

Now it happened that, as he there sat, he saw a man with very suspicious movements, creep down the street, and when he came near the pump before mentioned, make a great rush and dodge behind it, as if he had suddenly achieved something very wonderful, and executed some feat of exceeding cleverness.

"What's the meaning of that, I wonder?" muttered the officer. "There's something going on now, I'll be bound. If this infernally provoking Miss What's-her-name won't come out, I may find out something else quite as well worth looking after."

He saw the man behind the pump slowly and carefully peep out several times in the direction of the door of Miranda's house, and then suddenly draw back his head again, as if he expected a knock upon it from some invisible agency, if he kept it too long in that extremely artful position.

"I'll learn what he's bobbing about there

for," said the officer; "or else I'll know the reason why"

Advancing, then, carefully under cover of the pump itself, until he stood close to it, he waited till the head should again peer forth, and the moment it did he gave it a little rap with the stick he held in his hand, which so alarmed the owner that, with a cry of murder, he fell in a very complicated manner into the sink, producing a great rattling with the chain and the ladle, which, having been put up the week before, had not yet been stolen for old iron, as is the general fate of such public conveniences.

Immediately upon this successful achievement, the officer rushed round the pump, and seized the mysterious individual, crying:

"Hilloa! hilloa! my man, what do you do here? Come, let me see your face; perhaps I may know you. I suppose there's some robbery put up to-night?"

"Bless my heart and soul, is that you, Green?" said the man.

"Yes, I am Green," said the officer; "who are you?"

"Kiggs—Kiggs—don't you know me? I'm Kiggs."

"Cuss it," said the officer, "I know you now; but what are you skulking about here for? making yourself ridiculous by playing at bo-peep with the pump. Kiggs, old fellow, I'm afraid you're arter no good."

"No good, ain't I?" said Kiggs. "Half-a-guinea a day, and skulk as much as you like."

"Why, what do you mean?"

"Just this," replied Kiggs, confidentially. "I heard that Mr. Varley wanted someone to keep an eye on the young woman as lives here—she who got the chap, who was a-going to be hanged, out of the condemned cell. So I called upon him, and told him I had been occasional messenger about the courts for some time, and was up to a thing or two, and he gave me the situation."

"Indeed!"

"And it's not so bad, neither—is it?"

"I wish mine was half as good. Here have I been watching all day long almost, and it only comes into regular duty."

"More flat you," said Kiggs. "I took my situation this morning; and, when I did, Mr. Varley he says to me, 'I will come between eleven and twelve myself and relieve your watch, while you go home and take a few hours' repose.' So, you see, I've just come to meet him, for I haven't been here afore. Let him watch himself—let him look after the young woman himself—let him——"

"But you forget the half-guinea a-day, Kiggs," said the officer.

"Do I?" said Kiggs. "Catch me forgetting it, that's all. Hilloa! hilloa! hi! hi! look! look!——"

"What's the matter?" said the officer, turning round twice or thrice, like a man about to play at blind man's buff.

"On the steps," said Kiggs.

"The deuce!" said the officer.

"Much the same—a woman," said Kiggs.

"A fine woman, I should say. Blessed if she didn't shake the area rails when she sat down."

"The deuce she did!" said the officer.

Mr. Kiggs and Mr. Green then both hid themselves behind the pump, and, peeping one from each side of it, kept up a steady stare at Mr. Jones, who sat with great composure on Miranda's door-step.

CHAPTER LXXXIX.

MR. JONES AND THE OFFICERS—A DELICATE FEMALE—THE ATTACK AND THE ESCAPE.

"Who is it?" said Kiggs, in a mysterious manner.

"Don't know," replied Green. "Hark! she's a-singing."

To relieve the tedium of his waiting for Miranda, Mr. Jones hummed an air.

"Is it the young lady?" said Kiggs.

"Don't be a fool," said Green. "That female horse-marine could put Miss Miranda Rankley in her pocket."

"Hark!" said Kiggs. "She's a-singing again."

"Stash his whining, tap his nob;
Grab his ticker, it's in his fob.
Fal de ral, te tidy, tidy,
Kim up, fol de ridy,"

said Jones.

"What an extraordinary song for a female," said Kiggs.

"Rather," said Green; "but what a voice, too."

"I say," said Kiggs, "let's go over to the other side of the way, under *kiver* of the pump, and then cross over the end of the street, and walk past her as if we were thinking of nothink, and have a look at her."

Mr. Green thought this a good and reasonable proposal, so he accordingly adopted it, and he and Mr. Kiggs crossed over the road, as had been suggested by the latter gentleman.

Some good fortune did appear to be waiting on Miranda's flight, for it was just then that she opened the door, and held the short conversation with Mr. Jones which we have recorded in the preceding chapter.

By the time Kiggs and Green arrived at the door, Mr. Jones was again seated upon the step, but this time he had drawn a black veil partially over his face, and, exactly as they passed, he made a singular sound with his mouth, which sounded more like "kick" than anything else, and added, whilst he saluted Mr. Green across the ankles with a stick:

"My dear, are you good-natured?"

"Cuss you!" said Green, rubbing his shins; "what do you mean by that? I'll have you taken up."

"Oh, don't—oh, don't!" said Mr. Jones, in a tone of affected dismay. "I'm an unfortunate female—oh, don't!"

"What an extraordinary creature," said

Kiggs. "Come, get up. You can't sit there."

"Oh, you little sneaking, snivelling, never-grow-fat-must-be-hung-parish-brought-up wretch. Is that the way you speak to the fair sex?"

"Who are you?" asked Green.

"Larn politeness, and ax my elbow," said Jones.

"I'll be hanged," said Kiggs, "if I don't think it's a man."

"Oh, oh, oh!" said Jones, with great affected horror, "to even me with a male cretur, and make me out an anti-female perduction. You murdering wretch, I'll be down upon you in a minute, kivey, kim up."

So saying, Mr Jones rose and presented to Kiggs such Amazonian proportions, that he fairly ran away, leaving Mr. Green to stand the brunt of the contest as best he might.

Even he retreated two or three doors off, and had a passing thought that he had better leave the unfortunate female alone, but before he could settle his reflections into any form of action, Mr. Jones made a rush at him, at the same time that he made so exact an imitation of a dog being run over, that the officer was fairly bewildered, and knew not how, or when it occurred, but he found himself suddenly seized by the arms and legs, and carried with great rapidity down the street by two men, who had started from Heaven knows where.

"Ri fol-de-di-di-dol-di-di," said Mr. Jones, "their geeses is cooked."

"Thieves! thieves!"

"What's the matter?" said a voice from a window.

"Nothing," said Jones, as he threw a handful of mud in the speaker's face; "it's rather a dirty night, mum, that's all."

The head withdrew with a faint scream, and down went the window.

"Curiosity," soliloquized Mr. Jones, "is a very great failing—people often brings themselves to the dirt by that ere, and if they doesn't, why it's wery proper that the dirt should be brought to them. All's right now, and Miss Miranda may now be off without nobody seeing of her. I didn't think I could have come it half so well. One-eyed Bill says as how I wasn't delicate enough for a female, and what's the consekins, I have done it quite astonishing, and there's flukey Joe and the badger will carry that unfortunate officer to the blessed sewer as is under repair; it's not above five feet-six deep, and I think he is about five feet-eight, so he cannot come to much harm—a miss is as good as a mile I have heard say, and two inches is a pretty good miss."

Thus speaking, Mr. Jones reached Miranda's door, at which he tapped carefully with his knuckles.

Miranda heard him, and then immediately answered the summons.

"All's right," said Jones. "Come out, now, and take the direct road to London. You won't be quite deserted, for a friend of mine will keep on your track, just to give anyone a nobbler who may make themselves disagreeable the first mile or two."

"I am much beholden to you," said Miranda, "and shall never forget the service you have rendered me."

"Bother that," said Jones; "good-night, and good luck to you."

Miranda turned to Mr Percy, and taking him by the arm, said:

"Come, Mr. Percy, we will now go and seek for Rowland."

"Yes, yes," muttered the old man, "we will seek Rowland—my boy Rowland—we will seek him and save him from his enemies."

Mr. Jones darted away, and in another moment Miranda and her helpless companion stood houseless wanderers beneath the canopy of Heaven.

———

CHAPTER XC.

THE SLUMBERING CITY—THE WANDERERS— THE WALK FROM YORK—THE ALARM.

THE street was very dull and quiet. Scarcely a breath of air was stirring, and Miranda assured herself, by one glance, that she and her aged companion were the only living beings within sight.

She placed her arm within that of Mr. Percy, and gently led him down the street, now and then, as she went, talking to him of Rowland, in order to keep him still assured of the object of the journey.

"You know where to find him, Miranda?" he said. "You are quite sure you know where to find Rowland?"

"I am," was her reply. "It will take us a long while, Mr. Percy; but that matters little—we have ample time before us."

"Yes, we have," he said. "You are right, Miranda; we have ample time. Wherefore should we not? Who should control our actions?"

"No one," said Miranda. "See, Mr. Percy, the night is brightening, and we shall have pleasant weather for our journey."

"But, Miranda," said Mr. Percy, "I must still think of your father. You know he is scornful and proud of heart. Will not his anger be great to find that you have gone without his knowledge?"

It was a terrible grief to Miranda to hear this constant allusion to her father, whose unhappy fate she would fain have forgotten; but she controlled all expression of her own feelings, merely saying:

"No, Mr. Percy, there will be no danger from him. Think no more on that subject—let all your attention be directed to Rowland. There will be no anger from my father."

"I am glad to have that assurance," said Mr. Percy, "for he is apt to be choleric; and was ever proud of heart—so much so as to obscure at times some of his better qualities. But which of us is perfect?"

"Which, indeed," she said, mournfully; "but, thank Heaven, we are unpursued, and the night is brightening. Come, Mr. Percy,

THE QUAKER BARS THE PROGRESS OF MIRANDA AND MR. PERCY.

can you hasten for a short space, that we may get beyond the suburbs of this old city, and walk onwards more freely in the open country?"

Mr. Percy made no reply, but walked quietly and sadly by the side of Miranda. Now and then he murmured something about his Rowland—remarks that needed no reply, although his dejected companion invariably made some gentle answer, calculated to soothe his perturbed feelings, and cheer him with renewed hopes—hopes which she scarcely felt herself, but which certainly grew more full of reality as she uttered them to him.

There was evidently no pursuit, for, as the strangely-assorted pair passed from street to street in the outskirts of the city, Miranda often looked back, and as often felt assured that they were unobserved.

It was a weary time before the houses diminished in numbers, and becoming interspersed here and there with garden walls and patches of sweet, green verdure, announced that the city was being left behind, and that the open country was near at hand.

Miranda felt her spirits grow lighter the further she proceeded from York, for what had that ancient city presented to her lately but scenes of unhappiness and terror? Soon, too soon, however, the saddest reflections began to cross her mind concerning the depressed state of her fortunes, and as she felt in the breast of her clothing to assure herself of the safety of the little purse—a gift from Rowland Percy in happier days—in which she had placed the thirteen shillings, which comprised now all her worldly wealth, except a few half-pence, for some petty expenses during the day had swallowed up the small sum she had calculated upon over the five-pound note, she asked herself the often-repeated question of:

"How shall we travel nearly two hundred miles upon this small sum?" And with an additional pang to her already burthened heart, she told herself that it must surely happen that her father's ring must be parted with to provide the exigencies of the journey.

Slowly and wearily Miranda and old Mr. Percy made their way along the broad highroad, until at length a dim streak of gray light could be observed on the eastern horizon.

Mr. Percy gazed long and earnestly at this first dim intimation of the coming day, and then, in the same saddened, quiet tone in which he usually addressed Miranda, he said:

"Have we far to go, Miranda, to seek my boy? I am weary, I pray you let me rest awhile—the pleasant and beautiful day is coming; let us watch it, Miranda, it will well repay the trouble."

"Nay, you forget," said Miranda, "we have very far to go. Very—very few of the many weary miles that we must traverse, ere we reach Rowland, are already passed. Oh, bethink you, Mr. Percy, how far we have to go, and let us walk on, however gently."

"Hark, hark!" said Mr. Percy, whose external senses, like those of many persons in his unhappy state of mind, seemed preternaturally acute—"Hark! I hear the sound of horses' feet; the trot is a sharp one, just such a goaded trot as when the rider is in haste, or angry."

"I hear nothing," said Miranda. "Whence comes the sound?"

"There," said Mr. Percy, as he pointed up the road in the direction of London; "it comes from there."

"Thank Heaven," said Miranda, "if there really be horsemen approaching; so that they do not come from York, I have no apprehensions."

"But hark!" again said the old man; "there come sounds from York."

Almost at the same moment Miranda heard the sound of wheels from the neighbourhood of the city, and the heavy beat of the horses' feet, which Mr. Percy's acuter perceptions enabled him to hear before her, rapidly approaching in the opposite direction.

"Let us draw aside," she said. "It is unlikely that these persons are either friends or foes to us; they will pass us as mere wayfarers on the road, heeding not whence we come nor whither we are going."

The sky was just sufficiently light to enable Miranda, as she looked in the direction of York, to be aware that some vehicle was approaching, but what it was she could not ascertain, although from the dreadful rattle it kept up, and the occasional screaming of the wheels, and a perpetual jolt, jolt, jolt, at each trot of the horse, she guessed that it was of a very common description, and most probably belonged to some of the market people, going from York to the large orchards in the vicinity.

The sound of the horses' feet became suddenly much more subdued, for the mounted party were ascending an eminence at a walk, which enabled the small, dilapidated cart, for such it was that was coming from York, to reach Miranda and Mr. Percy some few minutes before the horsemen who were approaching from the opposite direction.

Whoever was driving the miserable horse, that with a convulsive sort of trot, as if kept in a perpetual state of galvanism, was approaching, seemed extremely jolly over it, for he was bellowing forth, with great strength of lungs, a popular ballad.

There was something about the tones of the voice which Miranda thought she knew, and as the vehicle came still nearer, she became convinced that it could be no other than Mr. Jones himself, who was proceeding with such glee.

Rough and uncouth as he was, a sense of pleasure came over Miranda's mind as she heard him approaching, for she felt sure then that there was one friendly heart at hand, although what was his errand out of York she knew not, but that it in some manner concerned her and her fortunes, she at once supposed.

"There is, at all events, one friendly person approaching," she said, to Mr. Percy; "one from whom we shall receive as much active sympathy and good will as it may be in his power to render us."

Mr. Jones, for it was, indeed, he, appeared to have seen Miranda and Mr. Percy, and he made an attempt to bring his sorry steed up to the spot where they stood, with some degree of *éclat*, and rather sharply; but the horse had not understood anything of that kind for many years, and resisted with all his might and main, sometimes backing a little towards York, then dodging from one side of the road to the other, and altogether exhibiting in the most determined manner his indisposition to proceed otherwise than by the spasmodic looking jerks, which he no doubt considered a famous trot, and one fully entitling him to great admiration and a handful of beans.

"Cuss you!" said Mr. Jones. "Do you think I stole yer? Infernal wretch! I only borrowed yer for a mile or two. You've had it all your own way, and be hanged to yer! and made my wery inside sore with that ere patent trot of yourn. What a invention that is! You shouldn't be so ingenious. Cuss yer! take that, and be hanged to yer. Oh, you wretch! I suppose you're over forty, if yer a bit."

Whether it was Mr. Jones's verbal remonstrances, or the application of a stick which had the effect, we cannot say; but certain it was that suddenly the horse made a great dart forwards, and so unexpected was that dart to Mr. Jones, that sitting, as he had been, upon a little piece of board, suspended by two straps, he, in the most scientific manner, as regarded the laws of momentum and inertia, lifted up his feet in front, as if he was doing it on purpose, and fell on the flat of his back in the cart.

The horse incontestibly would have had it all his own way now had he chosen to indulge in any vagaries; but, as the height of his ambition was to strike work whenever he could, he stopped exactly by a milestone, which, by the drooping of his head, and the watery twinkle of his one eye, he appeared to be reading attentively.

"Well, I'm blowed!" said Mr. Jones, struggling to his feet, and rubbing the back of his head, "there's blood for yer. I supposes, old boy, as you used up the last drop of that ere in executing this manoeuvre. Oh, cuss yer! Another time just cut up that ere bolt into small bits, and make a trot of it. Miss Miranda, mum! I thought I'd catch yer. I've been a-taking off my female toggery, and I's no longer the delicate cretur I was. 'I am rough and ready,' as the file remarked to the old nail. This ere's my carriage—leastways, it is mine, only the owner keeps me out of it, and is vexatious enough to carry his own greens and 'taters in it, just as if there was no such indiwidual as me breathing. I thought you and the old gentleman would like a lift just as far as this ere rum combination of an old door-mat and a bundle of sticks they call a hoss is capable of taking yer. Hallo! what's that?"

The horsemen, who were approaching from the direction of London, had now ascended the brow of the hill, and, suddenly increasing their speed, were coming, at a rapid pace, in the direction where Miranda and Mr. Percy were standing.

"Somebody's coming in a hurry," added Mr. Jones. "Woa, Buonaparte, don't you be arter being too fiery. I call him Buonaparte, mum, because it strikes me he's used up his inside, mum."

"If," said Miranda, "you can expedite us even a mile upon our journey, we shall be grateful, more especially so near York as we still are."

"I doesn't make the smallest doubt, mum, that Buonaparte will manage a mile if he's well walloped, and we must manage to do that ere among us. Just get in, mum."

"Let those horsemen," said Miranda, "pass us first. I do not know that it is so, but something seems to whisper to me that there is danger from them."

"Danger," said Mr. Jones, "they're not coming the right road for that, Miss Miranda."

"I do not know," said Miranda: "but I have a presentiment of evil from their approach."

"They're in a passion, howsomdever," said Mr. Jones. "Hark how they are a cussing."

CHAPTER XCI.

THE RETURN OF THE OFFICERS—ROWLAND IN SAFETY—MR. JONES AND BUONAPARTE A BIT OF BLOOD.

THE horsemen were, in a few moments, close to Mr. Jones and his cart, when, drawing up, the foremost of them cried, in a loud voice:

"Hilloa—do you come from York?"

"Yes, spoony," said Jones, "I do; where do you come from?"

"Come, come," said the man, "no insolence nor nonsense. What's the news?"

"'Taters is riz," said Jones, "and greens is fell."

"Curse your impertinence," said the horseman: "I want to know if anything's been heard of Rowland Percy, the murderer?"

"I believe yer," said Jones, "ever such a lot."

"Indeed!" said the horseman: "and here have we been on a fool's errand half-way to London."

"Well, if I didn't think as much," said Jones. "I judges of people wery much by their looks, and I should say that's just the way you does your messages, old feller."

"Come, come, my man," said the officer, "you may earn a crown, and perhaps more, by being civil. What is known as regards Rowland Percy at York?"

"You want to know what's know'd?" said Jones.

"Of course I do," said the officer.

"Ah, then, there you have me," said Jones. "You asked me what has been heard. There has lots o' things been heard, and nothink knowed."

"You're an impertinent fellow," said the officer.

"Yes," said Jones, dryly, "I comes from York. You're a clever, bustling sort of fellow in your way, but your ears are so precious long, and, when yer brays into the bargain, people thinks as yer a hass—that's yer way—the first public-house as yer comes to is the 'Cat's Tail and a Drumstick'—get yourself a pint, and tell 'em to score it up to nobody. Who did yer steal that ere hoss from? Is yer mother out of jail yet? What did yer get for that ere copper? Did they bone yer father's toggery when he was hung? How about them silver candlesticks?"

The officer could make no head against this, which Mr. Jones denominated chaff, but shouting "Come on!" to his companions, he merely added, in a threatening tone to Jones:

"If I were not better engaged, my man, I'd take you up."

To this Mr. Jones's only reply was an imitation of the braying of a donkey, which awakened echo far and wide, and so alarmed the old horse in the cart, that he suddenly woke up, and nearly shook his head.

"Now, Miss Miranda," said Jones, "I'm glad I was with yer when we met those chaps, or perhaps you wouldn't have found out that they had been to London, or nearly as far, after Rowland Percy."

"Indeed!" said Miranda; "then, of course, they have missed him. How could that be? for, doubtless, they have ridden harder than he could hope to travel."

"Dick Palmer must have managed that somehow," said Jones; "leave him alone for a bit of cleverness of that kind; there ain't much danger now, for this chap that spoke to me, though he asked such green questions, is about as good an officer as they have in York."

"Then you think he will escape?" said Miranda.

"He has a better chance than ever. The chase to London is given up, that's quite clear, and they'll be hunting in every hole and corner in York, while he's as safe as he can be."

"Is it of my son Rowland you speak?" said Mr. Percy.

"Yes, old gentleman," said Jones.

"Go to my house, then, and tell them to give you of the best—tell them to stint nothing in your entertainment. I'm going now to find my son Rowland, of whom you have just spoken; when I return, you shall be amply rewarded. You have an honest countenance."

"You mustn't take folks by their looks," replied Jones. "It's true I isn't a lawyer, or a parson, or any of them ere perlite perfessions, but I don't purtend to be more honester than my neighbours; but just please to get into this ere cart, and arter that I'll give you a leg up, Miss Miranda, and we may, by dint of uncommon persuasion, get Buonaparte to toddle."

With the assistance of Mr. Jones, Miranda and old Mr. Percy were seated in the frail vehicle, and Buonaparte, after some active persuasions, was induced to start at the extraordinary rate of three miles and a-half an hour.

Miranda felt the cold morning air acutely in that vehicle—the child of luxury as she had been so long, and accustomed to have every and the slightest wish gratified. Even at the slow rate they were then travelling, she felt the air blow keenly and sharply around her, and she shuddered several times.

Poor old Mr. Percy, although his mind was so dreadfully shattered by the misfortunes he had gone through, and the ruin which had fallen upon him and his, was still alive to anything that affected Miranda, and taking off his cloak, he insisted upon wrapping it round her, which she reluctantly permitted him to do, for he was otherwise but lightly clad.

"Here's a potato sack," said Jones, raking about in the bottom of the cart till he found one; "put that on, old gentleman, I'm blest if you won't look like an ancient Roman."

"I will," said Mr. Percy, "I will. It will be a disguise, too, against my enemies. Yon horsemen were seeking our lives, Miranda, and how thankful should we be that they were not successful in finding Rowland."

"Now, Miss Miranda," said Jones, in a low voice, so that Mr. Percy should not hear—"now that Buonaparte is taking it easy up this ere hill, tell me how are you off for the mopuses?"

"The what?" said Miranda.

"The tin—the dust—the coal—the pony, I mean."

"Do you mean money?" inquired Miranda, having an indistinct recollection of hearing it called tin once before.

"Yes, I does."

"Then I have very little, indeed, and must husband well my small resources."

"Have you got enough to get to London with?"

"Far from it, without parting with a ring of my father's, which—which I would fain keep, at least, until some very great exigency indeed."

"Oh, bother selling the ring," said Mr. Jones.

"But what else am I to do?"

"Wery good, we'll take a thought of that ere. Kim up, Buonaparte. Oh, you wretch, don't be purtending as you haven't got on the level. Now, what do yer see down that ere blessed drain? nothing, I'll be bound—it's only one of your wicious excuses."

Buonaparte seemed to have acquired a kind of dread of Jones, and upon the urgent remonstrances used to him, actually boldly stepped out six paces.

"This here wehicle," said Mr. Jones to Miranda, with the most unconcerned air imaginable, "and the singular cretur as walks afore it, was a standing at the corner of a street, so I guv the boy as was a minding on him a penny, and a bonneter, along with a solemn promise of tuppence, if he ever seed me agin—that ere being involved in great doubt; but I didn't diskiver as Buonaparte was such a rum 'un to go, till I got into the wehicle, and begun to wallop him."

"Good Heavens, Mr. Jones," said Miranda, "you don't mean to say that you stole this horse and cart?"

"Stole it, mum?" cried Jones. "I steal a consarn like this ere? I'd be ashamed to do it."

"But, Mr. Jones, you've confessed taking it from its owner."

"Wery good," said Jones. "I have sartinly took a loan of Buonaparte, and the bundle of old sticks as is miraculously holding together arter his tail, but as to stealing on 'em, oh, dear, no. If I stealed a horse and cart, I take care as they was genuine, and not a blessed one like this ere."

"But what will the owner do?" said Miranda.

"That's a curious speculation," said Mr. Jones. "My opinion is, he ought to be grateful, but I rayther think he'll run about like mad till Buonaparte comes back."

"Do you know who he is?" said Miranda.

"No, I don't; but, according to law, the name ought to be on the cart. But, if it isn't, I'll lay an information against the beast, and we'll divide the blessed penalty. Now, Buonaparte, what's the row? I'm blessed if he ain't getting aggrawated, and throwing his shoes away; there's one of 'em gone into that ere field just now."

The extreme coolness with which Mr. Jones took the capital felony he had committed, by the abstraction of Buonaparte and the vehicle, did not tend to assuage the alarm of Miranda, when she found that such was really the case; and to Mr. Jones's surprise, who thought her extremely fastidious, she expressed an earnest wish to quit the conveyance which had been so singularly obtained.

"Lor! bless you!" said Mr. Jones, "these ere things happen every day. I only wishes I had come across something worth borrowing, instead of this ere wretch. I had popped yer twenty or thirty miles on yer road in a twinkling. There goes another shoe. Cuss yer! You tried to throw that at my head, I know."

"I implore you to let us alight from this vehicle!" said Miranda. "My terror of pursuit is doubly increased by being here, and I do believe that the danger is far greater."

"Well, if so be you think so," said Jones, "you can get out. Let me see, we've been an 'our and three-quarters coming a matter of four miles. Well done, Buonaparte! If you don't die arter that ere unnatural exertion, you are an astonishing cretur."

Jones then assisted Miranda to alight, and when she and Mr. Percy were again on the roadside, he turned Buonaparte's head towards York. saying:

"Now, my high-mettled racer, you had better pick up yer shoes as yer go home, or you'll be accused of disposing of 'em in wice— you will. There, now cut."

Buonaparte seemed to understand this speech tolerably well, and at the same deliberate pace which there was no getting him out of, he went leisurely back to York.

"There's a willage," said Jones, "a couple of miles further ahead. You had better rest there, and take some breakfast; then walk on if I don't come. Depend upon seeing me again before long, however."

So saying, Mr. Jones pushed through a hedge, and walked off at a brisk pace across the fields to the right of the road.

CHAPTER XCII.

THE BREAKFAST AT THE VILLAGE INN— TOBIAS POPPLETON, ESQ., AND THE RIGHT OF PATHWAY—MIRANDA'S PROGRESS.

It was with a feeling of desolation that Miranda found herself again dependent upon her own resources and her own courage, with that aged and mind-stricken man. She determined, however, to follow the advice of Jones, and seek the village he mentioned.

On the whole, however, she found Mr. Percy bear up much better than she expected, under the fatigues of the journey. His debility began to leave him, and, by exercise, his physical powers seemed, in a great measure, to improve, instead of lessen.

He still, however, talked very incoherently, and in a low tone, as if communing with himself, rather than asking a question of Miranda. He would often say:

"Where is my boy Rowland? I wonder if we have far to go? It seems a weary way —a weary way."

Then Miranda would strive to cheer him, by directing his mind to other objects— although it is, indeed, a sad and heavy task for those who are careworn and full of anxiety themselves to minister comfort and consolation to others. It is only such noble natures as Miranda Rankley's that are equal to the task.

"Mr. Percy," she said, "you have been in London?"

"In London?—yes," he replied; "but that is very far from York."

"It is," she said. "Yet there must we go to meet Rowland. His enemies have forced him so far."

"To London—to London," muttered the old man—"a weary distance, indeed. Ah, Miranda, let us send for him. Nay, I will speak to your father myself. I will tell him to subdue the pride which has separated neighbours and friends. Yes, I will speak to him."

"Alas!" said Miranda, "let me tell you, Mr. Percy—once again, let me tell you—my poor father is not of this world."

"Sir George dead—Sir George dead!" said Mr. Percy—"impossible! But if so grievous a thing has happened, Miranda, you shall live with us, and we will make up to you in love for all the tenderness you have lost. But, see, someone is approaching. What manner of man is that?"

A singular-looking being was coming down the road, in the opposite direction from Miranda and Percy.

His attire was of that order which proclaims in every article the most elaborate and costly self-denial. His collarless coat proclaimed him a quaker, and his demure aspect, of course, showed how far above the vanities of the world he was.

Although it is possible that anyone inclined to be censorious might have detected in the general appointments of the man, and in his round, bluff face, abundant evidence that he had not wholly neglected the creature comforts, and had he (the censorious person) been quite wickedly inclined, he might have even gone so far as to intimate a suspicion which, of course, must be wrong, as quite opposed to the generally-received opinion, that the aforesaid quaker, like many of his brethren, was a painstaking humbug, making a trade of his piety and collarless coat, and succeeding wonderfully in taking in huge numbers of the population on the strength of a broad-brimmed hat.

In fact, we once heard a wicked and malevolent person say that quakers had so high a character for honest and upright dealing, that they could afford to be rogues for the next half-century, without being found out, except it was by troublesome and fidgety persons, who were always finding out everything, seeing farther into a mill-stone than their neighbours—persons wearing a kind of moral spectacles, that enables them quite to overlook a collarless coat and a broad-brimmed hat—persons who, with a species of mental gimlet, bore deep holes beneath the surface of society, and, peeping therein, make sad discoveries with regard to what things really are in point of distinction to what they seem.

These persons are apt, now and then, to proclaim that piety, whether real or assumed, covereth a multitude of sins—that there lurks many times under a white neckcloth, tied in the most evangelical manner, the most deadly hypocrisy; and that it is just possible a man who would not wear a collar to his coat on any account, nor have his garments of other colours than sober brown or black, may be a thundering rogue.

But people of this kind are very properly scouted by society at large, and considered very troublesome and disagreeable members thereof.

But to return from this digression:

The sombre-looking personage approached Miranda and Mr. Percy, saying to the latter:

"Friend, when thou gettest a little farther on thou wilt see a small gate, which leadeth across a dry path, and as it is in thy way, friend, thee may take that path unadvisedly, seeing that the road is uncommonly muddy and dirty. Now, friend, that path leadeth by a circumbendibus to my house, although it hath a branch which leadeth to the high-road again. Now, I desire that thee and the young maiden will walk in the road, instead of using that path; for, truly, I wish to keep it clean for my own feet, for, verily, as thee are already muddy, thee might as well go on in the road."

"Can you be so selfish," said Miranda, "wearing the garb you do, and professing such great charity as you do, as to wish to turn us from a few hundred yards of pleasant walking?"

"Oh," said the quaker, turning up his eyes in great horror, "I perceive, maiden, that thee art one of the scoffers and the mockers, although my worldly eyes do tell me thee art beautiful, and thee mayest walk with me up the path, while the old sinner who is with thee may walk in the road."

"Who are you, man," said Mr. Percy, "that you dare speak thus to one who, although she considers not that piety and the love of Heaven may be expressed by the colour and cut of the apparel, is as far above you as are the heavens above the earth. You are one of my boy Rowland's enemies, or you would not talk in such a strain."

"Come, come," said Miranda. "Come, Mr. Percy, do not speak to him."

"Tarry a moment," said Mr. Percy, as if in deep thought. "The world is taught many things by examples, and now I will make an example of this man, to teach them to despise mock piety."

"Murder—help—police!" said the quaker, as Mr. Percy advanced a step towards him, and then turning round, he set off at a most unquakerly speed—for they never drive anything hard but a horse or a bargain—towards his own house.

"How dare that man," said Mr. Percy, with great vehemence, "insult us thus! How dare he address us as he has done! He has gone to injure Rowland, and I must after him and slay him—death—death——"

Miranda was greatly alarmed at the excited manner of Mr. Percy, and it took her much pains to soothe and subdue the irritation which had been produced in his mind by the man of peace, who, with such rare philanthropy, wished to turn them into the road from the pleasant path.

The distance to the village mentioned by Mr. Jones was now not great, and it was with a thankful heart that Miranda saw the little cluster of houses peeping among the trees, and showing their white fronts and old gable ends.

"We shall rest there," she said. "We shall rest in yonder village, Mr. Percy; for there the only friend on whom we can rely has promised to meet us."

The village was soon gained, and the wayfarers sat down in the neatly-sanded parlour in the one ale-house to partake of the morning meal, which, after the, to them, long walk, they were much in need of.

The exercise seemed materially to have benefited Mr. Percy's health, and Miranda thought, with deep thankfulness to Heaven, that she detected less incoherence in his manner than while he was in York.

She was most anxious for the arrival of Jones, as expedition upon their journey was to her a matter of vast importance.

And not long had she to await him; for, within half-an-hour after their own arrival in the village, he walked into the parlour.

There was an air of disappointment about Mr. Jones which was fully observable to Miranda, and to her it was a great relief that she found it proceeded only from an inability on his part to supply them with money, for Miranda had been fearful that something had arisen in York to increase the peril of Rowland Percy, or render her own going more hazardous.

"I did hope, mum," said Jones, "to have downed with some dust when I seed you, but half-a-bull is the outside as I have got, and that won't go very far. Howsomdever, it'll cut up into two or three chops, and make an out-an'-out breakfast and lunch. There's a waggon coming by here in about an hour. He's not much of a spirit the feller as drives it, and he'd guv yer a lift if you was to frighten him into it; but, perhaps you objects to wiolence?"

"I certainly do," said Miranda: "and, I must say that I scarcely understand what you have been speaking about."

"Oh, I forget," said Mr. Jones. "That's the worst of not recollecting nothink. What I means is, I have only got half-a-crown; but, if you waits here for an hour or two, I shouldn't wonder but somebody will come along the road as'll lend me a trifle; leastways, you had better wait for the waggoner, and see if he'll give you a lift."

"We will wait for you," said Miranda; "we have too few friends not to heed the advice of those who still cling to us."

"How did you get this far?" said Mr. Jones, "for you have come a mile or two since I left you."

"We met with but one interruption," said Miranda, "and that was a quaker."

"A quaker!" cried Jones.

"Yes, he stopped us to prevent us taking a dry path, instead of the road, which was heavy and dirty."

"Confound his cat's meat," said Jones, "I know him, then; it's Tobias Poppleton; he's got an estate hereby, and makes an uncommonly good thing of being sleeping partner in half-a-dozen taverns in London."

"Indeed!" said Miranda; "it is strange, indeed, that there should be such a difference between what people profess and what people really do."

"Is it?" said Jones. "It strikes me it would be rayther unkimmon the other way; but, howsomdever, that quaker's guved me an idea, and not a bad one, neither. You wait here, Miss Miranda, until I come to you. I sha'n't be very long. How do yer get on, old gentleman?" to Mr. Percy. "Do you find yourself any better?"

"You are a rough, hardy fellow," said Mr. Percy. "I will give you a situation on my estate, for I think you mean well by Miranda; would you like to be a gamekeeper?"

"Yes, I should," said Jones; "but I am afeard I should keep all the fur and feather, so I begs to decline the situation at the present time, and thank you all the same, old commodore;" then turning to Miranda, in a low tone, he added: "There's nothing like humouring on him. I goes on the soothing system."

After that he hastily left the little alehouse, and proceeded rapidly on the road to York again.

Mr. Jones was not absent above an hour; but as, during that hour, his proceedings were more active and more amusing than Miranda's at the little ale-house, we will jog on pleasantly with him, in order to discover what was the idea which the mention of Mr. Tobias Poppleton had given rise to.

"The idea," he muttered, "of them ere quakers being such out-an'-out humbugs; it's enough to make a fellow savage, it is. I am bad enough, I daresay; but I ain't a quaker, at all events. I ain't come to that yet. There's a difference atween borrowing a trifle off people, whether they like it or not, and being an out-an'-out humbug, like Tobias Poppleton."

Mr. Jones, then, as he neared the quaker's

estate, saw no less a person than Tobias himself, sauntering up and down, acting as his own scarecrow in keeping people off the path, which was quite a public one, and no more for his private use than the King's highway.

"Oh, there he is," said Jones, "and a precious old pump he looks."

CHAPTER XCIII.

THE GIGANTIC WOMAN—THE HIGHWAY ROBBERY—THE SEASONABLE RELIEF—THE LIFT IN THE WAGGON.

As Mr. Jones uttered these words, he made his way through a gap in a hedge, and, being tolerably well screened from observation on the other side, he undid a bundle, which he had been carrying on a stick across his shoulders, and took out of it the female apparel in which he had figured so conspicuously in York.

There was the bonnet, too, but wrapped up to a perfectly flat shape, so that its appearance was by no means improved, and it had a very singular look indeed, when Mr. Jones bent about some of the wires with which it was provided, to make it what he called remarkably nobby.

The gown was easily slipped on, only, for the sake of convenience, it was hind part before, as Mr. Jones was not provided with a lady's maid to fasten the hooks and eyes; by the assistance, then, of a variety of handkerchiefs, which, by some means, Mr. Jones had become possessed of at the smallest possible expense, he contrived to hide his face and to tie on his bonnet.

"I wonder," he muttered, "if that ere Tobias Poppleton would mind lending a trifle to a distressed female. I don't see why I shouldn't try it on—so ere goes."

Mr. Jones recrossed the hedge, and appeared on the roadway as a gigantic female, a supplementary skirt of a different colour having been sewn on the dress, to make it long enough for him.

He then made directly up to Tobias Poppleton, who, being deeply engaged with his own thoughts, did not, for some minutes, perceive the singular apparition that was approaching him.

When, however, Tobias Poppleton did see him, he gave a great start, saying:

"Verily, in all my experience, I never saw such a woman; truly, she is nigh unto six feet high, and will make hideous marks upon the new path."

"How is you this blessed morning, sir?" said Jones. "Is this ere a civilized country? and do you think of letting a female like me pass you without so much as saying—'Oh, lady fair, where is you going?'"

"Begone, woman, begone," said Tobias, holding out his hands in horror.

"What, don't you know me?" said Jones. "Oh, you deceiver, I shall cry myself into fits. Don't you recollect Susanna?—how can you be such a brute—lend me a guinea."

"Verily, I know thee not," said the alarmed quaker; "go thy ways."

"You needn't look about you, Tobias," said Jones, "there's nobody near; and if you attempts to set up a shout, I shall put your head in Chancery in a minute. Just sit down and let's talk it over."

Here Mr. Jones introduced his stick so rapidly between Tobias's ankles, that that pious individual forthwith sat down with a great plump in some moist clay, while he looked at Mr. Jones with a rueful face, and muttered:

"Dreadful female! Art thee going to murder me?"

"No, I arn't," said Jones; "but I want to borrow a trifle. It's towards having the road scraped, so that the pathway as leads up to your house may not be trod upon; people must pay for their luxuries. Give us a guinea, or get up and be kicked."

"Yea, it striketh me," said Tobias, "that thee art on the high-road to the gallows."

"Never you mind about that ere," said Jones. "There's a good many little cross-footpaths as goes to that same spot; but here's somebody coming. Now, I tells you what, Mr. Tobias. If so be as you opens your mouth by way of saying anything but just what I tells you, there won't be so many quakers by one in this ere world. You understands me?"

To make his meaning more clear, Mr. Jones took from his pocket a clasp knife, which he opened with his teeth, and drew suddenly across the neckcloth of Mr. Tobias Poppleton with a threatening gesture.

"Mur—murder! Oh, spare my life!" said Mr. Tobias Poppleton.

"Very good," said Jones. "There's a fellow coming up on horseback, and if you don't say arter me just what I says, I'll cut your throat first, and manage him arterwards."

"I will—verily I will!" said Mr. Tobias Poppleton, with a groan; "for the preservation of my life, friend, I will even say after thee whatever profane things thee mayest put into my mouth."

The horseman who was coming up happened to know Tobias very well by sight, and his surprise was great on seeing the scrupulously-attired quaker sitting down in so miry a spot, to the great detriment of his drab inexpressibles, and he stared for some moments in astonishment at Tobias and Jones, neither of whom spoke.

At length the horseman ventured to say:

"How do you do, Mr. Poppleton?"

"Speak arter me," growled Jones, "or I'll cut your head off. Tell him to ax your elbow."

"Thee mayest ax my elbow, friend," said Tobias Poppleton, to the intense surprise of the horseman.

And he said "Sir?" with an inquiring tone, for he could scarcely believe his own ears.

"Has your mother sold her mangle?" whispered Jones.

"Hast thee mother parted with her mangle, friend?" said Tobias, in a groaning voice that betrayed great agony of mind.

"Bless my heart and soul, he must have taken a drop too much," said the horseman; "I never heard such a thing, or perhaps he's ill. How long has he been in this way, mum?" addressing Jones.

"As long as my arm, spoony," said Jones. "Where did you steal that ere hoss?"

"As long as my arm, friend," said Tobias, who thought himself bound to repeat what Jones said, on pain of having his throat cut. "Where did thee purloin that animal?"

"Ah, they are both drunk," said the man on horseback. "Mr. Tobias Poppleton, I couldn't have believed it of you, and nobody'll believe it when I tell them."

"Mizzle, you humbug. There you go with your eye out," said Jones.

"Thee must mizzle," said Tobias, "and proceed with thee eye out."

> "Oh, what's the use of grieving,
>   Since all the world—since all the world
> Must surely live by thieving.
>   To la looral, to la looral."

"Friend," said Tobias, with a groan:

> "What is the utility of grieving,
>   Since all the world, friend,
> Have to la rooral, friend, taken to thieving?"

"Now get up and dance," said Jones.

"Verily, I cannot," said Tobias, "for I have stuck deep into the clay."

"Gracious!" cried the man, "who would have believed it? Mr. Tobias Poppleton is undoubtedly drunk."

"Oh, he's all right," said Jones; "I am his new housekeeper, and we hob and nob a little now and then. It's as right as a trivet, ain't it, Toby?"

"Ay, truly," said Tobias, "as correct as a trivet."

"Well," said the horseman, "it's no business of mine. Good-morning."

"Call him back," said Jones.

"Friend—friend," cried Tobias, "wilt thee come back?"

"Well, what is it?" said the man.

"Are you sure you shut the door?" said Jones.

"Confound you both," said the man, as he stopped, and putting spurs to his horse, galloped away.

"Now, Mr. Tobias Poppleton," said Jones, "I advises you to make the best of this ere business by just handing out to me what tinklers you have about you, and saying nothing to nobody."

"Friend, I know not thy meaning," said Tobias.

"Money," said Jones; "and, mark me, if you say anything about it, or kick up any disturbance, don't show your sanctified mug on this road again; for, so sure as you do, I'll be down upon you, and you'll find me a dangerous female."

With a deep groan Mr. Poppleton produced his purse, and gave it to Jones, saying:

"Friend, I would gladly have given thee

ten times as much if thee had not made me say, ' ax my elbow,' and other profane words; but it will become known now that I did say so, and truly my brethren will cast me out, for verily they have no mercy upon those who cannot keep their frailties from public observation; ' if thee have a rent in thy garment,' they will say to me, ' under the sleeve of thy coat, keep thy arm down, and we will say nothing to thee about it, but if thee lettest it be seen, we will cast thee out.'"

"Twelve pounds," muttered Jones, as he counted over the quaker's money; "you may take your purse back again, old stick in the mud, and remember mum's the word."

"Verily, mum, I shall remember thee as long as I live," said the quaker.

Mr. Jones then left Tobias Poppleton seated among the clay, and hurrying forward till he came to a turn in the road, he took off his female habiliments, and tying them up again in the same bundle as before, he walked on at a rapid pace to the village.

An hour had not elapsed when he again entered the neat little sanded parlour of the village inn.

"Miss Miranda," he said, " here's luck in a bag, and take it out as you want it." At the same time he handed Miranda a small leathern bag, in which he had placed the greater portion of Tobias Poppleton's twelve pounds.

A slight flush came over Miranda's face as she said, timidly:

"May I hope, Mr. Jones, without offending you, that this money was come by honestly?"

"Honestly, Miss Miranda!" said Jones; " in course. I never did anything so outrageous honest in all my life. It's quite a hact of piety."

"I will take your word," said Miranda, " and thank you for this most seasonable relief. I have still hopes—very great hopes—that the day may come when I shall be able to repay all those who have so generously assisted me in my distress; but, till then, I must remain your grateful debtor."

"Never mind that," said Jones; " here comes the waggon. Don't you hear the horses' bells? It's not going to London, but it's going on forty miles of the road, and that's a good long lift. Offer the man a shilling a-piece, and he won't refuse it."

"And shall I not see you again?" asked Miranda.

"You may or you may not, as the case may turn out; but I intend to take easy stages to London, and borrow a little money as I go on. I rather think, though, that you will see me often enough, and, if you do not, go right on without me. Be sure you never make any inquiries after me, and remember that ere address as I guved you where to find Dick Palmer."

"I will remember," said Miranda, " with many, many thanks to you for all you have done for us."

The tinkle of the bells which adorned the heads of the waggon-horses, and which were placed there for the purpose of keeping them awake, but, notwithstanding which, the whole train was in a state of somnambulism by the time they reached the village, was now plainly heard, and Miranda, turning to Mr. Percy, said:

"Let us come now; forty miles will, indeed, be a long lift on our weary journey."

He followed her to the door, and there the waggon was slowly dragging its length along through the one street of the village.

The waggoner seemed as fast asleep as his horses, for he was going along with a monotonous trudge, neither looking to the right nor to the left, nor upwards, nor straight-forwards, but intently on the ground, as if, on his last journey, he had lost some small coin, and he was in hopes of picking it up on this.

Mr. Jones went up to the leading-horse, and, taking hold of it by the ear, bellowed into it " Woa!" upon which the leading horse shook his head, and came to a standstill, whilst the others, bumping up against him, took that as a hint to stop also; so that at length, after much creaking, and wheezing, and groaning, the waggon came to a stand; while the waggoner, who was totally oblivious of the whole circumstance, walked on as if nothing was the matter; and it was not until Mr. Jones commenced pelting him with stones—at which exercise he seemed quite an adept, for he hit the waggoner almost every time—that the latter, after saying " Woa!" several times, stopped, and became aware that he had shot ahead of the amazing bits of blood that were dragging his waggon.

He then walked back, and looked wildly about him for a few seconds, after which he said, fancying he was at a turnpike:

"Number thirty-seven."

"Two passengers," cried Jones; " an old gentleman and a young lady. Four quarts of threepenny a-piece."

"Ah—ah—ah!" said the waggoner.

"That'll do!" roared Jones.

"Ah!" said the waggoner.

"Get in," said Jones to Miranda. " You and the old gentleman will find yourselves comfortable enough, although it is tedious travelling."

Mr. Jones then went again to the leading horse, and, laying hold of his ear, as he did before, he screamed in it:

"Gee-up!"

And in about a minute the horse took it into consideration, and began walking on, the others all being roused by the process, and stepping out at the amazing pace of two miles and three-quarters an hour, while the bells kept up their monotonous tinkle, tinkle, and the waggoner resumed his dreamy career.

———

CHAPTER XCIV.

VARLEY AND HIS SPY—THE WATCH-HOUSE AT YORK—MARTIN, THE IDIOT, AND THE PISTOL-SHOT.

MIRANDA was gone, and the tumult and excitement which had reigned in the little street where she had resided in York was over before, like an apparition of evil, Bernard Varley arrived at the spot, and, as he gazed around him, he muttered indistinct imprecations upon the head of his spy.

"Where can the hound be?" he said. "Confusion! he's off his guard! How dare he leave without my express permission? Who knows what might happen, even in a temporary absence? I'll brain him if he has let her escape—I'll brain him. He's not here—'tis certain he is not here."

By this time he had arrived opposite the house in which Miranda had occupied apartments, and, for a while, his attention was taken from the consideration of the delinquency of his spy, in gazing with a wild rush of mingled feelings upon that house, which he believed contained the being who had cast such a spell of fascination around him, and whom, by a strong contradiction of feeling, he loved so intensely, and had injured so deeply.

"There is a light at the window," he muttered, "and I see a shadow flit across the casement. It must be hers. Miranda! Miranda! Even yet, methinks you could save my soul from the deep perdition that awaits it; in your hands I could be a slave—a willing slave; and I think, even terrible as death is to me, even in thought, I could consent to die soon, provided, in the interim, you would be mine, and light up my soul with some of those sunny smiles thou art so lavish of to others, but never—never allow to beam upon me. Oh, Miranda! even now look down with pity upon the wreck you have made!"

How common it is for such men as Bernard Varley, after a career of crime and villainy, to attempt to shift the onus of their guilt upon the shoulders of some innocent person, who could have nothing whatever to do directly with their iniquities.

Thus the thief, when sentenced to a trifling punishment for his first offence, would say that, if the judge, who, in his impartial administration of the law, was compelled to sentence him, had spared him, he might have become a useful member of society, instead of persevering in a course of crime. The housebreaker who, when meeting with resistance, murders the person whom he came but to rob, might as well attempt to shift the onus of the crime upon that person's head, and say that he himself brought on his death.

It was quite as absurd for Bernard Varley to accuse Miranda of being indirectly the cause of his iniquity, because she could not love him; but the o'erburthened conscience will catch at straws to float itself upon the sea of hope, and, strong-minded as Bernard Varley was, he would fain have cheated him-

self into the idea that he was not personally answerable for his own iniquities.

For a considerable time he remained, musing and gazing up at the window of the room, which he still supposed Miranda inhabited.

At last one o'clock sounded from the various steeples of the ancient city.

He then started from his dreamy posture, and, in an angry tone, said:

"So, I have paid well for being duped: the rascal whom I set here to watch, has utterly and wholly neglected his duty. It will yet be some hours before the city is alive again, and, during that time, what better occupation can I have than in watching your window, within which is all I ever loved on earth."

As he spoke, he became conscious of someone slinking down the street on the other side of the way, and, ever suspicious as he was, that where there was secrecy and caution, there must be danger to him, he stepped beneath a doorway, and stood in the deep shadow, watching the actions of the person approaching.

That person was Kiggs, who, having run home to Mrs. Kiggs, and informed her of the singular circumstances by which his watch had been disturbed, was duly advised by that careful and exemplary woman to return to the scene of action, and earn his money, a piece of advice that was rendered wonderfully practicable by a blow with the fire-tongs, so that Kiggs, who had begun somewhat to recover from his fright abroad, thought it best to flee from the wrath at home, and he accordingly hastened back to the street, to see what was going on there.

Now Mr. Kiggs was a politic man in his way, and he thought that if Mr. Varley should have been there, and duly missed him, that he, Kiggs, might still have a chance of saving himself from reproach by slipping behind the pump, and suddenly appearing with a "Lor! bless me, sir, is it you? why, I have been watching yer ever so long, and I didn't know you!"

It was in pursuance of this clever scheme, that Mr. Kiggs slinked down the street in the manner we have described, and then screened himself behind the pump, all of which Bernard Varley saw clearly, looking, as he was, from darkness to comparative light.

"What is the meaning of this?" he said: "the manner and general bearing of that man lead me to think it is he whom I employed to keep strict watch upon this house, and the scoundrel has deceived me, and thinks now to make some lying boast of his acuteness."

Varley then advanced to the pump with slow and cautious steps.

When he was sufficiently near, he bolted round it, and, seizing Kiggs by the collar, said:

"Scoundrel—you have deceived me."

"Lor! sir, is it you?" said Kiggs, who could think of nothing but the speech he had determined to make: "well, I never, I've been watching you ever so long. There hasn't a mouse been moving, sir, at the young lady's house; to be sure, I've had some of my clothes torn off my back by a mad woman, but your worship will, no doubt, make them good. Says I, to myself, says I, 'Mr. Varley's a gentleman, and he'll make everything square.' Oh! murder—murder!"

These exclamations arose from Varley kicking Mr. Kiggs down the street, who was thus doomed on that eventful night to receive another practical opinion as regarded his attainments.

As fortune then would have it, Mr. Green, who by this time had been rescued from the sewer, arrived, nearly red hot with fury, accompanied by half-a-dozen other constables in the street, resolved to find the gigantic female, if possible, or, at all events, wreak his vengeance upon somebody.

The first sight that met his anger-flashing eyes was Kiggs, being kicked ferociously down the street by a tall figure.

"Seize him! seize him!" he cried, and Bernard Varley was in a moment in the hands of the officers, and, in another, the whole party was rolling in the street, for Bernard Varley was not the kind of man to be taken quietly, nor was he, just then, in the sort of humour to be interfered with at all.

Nevertheless, no effectual resistance could be made against so many, and, the consequence was, that Varley, in defiance of all explanation, was dragged off, with scarcely a whole rag on his back, to the nearest watch-house.

There, however, a general explanation ensued, and Mr. Kiggs, after some hard pressing, confessed his delinquency, while Green explained how he had been maltreated by some fiend in petticoats, who had a dozen imps to do what she thought fit.

From all this Bernard Varley gathered abundant food for suspicion that something was going on as regarded Miranda, which he should miss the knowledge of, and, with frenzied gestures, he hastened back to the street in which she resided.

It was a little before three o'clock, but, without reflecting a moment about the unseasonableness of the hour, he knocked loudly at the door, nor ceased, notwithstanding he alarmed the whole street, until the woman of the house opened the window and appeared at it with a candle in one hand, and a watchman's rattle in the other.

"Woman!" shrieked Varley; "tell me this instant, is Miranda Rankley here, or not?"

"Gracious powers!" cried the woman, trying to spring the candle instead of the rattle; "who are you?"

"Answer my question," shouted Bernard Varley, "or I'll not leave a whole pane of glass in your house."

"She is gone," cried the woman, "and I am very glad of it; and if you don't go, too, I'll give you to the watch."

"Gone—gone!" said Varley, as he staggered across the street with clasped hands, not hearing or heeding the loud springing of the rattle, which the woman then really commenced. "Gone—gone! she is gone, and I have missed her. Oh! fool, fool, to lose sight for one brief moment of her—to delegate a watch to others which only I myself could keep with fitting diligence. Whither has she gone? Her progress must be slow, for it is cramped by want of means, and the company of the elder Percy, whom I am certain she would not forsake. London—that must be her destination, and where she is, there will be Rowland Percy. Where would he be likely to seek for refuge but in that great city—that grave of individuality, where one man may live entombed among the living, hidden amidst moving masses, so that it would be impossible for the most practised seeker to lay hands upon him, and point out his whereabouts? Where should I go but to London, if I wished to hide from the consequences of some great crime?—if—if those consequences were pursuing me, as, of course, they never will, they never can; for I have fenced myself too well round with precautions—my guilt is known but to one, and he dare not reveal it. Blood is upon my hands, but they will look pure in the eyes of men; for who but Samuel Twitter could point out the ensanguined stains, and he dare not. It would be to sign his own death-warrant."

He stood at the corner of the street, and breathed laboriously for several seconds.

When he again spoke, it was in a lower tone, and his steps became more languid, for Bernard Varley's health was sadly failing him, and he was only powerful and violent by fits and starts, like the gusty wind which one moment would rush on its career with headlong violence and fury, and the next subside into placidity and calm repose.

"To London," he muttered. "To London at once. I may overtake them on the road—I shall overtake them on the road, and never again will I lose the track of Miranda Rankley. The Grange shall be sold. It is mine, indisputably mine. My title to it is as good as Sir George Rankley's, for no one doubts the authenticity of the will by which he bequeathed it to me. It shall be sold by auction, and I will never again, while I live, sear my eyes with the sight of it or York."

"Never again—never again!" shrieked a voice in Varley's ear. "Ah! ah! a wild, stray thought. Bernard Varley will be hanged at York—hanged in the presence of thousands—hanged at York—hanged at York! They call me an idiot, but that is the prophecy. You sped the bullet well at me, Bernard Varley, but it would not do its work, for you are to be hanged at York, and I am to see it."

"Fiend!" cried Varley, as he aimed a blow at the retreating figure of poor Martin, the maniac. "Am I in my bitterest moments to be tormented by such as thou art? 'Tis a fair chance, and I will now rid myself of at least one of the curses of my existence."

He drew a brace of pistols from his pocket, and pursued the figure of the flying idiot.

Rage lent to Bernard Varley the fleetness

which he was far from ordinarily possessing, and he gained rapidly upon poor Martin, although the latter was no despicable runner.

Varley, however, had not patience to wait until he was close to his victim, but levelling one of his pistols, he fired at the retreating form, which fell with a loud cry to the pavement.

"'Tis done," muttered Bernard Varley, between his teeth, as he placed the other weapon in his pocket, "'tis done. Who dare cross my path, idiot or sane man, he shall perish."

A loud clapping of hands attracted his attention, and looking hastily in the direction from which the sounds proceeded, he saw, to his surprise, the idiot standing at the entrance of a narrow court, and when he saw that Bernard Varley's eyes were fixed upon him, he shrieked in wild accents that rang far and wide:

"Hanged at York—hanged at York—with a crowd to see it! Ah! ah! ah! Bernard Varley will be hanged at York!"

Upon the moment, then, he disappeared with extreme rapidity down the dark passage, and Bernard Varley felt that in the intricacies of the market-place to which it led, pursuit would be fruitless.

Uttering deep execrations, he wrapped his cloak hurriedly around him, and hearing many windows open, and that a general alarm was created in the street by the firing of the shot, he hurried on with great speed, and in a nearly frantic state of mind, towards the hotel at which he had temporarily taken up his abode.

CHAPTER XCV.

ROWLAND'S JOURNEY—THE TURNIPS—THE TURNPIKE GATE—THE ORDEAL PASSED—SUSPICION, AND THE CHASE.

WE left Rowland Percy in far from a very enviable position as regarded his mode of transit to London, although it had the great charm of being a tolerably safe one.

His acquaintanceship with turnips in the chaise-cart was by far too intimate to promote warmth or comfort, and as those vegetable productions had been, at the requisition of Palmer, newly pulled from the parent soil by the landlord of the roadside inn, they brought with them various accompaniments of lumps of mould, &c., which by no means tended to make them agreeable travelling companions.

Still, while there was no danger there would be no necessity for Rowland's being entirely covered up with cold vegetable matter, and they jogged on for some time without anything arising to necessitate such a measure.

"As I said," remarked Palmer, "the officers are sure to proceed a good way ahead until they are quite certain that you are not before them, for they will inquire diligently what travellers have passed through every turnpike."

"And then, I presume, they will return?" said Rowland.

"They will, and carefully, too, stopping every vehicle they meet on the road coming from York. If we escape them, then we shall be safe enough, for each moment will be increasing our distance from them."

"It may be premature," said Rowland, in a saddened voice, "for of course I am yet far from safe, but the thought will obtrude itself upon me, of what on earth am I to do when I get to London.—All the frightful misfortunes, under, certainly, the severest of which I was near sinking, have come together upon my own family and upon Sir George Rankley's. My own father became destitute at the same time that by a singular caprice of Sir George Rankley's, or by some deep-laid villainy, yet to be discovered, Bernard Varley, my bitterest enemy, claimed everything which should have been Miranda's."

"Your position in London is certainly bad," said Palmer, "because by the peculiarity of your situation you are deprived of your proper chances; but you, Mr. Percy, who have been brought up luxuriously, never knowing what want was, and, I daresay, scarcely the cost of any one article of your daily consumption, can scarcely have a notion of how small a sum will supply a person's mere physical wants in London."

"Indeed!" said Percy.

"Yes; your peculiar situation, until your innocence is established, if it ever should be, would prevent you from spending much money, unless you sat down and got drunk every day, or sent yourself into an apoplexy. I will undertake to get you boarded and lodged safely in London for a sum that will be to me very trifling indeed, until some change for the better takes place in your fortunes."

"My generous friend," said Rowland, "am I not only to owe to you my life, and my rescue from a death which, I will own, now, was most frightful to my imagination, but am I to make myself a perpetual burthen to you?"

"Oh, nonsense about perpetual burden," said Palmer; "lightly come, you know, Mr. Percy, lightly go. You know my profession; we have ups and downs, as there are in all trades. Sometimes we are overflowing with wealth; at another, we are poor, miserable wretches, with scarcely a farthing to help ourselves; but where I mean to place you, they know me, and will have confidence for a few weeks at any time. So cheer up, for it seems to me you have got out of the fire pretty well."

"Thanks to you, indeed," said Percy, "I have; but what—oh! what is to become of Miranda?"

"Be under no anxiety on that score," said Palmer. "I saw enough to convince me, before I left York, that Miranda was surrounded by good and warm-hearted friends, and friends, too, capable of helping her. She will want for nothing this world can afford, you may depend."

"I thank Heaven it is so," said Percy. "But hark! do I not hear horses' feet?"

MR. JONES COMPELS THE QUAKER TO PLAY AN UNSEEMLY PART.

Dick Palmer pulled up instantly, and they both listened with the greatest attention.

From afar off on the road they were taking, came the unmistakable sound of horses' feet at an easy trot.

"It may be them," said Palmer.

"The officers?"

"Yes; they'll be sure to return this way, and we had better provide against all chances. You must get down among the turnips, and we must see what a little bamboozling will do."

While Percy held the reins, Dick Palmer busied himself in making a hollow place among the turnips, where Rowland could lie down in a crouched-up position, and be easily and completely covered up by them.

"You'll have lots of room to breathe," said Palmer; "but, hear what you will as to any proposition for searching the cart, or taking us back to York, do not be alarmed, but remain perfectly quiet."

"I will," said Rowland; "although, believe me, rather than again fall into the hands of my enemies, I would die resisting them."

"If the worst comes to the worst," said Palmer, "I won't tamely give you up. You are an innocent man, and you have a right to defend your life. Place these pistols in your breast, but do not use them except in great extremity. If they should insist upon moving the turnips, we'll give them a chase for it to the darkest part of the road we can find, and then trust to our luck; but we had better talk no more, lest our voices should be carried on the air, and they'll never believe I have been holding a conversation with the horse."

"I think that will do," said Rowland, as Palmer placed an amazing bunch of turnips on his face; "it's wretchedly cold, and something like being buried alive, I think."

"Hush—hush!" said Palmer—"not another word."

Dick then allowed the horse to go forward at an easy trot, while he hummed a provincial air, and occasionally smacked his whip as the burden of the tune.

There was a toll-bar about a quarter-of-a-mile ahead, and from this there came a sound of voices, proceeding, as Palmer rightly enough guessed, from the returning officers, who were stopping to have a parley with the gatekeeper. Dick would rather not have passed through the ordeal which he felt was at hand under the glare of light from the toll-house; but the sound of the wheels of his cart must have reached the ears of the officers, and to stop then would be to create the very suspicion he wished so particularly to avoid.

Less than five minutes more driving brought them to the toll-bar.

Around the door of the little tenement connected therewith were several horsemen, one of whom had dismounted, and was doing something to his saddle-girths.

"Now, stupid," said the toll-man to Palmer, who was jogging through without taking any notice.

"What's the row?" said Palmer. "Don't the Thorn-end ticket clear this ere gate?"

"No, it don't, and you know that well enough, I'll be bound. Thruppence, stupid; perhaps you think it's hard?"

"Yeas," said Palmer; "de yow?"

At the same time he gave the man a hard rap on the head with three penny pieces, that made him jump back, and rub the afflicted part with great fervour.

"Confound you," said the man, "what did you do that for? You're an idiot, I suppose?"

"Eh! eh! I coomes from Yark."

"So, friend, you come from York," said one of the mounted officers. "Have you heard of Rowland Percy?"

"Chap as hoong?" said Palmer.

"No, the chap who was to have been hung, but who contrived to get away."

"Eh! eh!" said Palmer; "where did he coome froom?"

"The fellow's an ass," said the officer. "Where are you going to?"

"Next fair, with these ere nips."

The officer rode to the side of the cart, and looked somewhat curiously into it, as he said:

"Why, you have not brought them all the way from York?"

"Yeas, I have, though," said Palmer "They're fine 'uns, ain't they?"

"They seem of the right sort. Are you sure you saw no suspicious characters on the road?"

"Noa," said Palmer, "not till I seed some chaps round a pike, as seemed arter no good."

"Oh, the fellow's a fool," said the officer, turning away.

"Thank ye," said Palmer; "we are all fools as come froom Yark."

With that, he spoke to the horse, and jogged on at a very slow pace, while Rowland Percy blessed his stars that the investigation was over.

"Did you see the horse that fellow had?" said the dismounted officer to him who had ridden up to the side of the cart.

"No," was the reply, "I didn't notice it."

"On my soul!" said the other, "it was as fine a creature as ever stepped, and never cost less than a hundred guineas."

"You don't say so; that don't look a likely thing for a turnip cart."

"Look how he's stepping out now," said another.

This was a fact, for Dick Palmer really believed then that they had not the remotest suspicion, and when he got about a quarter-of-a-mile off, he just put the horse to a swift trot, and away they went at a good eleven miles an hour.

This was certainly injudicious of Palmer; but the idea of his pace making any difference to the officers never occurred to him, nor would it have occurred to them, had not the question been raised about the value of his horse.

There was a moment or two's hesitation among the officers, and several of them spoke together, saying:

"Is it worth while to go after him?" Then, by one accord, they said "Yes;" and, turning their horses' heads towards London, were soon in full gallop after Dick Palmer.

It was some minutes after Dick Palmer had increased his speed in the manner we have related, before he thought it prudent to speak to Rowland Percy, and then he leaned down, and said:

"I think all's safe, but I'll keep on at this pace for a few miles; and until we have put that distance between us and the toll-bar, we may as well speak low."

"I think you managed it amazingly well, Palmer," said Percy. "The few moments we remained in suspense were far from pleasant ones."

"We are safer now than ever we were," said Palmer: "and if the magistrates should take it into their heads to send a party again up the road, we shall have got a good start, and—what's that—what's that?"

"What?" said Percy, as Palmer drew up abruptly.

"Pursued, by Heavens!" said Palmer—"and at a slashing pace, too."

CHAPTER XCVI.

THE CHASE CONTINUED—THE PARTING—AN
HOUR OF DESPAIR—THE VILLAGE BELLS—
A BETTER RESOLUTION.

As Dick Palmer spoke, he gave his horse the rein, and the animal immediately broke into a prodigious gallop, the turnips flying about in all directions.

For some moments Percy said nothing, for the speed at which they went was so great, that it was as much as he could do to keep his place in the cart. At length he exclaimed:

"Surely, Palmer, mounted men must overtake us. I will sell my life as dearly as possible, for, by the Heaven above me, I will not be taken back to that cell from which I have so lately emerged."

"Make yourself comfortable," said Palmer, through his set teeth, as he held the reins slackly with both hands. "The road's like a bowling-green for the next dozen miles. I know that we are beating them now, although we sha'n't be able to keep it up."

"And then what is to become of me?" said Rowland.

"Why," said Palmer, "I have an opinion that you won't get to London as quickly as I thought. I tell you what you must do. There's a place some miles ahead called Wickford Hollow; it lies low, and is as dark a bit of the road as we could wish. As I say, we are beating them now, and by the time we arrive there we shall have about five minutes to spare. Your only chance, then, will be to get out, and hide yourself on the roadside, while I gallop on. They are safe to pass you then, and your plan will be to walk on leisurely; you will then come to a roadside public-house, called the 'Raven,' where you can wait till you see or hear of me. Tell them you are a friend of mine, and all will be right."

It may be supposed this speech of Palmer's was spoken under considerable disadvantages, and came jolting out of his mouth in rather an unconnected manner, as the horse galloped on.

Nevertheless, it was sufficiently explicit for Rowland Percy fully to understand it, and his immediate reply was:

"But, my good friend, do you not expose yourself to considerable risk and suspicion from such a course; for, when they overtake you, may they not arrest you on suspicion of aiding me in my escape?"

"I think not," said Palmer. "I shall go at my own pace, and they can't quarrel with me for galloping on the road from York to London, since they are doing the same themselves. I rather think it will be a long job to catch me, and, when they do, what can they find but a chaise-cart with a few turnips at the bottom, which they may take into custody if they like, and much good may they do them."

"Certainly," said Percy, "that presents a feasible aspect of escape; but, in good or evil fortune, whether we overtake each other or not, I shall never forget how much I owe to you."

"Never mind that," said Dick Palmer. "The man who would not assist such a noble-hearted creature as Miranda Rankley, must be a brute indeed, and I know by assisting you I am assisting her, not to mention my dislike and unwillingness to see an innocent man sacrificed to such an infernal scoundrel as Bernard Varley."

"I am deeply indebted to you."

"And then, again," continued Palmer, "we gentlemen of the road are the natural enemies of the law, and all its paraphernalia of judges and officers. But hark!—by Heaven, they are coming at a slashing pace. They've good cattle, but it strikes me that, lumbered as our horse is with two persons and a cart, he's beating them. His reach in a gallop is tremendous. I'd draw up in a moment if I thought they were gaining six inches in a mile upon us."

Percy could now plainly hear the loud and regular beat of the horses' hoofs which were in such hot pursuit of him, and as, occasionally, the road wound about in different directions, those sounds would appear to be nearer or further off as the vibrations of the air came directly to their ears, or were interrupted by intervening obstacles.

Their own steed showed not the slightest distress, but seemed rather to improve upon his speed than otherwise, galloping on at a rate which soon left nothing but the under stratum of turnips, and perfectly astounding the drivers of the few stray vehicles they passed.

There was something pleasurable in the excitement of that wild chase, notwithstanding its result was of such fearful import to Rowland Percy; and the cool air of the early morning, as it blew freshly in Rowland's face —for the speed they were going at created a tremendous artificial current—felt invigorating and delightful.

On, on they sped, past meadows, villas, cottages, and through long avenues of trees, at undiminished speed, until at a considerable distance ahead, Rowland Percy could perceive what appeared to him from so far off, a perfect wood, to which they were dashing with such tremendous speed.

"There," said Palmer, "there, right ahead you will see Wickford Hollow. There we will draw up for one moment to permit you to alight."

"It seems quite an impervious wood," said Rowland.

"Yes, but there is not a bad road going through it, although, except in the very height of summer, a damp one. Remember the 'Raven.' Say you are to meet me there, and do not think of moving until I come to you, except something very urgent should arise, and then do not let me pass you as you proceed towards London, for I suppose you will hardly turn your face to York."

"Hardly, indeed," said Rowland. "What an extremely dark place this is."

They had now plunged into that part of the road where Palmer intended to draw up, and he began gently to moderate the speed of the horse, saying:

"Creep out at the back, Mr. Percy, and then hide yourself among the brushwood—less than five minutes will bring them here."

Percy did as he was desired, and clambering over the back of the cart, hung for a moment to it until Palmer very nearly stopped the horse.

"All's right," he said, as he dropped into the road.

"Good luck to you," cried Palmer, and giving a cheering whistle to the horse, he again started off at the same tremendous gallop that for the last half-hour had carried them over so many miles of country.

The sudden transition from the rapid motion of the cart to perfect quietude and inaction, felt very strange for a moment or two to Percy, and he stood, as if half-bewildered, in the road, and incapable of action.

Then came upon his ears the fearful and tremendous beat of the horses' hoofs that were pursuing him for his destruction.

Death and disgrace came in the sound, and, excited as his imagination was, it was with a cry of terror that he rushed to the side of the road, and cowered down among the tall brushwood that grew there in such wild luxuriance.

Nearer and nearer came his pursuers, making the earth echo again with the loud tramp of their horses' feet; then, upon the dense morning air, he could hear their voices as they encouraged each other to the pursuit, some minutes before the purport of their words could reach his ears.

It was, however, with great gratification that he noticed the gradual decrease in the sound of Palmer's horse's feet, and felt that that faithful friend was in all probability still gaining ground upon the half-maddened officers, who did not entertain the shadow of a doubt but that their victim was really before them.

There was little time, however, for reflection before the officers came on with a speed almost equal to that of the fabled wild huntsman of the German forest.

He heard the voice of the foremost of them saying to his comrades:

"On—on—on! Never mind horse-flesh. We'll have him yet—we'll have him yet—they can't keep it up. On—on—on!"

Then there was one rush, as if a hurricane was sweeping through some trees.

The pursuers were passing him, and for the moment Rowland Percy was safe.

With a bewildered feeling he half-walked, half-staggered into the road, and strove to pierce with his eyes the deep obscurity of the shaded hollow through which the horsemen had disappeared.

Fainter and fainter came the heavy beat of the horses' hoofs upon his ear, and then, like a glimmering light which, after it has been extinguished, leaves its faint spectrum upon the eye, cheating the imagination into a belief of its continued existence, Rowland Percy thought he still heard, from afar off, the monotonous beat of those horses' hoofs, when they were too far off for the faintest sounds to reach his ears.

A few moments more, and even that delusion vanished.

He felt himself utterly alone—a wanderer on the earth's surface—friendless, or, at all events, those who would have befriended him were helpless—houseless, proscribed, and a price upon his head.

A deep sigh burst from his labouring breast, and lifting his arms to Heaven, he said:

"When, oh! when am I to know again that dear heart's security that was mine, in times gone by?—when can I again take my place among my fellow-men, as free as they, and as little obnoxious to death and ignominy as the best and bravest, with all the feeling to make one, and that not the least kindly one, of the family of man? Why am I picked out by cruel fortune for such a fate as that which I have narrowly escaped, and cast off from that society which I have never injured, for an alleged crime, at which my nature shudders, and which the world's wealth, and the world's power, would not have tempted me to commit? Miranda, too —Miranda, the pure and the beautiful—the sinless, innocent being in whose composition the diviner elements of nature seemed to have centred—what a fate has been her's! God of Heaven! is it possible that one bad man is endowed with a fiend-like power of crushing so many trusting, loving hearts? What will become of me—what will become of me?"

As he spoke he crossed his arms upon his breast, by which action he felt the pistols which Palmer had given to him, and forgotten to ask back.

"Ha!" he cried, "these are friends, indeed. While I have these I need not fear the felon's cell, for I can tempt those who would take me, to destroy me; and, oh! what would death be in comparison with again encountering the gloom of that prison-house, with the consciousness that but a few short hours were between me and death upon the scaffold."

The wind swept past him with a howling and melancholy sound, and the darkness of that nearly impervious shadow in which he was, seemed momentarily to deepen around him.

A cold and shuddering feeling came across his heart, and it seemed to him as if nature was assuming around him a more stern and forbidding aspect—as if the natural elements of creation, as well as his fellow-creatures, were arraying themselves against him.

"Am I repudiated," he cried, "by all? Am I to be alike cast off by heaven and earth? What deep sin have I unknowingly committed that I should be made the wretch I am, shrinking at every footstep, and trembling at the sound of the human voice?"

The dark feelings then, that for a time had swept across his soul when in the condemned cell, found a place again in his heart, and the one frightful word suicide rose to his lips.

He plunged among the brushwood again, and sat himself down against the trunk of an aged tree. He tried to extract hope from his position, but the feeling was dead within him. He tried to tell himself that all was not lost; but the reply he gave his own heart was, "All—all."

"If ever," he said, in a low, shrinking voice, "a mortal soul might be excused for standing unbidden before its Creator, it would be one placed in such circumstances as mine —persecuted without crime, hunted without cause, condemned though innocent."

The rapt stillness that reigned around—the entire absence of any sounds that would bring his thoughts back to earth and earthly feelings much assisted in nourishing the emotions which at that dread moment found a place in Rowland Percy's heart; everything was forgotten but his own hopelessness—his own fearfully critical situation, and his despair.

For a time he covered his face with his hands; a convulsive sob shook his frame; then he gazed wildly about him for a moment, and cried, in a loud voice:

"Farewell!"

It was his adieu to earth. In another moment the deadly weapon of destruction was in his hand. It was levelled at his head; but ere he could complete his fatal purpose amid that deep stillness of nature, some sounds fell upon his ear, which he felt as if compelled to listen to, and which seemed one by one to be drawing him back with a gentle and sweet compulsion to earth—to hope—and to happiness.

The sounds were those of the bells of some distant church, which, mellowed by distance, came with a silvery and softened tone to his ears. It was but a rude attempt on the part of the ringers of those bells to perpetrate a simple melody; but it was a melody which Rowland Percy had heard and loved in his childhood, when all was bright and beautiful around him, when the summer sun shone for him with a more than heavenly lustre, and when the sunshine of the heart, and the jocund merriment of a happy home, carried him fleetly through the winter, making it but the shadow to the otherwise too bright and lustrous picture of his happiness.

Now, each note of that simple melody fell upon his heart like the voice of a friend long lost; the dear companions of his early days seemed rising in thronging groups from the dim and fading past; all the bright—all the beautiful associations of his existence crowded about his heart, and then, with a gasping sob and a gush of tears, he cried:

"Miranda—Miranda! I am saved again!"

More sweetly, and with an evener cadence, came the witching of that sound across his soul. It seemed to fill the air with a chastening and holy influence.

The mists of despair cleared from the brain of Rowland Percy, and he arose from the foot of that aged tree with deep thankfulness to Heaven that had saved him from himself, and made him a wiser and a better man.

"Hope—radiant and beautiful hope!" he said, "I will not peep too curiously into thy airy structure. Thou shalt be to my cheering fancy as beautiful as rainbow tints, but not so fleeting; I will cling to thee, and in whatever depth of misery the malignant fates may place me, I will not only be hopeful of emerging from it, but I will imagine a still lower depth, and, raising my voice to Heaven, I will thank its mercy for that which it has saved me from, and not question the wisdom in which it is inflicted. For thee, Miranda, for thee I will live! Ah! how could I call myself lonely and desolate when such a heart as yours was mine—when I had such a pure spirit to cling to me in the dark hour of my fate? Miranda —Miranda! my beautiful—my best! A gift of God, which should fill my heart with thankfulness, instead of murmuring."

CHAPTER XCVII.

THE JADED STEEDS—THE OFFICER'S MISHAP —THE STAGE-COACH, AND THE MEETING.

DICK PALMER smiled to himself when he heard the horsemen in full pursuit of him and the few turnips that still remained in the chaise-cart, and with a malicious satisfaction he determined upon leading them a long and useless chase.

"I will not distress my horse," he said, "for that I wouldn't do for the whole lot of them; but I can lead them a tolerable distance on the London road without doing so— as for poor Percy, he's safe for the present; they'll be ready to gnaw their own heads off when they catch me, just to find they have been scouring somewhere between thirty and forty miles across the country after a man in a cart, whom they dare not interfere with when they catch him, and about two score bunches of turnips."

At the end of Wickford Hollow there was a turnpike, but Dick Palmer's pursuers were not sufficiently near to him to give any alarm to the pikeman to shut the gate; so, shouting out the number which enabled him to pass, he dashed through it without abating a jot of his speed.

The turnips made a terrible riot at the bottom of the cart, keeping up a constant dance, as if they had been instinct with life; but Dick Palmer would not waste time by stopping to throw them out, and the road, being now more level, and a great deal harder, he got on for five miles with amazing quickness.

Meanwhile, the horses of his pursuers became frightfully jaded, for, although good cattle, they by no means started fresh to their work, having had a good share of hard riding before the chase commenced.

The consequence of this was, that, getting up the rise on the opposite side of the hollow, nearly foundered them altogether; so that while Palmer was dashing on at a considerably increased pace, the only hope of his pursuers was to reach the next town, and there get fresh horses.

"This won't do," cried the senior officer; "I have no doubt on earth but our man is before us; we shall be able to get fresh horses in another six miles, and that six miles we must push on by some means or another."

"I doubt," said one, "if it be possible—whip and spur will never get my horse half the distance."

"Try it," cried the senior officer, "and don't spare him. I warrant you I'll get my brute on—I never saw the horse yet that I couldn't make go till he dropped."

The horse seemed upon this to conclude it would be better to do so at once, so he picked out the next little hole he came to, and stumbled.

Away went the officer over his head into the hedge at the roadside, performing, in his progress, several very curious gymnastic feats, and then embedding himself head foremost, like a congreve rocket, into the most vindictive quick-set hedge that ever was planted, for all the prickles by general consent seemed to assail the luckless officer at once.

"Murder — murder!" he cried. "Help, curse it, where am I going to? Pull me out—was there ever such a beast?"

It took the united exertions of the whole party to drag their leader from the hedge, and the process of so doing was torture of an infinitely worse character than getting into it, for the one was slow and protracted, while the other had been so sudden an operation, that he was wounded fearfully before he scarcely knew it, or could think of what was happening to him.

When rescued, he looked in the most pitiable plight—his face and hands were streaming with blood, and his clothes torn in many places.

His first fury seemed to be directed against the horse, and, with the exclamation of—"Where's that infernal beast?" he rushed towards the animal, who, however, was not to be so easily caught, for, after tantalizing his late rider by dancing round him twice, he set off at a tolerably smart trot towards York.

"Catch him—catch him!" said the officer; "what am I to do?"

But the moment the other horsemen set their steeds in action, the animal, who found himself unencumbered by a rider, increased his trot to a canter, and then the canter to a gallop, so that there was a fair chance, had they chosen to embrace it, of a gallop back again to York after the runaway steed.

This, however, they gave up as hopeless, and the officer who had been so anxious to push on, found himself most uncomfortably situated on foot and the prospect of a six miles walk lying before him.

Fortune, however, for once befriended him, for scarcely had he rubbed his face down with his handkerchief, and propounded the question

of "what's to be done now?" than the sound of a horn announced the approach of a coach.

"All's right—all's right!" he cried; "I'll get on the coach and stop at the next town, where, if you have not arrived, I'll order the horses in readiness, and we shall catch our man for certain. The pace he was going at can't last many hours."

The coach soon reached the spot, and being hailed by the officers, it drew up, while their unlucky principal mounted on its roof, smarting most woefully from the scratches he had received, and feeling a great degree of personal indignation against Rowland Percy, whom he heartily cursed as the author of all his misfortunes.

The other officers followed the coach in a straggling and disorderly manner, the whole party reaching the market-town, six miles off, at somewhere about the same period of time, although the horses were ready to drop from fatigue, and the riders themselves were more fit for bed than continued exertion.

Nevertheless, there was one circumstance that spurred them on.

At least, a dozen persons certified to the fact, that a man in a chaise-cart, with some turnips, had galloped through the town, at headlong speed.

"He must be ahead of us," cried the officer, "don't let us relax—remember the reward, besides the honour of the thing. The York police will be laughed at for ever, if we don't catch him."

Fresh horses, and tolerably good roadsters, too, were easily procured, and within ten minutes of their arrival, the whole party were again in the saddle, intent upon reaching the next turnpike, where another inquiry could be made to satisfy them, whether he, whom they were pursuing, was still on the high-road or not.

The answer convinced them that they were all right, for the turnpike man said, "that nearly an hour before such a vehicle had passed the gate."

"Was there one man or two?" was the question.

"One man, and some turnips," replied the turnpike-keeper; "and as nice a horse as ever I seed. I asked him how far he had come, but the chap only laughed in my face, and said 'as there was some people coming behind him as would be able to tell me,' and I suppose you are them?"

"Come on," cried the officer, and without another word he galloped forward.

Now Dick Palmer, for the last hour, began seriously to think that the chase was abandoned, although he was by no means unmindful of the fact, that the officers might have stopped to change horses, relying upon the extra speed they would afterwards be able to make to compensate for the trifling delay.

"But then, after all," he said to himself, "it was only a suspicion they had of me, and, it is possible enough, they may have abandoned it. I'll lead them another dozen miles, and then trot gently back, when, if they are coming after me, we shall soon meet. I must not forget Rowland Percy, and the precarious situation in which he is placed."

It was in consequence of this reasoning that Dick Palmer slackened his speed considerably, and even waited some time at a little roadside inn, to refresh both himself and his steed. Then he gave away the remainder of the turnips.

"Why, friend," said the landlord, "these are prime ones, and, if you have been to market, I wonder that they were left."

"I was going to market," said Palmer, "and had a cart full, but my horse took fright, owing to having something ugly behind him—and most of the turnips were left on the roadside for the lord of the manor, so you are welcome to the remainder if you like."

"Very good," said the landlord. "I'll swap a jug of my old October for them."

The old October was duly discussed, and the horse being refreshed considerably by his temporary halt, and the attention which Palmer paid to his wants, they started on the road back to York, at a comfortable and easy pace, which, the burden behind him being considerably lightened, was no hardship, and, perhaps, better than sending him at once to a stable.

The great speed which the officers were now making was to be added to the pace at which Palmer was travelling, and the two combined, presented a very early prospect of the parties meeting.

In fact, half-an-hour had scarcely elapsed, when Palmer saw his pursuers attain the brow of the hill, and come sweeping down the declivity at a great rate.

"Now for it," said Palmer. "I shall see what sort of a humour they are in—if they ride terribly rusty, and think of arresting me, I'll try to get a little start of them, and give them another gallop on their road home; but, in case they shouldn't recognize me now, I will just give them a taste of the quality of my horse, for I wouldn't miss the fun on any account."

Palmer then spoke to the horse, which immediately commenced stepping-out in that tremendous trot of which some horses are capable.

"Halt!" cried the senior officer; "halt! That's our man for a hundred pounds!"

"That's the horse—that's the horse!" cried another. "I should know him again among a thousand."

The horsemen immediately drew themselves up across the road, and Dick Palmer, bringing his horse to a walk, said:

"Gentlemen, I presume you are highwaymen; but it is of no use your stopping me, for I have not five shillings about me."

"Come—come!" cried the senior officer, galloping up to the side of the chaise-cart, "where's all your turnips?"

"Why, the chap as I'm taking home this cart for," said Palmer, coolly, "tells me the horse took fright, after shying at some ill-looking rascals that he saw near a turnpike-gate."

The officer bit his lip as he saw the empty cart, and felt an uneasy conviction that Dick Palmer was not the man he sought.

"Done again, confound it!" he muttered to himself. Then, in a loud voice, he added:

"Hark you, my friend! I don't know who you are; but I very much suspect you had somebody with you when you passed this way before."

"Ah!" said Palmer, calmly, "you look a suspicious chap."

"What have you done with the turnips?"

"Partly give 'em away, and partly swapped 'em. How came you and the cat to fall out—have you seen your own face lately?"

"We will take this fellow into custody, at all events," said the officer.

"May I humbly ask," said Dick Palmer, "what for?"

"Suspicious circumstances," said the officer. "You have a suspicious look, my friend."

"Lor! bless you!" said Palmer, "it would never do to take up people for that reason."

"And why not?" said the officer. "You seem a remarkably clever fellow in your way."

"Because you'd never be out of jail," said Palmer.

The officers who were not engaged in the controversy seemed fully to appreciate the joke of this retort of Palmer's, although the one against whom it was directed did not. Reddening with anger he turned to his companions, saying:

"Ho! my men, help me to lay hold of this vagabond. He's after no good, I'll warrant; and by laying hold of him, we shan't, at all events, return to York empty handed."

At the same moment that he spoke, he made an attempt to grasp the horse's rein; but Palmer, by a sudden movement, eluded him, and then, before the other officers could move nearer, he said:

"Harkye, my friends—a joke's a joke, and I know what you can do, and what you can't, as well as yourselves. You have no charge against me—not the shadow of one. You can't take me either unless I choose to let you. I don't see why I should put myself out of the way upon the subject; and I tell you candidly, that I have both money and inclination to trounce you soundly, if you attempt to lay hands upon me."

The officers drew back, leaving their principal to contest the matter alone, one of them remarking to the other:

"It's no joke taking up a man for nothing. Bill White was let in for a hundred pounds damages on such a score."

"And who may you be?" cried the senior officer. "You talk big enough."

"I am not bound to tell you on the King's highway," said Palmer, "who, or what I am. Go to school again, stupid, and persuade your mother to pay the extra twopence for you to learn manners."

The officer ground his teeth with rage, and shaking his riding-whip, said:

"You are on the high-road back to York now, my man, and so are we. If there be law to prevent my taking you into custody—which I am not quite sure of, only I wouldn't give a fellow like you an advantage—there's none to prevent me from keeping an eye on you."

"Oh! none in the world," said Palmer. "Would you like to go behind or before; a change would be desirable, as you are all on one side now."

Dick Palmer, then, at a sharp trot, proceeded on his road, followed by the officers, who kept within a dozen yards of the back of the chaise-cart, their principal being determined to see him into York, and ascertain really who and what he was

It was no part, however, of Dick Palmer's intention that such should be the case, and although he could, probably, have easily avoided the pursuit by turning his horse's head and going the opposite direction—whither the officers, after their long ride, would have no disposition to follow him—the spirit of fun took possession of him, and forgetting for a brief space Rowland Percy and his perils, he annoyed the officers beyond description by his singular mode of travelling.

For a few moments he would start off at a gallop, when they would all clap spurs to their steeds to keep up with him: but as soon as he found they had fairly got into the pace, he would draw the horse into a walk, or, perhaps, stop altogether, and whistle a tune throughout, with a great many variations, while the officers were fain to wait cursing and swearing the whole time, until the melody was finished.

This kind of thing lasted for about half-an-hour, and then Dick Palmer suddenly drew up, and clapping his hand over his mouth, exclaimed.

"Bless my soul. I have dropped one of my eye-teeth. and now I shall be obliged to go all the way back again."

Upon the word he wheeled the horse round, and, giving it a long whistle, he started it off again at a smart trot, leaving the officers in the middle of the road, looking at each other in bewilderment.

"After him—after him!" cried the senior officer. "Curse him, I'll take him handcuffed to York if it cost me a hundred pounds."

The others, however, hung back, and one of them said, shaking his head gravely:

"It's better to leave him alone, sir; he's only poking his fun at us. If it should turn out to be some sporting gentleman, after all—which, when you come to look at his nag, isn't at all unlikely—we shall get into a pretty mess."

"Mess be hanged," cried the angry officer. "Follow—I say follow. Confound the fellow, he'll be out of sight in five minutes."

He seemed to make no doubt, then, but his companions must of necessity follow him.

Such a supposition, however, was an error in judgment, for, although he started after Palmer at a good round pace, they made no movement to follow, but continued in the middle of the road gazing after him, as if they were quite unconcerned spectators.

"I say," said one to another, "what shall we do now?"

"Oh," was the reply, "I don't see that we are called upon to gallop off on every fool's errand. Here has been something like a chaffing match, and he who has had the worst of it would get us all into a pretty scrape, because he happens to be in a passion. I vote for a quiet canter back to York."

This suggestion met with general approval, and, rather to the consternation of the senior officer, far from being backed up by his companions, he found his distance increasing from them in a duplicate ratio.

Had he consulted his own inclinations, he would most certainly have turned his horse's head towards York; but pride and anger got the better of prudence. He dreaded the laugh which would ensue on his return—a laugh which, although from prudential motives it might be hidden from him, would be none the less indulged in; and, with a bitter curse against the man who had been the cause of his getting into so disagreeable a predicament, he determined to follow up the chase at all risks.

"It is but man to man," he muttered, "and I am armed. He would never be fool enough to resist me."

CHAPTER XCVIII.

ROWLAND'S PROGRESS—AN ANCIENT ENGLISH INN—THE LEGACY.

ROWLAND PERCY had perhaps never felt in so calm and clear a state of mind since he was first falsely accused of the dreadful crime of murder, as he did when his better reason had triumphed over the frightful suggestion to commit suicide, and he emerged from the copse into the high-road.

It seemed as if some accumulating mental vapour had been suddenly dispersed from before his soul, enabling him to see his situation more clearly in all its various bearings than he had been able to do before.

"I have numerous chances," he thought, "of yet emerging from the painful circumstances that surround me; and as yet what have I suffered in comparison with poor Miranda, who has supported herself amidst it all with an heroic resolution, which should have been a pattern to me, and enabled me to bear with my lighter ills most patiently.

"Has she not lost a father—a father whom she loved with an intensity of affection that, for many years, had no other object on which to expend its sweet impulses—lost him, too, in a manner calculated to rend her very heart-strings, and plunge her into the profoundest melancholy; yet, for my sake, for my sake alone, she fought bravely against all the accumulated evils that would have crushed a weaker spirit, and, discarding her own miseries, risked all, dared all, to save me from the unjust death that threatened me.

"True, the hand of man is raised against me, and I am a hunted, proscribed being; but, if I have lost one world, have I not gained another in the dear love of Miranda Rankley, and have I not escaped a death which the most sanguine heart that ever beat would have pronounced inevitable?

"Let me be thankful, then, for what I have, and the dear gifts that Providence has bestowed upon me, murmuring not that affliction has visited me, but seeking with a philosophy which shall surely be sublime to extract good from everything."

It was in a frame of mind such as this, and with a comparatively light and buoyant heart, that Rowland Percy walked rapidly forward in the direction where Palmer had told him he would find the roadside public-house, the landlord of which, for his (Palmer's) sake, would afford him food and shelter until he should arrive.

The clear and beautiful morning air imparted a strength to his frame, and a tension to his muscles, such as he had not experienced since his weary imprisonment, and the pace at which he walked was an extremely rapid one, so rapid that in much less time than he had expected, he arrived in front of the low, long-looking, straggling house, the swinging-sign of which proclaimed it the "Raven."

It was a very pattern of an old English roadside public-house, containing such a singular collection of architectural orders as would look absurd in a modern residence, but tinctured with age, and covered with the green crust of antiquity, it afforded a pleasing variety to the eye.

There were no end of gable-ends, and multitudes of little windows peeping out here and there from sly corners and odd places; sometimes struggling to show themselves amid an overgrowth of ivy, and at others, appearing as if jutting out from the house in order to find an additional support among the boughs of an adjacent tree.

Each succeeding generation seemed to have added something in its own peculiar taste and style to that ancient and most interesting structure, while Nature, ever bountiful, had aided largely by its multitude of creeping plants in connecting the whole together, so as to make the structure as pretty and romantic a piece of habitable confusion as the most ardent lover of the picturesque could wish to see.

Then there was the fantastic porch, still beautiful and sturdy in its old age—still admired for its blackened and ancient carvings that had resisted successfully the encroaching hand of time, and the clasp-knives of the topers, who, for nearly three hundred years, had quaffed old ale beneath its tempting shadow.

Oh, how many a portly man of iron-frame, and of such sinewy strength, that it would seem as if he could laugh at time and all its doings, had sat beneath that ancient porch, making the welkin ring with his loud and hearty merriment, but over whom now waved the long, rank grass of the silent churchyard.

But then, as the stout forest leaves fall before the autumnal blasts, and are succeeded again by the pure freshness of the spring-tide vegetation, which, in turn, becomes the glory and beauty of the forest, so as each three-quarters of a century rolled over the head of this ancient house, the song and the jest would still be heard beneath the ancient porch, although coming from new voices.

Rowland Percy could not but pause to admire the fine old structure ere he entered its portals. It was a pleasant and cheering thing to his heart, dear lover of the picturesque and the beautiful as he was, to find that his temporary sojourn was to be in a house the very exterior of which afforded him such ample food for pleasurable reflection.

"Ay," he cried, "I think I could be happy here, if free from the storms of fate; and, with my own beautiful Miranda by my side, I think I could be happy here—the world forgetting, by the world forgot."

It was rather *mal apropos*, though Percy was pleased to hear it, but at that instant such a peal of jovial laughter came from the ancient porch, that it was evident some joke of a most titillating character had been perpetrated, and a big, stout man, with a face as red and as round as a warming-pan, rushed out into the road, and danced again in the very ecstasy of his mirth.

Rowland was forced to smile in spite of himself, and, as he walked up to the porch of the "Raven," he said:

"A pleasant morning, friends. It does one good to see you so merry."

"Merry," cried the man with the warming-pan face, who, having recovered a little from his convulsive mirth, had followed Rowland within the porch, "merry, danged if we ain't! My ould aunt, poor creatur, worse luck, she's dead, and left me three hundred and twenty-seven quarts—danged if we haven't begun to drink 'em."

"Perhaps, sir," said a thin, lanky-looking man, who held a fast clutch of one of the quarts, "you will allow me to attempt an exemplification, as Lindley Murray says. I am the schoolmaster of the village close at hand here."

"Ay, ay," roared the fortunate legatee, "exploficate it, will ye;" and, at the same time, he dealt the schoolmaster such a blow between the shoulders, by way of encouragement, that he could scarcely draw his breath for three minutes.

"His aunt," continued the schoolmaster, "left him some chairs and tables, and what they come to just produces, according to an arithmetical sum I have made on the occasion, to the number of quarts he mentions, which quarts are a-going. My services to you, sir."

The schoolmaster, upon this, made a great vacuum in one of the quarts, and the man with the warming-pan face, shouted:

"Danged if that schoolmeaster ain't a clever fellow. Take a quart, my lad," to Rowland, "and we'll drink good luck to old Tabby Bullpitt, my aunt, and the 'Old Raven,' too, bless it."

Rowland did not refuse the draught, for, in truth, he was thirsty after his walk, and, when he removed the tankard from his lips, he said :

"I wish to see the landlord, if he's anywhere here about."

"Oh—ay," cried the legatee, "he's asleep in some corner, I'll be bound. Hedges! Hedges! Hedges! here be someone wanting thee."

Upon this an indistinct rumbling sound came from the passage, and, in a moment, an enormously fat man got through the door with a side wrench, which he could only have accomplished by long practice, but in the accomplishment of which he was fain to screw up his features into an agonized expression, which showed that it was an effort of no ordinary character.

"What's the row?" said Hedges.

"Are you the landlord?" asked Rowland.

"Yees."

"Then I wish to speak to you a moment in private."

"It be no use," said Hedges, "t'other 'size-man called last week. Stump."

"You mistake me," said Rowland Percy ; and, coming as close to the landlord as his rotundity would permit him, he whispered :

"Dick Palmer, known sometimes as the Slashing Squire, told me I might wait at the 'Raven,' and meet with a kind reception, till he came."

The landlord took a long, steady stare in Rowland's face, and then he looked right down him, beginning at the top of his head, and finishing at his boots, after which he gradually brought his eyes up again. He then began to make such extraordinary faces that Rowland became alarmed, and thought he was choking ; but, before he could interfere, the landlord seemed to recover, and, shaking his head, said :

"No go, no go—haven't succeeded in getting up a regular wink for a matter of thirty year; howsomdever, they say a nod's as good as a wink, and that's unkimmon easy. All's right—no gab or gaffery here ; stay as long as you like, young 'un, and you'll see as much rollicking, roaring, tearing, swearing, at the 'Raven,' as will do your heart good. All's right—curse this door, it gets narrower every day."

The fat landlord, with a dreadful effort—during which he stamped furiously upon the oaken flooring, to the immeasurable amusement of the topers in the porch—succeeded in forcing his way into the house again, whither Rowland followed him, as he was anxious to tell him more at leisure how much his circumstances required secrecy and caution.

Having thus seen the persecuted Percy safely housed beneath the hospitable roof of the "Old Raven," we will return to Dick Palmer, who very soon became aware of the fact that he was being followed by the officer, and he guessed, likewise, pretty correctly, that it was more from anger and spite, than from reflection, that such was the case ; for, first of all, there could be no charge against him ; and, secondly, it is very seldom that the police authorities place themselves absolutely upon equal terms, in point of strength, with those they wish to apprehend.

It was, then, rather with vexation than alarm that Dick became aware of the fact that he was still pursued, and he said to himself :

"What on earth can the fool mean by coming after me alone? He must be mad to think I'd let him interfere with me, when it is but man to man. His anger must have got the better of his judgment ; but still he may prove a serious inconvenience to me, if he chooses to keep following wherever I go. Rowland Percy is still but in a very precarious situation, and his escape, after all, depends upon a series of lucky accidents which may or may not occur. Curse the fellow, he's getting his horse warm to the work, and making more speed."

Dick Palmer set himself seriously to consider how he could get rid of the officer, and at last came to an extremely natural conclusion for a man like him, and that was, to accomplish by violence what might be a very slow process by any other means.

"If he will come," said Palmer, "he must stand the consequences, for I cannot be pestered with him any longer. He seems determined on an encounter, and he shall have one—the sooner the better."

When Palmer had once made this determination, he lost no time in putting it into execution, and turning round his horse's head again towards York, he advanced rapidly to meet his pursuer.

"I have turned him at all events," muttered the officer, as he saw this manœuvre. "He knows I must have had him the next place he passed through, and he seems willing to spare himself the trouble. It will be a feather in my cap to capture the blade, come of it what may, and I'll trust to my own luck and reputation to set things right with the magistrates, even if it is a mistake."

The officer then planted his horse exactly in the middle of the road, and, drawing a holster-pistol from the pocket of his overcoat, he presented it at Palmer, saying, as he approached sufficiently near to hear him :

"Hark ye, my man, I intend making you my prisoner, by foul means or fair, so you had better take it quietly, and give in at once. If you are an innocent man, there is no harm done, and you know your remedy ; but if a rogue, as I suspect you are, it is my duty to make you prisoner."

Palmer made no answer whatever, but came slashing on in the cart, keeping in the middle of the road, as if the officer was not there at all, so that the latter was compelled, for his own safety's sake, to get out of the way of the wheel, which otherwise would have inflicted upon him serious injury.

This contemptuous conduct on the part of

Palmer increased his anger wonderfully, and he cried, in a voice hoarse with rage:

"Surrender—confound you, surrender! If you hesitate another moment, I will fire!"

"Fire away!" said Palmer.

Even as he spoke bang went the pistol of the officer; but it was very unlikely he should hit so shifting a mark as was Dick Palmer, who had not failed to see the pistol, and whose great object was to get it discharged.

The moment he heard the report, he wheeled round his horse, and was in a moment by the side of the officer, to whom he dealt so heavy a blow on the head with the crab-stick he had, that it nearly knocked him from his horse, then taking immediate advantage of his temporary confusion, Dick Palmer sprang from the cart, and dragged his opponent to the ground.

The officer, however, was not so far stunned as to be incapable of resistance, and being far from a weak man, a tremendous struggle ensued between the two.

It was, however, soon manifest that he was no match for the sturdy highwayman, who, although not so muscular as the officer, was taller, and much more powerful. The consequence of this was, that in a few minutes Dick Palmer was uppermost, and had his antagonist fast by the throat, and within a hair's breadth of choking.

"Mur—mur—murder!" gasped the officer.

"You are a very troublesome, meddling fellow," said Palmer. "What on earth possessed you to put your neck into this noose?"

"Help—help! I am choking."

"Choke and be hanged," said Palmer. "You tried to take my life, and if I was as passionate a fool as you are, I should just knock your brains out. Come, answer me; if you don't, it will be the worse for you. Have you any information respecting Rowland Percy?"

"None—none!" gasped the officer. "I—I can't speak—you are choking me."

"Have you got any handcuffs about you?"

"Coat pocket," gasped the officer.

Dick Palmer, holding him by the throat with one hand, plunged the other into his coat pocket, and there, sure enough, he found a pair of very well-made, new-looking handcuffs, which shut by a spring as comfortably as possible.

The officer made a desperate attempt to rise, when he found that it was Palmer's intention to place the handcuffs upon him; but the latter was determined to secure his enemy, for some time, at least, and, as he continued his resistance, kicking and plunging in all directions, Dick laid down the handcuffs for a moment, and dealt him two such tremendous openhanded whacks on each side of the head, that his face tingled again, and the tears started into his eyes in spite of himself.

After this, the officer's spirit seemed completely subdued, and he allowed Palmer to put on the handcuffs, without the least attempt to hinder him.

Dick's next movement was to take from him a pocket-book and a purse, each containing a good round sum, after which, with a hearty kick, he said:

"Now, get up. I'll trouble you to get on the other side of the hedge."

The officer could not have got up himself; but Dick lent him assistance by a tremendous pull at his collar, and, when he was on his feet, he pointed to a gap in the hedge at some distance off, saying:

"You'll just be pleased to walk through there, and, as I am in a hurry, pray, sir, be quick."

Dick walked behind the officer, bestowing upon him each moment an accelerating kick, so that they were both of them in a meadow, adjoining the road, in a few minutes; but Dick made him cross that and enter the field beyond, after which he took a handkerchief and tied his elbows together at his back, which, combined with the handcuffs in front, as totally deprived him of all use of his hands and arms, as if he had not possessed those members.

A second handkerchief he then tied tightly round his eyes, after which, giving him another kick to bespeak attention, he said:

"Perhaps you'd like to know who I am now, after all this?"

A groan was the officer's only answer.

"Well," continued Palmer, "whether you do or not, I'll tell you: Did you never hear of the Slashing Squire?"

"The highwayman!" cried the officer; "the highwayman that the Rector of Elwinkle offered two hundred pounds reward for, because he robbed him one evening when he was trotting home from a charity sermon?"

"Yes," said Dick, "I'm the man."

"Oh, what an ass I have been."

"There you are right, and it strikes me that, for a little while, an ass you will remain."

So saying, Dick tripped up the officer's heels, bringing him down on his back with such a thump on the soft meadow, that he made quite an indentation in the turf, and there he lay, as helpless as could possibly be, for, not being a tumbler, and the grass being very slippery, his efforts to get up without the assistance of his hands were for a long while perfectly useless.

When Dick reached the road, he found that the officer's horse had trotted quietly off somewhere, while his own was nibbling the scant herbage that grew by the hedge-side.

"Now for the 'Old Raven' and Rowland Percy," he exclaimed, as he jumped into the cart and drove away.

———

CHAPTER XCIX.

VARLEY'S MEDITATIONS—WILD LOVE—THE SALE OF THE GRANGE.

IT was on the morning of the third day after the departure of Miranda from York, on her long and perilous journey to London, to meet with Rowland Percy, that Varley rose from a sleepless couch and proceeded, long before daylight, to the Grange estate.

He thought the cool air of the early morning would refresh his wearied body and heated blood—perhaps calm the harassing agitation of his spirits also.

No one was visible, and he proceeded unmolested towards the spot he sought. He wished to behold it once more, ere he parted with that which he had dyed his hands in blood to acquire, and which he now ardently wished to get rid of.

He was soon out of York, and in the green lanes which led towards the Grange—he, however, avoided the mansion, and sought a gentle eminence covered with verdure, from which he could see to a great distance.

It was still dark, but by the time he arrived, the gray tints of morning peeped up from the east, and proclaimed the earliest dawn—the chilliness and gloom of night would soon give place to the light of glorious day, and all creatures would rejoice in the warmth of the sun's beams. The cawing of the rooks in a distant rookery heralded the approach of day.

All else as yet was still and quiet—nature reposed—but ere long the teeming earth would be filled with life and motion, and every living creature would be endued with cheerfulness and gladness.

The feathered tribe began to twitter in the hedge-rows, and on the trees, as the light became stronger, and before the sun's beams had well illumined the hemisphere, the lark had risen to its giddy height, and hailed the coming morn.

Soon the face of nature changed, and what but a few hours since was silence, was now quickened into active life.

Such a sight as this casts over the most gloomy mind a sense of pleasure—earth and air contribute to fill him with emotions to which he may have been a stranger.

But the heart of him who now gazed upon that calm and beautiful scene was but little adapted to appreciate its varied beauties, and the claims it would have presented to the admiration of a better nature.

We will not libel common-sense, even to pay a compliment to human nature, by saying that no one could be found less calculated than Bernard Varley to admire and look with a kindly eye upon the glories of inanimate existence. There are many such, although we rejoice to say, few in comparison with the mass of mankind.

Situated as he was, he could take in at a glance the whole of those broad lands and that splendid mansion, for the acquisition of which he had risked his very soul's salvation, and now that he had gained all, now the glory of possession had departed, he would have trembled, and been possessed with a thousand terrors in walking over that estate, and entering the apartments of that splendid house, which he had coveted so fearfully as to dip his hands in human blood to obtain.

For some time he remained silent, with his arms folded across his breast; then deep sighs burst from his labouring heart, and he cried, in a despairing voice:

"I might have known—experience should have taught me—that it is not possession, but successful pursuit, which brings content. Am I the happier that all this is mine own?"

As he spoke, he made a sweeping gesture with his arm, then allowed it to fall to his side, and, uttering a deep groan, he added:

"No—no; did I say happier? Can I ever know even a negative state of repose? Will there ever occur a moment during which I shall not be haunted by the frightful images that now assail my soul? Will it ever be that I can lay my hand upon my heart, saying, 'Here is peace.' Oh, how I have lingered upon that estate, prying into every corner, counting its very trees, admiring its beauties, giving myself up to dreaming contemplation of its soft shadows, and basking in the mid-day sun, that shone upon its fruitful fields, until the wish that it should all be mine grew into a raging fever. It took possession of my heart and soul; withering all reflection, shutting out all feeling, and making itself the sole object of my thoughts by day, and of my dreams by night.

"Then came the murder—the deed of blood that gave me all I coveted; and no sooner was all mine—no sooner could I smile at the storms of fate, and tell myself that I was far above every ordinary contingency of existence, than a new passion—strange, wild, and wonderful—arose within my soul, and I would have given all again for one smile from her who is, and ever will be, the lodestar of my existence—Miranda Rankley."

It was a moment of wild and ungovernable passion with Varley, with the consciousness that he was alone, and no human eye was a witness to his emotion.

He felt no restraint in giving utterance to the terrible feelings that possessed him. Deep sobs burst from his lips; he struck his forehead frantically with his clenched hands, and shouted the name of Miranda, till far and near the fields and trees re-echoed the sound.

Anyone who heard him would have considered him a maniac in one of his most dangerous paroxysms, for he addressed wild and strange arguments and appeals to Miranda, as if she had actually been there to listen to him.

"Where—where can you find a love like mine? Where could you find a heart that, for the privilege of being beloved by you for one short week, would consent to be torn from its home and consigned to everlasting per-

DICK PALMER CAPTURES THE POLICE OFFICER.

dition? Will the puny passion of Rowland Percy bear comparison with such idolatry? Miranda, are you mad, that you reject a love like mine for the cold feeling which with the mass of mankind goes by such a name?

"Love! What do they know of the glorious impulse? What do they know of the god-like feeling, which has its true manifestations in such self-sacrifices as they would shrink from aghast? They call a preference for one being above another, love, and their feelings glide on in peaceable and quiet obscurity, like an overcharged puddle by a quickset hedge.

"But my love is like a torrent—foaming and whirling on its course, leaping from crag to rock in the wild delirium of its progress, and dashing itself madly into millions of bright, sparkling drops, rather than not reach the object of its destination; or, it is like the seething lava from a burning mountain—scorching in its progress, and full of fiercest fire. Oh, Miranda! would I could repay scorn with scorn—hate with hate. But, no, I must love you—adore you—even when you trample upon my very heartstrings."

A solemn sound came across the expanse of nature to his ears. It was the Minster clock. Eight pealed forth, and Varley cast his eyes hurriedly over the Grange estate, muttering to himself:

"Time warns me. I came not to rave and hold communion with my convulsed heart; but to take a long, last farewell glance of this spot, which I feel assured I shall never—never behold again. 'Tis fair and beautiful, if it were not full of such reminiscences as would soon drive my soul to madness.

"Besides, I have now a pursuit—the one only pursuit of my future life. I must find Miranda. I must see her—I must be near her, though she load me with execrations— though she revile me in the bitterest language that the human mind can conceive, and the human tongue utter. Still, I must be near her."

He was silent then for some time, after which he said, evidently pursuing a new train of thought that had arisen in his mind:

"The Grange estates should fetch a goodly sum; that sum I will securely invest, but not in English funds; for something I little expect may possibly arise some day to make it advisable for me to avail myself of the yacht I have purchased, and so make my escape. My money shall be in the Dutch funds; in my yacht, then, I can go to Rotterdam, make my own financial arrangements, and provide for my personal safety as circumstances may prompt. As for Samuel Twitter—my only incumbrance now—if it should happen that I have to fly the country, why, of course, I would leave him to his fate. Let them hang him, or do what they will with him, it matters not to me.

"In the event, however, of no danger occurring, he may follow me as my valet, and most abject slave; but, upon the first suspicion I have of any scheme on his part contrary to my interests, he shall die. It would become a measure of self-defence, and I shall not scruple to put it into execution. The Grange shall be sold to-morrow, agreeably to my instructions—sold without reservation to the highest bidder, be he whom he may—and then my life shall be devoted to a pursuit of Miranda."

———

CHAPTER C.

THE AUCTION—THE INTERRUPTED SALE— VARLEY'S RAGE—THE AUCTIONEER.

BERNARD VARLEY had pursued his original intention of applying to the attorney, who had assisted him in some of his machinations, to give a price for the Grange estates; but that wily practitioner—who, in his own mind, never entertained the shadow of a doubt of Varley's guilt as regarded the murder of Sir George Rankley—shook his head at the proposition, saying:

"Why, you see, Mr. Varley, if young Rowland Percy had stayed in prison, and been hanged comfortably, as he ought to have been, I should have had no objection; for, although I have not enough money of my own to buy the Grange estates, even at a bargain, yet I could have procured the means, and paid cash down. Now, however, the case is widely different, for, by the escape of young Mr. Percy, the subject is not allowed to sleep in the public mind, and really there's no knowing who may be hanged eventually for the murder, or what disputation there might be years hence respecting your title to the estates."

"Dare you insinuate?" cried Bernard Varley.

"Oh, dear, no, sir, I insinuate nothing—very far from it. There is a law of libel, and I know it—it's voluminous and comprehensive. I would not insinuate, or say anything for all the world, and being unusually busy, I must really wish you an extremely good-morning."

The fact is, that Twitter had paid the attorney a visit, and from what he had related to him concerning Varley's mad pursuit of Miranda, the professional gentleman, instead of thinking Varley the clever scoundrel he once believed him, began to be of Twitter's opinion, that his wits were a little deranged, and that he would be anything but a desirable acquisition.

Thus was Varley foiled in his original attempt to dispose of the Grange property, and, cursing the attorney in his heart, he proceeded to an auctioneer, who was in a large way of business in the city, and requested him to undertake the disposal of the Grange estates for whatever they would fetch in the then state of the market.

As a matter of business, the job was readily accepted, and for some days past the provincial and London papers had teemed with attractive descriptions of the property, setting forth in the most glowing colours what the Grange was, and, in a great number of instances, what it was not; but, at all events, there was certain to be some good bidders for so importantly-situated a property, although many capitalists would be deterred from attempting the purchase as a speculation, in consequence of the circumstances attending the death of its last occupier, and the unpleasant notoriety thereby created.

The ample revenue of the Grange estates, however, and its noble mansion, were not likely to go a-begging because one of its owners had been murdered, and by twelve o'clock—the hour appointed for the sale— there was a crowded room full of persons ready, some to witness the proceedings merely out of curiosity, and others really to bid for the important property.

By far the greater number, however, were strangers, come there for mere amusement, for the murder of Sir George Rankley, together with the criminal proceedings consequent thereon, had not a little added to the curiosity ordinarily felt in such cases.

There is ever a great interest and a morbid desire on the part of the public to be present at any proceedings which have grown out of others presenting features of peculiar atrocity. Thus there is no doubt if the furniture in the Grange had been sold by auction, it would have fetched enormous prices, and most probably the bed on which Sir George Rankley was murdered would have sold for ten times its value.

The price, however, at which the Grange estates must inevitably go at precluded the possibility of an exercise of this absurd feeling, which, to use a popular phrase of the day, might be called morbidity for the million. So those who attended from this feeling could only take an interest in preserving one of the catalogues, glaring at the auctioneer, and staring intently into the faces of those who bid for the property, as if by so doing they became in a remote degree connected with the murder—and so an object of popular interest themselves.

Half-past twelve o'clock came, and the auctioneer mounted the rostrum.

All was breathless attention, and a shade of care seemed to pass over the rubicund countenance of the knight of the hammer—his very whiskers seemed to quiver with anxiety, and it was observed that he turned his little gray eyes in a very singular manner to all parts of the room before he ventured to speak.

Then a cadaverous expression crossed his face, and pointing with his ivory-hammer, tremblingly, to a corner of the room, he said:

"You don't mean it; you don't mean it?"

"I do mean it," cried Mr. Anderson, stepping forward, and standing upon a chair, so that he could command a view of, and likewise be seen by the whole assemblage. "I do mean it. Ladies and gentlemen, I have something very important to say before this sale is allowed to be proceeded with."

"Oh! pho, pho—pish—pshaw," said the auctioneer.

"Ladies and gentlemen," continued Mr. Anderson, "many of you in this room know me; my name is Anderson, and I am sure I need not ask twice for a patient hearing while I make a few remarks of the first importance to those who may be interested in the disposal of the property now about to be put up for auction."

"Oh, rubbish—stuff—pho, pho," cried the auctioneer; "he came to me last night, and I know all about it—pho, pho."

"Hear him—hear him," cried several voices.

"No, no," cried others; "let the sale proceed."

"Anderson, Anderson—hear Anderson," was loudly cried; "down with him—hear him —the sale—police—shame—knock him down —turn him out."

The auctioneer flourished his hammer, and turned redder in the face, until he looked like a new copper caldron, while Mr. Anderson made repeated efforts to be heard in the midst of the confusion, which was every moment increasing.

Then, when the riot was at its height, Bernard Varley suddenly stepped forward, and, exerting his voice to the utmost, he cried "Silence!" in so tremendous a tone, that the tumult of sounds was stilled, as if by the voice of some enchanter; each one pausing, involuntarily, in the noise he was making to look upon the pale face, distorted with passion,

of the man who had so lately, in York, gained such an unenviable notoriety.

"I am glad you are here, Mr. Varley," said Mr. Anderson, "as you will now hear truly what I say, without being possessed of any garbled statements upon the subject."

"How dare you," cried Varley, in a tremendous voice, "interrupt these proceedings? Five pounds to the man who will bring me a police officer to turn this scoundrel out of the room."

"Hard words break no bones, Bernard Varley," cried Mr. Anderson, "and I would rather be abused wrongfully than deserve it, and escape."

"Proceed with the sale," cried Varley to the auctioneer; "time is a little too valuable to have it wasted in listening to this mad attorney and his musty proverbs."

"True," cried Mr. Anderson, "and that puts me in mind that I came here in order to stop this sale."

"Stop the sale," cried the auctioneer; "oh, pho, pho—rubbish."

"Don't be a fool, copper-nose," cried somebody from the lower end of the room, and a roar of laughter, at the auctioneer's expense, succeeded.

"Stop the sale!" shrieked Bernard Varley. "How dare you attempt to stop the sale of my property? police—police."

"Mad or sane, Bernard Varley," continued Mr. Anderson, "I mean to attempt it, and, I believe, with every hope of success. At all events, it will not be the threats of such a man as Bernard Varley that will deter me. I stand here as the champion, although, perhaps, an inefficient one, of the innocent and oppressed, but I hope that God will give me strength to support my cause."

Loud cries of "Bravo, Anderson! bravo, Anderson!" resounded through the room; "hear him—hear him—let him speak."

Mr. Anderson had fairly got the ear of the assemblage, but Varley made another desperate attempt to stop him, by crying:

"This man is my enemy; it is well known he is my enemy—my avowed enemy—and now he wants to prevent my selling the estate which was bequeathed to me by my friend, and which my feelings will not permit me, myself, to inhabit."

"As God is my judge," cried Mr. Anderson, solemnly, "I have but one object, and that is, to save, if possible, any gentleman here present from incurring heavy losses by purchasing an estate, the title of which may be disputed."

"Disputed!" cried Varley.

"Ay, disputed!" cried Mr. Anderson. "I dispute it, and I advise all here present to abstain from bidding for a property which has been acquired at the expense of the destitute, the innocent, and the orphan—Miranda Rankley."

A loud burst of applause followed from those who merely came as lookers-on, and even those who came to buy looked doubtful and dispirited.

"Ladies and gentlemen," continued Mr.

Anderson, for he saw popular sympathy was on his side, " I would fain have spared all of you the trouble of coming here to-day, and I called upon the auctioneer last night to tell him that I was determined to make this attempt to stop the proceedings. The circumstances under which these estates have passed to that man, Bernard Varley, are full of suspicion, and I warn anyone against taking the property off his hands, even at the lowest and most nominal price. Let him hold possession, ladies and gentlemen, while he can; but do not let him, after reducing to destitution the gentlest and noblest creature——"

Here there was a loud burst of applause, and, when it subsided, Mr. Anderson continued :

" Do not, I say, let him walk off in triumph after converting that estate into money. No, ladies and gentlemen, let it be a clog to his foot, a galling collar round his neck, a torment to him by day and by night, so long as he keeps it from that innocent and heroic girl, who has shown an example of courage and heroism that will for ages to come be talked of, as, along with her beauty (one of the characteristics of the ladies of York)——"

This was a most politic sentence of Mr. Anderson's, for it at once enlisted in his cause every female in the room, and several meek-looking men, who had rather hung back till now, were pushed into the front by their wives and daughters, and made to shout " Hurrah ! bravo !" and " Go it !" till they almost terrified themselves.

In vain did Bernard Varley try to make himself heard.

He grew hoarse with passion, and almost foamed at the mouth with his impotent rage. He sprang upon a chair in order to raise himself above the multitude; but it was kicked from under him in an instant, and he found that if there was the slightest chance of his being allowed to remain in the room, it was only by being on his good behaviour.

As for the auctioneer, he kept up a continual knocking with his hammer, and looked quite bewildered, until somebody threw another man's hat at him, and then he disappeared altogether, sinking down to the bottom of the pulpit, fully convinced that the end of the world was close at hand.

As the hat went down with him in a most singular manner, the occurrence produced a perfect shriek of laughter, and a variety of loose articles, which lay at hand, were pitched into the pulpit, producing almost a state of delirium in the auctioneer, who could not conceive what was taking place, and when at last somebody shut up the writing-desk which was before the clerk, and taking it from him by force of arms, dropped that in, there was such a shout as transcends all description.

" I think the sale's over," whispered Mr. Anderson to the two or three friends by whom he was surrounded, and who had accompanied him to the auction for fear of any personal collision with Varley.

" Quite—quite," said the young barrister, who was one of the party. " You need say no more. Our friend the auctioneer must fancy there is an earthquake, and that he is buried alive among miscellaneous property."

" I think so, too," said Mr. Anderson, as he stepped down from the chair on which he stood.

" On my word," said the governor of the prison, who made one of the party, and wiping his eyes as he spoke, " I never was so amused in all my life. That auctioneer is a perfect treasure for a joke. Who could have supposed he would have gone in again so curiously; but come away, Mr. Anderson, the sooner now we leave this place the better."

By this time Bernard Varley had somewhat recovered from the shock he had sustained in being canted off the chair so suddenly, and he roared out :

" Auctioneer, do your duty. I will not have this sale stopped. The Grange estates are at auction. Do your duty, sir. As for you," turning to Mr. Anderson, " I will prosecute you for your interference, in the proper quarter."

" And I will defend him," cried the young barrister; " and my first endeavour shall be to discover if the plaintiff comes into court with clean hands."

" I understand you all," said Varley. " This is a conspiracy against me. Was there ever yet a man prosperous by his own industry, or the kindness of another, who did not make hosts of enemies ? But I will indict you all for a conspiracy, and this day's work shall be the worst you ever did in all your lives."

" I should be glad, indeed," said Mr. Anderson, " to get you into court. You would cut no very enviable figure at the Assizes, and I don't think, for my own part, that you will relish another cross-examination."

" I despise you !" cried Varley, " and your insane remarks.—Auctioneer, do your duty !"

The auctioneer, however, was quite deaf to the repeated calls which Varley made upon him; for the room was getting rapidly clear of persons, the crowd following Mr. Anderson and his party into the street, cheering him as they went.

Even Varley began to see that there would, indeed, be no auction that day.

Then he took it into his head that if the auctioneer had acted with firmness, the sale might have proceeded; and, impressed with that conviction, he strode towards the rostrum, mounted the steps leading to it, and, looking in, shouted to the auctioneer :

" Idiot ! I shall make you answerable, by bringing an action against you, for this day's disappointment."

" Oh, have mercy upon me !" said the auctioneer; " where am I ?"

" Curse you !" cried Varley, making a blow with the heavy riding-whip he carried, on the top of the miscellaneous property, which, hitting the writing-desk, brought it in more violent contact with the auctioneer's head, making him believe he was in the other world, and the sport of malignant demons.

"Stay, stay," cried Varley, to the retreating throng of persons, "why are you going?"

"Ah! I hear him," said the auctioneer, "he says going; Satan is knocking down human souls, and I am gone."

The crowd of persons would not be stayed, for they saw no further amusement, or profit, by remaining in the auction-room, so that, in a few moments more, there was nobody left but the half-dead auctioneer, his clerk, and Bernard Varley.

"Now," said Mr. Anderson, when he gained the street, "come to my house, gentlemen, and let us think of some means of finding out where Miranda Rankley has gone."

"Ah!" said the young barrister, "I can well guess her feelings; she has that true nobility of soul which shrinks from being a burden upon anyone. I declare to you, gentlemen, that if her heart were free at this moment, I should glory in making that girl my wife."

"A better one," said Mr. Anderson, "could never be found to make a happy home, and I long to see the day, should it ever come, when she and her first and only love, Rowland Percy, for whom she has suffered so much, done so much, may meet, never to part again."

"Amen," said the Governor; "I never met or heard of her equal; the praises of her courage and heroism are upon every unprejudiced tongue in York. She deserves the happiest of fates; and it cuts me to the soul to think that she may be, even now, suffering great poverty, if not absolute want."

———

CHAPTER CI.

MIRANDA IN THE WAGGON—THE JEW PEDLAR —THE ROBBERY AND THE DIAMOND RING.

It was a slow and dreary mode of conveyance, that by the waggon, which Miranda, for the want of a better, had been forced to avail herself of; but, still, it was preferable to being exposed to wind and weather, and the chance accidents of the road.

If her progress was slow, it was certain; and, while old Mr. Percy fell into a dreamy and disturbed sleep, she pleased herself with the idea that she was each moment approaching nearer and nearer to Rowland Percy.

And, oh, how delightful would be their first interview, after so long a time—for long, indeed, did it appear to Miranda, although it had been short in reality.

The multitude of events which had been crowded into it, would have sufficed for the incidents of half a lifetime; and it seemed to her, since that night in the condemned cell, when her heart was fluttering between hope and fear, that a long and weary time must have elapsed.

She knew not how far she had travelled in the waggon, but her chequered imaginations were suddenly put an end to by the stoppage of the vehicle—some conversation then took place outside, and, in another moment, a man scrambled into the interior.

His aspect was far from pleasing—he had that indescribable look which belongs to a Jewish countenance of the worst order; and a small brass-bound box he had with him, not much larger than a writing-desk, would at once have proclaimed to any more practised eyes than Miranda's, that he was one of those itinerant hawkers of mock jewellery, who make the exhibition of their wares an excuse, in many cases, for committing petty larcenies, and, in others, for obtaining information which leads to more serious robberies.

Miranda shrank as far as possible away from the man, for his looks were repulsive in the extreme, and she was not a little annoyed by feeling confident that, for the next half-hour, he never took his eyes off her.

At length he spoke, and it was in a tone of insolent inquiry that he said:

"Going far, miss—eh?"

"I do not wish to awaken my companion," replied Miranda, pointing to the sleeping Mr. Percy, "and, therefore, decline conversation."

"Oh, you decline, do you?" said the man; "that's civil, anyhow. I didn't mean any offence, miss. Oh, Moses! what a handsome ring!"

As he spoke, he advanced so suddenly to Miranda, in order to look at the ring which she wore on her finger, as the safest place to keep that last memento of her father, that he was close to her side for a moment, but only for a moment, for she shrank back, crying:

"Help! Mr. Percy, help!"

The cry acted like magic upon the slumbering senses of Mr. Percy. All the maniac in his disposition seemed aroused, and springing to his feet, he seized the man by the throat with a grip of iron, and flung him on his back in an instant, shouting:

"Fiend! fiend! monster! have I caught you! So you would condemn my innocent boy Rowland to death—you would bear false witness against him, wretch!—you would see him writhing on the scaffold, and exult in his pangs. Fiend—villain, I will try if I cannot kill you."

He then bumped the man's head with such frightful violence and rapidity against the bottom of the waggon, that it sounded as if someone was performing a succession of double knocks at a street-door.

"Murder! murder!" cried the man; but the waggoner was fast asleep, and all the horses likewise, so that no attention was paid to the outcries of the pedlar, and he would in all probability have paid with his life for his unwarrantable insolence, had not Miranda sprung forward, and clinging to the arm of Mr. Percy, cried:

"Spare him! spare him! It is enough—spare him, Mr. Percy! Spare him!—I implore you to spare him!"

Her voice acted like a charm upon the troubled spirit which had been aroused to such an ungovernable pitch of fury, and, with a smile, he let go his hold of the terrified man, saying:

"Ay, Miranda, at your bidding. Yes, my beautiful child, at your bidding. Yes, he shall live—the wretch shall live. But is he not one of my Rowland's enemies?"

"No—no! let him be now," cried Miranda; "let him be now, Mr. Percy. He is not—do not heed him—he is not."

Miranda clung to Mr. Percy's arm, and was quite as much terrified at the scene which ensued as was the Jew pedlar himself, who slowly rose to his feet, as pale as a corpse, rubbing his head with great vehemence.

"You see," said Miranda, turning to him, "what your own folly brought upon your head?"

"Upon my head!" muttered the man; "he's nearly knocked it off. Is he a madman?"

"Hush! Yes," whispered Miranda.

"Oh, Moses!" ejaculated the pedlar, as he sprang to the tail of the waggon.

"Again—again!" cried Mr. Percy, in a loud voice.

"No—no!" cried the pedlar, "it's all right. I didn't mean anything. How do you do, old gentleman? I hope you'll be better soon. I never had such a bump in my life. When one gets into a waggon, one doesn't expect to get into a wild beast show."

"Is he an enemy now?" said Mr. Percy, turning to Miranda.

"No—no," cried the pedlar. "Tell him no, young woman. It's all right, old gentleman—I tell you it's all right."

"Peace!" cried Miranda, taking Mr. Percy by the hand; "there is no danger. Will you sleep again?"

"Yes—sleep," he muttered. "I was dreaming of my boy. Wake me, Miranda, if the enemy should come. I will tear them limb from limb, and tread down the pulsation of their hearts with my heel."

"Good gracious!" said the pedlar, suddenly dropping his brass-bound box, and, then, fearful that the noise would arouse Mr. Percy's fury, he said, in a whining tone: "Heaven bless you, sir, and all your family. It's a fine day, sir. I hope you're well, sir."

"We will let him," said Mr. Percy to Miranda, "we will let him live for a little while. Now, I will go to sleep for awhile, and dream of my boy, Rowland, and of you, my beautiful Miranda. Heaven have mercy on those who look awry on you, for I will have none."

"What a murderous old rascal!" muttered the pedlar; "but if I don't have that ring, my name is not Ikey Samuels."

The journey now proceeded some miles without interruption, no sound disturbing the stillness around, but the monotonous tinkle-tinkle of the horses' bells, which they were so accustomed to, that the sound rather acted as a gentle lullaby than otherwise, and it is probable that if the bells had suddenly been taken away they would have all started, wide awake, in wonder and astonishment to know what had happened.

The Jew, however, was too good a judge of the value of Miranda's ring, and of too avaricious and dishonest a disposition to allow even his dread of the violence of Mr. Percy to stand in the way of an attempt to possess himself of it.

"Miss," he said, in a low, cringing tone, "I've got a pair of earrings as is the very pattern and model of that ring you have on your finger."

"I do not wear such ornaments," said Miranda, shortly.

"But," added the Jew, "as it would match my earrings, I could, perhaps, sell the lot together, and as well to make up the little offence I gave you, my dear, as well as for that reason, I will give you a more valuable ring in exchange for yours."

"I want no exchanges," said Miranda; "there is no ring to me so valuable as this, and nothing short of absolute necessity to provide for the wants of my aged companion and myself shall ever induce me to part with it."

"But——"

"Nay—nay," said Miranda, "I wish for no offers, and no conversation concerning it."

"I humbly beg your pardon," said the Jew, "and am glad you are so well provided for the journey you are going on."

Miranda instinctively put her hand in her pocket, and felt for her purse.

With a pang of alarm she assured herself that the purse was gone, and, as the expression of her features could not be mistaken for a moment, the Jew said, in a low tone:

"Have you lost anything, miss?"

"My purse—my purse!" said Miranda, clasping her hands. "We are destitute, now!"

"Nay—nay," said the Jew, with repressed eagerness, "you—you have the ring, my dear, which, although of small value, will still, if given an honest and conscientious price for, carry you far on your journey."

"Small value," said Miranda. "I know well it is of large value."

"Indeed!" said the Jew; "let me look again. Ah! you are right—it is worth a hundred pounds, and, if you part with it for less, he who purchases it of you will be taking an undue advantage of you."

"I have heard that sum named as its value," sighed Miranda; "but it—it—is almost like parting with my dear father again, to part with this——"

"But, my dear," said the Jew, "you are destitute, friendless—that is to say, you have no rich friends, my dear, and poor ones are not worth having at all; besides, I dare say the violent old gentleman is quite depending upon you, my dear."

"He is," sighed Miranda. "Oh, Heavens! what will become of us now?"

"Why—why," said the Jew, speaking eagerly, and creeping nearer to her at each word, "you can sell the ring to me."

"To you?"

"Yes, my dear; rather than you should fall into dishonest hands, I will give you the full value for it—the hundred pounds, as I am a sinner."

"My father's ring—my dear father's ring!" cried Miranda, as she pressed it to her lips.

"Ah!" said the Jew, "I have a soft heart. Don't look at me—I am crying, my dear."

"If—if," said Miranda, in low, trembling accents, "if I sell it to you, will you tell me where I can find you, and promise me, in the name of Heaven, that you will keep it at least one year, in case I should be able to reclaim it of you."

"Oh, certainly—certainly, my dear," said the Jew; "as many years as you like. Do you think I have no feeling? I had a father myself: he was hanged—no, I mean he was drowned. You shall have it of me whenever you please, and without a farthing of interest, too."

"That," said Miranda, mournfully, "would be a great consideration. I could part with it with less regret if I thought that, when fortune smiled upon me again, should such ever be the case, I could reclaim it."

"Reclaim it—of course, my dear. Do you think I would keep your ring from you—your father's ring, too?"

"But how should I find you," said Miranda, "if I were to part with it to you?"

"Have you ever been in London?" said the Jew.

"Never," replied Miranda.

"Oh, then," said the Jew, "my dear, I live in London, and you have nothing to do at any time but to ask the first person you meet for Ikey Samuels, and they will direct you to me."

"May I depend upon you?" said Miranda.

"On my word," said the Jew; "and you may well believe me when I offer you the full value for your ring—the full value, my dear, that you have heard set upon it. Abraham forbid, my dear, that I should make a profit of you in your distress."

Miranda was silent for some moments, and it was evident that, during that brief space of time, her feelings were of the most painful nature; but then, when she thought of the heavy charge she had in Mr. Percy, who seemed committed solely to her care by Providence, and, likewise, how probable it was that, when she reached poor Rowland, his circumstances would be far from flourishing, she chid herself for hesitating, and being sentimental, about a ring, when so many more important feelings and interests were at stake.

"I will let it go," she thought. "A hundred pounds is a large sum, and it will be a cheering thing in the great city to which I am making my way to have such a sum to present to Rowland Percy. Moreover, it will enable me to pay the man, Jones, who has so kindly assisted me with money. Yes, I will let it go. How could I hesitate when such considerations are at stake?"

Then, turning to the Jew, she said:

"On your solemn promise to restore me the ring again, if it should be in my power to

make you ample restitution for so doing, I will sell it."

"I swear—I swear," cried the Jew, with eagerness, "I swear to restore it to you. My name is Ikey Samuels, and I would not break my oath for a thousand pounds, though, if you knew me, you would take my word just as easily. My word, my bond, and my oath, are all alike. Did you ever know, miss, a Jew that was dishonest?"

"I know nothing upon the subject," said Miranda; "but, with pain, I consent to part with my ring for what I have heard as its value—namely, one hundred pounds."

"And you shall have it—and you shall have it, miss. A Bank of England note for the amount you shall have, and here it is. How fortunate I have one about me."

As he spoke, he produced an ancient-looking pocket-book, and, after a great deal of fumbling about its contents, he produced a hundred-pound note, which he handed to Miranda.

"Can you not give me gold?" said Miranda. "I want money for current expenses, and not in this condensed form."

"My dear," said the Jew, "you'll get change at the first turnpike you come to. They always keep plenty of gold and silver to give change to chance travellers."

Miranda hesitated still for a moment, and then she blamed herself for her suspicions.

With a deep sigh she took the ring from her finger, and, handing it to the Jew, said:

"Take it, and pray preserve it. You do not—cannot, know how dear it is to me."

"I will preserve it with my life," said the Jew. "You have made a good bargain, miss. It is a diamond, certainly, and yet scarcely worth the hundred. A good bargain, miss, on my word, a good bargain."

He placed the ring, after carefully wrapping it in a piece of paper, deep in his pocket, and then he could ill suppress the chuckle of conscious knavery, that would make itself heard in spite of him.

Miranda placed the note in her pocket, and then, forgetting the very existence of the Jew, she fell into a deep reverie, in which painful reminiscences of the past, and hopes and fears of the future, mingled together in her mind.

She was aroused from this by hearing the voice of the Jew calling loudly to the waggoner to stop, and, glancing towards him, she saw that he was getting out at the back of the waggon.

When he saw her eyes fixed upon him, he said:

"Good-day, my dear—good-day. Be assured I will keep the ring. It is safer, a great deal safer, than if you had it yourself, for you might meet, you know, my dear, with some rogue on the road that might deprive you of it. He! he! he! Good-day, my dear—good day. Take care of the old gentleman—bless his heart."

"Good-day," said Miranda, and, with another disagreeable chuckle, the Jew left the waggon.

CHAPTER CII.

THE ATTEMPT TO CHANGE THE NOTE—MR. JONES'S ARRIVAL—THE DISTRESSING DISCOVERY—MIRANDA'S SACRIFICE IN VAIN.

MIRANDA was extremely anxious to get change for the hundred-pound note, for she had not, besides, a sixpence in the world; and it showed a very limited knowledge of society and its usages, to suppose for a moment that she could get change for it at a turnpike-gate.

An opportunity occurred of testing the accuracy of the Jew's information during the next hour, when the leading horse, after running his head against the gate, and producing an extra peal of all his little bells, came to a standstill, and succeeded, as before, in stopping the whole team.

The waggoner then opened his eyes, and, after rubbing them vigorously, said:

"Thirty-six."

"All right," replied the toll-man.

"Stop a moment," cried Miranda—"stop."

"Woa!" said the waggoner, and the old leading horse, who had slowly lifted up one leg, put it down again.

"What's the row?" said the turnpike-keeper.

"I wish to ask a favour of you," said Miranda.

"Sartenly, miss. What is it?"

"Can you give me change for a hundred pound note?"

"There's a jumping sell," said the turnpike-keeper, angrily, as he rushed into his little house.

"What does he mean?" said Miranda to the waggoner.

The waggoner shook his head, and then, giving a crack with his whip, shouted—

"Kim up—gee."

A rattling of chains ensued, followed by a tinkling of bells, and the whole team was in motion.

As Miranda looked from the back of the waggon, she saw the turnpike-man shaking his fist, and looking as angry as if somebody had just jumped on his corns.

Poor Miranda was quite at a loss to understand the meaning of all this, and she asked herself over and over again how she could possibly get change now for the hundred pound note; for, after the extraordinary conduct of the turnpike-man—unless it could be accounted for by insanity, engendered by the loneliness of his situation—she dreaded to ask another of the same class for the accommodation.

An hour and more passed away in uneasy thoughts, when a loud shout at some distance on the road attracted her attention, roused up Mr. Percy, and very nearly awakened the shaft horse.

"Hilloa! hilloa!" cried the voice. "Woa, there—woa. Stop the hunt. Good gracious! what a state you must all be in. You'll break all your blessed necks going at that speed. I never seed such coursing in all my life—neck or nothing—fifteen miles an hour—walk two on 'em, and dream the rest."

"That is Jones's voice," said Miranda. "He will assist me in my dilemma."

In another moment Jones appeared at the tail of the waggon.

He scrambled into the vehicle, and was out of sight before the waggoner had become thoroughly aware that there was a voice somewhere. When he did, however, his impression was that somebody had been run over, so he stopped the whole team, by spreading out his arms, and catching the leading horse round the neck.

Then he looked for five minutes under the waggon, by the end of which time he became satisfied that there was nothing to be seen but the wheels, the dirty road, the drag chain, and some turnip-tops.

"Kim up—gee," he said, and again the cumbrous affair crawled on in total unconsciousness of the addition of Mr. Jones to the party.

"Well, mum," said Jones, "how is you and the old gentleman? I hopes as you is tolderido."

"We are very well, Mr. Jones," said Miranda.

"Nothing happened, I presume?"

"I have been very careless," said Miranda, "for the money with which you so kindly supplied me, I have by some accident lost."

Mr. Jones gave a long whistle, and then added:

"Ah, well, it wasn't altogether unpleasantly 'arned. I have got a few more of them same little tinkling goldfinches; some wagabone, I suppose, seeing as you was werdant, boned the mopuses."

"I think less of the loss," said Miranda, who had got into the habit of guessing at Mr. Jones's meaning, rather than trouble him to explain each word he uttered. "I think the less of it, because, by a sacrifice, which I ought not, perhaps, to have hesitated about before, I am enabled to provide amply for my present exigencies, as well as repay you the sums you have so kindly lent me."

"The deuce!" said Mr. Jones; "what's up now?"

"I have sold my father's ring."

"Sold it? My eye!—who to?"

"A Mr. Ikey Samuels."

Jones gave a comic sort of shriek, and then exclaimed:

"What a captivating name—done brown—done brown! Tell us the peticulars. Oh, crikey! here's a go!"

"He came, like myself," said Miranda, "to have a lift in the waggon."

"'Twas arter that," interrupted Mr. Jones, "you found as your tin had lewanted."

"Found what?" said Miranda.

"As the poney had cut his stick — the mopuses mizzled—the goldfinches emigrated."

"Oh!" said Miranda, "you mean the money? Yes, it was after that I missed my money."

"Oh, in course," said Jones, screwing up a terrible face. "Resoom—resoom."

"When I made known my loss," continued Miranda, "he offered to buy my ring; but I was very cautious, as you had warned me there were dishonest persons about."

Mr. Jones gave a singular sort of howl, and kicked the straw at the bottom of the waggon desperately, after which he cried:

"Resoom—resoom!"

"I could not go wrong," said Miranda, "because I have often heard that a hundred pounds was the extreme value of the ring. and I resolved that I would not take a less sum than one which should come near that amount, and when he offered that price in full, and at the same time promised to keep the ring for me in case I should be able to redeem it, I could no longer doubt the sincerity of his intentions."

"Fake away," said Mr. Jones, placing the tip of his thumb on the extreme point of his nose, and agitating his fingers in a significant manner.

"So," continued Miranda, "I let him have the ring on those conditions."

"Where's the tippery?" said Jones.

"He paid me with this hundred-pound note."

"That's the dodge," said Jones.

"I have been trying to get it changed, but the turnpike-man refused the trifling accommodation, behaving very insolently, likewise, upon the occasion."

"What a ass he must have been," said Jones, unfolding the note, and putting it carefully on his knee. "Here's an out-an'-out do: 'Bank of Noland—I promises to humbug whosoever's as green as grass, and doesn't know B from a bull's-foot.'"

"B what?" said Miranda.

"What, didn't you read it?"

"No, I did not."

"My eye, what a extent of werdant wegetation you must carry about along of you—why, it's an out-an'-out do; he's not only boned them ere mopuses as I guved yer, but this here note's just the walley of any other little bit of crumpled paper. It's a outrageous do."

"Gracious powers!" cried Miranda, "am I deceived?"

"Gracious powers, you are regularly done brown," said Jones. "I never know'd such a splendiferous, flabbergasterous sort of do in all my life. Was he a feller with a little mahogany box, with brass edges?"

"Yes," said Miranda; "he said his name was Ikey Samuels. Oh! how could I be so heedless as to lose my poor father's ring in such a manner?"

"It's never no use of taking on," said Jones. "I meant to have gone the remainder of this here way with yer, but it's no go now. Howsomdever, I'll try to overtake yer yet; but if I don't, stick to the waggon till it's loaded, and come back with it, when I shall be sure to meet you. Here's something as'll do till I sees you again; and, goodness gracious, Miss

Miranda, whatever you does, don't be so outrageous green—its puffictly putrifying."

"Where are you going now?" said Miranda.

"To ax for change for the flimsey," said Jones. "Ikey and me must settle this ere affair somehow or another."

So saying, Jones, after thrusting the note into his breeches pocket, jumped from the waggon, and hastened off at a sharp walk in the opposite direction.

Poor Miranda felt this misfortune connected with the ring most acutely.

She had only parted with it at the greatest possible sacrifice to her own feelings, with the higher and nobler object of providing first of all for the wants of him who had been so strangely thrown upon her hands for support, and the pleasure it would be to her to place in the hands of Rowland Percy a sum, at all events, that would rescue him for a time from poverty and its series of attendant evils.

But now to feel that she had made all that sacrifice in vain—to feel that she had lost that last and only memento of her father, and that her mind had nothing to fall back upon and console her for the deprivation—was grievous and heart-sickening in the extreme.

The only thing that supported her was the hope, distant though it was, that Jones might be able to discover the man who had so heartlessly deceived her, and, before he could have disposed of the ring in any way, procure it for her, and once more give her the pleasure of having it in her possession.

The supposition that the note was not a genuine one had never for an instant occurred to her mind; but now that she felt its full force, she trembled at the danger she had unwittingly run into in attempting to change it.

"I ought to be thankful," she thought, "that I have escaped from this circumstance even as I have; for what horrors might have been in store for me had I been arrested on what surely would have been the criminal charge of attempting to pass a false note; what great delays my release might have been subjected to, while the safety of Rowland would have been greatly endangered by the very steps I should have been forced to take in order to free myself from the frightful suspicion which would otherwise have attached to me. Ought I not, indeed, to be thankful—most thankful?"

These were, however, but poor and sad reflections for Miranda as she proceeded on her weary and toilsome journey, yet they were the only ones with which her imagination furnished her.

The day was cold, but still fair, and occasionally bright, although anyone not particularly weatherwise would have prognosticated a change towards sunset.

It was a relief to Miranda's feelings that old Mr. Percy slept so much as he did, for she was hardly in spirits to have talked to him; the anxiety she felt concerning her ring, added to her other sources of discomfort, completely distracting her mind.

The horses that drew the waggon seemed to be well accustomed to the road, and to be perfectly well acquainted with the different roadside public-houses, at which it was usual to stop for refreshment, for they drew up as sagaciously as possible every time they came to one, and the waggoner, whenever he was thoroughly awake, would come now and then to the tail of the waggon to ask if Miranda and Mr. Percy wanted anything.

But slight refreshments, however, sufficed for those care-worn travellers, and they did not take, during the whole day, as much as was scarcely enough to suffice the waggoner himself at one of his numerous little halts.

As hour after hour passed away, Miranda became more and more anxious for the re-appearance of Jones; but he came not, and a deeper feeling of melancholy than had oppressed her for some time crept into her heart.

Towards evening the wind, which had blown freshly and in sudden squalls, fell; the whole atmosphere became charged with moisture, which spread its leaden-colour vapour over the country, and began to descend in the form of a dense mist, which, towards night, turned to a heavy rain.

Nature wore her sombrest hues, and assumed her most melancholy garb, as the light of day departed, and darkness shrouded the earth.

The rain continued to fall, while neither the light of the moon, nor of the stars, shed a solitary gleam of light to cheer the road of the weary travellers, or give them hopes of an amendment in the weather.

True it was that it was not so utterly dark that no object could be seen. But for the intervention of the clouds there would have been moonlight; as it was, sufficient illumination reached the earth to enable anyone who might be abroad to distinguish objects, though but dimly, and thus enable the peasant to plod over common and through field to his lonely home.

Gloomy and desolate was all around—no cheering sight or sound struck upon the senses—the dull, hoarse howling of the wind which came up in gusts, swept the shower in one direction, then suddenly ceasing, naught was heard but the sullen pattering of the rain as it fell fast in heavy drops.

Such a night would chill the heart of the boldest and stoutest, and gladly would they select the first shelter that afforded them warmth and the presence of their fellow creatures, for all else was so lonely—so dreary—and exquisitely uncomfortable.

The road was now beginning to assume a more lively character, and Miranda, on creeping to the front of the waggon, and looking out, saw some half a mile or more before her, the numerous lights of what appeared to be a large town.

"I shall soon have," she thought, "to leave this friendly shelter for awhile. Oh, that he would come! oh, that he would come!"

CHAPTER CIII.

JONES AND THE JEW—IKEY SAMUELS' DESPAIR—COGENT REASONING.

"WHAT an aggrawation this is, to be sure," was Mr. Jones' soliloquy, after he had parted from Miranda. "The idea of that infernal Ikey Samuels a boning that ere ring—what wice there is in the world—there is people as thinks nothing of dishonesty, and has no more notion of what belongs to 'em, and what doesn't, than a pig in a turnip field."

Having thus declared to himself his opinion of Mr. Ikey Samuels' rascality, Jones proceeded at a very rapid pace in a contrary direction from that in which the waggon was proceeding, for he had no doubt the Jew would choose to put as great a distance between himself and his victim as possible.

It did not take very long for Mr. Jones to reach the turnpike, and when he did, he entered the small dwelling without any ceremony.

"Hilloa, friend," he said to the turnpike man, "who's been through here lately—a fellow with a brass-bound box?"

"No," said the pikeman, "there's been nobody of the kind: mine's a dog sleep; I always looks on foot passengers with one eye, and anything on four legs or wheels with two."

"Thank yer," said Jones, "thank yer."

He then walked on, saying to himself:

"I'm after him, for a certainty; it was just possible he might have doubled on his track after going some distance this way to let the waggon get ahead of him, and I am quite sure and certain that, if that had been the manœuvre, he would have gone just as far as that public-house, and no farther."

Now the Jew pedlar congratulated himself extremely upon his meeting with Miranda, and the ease with which he had played upon her so heartless a trick.

Danger he never dreamt of for a moment, for two beings more thoroughly isolated from society or friends than were that beautiful girl and her aged companion he thought he had never met; and certainly without a knowledge of the very peculiar circumstances which had brought Miranda into her present situation, it would, indeed, seem as if she were utterly friendless, and, with that old man, thrown completely destitute upon the world.

He laughed repeatedly to himself at what he considered his own cleverness in the execution of the trick.

"Not a bad day's work," he cried; "ha, ha! far from a bad day's work. How she came by the ring it matters not to me. I have it now, and that is amply sufficient and satisfactory. It will be hard, indeed, if I can't make fifty or sixty pounds of it. Thanks to my apprenticeship to the old lapidary of Hamburg, I know a real diamond at a glance, and this is one of the first water—a fine day's work, a brave day's work, ah, and a safe day's work, for I'd swear she came honestly by the ring, or she would never have parted with it so foolishly. Well, Ikey Samuels, you are a clever boy, a very clever boy; what would Solomans, in Duke's Place, say to this?—I shall be made an elder of the synagogue."

Here Mr. Ikey Samuels rapped his brass-bound box with his knuckles, and laughed again, in the most exulting manner, as he said:

"I have it, I have it safe—safe and firm, and Old Nick himself sha'n't get it away from me."

"How do you do, Ikey?" said a voice behind him.

"So help me, Abraham!—who's that?" cried Ikey, giving a sudden jump forwards, and then, turning round, he saw the athletic form of Mr. Jones within a few paces of him.

"I don't know you," said Ikey Samuels, "so help my honesty, I don't know you."

"Not know me," said Jones; "lor! Why I thought everybody know'd me, and, if you doesn't, you are the only one as is in such a state of werdant ignorance, and we must alter that ere afore we parts. How is business, Ikey?"

"It's no business of yours," said Ikey Samuels, walking on doggedly, with a determination to get rid, as soon as possible, of his chance acquaintance.

"No, but it's a pleasure," said Jones, "you can't think how far I have come on purpose to see you."

"What do you want with me?" said the Jew, hurriedly, and looking round him in some dismay, as he recognized he was on a part of the road three miles from a public-house, and six from a private one.

"Why, to tell you the truth," said Jones, "I am distressed for change."

"Change! what do you mean?" cried the Jew, as he plunged his hand into his pocket, and brought it out again with a clasp-knife, the blade of which sprang up upon touching a spring, making it, indeed, a most deadly weapon in a close encounter.

"Ah," said Jones, "that's it, is it?" and he made a dart at the Jew so suddenly, that he succeeded in laying hold of his wrist with one hand, and his collar with the other.

"Murder!" cried the Jew.

"No," said Jones; "it's only a swindle. I doesn't accuse you of murder yet, whatever you might ha' done with that clasp knife if you had been able. Now, drop it, will you?"

The Jew aimed a savage kick at Jones, which, however, the latter adroitly avoided, and returned with such interest that Ikey Samuels set up a yell of despair, and danced again in agony.

"Drop it!" cried Jones. "Drop it, I say!"

The knife fell at his feet, and the Jew, sinking on his knees, cried:

"Mercy—mercy! Spare my life! I suppose you are a highwayman?"

"If I am," said Jones, "I am not a sneak. Do you know this?"

As he spoke, he unfolded the note within an inch of the Jew's nose.

Ikey Samuels replied in the negative, with a deep groan.

"Not know it!" cried Jones. "How can you say so to my face? Come, I'll let you off easy. Bolt the note whole, and give up the ring and purse, and then you may go."

"On my conscience," said the Jew, "I do not understand you. I am an innocent man, a poor hawker of Brummagem jewellery, and haven't five shillings in the world."

"What a shocking thing a bad memory is," said Jones. "Just sit down, will you?"

The Jew obeyed, and, with a face of absolute despair, sat down by the road-side, devoutly wishing that someone would come past to relieve him from his distressing situation.

"Now, you scoundrel," said Jones, "what I have to say to you is just this. You have a choice, either quietly to give up a ring which you got from a young lady in a waggon, who is a friend of mine, or to make a trouble of the matter, and place me under what people calls the pressure o' circumstances, which means as I shall have to break your neck."

The Jew wrung his hands, as he thought:

"There goes the result of all my cleverness in a moment."

Then, however, a sudden thought, which conveyed a very faint hope, struck him, and he said:

"I have not the ring here. I have sold it. On my conscience I have, and know not where it is."

"Oh, indeed!"

"Yes—yes. As I am an honest man, I have parted with it to a man who has gone on to London, and all I can offer you, as I'm a sinner, is the amount he gave me for it."

"How much is that?"

"Twenty pounds."

"Why, you just now swore as you wasn't worth five shillings in the blessed world. I'm afeard, Ikey Samuels, as you sometimes gives yer mind to saying what isn't exactly the blessed and out-and-out truth."

"But I was confused, and knew not what I said. You will take the twenty pounds, and let me go?"

"Yes, I will take the twenty pounds," said Jones.

The Jew's face brightened up in a moment, and he said:

"You shall have the money. I am very sorry the young lady was a friend of yours. You see I make nothing by the whole transaction."

"Absolutely nothink," said Jones. "I made up my mind as you shouldn't when first I heard of it, and so to make quite sure o' such a state o' things, I shall take the liberty o' overhauling that nice-looking box of yours."

"No—no—murder!" cried the Jew. "You don't know how dreadfully perishable the articles I have there are. The open air hurts them very much."

"I should say it would make some on 'em wanish quite outright," said Jones, as ho seized the box, despite the frantic struggles of Ikey Samuels, who felt that his defeat was now quite certain, and that, in addition to losing the produce of his robbery, he should himself be a considerable sufferer.

"In the name of Abraham," he groaned, "who are you?"

"A cracksman," was the brief response.

"Then—then," said the Jew, "you ought to have some feeling for me, as we are both of a trade."

"What do you mean, you humbug?"

"I never did an honest action in my life—I assure you—I'm a terrible thief, and surely we oughtn't to make war upon each other? You will spare me?"

"It's one o' my opinions," said Jones, "as all the world is thieves, only there's a precious difference as to how they does the prigging. Some is sneaks, and some is slashers, and if you takes upon yourself all for to try to make out as I'm as bad as you, I'll just break this box over your head, instead of over that ere milestone."

"Break my box!" shrieked the Jew. "Oh! for mercy's sake, don't. Here's the key."

"Bother the key," said Jones, and proceeding to the milestone, he dealt the Jew's box such a whack against it that it fell into pieces, scattering the "Brummagem jewellery" in all directions.

It did not take Jones many minutes to find among the mock gems the real diamond-ring of Miranda, and, placing it upon his little finger, he said:

"All's right, Ikey. Your friend as guv'd you the twenty pound for this here must have been an uncommonly careless fellow, for he's left it behind him. Now, I tell you what I'll do. I'll take both the twenty pounds and the ring, so when I meet him, you know, I can give him back his blunt in a honest way."

Foiled in all his tricks, and rendered nearly desperate by seeing his stock-in-trade scattered upon the public road, Ikey Samuels actually yelled with rage, and would have rushed away in hopes of procuring assistance, had it not been that he could not possibly tear himself away from his beloved box, in a secret drawer of which was some money, which he yet hoped would escape Mr. Jones' scrutiny.

In this expectation, however, he hugely miscalculated, for Jones was too practised a hand to allow any part of the box to remain unsearched.

With a cry of despair, the Jew saw his secret hoard discovered, and transported to Mr. Jones' pockets.

"I'm a ruined man!" cried Ikey Samuels. "What will become of me now? I shall be cast off by my people, and come again to selling black-lead pencils without lead in them. Oh, dear—oh, dear!"

"Hold your noise, and listen to me," said Jones. "This here affair is all in the way of business. It's diamond cut diamond, you know, for me to get the better of you, and now let me give you a warnin', Ikey Samuels. You may make a hue and cry after me for robbing you, but so sure as you do, you won't catch me; and if I hear that you so much as grumbles in your sleep about the matter, I'll take care that the young lady as you robbed shall prosecute you; and a defence which only says as you was robbed of your swag arter you had boned it you'll find is somewhere about pleading guilty. So, you see, Ikey, in this blessed business, the least as is said is the soonest mended."

To say that the Jew did not feel the full force of this course of argument would be to libel the cunning of his whole tribe.

He saw his position just as Jones painted it, and, with a deep groan, he replied:

"You are right enough; but do give me something to save me from starvation."

"Lying again!" cried Jones. "Why, you've got the purse now that you stole. Come, fork—fork."

Ikey Samuels showed so much reluctance to comply with the demand to "fork," that Jones took up the knife, and commenced whetting it upon his boot.

"What are you doing that for?" inquired the Jew.

"To cut your throat," was the reply. "I see I shall have to do it, and I may as well do it clean and nice as not."

"There's the purse; and now you leave me quite a ruined man."

"Very good," said Jones, as he coolly took the purse and walked away, without bestowing another word or look upon the half-distracted Ikey Samuels.

CHAPTER CIV.

THE QUARREL BETWEEN VARLEY AND TWITTER—THE COMPROMISE—THE JOURNEY TO LONDON.

STUNG nearly to madness with the agony of his feelings, and the successful opposition he had met with in the prosecution of his plans, Bernard Varley repaired from the auction-room to the hotel, where, for some short time now, he had taken up his abode.

Truly did he begin to feel that the possession of the Grange estates was not equivalent to a power of doing what he pleased with the property, and the more he thought over the circumstances of the last few days, the greater grew his rage at everybody and at everything.

He felt that if the whole human race had but one head, he would glory in striking it off. He raved at Providence—at what he called fate and destiny—continuing for some hours in an irrational state of mind, which knew but one strong feeling, and that was an intense desire to inflict upon someone, he scarcely cared whom, some exquisite kind of suffering.

His oaths and imprecations were terrible, and it was not until they could hear, by the comparative silence, that the wild storm of passion was abating, that any of the establishment would venture into the room,

MR. JONES MEETS UNEXPECTEDLY WITH AN OLD ACQUAINTANCE.

although he had repeatedly rung the bell for wine.

In this state of mind was he when Samuel Twitter was announced to him, and, with a shout of satisfaction that he should now have someone upon whom he could vent the utmost bitterness of his spirit, Varley ordered him to be at once shown into the room.

Twitter started when he saw the demoniac-looking countenance of Varley, and for the moment thought the catastrophe which he had prognosticated had actually occurred, namely, that Varley, by excessive brooding over his passion for Miranda, and its utter hopelessness, had gone mad.

With a pang of alarm, he said:

"Good Heavens! what has occurred?"

"Occurred?" cried Varley, glaring at him like a wild animal preparing for a deadly spring. "Sneaking hound—can you—dare you ask?"

"I—I—really don't know," said Twitter, keeping as near the door as possible. "I hope nothing particular has gone wrong?"

"How could things go right," cried Varley, "when I yoked myself to a man like you, with all the villainy to——"

"Hush—hush!" interrupted Twitter; "we may be overheard. Oh, Varley, think of the great danger you run by these bursts of passion! If indulged in at all, you should be far from sight or sound of human beings."

"Yes—yes," said Varley, "you are cautious —very cautious, Samuel Twitter. You excel in fear—that is your master passion—at least, with avarice. The one tempts you to crime, the other, to tremble at its commission."

"If," said Twitter, in a low tone, and turning supernaturally pale as he spoke, "if avarice tempted me to crime—what tempted you? Surely that feeling to a still greater degree, Bernard Varley, for, were I you, and you me, I should not refuse you your share in the profits of a deed which, although it might have been done single-handed, could not have been done so safely."

This was, perhaps, the boldest speech that Twitter had ever made to Bernard Varley, and, for a moment, the latter was quite silent from intense surprise.

Then rage became doubly increased, and he seized Twitter by the collar before he could get out of his way, saying, through his clenched teeth—for Twitter's caution respecting loud speaking had not been totally unheeded:

"Wretch! dare you presume so to address me? At least, I will satisfy one item of vengeance, by taking your worthless life."

"Help!—help!—murder!" cried Twitter, as loudly as he could.

In a few moments the room was half-full of people, and the alarmed Twitter was torn from the grasp of Bernard Varley, who began to feel terrified himself at the length he had allowed his passions, in this wild excitement, to carry him.

"What's the matter?" cried the landlord of the house. "What's the matter?"

"Ask him," said Twitter, pointing to Varley. "Ask him."

"It is past," said Varley. "This is my apartment. How dare anyone enter it without my permission?"

"They were summoned by my cries of murder!" said Twitter, who, for once in his life, found a little courage.

"Fool!" said Varley, "what's your worthless life to me?"

"I call upon all here present to witness," said Twitter, "that I have been compelled to summon assistance against the violence of Mr. Varley. If anything should happen to me, remember, it will be his doing."

"Are you mad?" cried Varley.

"No," added Twitter, who was never in such a state of excitement in his life before. "No—but I am determined to protect myself. This is no ordinary quarrel, and I will not for the future endure threats against my life."

"This—this is a matter between me and my servant," said Varley, rising from the sofa, on which he had sunk after his sudden burst of passion. "I had cause—ample cause for anger against him, and he knows it; but as for any serious intention of doing any harm, he is perfectly aware I should never entertain it."

"It's all very well, sir," said the landlord, "and you and your friends, or servants, may settle your own quarrels as you please; but all I've got to say in the matter is, that the sooner you leave my house the better I and all my other guests will be pleased."

The landlord did not wait for a reply to this speech, but walked out of the room immediately, in a great fluster, for he was really enraged at the disturbance, which was by no means calculated to do his establishment any good.

It was Twitter who first broke the silence which ensued for a few moments after he and Varley were alone.

"Mr. Varley," he said, "if you are not mad yourself, you will drive me so, if you go on in this way. Surely I am much ill-used by you in not having faith kept with me as regards what I was to have for assisting you, and when you add to that violence and threats, you may drive me to some course which will eventually destroy us both."

Twitter then sat down, and trembled like an aspen leaf, while a dread of what Bernard Varley might do or say lay heavy at his heart.

Varley's thoughts were by no means idle for some minutes; and, as the paroxysm of his rage rapidly subsided, he began to think that it would be absolutely necessary to adopt another course of conduct towards Twitter, or to take his life at the first convenient opportunity. The latter mental proposition, however, was one for more mature thought; but the former required instant decision, and Varley said, in a temporizing tone, which Twitter was delighted to hear:

"Twitter, are you a man who can make no allowances for a distracted temper? You must feel assured that I should, for my own sake, be the very last person really to harbour against you any ill design."

"Bernard Varley," said Twitter, "I only know that you have made my life a positive burthen to me. I only know that I am poor and wretched."

"There is a hundred-pound note for you," said Varley, as he took one from what appeared to Twitter's gloating eyes a well-filled pocket-book. "Let what has passed be forgotten. The impolicy of our quarrelling needs no sort of argument."

"Now, Varley," said Twitter, "you are more yourself; but tell me what had occurred to give you so much uneasiness."

"Simply this," said Varley, "that I thought the Grange estates were really mine, and now I find that such is not the case."

"Not yours?"

"No; I made an attempt to-day to sell them, which attempt was most audaciously resisted."

"Think nothing," replied Twitter, "about the hindrance of the sale. In London there are people who will buy anything, provided they get it a bargain."

"Ay," said Varley, "London is the place. This day, Twitter, we will post to the metropolis, for I feel convinced that thither

Miranda must have flown, notwithstanding the absence of any positive proof upon the subject."

"Shall I make the necessary arrangements?"

"Yes, assuredly; and remember, Twitter, we understand each other better than we did."

"Much better," replied Twitter; "and I sincerely hope the good understanding will never be broken in upon."

* * * *

"I will kill him!" muttered Varley, when he was alone; "I will kill him on the very first opportunity. He shall feel what it is to have braved me. He shall surely die! It is but another murder—only another. Let his blood mingle with that which already stains my soul. I will sell the Grange estates in London. Oh! how I detest their very name; and never, never again will I torment myself by a sight of that house which once I so much coveted to call my own. I have now but one hope—one pursuit in life, and that is thee, Miranda, thee!"

"Well done—well done," said Samuel Twitter, when he reached the street; "Varley *is* to be braved after all, if one can but muster up the resolution to do it. Oh, what a fool I have been! Henceforward I will threaten, and talk big to him. He evidently fears me. A hundred pounds to lull the remembrance of the little fracas which I am rejoiced I treated as I did! 'Tis well—'tis a glorious beginning. Now, Bernard Varley, I will stay by you while you have a guinea left."

That evening Bernard Varley, accompanied by Twitter, started from York to London, in a post-chaise, drawn by four horses.

CHAPTER CV.

THE MEETING AT THE INN — DICK PALMER'S ADVICE—THE JOVIAL COMPANY AT THE "OLD RAVEN."

JONES had been for a longer period of time away from Miranda than he had calculated upon, for Ikey Samuels had made good speed on his way back to York, and the little agreeable interview which Mr. Jones had had with him, had helped to prolong the time.

Nevertheless his success in getting back the ring was sufficiently gratifying to Jones to induce him to overlook other and more minor considerations.

He would gladly have taken some conveyance could such have been procured, in order to follow Miranda with greater expedition, for he was vexed at the idea that she should be left in the streets of the next market town, with her aged companion, and nearly destitute of means.

There was, however, no resource left him but to push on as quickly as he could, and this he did, not without a hope that some passing vehicle would give him a lift on his journey.

Slow as had been the progress of the waggon, when added to the distance that Jones had gone in the opposite direction, a good five or six miles had been placed between him and the objects of his care.

It was hard work to walk this in the hour, but being unobstructed on the even country road, Jones actually came in sight of the town which had attracted Miranda's attention, within that period of time.

That town, he knew, was the destination of the waggon, and he quickened his pace, with the expectation of speedily coming up with the heroic girl, who for truth and justice had suffered so much at the same time that she had achieved so much.

Mr. Jones' encounter with the Jew, added to his long walk, produced a sensation of thirst, and an ardent desire to imbibe something a little stronger than the purest element of nature.

"Well, she won't have to wait for me long," soliloquized Jones; "I am as dry as a methody parson, and I don't see no reason why I shouldn't break bulk of that ere blessed twenty pounds as Ikey Samuels was so particular about; what an agreeable sight a swinging sign is, to be sure, when one's blessed clay is nearly cracking, like a common in July for want of a moistening. There it is, a creaking now and then, as much as to say, walk in ladies and gentlemen, and taste of the wonders of nature in the way of gin and other things. What would this ere world be if it wasn't for public-houses—an out-an'-out bit of the infernal."

With these sentiments Mr. Jones arrived beneath the swinging sign of a public-house, which was the first tenement in the town, the lights from which Miranda had seen in the waggon.

Before, however, he could enter, the door of a stable, which was adjoining, opened, and a boy, with a head of hair that resembled greatly some superfluous piece of an old flock bed, led forth a horse, crying alternately, "woa," and "cum up," with a view, it is to be supposed, of keeping the animal quiet, and in one spot, by involving his mind in great doubt whether he was to "woa" or "cum up."

"Well, my kidney-bean," said Jones, "what's the sign of this ere house, for I can't make it how no how?"

"It's the 'Shovel and Shoe-brush,'" said the boy, "and I ain't the kidney-bean.— Woa, will yer; cum up—gee up—woa, woa, —gee up."

Mr. Jones walked to the front of the horse, and looking him intently in the face, he raised a kind of congratulatory shout that so alarmed the boy with the flock head, that he ran into the stable forthwith, and bolted the door.

"Why, how is you, yer love," said Jones, embracing the horse with great cordiality; "bless yer, you warigated tulip, the sight on yer is quite a treat—hurray, here's a meeting."

In his exultation, then, Mr. Jones laughed so uproariously that several people sallied out of the public-house, with a conviction that some admirable joke must be taking place.

"Hurrah, for the squire!" said Jones; "here's the horse, and where's his master?"

"Jones," cried Palmer, rushing forward, "how came you here?"

"Dreadfully dry," said Jones; "perfectly gasping."

Dick took him by the arm, and led him into the public-house, saying, in a whisper, as he went:

"Tell me of Miranda, Jones; where have you left Miranda?"

"Dry as dust," said Jones.

"And old Mr. Percy, Jones. Are they still at York, or where?—tell me at once."

"Baked as a pipkin," said Jones; "hav'n't had nothing to drink for so long that I have quite lost the blessed calculation."

"How can you be such a sot, Jones, as to think of nothing but drinking—order what you like at once, and answer me the questions I put to you."

"There's gratitude!" said Jones. "A pot of ale. Where's Rowland Percy? I thought you and him had been in London long ago. Here's a unexpected meeting, as the fox said when he crept into the dog-kennel. Miss Miranda ain't fur off, and, I daresay, is quite alive and kicking—you see, she wouldn't stay in York no how, and we've been on the road now some time. We've had a few little ups and downs; but, taking it altogether, we've rather done the knowing ones."

"Do you mean to say that Miranda is on her road to London?"

"That's the werdict. She's had a lift in a waggon, and has been a-coming it at the astonishing rate of a mile-and-a-half a hour. I hain't been able to keep by her, you see, all the while, cos you see, some on us must 'arn a living as we go on; and, I believe, I have only now got to prig something of old Nick himself, when I should have got over three of the most downy characters as is."

"What do you mean?"

"Why, we've been a receiving woluntary contributions from a Quaker and a Jew—they is rum uns, as you well know, to get the better on."

"I trust," said Palmer, "you have not committed Miranda in any of your heedless robberies?"

"I never commits nobody," said Jones. "Some of these ere days, when I retires from business, and becomes a country justice, I shall go on committing all sorts of people, and myself too, as well as the best of them; but is young Mr. Percy here?"

"No," said Palmer; "he is at the 'Old Raven,' some miles farther on; but you give me great uneasiness, Jones, when you talk of having committed robberies, while having escorted Miranda. You know not the frightful mischief you might do to her, by implicating her in such transactions. You must be aware, that she regards with a very different eye from what we do, the rights of property and the usages of society."

"Oh, indeed!" said Jones. "Where did you pick up that fine sentiment? I tell you

what it is, Dicky Palmer—there was a boy as was at the door with your hoss, and he was reading a astonishing moral lesson—he was—a lesson as just put me in mind of us, and society, as you speaks on."

"Indeed!" said Palmer; "how do you make that out?"

"This ere way, quite easy, unkimmon. That ere boy reminded me of society and us—one minute it says woa, and another minute it says kim up. Woa—says society when we prigs something, and, then, if we was to woa—society leaves us to starve, and human nature says kim up. What, then, is we to do? Of course, we kims up, and cracks a crib, or stops some confiding individual on the highway."

"There is, certainly, some philosophy in what you say," said Palmer, "and I confess to taking a similar view of our position. I regret much that Miranda did not see the policy of remaining at York, where she was surrounded by so many attached friends, instead of throwing herself upon the world, and, I must say, adding greatly to Rowland Percy's danger."

"I have hinted all that ere to her," said Jones, "and it wasn't of no use. I just advises you to say nothing to her about it—women is women, and the best on 'em is as obstinate as blazes."

"I shall certainly not endeavour to make her unhappy," said Palmer, "imprudent as I consider the course she has adopted. She is made up of high and noble sentiments, and I can well understand, though I deeply regret, the feeling that has induced her to fly from those in York, who would gladly have given her a home."

"Wery good," said Jones. "She came here in a waggon along with the old gentleman, and, as I told her to stick by it till she seed me, there ain't never a doubt but we shall easily find her."

Palmer looked embarrassed for some moments, and a shade of great care and anxiety was visible upon his brow.

"It's an unfortunate circumstance," he said, "and certainly increases most fearfully the risks Rowland Percy is compelled to run. It is quite impossible that we should all proceed to London in a body; such a step would be to ensure detection. You must continue your guardianship of Miranda, Jones, while I proceed by a different route with Percy."

"I sees all that ere," said Jones; "but it's difficult reasoning with her; just you come along with me, and tell her in your own way what you thinks of the proceeding. She doesn't always seem to understand me when I speaks to her, in consekens, I suppose, of learning too many 'complishments, instead of being teached some of the beauties of the language."

By this time Mr. Jones had finished his pot of ale, and feeling wonderfully refreshed, he was therefore willing to proceed at once after Miranda, and in a few moments Dick was mounted, and, with Jones at his side, proceeded at an easy pace through the high street of the town.

In the meantime Miranda's anxiety had considerably increased, as minute after minute passed without the return of Jones, and she began to think how difficult it would be to follow his advice, and keep by the waggon, should it be put up for the night in any inn-yard, into which she had no pretext for demanding entrance.

This proved to be very much the case, for the horses of their own accord turned under a narrow roofed way, which led into a large, badly-paved yard, littered with all kinds of lumber and merchandise, and then they all stopped, some of them shaking their heads, and producing an extra tinkling of the bells, as if in gratulation that their journey was over.

When the waggoner came to the back of the vehicle and looked at Miranda, it was with as great a stare of astonishment as if he had never seen her before; in fact, he had slept and awoke so many times since she first got into the vehicle, that had he been on his oath he could not have told upon which of his journeys it was that he had taken up a young female and an old man as passengers.

"Do you go no further than here?" said Miranda.

"No," was the reply; "here we be's."

"Then I presume I must alight. Come, Mr. Percy, we must now leave this friendly shelter."

"Yes," said the old man, "yes. But where is Rowland?"

"We are yet far from him, and we must wait here a short time, if we are permitted, until the friend arrives who has already done us so much good service."

The inn-yard was an old and picturesque place, oddly built, but commodious. It was some distance up the entrance ere you reached the yard, which opened into a wide space, around three sides of which ran the rambling old inn itself, and a large shed occupied the other.

Under this shed were stowed several waggons, for the most part laden with goods, others in the process of lading with bales of merchandise, crates of goods, and sacks without end or number. From under this shed appeared, every here and there, doors, from which, when opened, an odour escaped that at once proclaimed that they communicated with the stables.

From out of these doors would peep some curious faces, as if in anxious inquiry as to who it was that had now entered the yard, and whose services would be required next to take charge of the freshly-arrived cattle.

On the other sides, formed by the inn itself, ran an old-fashioned gallery, along what is called the first floor, and which was accessible from the yard by means of a wide flight of steps, and from the house by various little doors from the several sides. Besides this, it was conveniently protected from the weather by means of a covering, which was supported by little wooden pillars that took their rise from the old oaken balustrades that surrounded the gallery.

On this gallery were, as is invariably the case, several articles, such as clothes and linen, a collection of boots and shoes; and, of course, several female heads peering over, watching what was going on most attentively.

It was in the midst of this comfortless confusion that Miranda stood looking anxiously around her, and counting sadly each weary minute as it passed; but time brought not to her the only friend she could calculate upon, who would really do his utmost to expedite her on her journey.

———

CHAPTER CVI.

THE TRANSACTIONS ON THE ROAD—ROWLAND'S DANGER THICKENS — A LITTLE MORALITY.

THE impatience of old Mr. Percy was each moment growing greater, and it required an exercise of all the gentle influence which Miranda had over him to induce him to wait in the inn-yard.

She feared to go into the house, lest, by so doing, she should miss Jones; moreover, she dreaded the eccentricities of poor Mr. Percy becoming a subject of remark, as they undoubtedly would, if she entered with him into any of the public rooms belonging to the inn; and the state of her finances, dependent, too, as she was for them, upon the kindness of others, prevented her from dreaming for a moment of incurring the expense of engaging a private room.

How slowly and deliberately do the minutes pass to those who are in anxious expectation; those same minutes, if of a pleasurable character, would be more swiftly fleeting than the most evanescent vapour of creation, lingering, apparently, not half their allotted space, lest too much pleasure should live too long in the imagination.

Poor Miranda had waited nearly half-an-hour, and she began to think that perforce she should be compelled to enter the inn, more especially as old Mr. Percy was complaining bitterly of the cold, when, to her joy, she heard the voice of Jones, as he and Dick Palmer entered the archway leading to the inn-yard.

"You'll find her here," said Jones, "to a certainty; she won't stray from the waggon, it puts up in this yard."

"I am here," said Miranda, rushing forward.

"And well, I hope, Miss Rankley?" said Dick Palmer.

"You here, my good friend?" said Miranda; and then a sudden flush of terror came across her, as she thought that something surely must have happened to Rowland Percy, to account for the appearance of his generous protector without him.

An inquiry which she dreaded to make,

trembled upon her lips, and it was some moments before she could muster courage enough to say:

"Rowland—Rowland Percy—what has happened to him? Oh, tell me, is he safe?"

"Quite so, I trust and expect," said Palmer; "do not be alarmed at seeing me without him. We have met with some little accidents and difficulties upon our road, but nothing of half so serious a character as might fairly have been expected. He is in good hands now, and it was only as a measure of precaution for a short time that he and I separated."

"Thank Heaven," said Miranda. "Then all is well. Your appearance alone did certainly give me a pang of uneasiness, but I am amply repaid by the assurance that you have now afforded me."

"Miss Rankley," said Palmer, in a tone of sorrowful expostulation, and forgetting for a moment the promise he had given to Jones, not to annoy her by any strictures upon her conduct, "I implore you to think calmly and dispassionately of the circumstances by which you are surrounded. Let me beg of you to return to York, to remain with those friends, to whom it would be a pride, as well as a pleasure, to give you a welcome."

"Hush!" said Miranda; "I implore you upon that point not to urge me; do not, I pray you—my mind is fixed, and it is ever grievous to hear censure from those we esteem."

"I will say no more. Heaven help both you and Mr. Percy! He is not in London yet, but awaiting me at a very short distance from this place. If you insist upon seeing him, Miranda, let it be but a short interview, for I must urge you by every feeling of reason and reflection to abandon the intention, if ever you had such, of proceeding to London with him."

"Except as regards my return to York," said Miranda, "I will follow your advice most implicitly. I fear that, in this world, it will never be in my power—not to repay you, for that is impossible altogether—but even to give sufficient expression to my gratitude for the great service you have done to me and to Rowland."

"Oh, that's all gammon," said Jones; "I doesn't like to hear nothing about gratitude; it's out-an'-out affecting, and, if I wants to cry, I can always buy an ingon."

"Rowland Percy," said Dick Palmer, "is at an old roadside inn, called the 'Raven,' some distance further on the road to London. He is awaiting my coming with no little anxiety, I believe. My counsel to you is this: to get forward on your road to-morrow morning as quickly as you can, while Rowland and I will make a return of a few miles, in order to meet you; have, then, Miss Miranda, a brief interview with him. I know it will be a great pleasure to you both, and I would not baulk it for a thousand pounds. After that, you can still proceed under the protection of Jones, while Rowland and I can, of course, push on at a quicker rate towards the metropolis."

"It shall be so," said Miranda; "I will implicitly follow your directions. You know, my friend, I have not seen him since that dreadful night when he left me a prisoner in the condemned cell at York."

"I know it, and can well appreciate your feelings. Sleep at this inn to-night, and in the morning Jones will endeavour to get some conveyance that will convey you some distance on the London road. Be assured you shall meet us; but, as we are surrounded by dangers, and I may be aware of circumstances that you are not, when you do meet us, wait for the first salutation to come from me; there may be strangers on the part of the road we meet at, or sufficiently near to make a sudden recognition dangerous. Jones, be cautious and discreet."

"Unkimmon," said Jones—"a weasel in a rat-hole shall be a fool to me."

"And now as to money," said Palmer; "my exchequer is not very well stocked at present, but I can supply you with some."

"Oh!" said Jones, "we've been doing the rig as we com'd along, and we can lend you a few pounds, if you want it."

"No, no, I will now be off, for it is dangerous for us even to be seen conversing together. We shall meet to-morrow. Adieu, Miss Rankley, and Heaven bless you!"

"There's a fellow for you," said Jones, when Palmer was gone—"an out-an'-out natural philosopher. Lor! bless you, that fellow tried to be honest for a matter of ten or a dozen year afore he found out what the world was, and then he seed the error of his ways, and became the owdacious family cove he is. He's made up of feeling, and he never robs nobody as can't spare it—and that's more than your moral-going coves does, for the only people they robs is the poor, as haven't the means of making head against such outrageous piety. Why, bless yer! I know'd a feller as let his own child, a girl of some seventeen year old,—cos she'd gone a little astray, poor thing!—die in the streets; and then he gave a thousand pounds to translate the blessed scriptures for the King of the Cannibal Islands, or some such outrageous humbug. Piety wersus feeling!—cant wersus charity! Thank goodness! I am a prig, and not a beast."

* * * *

The police officer, who was left in so uncomfortable a position by Dick Palmer, was in too great a rage for a long while to reflect at all calmly upon his situation—but that first ebullition was sure to pass away; and, when it did, he assured himself, over and over again, that he was most certainly on the right track for the discovery of his prisoner, or he never would have been handled in so systematic and rough a manner as he had been.

He, therefore, lay upon his back, muttering a great many curses, and resolving, in his own mind, that the moment he got free of his present dilemma he would take up the pursuit, with still a hope of achieving something of a more satisfactory character on the road between York and London.

It was after a great many ineffectual struggles and plunges that he at length got upon his feet, and, after that, liberation was not far distant, for he contrived to make himself seen by some of the labourers belonging to the farm; and, being freed from his bondage, he thought his safest and best way of getting back to York was to wait on the London road for a coach, which he did, and in not many hours was once again set down in the ancient cathedral city.

We need not follow this worthy in the steps he took to get up a considerable force, with which he proposed to ride all the way from York to London, but, suffice it to say, that within six hours he again started on the errand which had been before so full of peril and misadventure to him.

It was strange, thus, that all our characters should be upon the road.

Bernard Varley was posting to London. The police-officers were riding at a hard pace; and our persecuted friends were, with deep anxiety, waiting the chance of events which should place them in a condition less full of moving accidents.

If Rowland Percy's mind had been disengaged, and if he could have got rid of the many deep anxieties, both for himself and others, that oppressed him, he could have much enjoyed his residence at that ancient and venerable hostel.

It was just the place which, at another time, and under happier circumstances, he would have gloried in visiting and thoroughly exploring. The exquisite irregularity of its structure, and the constant surprises which awaited anyone who might be rummaging over it in the shape of unexpected staircases, little odd, quaint-looking rooms, and dark, tortuous corridors, in out-of-the-way corners, was just the thing to keep the mind in a state of pleasurable occupation.

But poor Rowland had too many corroding cares and anxieties to give more than a passing meed of pleasurable admiration to the old house.

He thought once or twice, with almost a smile of anticipated delight, how happy he should be to visit it some day with Miranda—some day, perhaps, after his innocence had become discovered, and admitted by all men, when he could point out to her with a sigh for the past, and paint to her, in love's own glowing language, the mental suffering he endured upon his first visit beneath its romantic roof.

Such feelings as these were like glimpses of sunshine in November, beautiful, but so transient, that they made the gloom that had for the moment vanished, look afterwards doubly dark and mournful.

The landlord was extremely attentive to Rowland Percy, absolutely forcing him with rough hospitality to partake of many things, which he would have avoided. Then he

amused him during the day by telling of some kindly acts of Dick Palmer, concluding with a sigh that seemed to shake the whole of his ponderous bulk.

"Ah, sir, there's very few of the real knights of the road left now. Highway robbery, like everything else, has had its day; and gentlemen don't take to it now as they used to do, as a profession, without any malice or savageness at all. No, sir, it's only some rogue now and then who gets desperate, and tries to knock on the head a fat grazier or a commercial traveller. I look upon Dick Palmer, sir, as the last of his race—he's a real old English highwayman. One as ready to salute a fair lady, as to rob a fat parson."

"Of course," said Rowland, with a smile, "you sink the morality of the thing."

"Morality," said the landlord, "is a very nice thing for independent people, who are born with silver spoons in their mouths, and continue to keep them there."

Rowland Percy was not anxious to prolong such discussions as these, for he was getting angry with himself, as he found himself now and then, in the free and easy manner of a Jones or a Palmer, making excuses in his own mind for lapses of integrity that he had always been taught to consider as great enormities.

"At all events," he thought, "I have learned one thing by my association with these men, and that is charity towards my fellow-creatures, and a conviction that one departure from the strict line of moral rectitude by no means necessarily implies that he who so departs is a bad man, or destitute of human feelings."

* * * *

The ancient inn looked more lonely and isolated than it really was, for behind it, and out of sight—unless the traveller looked out of the back windows—was a thriving, pleasant little village, some of the inhabitants of which made a regular practice of spending an hour or two in the evening in the parlour of the "Old Raven."

Rowland Percy was so vociferously requested to join these worthies by the landlord, that he could not resist, nor did he regret that he yielded, when he found himself within the sphere of the ruddy heat from a blazing fire, and surrounded by the hearty bronzed English faces of some of the neighbouring farmer's men, who seemed to enjoy life as a rich boon of itself, and to be so gloriously obtuse to all care, that Rowland Percy felt a most unchristian feeling of envy taking possession of his breast, as he looked at them, and listened to their boisterous dialogues.

—

CHAPTER CVII.

THE INN PARLOUR—THE MYSTERIOUS TRAVELLER—THE BLUE BEDROOM.

ROWLAND PERCY had no reason to regret the good-tempered compulsion which had forced him into the parlour of the "Old Raven;" for, although the hilarity and mirth was of rather a boisterous description, yet there was no mistake in it. It was real, genuine, hearty good humour, and more than once he envied those unrefined, but happy yeomen, who, alas! are fast disappearing from the face of merry England, before the demon of manufacturing monopoly.

There were over a dozen guests in the old parlour, and, although the conversation was not of the most refined order, it lacked neither energy nor sincerity; if it wanted some of the courtesies of more elegant society, it escaped its duplicities, and both the novelty and nature of the talk amused Rowland amazingly.

The weather, of course, formed a principal topic for some time, and it was handled with great wisdom and vigour, as it related to agricultural produce, the only shadow of a difference of sentiment being between two extremely fat men, one of whom wanted it to rain, and the other didn't.

It seemed, too, as if the elements themselves were intent upon supplying matter for further conversation to the inmates of the parlour of the "Old Raven;" for the wind was getting up, and beginning to sweep round the old house, rustling among the ivy, and shaking the ancient casements, as if anxious to find some place of ingress through which it might make its way, and blow about the tables and chairs in the old inn at its pleasure.

"The wind's a-blowing," said a little, hard-featured old man, the skin of whose face appeared at one time to have been a great deal too large, and, rather than hang about in an unsightly manner, had done itself up into little crinkles. "The wind's a-blowing, and, for all the world, it reminds me of how I have been told it blowed when a sarcumstance took place at this here very inn a many years ago."

The little old man looked with such a solemn and fixed stare in the face of Rowland Percy, that the latter felt himself compelled to say something, if it were only "Ay, indeed."

"Oh, we know all about that," said the fat man, who wanted it to rain.

Upon this, the little old man pointed triumphantly with the stem of his pipe to Rowland, as much as to say: "He doesn't." And that being an unanswerable argument in favour of telling the story, the fat man, who wanted rain, felt himself very small, and said no more about it.

The little old man then, having first taken a few whiffs from his pipe, gently tapped the bowl on the toe of his boot, and kicked the ashes into the fire in a manner that told he had often done so before; and, laying it down, he said, slightly elevating himself, to look on all around, to make sure that nobody was inattentive:

"You must know that this occurred in my father's time. He was sexton, and buried him."

"Buried who?" said one of the guests.

"You'll know all in good time," replied the old man; "you must hear the beginning before you know the end.

"It was about fifty years since that my poor father—poor man, he's dead and gone!—was sitting one night, as I am in this parlour. It was a stormy night, I can tell you, for the wind howled and roared in the chimney of the 'Old Raven,' while the rain beat against the outside with fury.

"It was growing late, too, and many of those that were sitting round the blazing fire thought it was time they should return home; but the rain came down so heavily, that they did not like to leave good shelter, good fire, and good liquor, to encounter the inclemency without, when suddenly there was a sharp rap at the inn door, as if with the butt-end of a riding-whip, and somebody called, in strange accents: 'House—house! Here, house!'

"Well, they were all very much startled, not so much at the mere fact that a traveller desired shelter hastily — it was late and sudden it was true—but it was at the singular, and almost painful, tone in which the demand was made, and then a dead silence ensued. Each one looked at his neighbour, in doubt if he should break it, or was desirous of hearing somebody else's voice but his own.

"While they were thus looking at each other in something more than mere amazement, the knocking was repeated, and the same voice said, in louder but almost despairing accents:

"'Hilloa, house! house! hilloa!'

"The landlord then jumped up from his seat, for he was dozing by the fire when the first call was heard, and went to the door, and, in a few moments, returned with a traveller, who wore a horseman's cloak and slouched hat, sword, and holster pistols, which he brought in with him.

"He threw off his cloak, and seated himself near the fire, as if to warm and dry himself.

"The guests looked at him with much curiosity, not to say awe, for they knew not what to think of him. He was tall and well-made, and scarcely more than thirty years of age. But what interested them most was the peculiar air of melancholy that sat upon his strongly-marked and handsome features, and he remained for several minutes without uttering a word.

"This silence was particularly painful, and the landlord said, respectfully:

"'Your horse, your honour, is well taken care of—'tis a noble beast.'

"The stranger looked up as if he did not comprehend what was said.

"'I was saying,' repeated the landlord, 'that that's a handsome horse, sir, and well deserves to be taken care of; you could not come to a better inn, though I say it, to have your cattle looked after.'

" 'Ay, that is right,' said the stranger, slowly. 'He has come far and quickly—see to him.'

" 'I have, your honour.'

" ''Tis well; can I have a bed here to-night? I would not travel further in such weather.'

" 'You can, your honour—you can, and a better——'

" 'Hold,' said the stranger, 'I am content to take it for what it is; and, be it what it may, it will be all that I shall require.'

" 'Won't your honour take no refreshments?' said the landlord, who began to think his guest had been long enough enjoying the warmth of the fire to order something without being spurred on.

" 'No,' was the short reply; 'but you may draw what you like, and charge me with it.'

" 'Well,' muttered the landlord, 'this beats Akibo, and he beats What-d'ye-callum.'

"There was now another long pause, during which no one spoke, though several had made up their minds to be easy, and converse about commonplace things; and yet, think as hard as they could, they were unable to find anything to say; so they sat staring at each other in perfect silence, and stealing side-long glances at the stranger, whose mind appeared to be ill at ease, for his breast now and then rose with a long inspiration, as if he were about to sigh heavily, and then recollecting himself, he would suppress it.

"He sat before the fire, leaning his head on his hand, with his elbow on the table, gazing with a vacant eye upon the blazing logs.

" 'He is surely crazed,' said the landlord to my father.

" 'Yes, and had you seen his eyes as I did when you spoke to him, you would have seen them like living fire—he must be mad.'

" 'Bless me!' said the landlord. 'What shall I do when I show him to his room; he'll become outrageous, for there is no hangings to the bed.'

" 'Indeed,' said my father; 'what room do you intend to show him into?'

" 'Why, the blue room, to be sure.'

" 'The blue room? I have heard you say that nobody has slept in that old rambling room since the death of the squire, who broke his skull while taking a leap after the hounds.'

" 'Hush! say nothing about that. That is one reason why I want to have somebody to sleep in it, otherwise the place will get a bad name, for nobody likes to occupy it; besides, it's easiest got ready.'

" 'I have heard my father say,' continued the little old man, 'that he was upon the point of saying something by way of reply when the stranger suddenly turned round to the landlord, and said:

" 'Will you show me into my room?'

" 'Yes, your honour, certainly. I have ordered a fire, and in a few minutes the room will be well-aired. It will be warm and comfortable.'

" 'Never mind about that,' said the stranger, interrupting him. 'All I want is the room; but if there be a fire there already, well and good—let it remain—but, if not, you need not light one.'

" 'Not—not a fire—such a night as this, too,' said the landlord, very much bewildered.

" 'No,' said the stranger, in a sudden stern voice, so different from the painfully melancholy tones in which he had hitherto spoken, that the landlord gave a sudden start, in common with everyone present.

" 'But—but there is one,' was the reply.

" 'Show me to the room at once,' said the stranger, who evidently neither liked company nor conversation, 'and I will thank you.'

"The landlord was much puzzled at the conduct of his guest, but led the way out of the room.

"The stranger rose and followed him with a faltering step.

"In a few minutes the landlord returned and threw himself into a chair near the fire, drew a long breath, like a man who is suddenly relieved from some load of misery, and seizing the poker, began to stir the fire, as if actuated by an insane desire to destroy the fuel.

" 'What's the matter?' said one. 'What have you seen?' said another. 'Who is it?' said a third.

" 'I don't know. Nothing—nothing,' said the landlord; 'but I never came near his like before—that's all. Why, hark how the wind howls, and how the rain beats, and he wants nothing—is that natural?'

"There was a moment's pause before any one replied, during which the howling of the wind seemed to increase, and they thought it sounded more dismally than ever in the old chimney, while the rain beat fearfully against the closed window.

" 'It is not natural,' said one of the guests, 'for any man—mind I said man—who has been riding far in such weather, and on such a night as this, to go to bed supperless. I wouldn't do so.'

" 'And I could not, if I would,' said another.

" 'No,' continued the landlord, 'I am sure I could not; but I have left him in the blue-room—that's some satisfaction.'

" 'You don't mean that?' said one.

" 'I do, though, and it's quite good enough for the occasion. Moreover, it's the best room in the house.'

" 'How did you leave him? What did he say?' inquired one or two, in a breath.

" 'Nothing—nothing; he walked in, just looked round the place, took his hat off his head, and threw it on the bed; he seems to have something that weighs heavy on his mind—some load of guilt, I am sure.'

" 'He is a very strange man,' said one; 'but what makes you think that?'

" 'Because he trembled, and, clasping his hands together, fell rather than sat down in a chair opposite the fire, as if in great agony, exclaiming, in a dreadful whisper:

"'Oh, Agatha—Agatha, and has it come to this at last? Lost! lost!'

"'Poor soul,' said one, 'he is to be pitied.'

"'I don't know that,' said the clerk. 'You know, neighbours, that a lost soul may not be deserving of pity. He may have sold himself, and now repents.'

"'You don't think he has sold himself to the devil,' said one, who was compelled to jerk the last word out, else it had remained unsaid, to the great danger of choking the speaker.

"'He may be the—the—the——'

"'Bless me!' exclaimed the landlord, jumping up and overturning his seat at the same time.

"This exclamation was called forth by the stunning report of a pistol, which was discharged in the 'Old Raven.' The sound found many echoes in the rambling building, and to the fear of many of the guests, it seemed as if a regular discharge of small arms had taken place.

"Terror sat on every face—no one moved; they appeared like human beings turned by the wand of some demon enchanter into blocks of marble, so silent and so motionless they sat, with their eyes protruding with intense and fearful anxiety from their sockets.

CHAPTER CVIII.

THE REMARKABLE DISAPPEARANCE—A NEW ALARM—A FRESH ARRIVAL.

"How long this state of things might have lasted, it is impossible to say.

"After a while, and before a syllable was uttered, they began to recover from the shock and to think, but no sooner had their faculties become a little thawed than they were again driven to their wits' ends by a loud and continued knocking.

"It was long ere anyone spoke, but all looked at the landlord, who was wiping the perspiration from his face, and at length he said:

"'Will anyone go to the door for me?'

"No one, however, stirred hand or foot, or offered a word in reply, and by the time the knocks had been repeated for about the fourteenth time, he rose to his feet, and, without saying a word, slowly went to the door, and demanded who was there, and having received an answer from without, in a mortal voice—as they thought, of a woman—a horseman entered, dressed precisely as the former, but of a different form and feature. He was short and slim, his clothes loose, but with hat, cloak, sword, and pistols the same as the former horseman.

"The landlord recoiled in terror, when the traveller said, seriously:

"'Are you deaf, that you keep me waiting outside on such a night as this? Why, what ails you? You look frightened.'

"'The traveller—the pistol!'

"'What does all this mean?' said the stranger, turning to the guests.

"'Somebody fired a pistol upstairs.'

"'Indeed! Then why not go upstairs, and see who it is.'

"The guests all shook their heads, and the landlord evinced no desire to do so, when the stranger inquired further about the occurrence, and, appearing to be deeply interested, at length offered to go up to the blue room, if anyone would accompany him; but one and all refused.

"The traveller then took a light, and, being directed by the landlord, walked upstairs alone.

"During the traveller's absence not a sound was uttered, for all were too deeply engaged in speculating upon the result of the stranger's search, and their expectation was painfully wrought upon by the time he remained above; but presently they heard him descending the stairs slowly, and immediately afterwards he entered the room.

"Every eye was fixed upon his features, which were, though beautiful, deathly pale, and his lips of an ashy hue.

"He slowly turned to the landlord, saying:

"'There is no one there.'

"'No one there!' shouted the landlord, surprise getting the better of his terror for the moment.

"'No one,' replied the stranger, with a sad and powerful accent, as he turned on his heel, and left the house.

"When they heard the clatter of his horse's hoofs die away in the distance, the landlord said:

"'A pretty pass things have come to, indeed! He was certainly the evil one himself. I shall not go to see till to-morrow, nor shall I go to bed while I have a good fire; and if you'll all stop and keep me company till morning, you shall have what you like free of all charge.'

"This was agreed to, and they sat up all night.

"In the morning they went to the blue bedroom; but there was no one there, but traces of blood were visible.

"This was a most mysterious affair; but the strangest part of all was, perhaps, the existence of a most abominable odour that was ever after smelt in that room, though the windows were always open, but its cause could never be ascertained.

"Ever after, on that day twelvemonths, noises were heard in the blue chamber, and it has been said that a figure appears, but its features are always smeared so with blood as not to be recognizable, and the knocking at the outer door always continues for some time.

"Some years after this, my father got me a place in London to attend on a lady. I was a page, you must know, and seldom came to these parts, except once in a year or two, to see my father, and, of course, knew but little of what occurred here.

"I was one day attending upon my lady in the drawing-room, when my master drew his lady's attention to a paragraph in a paper, which related how a dead body had been found in a concealed cupboard of an old inn—it had lain there for many years, and was discovered in consequence of some repairs, when it fell forwards, a mass of bones and festering flesh. That was the body found here in the 'Old Raven'—the missing traveller.

"It then said that there was merely a letter addressed to the unfortunate man by his unfaithful wife. According to the letter, his name was Walter Montrose, and the letter was signed Agatha.

"My mistress no sooner read it, than she sprang to her feet, clasping her hands, and shrieking:

"'I dragged him there—I dragged him!' and then fell dead on the carpet.

"From all I could learn, she had been living, and was then with her betrayer, who had been her first lover. She had followed her husband, with the hope of making peace, or obtaining his forgiveness; but he had committed the rash act that placed it beyond his power to do so. She found him as I have told you, and being desirous of saving his body from the suicide's dishonoured grave, exerted her strength to conceal the body, which she did, and then left the house.

"A fit of illness afterwards occurring, she lay bereft of reflection for many months, and then, upon the solicitation of her lover and tempter, she returned to his arms. But the occurrence was only known to herself and the maid, who attended her through her illness, and from whom I learned all."

"I suppose the ghost was laid, and the knocking discontinued after that?" said one, inquiringly.

"I believe not," said the narrator, solemnly; "for I have heard that to this day, no one will venture to sleep in the blue room, at least, on the anniversary of that night, for strange, unearthly voices have been heard; and it is said that the spirit of the man still haunts the place, and will do so until a hundred years have expired."

"And the knocking, does that continue too?" said one, who was determined to obtain all the information he could upon so interesting a matter.

"Yes, and the——"

Here the speaker paused suddenly, for, just as he was about to say something more, a tremendous rapping was heard at the old inn door, and a voice cried out in stentorian tones:

"Hilloa! house! house! here—hilloa!"

The sounds acted like an electric shock upon those present, including the narrator. None dared move, or so much as breathe, and a universal panic pervaded every mind.

The greatest effect, however, seemed to be produced upon the fat man who wanted rain, for he slipped off his chair with a great dab on the floor, and, in doing so, tilted it forward in such a manner, that the back of it gave him, naturally, a blow on the head, and, not being quick at ascertaining cause and effect,

the fat man who wanted rain bellowed murder most lustily, and ever afterwards believed that the fat man who didn't want rain had done it.

As for the landlord, he certainly made an effort to move from the great arm-chair in which he sat, but it was only a preliminary one, consisting of a sort of convulsive movement of his fat, which, like a piece of blancmange in a state of agitation, gradually subsided.

Again the tremendous knocking came at the inn door, and the voice, in still louder accents, cried:

"House! house! Are you all asleep? Hilloa! It's trouble enough to reach the 'Raven,' and one might as well be let in at once. Come, old breeches and gaiters, open the door."

"He means me," gasped the landlord; "he means me," and he gave himself a terrible wrench, which brought him to his feet.

"Don't—don't!" cried four or five of the guests at once; "don't let him in; it's the ghost of the blue chamber!"

"If it is," said the landlord, "I can't have the door of the 'Old Raven' knocked in."

He made a movement towards the door, but the fat man who didn't want rain interposed, and the greatest confusion prevailed.

Everyone spoke at once, which certainly saved time, though it did not add to the general clearness of the conversation, while the knocking at the inn-door sounded like an accompaniment on a cracked drum to the tumult within.

Suddenly, then, the knocking ceased, and a rush of cold air, accompanied by a general slamming of doors in the upper part of the house, proclaimed that the outer door was open, and that the ghost—if such he was—accompanied by a great gust of wind, had found his way into the house.

Some then sat down behind chairs; one tried to clamber up the chimney, and four or five more made a rush to get under the table, which at once upset it, together with the lights and everything else that was upon it.

The scene of riot and confusion was at its height, when the parlour-door was dashed open, and the gleam of a lantern, carried by the ostler, shone into the room.

Behind him was a tall man, enveloped in a riding-cloak, who, after looking about him for a moment in surprise, said:

"Why—what on earth's the matter? Have you all gone crazy?"

"Gracious!" said the landlord, "it's the squire;" and snatching the lantern from the ostler, he held it up to the face of the new arrival, and discovered the well-known features of Dick Palmer, who unconsciously had created so much alarm at the "Old Raven."

"Why, Dick, is it you, after all?" said the landlord; "who would have thought it? Here's been a skrimmage about nothing. I tell you what it is, Peter Smuggs. If ever you tells that ere story here again I'll take an opportunity of treading on yer some day, and smashing of yer, an' at the crowner's quest I'll purtend as I mistook you for a black-beetle which we is haunted with, as will be well-known to the blessed jewry, no doubt, seeing as they have all on 'em found 'em occasionally in their ale."

Dick Palmer cast an anxious glance around him, in search of Rowland Percy, and when his eye fell upon him, he held out his hand, saying:

"I am glad to see you; the 'Old Raven' has done you good; you are looking a thousand times better than when we parted. Come this way."

So saying, he took Rowland by the arm, and led him from the oak-parlour, leaving the guests to recover from their consternation as best they might, and to alarm themselves, which they did, by ghost stories for the rest of the evening.

The fat landlord followed Rowland and Dick Palmer from the parlour, and the three were soon together in a room on the first floor of the old inn, which, although it had none of the comforts of the apartment they had just left, was much better calculated for a private conference.

"Well, Mr. Percy," said Dick Palmer, "we've been much longer on the road from York to London than I could have wished, and I think we've been the victims of as many accidents and crosses as could possibly be crowded into so small a space of time."

"We have, indeed," said Rowland, "and most certainly I should by this time have been in the hands of my enemies had it not been for the advice and assistance I have received from you. I hope now, however, we may continue our course uninterrupted; and believe me, I hope it for your sake, as much as my own, being far from unconscious what a trouble-some acquaintance I must be."

"Ah, well, well," cried the fat landlord, "we all have our ups and downs in this 'ere world. Human nature is a good 'un to look at, but a rum 'un to go. I suppose you've been on the roadside, and met with some ugly mischance. When I was young, and not quite so stout as I am—for you see I'm rather in-clined that way—I used to do a little business on the highway myself. It was an active, stirring sort of life, and suited me well, till I became not quite so active as I ought to be, and I was thinking of some genteel retire-ment, when my uncle, who kept the 'Old Raven' here, died, leaving me all his sticks; so, as the things fitted the house, I thought I had better rent it as well, and here I is."

"You are mistaken in me," said Rowland Percy. "I am not flying from justice, I am endeavouring to save my life from the most cruel persecution that ever man endured; accused and convicted of a murder, of which I am entirely innocent—even in thought. By rare good fortune, I have thus far escaped the malice of my enemies, and the ill-directed vengeance of the laws. My name is Rowland Percy."

The landlord gave a long whistle, and then said:

"Oh! oh! you're the chap there's been all the riot about in York. I've heard of you; but, howsomdever, you are quite as welcome as if you'd been the most dashing high-toby-man that ever stepped."

"I am obliged to you for the compliment," said Rowland, with a smile; "and I presume, Palmer, we shall now start at once."

"No," said Dick, "another delay has inter-posed itself; we cannot start till to-morrow morning, and then it must be towards York."

"Towards York?" cried Rowland, in sur-prise.

"Yes, to meet Miranda, who is on her journey hither."

"Miranda! to meet Miranda! Can it be possible that she is on the road, trusting her-self to all its dangers and disagreeables for my sake?"

"It's not only possible, but true," replied Palmer. "She has forsaken every friend she had at York, she has rejected the friendship and offers of assistance from those who would have felt a pride in rendering it; and, with a noble heroism, the discretion of which I can-not praise, but which, at the same time, I cannot help honouring greatly, she has re-solved to join her fortunes to yours, and to share with you in London whatever fate may have in store for you."

"Noble, generous girl," said Rowland. "Oh, how richly has Heaven repaid me by bestowing upon me such a heart as Miranda's, for all my sufferings. I should be insensible, indeed, did I not feel conscious, from the very bottom of my heart, of the value of the rich treasure which is mine."

Dick Palmer then explained to Percy the arrangement he had made with Miranda, as to meeting them on the road, as well as inform-ing him of the events which had occurred during their separation, concluding by saying, that he himself would take at the "Old Raven" what he was in so much need of, namely, a night's rest, advising Percy to do the same; when, early in the morning, he would move slowly down the road to meet Miranda and Mr. Percy.

As the hour was getting late, Percy and Dick Palmer each retired to a well-appointed chamber in the old inn. The latter to sleep away his fatigues, and the former to lie long in thought upon the beauty and excellence of Miranda, and, when fairly exhausted and overcome by sleep, to dream but of her, and the happy days which he still trusted were in store for them both.

Rowland Percy slept heavily, until he was startled by a hand that was laid upon his shoulder. It was Dick Palmer's.

"Up, up!" he cried. "We shall have just time to do some justice to the morning cheer of the 'Old Raven,' and then we must start off upon our expedition."

"I shall be ready in a few moments," cried Rowland, springing to his feet. He had only taken off some of his outer garments, for the

CONSTERNATION CAUSED BY THE UNEXPECTED APPEARANCE OF DICK PALMER.

feeling that he was surrounded by danger, prevented him from lying down with that feeling of security which is so delightful, and which people never appreciate fully until, by some untoward circumstances, they are deprived of it.

A substantial breakfast awaited them in the room below, and, after partaking of it, and shaking hands heartily with the fat landlord, they repaired to the inn door, where Palmer's own horse was waiting, and another, which he had borrowed of the landlord, for Rowland's use.

"I regret," said Dick Palmer, "that I could not provide you with a better steed than this.

In the event of a hard chase, he will be of very little service to you. I do not, however, anticipate further disagreeables on our road and, in that case, we shall do very well, for I can accommodate my horse's speed to yours.'

"At all events," said Rowland, as he mounted, "I shall feel myself far more secure, and capable of resistance, than I did before."

They went down the road from the inn door at an easy trot, and, absorbed as he was with many painful reflections, still Rowland could not be entirely dead to the beauties of the scenery through which he was passing; and although, in his conversation, he kept continually reverting to Miranda, and the probability of soon meeting her, he showed himself fully alive to the varied charms of the sylvan scene that greeted them on every side.

Rowland pictured to himself what was Miranda's state of mind on that eventful morning, and, in doing so, he was very far from exaggerating the state of anxious suspense she was really in.

She obeyed Palmer's directions faithfully, and at very nearly the same hour which witnessed the departure of Rowland from the door of the inn, she started with Mr. Percy and Jones from the place where they had succeeded in obtaining shelter for the night.

Miranda thought it would be imprudent to say anything to Mr. Percy in his peculiar state of mind, with regard to the probable immediate meeting with Rowland; she knew not what enemies they might have the ill-fortune to encounter before that meeting took place, in which case an imprudent word or two from the old man might be productive of the most fatal consequences to him, who held existence upon so frail a tenure as his escape, day by day, from the dread ministers of the law.

Both Miranda and Mr. Percy felt much invigorated by the comparatively quiet night's repose they had had; and, although the road seemed long to the tenderly-nurtured girl, that feeling arose from her state of anxious expectation, for, if anything, she felt herself more capable of undergoing the fatigue of walking than on the preceding days of her pilgrimage.

As for Mr. Jones, he now and then amused himself with a song, interspersed occasionally with scraps of his own peculiar philosophy, and many curious remarks concerning Ikey Samuels, and the peculiar interview he recently had with him.

There were but few passengers on the road, and although, when they both first started, the actual distance between Miranda and Percy exceeded five or six miles, yet it must be recollected that that distance was being decreased in a double ratio, so that something very far short of an hour would abundantly suffice to bring them together; but, oh, on what leaden pinions the moments move, when expectation is at its height, and some event is looked forward to, which engrosses the whole heart and soul of its anxious expectants. Miranda had never felt so short a distance so long, so weary, and so monotonous.

As for Mr. Percy, he walked on listlessly, now and then muttering to himself some surmises or expressions little in accordance with his real situation.

Miranda saw that, about half-a-mile in advance of where she was, there was a sudden turn in the road; and a fluttering sensation at her heart led her to suspect, she knew not why, that, at that turn, she should surely meet with Rowland Percy. She had no particular reason for so thinking, but a kind of perception came over her that such would be the case.

"He will be there," she said to herself; "I feel that he will be there. I shall see him again free from the terrors that surrounded him in his dungeon—that frightful condemned cell, to enter which was sufficient to cast a deadly gloom over any mind. Whatever dangers—whatever perils—I pray to Heaven we may be permitted to suffer them together, and not left to a conjecture of each other's sorrows and dangers. Rowland—Rowland! I shall surely know a moment of exquisite joy when I look upon your face again."

The sound of horses' feet came upon her ears, and now that she thought she was surely about to meet with Rowland Percy, all her courage, all her fortitude forsook her; and but that she clung to the arm of Mr. Percy, she thought she must have fallen to the earth.

She could not proceed another step, but, with her eyes riveted upon the turn of the road, she waited until two horsemen came in sight.

With a cry of joy, she uttered the name of Rowland, and then stood as pale as a marble statue awaiting his advance.

CHAPTER CIX.

THE MEETING—A SCENE OF PURE AFFECTION —THE ALARM—THE DANGER OF THE FUGITIVES.

THE recognition between Rowland and Miranda was simultaneous. Not less hopeful was he, at that turn of the road, of catching a glimpse of her than she had been of him, although he had scarcely expected to find her so very short a distance from him.

"'Tis she!" he cried, and he urged his horse to its utmost speed. Then, by a sudden impulse, he drew up, and hurriedly dismounted, preferring to rush forward on foot to meet her who was the one great object of his existence.

Two or three minutes brought him to her side. Pleasure beamed from his eyes, and, heedless of the presence of others, forgetting everything but that he saw again the dear object of his heart's idolatry, he clasped her to his breast.

Let those who prefer the cold proprieties of existence to its most exquisite feelings censure that embrace. It was one of the purest and tenderest affection.

An exclamation of joy escaped old Mr. Percy, and he clasped one of the hands of Rowland, while the tears fell fast down his furrowed cheeks.

"Found—found!" he cried. "My boy Rowland—he is found at last—long sought for as he has been. We shall all be happy now, for he is found at last! His enemies could not slay him. See, Miranda, he is unhurt! He is saved! Yes, he is saved!"

"Father—Miranda!" was all that Rowland could utter at the moment in the excitement of his feelings; and, had not a few tears come to his relief, he felt that he should almost have been choked by his emotions.

Any stranger would have wondered what could have been the circumstances under which this party met; there was so little for some time said, and yet such evidently deep emotion in the hearts of them all. Under such circumstances, words seemed too weak to give expression to the feelings that filled the heart, and their first gush must in some measure subside, before language can step in to the aid of the excited spirit.

How long Miranda and Rowland Percy would have continued gazing at each other, unheedful of everything but the intense pleasure they derived from such a process, it is hard to say, had not a warning intimation been given to them by Palmer that time was on the wing.

Being on horseback, he commanded a view to a considerable distance on the road towards London, in which direction he kept his eyes fixed; while, agreeably to his directions, Jones had mounted a high bank in the immediate vicinity of the place of meeting, and kept a good watch towards York.

"Mr. Percy," cried Palmer, "I am sure I need not warn you that this interview must needs be brief. Part soon, with a better hope of meeting again ere long."

Both Rowland and Miranda started at the warning voice, and the former said:

"Yes, Miranda, it is even as he says. We meet in difficulty and in danger, to part only with a hope of happier days, and we must part so very soon, that this meeting will appear to me like a glimpse of Heaven in a dream."

"But the time will come, Rowland," whispered Miranda, "I feel assured it will, when we shall meet to part no more; when danger and suspicion will no longer hover over you, and when you will be free and honoured, as you so amply deserve to be."

"My own Miranda, it rejoices me to find you so hopeful. If from any source I can derive pleasurable feelings in my unfortunate condition, it must be from your lips."

"Then be assured, dear Rowland, that I am full of hope. Does not everything which has occurred tend to the creation of such a feeling? Have you not escaped almost miraculously from death, and has not Heaven shown its care of you, by giving me, a weak girl, power to snatch you from a prison, where you were surrounded by all the care, the caution, and the strength which could be expended upon its defence? Let us be full of hope Rowland, and derive even from the calamitous circumstances you think of, holy and cheering consolation. Your accusation, your condemnation, and the ultimate triumph of your innocence—for that it will ultimately triumph, I feel most certain—will be a great practical lesson to mankind, and induce judges to be careful how they sacrifice a human life to the evidences of an act, which is in direct contradiction to all its former tenor. Moreover, Rowland, could any circumstances of prosperity have bound us to each other, as we are now bound to each other by misfortune? could any other circumstances have shown to us each other's hearts, as we now see them? none, Rowland, none. Let us, then, from out of this calamity extract some good, and while we have a hope of extrication from circumstances that cannot be otherwise than deeply painful, let us assure ourselves that the evil is not unmixed, but that when the day of tribulation shall have passed away, we shall find that we have not suffered altogether in vain."

It was soothing and delightful to Rowland Percy's heart—it must have been pleasing in the sight of Heaven, to hear that young and innocent girl breathing such pure piety, and uttering such sentences of firm reliance in the even-handed justice of that Providence, which can turn afflictions to blessings, and make the wounded heart radiant with joy.

"Let us go home," cried Mr. Percy; "we have surely now wandered far enough from York. Rowland is saved. What more have we to do?"

"Much," said Miranda; "leave him to me, Rowland, he attends greatly to my words. We have much yet to do, Mr. Percy; Rowland, although safe at present, cannot be called saved. He is still environed by snares for his destruction; and although I have a fervent hope, amounting to a conviction, that he will be saved at last, we have yet still much to do. We must go to London, and Rowland must precede us. You know that, when I say so, Mr. Percy, there are ample reasons for the act."

"Ample, I am certain," said the old man; "you are always right. Can an angel err?"

"You hear," said Miranda to Rowland; "he will accompany me cheerfully. We will submit ourselves entirely to the counsel of our good friend, Palmer, and as he considers that we had better not proceed to London together, we will satisfy ourselves with this brief interview, in the hope that a more lasting one awaits us when we meet again."

"You are right," Miranda," said Rowland. "Life and liberty to me now are ten times more precious than they could be under any other circumstances; when I see you, Miranda, full of hope and expectation, that a period will be put to our calamities, I ought to be the last to despair. You have ever been, and ever will be, dearest, my guardian angel; one who not only finds power to step between me and my enemies, but who likewise weans me from my own sad and sinful thoughts, winning me back again by your own gentleness and goodness, to a better frame of mind. Ah, Miranda, amid all these circumstances of pain, and toil, and trouble, what should I have been without thee?"

"And what," said Miranda, in a whisper, "what other feeling than that I have for you, Rowland, could have nerved me to do what I have done? We will mutually assist and support each other, trusting the while to Heaven to help us both."

"Mr. Percy," cried Palmer, "you must be brief. We know not even now what danger may come upon us."

"I will," said Rowland, "I will; but spare me yet a moment."

"Don't you wish you may get it," said Jones; "I expects as how we shall be in an out-an-out fix in a little while."

"What do you mean, Jones?" cried Palmer, "is anyone coming?"

"I wish it was one as is coming," said Jones, "but it seems to me somewhere about thirteen to the dozen. There'll be a spree, as sure as my name's Jones. They are coming."

"But who are they?" said Palmer; "for Heaven's sake be more explicit, Jones."

"More 'plicit—the only 'plicit as I knows is, I'm more 'elevated than you is, and sees 'em when you doesn't. There's a lot of fellows on horses; they've just turned the top of one of the hills, and all I can say is they're a-coming."

Palmer immediately dismounted from his horse, which stood as quiet as possible while he left it; then springing up the bank upon which Jones stood, with such suddenness as to disturb the latter's centre of gravity, and cause him to roll down into the roadway, he took a searching and anxious glance towards York.

"Enemies," he exclaimed, "they are enemies. By Heavens, Jones, they are coming!"

"I told you so," said Jones; "and you might just as well have said as you was a-coming just now, and not make a fellow fall down, with the hind part of him in a ditch. But what's to be done, Dicky, my boy? I forgives you; but what's to be done?"

"I know not," said Palmer; "the danger is great. I could swear to those men being officers from York; and what fresh information has induced them again to take to the road I know not. Our danger was never so great as now. They'll be upon us in ten minutes."

"Farewell, Miranda," said Percy, who had paid but little or no attention to what was passing between Jones and Palmer—"farewell, dearest; but I pray Heaven we may soon meet again."

"There is little utility in parting now," said Palmer. "Danger thickens; and there are now on the road twelve or thirteen officers from York, all, no doubt, bent upon your capture. They are not riding fast, but still something less than ten minutes must bring them to this spot."

A flush of colour came over Rowland Percy's face as he said:

"Is the danger, indeed, so near? Alas! Miranda, there may even yet be more sorrow in store for us. But, now, do not mourn for me. I will die, fighting for my life with those who would deprive me of it, rather than be dragged back again to that cell from which you rescued me."

"Then, Rowland, we will live and die together," said Miranda.

"Who talks of dying," said old Mr. Percy; "who talks of danger to you, Rowland or Miranda? Fools! do they know what it is to face desperation itself? Unarmed though I am, they shall find me more than their equal. Heed them not. You shall see this roadway dyed with their blood. Let them come—yes, let them come."

"That's all very fine, old gentleman," said Jones, "and I have no doubt you means the pleasant little theatrical performance, as you mentions, only some people's bow-wow is ever such a lot worserer than their bite, no exparagement to you, old gentleman; but I'd rather not put you to the inconvenience o' eating all these ere dozen officers as is coming."

"I do not understand you," said old Mr. Percy.

"Oh, it's all the same. Now, Dicky, I tell you what, it strikes me we must come the artful."

"How do you mean?" said Palmer.

"Why, there's a ditch on the other side o' that ere hedge, and I moves as we all lays down on the bottom on it, and trust to Providence and quickset."

"But the horses!" said Palmer; "the horses!"

"Why, your own will lay just on his back whensoever he's axed; and, as for the t'other one, I moves as we gives him a whack as'll start him off."

"Ay, and so excite suspicion that his rider has hidden himself close at hand," cried Palmer. "That will not do; and you must bear in mind, also, Jones, that you and I are likewise obnoxious to the officers, and they would not scruple an instant in arresting us, and lodging us in jail at the next market-town. However, your plan, I fear, is the only one which presents the least chance of escape. But Mr. Rowland's hack must learn a lesson in training on the spur of the moment, and he must hide himself, whether he likes it or not. Come on to the hedge in the hope that it will afford us efficient shelter."

CHAPTER CX.

THE CONCEALMENT FROM THE OFFICERS— THE PURSUERS OUTWITTED—THE CONTINUED JOURNEY.

ALL but old Mr. Percy followed Palmer to a high gate, which led into a meadow adjoining the road-side, which otherwise was skirted by an impervious hedge, at the foot of which was the ditch Jones had mentioned as likely to afford a shelter to those who were anxious to conceal themselves from the approaching horsemen.

The plan seemed feasible enough, had it not been for the horses, whose bulk it was difficult to conceal, and whose discretion could not altogether be relied upon.

"We could hide in the ditch, for it is nearly dry," said Palmer, "with every chance of escape; but, for the horses! there, I think, is an insurmountable difficulty."

"Why not," said Miranda, "strip them of

their bridles and saddles, and turn them into the meadow? It is no extraordinary thing to see two horses grazing in a road-side field."

Palmer and Jones looked at each other for some seconds in silence, and then the latter said:

"You punch my head, and I'll punch yours, then we shall both be properly served out for being two such fools as never to think of that afore; to be sure, that's the very plan, Miss Miranda. I beg to remark, as in some things you is as green as possible, while in t'others you is positively downy; in course, it ain't extraordinary to see horses a-grazing. Dicky, what two spoons we is. Hilloa! how he's a-working?"

Dick Palmer was busy, with a false key, unlocking a padlock, which fastened a gate. This accomplished, he led in both the horses, and commenced hastily divesting them of their trappings, in which he was assisted by Jones and Rowland.

In a few moments the horses, turned out into the meadow, began, as Mr. Jones remarked, in the most natural manner in the world, to crop the sweet herbage that grew in abundance at their feet.

"Now to the ditch!" he cried, "we've not a moment to lose!"

Even as he spoke, the sound of horses' feet, and even the voices of their pursuers, came, with painful distinctness, upon their ears.

Miranda took old Mr. Percy by the arm, saying to him:

"Follow me, and do as I do."

Then she crept close to the hedge, and lay almost completely hidden among the brush-wood and mass of decayed leaves that formed the base of the ditch.

In an instant they were all concealed in a similar manner.

"Hush!" said Palmer; "now, not another word."

"Mute as a coffin," murmured Jones; and then all was silent.

On came the horsemen, not at an extraordinary pace, but at one which, without distressing their horses, would carry them over a long stretch of ground in a few hours. Several of them were talking loudly, and, so near were they now, that their words came distinctly upon the ears of those who were so anxious to escape their observation.

"Well, if we don't come up with him," said one, "or, if he takes any of the cross-roads, instead of keeping to this one, we shall, at least, reach London time enough to raise a pretty hue and cry about him."

"We shall; I must have him!" cried the leader. "And, if Rowland Percy escape us, I shall think myself well paid if I catch the scoundrel who took me so much at unawares yesterday. Mind, I stand twenty pounds out of my own pocket to any one of you that places a pair of handcuffs on him: he is a tall, thinnish, sinewy-looking man, with a slightly aquiline nose."

"By-the-by," said another, "didn't you say, Viggers, when we were on the brow of the hill, that you saw some people hereabouts?"

"Upon my soul I did!" said the officer, suddenly checking his horse, and wheeling round to his companions; "I certainly did see four or five people hereabouts, but how they have disappeared I can't think, for there's no house near that I can see."

"Oh!" cried another, "don't you see what a twist there is in the road? They've gone on, of course, whoever they were, and, to set that question at rest, we'd better push after them."

"I say, one of those horses in yon field is a good 'un," remarked one of the officers to his companion.

"Yes, a beauty," was the reply; "come on —I only wish I had him instead of the beast I am upon."

This short colloquy took place exactly opposite to where the party lay concealed, and there can be no question but that it was listened to by them with an interest amounting to the deepest anxiety, particularly when Palmer's horse became a subject of remark; for, if Viggers, the constable, had looked at it —which he did not—there was every probability of his knowing it again, and at once suspecting that its rider, against whom he felt so much animosity, could not be far off.

In such an event, detection would have been almost certain, and through Rowland's determination not to give himself up to his enemies alive, blood would, in all probability, have been shed in the scene of violence that must have ensued.

Such, however, happily was not the case; and the ears of our friends were in a few moments blessed by the sound of the retreating footsteps of those who, by their superiority of numbers, must have been victorious over them, however gallant the resistance might have been.

"They are gone," said old Mr. Percy.

"Stow that ere gab," muttered Jones.

"Hush, for Heaven's sake, hush!" said Palmer.

"Nay, I will rise and go after them," said old Mr. Percy. "I wish them to know how dangerous it is to become enemies of my son Rowland. I will go after them and slay them. Nay, Miranda, stay me not. It is my duty—a sacred duty. Rowland will always have enemies unless I slay them; the dead can do no injury—therefore must I kill them. Let me go. Do not attempt to stay me from my just revenge."

"Mr. Percy, I charge you to remain where you are. Believe me, you are doing more for Rowland by quietness now than by violence."

"Ah, say you so? Hush, then—not a word."

"They are far enough off now," said Jones; "and I don't see as we need be so particular about holding our tongues; only it wouldn't be just the prudent thing for the old gentleman to go arter them, and make a kick up; for he'd do himself harm, and us no good; which I take it is somewhere about the same sort of thing."

"He will be still," said Miranda. "Thank Heaven, we have escaped!"

"Yet remain quiet awhile," said Palmer, "while I cautiously reconnoitre the road these horsemen have taken. Although the officers of York could not hold a prisoner when they had him, they seem determined to repair their error."

Dick Palmer then crept along the hedge, until he came to a lower portion of it, and raising himself then only so high as his eyes, to obtain a clear view over its top, he gazed after the retreating horsemen, who little suspected that they were really exerting themselves to increase the distance between themselves and the object of their pursuit.

"'Tis well," muttered Dick. "In the chances of escape, the greatest thing is always to be fully cognizant of the whereabouts of our enemies. Ride on to London, most sapient officers; if you will, you shall have the road to yourselves, and no hindrance to its full enjoyment, if it can produce you any. This, I take it, is about the narrowest escape we have yet had—our danger being so much the greater, in consequence of the number of our party."

He waited until the officers were nearly hidden from his sight, and then, abandoning the caution that was no longer necessary, he walked boldly back to the ditch, saying:

"The danger is passed; and with a feeling of relief we can at least tell ourselves that we need not expect an enemy in every chance person that may cross our path. Out of the worst circumstances we may gather some good; and the benefit we shall derive from this little dangerous *rencontre* is, that we know the tactics of our enemies."

"And I have one consolation," said Rowland Percy, "that if the worst comes to the worst, they would surely be satisfied with my destruction, as the principal party involved in all these transactions."

"Indeed, Mr. Percy, I don't know that," said Palmer. "I think I may make common cause with you now most fairly; for Viggers, the officer, seems as intent upon my capture as upon yours—nay, probably more so, for people's revenges are always more dear to them than their public duties. After what we heard Viggers say, I shall begin to think that he comes after me as much as after you. Help me to saddle the horses, Jones; and although I believe we are tolerably safe just now, yet I counsel an immediate separation."

The horses were soon in a fit state again for the road, and the whole party passed from the meadow which had afforded them so timely a shelter—each with a feeling of thankfulness at the escape, with the exception of poor Mr. Percy, whose state of mind would not permit him fully to appreciate the circumstances.

Miranda and Rowland Percy looked in each other's faces with the greatest tenderness.

Every new danger seemed to draw them closer together, and they felt to the full as unwilling to part as they had been before.

Stern necessity, however, admitted of no other course, and, with a few hurried sentences of affection, they bade each other farewell—that sort of painful, indefinite farewell with which persons involved in difficulty and danger separate, when their meeting again is a matter of doubt and uncertainty, and when much misery may befall them, ere they can look into the light of each other's eyes, and, with a thrill of joy, exclaim:

"Thank Heaven, we have met again!"

Palmer was standing with the bridle of his horse over his arm, while Jones held Rowland's steed ready for him to mount.

"Now, Miss Rankley," said Palmer, "mind you keep to the high-road; for even if the officers should recognize you they have no power to molest you, or obstruct your proceedings in any way. Nevertheless, I should say, keep out of the way, if you can; and if you should come across them, try, with the assistance of Jones, to puzzle them as to the track you are pursuing. I do not think that Mr. Percy and I will reach London much before you do yourself, for we shall take a course far out of the high-road, unless at intervals we succeed in ascertaining exactly that the officers are many miles ahead of us. Do not forget the address in London, where you are to inquire for me."

"I'll see that that ere dodge is all right," said Jones. "We shall soon be at the 'Star and Tinder-box,' in Steeple Court; and when we does get there, we rayther knows what to say. I doesn't make no sort of doubt, but we shall get on uncommon well on the road. I think as how we've got enough for our expenses in a moderate kind of way, and if we wants any more, I ain't such a fool as not to know somethink about what people call the rights of property, which means, in my very humble opinion, as you are to grab all you can."

"A comprehensive doctrine, truly," laughed Palmer, as he sprang upon his horse. "Ah, Jones, I'm afraid you'll never mend your life."

"It ain't broke yet," said Jones; "and if so be as there's anything wrong, there's two on us, you know, Dicky."

"Farewell!" said Rowland to Miranda. "May Heaven have you in its choicest keeping!"

"And you," said Miranda; "for if you are well, all is well."

There was a silent pressure of their hands, and then Rowland turned to his father:

"We shall meet again soon," he said; "but, in the meantime, I must leave you with my heart's best treasure—Miranda."

"What," said the old man, as a tear rose to his eye, "will you leave us so soon, Rowland? Oh! come home—at once! It seems to me that we are far from York—the pleasant meadows and the little wooded park, which is all our own—which will all be yours, Rowland, when death has taken me from you, and I can no longer love you with the love of a mortal heart—a heart which, until it ceases its painful pulsations, is all your own and Miranda's.

I have hopes, Rowland, great hopes, of procuring the full and entire consent of Sir George Rankley to your marriage."

"Father! think again," said Rowland, "and you will surely remember that he is dead?"

"That is a delusion," said Mr. Percy, quickly—"a delusion which the whole world is labouring under, except myself. Leave all that to me, Rowland, and, in the meantime, come home. Why, you were born in the old house, and have passed your happiest days in it. Why, then, should you wander from it now?"

"I have no choice, father. Even now moments may be precious; and although in the wide world there is but yourself and Miranda, for whom my heart feels most specially, yet must I leave you, although with greater ease and confidence, because you have with you the angelic spirit, which surely must be under Heaven's own care."

"You mean Miranda?"

"I do, father. Remain with her, and be all that kindness can dictate; but, as you love her and myself, do not mention to her Sir George Rankley, for indeed he is dead. Farewell."

Rowland then mounted his horse, and he and Palmer were ready again to proceed on their toilsome and dangerous journey. He waved his hand once more to Miranda, but could not trust himself to speak.

"On—on," said Palmer, and in another moment they were going at a sharp trot up the road.

Poor Miranda felt as if a sudden change had come over the face of nature, when Rowland Percy was gone.

She had felt a sense of security and freedom from harm when he was by, which seemed now to desert her.

It required all the really strong mind she possessed to be able to bear, with even outward composure, the sadness of her heart, and it was only by reflecting upon the important trust she had in the protection of him whose wandering intellect forbade him to control his own actions, that nerved her to undergo whatever further trials might be in store for her.

Jones first broke the silence, by saying:

"Miss Miranda, I have got a scheme of my own, which I didn't say nothing of to Dicky, cause he, perhaps, would have kicked at the way in which I wanted to compass the browns. It appears to me as we should have a much better chance of getting to London quick and easy by coming the bold caper."

"What do you mean, Jones?"

"Why, I means this ere, Miss Miranda. I takes it we are a third of the way between York and London, that is to say, we haven't much above a hundred miles to go; but that is a tolerable long way to foot it, with only the chance of a waggon, or something of that ere sort, to give us a lift. Now I propose we goes to the next town and waits comfortably for the mail or a coach, when we can get a lift as far as we like, or all the way, for the

matter of that ere; or, if you likes it better, we'll come it more out-and-out, and take a chaise, only, as I haven't got quite tin enough for that caper, I should be obligated to borrow some of a gentleman afore we could come it, cause we mustn't be in London without no tin for a start."

"I can really see no objection," said Miranda, "to our taking a coach, except the one which would most likely occur even under any circumstances—that is, the meeting of those whom we would fain avoid, and their consequent discovery that I was bound to the metropolis, from which they would infer that Rowland was there likewise."

"If you and the old gentleman can get inside places, it seems to me as if there isn't much to be feared. I'll warrant they sha'n't know me on the roof. To be sure, we should get to London before Dicky and Mr. Percy; but where's the odds, you can make yourself comfortable when they comes."

"True," said Miranda, "and, after all, in London we may succeed in hiding ourselves from any spies that might be set to watch us; for the great object, of course, will be to avoid being dangerous to Rowland, in consequence of making inquiry for him, and being traced to the house where we are to hear news of Palmer."

"The wery ticket," said Jones, "leave me to arrange all that; they'll be rum 'uns if they finds me out in going backwards and forards in London. I knows too many ins and outs there to be easy tooked in, and if they tries to follow me, I'll lead 'em a dance they'll be sick on before they've done with it."

"Then let us at once resolve," said Miranda, "upon that course of action. I am willing to risk it, if there be any risk in it."

"Kim on then," said Jones, "and I hopes we shall have the pleasure of seeing the most beautifulest and most romantic spot in all London afore we is twenty-four hours older."

"What spot is that?"

"Drury Lane, especially on a wet day. You should see the ins and outs as is there, Miss Miranda—nothing werdent, and no mistake—lots of conweniences of all sorts and descriptions. Hot saveloys at a ha'penny a piece, and baked 'taters for nothink, only you must be up to the dodge of grabbing of them when the fellow's looking another way in a fit of confidence. Then it's not like here, where you may go never so many miles without so much as seeing of a public-house—lor! no, it's quite the rewerse—if you wants a glass of gin, you've nothink to say but 'give us a penn'orth.' What do you think of all that, old gentleman?"

"I am thinking of the stars," said Mr. Percy.

"Do you mean the 'Seven Stars,' in Russell Court?"

"No, no—the heavenly bodies."

"Oh! that's another thing—they is all earthly bodies as is there—the only thing as is heavenly is the gin, and that is out-and-out."

CHAPTER CXI.

THE PLAN OF THE OFFICERS—MR. JONES'S
DISGUISE, AND THE COACH FROM YORK.

DICK PALMER explained to Rowland Percy his plan of reaching London without encountering the officers, by taking cross-roads, and out-of-the-way bridle-paths, with which he, Palmer, was familiar, and although such a mode of operation must necessarily consume considerable time, yet it presented such great claims of safety, that they both determined to adopt it, and accordingly started off at the first turning they came to with the resolution to go near the high-road as little as possible, and to obtain what refreshments they required, if it could be so managed, at cottages by the road-side, instead of at inns or public-houses.

Palmer could not but observe Rowland's intense anxiety as regarded Miranda, and he took occasion to assure him that she could not possibly come to any harm.

"Jones," he said, "with all his peculiarities, is courageous and full of expedients. He is tolerably well known on the road, and liked for a certain rough humour that characterizes his sayings and doings. I have every expectation that he will bring Miranda to London in perfect safety, and although I have warned him, as you heard, to be particularly careful not to involve her in any of his peculations on the road, I believe such warning was not required."

"I am rejoiced," replied Rowland, "to hear you talk so cheeringly upon the subject, which, of course, must be uppermost in my heart. Heaven knows what may eventually become of me, or whether my innocence will ever become apparent to the minds of men! I hope that it will, or I shall soon die, for I should be, even in London, like a man sent to seek his bread while manacled. I could not even be industrious, for I dare not show myself to those who would purchase the labour of my hands, or my head."

"Sufficient for the day," said Dick Palmer, "is the evil thereof. We will think of all that when we get to London. Your escape is now the one grand object in view."

The plan of the officers, who were so anxious to recapture the convicted murderer, as they called poor Rowland, was not a bad one.

They rightly enough conjectured that his progress would be slow, on account of the many shifts and manoeuvres to which he would be compelled to resort in order to escape recognition, and consequent capture.

They, therefore, considered that their safest way would be to take the high-road to London as quickly as possible, with the remote chance of finding him they sought on the road, but the greater probability of leaving him on it.

Viggers then intended to make arrangements with the London police, so that every avenue to the metropolis would be watched for a few days, and then his party, being a powerful one, could separate itself, and, taking different routes back again, stand possibly a chance of meeting Rowland.

How they sped upon their errand our readers will discover as we proceed, for a very short time must now suffice to bring those in whose fate we are so much interested, as well as their enemies, to the metropolis.

In fact, the road was clear, and it would have required some out-of-the-way accident to involve Rowland in such danger now that the York officers were several miles ahead of him on the high-road, while he was making various divarications from his course, each of which enabled them to gain a still greater distance in advance.

As for Miranda, she had not to go above three or four miles, at the very utmost, before reaching a straggling village, through which, Jones ascertained, all the coaches between York and London must necessarily pass; and there they resolved to wait, as they were told one would be by in the course of an hour and a-half, which had started at a very early hour from York.

In the neat, sanded parlour of the half-farmhouse, half-inn, at which they had made the inquiries, Miranda and old Mr. Percy rested themselves from the fatigues of the morning; while Jones went through the village, until he came to the barber's shop, into which he entered with an air of great familiarity, saying:

"How is yer? How do you find business?"

"Really, sir, upon my honour and conscience," said the barber, "you have the advantage of me."

"Lor!" said Jones, "you don't mean to say that! Why, I had my hair cut here seven years ago. What a memory you must have to be sure."

"Ah, my dear sir," said the barber, "seven years, you know, is a long time; we can't remember every gentleman who does us the honour of having his hair cut here. But, perhaps, you will like to do so now, sir?"

"No, I wants a wig."

"A wig, sir; certainly, sir. I believe, sir, my stock of wigs, consisting of seven, to be the finest in this part of the country; and I have got one, sir, that will match the colour of your hair to a T."

"Thank you for nothing," said Jones; "that's just what I don't want. I am tired of my own head of hair, and wants a change."

The barber produced his stock of wigs, and Jones chose one which differed as materially as possible from the colour of his own hair; then, borrowing the barber's scissors, he, to the astonishment of that functionary, cut his hair off in great masses, so that, when the wig was on his head, no trace of his own hair could be seen.

Having honestly, then, paid for his purchase—for Mr. Jones, in his refinements upon philosophy, would have thought it a very low thing indeed, not to pay for anything he had fairly offered to buy—he hastened back to Miranda, to show her the effect the singular-coloured wig produced upon his physiognomical expression.

"I don't mean to say for sartin, Miss Miranda," he remarked, "that I should be tooked up, even if they was to see me, only you see, it's just possible, as I had rayther a skrimmage with one of the magistrates when you was in quod, about what they called the Riot Act, which you may have heard as I boned; he may have turned wicious, and offered the officers something to lay hands on me, so I wishes to keep myself snug and quiet, rayther than trouble him, which is the reason of this ere wig. Now, if there's room inside, when the coach does come, you and the old gentleman shall get in, and I'll take care of myself on the roof; and pervided there should be a skrimmage of any kind, I can always get down, and put my spoke in the wheel. What have yer had to drink?"

"This ale," said Miranda, "suits my appetite well, though it may not yours. You will, doubtless, call it weak."

Mr. Jones tasted the ale, and then made a hideous face.

"Weak be blowed," he said, "I calls it strong, only it's strong of the wrong thing—the water, I mean. This ere ale has a very slight acquaintance with malt and hops."

Mr. Jones then went and made such a clatter in the house respecting the quality of the beverage which had been supplied, that, as is almost always the case in public-houses, large or small, a better article was produced, an article usually kept for guests who make a disturbance, and who will not be put off with inferior commodities.

The coach came pretty nearly about the time which had been mentioned, and, upon hailing it, Mr. Jones found that there were two inside places, and only two, vacant. Mr. Percy and Miranda were soon installed into the vehicle: and Jones, by the special invitation of the coachman, had the box seat, which gave him an opportunity of discoursing with that worthy, and beguiling the tedium of the way wonderfully.

In fact, the coachman thought Jones so extraordinary a person, that he treated him wherever they changed horses, and listened to the outrageous inventions, with which he was amused, with the fullest belief and the most unbounded satisfaction.

Thus are all our *dramatis personæ* fairly, without let or hindrance, on the road to London, where, let us hope—though it may be after many changing scenes and vicissitudes of fortune—Rowland Percy, with his faithful and beautiful Miranda, may meet the reward of their innocence, their rare fidelity, and their many trials of fortitude, by being blessed with the society of each other, never again to part, until death shall prepare them for a meeting of an eternal character, in those realms where the judgment of the Judge is infallible, and sorrow is a thing unknown.

CHAPTER CXII.

THE ARRIVAL IN LONDON—EVENING IN THE METROPOLIS—THE INN YARD.

OF the four separate parties—some of whom were so anxious to meet each other, others to avoid a collision—that were proceeding towards the metropolis, the one which comprised Bernard Varley and Samuel Twitter was the first to arrive at its journey's end.

Regardless of expense Varley travelled post, and, of course, secured the best relays of horses that could be had on the road; the consequence of which was, that he reached the metropolis in an exceedingly short space of time, considering the distance he had to traverse.

Twitter sat with him; for, although Varley took good care to let him know and thoroughly feel the difference in their positions, yet, like most men with an overburdened conscience, he would consent to any companionship rather than be alone, and, therefore, he admitted Twitter to a seat inside the carriage, with a view of conversing with him, when dark and desperate thoughts should come crowding on his brain, and he should feel the want of some human companionship, even if it were that of the man whom he most hated and abhorred.

After their recent quarrel, the reader is aware that a better understanding existed between these worthies, or, at all events, the semblance of one, which answered the same purpose, so far as they were mutually concerned.

It was upon the strength of this, and the elation of mind, arising from the possession of the hundred-pound note, that Twitter, during the journey, sought several times to wean Varley from the desperate pursuit in which he was engaged, and to lead him to more rational resolutions as concerned his future life.

It was curious to note how the half imbecile, weak-minded man rose, under the peculiar circumstances, far above him of an acuter intellect in, at all events, the one quality—discretion.

Samuel Twitter had not the mind to be diverted from his own petty avarice and considerations for his personal safety by any such passion as that which inflamed the breast of Bernard Varley.

Miranda might have been more beautiful, more innocent, more full of angelic qualities than she really was, without disturbing the mind of Samuel Twitter from its deep selfishness; but Bernard Varley was composed of more penetrable stuff, and, hardened villain as he was, he had a perception of the good and the beautiful, which induced him to covet the possession of the angelic being whom he had deprived of fortune and friends, and from whose very destitution he had gathered his greatest hopes of a successful result to his wild passion.

We cannot but believe, likewise, that Heaven's atoning justice shone conspicuously in the person of Bernard Varley, and that a part of his punishment in this world for the frightful and ungrateful murder of the father was a soul-consuming and hopeless passion for the child.

But be this as it may, not a day, not an hour, not a minute passed over the head of Bernard Varley without adding fresh fuel from the depths of his own reflections to that master feeling of his mind, which Samuel Twitter, with a groaning horror, foretold would be his ultimate destruction.

Ever dreading Varley's violence as he did, and knowing that he was about to touch upon a topic that would arouse his fiercest passions, they had not proceeded twenty miles upon their journey, when, with cringing accents, Twitter again implored him to reconsider the labyrinth of chances into which he was about to plunge himself.

"Remember, Varley," he said, "you have gained all—ay, more than all you ever expected. Let your exertions be for the death of Rowland Percy, but leave Miranda alone. I pray you, leave her to whatever fate may await her. Can you indulge even the faintest shadow of a hope that she will ever be yours?"

"I have three means before me," said Varley, gloomily—"entreaty, fraud, and force. I have placed them in their proper order. If one will not succeed, another shall."

"But neither will—neither can, and I repeat what I have before urged, that in some of your wild and vain appeals to Miranda, you will say something that will bring us both to——"

"To what?"

"To a scaffold. Hush!—speak low. Oh! Varley, think of what you might be, and what you are risking to become. Suppose the Grange estates will not be purchased by any-one, is not the income derivable from them most ample and satisfactory—satisfactory alike to you as to me; for, upon mature reflection, I believe, Varley, you were only joking when you talked of not giving me my full share of the proceeds; I am confident you were only joking."

"Samuel Twitter," said Varley, putting his hand into his pocket, and drawing it out again very slowly, with a pistol, "there are two things, it appears to me, that step between you and your wits: the one is a love of money; the other, a horror of my pursuit of Miranda Rankley. I have warned you often before; now be warned again, for let me tell you that in some unhappy moment you will say too much upon these subjects, and I shall be compelled to blow your brains out. After which I will place the weapon with which the deed was accomplished in your dead hand, so that before the muscles become rigid you shall grasp it tightly, and be deemed the author of your own death."

"Gracious powers!" cried Twitter, "what a horrible plan! I will be silent, since it is no use to speak; it was for your own good I addressed you; but I will be silent—I will not speak of it again."

"When we arrive in London," added Varley, "you will want for nothing; but unless you fully aid and assist me in my pursuit of Miranda, I shall be apt to consider you an incumbrance, and such a thought on my part might be dangerous. You understand me, Samuel Twitter?"

Twitter only replied by a groan; and the subject was not renewed during the remainder of the rapid journey which ushered them into London.

The coach which conveyed Miranda and her two companions was not very far behind the post-chaise, which carried him who had worked her so much woe and wretchedness, and Mr. Jones hailed with no little pleasure distant glimpses of the great city, which, to him, contained all human enjoyments, and in which he had passed, most certainly, his happiest days; but it was not until he came considerably nearer that he thought proper, by tapping on the glass of the coach, to give Miranda an intimation that they were so near their journey's end.

"Hilloa!" he cried, "we ain't far off now; we've come it out-and-out, miss—mum, I mean—and shall soon take a look at the jolly great hive."

It was towards the close of a fine, though wintry, day, that our travellers neared the great metropolis, such a day that brings to our minds spring and its gaily clothed hedge-rows and gardens.

The air was cold, and the wind blew keenly, yet the sun, for a few short hours, cast a gleam of gladness upon the country round within the reach of vision; but the sunshine of autumn and winter has but little effect upon the cold earth in comparison to its cheering effects upon the mind.

The destination of the coach was one of the oldest and best inns in London, and here Miranda alighted, not a little surprised at the tremendous bustle around her, and, had her mind been free from anxieties, she would have derived, from the new scene in which she found herself, much food for amusing speculation.

CHAPTER CXIII.

THE ILLNESS OF MR. PERCY—THE HOSPITAL— VARLEY AND TWITTER IN SMITHFIELD.

"WELL!" said Jones, when he had paid the fare, and Miranda and old Mr. Percy were standing beside him, as little regarded in the inn-yard as if they had been two bales of merchandize. "Well, here we is, at last. Isn't it pleasant? There's a constant skrimmage going on in London, which you can't get up nohow in the country. There's something for everybody to do, and you'd open your eyes, Miss Miranda, if you knew what a precious sight of cribs is cracked in one night in this 'ere city."

"Surely," said Miranda, "there is some unusual tumult in the streets. Let us wait until it has passed away before we venture out of this place of shelter."

"A row, do you mean? Lor! bless you, there's nothing of the kind. The sort of imitation of a shindy as you now sees goes on all day, without never a stop. But what's the matter with the old gentleman, he doesn't seem altogether the thing?"

Miranda turned hastily, and looked in the face of old Mr. Percy, in which she was shocked to observe a change as sudden as it was unexpected.

A death-like paleness was spreading itself over his countenance.

It seemed as if the very air of London was inimical to his existence, and that he could not breathe freely in the pent-up atmosphere of the great city.

"He is ill!" said Miranda. "What shall we do now? Ah! this is a new calamity, and one that I did not expect. Mr. Percy, speak to me; you are not well."

"Not well," he said, "and yet scarcely ill. My strength seems to have given way for several hours. Where—where is Rowland?—my boy, Rowland?"

His languor seemed to increase each moment, and, but for the timely interposition of Jones, it is probable he would have fallen.

"Hilloa! old gentleman," said Jones. "Take things easy—what's the dodge?"

"I fear I am not well," he said. "Miranda—how came we here?"

Miranda bent eagerly over him, watching every change in his countenance, while a throng of idlers began to gather round the little, anxious group.

"Can't you keep out of the way?" said Jones. "I'm blessed if that isn't always the case; if anybody feels a little faint, he's a'most smothered outright by a crowd of fools as seem to want to get down his wery throat. Come, now, you with the fur cap and the cribbage-board countenance, just be so good as to draw a jug of water from that ere pump, and make yourself useful, as nature won't let you be an ornament."

The man so appealed to stared at Jones in astonishment, and then went, with some alacrity, to do as he was bidden, apparently quite amused at the jest which had been made at his own personal appearance.

A draught of the water seemed to revive Mr. Percy, at least, so far as his fainting was concerned; but an occasional shiver would pass across his frame, which alarmed Miranda, and induced her to press Jones to let a medical man see him.

"Wery good," said Jones. "There's no want o' doctors in London; why, you might walk on their wery heads. The old gentleman had better go inside the house, while I goes and fetches one; but, between you and me, Miss Miranda, I'll have a wetter-and-hairy."

"A what?" exclaimed Miranda, in some surprise.

"I means a doctor as is used to horses. I never was outrageous ill but once; and then the doctors all gured me up, and said as how I was going to kick the bucket; but arter

that, just as I was really beginning to think o' croaking, there comes a wetter-and-hairy chap, as knowed me many years ago, and he says to me:

"Do you recollect that ere mare as I had once—she with a white spot on her nose, as won the silver cup and the kiver?"

"Oh! go at once," said Miranda. "I fear he is getting worse; I will see that he is assisted into the house while you are gone."

"Wery good," said Jones; "recollect, I left off at kiver. I'll tell you the rest at another time."

Jones was right enough when he alluded to the number of medical men, for there were three or four within a stone's throw of the inn, and he soon returned with a sensible-looking, middle-aged man, who, by great good luck, was a clever practitioner, as well as one above the necessity of making a patient.

Mr. Percy had been kindly helped into a spare room, adjoining the parlour of the inn, and the medical man, after an examination of the symptoms that oppressed him, said:

"I would advise you, miss, to get the gentleman home as quickly as possible; there are signs of fever about him which, if not checked, may do serious mischief. Pray get him home immediately."

"Home!" said Miranda, rather impulsively than from reflection. "Home!—we have no home."

"No home?" said the surgeon, looking with surprise at the party.

"Why, we've just come from the country," said Jones, "and our town-house ain't quite ready. We likes it to be well whitewashed, you see, sir, before we goes into it. Servants is nasty beasts, unless one is always abusing of 'em."

"If you've not a comfortable place immediately to take him to," said the surgeon, "I would strongly advise you to try one of the hospitals."

Miranda shrank from the name of hospital, and the surgeon, observing it, added:

"I can see such a course is repugnant to your feelings, and although I admit all the abuses of the hospital system, yet I must repeat my advice. You had better let your father be taken to one at once."

"He is not my father," said Miranda, "except by adoption."

"Then I the more strenuously urge my advice."

"And wery good advice, too," said Jones. "What do you say to it, old gentleman?"

"Miranda," said Mr. Percy, "it seems to me that I have been in a dream for some time, and knew not my real situation. I am willing to go, for I feel sickness coming fast upon me."

"His reason has returned!" exclaimed Miranda; "that look and tone assure me of it! Thank Heaven for its mercies! I know nothing of hospitals, further than that they are medical institutions for the relief of the necessitous; but Heaven forbid that I should stand in the way, from, perhaps, false feeling, of anything which is for the benefit of Mr Percy."

"Ahem!" said Jones, with a warning look not to pronounce the name again. "I'll get a coach. — What's to pay, sir?"

"Oh! there's nothing to pay," said the medical man, "I have done nothing; but you must come to my house again, to get a letter, without which the patient will not be admitted."

This was done, and nearly an hour of painful anxiety passed, before poor Mr. Percy, whose mind was still weak—although the sudden accession of physical indisposition seemed to have restored it in a measure—was placed in Saint Bartholomew's Hospital.

*   *   *   *

Poor Miranda felt as if her misfortunes were thickening around her, for wearisome as would have been—to anyone but herself—the close attendance that was necessary upon old Mr. Percy, still, for Rowland's sake, she could endure it cheerfully, and without a murmur bend her energies to the service of him whose mind misfortune had stricken, but who was dear to her from the very name he bore.

She stood in Smithfield, along with her strange companion, Jones, and it would almost seem as if he guessed the purport of the thoughts that were crowding round her heart.

"Miss Miranda," he said, "I daresay the old gentleman will get better, and if he doesn't don't you be taking on about it, for, sooner or later, you know, we must all give in to the enemy; and it's natural that the old should go first, to make way for the young 'uns as is to come; so pluck up a good heart, Miss Miranda—laugh at care, and it's ten to one but he gets so indignant that he cuts away."

"It is good philosophy, but the saddened bosom recognizes nothing but its own griefs. What now will become of me in this labyrinth of streets and houses, until Rowland shall arrive! Methinks it would have been almost better to have lingered on the road."

At this moment Miranda was surprised at Jones suddenly seizing her by the arm, and whispering in eager tones:

"Back, Miss Miranda—back, back. Here's a go. Don't speak now, miss. Don't think or move for a minute, till he's gone past. Well, I never. What an ugly-looking thief, to be sure. Who'd a thought it. There's a phisigogonemy."

Miranda retreated into a door-way, which was very dark, and the next moment she saw Bernard Varley pace slowly by, with a melancholy and abstracted air.

He was enveloped in a long, brown cloak, which made him look even taller than usual, and his face was cadaverous and ghastly in the extreme.

He seemed like a man soul-stricken by misfortunes, one on whom the hand of Heaven had pressed heavily, and who had almost lost hope from the dull weight of afflictions.

"There, there," said Jones, as he looked after the retreating figure. "Talk of people being misfortunate, and all that kind of thing! There's a wretch for you. I wouldn't be him for a guinea and a clean shirt a day."

"Hush, hush!" said Miranda; "look again."

"Gracious—preserve us!" said Jones, as he drew back, and nearly fell over the scraper.

Creeping along in a stooping posture, as if he would willingly have made his way under the pavement, instead of over it, provided a passage had been practicable, came Samuel Twitter.

His eyes were fixed upon Varley—whom he was evidently dogging—with all the suspicions and alarm that were characteristics of his character.

Had Miranda stood fully in his way, he would scarcely have seen her, so absorbed was he in the feeling of necessity of watching his companion in guilt, to see if he were bent on any desperate means prejudicial to the safety of both.

It was quite a study to see how Twitter glided along with his body bent, and his eyes so fixed upon the tall, dark figure which preceded him.

In fact, full of ample food for philosophical reflection, was the mere appearance of those two men, one of whom, at least, had reaped the full fruits of his villainy, but who was yet as unhappy, if not more so—as intolerably wretched as his companion in guilt, who fancied then that his chief care and anxiety was to possess himself of money, that he might fly from possible dangers to his personal safety.

"There's a couple of tidy nuts for Beelzebub to crack," said Jones. "We needn't ax for no vengeance against them, Miss Miranda, for, as the man said in the play I seed one night, they've got that there inside which isn't out. There they goes—what a kipple. I should like to drive 'em in a tandem to the gallows."

A deep sigh escaped Miranda, as she said:

"So, even here I am to be haunted by that fearful man; even here, nearly two hundred miles from where he first commenced his persecutions, I am still to feel the consciousness of his dreadful presence, and to look for fresh evils at his hands. Heaven help me! I will endeavour to submit myself to Thy holy will, but forgive me if I am impatient of much misery, and implore in the bitterness of my heart for mercy—mercy."

"Wery good," said Jones, looking intently at the sky, just above Giltspur Street Compter.

———

THE REWARD FOR THE ARREST OF ROWLAND PERCY.

CHAPTER CXIV.

MIRANDA IN SEARCH OF A LODGING—A FEW
WORDS ABOUT GENTEEL PEOPLE, AND
THEIR MANNERS AND CUSTOMS.

THE evening was rapidly advancing, and of
course Miranda's first object was to secure
some respectable lodging where she could remain, until there was a chance of Rowland
Percy's arrival.

Turning to Jones, she said:

"What will become of me now? Notwithstanding the heavy charge which Mr.
Percy in his afflicted state was to me, I feel
ten times more lonely now and desolate at my
heart, than I did when he was my companion."

"Why, Miss Miranda," replied Jones,
"what's the use of grieving, as the song says;
just you make yourself comfortable till Mr.
Percy and Dicky shows themselves in Drury
Lane. There's a few pounds yet left, and if
there wasn't, why there's ways and means of
getting more. Now, my advice is, that you
become Miss Jones."

"How do you mean?"

"Why just tuck your arm under mine, and
we'll go and look for a lodging; I'll say as
you're my sister, and that I'll pay the blessed

rent; but, being myself a traveller in the hardware line—and, gracious knows, precious hard wear it is sometimes—I can only come to see you now and then. When they axes us for a reference, we can tell 'em to go to blazes, and we'll pay a week's rent in advance, which is something ekal to being seven days afore the rest of the world in honesty."

"I think," said Miranda, "the plan seems feasible. My own name I certainly object to using, as it has become, unhappily, too notorious through the public Press, in consequence of the unhappy circumstances in which I have been involved."

"Call yourself Miss Jones, mum, it's an out-and-out good travelling name. I sometimes waries it myself, by being Smith for a year or two; but I never troubles my real name if I can help it. I am afeard as my relations would be continually inwiting of me, and axing on me to be godfather to all their babbies."

"I would," said Miranda, "that I knew in what part of London Bernard Varley resides, in order that I might keep at as great a distance from his locality as possible."

"I'll find out the warmint," said Jones. "You make yourself as comfortable as possible to-night. Think o' nothing but snoozing, and, depend upon it, everything will be as right as ninepence."

Mr. Jones, with his peculiarity of apparel, was not the most pleasant figure to parade the streets of London with; but Miranda was far from being hypercritical about the appearance of anyone whose heart she knew to be in the right place, and of the purity and kindness of Mr. Jones' intentions towards herself, she felt she should be doing him the greatest injustice for a moment to doubt.

Therefore, arm-in-arm did this strangely-assorted couple proceed through Smithfield towards the dense mass of houses lying about the neighbourhood of the City Road—a complete town in itself, where anyone might remain concealed for years amid the intricacies of hundreds of streets.

The first house to which they applied for a lodging was in a street which came fully up to the popular notion of the shabby genteel, and that particular house by no means set itself up as a contrast to its neighbours.

It was one of those streets which, in the most ridiculous manner, is always affecting to be what it is impossible for it to be—namely, quite noble, while its inherent meanness can never be got rid of. The houses were inhabited by persons who affected thorough gentility upon extremely limited resources, who hated everything low with a violent hatred; of people who were up to their necks in shabbiness, and who, avoiding the onus of a really large respectable house, as much as they shrank from the little residence consistent with their means, plunged into a genteel street, and let lodgings.

"I doesn't like this here house," said Jones, before he knocked at the door of the first one he came to, in which was the announcement of "Apartments furnished." "I doesn't much like this here house, Miss Miranda. It's like trying to make the condemned cell look cheerful; it's so outrageous nice, and there's such a blessed air of propriety about it."

"We must not always judge by appearances," said Miranda, gently. "Kindly people may be living here."

"Oh, as for that," said Jones, "it's wery much the same. So long as you pays 'em, and doesn't give 'em much trouble, and puts up with all sorts of impositions, it will be wery well, and nothink the matter. Howsomdever here goes, we'll let 'em see as we knows what's what, and be's as genteel as they is."

Mr. Jones then perpetrated what he considered a very genteel knock, which first of all consisted of a couple of postman's peals, followed by a running fire of small knocks, and then finished off with such a dab that he alarmed the whole street.

In a few moments the door was opened by the usual dirty servant, common to all lodging houses; and why? Because the mistress being only a degree cleaner herself all the morning, wishes to keep up the proper social distinctions.

"We wants to look at the crib," said Jones. "What's the damage?"

"The apartments," said Miranda.

"Please to walk in," said the girl, "and I'll call Mrs. Flint."

"Flint," said Jones, when they were ushered into the little parlour, "what a name for one of the soft sex. I thinks I sees her, just like a bundle of tangled wire, set up on end."

"Hush! hush!" said Miranda, "pray allow me to speak, for they will scarcely understand your meaning."

"Wery good," said Jones, "I'll make my own observations, while you converses with the Flint."

The door opened, and a very genteel-looking female entered the room.

Her thin lips were compressed as closely together as if she suspected the visitors of a design to purloin her teeth; and there was that air of general suspicion about her, which is a characteristic of genteel people.

"We have come," said Miranda, "to inquire concerning the apartments you have to let. I want accommodation for myself alone."

"Oh," said Mrs. Flint, "of course, we exchange references, always."

"Oh, mum," said Jones, "we couldn't think of doing that ere! we think so much of our references, we couldn't change 'em for nobody's. We pays our tin like bricks, and, if anybody objects, we tells 'em to take it out of that."

Mr. Jones tapped his elbow a great many times, to the unspeakable horror of Mrs. Flint, who, in her surprise, nearly sat down on one of the impracticable sofas.

"We've come a long distance—from the country," said Miranda. "If I can find a suitable home here, the rent will be paid in advance, as I have no friends or connections in London."

"We have a first floor," said Mrs. Flint; "the front room is very genteel, and the rent is eight-and-twenty shillings a-week."

"We'll see it, old lady," said Jones. "We doesn't mind the tin, but, as you sees, we's out-an'-out genteel people, we ain't a-going to put up with nothing rummy."

"Gracious powers!" thought Mrs. Flint, "this must be some country gentleman, unused to the ways of London. Why didn't I say thirty shillings; but I can make it up in extras."

And with quite a seraphic smile, she led the way upstairs.

The first floor was a very pattern of gentility; everything was so abominably small, and so frightfully clean; then there were little ornaments here, and there, and everywhere, such as mussel-shells, watch-pockets, pincushions, artificial flowers, and two or three nice little evangelical books, the very covers of which looked like a reproof to sinners, they wore so nice and stainless an aspect—moreover, nothing was covered up. Oh, no, that process was gone through after the victim was entrapped.

The bedroom was adjoining, and into that Miranda just looked, sufficiently to see that it was very small, but clean.

"I think this will do," she said, appealing to Jones.

"Wery good," was the reply. "I suppose, mum, that the place is quite—respectable. Eh, mum?"

There's no knowing what effect this question might have had on Mrs. Flint, if Jones had not, as he spoke, produced a couple of sovereigns, which acted as such a balm to her wounded feelings, that she very nearly smiled, and immediately made up her mind that Mr. Jones was only a little eccentric; but, taking everything into consideration, quite the gentleman.

The negotiations now proceeded without any hindrance, and Miranda, with some pounds in her pocket, found herself fairly installed in her new home.

CHAPTER CXV.

THE ARRIVAL OF ROWLAND PERCY IN LONDON—THE "STAR AND TINDER-BOX" IN STEEPLE COURT—THE REWARD FOR ROWLAND'S APPREHENSION.

DICK PALMER'S intimate acquaintance with the topography of the country, saved him and Rowland Percy from traversing many a useless bit of road, so that, after all, their progress, although, certainly, considerably slower towards London, than if they had been at liberty to take the high-road, did not throw them above a day behindhand; and at a somewhat later hour than Miranda, on the preceding evening, had reached the metropolis, Rowland and his friend looked upon the glancing lights of London.

It was only now and then, by turns in the road, that the distant glitter of the lamps became visible, and ere they had proceeded much nearer, Dick Palmer turned his horse's head down a narrow green lane, saying to Rowland:

"We must do the remainder of our journey on foot, as well as make some alterations in our appearance, for we must not forget that our enemies are already in London, and have, of course, taken care to describe us to the metropolitan police. I know a house at the bottom of this lane, where we can receive temporary accommodation, although it would not be safe for us to remain there for any length of time."

"Heaven be thanked," said Rowland, "we are so near our journey's end! I shall feel a sense of security amid the mass of humanity congregated in London, which I could nowhere feel but in a large capital."

The house to which Dick alluded had once been a flourishing one, but its fortunes had sadly changed, and, but for its peculiar connection, would have been scarcely worth keeping open.

In its ample stables they left their horses, and, from a miscellaneous collection of wearing apparel, which was freely offered for their selection, they both succeeded in equipping themselves as decent-looking mechanics, and, after a brief rest, hurried on towards the metropolis.

Rowland Percy had never before visited the great city; and, consequently, everything was new and strange to him.

Had his mind been disentangled from the circumstances which clung to it with such a withering blight, he would have experienced the most intense pleasure in watching the great human movement which was taking place in the vast metropolis, in the midst of which his evil fortune had thrown him.

Dick Palmer guessed his thoughts, and said, in a kindly tone of voice:

"Mr. Percy, there will come a time, I confidently trust and hope, when you will be able, as a free and acknowledged innocent man, to traverse the streets of London, and visit its extraordinary buildings and monuments; till then, I fear, you must be satisfied with but a transient glimpse of the great world into which you are thrown."

"I will live on," said Rowland, "with a fervent hope that some day I shall take my place among my fellow-men, without a price being set upon my head, and without my name awakening the indignation of that society which, Heaven truly knows, I have never outraged; when that shall happen, I have another hope, which has been latterly, day by day, growing stronger in my breast—the realization of which will give me as great a satisfaction as anything that could possibly confer a personal benefit to myself."

"Indeed," said Palmer; "and what hope is that?"

"It is the hope that ample opportunity may be afforded you of embracing a different course of life, and that, in a new arena, which will bring you ample honour and reward, you will exercise those abilities of intellect, and those excellences of heart, for which you are conspicuous."

Dick Palmer was silent for a moment, and then it was in a tone of emotion that he replied:

"Mr. Percy, for your kind words I give you my warmest thanks, and the more so because I am really unused to such from anyone; but my day is passed, and I have no hope of being other than what I am. The circumstances that have driven me to my present course of life lie buried in my own heart. There may come a day when I shall not shrink from communicating them to you; but I think, when I do so, I shall be near quitting a world which, perhaps, after all, I wrongly accuse of not using me well. But let us waive the subject; other and weightier cares assail us now. I dread every moment that you are in the open streets. Let us hasten at once to Drury Lane, where, I have every reason to believe, I can procure you a safe asylum."

The "Star and Tinder-Box," in Steeple Court, Drury Lane, was a very famous house.

Indeed, some malicious people made the adjective a syllable longer, and called it an infamous house; but those were what Mr. Jones would call strait-laced people, who did their thieving all on the sly, and hadn't pluck enough to go on the highway, like reputable folks.

The court in which it was situated was sufficiently narrow to be called a passage, and the "Star and Tinder-Box" was down a narrow entry out of that again, so that it could scarcely be said to be in Steeple Court, although the passage, which abutted upon that beautiful locality, was the exclusive property of the "Star and Tinder-Box," to all intents and purposes; and an admirable place for concealment and secrecy was that "Star and Tinder-Box," for, so dark and dingy was it, that one might well assimilate it to the tinder-box, without troubling the star at all about the matter.

"You will find this rather different," whispered Palmer, as they dived down the dark entry, "from the free, open meadows of your father's estate at York."

"Indeed," said Percy, "I do not compare it with them. In my mind, it only contrasts most favourably with the condemned cell in York Castle."

In another moment they were standing at the bar of the public-house, and Palmer, leaning over, looked into a little parlour beyond, where a man sat, either in deep thought or half-asleep, and cried:

"Bill! Bill! What's the dodge?"

"Eh—eh?" cried the man, starting up, and rubbing his eyes. "The old caper, to be sure. Who the deuce are you?"

"Look again," said Palmer. "How's the old woman?"

"Do me up in heaps!" ejaculated the man. "To think that I shouldn't know you. Come in directly. Bless us, where have you been? Split me into gold-leaf, if I've seen you for

two months. I was afeared you were nabbed, and had come an alias over the grabs. My eye and Elizabeth Martin, I supposes as you've been the grand tower, as they calls it? Strike me unfortunate, and kick me into the middle of the new moon, if I know'd yer at the first glance. Hilloa! who's that?"

"A friend of mine," said Dick Palmer, as he took Rowland by the arm, and ushered him into the parlour at the back of the bar.

"Oh, well, if he's a friend of yourn, it's all right. Has he been on the moonlight lay?"

"For aught I know, Bill," said Palmer, "time may be precious, and you may as well know at once that this is Mr. Rowland Percy, who was convicted at York for murder; but who, I pledge you my word, is innocent. He has escaped almost by a miracle; but, of course, for a time, there'll be a hue and cry after him, and, in one word, I have brought him here for safety.'

The landlord walked into the bar without a word, and called loudly to somebody of the name of Joe to look to it.

He then returned to the parlour, and locked the door on the inside, after which he drew a curtain across the upper part, which was glass, and turning to Palmer, said:

"It's no go. Not the remotest insignification of a go; and I'll tell you why. First of all, look here."

He took from behind the looking-glass a printed bill, which he handed to Palmer, which was headed with the ominous words of "Five hundred pounds reward!"

Dick passed it in silence to Rowland Percy, who read the following words:

"Five hundred pounds reward! Whereas, one Rowland Percy, convicted of murder at the last York Assizes, escaped from custody on the eve of his execution. This is to give notice, that the above reward will be paid to anyone who will lodge him in any one of His Majesty's jails. The said Rowland Percy is——"

Here followed an accurate description of his person, and, before he could finish the perusal of it, the paper dropped from Rowland's hands.

———

CHAPTER CXVI.

THE OFFICER IN PURSUIT OF ROWLAND—THE ESCAPE FROM THE PUBLIC-HOUSE—THE DRIVE TO SOMERS TOWN—THE SECRET PANEL IN THE WIDOW'S HOUSE.

DICK PALMER picked up the handbill which Rowland had dropped, and read it attentively; after which he said:

"Mr. Percy, you need not be surprised at this. Your enemies are sure to be active for some time to come. You must recollect that private hatred is leagued against you along with the law; but this virulence of pursuit will wear itself out; and if we can but keep you concealed until such is the case, you will be safe from further interruption."

"Listen to me, Dicky," said the landlord.

"I don't know why it is so, but my house has been regularly set upon about this matter. I rather think the police must have an inkling that you have a hand in it, and it's my decided opinion that there are spies lodging here at the present time, with the hope that Mr. Percy will make this his home."

"Lodging here?" said Palmer, in surprise.

"Yes, and I can't help it. We've beds to let, and it is impossible for me to pick and choose my customers, for, sometimes, I almost feel convinced they are set on me by the police. All I can do is to let them come, and warn other parties, as I now warn you, and I candidly say, I think a more unsafe place than the 'Star and Tinder-box' for you isn't to be found in London."

"When you say so much," said Palmer, "I know it can be relied upon. Mr. Percy, we must seek some other shelter. I had hoped that you would have remained here in security; but as such is not the case the sooner we decamp the better."

"I should say so," remarked the landlord; "and all the good I can do you is to offer you any assistance in the way of money you may want, so don't scruple to ask me for it if it should be serviceable. Take a glass of something with me, Percy, and be off with you, in Heaven's name, for I assure you, you can't be in a worse place than this."

Rowland Percy declined the something to drink, but intimated that he was quite ready to go.

"Very well, then," said Palmer. "I know well, Bill, you are not the one to make the most of danger, and a hint from you is as good as a long speech from anyone else."

"Hush!" said the landlord—"hush! Do you hear that?"

As he spoke, the sound of a man's voice was heard from the outer side of the bar, and Dick Palmer immediately said:

"Indeed, I do hear it; it's Fletcher, the Bow Street officer."

The landlord opened another door in the little parlour, beyond which all appeared darkness.

"You can get out that way," he said, "which will take you into the court. I will keep Fletcher in talk till you are clean off."

He then, himself, passed into the bar; and Palmer, placing his hand upon Percy's arm, said:

"Wait a moment; there can be no danger, and there may be some good in hearing what the officer says."

Percy assented, and in a moment the landlord's voice was heard.

"Well, Fletcher," he said, "what's the news?"

"Once for all, Bill," said the voice of the officer, "don't be a fool, but look to your own interests. Among your set you are sure to find out something of this fellow that we want, and when I tell you I want him very particularly indeed, you may guess there's something to be made by the affair past common, and, of course, I can afford to be liberal to you."

"I tells yer," said the landlord, "I knows nothing about it, if so be as it's the young chap about the murder at York."

"Oh, nonsense!" said the officer. "We are quite sure that some of the knowing ones from London must have helped him out of the scrape."

"I tell you, Fletcher, I knows nothing about it, and you needn't bother me."

"You shall have a hundred pounds down to-morrow morning, if you promise to assist. Mr. Varley, the prosecutor, is red-hot about it, and will stand any sum in reason."

"That is enough," whispered Palmer to Rowland Percy. "Let us go now."

He took Rowland by the arm, and led him through the dark doorway down a long narrow passage, which then took an abrupt turn, that brought them within view of a glare of light, and in another moment they emerged into the upper part of the court, close by the flare of an oil-lamp in Drury Lane.

"I must house you somewhere," said Palmer; "but really where I can scarcely at present determine. There are, certainly, persons in London who are under sufficient obligations to me, but in such a matter as this I know not whom I can trust; yet now, I bethink me, there is one who has ever expressed so anxious a wish to repay the deep obligation under which I was enabled at one time to lay her, that I think I may be safe to take you there. However, we will get into a coach, and drive to the locality. While we are so doing, I can explain some necessary particulars."

A coach was quickly procured, and Palmer desired to be driven to the end of Chalton Street, in the New Road.

"The street I have named," he said to Rowland Percy, "leads into a densely populated district, called Somers Town, which, although I cannot recommend it for salubrity or beauty, may answer your purpose very well as a place of concealment, if everything has gone on smoothly with the person to whom I wish to introduce you."

"Of the two," said Rowland, "I should certainly prefer a refuge in some private dwelling to one in a public-house; but I implore you to take steps so that Miranda may not be disappointed when she makes inquiry for me."

"Leave all that to me," said Palmer, "it shall be arranged properly. The person I am now taking you to is a Mrs. Howell, whose son fell into unhappy circumstances, although innocent, the particulars of which I shall get her to relate to you the first thing, in order to give you the consolation of knowing that there are others who are quite as misused as yourself."

When they alighted from the coach, Palmer led Percy through a number of intricate streets, until they came to one branching off to the northward of the Polygon. He knocked at the door of a small, but neat house, and inquired of the girl who presented herself, if Mrs. Howell was within.

The answer was in the affirmative, and an elderly lady, with a widow's cap, made her appearance, who greeted Dick Palmer in as affectionate terms as if he had been her own son, and immediately ushered him into her parlour, where the tea-things were all laid, preparatory to the evening meal.

"You have just come at the right moment, Mr. Palmer," said Mrs. Howell. "Sit down, and this gentleman, too. You appear tired, and will have some tea with me."

"I will, Mrs. Howell; but, first, this gentleman is Mr. Percy. He has many troubles to contend against. You know what misfortune is, and, to give him some hope, you will be pleased to relate the affair of your son, who was so full of hope, but suffered so great a reverse, while we solace ourselves with your tea."

"That I will: pray be seated; but I am always sorry to hear of anyone's misfortunes."

"And mine are of no ordinary character, I assure you, madam," said Percy, as he took the cup that was offered him.

"Ah, well, Mr. Percy," said the widow, "we've all our troubles: there are none of us without them, and they are best off who have the fewest."

"It certainly is so, Mrs. Howell, though I must confess that I am sometimes impatient of mine," replied Percy, setting down his tea-cup, and looking at the blazing fire, which threw a bright reflection over the room.

The apartment was a small one, possessing more furniture than was necessary, and that not of the most modern description; but there was an air of homeliness and comfort thrown over all that insensibly imparted similar feelings to Rowland Percy.

The widow herself had been a painstaking, hard-working woman in her time, though for the latter quality she had no present necessity, yet, from acquired habit, she busied herself in all matters connected with her house.

She was past the middle age of life; indeed, she must have been over fifty, tolerably stout, at one time pretty and attractive, but the fire of her eye was sobered down to an occasional twinkle of satisfaction.

She sipped her tea, and ate her toast, with a pleasure so evident, that Percy, as he looked at her, could not forbear a smile.

"You have been many years here?" said Percy, inquiringly, after a long pause, by way of breaking silence.

"Yes, sir. It's twenty years ago since I first came here, sir. Ah, this place is not what it was, I assure you; there were but very few houses in these parts then—we were quite in the fields. My husband, that's dead and gone, bought it, saying he would have a house to live in without paying rent for it, and the little money he had should not be thrown away in business, more especially as he was only at home once in a way."

"What was your husband's employment, then?" inquired Percy.

"He was a sailor for many years, and, at last, he was made a boatswain. Poor fellow, he was killed in battle, and the Government granted me a small pension. Ah, Mr. Percy, I was a lone woman then. I was left with only one child, and he, I am sorry to say, is not here."

"Yes," said Percy, "I have heard Palmer speak of him. He, like myself, has suffered from the deep-laid villainy of others, and was obliged to fly for his life."

"Yes," replied the widow, with a sigh; "he was indeed the object of another man's hatred. He stood in his way, and my poor boy was ruined—totally ruined. I fear I shall never see him again. He's the only relation I have living, and the only tie that binds me to earth."

The poor woman took the corner of her apron to wipe away the starting tear, which had risen unbidden to her eyes.

"Be comforted, Mrs. Howell," said Percy, in a kind, though saddened, tone, for his own unhappy fate rushed across his mind. "He may yet come back to you, when there will no longer be any danger. I did not have the particulars from Dick Palmer, and should like to hear them, if the subject be not a painful one."

"It is painful, sir; but not more so to repeat the story to you, than to think of it in my own mind," said the widow, who dearly loved to talk of her son, though it occasionally cost her a tear; and her lodger was so kind, and an ill-used man himself, that she longed for an opportunity to unburden her mind of her heavy sorrows to one who was, by his own unfortunate situation, in a position well calculated to enable him to appreciate them justly.

"Henry, sir, was my only child. He was young when his father died, and I kept him at school, though many said that I ought to put him out to place, where he would, at least, be earning something towards his own support; but I said that I would keep him at school, and then he would be better able to get on in life afterwards, if he acted properly, than if I made an errand-boy of him when very young. Besides, he was not so strong and robust a lad as many are, and, for that reason alone, I was afraid to let him go anywhere where his strength would have been tried. He was a good boy, and a quick one at his letters, which repaid me.

"When he was fourteen, a gentleman who lodged in this house said he could, likely enough, hear of something in a counting-house that would suit Harry, if I would like to let him go.

"Of course I was glad, and said I should be very much obliged to him if he could get any employment which would be an opening in life for him. This he promised to do, and, before a month had passed over, the gentleman called me upstairs, and said:

"'Mrs. Howell, if your son Henry will go with me to the city to-morrow, I will take him to some gentlemen, who will most probably place him in their counting-house, where, if he minds what he is about, he may stay all his life, and be very comfortable.'

"Of course, sir, I was well pleased at such a chance as this, one that I could not hope for from myself, for I had no connections that way.

"I sent him in the morning—I remember it as if it were only yesterday; he had a new suit of clothes on, and he looked very well. I was all anxiety until my lodger should return, for he would keep him until he came home at night. When evening came, I knew hardly how to await their arrival with patience. I listened to every footfall that approached the door, and felt disappointed at every one that died away in the distance.

"At length they came. No sooner did I hear them on the step than I had the door open to receive them, and, by my Henry's sparkling eyes, I knew that he must have succeeded, for he had often talked of being able to earn me money, so that I should not be obliged to work so hard.

"'We have succeeded, Mrs. Howell,' said my lodger, good-naturedly, as he entered the house; 'Henry is bursting to tell you all about it, so, when you have heard all that he has to tell you, I'll give you any information you may want.'

"I thanked him for his goodness, and brought my son into my room, when he related to me all that had happened. The gentlemen seemed so pleased with his appearance, and the manner in which he answered the questions they put to him, that they at once agreed to take him into their counting-house—of course, in the lowest capacity, as he was the youngest, and last there; but, still, he would rise in rotation with the rest.

"He had to go next morning, for they took him from the first day of his appearance at the office.

"It was a happy time that for me, Mr. Percy. He was my only hope—the only being I had to look to for love and affection, and his conduct deserved all that I did for him, for, as regularly as he received his money, so regularly did he bring the whole of it to me. He never stayed out with companions at any time, but always came home direct to me.

"This went on for several years; till, indeed, he was between nineteen and twenty.

"One day he came home in a very thoughtful manner—a most unusual thing with him; he looked very serious and sad. I could not bear this, and at once inquired what was the cause of his thoughtful and melancholy look. At first he evaded me, but at length he said:

"'I am afraid all is not right with our head clerk, mother, and I don't know what to do about it.'

"'All right, Henry?' said I. 'What do you mean?'

"'I think our head clerk's accounts are not right, or that he has appropriated money to his own use that he ought not to have touched, but which belongs to his employers.'

"'Are you sure of it?' I inquired.

"'Not so sure of it,' he replied, 'but that I may be mistaken, and, therefore, I do not like to make any accusation against him.'

"'Certainly not,' I replied, 'for by that you may make many enemies, and no friends.'

"'I know that,' he replied, 'but there can be no harm in my drawing his attention to it, and by that means, if it be merely an error, he can correct it, and if not, he will use what exertion he can to make good any defalcation into which he may have fallen.'

"'That will undoubtedly be the best plan,' I replied, 'for it will give him a chance of retrieving himself before he is utterly lost.'

"Having made up his mind to this course, he promised to do so the next day, and it was with a sense of sadness that made me feel impatient for his return. I began to feel sorry that I had given him the counsel I had. I regretted I had not begged him to leave the affair alone, and let the whole thing take its own course. Some undefined notion of what was to follow appeared to depress my mind, and I was only relieved from it by hearing his step at the door. When I let him in, I saw he was vexed about something; but I said nothing until he had had his tea, and I then inquired how he had got on with the affair he had been speaking about the day before.

"'Rather badly,' was his reply; 'Mr. Crosby, the head clerk, has taken it all in bad part, and we have had a quarrel.'

"'I am sorry for that, Henry,' was my answer, 'for I fear that it will make you uncomfortable.'

"'Oh! no,' he replied, 'I have nothing to fear on that score—he cannot prejudice me, or hurt me in any way, though he as good as said he would do both.'

"'Indeed! Tell me what he did say?' I asked.

"'Do not be alarmed, mother. You look serious, and there is no need of your doing so. I showed Mr. Crosby what I believed to be errors, and he flew into a great rage about my meddling with things that did not concern me, though at first he trembled in every limb, and was as pale as the paper upon which he was writing. I merely replied that, thinking there was something wrong, I thought it better to name it first to him. I shall not forget easily the expression of his face when I said this, and he answered me by saying that I should know what it was to interfere with him, and that, too, upon such a subject. He understood his business, and begged me to keep a strict eye upon my own accounts, as it was possible I might find errors there.'

"'What does he mean, Henry?' said I.

"'I know not,' he replied, 'nor do I much care, as I have nothing to fear, and so I told him. And he said to me that my impertinence would cost me dear—there would be a day when I should remember this. I was then called away, and nothing more has been said.'

"'Be careful, my dear boy,' said I, 'lest he should have it in his power to do you an injury.'

"This was all that passed, and no more was heard about the matter, save that my son and Mr. Crosby were ill-friends, and Henry was determined to keep a strict eye on the other's motions, and also the accounts, at which he seemed much annoyed.

"Some months after this, my Henry returned home much earlier than his wont. He entered the house without saying a word, which was unusual with him. It was dark, and I had no light with me, and did not see his face; but when I did, I was much shocked at the sudden alteration that had taken place in his features.

"He was dreadfully pale and haggard, his eyes almost fixed, while his whole frame seemed agitated by something dreadful. I was so alarmed, that I could not muster courage to speak for several seconds; at length I did contrive to say:

"'Henry—Henry! what can be the matter? Are you ill? Pray—pray speak to me.'

"'Oh, mother,' he said, but in such an altered voice, 'I am ruined—lost—quite lost!'

"'Ruined! How? Tell me all, Henry—tell me all. Keep nothing from me, I command you.'

"'It is all true, I am ruined—entirely ruined; that Crosby has kept his word. It is his fiendish malice that has caused all this. I saw him smile horribly, as if he felt all the pleasure of a demon at my early downfall.'

"'What is all this about, my dear Henry—you talk of ruin and downfall? What does it all mean?'

"'Why, this, mother—I am accused of forgery, and appropriation of money so obtained to my own use.'

"'Good Heavens, my son, you—you have not done this—tell me you are innocent.'

"'Yes, I am innocent, as I hope for grace. I am, indeed, innocent; but I am accused, and shall not be able to prove it, I know, for a most cunning device has been laid to entrap me, and it has proved successful. I will tell you all about it.

"'About two months back, I was desired by Mr. Crosby to take a bill to a certain party and get it cashed, and bring the money to him, less the discount. This was an ordinary occurrence, so I did as I was desired, without any hesitation whatever, and thought no more of the matter; I acted merely the part of a messenger on the occasion, and, therefore, I made no entry of the transaction, but delivered the money to Mr. Crosby, who received it, and appeared to me to enter it.

"'To-day a bill was presented at the house—it was the same one that I had carried to the holder, and obtained the cash for; for two hundred pounds, and payment demanded. The gentlemen were much surprised, said they knew nothing of it, and declared it to be a forgery.

"'That must be a mistake,' was the reply, 'because one of your own clerks came and cashed it at our office.'

"'Mr. Crosby was called, but he declared he had never seen the bill before, and had no note of it, or entry of any kind; and more, he declared he believed that the signature was forged.

"'The person who had called was desired to point out the clerk who came to him, and I happened to enter at the moment.

"'That is the young man,' was his immediate answer. 'Don't you remember coming to me to get a bill cashed about two months since?'

"'Yes,' I replied.

"'Then where is the money?'

"'I gave it to Mr. Crosby.'

"'I never received any such money,' replied Crosby, coolly. 'It is a wicked falsehood.'

"'I not only gave it to you, but I received the bill from you in the usual course of business.'

"'That is too gross and improbable,' replied Crosby. 'I believe the bill to be a forgery, and the more I look upon the signature, the more I am inclined to think that Henry Howard is the man who forged it.'

"'Several specimens of my handwriting were immediately procured, and they were compared, when they all concurred in the opinion that I had done the deed. The holder of the bill demanded the money—my employers refused to pay what they did not owe, and then they all turned upon me, saying, that if I would produce the money by to-morrow, I should escape with life, but, if not, I must expect the worst.'

"Picture to yourself, Mr. Percy, what were my feelings when my son related all this to me. I was more dead than alive, and knew not what to do or what to advise. The money I could not obtain, nor a tithe of it, and even that small sum I could not get until I had sold all that I had.

"There was no resource left except of waiting till time should establish his innocence, and, in the meanwhile, he must hide from the officers of justice. It was a terrible time for me. The officers came next day, and searched my house, and all around; but Henry had gone away for a few weeks, with what little money I could spare, until the heat of the affair had blown off.

"About six weeks after, and late one night, he came back to me, and, for a few days, he was hidden upstairs, and, during this time, he contrived to move some panelling, which exposed a large recess in one corner of the room, which had not been observed before. This he caused to slide backwards and forwards, so that he could easily go in or out as he pleased, and, if need be, could stay in for a day or two, having food put in for his use.

"It was lucky that this was done, for it seems the officers had some notion of his being about the house. They came in one day, and, before I was aware of it, commenced a search for him. However, Henry caught sight of them without being seen, and escaped to his place of concealment, where he remained till they had gone. This happened several times, but they never discovered the secret hiding-place.

"He remained at home for more than two years, when, finding all chance of establishing his innocence to be distant, or very improbable, he quitted this country for America, where he is doing very well; but I shall never see him more, I fear I shall never see his face again."

"And that place of concealment, which served so well for Henry, is still in existence, Mrs. Howell?"

"It is," she said. "I would never have it altered, though the sight of it always produces a sad feeling in my mind, when I reflect how hardly used was my poor boy, Henry."

"Mrs. Howell," said Palmer, "this gentleman has been accused, convicted, and actually condemned to death for a murder of which he is as innocent as you are."

"A murder!" exclaimed Mrs. Howell.

"Yes, and he requires, until the eagerness of pursuit has abated, just such a place of concealment as that you have in your house."

"Heaven forbid that I should refuse to succour him in his misfortunes," said the widow. "What would have been my feelings if my poor boy had appealed to anyone in vain?"

"Then, Mr. Percy," said Palmer, rising, "I feel confident I leave you in safe hands. Expect to see me to-morrow, and now I shall hasten back to the 'Star and Tinder-box,' to make arrangements concerning Miss Rankley."

"Heaven bless you!" said Mrs. Howell, as she rose to light him from the room. "To you, mainly, I owe the safety of Henry, and Heaven forbid that I should not do my duty by a friend of yours. It seems like paying a small portion of the debt I owe you."

CHAPTER CXVII.

TWITTER'S DEMAND UPON VARLEY—AN UN-EXPECTED CHANGE OF DEMEANOUR — MUTUAL DISTRUST.

BERNARD VARLEY had put up at one of the most expensive and magnificent hotels he could think of in London.

He could not get rid of the idea that, by surrounding himself with the magnificent and the beautiful, he should, to a certain extent, succeed in stilling those pangs of conscience which would ever make themselves felt in such a breast as his.

He fancied that the glitter of decoration around him would war successfully with the dungeon-like gloom of his own heart.

How vain an idea!

The more of elegance, the more of beauty he saw around him, the more dark and wretched by contrast did his own feelings appear; and any momentary feeling of satisfaction was but the precursor of an acute pang, and the forerunner of more misery than could be repaid to him by the brightest gleam of sunlight that had danced upon his spirits.

When he had made all the arrangements in his power with the police, and had done all that he could possibly think of to ensure the capture of Rowland Percy, he turned the whole attention of his mind to the pursuit of Miranda, and, although he had no clue whatever to her place of concealment, yet he thought that, with his great resources, he should surely be able to ferret out one who would be compelled, for the sake of an existence, to mingle with the world, and make herself known to many persons.

"She has not yet," he said, "felt the acute sting of poverty. Cradled in the lap of luxury in early life, and then, when misfortune came upon her, surrounded by sympathizing friends, she has not yet endured that poverty, that destitution which, like mental poison, preys upon the intellect, destroying its best energies, and fitting it for the reception of thoughts, that in a more easy and pleasant state of existence it would have scorned as far beneath it. The sympathies of friends soon wear out, or become cold, and Miranda will be left to her own resources. Her pride, too, will step in to hasten such a result, and then, in some sad hour, when her experience in the world has deepened into terror, I shall come to her with an offer of wealth and an unvarying round of pleasure. Surely she will then be mine, and, shrinking from the abyss of poverty into which she had plunged, would be glad again to ascend to the height of prosperity. Yes, she must be mine, or I must perish in the pursuit of so much beauty. Whether Rowland Percy live or die, Miranda shall be mine, and, in the pursuit of her, too, will I pursue him. I have now a fixed determination, that let me but catch a glimpse of his person, I'll kill him, and plead as my justification for the act that my own life was in jeopardy on account of his resistance to being captured. Always armed as I am with weapons upon which I can depend, his death, should we chance to meet, shall be certain.—Well, Twitter, what now?"

With the usual snake-like movement that characterized his steps, Twitter had glided into the room, and stood peering at Varley out of his small eyes as if he had something to say which he yet could scarcely give utterance to.

"Well, Twitter," added Varley, "I did not ring for you."

"You're considerate," said Twitter, "and you ring for me so seldom, that I do not feel my servitude very heavy, although you have compelled me to become your valet. I almost think, Varley, sometimes, that you would quite as soon be without me altogether."

"Indeed!" sneered Varley.

"Yes; and you would scarcely regret it if I were to remove myself."

"Not at all—far from it, Samuel Twitter; only I wish to dictate the place to which you are to remove if you leave me; that is a point I must reserve to myself."

"And where should that be?"

"Into your grave, Samuel Twitter:—remove there when you please, and I will bid you adieu upon its brink. You understand me, Twitter? No more of these attacks upon my purse, for such they are."

"But you promised me."

"Pshaw! promises to you! Why do men

keep promises but for special reasons, which can never exist between us. Some will keep a promise for what they call character sake; others, to beget confidence which will enable them to break one of more importance at another opportunity; but, Twitter, we have no such motives, and I can make and break promises to you at my own good pleasure."

"Cursed thief!" muttered Twitter, in too low a tone to be heard; and then he added, aloud: "Well—well, I came to make a trifling request. As we are now in London, Mr. Varley, I would fain see some old friends that I have not visited for many a year, and as I would wish to make a liberal appearance, and be very gracious to them, lend me a hundred pounds."

"Lend you a hundred pounds!"

"Yes, I say lend, because you can pay yourself out of my share of the Grange estates whenever you like."

"Are you tired of your life," said Varley, "that you insult me with such propositions?"

"Nearly," said Twitter; "aren't you?"

"Now, by Heavens!" said Varley, rising, "this insolence shall not go unpunished. Samuel Twitter, if you have taken the absurd notion into your head that you can acquire any mastery over me by intimidation, or threats, or coarse insolence of conduct, you shall find yourself most woefully mistaken."

"I threaten nothing," said Twitter, who, certainly, since the quarrel when he had called for assistance, had presumed upon Varley's fears, and with a dogged kind of resolution not given way so completely to the other's threats. "I threaten nothing, and know not what you mean. I only ask for a hundred pounds on account, Mr. Varley; surely that is moderate out of I know not how many thousands which are my due. As for threatening, we neither of us can threaten the other. The fact is, when there are two men who can——" Twitter walked to the door, and looked out to assure himself that no one was listening, then coming back, added: "hang each other, it behoves them to be civil."

Varley felt annoyed, for Twitter had never ventured upon quite so much boldness before, and was looking anxiously in his face to see how it was received.

"Samuel Twitter," said Varley, "have you totally forgot the desperate man you have to deal with?"

"I am more desperate still," said Twitter. "Try you and be my valet for a month, and let me have the disposal of the whole of the Grange revenues; you will then be able better to speak of what it is to be a desperate man."

"Did you say a hundred pounds?" said Varley, with a calmness that made Twitter give a jump towards the door, for it alarmed him much more than any ebullition of rage would have done, on the principle that a violent man is always more dangerous when he thinks proper to smother his passion for a time.

"Did you say a hundred pounds, Samuel Twitter?"

"Yes, I did. Come, now, Mr. Varley—no—no outbreak. We—we are bound together by mutual interest; danger to one of us is danger to the other. Only a hundred. I am sure my request is reasonable. I threaten nothing, and never attempted to threaten anything. I only wished that we should mutually have a good understanding."

"Oh, certainly," said Varley. "I daresay you are quite right. When you have expended the hundred pounds I shall now give you, pray come to me for another. I begin to feel, Samuel Twitter, that my conduct must have been faulty towards you, and that you have a claim which must be satisfied."

"You—you are not joking, Varley?" said Twitter.

"Joking! Heaven forbid! You'll find by the result that there isn't the shadow of a jest lurking in the whole affair. I am extremely serious."

Twitter looked anxiously into the countenance of his associate in crime, but he could detect nothing but cold austerity, and he was puzzled, as well as alarmed, at the remarkable change in Varley's manner towards him.

"I do not wish to annoy you, Varley," he said; "very far from it. You know I would do anything for you, and, in fact, as I have remarked, our interests are identical."

"Admirably reasoned," said Varley, "but quite a work of supererogation, for I am already convinced that I have been proceeding upon a mistake. I am quite clear now with respect to the claim you have upon me, and be assured, upon the first convenient opportunity, you shall be settled with in full; but the complete wind-up of an account, you know, Samuel Twitter, requires some little careful consideration of one's ways and means, even after the act itself is quite determined upon. Is a hundred pounds quite enough for the present?"

Twitter was getting in a perspiration at this unexpected change in Varley's manner.

It was something out of all calculation—a state of things for which he was not prepared; he was full of suspicion, although he could not tell in which way his danger lay.

If Varley had but got into a great passion, Twitter could have understood him, and all would have been well; but that he should so suddenly become polite, civil, and considerate, was perfectly horrible, and put him in a state of alarm that almost took away his breath.

"Varley!" he gasped, "what on earth do you mean? Why aren't you in one of your furies? Explain your meaning, Varley! Why this unnatural calmness? It—it is terrifying!"

"Nay, now," said Varley, "what a hard matter it is to please you! If I storm at you and get angry, you think yourself mightily ill-used, and wonder that I should so treat you. Then, again, now that I am calm and considerate, and candidly confess that I have treated you in a mistaken way, which shall be amended for the future, you are angry because I am not angry. Really, Samuel Twitter, you are a most inconsistent person."

"Nay; but, Varley, do you really mean what you say?—or are you, with a frightful irony, deceiving me?"

"I never was so clear in my intentions regarding you," said Varley; "if you doubt my words, time alone can show my sincerity."

Twitter gave a deep groan as he folded up the hundred-pound note which Varley handed him.

"Well, Varley," he said, "I hope that for the future no harsh words need ever pass between us. You will do me justice—I feel assured you will do me justice."

"Most ample justice, you may feel assured. I will not deny that at times your principal claim upon me has come forcibly upon my mind; but I never felt so thoroughly convinced that it ought to be paid in full, as now; but, then, as I said before, Twitter, one must take one's opportunity. Good-morning to you; a pleasant day with your friends, Samuel Twitter."

Twitter shrank to the door, and, trembling in every limb, passed out of the room.

"Yes," cried Varley, stamping vehemently, when Twitter was out of the room, "by Heaven! he shall have his claim — he shall!"

"Eh?" said Twitter, putting in his head at the door.

"What now?" said Varley, suddenly dropping his voice.

"Nothing," said Twitter, "only I thought you spoke."

"No—no; you are a man of imagination, and fancied it."

"Oh!" said Twitter. "Good-morning."

This time Varley held the door in his hand, while Twitter descended the staircase, after which he closed it, muttering to himself:

"He courts death at my hands, and he shall receive it. While he continued the low, cringing villain, upon whose neck I could place my foot, I was content to let him live; but now he has begun to resist, he is finding out his real strength, and, like all cowards, under such circumstances, he will use it recklessly. I am decided upon his death. The manner of its execution I must think upon. The means must be safe, and certain, and noiseless—yes, noiseless, if possible."

He sat down, and fell into a long train of thought with regard to the means of taking the life of his associate in crime.

As for Twitter himself, no course of conduct which Varley could possibly have pursued would have entailed upon him such absolute misery as that he now suffered from the mass of conjectures that rose upon his mind, in consequence of the sudden alteration in the conduct of him who had always shown himself to be of the most violent disposition, and ever ready at a moment to break out into the most angry denunciations.

The real truth did certainly cross Twitter's mind more than once; but, strange to say, he discarded the supposition, more than any other, that Varley intended to murder him.

First of all he shrank from it, and strove to shake it off, as weak-minded people commonly do any idea that is of an extremely distressing nature to them. Then he thought of what great difficulties Varley would have to encounter in the accomplishment of such a purpose—difficulties nearly insurmountable—for would he (Twitter) be so foolish as to trust himself with Varley under any circumstances which would give him a fair opportunity of executing so terrible a purpose.

"No, surely," he muttered, "he cannot mean my murder. To put me to a violent death he shall have no chance, for I will never meet him but in the populous haunts of men, where his instant apprehension for the deed, or the attempted deed, would be certain. Dare he poison me? No; for what poison is there that he could administer so quick in its effects that it would not leave me time ere I died to denounce him as the murderer of Sir George Rankley? No, I do not—cannot think he means to take my life."

Having, as he thought, disposed of this conjecture, another rose up in Samuel Twitter's mind, which, bad as was the former, was of a still more agonizing description.

That was that Bernard Varley was maturing some scheme for escaping from England, and leaving him (Twitter) to take the consequences of the crime they had jointly committed.

From the moment this idea suggested itself to the mind of Twitter, the stronger and more feasible it grew, and he fancied he saw confirmatory reasons in every word which had fallen from Varley's lips.

"His first wild excitement," he thought, "has died away, and no doubt he has resolved to give up the mad pursuit of Miranda; he has probably got some offer for the Grange estates, which he will close with, and then, repairing to the yacht which he has purchased—the existence of which I became aware of by so strange a chance—he will sail, Heaven only knows whither, denouncing me, in the meantime, for my share in his crime, and so, in his own language, pay me the debt he owes me."

Samuel Twitter quite satisfied himself that he had found out Varley's real meaning, and the course of conduct he pursued thereon will be quickly made manifest, a course of conduct eminently calculated to ensure the destruction of both of those men who, had they but held together in their iniquities, deeply dyed with guilt as they were, might have defied the hand of justice; but, how true is it, that great criminals are their own greatest enemies, and that a chain of union, forged in iniquity, has not the strength of a hair to hold its links together.

CHAPTER CXVIII.

THE DELIGHTS OF DRURY LANE—THE SPY
—THE MEETING BETWEEN PALMER AND
JONES.

THE large rewards which had accumulated upon the head of the unfortunate Rowland Percy, induced an unprecedented activity among the London police for his detection.

The Government had offered five hundred pounds for his capture, Bernard Varley five hundred more, and the magistracy of York, feeling themselves in a very peculiar situation, in consequence of letting slip the only great criminal that had been in their hands for the last four or five assizes, offered three hundred; so the total reward for the recapture of the innocent Rowland Percy amounted to the large sum of thirteen hundred pounds, and, it will be recollected this sum was only for the seizure of his person, and not, as is ordinarily the case in such money matters, contingent upon the conviction of the accused, for Rowland had but to be identified, in order to make him amenable immediately to the last dread sentence of the law.

The most incredible exertions were made to secure him; and, had he not been in the extremely unsuspicious place he was, in the first flush of the active search, he would surely have fallen into the hands of the police; the avenues of London were well watched; the passengers on every coach coming from York, or its direction, scrutinized; and persons, having the appearance of quiet, harmless sojourners in the metropolis, were placed as lodgers in those public-houses where it was well known to the police any criminal, however grave his offence might be, could obtain shelter and assistance.

The metropolis was placarded with bills, giving a description of Rowland Percy, and detailing the rewards offered for his apprehension; while the newspaper Press, of course, added to the hue and cry which was raised against him.

Happily, perhaps, for his peace, Rowland knew not of the extensive arrangements that were made for his apprehension; true, he saw the newspapers, but their information being notoriously defective, they contradicted each other so completely, that he placed no reliance upon any of their statements.

The "Star and Tinder-Box" was more watched by the police than any other house in the metropolis; and, had Dick Palmer been thoroughly aware of the great exertions that would be made for the recapture of Rowland Percy, he would have quite altered his mind as to the propriety of taking him to Drury Lane; for not only was the house what is termed a flash one, but the landlord, being a Yorkshireman himself, was well known to the police for his sympathy for offenders from that part of the country.

He was quite right in the information he had given to Palmer and Rowland, that parties came to his house on the look-out for the latter, and it was most fortunate that the persecuted young man and his friend, the highwayman, left as early as they did.

Mr. Jones, upon leaving Miranda in the genteel establishment which we have taken some pains to describe, hastened to the "Star and Tinder-Box"—a house much more congenial to his tastes and habits.

A sort of cheerful expansion came over Jones' face as he neared the purlieus of Drury Lane, spots as dear and hallowed to his memory as are the arcadian groves of Italy to the worshipper of classicality and romantic beauty.

"Drury Lane!" cried Mr. Jones, when he arrived at the corner of Broad Street. "Here yer is, bless yer. Talk o' streets, and squares, and willas, and all them ere things, they're none on 'em ekal to Drury Lane. If I was ever to retire from business, I should just like a willa up some of them ere courts. There's no air as comes near the air of Drury Lane. Sometimes it's pork-sassengers, then there's a wariation of fried-fish and tripe, and, above all, there's aromatic odour, as people calls it, and nothing disagrees with nobody, cause of the particles of gin as is floating in the air. Then what's to come near them courts and alleys, running quite beautiful into St. Giles's, and out on it again, quite natural, where a fellow might dodge the grabs for a month, and pop in and out like a dog in a fair. Then there's the fences and the flash kens. Drury Lane, you is a beauty! Some people says the smell on yer is rather strong, but it's wery pleasant for all that, and here's Steeple Court, too. Was there ever such an out-an'-out rummy, little, dark, down-hill alley as this here; it's quite romantic and lovely. If I was a great monarch, I'd have that ere 'Star and Tinder-Box' as one of my royal residences, that I would. Why, there's baccy smoke in every room on it, 'cause it creeps up the staircases just like a live creature."

By this time Mr. Jones had arrived at the "Star and Tinder-Box," where the landlord was not visible; but he quickly summoned him by leaning over the bar with an air of great familiarity, and shouting, "Vell!" in a voice that quickly reached mine host.

"Why, pipes and quarterns," said the landlord, "is it you? you are an inch too late."

"Guv us six foot of explanation," said Jones. "What sing'lar noise is that ere?"

"Well! if somebody hasn't left the old Tom tap running," said the landlord, in a rage, not at all expecting that Jones, by way of a practical joke, had just accomplished that feat.

"That ere was wilful waste," said Jones. "Guv us half a pint to begin with. Have you seen Dicky? How does times go? York, eh? Tow-row. All right—somewhere upstairs?"

The landlord placed his finger mysteriously by the side of his nose, and said "Hush!"

Behind mine host was a looking-glass, which reflected a good view of the parlour-door,

TWITTER IS ALARMED AT VARLEY'S GENEROSITY.

which, by that means, Jones saw slowly open, and a head protruded, in the act of listening.

"Sneaks about?" inquired Jones.

"Wery," said the landlord.

By a dexterous fling of his hand, then, Jones threw the whole half-pint of gin over his shoulder, exactly into the eyes of the prying listener, who immediately disappeared into the parlour with a howl of pain, and such a volley of curses, as quite delighted Mr. Jones, some of them being of a very original character.

As for the landlord, he sat down in his little parlour, and roared again with laughter. After which he upset several glasses, in lean-ing over the beer-engine to touch Mr. Jones on the back, in token of his high approbation of his conduct.

"Bless yer!" he cried, "I always said you was a ornament to sossyiety, and so you is. That feller's been here for a week a-prying and poking about. Come in, yer amusing wretch; I could quite swaller yer."

The feelings of the gentleman who had had the gin thrown in his eyes appeared to have been rather excited by the circumstance—an excitement which was most probably added to by the roar of laughter with which he was greeted in the parlour; for, after executing a grotesque dance, in great agony, from the gin in his eyes, he rushed to the bar, looking as if he had been crying for a week, and, in a voice compounded of rage, fear, and pain, he shouted:

"What villain did that?—what infernal scoundrel did that? Help—murder! I can hardly see. Who threw gin in my face? Who dared to half-blind me in this way? Tell me who it was, and I'll be the death of him."

"Why, you're drunk," said Jones. "What do yer mean, poor cretur? You've had so much gin, that it's running out of yer eyes."

"Was it you threw gin at me?" shouted the man.

"Over the left," said Jones.

"Hark yer, my friend," said the landlord; "I know yer. They say listeners never hear no good of themselves; but you've done better, for you've had half-a-pint of gin for nothing. I shan't charge yer for it. Now mizzle. A spy's business is over when he's found out. Take a hint; it wouldn't be good for your health to stay here to-night."

"Exactly," said Jones. "Something might happen uncomfortable before mornin'."

"Curse you all!" said the man; "you'll do yourself a deal of good by all this. I'll give a report of the house, that you may hear of next licensing day."

He then rushed into the street, with a very despairing look, feeling, indeed, according to the landlord's dictum, that his occupation was over.

"What is the news?" said Jones to the landlord. "Is Percy here with you as escaped from York scragging?"

"He's been here, but he ain't here now. I advised Dick to take him away, as I knew there was a dead set made here for him; and so, you see, Dick knows when I adwises anything I means it. He took him away, and where he's stowed him I can't say."

"Safe and sound somewhere, I'll be bound."

"Why, Dick isn't the man exactly to do things half ways. I'd say as much of him behind his back as I would before his face, that a better fellow never stepped in shoe leather; he's too good for this ere world, Mr. Jones. I respects him as if he was my own babby; and, come what may, I'll stick to him like bricks, through thick and thin, odd or even, and all sorts of luck; I'm not the man to turn tail on an old acquaintance; and as long as the 'Star and Tinder-Box' has a bit of flint in its lockers, hurrah for Dicky!"

"Thank you," said Palmer, who at that moment appeared in front of the bar; "I owe you one for that. Jones, is she all safe?"

"I should think so," said Jones; "and snug as—ahem!"

"Thank Heaven!" said Palmer, as he walked inside the bar; "I think, then, there is a prospect of holding out until the ardour of pursuit is abated—a pursuit which I never could have believed would have been carried on with so much rancour. The aggregate rewards offered for the apprehension of poor Rowland Percy this day amount to thirteen hundred pounds."

"He may thank his stars he's not here, then," said the landlord, "for we have fellers come to this here crib as would make their own mothers into sassages, and then fry and eat 'em, for half the sum."

"Thirteen hundred," said Jones. "I should just like to meet the kiddy as was walking away with that 'ere sum in a rayther lonely place."

"Some of the rale," said the landlord, handing a glass to Palmer. "Drink it, my boy. Here's better luck, more friends, and less need of them. Lor bless yer, beaks and officers are but human *beans* after all. Some on 'em has a little cleverness, and some on 'em hasn't; but take 'em at the best, we generally gets the better on 'em; so never fear, all will be right, and the young chap will give 'em the double. Here's luck to him; and may willainy meet with its just reward."

"I trust it may," said Palmer. "I have heard, during my brief life, many instances of oppression and false accusation, but I never, even in a romance, could have expected to meet with such a systematic course of villainy as that which consigned Rowland Percy to a dungeon, and precipitated one of the most beautiful and innocent of her sex from the very height of prosperity to the lowest depths of despair and destitution. Heaven cannot, will not, look calmly on such frightful wrongs; and the day must soon come when the oppressor shall fall, and innocence rise more triumphant still upon the ashes of its former glory."

"Knock my back!" said Jones to the landlord; "thank yer, I've swallowed it now. Give us that another time, Dicky, in little pieces, and lend us a dictionary as you goes on. Blessed if ever I heared anything so strong in my life. One's forced to swallow it all at once, for fear it should ewaporate."

CHAPTER CXIX.

THE ATTEMPTED CAPTURE—THE SEARCH BY THE OFFICERS, AND THE DREADFUL DISAPPOINTMENT.

IN a few minutes the discourse assumed a much more serious aspect between Jones and Palmer, and they mutually communicated to each other the particulars concerning Rowland Percy and Miranda, with the urgently expressed desire of each of those persons to have another interview.

"Mr. Percy, I believe," said Palmer, "is perfectly safe for the present; in fact, I feel quite sure that no inducement upon earth would get the person he is with to betray him. His subsistence must be my care, and I must, as well, do what I can for Miranda, who must surely claim the tenderest sympathy of every man of true feeling. She has borne herself most nobly under the acutest trials, and one cannot but respect the fortitude and courage which has raised that young, shrinking, and timid girl, to be a perfect heroine."

"Wery good, Dicky," said Jones; "wery good. All I can say is, as she is in a wery genteel house, in a wery genteel street. I never was genteel, thank goodness, and never shall be. Blessed if I don't think it's another name for being uncomfortable. Howsomdever, you know, Dicky, she may like it, as she's been brought up in the young-lady way, which I wasn't. Now and then she takes on a little melancholy, and then she picks up a bit, and she wants to see that sweetheart of hers, young Mr. Percy; and, as it's a wery genteel house she lives in, and nobody would suspect as anybody worth a curse would live in it, or wisited at it, I don't see why he shouldn't go and see her. It'll make 'em both more comfortable. What do you think of it, Dicky?"

"I would, gladly," said Palmer, "assist in procuring an interview between them; but you've really no notion, Jones, of the hot pursuit that's made after him. Believe me, he cannot, for a short time, leave the widow's house with any degree of safety, and, when they meet, I should advise that she should go to him, instead of he visiting her."

"Wery good," said Jones; "but I should like you to see that ere genteel house. It's out-and-out nobby in its way. I wouldn't live in it if you'd give me never so much. Talk of comfort—oh, lawks! I daresay, if you and me were to smoke a pipe on the roof, they'd think themselves ruined for ever."

"With Miss Rankley's permission," said Palmer, "I shall certainly call and see her; and obviously the danger of her visiting Mr. Percy at the widow's is not near so great as his visiting her, for even—which is very unlikely—should she be seen and followed, still the discovery of his hiding-place is not a necessary consequence."

"Sartenly not."

"Yet, Jones, I should advise, that a day or two be allowed to elapse. We cannot be too prudent. Only consider the dangers we have already passed through, and the great hopes that Mr. Percy still has of some circumstance happening to prove his innocence. Were he really a guilty man, I own the case would be widely different, even if we wished to save him."

"That's all wery true," said Jones, "and I needn't say, Dick, that I leaves the affair in your hands; and, now, as to the keep of these ere unfortunate creters as can't keep themselves. You knows my business as you knows your own. There's a little unsartenty in all speculations; I may crack a crib as is worth the cracking, or I mayn't. I tell you what we'll do, Dick, we'll meet once a blessed week, and calculate what's wanted. If you haven't it, perhaps I shall; if I haven't it, perhaps you may. I think that ere 'll be the way to work the oracle?"

"I see no objection to the plan," said Palmer; "but mind, Jones, I implore you to be careful not to bring suspicion on the innocent Miranda, by visiting her after any of your professional avocations. You know not what might result from one such act of imprudence."

"Leave me alone; I'll be as prudent as the Lord Chancellor when he won't decide a case, because he does not know what to think of it. If I think all isn't right, when I want to send her any blunt, I'll pop it in a letter, and she'll get it, and nobody suspect it nohow."

"Hilloa!" said the landlord, "visitors;" and, in another moment, three men lounged to the front of the bar.

"Your sarvant, gentlemen," said the landlord, who knew them at once as Bow Street officers. "What's the row?"

"Game's up," said one of the officers. "We must have him—it's a serious case—so make no bones about it."

"Have who?" said the landlord. "I never was good at riddles; if my grandmother had been alive, she'd have given you an answer quite pat."

"Come, come, no nonsense," said the spokesman of the party. "Rowland Percy, the murderer, from York, has been traced here. We have a warrant, and it includes the Slashing Squire, for aiding and abetting him. Come, now, don't put on such a phiz as that, it won't do any longer; we must have both on 'em. As for the Slashing Squire, he's booked, too; for there is two or three highway robberies waiting to be down upon him as soon as he's nabbed."

"Perhaps you'd like to get me first?" said Palmer, making his appearance from behind the landlord and Jones.

"Here goes for a try," said the officer, as he stretched his hand over the bar, in which was his little brass staff, and made an attempt to seize Palmer.

The latter, however, struck up the officer's arm, and wrenching the staff from his hand at the same moment, disappeared through the door leading into the back-alley, by which he and Rowland had made their exit from the "Star and Tinder-Box."

"It's no matter—it's no matter," cried the discomfited officer, as he tried to scramble over the bar. "He'll be nabbed at the end of the alley."

"In the meantime," said the landlord, taking up a large toasting-fork, "there is no occasion for you to come into my bar. I haven't seen your search warrant, and I don't mean to take your word for it."

Several vigorous thrusts of the toasting-fork, induced the officer to withdraw his leg.

"Where's the warrant—where's the warrant? Show this fellow the warrant, and then let him resist if he dares."

While the landlord affected to be very seriously looking at the warrant, Dick Palmer walked hastily down the dark passage, until he was suddenly seized by someone, who cried:

"Hold! not so fast," and the gleam of a dark lantern immediately illuminated the place.

Dick saw in a moment that the officer was a new hand, and did not know him.

"My good fellow," he said, "are you an

officer? because if you are, I am one of the York police, and am come to tell you you are particularly wanted in the house; we've nabbed our men, but there's something of a row going on."

Dick showed him the officer's staff as he spoke, which completely silenced his scruples, and exclaiming: "The deuce there is," he rushed up the alley, leaving Palmer at perfect liberty, who, darting into Drury Lane, crossed it, and was soon lost in the intricacies of a maze of courts which branched from its opposite side.

The officer who had been so outwitted, rushed breathlessly into the bar, exclaiming: "Here I am—here I am; what's the matter?"

"The matter!" cried the others. "Where's your prisoner?"

"Prisoner? I've seen nobody but the York officer, a big fellow, with his staff. He told me you wanted me."

"Done," said the officers, looking at each other. "You're an ass, Fredericks. One of the birds has flown."

"Yes, but we'll have the other and the principal one," exclaimed one of the officers. "The front door is well guarded; and now, Fredericks, do you stick your broad back against the door you have just come through. Let this be a lesson to you, and don't let a prisoner go because he happens to show you a constable's staff."

"What a skrimmage!" said Jones. "Really, gentlemen, you turned all my milk. Do you want to take anybody up, or are you only in joke?"

"You mind your own business," said the senior officer; "when we want you, we'll call for you."

"Oh, thank you," said Jones. "If I shouldn't happen to be at home, you can leave your card, you know. You won't take anything to drink now, I suppose, as you're rayther in a hurry?"

The officers disdained to make any reply to this invitation, but commenced a vigorous search through the house, with, as they thought, the certainty of finding the man they sought; and, indeed, they had taken their measures very well for the accomplishment of that result, had Rowland Percy been so unfortunate and ill-advised as really to have taken up his abode at the "Star and Tinder-Box."

They had placed the man Fredericks—who, although but a young officer, possessed remarkable muscular power—in the narrow passage by the back alley, with instructions to make prisoner anyone who attempted to pass from the public-house. How he acquitted himself we have seen.

Then, at the front door an officer was stationed, and another one on the roof of the opposite house, in order to watch if any attempt were made by Rowland Percy to escape over the roof of the "Star and Tinder-Box."

From the description of the York officers,

they had been quite able to identify Dick Palmer as the person who appeared to have assisted Rowland Percy in his flight; hence was it that his name was included in the warrant.

From a woman who kept a little shop opposite to the "Star and Tinder-Box," they had been told that two persons, answering the descriptions of Percy and Dick Palmer, had been seen to enter the public-house, but not to leave it.

This was the whole of their information; but, coupled with their previous suspicions, it was amply sufficient to enable them to obtain a warrant upon, and to serve as a foundation for a tolerably well-grounded belief that an active search in the "Star and Tinder-Box" would discover Rowland Percy.

The landlord, feeling so very conscious as he was that the search throughout his house would be fruitless, had the malice to amuse himself at the officers' expense, by expressing great fear and anxiety, as they entered into every room, calling frequently upon his lucky stars to save him from the consequences, if they looked into this cupboard or that, so that he kept the officers in a perpetual state of fidget during the whole time of the search, for they were always expecting something, and finding nothing to repay them for their labours.

It took a long while to go over the "Star and Tinder-Box," for it was an old rambling house, with a great number of odd nooks and curious corners.

There were deep, out-of-the-way cupboards here and there, where they would have been least expected, so that to perform the search thoroughly, even to those practised men, occupied much time.

Doubly toilsome, too, did it become, as floor after floor, room after room, cupboard after cupboard, were searched in vain, and at the end of about an hour they stood in the attic, weary and discomfited.

The last attic, too, they had to search— and, Heaven knows, that was done easily enough—it presented nothing to their gaze but four bare whitewashed walls, not even relieved by the wretchedest skeleton grate.

They were begrimed with dust and dirt, for such a rout-out of all the old holes and corners in the "Star and Tinder-Box" had not taken place for many years; in fact, as the landlord himself emphatically declared, he wasn't aware of half the conveniences of the ancient house until they were so kindly pointed out to him by the officers.

"Well, gentlemen," he said, when they took a despairing look round the miserable attic, "you would persist in taking all this trouble, you know, and it's no fault of mine; you wouldn't be satisfied without poking your noses into every hole and corner in the old house, and making yourselves more like a set of chimney-sweeps than respectable Bow Street runners."

"He isn't here," said the senior officer, "unless there's some hiding-place we can't find out. Now, remember," turning to the landlord, "this is a serious affair, and one which may do you a good deal of good or a good deal of harm. You know we don't trouble your house oftener than we can help; but, when we do, it must be to some purpose. A poor, miserable housebreaker is one thing, and a fellow convicted of murder is another; besides, here's thirteen hundred pounds reward. Come, now, say the word, of where he is, and you shall have the odd money—the three hundred, I mean."

"You must think me a precious ass," said the landlord, "to hand over to you a thousand pounds if I had the means and inclination to pitch upon a poor cretur who was playing hide-and-seek with the law. I tell you, as I told you before, he ain't here; if he was, and I wished to do the sneak, do you think I'd do it for three hundred pounds, when I could get thirteen for the job? Bah! you've gone to sleep."

"Oh, that's all very well," said the senior officer; "but you know what I mean as well as I do myself. It isn't three hundred pounds, or thirteen either, that would pay you for losing the confidence of the *family*—you know that as well as I. When I spoke of the three hundred, I meant that I'd hold you harmless in the affair, and nobody would know that you had given us the office."

"Lor! bless me," said the landlord, "how some people make money like dirt! You may depend upon it, gentlemen, I'll look for him high and low, and, if I should find him, I'll come to you for the three hundred, never fear, it's so very kind of you to hold me harmless. It's enough to bring tears into my eyes."

"Come along," said the officer to his companions, "it's no go. If he's been here he's gone again. But, hark ye, master landlord, when it comes to light—which it will some day—that you knew more of this matter than you'd tell, look out for squalls, that's all."

"Certainly, gentlemen, I'll look out for anything you like to mention. Mind how you go down the stairs. If one of you were to slip and break his neck, what a thing it would be. I think I should never look up again."

The officers went down the stairs muttering curses to themselves.

At the bottom of the first flight was an old cupboard, which wound a good deal under the staircase, and which they had been at great pains thoroughly to explore; now, however, as they came opposite to it, they all made a dead stand, for the door moved perceptibly, though slightly.

"Ah!" said the senior officer, as he folded his arms, and placed his back against it, "will you take the three hundred now, landlord? Come, say the word."

"Ah!" said the landlord, "it's better to be born lucky than rich. It's a great offer, gentlemen, and, when I find him, I'll run and let you know, without stopping to put on my hat."

"Then, my man," said the officer. "I strongly suspect you're a fool."

"Do you, indeed! I suspected that of you when you first showed your nose here to-day, but now it's come to a dead certainty."

"Very good—very good, have your grin; perhaps it'll change to the other side of your mouth in a little while. You won't take the three hundred now, and tell us where he is, candidly?"

"There you go," said the landlord, "poking your fun at a poor fellow; upon my soul, it's aggravating."

The officer laughed, and rubbed his hands together, and then he laughed again, in the most joyous manner imaginable. Altogether a more happy-looking man than the officer could scarcely have been found within the bills of mortality.

Various smiles passed across the faces of his companions, and they winked at each other, as much as to say that their chief was a wonderfully clever fellow, and was quizzing the landlord amazingly.

"Upon my life," said the senior officer to the landlord, "you carry it off remarkably well. Ah! ah! ah! I never saw such a face in my life, it's positively quite rich, but it won't do; oh, dear, no, not at all. It's a lot of cleverness all thrown away—an amazing lot of cleverness. Ah! ah! ah!"

The other officers laughed, as in duty bound, and, altogether, the landlord was made quite a butt among them. It seemed cruel and heartless; but such indeed was the fact.

"Now," said the senior officer, drawing out his staff; "hocus pocus. I'm a conjuror. Stand off a moment! Now, in upon him—hold him—that's the ticket."

Uttering these, and such warlike expressions, he pulled open the cupboard-door, and—discovered Mr. Jones, sitting very composedly in a chair, smoking a long pipe.

"What's all that blessed talking been about?" said Jones. "What an out-an'-out sanguinary disturbance."

"You infernal scoundrel!" said the enraged officer.

"Hi!—hi!" said Jones, "fetch us a strait waistcoat! There's a skrimmage."

The officer, stamping and swearing for a few moments, rushed down the remainder of the staircase, nor paused in his career till he had gained the open street.

After which, with a volley of abuse against the "Star and Tinder-Box," he walked in a very melodramatic manner to the Bow Street police-office.

———

CHAPTER CXX.

MIRANDA AT HOME—HOW TO GET "FOUND" IN LONDON LODGINGS—NIGHT AND MORNING.

MIRANDA felt very sad and lonely in her new home, situated as she was. It was cheerless and wretched in the extreme, to have no one who would address to her a kind word, or to whom she could discourse upon those subjects nearest and dearest to her heart.

Even the rough kindness and strange courtesies of Jones would have been very acceptable to her in her isolated condition; but he was gone, and she felt herself truly and sadly alone in every sense of the word.

Moreover, there was nothing cheering in the place, which she felt compelled to make her temporary home, and it was with a sigh of regret that she told herself that she would much rather have taken up her abode in some more homely and domesticated place, but she soon checked these mental aspirations, by exclaiming:

"Ought I not to be thankful, most thankful, for any home, situated as I am, in such melancholy circumstances, instead of being critical as to its advantages and disadvantages? If I have much to sigh for, at least I have much to be thankful for; Heaven forgive me for repining for a moment."

But if poor Miranda thus early found her home in the lodging-house cold, sterile, and disagreeable, what would be her feelings when she should eventually discover the heartless selfishness that would dictate every word that was spoken to her, and influence every action that was done, that was in relation to her.

She little imagined that the lodging-house keeper's creed was to look upon everyone, who by evil destiny came to reside on the genteel premises, as a special victim to the altar of avarice. One who is to be robbed, annoyed, unsettled, victimized in every possible manner, until driven out of the place to make way for some new comer, who might not be fully aware of the region of rascality into which he or she was plunged.

Jones had not left many minutes, when the landlady made her appearance on a voyage of discovery, to ascertain to what extent her new lodger would submit to be fleeced.

Upon Miranda's saying "Come in," in answer to a knock, she entered with a true lodging-house keeper's hypocritical smile.

"Miss Jones," she said, "I have just taken the liberty to come to inquire whether you mean to find yourself or not. I generally find my lodgers—particularly the first floor. By-the-by, you'll find the parlour very quiet—the second-floor back is out of town, and we have never allowed keys, since we had a first-floor come home drunk."

"I do not understand you," said Miranda, "when you talk of finding me. If you'll have the kindness to explain your meaning, I shall be obliged to you."

"Oh, very good," thought the landlady.

Then she added aloud:

"Perhaps you never were in a lodging-house before?"

"Once, and then only for a very short time," said Miranda, as she thought of her humble abode in York, with old Mr. Percy; "but it was far away from here, and the same usages may not exist in London."

"Why, finding you," said the landlady, looking very benign, "means saving you a deal of trouble in buying little odd matters, such as candles, and coals, and wood, and soap, and blacking, and so on, which can all be done up in a little weekly bill."

"You're very kind," said Miranda, "but it would be giving you a deal of trouble to spare me some."

"Oh, not at all great. Of course, I must buy these little things for myself, and I can oblige you at the same time. I have no objection to finding respectable lodgers."

"Very well," said Miranda; "if you will do so much for me, I am greatly beholden to you."

"Perhaps I had better find you everything else besides? Because I am sure, when I go and buy my own tea and sugar, it will be no trouble to buy you some. As I say, I generally find the first floor."

"If you please," said Miranda, "I will leave all those matters to your kind superintendence."

The landlady was amazed, and went down into the kitchen with the firm conviction that Miranda was a fool, and certainly had never been "found" in a London lodging before.

Great fatigue as the persecuted girl had suffered, it is no wonder she slept soundly, even under the cold and cheerless roof of the lodging-house, and, with a prayer for the safety of him who had already escaped so much danger, upon whose head the error of human judgment had put a price, she lay down in all her innocence and virtue, and all her troubles, to enjoy a purer and more refreshing sleep than would visit the couch of luxury, or the tapestried beds of the great.

It is true that some faint visions crossed her gentle slumbers; she thought she was again in her dainty little chamber in the old Grange. The sweet odours of the honeysuckle that twined round the window, came upon her senses. She heard the well-known songs of the birds that used to welcome her to morning, to joy, and hours of quiet happiness, to such as she had not now known for many a weary day.

Then she would be wandering with Rowland Percy in deep wildernesses, made beautiful, and full of life-like beauty, by the presence of him she loved.

It was from such soft visions that Miranda, at a very early hour, awoke in the lodging-house, but little knew she of the great change which morning produces in the gigantic metropolis.

A bright gleam of sunshine stole into her room, and played sweetly on her innocent face.

"Thank Heaven!" she cried, "for, amidst all my other troubles, yet another day of health and life." ——

CHAPTER CXXXI.

PALMER'S INTERVIEW WITH MIRANDA AT THE GENTEEL LODGINGS—THE SPY, AND THE CONSEQUENCES OF LISTENING AT A KEY-HOLE.

A STRANGER as she was in London, poor Miranda felt the painful consciousness, that, were she to leave her temporary abode alone, she would not be able to fulfil her first intention in the morning, namely, that of seeing old Mr. Percy, and ascertaining the state of his health.

In the whirl of events of the preceding day, she had forgotten to ask for a particular direction to the hospital whither he had been conveyed. Indeed, she did not even know it by name, so that she was not in a condition to ask her way, had she chosen to risk wandering about the great metropolis alone.

But still she thought there could not be many institutions of the kind, to one of which Mr. Percy had been conveyed, even in London, and had it not been for the dread of encountering Bernard Varley, and affording him, perhaps, a clue to her own place of abode, which might ultimately lead to a discovery of Rowland, she would have ventured, ignorant as she was of the localities of the city, alone into its streets, in search of the afflicted old man, who had been, by so strange a combination of circumstances, committed to her care.

In the present state of things then, she felt that prudence, if not downright necessity, compelled her to await another visit from Jones, ere she should stir from the lodging-house; and more strongly than ever came over her mind the wish for some domestic companionship, which would have beguiled the tedious hours of what might have been called her imprisonment.

Such, however, was not to be had, and poor Miranda, after partaking of a lonely and cheerless breakfast, which was "found" her by the landlady, with the trifling addition of about a hundred and twenty per cent. for so doing, sat with a forlorn feeling by the window, with no other amusement than that of looking into the genteel street, and seeing the occasional visitors that knocked at the highly respectable houses.

She asked her landlady for the loan of some books, but genteel people never have any light or profane literature by them; and even had the gilt-edged prayer-book been offered, which it certainly was not, Miranda was by no means in a frame of mind to sit down and peruse it with the purpose of whiling away a few tedious hours, so that she had no resource eventually but to sit brooding over her own sorrows—a sad employment, for there were but a few faint streaks of light in the gloom that surrounded her.

It was about ten o'clock in the day, when the first application was made to the knocker of the genteel house, and startled Miranda from her meditations.

Her heart beat quickly with pleasurable emotion at the thought that it might possibly be one or other of her friends, come to speak comfort to her, and to take her not only to old Mr. Percy, but, perchance, to Rowland, whom she longed to see, now that the great dangers on the road from York to London were over.

The suspense of the next few minutes was painful in the extreme, and when the door of her room was opened, she could scarcely speak from eagerness to inquire who it was that wished to see her.

"Here's a gentleman, mum," said the dirty servant.

"And his name?" said Miranda.

"I don't know his name, mum."

It is not one lodging-house servant in a hundred that can be drilled into asking the name of a visitor, and this one thought Miranda mighty particular in asking such a question—a question, however, which was speedily set at rest, by Miranda observing the friendly face of Dick Palmer, as he ascended the staircase.

With a flush of pleasure mantling in her cheeks, she advanced to meet him.

"Miss Rankley," said Palmer, "I should have been with you earlier, but, to tell the truth, I am not so well acquainted with London as to have found out this street very easily."

"You are truly welcome," said Miranda; "I feel myself quite solitary and prisoner-like in this place. I have been for some hours longing for a friendly face to make it look home-like. Is Rowland safe?"

"I think I may say quite safe from all ordinary accidents. It must be something very far out of the usual course of events that can bring to him any danger, situated as he is at present. That he suffers much mental anxiety cannot be denied, and chiefly, too, upon your account, for the more he feels what you have done for him, the more uneasiness seems to mingle with his thankfulness to Heaven, for bestowing upon him so pure a gift as your own spotless heart."

"Alas!" said Miranda, "we seem both the children of misfortune; but if, by aiding each other, we can ward off some of the bitterest blows of fate, we should be thankful to Heaven for permitting us."

"I have seen our friend Jones," said Dick Palmer, "and he has acquainted me with all the circumstances that have occurred since last I saw you."

"And Mr. Percy," inquired Miranda, "have you ascertained his condition?"

"I have, and I am sorry the report I have to give is not a favourable one. It is the opinion of the medical men at the hospital that a complete break-up of the physical powers is taking place."

"Alas—alas!" said Miranda, "this will be another severe blow to poor Rowland."

"Nay, Miss Rankley," said Palmer, "death has ever appeared to me an evil that ought to be borne with greater fortitude than many which afflict us during life. It is the end of all sorrows, instead of being, as is too generally supposed, the greatest sorrow of all."

"You are right," said Miranda. "What thinking mind could say otherwise? But when did philosophy ever yet succeed in successfully combating the feelings?"

"Never, indeed. And now, Miss Rankley, I have called to make with you some definitive arrangements for the future. I have great hope that the time is not far distant when the innocence of Mr. Percy will be established, and you and he will no longer be in a position to require advice or assistance from Dick Palmer; but till then I beg of you to relieve your mind from all anxiety with regard to the means of living. Rowland shall want for nothing, and I will likewise take care that no claim upon you shall be unsatisfied. I rather question Jones' discretion in bringing you here; there is an appearance of very cold comfort about this place that does not recommend it to me as even a temporary home for you. I think you would have been happier in some quiet, pleasant, domestic circle, instead of being shut up here with such a few real comforts about you."

"I cannot say I like the place," said Miranda, "nor do I like the people."

"Very well, then," said Palmer; "that being conceded, I will look out for a more comfortable home for you; this can be left at any moment."

"Would there be danger," said Miranda, "in my seeing Rowland?"

"I cannot say that your visiting him in his place of concealment would be entirely destitute of risk, and yet when I come to consider how very safely he is housed, and how unlikely it is that anyone who knew you should see you and follow you, I am tempted to make arrangements between you this very evening. I have combated with Jones the notion of your meeting for some time; but, upon reconsidering, I cannot say the danger is greater now than it would be a few days hence."

Miranda's eyes sparkled with pleasure at the near prospect of once again holding communion with him she loved, and who had become, if possible, still dearer to her for the disasters and dangers he had passed through.

"This evening, then," she said, "I will expect you; you will not disappoint me?"

"On my sacred word," said Palmer; "expect me here, and we will walk quietly together to the house in which Rowland is concealed. The distance is but short, and there is one desirable feature in the circumstances—namely, that both your own situation and Rowland's are known, and probably sympathized with, by the party in whose house he has taken refuge, so that, when there, there will be no need of concealment—no dread of being overheard."

These words had scarcely escaped Dick Palmer's lips, when a sudden thought seemed to strike him, and rising so as not to make the least noise, he approached the door of the room, which he suddenly flung wide open.

The landlady, who had been listening at the keyhole, rolled into the room on the floor, uttering a loud scream.

"Oh, indeed," said Dick, as he strode over her, and locked the door on the inside; "you are a nice article, madam. Look here! I have a trowel in one pocket, and a double-barrelled pistol in the other, and if you attempt to say one word, or to raise the least alarm, I'll blow out your brains with the pistol, and plaster them up against yonder wall with the trowel, as an example for the future to all prying lodging-house listeners. I am a man of my word, and one cry will be equivalent to sentence of death upon you."

The word murder died away on the landlady's lips into an indistinct whisper, and she glared at Dick with frantic dismay, as she pictured to herself the process of plastering the wall with her brains, and for ever ruining the paper.

"'Tis hard, indeed," said Palmer, "that persons cannot converse freely in rooms, for which, I have no doubt, they have well paid, without being subject to the prying curiosity of those who should be the last to practice such meanness. Miss Rankley, I advise you at once to leave this place with me."

"I must have a proper warning," said the landlady. "I'm not going to be imposed upon because I am a lone woman. I insist upon a proper warning, or——"

"Hush—hush!" interrupted Dick. "I mean you to have a proper warning, and one which I hope you will never forget. I only wish you were a man, for, in that case, the proper warning should partake of a more violent character than you would consider at all pleasant. As it is, however, madam, you have placed both yourself and me in a disagreeable situation. Speaking candidly, I don't know anything I have said that I should fear to hear repeated; but, in case I should, and by way of giving you the warning you require, I shall trouble you to remain in this apartment for the space of one hour from this time, during which hour, if you move or speak in the slightest, I shall feel it to be a duty I owe myself and society to take your life. I am perfectly serious, madam."

As a convincing proof to the landlady that her danger was great, Dick produced a horseman's pistol from his coat pocket, the sight of which put her in a perfect agony: for although Dick held the butt end of it towards her, it was still a pistol, and, to her mind, just as dangerous as it would have been had he presented the muzzle towards her instead.

"Oh! have mercy upon me," she said. "I didn't hear anything, sir. I was only passing the door accidentally, and my foot slipped as you opened it. Besides, the man you was speaking of mayn't be the York murderer after all, although it is the same name as we have all of us read in the newspapers."

Dick looked much vexed as he said, in a low tone to Miranda:

"You will scarcely forgive me for the folly I have been guilty of, in talking so freely in a strange house. I will do, however, my best to repair my error, and in the meantime attire yourself for the streets, for you must leave this place immediately. Another moment would be fraught with danger."

Miranda, without another word, entered the inner room, and began hastily putting on her cloak and bonnet, in order to accompany the highwayman.

Dick then, in a low but serious tone, said to the landlady:

"If you do not in all respects conform yourself to the directions I shall give you, be assured you had better have had your winding-sheet ready, for you'll be a dead woman before an hour shall have elapsed."

"Have mercy upon us, miserable sinners! Amen!"

Dick placed an arm-chair close to one of the walls, and then added:

"You will sit in that chair, in which I shall bind you, and not dare to speak or turn your head for the next hour. I shall be in waiting myself at the head of the staircase, and should assuredly hear you, and then it will become my duty to myself and others to put my threat into instant execution."

If avarice be a master passion, strong in death, or even with the prospect of decease, it is to be found in all its strength and mastership in a genteel lodging-house keeper.

"I—I 'found' the young lady," she gasped, in the midst of her fears; "I've only been paid a week's rent. I 'found' the young lady, and that, with a week's warning, makes three pounds seventeen and twopence."

Dick made no answer, but getting upon a chair, took down the bell-ropes, and the terrified landlady, being already seated in the arm-chair as he had directed, he proceeded to bind her therein with the cords he had so obtained.

One he tied round her neck, and then secured it in an elaborate manner to the legs of the chair, intimating to her at the same time that even when the hour had expired, if she made much effort at liberation, she would, in all probability, hang herself—a consummation which, he said, for his part, he devoutly wished.

The other rope he tied round her ankles, and then, passing it under the chair, secured it to the back, so that it would require a great deal more ingenuity than the genteel landlady possessed to have liberated anyone else under such circumstances had she herself been free.

Miranda was by this time ready to depart, and made her appearance in the front room.

"Now, madam," said Dick, "this lady will leave your house, and I shall keep guard at the head of the stairs—move or speak at your peril."

A half-stifled groan came from the terrified woman, and then Dick and Miranda left the room—the former locking the door on the outside, and putting the key in his pocket.

In a few moments they were in the street, when Dick Palmer said:

"Miss Rankley, I was nearly leading you into a great danger, but I hope I have rescued you from it. Here is money. Go into the first shop you come to, and purchase a shawl or some other article of wearing apparel, which shall be different from what you have on, for no doubt your dress has been accurately described by Varley to his numerous spies, who, I believe, are hunting over London in all directions."

As he spoke he placed some gold in Miranda's hand.

She was only able to thank him with an expressive glance, and, a draper's shop being near at hand, she purchased a large shawl, which, although far from being to her own taste, was probably all the better calculated for the purpose of concealment.

"As we are in the street, we will take a hackney-coach, and go and see Rowland Percy at once."

"Oh, I am thankful," said Miranda, with fervour, "for the slight mischance that has happened to procure me so much happiness. I shall see Rowland once again out of the gloom of a prison."

CHAPTER CXXII.

THE VISIT TO ROWLAND PERCY—THE WIDOW'S HOUSE—AN UNEXPECTED AND AWFUL DENOUEMENT.

THE street in which the kind-hearted widow, Mrs. Howell, lived—she with whom Rowland Percy found refuge—although not a very secluded one, was still sufficiently narrow and sufficiently quiet for any unusual circumstance in it to create a considerable degree of attention on the part of its inhabitants, who were ever ready, as is so generally the case in such localities, to pop their heads out of window on a very slight provocation.

Dick Palmer was well aware of this amiable peculiarity on the part of the dwellers in narrow streets towards the suburbs of the metropolis, so he would not, on any account, allow the coach, into which he had handed Miranda, to be driven to Mrs. Howell's door; but he ordered the driver to stop at the Catholic chapel in the Polygon, where he paid him, and saw him out of sight before he would walk with Miranda direct to Mrs. Howell's.

"You see, Miss Rankley," he remarked, "that, considering the vast size of London, you were not so very far from Mr. Percy. His place of concealment is in a street only a very short distance from where we now are. On any other occasion I should, perhaps, have advised you that the visit should be brief; but now, as you have come here in daylight, I think it would be more prudent for you to remain till the dusk of evening."

This was a pleasant and welcome piece of advice to Miranda. She knew that it was dictated by sincerity, and, consequently, she felt doubly grateful to find that it accorded so well with her heart's dearest wishes.

A long and confidential conversation with Rowland Percy was what she most ardently desired, as not once, since her father's death, had she been able to talk freely about the various circumstances that had occurred to separate them.

The longest interviews she had had with him were during his confinement at York, and then so many hopes and fears connected with his own actual position had pressed upon their attention, that no time had been spared for retrospective glances or anticipations of the future; but now, in her great faith in Dick Palmer's skill and management, the present did not appear to her mind so engrossing, and she wished to compare her own hopes of the future with those of Percy, from which free communion, perhaps, both of them might gather fresh courage and hope for the time to come.

Miranda trembled, and leant more heavily upon the arm of Dick Palmer, as she felt that each step drew her nearer to her heart's only treasure, for, since her father's death, there had been no one on whom she could expend any portion of her affection but Rowland Percy; he was the one sole tie that bound her to existence; it was the love of him that armed her with fortitude to bear the heavy trials she had passed through, and which had changed her, as Dick Palmer had truly remarked, from a timid, shrinking girl, to a heroine of romance—a heroine not surpassed in fortitude and noble courage by any that have figured in the world's great history.

"While you remain here," said Dick, as they neared the door, "I will find some other home for you of, I hope, a more agreeable character than the one you have just left. If it were prudent for you, under the circumstances, to become an inmate of this house, I should rejoice exceedingly, but, believe me, it is not. By you and Rowland living separately until the ardour of pursuit is abated, his danger will be considerably lessened. There are means of concealment for him which could not be made available for both of you; and although, if your residence in London was known to the whole world, no one could interfere with you, yet it might, you see, if you resided here, afford a dangerous clue to Mr. Percy's whereabouts."

"The idea," said Miranda, "did rise in my mind of how pleased I should be to be an inmate of the same house with Rowland, but I have dismissed it for the very reasons you have yourself urged upon me."

Dick cast a hasty glance about the street to ascertain if they were observed, and then he knocked lightly at the widow's door.

Mrs. Howell herself admitted him, and guessing in a moment who was his companion, took Miranda affectionately by the hand, and led her into the homely little parlour.

Oh, how delightful and full of excellence did that humble home seem to Miranda, since, beneath its roof was sheltered her lover, who had passed through so many dangers and vicissitudes of evil fortune.

We have always thought there is something in keeping between people and their houses, and that the one might be judged of by the other quite separately. It was particularly so with regard to Miranda's last place of abode, the mean gentility of which seemed only equalled by that of its landlady.

If Miranda was not struck by such a coincidence then, she was wonderfully so with it at Mrs. Howell's. The poor widow and her little neat parlour, about which there was no vain parade, seemed quite to be made for each other; there was none of the flimsy striving for effect, and flourish upon scanty means, that had characterized everything at the genteel house; but, oh, what a world of comfort and homely fireside enjoyment was there, instead of that cold attempt to be something, for which there were neither the means nor the mind.

The very fire threw out a warmer and kindlier beam than it did at the shabby-genteel lodging-house, over everything connected with which a moral winter seemed to reign, rendering what otherwise would have been cheering and pleasant, cold and drear.

And in what admirable keeping was the widow Howell herself with her home? One might look at her, and then, glancing round, feel assured that the cosy little apartment was hers, and that she had long had the ordering and management of its contents.

Dick Palmer could hardly have taken Miranda to a place more in unison with her feelings. It was a home which had produced kindly and gentle effects upon the saddened mind of Rowland Percy; for it must not be supposed that there always existed a necessity for his continuing in the place of concealment which had proved of such service to the widow's son.

Mrs. Howell's household consisted only of herself and a young girl, the daughter of a poorer neighbour, who was in the habit of coming in the morning as a domestic assistant, and going to her own home at night, so that, by a little management on the part of Mrs. Howell, the girl was got rid of at a much earlier hour than usual, and then Rowland could emerge from his place of concealment, and sit down by the fireside in the old-fashioned, but comfortable, little parlour.

Upon the whole, therefore, his abode at the widow's promised to be far less irksome than it had at first appeared; besides, she reasoned, rationally enough, that he might enjoy considerable liberty in the house without much fear for his safety, for she would say:

"You are much safer here, Mr. Percy, than was my poor boy; there was no place where a search would more naturally be made for him than in his mother's house; so that I was kept, and he, too, poor fellow, in a constant state of alarm; but it is different with you, you see, Mr. Percy, for there is nothing to point out my house as your hiding-place more than any one of all the thousands in London."

Rowland could not but assent to the justness of this reasoning; and, although he made up his mind always to retire to his place of concealment when a knock came at the door, yet he did so without any very great nervousness as to the result.

Then, it was soothing and pleasant to him to have such a one as Mrs. Howell to whom he could speak of Miranda, and who, kind soul, quite agreed—although she had never seen her—in every word Rowland uttered in praise of her.

"Oh, Mrs. Howell," he would say, "many and many a time I could have given up all human hope, and let them, innocent as I was, drag me to an instant and ignominious death, had it not been for that dear, better angel, who stepped between me and my rash resolves, winning me back, by her beauty and innocence, to better hopes, and a firmer reliance upon that Providence it was so sinful to doubt."

* * * *

It is not to be supposed that poor Miranda, oppressed with so many hopes and so many fears, could take the notice we have done of the widow and her home; but we ourselves love the picture of humble and cheerful poverty, as a contrast to the detestable shabby gentility of the house from which Miranda had just escaped so strangely.

"Cheer up," whispered Dick Palmer to Miranda; "you are looking pale and ill."

A languid smile played across Miranda's beautiful features, as she replied faintly:

"I believe it is the fault of my nature never to feel bold and confident, unless I am oppressed, or at war with someone. Surround me by friendly faces, let me hear kind voices making sweet music to my heart, and I know not why it is, but I then always wish for tears to relieve my sinking spirits."

"The feeling is natural."

"And yet I ought to be happy now—very, very happy."

"And I, too," said Palmer, "for at a busy time of the day, when I should not have advised you coming through the streets, I think we have succeeded in doing so in perfect safety."

This short conversation, spoken in a gentle voice, took place in far less time than it takes us to record it, and it was uninterrupted by Mrs. Howell, who was too intent upon gazing upon the beautiful face of Miranda, to attend to anything Palmer might be saying.

The widow was one of those rare females who can bear to look on female loveliness without a pang of envy, and she received real pleasure from the contemplation of the innocent beauty of Miranda, mingled as it was with an expression of nobility of soul, as rare as it is admirable.

"My dear young lady," she said, "you are Miss Rankley. I have heard sufficient of you to have pictured you in my own mind, and you are very much like that picture, only much more beautiful. Trust all to Heaven, my dear young lady, and, in the end, innocence must prevail."

"There was a time," said Miranda, "when to have heard words of kindness such as these being spoken to me in my forlorn and calamitous state, would have brought the ready tears to my eyes; but I have not wept since—since—since my poor father became no more."

"Now, my dear girl," said the widow, "do not distress yourself by mournful recollections. You have come here to have an uninterrupted and happy interview with one, of whom it is no slight praise to say, I think is deserving of you."

"Mrs. Howell," said Dick, for he saw that Miranda was distressed, and scarcely knew what to reply, "Mrs. Howell, I will leave Miss Rankley here until sunset, if you please, for it has become necessary for me to seek another lodging for her."

"Would to Heaven," said Mrs. Howell, "she could stay here altogether; but I quite understand how dangerous that would be. Why, bless you, my dear, with your sweet, innocent face, you would soon be the talk of the whole street, and then it might get to ears that we specially wish to keep it from."

"I am quite convinced," said Miranda; "quite—quite, and very thankful for all the kindness which is being shown to me."

"Miss Rankley," said Dick Palmer, "by Heavens, if I thought the world was so bad as not to contain many hearts that would truly sympathize with you, and admire your courageous conduct, I would not care how soon I left it. I will anticipate no danger while I am gone. Farewell! and Heaven protect you."

Dick Palmer left the house, and Mrs. Howell, after kindly assisting Miranda to take off her bonnet and shawl, seated her upon a sofa, and, after a few more gentle words, left the room.

Miranda's heart told her that the good woman's errand was to fetch Percy, and such was the excitement of her feelings, that, for a moment, every object swam before her.

Her heart beat with tumultuous emotion, as she sat, in a state of breathless agitation, with her eyes fixed upon the door.

In a few moments the door opened, and— Bernard Varley, the author of all her misfortunes, stood, with the smile of a fiend, upon the threshold!

CHAPTER CXXIII.

VARLEY'S PROPOSAL—DANGER THICKENS— THE MELEE AND THE SEARCH FOR ROWLAND.

To describe the surprise, mingled with terror, of Miranda, at the sudden and inexplicable appearance of Bernard Varley in the parlour of the widow, would be a hopeless task.

For a moment she actually doubted the evidence of her own senses, for she would have as little expected to see the apparition of someone who had been in life a thousand years before, at that moment, and in that place, as the man who had wrought her so much woe, and who still seemed following her with a determination and malice perfectly fiend-like.

An utter prostration of strength came over her; she felt like one, who, afflicted by a nightmare, tries to scream, but finds scarcely voice enough to utter the faintest sigh.

The various objects in the parlour seemed to whirl before her eyes, as if instinct with life.

By a strong effort, however, she kept herself from fainting, and then her frame slowly recovered from the shock it had received, and she became assured of the reality of the appearance before her.

It was, in truth, no other than Bernard Varley!

There could be no mistaking that ferocious, yet pale and haggard countenance, and those dark, lustrous eyes, that were bent upon her with a wild and fearful gaze, that seemed not of the earth.

Slowly he paced into the room, closing the door behind him, and turning the key in the lock.

He stood still within a few paces of her, but still he spoke not; nor could she command voice enough to call for help in that frightful emergency.

He folded his arms across his breast, and gazed with a deep earnestness in her face, as if it were a feast even to his eyes to look again upon so much loveliness.

When he did speak, it was in hoarse, guttural tones, as if he were making an effort to be calm, while a tempest of passion was raging in his breast.

"Miranda Rankley," he said, slowly drawing a watch from his pocket, and holding the dial before her face; "Miranda Rankley, do you note the hour?"

He pressed a spring, and, with a sweet, silvery chime—so much at variance with his own voice, and the harshness of his general demeanour, that Miranda might well shudder and start at the contrast—the repeater struck twelve; then the three-quarters past were proclaimed by the fairy-like bell within the rich encasement.

"Do you note the hour?" said Bernard Varley. "Miranda Rankley, do you note the hour?"

A cold chill struck Miranda's heart.

She felt as if something was about to happen, transcending all the miseries she had yet experienced—a blight seemed to have fallen upon her mind. She could see nothing but the dial of that watch, hear nothing but the echo of the soft sounds that had proclaimed the lapse of time.

"'Tis well," said Bernard Varley, "you feel my power. That power you have mocked at, Miranda Rankley. It has reached a fearful height—a height only equalled by yours. The life of Rowland Percy is in my hands. Miranda Rankley, it is likewise in yours. We two, and we two only, can save or destroy him."

Miranda sprang to her feet. The spell that entranced her faculties seemed broken.

"Help—help!" she cried. "Rowland—Rowland! help!"

"Ah—ah!" laughed Bernard Varley. "You but expedite the doom you might avert. This is no child's play—no affectation of doing something which will fail in its execution. My information is ample. Rowland Percy is concealed in this house; the door is watched by an emissary of mine. At one o'clock officers will be prepared for his apprehension. He cannot—cannot escape, unless—ay, unless—Do you note the time, Miranda Rankley? I ask again, do you note the time?"

A fearful thought rushed across Miranda's mind.

It was, that poor Rowland had been betrayed by the widow, and that, innocent though he was, he had been sacrificed for money.

Hope seemed extinguished for ever, and the appalling power of Bernard Varley rose giant-like before her imagination, for a time benumbing her faculties by its greatness.

With frightful rapidity her mind ran over all the circumstances of her position, and that process only served to augment the despair which was sufficiently depicted in her countenance.

"Monster!" she gasped; "is your soul dead to every spark of feeling? Bernard Varley, have you no compunctions for the past, that will now stay your murderous hand?"

"But ten minutes remain," said Bernard Varley. "Do you note the hour? I tell you again, his life is in my own hands. Give me—even now—your sacred promise, in the name of that Heaven which I know you hold so sacred, to become my wife, and I myself will open the door of this house, allowing Rowland Percy freely to walk forth, as well as providing him with ample means—carriages, horses, and faithful attendants, to convey him to the sea-coast, where he may embark on board a vessel of my own, and so ensure his safety. On the other hand there is an ignominious death, the writhings of a criminal at his execution, and he will be heralded to another world by the shouts and execrations of all who witness the painful and horrible death of the murderer! Miranda Rankley! Once more, do you note the time?"

Miranda clasped her hands.

"Heaven," she said, "has boundless mercy yet."

"You consent?" cried Varley, "you consent?"

"Never!"

The handle of the door was now turned by someone from without, and the voice of Rowland cried:

"Miranda!—Miranda!"

"Rowland!" she cried, "save yourself! Fly—fly—fly—Rowland—fly!"

"Ah! ah! ah!" said Varley, "for but one kiss from those pouting lips I will give him a chance to gain the street, and yet not fear to hunt him down. Miranda Rankley, are you mad in your wild obstinacy? His death, and the last shriek of his agony are upon your head."

"Fly—Rowland—fly!"

"YOU NOTE THE TIME!" CRIED BERNARD VARLEY, EXULTINGLY.

A heavy knock on the street-door at this moment resounded through the passage.

"You note the time!" cried Bernard Varley, exultingly. "Truly, they are more than punctual. You might have saved him, Miranda, but now——"

"Miranda—Miranda," cried the voice of Rowland again; "what is the meaning of this? Who is with you?"

"Ask not, but fly, Rowland, fly!" shrieked Miranda.

"'Tis I—Varley," cried the villain, in a loud, hoarse tone.

Bang went the knocker again, at the same moment that Rowland made a violent, but ineffectual effort, to burst open the door of the room.

"Even yet—even yet," said Varley, seizing Miranda so forcibly by the wrist that he left the mark of his fingers upon her fair skin; "even yet I can save him, if you consent. These are London officers, who know him not, and there is no one who can identify him but myself. Will you swear by all that you hold sacred to be mine?"

Bang went the parlour-door into fragments, and Mr. Jones, by the suddenness of his entrance, rolled on to the floor, as if he were performing a somersault.

"Wery good," he said, as, without rising, he

took hold of Varley by the ankles, and brought him down on his back, with a force that seemed enough to dislocate every bone in his body, not to speak of his head coming in contact with the fender, which it actually bent.

"Rowland!" cried Miranda, and in another moment she was in her lover's arms.

Tearing herself, then, from his embrace, she cried, in almost inarticulate accents:

"Save yourself, Rowland! Fly—fly—lose not a moment! They—they are coming—the officers—the officers. Fly, Rowland, fly! I implore, I entreat—Rowland, fly—fly!"

"Wery good advice," said Jones; "but don't think of flying out of the front door, for I'm blest if there isn't that immortal thief, Twitter, on the spy, and any fool can cry 'Stop him.'—Be quiet, will yer?"

This last remark was addressed to Varley, and was accompanied by such a punch on the jaw, that, added to the blow he had received on the back of the head, quite bewildered him.

"Cuss you," added Jones; "I've thought of a scheme."

Turning Varley upon his face, he sat down on the middle of his back, and Mr. Jones being no trifling weight, Varley was as effectually pinned down as a grasshopper with a pin through his back in the cabinet of an entomologist.

"Rowland, why delay a moment?" still cried Miranda. "Surely there must be some means of escape, so that you fly from here. You have been betrayed."

"As Heaven is my judge, not by me," said Mrs. Howell, wringing her hands and weeping bitterly.

"Gracious Heavens!" cried Rowland, "what can I do? I am helpless, save this last, only friend. In life they shall not take me."

He drew a pistol from his pocket, and at the same moment a voice shouted through the keyhole of the door:

"Open, open; 'tis I."

Rowland himself opened the door, and Dick Palmer, without a moment's pause, dragged his arm within his, saying:

"Away—away; come with me this instant. This house is watched, but I believe by one spy only. I have just knocked down Samuel Twitter, on the other side of the way, and while he lies insensible you may escape."

"Bravo!" said Jones; "here's t'other beauty, he's wriggling about like a blessed old snake, but it's no go. Be quiet, will yer?"

Jones took hold of the hair of Varley's head behind, and gave his nose two hard knocks against the floor, which appeared to have the desired effect, for Varley became quite quiet; he was, in fact, insensible for some short time.

Dick Palmer's conduct now became rather of a contradictory character, for after dragging Rowland Percy on to the step in the manner we have described, he as suddenly pulled him into the house again, banged the door shut, put up the chain, and shot two bolts into their sockets with marvellous rapidity.

"You've been betrayed, Mr. Percy," he said. "Four Bow Street officers have but this moment turned the corner of the street. All's up, I fear!"

"Rowland—Rowland, my Rowland!" cried Miranda, as she flung herself upon his neck.

"If my last hour has come," said Rowland Percy, "I will meet it like a man. Farewell, Miranda, may Heaven shower blessings on you. They may take me, but their triumph will be a poor one, for it shall be over the lifeless, and not over the living."

"Walker," said Jones; "never say die. You are worth a dozen stiff 'uns yet. I say, Mother What'soname, don't be wringing your hands and turning on the main there, come and sit on this gentleman's back, while I makes myself a little more active, and if you've got such a thing as a carving fork, just hold that in your hand, and jab it into him if he gets obstropulous. Is there a sky peeper atop of your roof?"

"He means a trap-door," said Palmer. "It is the only chance, poor though it be. We must not trust to the place of concealment you have in this house, Mrs. Howell. Whoever has betrayed Mr. Percy's residence here is most probably aware of that likewise—there——"

A loud rat-tat at the door announced the arrival of the officers.

"Vy don't you ring?" said Jones; "we never hears knocks here. Dicky, look arter affairs down below, while Mr. Percy and me tries what we can do through the trap."

"There is one," said Mrs. Howell. "Heaven speed you."

"Then go, Jones," said Palmer. "Do the best you can, and I will keep the officers out of the house for some time, at least."

Jones sprang to his feet.

Varley, with a deep groan, rolled over on to his back, but Dick took some cord from his pocket, and tied his hands, so that he could make no use of them. The shock that he had received in his fall made him too confused to feel the necessity for calling out for help.

Another loud appeal to the knocker announced the impatience of the officers; and, after a few kind words, Miranda and Rowland parted again in circumstances of greater trouble and danger, probably, than they had ever experienced before.

"Come into the parlour, everybody," said Palmer, "and we will leave these gentlemen outside to get in as best they may. You, Miss Miranda, they will not interfere with. If I escape—which I intend trying, although the chance is small—I will meet you to-night, at nine o'clock, in Whitehall, opposite the Horse Guards—you can easily inquire your way; but, on your road there, be careful you are not watched. Go down one of the streets in the Strand, get into a boat, and cross the river; take a coach on the other side, and drive to Whitehall, and be sure you are not observed. Here is money; and now, Mrs. Howell, remember you know nothing about

Mr. Percy, but merely had a young man lodging here, whose name you believe to be Smith, and that just now you can't open the door to the officers, because you are coerced by me."

The knocking at the door by this time was perfectly furious, so noisy, in fact, as to drown all further conversation.

Poor Miranda sat down, looking as pale as one newly risen from the dead, while Bernard Varley gazed vacantly around him, like a man half asleep, and not able to distinguish realities from visions.

With amazing strength and quickness, Dick Palmer drew some heavy pieces of furniture to block up the doorway, and constructed a very tolerable barricade.

He then darkened the room by drawing the curtains close, and scarcely were his arrangements completed when a harsh grating noise at the outer door proclaimed that it was being forced from its hinges.

"They are using crowbars," said Dick Palmer; "but yet it will be some time before they can gain an entrance, and moments are like drops of blood to Mr. Percy."

CHAPTER CXXIV.

THE ESCAPE OF PALMER—THE TRAP-DOOR IN THE ROOF—JONES' ADMIRABLE SCHEME, AND TOTAL DEFEAT OF THE OFFICERS.

THE officers worked with might and main to gain an entrance into the widow's house, for visions of the thirteen hundred pounds reward were vividly present to their imaginations, and so therefore they were not very scrupulous about breaking through a door, provided they could share so very desirable an amount among them.

The alarm in the street was tremendous, and a dense crowd was rapidly collecting.

The rumour ran from mouth to mouth that a dreadful murder had been committed at the widow's, and the excitement was each moment on the increase, when the officers succeeded in dashing open the door, and rushing into the passage.

The moment they did so, Dick Palmer, without much noise, opened one of the parlour-windows as far as it would go, and got upon the ledge, in a crouching attitude.

It looked a fearful leap to clear the area-rails, but to hesitate was not a part of Dick's nature, and before a cry of alarm could arise from the multitude, he took the spring, and alighted safely upon the pavement.

His danger, however, was not over; for, before he could advance above half-a-dozen steps, he was collared by several of the mob, who, seeing him make such a singular exit from the house, at once believed him to be the person of whom the officers were in pursuit.

"Thank you," said Dick, calmly, "but you are mistaken, my good friends. Catch the right man, if you please, but don't impede me. We want more force, and I must be off to Bow Street as fast as possible."

As he spoke he took from his pocket the constable's staff he had wrested from the officer in the back passage in the "Star and Tinder-Box."

"Hurrah!" shouted the mob, as they let him go. "Be off with yer. We'll take care nobody gets out. Who's murdered?"

"A woman and six children," said Dick Palmer; "and, added to it, is the most desperate swindle ever conceived."

In a moment or two he was out of sight, and the officers, little suspecting that one of their victims had escaped them, placed one of their number as a sentinel upon the door-mat, whilst the others commenced busily removing the articles of furniture with which Palmer had barricaded the parlour-door.

This was soon accomplished, as, of course, there was no resistance offered from the inside, and, to the disappointment of the officers, they at first saw no persons but Mrs. Howell and Miranda.

In a moment, however, they pounced upon Varley, who, having a chair overturned upon him, they thought was one of their prisoners, making an insane and stupid attempt to conceal himself.

He was recognized, however, the moment they raised him to his feet, for there was not one of the principal officers of Bow Street whom Varley had not himself seen and conversed with upon the subject of Rowland Percy's apprehension.

"Mr. Varley," cried one, "is it you, sir?"

Varley glared about him like a madman, and then espying Miranda he cried, in hoarse and terrible accents:

"Tremble, Miranda Rankley, for this day's work shall lie at your door; you are in my power, if others have escaped. Search the house—death and fury! search the house. Leave not a hole or corner unexplored. A hundred pounds on the spot to him who first lays hands on the convicted murderer or any of his associates. I—I—I—curses on them all—they've nearly killed me!"

He reeled and sank into a chair as he spoke.

His brain was much bewildered by the usage he had received; and his sudden energy was merely the result of a burst of passion, which had lent him a momentary strength.

"You hear that man?" said Miranda Rankley, appealing to the officers. "I charge you to take notice of the threats he makes use of towards me, as I may choose to make them a subject of inquiry. Bernard Varley, with indignation and contempt, I defy you! Heaven preserve Rowland Percy from your machinations!"

The officers knew not what to make of this strangely recriminatory conversation; and having satisfied themselves that neither of the men they came to seek were then in the parlour, they hastily proceeded to search the house.

Their information must have been tolerably precise, for they at once proceeded to that part of the room above them, where was the sliding panel, which, after some difficulty, they succeeded in opening, although, to their great chagrin, they found nothing but one old chair, which just fitted into the narrow space between the two walls.

"Here's the nest," said one, "but the bird's flown. We are done as safe as ninepins, and I'll be hanged if I didn't think we should be, when I heard the Slashing Squire had something to do with the business. He's an out-and-out fellow that—I've often told Sir Richard that he'd make a splendid police officer."

"Never despair," said another; "let's search the house thoroughly; hilloa! what's this?"

Lying upon the stairs leading to the upper story, was a small step-ladder, and the officers were too used to escapes of all kinds not to feel at once assured that it had been used in reaching a trap-door at the top of the house.

"We have him now," they cried, and upon arriving at the head of the staircase, they saw that the trap-door admitted a beam of light, thus giving clear evidence of having been recently disturbed.

They immediately placed the step-ladder against the opening, and felt quite certain they should find those they sought on the roof of the house.

They all three ascended with great rapidity.

No sooner had the last man disappeared through the narrow opening, than Jones walked out from the front-attic, and, ascending the ladder, he, without a word, shut the trap-door, and firmly bolted it within.

"Just wait there till you are wanted, my tulips," he remarked; "it's a fine airy situation, and will do you a vorld of good—you can make speeches to the mob from the blessed parapet, for as these ere houses are built, blow me if you can get into any of the attic windows—out-and-out knowing blades these ere officers is, to be sure. Come along, Mr. Percy, but mind your eye, for there's one on 'em downstairs, seeing as there's only three been so obliging as to get on to the roof."

Rowland Percy, with a pistol in his hand, appeared from the attic.

"Escape must be impossible. Save yourself, Jones, and risk no more on my account."

"Gammon," said Jones. "Stow that ere guffery, and foller me. Never say die. I tells yer what you'd better do, Mr. Percy. Walk down to the first floor, and just stay in the room till we sees what will happen next."

"I will obey your directions, although I am altogether hopeless;" and the two descended the staircase together.

The street-door was not broken entirely off its hinges, and the officer who was left on guard there thought it his wisest plan to shut it as close as he could, so that if anyone was to attempt to rush past him, their manœuvre would be foiled.

So there he stood with his staff in his hand, looking as vigilant as half-a-dozen officers rolled into one, reckoning up in his own mind

what a windfall his share in the rewards would be, and cursing his luck for not having a chance of the hundred pounds down upon the nail in addition.

Mr. Jones and Percy of course reached the landing without any hindrance.

"Just step into the back-room for a moment," said Jones; "it's hit or miss."

Rowland obeyed him, and then Jones took a sudden run about half-way down the staircase, when he pretended to see the officer for the first time, and exclaiming, "Lor! I'm nabbed!" ran nimbly up again.

Now, if Bernard Varley had not been so ready with the offer of his hundred pounds, in addition to the high rewards already heaped upon poor Rowland Percy's head, the officer would, in all likelihood, have remained where he was, with perfect confidence that his companions above stairs would catch the man who had so suddenly appeared, and run off again.

That extra hundred pounds, however, did the business, and he darted upstairs after Jones like lightning—a measure which Mr. Jones was, in his own mind, devoutly wishing and expecting.

"Come, my fine fellow," cried the officer, rushing into the room after him, "no nonsense."

"Not the least little bit," said Jones, as, stepping from behind the door, he dealt the officer such a tremendous facer, that the officer reeled again.

The advantage of a first blow between two strong men is immense, and, in this case, it was everything, for Jones took care to follow it up by another, which he denominated "a stunner," that sent the officer sprawling, and deprived him of all sense and consciousness.

"That'll do," said Jones. "There's a muff.—Mr. Percy, now for it—a clear stage, and no favour. I think we've nothing to do but to walk out, take it easy, and nobody will suspect us. Where the deuce is your hat?"

"I really don't know," said Rowland.

"Then take this 'ere," remarked Jones, pointing to the officer's hat, which had rolled on to the landing. "Yet, stop a minute. There's such a blessed crowd in the street, that some officious fellow will be stopping us—I have thought of a move."

He possessed him, in a moment, of the officer's staff, and, collaring Rowland in a very scientific manner, he added:

"Now, come on! Mind, you are in custody."

When they reached the door in this manner, there was such a shout from the crowd, that Rowland involuntarily shrank back for a moment, but Jones pulled him down the steps, saying, "Kim on, yer warmint, no shying," and he held the staff in a very threatening manner close to Rowland's nose—to the immense delight of the mob, who cheered again vociferously.

It was pleasant to see the three officers on the roof making what appeared to be, from their gestures, highly inflammatory speeches to the mob, scarcely a word of which, however, was heard by those below, in consequence of the uproar in the street.

"A coach—a coach!" cried Jones; "a tanner for a coach—now, then, yer cripples, be quick!"

Nearly one-half of the mob ran for a coach, while the remainder set up a tremendous hoot of execration at Rowland, the supposed murderer of the woman and six children; and Jones kept making him wink again by flourishing the constable's staff in his face.

Before the coach arrived, a very fat man, in a tremendous perspiration, bustled on to the step of the door, carrying in his hand a huge painted constable's staff.

"Hilloa! have you caught the willain? I'm a constable in my own right, and landlord of the 'Magpie and Stump.' Have yer cotched the willain?"

"Yes, little 'un," said Jones. "Will you lend us your vescoat for a great coat? How are you off for tallow?"

The constable in his own right looked rather amazed at this sally, which greatly amused the mob, who thought Jones a capital fellow, and a most enterprising officer.

One of the officers on the roof now raised his voice to an extraordinary pitch, so that the people below heard the words:

"Somebody's bolted——" but nothing else.

"Well," said Jones, looking up, "why don't you bolt arter 'em, instead of speechifying up there. Pretty gemmens you is. Just step over, and I'll give you a leg down."

"The trap!" shouted one of the officers, swinging his arms about like the sails of a windmill.

"Wery good," said Jones. "They've found a trap up there—there's a discovery! They only want a bat, and either of them's capable of getting up a ball at a moment's notice."

At this moment, escorted by an immense crowd, as if it had been some wonderful natural curiosity, the hackney-coach arrived.

"Now, jarvey," said Jones, "just crawl down with all them ere wonderful coats of yourn, and open the door. This chap's like an eel as I've got hold on."

"Stop the murderer!" shouted one of the officers from the roof of the house, getting very red in the face from the exertion.

To this Mr. Jones replied with such an admirable imitation of the braying of an ass, that the mob, in its intense satisfaction, would have let off anybody.

In the desperation of their rage, the officers took the ill-advised step of throwing their hats upon the heads of the mob, which, of course, produced a retaliation in the shape of stones; so that in a few moments they were forced to disappear altogether—two of them hiding behind the chimney-pots, and the third lying flat in the gutter.

"Vere to?" said the coachman, as he banged the door.

"To Bow Street," said Jones, and off they went amid the cheers of the assembled multitude.

CHAPTER CXXV.

ROWLAND PERCY'S PLACE OF REFUGE—THE SECOND FLOOR OF THE "STAR AND TINDER-BOX,' DRURY LANE.

WHEN the hackney-coach containing Percy and Jones had got thoroughly clear of the mob, and was about half-way to Bow Street, the latter pulled the check-string.

The coachman stopped and looked inquiringly through one of the glasses.

"We won't trouble you to go quite so far, old brick," said Jones. "Charge your full fare, and we'll get out here."

This was an arrangement to which the coachman was not at all likely to object, so he rolled off his box and opened the coach-door, permitting, if he had but known it, thirteen hundred pounds to slip through his fingers as comfortably as possible; but Providence was merciful, and the jarvey never did know it, or, Heaven knows what desperate act he might have committed upon the horror of discovering such a loss.

Thus, then, was the hunted and persecuted Percy in the streets of London—free, certainly, but still surrounded by dangers—dependent for food, shelter, and sympathy, upon strangers, with a price set upon his capture, that would have tempted many a sleek, well-fed, highly moral man in the world's opinion, to have surrendered him to death.

But such men as Jones and Palmer certainly do not set that high and startling value upon money which many persons do. They are accustomed to the extremes of affluence and poverty, they make no calculations for the future; they are not hoarding for this or that particular object, and the temptation to betray Rowland for money certainly did not present itself very strongly to either of them.

"Vell," said Jones. "here we is. Now I tells you what, Mr. Percy, it strikes me as the safest place you can go to now, is the 'Star and Tinder-box.' It's been out-and-out rummaged by the officers, and they have made up their minds that you are not there. Give them the double, say I, and go there now. The nearer to the church, they say, the further from the great Being what rules everything; and if a gentleman of the road, or a cracksman wants to hide, I am convinced it ought to be very near Bow Street."

"Ignorant of London, as I am," said Rowland Percy, "and utterly destitute of resources, I am but too thankful to you that you will guide my steps."

"Wery good," said Jones; "but don't guv up jist yet. It's a wery extensive out of town thoroughfare as hasn't a turning; and some of these ere days it will be Percy's riz and Varley's fell."

"This is but a sad life to lead," said Rowland, mournfully. "If poor Miranda and I could leave England, perhaps, after all, it would be our best plan. By the exercise of our unfettered industry in some foreign land, we should no longer be a burden upon those kind friends who have already done so much for us."

"Burden, be bothered," said Jones. "This here's the state of the case. Society hunts you about, here and there, and round and about, just like a dog in a fair, because they fell into a mistake that you smothered an old gentleman. Now that ere is a blunder of society, 'cause you knows you didn't."

"As Heaven is my judge, I am innocent."

"Stow that, I knows it. Well, in course, if individuals makes blunders they has to pay for 'em: so as society won't let you get your living, Dicky and I means to make 'em keep you. Lor! bless you, two or three good family jobs will keep us all like game-cocks for a twelvemonth. But here we are in Holborn. Just step out, and we'll be housed in the 'Star and Tinder-Box' in something under ten minutes."

How would Rowland Percy, a few short months before, have scorned, as an affront upon his understanding, a prophecy that he would have been indebted for his means of existence to the indiscriminate depredations of a housebreaker and a highwayman, and yet circumstances were now such that he could almost invent excuses to himself for so doing, and, at all events, if he had rejected such aid, he must have become a beggar in the public streets, and, most probably, a far greater social evil would have been perpetrated by his apprehension and execution upon a charge of which he was innocent.

Unwelcome to his mind, and startling to all his previous notions, as was the proposition, he began almost to think with Jones and Dick Palmer, that criminality was scarcely anything of itself, but a circumstance altogether dependent upon other circumstances for its complexion.

Rowland Percy, however, required the lesson he was receiving in the rude school of adversity before such a sentiment could have entered into his brain; but now he said to himself:

"If once the cloud which hangs over me and my fortunes should dissipate, and I should once more attain that position in society from which I have been so roughly driven, I shall look with a kindlier eye upon human frailties, and upon that sad class of humanity called criminal by its fellows. I shall ever be tempted to look deeper than the crime itself, and endeavour to ascertain what circumstances have given rise to it, always remembering that in my own misfortunes the principal sympathy I met with was from persons amenable to the laws, and that every piece of bread I put into my mouth was part of the produce of a robbery."

The 'Star and Tinder-Box' was reached some minutes before the time Jones had mentioned.

With all speed Jones conducted Rowland Percy through the narrow back entrance, which terminated at the door leading into the landlord's little private room behind the bar, at which he gave a peculiar knock, which was immediately answered with the loudly expressed question of:

"Hilloa! what's the dodge?"

"The old caper," said Jones.

"I have a gentleman's fancy, fair and free;
  The 'Star and Tinder-Box' does for me,
When I'm out on a rollicking, roaring spree.
                 Tooraloo, slash away."

The door was opened, and the landlord, shading his eyes with his hands, said:

"Walker's the dodge for five minutes."

"Scooped out?" said Jones.

"Tow-row," rejoined the landlord, and the door was immediately shut.

"Will he not admit us?" whispered Rowland.

"Yes, suttenly; but didn't yer hear him? He said it wasn't safe for five minutes, 'cos somebody was lounging about the bar as he didn't know, but rather suspected."

"Oh," said Rowland, "I certainly did not understand the singular little bit of dialogue which you exchanged."

"Defects of edication," said Jones, "isn't people's own faults. If you doesn't understand all that the English langivedge can do, it's yer broughtins up, and not you, that should have a hit in the eye for that 'ere neglect."

"Flicks, away," said the landlord, opening the door.

"Crush the downy," said Jones, and taking Rowland by the arm, he led him into the little bar parlour.

The landlord immediately opened another door, leading to an inner room, of tolerably ample dimensions, which, from the general decorations and furniture, was evidently used for what are called convivial purposes, although at that time of the day it was completely empty.

The landlord further secured this room from interruption by locking a door which led into the passage, and was the usual entrance; after which, turning to Jones and Percy, he said:

"What's the row now?"

"You knows him?" said Jones, pointing to Percy.

"I does," said the landlord. "That is Mr. Percy. They've put a good price on you, sir, and, upon my word, I think it's imprudent of you to be walking about in this way."

"In course it is," said Jones; "but what's a chap to do when he's bowled out? The hawks have been down upon him. He was as near nabbed as possible, and the last nest is a great deal too hot to hold him. Now, there's been a thorough hunt in every hole and corner of the 'Star and Tinder-Box,' so it strikes me now outrageous forcible, that this is his safest place."

"It's hard to say," replied the landlord; "but if you like to stay here, we'll do the best we can for you; and, for Dick Palmer's sake, you shall be as welcome as flowers in May."

"Hasn't Dicky been here?" said Jones.

"No."

"Then he will show up soon, for he's had to make an extraordinary cut of it himself. The grabs are sharp after him, and he'll have to make up his mind uncommon clear what he's going to do next."

"In truth, as far as I am concerned," answered Percy, in reply to the landlord, "I'm thankful for any shelter, proscribed and hunted as I am. If you'll permit me to remain here until I decide upon some line of conduct, I shall be your debtor for a great kindness."

"Oh, never think of that," said the landlord; "It's quite understood among us all that you didn't do the murder. We decide upon those things much better than juries, and we all of us feel as certain that Bernard Varley murdered Sir George Rankley, as if we had seen him do it."

"In truth, your opinion coincides with my own," said Percy, "and I am scarcely more assured of my own innocence, than I am of his guilt. Heaven help the innocent Miranda, and save her from his machinations."

"Wery good," said Jones. "And now let's come upstairs, for that's the place to hide in."

The second floor of the "Star and Tinder-Box" consisted of a number of rooms, connected with each other by so many doors, that had it not possessed numerous hiding-places, in the shape of curious closets and cupboards, a more admirable place to play hide-and-seek could scarcely have been found ; and it would require someone exceedingly intimate with the localities to run the slightest chance of successfully pursuing anyone through such a labyrinth.

"Now," said the landlord, turning to Rowland, "we've been searched here once, and we may be again. I can't put you into a hiding-place where you can lay down on your back, and take your chance to see if you are found. We never tried to get up such a thing here, and, if we had, I don't think we could have done it. Yet, notwithstanding all that, many a chap that's been hard pushed has held out for weeks together on this second floor."

"Ah, I knows it," said Jones. "There was Conkey Joe, as stopped somewhere by Kennington a parson feller, as they calls a wicker, and took nigh a thousand pounds out of his pocket, besides putting him in what they call bodily fear. Well, Mr. Percy, this here wicker got wicious, and, arter cussing Conkey Joe as none but a wicker could cuss him, he offers five hundred pound to anyone who could grab him. Well, Conkey Joe was hard pushed, and he comes here, and the grabs searched this here floor three times, and went into every hole and corner of it, but Conkey Joe guv them the go-by."

"So he did," said the landlord ; "so he did. And you must do it the same way, or no ways at all, Mr. Percy."

"What way's that?"

"Why, the rooms go in and out of each other curious, and the only way was, first of all, to get into a cupboard of one of the further ones, and wait there till they have poked their noses into some of the outer ones. The caper then is, to know the rooms well, and double upon the officers as they are going through them, by which means you get into one of the cupboards they have searched, where they are not at all likely to look again."

"That's the way Conkey Joe did it," said Jones ; "three times the officers passed him in a cupboard at the head of the stairs, the door of which he left ajar, but then they knowed they'd looked into it afore, and never dreamed of wasting time by a second search."

"Then," said Rowland, "I must run that risk for the present, or, at all events, until I see my friend Palmer, under whose guidance I have placed myself, and upon whose judgment I have so firm and entire a reliance."

"Come on, then," said the landlord; "keep your eyes about you, and I'll walk you through the rooms to show you how you may manage the doubling dodge should there be occasion for it."

Rowland saw that the scheme was practicable, although certainly attended with great risks.

He followed the landlord through the various apartments, taking the most careful notice of each, and as he did so, he was perfectly amazed at the multitude of cupboards and little secret places with which that floor abounded.

"No one comes up here," said the landlord, "and although there are several bedrooms, as you perceive, we do not let any of them. This floor is specially kept for private use, and I only hope it may serve your turn as well as it has others."

"Mind," said Jones, "if you should be forced to come the double upon the grabs here take off your shoes, and slip along without them, for the least sound would be ekal to your death-warrant."

"I shall be very cautious," replied Rowland, "but I do not believe I shall be here long. It seems to be my fate to be hunted from place to place, and since I have left York I have had so many hair-breadth escapes that I believe I am almost getting reckless, and care not what I do."

"Reckless—nonsense," cried Jones; "recollect your young woman, and if you don't care for yourself, keep up a stout heart for her sake."

"Bah," said the landlord, "people with ropes round their necks shouldn't think about young women."

"Don't be making yourself a ass now," said Jones, "by talking about what you don't understand. You knows nothing about it, so jest hold yer mag. As for me I shall wait here till Dicky comes, which won't be long, I guess. I do long to know from somebody how them ere fellows got off the roof, and I believe I must make an expedition to-night to Somers Town to find out the blessed particulars. Oh, that was a go! I think I sees 'em now a preaching from that ere blessed parapet, and the out-an-out congregation pelting them with stones like mad. Then there was the feller, too, that took care of the street door, and thought himself so cunning—Lor! bless you, some people is very green!"

The tinkling of a little bell on the landing stopped Mr. Jones in his felicitations, and the landlord immediately said:

"I am wanted below. Mr. Percy, I must leave you to take care of yourself; only if I should have any unwelcome visitors, I'll take good care to let you know in time."

CHAPTER CXXVI.

MIRANDA'S ESCAPE FROM VARLEY—MOB SYMPATHIES AND THEIR RESULTS—A DESPERATE CONFLICT.

IT was some time after Jones and Percy had left Mrs. Howell's house that the officers got liberated from their disagreeable position on the roof, which chivalrous feat was executed by the fat landlord of the "Magpie and Stump," who boasted so much of being a constable in his own right, and who had been so very unceremoniously put down by Jones.

They then pretty accurately guessed the state of things below, and, having learned from their stupefied comrade, who was lying with a most dolorous aspect where Jones had thrown him, what had happened, as far as he was concerned, they gave up the affair, for the time being, as hopeless, feeling all the intense mortification of men who have allowed themselves to be thoroughly outwitted in quite a professional matter, and, with the additional aggravation, as in the present case, that the reward of success would have been so great.

They looked at each other with the most ludicrous and dolorous expression.

"Well," said one, "we three have lost our hats, which I don't know what in the world induced us to throw them among the mob; but we are better off than Godfrey, for he seems to have lost his nose—at least, it won't be near the feature it was."

"And my staff, too," said Godfrey; "I can't find it anywhere; but we will arrest the woman of the house as an accessory to the escape of our prisoners."

"There now, you spoke in a hurry," said the oldest and most experienced of the party; "if anybody had told me as I should have been such an ass as to get on the roof of a house without securing my retreat, I shouldn't have believed him. I did it, though, and there's an end of it. I knew we were done the moment I heard the bolt shot underneath. Now, take my advice; come away, and don't say anything about the affair. We can plant a spy upon this house, and it's odd to me but something will come of it; but, for my sake, don't let it get wind that there's been such a regular do."

A moment's consideration convinced the others that this was a proper view to take of the subject, and, although it diminished not a bit of their vexation, they acceded to the proposition, and walked in a body down the staircase, in order to put it in immediate execution.

It was some few minutes before the officers arrived at this sage conclusion, that Miranda thought she would leave the house, for the presence of Bernard Varley was a source of great annoyance to her; and, although she despised him as much as her gentle heart could despise anyone, yet she could not but look with fear upon the dark, scowling countenance, and the wild, glaring eyes that were fixed upon her face.

Her slight movement towards the door, however, seemed to rouse Varley from the moody reverie into which he had fallen, and, springing to his feet, he opposed her passage, saying:

"No, Miranda; with pain, toil, trouble, and expense, I have sought you, and found you—we part not again thus easily."

"Murderer of my father!" cried Miranda, "what right have you to bar my progress?"

"Call me what you will," cried Varley, "heap whatever charges on my head your imagination may suggest to you—I have found you, Miranda, and I will cling to your very shadow."

"Villain!" said Miranda, "you dare not. I will pass were you ten times the monster you are. Raise against me your guilty hands if you dare!"

"Hold!" cried Varley, "another step, and you are in my arms. Ah! ah! ah! It would be ample payment for all I have suffered, to grasp, even for a moment, such peerless charms. Advance, Miranda, advance. Welcome—welcome!"

Miranda shrank back instinctively, and, at that moment, the officers appeared in the passage.

"What's this?" cried one. "What's this?"

"I claim protection," cried Miranda, "against this man—this villain—Bernard Varley. You are men, and be you whom or what you may, you cannot have such hearts as his. I claim your protection from him. Why should he prevent me going forth?"

"Oh, Mr. Varley, is it you?" said the senior officer. "What's the young woman done?"

"I answer no questions," answered Varley, furiously, "and ask them at your peril."

"Come—come!" said the landlord of the "Magpie and Stump." "What's the row? Mrs. Howell, what's the matter? You have your beer of me, Mrs. Howell, and I am sure you are quite a respectable woman. Ahem! What's the matter, ma'am?"

"This young lady," said Mrs. Howell, "is a friend of mine, and on a visit to me. How this man "—pointing to Varley—"came into my house, I know not, but surely I can make him leave it?"

"Ah, to be sure," said the landlord. "Not a doubt—not a doubt. What a thing it is to have a constable in his own right in the street. A precious vagabond he looks. There's not a jury in England, Mrs. Howell, that wouldn't have him hung on the least suspicion. Count your silver spoons, Mrs. Howell, and if you find one missing, I'll take him into custody directly. Hilloa — hilloa! No resistance! Hilloa—hilloa! Somebody outside there run to the 'Magpie and Stump,' and tell my big pot-boy, Tom, to come here. He'll collar the warmint, while I make the end of my staff acquainted with his ribs."

"Miranda Rankley," said Varley, "while you stay here, I stay here—there!" stepping aside. "Your passage out is free, but I will follow you as closely as your shadow."

"Gracious Heavens!" cried Miranda. "Can I have no protection from this man?"

"Lots—lots!" cried the constable in his own right. "We've no half measures here. Everything tip-top, with a head on it."

"Mr. Varley," said one of the officers, "I think you had better leave the young lady alone."

"You think," said Varley, with ineffable scorn; and, crossing his arms upon his breast, he leaned back against the door-post with apparently quite a fixed determination of carrying out his declared intention.

"Come, toddle," cried the constable in his own right, flourishing his staff. "Just move your long legs out of this place; we can't have you here, you know. You had better make a virtue of necessity, and go before my great pot-boy, Tom, comes. There's the 'Magpie and Stump' at the end of the street. You look thirsty. Why don't you go and stay there? Barclay and Perkins' entire; genuine wines and neat compounds. The celebrated house for a glass of stout and fine cordial gin. Come, don't be a fool."

"You'll get yourself into a mess, master constable," said one of the officers; "you can't turn him out unless he's given in charge to you on suspicion of being here to commit a felony, or the occupier of the house attempts to do it, and he resists—that's the law."

"Blow the law," said the landlord; "what's the use of a constable?"

"None at all when he's such an overgrown porpoise as you are."

"Heaven and earth! where's my pot-boy, Tom?"

"And do you mean to tell me," said Mrs. Howell, "that I, a weak woman, am to risk a blow from that ruffian, in an attempt to put him from my house, while all you men stand by, and lend me no assistance?"

The officers looked at each other rather curiously at this appeal, and Miranda stepping forward, said firmly:

"I will end this difficulty; I have heard that the slightest touch is sufficient to constitute an assault in law."

"Certainly," said the officers, "if Mr. Varley touches you, miss, you can give him in custody."

Miranda stepped boldly forward, and he shrank back, and allowed her to pass out.

Varley then darted after her, and reached the step of the door at the same moment.

Miranda was in despair.

Where to go, or what to do, she knew not; and there stood Varley, with his fierce, sparkling eyes fixed upon her face, as if he would read her very soul, while a triumphant expression spread itself over his features as he perceived the dilemma in which she was.

The crowd in the street was still very great, and Miranda's beauty became in a moment the theme of universal admiration.

A sudden thought struck her that she might succeed in ridding herself of Varley by throwing herself upon public sympathy.

A flush of colour gradually spread itself over her pale countenance, and her agitation as she began to speak, was painfully observable.

The mob seemed intently interested in what she was about to say, and a dead silence ensued while she spoke the following words:

"Good people, I am an orphan, and, at this moment, friendless. This man," pointing to Varley, "who, I believe, from my heart, to be the murderer of my father, threatens to pursue me wherever I may go, because I will not receive his fulsome addresses. Is there a father, a brother, or a pitying heart in this crowd that will step between me and his dreadful oppression?"

A great shout arose from the crowd, and Miranda descended to the pavement.

Varley made an effort to follow her, and then a tremendous rush took place, headed by a gigantic dustman, with a short pipe in his mouth, who pushed himself between Varley and Miranda, crying:

"Take it easy, my little wench—take it easy. We'll soon clear out this ere bin. Well, my grand Turk, what now?"

Varley tried to dodge him, but the effort was in vain, and he only got his toes desperately trodden on by the dustman, while Miranda was each moment increasing her distance from the house, pushing through a lane of the people, who were cheering vociferously, while the constable in his own right was standing on his tip-toes, making a very eloquent harangue, which nobody heard a word of, and getting dreadfully red in the face, from the depth of the sentiments he was uttering.

Rage got the better of all discretion in the breast of Varley, and he seized the collar of the dustman with both hands, dashing his pipe out of his mouth in the effort.

He might, however, as well have tried to shake a great tree by laying hold of its trunk as to move the mass of bone and muscle opposed to him, and he became soon painfully aware that dustmen wore dreadful heavy shoes, for he received a kick on the shins that made him release his hold in a moment, and execute quite a dance in his agony, of course, to the intense gratification of the mob, which unfeelingly laughed, like a great hyena.

Then the fat landlord, having arrived at a climax in his discourse, which might possibly call for such movement, gave Varley a push behind, which sent him right among the mob.

Then someone bonneted him, another kicked him, and another cuffed him.

Several women, of more energy than gentility, scratched his face, and he was hustled about so dreadfully, that in the course of five minutes he had but half a coat and no cravat, and was in such a state of rags and bewilderment, that, although he fought like a maniac, he must soon have dropped from sheer exhaustion, had not the officers rushed to his rescue.

Four men acting together will do wonders, even in a dense crowd, which is always a dis-organized body; and the officers succeeded in a very few minutes in reaching Bernard Varley, who, more dead than alive, fell into their arms, and was conveyed into the very "Magpie and Stump" he had been advised originally to go to by the fat landlord; an advice, could he have foreseen what was to have occurred, it would have been so much better to have followed than disregarded.

— —

CHAPTER CXXVII.

THE DEATH OF MR. PERCY—OFFICIAL IN-DIFFERENCE, AND MIRANDA'S DESPAIR.

FOR the first time, Miranda found herself utterly alone in the streets of the mighty city, whither she had come for refuge from a series of persecutions unparalleled in private life, and the endurance of which, as she had en-dured them, should certainly make her a heroine of no ordinary character.

At first, of course, her feelings were of a pleasurable character, because she was hasten-ing away from the dreaded presence of Ber-nard Varley; and she had seen him, in whose safety she was so deeply interested, escape from, perhaps, the greatest danger to which he had hitherto been exposed.

A pleasant feeling of excitement pervaded her frame as she walked rapidly through the streets, heedless of what direction she was taking, so long as she increased her distance from Varley, who she little suspected was re-ceiving such rough usage at the hands of the mob on which she had called for sympathy.

She walked onwards for about an hour, and then feeling wearied and exhausted, she slackened her pace, and stood gazing with admiration, not unmingled with awe, at a massive and splendid cathedral, which spread itself out far and wide before her eyes.

To her left she saw, what she supposed to be, the river Thames, spanned by an ancient bridge, on which was such a mass of people and carriages, moving along in regular order, that she could not but believe that some extra-ordinary circumstance had just occurred, or was about to happen.

But most of all did the venerable pile with its splendid architecture attract her steadfast gaze; and so little acquainted with London was Miranda Rankley, that she could only hazard a guess that it was the ancient and noble Abbey of Westminster upon which she gazed.

A clock at the moment struck three, and, with a sigh, she asked herself what she was to do with herself for the six hours that were to intervene before she could meet Dick Palmer according to the appointment that he had made with her; then a sudden thought struck her, and she cried:

"Alas, alas! how one great anxiety blots out another from the memory. In all this terror and tumult connected with Rowland's escape, I had for a moment forgotten that there was one other who claimed my tenderest sympathy. Poor Mr. Percy is pining alone, sick and wretched, with none to whisper a word of consolation to him, surrounded by strangers, whose attentions are those of cold custom. I had for the time forgotten him; be it my task now, hopeless though it may appear, to seek him in this gigantic city, and ascertain his true state; even now he may be accusing me of breaking the pledge which I made to consider him as my second father, and to cling to him in sickness and in sorrow."

It was easy, however, whilst standing by Westminster Abbey, to make a determination to visit Mr. Percy, but not at all so easy to carry it into effect; and a moment's thought con-vinced Miranda that a hospital in London was rather a vague address, when so many of those establishments existed, and she blamed her-self exceedingly for not procuring of Palmer or Jones, at the widow's house, the requisite information with regard to the precise name of the establishment to which he had been conveyed; but then her mind had been so in-tensely occupied during that period, that in-deed it was next to impossible she should be able to think of anything but Rowland Percy's excessive danger.

"Surely, however," she said, to herself, "there cannot be so many hospitals in London but what I may make a tour of them in the time I yet have, before it is necessary for me to inquire my way to the place of meeting with Palmer."

The money which Dick had handed to her she felt conscious would be more than sufficient to carry such an intention into effect; and her object now was to hire a coach, and desire to be driven to the nearest hospital, where, if unsuccessful, she could re-pair to another and another, until she found the object of her search.

There was a stand of vehicles where she paused to gaze at the solemn and beautiful abbey, so that she had no difficulty in procuring a hackney-coach; in fact, the difficulty was to procure *one* only, for there ensued quite a con-test between some half-dozen drivers as to which should have the job, so that Miranda ran a risk of being almost torn to pieces by the rival candidates.

"Don't go into his vehicle, mum," said one; "it's quite celebrated for carrying corpses. Von of the cushions has the small-pox, and t'other the measles, mum, and there's typhus fever among the straw."

"Oh, you're a nice warmint," said the man whose carriage was thus libelled, "to begin to talk of coaches; yer knows quite well that the last lady as had the misfortune to get into your wehicle was eaten up alive, and when yer came to open the door yer found nothink but her teeth."

A third candidate for Miranda's patronage succeeded in getting it, for he had the wisdom to say nothing.

Preferring deeds to words, he seized Miranda by the arm, and pushed her into his coach before she was aware of where she was going.

"Vere to, mum?" said a singular-looking man, with a wisp of straw round his hat, and attired in so strange a collection of cast-off garments, most of which were too long for him, that he seemed as if he could have withdrawn his face at any time altogether, and hidden it among the mass of clothing; "vere to, mum? Please to remember the vaterman."

"Certainly," said Miranda. "I want to go to the nearest hospital. I want to discover someone who has been taken to a hospital."

"Yes, mum—remember the vaterman."

"Certainly—certainly."

"Done again," said the man, as he slammed the coach-door. "It's bad enough to be refused a copper, without being made fun on into the bargain. Bill, you've got to go on your travels, a grand tour to the hospitals, and it strikes me you've got a fat customer inside. I've had some gammon pushed down my throat, instead of a copper. Suttenly be blowed! Some people's mean, and wicious, too. Suttenly—suttenly! Oh, cuss yer, why didn't yer say yer would see me blowed first?"

The hackney-coach now made a violent demonstration of an intention to proceed, and, after some most formidable oscillations, it proceeded at a very leisurely pace up Parliament Street, the coachman fully making up his mind to visit the metropolitan hospitals in such order as should cover the greatest quantity of ground.

But the schemes of mankind are sadly liable to derangement, for while he was congratulating himself upon nearly a day's work, the fates were so ordering it that he should, in the first instance, proceed to St. Bartholomew's Hospital, where Mr. Percy really lay; and so great was his disappointment, when in answer to Miranda's inquiry of the porter, he was informed there was such a person in the establishment as Mr. Percy, that, in a fit of absence of mind, he charged only his proper fare; and, upon discovering how frightfully honest he had been, he drove to the next public-house, and got drunk *instanter*—all of which terminated in the coach being taken to an uncomfortable place called the green-yard, because there's nothing green about it, and the coachman himself being provided for till next morning in the nearest watch-house.

The porter could give Miranda no information with respect to the condition of Mr. Percy. All he knew was from the list he had, that such a person had been received; but he told her she would soon find which ward he

was in by walking into the building, and making inquiries of some of the nurses.

Miranda obeyed his directions, and meeting an elderly female, she inquired of her in which ward was placed Mr. Percy—an elderly gentleman, who had been recently brought into the hospital.

"Percy—Percy!" said the woman. "Oh, I recollect. Go through that door, and you will find him at the further end."

Miranda slightly paused at the door, but duty conquered her repugnance to enter that long apartment, where so many strange eyes from the occupants of various little truckle-beds were gazing upon her.

"This is not a time," she said, "for idle scruples. I have a duty to perform, and it shall be done."

At the further end of the room a screen was placed round a particular bed, and a chilly sensation came over the heart of Miranda. She knew not why, for she was new to the habits and customs of such a place.

She could not see Mr. Percy anywhere; so accosting another female, she said, in tremulous accents:

"I have come to see Mr. Percy, who, I understand, is in this apartment."

"Oh! a tall, elderly gentleman?"

"Yes—yes."

"Really, I don't know, but I daresay he's dead."

"Dead!" cried Miranda, clasping her hands.

"Yes, Mr. Fergusson's just felt his feet, and says they are getting colder. He's behind that screen."

Miranda looked for a moment in the calm, undisturbed countenance of the woman, and wondered at the want of feeling, that could so speak of a fellow-creature in his last moments.

She then tottered to the bed, which was inclosed by what might appropriately be called "the death screen."

She passed round it, and, in another moment, gazed on the pale and ghastly features of Mr. Percy.

"Speak, speak!" she said, "I am here—Miranda is here!"

There was a strange noise in the throat of the dying man.

He made a painful effort to articulate, pronounced the one word "God," and instantly expired.

"I think he's gone," said the nurse, peeping round the corner of the screen with a shovelful of coals in her hand. "Isn't he gone?"

Miranda felt for a moment as if she could scarcely stand.

She spoke not, but tottering down the ward with a face as pale as one newly risen from the grave, she reached the door.

All strength then deserted her; she could just say "help," and then she fainted upon the threshold.

"Well, I am sure," said the nurse, as she flung the coals on the fire, "fine feelings are all very well in their way, but they don't do in hospitals." ———

CHAPTER CXXVIII.

VARLEY'S LEVEE—THE FALSE STAIR, AND
THE CAPTURE.

VARLEY had held quite a levee of spies,
police-officers, and informers every day since
his arrival in London; but, on the morning
following his disagreeable adventure in
Somers Town, he was by far too ill and
exhausted to give so early a reception to that
class of visitors as he had been accustomed to
do.

The consequence was, that they had all
dropped off, with the exception of two of the
officers, who had made so unsuccessful an attempt to capture Rowland Percy, and these remained, being resolved to see Bernard Varley,
in order to get his sanction for the employment of more spies, and to obtain an advance
of money to pay them, for they were not the
sort of gentry to give long credit, or, in fact,
any at all; so they exerted what patience was
in them, until their dastardly employer should
be visible.

It was early. Bernard Varley was not yet
up, and the two officers were shown into a
small waiting-room.

It was just such a room as is usually set
apart for the reception of strangers, until they
can be otherwise disposed of. In form, it
came as near a parallelogram as possible, with
two long windows on one side, a bare wall,
garnished with two maps—the one of London,
and the other of the country a few miles round
it—a door at one end, and a fireplace at the
other.

It had, besides, a table, on which were
placed writing materials of not the best
quality—several chairs, with uncomfortably
hard seats, a carpet, the pattern of which
had long since departed, and a hearthrug, on
which the two ears, tail, and hind leg of a
leopard were still visible.

"Well," said the senior officer, to his companion, "I suppose we must wait his leisure;
though, having fixed the time himself, he
ought to have kept his appointment, for he
must know that our time is valuable, and can
be spent to more advantage than being cooped
up in this place."

"Why, yes," replied his companion, "it
may be a grand and a respectable place, but
this room is not too comfortable, anyhow. It
strikes me that it takes but little to make a
place respectable, and uncomfortable, too, eh?"

"Yes; but we can make ourselves tolerably
easy, I daresay. Here's a fire and a seat. We
are by ourselves, and can chat for half-an-
hour, and so pass the time."

"With all my heart; anything for a quiet
life, as the man said when his wife made him
get up in the middle of the night to nurse the
babby. What do you think of this affair we
have on hand?"

"It's no matter of ours that we should
think at all about it," replied the first; "but
Mr. Varley seems bent upon the recapture of
this young fellow. I can't understand it, but

it is clear he bears great ill-will towards him,
because he is a successful lover of the girl.
Jealousy may aid his desire for public justice,
you know."

"Ay, I think it does; though, if that be
the case, it would go far to render his evidence
suspicious."

"Oh, no. He's a gentleman, and would
hardly go to such lengths as perjury; besides,
the jury on the spot did not hesitate in returning their verdict."

"No; but it was a strange escape, not only
from York jail, but from York, too. Indeed,
the whole affair must have been cleverly conducted."

"You may say that; there were old hands
engaged upon it. Much, however, depended
upon accident in such a protracted affair; but
that was an unlucky escape from the 'Star
and Tinder-Box' last night."

"There may be more chances yet."

"No doubt. I have spoiled better laid plans
than even theirs, I can tell you. I've ferreted
men out of strange holes and corners, such as
you would hardly ever dream of, and such as
I should never have thought of, but for some
trifling thing or event, which no one could
calculate upon happening."

"You may as well relate one or two of
your experiences, you know, for we have
time, and it may be useful to learn a little.
A good trick may some day be repeated."

"True," replied the senior officer, pleased
with the attention of his junior. "Well, it's
not many years ago that a desperate gang
of housebreakers infested London and the
country for many miles round. At first they
spread great terror through the whole metropolis, and many complaints were lodged at
Bow Street; but there was no great stir
about them, though the men were pretty well
known who were suspected of forming the
gang. There were five of them, as resolute
and desperate a set of men as you would wish
to meet with; they were all young and strong
fellows, so that resistance was vain, and
never attempted, or murder would, no doubt,
have been the result, as, indeed, it was in the
end.

"As I was saying, we did not at first make
much stir after them, for there was no great
temptation, till so many daring robberies had
been committed with impunity, that it began
to reflect upon the office, and a search was
ordered.

"Well, we did look out pretty sharp. I
had my eye on one of the gang; I was but
lately in the line then—I had my eye on one
of them, the head man of the gang—a carpenter by trade, a clever fellow; his name
was Charles Hardman, or Hammering Charlie,
as he was nick-named, from his desperate
fighting qualities; but I could catch him at
nothing—the whole of them were so wary and
watchful, that you might as well have tried
to catch a weasel asleep, as to trap them. No,
no; they were knowing coves, and not to be
had for a trifle.

"Soon after this a desperate robbery took

MIRANDA ARRIVES IN TIME TO SEE OLD MR. PERCY DIE.

place at Sir Philip Heatheridge's, near the New Road, and the 'Adam and Eve,' in St. Pancras Fields. Well, the old knight, having served in the wars, I suppose, could not bring his mind to be quiet; but, rising hastily, seized his sword which hung by his bed; drew it, and attempted to make a stand against the thieves, who, not used to this kind of reception, at first knew not what to make of it; but he gave them no time to consider, for, seeing them hesitate, he rushed at them, brandishing his sword, and would have cut one, at least, down, had he not been shot dead through the heart by—it was supposed—Hammering Charlie.

"This, as you may imagine, created no end of a row. The people were up in arms about it, and the Secretary of State offered a reward of three hundred pounds, and his family a further reward of two hundred pounds, for the apprehension and conviction of the murderers.

"You may be sure we went to work in earnest now, and, notwithstanding the carefulness of the gang, they had been seen and recognized in the house; especially Charlie, who had been at work there some time previously as a carpenter. This is how it was he came to plan the attack upon the house, knowing the quantity of plate, jewels, and money they kept in it.

"He was advertised for by name and description, but he appeared to have vanished, for no one could tell of his whereabouts. I knew his haunts well, having kept my eye upon him, thinking that some day he would be worth a heavy sum to the public, and now he was, and I set about capturing him if I could; but this was a matter more easily thought of and said than done.

"I am no chicken, and then I was in the pride of my strength, as they say in the plays: but I felt that if we ever did meet, and a skrimmage was to ensue, and that Charlie would not be taken—and I could not expect he would, for the charge affected his life, and hanged he would be—I felt it would be a doubtful and desperate affair. I cared for nothing, however, but determined to brave all for such a sum.

"Several of his companions had been taken, and one had been fortunate enough to escape from the country; but not so Charlie. We knew he was in London, and from information I had received, and several hints I had heard among his own friends, I felt convinced that he was near his old haunt in St. Giles'.

"I told you he was a carpenter, and a clever one. This made me feel convinced that he was secreted in the house where he usually lived; but I could see no trace of him. However, I mentioned my suspicions to the magistrate, and got a search warrant immediately, and with two assistants, I determined to make a sudden rush into the house, when least expected by the inmates, and, if possible, secure my prisoner.

"Well, then, I thought it of no use to pounce upon them either in the daytime or night; Charlie would be too wide-awake for that, and I determined to go before daybreak one bleak, cold morning. I did so, and got into the house readily enough, searched through every room, every cupboard, and every nook and corner of it that you could think big enough to conceal a cat; but no, he was not there.

"We stood staring at each other in vexation and shame, for we could easily perceive the anxious faces of some of the inmates were bent upon us, while others jeered at us for our non-success. However, we were compelled reluctantly to quit the premises.

"Having got into the street, I said to one of my mates:

"'It strikes me that our man is in that house now, notwithstanding we have not been able to find his hiding-place.'

"'He must have doubled himself up into an uncommon small compass, then: for we have not left a place unexplored in which I could find room for my hat,' said he; 'but yet some of the women looked anxious and troubled.'

"'They did,' I replied, 'and that's what makes me pretty sure that he is hidden there, and I have a great mind to return to them, and make another search.'

"'I think it would be useless,' he replied.

"'Why useless? They think we are gone, and will not expect to see us again so soon.'

"'No such thing—we are watched now,' he said, 'there can be no doubt; but we can return at another time, setting a watch upon the door, to see who goes in and out.'

"'That's very good advice,' I replied; 'but yet he may be carried out in a piece of furniture, or some such scheme as that. I suppose it can't be helped, but I'll have another rummage over that house before long.'

"Well, that passed over, and I was then engaged in tracing the stolen property. The plate was no doubt melted soon after the robbery was committed, and turned to cash; but not so the jewellery—that, I believed, had not been touched, as thereby its value would be much lessened.

"I made careful inquiries among the Jews, but could learn nothing. These people have great advantages in the disposal of stolen property—they have so large and confidential a connection, that what they do seldom, if ever, comes to light. My own belief was, that they had been turned into money, and at once sent out of the country.

"I had placed a man to keep watch near the house in which I suspected that he was concealed, to keep a good look-out, and inform me of whatever he saw of a suspicious tendency; and from him I learned that the family, though very poor, were doing extremely well, and none of them had any work of any kind: they paid for all they got, and, besides, they had all got new clothing.

"I had myself learned that Charlie had been among the Jews lately, and he had received large sums of money. No doubt he was lying by until a safe opportunity occurred of allowing him to escape to France or America.

"Taking all these things together, I determined to make another attempt to catch him.

"It was about midnight that I and two more again sought the house with this intention. We gained admittance after some little delay and wrangle.

"We commenced our search carefully, from the kitchens upwards. We proceeded slowly and with great care, not missing a square foot of either brickwork or woodwork; but all to no purpose. I could not see anything that would lead me to a conclusion that he was present in the house, and yet I felt certain that he was.

"It was vexatious enough to be thus foiled a second time, more especially as everything tended to increase my suspicions that he was there, for we found his clothes, some of which appeared to have been recently worn, and had marks or stains on them as if they had been near bricks or mortar.

"This made me positive of his presence, and I pointed out the marks to my companions, who thought as I did. The family did not like it, but began to grow serious and angry. They complained of my presence. I showed them my search warrant. They admitted my right, but added that I was wantonly breaking in upon and destroying the liberty of the subject by my intrusion into their house.

"'That is my object,' said I. 'I do wish to abridge liberties such as these, hang them. It's too great a liberty for one man to take the life of another. But he's not here, and I'll leave you now; but you may be sure we'll have him despite of all he can do.'

"'You have tried,' said one of his family, 'and had better try again.'

"'I will,' said I, 'but not just now; I shall see you on another occasion.'

"So saying, I walked down the stairs. I was in no good humour, and strode down the stairs in anger. When I got to a very dark part, I thought I felt the stairs spring, as if they were supported on some soft body.

"'Hilloa!' said I, 'what is the matter now?' and on examining the spot, I could see that the top of the landing did not consist of boards that ran from side to side and under the skirting, but that there was a clean cut all along. I instantly lifted up the boards; it came up easily enough, and there lay my prisoner. The hollow place in which he lay was scarcely deep enough for his body, which would hardly allow the board to shut flat down, and having been seized with the cramp during our search, he was forced to turn his body, and hence the discovery.

"No sooner was he conscious of being detected, than he sprang up and attempted to escape; but I seized him, and a desperate struggle ensued, for the rest of the people took his part, and we were terribly beaten and thrust from the house; but yet I still retained my grasp of my man.

"Outside, the struggle was renewed with greater desperation than ever, for he was assisted by some more of his people, and I had a narrow escape of my life. During all this, Charlie kept biting and kicking most violently. I was losing strength, and soon should have been overpowered; moreover, to add to my distress, I could not get the handcuffs on. I had him fast by one hand, but the shower of blows I was enduring would, I knew, soon disable me, and, with a last effort, I fastened the other half of the handcuff to an iron staple by the area-railings, and so secured him.

"I then got up with some difficulty, and sprang my rattle. Assistance soon arrived. My man was safe; but I fainted after I saw him housed, and I was on the sick-list for a long time after. But I got the rewards, which made the matter not so bad after all."

"No; but it would not do to have such often repeated," replied his companion, who had been listening attentively.

"It would not; but it was a feather in my cap, and my promotion quickly followed."

* * * *

A servant, at this moment, summoned them into the presence of Varley, who spoke with great pain and difficulty, for, although he had received no one serious injury from the rough treatment of the mob, yet he had been terribly shaken. ——

CHAPTER CXXIX.

TWITTER AND VARLEY—THE PLOT FOR THE MURDER—TWITTER IN TWO MINDS—THE CONSENT.

THE interview between Bernard Varley and the officers was very brief; it consisted of a wild kind of harangue upon his part, the purport of which was, to authorize them to go to any expense whatever, provided it presented them with a good chance of apprehending either Rowland Percy, Palmer, or the third person, who was evidently rendering assistance to the fugitives—Mr. Jones, to wit, whose name, however, was unknown to the officers, although they declared they could readily recognize him again, from the view they had had of him during the recent proceedings; and they would take care to have him included in a warrant, which they would immediately apply for.

So far, all was satisfactory to the officers, for they were making immediate cash by the transaction, as well as chancing the large reward that was offered for Rowland's apprehension.

Very far, though, was Bernard Varley from sharing in that satisfaction, for he could not conceal from himself that, hitherto, he had been signally unsuccessful in his pursuit of the innocent parties, whom he hated much more for their innocence than if they had been guilty, since all his endeavours had resulted in nothing but derision, annoyance, vexation, and personal injury.

He was suffering, too, considerable bodily pain during the interview with the officers, and that circumstance imparted an acerbity to his tone, which made them think that his reason was certainly a little deranged, and gave rise to many grave suspicions among themselves as to his real connection with the events which had produced so much troublesome excitement.

But this they wisely considered was no business of theirs; and, although they had made the subject a matter of free discourse among themselves, their doubts of Rowland Percy's guilt made them not a whit the less anxious for his apprehension, the effecting of which they looked upon quite as a matter of business, his guilt or innocence having nothing whatever to do with their part of the work.

With full instructions, then, to spare no expense, and to leave no means untried for the destruction of Rowland, the officers left Bernard Varley, whose passions had reached a height that quite threatened his mental alienation.

With a deep groan, then, he threw himself upon a sofa, and tortured by pain, he—interspersed with groans—gave utterance to the agonizing thoughts of his half-distracted mind.

"Fate seems to fight against me," he muttered. "Miranda—dear Miranda! I have seen you once again, and you have been snatched from me at a moment when I thought it impossible you could escape. Some accursed train of circumstances seems ever to come between me and the accomplishment of the fixed purposes of my soul: the nearer I seem to approach the full realization of my wishes, the further I may calculate, by some unlucky movement, to be hurled to a distance, enough to deprive me of all hope of future success—foiled—foiled—for ever. But I will live alone now for those two great objects of my soul—revenge on Rowland Percy, and the love of Miranda. There shall interpose nothing to prevent my continuing those two pursuits to their successful termination; I will devote to this end the large fortune that has come into my hands, as well as my life. Opposition may depress me, but it shall not daunt me. I will either live to accomplish my desires, or not live at all. Death were a thousand times more welcome than this frightful state of painful expectation, and still more painful disappointment."

With a noiseless tread, Samuel Twitter glided into the apartment.

"Oh, good morning!" said Varley, in a bland tone, much at variance with that in which he had been muttering the resolves of his dark and troubled spirit. "Good-morning, friend Twitter. I regret—very much regret—that you did not escape scathless yesterday."

"Scathless," said Twitter, as he lifted up a green shade that was over one eye, and exhibited that organ surrounded by a variety of colours.

"Ay, I perceive, my good Twitter," said Varley, "someone hath struck you in the eye; you have my most poignant regrets and deep commiseration. We were assailed by terrible ruffians, Samuel Twitter, persons quite destitute of humanity and conscience."

"For Heaven's sake," said Twitter, with a prefatory groan, "don't speak in that way, Mr. Varley. I would rather, on my soul I would rather ten times that you abused me, as you used to do, than speak to me in that tone of mock civility and consideration, which makes me almost think — that — that——"

"That what?"

"That some day you would take my life!"

"Oh, what a libel," said Varley, holding up his hands.

"The truth's a libel," remarked Twitter, with an uneasy shuffle in the chair. "You know the truth's a libel, Varley, in this country. Do you mean that?"

"Really, now, my dear friend, you allow your perverted imagination to picture to you evils that have no foundation."

"Dear friend!" ejaculated Twitter, with a tone of surprise. "Don't—oh, don't——"

"Do you want any money?" said Varley. "Pray draw upon me for as much as your necessities require. Between friends, what are a few pounds?"

"I should like to have fifty," said Twitter, "if quite convenient."

"My dear Samuel, take a hundred," said Varley; "you find me in an agreeable mood this morning; and I confess my mind is rather elated by some agreeable intelligence that I have received."

"Indeed!"

"Yes, the principal drawback upon my satisfaction, in fact, is that blow you have had on your eye."

"Infernal hypocrite!" said Twitter, jumping up, and making for the door.

"Nay," said Varley, "my dear Twitter, lend me your attention for a brief space, while I explain to you that I have, this morning, received intelligence that Rowland Percy and Miranda have found refuge in a house some little distance from a place called Richmond, on the banks of the river. I have made an agreement with a strong posse of officers to meet us at a particular landing-place, about half-a-mile from the house. The shortest route is unquestionably by water, so you and I will take a boat, and row ourselves up to where we are to meet the officers. I have thought over the matter well, and I have quite convinced myself that the shortest route, as well as the easiest, is by water—to your grave," he added, to himself.

"Oh," remarked Twitter; "did you say a boat on the water?"

"Yes," said Varley, unconcernedly fixing his eyes upon the ceiling.

"Don't you think that rather dangerous?"

"I don't see any danger, if the thing is properly managed."

"Then I tell you what," said Twitter. "Bernard Varley, you may be as civil and pleasant-spoken as you like; but, before I trust myself with you in a boat on the river, I'll see you hanged first."

"Not trust yourself with me, Samuel Twitter, your old friend—your well-tried faithful friend and confidant. How is it that you have given yourself up to such degrading suspicions? Oh, Twitter—Twitter, am I deceived in you?—and are you not the open-hearted, candid character I took you for?"

"Give me the money," said Twitter, "and let me go. You want to drive me mad, I know you do."

"Well, well, I will have no more suspicions," said Varley. "We will meet at Blackfriars Bridge."

"We will do no such thing."

"At the stairs to the right hand."

"No—no—no!"

"At half-past eight o'clock this evening, when the silver moon is rising, and shedding its refulgent light upon the waters. 'Tis pleasant to be at such a time in an open boat, with an attached friend, from whom one has no secrets."

"I won't come!" cried Twitter, knocking the table with his knuckles vehemently. "It's no use tormenting me, Varley. I won't, and there's an end of it."

"Nay, now, but you will. Why force me to the disagreeable alternative of saying that you shall? For, if you do not, I shall stop the supplies, Samuel Twitter, and not another farthing do you procure from me."

"Reduce me to destitution," said Twitter, "and I will confess the murder at York."

"Indeed!" said Varley, in the same bland tone he had used throughout the interview. Then, it behoves me, in a friendly way, to save you from that inconvenience."

"Save me! How?"

"By blowing your brains out before you could carry that pleasant little intention into effect."

"Murder! murder!" said Twitter, as Varley, upon the moment, took a pistol from his pocket, and held it within an inch of his head.

"Will you come?" said Varley.

"You—you dare not kill me here! The noise—the excitement—suspicion would be sure to be directed against you. You dare not kill me here, Varley!"

"Nay, do not make too sure; but, to convince you that your suspicions are groundless, I will excuse your attendance upon the occasion I have hinted to you; but, by so doing, you force me to an alternative I would gladly have avoided—you will no longer be useful in bringing Rowland Percy to a scaffold, and so quieting suspicion once and for ever of the murder of Sir George Rankley. I shall be compelled to make a confidant of some other person, Twitter, a measure fraught with frightful danger to us both, for I must have somebody to assist me in my schemes; that somebody should be you, but since you refuse, I am thrown upon the consideration of strangers, and our danger will be not a little increased by my taking to myself, into my full and free confidence—for full and free it must be, or not at all——"

"Varley—Varley," said Twitter, "you cannot mean to be so mad!"

"The result must speak for my sincerity."

"In town, and where there are people about, I don't mind going with you; but, in lonely situations, I confess I always feel unhappy, and I cannot bear them; so do not ask me, Varley—do not ask me."

"Twitter, your services to me—in fact, I may say, our services to each other—must be unfettered by foolish conditions. You fancy that I have a design upon your life. What folly is that, when I have so much need of a confidant, and have in you a perfectly safe one, because implicated, ready to my hand. What one object on earth would your death avail me, especially now that we are upon such civil and pleasant terms, and understand each other so fully and so completely?"

"I know not," said Twitter; "but I have horrid suspicions. To speak candidly, Varley, I am very—very much afraid that you thirst for my death."

"Twitter, my dear friend, such a thought is quite unworthy of you. It is foolish, because not based upon reason. Ask yourself, for one moment, what advantage could accrue to me from your decease. What possible good could it do me, if by a word I could hurry you into eternity? On the contrary, you have been very useful to me, and you may, in all

human probability, be more useful still. You fancy me mad in my passion for Miranda, but I am not so mad, Samuel Twitter, as not to know what I am about. Do not expose me to the danger of employing strangers, and I promise you that if Rowland Percy be brought to a scaffold—as I think he may, by your assistance—that I will sell the Grange by auction in London here, and give you a large sum from the proceeds—a sum that shall at once enable you to take what course you please, and place you far above the reach of pecuniary difficulties."

"Oh, if I could but trust you!" said Twitter; "but I cannot, Varley—you know I cannot—you know I dare not."

"Twitter," said Varley, "we have so long, figuratively speaking, rowed in the same boat together, and now you shrink from doing so actually for the space of about an hour. Excuse me for saying that such a course of conduct is quite unworthy of your high reputation for sagacity and courage."

"My reputation!" said Twitter. "Oh, dear, if you would not say such things as that I might almost believe you, but how can I when you talk in such a strain? I repeat, how can I? You know well that your conviction goes not with your words, and that were you to speak what you would consider the truth, you would absolutely deny me the possession of any of the qualities you mention. I would go with you freely, if I could really trust you—if I could really rid myself of the frightful supposition that you seek my life."

"Rid yourself of it, Samuel Twitter, once and for ever," said Varley, with such an air of sincerity that Twitter was absolutely staggered, and half believed him. "Accompany me this evening upon the expedition I mention, and which I honestly believe will be crowned with the most perfect success, then the other occurrences, such as the sale of the Grange, and the possession by you of a large portion of the proceeds, would follow as things of course, and you would reach the consummation of your wishes, without any further doubt, danger, or difficulty."

"I—I think," said Twitter, "I will venture—I think I will try to venture. At half-past eight, you say, Varley?"

"At half-past eight," said Varley, in an indifferent tone. "On the steps by the right-hand side of Blackfriars Bridge."

"I will think of it between this and then."

"No," said Varley, "you must decide now, for between this and then I must procure someone to accompany me, in case of failing to meet with the officers, or any other accident which would leave me alone otherwise."

"I—I will come—I will meet you, Varley. You will really sell the Grange estates, and let me have my share?"

"I will; but, of course, you know, it must be subject to the deduction of what you have already received. That must be considered, you know, Samuel Twitter."

"Certainly—oh, yes, certainly."

This seeming urgency in the reduction of

his demand by the amount he had already received, went a long way with Twitter in convincing him of the sincerity of Bernard Varley. He thought to himself "he surely would not be so anxious in making such a condition, if he intended any foul play, for he would be too ready to promise me anything, rather than I should refuse to accompany him on this expedition, which, after all, may be, as he says, a means of ridding us entirely of Rowland Percy, who, while he lives, will ever be to us the greatest possible enemy, because, if his innocence should become apparent, guilt must be sought for elsewhere."

Alike fearful of refusing, and of going to meet Varley, Samuel Twitter at length gave a reluctant consent, and advancing his claim upon Varley from fifty to a hundred pounds, he left the hotel, scarcely quite clear in his own mind whether he meant to keep his word or not.

CHAPTER CXXX.

MIRANDA'S ADVENTURES IN THE STREETS OF LONDON—THE HOSPITAL—THE MEETING WITH DICK PALMER AT WHITEHALL.

WHEN Miranda recovered, after fainting at the door of the hospital-ward in which poor old Mr. Percy lay a corpse, she found herself in a little, dingy apartment, surrounded by several persons.

It was some moments before she recovered consciousness sufficiently to remember what had occurred to her; but when once the memory reasserted its power, nothing was forgotten, and, like a flash of lightning illumining a dreary waste, her mind became fully alive to her painful situation.

"Ah!" she heard someone say, "it's over now!"

She tried to rise from her seat, but found her strength almost inadequate to the task.

"You had better remain here for some time," said a gentlemanly-looking man. "Here, drink this."

Miranda instinctively drank the contents of a small glass that was placed to her lips, and almost instantly she felt the reviving effects of the stimulant that had been administered to her.

"Alas! alas!" she said; "he's dead! he's dead!"

"Ah, you mean the old gentleman in the ward," said the same person who had addressed her; "there wasn't a chance for him from the first; he was sinking when he came in, and never rallied."

"Perhaps it is a great mercy," added Miranda, clasping her hands. "Heaven only knows what he might yet have had to struggle with."

"About the body," said another person; "do you mean to claim it?"

"Claim it!" said Miranda; "what mean you?"

"Oh, nothing particular; but we'll take the trouble off your hands of the funeral, and

that kind of thing, provided you have no particular objection to a slight, nay, almost nominal, *post-mortem* examination, for the purposes of science."

"The body," said Miranda, as she rose, and moved to the door, "will be claimed, and not left for the purposes of dissection. I quite understand you, sir."

"Oh, very well, very well; but, mind, it must be done within four-and-twenty hours."

Choking back her tears, poor, sorrow-stricken Miranda made her way to the outer gates, and emerged into Smithfield.

She was pleased to see by the lengthening shadows, and the dim evenness of colour that pervaded all objects, that the evening was rapidly approaching. Still, however, it wanted some hours to the time of meeting with Palmer, and she felt herself greatly in need of some bodily refreshment in order to sustain her exhausted steps.

Where or how safely to procure such she knew not, but her increasing faintness warned her that she would be exposing herself to the absolute peril of again fainting if she did not hasten to procure food of some description.

She turned down a narrow street in the immediate vicinity of the hospital, and soon observed a small shop, which she was encouraged to enter, because she saw no person but a woman in it, although the display of eatables of all kinds and descriptions was not of the most inviting character.

There were pickled herrings, Flanders bricks, butter, soap, kitchen-stuff, tobacco, hearth-stone, split peas, snuff, cabbages, sugar, birch-brooms, soda, starch, table-beer, and blacking, candles, tea, and the best white linen rags, etc., etc.

Into this *olla podrida* of a shop, Miranda, with some reluctance, entered, and inquired if she could have some bread, when, to her surprise, the woman replied:

"Certainly. Would you like a Frenchman, or a buster?"

"I really don't know," said Miranda. "A small loaf will suffice."

A twopenny loaf was handed to her, and the woman stared when she asked leave to eat some of it in the shop.

"We've small-beer at a penny a pint."

"Have you any milk?" said Miranda. "I should prefer it."

"Yes," was the reply; "we are forced to sell everything to get a living in this world."

A suspicious-looking liquid, which, by the courtesy of the inhabitants of London, is denominated milk, was handed to Miranda in a cracked mug, and, having partaken of some of it, and eaten a small portion of the bread, she paid threepence for her frugal repast, and left the shop.

As she did so, she heard seven o'clock striking from some neighbouring church, and, not knowing how great a space she might have to traverse in order to obey the injunctions of Palmer before meeting him, she resolved at once to start on the undertaking, and, as a preparatory step, she called a hackney-coach, and desired to be driven to the Strand, to which the reader will recollect that Palmer had told her to go, for the purpose of procuring a boat at some of the stairs at the bottom of the numerous streets running from its southern side towards the river.

A very short drive sufficed to place Miranda in that bustling thoroughfare, and she required not to make many inquiries before she found herself on the banks of the river, at the bottom of a flight of wooden stairs, where a number of wherries lay moored ready for hire.

In answer to the repeated inquiries of " Boat, mum ?—boat, mum ?" from a lot of idlers on the stairs, she desired to be conveyed across the river, and after agreeing, to the great surprise of the waterman, to pay sixpence for the accommodation, she stepped into a wherry, which was soon gliding along on the surface of the water with that pleasant, easy motion which is so delightfully superior to every other artificial mode of progression, and which, were it not for the mass of sputtering steamers that make the Thames a highway, and the disgraceful condition of the river itself, would form one of the most agreeable pleasures in the summer season which London could present to its inhabitants.

A very few minutes sufficed to land Miranda on the opposite side of the stream, and she ascended some steps very similar to those she had descended on the Middlesex shore.

Reaching the top, she found herself in a dirty, narrow street, which, after pursuing some time, conducted her into a large, rambling thoroughfare, where the houses were of a miscellaneous character; shops of all kinds and descriptions and private dwellings being jumbled together in disorder.

To procure a coach in such a thoroughfare was by no means a difficult matter; and Miranda directed that she should be driven to Whitehall, looking carefully about her previously to stepping into the vehicle, and being quite assured she was unwatched.

Indeed, the mere fact of crossing the river alone was a sufficient guarantee that no one was upon her track; and, in the midst of all her misery, she felt a glow of satisfaction pervade her frame at the thought that she should soon meet a friend, even although that friend was of so doubtful a social cast as Dick Palmer, the highwayman.

She ascertained when she reached Whitehall that she would have still very nearly an hour to wait.

She asked the name of the large building opposite to where she had alighted from the coach, and being informed it was called the Horse Guards, leading into St. James's Park, she thought that, in preference to loitering about in the open streets, she would walk into the park, of which she had read a great deal, and which, to her mind, was full of historical recollections.

In a few moments she was standing in the broad expanse opposite the park front of the Horse Guards, but the darkness had increased greatly, and she could only faintly see those

objects which would have been of great interest in consequence of their being mingled with memorable realities.

Here she lingered until half-past eight was chimed from the Horse Guards' clock. Then she passed again through the gloomy-looking archway, and, crossing the road, stood close to that building which had been the prison and witnessed the execution of Charles the First, who allowed his resources to get weaker while his enemies were gaining strength, instead of crushing, as he should have done in the germ, a political movement which brought years of distress.

" Miranda," said a voice behind her, while a slight touch caused her to start suddenly, and she beheld the friendly face of Dick Palmer.

" Thank Heaven," cried Miranda, " you have come. Oh, what a weary day I have passed. I seem to live again now that I have met you. Tell me of Rowland. Is he well ?—is he safe ?"

" Yes, Miss Rankley, he is well, and he is as happy as circumstances will permit him to be. He wished me particularly to inquire of you concerning his father."

A grief-like shadow passed over the countenance of Miranda, and, shaking her head, she said, sadly :

" Alas, he is gone—gone !"

" Dead !" exclaimed Palmer, " can it be possible ?"

" It is true. The satisfaction was a melancholy one of being with him at his death. but such as it was I had it. He is now far removed from earthly cares and earthly miseries. Heaven receive him."

" Amen !" said Palmer. " This will be a sad blow to poor Rowland, for he never believed his father in any danger. Well—well, we must reason with him upon the subject, and endeavour to convince him that all is for the best, though that is a philosophy very difficult to convince people of when suffering from the severe hand of misfortune."

" That is too true," said Miranda, " it is the wealthy alone that, in the midst of their luxuries and socialities, can treat misfortune as an abstraction, reasoning calmly and dispassionately upon it ; but let those same persons feel the biting of real sorrow, and they shall be the first to shrink aghast from its presence."

" You have learned some home truths early in life, Miss Rankley," remarked Palmer. " Heaven send they may conduce to your future happiness. But now, tell me, are you quite certain that throughout the day no one has dogged your footsteps ?"

" Quite certain," said Miranda. " I escaped from Bernard Varley by a miracle."

" You shall tell me all particulars as we proceed to where I hope you will enjoy an uninterrupted interview with Rowland Percy, but we must be perfectly sure we are not followed. If anyone is watching me now, I shall be pounced upon before I can get into a hackney-coach."

As he spoke, he beckoned a coach from a stand which was near, and, handing Miranda into the vehicle, he himself followed, desiring the coachman to drive to St. Paul's Cathedral.

"I think we are safe," he said; "but, in order to make assurance doubly sure, we will ride about a little in an opposite direction to that in which we really wish to go."

The coach started, and during the drive Miranda related to Dick Palmer the daring attempt Varley had made to stay by her, and the very singular manner in which it had been frustrated.

———

CHAPTER CXXXI.

THE SPY AND THE LETTER—MIRANDA AND THE LANDLORD OF THE "STAR AND TINDER-BOX"—THE MEETING.

In St. Paul's Churchyard, Dick Palmer and Miranda alighted from the hackney coach, and after the coachman was paid, the former said to the latter:

"If we were being watched at all, the number of this coach would have been taken, because it would be a greater object, of course, to follow me to Mr. Percy's place of concealment than to affect my apprehension in the street. I feel quite assured that we have not been followed, for, if so, it must have been in a vehicle; and now let us walk round the cathedral, and make sure that our late coachman does not see the number of the next vehicle we get into."

This was easily accomplished, for the coachman evidently took no notice whatever, and, stepping into another coach, which was plying for hire at the top of Cheapside, Dick Palmer at once desired to be driven to Holborn, and he drew the check-string within about a hundred paces of the top of Drury Lane.

"Now," he said to Miranda, when they were in the street, "comes our greatest peril. We must walk down Drury Lane, and, of course, it is just possible it may be well watched. A few moments, however, must decide that question, and I only speak to you now in case it should be necessary for us to part company, which I beg of you to do without ceremony, should I see occasion to give you such a hint. Rowland Percy is at the house I mentioned to you. Should I be apprehended, you will be untouched, and when the row and excitement have subsided, you can proceed quietly and ask for him of the landlord."

"Do not run the risk," said Miranda. "Why walk down this dread thoroughfare at all? Let me proceed alone."

"Nay," replied Dick; "I want a day and night's rest at the 'Star and Tinder-Box.' I think if I can once get into the house undiscovered, I shall be comparatively safe. It is the passsage to it which alone is dangerous. Let us hope for the best."

With Miranda Rankley upon his arm, Dick Palmer walked boldly down Drury Lane.

The night was dark, and, consequently, he was so far favoured by circumstances, and when he and the beautiful being who accompanied him turned into Steeple Court, he remarked:

"I think, Miss Rankley, we have performed the perilous voyage with safety; but let us pause in this old doorway a little while. If we have been dogged hither, the party or parties who have followed us will soon appear."

Some minutes of very anxious suspense passed to Miranda, but all was still, the only person passing up Steeple Court being a slip-shod girl with a mug for some beer, who was about as unlike a police spy as could well be imagined.

"We are surely safe?" whispered Miranda.

"Yes, I think so. Now, go to the bar, and ask for the landlord. He's a stout, rather rough-featured man, but good-humoured withal. Say to him when you see him: 'Is there a loose box for a hunter in the "Star and Tinder-Box?"' If he says yes, and there's nobody by, you can come and tell me directly; but, should there be persons about when he says yes, just add: 'He's nearly dead beat, and shy of the crows.' He will understand you, and get rid of any obnoxious personages if they be loitering about."

"I will recollect," said Miranda; "you may depend upon my doing your bidding carefully."

Poor Miranda stepped on towards the public-house.

When she reached the bar there were two persons standing at it—one was the girl who had recently passed her and Palmer in the narrow passage, the other was a young man of the class denominated "shabby-genteel," and he was smoking a cigar with an air of great nonchalance, as he leaned idly against the bar, with his hands in his pockets.

After a hard stare at Miranda, he continued apparently some remarks that he had been before making, for he said:

"Yes, it's my decided opinion that the laws are often and often too hard upon a fellow, and don't take into consideration that one chap must live as well as another."

"Oh, sir," said the landlord, "I know that dishonesty's a dreadful vice, and I really think thieves and vagabonds ought to be punished most dreadfully."

"Oh, pho—pho—pho!" cried the man. "Come, now, no reserve with me; I'm on the lay myself. How is business?"

"Why, we've drawn half-a-butt to-day," said the landlord, considering; "but really, sir, if you begin talking slang to me, you'll puzzle me completely, and if you mean to insinuate that you are not strictly honest and honourable, I must beg that you will leave my house."

Miranda was quite delighted to hear such a sentiment, but she little imagined that the shabby-genteel man was strongly suspected by the landlord of being what is called a "plant" upon him, and that the landlord himself was the greatest proficient in slang London could produce.

She was just about to speak, when the little girl, poking a jug upon the bar, said:

"A pint-and-a-half of the sixpenny ale, and mother says please draw it mild. A gentleman in the street's given me this ere letter to bring you; it's all right, sir, cos he guved me twopence for bringing it."

The landlord took the letter, and read aloud the address, as follows:

"Mr. Rowland Percy, care of George Frith, landlord of the 'Star and Tinder-Box,' Drury Lane."

"What!" cried Miranda, stepping forward, hurriedly; "did you say Rowland Percy?"

"Eh!" said the shabby-genteel man, taking the cigar out of his mouth, and looking deeply interested.

"Yes, I did," said the landlord, loudly; "but as I don't happen to know the gentleman, I think, my little girl, you had better take the letter back to the person who gave it you, or swallow it, as you think proper."

"Oh!" said the little girl, as she took the letter again.

"Rowland Percy—Rowland Percy!" remarked the shabby-genteel man; "why, that's the same name as the murderer from York—ain't it?"

"I daresay you know best," said the landlord; "perhaps you had better take the note; you might find him out before I do."

"Oh, I—I have nothing to do with it," said the man.

"Pshaw!" said the landlord; "you are as shallow as a saucer. Go and tell your employers that I have nothing to do with Rowland Percy, and I don't mean. You may say, too, it's no use sending every hour in the day a fool like yourself on the spy; there, now, go away, my good man, the little girl's waiting for you outside with the sham note. I tell you Percy is not one of my sort, from all I can hear of him, and if he was to come in here, I should just say, my good fellow, bolt—this house is too hot to hold you, for I've been doing a roaring trade this last week among spies and informers. Now, will that do, or must you have a kick?"

"Really," said the shabby-genteel man, "I don't know what you mean; and as for Godfrey employing me, I don't even know him by sight."

"Ah!" remarked the landlord, "you may know a goose by its gabble. Who spoke of Godfrey but yourself, spoony? I really think when the police want a spy, they go through London for an idiot."

The shabby-genteel young man muttered something that was quite unintelligible except to himself, and then sneaked out of the house like a cur that has been unexpectedly found under a dining-room table.

"Well," remarked the landlord, "I can forgive a rogue, but I've no patience with a fool. There's that fellow drunk four shillings-worth of mulled port and smoked three cigars just to expose his own want of the common assortment of brains. Well, hurrah's all I have to say."

"Are you the landlord," said Miranda, "of this house?"

"So they say."

"Then have you a loose box for a hunter in the 'Star and Tinder-box?'"

The landlord placed his elbows on the bar, and looked long and steadfastly in the face of his fair questioner.

"I don't know you, my dear," he said; "but you've as pretty a face for all that, as I've seen for many a year. Yes, I have got a loose box for a hunter in the 'Star and Tinder-Box,' and, for your sake, it shall be a snug one. Now, tell me, as there's nobody here, who is the out-of-the-way lucky dog to own you?"

Miranda shrank a little from the familiarity of this address, and then said in a low voice:

"I have been told I might trust you. My name is Miranda Rankley. I am the daughter of Sir George Rankley, who was basely murdered. My errand here is to see the innocent Rowland Percy. My companion now waiting in the court is named Palmer."

The landlord gave a long whistle, and then opening the little wicket that led into the bar, he said:

"Come in, Miss Rankley. Of course, I couldn't know you. Excuse me and my odd manner; I am rough and ready, like a Scotch terrier."

"Nay," she said, "I must go back with the news that all is safe."

"Leave that to me; I'll fetch Palmer in. Walk in here yourself, for it's seldom that the bar of the 'Star and Tinder-Box' is as clear as it is now. We don't know a minute but that we may have some ugly customer walk in."

Miranda no longer hesitated, but, passing the little bar, accepted a proffered seat in the parlour beyond it, with a feeling of great relief.

A glance around her let her see that Rowland Percy was not in the apartment; but she could scarcely be said to be disappointed, for a moment's reflection told her how unlikely it was that he should be so readily accessible in his place of concealment.

She heard the boisterous mirth of some topers who were making merry in the parlour in the ancient hostelry, and, rude and coarse as those sounds were, they came with a chastened effect upon her ear, because she felt that she was under the same roof with Rowland Percy—a conviction which gave beauty to every object around her, and made that house of entertainment an object in her eyes dearer than a palace.

"Now, at least," she thought, "we shall meet without the accompaniment of those calamitous circumstances which followed so hard upon our last attempt at a conference. Oh, Rowland—Rowland! surely some day the clouds of misfortune which now overshadow us will roll away, and we shall see the future more clear and bright, perhaps, than ever was the past. While I have faith in Heaven, and its justice, I will not desert hope—a hope of happier times, which will yet dawn upon us when we least expect it. We shall yet live, I feel a conviction, to look back upon the past as the troubled phantasma of a dream, from which we have escaped, but which has not been altogether full of evil, inasmuch as while it has chastened us, it has taught us the true value of many things and many persons which, in the palmy days of prosperity, we could never have arrived at."

Minute after minute passed slowly, and no one came to her in her solitude.

An irrepressible feeling of loneliness began to oppress her, and she exhausted her mind in endless conjectures as to what could be the occasion of the long delay.

Suddenly, then, she heard a door slightly creak upon its hinges, and, turning hastily in the direction whence the sound proceeded, with a cry of joy she recognized Rowland Percy, who in a moment sprang towards her, and clasped her in his arms.

"Once again—yet once again, my noble—my heroic Miranda," he said; "once again we have met. Fate persecutes us, dearest; but it leaves our own hearts untouched."

"Ah, Rowland," replied Miranda, "misfortune is real love's only test. We will have faith in each other, and stand it bravely. You are looking wearied and ill, Rowland. Oh, that this life of incessant disquietude and harassment would cease."

"We will bear it, Miranda, as best we may, gazing upon the future as upon some bright, particular star, dearest, which we may hope to reach in the fulness of time; but the roses have deserted your cheek, Miranda, and I feel myself too much the cause."

"No, no, Rowland; do not add any self-accusation to the already more than sufficient oppression that must be upon your mind. Trains of circumstances, as unprecedented as terrible, have given us much suffering, and may give us much more; but always remember, Rowland, we are but passive instruments in the hands of that Providence which, in its own good time, will release us from our thraldom, and permit us, dear Rowland——"

"To live and love together," added Percy. "To be all the world to each other, my Miranda."

"As we are now, Rowland. We are both orphans, and our hopes in this world must be centred in each other."

"Both orphans!" exclaimed Rowland; "my —my father——"

"Is in Heaven."

Rowland Percy clasped his hands, and tears glistened in his eyes.

Then, by a great effort, he in part controlled his feelings, saying, in a voice of emotion:

"I will not weep; he is the happiest. But, tell me, Miranda, how happened this?"

"His end was peaceful," said Miranda, hurriedly giving him the particulars.

"I will strive to be content," said Rowland, with a deep sigh; "but this is a blow I did not look for. I—I—I thought—but no matter, Heaven's will be done."

"Yes, Rowland; let us now look to the future. Tell me what is to be done, and how are you to free yourself from the frightful entanglements that surround you?"

"I am as helpless, Miranda, as an infant, and the few energies I possess are all locked up in that one deadly circumstance that a price is set upon my head by my accusers, and, innocent though I am, I dare not show myself in the face of day, for my very life's sake. Thus you see, dearest, I have become dependent upon those I would fain not hamper with such a charge."

"And yet," said Miranda, "amid all our misfortunes, all the false accusations that have been heaped upon you, and all the malignant persecutions we have endured, how wonderfully and strangely have friends sprung up around us; and even among those, where, perhaps, we should hardly have looked for sympathy and sorrow, we have found such warm hearts, that they are sufficient to redeem human nature from any stigma of universal selfishness that might be cast upon it."

"True—true; in the darkest storms of fate there are some rays of light, bright and beautiful, that bring comfort to the distressed soul, and bid the aching heart not quake in despair."

At this moment, the door of the room leading from the little bar was flung open, and Dick Palmer, with the landlord, entered the apartment.

"There is danger, Mr. Percy," cried Dick—"immediate danger, though what may be its extent I know not."

"The old 'Star and Tinder-Box,'" said the landlord, "is beleaguered at last, and, for once in a way, I'm nearly at my wits' end."

"Rowland—Rowland," cried Miranda, as she flung herself upon his neck in a paroxysm of apprehension, "I am doomed ever to be to you the harbinger of danger!"

"Hush—hush!" said Rowland, "my only hope—my only joy!"

CHAPTER CXXXII.

THE INTERRUPTION, AND ARRIVAL OF MR. JONES—MEDITATED SACRIFICE, AND ESCAPE —DESPERATE CONFLICT WITH THE OFFICERS.

SCARCELY ever had Dick Palmer worn such a face of alarm as he did upon the present occasion; or, rather, it should be called excitement, instead of alarm, for there was not the remotest indication of timidity in his words, looks, or actions; the landlord, too, seemed quite possessed with the idea that no common danger was a-foot, and locked the door through which he and Palmer had passed, as well as the one at which Rowland had entered, and said:

"Now, some of you just have the goodness to tell me what I am to do. I'm stumped for an idea, and don't know which way to turn myself. It seems to me that we are all rather in for it."

"Affairs are desperate," said Palmer, "and yet not quite so bad but they might be worse. I do not think, Mr. Percy, that we can both save ourselves; the house is guarded at every available point of egress by officers; nevertheless, I think that by making up my own mind to be taken, I can make an outlet for you."

"Never!" cried Rowland, "never! Let the consequences be what they may, I never can permit such a self-sacrifice upon your part. I will stand or fall by my own evil destiny. Accept the thanks and admiration of my heart. I should despise myself, as well as be despised by all of you, were I to accept safety upon such terms."

"Right, Rowland," cried Miranda, with a firmness that perfectly astonished Palmer and the landlord; "we may suffer, but it shall be with clear breasts. Never shall it be said that, even in the greatest extremity of evil fortune, you consented to the sacrifice of another to save yourself—death with honour is more noble, more glorious, than life with infamy. Rowland Percy, dearly as I love you, I would stand by your grave, rather than purchase your safety with one act that you could look back upon with the blush of shame!"

The landlord opened his eyes and mouth so wide that it seemed doubtful if they would ever close again, and as for Palmer, such a glow of pleasurable admiration shone upon his face, that anyone would have thought him a man just apprised of some bright and pleasant destiny, instead of being on the brink of capture for infringing laws that would show him but little mercy.

"Mum—miss," said the landlord, when he recovered his speech, "all I have got to say is this ere—you are the out-and-outest female trump as ever I heard on, and afore anybody should so much as wag a little finger at you, they should walk bang over my carcass with rough nailed shoes. I'd guv myself up—I'd guv up the 'Star and Tinder-box'—I'd guv up everybody, rather than a hair of your head should be placed awry. I've been married once, and, consequently, always misdoubted such things as female trumps; but now I'm convinced."

"My heart's best treasure!" cried Rowland, "how admirably have you spoken for me that which I feel, and should myself have said."

"For the love of right, justice, mercy, and Heaven," said Dick Palmer, "hear me. You take a wrong view of this case—the sacrifice on my part is nothing near the sacrifice on yours. I am hunted by the officers of the law for what I have done, you for that of which you are entirely innocent. Sooner or later I must be taken. Moreover, if I am, there are a great many chances in my favour, and not one in yours; for what I am known to be guilty of is of far less importance than that of which you are so wrongfully accused. For Heaven's sake, Miss Miranda, listen to reason, and allow me to act as I propose."

"I cannot—I cannot," said Miranda.

"Moments are precious—I have means of escape, Rowland Percy has none. The narrow passage at the back of this house is guarded by officers. If I make a rush through them they will pursue me, and this is his only chance, for so strong a party of our enemies will take possession of the house, that I fear the upstairs rooms will be of no avail, however skilfully they might be used."

A loud knocking at the bar now attracted their attention, and the landlord, with a sort of half-groan, said:

"There, it's all up now—we are done. They've taken their measures, and won't wait any longer, so there's an end of that caper."

The knocking continued furiously; and, while Palmer laid his hand upon Miranda's arm, and earnestly besought her to reason with Percy, and induce him to act as he advised, the landlord left the room to see who the impatient person was that seemed so intent on attracting attention at the bar.

"Once for all," cried Dick Palmer, "I tell you you will be sacrificing yourself for no earthly object. One of us must be taken, and you could only save me by the same manœuvre that I propose for your benefit. You must recollect, too, Mr. Percy, that, without any disparagement to you, you are not so capable of executing that manœuvre as I am. My firm conviction is, that you are throwing away your only chance of escape for a mere chimera; for, if you do not accept of my proposition, we must both inevitably be captured."

"Palmer," said Miranda, "on your soul, tell me, do you speak from your true conviction, or from your noble and disinterested desire to serve the unfortunate?"

"From my true conviction, as I am a living man, Miss Rankley," exclaimed Dick.

The door of the apartment was opened, and the landlord entered with Jones, who was carrying a bundle, and who without a word went up to Rowland, and began hauling off his coat.

"Good Heavens!" said Percy, "what's the meaning of this?"

"Hold yer gab," said Jones; "I'm agoing to try to make a honest woman of yer. All the fat's in the fire, and we shall have a skrimmage here as'll beat the battle of Waterloo into fits. Just open that ere bundle for me, Dicky; you'll find a gown and a cap there. Mind, Mr. Percy, you are to be for the future a respectable young woman, in search of a place; don't speak to the fellows. Miss Miranda, mum, just give us a help."

"Jones," said Dick, shaking his head, "I fear such a disguise will not evade the eager eyes of Bow Street runners."

"Dicky," said Jones, "Bow Street runners is human beings, and they is do-able as well as other people. Have you got any hot water, landlord?"

"Ah! to be sure."

"Then I tells you what, Mr Percy; when you have got on these ere female togs, just you go into the wash-house, and we'll bring you a tub of hot water and some clothes, and do you pretend to be washing away like bricks. As for you, Dicky, I shall make a diwershun in your favour; there's no warrant agin me as yet. Just lend me that ere swell tile of yours, and the out-an'-out cutaway coat, and I'll try and bother them ere officers' notions of 'dentity."

A tremendous smash, at this moment, occurred at the bar.

It seemed as if every bottle and glass had made up their minds at one instant to commit suicide, and the little party in the inner parlour looked at each other speechless and aghast.

"They are coming it now," said the landlord; and he placed his back against the door as he spoke.

Mr. Jones began whistling a popular air, at the same time turning up his cuffs very deliberately.

"Lots o' work," he said; "jist say what's to be done, and then a fellow has a chance of doing it; this ere washing-tub business as I was a-speaking of, looks now remarkably like no go."

Such a drive came at the door, against which was the landlord's back, that, had he not been of a tolerable, or, rather, an intolerable weight, it must have been burst open.

"Now, Mr. Percy," said Dick Palmer, "can you hesitate? Clear the doorway; and, while I am in the midst of them, by a little activity you may get clear of the house."

The landlord moved from the door, keeping his hand upon the key.

"Are you ready, Dick?" he said.

"Quite."

"And," said Rowland, "we will both attempt this desperate adventure, and, let either of us escape, as chances may direct. Miranda, farewell! Something at my heart tells me we shall meet again."

"Open this door, or we force it," cried a voice from without.

"Oh! the door!" said the landlord; "certainly," and he turned the key, and flung it wide open.

Three stout men made a rush into the room, but they were met on the threshold by Rowland Percy, Jones, and Dick Palmer.

Not a word was spoken, but a desperate struggle ensued, which lasted for several minutes.

The critical nature of his situation, and the awful consequences of being captured, armed Rowland Percy with preternatural strength; so that, although the man he had to contend with was his superior in weight and strength, he fought with a desperation that the officer could make no head against.

They fell heavily to the floor together, but Rowland Percy was uppermost, holding the officer's throat with such a grasp that his strength was evidently fast failing, and a bluish hue began to spread over his face.

In the meantime Palmer had given his antagonist a heavy fall, which brought him upon his head with one of those frightful dabs which experienced wrestlers know how to present to those who are opposed to them.

The third officer who had come into collision with Mr. Jones seemed not to like the turn events were taking.

Drawing a small pistol from his pocket, he placed the muzzle within half-an-inch of Jones' ear, and pulled the trigger; the weapon missed fire, or his destruction must have been certain.

"Thank you all the same," said Jones; and, taking the opportunity of the moment, he drew back his left hand, and gave the officer a crashing blow on the jaw.

It would appear that the officers had made some arrangements with their companions concerning an accession of force, in case any disturbance should be made, for two more Bow Street runners made their appearance at this identical moment at the door of the room.

"Help!" gurgled the man who was held in such an iron grip by Rowland Percy, and, in a moment, the two fresh arrivals threw themselves upon Rowland, and his capture seemed certain.

A second blow, however, on the ear of the man who had attempted to shoot Jones put him *hors de combat*, and, in an instant, Palmer and he threw themselves upon the fresh arrivals, with the view of rescuing Percy from them, and giving him a chance of a rush from the house.

The struggle was a terrible one between those five men; but, as Palmer's object was to free Percy from the entanglements of the fight, and not himself, he was more likely to succeed than if his own safety had been his sole object.

At the expense of a considerable portion of Rowland's coat, and the whole of his cravat, the officers were dragged from him.

"Now, now," shouted Dick Palmer; "scruples are madness; fly—fly!"

This was not so easy, however, as it appeared, for the half-strangled officer had recovered his faculties, and scrambled to his feet with an exclamation of:

"Not so fast, young fellow; you must get yourself some better wings before you can fly yet—you are a prisoner."

Poor Miranda, who had been an agonized spectator of the fray, saw that now all was lost, unless she could do something more than sympathize with the unfortunate Rowland Percy.

There was no time for hesitation, and, on the impulse of the moment, seizing the poker from the fireplace, she dealt the officer, who was scrambling to his feet, a blow on the head that laid him flat again in an instant.

With one bound Rowland was over the bar; a few moments brought him into Drury Lane, which he immediately crossed, and, diving into a mass of courts on the opposite side of the way, disappeared from the astonished gaze of the passers by, who, by his disordered appearance and torn apparel, took him for a madman. ———

TWITTER DIVINES VARLEY'S MURDEROUS INTENTIONS.

CHAPTER CXXXIII.

THE APPOINTMENT BETWEEN TWITTER AND
VARLEY — THE THAMES AT NIGHT — THE
LONELY SPOT.

BLACKFRIARS BRIDGE, on a dark night, when
a light east wind sweeps the principal thor-
oughfares and the river for its whole length,
is not the warmest, nor the most comfortable
spot whereon to wait, or stroll about; but
yet, up to the hour of eight, there had been
waiting, near the centre of the bridge, a tall,
gaunt man, wrapped in a cloak. As soon as
the hour struck, he slowly left the roadway,
and descended the stairs leading to the water's
edge. He stopped on the first landing, about
half-way down.

There he mused for a time; a dark smile
crossed his sallow features, and an expression
shot from his eyes that would have appalled
the soul of any man who had suddenly witnessed it.

This was Bernard Varley, who, not knowing how soon Samuel Twitter might, in the
agony of his spirit, arrive at the rendezvous,
came much before the time in order to prevent
his accomplice from cooling over his half-
made promise. The untempting appearance
of the night and water, he thought, might in-

duce Twitter to repent, and quit the spot, which Varley, if present, might possibly prevent.

Twitter had not yet come, and Bernard Varley paced the few yards backwards and forwards for some time in deep thought; then, leaning with his back against the bridge, became lost in contemplation.

"The night is dark and cold," he muttered: "so much the better—we shall meet with fewer obstacles—fewer craft will be on the river, and the gloom that shrouds everything around will strike terror to the heart of the cowardly wretch, and he will be an easier victim than I expected him to be. The tide is running up, and the wind blows up the river—it will be easy work—a sail—ay, that must be it—oars will not do; I will steer the boat, and Master Samuel Twitter shall mind the sail—yes, he can trim a sail, doubtless. This night appears as if specially appointed for such purposes as that which I have in hand."

He walked down to the water's edge, and looked on the stream as it silently glided by, its deep, calm bosom here and there slightly ruffled, as the waters struck against some impediment in their course.

"Yes," resumed Varley, "a better night for such a work could scarcely be found. I trust he will not fail—it is a pity he should miss so fair an opportunity of quieting all his fears and troubles for the future."

Varley turned towards the stairs, and, re-ascending them, gazed around him. The distant lights appeared to burn more brightly, and seemed to throw out a more ruddy glare since he looked upon the dark and silent stream below.

"He comes," he muttered to himself, but in such a tone of inward satisfaction that at once betrayed the deep-set resolution of his heart, and a brighter gleam of fiendish gladness shot from his eyes, as he crept close beneath the shadow of the balustrades.

At some distance was the figure of a man, whose irresolution was apparent from the very mode in which he made his way towards the spot where Varley stood, but where he was not seen.

He walked forward for a few yards, but at a slow, varying pace, and ever and anon he would come to a halt, as if he debated in his own mind the propriety of returning.

But again he would move forward, and again the same process would be gone through ere he would advance many paces, and all this was done with such an air of secrecy, as if he were fearful lest he should be seen, which induced many persons to look after him with curiosity, to know what a man so acting could mean.

At length, however, Samuel Twitter arrived at the head of the stairs, and peered down towards the water. Seeing no one, he said:

"I wonder if Varley will come—he's not here. Well, I'm glad of it. I have kept my promise, and he cannot complain if I refuse to come again, since he keeps not his time. It is dark, cold, and gloomy. I am very glad he is not come."

"But I am come, Samuel Twitter," said Varley, stepping out from his place of concealment.

Twitter started back with a half-scream, and showed an inclination to quit the spot with much precipitation; but Varley said:

"I am glad, too, to see that you are so punctual and ready, Samuel Twitter. It will be a matter of congratulation to yourself at a future time, if ever you think of this night again, to know it was the means of rescuing us both from many difficulties and dangers, and that this night's work enabled me to settle definitely with you."

"True, Varley, very true," replied Twitter, whose teeth chattered with cold and fear; "but do you intend to go upon the river such a night as this—so cold, so dark, and so severe?"

"Yes, Samuel Twitter; do you think that Rowland Percy would wait where he is if he had to keep an appointment with me for his own benefit, instead of being hanged, as he assuredly will, if, with your assistance, I can secure him, and safely bring him to town?"

"With my assistance, Varley? I cannot do much, and it's so cold that I can scarce stand. Think better of it, and let the officers take him themselves—it is their business, not ours; what else are they for?"

"Samuel Twitter, do you not know that so long as Rowland Percy is at large so long are we in danger of being hanged—ay, hanged—would that have any charms for your mind, Samuel Twitter?"

Twitter shook his head with a groan, and Varley then went on:

"Besides, were he safely disposed of, I tell you again, that the Grange estates shall be sold for what they will fetch, and then I shall settle my account with you, which, you know, Samuel Twitter, I could not do otherwise."

"But will you really sell the Grange estates? If I could believe that you meant me fairly, Varley, with what pleasure could I go with you. I fear—I fear——"

"What can you possibly fear from me, Samuel Twitter—are we not as brothers?"

"Brothers, Varley, brothers?"

"Ay, brothers in crime, you know, at least."

"I didn't do the—the——"

"Murder," added Varley; "no—I know you did not; but you could not well tell what my share was, save at the expense of your life or liberty, which would be the same in a short time; we are both, therefore, deep enough in this affair to make it desirable that we should act fairly towards each other, so that we may, if we choose, part from each other, and have the choice of living in separate countries, and thus put it out of the power of either to injure the other by accident or design. This, I believe, is for the good of us both. Your intellect, Samuel Twitter, must surely at once, and in strong colours, show you that I am acting for your benefit equally with my own."

"Well," said Twitter, "when shall we go?

But you are sure that you will sell the Grange, and give me my share of the proceeds?"

"I will—I will, by all that I hold, or ever did hold sacred, do as I have promised you, if you fairly assist me as I require of you."

They turned down the steps, and proceeded to the foot of the stairs, and getting into a boat, desired to be taken to Searle's boat-house, Lambeth.

They now silently glided over the bosom of the Thames towards their destination, which they were not long in reaching, as the tide went with them.

"Now," said Varley to Twitter, as they quitted the boat, "we will have a sail, you can manage that very well, and I will steer; there is only a light breeze, which will render it perfectly safe."

To this arrangement, Twitter proposed no objection—indeed, he would rather it were so, since the labour was less, and Samuel Twitter hated labour. Ere long they were suited, and a sail was hoisted for them. Twitter stepped into the boat, and Varley followed, seating himself in the stern to take the rudder. In a few moments more they had gained the stream, the light wind filled their sail, and away they went towards Richmond.

The night was very cold and dark, the red glare of the buoys, and the lights from the shore looked dim and distant, making their position lonely and cheerless.

There were but few craft on the water, and after they passed Vauxhall Bridge, they met with scarcely a boat of any denomination.

Twitter's mind was a prey to a thousand torturing reflections; he noted all that would conduce or assist in the commission of such a crime as that which Varley meditated, while Varley himself was well noting all that passed around—the position he occupied on the river—the spot—the lamps—and, lastly, Twitter himself, engaged no small share of his thoughts; for he had seen, by the light at the boat-house, the stock of a pistol protruding from under his waistcoat; of this, however, he took no notice.

They soon passed Battersea Bridge—here the river was very wide, and not a boat was to be seen. On the right lay a piece of low, swampy ground, on which grew tall trees, and, in the summer, parts were cultivated with vegetables, but which was now scarcely to be approached. On this spot Varley fixed his eyes, and calculated chances.

CHAPTER CXXXIV.

THE MURDER—THE DEATH STRUGGLE—THE LAST SHRIEK.

TWITTER'S uneasiness had evidently been on the increase from the moment of starting until the present time. In his heart he cursed his folly for trusting himself with Bernard Varley under such favourable circumstances for the commission of an act of desperation, which should at once hurry him from the world and all its anxieties, a consummation which Twitter by no means devoutly wished; for, like most men who have perpetrated, or assisted in the perpetration of great crimes, he shrank from death as the greatest of all possible evils.

Moreover there was—or he thought there was, which was quite sufficient—a lurking, mysterious meaning in every word Varley uttered. Once or twice, too, he caught the dark, flashing eyes of his master in iniquity glaring upon him, so that, altogether, Samuel Twitter was about as uncomfortable during his aquatic excursion, as anyone could very well be under any circumstances whatever, and most devoutly did he wish it over.

That part of the river they had reached was not overburdened with houses on its banks, so that it was only occasionally that a gleam of light shone upon the water, and gave poor Twitter a ray of comfort, for he thought that Varley would surely attempt nothing while there were human beings sufficiently near to be cognizant of any cry of distress.

"This is rather a lonely spot," remarked Twitter. "Are we near the place of our destination?"

"I trust so," was the reply. "The inquiry, Twitter, is a more profound one than you intended it."

"Profound!"

"Yes, Samuel Twitter; for putting aside the fact, that we are all near our destination—I mean the grave—some of us may be much nearer to it than others. The most cunning of us, Samuel Twitter, in a moment of incaution, will do things that life would be too short to repent of."

"Yes," groaned Twitter; "you've grown quite metaphysical lately, it's not a pleasant subject."

"And yet," said Varley, as if pursuing quite an abstract chain of reasoning—"what is death but a release from worldly troubles—and which of us is without troubles?"

"Very true," said Twitter, trembling so violently that he shook the sail. "I don't mind putting up with my troubles a little longer, however; besides, you know, Varley, it's very unmanly indeed, to fly from one's troubles."

"Ay, true—but why do you keep your hand so constantly in the breast of your coat?"

"My hand—the breast of my coat? Oh, oh! for nothing."

"You look suspicious, Samuel Twitter. What a curious calculation it would be to consider if you could gain most by murdering me, or I the most by murdering you."

"Very," cried Twitter, with a deep groan; "more curious than pleasant a great deal."

"Indeed!"

"Why — why — where are you going, Varley; why—why don't you keep the middle of the river? Good gracious! where are you steering?"

"I like this side of the river, especially in a quiet spot like this, where one can indulge in pleasant imaginations without interruption."

The boat now moved slowly and languidly through the tangled weeds, among which Varley had steered it, and Twitter half-drew the pistol from his bosom, as if he expected each moment that a desperate attempt was about to be made against his life.

The spot was very dark, but the distance between those two guilty men in the boat was so short that Varley could easily perceive the action of Twitter, and, if he persevered in his intention of attempting his destruction, he felt the necessity of securing the weapon with which Twitter was armed, as a preliminary to any other hostile movement.

"Nay, now," he said, "I was foolish to steer in here, for we have got entangled among the weeds, and I must use the sculls, with which we are happily provided, to row us out. Step over here, Twitter; you take the rudder."

"Eh? step over there? I'm rather nervous, and I'm afraid I can't."

"You think you cannot?"

"Ye—yes, Varley; just manage the rudder yourself; I am so cold I couldn't move on any account, besides you are——that is nothing."

By what he thought a very dexterous movement, Twitter got the pistol completely from his breast, and hid it beneath the skirts of his coat, but the manœuvre was not executed so quickly as to escape Varley's notice, and he said:

"Well, Twitter, at least the sail must come down, so let us see your seamanship in accomplishing that."

Twitter looked up hopelessly at the sail, for he had about as much idea of how to pull it down, as he had how to manage a man-of-war.

"Ah, now, Twitter," said Varley, as by a movement of one of the sculls he hit him a hard rap on one side of his head. "You're but a clumsy sailor, but, perhaps, you think life is too short to make it worth while to learn everything."

"Keep off—keep off," cried Twitter, in an agony of terror and pain; "keep off, Bernard Varley, keep off. I may be a fool for trusting myself here with you, but I am a desperate and dangerous man. Keep off, I say, keep off."

He held out the pistol as he spoke, steadying it with both hands, and pointing it as correctly at Bernard Varley's head as his nerves, and the little light there was, would permit him.

"Why, Twitter," said Varley, "are you mad? What is the meaning of all this show of violence?"

"It's loaded to the muzzle," yelled Twitter; "get out of the weeds—go home, no nonsense, Varley: I tell you it's loaded to the muzzle."

"This is strange conduct," added Varley, as he pretended to make great efforts to get out into the middle of the river; "this is very strange and ungrateful conduct. I really——"

While he spoke, Varley had been artfully getting one of the sculls into position for effective use, and, at this moment, with a sudden swing of it, he struck Twitter's arm,

throwing himself back in the boat simultaneously, or rather a little before the blow.

Partly with the sudden fright, and partly under the influence of pain, for the edge of the scull had struck his wrist very sharply, Twitter pulled the trigger of the pistol.

A tremendous report followed, and a strange shower of some sort of missiles from the weapon—for Twitter had really loaded it to the muzzle—passed over Varley's face, within an inch of his most prominent feature.

This was just what Varley wanted; that is to say, that Twitter's pistol should be discharged, and harmlessly. It screwed up his courage to the sticking-place, and it took away, too, from the murder he contemplated, much, if not all, of its cool-blooded atrocity, since he could now almost persuade himself that Twitter was the aggressor, and had tried first to take his life before he, Varley, made any hostile movement whatever.

Abandoning rudder and sculls, he rushed upon Twitter, and, in an instant, had him by the throat.

"Villain!" he cried; "no power on earth shall save you; you are a dead man!"

"Help! help! murder!" shrieked Twitter.

His voice rang over the water wildly and fearfully; but no help was near, and Varley laughed aloud at the impotence of his rage.

"Ay, shriek on," he cried, "Samuel Twitter, shriek on; your cries are music to my ears. Wretch, did you think, for one moment, you had subdued such a man as I am? You have courted your own destruction, and nothing, now, can save you."

He tightened his grasp upon the throat of the terrified wretch.

Twitter felt, indeed, that his last moments had come, and yet, with what little breath was left him by Varley's tightening grasp, he shrieked for mercy—that mercy which he would not have shown himself, and which was equally a stranger to the breast of his ruthless companion in guilt.

"Varley—Varley!" he cried; "you would not kill me! you cannot, would not, kill me! I will be your slave, your abject slave; I will ask for no money, and desire none. You shall command me to what you please, direct me to what you please, and I will not demur. Varley, you do not mean it—tell me you do not mean to kill me. Mercy—mercy—let me live! I ask but for life—life!"

"And you ask in vain," growled Varley, as he tightened his hold, and dashed his victim's head against the gunwale of the boat. "You ask in vain; I have made myself a promise that this night shall be your last, and I will keep my word."

"No, no—mercy! mercy!"

"Have you no prayer, Samuel Twitter—no last wish—no hope?"

"Yes; a prayer for mercy—mercy!"

"None other?"

"Give me life, and I will pray for you."

"Ah! ah! ah!" laughed Varley; "I am past praying for."

There came over the surface of the water at

this moment the sound of a distant voice chanting some merry air, which, after a moment, had its burden taken up by others; and then there was a wild and boisterous shout of laughter, which came strangely and discordantly upon the ears of that terrified man, who believed himself, correctly enough, at his last gasp, for never had mortal man so determined upon a fiend-like act with more resolution than had Bernard Varley made up his mind to the death of Samuel Twitter.

The voices were far distant.

"But, still," muttered Varley, "if I can hear them, they may hear Twitter—no time is to be lost."

Placing his other hand upon his throat, so as to have a desperate clutch, he struck his head against the side of the boat again and again, with the hope of producing immediate insensibility; but such was not the case, for Twitter raised another shriek of such intensity, that it alarmed Varley beyond measure, and he dashed down the head of his victim twice more with fearful violence.

To cast him over the boat's side was the work of a moment, and Varley believed then that he had got rid, once and for ever, of the greatest enemy to his peace.

Such, however, was not at once the fact.

It might have been the sudden immersion in the cold water, or it might have been that Nature herself rallied at the moment with one desperate effort to cling to life; for Twitter, although he was immersed completely in the river, clung, with a desperate energy, by both hands, to the side of the boat, near the stern.

His faculties seemed too confused to allow him to speak; but, by the dim light that came from the heavens, Varley could see the horrible countenance of his victim—white and awful, with here and there a spot of blood upon it, and the eyes bent upon him with so wild and frantic a glare, that even he, heartless ruffian as he was, shrank for a moment aghast from the horrible apparition.

It was, though, but for a moment.

A fear came over him that Twitter would find voice to cry for help, and that the persons he had heard singing might hear him, and come to his assistance.

Springing upon him, he strove to force him to disengage his hold; this, however, was more difficult to accomplish than he imagined, for not even the most savage blows would suffice, and what he apprehended did take place; for, while he still clung with desperate energy to the boat, Twitter again found voice to speak.

"Heaven have mercy upon me!" he said; "I am guilty—guilty!"

"Down—down!" shrieked Varley; "down, I say!"

He struck the hands of the wretched man violently with the movable seat of the boat.

They were crushed and bleeding, but still Twitter kept a desperate hold: it seemed that only with life itself would he part from that one poor chance of saving himself.

Then Varley suddenly thought of an expedient as ferocious as it was effective.

Taking a clasp-knife from his pocket, he opened its largest blade, and commenced drawing it across the fingers of Twitter until he severed the tendons, when, with one loud, gurgling shriek, the unhappy wretch fell backward into the stream.

CHAPTER CXXXV.

AFTER THE MURDER—VARLEY'S DANGER—THE BARGE, AND THE FINDING OF THE MURDERED BODY.

THE perspiration stood upon the brow of Bernard Varley, as he plied his sculls with desperate energy, and rowed from that lonely spot, which would ever be frightful to his imagination, fancying, as his only one source of satisfaction, that now, indeed, he was a free man, and that the only secret that could consign him to the gallows was locked in his own breast.

"Curses on him!" he muttered. "With what a desperate energy he clung to life! I had hoped to have quietly cast him, stunned, into the river, with such injuries upon his body as could be accounted for by accident alone; but now, of course, if the body is found, there will be no end of troublesome inquiry. Well—well, I am at least safe, for I have not now that besetting curse upon all dangerous enterprises—an accomplice."

The river was unusually dark, and Varley was anything but well acquainted with it; still he rowed on, having but one feeling on the subject of his progress, and that was, to get as far away as possible from the spot where the murdered body of Samuel Twitter might soon float.

He, in the course of a few minutes, heard again the voices of those who had been singing; and, in the dim obscurity, as he looked now and then over his shoulder, he saw a large boat approaching, apparently full of people, and with a lantern at its prow.

As his boat glided past, he was hailed by a man, who spoke as if he had been liberally sacrificing to the rosy god, for his voice was thick, and he tripped over his words now and then rather curiously.

"Hilloa!" he said. "Where have you come from?"

"Not from a pot-house," replied Varley, who would not have condescended an answer at all, only that he was anxious to know if Twitter's cries had been heard by those whose voices had come so plainly to his ears.

"Oh, curse you!" added the man. "I suppose Old Nick got hold of you, and made you squall out so as you have been doing."

"Did you hear anything?"

"Yes, to be sure, I am not deaf."

"And yet drunk," said Varley, who, having now ascertained that Samuel Twitter's cries had been heard, desired no further parley with the riotous party in the boat, and plied his sculls accordingly, with a quickness and energy that soon took him a considerable distance in the other direction.

He heard, as he went, a violent dispute going on as to whether he should be followed or not, for the gentleman who was in a state of vinous stultification—as all gentlemen do under such circumstances—felt grievously insulted at being told so.

The angry sounds, however, gradually decreased, until they came to Varley's ears only in indistinct murmurs.

"Curses on the unfortunate management of this affair!" he muttered. "The cries of Twitter have been heard, and, if the body is found, the injuries on it will proclaim in a moment that murder, and not accident, has brought him to death. If suspicion should fall upon me, what can I do? How endeavour to get rid of the fact that I was on the river? If I could hit upon any plan of obtaining evidence that I was elsewhere, all might be well yet."

The chimes of some distant clock now came upon his ears, and he was astonished to find it was so late as eleven, for he had taken no account of the long time that had been consumed in getting so far up the river as he had gone.

The thought then struck him that it would be imprudent to return direct to the boat-builder's at Lambeth with the wherry, as it would but afford another opportunity of identifying him, and likewise excite some observations, from the fact that he had gone out in company with another, and come back alone.

"No," he added, " I will not go back there. Let them find their wherry where they may, and how they may; I will land myself, and turn it adrift into the river."

With this object, he slackened his speed, and turned the head of the boat towards shore, preferring the Middlesex bank as being by far the most convenient for him.

In executing this manœuvre, he did not notice that very near to him was a barge which had just left her moorings, and was slowly emerging from a wharf into the middle of the stream.

So mingled was its black hulk with the dingy hue of the houses on the bank, that he saw it not until he was warned by a loud voice, shouting:

"Wherry ahoy, there! Ahoy!—ahoy!"

In another moment there was a loud crash, the sculls were dashed from his hands, and he found himself struggling in the river.

"Help—help!" he cried, in quite as frantic accents as those which had come from Samuel Twitter in his death agony.

Then something struck him across the arms, and he instinctively seized the object.

It was a rope which had been accidentally towing from the stern of the barge.

With desperate energy he clung to it, but his weight caused it to run out further; and Varley, amid such a whirl of ideas, and a flashing of lights, that he knew not if he were dead or alive, felt himself actually touch the bed of the river.

He could swim, although he was not practised in the art, and the extreme suddenness of his immersion had deprived him of all thought for the moment.

In another instant, however, he was on the surface, and, collecting all his breath, in one loud shout he again cried:

"Help—help! I have the rope—draw in! Help!"

"Ay, ay," said a voice from the barge, and then he felt himself drawn through the water by the rope.

In half-a-minute he was at the side of the barge again, from which the current, during his descent and ascent, had hurried him.

"Hold on!" shouted the man on board.

"Yes," gasped Varley, "yes;" and his knuckles cracked again as he clung to the rope.

Then there was a desperate pull, and he was in safety on a heap of coals in the barge.

He staggered, and fell with a deep groan, for his fears that his last hour had come, as well as the exertion he had been compelled to make, had terribly exhausted him.

The man got a lantern, and held it close to his face for a few seconds.

"Saved—saved!" muttered Varley.

"Yes, you're saved; but how comes it you ventured on the river, when you don't know a barge by sight?"

"The darkness—I did not see it. I am very cold—very cold."

He shook fearfully, and the man, after rummaging for some moments in his pockets, produced a little flask-bottle, which, after uncorking, he placed to Varley's lips, saying:

"There, drink a drop o' that—it's the right stuff. If that don't warm you, nothing will."

Varley drank some of the burning liquor, which was of tremendous strength, and he felt for some minutes as if a red-hot iron heater was in his stomach.

It had its effect, though, for the circulation of his blood quickened, and the shivering, which had made his very teeth chatter, subsided.

"Better?" asked the man.

"Yes, yes—much better. I owe you many thanks, friend."

"Whose wherry was it?"

"I hired it at Lambeth."

"Well, you'll have the pleasure of paying for it, then; for it don't do to run wherries agin barges. I'm going to Limehouse, but I s'pose as you'd like to be put ashore somewhere?"

"I should, indeed."

"Very well. You can hail a boat at the first stairs we come to."

"What reward can I give you, for saving my life?"

"Reward! Oh, I can do as my pal, Ben, did."

"How was that?"

"Why, he saved the life of a child some twelve months or more ago, and he got, after a great deal of trouble, a reward of quite an out-and-out magnificent kind."

"Indeed !"

"Yes. The Humane Society sent him what they calls a medal. It looked for all the world like a bad penny, and Ben had a great deal of trouble to pass it. At last he did though, when he gave change for sixpence once. I hear as they gives away nearly half-a-crown's worth of medals in the course of a year. Somebody tells me as they gave two pounds once to a man who jumped into the London Docks and saved another ; but we mustn't believe all we hears or sees in the papers."

"Take that," said Varley, as he handed a bank-note for fifty pounds to the man. " You need not trouble yourself about a penny medal."

The man held the note up to the lantern, and, when he saw the amount, his eyes opened wide with astonishment.

"Why—why," he said—"do you know what this is ? Who are you ?"

"My name is John Smith," said Varley. "That is a fifty-pound note, I believe, to which you are heartily welcome."

A tear started to the man's eyes, as he said :

"My old mother and father are fighting hard for a few comforts in their old age. This will last 'em out as long as they live, poor old folks. I—I don't know how to say thank you for a fifty-pound note. If it had been half-a-crown now, I could have done it."

"I want no thanks. Hail me a boat. You drew me from the water, where, probably, I should have perished."

"Boat ahoy !" cried the man.

"Ay, ay," responded a voice from the stairs opposite, and a wherry shot out in the centre of the stream.

"Farewell !" said Varley. "My name is John Smith."

"Good-night to you, sir, good-night. I never had such an evening's work as this. My old mother will write John Smith on the inside of the kiver of her Bible, I know."

Varley dropped into the wherry, but scarcely was its head turned to the shore, when he heard a loud shouting from the direction whence the barge had come, and he recognized the voice as that of the half-drunken man with whom he had held a few words of discourse immediately after the murder of Samuel Twitter.

His heart leaped to his mouth, and he sat trembling in every limb as he heard the words :

"Hilloa ! Boat — boat ! We've found a dead body in the river. A fellow has been murdered. Boat—boat !"

The waterman, who had taken Varley, hesitated for a moment, and said :

"A murder !"

"Confusion !" growled Varley. "Do you think I can wait here all night ?"

"But you hear, sir, there's been a murder !"

"What is that to me ? Place me on shore, and you shall have five shillings for your trouble."

The man rowed hard upon this promise, and the boat shot along with great rapidity towards the landing-place.

The party that had been out merry-making kept on shouting for a boat, and exclaiming that they had picked up a body, in accents that came upon Bernard Varley's ear with awful distinctness and meaning.

If by one word he could have annihilated the man who was so persevering in making the announcement, how gladly he would have spoken it !

The boat now grated on the shore, and, throwing a crown piece to the waterman, Varley sprang from the wherry and disappeared in a minute in the darkness that reigned around.

Saturated with wet, as were all his clothes, he felt far from comfortable, and yet he dreaded going into any house of entertainment ; for he told himself with a groan that he had already unfortunately been looked at by too many persons for his safety on that eventful night.

His object was to get back to his hotel, and slip in, if possible, quite unobserved, to the rooms he occupied, when he might, if such a measure were skilfully managed, be supposed to have been there some time.

Getting into the first hackney-carriage he could find, he had himself driven to the street adjoining that in which his hotel was situated, and then, alighting, he walked the remainder of his way, and succeeded in reaching his rooms unobserved, as he thought, by anyone.

Undressing himself rapidly, he got into bed, and then rang the bell.

When a waiter appeared, he said :

"What is the time ? I have been in bed a long while, I think ; for it was daylight when I retired—not feeling very well."

"Past twelve, sir," was the reply. " We didn't know you were at home, sir."

"I have not been out since dinner," said Varley.

CHAPTER CXXXVI.

THE TEMPORARY SHELTER—MATRIMONIAL JARS AND DIFFICULTIES—THE VISIT TO THE HOSPITAL.

ROWLAND PERCY no sooner got clear of the "Star and Tinder-Box," than he rushed into a labyrinth of courts, on the opposite side of Drury Lane, where we left him.

Here he ran from one part to another, with a wild vehemence that excited the curiosity of the passers by.

At length, after he had lost much time in this manner, he fancied he perceived someone following him, and, with a feeling of terror, dashed down a narrow passage, where a door stood open.

In here he went, closing the door softly, and then looked around him to see if he could find any spot in which he could conceal himself ; but all was darkness, and, after a few moments' reflection, he determined to attract someone's attention, and beg refuge for a time.

He felt about until he found the stair-rails, and then ascended a few stairs; he had not, however, gone up many, when a room-door opened on the first-floor, and a woman stepped out, who said, in a tremulous tone:

"Is that you, Robert?"

"No," replied Percy, "it is not; but it is one who needs a few moments' shelter and concealment from his enemies. I have heard it said, that a woman never yet refused such a prayer. I am hunted from house to house—from one place of concealment to another, and yet, as I am a living man, I have committed no crime to deserve it."

The woman at first stepped back with a half-scream, when she saw Percy and heard his voice; but she presently recovered herself, and, when he finished, she said:

"If such be really the strait you are reduced to, come in here for a short time; and, if I do wrong, may God forgive me—I mean well."

"You cannot do wrong in sheltering an innocent man, though others hunt me as a guilty one. Your reward will one day be that of knowing you sheltered an innocent man in the utmost need and distress."

As he said this, Percy walked into the room, which bore but a wretched appearance.

There was a small fire in the grate; a table, on which were spread some plates and tea-things. At one end of the room stood a bedstead and bedding, while, in an opposite corner, was a large chest of drawers.

"You can remain here for a short time," said the woman; "my husband will not be in yet, and, if he should come suddenly, you must conceal yourself, otherwise you would run much danger from him."

"Thanks," replied Percy; "I have been hardly dealt with; life is scarce worth preserving to be hunted about in this manner, and yet one clings to it."

"Do not speak so," replied the woman; "I have had years of trouble, years of hopeless misery—misery which I never hope to be at an end. It is our lot, and repining is useless. I used, at one time, to grieve, and so I do now; who could help it. But sorrow has grown familiar to me."

"But you are not alone; your life is not sought; you have a husband, one who should protect and support you, and shield you from harm."

"Ay, sir, what should be done, and what is done, are very different things," said the woman, shaking her head; "but my husband is not such. Drunkenness is his vice—I may say, passion—and, when in that state, I am the object of his greatest enmity and hate."

"Good Heavens!" exclaimed Percy; "no man can surely act in the manner you describe, and yet be sane enough to be allowed to go about all the ordinary affairs of life!"

"It is true," replied the woman, sadly, "too true; and I am not the only unfortunate creature who has the same kind of evil to go through—not once, or twice, but all my life.

I sometimes think if I were dead I should be happier, and am almost tempted to take means to ensure my destruction; but I shrink from it—I cannot do it."

"Think not of it," said Percy, insensibly offering consolation, and forgetting his own danger, "think not of it. Fortune will yet change, and happier days will yet visit you."

"No, no," said the woman, "no hope, no hope. It is a dreary prospect for me, and I must go through my allotted task, though I sink down and die under it. God loads His creatures with misery for a wise purpose, though we do not always see it."

Percy started—his own case recurred to his mind.

A heavy knock was heard at the street-door, which was opened by someone going out, and a man came blundering upstairs, and stumbling at every second stair, cursing and swearing at every alternate step.

"It is my husband," said the woman, noticing Percy's look of alarm and excitement; "he is in his usual state, and I shall be abused for not having food that he likes in the house, while he spends all he earns at a public-house. You must hide yourself, sir, or there will be danger."

Percy rose, and secreted himself behind some utensils and a table that lay in one corner, out of the way; and he had scarcely done so when the door was flung open by the man, who said:

"You lazy jade, why d—d—didn't you show me a light u—u—upstairs, eh? Answer me that, curse you!"

"I couldn't get to you in time, Robert, or I should," replied the wife, in a submissive tone.

"B—b—but you ought to have g—g—got to me in time; it was your place to do so, your d—d—duty to do so. But that's how it is nobody thinks of me. Here have I—I been all d—d—day long work—ing hard, and, now I c—c—come home at night, you c—c—can't show me a light."

"Come and sit down, Robert," said his wife, endeavouring to get him near the fire.

"I shan't sit down if I don't like. Can't a man st—st—stand in his own room if he likes —without b—b—being told to sit down—by a woman? B—b—but where's my—supper, you jade, where's m—m—my supper?"

"There is none, Robert; you know you left me none at all when you went out this morning."

"Nor none you wanted," said the man, with a sullen, dogged air, as he sat down. "I must have supper; I—c—c—can't work hard all day, and go without my supper. Do you hear?—go and get something to eat."

"I will," said the woman, submissively.

"Then why don't you go?"

"I must have money, Robert; I cannot get things without you give me the means."

"Money be hanged! where do you think I can get money from? People won't give me money."

"But you work for it, Robert, and people

won't let me have things unless I have money to give them in return."

"You won't go and get what I—I want?" roared the drunken fellow, with a coarse oath. "Then I'll make you. If you don't go at once——"

"I cannot get what you want, Robert; indeed, I cannot. Don't strike me—don't strike me; indeed, it is not my fault. I will go and ask them, if you please."

"Curse you," said the brute; "I'll teach you a lesson; I'll learn you to be obedient, madam—I—I will; you shan't complain in this manner for nothing. When I come home, in—in—instead of finding all as it should be, there is nothing at all to be had; I'll teach you d—d—different."

As he said this he rose, and staggered towards her with a menacing aspect, and she in terror, and begging him for mercy sake to spare her, retreated towards the spot where Percy was concealed, until she could go no further, and Percy could see all that occurred.

"Mercy — mercy!" shrieked the woman; "you would not strike me? Oh, say, Robert, you would not strike me! Recollect all that has passed, and have mercy!"

"Curse you!" muttered the man between his clenched teeth, as he with one hand seized her shoulder, and was about to deal her a tremendous blow with the other, when Percy, who could remain in concealment no longer, rushed upon him, and striking up his arm, said:

"Detestable scoundrel! would you strike a woman, and that woman your own wife, and, above all, for no offence of any kind?"

"W—w—who are you?" exclaimed the astonished man, releasing his wife, and reeling backward with surprise.

Percy, however, made no answer, but seized him by the throat, and held him so tight that he could not speak; then, flinging him down, he rushed out of the room.

He had hardly gained the landing, however, ere the woman followed him, saying:

"You have saved me; thank you, and may Heaven reward you! Take this old coat, and throw it over yourself, otherwise you will be detected, for your own is torn to pieces."

"Thank you," replied Percy, as he took the proffered article, which was a brown greatcoat; and, before he could say more, the woman disappeared again upstairs.

He waited a moment or two and listened; but he heard no sound indicative of any renewal of the tumult.

He took the coat, and, opening it, put it on. It was somewhat too large, but not much, and would pass off very well. It was most essential, both as far as hiding his own tattered garments went and the concealment of his person from the view of those who might be inimical to him.

After a few moments spent in listening to the passengers who passed the end of the court, Rowland Percy opened cautiously and slowly the door, and peeped out.

All was still—not a soul was in this part of the court; it was no thoroughfare. At the other end another court crossed, and the passengers passed and re-passed; but Percy saw no signs of anyone watching the place, so, after a while, he ventured out, and, shutting the door after him, walked boldly down the court.

He was perfectly safe; and it is probable, even if the officers with whom he had had his late conflict had met him, that they would have passed him unrecognized. The coat was buttoned to the throat, and the collar turned up, so that his features were hidden from all casual observation.

"Where shall I, where can I now go?" he said to himself; "all, all are parted from me, and my poor father, he is gone. Well, his troubles are over; but, oh! what a parting—what a moment to quit the world in—himself in distress, and afflicted with disease; his son a proscribed man, and flying from those who would take his life; no friendly hand to close his dying eyes, none whom he loved were by to receive his last breath."

A sudden thought flashed across his mind, and he suddenly muttered:

"Ay, ay, I will go and see him—it is strange that I thought not of it before; but grief deprives the mind of its perceptions, and one's heart becomes hardened to all, save one's own sorrows. It shall not be said, though, that the fear of danger prevented me from seeing the last sad remains of my kind and affectionate parent."

He turned down Drury Lane, and pursued his course until he arrived at that part of the Strand by St. Clement Danes and Temple Bar.

After some hesitation, he entered a shop, and inquired the way to St. Bartholomew's Hospital, to which he was directed, and then he made what haste he could thither, on account of the lateness of the hour, fearful lest he should be denied admission.

When he arrived, the place was closed against the admission of strangers or visitors, and he was denied permission to enter.

"You can't come here, sir, unless you've a broken arm, or a back, or a head, and then we can admit you at all times."

"I am not so afflicted," replied Percy; "but I want to see a Mr. Percy, who has died here; I am a near relative, and wish to see his sad remains."

"Ah! sad," said the man. "Well, it's a matter of taste; no harm's done when the old un's out of the way; but what relation are you to him?"

"His son," replied Percy, reluctantly.

"Wery good; then the surgeon will let you in, so you may as well follow me till I get you permission to enter."

Percy did as he was desired, and in a few moments more he entered the apartment where the remains of his father had been deposited.

———

CHAPTER CXXXVII.

THE RESUSCITATION OF TWITTER—THE PLAN OF FORGERY.

WHEN Varley rose on the following morning, he eagerly ran his eye over the newspaper which lay upon the breakfast-table, and, with a flashing eye and burning cheek, read the following paragraph:

"ATTEMPTED MURDER ON THE RIVER.— Last night the attention of a party on the river was attracted by cries of 'Help!' arising from someone apparently suffering violence, but, before they could reach the spot from which the sounds proceeded, all was still. Some time afterwards, however, the neighbourhood of the crime was thrown into a state of indescribable consternation by the finding of the bleeding and inanimate form of a man in the water. The vital spark was not quite extinct; and, by the praiseworthy and active exertions of Mr. M'Fudge, a medical gentleman in extensive practice, he was restored. We have ascertained from the very best authority that his name is Twitter, and the first word he uttered when he recovered consciousness was Harley, and something about the Mange at York. At present the affair is involved in considerable mystery, and a great number of rumours keep perpetually floating about concerning it. The active inspector, Gobbles, assisted by the enterprising officer, A 227, who is further associated with B 122, will, no doubt, ascertain some interesting particulars in time for our next impression."

"Alive—alive!" groaned Varley. "Curses on him—water will not drown him; he is born to be hanged."

A shudder came over Varley's frame as he pronounced these words, for they had a disagreeable significance as concerned himself.

He again read the paragraph; after which he began to calculate the chances of what Twitter would do.

"Dare he, for his own sake, confess all?" he muttered. "No, surely not. In a crime of such magnitude as that which we have together committed, there can be no mercy shown to either party. Perhaps, after all, this attempt upon his life, may convince him how dangerous it is to hold any further communication with me; and I may never see him again, while, at the same time, the fear of compromising himself fatally will prevent him from implicating me in any way."

This was a consoling train of reflection, and Varley resolved that he would not, as had been his first impulse, seek safety in flight, but remain where he was, trusting to the fears of Twitter for his safety.

And so far Varley exercised a sound discretion; for, whatever efforts Twitter might make to be revenged upon him would necessarily require some time to arrange, seeing that he must place himself first in some foreign country, before he could make a charge against Varley, and then such charge must fall to the ground for want of evidence of a legal character to support it, since a mere assertion on the part of Twitter could not suffice for the temporary detention of Varley; and, to come into court to substantiate his accusation, would be to place himself as a prisoner by Varley's side.

"I will not fly even from this danger," he muttered; "I will still persevere in hunting Rowland Percy, and in my pursuit of Miranda, whose scorn only adds to the passion which was already sufficiently consuming. I will spend the Grange estates ere I relinquish my pursuit of her, and then, if I have been unsuccessful, I am content to die."

During that day he doubled his spies, and gave *carte blanche* to the officers, who were immediately in his employment, to spare no expense whatever in pursuing the inquiry. In fact, the spirit of vindictiveness he exhibited surprised even them, and they were not without their suspicions that there was a great deal more in the whole affair than met the eye.

Nevertheless, they were not going to be too curious in inquiring into the motives of a man who paid so liberally, and from whom they got more money from a run of ill-success than under ordinary circumstances they succeeded in handling when most successful.

In the meantime, Twitter was lying at a little public-house, whither he had been conveyed after being taken from the river.

There he was restored to consciousness, or, at least, to life, for it was not until he had awakened from a long sleep that he became aware of what had occurred to him, and could link circumstance to circumstance, until he found himself rescued from a death which seemed inevitable.

"The villain, Varley, would have murdered me," he thought. "Oh, what an escape I have had!"

A sudden accession of pain from the wounds he had experienced, caused him to utter deep groans, and he was advised by one who was watching in his room, to keep himself quiet.

Not only had he received serious scalp wounds, but the barbarous manner in which Varley had cut his hand had, in all likelihood, disabled that member completely, for the tendons had been divided.

A wandering thought did occur to Twitter that it might have been better if he had been killed outright, but only for a moment such an idea found a haven in his breast, and, with a shudder, he told himself:

"Yes, it is something to live. Let me have life, and I will endure anything."

The amount of that endurance, however, presented itself to him in alarming colours when he came fairly to think of it, and he asked himself a variety of pertinent questions with regard to his ways and means for the future.

Could he possibly, knowing what had occurred, ever again appeal to Varley for that assistance which he had no means of getting elsewhere? No; that would be to place his life again in the most imminent jeopardy; for he who had once attempted his destruction was likely to repeat the attempt with a greater prospect of success, arising from the experience of his first defeat.

"What am I to do?" groaned Twitter; "what am I to do? What will become of me? Friendless, homeless, with but a few pounds in my possession, and prohibited, by a fear of actual murder, from applying to him, upon whom alone I have any claim in this world."

These sad reflections were by no means of assistance in recovering Twitter from the effects of his wounds and his immersion in the river; a deep melancholy came over him, and, when the active Inspector Gobbles called again at the public-house, in order to get the full and interesting particulars of the attempted murder from the mouth of the rescued victim, he was amazed to find that victim most unwilling to hold any communication upon the subject, and, apparently, as anxious to bury the whole affair in oblivion, as if, instead of being the attacked party, he had compromised himself by a considerable amount of criminality.

"But," said Gobbles, "you'll tell me who did it? Consider the ends of public justice, and the reputation of the Metropolitan police."

"Don't trouble me," said Twitter; "I don't care about public justice, or the Metropolitan police either."

"But," urged Gobbles, "you said somebody tried to murder you."

"But I didn't say who."

"Ah, but you did though; you said it was Harley, or Larley, or Barley, I don't know which; you see, we inspectors of the Metropolitan police know everything."

"Then you may decide between Harley, Larley, and Barley, at your leisure," said Twitter.

"But, my dear sir, we must take up somebody."

"Very well," said Twitter.

"Very well! yes, it's all very fine to say very well, but you must tell us who to take up. Come, come; are you aware that you are compounding a felony, and we inspectors of the Metropolitan police never suffer that."

"You may all be hanged," said Twitter, who was fairly provoked, thinking it was hard enough that he was placed in a position to be nearly murdered, and yet dared not accuse his enemy without being pestered to death by the active Inspector Gobbles upon the subject.

"Hilloa, hilloa!" cried Gobbles, feeling for his staff; "do you mean to say you won't say anything more about it?"

"I do—go to the deuce."

"I shall go to Bow Street," said the inspector, jumping up and stamping with great fury. "Ay, I shall go to the commissioners—I shall go to all the magistrates—confound it all, I have never had a case of murder since I have been an active and exemplary inspector. I shall go mad. What do you say to that, eh?"

Twitter had coiled himself up in the bedclothes, and would say nothing, so that the inspector, after shouting out "eh, eh, eh!" four or five times, was compelled to jam his hat violently on his head, and leave the house in a most unsatisfactory state of mind, which he resented upon the first police-officer he met, declared that he smelt a mile off that he had been drinking gin, and when the unhappy lobster ventured to insinuate that such was not the fact, and that he only wished he could smell some gin, he was reported for insolence to his superiors, to be made a great example of.

When Twitter was alone, he groaned out:

"Oh, if I only dared accuse him! If I only dared have him put into jail and hanged afterwards! but I dare not; he might keep the secret until the morning of his execution, till he saw that there was no hope, and then he would tell all about the murder at the Grange, and I should be hanged, too. Revenge is sweet, but sometimes too expensive."

Twitter then felt exhausted, and fell into a deep sleep, after which he awoke, greatly refreshed both in mind and body, and more capable, in a great degree, of coming to some accurate conclusion as regarded his peculiar position than he had been.

"I must put," he said, "my long-cherished scheme into execution, and avail myself of the means which Varley has taken to secure his own safety. That yacht which he has purchased so wisely, and the particulars concerning which I so strangely, but fortunately became acquainted with, shall be put to my own use. When I am in some foreign land, then I can take active measures against him; nay, what is to hinder me writing a full statement of the murder at the Grange, and placing it in the Liverpool Post-office before my own departure, but only so short a time before it, as shall ensure to me the advantage of many hours start before it can reach its destination. Yes, that will be a good scheme, a most admirable scheme, and one which surely cannot fail of success. All I require is a sum of money to support me abroad, and free me from the necessity of striving for a subsistence. I have before thought of a plan of procuring that—a plan, which, under ordinary circumstances, would be attended with much danger, but which, as I am situated, can do me no harm if it does me no good. I can commit a forgery upon Bernard Varley, and dare he accuse me of it? No, certainly not. If I am so situated with regard to him that I dare not accuse him of an attempt to murder me, he dare not charge me with the crime of forgery—nay, he must admit the signature to be his own. I have taken the opportunity of possessing myself of blank cheques from his cheque-book, and well I know his handwriting—what is to hinder me from filling up one for a large sum?"

This was so pleasant an idea to Samuel Twitter, that in the contemplation of it, he almost forgot his numerous wounds.

He eagerly ran over in his mind all the

probabilities and possibilities connected with the scheme, and he wondered to himself that he had not concocted it before, for he saw how very safe it must be.

"What risk can I run?" he muttered; "none at all. Let them at the banking-house suspect the cheque and refuse to pay it, well, what then? I offer to wait there until Bernard Varley be sent for—he is sent for—what then? Dare he repudiate the cheque? No, a glance of mine will be sufficient to assure him, that my being given into custody on a charge of so serious a nature, will be the signal to me to tell at once all the particulars of the murder at the Grange. Oh, the plan is an admirable one, and very safe indeed."

Twitter then amused himself by considering for what sum he should draw the cheque. Varley's account at the bankers he knew to be very large, and he had no fear of overdrawing it.

After much consideration he resolved that the cheque should be drawn for eight thousand pounds.

"As well that as eight hundred," he thought, "so far as the safety of the proceeding is concerned. Tremble, Varley, I have you now in my grasp—you cannot escape me. Not only shall you pay me handsomely for the assistance you have had from me, but you shall suffer, and that at once, too, the full penalty of murder."

CHAPTER CXXXVIII.

THE ARREST OF JONES AND PALMER—THE DETERMINATION OF MIRANDA.

WE left Miranda and her friends, Palmer and Jones, in a very precarious and awkward predicament at the "Star and Tinder-Box," in Drury Lane, after Rowland Percy had escaped from the officers who had so very nearly succeeded in capturing him.

After Miranda had made the exertion we are aware of, in order to rescue Rowland from the grasp of the officer who held him, she abandoned all resistance, and suffered herself to be seized, which was done rather roughly by one of the Bow Street runners, while two of them rushed into Drury Lane in pursuit of the fugitive.

When they had got there, however, they had not the remotest idea which way he had gone, and they were compelled, after making inquiries of several persons, and receiving no satisfactory information, to admit to each other that, at all events, for the present, the attempted capture had failed.

During this absence Jones made an effort which said more for his generosity than his prudence.

There was quite sufficient force remaining to prevent him and Palmer from both escaping; but he would have done everything to secure the freedom of Palmer, and, watching his opportunity, he closed with the officers who were left, and engaged them so completely in a desperate struggle with him that

Palmer was comparatively free to go or stay, as he pleased.

"Bolt, Dicky, bolt!" shouted Jones.

"And leave you? No."

"Don't be a fool. Cut—cut!"

Palmer did make a rush to the door; for, although he was as full of generosity and good feeling in such a matter as could be, his reason told him that there was no policy in two being taken when one would suffice; and, besides, he knew he could do a great deal for Jones out of prison, and nothing in.

These thoughts darted through his mind in an instant, and he would unquestionably have effected his escape, had he not, at the very door, encountered the two officers who had gone in pursuit of Rowland Percy, and were returning so much disappointed.

These pounced upon Dick Palmer in a moment, and, exhausted as he was by the previous struggle, he was no match for the sudden attack of two powerful men.

After one desperate attempt to pass them, he was compelled to surrender himself a prisoner.

He was brought back into the bar of the public-house; and when Jones saw him, he shook his head, saying:

"Well, Dicky, it wouldn't do—better luck another time. What's the odds as long as you are happy."

"I have still to thank you, Jones."

"Thanks be blowed!"

"Thank you both for nothing," said one of the officers, wiping the perspiration from his forehead.

Handcuffs were expeditiously placed upon both the prisoners, and then a consultation ensued as to what was to be done with Miranda.

"Take her to Bow Street," suggested one; "I'll charge her for obstructing me in my duty, and be hanged to her. Here's a lump on my head as big as a turnip."

"I've seen little turnips," remarked Jones, "striking agin big ones, and that accounts for it. Now, I tells you what: you are all very clever fellows in your way, but you've been rather done to-day, and you knows it. Least said is soonest mended, you know. Now, if you are such out-and-out flats as to interfere with this young lady, because she laid the poker over your heads, you'll never hear the last of it. Leave her alone, and nobody will know much about it. Don't be fools. What will you take to drink?"

"There's some truth in that," remarked one of the officers to another.

"Besides," whispered his companion, "this, you may depend, is the identical girl that Mr. Varley wants to find out. You know, he offers a cool fifty to whoever will bring him word where she lives."

"So he does."

"Well, then, let's allow her to go, and one of us can watch her. Who knows but we may light upon Percy by so doing, for she's a bit of a sweetheart of his, as we have all heard."

ROWLAND PERCY LISTENS TO THE CONVERSATION IN THE TAVERN.

This little conference was, of course, carried on in a whisper, so that it did not reach the ears of the prisoners; but they tolerably well guessed what its purport was by one of the officers suddenly saying:

"Well, well, let the girl go. We don't want to trouble her for all she has done."

"Miss Rankley," said Palmer, "beware. Your footsteps will be dogged—your every action will be watched—beware!"

Miranda clasped her hands, and, with a despairing look, said:

"What will now become of me? Are all my friends lost to me? Alas! alas! where now shall I find succour?"

"My advice, miss, now," said Jones, "is to go to York."

"And good advice, too," cried Palmer. "Follow it, Miss Rankley, I implore you. At York you will find, as you well know, dear friends, who will warmly welcome you. Do not hesitate. The landlord of the house will, I am sure, on my account, furnish you with the means. Do not, I pray you, sleep another night in London."

"That's the dodge," said Jones.

Miranda looked inexpressibly distressed.

The idea of leaving Rowland in more difficulty and danger than he had ever yet been was terrible to her, and yet her reason assured her how powerless she was to do him any good, while she felt what injury she might inflict by any attempt, closely watched as Palmer assured her she would be, to find him out, and breathe one word of consolation in his ear.

"I will go," she said; "I will follow advice which, I know, is given me by true friends. I will go to York. Farewell to you both!—Heaven help you; I have nothing but prayers to offer in your behalf."

"We don't want nothink," said Jones. "Just you take care of yourself, Miss Miranda. Don't bother yourself with nobody; and when you feels queerish and uncomfortable, in consekence o' things not toddling on just as they ought, don't take to gin, as I did, but console yourself with a *hidea*, which is that it's all the same a hundred years arter."

"God bless you, Miss Rankley," said Palmer. "Something even now tells me that happier days are in store for you, and that the clouds which have hitherto obscured your destiny will dissipate, leaving a brighter sun behind them than has ever yet shone upon your fortunes."

"Lawks!" said Jones, "there's a speech. Well, well—it's all the same. I wishes you luck in a bag, and shake it out as yer wants it."

"Thanks—thanks to you both," said Miranda, mournfully. "I have nothing else to offer."

"Didn't you mention about something to drink?" remarked one of the officers.

"Yes, I did," said Jones. "What's it to be?"

"Oh, anything mild. Suppose we have some hot brandy-and-water."

"Wery good."

Miranda slowly left the room, in obedience to the beckoning of the landlord, and when she reached the next apartment, he said to her:

"Never mind what's happened, my dear. Percy has got away again. It seems as if he wasn't to be nabbed. You wait here till these chaps are out of the house, and then, if so be as you do wish to go to York, I'll put you in the coach to-night, and see you off."

He then left her, and proceeded to the bar, where divers glasses of brandy-and-water were brewed and discussed, during which all sorts of disagreeable feeling were washed down.

"This won't do, you know," remarked one of the officers to the landlord, in a tone of voice half-jocular and half-earnest. "How you go on balking us continually."

"Balking you? Nonsense! What could you do without my house, I should like to know. Look you, now, the matter stands this here way. You are like sportsmen after game. Well, my house is a preserve; and when you want to bring down any particular bird, you naturally come here, thinking you have a good chance."

"There's something in that."

"Something? There's everything in it. You'd be all abroad without houses like mine, and wouldn't know when and where to light on anybody."

"Well, I suppose—that is—just fill this glass again."

"Certainly; and, you see, you must not grumble if now and then I take a fancy to someone, and try to keep him out of the fire. Any more sugar?"

"No—yes, of course. It's all right."

"I knowed it was," said Jones. "Now, I'll tell you what. You are all of you getting tin from that wagabond, Bernard Varley, to carry on the war. Now, I can tell you there isn't such a rascal unhung, and some day he will be hung."

"Well, what's the odds to us? Here's luck. Come, we must be off now."

Jones drank freely enough of the brandy and water, but Palmer could not be induced to touch it.

A gloomy depression seemed to have come over him, and he scarcely spoke in answer to the various remarks which were made to him.

"Come, come, Dicky," said Jones, "don't be downhearted, man. All isn't lost as is in danger."

"It is not for myself," said Palmer. "But no matter—no matter."

The party now proceeded to Bow Street, where both prisoners were, after a very slight examination, remanded till the morrow, in consequence of the officers stating that by then they would be prepared with more serious charges against them than merely obstructing the apprehension of a criminal, and harbouring and aiding a condemned felon.

Palmer said nothing at all; but Jones, when asked if he had any statement to make, replied:

"What's o'clock?"

"Come, come," said the magistrate. "You will do yourself no good by any low impertinence here."

"I only asked," added Jones, "cos it will take some time for me to make the speech as I intend to make, and I don't want to hinterfere with your worship's dinner time."

"Remove him, officers," cried the indignant magistrate. "We cannot have the public time wasted in this wilful manner."

"Here's injustice," cried Jones. "He axes me what I've got to say, and then won't hear it. I tell you what it is, old *habeas corpus*, I'll have you removed from the bench. Mind what you're arter, or I shall be forced to do it."

CHAPTER CXXXIX.

ROWLAND PERCY AT THE HOSPITAL—THE ATTEMPTED CAPTURE BY THE FAT PORTER—A NEW PLOT.

WHEN Rowland Percy entered the room in which the sad remains of his father had been placed, his mind felt the full force of the misfortune that had befallen him.

Up to this moment self-preservation and active exertion had engrossed much of his thoughts—they, indeed, forced him from the indulgence of gloomy and melancholy images.

But grief, sooner or later, will have its way,

and indulgence in sorrow is, perhaps, the safest means of ultimately banishing the painful reminiscence from the mind. It exhausts itself—the well of grief becomes dry, the elasticity of the mind is gradually restored, and, though the event be never banished from the mind, or forgotten, yet the recurrence of sad images seldom brings back the full tide of grief as when it first exerts its influence upon the mind.

Rowland's thoughts, for some hours, had been directed into a different channel; indeed, instinct was the most active principle within him from necessity; but this had now ceased, his mind now came, for the first time, fully to contemplate his heavy bereavement, and his present situation.

These were no happy topics for thought. Despair seized his soul, and dried his tears—his heart beat violently, and his head swam as he neared a part of the room where a screen had been drawn round at some distance from a truck bedstead.

"This," he thought, "then, is the spot where they have placed the remains of him to whom I owe life."

He turned round the screen, and, with a slight tremor—a slight quiver of the lip, and moisture of the eye, approached the body.

Meagre and thin, the poor old man had evidently suffered much from exhaustion, for now Percy saw him, he appeared emaciated, and brought to a mere skeleton.

"It is my father," he murmured, when he lifted the sheet from off the features of the corpse, and gazed at it intently for several minutes in silence, during which his heart heaved with inward emotion; "and I have brought him to this. I have been the cause of this sad end of one who would willingly have laid down his life to save mine. Oh, it is a hard thing to bear, and yet I am told to submit in silence. Can there be such a superintending Providence as we are sometimes told of, and yet such deeds allowed to be enacted? The good and great to be a sacrifice to the unjust and the vicious; the real criminal allowed to lie in peace and security, to enjoy the fruits of crime, while the innocent are hunted from spot to spot, and the fear of death and ignominy ever present to the mind. It cannot—it cannot be."

"Oh, father, forgive me—forgive your proscribed but innocent son, for all the misery he has caused you, and, should it ever be in his power, a terrible vengeance shall be exacted from your enemies.

"I live but to exact it. I live but to protect that dear angel, Miranda. To protect her—no, that were, indeed, too much to expect from me. I—protect anyone! I have not a home—not a shed that I can call my own to lay my head under. I am an incumbrance to her. She, the young, beauteous, and good, will ever find protection. So much innocence and angelic beauty can never be at the mercy of villainy.

"Oh, Bernard Varley, what a terrible day of reckoning will one day come upon you!

Here is more blood upon your hands—hands already deeply stained with the murder of Sir George Rankley."

For a few moments the thoughts that crowded fast upon his brain almost drove him to frenzy, and, with blood-shot eyes, he stood gazing on the cold, inanimate form of old Mr. Percy.

How long he might have remained in this state, it is impossible to say—nay, he knew not how long he had been there himself; but he was suddenly awakened to a sense of his own precarious situation, and he started on hearing his own name pronounced in a whisper, on the outside of the door.

He listened attentively for a few moments—a shuffling of feet ensued—a voice said:

"It must be him—there can be no harm done if it be a mistake, so go in, Jobbins, and seize him—you are big enough, and ugly enough."

"Very like, sir; but you will hold me harmless with the governors, if it should turn out wrong!"

"I will. Remember, I will reward you handsomely, if I get all they have offered."

"He's a desperate man—eh?"

"You are big enough," replied the other.

"I know that; but I am not so slim as I was twenty years back, and I can't run, so you must stop him from coming out."

"Oh, yes, I'll shut you both in, and then you must have him anyhow."

"Oh, lor, no—don't do that, he'll be having me. I can't abide being shut up with a murderer. You know he may be used to it, and then he'd make no bones in cutting my throttle."

"Well, I'll undertake to sew it up for you, and all will be well again, I daresay."

"Oh, yes; but I'd rather somebody else's throat were cut than mine, and the idea of a needle being run through my flesh, makes me nervous and chilly. I recollect seeing a man's throat sewn up once—it was done by a young gentleman—one of your pupils, who——"

"There—there—go in and take him," said the other, interrupting him; and opening the door, the fat porter entered; but was at first staggered to see Percy within a few paces of him.

After the first start, he made a rush at Rowland, saying:

"Surrender—you're my prisoner. I've got——"

He had got so far, when a catastrophe occurred that stopped his exclamation, and rendered him incapable of finishing, for, as he rushed at Rowland Percy, who, when he saw the other's situation, stepped back, the fat porter came in violent contact with the screen, with which he got mysteriously entangled, and falling down, the screen fell over him, and completely hid him from sight.

"Murder—help—fire—oh! oh!" screamed the fat porter.

But Rowland Percy heeded not his cries, and instantly stepped on him, and made towards the door, which was being opened by the house-surgeon, who was coming to the assistance of the porter, who appeared to be in such peril.

"Hold him, Jobbins—be quiet, my——"

His further converse was cut short by a tremendous blow in the face, which Percy dealt him.

The house-surgeon's eyes flashed a thousand lights, and he fell heavily to the floor.

Percy immediately rushed down the stone stairs that led to the hall-door, which, by good fortune, had been only left latched, and thence across the yard, where, after a moment's delay, he passed the iron gates, and emerged into Smithfield.

Rowland Percy was once more free—another escape had been effected. A second time that night had his capture been considered certain by his enemies, and a second time had their schemes been rendered abortive. The pursuit was long and hot, how much longer it was to continue, and how much longer he was, by strange good fortune, to be able to baffle his enemies, he knew not; but the day must speedily come when all would be unavailing, and when he would probably fall into the hands of his persecutors.

He felt harassed and fatigued, careless and indifferent as to where he went, and what he did.

After walking about for a short time, he entered a public-house, and, seating himself in the first room that presented itself to him, he called for some refreshments, with the determination to stay there for an hour or two.

"I am not known to anyone save the officers who have seen me, and Varley and Twitter; I may pass through London, and never be detected—at least, I shall run no more risk than when I was hiding in places supposed to be safe, but upon which the officers of justice always have their eyes, and are carefully watching."

While these thoughts were occupying his mind, the people around were engaged in earnest conversation, but in too low a tone for Percy to hear distinctly what was said, and, there being many others in the room, he did not attempt to listen.

The room itself was large and low-roofed, divided off into several compartments, or boxes, as they are called; on the top of these partitions were small brass rails, on which hung little dingy curtains, so that the occupant of one box could, by drawing these, render himself invisible to the occupants of the next.

It was in the smallest of these that Rowland Percy had ensconced himself, scarcely noticed by the numerous guests, many of whom, indeed, had departed, leaving only the more inveterate topers behind.

Percy's state of mind was such that he heeded little what passed around him. His thoughts were with the dead. The decease of his father preyed upon him—it was a chill to his heart beyond what he had yet felt, a heavier blow than he had yet experienced. Relentless was the fate that pursued him.

Beggared and proscribed—his dearest ties—those whom the bonds of blood and affection drew closer to his heart than all the world besides, were all suffering alike; one deep gulf seemed about to swallow them up, the extreme of suffering and despair sat heavy on their hearts, and yet he, Rowland, was unable to help them, to aid them in any way; nay, he was the greatest bar to their happiness; he it was who caused the suffering of the beauteous and heroic Miranda Rankley.

That name acted like a charm upon his mind, it seemed real; the very thought rushed through his frame, and appeared palpable to his senses, as if it had been uttered by someone present. He awoke from his dreamy trance, and listened to the conversation that was being carried on by several individuals in the next box to his own.

It was no delusion, the name of Miranda Rankley had been uttered. Nay, it was with almost a start of surprise that he heard it coupled with his own.

"I tell you," replied one, "we should run as fair a chance of finding him as the officers themselves."

"That is very doubtful," remarked another, "but I don't mind making one; I have time on my hands, and so we all have."

"Yes, and the reward is heavy, very heavy, and would be an object to us."

"Of course, it would be the only object that we should have in view; to seize him would be merely the means of obtaining that object; other considerations apart, I'd rather the young fellow escaped than not; he has tried hard for his life, and well deserves to save it, after the efforts he has made, especially as I think his guilt is doubtful."

"Yes; but we have nothing to do with that. You know that an attentive and respectable jury of twelve enlightened and intellectual human animals have declared him guilty, and that is enough for us. There's no gainsaying that, I believe."

"Of course there isn't. Let me see, there are five of us; well, we will all take our chance of meeting with him somewhere; we will walk about, look and pry into everything, and, should one of us succeed, the reward is to be divided among the lot—the whole five are to have equal shares in the amount."

"Agreed, agreed," said several voices, and then the subject was, with one consent, dropped, and other topics resumed.

"So," thought Rowland Percy, "my danger thickens as the number of those intent upon my capture increases. Well, well, it must come to that at last. I begin to fear that Heaven and earth have alike deserted me; but I have one resource yet, I will not be taken alive—my disfigured corpse they may indeed insult and degrade, but life itself will be beyond the reach of their malice. These men, however, know me not; they have already seen me, and I will wait here until they have gone."

CHAPTER CXL.

MIRANDA AND THE LANDLORD OF THE "STAR AND TINDER-BOX"—THE DEPARTURE FROM LONDON, AND THE HEAVY OUTSIDER.

IT would have been a singular sight to anyone who had known Miranda Rankley in her palmy days of wealth and happiness, when she had but to form a wish and it was gratified, and who had also been acquainted with the landlord of the "Star and Tinder-Box," his mode of life, and his associates, to have seen these two walking arm-in-arm through the streets of London, much in the guise of father and daughter.

Could Sir George Rankley, a baronet, have returned to this life, he would, indeed, have been surprised at this association of his beautiful and dearly-loved daughter with the companion of thieves, and the worst characters in the metropolis.

But these men are not lost to all sense of justice, and it often happens that they display more untiring sympathy towards the oppressed than those who, from their wealth and station, are better qualified to afford it, yet who lack the desire to do that good which they are so well able to bestow.

Poor Miranda Rankley felt but too glad to have the arm of the kind-hearted landlord to lean upon, for she was nearly worn out with fatigue and the harassing anxieties that she had been compelled to bear up against. Her whole frame seemed bowed down. Since Rowland's escape her spirits, indeed, were better—her heart felt a little less of the load it bore, but she could not hide from herself the fact that Percy was in a precarious position.

The landlord of the "Star and Tinder-Box" had allowed her to walk by his side for some time in silence. He thought that it would not lessen her sorrows should he attempt to divert her attention from them, and in which he felt he should neither be doing a good or a kind action if he succeeded, which he would not have done.

Now, however, that they had nearly reached the coach-office, he thought he should no longer be acting for the best if he remained silent; so he proceeded to give her some advice.

"Miss Rankley," he said, "now that we are nearly at the spot you will start from, excuse me if I give you a little advice. I have lived some years. No matter how I came by it, but I have had much experience in the world, and its ways. Have as little communication with those who may be your fellow-travellers as possible; but as soon as you arrive at York, seek out your friends, and remain with them till some event or other calls you imperiously away again; but, believe me, it will be safer for Rowland Percy that you should be no longer in London."

"I will be guided by what you say," replied Miranda, "as I am sure your advice is the best, for you are well qualified to give it. I see I can be no longer useful here; my

presence only endangers him I would sacrifice my life to preserve."

"Exactly," replied her companion, "and hope for the best. Stay there until something happens that shall change the aspect of affairs. The desperate efforts that are made to capture Rowland Percy are, in my mind, so much evidence of his innocence, and that those who accuse him well know it—they think, were he once executed, they would have nothing to fear."

"Do you think so?" inquired Miranda.

"I do indeed, and you may rest assured, that should he succeed in escaping the search that is making for him, he will yet live to see his innocence established."

"Thank you, thank you," replied Miranda, "for those words; they convey comfort to my mind, though it be but small. The risk he runs is fearfully great—I pray to Heaven that it will befriend him—that it will protect the innocent from the machinations of the wicked, for poor Rowland Percy is as innocent of the horrid crime imputed to him as Heaven itself, and as sure is it that Bernard Varley is the real criminal."

"In my mind, Miss Rankley, there is no kind of doubt respecting the share these two men, Varley and Twitter, had in the death of the unfortunate Sir George Rankley—they are guilty."

"They are; and yet the one professed to be the bosom friend of my father, and the other was indebted to him on the score of gratitude, for Sir George was a kind and liberal master."

"Well, Miss Rankley," replied the landlord, "we will not speculate upon their motives, but the fact is evident, and will be, I hope, apparent to everybody, one of these days. Here we are now at the office—follow me, and I will inquire if there be a place vacant."

The landlord now entered a gateway, from which opened a door into the booking-office, and entering this, he inquired of the clerk if there was an inside place vacant for York; being answered in the affirmative, he immediately secured it, and turning to Miranda, said:

"Your place is now secured, you had better come and at once take your seat, as I saw that the coach was being got ready outside."

It was indeed quite ready, merely waiting for the coachman to ascend and assume the sovereign control of the whole machine. The landlord, therefore, handed her in, and saw that she was safely bestowed, at the same time he gave her a small parcel, which he desired her to take care of, as she would need it on the road.

She had barely time to thank him and express a hope that Rowland Percy would be safe, when the coach began to move slowly away.

"Have no fear of that," replied the landlord, still holding by the door, and willing to give what comfort he could; "he shall not want a friend while I have it in my power to be one to him."

He could not hear the reply, for he was compelled to let go his hold of the door, and the coach drove off.

Thus was Miranda now fairly on her way back to the very place from which she had escaped with so much difficulty and danger.

Under what singular and different circumstances did she leave the metropolis, and journey towards York! And what changes had taken place since she first set out from her native city!

Since then many hair-breadth escapes had happened, and poor Mr. Percy had died, and still lay an unburied corpse in a public hospital. These were sad and dismal thoughts to pass through the mind of a young and beautiful girl, one who had barely touched the cup of life.

The coach rattled on through the streets, and attracted her attention to many objects that she now saw as they passed them at a quickened pace. The lights and shops appeared more numerous than ever, and the people more busy, and in greater numbers; the fact was, the pace at which she was going through the streets brought her a quicker succession of objects, and their number hence appeared to be increased.

After stopping at one or two places for more parcels and passengers, they fairly set off at a travelling speed; yet it was some time ere they were entirely free from London, either its shops or its lights; they lined the road-side for some miles, and it was not until the first change of horses took place that Miranda opened the small parcel the landlord of the "Star and Tinder-Box" had given her, the contents of which she found to be a silk purse, somewhat the worse for wear, but well filled with cash.

Miranda looked at the purse and its contents. Tears of gratitude started to her eyes as she thought of the sympathy and kindness she had experienced from people who could scarcely have been expected to show any. This last act of kindness from one whom she had never seen but once, and who probably she would never see again, came forcibly to her mind.

The horses were quickly changed, and off they started at a good, rattling pace, passing objects in the dark roads at a great speed; but these were invisible, or mostly so, to the inside passengers.

The night was very dark, the wind blew very keenly over the fields, over heath, and over moors; the old trees rustled to the sound of the eastern tyrant, who stripped the branches of their last leaves, leaving but the bare and naked trunks.

It was a cold night, and the outsiders must have felt it. Many of them wrapped themselves up in a wonderful quantity of great coats and shawls, continuing, nevertheless, to dismount and refresh at every inn the coach stopped at to change.

Thus they travelled onwards till daybreak. Miranda felt the position to cramp her much; she had never seated herself in one place for so many hours before this; the weather was bitterly cold, and she drew her shawl around her closely, to screen herself from the weather.

They stopped, and had an early breakfast, and at several other inns Miranda had the opportunity of alighting, refreshing and warming herself at a good fire.

It was near night ere they reached York. The Minster spire she could just see before they reached the town; and, when she felt the coach rattling over the stones, she said:

"So here I am again at York! What events now will happen to disturb the peace and repose of this now quiet city?"

The coach now stopped; it had reached its destination.

CHAPTER CXLI.

PALMER IN NEWGATE—THE FRIENDLY VISIT —THE BLACK HOLE.

DICK PALMER'S capture was, perhaps, the severest blow which a malignant destiny had still to give to Rowland Percy. It deprived him not only of a sincere friend, but one of almost boundless resources.

Palmer himself felt as keenly as anyone could the situation in which he was placed. We need scarcely now inform our readers that, however he had determined never to exhibit such a sentiment—however he had resolved that he would never, by word or action, let his heart's secret be known, he loved Miranda Rankley!

How different, though, was his love in its manifestation from the wild passion which Bernard Varley affected to feel for the beautiful girl, who, through his vices, had been "toppled from her high estate," and reduced to such dire extremities of evil fortune. Varley's passion was a purely selfish one, looking only to its own gratification, heedless if its object were its victim or not. With poor Dick, the case was widely different. From a knowledge of her noble endurance of the many trials she had gone through—from an appreciation of her heroic virtues—from an admiration of her more than mortal beauty— he loved her—but his love was a pure and holy passion, seeking unselfishly the happiness of its object only. He never dreamed of attempting to disturb the feeling which he knew was deeply rooted in Miranda's breast for Rowland Percy, because he thought Rowland Percy deserving of such a feeling.

"No," he told himself, "he shall never know a pang by being made acquainted with my hopeless passion. Blessings on her! may she be happy with the object of her choice, and I shall think some of my own misdeeds in some measure compensated, and my life altogether not idly spent, if I succeed in rescuing her from the calamitous circumstances in which she is placed, and uniting her to him in whom I am convinced her happiness is so much bound up."

From such reasoning Dick Palmer had come quite to devote himself, in the manner we have seen, to Miranda's service; he thought that he could be of great assistance, and truly he was; he knew there was no other one, if he had the ability, who could act for her as he had, because sympathy in his breast had really ripened into love, and what will not that feeling inspire its votaries to do or dare?

Under ordinary circumstances, Dick Palmer would have considered his imprisonment as one of the natural chances of the dangerous profession in which he was engaged, and so considering it, he would have endeavoured to arm himself with patience to endure his seclusion from the world when he had nothing very particular to do in it. But in his present circumstances the case differed much, and when he found himself utterly powerless for Miranda, when he found his liberty of action gone, and that he was immured in the cell of a prison, a feeling of such impatience took possession of his mind, that for four-and-twenty hours his sufferings were extreme.

At the expiration of that time they only received some slight amelioration from the fact that his imagination became absorbed in devising some means of escape from the misery and gloom of his confinement.

He had been again examined much earlier than he had anticipated, and fully committed to take his trial for several daring highway robberies, the magistrate intimating that, should those charges fail, which was next to impossible, he could be criminally arraigned for aiding and assisting in the escape of a felon.

He was then conveyed to Newgate, that awful building, at the portals of which hope seems to leave the unhappy wretches who are compelled to enter it, and from which so very few have been able to escape. Still his good heart did not fail him, and although he felt that his attempt would be more difficult, he was not, on that account, inclined to give it up.

"There have been escapes from Newgate," he thought, "by persons who were only actuated by a desire of avoiding punishment; surely I, who have a stronger and better motive—namely, the intense desire to aid Miranda Rankley in the present sad state of her fortunes—may succeed."

He would fain have had Jones with him, for he knew well he could have implicitly relied upon his courage, fidelity, and abundant ingenious resources. But such good company was denied to him, for it appeared more difficult to fix any particular overt act upon Jones, beyond aiding in Percy's escape, so that he was still kept in the prison at Clerkenwell, pending the inquiries of the officers concerning him.

"If I were but alone," thought Palmer, "for a night, I would see what could be done by perseverance, and a strong arm, towards freeing myself from this horrible abode, and lending some assistance to Miranda Rankley. In this crowd, among which I am condemned

to live and wander, I can scarcely think, far less adopt any efficient course of action."

He then got into converse with some twenty or thirty more prisoners awaiting trial, who slept in a large ward, in which they were locked at night, while in the daytime they were allowed to perambulate a yard of confined dimensions for the purpose of air (such as it was) and exercise. Under these circumstances, and with so many jealous eyes upon him, to attempt an escape would have been madness, and he much longed for the system which would have left every prisoner to the silence of his own dungeon, and the company of his own thoughts.

While in this state of mind, he was accosted by a fellow-prisoner, who said:

"So they have you in for coming the old dodge on the highway?"

"Exactly," said Palmer.

"Well, when I once get out, I'll do the same. I've been a cracksman, but the latter is more gentlemanly. You haven't been served out though, as I have."

"How was that?"

"I have been in the black hole."

"Indeed?"

"Yes; one of the turnkeys called me an ugly name, and I called him another, so they put me all alone into the black hole."

"All alone," murmured Palmer; "for how long?"

"For twenty-four hours, and only left me a pitcher of water and a quartern loaf."

"Where is the black hole?"

"It's a dismal place. Rather dark, you may suppose, and not over cheerful. It seems to me to be somewhere underneath the chapel, or thereabouts."

"Well, well, one must keep oneself out of it as long as possible, I suppose."

"You are wanted," said a turnkey, laying his hand on Dick Palmer's shoulder. "Your brother has brought you something or another."

"My brother?"

"Ah, we understand that kind of thing. It's a pal, of course; but, if you say nothing, we won't. Come along. You'll find him at the grate."

Dick said no more; but, following the turnkey, found himself placed against a grating, beyond which there was a space of about four feet, and then another grating, behind which was his visitor, whom he at once recognized as the landlord of the "Star and Tinder-Box," in Drury Lane.

"Well, Dick," he said, "how are you?"

"As well as I can be here. Is *she* safe?"

"Quite. It's very ridiculous, but I've brought you a pie."

"A what?"

The landlord made a significant sign, to imply that he (Palmer) should not contradict him, and then continued:

"I've brought you a pie, as you used to be so fond of it. It's nearly spoilt, though, for they lifted off the crust, and had a regular rummage among the fruit, to find if I had concealed any small, well-tempered saws there, you see; but, lor bless me! I never thought of such a thing as concealing a saw among the *fruit*, Dicky—the *fruit*. A-hem!"

"Now then," said the officer, coming up, "where's your confounded pie?"

"Here you are," said the landlord, pushing it into his face. "It ain't over delicate now it's had the crust lifted off, and been stirred about with an old key."

"Then you shouldn't bring such things here. Baccy and spirits we doesn't let in, and, in consequence, we're bored to death with rubbish like this here. Oh, cuss it!"

"How amiable you are," said the landlord. "Don't you see me a-weeping?"

The officer muttered an oath as he unlocked a little wicket-gate in the grating next to the visitor, and then another where Palmer was standing, and handed him the pie.

"Don't eat it now," said the landlord. "Good-bye, Dicky. The idea that I should hide a saw or anything among the *fruit* of a pie. Oh, gracious! It's agin all law. The idea!"

Dick Palmer felt quite certain that the pie contained something, and he took the very first opportunity of getting into a corner unperceived, thoroughly to examine it.

Buried in the crust were three hair-saws of exquisite sharpness and temper, capable, in the hands of a skilful operator, of sawing through, noiselessly, the thickest bar of iron, perhaps, that Newgate could boast of.

In a moment Dick concealed them, and then shared his pie with some of his fellow-prisoners, after which he set himself seriously to think how he could render available the efficient instruments he had now in his possession. It struck him that if he were to make the attempt at all, it must be done alone, for not only could his fellow-prisoners not be trusted, but the love of liberty was equally strong in their breasts as in his own, and if he should be able to make one successful step towards escape, he was sure they would ruin everything by promptly trying to take advantage of it.

"Cannot I," he thought, "get easily enough placed in this black hole they talk of, for four-and-twenty hours, and from there make my attempt? It must lead somewhere, and surely in that time something may be done."

The more he thought of this project the more feasible it appeared, and even its failure he considered could not possibly place him in a worse position than he was, for, after all, they could but imprison him; and, on the whole, he considered solitary confinement as more congenial to his thoughts and feelings than being mixed up in the coarse companionship he was then compelled to endure.

"I will try it," he said to himself. "These saws have not been supplied to me for nothing. If my escape seems possible to one outside of the prison, it shall not seem impossible to me that am within it."

With this view he waited until one of the officers was passing through the yard, and then walking up to him with the remains of the pie in his hand, he said:

"Was it you who stirred my pie with an old key?"

"Eh?"

"Was it you who had the infernal impudence to stir the fruit in my pie with an old key?"

"You be——!"

"Take that," said Palmer, and smash went the remnants of the fruity compound in the officer's face, who spluttered, and stamped, and swore, and finally rushed off to lodge a formal complaint against Palmer for insubordination, exhibiting his face in corroboration, which, being covered all over with smashed red and black currants, had certainly rather an awful appearance.

The result of the *fracas* was predicted to Palmer by the other prisoners; who, nevertheless, much admired the manner in which he had acted.

"You'll be put in the black hole, old cockalorum," said one, "as safe as the bank, and safer, too, for this. Never mind, though. It will be all one in the end. Lagged, scragged, or let off, it all comes to the same thing in a hundred years."

"Ah," said another, "Queen Anne's dead. Here come the grabs."

A couple of officers entered the yard, and laid hold of Dick Palmer.

"What now?" he said.

"The black hole, my gentleman," said one. "You'd better have eaten yer pie than wasted it."

"What, the black hole for twelve hours, I suppose, for throwing a bit of pie in a man's face?"

"Four-and-twenty hours will be a precious sight nearer the mark," was the reply, "so come along."

Another moment and Dick Palmer was on the damp floor of a dismal cell in nearly utter darkness.

He had, however, taken the first step, he thought, towards escape, and his heart felt lighter, even in that dismal abode, which was intended as a terror to the refractory, than it had done when comparatively in freedom and association with his fellow unfortunates in that prison-house.

"For thee, Miranda, for thee," he cried, "I will risk all—dare all. There have been wonderful prison escapes ere now, and why should not I, with health, strength, energy, and a powerful motive of action, add one to the list?"

CHAPTER CXLII.

THE ATTEMPTED ESCAPE—DANGERS AND DIFFICULTIES—THE TURNKEY'S CAROUSAL.

THE black hole at Newgate, in which refractory criminals who were waiting trial were placed, was very comfortless indeed. It was not entirely dark; perhaps it would not have been quite so bad if it had been, for the light that was there only sufficed in a dim spectral-like manner to show the wretchedness of the dungeon, and point out the whereabouts of a pitcher of water, and a loaf of not the most delicate bread in the world.

This light came in between some rusty iron bars, which were let in near the roof, and towards which there came a borrowed light from some other place. Truly that black hole was amply sufficient to quell any ambitious strivings at an escape, and to make the boldest tremble at the hopelessness of emerging therefrom, save by the entire and full consent of the outraged authorities who might have placed him there.

Still, Dick Palmer was not discouraged. His first object was thoroughly to accustom himself to the darkness of the dungeon-like place, and this he did by shutting his eyes for some time, so that, after all light had been, for some moments, excluded, the little that found its way into that gloomy place became to the senses much more visible than it had at first appeared.

Palmer then found that the floor was of earth, and the walls of stone, dripping with moisture. The slightest investigation assured him that, to move even one of the huge blocks that formed the sides of his cell, would be quite out of the question. Then he thought of undermining the wall, but he had heard of the amazing depth of the foundations of Newgate, and he shook his head, as he said, with a sigh:

"No, I will not attempt that desperate piece of work. Heaven knows how long it would take me to dig with my inefficient means below the foundation. I have but one hope, and that must be the removal of those bars."

It was easy to determine upon the removal of the iron bars, and it was easy to imagine that the highly-tempered and exquisitely finished saws he had would suffice for that purpose; but it was far, very far from easy to imagine some means of getting from the damp, slippery floor of that cell, a height of somewhere about fifteen feet, in order to obtain a hold of the iron bars at all, situated as they were.

For a considerable time Dick remained in deep thought. Then he approached the large earthen pitcher, in which was the water that was to suffice him for four-and-twenty hours.

He took a deep draught of the liquid, and then saying:

"It is the last drop I shall have to recruit my strength for many hours," he, with one kick, smashed the pitcher into many pieces.

He then selected from among the fragments those which were the strongest, and with one of them he felt carefully between the masonry of the wall, immediately under the iron bars, but, to his chagrin, he found that he could not insert it sufficiently to afford the least prospect of its making a step sufficiently strong to support him.

Yet he would not abandon his idea, but with incredible labour, by the aid of one of the saws, succeeded in cutting between two of the stones an opening, that admitted two strong pieces of the broken pitcher, just leaving them standing out sufficiently to make a step for his foot. It is said that the first step in any enterprise is the only difficulty, but Dick Palmer found such a statement extremely fallacious so far as he was concerned, for to make another step above the one he had already achieved, was, indeed, a most troublesome piece of work, although, by dint of hard labour, during which he scratched and tore his hands frightfully, he succeeded.

These two steps raised him about four feet from the earthen flooring of his cell. Being a tall man, he could reach nearly another seven feet, but all that brought him still some distance under the bars, and what was more provoking, his standing upon the inserted pieces of earthenware was far too insecure to enable him to jump the distance, and make a snatch at the bars, which otherwise he certainly would have attempted.

There was no resource but to manufacture another step, and that he had to do standing upon the first one, expecting each moment that it would give way under him, and precipitate him to the ground. Such an accident, however, did not occur, and he felt thankful when he had succeeded in making another step, which he did higher than the other, as well as broader, although he had his doubts about its stability. To get up to it was a task of the greatest difficulty, and only to be achieved by inserting his fingers as far as possible between the blocks of stone, and so drawing himself up the face of the wall.

With a sense of great relief he at length got hold of one of the iron bars, which eased his weight from the frail support on which he stood.

With one hand he disengaged from his neck a stout silk handkerchief, and then tied it firmly to one of the bars, and round his waist, so that he had another support quite independent of his hands.

He then considered himself tolerably safe for commencing operations upon the bars themselves. He calculated that if he got away two of them, he should be able to squeeze himself through the aperture, and, although much fatigued, and his hands dripping with blood, he began slowly, but surely, to saw the bar nearest to him, close to its insertion in the solid masonry.

He was astonished before he had got half through the huge piece of iron, to hear a clock faintly in the distance strike eight.

"Have I already," he asked himself, "been nearly four hours getting thus far in my task? Heaven aid me, not for my own sake, but for Miranda Rankley's. I can help her and hers, although I have no hope for myself in a world with which I have been at war too long to expect it to show me any mercy."

He renewed his work with fresh vigour, and, in ten minutes more, the low grating sound of the saw ceased, and it passed through the iron bar completely.

By cutting it where he had done, he obtained a powerful leverage against the other extremity of it, and, with one effort, he succeeded in wrenching it altogether from its hold. That bar he cast to the floor of his cell, and, scarcely pausing a moment, attacked the one next to it with like success; but that he kept, for a more powerful weapon he could not well have had to aid him in his further operations.

By a tremendous exertion of strength, he next drew himself through the grating, and found himself overlooking a passage, while above him was quite a perpendicular wall, the sloping appearance of the bars being managed by making them jut out on to a stone sill, which afforded him an excellent foothold.

By the dim light which now remained, for the last gleam of daylight was nearly gone, he thought the depth into the passage did not exceed the depth of his cell floor from where he was. To attempt scaling the wall was out of the question, and he must either remain where he was, or drop into the passage. He adopted, of course, the latter alternative, and, hanging by the stone sill to which one end of the bars had been attached, he dropped as lightly as he could into a paved narrow passage.

The moment he did so, he saw a flash of light, and he heard footsteps approaching. Springing to his feet, he moved on in the opposite direction to the sounds, feeling the wall carefully as he went. He had not so proceeded many moments when a door gave way under his touch, and that so suddenly, too, that he could not recover himself, and, hearing footsteps close upon him, as well as the sound of voices, he passed through the doorway, finding himself immediately in a little room in which was a bright fire burning, but no other light.

The thought struck him, then, that into that very room the men whose voices he heard might be coming. There was no other door but the one he had entered at that he could perceive, and he made a desperate effort again to pass through it, and recover the ground he had lost. To do so, he saw in a moment would be instant detection, for the men were close at hand. With a sensation of utter abandonment of all hope, he recoiled into the room again, and crept under the table just as the men reached the threshold of the door.

One of these carried a light, and the other had a quart pot full of some enticing liquor in his hand. They seemed extremely sociable, and were laughing very much, as if they had achieved something that was quite of a desirable character.

"Ha! ha!" said one, as he placed the candle on the table, "it's all very fine, but I'll have my pot and my pipe if twenty governors were to say nay to it."

"Well, Billy, you're right enough, you is; and, if there's a pipe and a pot to be got into the gate arter hours, you are the covey to get that same."

"I believe you; here's luck."

"Amen. Do you want to see the bottom o' that quart pot afore you're done?"

"No—got it? 'pon my soul it's out-and-out, that half-and-half. It's meat and drink, ah!"

"It ain't to be sneezed at, ah!"

After these two hearty pulls at the quart of half-and-half, it was placed upon the table considerably lightened, and the two men drawing chairs, sat down, one of them remarking, as if in continuation of what they had been talking about in the passage:

"Well, as I was saying, there was, to my mind, something more in that smacking the pie into Wilkins' face than there looked. The fellow as did it wasn't the sort o' fellow to do it, mind you."

"Ah—yes—no."

"You see, he was one o' your old-fashioned, out-and-out highwaymen as have gone down, you see."

"Ah—won't you take a pipe?"

"Thank you. Well, as I was a-saying, I think, and I said as much to Wilkins, I think there's a-something in it as wants a magnifier to see it."

"You do, do you?"

"I do. Take my davy."

"Now, don't be a goose. You're always a-supposing this, and supposing t'other about the prisoners, whereas, with me, it's quite t'other. All I thinks of, from morning to night, is how many——"

"Hilloa! are you going to finish it? Leave a drop."

"Ah, pots of half-and-half I can get inside the walls more than the Governor says shall be reglar."

The other turnkey knocked his knuckles ruefully against the bottom of the empty pot, as he said:

"It's all very fine, but I'm blessed if you haven't had a pint and a-half out of it."

"Never mind. *Genus* must have its reward, though it's very seldom as it gets it in anything so substantial as half-and-half. Hush! you wait here, and, if I don't get in another quart, call me a goose, that's all."

He rose, and immediately left the room.

"Man to man," thought Palmer, "what is to hinder me securing this fellow, who is now without assistance."

CHAPTER CXLIII.

THE ATTACK ON THE TURNKEY—THE GOVERNOR'S LADY—THE ESCAPE.

IF such an idea as making an attack upon the one man who was left in the room was worth anything at all, such value could only arise from the rapidity with which it might be carried into execution.

Moments were precious.

The other turnkey would, doubtless, return as quickly as possible to the comfortable fireside he had left, and the noise consequent upon overcoming two men, should he be so fortunate as to do so, would render his victory of no account to Dick Palmer within the precincts of those walls, where the least alarm would a-suredly bring him an overwhelming host to contend with.

These thoughts passed rapidly through the

mind of Dick Palmer, and, even as they did so, he slowly extricated himself from under the table.

The man who had left the room had taken the light with him; but the fire was burning cheerfully, and sending forth a glaring lustre upon every article in that little, snug room, making the face of the turnkey, who sat by it, look like burnished copper, and lending a warmth to the otherwise cold-looking walls.

"Ah!" soliloquized the man. "He is a famous hand at getting half-and-half into the prison. He thinks of nothing else. Now I do, and, as I said before, something strikes me uncommonly hard——"

These words had no sooner passed his lips when something did strike him uncommonly hard, and that something, as the reader may surmise, was the fist of Dick Palmer, which came against the side of his head with a momentum that sent him sprawling, chair and all.

One glance upon the table showed Dick a bunch of keys and a pair of pocket-pistols.

He secured them in a moment, and darted from the room before the bewildered and partially-stunned turnkey knew what had happened.

In fact, when his comrade returned triumphant with another pot of half-and-half, he could not exactly tell how it had occurred that he was sitting on the floor, and there was a great lump on the side of his head, which, like the blood upon Macbeth's air-drawn dagger, "was not there before."

When Dick reached the passage he took the contrary direction from that whence the turnkeys had come, as more likely to lead away from the regular entrance to the jail than towards it.

The passage was long and tortuous.

Here and there it was lit by a small, dismal-looking lamp placed in a little bracket.

The walls were of stone, and the flooring of small red bricks, through the interstices of which a dampness was continually exuding.

Doorway or branch passage he could not find for some time, and he began much to wonder where the long corridor would lead him, when he came upon the opening of another passage exactly at right angles to the one he had been so long pursuing.

He turned down the new passage without a moment's hesitation, and a little in advance of him he saw a door, above which was one of the small lamps which seemed to be generally used for lighting the interior of the prison.

He placed his hand on the lock of the door, and it yielded directly.

He had made one step into just such another little room as the one in which he had been concealed, before he saw that a man was there, apparently half-asleep, by a fire, while a candle, with an enormous wick, showed the inattention it had received.

The sleep of the man—if sleep it could be called—must have been very light, for the slight noise that Dick made in opening the door aroused him, and he started to his feet in an instant, crying loudly:

"Hilloa—hilloa! who are you?"

Dick Palmer was out of the room in a moment, and slammed shut the door.

A key was in the lock; to turn it was the work of a moment, and then Dick darted off.

The dangers he had already gone through would have been amply sufficient to appal many men, but they only served to excite Dick Palmer to still greater exertions, and he thought to himself:

"Surely I shall scarcely be so unfortunate again as I have been. Here have I encountered no less than three turnkeys, and yet escaped a capture. I would to Heaven I had the least idea of where the passage leads to."

With increased caution he continued to pursue the narrow way, determined to be more careful before he again opened any door which might present itself to him.

In fact, he began to think the safest plan would be to lock all doors where he saw a key, as by such means he might be allowing himself much longer time to proceed while his foes were trying to escape from their places of confinement.

As these thoughts were passing through his mind, he came to a flight of stairs, which he ascended to a landing, from which opened two doors.

They were both fast, as he ascertained by carefully trying them.

Above him the staircase continued, and he stood for a moment or two considering whether he should try the keys he had upon one of the doors, or ascend the remainder of the staircase, when a strange, hollow sound, like the deep toll of a bell from underground, met his ears.

It only sounded twice, and then he fancied that a murmur of voices, and a rushing of feet succeeded.

"What can that mean?" he said. "Is it an alarm?"

It was an alarm.

The turnkey who had been locked in his room by Dick Palmer had succeeded in making himself heard, and, being liberated, had declared that a prisoner must have attacked him, as the locking one of the night-watch in his room was much too serious a joke for any of the officials to perpetrate.

An immediate alarm was given throughout the prison, and the Governor was at once aroused with the intelligence that there was something wrong, although they, the turnkeys, did not know exactly what.

Before Dick had time to decide upon what he should do, he heard a key placed in the lock of the door before which he stood, and he had just time to spring up half-a-dozen of the stairs above him, when the door was flung open, and a glare of light shot out from a large lantern carried by a man, after whom came two others well-armed, and then one who, from his dress and general appearance, Dick Palmer at once guessed to be the Governor.

"Here, Burdon," said the Governor, for it was indeed he, "you keep this door; I don't believe anything is the matter, after all."

The man he had addressed as Burdon stationed himself at the doorway, which Dick at once presumed led into the Governor's apartments, and the others, accompanied by that official personage, rapidly descended the staircase.

"Humph!" said Burdon, as he cast a knowing glance round him; "it's all gammon, I daresay. It's impossible for anybody to get out o' any o' the wards without a reglar row, and there's nobody in the cells at all; if there was, I'd give 'em leave to get out, if they could."

With these remarks, Burdon, who was a man of immense size and strength, stuck his back against the door-post, and, putting his hands in his pockets, looked the picture of patience while he whistled a tune.

"Man to man again," thought Palmer; "this is my best—last—only chance. I must overcome him, if possible."

The principal difficulty to Dick's mind in making an attack upon Burdon was to descend the stairs quickly enough to be upon him before he should be aware of the danger.

As Burdon stood, the side of his face was turned towards the upper staircase; but, then, the slightest noise would have induced him to turn his head, when he would inevitably see Dick, and have him at a disadvantage.

Each moment appeared an age as it flew past, and Palmer could not make up his mind what to do.

At length he thought he would creep down about two steps, and then jump the rest, which would give him all the advantage of a good spring upon Burdon, whom he might so overcome, powerful as he was.

The determination to adopt this course was strengthened by his fancying he heard the sound of returning footsteps in the passage below the first flight of stairs.

"They are returning," he thought. "This is the crisis of my fate. Good fortune assist me!"

He crept down the two steps, and then, gathering all his energies, made a desperate spring full against Burdon, whose throat he succeeded in grasping with both hands, at the same moment that he nearly knocked all the breath out of his body by the violence of the concussion.

Before, then, Burdon could recover from the shock, Dick gave the back of his head such a bump against the door-post, that when he left go of him, Mr. Burdon slipped down quite stunned, and went bundling down the staircase like a great log of wood.

Dick was not wrong in his supposition that the Governor was returning; for at the instant that he had got rid of Burdon, the flash of the lights, carried by a strong body who had joined the Governor, came up the staircase, and it was clear that they saw Burdon, for the Governor cried out:

"Come on, he's upstairs, and has killed Burdon. Fire on him—fire!"

The report of several pistols succeeded; but Dick darted through the door, and immediately locked it on the inside, where the key had been left.

A green-baize swing-door next presented itself, and then a short passage, after which there was a strong door partially open.

Dick dashed through it, and found himself in a handsome bedroom.

A scream came from a lady who was in bed, and she pulled a bell-rope violently.

"I really beg your pardon, madam, for this intrusion," said Palmer; "but it's quite unavoidable; I have the honour to bid you a very good-night."

He darted from the room by an opposite door, at the same moment that the bell-rope came away in the lady's hands.

A well-carpeted staircase presented itself, which he was rapidly descending, when he met a woman carrying a light, who, the moment she saw him, cried:

"Thieves—thieves! Help! Fire! Murder!"

Dick seized her arm with one hand; and, placing the muzzle of one of the pistols he had in her mouth, he said:

"If you speak another word, I'll blow your head off."

She dropped the candle, and stood aghast.

Some light from below, however, afforded an ample illumination to the staircase, and Dick added:

"If you want to save your life, show me the way to the outer door directly."

She could just gasp "Yes," and, trembling dreadfully, led him down the staircase, which terminated in a long, narrow passage, at the end of which was a heavy door.

That she opened, and, holding it in her hand, said:

"For Heaven's sake, go!"

"Good-night," said Dick Palmer.

And, springing over a little iron gate that was at the bottom of some stone steps, he found himself in the Old Bailey, exactly in front of the Governor's house.

CHAPTER CXLIV.

MOONLIGHT AT NEWGATE—THE ESCAPE OF JACK SHEPPARD TRULY RENDERED—THE PURSUIT.

It seemed to Dick Palmer as if a new existence had been suddenly given to him the moment he set his foot beyond the walls of that dismal prison-house from which he, with such toil, trouble, and danger, had escaped.

He drew a long breath, as he exclaimed:

"Free—free at last! Thank Heaven, I am free!"

Then, darting across the road, he dived into the darkness of an inn-yard, and there took counsel with himself as to what course he should immediately pursue to ensure his safety, and prevent, if possible, the risk of recapture.

The little likelihood of their looking for him

TWITTER PRESENTS THE FORGED CHEQUE AT THE BANK.

anywhere in the Old Bailey made him believe himself secure where he was for a few minutes; besides, his position commanded a view of the prison, and, if any parties emerged from it in pursuit of him, he could note which way they took, so that he might be better enabled to avoid them.

A delicious calm seemed to have spread itself over the face of nature. By the aspect of every object, Dick thought it must be very late indeed, but he had no means of accurately ascertaining the time; for so excited had he been during the progress of his escape, that, for all he knew, he might have been one hour or ten in getting clear of Newgate; still,

he could not but admire the beauty of the night.

The moon shone upon the slumbering city in silent splendour, but was often obscured by passing clouds; but they would presently pass over, and all again appeared visible in the strong contrast of shadow and light.

Newgate, the giant building of that extremity of the city, from which it has derived its name, shone in these occasional moments of splendour in all the gloomy majesty that could be imagined of a strong and extensive prison.

Its blackened stone front, its massive doors, and iron-stanchioned windows, were enough to strike terror to the heart of the unfortunate captive that for the first time was brought to this abode of sin and sorrow.

Dick Palmer was suddenly aroused from his reverie by seeing the Governor's door open, and six or eight persons rapidly descend the steps.

They paused in the street, and appeared to be consulting a moment or two. Then in couples they separated—some going towards the heart of the city, while others went westward. In a few moments all had disappeared.

Dick then crossed the road, and walked slowly up Newgate Street. He had got past the wall of the prison, and was going leisurely on, when from a doorway two men pounced upon him.

"So, my fine fellow," cried one, "we are as artful as you, are we?"

"Not quite," said Dick, and the foremost one he knocked down with a blow. Before, then, the other could lay hold of him, he darted off, and turned into Newgate Market.

He could hear that he was hotly pursued, and he paused an instant when he found that more than one man was after him, not only by the sound of their footsteps, but by the voices that came upon his ears. He felt much exhausted, and a feeling seized him that it would be impossible for him to keep up such a chase long.

"I must find some place of shelter," he thought, "be it where it may."

A glare of light down a narrow turning attracted his attention, and, without any defined object, he darted towards it.

It proceeded from a slaughter-house, where several men were engaged at that silent hour in their vocation in order to be ready for the morrow.

A desperate expedient suggested itself to Dick.

It was his only chance.

Darting in among the men, he said:

"The bailiffs are after me, my men. Will you see a poor fellow hauled off if you can help it?"

"No," said one. "I laid in Whitecross Street a year myself."

"Can you hide me?"

"No. But this is better."

The man took off his own apron and worsted nightcap, in which he hastily attired Dick. Then, giving him a knife, he said:

"Stoop down by that bullock. Leave the rest to us."

The other slaughtermen laughed outrageously, and, when the officers arrived panting at the spot, and inquired if anyone had passed, they were most solemnly assured to the contrary, and they went on with sad misgivings that they had lost their man.

The consternation in Newgate at Dick Palmer's escape was immense.

Every turnkey on duty was suspended till an inquiry should take place, and the manner of the escape was a theme of gossip throughout the entire edifice.

"Well, he's gone, that's clear enough," said a fat turnkey, as he seated himself, puffing and blowing for want of breath from recent exertion and exercise.

"Gone, I should say so; there'll be a pretty row about it, I'll lay a wager. The Governor will be poking and prying about, asking this question, and wanting to know that, as if a fellow was one of the '*Delfy Oracles*,' and could tell everything they could find time or patience to ask."

"It's a sad thing, Master Nightingale, that His Majesty's jail of Newgate should thus be set at naught, and people what we locked up should get out again by any means at all. I am scandalized, I am, indeed."

"Oh! pho—pho. What's the odds—hold your tongue about being scandalized, except you want to revive that 'ere story of the young woman who lodged at your mother's. Oh! you shocking old man."

"Come, come, Master Nightingale, none of your chaff; I am down upon you if you don't. I mean as how it's a dead do, a regular swindle upon us all. It's as bad as that there business of Jack Sheppard."

"Jack Sheppard—nonsense; he never did anything half so clever—he hadn't got it in him—he hadn't strength enough. Indeed, he was little more than a boy."

"I say that Jack Sheppard's escape was much more wonderful than that which has just occurred. Didn't he break through almost every door and wall in the old building? Was there any place that was free from his visits? Tell me that, I say."

"And so I will," replied Nightingale. "It's all moonshine. Jack Sheppard never did one-half that fools now say he did do; and what he really is believed to have done, he was greatly assisted in by others."

"How, Master Nightingale, how? Tell us that—come to the point, and bring your proof, that's all; we want to be reasonable—come to the point."

"That's easily done," replied Nightingale; "my father knew all about it. He knew the turnkey who was here when Jack Sheppard was hanged."

"Did he now?"

"Yes, he did; he was a very old man when my father was but a very young one, and he assured him that it was a put up job between him and the turnkey, who was here at the time."

"I'll never believe it."

"You are an unbelieving brute, then, that's all I have to say," replied Nightingale; "but I'll tell you how it happened, nevertheless, that you may know better for the future.

"Jack Sheppard had been taken by Jonathan Wild, and contrived to escape him very cleverly, and got clear off. There was an officer named Inglis, a clever, enterprising fellow, who knew a few things, and among them the way to catch a runaway jail-bird. Wild set him on, and left the whole management of the recapture with Inglis, save that he walked about, and endeavoured to meet him; and, had he done so, it was likely he would have taken him.

"Inglis, however, got scent of Jack, and, after much dodging about, and going to one place, and then to another, contrived to come up with him near Leadenhall Market. To make sure of his man, Inglis contrived to obtain the aid of a butcher who lived there —a big, active fellow.

"The two, you may be sure, were more than a match for little Jack; they both pounced upon him, and, after a short struggle, they managed to secure him, and clapped the darbies upon him, bundled him into a coach, and were soon at the wicket of Newgate.

"Jack was very dull when he was brought back; he appeared to think that it was no joke, and stood in the lobby in rather a melancholy and sulky humour, till the turnkey, who I told you of, went up to him, and slyly squeezed his hand.

"The hint was not lost, and Jack's countenance soon grew bright. He chatted with one and the other with the freedom of an old acquaintance; and little did they think that they would have been so cleverly done by one of their own pals, and that all the credit was to be given to Jack Sheppard."

"Don't tell me that," remarked the fat turnkey, who had, like many others, pinned his faith to some popular ballad, or tale, and could not be reasoned out of it, though the truth glared as brightly in his eyes as the sun at noon-day; "don't tell me about your father's, or your grandfather's tale. I have heard all my life that Jack Sheppard did it— and so he did—I'll swear to it any day against any man."

"I daresay you would," replied Nightingale, "and swear through one of the stone walls, too, if it pleased you; but, yet, what I tell you is truth, in spite of all your disbelief. His friend, the turnkey, did not forget him; on the contrary, he gave him tools very different from those which are usually spoken of, that would scarce have made a scratch upon a piece of plaster; and, more, he unlocked his cell, and enabled him to break through places from the outside instead of the in, so that his friend, the turnkey, should not be put in disgrace.

"He did more than that, too, for he obtained some stuff, and put it in his comrades' drink, and hocussed them, so that they slept sound, and were unable to hear the din of the crow-bars and falling pieces of brick and plaster.

"Jack did much, I will allow, but his friend did more. This, however, is the case with all things—the saddle's put on the wrong horse— it's like tying up the wrong man.

"My father has told me, often enough, that Jack warn't strong enough, there warn't enough of him to do all that he is said to have done; his will might have been good, but it's no use of people talking and heaping up a lot of impossible adventures upon Jack Sheppard.

"The turnkey, when he found all was right below, threw off his coat, and went to work in earnest, and their two crow-bars did wonders, for Jack's friend was a big man, and a strong one to boot.

"It did not take them long to get to the roof; and here he again befriended Jack, by helping him over, and lending him a ladder. When Jack Sheppard was gone, and fairly clear of the prison, then his friend returned, carefully arranging all things, so that the escape would appear as if effected by Jack himself, unaided by anybody.

"There was a desperate rumpus when it was discovered that the cell was empty: at first it was supposed he must be secreted in the jail, merely waiting an opportunity to escape: but their astonishment was great when they found the mischief that had happened in the upper part of the building.

"Of course, all that had been done was placed to the account of Sheppard; the whole town rang with the fame of his exploits, and even to this day there are those who know no better, and can think of nothing better or more novel than Jack Sheppard and his deeds."

Having delivered this oration, Master Nightingale left the lobby to go his rounds, and see that his department was all secure and safe.

The big turnkey sighed deeply, and said, solemnly:

"Well, I am flummoxed; to think as how all the story-books ain't true—all them ere rollicking novels is all gammon, and ain't true, either. I'll never believe in the Newgate Calendar arter this—no, I won't."

"Don't."

CHAPTER CXLV.

BERNARD VARLEY'S APPLICATION TO THE AUCTIONEER—THE SOLICITOR'S LETTER— VARLEY'S DISAPPOINTMENT.

VARLEY, although he could not bring himself to think that even his last atrocious attempt upon the life of Samuel Twitter would induce that sagacious individual to attempt anything against his personal safety, inasmuch as he could not well do so without grievously committing himself, still began to be extremely uneasy at the whole aspect of affairs.

The great difficulty of apprehending Rowland Percy—a difficulty which appeared really insurmountable, filled him with superstitious alarm.

Then how utterly had he failed in his pursuit of Miranda. How much more detestable and abominable had he made himself in her eyes by the very means he had adopted for the purpose of winning her to him.

Even he, half-blinded as he was on the subject by passion, began to think his pursuit of the beautiful orphan one of the most hopeless of projects.

He now knew well that no persuasion would avail to induce her for one moment to listen to his suit—not even the jeopardized life of her lover could wring from her one word of concession.

Truly did Bernard Varley feel himself defied by one who—with all his intellect, with all his wealth, and with all his most unscrupulous manœuvring—he thought he should surely succeed in easily triumphing over.

"What is to be done?" was the question he continually asked himself, but he could find no satisfactory answer to it, and became completely involved in a labyrinth of painful thoughts and emotions.

Slowly, then, but surely, the notion forced itself upon his consideration, that he would at last be compelled to seek safety and reputation in some country where his name was unknown, and where none could point to him as the despoiler of the orphan.

"It must be so," he muttered; "Twitter is quite harmless from his want of resources. Had I given him a large sum of money, he might have proved very dangerous, for he could have placed himself in some situation of safety, from which he could have made accusations against me. But, as it is, he would gain nothing by my destruction; on the contrary, he would give himself much trouble, and bring upon himself much detestation, even if his evidence against me was employed at the price of his own safety. I am quite free from any danger on Samuel Twitter's account; I have acted most wisely in holding my purse-strings tight against his large demands."

This point settled, Varley next thought it would be extremely desirable to carry into execution the plan in which he had been so signally foiled at York, namely, to sell the Grange estates.

"They will produce me," he thought, "a large sum in ready money, which I will invest in some foreign funds. The amount will be tolerably safe anywhere but in America; and then, should anything suddenly occur here to make it prudent for me to leave England quickly, I do not do so a beggar, but retain at least one of the objects I proposed to myself by the death of Sir George Rankley. If I cannot procure smiles from Miranda, I can purchase them from others."

As Varley uttered this sentiment, he groaned aloud, for it was really quite different from his real feelings.

Even then he would have given up all his wealth—all his hopes of revenge against Rowland Percy—for by that name he called his persecution of the young man—if he could but have received in exchange the hand of the beautiful girl upon whose innocent head he had heaped so much distress, and who had so much cause to think him a very fiend in the prosecution of his evil passions.

Putting aside, however, for the present, his pursuit of Miranda, and his hatred of Twitter and Rowland Percy, Varley left his hotel, for the purpose of at once putting in hand the sale of the Grange estates.

Naturally, he went to the most celebrated auctioneer in London; a man who, by vulgar impertinence, ignorance, and a large person, had raised himself to the top of his profession, and acquired a large fortune.

This man Varley had frequently heard of; he knew, as a fact, that he procured larger sums for property placed in his hands than any other of his profession. To him, therefore, he went, knowing nothing further of the man than his widely-spread celebrity as an auctioneer—a celebrity which the curious in such matters may indulge themselves in endeavouring to account for in vain, as we have often done.

It is one of the phenomena of all ages, and all countries, that some men may do and say things broadly, and fill their coffers thereby, while other men would be ruined at the remotest approach to such conduct.

Thus this great auctioneer seemed to owe much of his success to coarse buffoonery, and insulting the very people who came to purchase the properties that change hands at the fall of his hammer.

It may be that they consider him something in the light of the Court fools, or *righte merrie jesters* of ancient times, who were at liberty to say what they pleased to anyone, from the throned monarch to the tattered mendicant, and to take offence at whom would be as absurd and *infra dig.* as to pass over an insult from a gentleman.

But, be this as it may, Bernard Varley repaired to this portly individual, and, in his cold, distant manner, demanded an interview.

It was in an outer office that Varley propounded his request, and he did not know that the great man was himself there, for he could not imagine that the big individual he saw bustling about, and talking with great rapidity on all matters, was the real magician of the hammer.

"Bless my soul!" exclaimed the great man to a bewildered-looking boy who was present, "what are you about, what have you been doing, and what are you going to do? It would be positively refreshing to see you doing something. There, move those pedestals, fill those lamps, sweep out the office, take those letters. Come—come—come—really—bless my soul!"

"I wish to see," said Varley, "Mr. Bobbins."

"Well, bless my soul! I'm Mr. Bobbins; don't you see me? What is it? My time's valuable, if yours ain't. Come, out with it, what do you want?"

"You sell estates by auction?"

"My good sir, I sell anything by auction, and everything by auction, from peg-tops to palaces. I'll sell you, if you like. Bless my soul! I sell everything and everybody."

"Indeed! I wish to place in your hands a large estate near York for public competition."

"Very good—that'll do. Come in. Now for the particulars. Here goes. York to wit; do you take—eh? Come along, this way—private room. How much do you think it's worth?"

"Not much," said Varley, looking round him, "if I may judge from its style of decoration."

"Pho—pho! I mean the estate, not the room. Come, what's its name? Out with it."

"It is called the Grange estate, and was formerly the property of Sir George Rankley, now deceased."

"Eh?—what is your name—Harley?"

"No."

"Barley?"

"No."

"Bless my soul! what is your name?"

"Varley."

"That'll do, it's all the same—here goes. Read that. Business is business. If your time ain't valuable, mine is."

He took from a file a letter, which he placed in Varley's hands, who, with unfeigned astonishment, read as follows:

"Sir,—As a metropolitan auctioneer, I address you this circular, which has been transmitted to every gentleman of your profession in London, warning you against accepting instructions for the sale of an estate near to York, and lately the property of Sir George Rankley, Bart.

"The present holder is a Mr. Bernard Varley, and, as the solicitor of Miranda Rankley, the daughter of the deceased baronet, I am laboriously collecting evidence disputative of Bernard Varley's title to the estate in question. Should you, therefore, be waited upon by him with an offer to undertake the sale of the said estate, you will do so on your own responsibility, and the purchaser may afterwards find he has no title.

"I am, sir, your obedient servant,
"Charles Anderson, Solicitor,
"Mr. Bobbins. "York."

"Confusion!" cried Bernard Varley.

"Exactly. Good-morning. That's the way out. No go. If your time ain't valuable, mine is. Tom—Tom, show Mr. Farley out—eh? Good-morning. Bless my soul!"

Perfectly bewildered, and in a storm of passion, Bernard Varley found himself in the street.

CHAPTER CXLVI.

TWITTER'S RESOLVE — THE FORGED CHEQUE, AND THE DETECTION—VARLEY'S ATTEMPT TO POSSESS HIMSELF OF THE MONEY.

IT was in a perplexing and anxious state of mind that Samuel Twitter revolved in his thoughts the various modes of procedure.

Many things were desirable, he told himself, yet many were dubious or dangerous; the thing, therefore, that he endeavoured to compass was the most certain, and, at the same time, it involved the least possible amount of personal risk; for Samuel Twitter's recent adventures had but little tended to infuse a spirit of courage and adventure into his mind.

After much thought, he determined to provide against the next visit of the active and exemplary inspector, by decamping and leaving the nest empty.

He, therefore, rose early, while the people of the house were busily employed about ordinary affairs, dressed himself, and, after assuring himself, by carefully listening at the head of the stairs, that no one was at hand, he quietly descended the stairs, peering, as he came down, into every hole and corner, until he finally reached the front door, which he opened and closed without disturbing any one of the household.

"There," said Twitter, "Mr. Inspector can now settle the bill, if he likes, I shall not. I didn't go there of my own choice, nor did I order anything, so I ain't liable."

Twitter found that the exercise of walking was anything but pleasant; his limbs were stiff and sore, while his bruises required some attention, and, fearful of the consequences, he called a coach, and ordered the man to drive him to the hotel he had been living at, separately from Varley.

His appearance here was rather unexpected —at least, his personal appearance in such guise was scarcely looked for; and Twitter was much annoyed by being conscious that he was food for observation among the waiters.

He, however, immediately retired to his own apartment, and remained some time in communion with his own thoughts, and then he ordered a large box to be brought to him, and, when again alone, he opened it and began to make a careful search over its contents.

For some time Twitter's search appeared in vain, and his peevishness seemed upon the increase, for he turned the contents over in a hasty and angry manner, as if his patience and hopes were alike exhausted.

"I shouldn't wonder," said Twitter, in a low tone, "if I have lost them. I know I had some, for 1 always thought they would be useful, and now when they are most needed they are not to be found."

As he spoke, however, so much of Twitter's countenance as was capable of expressing satisfaction, did so, as he held in his hand a small piece of paper.

It was a blank cheque.

He hastily thrust back the contents of the box, and, drawing writing materials towards him, began to practice on a sheet of paper the name of Bernard Varley, imitating a signature he already possessed, written by Varley himself.

Many attempts were abortive, but at length he succeeded, and the signature was attached to the cheque, which was filled up with the amount of six thousand pounds.

Twitter would have demanded more, but he feared that so much might not be there, and then he would get none.

It was, however, much against his nature to seek a smaller sum, when he believed a larger one was to be obtained, even for safety sake, but he did do it, and the cheque was accordingly drawn for the sum of six thousand pounds.

"Now," thought Twitter, "the next thing will be to present it and obtain the money."

So greatly was he elated that he asked for some refreshments to be brought him; then, after a time, he ordered a coach, into which he stepped, instructing the coachman to drive to the bankers.

Twitter was not in the most imperturbable mood as he was driven along; on the contrary, now that his scheme was so near completion, he became slightly nervous as to the result, though he felt conscious that if he were detected, Varley dared not do aught to injure him.

Yet Varley was a desperate, bold, and bad man, altogether free from those fears which haunted Twitter's imagination.

While these thoughts crossed his mind the coach stopped, and the driver in another minute opened the door, saying:

"This is the house, yer honner."

"Very well," said Twitter. "Wait awhile till I return, as I shall want you to go back."

"Yes, yer honner," said the coachman, touching the brim of his hat.

Twitter entered the banking-house and made straight for the desk where he saw cheques were being cashed, and handed in his own.

Twitter's manner betrayed embarrassment; indeed, he had scarce breath enough to speak, and he watched the expression of the clerk's countenance with a nervousness that was quite painful to himself. The individual who took the cheque looked at the signature very hard, and then consulted a book, after which he left the room, and presently returned with another individual, who likewise consulted the book, and then they both came to Twitter.

"We cannot pay this cheque," said the clerk.

"Are there no funds?" inquired Twitter.

"Yes; but it does not appear genuine. The signature and filling up are different from what Mr. Varley usually adopts. I must detain the cheque and yourself."

"Very well," replied Twitter, with more composure than he thought himself capable of, but which no doubt arose from his belief in the inability of Bernard Varley to do anything to his detriment. "You had better send for Mr. Varley, as my time is of consequence."

"Certainly, sir," said the clerk, somewhat staggered by this cool request; "have the kindness to walk this way, and we will immediately dispatch someone for Mr. Varley."

Twitter entered a small room, evidently used as a waiting-room, and seated himself before the fire, there to wait until Varley came.

It was some time ere he could arrive, and Twitter took up the morning-paper, feigning to amuse himself during the interval he had to wait, but, however well to appearance he effected this, he felt but wretchedly at ease.

"I wonder what he will say," thought Twitter, with an uneasy shift in his chair: "he cannot let me be taken for forgery, that's clear, because, though he would be very glad, indeed, to see me hanged, yet he would know very well that his fate would be similar to my

own; for what motive should I have to keep the secret since my own life was no longer affected by it, and I could revenge myself upon him.

"No; he must admit the writing as his: but should they make the inquiries without my being present, then I am lost," thought Twitter, with a groan.

There was a slight bustle, and one of the clerks uttered the name of Varley.

"Ah! he is come," thought Twitter, and, in another moment, Varley entered the room.

There was a strange mixture of malice and pleasure perceptible on his face, as if he were glad that Samuel Twitter was thus safely lodged, and in his power.

He looked more pleasant than before, when he saw, too, the marks of violence Twitter bore upon his person—evidences of his own brutality—which seemed to give him much delight.

"Ah! Samuel Twitter," he said, with a triumphant air, "I had not expected this interview. It is pleasant when friends meet unexpectedly. It brings joy to my heart, Samuel Twitter."

"Ah! you're very good—good," groaned Twitter, "and would, I daresay, be happy to have seen me at the bottom of the Thames."

Varley's colour changed for a moment as he met Twitter's eye during this reply. It brought with it a disagreeable reminiscence.

"Not at all," replied Varley, "not at all. You are here upon business, I daresay; you did not desire my company, though, so much, perhaps, as I desired yours. Our meeting is unexpected, Samuel Twitter."

"Oh, yes, very; but the people here sent purposely for you upon business."

"Why is it that you sent for me?" he inquired of the clerk who was in attendance.

"A cheque has been presented to us, purporting to be drawn by you for six thousand pounds."

"Six thousand pounds!" echoed Varley, in a peculiar bland and subdued tone, that made Twitter groan internally.

"Yes, Mr. Varley; we were doubtful of the signature, and sent for you."

"You did very right," said Varley, in the same tone, but glancing at Twitter.

"Is it genuine?" inquired the clerk.

"Allow me to look at it," said Varley.

The clerk handed the cheque to him, and Varley carefully read it through, and, after curiously and minutely examining it, he laid it down before him, and was about to speak, when Twitter, fearful of the consequences, interfered, with the desperate attempt of silencing Varley, and even compelling him to acknowledge the signature, through fear of the consequences.

"Mr. Varley," he said, "knows that I would not commit such an act as your suspicions would imply; he knows, too, that I would not do anything that would cost me my life, especially as he is well aware that the existence of another person entirely depends upon my own."

This had all the effect that was intended.

Varley at once saw his imminent danger. He turned sick. The room appeared to swim round, when he made an effort to speak, and he said, in a faint voice:

"I recollect now—it is my signature. It is all right. You must cash it."

"Oh, certainly, Mr. Varley," replied the clerk, much puzzled, for he could not understand what had happened. In his own mind the forgery was clear, and he thought Varley knew it; but why he should suddenly admit the cheque to be genuine was beyond his comprehension.

There was, however, no room for hesitation, and he continued:

"I am very sorry for having given you so much trouble, Mr. Varley, and must apologize to this gentleman for the unpleasant occurrence of his detention; but it was our duty to make sure where a doubt existed."

"Oh, don't name it," cried Twitter, delighted at the turn events had taken, but yet nervously apprehensive of Varley. "It couldn't be helped, I daresay; but, as I have waited here long enough, perhaps you will have the goodness to give me the cash for this at once."

"Most certainly, sir," said the clerk. "Step this way."

Twitter entered the public part of the bank, and once more stood at the counter.

He was closely followed by Bernard Varley, who watched every movement he made, and fixed his eyes upon Twitter, who felt as uncomfortable beneath his basilisk-like gaze as it is possible to imagine, though he (Twitter) never once looked at Varley, or met his eyes.

He hastily counted over the change for the cheque, and carefully secured it about his person, and then turned to leave the bank.

In this he was followed by Bernard Varley, who kept close to his heels, until he came into the street, when the latter seized hold of him with a nervous grip of the throat, saying:

"Samuel Twitter, the money—the money! I must have it. Give it up quietly, and save your life, or all the help you may call for shall not save you."

"Help—help! Murder! Police!" cried Twitter, as he felt Varley's grasp, and his endeavours to possess himself of the booty he (Twitter) had about him, and a desperate struggle ensued between them.

CHAPTER CXLVII.

TWITTER'S ESCAPE—VARLEY'S ANGER AND DESPERATION—THE VISIT TO JONES IN THE NEW PRISON.

TWITTER'S cries for help soon brought a crowd of individuals round them, though no one seemed inclined to interfere, not knowing the nature of the quarrel, and, moreover, it appeared as if the superior had merely committed an assault on the inferior, which, as all the world knows, is a very venial offence; but just reverse the order of things, and the punishment is not yet invented that is suffi-

cient, as a punishment, for the audacious inferior who may be goaded by provocation to inflict a merited chastisement on his superior in society.

Thus, for some minutes they were left to themselves to fight it out as they could.

Twitter's outcries could not long remain unheard by the police; and Varley's attempts to introduce his hands into Twitter's pocket became evident to all the spectators.

This being a point that touched them all very closely, they soon began to give vent to their horror at the idea of one man's putting his hand into another man's pocket, and Bernard Varley, instead of being popular in the affray, which he was nigh becoming at first, ran some danger of being maltreated.

"Murder! murder!—help!—police!" cried Twitter, as he writhed and twisted in Varley's grasp, at the same time he kicked and bit very hard.

"Do you want to murder the man?" inquired one old gentleman, who was fat and short-winded. "Leave go his throat, you'll induce an apoplectic fit."

"Why, he's trying to pick the other's pocket," remarked another; "he deserves to be sent to the compter."

"Why don't you leave go, and fight it out like men?" interposed a brewer's drayman, who looked on both Twitter and Varley with great contempt.

"Give up the money," exclaimed Varley.

"Murder! police!" screamed Twitter.

"I'll kill you if you do not instantly give me the money you have robbed me of," exclaimed Bernard Varley.

"Murder! police! Save me from this man, who has before tried to murder——"

Here his voice became drowned in the exclamations of several persons, who said:

"Here's the police—here's the police!"

In another moment Bernard Varley was staved off Twitter by force of blows, and both combatants were secured by two stout city officers, either of whom would have made but little matter of a contention with the two belligerents at once.

"What's the matter?—what's the row?" exclaimed the officer who held Twitter.

"Come, sir, no violence—you must not resist the city police, or my Lord Mayor will have to deal with you," said the other to Varley, who made several demonstrations to renew the attack upon Twitter; but the policeman intimated that would not be allowed, by gently drawing him back by the collar, in a mode that rendered question as to the right of procedure useless.

"That man," cried Twitter, "has nearly killed me."

"Why, you don't look as if he had used you gently. What's the meaning of this?"

"That scoundrel has robbed me."

"It is a lie," screamed Twitter, furiously; "he knows it's a lie."

"Do you give him into custody for a robbery, sir?" exclaimed the officer to Varley.

"He dare not," vehemently exclaimed

Twitter, though he trembled violently in every limb from exertion and anxiety: "he dare not."

"I do; he knows he has robbed me."

"You know that you, Bernard Varley, are more likely to be hanged, than I am to commit a robbery, and that I see will be your fate before long."

"Why, bless me," exclaimed one of the officers; "is this Mr. Varley, from York?"

Bernard Varley trembled in every limb with passion, but by a strong effort he subdued it, for the last sentence and Twitter's growing violence and audacity showed him the brink of the precipice on which he stood, and in reply to the officer's demand, if he should lock Samuel Twitter up, he replied:

"No, no—never mind now; I have another way to deal with the scoundrel. Recollect, Samuel Twitter, life is short and uncertain—your new-found treasure may want an owner."

Though Twitter was nigh sinking when he met Bernard Varley's gaze, yet he replied:

"Remember, Bernard Varley, the slightest act of yours may bring ruin upon your own head, and then your long life of scheming becomes too short to enable you to enjoy the fruits of it."

"Farewell, Samuel Twitter," said Varley.

"Oh, don't trouble yourself about that," exclaimed Twitter; "I suppose we love each other—eh?"

Bernard Varley turned and left the spot.

Calling a coach, he was quickly on the road to his hotel, and Twitter followed his example, thinking it safest, and being desirous of digesting his other plans.

When Bernard Varley was alone in the coach, his thoughts were busy with the scene he had just passed through.

Samuel Twitter, with all his cowardice and all his want of intellect, had been a match for him, Varley, and had succeeded in possessing himself of money that he was most anxious to keep from him.

Twitter was no longer his slave; he had him no longer in his power; he could do nothing with him—he was independent.

Varley became sensible that he himself stood upon very insecure footing; day after day showed all his fairest schemes baffled and all his hopes annihilated, and his own safety threatened by the man of all others whom he affected to despise, and with whom he held himself to be in the safest keeping, and whom, if he chose, he could make subservient to himself in almost anything. Great, therefore, was his chagrin to find that he had been so completely and so thoroughly baffled in all his schemes respecting Twitter.

What to do he knew not; he was so completely at fault, and so much annoyed at Twitter's getting so large a sum in his possession, without his, Varley's, being able to deprive him of it.

During these reflections, the coach arrived at the door of the hotel, and, having dismissed it, he at once ascended to his own apartments, where he had been scarcely a minute when a waiter entered, saying:

"One of the police officers is waiting to see you, sir."

"Has he been here long?"

"Yes, sir; he came here just as you left."

"Then show him up to me immediately."

In another minute the officer entered the apartment, and, when the waiter retired, Varley said:

"You bring me some news, I suppose, of Rowland Percy?"

"Yes, sir, some news, certainly; but nothing particular as yet."

"Indeed! It's a long affair."

"And a very troublesome one, Mr. Varley," replied the officer, dryly. "The fact is this, there has been a regular conspiracy to secrete Rowland Percy from us; many individuals have assisted in it, and they have succeeded as yet."

"But I hope you will succeed better now you are aware of the means by which he has succeeded in eluding your vigilance."

"We shall, I believe, for we have succeeded in capturing the principal individuals, by whose aid and advice he has been so long able to escape us."

"That is at least something towards a better conclusion than I have had as yet. Your exertions, I trust, will not relax now; you are nearer than ever in succeeding in catching your man, and the rewards will be yours as a natural consequence."

"Thank you, sir," replied the officer; "the exertions and dangers we have run have been very great, and the capture of these two men has cost us some hard blows, I assure you, for the struggle was of the most desperate character."

"You secured them, however?"

"We did; and one of them is now in Newgate, and the other is in Coldbath Fields."

"Who are these men?" inquired Varley.

"The one is a highwayman, called the Slashing Squire, and whose name is, I believe, Dick Palmer."

"And the other?"

"His name is Jones."

"Is Jones at Coldbath Fields?" inquired Varley, after a few moments' thought.

"He is," replied the officer.

"What sort of a man is he?"

"A big, strong man, very powerful, and wonderfully active for his weight."

"Ay, but I mean what is he?"

"A thief and housebreaker by profession," said the officer, coolly.

"Then I daresay money would be acceptable to him. Do you think he could be bribed?"

"Money usually effects wonders with these people, and I daresay that Jones will do as much for money as any man of his class, and you can't find one much lower."

"Very well," said Varley, "I'll try the experiment; but what do you intend to do about Rowland Percy?"

"Catch him, if we can," replied the officer; "those by whose assistance he has as yet lived are now secured. He is at large, it is true, but he has neither knowledge nor means; he, therefore, cannot hold out long, and there is every chance of our meeting with him every day, as he cannot lie concealed."

"Indeed!"

"No; he has no one whom he can trust, or who will do a single act for him; he must be reduced to the alternative of begging."

"In that case," said Varley, "the ends of justice will not be long ere they are satisfied. I wish you good-morning."

"Good-morning," returned the officer, who then rose and quitted the room.

"So," thought Varley, "events are fast hurrying on. Rowland Percy, once in the hands of justice, I shall then have more leisure to consider other things; but this Jones must not be forgotten, I will go and see him. I may make him useful to me, and Twitter will yet learn to fear me once again."

He rang the hand-bell, and desired the waiter who answered it to summon a coach, which no sooner came than he entered it, desiring the driver to convey him to Clerkenwell prison, where he alighted.

It was not long ere he was informed in what part of the building Jones was imprisoned.

It was a dark and dismal cell, intended only for the refractory, to which class Mr. Jones, it appeared, belonged, and into that gentleman's presence he was speedily ushered.

CHAPTER CXLVIII.

THE OFFER OF VARLEY TO JONES—THE HORRIBLE FRIGHT—THE SINGULAR MEETING WITH ROWLAND PERCY.

THERE was but a dim light streaming through a narrow grating in the cell wherein Jones had been placed, and it was some moments after Varley had been ushered into it before he could manage to discern any object distinctly.

At length, however, his eyes got accustomed to the darkness of the place, and then he saw Jones with his arms folded across his breast, sitting very composedly on the pitcher which had contained water, but which he had turned bottom upwards in order to make a seat of it.

"Your name is Jones?" said Varley, when the door of the cell was closed upon him.

"That'll do," replied Jones; "who are you when you are at home?"

"Do you not know me?"

"Now I do. You are the handsome gentleman as handsome does, or else quite the rewerse. I won't ask you to take a seat, as the floor is rather damp. Howsomdever, you are out-and-out welcome, if you like, both to the seat and the best rheumatics the place affords. I suppose as you are sent in here as a aggrawation o' solitary confinement?"

"Cease this buffoonery," said Varley. "Have you any objection to a hundred pounds?"

"Not the least. You can't pison the money,

old bloke. Hand it over; I suppose you looks on it as a kind o' conscience money for the skrimmage we had at old mother what-do-ye-call-ems, at Somers' Town, eh? Is that it?"

"Psha! You should be a man of the world."

"I was; but this here place is rather out of sossiety, you see."

"Then you can have no objection to forwarding my views, provided you are well paid for your trouble."

"Let's see the views," said Jones; "I'll turn 'em over in my mind a bit, and guv 'em you back if I don't like 'em."

"I wish Rowland Percy to be brought to justice."

"So do I."

"You do?"

"On my davy. When's it to be done? You can have a pick of that loaf there, if you're hungry, and your finger-nails are long enough. They guvs us yesterday month's baking here to put off the time. Some o' the gentlemen in difficulties, as is here, practices knocking up Macadamized stones with the loaves. They come in two with a crack as is enough to stun you."

Varley made a gesture of impatience, and proceeded:

"You, from your companionship with the man Palmer, must be aware of the plans, and, probably, of the actual place of concealment of Rowland Percy. I will give you a hundred pounds for such information as shall enable me to have him apprehended."

"Apprehended, did you say?"

"Yes, apprehended and executed pursuant to his sentence, for the murder of Sir George Rankley."

"Lawks, here's a blessed mistake—what queer mortals we is!"

"What mean you?"

"Why, if you'd persevered another minute I should a told where he was; but now you've done it. Well, I never! Eggs is eggs."

"You speak in riddles, or are drunk."

"Drunk? Just ladle up in yer hand some o' that slop on the floor, and you'll soon taste whether what was in this here pitcher comed out of a cask or the New River. You said as you wanted to bring Percy to justice, didn't yer?"

"I did."

"Well, that's the way you imposed on my werdant innocence. Lor, bless me! I find I'm quite a baby yet in the wickedness o' the world. I thought you meant to give Miss Miranda back her sticks—let her marry the young man—make a full confession of what a thundering rogue you are—give me a cool hundred for promising to go to your funeral, and then hang yourself."

Rage seemed for the moment to get the better of Varley's discretion.

A bitter oath escaped his lips, and he gave a stamp on the wet floor of the cell that covered himself with dirty water.

"There now," remarked Jones, "just see what you've done! What possessed you to take a shower-bath that ere way? Don't do it agin, I begs on you. There's a drop comed in my eye already."

"Do you mean to say," cried Varley, "that you will be mad enough to refuse my offers for the sake of mere obstinacy in a cause which cannot really interest you?"

"We've been a-driving at cross purposes," said Jones. "You talked o' justice when you meant law. That makes all the difference. The *law* would hang Rowland Percy if so be it catched him. *Justice* some o' these here days will hang you. There's the difference, you see. It's enough to make one cry like a *hinfant* to think how nearly one was being riglarly tooked in."

"Fool!" said Varley. "You cannot be serious. Will two hundred pounds tempt you to assist me in discovering Rowland Percy?"

"Two hundred?" said Jones, affecting to consider. "I'll tell you what I'll do, now."

"What—what?"

"You confess as you did the murder and get yourself hanged, and then I'll swear I saw Percy assault you. He'll be fined a matter o' twenty bob, perhaps. There'll be wengeance."

"Idiot!" said Varley, and, turning to the door of the cell, he hammered loudly upon it with his clenched hand to be released.

"I tell you what it is," said Jones, "you are a prisoner here. There's been a fellow here this morning as confessed you killed Sir George yourself. You are nabbed, my tulip."

"No — no!" shrieked Varley. "Great Heaven! No! It's false—false! I did not do the deed! No—no! Have mercy! No!"

"Hurrah!" cried Jones. "Here's a go. It's true. Hurrah!"

The door of the cell was flung open, and a couple of turnkeys appeared with surprise depicted upon their countenances.

"What's all this about?" said one.

"No—no," shouted Varley, while his whole frame was convulsed with terror, and his face was perfectly ghastly to look upon. "It is false. I did not do the deed. Mercy—mercy. Let me go. Let me leave this place. I—I am stifled by the air here. I will bribe you all. A thousand pounds to let me reach the open street."

"Go it," cried Jones. "Here's a go. What a lark. How do you feel now, old boy? Pick up your hat. Hurrah!"

"What is the matter?" shouted the turnkey. "Are you mad, sir?"

"Am—am I?" gasped Varley. "Am I——"

"Are you what?"

"Your prisoner? Tell me, am I detained here?"

"Not as I know of. What put that into your head?"

"He—he" gasped Varley, pointing to Jones, and leaning heavily against the door-post for support. "Villain! You—you have unnerved me. I will make you suffer yet for this."

"What are you talking about?" said Jones. "I never seed such a old picture-card in my life as you are."

"Well," remarked the turnkey, "I'm blessed if I can understand what it's all about. Are you going to go, sir?"

"Yes—yes. I am free to go. Of course I am going. Who dare detain me? I am going now."

"Good-bye," cried Jones. "Take care of yourself. Mind the step. Well, I never. Of all the blokes ever I comed near, you beats 'em. What a go. Hurrah!"

Varley never had endured such agony in all his life; he could not even believe himself safe until he reached the exterior of the prison, and the wicket-gate was fairly closed upon him.

Then, when he could no longer doubt that he had been imposed upon by Jones, such a torrent of invective escaped his lips as would have frightened anyone to hear.

"The villain!" he muttered, when he had satisfied the first ebullition of his rage; "the desperate villain! to tamper with an imagination in the fearful state of excitement that mine is, in such a way. Oh, I will be revenged—I will be revenged!"

Varley rushed from the prison-gates, heedless of a wretched night that had set in.

He felt as if he had but just escaped from some terrible danger, and more and more did he, too, begin to feel the utter hopelessness of his pursuit both of Miranda and Rowland Percy.

The rain was now falling so thickly that he was fain to get into a doorway for refuge, where his reflections assumed as gloomy an aspect as the weather.

In the course of half-an-hour, however, the torrent of rain sensibly abated, and Varley was about to leave his place of shelter, and hurry to his hotel, when someone turned into the doorway, and commenced knocking the moisture from his clothes.

Varley made an effort to pass him.

They met face to face.

An exclamation simultaneously burst from each of them—Bernard Varley and the stranger.

"Rowland Percy!" shouted Varley.

CHAPTER CXLIX.

THE STRUGGLE FOR FREEDOM—THE PLACE OF REFUGE—ROWLAND'S CRITICAL SITUATION.

PERHAPS in the whole of London no two men could have encountered with the same feelings towards each other as Rowland Percy and Bernard Varley—feelings so very different in themselves, and yet so intense and vivid in their manifestation.

There was no man in the great city that Varley cared to meet but Rowland Percy; there was scarcely one that Percy cared to avoid but Varley. And yet, by one of those strange accidents which bring people together where such a circumstance might be least expected, here had they met, face to face, in a narrow doorway, as if by appointment.

After the first exclamations of surprise on each side, the energies of both seemed for a few moments paralyzed by the intense surprise of the sudden encounter.

Rowland was the first to recover himself, and, feeling in its full force the critical nature of his situation, he drew back, determined to rely for safety upon his speed, for the thought occurred to him that he might have been watched, and that, possibly, Varley had plenty of assistance at hand to ensure his capture.

"Villain!" he cried. "Heaven will save me yet!"

He, however, had to turn in the narrow doorway before he could fly from the spot, and before he could do so, Varley, with a cry of exultation, sprang upon him like an enraged tiger, and clasped him round the waist, shouting:

"Help! help!—help to seize the murderer, Rowland Percy. Help—police! A murderer—a murderer! Ha! ha! caught at last. Triumph—triumph. Help! help! help!"

The grasp was one of iron, for Bernard Varley's whole soul was bent upon the capture of Rowland.

In vain did the young man strive to shake him off—disadvantageously as he was with his back to Varley, it was next to impossible.

His danger was each moment frightfully increasing, for Varley never ceased his cries for assistance, and it was a mercy no one happened to be passing at the precise moment; but, then, in such a neighbourhood, the solitude of the street was not likely to last long, and Percy felt that each moment was a perfect age of agony while he continued in that serpent-like grasp, which rather tightened than loosened on him, compressing his chest, and almost depriving him of the power of breathing, or moving his arms.

It was not to be borne.

Instinctively, rather than from design, he lifted his foot, and with the heel of his boot, commenced kicking Varley with a power and rapidity which no mortal endurance could stand above a few moments.

With a perfect howl of rage and pain, Varley was compelled to relax his hold, and the instant he did so, Rowland faced him, and doubling his fists, struck out with a rapidity and desperation that set all resistance at defiance.

In a few seconds Varley's face was a mass of contusions, and he fell heavily upon his back in the narrow passage.

To turn, then, and dart from the passage was the work of an instant; but Varley's cries for help were not altogether in vain, and Rowland found himself opposed by a man with a constable's staff, about the size of a mop-stick, who said:

"Hilloa, my fine fellow, don't hurry yourself. You are my prisoner."

Rapidity of action does wonders, and, in this case, it overcame the constable in a moment, for Rowland seeing the staff held up so threateningly before his face, laid hold of it with such a sudden jerk that he whipped it out of the hand of the constable, and then, before he could recover himself, he brought it down on his head with such a stunning whack that it sounded as if he had struck a beer-barrel with a heavy mallet.

Down went the constable, and Rowland Percy, who was in too great a state of excitement to be very particular, walked over him, and rushed down the street.

His dangers, however, were not yet over, for Varley, although partially stunned by the shower of blows he had received in the face, had managed to scramble to his feet, and he, too, rushed over the constable, when the first object his half-closed eyes lighted upon, was the rapidly retreating figure of Rowland Percy.

With a shout that was enough to fill the whole neighbourhood with terror, he gave pursuit.

Rowland heard him, and increased his speed; but if he (Rowland) flew with desperation onwards to escape a fearful death for a crime of which he was entirely innocent, he was pursued by Bernard Varley with all the wild fury of inextinguishable hate.

A more than mortal speed seemed to be given at that time to the desperate ruffian.

Smarting with pain as he was, too, from Rowland's blows, every wild passion of his soul was in arms. Had Percy dashed over a precipice, "deeper than plummet ever sounded," Bernard Varley would, at that moment, have madly followed him.

His wild, hoarse voice, now and then breaking into frightful screaming accents, came fearfully upon Rowland's ear.

He could have well believed that he was pursued by some demon, instead of a mortal man, so strange and awful was the tone in which Varley shouted for help to secure the murderer.

"Help! help!" he cried. "Murder! Hold him! See, he flies—help! Secure the murderer — Rowland Percy — the murderer! A thousand pounds for him, alive or dead! Kill him! Help—help! Murder—murder!"

These cries brought many people from their houses, and quite appalled the few chance persons who heard him.

They could not help thinking that Bernard Varley was mad, or that the retreating man he pursued was some great criminal indeed.

At least a dozen pursuers joined in the chase, and added their shouts to those of Varley.

"Stop him — stop him!" sounded from many throats, and poor, innocent Rowland found himself thus fearfully hunted through the streets of London, as if he had been some wild beast of prey that had suddenly made its appearance in the haunts of man.

Flushed, heated, and excited, he rushed on with amazing swiftness, he knew not whither.

Down one street and up another he ran, heedless of his course, so that he kept ahead of those who would have brought him to death and despair.

A narrow turning now presented itself to

his view, which was very steep, but he would not swerve from it, as he had partially turned into it, and with increased speed from the descent, he darted on.

The place was of a dirty and squalid appearance, inhabited by low brokers, several of whom made a dart at the flying man, and, in consequence of his speed, got rolled in the mud for their pains, or shot on one side with a great crash among their furniture and crockery which were exposed for sale.

But if Rowland had the advantage of increased rapidity in descending this thoroughfare, he soon found that he had an ascent before him of a steep character.

He heard the loud shouts of his pursuers, and each moment he fancied those shouts came plainer to his ear, and that his capture was certain, although he was in reality increasing his distance from them by the tremendous speed with which he ran.

Indeed, had he known the neighbourhood well, and all its resources of courts and alleys, there is no doubt he would soon have thrown those who were hunting him off the scent, but he was in such knowledge woefully deficient, and the consequence was that, in taking a turning, he was solely guided by the chance impulse of the moment.

Thus, then, although many saw him pass without attempting his capture, or joining in the chase, they added to the clamour, and eagerly pointed out which way he had gone.

When Rowland reached the summit of the hill he had been compelled to climb, he found a choice of several streets open to him; but, now fully alive to the danger of being pounced upon and captured if he passed down a street of shops, he chose the quietest thoroughfare he could see, which happened to be Hatton Garden, and down that he darted at a tremendous rate.

He had got two-thirds of the way towards Holborn before his pursuers arrived at the corner of Hatton Garden, but there they were informed by several officious persons which way the fugitive had gone, and the chase was joined by several constables from the police-office near by, who, hearing the riot and alarm, eagerly took part in the business.

To reach Holborn did not take Rowland many minutes, and then, when he saw the steep hill and the wide thoroughfare before him, he thought it would be more prudent to dart across the carriage-way into some obscurer street, which might lead him from so very public a place.

This plan he immediately adopted, but it appeared that the clamours of his pursuers in Hatton Garden had reached the ears of the people passing in Holborn, and a little knot of persons had collected to see what was the matter.

None of them attempted to seize Rowland, and he got over the roadway in safety; but, the moment he did so, a rush was made from the watch-house close to St. Andrew's Church of several constables, who tried to seize him.

To escape them, he diverged a little from his course, and stumbled over the steps of the church.

One man seized him, but Rowland shook him off, and, with a feeling of desperation, rushed up the steps, and, finding the iron gates partially open, he went on, nor stopped till he reached the church door.

A man was standing just within the porch, with a lantern in one hand, and a large key in the other.

"Hilloa!" he said. "Who are you?"

"An innocent man," cried Rowland. "Aid me, as you hope for Heaven's mercy!"

"Hilloa! hilloa! You are a rogue—come, come, be off."

"Stop him—stop him!" cried dozens of voices. "Seize the murderer—seize him—the murderer!"

"Gracious!" cried the man with the key; "my flesh creeps—they mean you. Here he is—come on—fire! murder! thieves! Here he is—come up. I've cotched him."

With one blow Rowland dashed the lantern from his hand, at the same moment that he wrested the key from him.

"I'm a dead man," cried the beadle, for it was no other than that functionary himself, who had been making some visit to the church in the course of his onerous duties. "I'm a dead man—save my soul!"

He then threw himself down on his back, and commenced kicking with his feet like a crab newly captured.

Rowland found the church door unlocked, for, when he arrived so suddenly, the beadle had only just emerged, and had been on the point of locking it.

In a moment Rowland passed into the sacred edifice, and locked the massive door on the inside.

Oh! how sudden and how great was the transition from the noise and riot of the streets—the glare of the lights, and the eager shouts of his pursuers—to the calm and beautiful stillness of the church.

In an instant, the very atmosphere of that place of holiness appeared to spread a delicious calm over the heart of the poor fugitive.

There seemed to reign above, around, and about him, the spirit of gentleness and resignation.

The air, too, was delightfully cool, and, as it played sweetly upon the burning brow of the harassed Rowland, he could not help exclaiming:

"Surely, surely, Heaven, which knows my innocence, has, in its mercy, sent me here for succour and assistance."

The busy hum of the city seemed completely shut out, or came in such indistinct murmurs as made that deep solitude strikingly apparent.

A dim light came in from the windows, just enabling him, after a few moments, to see the objects around him, and to guide his course down the aisle easily.

He had scarcely any notion of what next could or would happen.

How to escape from where he now was, should a search be made through the sacred

BERNARD VARLEY VISITS JONES IN PRISON.

edifice, he had no idea; and yet he felt a sense of security in that building devoted to God, which only his innocence could impart to him, and from that moment he told himself that, come what would—let what apparent evil fortune environ him that night—Heaven would not allow him to suffer the death which it was sought by his erring fellow-creatures to inflict wrongfully upon him.

Impressed with the calm holiness of the place, and grateful for the relief it had afforded him, Rowland opened the little gate leading to the communion table, and there he knelt and offered up a prayer to Heaven—not a prayer of supplication for the future,

but a pure and holy acknowledgment of his reliance upon God's mercy and justice—such a prayer as a thinking man may offer to his Creator in his humbleness before the Majesty of power, goodness, and wisdom to which he is not arrogant enough to dictate.

The persecuted Rowland rose chastened, but happier in spirit, and better prepared for any fate than he had ever been since the commencement of his long career of trouble.

As he did so, he was astonished by hearing a solemn strain from the organ, which with its sweet sounds filled the whole church with a very atmosphere of melody.

CHAPTER CL.

THE ARREST—THE MANIAC FROM YORK— THE STORM.

WITH surprise and admiration, Rowland Percy listened to the strains of music that came from the organ.

For a moment a superstitious feeling crossed his mind that surely at such a time it was played by no mortal hand; but, full of enthusiasm as was his mind at that moment, he quickly dismissed such a supposition, and scarcely had he done so, when he was rudely recalled to the world and its concerns—its hopes and fears, its few joys and deep distresses—by a violent hammering against the church door, and the confused hum of voices in the porch.

"They come—they come!" he said, "and I shall assuredly be taken here. What means have I of escape from this sacred edifice? I am lost—lost!"

The music suddenly ceased, and a voice from the organ-loft cried, loudly:

"Who is there—who is there? Is that you, Bellamy? For Heaven's sake do not make that uproar. How can I practice here if you keep up that thumping?"

"Open the door—open the door," cried a voice from without.

"What?" cried the organist.

"Rowland Percy, you cannot escape, and may as well yield yourself quietly," added the voice.

"What?" screamed the organist. "Quietly—I was playing very quietly."

Rowland crept as close to the church door as he could.

It opened inwards, and should they force the lock, as doubtless they would, he thought there would be just a faint chance of escaping out of the building when, as was probable, his pursuers made a rush into it which would carry them past him.

This was a forlorn hope, but it was his only one, and a drowning man will eagerly snatch even at a straw.

"Surrender yourself," again cried the voice; "open the door, it will be better for you!"

"You can but be hanged, old chap," cried another voice, which produced a roar of laughter.

"Well, I never heard such an uproar in all my life," said the organist; and he commenced his descent from his exalted station, in order to inquire into the cause of the increasing tumult.

"Now, Mr. Locksmith," said one outside the door, "see what you can do."

"Stand back, then," replied a man, in rough tones; "why, you all press on so, I can't get at the lock at all."

"Stand back, all of you—don't you know me?—good gracious, am I beadle or ain't I? A pretty upset I've had, to be sure. You should have seen how the villain snapped a pistol twice at my head, which, by the special mercy of Providence, did not go off—ah!"

There was a strange rattling in the lock for some seconds, and then the door creaked on its hinges.

"There you are," said the locksmith.

"Seize him! all of you," cried the beadle, as he ran into Holborn, and never stopped till he got to the corner of Field Lane.

As Rowland anticipated, a rush was made into the body of the church; and that rush, too, was the more vehement, because the figure of the organist was just dimly discerned coming slowly up the aisle.

But there were more experienced officers now in pursuit of Rowland than those who went so headlong into the church, and such remained at the door quite satisfied that the prisoner could not escape, and content to take him should he, as they thought highly probable, dodge those within, and attempt to leave the building.

Rowland waited but for an instant.

He saw the organist seized, and then he thought himself in possession of a good chance of escape, and he made the rush he had projected.

Alas! 'twas in vain; in an instant he found himself seized by two powerful men, to shake off the hold of whom was a matter of impossibility.

With a deep sigh, he surrendered himself to his fate, and made no useless struggle for release.

He said but one word, and that was:

"Miranda!"

In another moment Bernard Varley pushed his way forward, and, folding his arms across his chest, he stood within three paces of Rowland Percy with such a diabolical expression of exultation upon his face, that it was terrible to look upon.

Moreover, he was smeared with blood and dirt; his apparel torn; and one side of his face, from the punishment Rowland had given him, was frightfully swollen.

A more awful-looking object could not be conceived.

His voice was thick and hoarse from the exertion of shouting, and, as he spoke, his whole frame quivered with emotion and excitement.

"At last—at last," he cried; "at last hunted down, Rowland Percy!—murderer, and my enemy! Ha, ha! at last caught. Death! death! Can you escape it now? Dream of the scaffold, and all its frightful paraphernalia, until the reality bursts upon your sight. Die!—die! and carry with you to the grave my curse!"

"Impious, wretched man!" replied Rowland. "A thousand deaths, or a thousand scaffolds, to the innocent man, could not make up the sum of the mental tortures which are yours now, which may be yours for all time to come. I am hunted down, Bernard Varley, and yet even now, in this extremity of my fortunes, I can shudder and pity you."

"Well spoken," cried Varley, clapping his hands. "Condemned felon, you pity me! Ha! ha!—'tis well and bravely spoken.

Curses on you! When I see your lifeless body swinging in the breeze, I will bring Miranda to look at it; and, as she does so, I will whisper such vows of love in her ear as would make your very spirit mad to hear."

"Miserable man," said Rowland, "your every word bespeaks your wretched state."

"Ha—ha—ha! That is good—very good. I will post to York to see you hanged, Rowland Percy; and ever afterwards I will hold the day as a gala day. Rare sport—hunted down at last! Ha—ha—ha!"

His wild laugh rang far and wide, and the officers looked at each other significantly, as if they would have said:

"He is quite mad, is this fellow—as mad as he can be."

Varley's frightful laugh had not subsided when it was taken up by another voice—a voice of so wild and fearful a character, that even he staggered back a pace or two as it came ringing on his ears so strangely and suddenly.

The voice came from a poor, tattered-looking wretch, attired in the coarsest and wretchedest-looking mendicant's garments, who crawled up the steps leading to the church, and then leaned back on his knees close by Varley's feet.

One glance was sufficient on the part of the guilty wretch to identify that man as the maniac who at York had so often darkly prophecied the end of Varley's and Twitter's career, and now, again, at that moment, when feelings of exultation had found a home in Varley's breast, and he thought the fall of the unhappy Rowland Percy certain, the words rang in his ears:

"And yet Bernard Varley will be hanged at York—hanged at York. Ha—ha—ha! Come weal, come woe, on all else, Bernard Varley will be hanged at York. The innocent may perish; the beautiful be sacrificed; right may be quenched; wrong triumph for a time—for a time! And at the end of all that Bernard Varley will be hanged at York. Hear it every one of you—he will be hanged at York!"

Varley's surprise — not unmingled with terror—at the sudden appearance of the maniac, prevented him from interrupting this speech; but when it was concluded, and he saw that the eyes of all were bent on him with astonishment, he stamped vehemently, crying:

"Seize him—seize this man! Am I to hear for ever these evil croakings? To prison with him!"

"On what charge?" said an officer.

"Did you not hear him? Can you ask me what charge? I will have his life!"

"Then you will make yourself amenable to the laws, and his prophecy will be fulfilled, with one exception, namely, that you will be hanged in London instead of York."

"Ha—ha!" laughed the idiot, "he knows it. In the depths of his own mind he knows it, and that makes him the wretch he is. Well he knows it."

"Wherefore do you turn against me?" said Varley to the officer.

"You have spoken to the prisoner as no man ought to speak to a prisoner. If he is Rowland Percy he will be hanged, and that's quite enough, especially as there are two opinions about his guilt in London, without the aggravation of your taunting him in the manner you have done."

"Dare you——"

"Ay, dare I. You are either drunk or mad. If you don't come now at once, and identify the prisoner, I shall let him go."

"On your life you dare not; but I do much demean myself by holding words with such as you are. Lead on; I am prepared to identify that man as Rowland Percy, the escaped convicted murderer, from York."

The officer kept a firm hold of Rowland Percy, for, notwithstanding all he had said in his indignation at Varley, for the manner in which he had addressed Rowland, he had not the slightest notion of letting his prisoner go, and the whole party repaired to the watch-house close to the church, where Varley formally gave Rowland into custody, declaring him to be the same Percy who had escaped from York on the eve of his execution, and for whose apprehension such unprecedentedly heavy rewards had been offered from time to time, and so much trouble taken.

"Do you admit the identity?" said the constable on duty to Rowland.

"I do," was the brief reply.

"Then," he added, "I certainly decline keeping such a customer here. I shall send you at once to Newgate for security."

"And I will make one of his escort," remarked Varley.

"And I one of yours," said the maniac, who had crept into the watch-house unobserved.

Varley muttered a curse, and strode to the door.

There he waited again, for a dense crowd had assembled, which, to his surprise, saluted him with a hoot that rent the very air.

He drew back into the watch-house, and said:

"You will do well to keep your prisoner here; for without is a mob formed, to all appearance, of the worst of characters."

A peal of thunder at this moment appeared to shake the very heavens, and the bad weather of the evening seemed to be resolved upon ending in a terrific storm.

The guardian of this abode of disorderlies involuntarily paused, and listened to the riot of the heavens, which he seemed to consider as a matter that could not be put down by police interference.

Indeed, a sharp and serious contention of elements took place; the rain rattled down heavily, soon clearing the streets of all stray persons who cared for a wetting, and, in the minds of Bernard Varley and the keeper of the watch-house, it would speedily disperse the mob on the outside.

In this, however, they were disappointed, for the mob did not disperse so rapidly as they anticipated, though it slowly diminished in numbers.

The thunder became louder and louder, pealing overhead with such horrible crashing and cracking sounds as had seldom been heard, while these terrible indications of the strife were preceded by many a broad and vivid flash of lightning that displayed each object with fearful distinctness.

Not a steeple, not a chimney, not an eminence of any kind, within the sphere of vision from that spot, but what became as distinctly visible as if it had been broad day, while the falling rain came down in torrents that soon filled the channels, and, rushing down Holborn Hill with great fury, filled with water the hole that used to exist, as if formed on purpose, by the end of Shoe Lane. The hill appeared as if it had been well washed.

The high wind, which appeared to come with the storm, seemed to have the effect of carrying it off again, for a general subsidence of the angry elements to something like peace and repose soon took place. The wind subsided to a gentle zephyr, the clouds cleared off, and the rain ceased. No traces in the heavens remained of the storm, nor on earth, save the whitened streets, which had been so thoroughly cleansed as to render human labour needless.

CHAPTER CLI.

THE ATTEMPTED RESCUE—PALMER'S DEVOTION TO PERCY—THE LODGMENT IN NEWGATE.

IT was strange, but no less strange than true, that the furious strife of the elements rather assuaged than increased the deep anxieties of Rowland Percy, in consequence of his arrest, and the awful fate which awaited him.

His imagination seemed lifted above the earth and its pursuits as he heard the incessant boom of "Heaven's artillery," and he sat perfectly calm, while Bernard Varley shrank into the farthest corner of the watch-house, and consternation was depicted upon the faces of the constables.

When the loud thunder-claps were not heard so frequently, and the dazzling flashes of forked lightning were not each moment bewildering the faculties of all who looked through the begrimed window-panes into the street, Varley made an effort to rouse himself from the mental disquietude that had come over him.

He strode towards the door, saying, as he went:

"It seems to me now that the storm is over, and the prisoner can be removed. Surely no mob could stand such a torrent of rain as has been falling within these ten minutes."

One of the constables opened the door cautiously, and looked out.

The gutters were swollen to petty brooks, and such torrents of water were rushing down the hill, that anyone might have supposed some river above had burst its bounds, and was sweeping headlong into the valley.

"I don't see nobody," said the officer.

"But if there was nobody," cried the beadle, who had become quickly heroic since Rowland's capture, "I'd face him. It isn't nobody as can defy a beadle."

"Come on with your prisoner," cried Varley; "I will know no rest to-night, nor shall refreshment pass my lips till this murderer is in prison."

"Murderer yourself," said Rowland; "once and for all, before those here present, I declare my innocence of the crime imputed to me, and with it my firm conviction that you, my accuser, and the false witness against me, are yourself the murderer of Sir George Rankley!"

"Indeed," said Varley; "you are going to be hanged, so it is scarcely worth while to prosecute you for libel; one of the privileges of a man condemned to the gallows is certainly that, until the drop falls from beneath his feet, he may say just whatever he pleases."

"Villain! you in vain strive to hide beneath that sneering exterior the torments of a conscience ill at ease."

"Rail on, Rowland Percy, rail on; you are quite at liberty to take that poor, but pleasant revenge upon those who have succeeded in surrendering you to justice."

"I cannot, will not, have my prisoner spoken of in such a strain by anyone," said the officer, who principally had assumed the charge of Rowland Percy. "Come on to Newgate, since Master Constable here appears not to like the responsibility of the charge of so serious a criminal, although I very much doubt if the Governor of Newgate will consider himself authorized to receive a prisoner, except upon a warrant committing him to his custody and safe keeping."

"Do try," said the watch-house keeper; "we really have no place sufficiently secure for a murderer. Besides, we shall have all sorts of night-charges, as well, which will mix him up, you know—very wrong, indeed. Murderers is murderers, and ought to have places all to themselves, in my uncommon, humble opinion."

"Why waste time here," cried Varley, "in chaffering about such a point? Come on, I say, come on."

"Come," said the officer to Rowland Percy; "my advice to you is that you hold no further conversation with that man; he seems your most determined enemy."

"You have my warmest thanks for your courtesy and good feeling," replied Rowland; "you could not perform an unwelcome office in a kindlier spirit."

The little party, which was strengthened by all the night-watch that could be spared from the watch-house, now proceeded to the door.

The thunder-storm had quite abated, and, although a heavy, misty rain was still falling, the sky was getting lighter, and people were beginning again to venture forth from the various places of refuge into which they had rushed.

The streets were beautifully clean, from the effects of the deluge of rain that had fallen; in fact, the beadle remarked:

"You might eat off them, and they was a world too good for paupers."

"The mob has gone," remarked Varley, with an air of satisfaction, as he ran his eye over the party, and found that Rowland was guarded by nine men in all, including himself and the beadle.

"A rescue would be impossible," he then said to the officer.

"You mind your business, and I'll mind mine," was the pithy and rather unpromising answer.

"You shall, some day, and that soon, too, repent this insolence," said Varley. "As it is, it is some hundreds of pounds out of your pocket."

The officer only laughed, and walked on, holding Rowland by the arm; and, although he hardly thought it at all likely he would try to get away from so many, yet he kept a most wary and vigilant eye upon his prisoner.

No interruption took place till they came opposite to Shoe Lane, and then, from that thoroughfare, there ran out a man who, throwing up his hat in the air, cried in a loud, clear voice, that must have been heard a long way off:

"Grabs—grabs—Newgate, a-hoy!"

The officers drew back a step, as if uncertain what was about to happen, and yet, thinking it something dangerous; and at the moment from Field Lane, there emerged a strong body of men, while from Shoe Lane came some four or five, who commenced hustling the constables and their prisoner.

The officer who held Rowland in an instant snatched a pistol from his pocket, and, placing its muzzle against Rowland's cheek, he cried:

"Dead or alive, I will have my man! You know me—my name is Hunter. Clear the way, or you will have his death at your doors —clear the way!"

"Rowland Percy," cried a voice, "can you free yourself?"

The voice was Palmer's, and at that moment he made a rush between the officer and Rowland.

The former turned the muzzle of his pistol full against Dick's breast.

"I know you," he said; "do you want an ounce of lead in your lungs? Come, come, Dick Palmer, don't be a fool; I will have my prisoner; and you know when I say I will, I will."

"Fly, Rowland, fly!" cried Palmer; "fire away, Hunter, but let him go!"

All this happened in the course of about half-a-minute, and Rowland Percy had just time to say:

"Palmer, I swear, if you sacrifice yourself for me, to deliver myself up at the door of Newgate," when a rush was made from behind to the officers' assistance by the remainder of the watch.

Probably, then, Mr. Bellamy, the beadle, did as good service as anybody; for, in his fright, he made a wild kind of rush across the road, right against the party that was advancing from Field Lane, and they were so pleased with the fun of bonneting the beadle, that time was afforded to the officers to get back to the watch-house with their prisoner, and once again Rowland found himself, after a futile attempt to save him, a prisoner, without a hope of rescue.

"This is sharp work," remarked the officer.

"I knew nothing of it," said Rowland; "and all I have to beg of you is, that nothing may be said of it to Palmer's prejudice. He well deserves a better fate than is his in this world—a better heart never beat in human bosom. The law will be satisfied in its blind vengeance against me. Let him reap no evil consequences from this rash attempt."

"Nobody will hear anything of it from me," said the officer; "I know him well."

"But from me they shall hear of it," cried Bernard Varley, who was quite wild with rage and disappointment that Rowland was not safely lodged in Newgate.

"Gracious worships!" said the watch-house keeper, "what can I do? He wouldn't be safe here all night. You know what a little bit of a crib this is. Why, we have enough to do sometimes with half-a-dozen disorderlies; we should be taken by storm in the middle of the night, and done for."

"I will write a note stating the particulars to the Governor of Newgate," said Hunter, the officer. "Under the circumstances, he will now, no doubt, receive the prisoner, as well as send an armed force to assist in his removal. I am thankful that this affair, as yet, has gone off without bloodshed."

The note was written and despatched by one of the watch, to whom Bernard Varley promised a guinea if he performed his errand quickly and safely.

The man started off, and the whole party remained in a state of the most painful suspense till his return.

As for Rowland, he looked upon any attempt to rescue him by force in the public streets as perfectly hopeless, and regretted that human life should be sacrificed, as in all probability it would, without leading to any good result, if Palmer should again try to save him on his route.

Bernard Varley paced the confined precincts of the watch-house like a caged tiger, impatient and nearly maddened by the circumstance of his confinement.

Half-an-hour passed in this state of disquietude, during which scarcely a word was spoken by anyone, and then a knock came at the outer door of the watch-house.

"Here he is!" cried the officer; and he was going towards the door, when Varley, in his impatience, anticipated him, and opened it.

"Ha! ha!" laughed the maniac from without, "you will be yet hanged at York."

"Confusion!" cried Varley, and he grasped him by the throat.

"Hold, sir," said the officer; "you had better be careful what you are about. Here are too many witnesses for you to perpetrate a deed of violence. You are not so safe as when you fired a pistol at this poor creature for looking through a drawing-room window at the Grange."

Varley nearly fell down, he was so taken by surprise, and he gasped out:

"How—how came you to know that?"

"Never mind. I know, perhaps, more than you think. But here are our men."

A party of about a dozen well-armed men reached the door of the watch-house, and their leader placed a small piece of paper in the hands of the officer, on which was written:

"Bring your prisoner at once to Newgate. Though contrary to rule, he shall be received."

This was signed by the Governor, and the additional force of resolute men now made escape out of the question.

Varley's eyes glistened with satisfaction, for he looked upon Rowland Percy's incarceration in Newgate as already safely accomplished.

He turned again to address some taunting observations to the unfortunate young man; but the officer checked him with such a stern look, that even he shrank back abashed.

"We shall not want you," said the officer, "till to-morrow. The prisoner will be taken to Bow Street to be identified, when you can attend if you like."

"Enough," said Varley. "Let him escape now at your peril. And yet I shall see him safely lodged in Newgate myself. I have sworn to do so, and I will keep my word."

The party now, with its strong reinforcement, once again started for the gloomy prison-house from which Dick Palmer had so recently, with so much toil and difficulty, escaped.

No opposition was offered—in fact, scarcely a chance passenger was in the street, for the aspect of the evening had driven everyone home who had a home to go to; and those who were compelled to wander in the streets had again, as the rain threatened, ensconced themselves under doorways, and within the entrances of stable-yards and coach-inns.

The dismal portals of Newgate were gained at last, and, in another moment, poor Rowland was a prisoner within its walls.

"Ha! ha!" laughed Bernard Varley. "I triumph—I triumph! Oh, I have dreamed of such a time as this!"

"Ha! ha!" cried the beadle, who thought Varley's manner uncommonly grand, "I've triumphed, too, and I have dreadful dreams. My wife often says——"

"Fool!" muttered Varley, as he pushed him on one side with a violence that made him sit down right in the kennel, and then he rushed from the spot.

CHAPTER CLII.

SAMUEL TWITTER'S RESOLVE AND WRITTEN CONFESSION—POSTING TO LIVERPOOL.

No sooner did Samuel Twitter get perfectly free from Bernard Varley, after his quarrel and fight in the street, and also of the mob, who, for some distance, continued to follow him, than he revolved over several circumstances in his mind, and he came to the resolution to put into execution the plan he had long since formed.

He felt certain that Varley would not cease to make desperate efforts to regain the money he, Twitter, had possessed himself of by means of the forged cheque. London, therefore, was the most dangerous spot he could choose for his residence.

Besides this, he felt the full desire for revenge against Varley, who had, in so many ways, attempted to do him deadly injury.

He had, more than once, attempted his, Twitter's, life, and, now that he had a chance of turning the tables against him, nothing could afford Twitter so much happiness as the knowledge that Varley himself was suffering the full penalty of his crime.

Full of these thoughts, he hastened to the nearest livery stables, and inquired how soon he could have a post-chaise and four to carry him to Liverpool, when he was informed that in less than an hour it would be ready for him.

"Then let it be got ready immediately, and sent round to the hotel, where I shall be waiting."

"Very well, sir," said the man who took the order, with great deference; "it shall be there punctual."

Twitter turned from the place, and was soon in his hotel, where he gave orders that no one should, on any account, be allowed to enter his apartments without he first knew the visitor's name and business, for he was fearful that Bernard Varley had watched him, and would attempt to re-possess himself of the money.

After he had arranged all for his immediate departure so soon as the post-chaise should be announced, he called for writing materials, and, after some hesitation, began to write.

That writing was his confession of the whole of the occurrences as they occurred at the Grange, and it ran as follows:

"I, Samuel Twitter, do make the following confession, not from any motive of fear, neither am I induced to do so at the suggestion of any other person, but because the man who has reduced me to the state I have lately been in, is the prime mover and principal actor in all the deeds of iniquity that I am about to relate, and on him ought all the punishment to fall; and a still stronger motive actuates me, namely, that he who is now persecuted for the murder of Sir George Rankley, may not escape the doom that awaits him, if I make not this confession—I mean Rowland Percy, who is innocent of the murder.

"I was valet to Sir George Rankley, who was a kind and generous master: however, I had been in the habit of stealing the plate belonging to Sir George, and sending it to London in the charge of a confederate of mine.

"This was no other than a man named Dick Palmer, who used to meet me at a particular part of the estate, near a shrubbery among some tall trees that grew near the roadside; here he used to come and meet me, and take what booty I had, carry it to London, and then dispose of it.

"Of course he kept a great portion for his own pains, and gave me the remainder.

"This went on for a long time, and no one suspected what was going on; until, indeed, Bernard Varley came down as a visitor to the Grange.

"This man appeared to be always prying about, and seemed to know much about Sir George Rankley and the house, beyond what anyone deemed likely.

"One day, just as I had had an interview with Palmer, and had given him some more plate, and received some cash of him, and Palmer was gone, whom should I meet but this Bernard Varley. I was much confused by his scrutinizing glance, and he said in a peculiar manner:

"'So, Samuel Twitter, you are not like the unworthy servant who hid his master's talent in the earth; but, on the contrary, you obtain something in the way of exchange.'

"I made no answer, for I knew not what to say, and he continued:

"'Pray how long has Sir George Rankley allowed you to effect a conversion of his plate into specie?'

"Still I was silent, for I was now fully aware of the extreme danger I ran, and that I was found out in my peculations. A cold perspiration came over me, and I dropped upon my knees, beseeching him not to inform Sir George Rankley of my doings.

"'Samuel Twitter,' he said, 'why should I not instantly explain to Sir George what you have done? You would then be transported for life.'

"I begged and entreated, and promised all that a man, under such circumstances only, could think of; nay, I even offered to be his slave.

"Bernard Varley paused a moment or two, and then he said:

"'Well, Samuel Twitter, there is one condition, and one only, upon which I will be silent upon what has passed.'

"'Name it—name it, Mr. Varley, and, depend upon it, if it be anything short of death or imprisonment, I'll do it.'

"'Well, then, attend to me. Can you be faithful?'

"'I can, and will.'

"'Then will you become my assistant in getting up certain schemes in the house against Sir George Rankley? I have designs of my own, which I will explain more fully by-and-by; but swear to me that, henceforth, you will be faithful to my person and interests.'

"I solemnly swore to be so, to do all that he desired, and to keep secret all that he said or did, or that I did for him.

"'Now, then, Samuel Twitter, attend to me. As we walk back to the Grange, I will unfold to you a few of my projects, in the fulfilling of which I shall require your assistance.'

"'I would have it happen,' he continued, 'that Sir George Rankley was dead.'

"'Dead!' I exclaimed.

"'Yes, dead. You understand me, Twitter?'

"'Yes; but not murder?'

"'It matters little, you know; for, should he not die as soon as I should wish him to die, you must assist me to dispose of him. Do you hear me? There will be no danger, except such as can only arise when you refuse to aid me, or to break my council.'

"I promised to do all he required of me, but I trembled excessively when he talked of murder in such a cool strain.

"'I wish,' he said, 'that, after that, there should be found a will by Sir George Rankley, bequeathing to me all his property, and a recommendation to marry his daughter. Now, when Miranda finds herself no longer possessed of anything like independence, and poverty treads close on her heels, she will become an easy conquest.'

"'But,' said I, 'there is young Mr. Percy. It is well known among the servants that they are attached to each other.'

"'It matters little,' he replied. 'I have been thinking over that matter, and I believe I can foment a quarrel between Sir George Rankley and the Squire of Larkswood; a duel will be the consequence, and, if Sir George falls, why, our work is the lighter.'

"'True,' I replied; 'that way, then, our work will be so much the lighter, for I own my nerves are not of the best, and I shrink from murder.'

"'You have not the liberty to shrink from anything,' replied Bernard Varley, with sternness and impatience, 'for, should he not fall, it will be necessary to put him out of the way, somehow or other; and, recollect, should you fail, you will certainly be consigned to a prison for life, while I offer you immunity for all that is past, and a sufficiency out of the funds the Grange estate will produce to me, to enable you to live independently for life—but, in the meantime, you must be both silent and cautious, for, should a word drop, that word will be your sentence to perpetual imprisonment.'

"Thus speaking, we both arrived at the Grange, and I retired to the apartment allotted to me, there, in silence, to meditate upon the strange conference that had passed between us.

"The principal events that I have now to relate, are already known. A quarrel was fomented between Sir George Rankley and the Squire of Larkswood, as Mr. Percy was called; they fought, and the former was wounded; that wound was trifling, but it gave Bernard Varley the opportunity he sought, for, stealing to his room, and relieving the nurse, he smothered him with his pillow. I was to have aided, but I fainted on the bed.

"Bernard Varley refused to give me my share of the produce of our iniquity, for he obtained a forged will, and all was his. I attempted to induce him to act fairly, but he made more than one attempt on my life. I have, now, a sufficiency, and am about to quit the country, and, before this confession can reach you, I shall be far away beyond your reach. I go to the East, there to spend the remainder of my days in seclusion, and to repent of the crimes I have been guilty of.

"Bernard Varley ought to be arrested, and confronted with my confession, without his having any knowledge that I have escaped. If he supposes I am in custody, you will speedily ascertain the truth of my words.

"Rowland Percy is innocent of the charge. Bernard Varley is guilty of it, and I was present, but unable to assist, in consequence of insensibility, induced by my fear of shedding blood. The will was forged, and Miss Miranda Rankley has been robbed of her inheritance.

"This confession is true, I solemnly declare, and my share of the dreadful transaction that I have detailed was forced upon me, for the only crimes I had ever committed amounted to no more than robbing—murder was against my nature. I now wish justice to be done to the innocent, and to the guilty. I do, now, all that I can do towards such an end, without my person being endangered—that I shrink from. I will live and repent ; but much more injury may be prevented by this confession.

"(Signed)   "SAMUEL TWITTER.
"To the Lord Mayor of the City
of York, and the Town Council."

Twitter carefully directed this paper and sealed it up, though he had written the body of it in great haste, and even perturbation of spirit, for every sound caused a start, and the recital of his own crimes brought beadlike drops of moisture upon his brow.

At length he secured the packet carefully in his bosom, and as he extinguished the taper he had used to seal it, a waiter entered the room, saying :

"Mr. Twitter."

"Well?"

"The travelling carriage is at the door, sir, and waits for you."

"I am ready," exclaimed Twitter, as he rose, and pointing to a portmanteau and trunk, desired that they should be placed in it, and then following after, was soon safely shut in.

No sooner was he inside, than he hastily pulled up the blinds on either side, fearful of meeting by accident his arch-enemy, Bernard Varley, and calling to the post-boy, he said :

"Drive on as fast as you can," and in another moment he was rattling over the stones at a rate that excited the attention of everybody who came in the road.

CHAPTER CLIII.

TWITTER'S JOY.—HIS JOURNEY TO LIVERPOOL
—THE "ROYAL GEORGE."

TWITTER'S spirits seemed gradually to rise, and his features betokened a lightness of heart that he had been a stranger to for many a day.

Whether this was from the sense of security arising from his knowledge that he was increasing the distance between himself and Bernard Varley, or the excitement of rapid riding, he could not have explained if he had been asked, but doubtless both these causes had something to do with it.

But those who knew Samuel Twitter as well as the reader now knows him, will easily perceive that these could not be the whole and sole causes of his excitement.

He exulted in two things besides his certain escape and possession of wealth—one of these was, that he had completely out-generalled Varley. He had, in Twitter's own words, "done him brown."

He was about to make use of the very means of escape that Varley had secretly, and at great expense, provided for his own use.

His cunning had been successful, he thought, on this point, and he hugged himself as he thought of the talismanic words that would enable him to take possession of a yacht.

"Ah, Bernard Varley," apostrophized Twitter, "after all your care and cunning, you see you are not the cleverest man in creation. You little thought I, whom you pretended to despise, would be able to foil you at your own weapons, that I should succeed in baffling your utmost efforts, defy you, and, in the end, do all you intended to do, and then a little more on my own account to pay off old scores, merely a private debt, which shall be posted to your account at Liverpool within a very short time."

As he uttered these words, he took his sealed confession from his breast, and looked at it, carefully examining the seals and the very edges to see that nothing peeped out that might betray its important contents.

"He! he! he!" laughed Twitter, as he gazed upon it, with half-gleeful and half-scared eyes; "he! he! he! Mr. Bernard Varley will hardly expect Samuel Twitter to be so punctual in the return of the obligations he owes him—no, no! he! he! he! it makes one laugh to think of it, and——"

After a pause, he replaced the letter in his bosom carefully, and continued :

"It makes one laugh, indeed. He who assumed so much superiority over me ; well, he may be bolder than I, and that brings people into trouble, and so it will Bernard Varley. What will he say when he first hears from the Mayor of York? He! he! he!"

Twitter's laugh became louder, and the post-boys, hearing it, turned their heads, to make sure of the nature of the sound.

Such a laugh they had never heard before; but, seeing Twitter's eyes fixed on them, they immediately turned, and spurred on their horses.

There was another motive, in addition to Twitter's pleasure, arising from mere cunning —he was an egotist in his way, but revenge took as strong a hold upon his narrow intellect, and the knowledge that all the ills that he had received from the hands of Varley were about to be repaid in such a manner, caused a sensation of glee and delight that cannot well be conceived, arising, not as in many cases it would, from intensity and depth of feeling, and giving a savage pleasure; but to him it appeared absolutely funny, and, save now and then, when he considered even the most distant chance of his ever being taken; then, like a timid hare, he would sit crouched up with a scared aspect, fearful of the slightest appearance, either in the heavens or on the earth.

The flight of a bird at such a moment would affright him, and the sound of horses would make him urge the post-boys to use greater exertions to reach their destination more speedily than they were doing.

At such moments the men would cause a great bustle with the horses, which, from long practice, they were well able to do, that gave Twitter the notion that he was literally flying over the ground.

Often would he place his hands upon various parts of his person where he had secreted his money, and congratulate himself upon the success of all his plans, and exult in the idea that he was a much better schemer than Bernard Varley after all, for his, Twitter's plans, would succeed, while Bernard Varley's would lead him to destruction.

"And then," thought Twitter, as the idea flashed across his mind, "and then the prediction of the idiot at York will be verified, and Bernard Varley will be hanged at York. He! he! he!"

As these cachinnations escaped his lips, Twitter's eyes glanced all around to detect, if possible, if any one heard him laugh, fearful that even the laugh might betray some hidden meaning; then a slight tremor would creep over him, which was speedily allayed by his looking upon the four horses in front at full pace, and the knowledge of the money he possessed.

Thus travelled Twitter, but, despite all their exertions, the distance was scarce a third accomplished ere night set in, and he was compelled to stay at an inn for a few hours, as the horses could travel no further that night, and had he wished he could not obtain more, therefore he determined to stay till early morning, and again dash onward, when he hoped to reach Liverpool before night.

That day he did not start till late, and, but for the heavy bribes he gave the postilions, he would not have accomplished half the distance, but money will do much in these cases.

The day had scarcely dawned ere Twitter had arisen from his sleepless couch, for sleep did not visit his eyes; his thoughts were too active, and his fears too numerous, so, after partaking of a hearty breakfast, he was on his road.

When he had nearly accomplished the distance, and by dusk he came within a few miles of Liverpool, his joy and exultation were great.

He was safe—he was now at the very acme of his wishes—all his hopes were about to be crowned—a few hours more and he would be beyond the reach of the law.

The weather was overcast, but what cared Samuel Twitter for that? He was travelling in a carriage—it was not often he did so as the principal person, and this knowledge was grateful to him, and he placed himself in various extraordinary postures, such as lying all along, and then with his feet up in front. Indeed, he was so restless and fidgety that the post-boys at length began to conceive they had either got some individual who was noble by descent, or an idiot; and, so impressed were they with this notion, that they behaved with extraordinary civility.

As night closed around them, the town of Liverpool came in sight, and, ere long, to Twitter's great joy, the post-chaise rattled over the stones, and stopped at one of the first inns, not far from the docks, called the "Royal George."

Here a host of waiters and others immediately rushed out to usher the distinguished individual who stopped there with four horses, and Twitter was soon splendidly lodged in the best room the house afforded, first having handsomely rewarded the postilions, who communicated this intelligence to the people at the "Royal George," who immediately gave extra attention and civility, which always precedes robbery and extortion at such places.

A splendid repast was ordered and partaken of by Twitter, who afterwards desired that the landlord might be sent to him.

In a few moments this individual appeared with a low obeisance, and inquired what he should have the pleasure to do for Mr. Twitter.

"Can you," replied Twitter, without deigning to thank him for his civility, "Can you obtain me a boat on the Mersey to-night?"

"Why, sir," replied the landlord, "this is a very bad night for the water, very windy and cold, and inclining for rain. If you desire a pleasure trip, allow me to advise the morrow to be taken for it, when you can see the shores and the shipping."

"Ay, that's all very well, you know," replied Twitter; "but there is a vessel that I desire to speak with particularly, lying in the Mersey."

"Very well, sir," replied the landlord, deferentially; "I will procure a boat and four stout rowers to carry you out, as it is a rough night."

"That will do," replied Twitter, "I will pay them well, expense is no object, and my business is most important."

Impressed with the idea that his guest was

someone of great consequence, the landlord immediately dispatched a messenger to a boatman whom he knew, with orders to get his boat in readiness, and manned in a short time for a row down the Mersey.

Twitter, in the meantime, revelled in all the luxuries the hotel could offer.

He marched up and down the well-lighted room; the soft carpets were grateful to his feet, and the mirrored walls reflected his person.

His littleness of mind, and extreme vanity, appeared to diverge from each other in opposite degrees of comparison; the one was very great, and the other small beyond comparison.

Samuel Twitter slapped his pockets, and took a gleeful glance at his own reflection in the mirror, a glance which for the moment scared him; but he quickly recovered himself, and his pleasurable looks returned, as he said to himself:

"Well, here am I at last, safe and rich. I am worth six thousand pounds odd. He! he! he! Oh, Samuel Twitter, this last stroke of yours has been admirably struck; it has smashed Bernard Varley, he who has always thought you were an ass. Who is the fool now, eh?" and as he spoke he drew forth his written confession from his bosom.

It was all right.

It was a fearful instrument, and Samuel Twitter appeared to think so, for his hand shook while it held the terrible sheet of paper, that contained in it matter which would not only hang Bernard Varley, but himself too, were it to be opened before the proper moment.

"No—no," at length exclaimed Twitter, putting it back in his bosom carefully. "It will not be sent until I am off for some hours; no danger can possibly happen to me, and Bernard Varley will be hanged at York—hurrah. I could almost cry for joy. I am worth six thousand pounds in hard cash."

Twitter again sat down to the table, and commenced another complicated attack upon the delicacies and wines; but in such an order that would have shocked many who only took these things by rule, and in regular rotation.

The fact was, Twitter was determined to enjoy himself, and so extravagant was his joy at what had happened, that he committed many absurd blunders.

"I won't eat any more," said Twitter, filling a glass of wine; "the victuals have a queer taste. Sours and sweets get mixed up in such a confusion, that it spoils one's appetite. Wine is the nourishment of gods and rich men. Hurrah! Bernard Varley and York Castle. Eight o'clock and a strong rope. Hurrah!"

Twitter's toast was uttered rather louder than he intended, and the waiter entered, saying:

"Beg pardon, sir: but did you call?"

"Call, no: who said I called?"

"Beg pardon, sir. I didn't: but I thought you did."

"No—no, I didn't say anything," said Twitter, rather alarmed.

"No, sir; the boat is ready, sir."

"I will be down immediately," replied Twitter. "Give the men my luggage, while I speak to the landlord."

In a few minutes more Twitter had settled his bill, and stood on the steps of the hotel, with the landlord bowing his leave at his elbow.

CHAPTER CLIV.

THE SEALED CONFESSION—THE MERSEY AT NIGHT—THE PERILS OF AN OPEN BOAT IN A STORM.

As Twitter made a motion to leave the doorsteps, he turned to the landlord as if he had suddenly recollected something he had forgotten, and putting his hand to his breast, he drew forth his written and sealed confession, directed to the Lord Mayor of the City of York.

"This letter," said Twitter, handing it to the landlord, "is of some consequence: will you have the goodness to take charge of it, and send it to-morrow by post to its destination?"

"Certainly," said the landlord, receiving the letter with a bow. "I can put it in the post immediately."

"No—no," replied Twitter, "to-morrow will do as well; and, indeed, I would rather that you sent it to-morrow than this evening, but be sure it does go."

"I'll vouch for it being safely delivered to the post, sir," replied the landlord.

"Then I am ready," said Twitter, to the men who carried his luggage, and they all at once started for the stairs at which the boat was awaiting them.

Twitter, since he left the hotel, appeared to be very anxious about making haste; he wanted to be on the river as quickly as possible; every moment appeared to be an age—moments that were laden with golden treasure, and which were being wasted by the necessary operations of locomotion, and the arrangement of the luggage in the boat.

"Now, sir," exclaimed the boatman. "Are you ready? we are."

"Yes, quite—quite, my good man," exclaimed Twitter, jumping into the boat, and tumbling over the thwarts, thereby bruising his shins most dreadfully. "Bless me, how hard the seats are. I do think I have broken my legs."

"Shall we put back and carry you to a doctor's?" inquired the master of the boat.

"No, no," hastily interposed Twitter; "it's nothing—drive on—row away, I mean. What do you stay for? Can't you go on?"

"Oh, yes, sir; but—but——"

"But what?" exclaimed Twitter, alarmed.

"Where are we going to, sir?"

"Down the Mersey here—towards—the Irish Sea, or what you call it."

"Oh, yes, sir; pull away, my lads; keep her along shore: the water runs smoother."

Acting upon this advice, the men pulled stoutly at their oars, in silence.

The night was very dark, and not a star was to be seen. True it was that there was sufficient of that uncertain light which enabled persons in company with each other to see and distinguish the expression of features; but you could see but a few yards at the utmost, and the boat made its way over the labouring water, which rose up from beneath it in swelling mounds, lifting the boat up at times without any previous indication of waves.

Twitter seemed not to notice these appearances; or, if he did, he did not understand their significance. He only endeavoured to pierce the gloom that surrounded him.

His anxiety to leave Liverpool was so great, that he had not as yet opened his lips as to the object he had in view in their rowing on the bosom of the Mersey in such darkness, and at such an hour; besides, he almost apprehended a pursuit from Bernard Varley.

He was, therefore, rather surprised when the owner of the boat said:

"What part of the river do you wish to go to, sir, this shore, or the Cheshire shore?"

"To neither," exclaimed Twitter; "I want to go on board a yacht."

"A yacht? I doubt if you will get on board of one on such a night as this—it is so dark."

"Oh!" said Twitter, "I will pay you handsomely—expense is no object."

"Very well, sir," replied the owner; "it's hard and dangerous work, especially as I think a storm is a-brewing, and deserves extra pay. What say you, lads, the gentleman will be generous; shall we pull after the boat he wants?"

"Ay, ay, sir," replied the men; and one of them said: "Do ye see, sir, money I don't valley—save money gets grog, and grog's what I like."

"You shall be paid liberally, I give you my word; a handsome sum shall be given to each of you, as soon as I am on board of the *Zephyr* —I am her owner."

"Oh! the *Zephyr*," said the boatman, with a blank expression of countenance; but instantly added: "We'll pull for her; I know she must lay somewhere hereabouts, for I was told so by a man who saw her a few days ago."

They now applied themselves to their oars, and rowed about for a long while—Twitter alternately cursing and praying.

He began to blame himself for his precipitancy in giving the sealed confession so early to the landlord of the "Royal George."

The night grew very cold; the wind rose and fell in heavy, moaning sounds, and a dense mist began to come down, so that Twitter, who sat exposed in the boat, soon became wet to the skin, cramped, and miserably cold.

"Is she far off?" he inquired.

"Don't know," replied the owner, winking at one of his men. "Do you know whereabouts she is?"

"Can't say," replied the man, pulling very hard, and trying to look a long way through the darkness and rain.

"Where did you see her last?" inquired Twitter. "Surely you can say or know something."

"I might say a great deal, sir; but, then, you see," replied the boatman, with a queer and important screw of the mouth, "I alus looks to the quality of what a man says afore quantity; I can't say as I knows much of the *Zephyr*, seeing she's been a-lying-to here, nobody knows why, nor her own crew, either; but, howsomdever, I see her, yesterday, drop down the horizon."

"Drop down where?" screamed Twitter. "She's not sunk, I hope?"

"Sunk! no; she went, I mean, clear out of sight."

"Where to?"

"Lord knows, sir, I don't; but it's out hereaway," replied the boatman, with great gravity, and, turning an immense quid in one of his cheeks, he winked with the opposite eye to the man next him.

"Then row after her," replied Twitter; "I must be on board of her to-night, at any risk."

"A starn chase is a long chase; but, hows'ever, a long pull, and a strong pull, will pull us there. Away, lads—eh?"

"Ay, ay, that it will," was the prompt reply.

"Pull, then, in Heaven's name!" replied Twitter; "and, if you put me on board safely, you shall be handsomely rewarded."

The men rowed for some time in silence, until they showed evident signs of fatigue, and they had got so far, that the surf ran strong, and the master of the boat said it was impossible to get on board that night, but had better put back till daylight assisted them.

For a long time Twitter would not hear of it, until they assured him of the inutility of remaining on the water, and the almost certainty of losing his life by wreck, if they attempted to remain out, and they would not stay if he wished it ever so.

Great was Twitter's rage and anger, which showed itself in many shapes: he was one moment cursing and scolding, the next breathing prayers, repentance, and shedding tears, till, at length, frantic in mind, and exhausted in body, he lay at the bottom of the boat, kicking dreadfully, and it was only by threatening to throw him overboard that he was kept at all quiet.

The boatmen had miscalculated their powers when they talked of getting back. The wind now blew off the shore, and the water was so rough they could not return.

In addition to this, the boat was fast filling with spray, which dashed over the boat every minute, and threatened to overwhelm and sink them. They then endeavoured to make Twitter sensible of their danger, upon which he got up, and again sat upon the seat, supporting himself against his luggage.

The wind howled most piteously, the rain

descended in a deluge, and the spray, dashing over them every moment, they were all speedily wet to the skin.

Twitter had been so for some time, but now he became more sensible of it. Sickness overtook him from the motion of the boat, which was carried hither and thither, without the men being in any manner able to control it, or even direct its course.

"Oh, dear—oh, dear!" exclaimed Twitter, half-audibly, "what will become of me—what will become of me? I shall surely be hanged—I shall surely be hanged!"

"I am glad to hear it, sir," replied one of the men, who had been baling the water out with an old saucepan.

"Are you? Curse you, what do you mean by that?" exclaimed Twitter, as fiercely as he could.

"Why, sir, it will insure us against drowning, for I have been on the Mersey these thirty odd years, and I never saw such a night. We are sure to be drowned, unless anybody here's under the protection of Providence, and 'specially booked for a place at the gallows."

"Come, come," exclaimed the owner of the boat, "leave off jawing, and pull away. Come, sir," he continued, to Twitter, "we are all alike now, Jack is as good as his master; we must make common cause."

"Must you?" growled Twitter, stupidly staring at him.

"Yes, sir. Come, pull away—you must take your turn, and help to keep her afloat."

"I shan't," exclaimed Twitter, passionately.

At the same time, his fears were so great that he scarcely knew what was going on, and, moreover, he became almost indifferent to his fate, and knew not whether he might not as well be drowned as be saved to be hanged.

"You must, sir. Our lives are all alike endangered. You must help to keep her afloat."

"I shan't," doggedly replied Twitter. "I hired you to row me to the *Zephyr*, and I'm not going to bale her out, as you call it. Good Heavens! what shall I do?" he exclaimed, as his mind returned to the consideration of the probable fate that awaited him ashore. "Still," he thought, "there may be time to escape before the letter could reach York, and a message return, should they send one."

These reflections were cut short by the master hitting him with the tin saucepan over the head, and then, seizing him by the collar, and declaring that he would pitch him over if he did not help to bale out the boat.

His terrors of immediate death were so great that they overcame all fears of the future, and Samuel Twitter, with his six thousand pounds in his pocket, was seated in a boat, nearly up to his knees in water, baling it out with an old saucepan, as if for very life.

The prospect around was cheerless indeed. The surf ran high, the billows were crested with a white foam, and the sea-breeze now

took this off in many cases, covering them with masses of water. The cold and darkness were intense, and their danger was terribly increased, for they were nearly run down by a Bristol vessel, which afterwards took them all on board, and, as they got up the side, they saw their frail vessel fill and sink.

They were all much exhausted, and immediately placed in hammocks, and every attention paid to them their condition required, the vessel still continuing its course to Bristol.

CHAPTER CLV.
PRISON REFLECTIONS—EXAMINATION AT BOW STREET—THE ROAD.

THE day broke to poor Rowland Percy in his cell in Newgate with all the horrors of hopeless imprisonment.

The dull, dreary routine of duty carried on throughout all the different parts of the prison were but so many means of recalling to the oppressed the full sense of their sad and unhappy condition.

To Rowland Percy it brought back the full knowledge of his present state, which he had forgotten in the slumbers that had settled upon him.

The felon's cell affords few topics of consolation, and the walls of Newgate to an innocent, helpless, and doomed man, present but little hope.

The locking and unlocking of wards, the closing of gates, the shooting of bolts, and the hoarse calling of names, were sounds that carried scant comfort to the heart of poor Rowland.

His morning meal was coarse and disgusting to him, though had he been at liberty he could have eaten a much worse; the knowledge that it is prison diet is poison.

However, Rowland Percy did eat; he knew on that day he should have to go through an ordeal that would, short as it was likely to be, require some little nerve, for, on that day, he would be brought up at Bow Street, for the purpose of being identified.

The hour came round, and with it the prison van.

Rowland Percy was not included in the number of prisoners to be sent away in it, but, shortly after, a body of select officers came for him, and, securing him with handcuffs, he was placed in a coach, and so conveyed to Bow Street.

Here a crowd was collected to see what was going forward, and Percy could not help noticing momentarily one or two singular-looking men, who were strangely attired, and who appeared to take an interest in him; but he was hurried past with so much rapidity that he could not bestow a second glance upon them, and then he was led through a long succession of passages, and, in company with several officers, compelled to await until the moment for his examination arrived.

SAMUEL TWITTER FINDS HIMSELF AT THE MERCY OF THE UNSCRUPULOUS CAPTAIN.

At length the time arrived, and one of the officers, who came to announce the fact, said:

"Bring him along; his worship waits, and Mr. Varley, the prosecutor, is in the court."

Percy was, therefore, conducted forward, and, soon afterwards, found himself in the court, and was quickly placed at the bar.

One of the officers explained to the presiding magistrate the state of the case—that the prisoner, Rowland Percy, had been convicted of murder at the York Assizes, and condemned to suffer death, but that he escaped from the condemned cell, and was now recaptured.

"Have you evidence of his identity?" inquired the magistrate of the officer.

"Yes, your worship, Mr. Varley, the prosecutor in the case, is here to swear to the man."

"Then let him be sworn."

Varley accordingly came forward, and, with a smile of fiendish malice, took his station in the witness-box.

Rowland stood up, and gazed upon the villain calmly, and said, in clear and distinct tones:

"Mark me: that man, Bernard Varley, is the murderer of Sir George Rankley—his motives being, first to obtain his property, and then to force his destitute child to wed him, for support. The day will come, and that before long, and yet too late, perhaps, to save me, that will make this apparent."

Bernard Varley turned deathly pale, as he listened to these words, but he answered them not; he kept his eyes fixed on that part of the court where the magistrate sat. He appeared to be unable to look towards the dock where Percy stood.

The presiding magistrate shook his head, and said, in an unconcerned tone:

"Do you know the prisoner, Mr. Varley?"

"Yes, I do. He is the same Rowland Percy who was condemned to death at York, and afterwards escaped from his prison."

"Well," said the magistrate, "then all I can do is to order his detention and return to York."

"He has escaped once, your worship," said Varley, deferentially to the magistrate, "and may do so again, especially as he is well known to be leagued with highwaymen and house-breakers, and others of desperate character."

"Then a sufficient escort must be provided; those who have any connection with the York police in London must look to that part of the affair. I can only order him to be sent to York under their care, and I would advise you yourself, Mr. Varley, to go with them, since your evidence may be required, when he reaches that place, to identify him anew, and then his execution will immediately follow."

Varley bowed and left the box, and Rowland Percy was removed from the bar.

All had occurred in a very short space of time, and Rowland found himself again in the coach before he could well understand how he had been disposed of.

Before many hours elapsed, a post-chaise and a strong escort were got ready.

The order for Rowland's removal, and the delivery of his body to the care of the York police, being produced, he was placed in the vehicle, securely handcuffed, with an officer on either side of him, while Bernard Varley and several mounted officers rode beside the carriage, all well armed.

It was towards the afternoon that they commenced the journey to York, leaving London as early as their departure could be effected, Bernard Varley having successfully combated the officers' objections to starting that day, as they wished to leave town the next morning early; but Varley appeared to be in great anxiety to have Rowland reconducted to York without a moment's delay, if possible.

Rowland Percy's thoughts were anything but cheerful or hopeful.

His life of late had been one scene of alternations of hope and despair, hair-breadth escapes and imminent dangers, and the excitation natural to this state of things had subsided as hope deserted him. He leaned back in the carriage, unable or unwilling to break the silence that reigned around, by conversing with his custodians.

The monotonous sound of the carriage-wheels, and the feet of the horses were, too, of a character likely to promote thought in preference to speech.

At the decline of day, ere the sun had by two hours approached the western limit of his influence, a travelling carriage came towards town at a rapid pace, and Bernard Varley's party drew to one side of the road, which was narrow, to allow them to pass, but in doing so the two carriages approached very closely, and Percy was aroused from his reverie by hearing his name pronounced. Looking up, he caught a momentary glance of the form of Miranda.

His first motion was to put his head out of the window: but in this he was restrained by the officers, who would not permit him to hold any communication with any person whatever.

It was, indeed, Miranda, who was accompanied by Mr. Anderson, fully bent upon making some effort for the benefit of Percy—their object being to petition for his pardon; but this unexpected meeting altered their plans, and Miranda determined to return to York with Percy, and not to lose sight of him while he was permitted to live.

In this Mr. Anderson concurred, and they attempted to gain speech of Percy, but were informed that they could not be permitted to communicate with the prisoner.

"Miranda," said Bernard Varley, riding up to the carriage, "I would speak with you."

"Monster! Murderer of my father! Insult me not with your presence, nor the air with your voice."

"You know who is yonder?" And Bernard Varley pointed triumphantly and significantly towards the carriage in which Rowland was a prisoner.

"Execrable villain! It is a victim of your crimes!" she said, in a voice that plainly spoke her abhorrence."

"'Tis well," replied Varley; "we travel towards York, and a second escape will not be easy. I have desired an interview with you, and you deny it; be it so; you may mourn the consequences. I have given you an alternative, which it may not yet be too late to accept—think of it."

As he said this, he rode forward, for he desired not to be drawn into a lengthened conversation in the presence of Mr. Anderson.

Miranda's feelings it would be difficult to describe; her despair and agony were great at thus again seeing Rowland Percy in the hands of his enemies, and had it not been for the knowledge that Bernard Varley was present to triumph in her misery, she could not have maintained even the appearance of calmness.

At this moment they were met by a horseman, who immediately turned into the road from the cross-road.

It was a servant in livery, attired as if he had been sent express to some distant part.

When he came up to the party, he rode close to the carriage, and endeavoured to look into it, when Bernard Varley cried:

"Stand off, fellow! you cannot come here; dare to approach that carriage, and I will have you punished."

"I am here, you see," replied the servant: "and, therefore, can go on any road, and as for your punishment that you threaten me with, you must have cause to give it me; but I warn you to be careful, for if it comes to my master's ears, he will punish you for interfering with me."

"How, scoundrel! dare you talk thus to me?"

"Yes, to a much better-looking man than you are," replied the man. "I am on the highway, and I don't expect to be stopped by you."

"Come, come, my good fellow," replied one of the officers, "we cannot have any of this."

"Certainly not, if you don't wish it; but why do you have such a quarrelsome helper with you?"

"You must keep clear of the carriage, or else we shall be obliged to do more than persuade you; we are officers, and have a prisoner."

"If you had said that at first, all would have been right. I don't wish to be troublesome, but company on a long road is desirable; as it's not wanted, however, I'll fall back."

So saying, he drew his bridle, and awaited the coming up of the carriage in which Miranda sat with Mr. Anderson.

He rode for a short time in silence, and then, coming close to the carriage, and looking hard at Miranda, he said:

"Miss Rankley must take no notice of me."

Miranda started, and, looking at the man who rode by the side of the carriage, she, after some scrutiny, recognized Dick Palmer, and, though despair sat heavy at her heart, yet a ray of pleasure beamed from her countenance at seeing at liberty one who had so much befriended her.

She was about to express her feelings, when he motioned silence to her, and said:

"Do not be alarmed if, at a turn in the road, a row should take place. I have a few friends below, and they will try to do something. Heaven knows if it will be effectual. Be silent, and do not mix yourself up in it. What can be done, will be done, and be sure that friends will be at hand all the way to York."

Miranda's heart beat with fear and hope alternately.

She dreaded the event she hoped would take place, yet feared the result.

Bernard Varley, she thought, would have provided against any such contingency, and, perhaps, Rowland Percy might fall by his hand, for no deed, she thought, was too bad or fiendish for Bernard Varley.

CHAPTER CLVI.

THE HORSEMAN—A MOONLIGHT NIGHT—THE ATTEMPTED RESCUE.

TOWARDS the evening, the whole party— Rowland Percy, his escort, and Bernard Varley, followed at a short distance by Miranda and Mr. Anderson in the carriage, reached a romantic and beautifully-wooded valley, through which meandered a quiet and placid steam, whose unruffled bosom was yet free from the swelling floods of winter.

Sad thoughts arose in the mind of Miranda Rankley, as the *cortège* descended into the valley, and the brilliancy of the moonlight was much diminished by the shadows thrown by the tall trees that grew in a plantation near the road.

They had proceeded thus for nearly the whole of the distance, when, near the bottom of the valley, they met with an interruption, in the shape of a felled tree laying across the road.

"It is strange," said one of the officers, "that it should be left here in such a position, for it stops the whole road."

"Look to your prisoner," said Bernard Varley, whose fears for Rowland's safe custody made him suspect every accidental circumstance as affording indications of design, and that design to balk him of his ungratified revenge.

To drive the carriage over the obstacle was out of the question, and to remove the tree equally hopeless.

All that remained was to lift the carriage over, which they did by using the force of four or five men to raise it by the axles, and thus put one end over at a time.

They had just got the hind wheels over this impediment, and they were once more involved in darkness by the temporary obscurity of the moon by the passing clouds, when a loud shout resounded in their ears, and a desperate attack was made upon the whole party.

Bernard Varley immediately rushed to the aid of the officers, and fought like a maniac, striking at he knew not whom, and receiving desperate blows in exchange, equally ignorant from whom.

The carriage that contained Rowland Percy was closely beset, and had he been in it at the moment, no doubt he would have been sacrificed to Bernard Varley's desire that he should not escape with life; for with maniacal fury, he fired full in the spot where Percy a moment before had sat, but he had alighted, to allow the carriage to be lifted over, and was on the other side.

The report of Varley's pistol was a signal for the discharge of several more, and the sound of firearms rang sharp and clear upon the midnight air.

The struggle was severe and obstinate, but never once had Percy the remotest chance of escape, for he was surrounded by eight desperate men, who were well used to strife, and who would have perilled their lives ere they would have missed the reward; besides these there were Varley and the drivers.

Several desperate rushes were made upon the officers by men with bludgeons and blackened faces, disguised in a variety of clothes, but they withstood the attempts, and fired upon their assailants repeatedly, though none seemed to fall, save one who was believed to be dead.

After many minutes' contention, the attempt was not persevered in, for it was found that the officers were too strong for their assailants, who were, with one or two exceptions, merely armed with bludgeons; not that the attempt was given up without some desperate hurts on either side; some of the officers could hardly stand under their injuries, and one man had his arm fractured.

Bernard Varley seemed to be a mark for their vengeance, for his bruises were neither few nor light, and when the assailants drew off, one of them fired a pistol full at him, but it missed its object, and he escaped the death that was intended for him.

"Mount! mount!" cried Varley, with frantic energy, "mount, and ride from this hollow, or the attempt will be renewed. Once in the open road, and the dogs shall meet with the death they deserve."

Obeying his directions rather as the impulse of their own nature, the officers thrust Rowland Percy into the carriage, and, mounting their horses, bade the driver proceed.

In less than ten minutes they had passed the valley, crossed the bridge that spanned the stream, and were once more on the open road, where they could see and effectually resist assailants if any offered opposition.

Shortly afterwards a road-side inn appeared in sight, and Bernard Varley said, pointing to it:

"We must stop there for the night, and secure the prisoner."

The officers were willing enough to agree to this proposal, for there were few who were not fatigued, and much bruised, and the whole party halted before the door of an old-fashioned road-side house.

CHAPTER CLVII.

THE SHIP—TWITTER'S GREAT DISTRESS—THE GALLANT CAPTAIN—THE LOSS OF THE MONEY.

UNDER any other circumstances, such a rescue from almost the certainty of a watery grave, would have been, to Samuel Twitter, a source of the most unbounded felicitation.

But now, when the first feeling of relief was over, and he had drawn two or three breaths on board the vessel which had picked up him and his companions, all the horrors of his situation, consequent upon his written communication to the Mayor of York, came, with frightful force, across his imagination.

When he reached the deck of the vessel, he glanced around with a look of dismay, and as some of the crew approached him, they thought, from the strange and terrified aspect of the man they had rescued, that his danger must have affected his mind.

It was some minutes before he spoke, and, when he did, it was to say, with terrified gestures:

"What ship is this?—what ship is this? Take me far away—where you please, so that you take me far away. I will pay any money; but take me away from England."

"What's the matter now?" said the master of the vessel—a rough-looking man, attired in still rougher garments. "Ain't you satisfied to be picked up?"

"Yes, yes; but—but—tell me where you are going?"

"To Bristol."

Twitter wrung his hands, and groaned.

"Why, what now?" shouted the captain. "One would think your wife was at Bristol, you seem to have such an objection to go there."

A laugh from the crew rewarded this brilliant sally of wit; and Twitter, looking around him in despair, said:

"But—but you wouldn't mind placing me on the French coast—would you?"

"Would Africa suit you?" was the answer.

"Listen to me, and do not jeer at what you cannot feel the importance of. Of course, you trade for money?"

"Rather."

"Well, well, I will pay you—pay you well. Place me on any land but English, and you shall receive ample payment from me."

"Indeed!"

"Yes, yes; you understand me; I don't wish to touch English ground. It's a mere whim—just a fancy; but I implore you to take me anywhere else; charge your own price, and, be it what it may, I will pay it."

"Why, you must be tolerably well off, then?"

"Yes, I have money—plenty of money. Of course, you will be reasonable. You will take me to—to anywhere but an English port. I will make it worth your while, believe me. You understand—I will make it personally well worth your while."

The captain began to think that it might indeed be personally worth his while, and he beckoned Twitter aside with him, after which, with his finger to the side of his nose, he said:

"Run away from creditors—eh?"

"Yes, yes," eagerly replied Twitter.

"Oh! plenty of money?"

"Enough to pay you very well; you will not be exorbitant?"

"Oh, dear, no; but consider the risk."

"Risk! why, it can be no risk to you. It would not take you one day out of your course."

"Ah! but if my owners were to find that out, I should have a row made about my ears. However, I like your looks, and wish to serve you, and, although you are most confoundedly out in your reckoning as to the distance, I don't mind taking you, for five hundred pounds, right on towards Brest, with the understanding that, if we can put you on board any foreign ship we may come across, it will do as well."

"Five hundred pounds!"

"Ah, to be sure; why, we are some four hundred miles from the nearest French port."

"So far?"

"Quite; so, you see, it's reasonable enough."

"Five hundred pounds!"

"Not a penny less."

Twitter groaned aloud, but still he thought to himself, if it were a thousand instead of five hundred pounds, it would be cheap to get free from England at such a price, with the remainder of his plunder from Varley safe in his pocket.

After some moments of painful consideration, he said:

"Well, well, I consent. 'Tis a very large sum, but I consent. You will make what speed you can?"

"I believe you. It will in all likelihood cost me my command; but, still, five hundred pounds in cash is a sort of set-off against a few disagreeables."

"I should think so."

"Come with me to my cabin, and we can count over the money without anybody being the wiser."

"What will you do with the men who were with me? They are extortionate rascals."

"Oh, I shall put them on board the first fishing-boat we come across. Well, here we are. Isn't this handsome? Quite a little palace, ain't it?"

The little palace consisted of a room about eight feet by six, full of the most abominable stenches that could be imagined, while the ceiling was so low that scarcely a moderate-sized man could stand upright in it.

Samuel Twitter, however, did not wish to disagree with his host, and he fully admitted the palace-like pretensions of the cabin, although he thought to live in it long would quite kill him.

"Come," cried the captain, "you have had a good sousing with spray. What will you take to drink?"

"Anything—anything you like."

"Very good, here's some prime Hollands—the real stuff—runs down the throat like melted lead. Famous—eh?"

The captain, to give confidence to Twitter, here drank a tolerable good quantity of the spirit raw, and, handing a glass to Twitter, said:

"There, now. Strong enough to scald a pig, and yet as soft as cream. Oh, 'tis lovely!"

Twitter took a small portion, which made him cough so terribly that he declined any more, unless freely diluted.

"Very good," said the captain, who seemed in a wonderful good humour at the near prospect of handling the five hundred pounds, so he ordered hot water with the other accessories of grog-making, in abundance.

Whether or not he ever really intended to fulfil his share of the transaction must remain a mystery, for the matter never reached so far. But we will not anticipate.

Twitter found the strong Hollands much more drinkable and palatable when diluted than in its purity, and he and the captain got, in the course of half-an-hour, on the most friendly terms.

"Well, now, shipmate," remarked the latter, as he mixed for himself another steaming glass

of the hot liquor, "short reckonings make long friends, you see."

"Exactly."

"Precisely. Well, we are going full sail for Bristol now."

"Gracious powers!"

"Oh, of course."

"Why—why—I made sure that you changed your course at once after our agreement. I don't understand ships, but I thought each moment was removing me from England."

"You did, did you?"

"Of course."

"Then that shows your ignorance. Hand over the five hundred pounds, and I'll go on deck and stop the ship's course to please you, upon my word."

"Why didn't you say so before?" groaned Twitter. "Minutes may be very precious to me."

"The money—the money," said the captain, laying his great, coarse hand on the table with a dab that made the glasses ring again. "The money."

"Oh, yes—yes."

Now, Twitter had very carefully concealed about him the amount of the cheque he had forged upon Bernard Varley's bankers; indeed, so carefully had he stowed away the notes in a small pocket he had in his waistcoat, and so nicely had he pinned them in, that he had considered them perfectly safe, and had given himself no further care about them.

Now, however, after a few moments' search, his hands began to tremble, then a cold perspiration broke out upon his brow, and his lips became of an ashy paleness.

"Good Heaven!" he gasped. "I—I—can't find my money—my money. Gracious Heaven! I—I—I shall go mad!"

"Why, what's in the wind now?" roared the captain, who began, in his turn, to feel apprehensive that his hopes of five hundred pounds were vanishing into thin air. "What's the matter, I say?"

"The—the matter?"

"Yes. What are you fumbling about?"

"I—I—hardly know. It strikes me I shall go mad, if I can't find my money."

"It strikes me I shall, too, and be hanged to you. You had better find five hundred pounds of it."

How hopelessly will a man search the same pocket over and over again for an article of such bulk, that it could not escape his detection—so was it with Twitter.

He felt quite sure his money was all gone, and yet with trembling hands he kept up the frightfully hopeless search.

But that could not last long, and in another minute he wrung his hands despairingly, exclaiming:

"Gone!—gone!—gone!"

"The money?" roared the captain.

"Yes—yes."

"All of it?"

"All—all."

"Curse you! Take that."

As he spoke, he flung the boiling hot glass of Hollands and water with a great smash, glass and all, into Twitter's face.

With a howl of pain, the unhappy, foiled wretch fell backwards with his chair, and striking his head against the corner of a large chest, became stunned, and for a time quite insensible to all his miseries.

The rage of the captain was beyond all bounds.

He stamped and swore with the energy of ten men, and dealt two or three such savage kicks upon the prostrate form of Samuel Twitter, that it was a wonder he did not do him some deadly injury, or even kill him outright.

Rushing, then, upon deck, he accused the boatmen of committing the robbery; but they, at once, stated how much money they had about them, and offered to be searched, which was done, without producing any satisfactory results.

In his rage, the captain would have willingly thrown Twitter overboard; but that was a feat he was afraid to perform, so he amused himself by swearing and stamping on the deck for the next half-hour, to the immeasurable delight and amusement of the crew.

"Curse you all!" he cried; "is this the way I am to be treated, eh? I'll sink the ship."

A broad grin was the only reply vouchsafed to this threat, and the captain, after another volley of oaths, retired again to his cabin, where lay the still insensible Samuel Twitter.

Then a sudden thought struck him, that just possibly his own search in Twitter's pockets might be more successful in its results than that which had already been made by Twitter himself.

He accordingly took a lamp from a bracket, and held it down to the prostrate form at his feet.

For a moment a pang of alarm came across his mind, as he muttered:

"Curse the fellow, I have killed him."

And in truth, Twitter as much resembled a dead man as any living one possibly could, for living he was, although, to the hurried examination of the captain, there were no signs whatever of anything like vitality.

"What shall I do now?" he added. "It was that grog that knocked him down—perhaps a little more would bring the life into him; but, first of all, here goes for a search."

He then, with some trouble, searched the whole of Twitter's pockets, finding various articles, which he coolly appropriated as waifs and strays; but beyond a sum in gold and silver, not in the whole amounting to five pounds—money there was none.

"What a rascal this must be," soliloquized the captain; "to run away from his creditors, and then lose the money, a part of which I ought to have had—ah!"

It is to be supposed, then, that while the captain mixed for himself another glass of grog, he was deeply immersed in speculations on the rascality of human nature, for when he had finished it he heaved a deep sigh, and said:

"It's my duty to give this fellow up to justice. He's got no money, and I'll do it. 'England expects every man to do his duty,' especially when he can get nothing by not doing it—a-hem! I'll give him up at the first port we come to."

CHAPTER CLVIII.

THE PACKET TO THE MAYOR OF YORK—THE STRANGE DELAY—TWITTER'S LANDING AND DESTITUTION.

"THERE is a tide in the affairs of man, which, taken at the flood, leads on to fortune," and there are accidents, rare and far between, but still accidents which marvellously interfere to save persons from apparent utter destruction.

One of these remarkable accidents, if Samuel Twitter had but known it, would have enabled him with perfect safety to go back to Liverpool any time during the day succeeding that on the evening of which he had placed in the hands of the landlord of the inn his important packet for the Mayor of York, and reclaim the said packet, for the truth was, it had not reached the post even then.

Mine host, when he received Twitter's packet, placed it at once, for safety, in the capacious pocket of a sort of shabby, comfortable, indoor coat he was in the habit of wearing, and, like many very cunning men, who put off everything, and forget everything, he said to himself, instead of sending the communication at once to the post-office:

"I must mind I don't forget this now."

Almost at the same moment, one of the stable-helps sang out, in a loud voice:

"Guvner, there's a private po chaises a-coming, and a hout rider. I'm jiggered if there ain't."

"Eh? what? Travelling-carriage and outriders. Bless my heart and life, really——"

"Yes. They is a driving up here. Here they comes."

"Hilloa! hilloa!" shouted the landlord, rushing into the house like a maniac innkeeper. "My coat—my best coat. Hilloa! Hang it all, my best coat."

By the time he had done shouting and screaming for his best coat, he had reached his own bedchamber, and thrown off the shabby old garment, with which he could not think of appearing to persons in their own travelling carriage and outriders.

On went the best coat, and away into a corner was thrown the objectionable indoor one.

In another minute the landlord was a little in advance of his door-step, bowing low before the Honourable Augustus Fitzmaurice Algernon Fuddle, who had been given the command of a frigate because he had an uncle who made a majority of one for Ministers on a strong question in "the House" the other night.

Who shall, then, feel surprised that the Honourable Augustus Fitzmaurice Algernon Fuddle should be appointed to command a frigate?

He once had a yacht which he never paid for, and who shall wonder that Samuel Twitter's letter to the Mayor of York lay quite forgotten in the indoor, comfortable coat which the landlord had thrown aside in order to do honour to his illustrious guest.

Thus, then, was there another chance given to the villain, Varley, of escape from the consequences of his crimes, through the fears of Twitter, had the latter but known that he could have walked safely into that inn, and claimed again his packet from the pocket of mine host's coat.

The Honourable Augustus Fitzmaurice Algernon Fuddle condescended to sleep that night at the "Royal George," and he further condescended to breakfast there in the morning, and even to come back to dinner after going to see the frigate he had condescended to accept the command of, so that the "Royal George" was kept in a state of commotion which prevented the landlord from bestowing a stray thought upon his old coat.

It was late in the evening when the noble guest left, and then, with a feeling of great relief that the honour which had been done him was over, the landlord called for this particular coat.

He put it on; he placed his hands in the pockets with a comfortable grunt, and then his heart misgave him, for he felt the packet that had been intrusted to him to place in the post-office.

The first result of this discovery was a long whistle, and then he took the rather bulky letter from his pocket.

"Well, I never!" he exclaimed. "What an odd thing that I should quite forget this here affair. 'To the Mayor of York.' Humph! Well, what's done can't be undone, that's clear. I couldn't help it. It all comes of changing one's coat; but, then, how could I tell I was going to change my coat? How could I tell that the Honourable Augustus Fitzmaurice Algernon Fuddle was a-coming here? Eh?—eh?"

The landlord looked round him quite triumphantly as he propounded these questions to vacancy, and, as he found no answer was returned, he took it for granted he was quite right—nay, he rather had a feeling than otherwise that somehow or another he was a little ill-used in some way.

However, he condescended to call a waiter, of the name of Charles, and to say to him:

"Here, Charles, just pop that into the post."

"Yezer," replied Charles, which the landlord put up with very quietly, translating it into "Yes, sir."

The letter was then duly posted, and Twitter's danger fairly begun, while Bernard Varley little dreamt of the damning com-

munication which was slowly making its way to the authorities of York, towards which place he, too, was hurrying with so much exultation and speed, in the full belief that at last he had hunted poor Rowland Percy to death, and that nothing now could possibly save him from the horrors of a public execution.

In the meantime, the virtuous captain of the trading vessel which had picked up Twitter in the extremity of his danger held a consultation with the men who had rowed him from Liverpool, and understanding from them that his behaviour had been very strange, and characterized by a degree of anxiety which seemed to bespeak more than a usual desire to get clear of England, he safely enough thought it possible that if nothing could be got by way of reward for aiding in Twitter's escape, something handsome might turn up for surrendering him to justice.

Reasoning thus, he shaped his course towards the nearest place to Liverpool he could readily reach.

After some consideration, he resolved to put him on shore at a place called Kirkdale, a few miles from Liverpool, where he knew he could give him into safe custody.

By the time these arrangements were concluded in the captain's mind, Twitter had so far recovered as to be sensible of surrounding objects, although for some time his mind was in a sad state of confusion as to what had happened, and where he was.

Slowly, however, but surely, there came to his recollection the knowledge of the circumstances in which he was placed—circumstances which looked amazingly like the heralds to inextricable ruin and despair, ending in a perspective view of the scaffold.

With a groan which might have trumpeted the departure of his soul from its earthly tenement, Twitter felt all this, and he wished most devoutly that the insensibility from which he had just recovered had lasted for ever, and merged into death itself.

"What's to become of me now?" he groaned. "Oh, fool—fool that I was, not to keep by me that fearful communication to the Mayor of York, until I was safe in some foreign land. I could then easily have sent it. Oh, what an error of judgment have I committed!"

He was sitting on the floor of the cabin as these painful reflections crossed his mind, and so overcome was he by their frightful tendency, that he fell back again with another groan, and again hit his head—though not with such stunning vehemence as before—against the chest.

Physical pain is the very best antidote for mental agony, and Twitter, when he hit his head against the chest, jumped up with an exclamation of anger, couched in a very different tone from what he had used when bemoaning his hard fortune.

Not for long, however, was he left to his own ruminations, for the captain descended to the cabin, and, with virtuous indignation, cried:

"Oh, so you are alive again, are you? A pretty rascal you are to run away from your creditors. You vagabond! Did you think I would screen you from the consequences of your villainy? Oh, no. I shall just put you on shore as near Liverpool as I can, and give you in charge to some constable."

"Oh, for Heaven's sake, do not!" said Twitter. "Believe me, although I have no money now, I can procure ample to reward you, if you will carry me elsewhere than to an English port."

"Gammon," was the unanswerable reply; and then the captain took him by the collar and dragged him upon deck without much studying the gentleness of the proceeding.

A boat was by the vessel's side, manned by two of the crew, and into that Twitter was thrown, as if he had been a sack of potatoes.

The captain himself followed, for he was resolved to be violently virtuous, and give Twitter up in due form on his own confession of having escaped from his creditors.

"Once more," groaned Twitter — "once more I implore you not to put me on shore."

"Go to the deuce," was the euphonious reply. "Pull away, men—pull away."

The boat cut swiftly through the water, which was now deliciously calm, and a landing-place appeared not half-a-mile in advance, towards which it shot rapidly.

Twitter lay in the bottom of the boat half dead from terror.

He gave himself up wholly and utterly to despair.

Once or twice, as he glanced over the side at the quiet, limpid water, as it lazily washed by the boat, he felt tempted to seek for peace and relief from all his terrors in its cold depths, but he had not courage to make the plunge, and in less than a quarter-of-an-hour the opportunity was gone.

In the neighbourhood of Kirkdale there is a prison, and there the captain had resolved to take Twitter, as it was not many minutes walk from a little creek where they could very conveniently land.

Twitter was dragged out of the boat and pushed on till they reached the prison, where the party was carefully surveyed, through a small wicket-gate, by a surly-looking man.

"Well, what now?" he cried.

"Here's a fellow," said the captain, "has been doing something or another, and I want you to nab him."

"Who are you?"

"Captain Smithers."

"Go to the deuce!"

Bang went the wicket-gate in the captain's face, and he looked both amazed and angry.

A stranger came up at the moment, and asked what was the matter, when, the affair being explained to him, he said:

"You cannot expect them here to take a man into custody without a warrant against him."

"The deuce they won't! Well—well, it can't be helped, then. I've half a mind to smash him for the trouble he's given me. He acknowledges he has bolted off from his creditors with ever such a lot of money."

"Indeed?"

"Yes, confound him. Oh, you wretch!"

A kick added point to the captain's reproaches, and Twitter got out of his way as quickly as he could.

In a few moments the captain had gone, and Twitter found himself alone, friendless and destitute, by the door of the jail, close to Kirkdale, and not three miles from Liverpool.

CHAPTER CLIX.

THE OLD INN—THE LANDLORD AND HIS
WIFE—THE SEARCH FOR THE WOUNDED.

BERNARD VARLEY directed one of the officers to alight and make an application for admittance, which he speedily did, by using the butt-end of a heavy riding whip on the door in such a manner, that in a very few moments a window was thrown up, and a head, ornamented with a white nightcap, accompanied by a large brass blunderbuss, was thrust out.

"Hilloa! hilloa! what's all the row about?" exclaimed the head. "Do you want to break into and rob the house? Hilloa! hilloa! I'll fire at you all if you don't get into the road."

And, suiting the action to the word, the weapon was duly poised and pointed at the officer, who immediately retreated, but Bernard Varley advanced, saying:

"We mean you no violence or wrong—open your doors, for we must remain here till daybreak."

"Ay, but it's easier to keep you out, than for you to get in—and such gentry as you do an honest man no good—none—I'm safe while I have a good oaken plank between you and me."

"Open the door, I say—else it shall be forced open. This is a party of officers with a prisoner. We must stay here—you'll be well paid."

"Blow'd if you ain't some of the right sort, after all, or 'tis a most woeful do. I'll be down directly."

Saying this the window was shut down, and a light was seen moving about. Presently it descended, and in a short time a terrible rattling of chains and bars ensued, and then the door was opened by a short, fat man.

"You have bolts and bars enough to secure the gates of a town against an enemy."

"Why, pretty well for that, sir," said the man. "You see, we takes care of ourselves in these parts; we don't like to give a chance away."

"Come," said Varley, impatiently, "show us the most secure room you have here. We have a prisoner to take care of, and one who has already once escaped from York."

"You shall see, sir, what we have presently; but things are not as they should be. You see, sir, we were all asleep."

"You were all! pray who is there besides yourself, for I see nobody?"

"My wife will be up directly, sir, and the

gals. My wife, you see, sir—and my wife's a prudent woman—won't let the men sleep on the premises. She says, gals is gals, and men is men; and then she says there is no keeping them separate, and so the men sleep out of the house."

"Rather an inconvenient plan when you require their aid suddenly."

"Yes, but we can't have all the advantages, as my wife says, as we could were everything as we should wish, or should order it."

"Then get us some refreshments, and show us a room where we can secure our prisoner."

"Come this way," said the landlord, preceding them with a light.

After passing through many passages, and through several doors, up and down short flights of steps, so that they scarcely knew whether they were upstairs or down, at length the landlord stopped at a door, which he opened with much effort.

"Walk in, gentlemen—that room you'll find safe and cosy."

The whole party entered, and the landlord followed, saying:

"This is a comfortable room, gentlemen, and very safe; nobody has been in it for years, since a gentleman died here very mysteriously in my father's time—nobody know'd how—and I never heard, though a many talked of it as knew nothing about it."

Bernard Varley looked round the apartment, and then, turning to the officers, said that he thought Rowland would scarcely be safe there without someone sitting up with him, and being heavily ironed, as an additional precaution.

Rowland Percy was at once introduced into the apartment, and the officers forthwith proceeded to place irons on his hands and feet, against which he remonstrated with much earnestness, declaring that he knew nothing of the attempted rescue, or by whom it was attempted.

"Can't help it," replied the officer, "you have once broken prison, and may do so again, and we should be blamed if we were not to secure you."

Upon this Rowland said no more, but submitted in silence to the operation.

The house was in a great bustle, the landlord's wife was in the full swing of her authority, and everything was done for the comfort of the guests who had so suddenly come upon them.

To return to Miranda and Mr. Anderson, whom we left in the coach following the party who had Rowland Percy in custody, and who could not so easily pass the impediment that had been placed across the road.

Their single driver could effect nothing by himself, and Miranda was reduced to a state of despair at not being able to follow Percy on his route to York.

It was only by much persuasion and kindness from Mr. Anderson that she could abstain from a violent outburst of grief.

Mr. Anderson himself got out and examined the road, and, by great good fortune, found that at one end of the tree the carriage might be driven over with care without incurring any great risk of upsetting it.

This was no sooner proposed than it was done, and the check to her pursuit of Rowland Percy was immediately removed.

Once more, therefore, Miranda and Mr. Anderson entered the carriage, and drove in the direction the officers took.

It was not long ere they reached the roadside inn, and, perceiving the lights moving about, they at once concluded that Bernard Varley and the unfortunate Rowland were there.

Drawing up, therefore, before the inn door, Mr. Anderson alighted, and proceeded to make inquiries respecting Rowland Percy, and soon found that their conjectures were correct, and he at once procured a room to which Miranda could retire for a few hours ere they again proceeded, Mr. Anderson taking care to keep such a vigilant watch that Bernard Varley could not possibly intrude himself upon her.

The officers, who had recovered somewhat from the surprise of the affair, now proposed to go back in a body to the spot where they were attacked, for one of them was certain that he shot one man, who fell, and, he thought, must have been killed.

This Varley opposed as being unnecessary, and risking the safety of the prisoner, but he was overruled by the officers, who, whatever their recklessness and daring might be, would not listen to the cool proposal of letting a fellow-creature perish for want of common attention.

Leaving three of their number well armed, and Bernard Varley with the prisoner, five of them rode back the last two miles, but met with no interruption, nor could they trace any human being until they arrived at the spot where they had been attacked.

Here the marks of blood were perceptible, and could be traced till lost near the roadside, which bordered a wood, and where the officers had no doubt the perpetrators of the outrage were concealed, or through which they had made their escape.

"Well," said one of the officers, "it was as sharp an affair as ever I saw. I could have sworn there would have been lives lost, and I am not so sure, even now, that there ain't."

"Very likely; but, dead or dying, they have carried them off, and we have nothing to do save to turn back, and get what we can in the shape of rest and food, for that Bernard Varley cares little for fatigue himself, and will hurry us on towards York, though we and the horses were to drop down dead on the journey."

"Yes, he seems terribly anxious about hanging this young fellow, and but for the reward that is offered, I would have nothing to do with him."

"Nor I; but we must do our duty in spite of all. I could have wished that he had been our man instead of the other poor fellow."

"Ay, and for all his brag and independence he would cut but a sorry figure if the darbies were once put on him. My belief is that he would be but a chicken-hearted one after all."

"I think so, too; but we must return, and bow to him, I suppose. The least said, soonest mended, and he has money, you know. He will bleed well, no doubt."

"He has done so already, and as long as he will keep at it, well and good. I am, as in duty bound, his slave, you know: but here we are at the old inn again."

Thus talking lightly, these men, to whom a life was of little or no consequence, but who merely had their likes and dislikes—as to who should be hanged and who should not—a mere preference—all sat down to the best the house could afford, at Bernard Varley's expense, and soon forgot their momentary dislike of the donor of the feast.

Yet though Varley treated these men to all that money could procure, he could not purchase their gratitude: but gratitude in a police officer is a rarity: they served him with outward show of respect, and cared but little for the man.

After a few hours' rest, they partook of another hearty meal, and were speedily again on the road to York, closely followed by the other carriage, in which were Miranda and Mr. Anderson, who tried every method he could to buoy up her spirits: but hope to her seemed gone, and tears coursed each other rapidly down her pale cheeks as she sat by his side.

All the hopes she had but lately possessed were now dead within her—the dreary prison at York rose before her eyes—the dreadful tolling of the bell rang in her ears—and the sight of her lover's corpse swinging from a gibbet in the air, appeared to her disordered mind with such startling distinctness, that she shrank back in the carriage to escape the dreadful sight.

But Miranda knew that Rowland Percy would need comfort and consolation, and this thought, and the knowledge that she was the only living being who yet remained to him that could or would impart it, enabled her to keep up better than at one time her extreme agitation and grief promised she would be able to do: but, by a great effort, she overcame her feelings, determined that when she should again be permitted to speak with him, that she would do so in a tone and manner that should not embitter his last moments.

Thus the time passed on their return to York.

Miranda was not allowed to hold any communication with Percy during the journey. This was probably at the instigation of Bernard Varley, who watched with malignancy of disposition every attempt on the part of Miranda to get near the carriage in which Rowland Percy was a prisoner.

CHAPTER CLX.

GLOOMY REFLECTIONS—DICK PALMER'S DESPAIR—NIGHT AND MORNING.

It was late in the evening when the whole party entered the precincts of York.

The sun had sunk beneath the western horizon, and the chill winds of evening had arisen after a bright sunset, the more melancholy to poor Percy, since he believed the beauties of nature were fast closing in for him.

He trembled to think of the future—he even questioned the justice of Heaven in his own case.

They soon after entered York, but, owing to the darkness that spread around, they were but little noticed: else the whole city would have flocked round them; as it was, a few individuals only saw them, and these were ignorant of who they were.

He was too late for an examination, and an immediate application was made to the chief magistrate to commit Rowland Percy to York Castle.

It is needless to say that this was immediately acceded to by that official personage, who congratulated the officers upon the vigilance they had displayed in the search which had occupied them so long.

In a very short time, Rowland Percy was an inmate of York Castle, and, on the morrow, he would be taken before the magistrates, and identified, then given over to the executioner.

Miranda and Mr. Anderson entered York nearly at the same time as the officers.

Mr. Anderson thought it unnecessary to attend, as the step was but a preliminary one, and one which must inevitably take place; besides, he did not wish to leave Miranda in her present state of mind.

How different was her mental condition when she last entered York.

She knew that Rowland Percy was at least free—knew that he had good and kind friends who would do their utmost to shelter him from the evil destiny that awaited him, until the time should arrive, as she told herself it would, when his innocence would be proclaimed.

But now he was again a prisoner—a victim of oppression—and nearer than ever to death.

Miranda shuddered at the thought, but she was aroused from her gloomy reverie by the stoppage of the carriage at Mr. Anderson's door.

Mr. Anderson had, with truly philanthropic humanity, insisted on Miranda becoming an inmate in his house, and used every argument he could think of to induce her to be calm, telling her she had better prepare herself for the worst, as it would be cruel in him to give her hope where none existed, and that upon her depended the consolation of the last hours of poor Percy.

Sad as the consolation was, and unlikely to produce calmness in most minds, yet in hers it had its effect.

Calm she was, to a certain degree, but it required an effort to be so, which would probably terminate in some great prostration of spirit and mental energy.

That night, too, was the moment of hopes and fears, the latter preponderating, in the breast of another heart in the city of York.

At a low public-house in one of the many dirty, narrow ways in which one part of York abounds, were assembled a number of men of no very inviting external appearance, and certainly of no high order of morality.

Few of these men had the humour of Jones, or any of his good qualities, or the kindness and thought of Dick Palmer, though they belonged to the same class, and were their intimates.

Their conversation was wholly confined to their own plans, either for robbery or revenge.

"What say you," asked Dick Palmer, who was one of the number, "will you all assist me?"

"What in?" inquired one who had but just entered the room.

"Why," said Dick, "Mr. Rowland Percy, whom we got off once, is again nabbed; now he will be brought up for re-committal to the condemned cell, and then he will immediately after suffer. Now, what I propose is, that a rescue should be attempted on the morning of the execution, when he is brought out."

"What! rescue him when he has the halter round his neck—and the dragoons in York, too—I would run some risk, Dick, but this is absolute madness—and if not, why should we risk our lives for a young fellow like this, innocent or guilty? we are sure to be taken, or shot, or cut down. No, no, that will never do."

This was so clearly the opinion of all present, that Dick forbore to press the plan further; indeed, he had previously urged all he could with the like result, and now turned from the room with feelings of sorrow and despair that had not for years visited his breast.

The tear stood in the highwayman's eye; he left his companions, sought solitude as the only relief he could experience in this as yet greatest trial of the heart that he had met with.

That night it was bruited about that Rowland Percy, the murderer, had been re-captured, and would be taken before the magistrates in the morning to be identified previous to his execution, and it was expected that there would be a great concourse of people assembled; to meet this the chief magistrate had dispatched orders for strong bodies of police to protect the town during the night, and that the military should be in readiness in case their presence should be required; this done, the city of York was once more in profound repose.

Early in the morning all the avenues leading to the court-house were crowded with human beings, anxious to catch even a transitory glimpse of one who had caused so much stir in York, and more especially one who had

broken from prison and eluded the most active officers.

Strong bodies of police were stationed at favourable points, and a strong party of the dragoons were ready to mount at a moment's notice; indeed, their bugles were distinctly heard by the crowd, for whose ears they were sounded, so that there might be no attempt at a riot.

A few unimportant proceedings were attended to first—while they were waiting for the appearance of Rowland Percy—for whom a strong body of police were despatched mounted, and a carriage was sent, into which Percy was conducted with an officer on either side of him.

The morning was one of more than ordinary beauty and serenity, the sun shone gaily, and Rowland Percy contrasted all the happy faces —for such he deemed them—with his own sad and miserable case.

Not much time was given him for thought; he was hurried forward with rapidity, and he soon arrived at the court-house, into which he was immediately ushered by the party who had the custody of his person.

CHAPTER CLXI.

THE IDENTIFICATION OF PERCY AT THE POLICE OFFICE—THE COMMITTAL TO THE CONDEMNED CELL—MIRANDA'S DESPAIR.

THE news of the apprehension of Rowland Percy had spread with a most marvellous rapidity throughout York.

His name was familiar to everyone, and his history had so much of romantic interest attached to it, that scarcely anyone in the county was so indifferent as not to have an ardent wish to see the man, concerning whose guilt or innocence there was such diversity of opinion, and who had, for so long a period, successfully resisted and set at nought a pursuit dictated by malice, revenge, and passion, and stimulated by enormous rewards.

The whole circumstances of the murder of Sir George Rankley had exercised a remarkable effect upon the lovers of the mysterious, and Miranda's strange devotion to him who had been declared by the laws the murderer of her father, enriched the story with a wild, romantic interest.

No wonder, then, that, when the news spread from mouth to mouth, that the celebrated Rowland Percy was again arrested, and brought to the original scene of his trial and condemnation, all who had leisure, or could call half-an-hour their own, should flock to the court to obtain a passing glance at the prisoner, and, if possible, too, of Miranda, who, it was likewise known, had followed him through all his dangers and wanderings with a degree of faithfulness that had no parallel.

We have recorded how hastily, and even rudely, Rowland was pushed into the presence of the assembled magistrates, and how very transient a glance the crowd outside the court must have had of the prisoner; and, perchance, the violence and roughness with which Rowland Percy found himself treated by the York police, arose, in some measure, from a feeling among them that they had, as Mr. Jones would have said, rather made a mess of the affair before, and let Percy escape from their hands a great deal easier than he should have been permitted to do.

Certainly it was a fact, that the Secretary of State had written a letter to the chief magistrate of the city, inquiring very politely whether some regulations might not be adopted to prevent the possibility of such an occurrence for the future, and such a letter, of course, had, to a certain extent, aggravated the chief officer, who had, in his turn, said something very aggravating to the head constable, who then had abused the turnkeys; so that a general feeling of discomfort, in consequence of Rowland Percy's escape, had pervaded for some time all the police authorities of York, and they looked upon his capture as a very desirable thing, and quite a triumph in its way.

It was a mere matter of form to bring poor Rowland before the court, for he was well-known to every officer who had him in custody, and thousands of persons in York could have sworn to his identity.

Yet it was necessary that he should be given formally into the custody of the authorities of York, by virtue of the warrant from the magistrate at Bow Street, and then sworn to by some one or more persons, as being the identical Rowland Percy who had escaped from the condemned cell on the evening prior to his intended execution.

Varley had shown too much malevolence of feeling throughout the whole proceedings connected with the trial and condemnation of Rowland Percy to be a favourite with the populace of York; and, indeed, he was shunned as much as possible, for they could not fail to perceive the animus with which he acted, and whatever might have been their abhorrence of the supposed criminality of Rowland Percy, they had a scarcely less abhorrence of anything like partizanship on the part of a witness.

To avoid the crowd they anticipated, the magistrates had ordered that Rowland should be brought to the court-house earlier than had been first appointed, for they dreaded the popular excitement which was evidently manifesting itself throughout the city on the subject.

Hence was it that poor Rowland, when he was ushered into the court-house, found himself without one friendly hand to greet him—without one friendly face to give him a glance of encouragement or sympathy.

Miranda had not arrived, and, alas! when she should come, how utterly powerless was she to aid him she loved in this sad and mournful extremity of his fortunes.

Bernard Varley, likewise, was not there; but had he known that his victim was present, he would, indeed, have hurried to the spot to gloat over the prospect of the completion of the monstrous injustice he had been such an important instrument in perpetrating.

Mr. Anderson, however, was very soon informed that Rowland was in the court, and he at once started on foot with Miranda, in order to be present at the brief but painful scene.

He was personally well known and respected in York, and more particularly so, as he had made himself so conspicuous in Rowland's affair, and had acted so noble and disinterested a part in the whole proceedings.

Miranda, too, was at once recognized by the populace, as, leaning upon Mr. Anderson's arm, she walked with slow and mournful steps towards the court, where, perhaps, she was to take a last glance of Rowland Percy, before, for the second time, an hour was announced when he was to be hurried into eternity for a crime of which she knew he was innocent.

Occasionally, as the mob cheered her as she passed, a choking feeling at her throat would almost deprive her of the power of progressing, and she could not refrain from asking herself:

"Can all this be possible—that the innocent shall be really sacrificed at last, and yet so many appear convinced of that innocence? Will all these people, who are uttering words of sympathy to me, permit a deliberate judicial murder to take place before their very faces, and contrary to their judgments and feelings?"

Mr. Anderson seemed to guess her thoughts, for he said:

"Is it not strange, Miranda, that, notwithstanding the general—nay, almost universal opinion of Percy's innocence, the power of social order should be so great, that thousands of persons will stand by and see a few men commit an act which they loudly condemn, and could stop on the instant."

"It is, indeed, strange and horrible to me."

Such a shout of execration at this moment burst from hundreds of voices, that Miranda involuntarily paused to see from what cause it had arisen, and, in an instant, she perceived, turning from a narrow street into the main thoroughfare, a person mounted upon a large and powerful black horse.

A glance was sufficient to show her it was Bernard Varley.

"My evil genius!" she said, with a shudder. "Mr. Anderson, I have sometimes doubted if that man be mortal."

"His actions are like those of a malignant demon; but see, Miranda, how he is hemmed in by the crowd, while a free passage is made for you. Hark at that sound again!"

Another roar of popular indignation arose as Varley, with an assumed air of indifference, walked his horse through the throng.

He carried in his hand a heavy riding-whip, which he seemed quite inclined to bring down on the head of the first person who should attempt to impede him in any way.

Mobs, however, are most harmless when they make the most noise.

The indignation of a multitude of persons evaporates, if permitted to expend itself in

JONES SETTLES SCORES WITH BERNARD VARLEY.

noisy vociferation, and, although Bernard Varley was impeded by the pressure of the throng, no one attempted to lay a hand on him, or the powerful horse he had got specially for the purpose of dashing through the crowd with, if necessary.

Miranda and Mr. Anderson reached the court first, although on foot.

It was evident that Varley had made an effort to gain the entrance at the same time with Miranda; but he could not do so unless he had at once declared war with the mob, and become the provoker of a conflict which, when once begun, it would have been difficult to say where it would have ended.

As it was, Miranda had effected an entrance, with the assistance of Mr. Anderson, into the crowded court, over which she ran her eyes till they rested on the pale, jaded-looking countenance of Rowland Percy, who seemed, by his expression, to have now given up all hope.

He saw her at once, and a momentary light seemed to beam over his face; but it was like the pale glimpse of sunshine which for an instant will gleam forth on a wintry landscape, reminding those who see it of the beauty and radiance of other days, and likewise the sadder for the comparison.

She would fain have reached the spot

where he stood; but she was firmly repulsed by the officers, who said their orders were to allow no one whatever to speak to their prisoner, and that particular instructions had been given that she was to be prevented from holding the slightest communication with him.

This was, indeed, a cruel blow to poor Miranda; although, had she reflected upon the subject, it was no more than she might fairly have expected, considering the part she had taken in his escape on the previous occasion.

In a few moments Bernard Varley entered the court, and that appeared to be a signal for the business to commence, which it did instantly, by one of the London officers stepping forward and producing the warrant from the Bow Street magistrate, empowering him to bring to York, and surrender into the hands of the authorities there, Rowland Percy, sworn to as an escaped convict.

"Very well," said the chief magistrate; "Mr. Sheriff, this prisoner belongs to you, having escaped from your custody. It would be as well that he should be sworn to before us. I believe that will be the regular course."

"I have plenty of witnesses," said the sheriff, "as to the identity of the prisoner at the bar with the Rowland Percy convicted of wilful murder at the last assizes, and sentenced to death. I, therefore, claim the prisoner, in order that the sentence of the law may be carried into effect."

"Very well; there is no doubt, I believe, as to his identity."

"The unhappy, persecuted young man at the bar," said Mr. Anderson, "is willing to admit that he is the Rowland Percy falsely charged with murder, and grievously wronged by a conviction."

"Is this regular?" said Varley, in a deep tone, that drew the eyes of everyone upon him.

"I am attorney for the prisoner," added Mr. Anderson, "and I presume that, according to custom and courtesy, the bench will allow me to make an application on behalf of my client."

The magistrates consulted together a moment, and then one said:

"The whole circumstances are of a novel character, and we are not aware of any precedents; but God forbid we should act harshly —we will hear you."

"I have to thank the court," said Mr. Anderson, "in the name of the object of my professional and private solicitude, as well as in the name of Miranda Rankley, the daughter of the murdered Sir George—she who, loving her father with an affection of the most intense character, asserts so boldly her belief in the entire innocence of Rowland Percy. Oh! sir, the hand of Heaven itself is manifest in these proceedings. The circumstances——"

"Really," said the chief magistrate, "however we may feel inclined to grant every indulgence to a person in the awful situation of the prisoner, we cannot listen now to more than your application, whatever it is. We are not trying the prisoner."

"Pardon me," added Mr. Anderson, "if, for a moment, feeling so strongly as I do in this case, I was betrayed into irrelevant matter to my application, which is simply this: that time be allowed the prisoner to set forth, in a memorial to the Secretary of State, all the circumstances which have occurred since his condemnation, many of which tend strongly against the evidence offered at his trial by the witnesses against him."

"What witnesses in particular?"

"Bernard Varley in particular."

A smile of derision crossed Varley's face; but that was assumed, although there was no mistake whatever about the glance of deadly hatred he shot at Mr. Anderson.

"Can you," said the magistrate, "give us any grounds to go upon which might enable us to accede to your request?"

"Yes. If Miranda Rankley be permitted on oath to make statements concerning circumstances that have occurred in London, and proposals that have been made to her by Bernard Varley, it appears to me your worships will see ample reason for granting my request."

"How long time do you want?"

"So long as shall permit affidavits to be made and forwarded to the Secretary of State, and his answer to be received."

The magistrates laid their heads together, and seemed rather confused by the novelty of the whole circumstances.

A breathless stillness pervaded the court, and a slight tinge of colour on the face of Rowland Percy betrayed that hope had revived in his before sinking bosom.

Too soon, however, was it quenched; for the chief magistrate, after nearly ten minutes had been spent in a whispered consultation with his colleagues, said:

"We are unanimously of opinion that we have no sort of jurisdiction in this matter. A prisoner has been tried at the assizes on a capital charge—convicted on evidence satisfactory to a jury, and sentenced to execution, which execution would have taken place some time since, but for the escape of the prisoner. He is now re-taken, and it is not in our power to re-try the case, because he has for some time succeeded in evading the sentence of the law."

"Am I to understand," said Mr. Anderson, "that my application is wholly refused?"

"Certainly."

"When, then, will the unhappy prisoner be ordered for death?"

"We are of opinion the sheriff is now bound to proceed to execution with all convenient dispatch."

"It was my duty," interposed the sheriff— "a most painful one, I fully admit, but still my duty—to have seen the sentence of the law carried into effect long since upon Rowland Percy. I am bound now to cause no unnecessary delay. He will have notice of the time appointed."

"Let me press for an answer now," added Mr. Anderson; "when will that time be? I wish to know if his friends can make an application to the Secretary of State?"

The sheriff shook his head.

"I dare not delay," he said. "The execution must take place to-morrow morning."

A stifled cry burst from Miranda, and Mr. Anderson turned instantly to her, saying:

"Hush! hush! For Heaven's sake, control your feelings. Be guided by me—say nothing."

With a low moan, Miranda sank into a seat, and covered her face with her hands, while Rowland Percy appeared quite unconscious of all else, as he kept his eyes riveted upon her with a painful interest.

"If," continued Mr. Anderson, "the sheriff feels it to be his painful duty to have execution done so quickly upon Rowland Percy, I beg that he may be allowed the consolation of visits from those who, through good and evil report, have still clung to him, and still believe him innocent."

"You can have access to him as his attorney," said the chief magistrate, "and any relative may claim admittance; but Miranda Rankley is decidedly objected to."

"What!" cried Rowland. "Even with death before my eyes, are you such barbarians as to deny me one farewell word with that noble soul which has indeed clung to me through all misfortune? You cannot mean what you have said."

"The peculiar part which was taken by Miss Rankley in your escape, determines us to refuse her admission to your prison. We are only surprised that any application on her behalf should be made. Mr. Sheriff, will you remove your prisoner?"

"Ay, to death!" cried Varley.

"Miranda! Miranda!" said Rowland, and he stretched forth his arms over the bar at which he stood.

She sprang towards him, and no one hindered her.

"Rowland! Rowland! They yet dare not murder you! Heaven is merciful, and just."

"Farewell, dearest—best——"

Everyone in the court was deeply affected, and, for about two minutes, no interruption was offered to the lovers.

Then the sheriff nodded to the officers, and Rowland was taken away.

With one piercing shriek, Miranda fainted on the floor of the court.

CHAPTER CLXII.

THE LAST PROPOSAL OF VARLEY—THE FIGHT.

ROWLAND was in a moment removed from the court by the officers, while the greatest confusion prevailed in consequence of Miranda's emotion.

She was immediately raised by Mr. Anderson, who called, loudly:

"Make way by the door. Make way—air—air."

Supporting her upon his arm, he half-carried her from the court through the dense throng of persons who jammed up the entrance, and it was quite marvellous how they contrived to make a passage for her at all, so closely wedged together were they.

Once out of the precincts of the crowded court, Miranda felt the influence of the cool, fresh air, and partially revived.

Mr. Anderson wished to get her to his own home as swiftly as possible, but he feared her weakness was too great, so he assisted her into a chemist's shop, which was near at hand, and from the owner of which she received every assistance.

After a few moments, she spoke, but it was in a tone of such utter grief and despondency, that it was painful, and enough to bring tears into anyone's eyes to hear her.

"He is lost—lost!" she said. "Lost—oh, Heaven! he is forsaken."

"Miranda, Miranda," expostulated Mr. Anderson, "do not speak so fearfully. Be calmer, I implore you."

"Heaven has given him to his enemies. Rowland—Rowland. So innocent, too."

"Nay, nay. View this dispensation more patiently. God knows what is best."

"Talk not to me of resignation—I will die to-morrow. To-morrow they will murder him. Oh, Heaven! why was I created to suffer so much misery? First my father, and then Rowland—both murdered."

"Will you," whispered Mr. Anderson to the chemist, "attend to her while I get a coach?"

"Yes, certainly."

"Thank you; I shall not be many minutes."

Mr. Anderson left the shop, and ran down the street to where he knew there was a stand of hackney carriages, but he had not been gone above a moment, when the chemist's door was darkened by a tall figure, and Bernard Varley entered the shop.

Without a word, he approached Miranda, and, inclining his face to her ear, he said, in a hissing whisper:

"I can save him yet!"

She started, as if a serpent had stung her, and sprang immediately to her feet.

"Demon!" she exclaimed. "Accursed evil spirit!"

"I can save him yet!" again said Varley, as he folded his arms across his breast.

"Monster! The death of Rowland Percy, whom you know to be innocent, will break my heart. We shall die together, and I—I——"

She could say no more, but sank again into the chair; and, while the chemist looked on in silent wonder, Varley again whispered in her ear:

"Be mine, and I can save him yet! Beautiful being, be mine, and I can save him yet!"

"Help—help!" cried Miranda.

"Nay, pause awhile. Think of to-morrow—the crowd—the hangman. I can save him yet!"

"Are you human?" cried Miranda. "Or is this some frightful dream?"

"You will find it too real," muttered Varley.

"Say the word, Miranda Rankley, and I will save him."

Miranda crossed the shop to where the chemist stood, and, laying her hand upon his arm, she said:

"Protect me from this man, or demon, as he is—protect me from him! My pulse beats languidly in his presence, and my heart almost ceases its pulsation. Save me from him!"

"I will thank you to leave my shop, sir," said the chemist, "whoever you are."

"Curse your shop!" cried Varley.

And he strode out without another word.

This was Varley's last effort, and, to judge by the expression of deep chagrin that sat upon his countenance as he emerged into the street, he had flattered himself it would be successful.

To add, likewise, to his discomforts, he found when he reached the door that his horse by some means had gone, and he was met by a large mob, which commenced hooting and groaning at him as large mobs only can hoot and groan at unpopular people.

His courage was never very good, and yet there was a kind of dogged obstinacy about him which always induced an appearance of courage.

On the present occasion it had all that effect, for he would not take refuge anywhere, preferring to walk on, determined in his own mind not to provoke an encounter, but to get to the hotel where he had taken up his quarters, as quickly as possible.

The fates, however, were decidedly malignant, and it appeared that Varley was doomed that day to be tormented both in body and mind.

At the first corner he reached he found himself pushed on by a throng of persons, who seemed acting with a greater degree of combination than mobs generally do, and he was on the point of making a vigorous effort to retreat, when he found himself jammed up against a wall suddenly, and a kind of ring made round him.

Then a man slipped into the open space left in front of him, whom Varley did not at once recognize, but when he spoke, he knew him directly.

It was our old friend Jones.

"How are you?" he said. "You ain't improved. The beaks have let me go, cos they couldn't prove nothing. They guved me what they calls a *hadmonition*, and I've come all the way here, old Marrowfat in conwulsions, to guv you one."

"Police—police!" cried Varley.

"Holler away," said Jones. "Hark ye, I owes you a towelling, so does Miss Miranda, so does Dicky, so does young Percy, and, be hanged, if I don't pay you now a tidy instalment."

Mr. Jones then commenced such a scientific attack upon Varley, that in a few moments he gave him two tremendous black eyes, and such severe punishment, that when those around let Varley go down, which they would not for some moments, he fell like a lump of lead.

"Come on, my pals," said Jones. "That's what religious people calls retributive justice. Providence is merciful. Come on."

The whole affair was over so quickly that no one came to Varley's assistance until too late, and when he was picked up, there was no mob at all, and everybody wondered who in so short a space of time had contrived to punish him so tremendously.

While this was taking place, Miranda was placed in a coach by Mr. Anderson, and in a nearly insensible state conveyed to his house.

CHAPTER CLXIII.

MIRANDA'S SAD PRESENTIMENTS—THE VISIT TO THE GRANGE—THE CHAMBER OF DEATH —THE OMEN.

WHEN Miranda reached Mr. Anderson's house, she appeared like one more dead than alive.

A remarkable change had taken place in her appearance.

The few hours of intense suffering she had undergone, since she became convinced that there was no hope for Rowland, seemed to have attacked the very springs of life, and her own sad prophecy that her heart was breaking, looked, indeed, as if it were about to be fulfilled.

She answered all questions that were put to her with such a mournful, painful pathos, that it was terrible to hear her.

It was worse, far worse, than loud complaining.

The awful resignation that had come over her looked, indeed, like the precursor of death itself.

Under all the previous circumstances in which she had been placed, there had been a something approaching to hope in her mind; she had never felt utterly abandoned to despair.

True, Rowland had once before been in a condemned cell—true, once before, the very morning of execution had arrived, but then she was supported by the hope of rescuing him—a hope which, as we are aware, was fully realized; but where, now, was such a hope?

She was denied even access to him—she was refused the sad consolation even of bidding him a last adieu.

What fortitude could she now call upon to sustain her under the trying circumstances in which she was placed?

Could she find, amid all her reflections, one point of consolation or support?

Not one—not one.

Mr. Anderson, too, found himself nearly struck dumb by the painful nature of the proceedings.

The common topics of conversation he felt would have been insulting to Miranda, and what could he say of another character?

Could he tell her there was still a hope for Rowland?

No; all was black despair.

Miranda kept continually, in a low, moaning voice, asking the time.

She seemed to be counting the very moments which were intervening between this and the following morning, which was to bring with it the awful tragedy of the execution of the innocent and devoted Rowland Percy.

By the persuasions of Mrs. Anderson, she lay down for some time; but the attitude of repose brought no repose with it.

She merely assumed it to please her generous benefactors; she was not conscious of the low moans which each moment came from her bursting heart; and when she saw tears standing in the eyes of Mrs. Anderson, she said:

"Do not weep for me; I am calmer; all will be over soon. You see I am calmer now."

Then she would moan again, like one lingering on the verge of life, and with painful emotion struggling to eternity.

Thus passed the half of that fearful day.

Towards one o'clock she rose, and requested to see Mr. Anderson.

With visible emotion in his countenance, he came to her.

She took his hand gently, and in a low, soft tone, said:

"I have much, very much, to thank you for. I am dying now; but I shall live till *he* is murdered. We shall leave this world of woe together, hoping for Heaven's mercy hereafter. Our prayers at the throne of God shall be offered up for those who have, like you, sought to alleviate some of the sad pangs of life, and to stay the hand of persecution. God bless you, sir."

"Nay, Miranda, do not talk so," said Mr. Anderson, in tones that faltered from deep emotion. "Do not say so. Still live to bless those who love you. You will find always an asylum here. Time may, and, I believe, will, clear the memory of Rowland Percy; and you will have the consolation of universal sympathy."

Miranda shuddered.

"Can sympathy restore the dead?" she said. "Can the sympathy of a world—a universe—heal such sorrow as mine?"

Mr. Anderson felt himself silenced; and he walked to the window to conceal the emotion which he could not control.

"What is the time now?" asked Miranda, with the same earnestness that had characterized her previous inquiries upon that subject, so momentous to her.

"Past one," replied Mr. Anderson.

"Past one. Less than nineteen hours—yes, less than nineteen. There is time. Mr. Anderson, I have a request to make to you. This is my last, with the exception of one."

"Anything you can request," said Mr. Anderson, "that is in my power, is a command to me."

"Before" she continued—"before the last scene of this eventful tragedy closes, I have a wish to look upon the home of my lost happiness—the house where I passed so many joyous hours—where my father died, and where my woes first began."

"You would visit the Grange?"

"Yes; I would pay a last farewell visit to the Grange. Is it occupied?"

"No. No one has been found to rent it of Varley, and he has been defeated in several attempts to sell it."

"It is empty, then, and desolate?"

"I believe some of your father's old servants still live in it. They are too aged to go into service again, and they still cling to their old abode, unknown to Varley, who else would soon clear them off the estate."

"Will you take me, Mr. Anderson?"

"Yes, most certainly. When would you wish to go?"

"I would wish to see the Grange at that sweet time when I have so often gloried in its beauties, when day is struggling with twilight, and the long shadows of evening are dappling sweetly the glades and meadows."

"I will make arrangements, Miranda, so that your wish shall be complied with."

"To-morrow—to-morrow!" cried Miranda, with a sudden burst of grief. "Oh, what an awful day will be to-morrow!"

* * * *

How shall we speak of Rowland Percy, in his dismal cell?

How shall we paint his sufferings—his absolute anguish, as he felt that, after all, falsehood and villainy were to triumph over him, consigning him to a terrible and ignominious death, from which there seemed now no possible escape.

A feeling of dreadful despair came over him when he was first placed in the cell; and hardly conscious of what he did, he seized the chaplain—who had just begun a psalm about being generally thankful for all things—by the throat—and nearly throttled that holy character.

The cool assumption of his (Rowland's) guilt, on the part of the reverend gentleman, quite infuriated Rowland, and he could not endure that such should be the case.

"Murder! Help!" roared the clerical functionary, and two turnkeys rescued him from the grasp of Rowland.

"I'll pray for you, you hardened rascal!" said the reverend gentleman, when he had rearranged his cravat. "I'll pray for you; but I cannot promise you that the 'ten thousand angels' I have before mentioned will have anything to say to you."

[*Vide* the Rev. — Carver, the chaplain of Newgate, who promised to murderers a welcome to that angelic amount, the "ten thousand angels," in the event of a profession of unlimited faith.]

The two turnkeys were ordered to remain with Rowland in his cell; for, in addition to suspecting that he might attempt suicide, the fact of his having once escaped alarmed the authorities so much that they could not think of leaving him alone for any length of time.

When this little burst of natural passion was over, a deep despondency, very similar to the despairing feeling which possessed Miranda, came over him, and he sat down in an attitude of great dejection.

Oh, how dark and terrible were the thoughts that chased each other through the mind of that innocently condemned man, during that awful night.

All the various incidents of his brief career came vividly before him.

His early love for Miranda—the delirious throb of joy when she accepted his ardent vows—the quarrel between their respective parents, and then that night, when, by such a strange coincidence of circumstances, he arrived at the Grange, as if just in time to be accused by Bernard Varley of the crime he knew not had been committed.

Then the trial—the condemnation—the escape—the shifting, uneasy, anxious life he had led for some time in London—the noble self-denial and heroism of Miranda—the disinterested and important friendship of Palmer, and the less judicious, but none the less sincere, partizanship of Jones, all—all flitted before his mental vision like the well-remembered incidents of some romance or drama which has made a strong impression upon the mind.

There appeared to him, after all, something so glaringly improbable in the fact of a perfectly innocent man being actually executed, in defiance of right and justice, that he could scarcely conceive, himself, that there really was no sort of hope of a release from the dreadful situation in which he was placed.

It was towards evening that he desired to see the Governor of the castle, and when that functionary appeared, he said:

"Did I hear aright, in the court-house, when I fancied a refusal was given to Miranda Rankley visiting me here, under the dreadful circumstances I am placed in?"

"It is true," said the Governor. "I have now no voice in the matter. Your recent escape, you will perceive, has made your case a peculiar one."

"Good Heavens!" said Rowland. "Am I then to be hurried to death, without even the poor consolation of bidding adieu to those I leave behind me?"

"I cannot help it."

"Well—well, God help me! So the authorities of York are afraid of a young, weak girl, and I am to be hurried to death like a dog, on the morrow, in perfect innocence. Oh, sir, tell me! Am I really awake, or is this some horrible vision of a tortured fancy? Is this a madhouse or a prison?"

"I feel for you deeply," said the Governor, in tones of emotion. "My whole conduct towards you has shown that I feel for you; but I am quite powerless to render you assistance. Myself and the chaplain are the only persons you will be allowed to see now."

"I thank you. Farewell! I thank you."

Rowland sat down again, with such a sigh of despair, that the Governor lingered in the cell for some minutes, in the hope that his prisoner might ask for some indulgence which in the course of his duty he could freely grant

him; but the persecuted young man said no more, and the humane Governor, with a sad heart—for he doubted much the guilt of Rowland, if he had not a strong personal impression of his innocence—left the place.

Dark, terrible, and mysterious thoughts then came over the mind of Percy.

He fancied himself deserted both by man and God, and a feeling rose up in his mind of indignation at the manner in which he considered himself picked out to undergo so much misery.

He pictured to himself the morrow, with all its hideous preparations to put him to death, and in his mind's eye he saw the mob, the scaffold, and the executioner.

He saw the fatal cord, and in fancy he heard the confused hum of the multitude, which came to make a holiday, in order to see a fellow-creature put to a death of torture and ignominy.

Then his bosom swelled with a sense of the injustice that was being done him, and he asked himself:

"Shall I submit to all this? Or shall I, if I cannot save myself, at least make some effort to disappoint my persecutors of to-morrow's show? Oh, that I could—oh, that I had the means of doing this, that when they come to drag me to execution, they might find that I had eluded their blind vengeance in the arms of death."

He glanced uneasily at the two men who were in his cell, and he saw that they were conversing together in whispers, and not paying any very particular attention to his actions.

"It may be done," he thought, "it surely may be done! 'Tis worth the trial. It would be more glorious than the death they contemplate. Let me think calmly how I may myself 'shuffle off this mortal coil.' I have heard that they refuse prisoners nothing in the way of sustenance they feel inclined to take, previous to their execution. What is to hinder me assuming great quietness and resignation? Asking for some food that requires a knife—ay, a knife—would it were in my heart! I will disappoint them; and, when the tale is told in after years of my false condemnation, it shall not be said that I yielded tamely. They shall add that I was goaded to such desperation, that at last I took my own life to escape the awful persecution and the threatened death that awaited me. I will try—yes—I am resolved!"

CHAPTER CLXIV.

THE VISIT TO HER ONCE HAPPY HOME BY MIRANDA—THE OLD SERVANT—THE OMEN.

AFTER her request to Mr. Anderson to take her to the Grange once again, Miranda scarcely spoke for several hours, and her friends entertained the greatest apprehensions for her health's sake.

She was really visibly sinking, and a more remarkable change than had taken place in that gentle, heroic girl within a few short hours could not have been conceived.

Years of happiness and contentment might

have passed over her head without producing a tithe of the alteration which had ensued on the morning of that day. Indeed, no mere changes produced by time could have given to her beautiful countenance such an aspect of the very abandonment of woe and despair.

She might have sat to a sculptor for a model of grief. Her face was terrible, in its calm agony, to look upon. There were no tears. Hers was not the grief that could find relief in weeping. She would have been happier if she could have wept, and wept freely, too; but, alas! tears were not for her!

It was towards sunset that Mr. Anderson came to tell her he had a carriage ready to convey her to the Grange.

At the same time, he begged her not to go unless she found her strength fully equal to the journey.

"Yes, yes," she replied, "I will go—I must go. I only wish to see my old, happy home once again. I wish to take a parting glance at some of the old trees. My thoughts will soon be all with the dead. To-morrow will be the end of all my misery. I am dying."

"Miranda—Miranda. Think of Heaven and its mercy yet."

"I think much of Heaven. I hope to meet my dear father and Rowland Percy there. I am quite ready, Mr. Anderson—quite ready. You see I am strong enough to walk well, and without assistance, too. Let us go. I long once again to look upon the Grange."

With tearful eyes, Mr. Anderson conducted her to the carriage, and, in a very short time —for the distance was not great—York was left behind, and some familiar objects in the neighbourhood of the Grange came into sight.

The beauties of the day, which was nearly over, appeared suddenly to shoot out, and beam upon the earth in dying splendour.

All was calm and serene.

Not a breath stirred to lift a leaf of the old trees that surrounded the Grange, and all the grounds around it.

Not a sound was to be heard; the notes of the feathered tribe seemed hushed as though they knew that the once proud heiress of all around was approaching the spot where she had dwelt and commanded—was approaching to take a last, fond, lingering look at, and to bid a farewell to the spot where she had tasted of happiness unalloyed.

The beams of the sinking sun shone through a mass of clouds that were illuminated by its rays, imparting a depth and variety of colour that made it a sublime and magnificent spectacle. It reminded Mr. Anderson strongly of the reflection of the sun's rays shining through a painted window on the stones, save that the colours ran more softly one into another.

It was at this moment, when the sun was just dipping below the horizon, that Miranda Rankley and Mr. Anderson came in view of the Grange.

She turned her eyes towards the sinking sun, and then upon the building before her.

A deep sigh escaped from her bosom.

Mr. Anderson saw and marked this; but he forbore to offer any topic of consolation, for he knew that for such grief as Miranda's there was no alleviation.

The many objects that surrounded the spot brought a host of agonizing reflections and remembrances to the mind of Miranda.

"The recollections of the past," said Miranda, "cause emotions as painful as if they were of a different character."

"It is," replied Mr. Anderson, "the situation in which you are placed that causes them to be painful; the contrast is great and lamentable."

They continued walking over the grounds until they neared the entrance to the Grange, from which Mr. Anderson was about to lead her, when she said, turning towards the door:

"I will endeavour to gain admission; the house cannot be entirely empty. I should like to see it once again."

"Bernard Varley is not here," replied Mr. Anderson, "and those who are, if any, cannot be so much his creatures as to refuse you that request."

They immediately ascended the steps, and, after some delay, were admitted by an old servant, whom Miranda recognized as having been long in the family, the only representative of which had been so cruelly deprived of her birthright.

The old man had sought the house, deserted as it was, as a shelter against the inclemency of the weather, being of opinion that Varley would scarce disturb him even if he came, which was unlikely.

His sorrow, when he saw Miranda, was re-awakened, and tears ran down the old man's face, as he looked upon her pallid countenance, tinged as it was with sorrow and deep dejection.

Their colloquy was brief—a few words, uttered with deep pathos and feeling, conveyed much meaning to the heart, and Miranda Rankley passed on, in company with Mr. Anderson.

Each room, as they came to it, they found in exactly the same state as when she quitted it.

Not an article of furniture had been touched, even the room in which the late Sir George Rankley died—the very bed on which he lay when the murderers came to him and deprived him of life, was in the same state as it was left.

Varley, it will be recollected, had but little delight in going through the house, and none in living there, and he had not succeeded in selling the estate; therefore, all was in an undisturbed confusion, consequent upon the sudden and complete clearance of the place which Bernard Varley had caused.

The room was dimly lighted, and the gloom of the night was rendering objects indistinct, though the moon was fast rising.

Miranda stood motionless as a statue for some minutes, and Mr. Anderson was fearful of disturbing the feeling which he knew must be, at that moment, rising in her breast.

The old man stood by trembling and gazing, with an expression of intense and painful interest, upon the pale face of his former young mistress.

It was a study worthy of any painter, that strange group—Miranda, with her exquisitely chiselled features, pale as monumental marble, unconsciously assuming an attitude of abounding grace, while, at the same time, it expressed the very ecstasy of grief. The old, white-haired man, too, trembling half from age and half from emotion, and Mr. Anderson turning aside to hide the emotion that would make itself too sadly visible in his countenance.

The silence was at length broken by the aged domestic, who said, in a faint, quivering voice :

"Miss Miranda, you—you recollect this room ?"

Miranda started.

The spell which had kept her so still and silent was broken.

"God help me," she said; "I do, indeed. 'Twas here I watched by what I thought the sleeping form of my father, when I little thought that sleep was the repose of death."

"Ay—ay," said the old man, "I recollect. It seems to me as if it were a long while ago now. Is Bernard Varley dead yet ?"

"No," said Mr. Anderson; "he still lives. You forget you have yourself spoken of him."

"My memory goes; but I see main well. Heugh!—heugh!—I don't fail much—heugh!"

"Will you come away now, Miranda ?"

"Yes," she said, with a shudder. "It is very cold. This place is more like a charnel-house."

Mr. Anderson gave her his arm, and, with a calmness that had something unnatural about it, she left the apartment.

Once only she paused on the threshold, and looked back, then she said, in a whisper, to Mr. Anderson :

"Do you think the dead can visit the scenes that were interesting to them in life ?"

"Do not," he replied, "talk on so melancholy a theme. The moon is rising, and you will have a rare opportunity of viewing the Grange. You will be better to-morrow."

"Much better. I shall be quite well and quite happy. Death is the end of all evils."

Mr. Anderson saw it was quite in vain to struggle with the strong presentiment she evidently had that she should not outlive Rowland Percy, and he resolved to say no more on the subject, but to get the advice of the best physicians the city afforded, for her on their return home, and he was now anxious that they should get there as quickly as possible.

"You will come, now ?" he said.

"Let me walk but for a few minutes on the lawn," Miranda replied. "I am giving you a world of trouble."

"Nay, do not think of that. The night air is beginning to blow keenly, and I did not wish you to linger in it."

They left the house, and stood by the side of a statue on the lawn, while the beautiful moon rose up above a bank of clouds, and spread such a sudden flood of radiance over the landscape, that every flower and every shrub was as visible as in mid-day.

"Alas !" moaned Miranda, "so have I often seen this place. I will go now."

A black cloud swept at that instant over the face of the moon, and all was darkness.

"Ominous !—ominous !" muttered Miranda. "I will go now."

CHAPTER CLXV.

TWITTER'S WRETCHED SITUATION—STARVATION—THE INN AT LIVERPOOL.—THE FRANTIC RACE—THE WAGGON.

THE morning brought no pleasing reflections or hopes to Samuel Twitter, for he was weary, wet, and hungry, and what was, perhaps, worse than all, penniless.

If ever Samuel Twitter felt human misery, it was at this moment. He knew not where to go—to what quarter to bend his steps.

"Oh, dear !" exclaimed Twitter, in the depth of his distress. "What shall I do? What will become of me? I would that I had never seen Varley, who must surely be the evil one in human form. All my plans have failed—all I have done has come to nothing, and here am I in difficulties and danger—ay, danger of starvation.

"Then there is the confession! Curse the confession. What did I write it for?—for revenge. What did I want revenge for?—But that hasn't failed. I daresay I shall be hanged alongside of Bernard Varley, according to the prediction of that idiot. I wish his tongue would drop out. Oh, dear! oh, dear!"

Twitter wrung his hands in despair, and scalding tears ran down his face.

Unable to go further, he seated himself on a bank for a few moments' repose, and to indulge his grief, which was extreme and loud; but at length a happy thought seemed to cross his mind, and he said :

"Ah! It may not be posted. They may have forgotten to post it, and I may be safe yet. I will go and endeavour to find out the place."

But he knew not where he was, and when he arose, he saw nothing but a dreary road, which appeared, as far as he could see, to lead anywhere or nowhere, and despair again sat heavy at his heart.

At a slow pace he crawled forward.

His clothes were hard, and stuck to him in a manner that was both uncomfortable and painful.

His feet were benumbed, and he dragged himself onwards at a slow and irresolute pace, each moment execrating his bad luck.

Hunger now rose above all other sensations; his fears vanished, for Samuel Twitter's stomach was most unequivocally empty, and he was without the means to stay the cravings of his appetite.

This feeling soon pinched him so sharply that he determined to beg.

"I must do it, or starve!" he at length uttered, in a melancholy voice. "Yes, it has come to begging at last! Well, and if begging will do, I may yet escape; for then I will try to excite the compassion of some kind and charitable person; but, oh, dear! how far shall I have to go on this infernal long road?"

The road was not so long as Twitter believed, but, in his then state of misery, a few yards became a mile in point of fatigue in travelling.

He walked some distance, but was unable to meet with any human being, except a few labourers, who were too poor to afford him the slightest hope of even a crust.

At last, Twitter came in sight of a public-house—a road-side inn, one with a seat and water-trough before it.

It was a small, neat house, but bore the appearance of plenty, and here Samuel Twitter determined to make his first attempt at begging.

For this purpose he went straight up to the house, then hesitated.

Hunger, however, soon admonished him that time was flying, and, with a desperate resolve, he crossed the threshold.

The first individual he encountered was the landlord, who was at once impressed with the idea that Twitter had a very suspicious appearance, and had come to make observations on the position of the premises.

"Now, my fine fellow," said that worthy personage, "what do you want?"

"I want everything," said Twitter.

"Ay, I daresay; but we don't sell it, and you'll get it further on. Come—come; be off with you, or I'll set Jowler at you."

"I am starving—I have been shipwrecked," said Twitter, rendered desperate by his condition. "For Heaven's sake be charitable, and give me a mouthful to eat. I am in great want."

"I daresay you are in great want, and so is Jowler, and he will make a breakfast off your legs, if you are not off directly."

Twitter trembled with fear, and was about to move off, when he again besought the aid of the landlord.

In another moment he was seized by the skirts of his coat by the aforesaid Jowler, who had been growling savagely.

Samuel Twitter no sooner felt the dog than, giving a loud scream, he rushed out of the house, leaving a part of his garment in the mouth of the ferocious brute.

It was not until he had left the inn some distance behind, that Twitter ventured to slacken his pace, which he had kept up for nearly a mile, notwithstanding his fatigue.

Utterly exhausted, he sank upon a bank, a prey to all the horrors of such a situation as that in which he was placed.

He groaned aloud, and wept bitterly.

"Oh, that I should be such a fool as to write that confession. I might as well have gone and given myself up at once. They might hang me, but they wouldn't starve me. No—no. I can't even get a bit of bread now. Begging is not a very good way of living. I shall die—I shall die! I hope so, and that will save me from a worse death. Oh, that I could kill myself! I would, but I can't. No—that's worse than starving. What will become of me?—what shall I do? I am starved!"

While Twitter was thus soliloquizing, a little girl happened to pass, with a pitcher of milk in her hand.

She stopped to look at him, and, apparently, felt pity for his misery, for, going up to him, she inquired what was the matter with him, and if he were not ill.

"I am dying of hunger and of thirst," said Twitter. "I have been shipwrecked, and have had nothing to eat for some time. Give me a draught of milk, for I am famishing."

The little creature took a slice of bread and butter from a pocket she had beneath her apron, and gave it him, and then offered him some milk when he had eaten it.

Samuel Twitter, when he placed the pitcher to his lips, never thought of quitting his hold of it until he had swallowed considerably more than half the contents.

The little girl looked into the pitcher with dismay.

"Oh, what will my mother say now?" she exclaimed, crying. "I shall be beaten. I didn't think you would have taken so much."

The poor little thing went off, weeping bitterly, from the effects of Samuel Twitter's greediness; while he, being somewhat refreshed, and having a dread of the girl's mother, rose, and started forward again, but at a slow pace.

"What hard-hearted creatures there are in the world," said Samuel Twitter, "who will not help a fellow creature in extreme distress. Even that child grudged me the draught of milk she offered me. Well—well; this is a dreadful world to live in."

With these reflections, and others like them, he wandered about till nearly sunset.

What to do he knew not.

Where to go, either for food or for shelter, he knew not.

He had made such an unsuccessful attempt at begging, that he believed it would be useless to try again.

Twitter had at one moment determined to return and attempt to rob the larder of the house where he had been so unceremoniously dismissed. It could be done, he thought, for it was easily approached, and not very well protected; but, then, Jowler was there, and acted like a guardian angel to the larder.

For some time Twitter knew not what to do; but at length resolved to make the attempt.

Hunger was the grand incentive to do a deed of so much boldness, and before Samuel Twitter was aware of his own temerity, he was in the neighbourhood of the public-house.

All was dark and still.

"Now," thought Twitter, "I will be revenged upon these people for the way they treated me this morning. I'll empty their larder, if I can."

With this amiable resolution, Samuel Twitter crept close to the house, and, after listening attentively, carefully groped his way into an out-house, or wash-house, and thence into the larder.

The wash-house door had been left open by the girl, who had gone out to speak to her sweetheart.

While Twitter was helping himself, she returned and bolted the door, then passed by the end of the larder to her own place of repose.

Twitter's agony cannot be described.

His fears of detection were intense, but of short endurance, for he heard her go into her apartment, and bolt herself in.

He then resumed his employment, and, having eaten heartily, and loaded himself, he sought for the means of gratifying his desire to drink.

A barrel of choice ale being near at hand, he attempted to drink, but the key of the tap was gone, and he was forced to pull the tap out.

At first he contrived to drink, but soon was compelled to desist, for the ale gushed out with great force.

As he could not put the tap in again in the dark, he commenced a hasty retreat, and had scarcely got the wash-house door open, when he heard the landlord's voice, saying:

"Why, cuss it! who's been at the ale in the larder? It's all running to waste."

Twitter stayed to hear no more, but took to his heels.

After a long run, he came to a kind of cattle-shed where there was some straw, and there he slept till the morning came, when he was thrust out with threats.

It was not long ere he reached the next town, which, upon inquiry, he found to be Liverpool; he then determined to go to the inn at which he had stayed, and, if possible, obtain assistance of the landlord by representing his condition to him.

Going up to the door, he espied him, and made inquiry after his letter, when he was assured, upon the landlord's honour, that it had been carefully posted.

Twitter had scarcely heard the answer when two men rode up to the door, and as one dismounted, an officer's staff was visible.

This was enough for Twitter, who believed them to be in search of himself, and instantly set off at full speed through the streets of Liverpool; indeed, many who witnessed his course believed him to be a madman, and carefully avoided getting in his way, until at length exhausted, he espied a waggon leaving the town; to this he rushed, and made a most abject appeal to the driver, to be permitted to creep in and rest himself.

After much persuasion, the driver consented, and Samuel Twitter crawled in and threw himself on a heap of straw, quite exhausted with fatigue and overcome with terror.

The officers he saw, he doubted not had been sent from York on purpose to capture him.

His agony of mind was intense, and so confused were his intellects, that he could think no longer, and fell into a troubled sleep.

CHAPTER CLXVI.

THE ROUTE TO YORK—THE IDIOT—TWITTER'S ALARMS.

WHEN Samuel Twitter sank down among the straw and litter that was in the waggon, he felt quite a sensation of relief, for he was wretchedly uneasy; moreover, beneath the ample canopy that was above his head, and nestled among the straw, he was secure from that curious observation with which he thought everybody regarded him.

"Thank Heaven!" he murmured, "I am alone here; there is no one to torture me by glances that have horrible suspicions in them. How—how awfully strange it is now that everyone seems to be able to see that I am a murderer!"

Twitter fully fancied that such was the case.

Since his adventures in attempting to escape, and since he had become aware of the horrible fact that his letter to the Mayor of York had been posted to that functionary, he had translated every casual glance of curiosity that was bent on him into a meditated seizure of him on the charge of murder, as well as upon that of having given false evidence against poor Rowland Percy.

Therefore was it that the gloom, darkness, and loneliness of the waggon, became so grateful to his feelings.

He lay for some hours without so much as moving from the position in which he had first cast himself; but what a world of bitter and awful thoughts passed through his burning brain during that short period.

The question so easily asked, but so difficult to answer, of "what shall I do—what shall I do?" escaped his lips frequently, in mournful and agonized accents.

"I am destitute—starving—friendless—homeless!" he thought, "and, moreover, I have accused myself of a crime, which, in a few hours more, will raise the whole country in arms against me, and place a price upon my head. What shall I do—what shall I do?"

The idea again crossed his mind of escaping from all his evils by suicide, and so leaving Bernard Varley still in the lurch; but the act of self-destruction required a degree of courage which Samuel Twitter never possessed, or a degree of insanity he had certainly not yet arrived at.

Soon, therefore, he banished from his mind all thought of self-destruction.

But what remained to present to him any feasible hope of escaping from the gallows?

"I am lost—lost!" he groaned. "What can I do? They would not take me for a soldier or a sailor; and if I attempt to beg for my bread through London or the country, I shall be in hourly expectation of recognition from someone. Oh! if I had ended all this horrible state by adopting a different plan, there might have been a chance of escape from death—if I had freely given myself up to Rowland Percy's friends, affected great repentance, and made reparation for what I had done, I might have been let off on becoming evidence against Bernard Varley; but now—now—oh, fool that I have been—I have criminated both him and myself for no consideration."

Twitter lay on his back and groaned aloud as these sad reflections crossed his mind; indeed, the waggoner was attracted by the noise, and looked in at the end of the waggon with a face of great curiosity.

"Hilloa!" he said, "what's 'e matter, eh?"

"Nothing, nothing!" cried Twitter, greatly alarmed, "nothing at all. I fell asleep, and was dreaming; that's all. I swear to you that's all."

"You needn't swear. I be main troubled with bad dreams myself. I once dreamt I saw the whole team run away, and upset a haystack—gee up!"

Twitter after this was more quiet, although none the less mentally tormented; he reflected as painfully and as intensely as before, but he took care the waggoner should not hear him.

Things went on thus until towards evening, which rapidly darkened into night, just as Twitter began to hear rain coming down heavily on the tarpaulin of the waggon.

A strong and vivid flash of lightning suddenly lit up the dark road, which in a few seconds was followed by a loud peal of thunder.

The wind sensibly increased, and ever and anon, upon the silence of the night, was carried the crashing sound of the rending of some strong limb from the trunk of an aged tree, or the destruction of such as were less able to bear up against the fury of the storm.

The heavy pelting of the rain continued for some time with unabated violence.

Upon the whole, Samuel Twitter rather liked the storm.

He was sheltered from its fury; there were not so many people abroad, and he therefore considered his danger of arrest lessened.

Suddenly the waggon stopped, and Twitter heard a conversation taking place between the waggoner and someone who appeared desirous of obtaining the same shelter from the storm he, Twitter, had enjoyed.

"Who are you?" he heard the waggoner say. "You gave me a bit of a fright coming out of the hedge in that kind of way."

"I'm mad Tom," was the reply, in a voice that Twitter knew well to belong to the maniac who had always so much annoyed Bernard Varley.

"Mad Tom, are you?"

"Yes. See, I am benumbed with the rain.

I'm going to York. Ha! ha! ha! Why don't you laugh?"

"'Cos I don't see the joke."

"But I do. There's a man to be hanged. I dreamt it, so I know it's true. There's a man to be hanged. Ain't it fine. He will kick and plunge. A strange, tall man to be hanged."

"You may like it, mad Tom, as you call yourself; but it's more than I do," said the waggoner. "Howsomdever, get in. I don't like to refuse a poor fellow a lift."

"Thank you. Oh! oh! oh! It's enough to make one laugh dreadfully to think of it. Bernard Varley will be hanged at York."

A cold sensation came over Twitter's heart as he heard these words.

He drew himself up into the further corner of the waggon, so that he was not seen by the maniac as he scrambled in.

"Who's to be hung, did you say?" said the waggoner.

"Bernard Varley. Do you know him? He's a fine fellow to hang. They'll have Samuel Twitter, too, the sleek villain. I know them both. They are to be hanged at York, and I cannot think of leaving the city when once I get to it, till I see the sight."

"Ah!" said the waggoner, "you don't know what you are talking about, and I don't understand you."

For the first time it came across Twitter's mind like a shock of electricity, that he had never thought to inquire where the waggoner was going, and that he might actually be conveying him slowly and surely to York—that city which, of all others, he had most now to dread showing his face in.

He was afraid to cross to that part of the waggon where the maniac was seated, so he crawled right up to the front, and removing a piece of the tarpaulin, said, in a low voice, to the waggoner, who was walking close to the shaft:

"Hi! hi! where are we going?"

"To York."

"Gracious Heaven!"

Twitter fell backwards among the straw, and in a moment, with a loud cry of alarm, the maniac sprang upon him, and clutched him by the throat.

CHAPTER CLXVII.

THE APPEAL TO THE SHERIFF—THE ATTEMPT TO BRIBE THE JAILER—THE SCAFFOLD— THE DRAGOONS.

AFTER Mr. Anderson had returned with Miranda Rankley from her visit to the Grange, he felt much affected by what had passed between them.

Her resignation, her beauty, and constancy, claimed his admiration.

He then began seriously to consider whether all hope was dead, and if there were no means of staying the execution of the sentence for a short time.

Late as it was, Mr. Anderson knew that if any attempt were made, it must be done at once, and he determined that he would instantly set about consulting the most influential people of the place.

Having obtained the ear of some of them, they listened attentively to his proposal, which, however hopeless, was by many thought to be too near the absurd to be useful, or even probable.

They all agreed, however, that Mr. Percy's execution ought to be put off for a few days, to give the parties an opportunity of petitioning the Crown, and of being able to revise the case against the unfortunate prisoner.

Feeling assured of his innocence as they did, it was no wonder that they all immediately assembled at Mr. Anderson's request, and quietly heard all that he said to them, eventually agreeing to go to the sheriffs in a body, to make the request that they would grant a delay of three days.

Mr. Anderson's name procured him an instant admission to their presence, and they inquired kindly what they could do to oblige him.

"I have come," said Mr. Anderson, to the principal and most active of the two sheriffs, "I have come, and with me these gentlemen, to pray you to exert your influence on behalf of the unfortunate man who now lies under sentence of death."

"You mean Rowland Percy?" said the sheriff, shaking his head.

"I do, sir."

"And upon what grounds?"

"I fear to name them; but we are assured of his innocence, and want but time to enable us to prove it. Should you grant our request, we will make application for a reprieve."

"These are really no grounds at all, Mr. Anderson, and you, as a lawyer, ought to know that; besides, under the peculiar circumstances, I dare not—I have really no power left."

"We will undertake to bear any responsibility that you could possibly incur; for we are convinced that time, and time only, is required to make the innocence of Rowland Percy evident."

"I can't help you," replied the sheriff. "You know he has had time; he has escaped from us, and been at liberty for many days; he has had friends, and yet nothing has been done to establish the fact of his innocence; and, however my private sympathy may be affected, yet I cannot exert it in his favour. He has been found guilty by a jury, and sentenced by the judge; were there any doubts, representations would have been made from these quarters."

"I want time to do so. I am convinced they will all assist me."

"I wish I could help you, Mr. Anderson; but my duty binds my hands, and I dare not go outside that duty. There has already been much disturbance in York about the prisoner and the authorities. I have been much blamed —I dare not, for that reason, grant the request you make."

"I have yet another request to make of you," said Mr. Anderson, with a sigh, "which I hope you will be better prepared to grant me."

"What is it, sir?" inquired the sheriff.

"That you will permit Miss Rankley to visit Rowland Percy in his cell."

"It cannot be done, sir; no one will be permitted to see him."

"That is very unusual, as well as a great hardship," said Mr. Anderson.

"Perhaps it is," replied the sheriff; "but it has been determined upon by the authorities. I am merely the agent, the responsible agent, and she cannot be permitted to see him, by a resolution they have come to upon the subject."

"Well," said Mr. Anderson, "I had hoped to be more successful, and I did think that in York the last request of a dying man would have been complied with."

"Do not think that I am to blame for your want of success, sir; it is with pain that the authorities have come to such a determination, but it is necessary for the ends of justice."

Mr. Anderson then, with a heavy heart, thanked those who had accompanied him to the sheriffs', but he determined to go alone to the prison and endeavour to make an impression upon the Governor, and obtain his consent to allow Miranda to visit Percy in his cell ere morning.

When he arrived, a man at the wicket let him in, and desired him to wait awhile, as he was at that moment alone, expecting the return of one of his companions.

"My friend," said Mr. Anderson, driven to despair and seizing any project that was likely to be available, "would you like to earn a few pounds easily and safely?"

"Yes, I should," replied the jailer; "but what's the dodge—it must be all right."

"Then I will give you a hundred pounds if you will allow Mr. Percy to escape; he is innocent, and as sure as he dies to-morrow, he is a murdered man!"

"I am very sorry, sir," said the man, "but I can't at any price have anything to do with that piece of business."

"He is innocent," said Mr. Anderson.

"Ah! sir, so we all are until the jury says we ain't; but his hash is settled. I wish it had been different, but there's no getting over such things."

"It is not enough, perhaps," suggested Mr. Anderson; "I will give you two hundred pounds down if you will assist him in getting free of this place."

"I wish I could, sir; but I have eyes enough on me now, and it's no use your trying it on. It can't be done."

"But it can if you will all agree; make them any offer—I will pay it all—so that Rowland Percy escapes free, I care not. You know me, and know that I would not make you a promise that I should not perform."

"Very well, sir, I'll go and see what I can do with some on 'em, but you remain quiet for a minute or two."

THE RESULT OF SAMUEL TWITTER'S FIRST ATTEMPT AT BEGGING.

Mr. Anderson remained seated, in much anxiety, while the jailer was gone, and it was with a palpitating heart that he followed the footsteps of another man who came and beckoned to him in a mysterious manner.

Presently they emerged into a small room, when the turnkey he had been following turned round, and taking hold of his arm, said, in a low tone:

"You are my prisoner."

"What do you mean?" said Mr. Anderson.

"Exactly what I say—you are my prisoner. You've been trying to corrupt one of our people to let Rowland Percy escape."

"Where's the Governor?" inquired Mr. Anderson. "Let me see him immediately; I have some urgent business to transact with him."

"The Governor will be here directly, sir," replied the man; "he has been sent for already."

"What noise is that?" inquired Mr. Anderson, as the sound of hammers and the working of mechanics was distinctly heard.

"Oh! that's the men getting the *gallus* ready," replied the man, coolly; "they always makes that ere row afore hanging mornings. Some people can't sleep for it, but it never disturbs me."

Mr. Anderson's heart sank within him as he listened to the ominous sound.

Death seemed to stare him in the face, and the terrors of such an end appeared more real to him than ever he thought they could possibly be.

The Governor now entered, and, bowing to Mr. Anderson, said:

"Mr. Anderson, I am sorry you have placed yourself in a disagreeable situation as well as myself. It is said you have attempted to bribe the jailers."

"You surely do not intend to detain me on such a charge?" said Mr. Anderson.

"I don't think I ought to do otherwise; my duty would induce me to do so, yet the unhappy cause of it excites my strongest sympathy, and I feel reluctant."

"I have seen the sheriffs and prayed of them to delay the execution."

"Which, of course, they did not agree to do, for they could not."

"That was the result of my interview," said Mr. Anderson, with emotion; "though, God knows, I am convinced that Rowland Percy is an innocent man."

"Whatever my private opinion may be, I cannot be supposed to do what is not consonant with my duty."

"Then all I wish," said Mr. Anderson, "is that you will permit Miranda Rankley to see the unfortunate man in his cell; his hours are few, and you cannot surely refuse to grant such a request."

"I am sorry to say that I cannot possibly grant you even that request. It has been determined that no one shall see him."

"That is very hard."

"It may be; but recent events render every precaution we can take necessary; this you, Mr. Anderson, must be well aware of."

"Well, then, she will not be allowed to see him again in life?"

"Yes, I can do this much, she may see him as he is passing through the prison to the place of execution."

"Is that all?"

"Yes, all."

"Then I must bid you adieu," said Mr. Anderson. "I suppose I can depart?"

"Yes, certainly; but make no more attempts of this sort."

"I will not. But what is that?"

"A troop of dragoons, that are to quarter themselves before the prison."

Mr. Anderson's heart sank within him, as he saw the troopers ride up and dismount, scatter litter for their horses, and prepare themselves to remain under arms during the night.

As he looked on these preparations with an aching heart, someone pressed his arm. He turned, and perceived Dick Palmer, who motioned Mr. Anderson to follow him.

CHAPTER CLXVIII.

THE ARREST—THE PARISH BEADLE—TWITTER'S ARTFUL PLAN OF ESCAPE — THE CHALK-PIT.

So tightly did the maniac hold Twitter, that he found himself unable even to raise a cry for help, and he truly thought his last hour was come.

All the incidents of his evil life flashed in a bewildering throng across his imagination, and holding a prominent place in the hideous images that crowded to his brain, was Sir George Rankley, as he, Twitter, had last seen him in life, struggling to free himself from the murderous grip of Bernard Varley, in the chamber at the Grange.

"Ha! ha!" shouted the maniac; "I have him now—I have him—my tormentor. He, the fiend, who has placed an imp in my brain to strike ding-dong for ever, till I could have wrenched my head off in despair. Ha! ha! ha! I have him, now. Death—death!"

So loudly did the maniac speak, that the waggoner, although half asleep, was attracted by the noise, and, coming to the end of the clumsy vehicle, threw the strong light of a lantern, which had been dangling by one of the shafts, into the interior.

In a moment, he saw, as he thought, one of his passengers murdering the other, and, with honest zeal, flew to the rescue.

By main force he dragged Twitter's assailant from him, and it was well he did so, for Twitter was almost insensible, and quite black in the face.

"Why, what art 'e at?" cried the waggoner. "Thee called theeself Mad Tom, and I see thee are."

The maniac pointed with both hands full in Twitter's face, and then burst into an uproarious fit of laughter.

He clapped his hands—he danced among the straw in the waggon—he shouted and exhibited such demoniac glee, that the waggoner was amazed, and Twitter, who was slowly recovering, could scarcely believe he was not under the influence of some nightmare.

"Ha! ha! ha!" roared the maniac. "'Tis one of them—one of them. Oh! that I should attempt to cheat the hangman. 'Tis one of them, and he is going to York to be hanged. He knows he must. He can't escape. Ho! ho! ho! glorious! He is going to York to be hanged, and I in the same waggon to see the sport. I shall be in good time after all. Ho! ho! ho! and I was so afraid of being late."

"Why—why, what is all this?" cried the waggoner.

"For mercy's sake, tell me," said Twitter. "Are you, indeed, going to York, or not?"

"I am going to York—I always goes to York—I've been a matter o' thirty years now, always going to York, or coming away from York."

"Then let me get out this moment."

"His name is Samuel Twitter," cried the maniac. "He and Bernard Varley murdered

Sir George Rankley. They will both be hanged for it. Ha! ha! ha!"

"Let me go—let me go," cried Twitter. "I do not like travelling with a madman. Let me go now."

"I will go with you. Where you go, I go—where you stop, I stop, because I wish to be in time for the execution. I would not leave you for worlds. Ho! ho! ho! Come on. Boon companions we shall make on the road to York."

"For the love of Heaven," cried Twitter to the waggoner, "save me from this man."

"I—I'm a-going to York," said the waggoner. "What can I do? I'm a-going to York."

"But you will not see me murdered by him?"

"He is a murderer!" cried the maniac. "I denounce him as a murderer! He committed a murder near York, and he must not be set at liberty. I know him. His name is Samuel Twitter."

"A murderer!" ejaculated the waggoner. "The Lord have mercy upon us!"

"I am not!" screamed Twitter. "I am not! Curses on you both! Curses—curses!"

He jumped from the waggon, and made an attempt to escape in the darkness, but this manœuvre only induced the waggoner to suspect more strongly that the accusation of the idiot had some sort of foundation.

Crying "Whoa!" to his team, he made a blundering effort to catch Twitter, who would unquestionably have escaped but for the maniac, who, with a bound and a whoop, sprang after him with such tremendous speed, and with such precision, that it placed Twitter in a few moments quite at his mercy.

"You thought to escape me," he shouted. "but you cannot. Folks say I am not so wise as the rest of mankind, so they hunt me from their houses, and I am forced to wander about roads, and fields, and woods at night, till my eyes have become accustomed to them, and I can see almost as well by night as by day. You cannot escape me, Samuel Twitter."

So saying, he held him with a grasp which there was no shaking off, and brought him in triumph back to the waggon.

Twitter only spoke once.

"Mercy—mercy!" he said.

"Ask it of Heaven!" cried the maniac, "and ask in vain, as I have, when some gleam of reason—ha—ha—ha! I am mad again—I am mad again!"

"I am lost," thought Twitter; "lost—lost. I shall be taken to York, and there immediately arrested, for the Mayor will have received my letter, and then there is but one step to the scaffold. I am lost—lost."

"Get in," said the maniac, when they reached the waggon. "You shall still go to York."

"No, no," cried the waggoner. "I'll have no murderers in my waggon further than I can help. I'll let him go to the next village, and then he may be guved to some authority sort o' person."

"Good," said the maniac, and he commenced kicking Twitter till the latter scrambled into the waggon to escape him.

Then he sprang in himself, and, sitting down close to the entrance, kept vigilant guard over his wretched prisoner.

Twitter quite, for a time, gave himself up to despair.

His evil star seemed to be in the ascendant, and he saw no hope of release from the circumstances in which he was placed.

He threw himself among the straw at the bottom of the waggon, and wished himself dead.

To be taken to York, of all places in the world—York, where he was well known—where he could be recognized by thousands of individuals, and where, if not already, in a few short hours, his presence would be so much desired! Oh, it was horrible! If Twitter had had the means in that time of dreadful despair, he might, indeed, have raised his hand against his own wretched life.

In the confusion of his thoughts, he could form no sort of idea as to how far they had gone, when the waggoner stopped; and, upon looking up, Twitter could see the glancing of lights through the canvas sides of the waggon.

He sprang to the seat, but was immediately pounced upon by the maniac, who held him with a grasp of iron, as he shouted:

"No, no; you shall not escape me. A village—a village. Secure the murderer!"

Then arose the confused murmur of a number of voices, and Twitter heard one man say, distinctly:

"If so be as there bees a murderer in the waggon, aren't I parochial? Bring him out. Hold him fast, and then you'll see how I'll mystify him. Am I a beadle, or am I not—eh?—eh? Nobody says no. I is."

"Ah! Mr. Fitch," said a thin, cracked, female voice, "you may be very good for a young vagrant, or a little boy as plays marbles on a Sunday, but don't you have anything to do with murderers, there's a good man."

"Woman," cried the insulted beadle, "you are a female, and kensequently ain't parochial. Show me the ruffian. Five or six of you hold him tight, and leave him to me. A-a-hem—a-hem—a-hem."

"I will surrender myself to that man," thought Twitter, "and get him to have confidence in my quietness, after which I can escape from him, if needs be, at the expense of his very life—but he won't resist me."

A crowd of people now appeared at the end of the waggon, and the maniac, suddenly jumping out among them, created so much consternation, that they rushed away in all directions, the most astonishing thing being the sudden disappearance of Mr. Fitch, the beadle, who, as we dislike mysteries, we may as well state at once, crept under the waggon, which, moreover, gave him all the appearance of having suddenly disappeared down some trap-door.

The maniac then reached his hand into the

waggon, and, before Twitter was aware, seized hold of his leg, and dragged him out.

"Mercy—mercy!" cried Twitter; "I surrender myself to the proper authorities. I am an innocent man, and I claim the protection of the proper authorities."

"Eh?" said the beadle, "that's me."

He slowly emerged from beneath the waggon, and then the maniac cried aloud:

"Who will take charge of a murderer? I accuse him. Who will carry him to York?"

"Me," said the beadle. "Look at me and shiver—I'm a beadle. I'll take him, of course. My name, Fitch, will be in all the newspapers. I shall be called that active and enterprising beadle, Fitch—ah!—hem."

"I'm an innocent man," said Twitter, "and a timid one. I yield to your authority—I yield."

"You are sure you are a timid one?"

"Very, sir, very."

"Good. Then I'm a perfect lion. Don't attempt to escape, or else woe—woe—woe—a-hem."

"I tell you what it is, Mr. Fitch," said the waggoner, "I suspect the fellow myself. He did go on so talking to himself when he got in the waggon."

"Ah! ah! It's only fifty miles to York, now, but I'll get all the authorities—all the road to give us a hoist. My chay-cart will do the job. Oh! if I should become the celebrated Fitch."

So inflamed was the beadle with the prospect of celebrity before him, that nothing would satisfy him but an immediate departure with Twitter.

Having procured a chaise-cart, he placed him in it, with much confidence in his timidity, and was about to start, when the maniac made an effort to go likewise, which Mr. Fitch by no means approved of, so whipping on the horse, he stopped the argument by the force of speed and distance.

* * * *

How hollow are human expectations—how short-lived are human glories—Mr. Fitch—alas! for a beadle's reputation! It was—but we will not anticipate—something serious did befall Mr. Fitch with his timid passenger, that must form part of another chapter.

CHAPTER CLXIX.

SAMUEL TWITTER'S ESCAPE FROM MR. FITCH, AND THAT GENTLEMAN'S FATE—TWITTER'S TERROR AND ARRIVAL IN THE VICINITY OF YORK.

THE situation of Samuel Twitter was one of some peril, and begat, by force of circumstances, which were imminent, a proportionate degree of cunning, or wisdom, as the reader shall determine.

Whatever reluctance he at first felt to get into the cart with Mr. Fitch, and be driven quietly to the next authorities, had now vanished, and his desire to accompany him was stronger than he thought it prudent to show.

He was soon seated, Mr. Fitch having charge of Samuel Twitter and the horse and chaise.

Now a constable may do either; but none save a Fitch could undertake to do both.

Mr. Fitch was anxious that his prisoner should not think him at all in an embarrassed situation, and to do this was a matter for serious thought, and, when once away from the crowd, he said, in an elevated tone, and easy, off-hand manner:

"Prisoner, are you a timid man?"

"Yes," said Samuel Twitter, "I am, very. Didn't you see how I trembled when they first pulled me out of the waggon?"

"Yes—yes, I noticed that. I am not at all timid or afraid myself, you see. Oh, dear no—no, not at all. It wouldn't do for Fitch the beadle to be afraid. Why, I could never keep our village in order, I tell you, if I were."

"I should think not," remarked Twitter. "Your horse won't run away, I hope?"

"Oh, dear, no; he's never been known to do such a thing, and upon parish business, too, with me inside; why—why, I'd impound the brute if he were so much as to cock his ears. But he's quiet enough, I'll go bail."

"I hope so," said Twitter, dubiously.

"Are you timid, nervous, frightened, and all that sort of thing? Well—well, I ain't surprised, considering how queerly you must feel. Your conscience must be like a dead weight."

"It is indeed," said Twitter; "how far have we come?"

"I don't know, not two miles; but, bless you, conscience never troubles me, that's because I'm strong; morally and 'tisically strong."

"Eh?" said Twitter.

"Why, you see, morally strong is having nothing on your mind. The mind, you see, is like a clean sheet, you see nothing on it. Now, 'tisically strong is wery much the same thing. Why, it relates to the corpus, the habeas corpus, I believe. So you see I am as good as two men, for I am strong in two ways."

"Ah!" said Twitter, "I wish I was like you. I think, in that case, they could only hang me morally and not 'tisically, as you see I have only moral faults and crimes to answer for."

Mr. Fitch was considerably embarrassed by this argument, and knew not how to answer it.

He gravely shook his head for some time in silence, but at length said:

"It's all wery well of you, prisoner, to talk after such a fashion; but them ere lawyers will tell you something like what they told the man who stole a halter with a horse at the end of it. It's no use your denying the deed, you took both instead of one, and you must be transported all the longer, so I expects they'll hang you all the longer."

Samuel Twitter felt somewhat uncomfortable under this intimation, and made a motion indicative of his extreme dislike to anything approaching familiarity towards his neck.

His object was to get to as lonely a spot on the road as possible, and escape from the custody of Mr. Fitch.

This he was pretty sure he could not effect, except partly by stratagem, and partly by force, though the latter was of such an easy character that none, save Samuel Twitter, could have hesitated or doubted for one minute.

They journeyed on for some time, and many spots were passed that would have served the purpose of a more resolute man than Samuel Twitter; but as each lonely spot was reached his heart sank within him, and, desperate as his condition was, he could not as yet become the assailant.

The morning was fine, though cold, and a sharp breeze sprang up, much to the annoyance of Mr. Fitch and his prisoner, the former decidedly voting driving with the wind in his teeth a bore, and the latter feeling anything but easy with an empty stomach, and as perilously placed as man could well be.

At length Twitter suggested the propriety of refreshment.

"Refreshment!" said Mr. Fitch, in astonishment. "A prisoner—a murderer captured by me, think of refreshment! What a state of mind you must be in—how horribly hardened! What will the world say of me, who have trusted myself in a cart with an impertinent (impenitent) murderer? My temerity will be the theme of future times."

"But I am hungry and cold," said Twitter, "and you have no right to starve me."

"No right? Why, what can you be thinking of? A murderer has no rights, save the prison, and maybe the gallows. You'll be refreshed when you get to York, and so shall I, but it will not be at the same shop."

They jogged on for some distance.

Mr. Fitch's importance increased with his sense of security, which was almost perfect, as Samuel Twitter exhibited no signs of resistance, or even a desire to escape, and Mr. Fitch, always a man of importance, was lifted up now into regions even far beyond the reach of his own conceit, which was extensive enough, and fear was a stranger to the great man's breast, because he saw not the remotest danger ahead.

They now approached a lonely and desolate spot near to some lime quarries that were, indeed, worked close to the road; or, rather, had been worked, for they were now deserted and overgrown with vegetation.

This, Samuel Twitter thought, would be a good spot to put his plan into execution; indeed, he became sensible, that unless it were done quickly, they would soon get so near to York that it would become, probably, impracticable, or near some village, where aid might be procured, all which reflections greatly urged upon Twitter's mind the necessity for immediate action.

With a desperate resolve, he determined to make an instant attack upon Mr. Fitch, which he did by starting up, and seizing Mr. Fitch by the collar.

The great man also rose to his feet, but this was quite an involuntary act, for he would much rather have lain down; but he recovered from his surprise, and said, in a loud, though tremulous voice, while he laid his hand on Twitter:

"Hilloa—hilloa, prisoner, what's the matter? Didn't you say you were a timid man? Leave go your hold, or I'll—I'll——"

"I want to get out," said Twitter. "I'll—I'll—yes, leave go, can't you?"

"Oh, you bloodthirsty wretch," thought Mr. Fitch. "Here's an encounter. His thoughts are too terrible for utterance. I say, prisoner," he added, aloud; "leave go, or I'll have you punished when we get to York."

"Ay, but I ain't a-going to York," said Twitter, trembling so excessively, that, to any one save Mr. Fitch, it would have been apparent.

Affairs had now come to a crisis, and one or the other must succumb.

Both were most dreadfully afraid of each other, and neither liked to give way; but one must, and Samuel Twitter being in by far the most desperate situation, despair supplied the place of the courage which nature had denied him.

A slight push sent Mr. Fitch flat on his back in the cart, crying out, in a piteous tone, to Samuel Twitter, not to strike a fallen man, and to spare him for the sake of his wife and the little Fitches.

Twitter did not wait to hear all Mr. Fitch's adjuration; but, scrambling out of the cart, he picked up the whip, and struck the horse a smart blow with it.

The animal made a swerve from the spot where Samuel Twitter stood, and thus came near the edge of the lime quarries, where it tottered for a moment, and then gently rolled over and over, till finally the whole concern came to a standstill, and the gallant Mr. Fitch was nowhere to be seen.

Samuel Twitter did not wait to render him any aid, or even to learn his fate; but, lest posterity should think the world lost the valuable services of such a functionary, they must know that being in the cart, and laying fast hold of the seat, he kept his position, and was finally compelled to do so, by being thrown on his back, with the cart on the top of him, where he lay like a hen in a gigantic coop.

On rushed Samuel Twitter across fields, woods, and roads, he knew not whither, but he had turned his back towards York.

He rushed on with a speed that would have astonished anybody, ay, even himself—but just then he was scarcely sensible of fatigue—until, at length, fatigue and hunger became so great that he was compelled to rest himself on the banks of a small stream, at which he assuaged his thirst, and then began to think how he should act.

Food was his first requisite, and he determined to take that, rather than ask for it; but, to do so, he was compelled to wait until nightfall.

It was then that Samuel Twitter went in search of food, like an obscure bird of night, whose deeds are hidden by darkness; but he was terribly frightened, for every noise, the cracking of a dry twig, caused a pang to his timid heart.

Again was he successful in a petty robbery; and he began to think he might be able to live a long while without detection.

Having obtained the supply he required, he next sought for a lodging, which he found in an out-house, but at some distance from the spot where he had committed the robbery.

Here he slept well, and long, but had a terrible dream, for he dreamed that he and Varley were being hanged at York, and the pain was so very great, that it was with a cry of horror he awoke, and found that he had been seized by a large dog by the throat, and two men were standing by, encouraging the animal.

He released himself from the dog, and made off with what speed he could; the men abused him, but he knew not what they said, so great were his fears.

At length he came near a large town.

Twitter knew not what place it was; but the roads were broad, and well made, and there was every indication of his being near a place where there was a large population.

Seeing a countryman coming towards him, Twitter went up to him, and said:

"What is the name of that town?" pointing in the direction.

"That, master, is no town, but the city of York."

Twitter was stunned.

At that moment the booming of the Minster clock struck with solemn sound upon his ears.

So great was the effect of this, that he staggered a few paces, and then sank beneath the hedge by the road-side.

CHAPTER CLXX.

PALMER'S PROPOSAL—THE RESOURCES OF DESPERATION—ROWLAND PERCY'S ATTEMPT AT SUICIDE DEFEATED.

WE left Mr. Anderson in despair at the utter failure of all his attempts to benefit Rowland Percy, and in the company of Dick Palmer, who had just accosted him after leaving the prison in which Rowland was confined.

The deep dejection of Mr. Anderson's countenance did not escape the eyes of Palmer, and he said:

"You have been striving to do something for our poor friend, young Percy, and I need not ask you if you have failed. Your looks sufficiently proclaim it."

"I have failed," reluctantly said Mr. Anderson. "His fate is now certain, inasmuch as he is a doomed man."

"I fear so. It is, indeed, a hard case. Have you asked for time, sir?"

"I have; but the sheriff is inexorable; yet I cannot blame him. Were I in his situation, I should feel myself, perhaps, bound to act as he is acting. A train of wretched circumstances seem intent upon sacrificing that young man, and I fear no human power can save him."

"If human power can save him," said Dick Palmer, "it must be by some desperate means."

"Impossible—impossible."

"What say you to a desperate combined attempt of a couple of hundred strong, determined men, to-morrow morning, to storm the very scaffold?"

"It would never do. Lives would be lost, and the attempt would be sure to fail."

"Nay, such things have been done, and have succeeded on account of their very desperation."

"Saw you the troop of dragoons?"

"I did. Of course, a regular contest with them would be out of the question. If anything were done successfully, it would depend upon the suddenness of the proceeding. If a dozen or two strong, active men were to spring upon the scaffold, and throw Percy among the mob, there might be just a possible chance of his escape."

"Do not attempt it, I implore you. Sufficient evil has been done already, and sufficient evil will be done, I fear, to-morrow morning, without adding to it a useless waste of life and limb. Your expedient is a desperate one."

"I own it is, but I am myself desperate. Mr. Anderson, you saw the glance of Miranda Rankley when she fell fainting in the court-house. You saw the look of utter despair which crossed her beautiful features. Was it not enough to turn one's heart to stone? I love her, sir—I adore her, but not with a selfish love—not with a common adoration which seeks its own gratification before the happiness of its object. No, sir, I would lay down my life to be sure of her becoming the happy wife of Rowland Percy."

There was pathos, as well as passionate sincerity in the manner in which these words were uttered, and Mr. Anderson replied, sadly:

"Your feelings do you honour; but, alas! poor Miranda, although beloved by many, can now be helped by none. I fear her mind will not stand the shock of to-morrow's proceedings. By Heaven! I would give all I possess, and freely sacrifice every fancied prospect of life I have, to save Rowland Percy."

"And I also. Can you think of no scheme whatever—no matter how dangerous in its execution or consequences, so that it looks promising of success?"

"None! I have racked my brain in vain. What you yourself propose is very little short of madness. I pray you not to persevere in it."

"Alas! sir. I know I am not in a state of mind to think calmly on this matter. You must excuse my emotion. I never thought to have been moved, as I am, by anything human."

"I can readily excuse you," said Mr. Anderson, "for I have myself made as mad and outrageous an attempt to save Rowland Percy as could be well imagined."

Dick Palmer walked on for some moments in silence, then, in a voice of deep emotion, he said:

"Sir, remember me to Miranda. You have always been very kind and good to her, but it would be some solace to me should you allow me to have a share in contributing to her comforts."

"Do not think of that," replied Mr. Anderson; "while I have a home, she shall have one. I fear, however, that she will not long require assistance or kindness from anyone. A most remarkable change has already taken place in her. I have the very worst fears on her account."

"God of Heaven!" exclaimed Palmer. "Can it be possible that one innocent life is to be taken, and an innocent heart broken, without some interposition of Thy mercy?"

"Hush, my friend—hush!" cried Mr. Anderson. "Let us not call into question the decrees of Heaven."

"Farewell—farewell. Will you do me one favour?"

"Yes, certainly."

"Mention me, then, to Miranda, and ask her to see me, if it is but for a minute, some time to-morrow. I wish to take leave of her. It will, in all human likelihood, be for ever."

"I will faithfully carry your message. Farewell."

At this moment a man touched Palmer on the shoulder.

Turning hastily, he saw Jones.

"Well, Dicky," said the latter, "what's the verdict? Is there to be never sich a blessed row to-morrow, or isn't there, eh?"

"There is no chance, Jones."

"Well, that's what I said; but I didn't want to throw a lot of cold water slap in your face. The game's up, and all we can do is to pray—I mean swear."

"Good-night to you both," said Mr. Anderson, "and accept from me my sincere thanks for what you have done for Rowland Percy and Miranda. Never hesitate about applying to me in any difficulty. I shall always be happy to see you, or hear of you."

"Wery much obligated," said Jones. "Just you tell Miss Miranda, from me, not to mind nothink, but to hold out like a brick, bless her."

"Alas! poor girl, she is dying."

"What — croak — croaking? You don't mean that? Come along, Dicky—he's a gammoning on us. Why, veres her ekal, I should like to know? I—I—somebody must have blowed some snuff in my eye—that's uncommon plain."

"Your good feelings, Jones," said Dick Palmer, mournfully, "bring a tear of sympathy to your eye."

"My good feelings be bothered. Don't go for to insinuate as I'm *guv to blubbering.* Don't insult me, Dicky. Call me a hass at once, will yer?"

The contortions of countenance which Jones made to conceal his emotion while he spoke, would have excited laughter under any other than the present mournful circumstances; but his audience were not in a laughing vein, and, after another brief adieu, Mr. Anderson went sorrowfully home.

"Alas!" he thought, "poor, poor Miranda, I have but small comfort to bring you. Oh, what a day will be to-morrow."

As for Jones and Palmer, they both repaired to a tavern, where they determined to remain till the morning came, that morning on which so fearful a tragedy was to be enacted.

* * * *

While these proceedings, so unsatisfactory in their result, were proceeding outside the walls of the prison, how frightfully and fearfully passed the hours to poor Rowland in the condemned cell, from which he so soon would be dragged to suffer a painful and ignominious death.

He knew not whether to wish the time between then and the fatal morning prolonged or shortened.

At one moment he would wish that all was over—at another he felt that wild, painful clinging to life, which will, however its manifestations may be smothered, come over the boldest spirits at such times.

And then, in the midst of all, he thought of Miranda; and what a world of agony was now concentrated in the mention of her very name to his own heart.

The wish to commit suicide, too, as hour after hour slowly winged its weary flight, came stronger and stronger upon him, until at length it assumed all the force of an awful and fixed determination.

He sat down, and leaned his head upon his hands on the table that had been placed in his cell, and he strove to concentrate all his thoughts upon the means he should adopt to get some weapon into his hands which should enable him to carry into effect his frightful purpose.

He thought if he asked for food, they would surely bring it to him; and that, if he seemed calm and resigned, they might trust him with a knife.

One moment of such a possession, and what was to hinder him from plunging it into his heart.

"Yes," he thought, "they shall have a barren triumph over me. I will not be dragged to the death that is preparing. They may say that I was hunted, goaded to destruction—that I was persecuted, until I laid violent hands upon myself; but the deep malice—the awful villainy that would make me die upon a scaffold, shall, if possible, be foiled."

He then rose, and in a perfectly calm voice, said to one of the men who had been placed in his cell:

"Can I have food?"

"Yes," was the reply. "You can have any food you like, and drink, too, in moderation."

"I wish, then, for some meat and bread, and water."

One of the men immediately left the cell to procure what was required, while Rowland could see that the other—who was by far the more athletic of the two—kept a watchful eye upon his movements.

Some time elapsed before the other returned—nearly half-an-hour, in fact.

When he did, he brought a tray with him, on which was meat, bread, cheese, some porter, and one fork—but no knife.

"How am I to manage," said Rowland, in as calm a tone as he could assume, "without a knife?"

"Knives are not allowed," was the reply. "You will find your meat cut up, and it is presumed you can help yourself to the cheese."

A pang of disappointment came over Rowland's heart, and he looked despairingly at the victuals.

Then he thought:

"Surely the prongs of a fork will reach deeply enough to find my heart. I may disappoint them yet."

He looked warily around him.

The two men were both watching him intently, and he found it necessary to take some of the food, in order, if possible, to throw them off their guard.

It was sorely against his inclination; but he swallowed a mouthful or two, and then took firm hold of the fork.

He uttered but one word — that was Miranda—and raising his arm, made a stab at his own breast.

The officers saw the movement, and threw themselves upon him in a moment.

He was uninjured, for the fork had been turned aside by a button of his clothing, and had only torn the skin of his side.

CHAPTER CLXXI.

THE MORNING OF THE EXECUTION—A SHORT RESPITE FROM SUFFERING—ROWLAND IN HIS CELL.

AFTER his attempt at self-destruction, Rowland had quite given himself up to despair. He would speak to no one. Even the Governor, who had shown so much sympathy for him, could only get a few words from him, and they contained a complaint of how much those who had lent themselves to his persecution increased the pangs even of death, by preventing him from breathing to Miranda a few last parting words.

This the Governor thought a needless aggravation of the prisoner's punishment, and an utterly needless precaution; for what other plan of escape for Rowland could Miranda possibly devise than the one which had already once proved so successful, and the very fact that it had been so successful, was quite sufficient to prevent it from being so again.

After turning the matter over in his own mind, the Governor resolved upon taking a step which, although it might throw some responsibility, and, possibly, some blame upon his own shoulders, would tend to give him the after reflection of having soothed some pangs, and possibly smoothed the passage of a fellow creature to the grave. That step was to invite Miranda Rankley to the prison as his guest, and so permit her, at a very early hour in the morning, to have an interview with Rowland Percy out of his cell.

With this object, about four o'clock in the morning, he sent a messenger to Mr. Anderson to say that the Governor wished to see him, a message which Mr. Anderson was by no means remiss in paying attention to, for he accompanied the messenger back again, hoping, and yet hardly daring to expect any communication which should hold out a ray of hope to the condemned prisoner.

He then learned at once what was the humane proposition of the Governor, and, warmly thanking him, he immediately returned home to awaken Miranda, and convey her to the prison.

Mrs. Anderson, at the request of her husband, immediately repaired to the chamber where Miranda had been persuaded to lie down for a brief space, and endeavour to obtain some rest.

This the gentle girl had done to please her kind friends, although she herself despaired of snatching one moment of repose while such harrowing thoughts as those that now possessed her were running riot in her brain.

Mrs. Anderson returned in a few minutes, and when her husband said, in a low tone, "Is she coming?" Mrs. Anderson could not speak; but sitting down in the first chair that presented itself, burst into a flood of tears.

"What has happened? Gracious Heavens! what has happened to Miranda?" cried Mr. Anderson.

"Hush! hush!—nothing," was the reply; "but I could not awaken her; she is sleeping soundly, and there is a smile upon her face as if God had granted to her at this sad time some pleasant images in slumber to cheat reality for a brief space of its abounding terrors. Oh, such a smile—so beautiful—so full of innocence—of purity—of joy. I could not awaken her. Indeed, I could not."

Mr. Anderson turned aside to hide his own emotion, and it was some moments before he could say:

"Let her sleep—let her sleep; if she is happy in that slumber, Heaven forbid that we should disturb it."

Mrs. Anderson then went and sat down by Miranda's bedside, resolved to wait until she should awaken from the temporary oblivion of sorrow that had so sweetly crept over her.

It was strange that at that very time a slumber should have stolen upon Rowland Percy, and that the visions which visited his sleep should be even as Miranda's were, bright, beautiful, and full of joy; but such was the fact, and at the very same time that Mrs. Anderson was watching by the couch of Miranda, the two men who had charge of Rowland Percy in the condemned cell, were looking on in silent wonder at the calm and joyous expression of his face while sleeping, and the bright smiles that occasionally, like sweet sunlight, broke over his features.

Oh! it was great and merciful of Heaven to grant such a respite to human suffering—to step between the criminal and the scaffold at the eleventh hour, and soothe his wounded spirit with beams of joy and Heavenly love. What to Rowland Percy and Miranda were then the frowns of a too bitter fortune?—what to them, while this sweet oblivion lasted, was the present with all its terrors?—a dream—a fleeting phantasy; but, alas! the time of awakening was at hand, and then what a revulsion of feeling would ensue. Could reason stand the shock? Would the pulses of life still beat, with such an awful prospect before them?

Four o'clock had come and gone. Then five, then six, and then—yes, then Rowland Percy awoke, with the name of Miranda upon his lips.

He sprang at once to his feet, and, for the space of about three fleeting moments, the truth of his awful position came not before him; when it did, with one short, sharp cry of mental agony, he sank down again, and buried his face in his hands, leaving his two guards gazing at each other in silent wonder and trembling terror.

They then whispered to each other, for it was a relief to them to hear their own voices.

A gleam of sunlight streamed through a narrow grating into the condemned cell, and one of the men extinguished the lamp that had been burning all the weary night long, saying to his companion, in a suppressed tone:

"It is morning, now. Our task will soon be over, and I don't care how soon."

The sunlight fell upon Rowland Percy's face, and again he sprang to his feet, saying:

"The time—the time? What is the time? Tell me, am I to be sacrificed, soon, innocent as I am, or have I yet a little space to commend myself, in my own fashion, to my Maker?"

CHAPTER CLXXII.

THE CHAPLAIN—MIRANDA'S APPEAL TO THE GOVERNOR—THE THREAT—THE INTERVIEW IN THE COMMON-ROOM.

MRS. ANDERSON kept her lonely watch by the bedside of Miranda for some time, and it was only when, upon gently rising to leave the room a moment, in order to consult with Mr. Anderson upon the propriety of awakening her, that a slight accidental movement of the chair upon which she had been sitting, aroused the sufferer from the sleep that had so beneficently come over her, and Miranda, with the same winning expression of joy she had worn in her sleep, gently unclosed her eyes.

Oh, how strange and awful, then, was the change that gradually swept over those beautiful features. It seemed as if, in the course of one minute, the usual work of years was being produced upon a human face.

Then she pressed her hands upon her heart, and said, in a tone of such exquisite mournfulness, that it brought tears again to the eyes of Mrs. Anderson:

"Oh, why did I awaken — why did I awaken? If that sleep had been the sleep of death, I might have been happy. Rowland—Rowland!"

"Hush! hush! For the love of Heaven!" cried Mrs. Anderson, "arm yourself with fortitude and calmness. Life itself is but a fleeting shadow. While it lasts, let us trust to God and His decrees."

"I—I will try. Rowland — Rowland — what are your thoughts now? I—I—the time—the time?"

She eagerly examined a watch that was close at hand.

It was half-past six.

Then she rose, and, without another word, she commenced rapidly replacing the few articles of dress she had taken off before lying down on the bed.

"My dear Miranda," said Mrs. Anderson, "let me implore of you to remain here."

"Remain here!" cried Miranda, in a strange, unnatural voice. "Remain here while Rowland Percy is being murdered. No—no! I dare not!"

"But — think again. You cannot save him."

"No. But I can still raise my voice against the frightful deed. I have still strength left to denounce those who, in cold blood, will take the life they cannot give. Oh! I will cry aloud to Heaven for justice! I want no mercy—no consideration—no miracle to make me more than grateful. No, I want justice—justice! Now I am ready. Let me go forth."

"Oh! where—where?"

"To the execution. You see I can pronounce the word. I am going to see the execution of—of—Rowland Percy, my betrothed husband. The innocent Rowland Percy, who is going to be gravely and calmly murdered, with all pomp and ceremony, by his fellow-men. Yes, God help me! I am going to the execution."

There was a wild vehemence about her manner that gave poor Mrs. Anderson the worst fears on account of her reason, and she hurried from the room to seek her husband, in order to implore his interposition to prevent Miranda from leaving the house in such a frame of mind as she appeared to be in.

"Hush! hush!" replied Mr. Anderson. "I will take charge of her. For the love of Heaven, let her go where she likes—do what she likes. I would not thwart her for worlds now. Where is she?"

"Here," said Miranda, entering the room. "You see I am very calm. I have had a dream. I thought Rowland and I stood upon the terrace steps of the Grange, and that he called me his wife, while a voice rang through the sunny air, saying, 'He is free—he is free!' but that is a delusion, for it was but a dream."

She shuddered a moment, and Mr. Anderson thought she would have fallen, but, by a great effort, she recovered herself, and, in a low, agonized voice, said:

"To the execution. Yes, to the execution. We—we shall be late."

"Miranda," said Mr. Anderson, "be calm. You shall go with me, and once more see Rowland Percy. Exert all your fortitude for this day, I pray you."

"I—am—calm," she said, "very calm - who would be so calm as I when all they loved on earth was being murdered? I tell you, since my poor father's death, such have been the horrors that have surrounded me—horrors, mind you—not mere griefs—that I have not shed a tear. I could not weep. Let sympathies and ordinary evils draw tears from tender eyes. My griefs lie deeper. Would that I could weep, but I cannot—I shall never weep again."

Suddenly, then, Miranda pointed to the window, past which hundreds of persons, who had arrived from all parts of the country, were hurrying, to be present at the execution.

She guessed the cause of the unusual throng, and said, in a hoarse whisper:

"See—see. They are all going to see Rowland murdered, and I am lingering here. Late—late—late."

She walked hurriedly to the door, and Mr. Anderson lost no time in following her.

In another moment they were in the street, and Mr. Anderson was on the point of turning out of the main thoroughfare, and proceeding by a less frequented route to the prison, when his progress was suddenly arrested by Jones, who stepped up to Miranda, and, taking off his hat, said, in a voice so different from its usual wild recklessness, that no one would have recognized him by it, even had they known him well:

"God bless you, Miss Miranda—God bless—bear up against it all. I—I—don't know what to say—because—because, you see—I can't see at all, somehow. God bless you, and good-bye!"

"My kind friend," said Miranda, "we shall yet meet again in Heaven—in Heaven—farewell. The blessing of God be upon you for all you have done for the innocent and persecuted!"

She held out her hand, and Jones took the small, taper fingers in his for a moment.

Then he dashed his hat on his head with a vehemence that sent it down over his eyes, and darted off.

"I am glad I have seen him," muttered Miranda, in a low tone, to herself, "before I die."

Mr. Anderson caught the last words, and said:

"I beseech—implore you to think more resignedly."

"I cannot help it," she replied. "Would you have me long outlive *him* who is to be sacrificed this morning? Ah, no! And yet understand; Heaven shall do its own work, I contemplate no unholy act. No—no. Oh, God! let it be soon; but I will go only with Thy warrant for my going."

The throng of persons now became so very great that Mr. Anderson found it extremely difficult to proceed with his charge, and, to add to his perplexity, he had been in constant dread ever since leaving his own door that someone might recognize Miranda, and turn the attention of the crowd upon her, which, whether sympathetic or not, could not be otherwise than distressing.

The time seemed passing rapidly, for before they reached a side entrance to the Governor's house, seven o'clock boomed forth from the sonorous bell of the Minster.

"Hark! hark!" cried Miranda.

"'Tis only seven."

"Only seven!" she repeated, with a shudder. "On—on. Oh, shall I yet see him, to tell him we shall meet soon again! Only seven! Another fleeting hour, and then!—oh, Heaven! support me, now!"

She hung heavily upon Mr. Anderson's arm, and they were close to the Governor's house, when a sudden movement took place in the crowd, and, pale and disfigured from the punishment he had received from Jones, Bernard Varley opposed Miranda's further progress.

She shrank back with a half shriek, as if the spirit of all evil stood before her.

Varley raised his hands, and at first Miranda thought he was going to touch her; but it was only to give urgency and force to the words he was about to utter—words which came with an awful quickness and energy from his lips, while his whole frame seemed convulsed with contending emotions as he uttered them.

"Miranda Rankley," he said, "once for all—for the last time, hear me!—I conjure you to hear me! Even yet—even with the fatal noose round his neck, while the last words of those about him are ringing in his ears, and the funeral knell is tolling, Rowland Percy may be saved—yes, saved—to life—to you—to joy!"

"Hence, monster! hence!" said Miranda.

She attempted to draw Mr. Anderson away; but he felt too much interested in Varley's words to move, and he cried in a voice of anger:

"Bernard Varley, man or fiend, say what you have just now said in the presence of the authorities of York, and Rowland Percy will not die this morning. Oh, if you do, indeed, repent of the false evidence you have given—that false evidence upon which a fellow-creature is at this moment trembling on the verge of an awful doom—save him, oh, save him, and lay up in Heaven one action that will plead trumpet-tongued for you at the throne of Grace."

Varley waved his arm, as if, by that one action, he threw aside all that Mr. Anderson had said, and then, again addressing Miranda, he said:

"Be mine, and he is saved."

She made no reply to Varley; but, in a low voice, said to Mr. Anderson:

"Come—come—oh, come. Time is flying fast. Come, I implore you."

"But—but—this fiend. He as good as declares his own villainy. How else than by a crimination of himself, such as must bring the vengeance of the law upon him, can he save Rowland Percy. Hear me, Varley. Let me tell you——"

"Peace!" thundered Varley. "I address no discourse to you. I ask you for no remarks upon my words. To you, Miranda Rankley—beautiful being—shrine of an angel spirit—divinity—miracle of earth, to you I sue. Be mine, and Rowland Percy is saved."

A solemn boom from a bell announced, at this moment, that preparations were actually commencing for the execution.

The sound seemed to cut into Miranda's heart, as if some deadly weapon had been suddenly plunged into it.

A half-suppressed cry escaped her lips, and clasping her hands, she said:

"Mr. Anderson, I go alone, or with you at once. I cannot—dare not delay. The execution!"

"May yet be stayed," said Varley, frantically. "Miranda, I plead as much for Rowland Percy—ay, more than for myself."

"Murderer!" said Miranda, and she passed on, while a wondering throng, attracted by his words and violent gestures, was beginning to collect, although, as it happened, those who were passing at the time, knew not personally any of the parties.

Then Bernard Varley, after all his persecution of Miranda, reluctantly admitted to himself that his deep-laid schemes had availed him nothing, and the change that came over his features was a more awful one than that which takes the place of vitality, when death has done its work upon a human form.

There was an expression of such utter despair, accompanied by such fiendish malice, that, at his glance around him, the many spectators who had been attracted to the spot, reeled into the roadway, as if surprised by some devilish incarnation.

He then gathered around him the cloak in which he was attired, and gasping out so awful a curse, that we cannot stain our pages with its record, he walked hastily after Miranda and Mr. Anderson.

CHAPTER CLXXIII.

TWITTER ON HIS ROAD TO YORK—THE VAN—A RADICAL REFORMER—THE FELICITATION OF THE GUILTY MAN—YORK.

WHEN Samuel Twitter, after his adventure with the beadle, heard the sound of the Minster bell of York, and found that, despite all his exertions to the contrary, he had been gradually approaching the city which was so dangerous to him, and where he expected, the moment he had set foot in it, to be apprehended upon his own confession, such a tremor came over him that, had his life, at that moment, depended upon proceeding half-a-dozen steps, he could not have done so, but must have met any death that anyone chose to subject him to.

His eyes became dim—a confused singing in his ears mingled strangely with the sound of the Minster bell, and he fell heavily to the ground, not quite insensible, but sufficiently so as to have but a very slight consciousness of where he was, or what had occurred to him.

His miserable-looking condition arrested the attention of several chance passengers, and they gathered round him as people do round any object of more than common-looking misery, to speculate upon what could have reduced a man to so awful a state.

Samuel Twitter was never, at the best of times, a healthy-looking mortal.

He always had, even when well-fed and well-lodged at the Grange, a strange, clammy, unwholesome look; but, now that he was suffering from want of food—now that mental anxiety had made deep ravages in his appearance, and his clothing was in tatters, while several long scratches upon his face and hands showed evidences of falls or squabbles, he did, indeed, look the very picture of wretchedness.

"Well," exclaimed one person, "I never did see anyone so thoroughly done up."

"Poor wretch!" remarked another, as he put his hand in his pocket, intending to give Twitter a halfpenny; but, finding nothing less than a penny, abandoned his benevolent project.

"It's a take-in," said a fat man, in a half-clerical costume. "Never encourage beggars—and—and then, you see, you will have no destitution, because it won't be worth while to beg, you see. I never give away anything."

"Mercy—mercy!" moaned Twitter.

The people shrank back a little, and looked at each other.

"I am starving," added Twitter, "starving. Oh, save me from death, and—and from York!"

"What does he say?" inquired one.

"He says he's going to York. Who'll give him a helping hand?"

"Here's my penny to begin with."

"Oh," cried several, "we have no change."

"And I shall be too late for the execution," cried one, "which I wouldn't miss for a crown piece. I've seen, do you know, every execution that has taken place for the last fifteen years in the county. I've got a piece of the rope that the celebrated Maggs was hung with. I've got one of Larkins', the murderer's, eye teeth. I wouldn't be late for a crown."

Twitter felt the cold pressure of a penny piece in the palm of his hand, and he looked down sorrowfully upon it, as he muttered:

"Bread—bread—I am starving!"

"Oh, you are a horrid-looking wretch," said a fat woman, who had bustled through the throng; "and I daresay you are no better than you should be, or you would have somebody to give you a helping hand. Howsomdever, drink some of this rum and milk."

She placed a bottle in Twitter's hands, and he drank greedily of the contents.

With each drop his strength revived, and by the time he had consumed half the contents of the bottle, he was able to look about him a little more confidently, and to wonder what had brought so many people out on to the highway, at so uncommonly early an hour of the morning.

"Thank you," he said. "I am much better. What is the meaning of all this? Where—what has happened? Let me go now. How far am I from York?"

"Not very far," cried a man; "and if you must know where we is a-going, why, we is a-going all for to see the hanging as is to be."

"Hanging—hanging?"

"Yes, to be sure."

"And you look," remarked one, "as if you'd been hung and cut down again."

A laugh from the crowd proclaimed its appreciation of this brilliant stroke of wit at Twitter's expense, and some of the people began to move off. In fact, the interest was fast diminishing, for Twitter was manifestly better. The rum-and-milk had done wonders.

"Tell me—for the love of Heaven, some of you tell me who is to be hanged?"

"Why, the murderer, to be sure."

"At—at York, say you, and this morning?"

"Yes—yes."

"His name; is—is it Varley?"

"No. Varley?—oh, no. Rowland Percy, that has led the officers such a dance after him. It will be a famous hanging."

Twitter passed his hand over his face several times, as he muttered to himself:

"Perhaps I am dreaming, after all. Rowland Percy hanged this morning at York—Rowland Percy! What—what has become of my written confession? Am I, after all, safe? Has it got lost, destroyed, or is no credence given to it? Rowland Percy, too, why—why, but a few days since and no one knew where he was. I am surely dreaming, or mad."

"What's the matter now?" cried one. "I tell you what, old chap, if you are going to York, I don't mind giving you a lift in my van. Come on."

"A hanging," said Twitter—"are you sure there is a hanging at York?"

"Sure enough. They have caught young Percy that murdered Sir George—what's his name?—a good while ago now, and they are going to hang him at last."

A dawn of hope began to brighten in Twitter's mind that, after all, he might be safe.

He felt certain that his communication to the Mayor of York must have reached its destination, if all had gone smoothly in its transit, long ere that hour; and, therefore, if Rowland Percy was about to be hanged, it must either have miscarried, or been received, and disregarded. One of those propositions must be the case. There was hope. Even yet, despite all his miseries and distresses, he might succeed in saving himself from the horrors of utter destitution by wringing a sum of money from Bernard Varley, with which he might leave England openly and promptly.

"If," he thought, "Rowland Percy is being hanged this morning at York, there is Bernard Varley—yes, of a surety, he will be there. I can see him, and, by threats, get money from him, he knowing nothing of the contents of my confession, or of the fact that I have made such an attempt at his destruction—an attempt which has so inexplicably failed, too. The letter must be lost. Yes, I am safe—safe for a time. In a few days it may be found. It may reach at last its destination, and still ruin Varley—still bring him to the scaffold; but, ere then, I may be far away and safe. I will—at least I think I will, go to York. Yes—yes, I will venture, and yet 'tis scarcely a venture—I am determined."

These thoughts passed much more rapidly through the mind of Samuel Twitter than one can read them, so that there was scarcely a perceptible delay between the offer of the man who had the van to give Twitter a lift, ere the latter replied:

"I shall thank, and be able, too, to pay you, when we reach York, for there is one there who will immediately supply me with money."

"Very well, jump in."

"But—but you are quite sure it is Rowland Percy who is to be hanged?"

"Oh, quite."

"And you have heard nothing to the contrary, no hint, no whisper of any circumstance having occurred to stay the execution—no doubt upon the subject, no surmise of any other person's guilt?"

"I'll be hanged if I can understand you," said the man. "Here's the van. I'm a-going to York to see the hanging. If you're a-going to get in, get in; if you ain't, don't."

"Yes—yes, I am—thank you, I am. Rowland Percy it is who is to be hanged?"

Twitter said these words aloud as he scrambled into the van in hopes of receiving an additional confirmation of them from the parties who were already in the vehicle, and he was not disappointed, for several said, "Yes, to be sure;" and one man, with an argumentative air, added:

"Look here; this here Rowland Percy ought to have been hanged ever so long ago; and I means for to say, a more out-and-out villain nor he is, isn't. 'Cos why?—that's the reason. There's reason in roastin' eggs, as my missus says. He puts hisself afore honest people as wants to yarn a honest penny—how—'cos why? Last time as he was to be hanged, I got up his dyin' speech and confession. Well, what does he do?—he breaks out o' quod; in course, the dyin' speech and the confession ain't no go, no how, and I gets precious well bonneted by the mob; 'cos why?

THE BIGOTED CHAPLAIN IS HORRIFIED AT THE CONDUCT OF MIRANDA.

—he'd got away. There's a wretch for you. Well, now he's a-going to be really hanged, and I'm a-going with this here bundle o' last dyin' speeches and confessions to try my luck; and all I means to say is this here—if, mind, he ain't hanged now, hang me!"

The people in the van appeared to think this very conclusive indeed, and not one seemed to imagine that there was the slightest incongruity in having the last dying speech and confession ready beforehand.

One woman, indeed, said:

"Oh, it's always the way. Poor people is never let earn a honest penny."

"That's true," exclaimed the argumentative vendor of last dying speeches and confessions. "It's all along o' the *anstickocracy* as grinds the poor. Is we freemen, or isn't we? No.—Has we our rights, or hasn't we? No.—Is we Englishmen? Yes.—Is we slaves. Rather. My opinion is down with everythink, and up with nothink! Hurrah! bonfires and bonneting for ever! Down with property, and divide it ekal. Let me ax who am I?—a Briton. Well, there's the consekence. I ain't well off. Why?—'cos I hasn't the rekisite tin. Well, somebody else has. Take it from him, guv it to them as hasn't; that's what I calls radical reform, and the only vun as will please the people. I knows it, and I says it, and 1 ends where 1 begins—down with everythink, and let's have a scramble."

The distance to York was not great, and in a very short time the suburbs of the ancient city were gained.

The progress of the van then became slow, on account of the vast throngs of people that were hurrying to the place of execution, and Samuel Twitter had the satisfaction of hearing from many mouths assurances of the, to him, gratifying fact that it was poor Rowland Percy who was about to be hanged for the crime he had never committed.

The spirits of the villain began to rise as he found himself in the streets of York, without hearing the least allusion to himself, or any doubt suggested by anyone of Rowland's guilt. He began to feel quite convinced that he was safe, and that, by some singular accident which would in time develop itself, his confession had never reached the Mayor of York.

The mind has an immense influence on the body, and Twitter looked so much better after he had succeeded in shaking off the horrible fears that had harassed him, that he looked quite a different creature, and began to gaze about him at the well-known buildings of York with feelings of satisfaction, instead of dismay, that he had been, by such a series of strange circumstances, brought there again, so contrary to all his expectations.

CHAPTER CLXXIV.

THE PRISON CHAPLAIN—THE LAST INTERVIEW—THE QUARREL AND THE THREAT—THE CROWD AND THE EXECUTIONER.

BERNARD VARLEY'S notion, when Miranda so abruptly, and with such evidences of abhorrence, left him, was to follow her, and, if possible (for his was a disposition in which hate held as high a place as the passion he dignified by the name of love), add to the painful mental sensations she must be experiencing, all the additional pangs he could in his base nature invent.

With this view, he quickened his steps, and would have carried his passionate resolve into effect, had he not observed Dick Palmer suddenly come from among the crowd and fix his eyes upon him with an expression that taught him (Varley) to think there might be absolute personal danger in pushing his resentment too far, for he recollected the severe punishment he had received from Jones, and he doubted not that Dick was quite ready to bestow a similar dose upon him.

As for Jones, he resolved, if he should see him after the execution, to give him into immediate custody, and prosecute him with relentless rigour. Before, however, Rowland Percy should be a dead man, Bernard Varley smothered all his pettier resentments, and resolved that nothing should withdraw him from seeing the sentence of the law carried into effect upon the man who had stood between him and his dearest hopes.

He was vain enough to think that, had Miranda never known Rowland Percy, he might have moved her heart to love for himself, as if it was necessary that she should, failing to bestow her heart upon one endowed with every manly quality she had ever held in estimation, give it to one whom she had always looked upon with a dislike amounting to absolute abhorrence.

Palmer, too, Bernard Varley resolved should find that he had brought upon himself vengeance. After the execution he fully intended to have him apprehended, offering ample rewards to all parties who could prefer charges against him in addition to that of his escape from Newgate; but such was Varley's terror lest some popular riot should yet save Rowland Percy, that now, although he saw Dick, he shrank from him, and gave no alarm whatever, nursing his vengeance until a more fitting opportunity.

The delay which had taken place in Miranda's route to the prison had fearfully dipped into that hour which appeared destined to be the last of poor persecuted Rowland Percy's existence; and when she, with Mr. Anderson, stood upon the stone steps of the Governor's house, it was not far from being half-past seven.

"Oh, let us hasten," said Miranda—" let us hasten. He will think himself at this, the last hour, deserted alike by earth and by Heaven. Let us hasten!"

The Governor had given orders to admit Mr. Anderson and Miranda, and he had been not a little surprised at their non-arrival.

He had, in fact, begun to think that something must have befallen Miranda, to prevent her appearance. She might actually have sunk under her severe griefs; and when seven o'clock came, and the awful preparations for the death of the unhappy man were nearly completed, without one person coming to bid him a last adieu, the humane Governor had himself gone to Rowland's cell to say some words of comfort to him, and to ask him if there was anything he could do that would give him any satisfaction in his last moments.

It was only a voice of so much kindness as that in which the Governor addressed him that could get a response from Rowland Percy; but, even in those awful moments that were swiftly intervening between him and a death he so little deserved, he could not be insensible to such sympathy as was thus voluntarily offered to him.

"I thank you," he said, sadly. " I am much beholden to your kindness. You have done all that you possibly could do to alleviate the wretchedness of a condition little susceptible of any alleviation whatever."

"Have you any request to make that can be attended to? Be assured that your wishes shall be to me sacred commands."

"Only one," replied Rowland, with emotion. "Tell Miranda that her name hovered on my lips when I was leaving life, and that my last, my only prayer, was for her."

"I will."

"I have been fearfully wronged. I am as innocent as you are of the crime imputed to me. Therefore, the strong urging to confess my guilt, on the part of the chaplain, has become to me insulting. He likewise has tormented me with set prayers, which, with badly-composed hymns, he wishes me continually to be repeating and singing. It is the will of God that I should be placed in the position I occupy now, and I cannot help it; but it would be the grossest hypocrisy of me to say I am resigned to my fate, when God knows I am not."

"Do you forgive those who have brought you to this sad end?" said the Governor.

"To forgive is divine," said Percy. "I am human."

"I regret I cannot help you. I believe, now, there is indeed no hope. God bless you in a world to come. It is not, as you know, with my sanction that the chaplain has been let loose upon you. He and I before have had serious disagreements on your account, and, in fact, it was only by the interposition of the magistracy that I consented to retain my situation while he retained his."

"I know you are free from the faults I find in the chaplain," said Rowland. "Once more accept the heartfelt thanks of one standing, as I am, on the threshold of eternity. I—I would fain once again have looked upon Miranda's face. Surely, it was a needless cruelty to prevent me."

"I hope you will see her yet, and you shall, if I can so manage it. I have sent for her on my own responsibility, and believe she will soon be here."

Rowland Percy wrung the hand of the Governor, as he said, with much emotion:

"You are a true friend. God bless you, sir."

The Governor was now informed that the sheriff had arrived, and that his presence was immediately required; upon which he left the condemned cell, in order to act according to his painful duty in the solemn arrangements that were in progress.

The two men still remained with Rowland in his cell; and, perhaps, the greatest aggravation of his imprisonment had been the fact that he was constantly watched so closely.

He now turned his back to them, and sat down, giving himself up to a review of his past life, interspersed with such bitter gushes of anguish as could not fail to attack the mind of one so young, condemned to an awful and degrading death upon false testimony.

Let none of our readers blame Rowland Percy for want of religious fervour in the awful moments preceding his expected execution. He was no bigot, nor had he been brought up with any doubts or fears of Heaven's goodness. He was one who had tried, through life, to do right. If he had, in some instances, failed, his failures were errors, not wilful wickednesses. All, therefore, he would have asked of Heaven, had he not deemed it impious to ask what could not be doubted, would have been justice. Consequently, he refused to subscribe to the fact implied by the clergyman, that he was a miserable sinner, deserving of everlasting torture, and only to be saved by howling appeals for mercy—psalm-singing, and wild rhapsodies, without force or reason, in the shape of prayer.

Rowland considered that

"He prayeth best who loveth best
All things both great and small,"

and having a conscience uncorrupted by wrong or injustice, he had no qualms about the future, and in his reliance upon the justice of the Almighty, he refused to listen to those persons who would

"Ring the Gospel gong in both his ears,
And, if he feared not, fill him full of fears."

* * * *

"Well, Mr. Governor," said the sheriff, "this is a painful duty we have to perform; but, thank Heaven, we are only portions of the executive in this case. I would not have been on the jury for a great deal of money, for I really have serious doubts as to this young man's guilt."

"And so have I."

It was at this moment that Miranda and Mr. Anderson arrived at the prison, and were announced by name to the Governor by one of the under-turnkeys.

"Admit them instantly," he said, and then turning to the sheriff, he added, "There can scarcely be an objection now to an interview between Miss Rankley and the prisoner."

"Do what you please," said the sheriff, "till eight o'clock. I will see nothing."

CHAPTER CLXXV.

HALF-PAST SEVEN—VARLEY'S ADMISSION TO THE PRISON—THE IDIOT AND THE CROWD—THE FUNERAL KNELL.

In a few moments Miranda was introduced into the room where were the sheriff and the Governor.

It was a small apartment, connecting the private rooms of the Governor with the other portion of the building, and went by the name of the common room, owing to its being made usually a waiting-room for parties coming with messages to the Governor.

Miranda had scarcely entered, and been kindly handed to a seat by the sheriff—who, despite his resolve to see nothing, had too much of the gentleman in him to be uncourteous — when the chaplain made his appearance by another door, fully attired in his canonicals.

He stood near the door by which he had entered, and it would seem as if he was on good terms with neither the sheriff nor the Governor, the latter of whom immediately approached Miranda, saying:

"You shall see him. I will have him brought here to you in a few minutes."

Miranda did not speak; but she looked up in the Governor's face with a thankful expression, combined with such an appearance of suffering, that it smote him to the heart.

"God help you!" he said, fervently.

"Amen!" was all Miranda could reply, and in a tone so different from that in which she usually spoke, that even Mr. Anderson started, and could hardly tell whether it was from her lips that the word had proceeded.

"If," said the sheriff, "the unhappy prisoner is innocent, Heaven have mercy on us all, and on his accusers!"

Miranda shuddered, and moaned audibly.

She had not the spirit to speak now; she could only suffer.

Here the chaplain advanced, and, standing a few paces from Miranda, said, in a nasal tone:

"Misguided young woman, if you have come to this prison-house to see the grievous sinner who is about to be launched into eternity, in order to fill his awfully sinful mind with yearnings for life, and things that belong to the earth, earthly, I tell you to be gone—avaunt! If you come to withdraw the mind of a wretched man from a contemplation of the awful original sin in which he was born, and for which he must suffer, except through atonement and everlasting torments, I again say avaunt! Get thee hence, agent of Satan—get behind me."

"Who is this man?" said Miranda, "who thus insults misfortune, and steps between Heaven and its creatures with such hideous denunciations?"

"This man," said the Governor, "is an intolerant bigot, whom I will at once remove from the room, if he dare address you contrary to your wishes."

"You dare not," cried the chaplain, turning most unchristianly angry. "I say you dare not. For your place, you dare not. It is my duty to attend upon criminals in this prison, and I insist upon being permitted to do so."

"You know me sufficiently," remarked the former, "to be aware, by this time, that considerations connected with what you call my place, would not prevent me from kicking you into the street, and you ought to know, if you do not, that, although you are paid for attending to the spiritual wants of prisoners, you have no right to force your presence or your doctrines upon anyone."

"You will hear of this in another place," said the chaplain. "I will make you repent of this."

"Hear him. How very meek and Christianlike is this holy man. He can, however, condescend to threaten. It is sufficient that Rowland Percy refuses your ministrations, and as for this young lady, she is my guest, and I will not have her annoyed by you."

The chaplain was in a great passion; but he seemed, at all events, to think discretion the better part of valour, for he no longer confronted Miranda; but, walking to the window put up an extemporaneous prayer, in which he begged he might not be made too proud, in consequence of the assurance he felt that he was one of what he called the elect, and hoped the Governor of the prison and Miranda Rankley might—albeit they were scoffers and mockers, and dared to use the reason God had given them in matters of belief—be saved from fire everlasting.

The prayer was couched in a form, and uttered in a tone which implied a strong conviction that it was of no use at all, and that Miranda and the Governor would both be burnt for ever, which we may fairly presume was a great consolation to the chaplain.

The same door by which the chaplain had entered the room was now opened, and preceded by one turnkey, while he was closely followed by another, Rowland Percy made his melancholy appearance.

Miranda and he saw each other at the same moment. To pronounce each other's names was the first impulse. In another instant she was lying on his bosom, alike indifferent of who was present, or what might be their opinions of her for so acting.

In her own innocence and sweet purity lay her strength.

The Governor and the sheriff were visibly affected.

As for the chaplain, he looked perfectly aghast, and, after lifting up his hands in horror, turned to the Governor, and said, indignantly:

"Do you—dare you allow such awful immorality to take place within these walls?"

"No," said the Governor.

"But look—look—the young woman embraceth the young man who is to be hanged."

"Oh, I don't call that immorality. The immorality lies wholly in your vicious mind, which puts an immoral construction upon the most innocent and pure actions that can be conceived."

"Miranda—my Miranda!" sighed Rowland; "am I, indeed, so blessed, as to see you once again?"

"Yes, Rowland, it is your own Miranda. She who even now would die to save you. Rowland, let me look upon your face. Let me see that you can meet, as a man, and an innocent one, even this misery, as becomes you. Rowland, dear—dear Rowland, dearer now than ever, I shall not be absent from you long. The world and I have done with each other now. Look up, Rowland, and let me see your face again."

"Call upon your Redeemer," said the chaplain. "Do not talk of love here."

"Silence, sir!" cried Miranda; "profane not the holy atmosphere of this place, made beautiful by the presence of guileless hearts. Remember, God hears you even as He hears us."

"My darling Miranda!" said Rowland Percy; "death's pangs will not have half their bitterness. I thought I should not see you again, and that, even now, without a last kind word from your lips, I was being hurried forth to die."

"No, Rowland, no. There are still hearts that feel for us; still voices that will breathe kind words of us when we are both gone. I have prayed to be permitted to follow you soon to that world where no false witness will avail—where an infallible judge is the only judge, and where we shall meet my dear father, too, and you, Rowland. Oh, that I could die to-day—this hour—now, Rowland—this moment—clasped to your breast—held to your heart—in your arms—my Rowland—my affianced husband—dearer to me for all your sufferings—closer to my heart for all your persecutions."

"Oh, this is a foretaste of Heaven," cried Rowland, with a cheerful voice.

"What wretches!" muttered the chaplain.

"You are happier, Rowland. Death is but a fleeting pang—would I could share it with you. And the time will come, too, when your name, in this world, will be rescued from the obloquy cast upon it, and your innocence will be made apparent. I should like to see that day; but still, even for such a triumph, I would not live."

"Nay, Miranda, live on, and if it be permitted for the spirits of those who have gone before to bring a blessing to the earth they have quitted, and breathe soft visions of happiness into the ears of those whom they loved while in life, I will be to you such a minister of joy, waiting, not with impatience, but hope, for the day when we shall meet to part no more."

Miranda led Rowland to the window, and then looked long and anxiously in his face.

Alas! it bore too evident marks of mental pain, and, with a deep sigh, she said:

"Rowland, you have suffered much. Surely your reward will be great."

"I have my reward," he replied. "The brightest, best, highest reward I can have is your love. These few moments, Miranda, repay me for all."

"Then fate, after all, has not succeeded in bowing completely our hearts to its stern decrees," said Miranda. "Rowland, I—I hope that my heart will break to-day."

The chaplain commenced a hymn entirely on his own account, in which nobody joined; then he took out his watch, and told the Governor it only wanted twenty minutes to eight, to which the Governor made no reply, but turned his back upon the chaplain, who then applied to the sheriff, who told him to mind his own business.

"Dearest!" whispered Rowland Percy, "allow me, now, to bid you farewell. Let me implore you to go home immediately with Mr. Anderson—I pray you to do so—now—now."

"Not yet, Rowland—not yet; I—I cannot leave you yet. Surely, they will not drag you from me. I feel strong, and will resist them. Rowland, do not look so sad; they shall not tear you from me."

"Oh, Miranda! Leave me now. As you love me, leave me now."

"No. As I love you, so will I remain.

Let them kill me in wresting you from me—then, and not till then, shall they separate us."

The door of the room was opened, and the Mayor of York made his appearance, arrayed in his robes of office.

Then came several other of the functionaries of the city—sad indices of the lapse of time.

Miranda tightened her grasp of Percy, who looked the living picture of despair.

She gazed around her like one distracted, and, with a voice that was perfectly appalling, said:

"No, no; you cannot—dare not kill him! Why do you all glare at him as if you would make him your prey? Think you he is guilty! Oh, no, you cannot; he never harmed you or yours. It is my father he is accused of killing, and I declare him innocent. Touch him, who dares! God knows he is innocent. You will not murder him? You are men; you have brave hearts, full of human and kindly sympathies. I tell you Rowland Percy is innocent—I swear it—before the Majesty of Heaven I swear it. Save him—save him! Give him to me. Let me take him home. Mercy! mercy! mercy!"

"This is terrible," said the Governor.

"A quarter to eight," said the chaplain.

The Mayor trembled, and turned towards the door, which was on the instant thrown wide open, disclosing two men with white wands, and a third behind them, who carried a coil of rope.

A shriek burst from Miranda's lips, and she twined her arms round Rowland so tightly that it seemed next to impossible to tear him from that wild embrace.

As for Rowland himself, he seemed distracted.

Every vestige of colour had left his cheeks—a dewy moisture stood upon his brow, and all he could do was to lift up his hands, and keep repeating one awful adjuration.

The scene was, indeed, a terrible one—one calculated to live, while life remained, in the memories of all who witnessed it.

Even the chaplain shrank back and looked terrified, while the book he carried dropped from his hands on to the floor of the room.

"It must be done," said the sheriff, in half-choked accents, to the Mayor. "It must be done."

Miranda heard him, and answered by an appalling shriek.

"Help—help!" she cried. "Palmer, is there no help? Off, murderers!—off. You shall not kill him."

She twined her arms still more tightly round the prisoner, and none liked to be the first to raise a hand to tear him from her grasp.

CHAPTER CLXXVI.

TWITTER IN THE CROWD—THE IDIOT—VAR-
LEY'S APPEARANCE AND DANGER—THE
PARTIAL RIOT—VARLEY'S ADMITTANCE TO
THE PRISON.

SAMUEL TWITTER was much relieved by the recent circumstances that had occurred to give his fate an apparently different complexion.

He felt quite certain now that his packet to the Mayor had been lost, and he almost laughed, as he congratulated himself upon the rare accident which had saved him from the evil consequences of his detention in England.

"So much for Providential circumstances," he muttered. "Providence works for me as well as for others. I may as well consider that I am saved by a special interposition, for who would have calculated upon the rare accident of a packet, addressed properly to the Mayor of York, never reaching its destination?"

He then smiled, as the van proceeded through the crowded streets, and he found himself getting comfortably on without the trouble of pushing his way.

Perhaps the full dose of rum-and-milk he had had contributed a little—having been thrown, as it was, upon an empty stomach—to make his reflections of a light-and-lively order; but, be that as it may, certainly Samuel Twitter—considering all things, his peculiar disposition included—never had been in better spirits than on that morning.

By degrees, however, as he neared the place of execution, his natural timidity asserted itself a little, and he began to think he would rather have been in a less conspicuous position than he was, and yet he reasoned with himself:

"Why should I care? I am free; and, moreover, I wish particularly to see Bernard Varley, for from him I must and will procure funds to carry me out of England, and then from some secure foreign land I can send another accusation of him to the proper authorities. What matters it to me that Rowland Percy, innocent though he be, is hanged first? It will not decrease Varley's danger; on the contrary, it will tend to make his crime appear the greater. Let Percy be hanged, then, by all means."

The progress of the van now was exceedingly slow, for the people were so closely wedged together in the principal streets leading to the place of execution, that any attempt to get on quickly would have been resented and unquestionably frustrated by the mob.

As it was, there was much swearing and tumult as the van proceeded, and Samuel Twitter crouched down low in the vehicle in order to escape observation as much as possible, for although he did not think he ran any danger by being seen, yet he thought it might be pleasanter if he were out of sight of the mob, some members of which might recognize him, and confer on him an unenviable notoriety.

At a sudden turning, the scaffold, with all its frightful appendages, came in view, and a cold shiver came over Twitter, as he gasped to himself:

"If—if now that scaffold was erected for me, instead of for him who is to suffer, I—I think I should drop down dead ere I reached it. I'm sure I should."

The van driver, after several ineffectual attempts to get a little nearer, was at length compelled to be content to remain where he was, and, turning to those he had brought with him to see the sight, he said, shaking his head:

"We shan't get a better place than this. We ought to have been sooner; but who would have expected such a crowd? Why, we might walk on the people's heads."

And such, indeed, was the fact, for from the spot where the van was compelled to halt, to the scaffold, was now one dense mass of human heads.

It seemed as if it would have been impossible to have wedged in another human being, so closely packed were those already there.

All eyes appeared turned towards the scaffold—a circumstance which gave Twitter more courage to stand up in the van, and look round him, for he was very near the outskirts of the crowd, and, consequently, not likely to be seen or recognized.

A confused noise pervaded the vast assemblage, and here and there, by undulations among the mass of humanity, it would seem as if some partial rioting was taking place, either in consequence of some person striving to force himself unduly forward, or, as was the real case in many instances, from the frantic efforts of somebody who had been long waiting, and was half dead from exhaustion, to escape from the terrific pressure of the mob around him.

There were women, too, in that vast assemblage, and if one place more than another was dangerous to get into, or troublesome to escape from, there to be sure were women, and some of them screamed till the crowd became sympathetic, and made a lane for them to escape by; but the sympathy was in many cases thrown away, for, after adjusting their disordered apparel, they again pressed forward, to get into the same difficulty as before.

Some of these—shall we say ladies?—had brought young children in their arms, and when they got into the middle of the crowd, they, with a mock feeling, asked those around them if they had the hearts to crush a baby.

Beyond this moving throng Twitter saw the uniforms of the dragoons, who were drawn up round the scaffold, so as to keep the pressure of the mob off it, which they succeeded in doing by now and then letting the horses tread on the toes of the most forward of the sight-lovers.

Oh, how Twitter congratulated himself that he was in a van, and free from the pressure and inconvenience of the mob.

That Varley would be there he did not doubt for a moment, for he well knew how his rascally coadjutor in villainy had set his heart upon the execution of Rowland, and he turned his eyes in all directions, and scrutinized the faces at every window with the hope of discovering him.

All his endeavours, however, were in vain —no Varley could he see; for, although that ruffian had secured a place from which he could see the execution, and had paid a high price for the exclusive use of a window, the attempt he had made to induce Miranda to listen to him at the last hour had so much delayed him in reaching it, that, after the most tremendous efforts, he began to think it impossible to force his way through such a mob as had assembled.

Still, in his attempt he succeeded so far as to wedge himself in the crowd to such an extent that it became doubtful whether it was not just as difficult to get back again as to go on.

Varley's height gave him an advantage in some respects; but, as the sequel showed, it was of great disadvantage in others, for it made him very conspicuous, and liable to be recognized by some of those very persons who, in their love of a riot more than their hatred to him, had before done him the honour of hunting him through the streets of York, to the great damage of his person, and near risk of his life; for mobs are not very particular, and whether their victim be a mad dog, an over-driven bullock, or a man, it's much the same. The only fact worthy of remark being, that the human animal is the only one that shows a strong disposition always to hunt down its own kind.

Varley, then, had hardly relaxed a little in his endeavours to push his way to the house where he had engaged a window from which he could see the execution, when a screaming shout from a short distance behind him came like some well-remembered tone to his ears, and in the next moment he heard the cry which had annoyed him so often.

"Bernard Varley. Ha! ha! ha! Hanged at York. Bernard Varley will be hanged at York yet. There—there goes the murderer; look at him well that you may know him again when he is hanged at York."

This was quite a treat for the mob, and in an instant Varley was greeted with a shout that struck terror to his heart, for he knew himself to be surrounded by many desperate men who had been waiting for amusement for some hours, and would gladly seize the first opportunity that presented itself for a little interlude prior to the execution.

The idiot was within half-a-dozen feet of him, and Varley's first impulse was to make a rush in his direction, and strike him down.

Oh, how pleased he would have been to have got him trampled to death, and so been rid for ever of his evil greeting.

In the attempt, however, he most signally failed, and only brought upon himself the resentment of those who were in his way.

Again the idiot raised his crazed voice, shouting:

"Hanged at York—hanged at York! Bernard Varley will be hanged at York, and I shall see it. Ho! ho! ho! A brave sight— a gallant, noble sight will be Bernard Varley's hanging at York."

Varley was not quite so unprepared for a personal encounter with either an individual or a mob as we have hitherto found him, for, since his little adventure with Mr. Jones, he had taken counsel with himself how he should best provide against such attacks for the future.

His first idea had been to provide himself constantly with loaded firearms, and shoot anyone who should attempt to meddle with him in any way. But there was one objection to the use of the pistol which did not escape Varley's penetration, which was, that when once discharged, and possibly the object missed, it was an utterly useless weapon.

Moreover, in a crowd such as that which was now beginning to hustle him, he could shoot only one person, which would be ample excuse for the others tearing him to pieces. No; Bernard Varley resolved upon not using pistols on every provocation; but he provided himself with two of those formidable weapons called self-protectors, and he made up his mind, that should he ever again have to battle for his life amongst an enraged multitude of persons, it should be with one of them in each hand.

When, therefore, he found that he was prevented from reaching the idiot, and wreaking his vengeance upon him, he drew out the two weapons with which he was provided, and commenced so desperate an attack upon all who opposed his progress, that he cut for himself a lane through the people, despite all their efforts to detain him.

Quite heedless of which direction he was taking, so that he kept on tolerably straight, he struck out right and left, inflicting serious wounds upon many persons, until a great riot ensued, accompanied by such shouts, cries, shrieks, and tumult, that a body of constables made an attempt to push through the crowd to the spot where they saw one man fighting apparently with such maddened desperation.

It was at this juncture that Twitter—who, in common with all the occupants of the van, had had his eyes drawn in the direction where such a riot seemed to be going on—recognized the tall, gaunt form of Bernard Varley as he who was fighting his way so desperately against a whole mob.

Twitter was much pleased to see that Varley was not a prisoner, for it at once put an end to any lingering doubts he might have had that some artful manœuvre had been concocted to catch him.

Now he felt quite certain that his letter had never reached the Mayor; and oh, what an amusement it was to Samuel Twitter to see, from the safe covert of the van, how Varley was forced to make such incredible exertions to get out of the mob.

The constables fighting in one direction,

and Varley fighting in the other, rather bothered the crowd, and the consequence was, that they and Varley very soon met, when he at once threw himself among them, crying:

"My name is Varley. Because I was a witness at the trial against Rowland Percy, his associates in the mob would murder me. I claim protection."

By this time he was within a few feet of the military cordon that surrounded the scaffold, and the chief of the police, seizing him by the arm, dragged him past the dragoons, where he was in perfect safety.

Varley, however, notwithstanding the desperate manner in which he was armed, and the fearful use he had made of those arms, had not escaped quite scathless from the mob.

On the contrary, he had received more kicks and cuffs than, at the time, he had noticed; and now he absolutely reeled from exhaustion, and was compelled to lean on one of the police-officers for support.

"You had better come into the prison," said the chief officer, "at once, and stay there till the execution is over. This way—this way."

Varley followed him, and in a few minutes was seated in a room, through which he was not aware Rowland Percy must pass on his way to the scaffold.

CHAPTER CLXXVII.

FIVE MINUTES TO EIGHT—THE SEPARATION —THE ROUTE TO THE SCAFFOLD—A PRIVATE SECRETARY IN A FLUSTER.

WE left poor Miranda clinging to him who was too soon to be separated from her. Oh, would that we could still leave him in such gentle custody; but the order of our narrative forbids it, and at whatever violence to our feelings, those fond lovers—who had maintained so pure and holy an attachment for each other through so much danger and difficulty—must be parted at last.

The very persons whose duty it was to interfere shrank from the task, although they had been used to scenes of misery, and had long lived in the very atmosphere of sighs and tears as attendants in that prison-house.

But shrink or not, the task must be performed. The scaffold was prepared.

The fatal noose was ready.

The clock had ten minutes since chimed the three-quarters past seven.

In five minutes more Rowland Percy must be judicially murdered.

The sheriff looked at the Governor, and the Governor at the sheriff, as if each wished to shift on to the shoulders of the other the uncomfortable duty that had to be performed.

"You—you will tell them," whispered the sheriff, "to—to separate them, if you please."

"He is your prisoner now," replied the Governor, "not mine. God help the poor girl! I never saw such a scene as t... and trust I may never see such another."

"Five minutes to eight," muttered the chaplain. "A-hem!—five minutes to eight."

An angry roar from the impatient crowd without reached the ears of those who were assembled in that room of horror—that room which had witnessed so many tears, echoed with so many sighs.

Then the sheriff stepped up to Mr. Anderson, and said:

"For Heaven's sake, sir, induce Miss Rankley to leave this place at once! Try your influence with her."

Mr. Anderson could not speak, but he approached Miranda, and gently laid his hand upon her arm.

She knew not who touched her, but she shrank from the touch, which she conjectured was meant as a prelude to a more violent effort to make her loose her hold of Rowland Percy.

A piercing shriek burst from her lips, and she cried:

"Save him—save him! Heaven! Is there no justice on earth, or in Heaven? Save him —save him!"

"I cannot—I cannot remove her," said Mr. Anderson; and he retired to the farther end of the room, where he sat down and covered his face with his hands, that he might not witness the scene that he knew must now ensue.

Moment after moment passed, and the sheriff felt that he could delay no longer.

He beckoned to the officials of the prison, who stood awaiting orders on the threshold of the door, and silently pointed to the prisoner.

Two men at once advanced and laid hands on Rowland, who, in a deep, hollow voice, said:

"Miranda—my Miranda, one long—one last farewell! Dearest, I must go now! Farewell—farewell!"

She looked up from his breast where she had been hiding her face, and, at the sight of the men who had hold of Percy, she shrieked again, and clung still closer to him.

Then one of them tried to disengage her hands.

Rowland averted his face as he said, in heart-breaking accents:

"Gently—gently."

Considerable force, however, had to be used before she could be dragged from him, and when she was, the expression of her pallid countenance was truly terrible.

As for Rowland himself, he seemed to have made up his mind not to trust himself to look at her again.

He walked a few steps to the door, but he could not find strength of mind to persevere in such an intention.

When within a few paces of the threshold, he turned, and with one long, gasping sob, he said:

"Miranda!"

She made a spring towards him, but one of the officers caught her by the waist ere she reached him, and the sheriff motioned with his hand that Percy should be immediately removed.

He was taken from the room in a moment, and the door closed behind him.

An officer stood on each side of the unhappy prisoner, and held each an arm; and then the mournful procession moved on until it reached a room, where a halt took place, and the sheriff, advancing to Rowland, said:

"Is there anything you wish done, in which, consistent with my duty, I can favour you?"

"Nothing," was the brief reply.

"Do you now repent?" urged the chaplain.

"No."

"Do you confess your guilt, and the justice of your sentence, unhappy young man?"

"No. I deny my guilt, and I cry out aloud against my sentence as unjust. My death will be a murder, for I am innocent of the crime imputed to me, so help me, Heaven."

"This is a painful declaration for us all to hear," remarked the Mayor. "I trust you will not persevere in it."

"It is the truth," said Rowland. "May I find that justice from God I am not receiving at the hands of my fellow-creatures. I am innocent."

Eight o'clock sounded from the Minster clock, and the funeral knell mingled strangely with the sound.

The executioner slipped behind Rowland, and began rapidly to pinion his arms, while the Governor said to him, in accents of deep emotion:

"Make your mind easy on one subject. Miranda Rankley shall never want a friend."

"Thank you," said Rowland, in a voice that had sunk almost to a whisper. "God will help her, although I am deserted. I am innocent."

The preparations were now nearly completed, and the various parties who were to make up the procession that was to herald Rowland to the scaffold took their places.

The chaplain read aloud the funeral service, while the deep tolling of the bell had an awful effect, amid the otherwise solemn stillness that reigned around.

Since eight o'clock had struck, a complete silence had come over the mob, for they knew that a few minutes would produce the unhappy man, whom they had come to see suffer so terrible a death.

Now the cavalcade moved from room to room.

Then it took its way along a winding passage, which terminated in a small apartment, separated only by a vestibule from the lowest step of the scaffold itself.

In this room sat Bernard Varley, and, when a door in it unexpectedly opened, he comprehended who was coming.

He sprang to his feet, and stood trembling with terror, unable to fly, and yet horrified to stay.

Rowland Percy saw him; and the fixed, stony glare he bent upon him pierced his very heart.

Varley held up his hands to hide the face of Rowland from him, and shuddered as he stepped back towards the wall.

"Man of blood!" said Rowland—"perjured villain!—false witness!—murderer! Dare you, at such an hour as this——"

"Let me go!" cried Varley—"let me go, or take him away! Why was I brought here?"

"By Heaven!" said Rowland, "to receive my dying malediction. Bernard Varley, may rest never sit again upon your eyelids, but your brain be tortured by such visions as shall sting you to despair!"

"No, no. Stop him from speaking!" shouted Varley. "I will hear no more!—take him away!—hang him!—hang him!—don't let him look at me with that—that dead glare. I shall go mad!"

A door was flung open, and a rush of cold air made its way into the room.

"Come," said the sheriff—"come."

The procession moved on, while Varley sank into a seat, trembling like an aspen leaf.

Another moment, and Rowland Percy saw the scaffold.

A confused murmur ran through the crowd, then there were some cries uttered, which were quickly suppressed.

The military and police redoubled their efforts to keep off the pressure of the mob.

Some persons fainted from over-excitement at the scene; and Samuel Twitter grasped the edge of the van till his fingers turned blue, and he drew his breath short and thick as he saw the door open, through which was to come the sacrificed man who, on his and Varley's testimony, had been so wrongfully condemned to death.

He heard nothing but the loud beating of his own heart—he saw nothing but that open doorway, and the faces that began slowly to appear at it.

His feelings were wound up to the highest pitch of excitement when eight struck, and no one appeared.

True, the door was opened at that hour by the officers who were placed at it; but from the peculiar circumstances that were taking place within the jail, no one was aware that more than ordinary delay was experienced in bringing the doomed man to the scaffold.

Rowland Percy had to be separated from Miranda. He had to be pinioned for death; and then came his own brief declaration of his innocence, and the strange but appalling interview with Bernard Varley, which left that man, villain as he was, to greater—far greater—pangs than any death could have inflicted upon the innocent, persecuted Percy.

There had arisen in Twitter's mind a feeling of horrible apprehension that something must have happened of an extraordinary nature to delay the execution, and it became to him a feeling of exquisite relief, when he saw the procession make its appearance, and he was convinced—quite convinced, that in a few moments more Rowland Percy would be a dead man.

The danger of Varley had rather gratified than alarmed him, for he thought he could see in it an additional argument to wrest money from him, for he would say:

"Already are you in such bad odour with the populace, that they are ready to tear you in pieces. What could control their fury were the slightest hint given of your real guilt?"

All this was uncommonly satisfactory to Twitter, and he looked fixedly, with quite a benign expression, upon the persons who ranged themselves on each side of the few steps leading to the scaffold, for he said to himself:

"My danger is over. However strange and unaccountable it is, my letter to the Mayor of York has never reached him, and it is not a little satisfactory from this green sward, with the river behind me, to be able to view the death of Rowland Percy on yonder platform, for the crime in the commission of which I have myself been so great a sharer."

CHAPTER CLXXVIII.

THE APPEARANCE ON THE SCAFFOLD—THE SECRETARY—THE UNEXPECTED DELAY—THE ANGER OF VARLEY.

WHEN Rowland Percy appeared on the scaffold, he, for a moment, and only for a moment, shrank back, as he looked down upon the sea of heads before him.

Then, as a confused murmur ran through the crowd, and he heard many voices saying, "That's he—that's he," he began to wish the awful scene was over, and that he had gained the shores of that other world, on the brink of which he believed himself now to stand.

Yet, even in that awful extremity of his fortunes, with death awaiting him, and while the executioner was slowly approaching him to perform his fell office, Rowland could not wholly divest himself of the natural indignation he had all along felt at being thus sacrificed to false testimony.

No sense of humility or resignation came over his proud spirit. As God had made him—innocent and indignant at wrong—there he was, and even a shameful death in immediate expectation could not lead him to tears, or lamentations, or that sickly sentimentality, compounded of tears, insanity, and superstition, which the chaplain was so exceedingly anxious to see exhibited.

Glancing for a moment over the multitude before him, he stepped to the extreme verge of the platform on which was the awful apparatus of death, and raising his voice so that it reached even to the ears of those farthest from him, he said, loudly and clearly:

"I am innocent!"

A great commotion took place in the crowd, and his words appeared to have had almost a magical effect.

The pressure towards the scaffold became tremendous, and loud cries issued from many mouths, of:

"Save him—save him! He is innocent!" while one fierce, shrieking voice, above all the din, was heard crying:

"Bernard Varley will be hanged at York!"

The authorities seemed for a moment staggered at the din, and then they became anxious that the awful scene should be as quickly over as possible.

The sheriff motioned to the executioner—who stood irresolute—to do his duty.

At this moment, Bernard Varley, to whose ears the unusual noise without had penetrated, appeared at the door in sight of the scaffold.

He fully expected to see his victim hanging, but when he perceived that, from some unaccountable cause, Rowland still lived, his face assumed a livid hue, and he cried:

"This is a mockery—kill him—slay him—to execution—are you waiting to have him rescued? Hang him—kill him! Are you all mad?"

The executioner was about to place the rope round the neck of Rowland Percy, when the Mayor of York was suddenly seized hold of by someone who had made his way to the scaffold, and who, in the vehemence with which he claimed the attention of that functionary, almost threw him down.

This man, who thus unceremoniously appeared, was heated and exhausted.

The perspiration was rolling down his face.

His clothes were torn, for he had had to force his way through some part of the mob before he could reach the prison, and his whole appearance bespoke so much agony, so much haste, and so much terror, that the Mayor might well, as he did, shrink back aghast, and scarcely recognize in him his own private secretary, who must have made such great exertions to come to him.

At Varley's appearance such a wild shout arose from the mob, who had begun to have a strong feeling in favour of Percy, that he had as immediately again retired, and now was out of view of the proceedings on the scaffold, although he was quite satisfied that in another minute Rowland would be a corpse.

"Sir—sir—my lord—sir!" gasped the Lord Mayor's private secretary, "I—I can't speak, sir—gentlemen. I've run so hard. I—I—sir——"

"Gracious Heaven! what has occurred?" said the Mayor.

The secretary, with trembling hands, took from his pocket a crumpled-up letter, and, still absolutely tottering from exhaustion, added:

"Stop—stop the execution! Save him! He didn't do it. I should never have forgiven myself. Save him—save him!"

"Hold!" cried the sheriff to the executioner. "Hold!"

For at the appearance of the Mayor's secretary, in such a state of haste and exhaustion, he had drawn near, and heard what was said.

"Dust to dust," said the chaplain, solemnly, "ashes to ashes."

Then he looked amazed, as the executioner stepped back from Rowland Percy, and omitted drawing the cap over his face, as was customary.

The mob could not make out what was going on, for they had seen nothing of the Mayor's secretary, their whole attention being fixed upon the prisoner and the executioner, who, with the clergyman, prevented either the Mayor or the sheriff from being seen, they being far back on the scaffold, and now that Rowland was left so strangely, still standing, and by some unaccountable means the execution was not proceeded with, the excitement became intense in the extreme, and such a hooting arose as was perfectly stunning, for many of the crowd were indignant at this supposed protraction of the sufferings of the criminal.

Rowland, himself, looked about him like a man newly awakened from some dream.

He could not divine what was the matter, and once more the name of Miranda came from his lips in accents of such an agonizing nature, that even the chaplain ceased his prayer, and stepped back a pace or two in terror.

All this was the work of about one minute, although it has necessarily taken us a longer time to record it, and the Mayor's secretary having partially recovered his breath, with trembling hands unfolded the letter he had brought, and while the sheriff listened to him in no small wonder, and the Governor of the prison formed one of the group, he said:

"This—this letter—you see—it came yesterday, and—and—I didn't know the seal. It seemed like some begging concern, you see, and—and in the pressure of more important business—it was only done up with a couple of wafers. I—I can hardly speak—I put it on one side, and never opened it till this morning. You understand? It's a confession from Samuel Twitter—one of the witnesses at the trial of Percy—that he and Bernard Varley murdered Sir George Rankley between them. It—it altogether exonerates Percy—on my soul it does! It bears the impress of truth on it. There, there it is. He might have been hanged through my neglect—and I—I——"

The secretary, uttering a deep groan, fainted at the feet of the Mayor, for he had really made incredible exertions to reach the place of execution, and was utterly exhausted in consequence.

The Mayor looked thoroughly confounded, and, on the impulse of the moment, was quite unable to act in any decisive manner; and, indeed, the sheriff turned very pale; he did not exactly seem to know what to make of it.

The Governor, however, was more accustomed to act and think promptly, and he said, at once:

"Bernard Varley is in the castle now. Let him be surrounded by officers, so that he may not escape, and, by watching his conduct, we may come to some opinion as to the truth of this confession. At all events, there is ample authority in it for staying the execution."

Rowland Percy was standing on the drop, and the chaplain was looking at him with surprise and consternation, when the Governor, having said these few words to the Mayor and the sheriff, darted forward, and laid hold of Rowland's arm, saying:

"Mr. Percy, do not think too much of it, for I don't know myself how far we can go, only you shall not be hanged this morning, unless they hang me too."

It was well the Governor was close to him, or Rowland might have had a heavy fall, for, somehow or another, the executioner's assistant, who was underneath the scaffold, thought it was time to draw the bolts which kept up the drop, and Rowland just escaped in time from falling through the yawning chasm that opened at his feet.

The sudden revulsion of feeling, then, that ensued in his mind, did more towards recovering him than had all his previous danger, and he leaned heavily on the arm of the Governor, as he said:

"Do—not—mock me—I—I pray you."

He then fainted, and would have fallen, but for the efficient support that was rendered to him.

The excitement among the crowd at this stage of the proceedings, beggared all description.

A rush was made to the scaffold, and it required all the exertions of the military to keep off the pressure.

As for Twitter, whose eyes had never for one moment been allowed to stray from Rowland Percy since he had made his appearance, he got into such an agony of terror when he saw that, from some cause or another, he was not hanged, that he relaxed his hold upon the side of the van, and fell backwards among the feet of the people who were standing in it.

He uttered a deep groan, and gave himself up completely for lost, as what but his confession, or a similar one from Varley, could possibly rescue Rowland Percy at that moment from the death which had been all but inflicted on him.

Bernard Varley, who had retired to the room through which Percy had passed on his route to the scaffold, heard the shouts of the multitude, and, springing to his feet, exclaimed in a tone of relief:

"It is over. Rowland Percy is no more. All is over now. He is dead—dead!"

At that moment an officer entered the room, and Varley eagerly questioned him as to the execution.

"Is all over?" he cried. "Tell me, is all over?"

"Yes," replied the officer; "all, I think."

"Then I will go. Yet no—the crowd. Tell me, is there any outlet from the prison by which I can leave secretly?"

"None; and I would not advise you to leave too soon, for they do not seem to be very favourably disposed towards you, sir."

So saying, the officer passed through the

room, and went directly to the apartment where Miranda had been left with Mr. Anderson.

The latter was weeping, but the former sat pale and motionless as a marble statue—she seemed, indeed, waiting for death.

An awful apathy had come over her, and when the officer entered the room, she bent no inquiring gaze at him.

A single shudder passed over her, and that was all.

Mr. Anderson had felt how utterly inadequate were all the ordinary topics of consolation to her, and when she had recovered from the insensibility that had for a brief period come over her, when she was torn from Rowland Percy's arms, he had said nothing to her, but had stood near her, painfully watching the changes of her sad countenance.

"I have been sent," said the officer, "by the sheriff, to say that a circumstance has occurred to stay the execution."

Miranda, with a cry of joy, sprang to her feet, and before either Mr. Anderson or the officer could interfere to prevent her, she had darted from the room.

There was no complexity of passages or doors, but one even course right on to the very scaffold, for to facilitate the progress of the mournful procession which was to conduct a fellow-creature to death, all the doors had been propped wide open, and an unencumbered passage left.

Still Miranda had to pass through the apartment in which was Bernard Varley, and she did so with such rapidity, that he could scarcely believe the evidence of his own senses, that it was, indeed, she who had flitted for an instant before his eyes.

He hesitated only for a moment, and then darted after her, muttering to himself:

"Who shall now stand between me and my pursuit of Miranda Rankley? She shall be mine—by fraud or by force, I swear it, she shall be mine."

Miranda's progress was by far too fleet for him, and, long ere he could reach the scaffold, she was on it.

Her sudden appearance gave such a surprise to the mob, that every feeling was hushed in a moment of anxious suspense to know what was about to happen next.

She cast one glance around her, and saw Rowland half supported by the Governor, for he was somewhat recovered from his fainting, and could just stand.

Miranda threw herself into his arms, as she shrieked:

"Saved!—saved!—Rowland—see—see—there are—tears—now!"

She burst into a passion of hysterical weeping.

Those were, indeed, the first tears she had shed since Rowland's accusation, and, oh, how abundantly did they relieve her oppressed heart—with every gushing drop of pearly moisture, a load of care appeared to dissipate, and, when she looked up again, the fond, old, familiar smile of happy girlhood beamed upon her face.

"One, two, three, hurrah!" shouted a man who had climbed a tree, and sat upon an overhanging branch. The mob took up the shout, and such a joyous cheer rang far and wide, as had not been heard in York for many and many a day.

It was at this very instant that Bernard Varley, who had followed Miranda, appeared on the scaffold, when the man in the tree, who seemed half-mad with exultation, and who was no other than Jones, shouted:

"A groan for Bernard Varley. There he is, the vagabond, with the ill-looking physog, and the patch on his nose."

The groan that succeeded was given most heartily, and then the mob began to ask each other what had happened, and why the man was not hanged.

Varley looked petrified with amazement.

He knew not whether to retreat or advance.

What had happened he could not imagine—a pardon for Rowland Percy was not in the order of things at all, and yet there he was, still alive, and clasped in the arms of Miranda, who was smiling like a cherub in his face, while her eyes glistened with tears that looked very much like those of joy.

CHAPTER CLXXIX.

THE ARREST OF VARLEY—HIS DESPERATE RESISTANCE—THE REWARD OFFERED FOR TWITTER—THE RIOT.

THE sheriff and the Mayor had been engaged in earnest conversation for a few moments, and the result was a determination, under all the circumstances, not to allow Bernard Varley to leave the castle.

"We cannot implicitly rely on this confession," said the sheriff; "but, as I have hinted, we may discover something from Varley's manner when arrested. As for Twitter, I daresay he has taken good care to get far enough off before this document reached you."

"No doubt of that. The officers can surround Varley so as to prevent his escape."

"Leave that to me," said the Governor, coming up to them, and just hearing the last remark. "I will manage it. Say no more. This matter will end more to all our satisfaction yet than ever we expected."

When the mob, at the instigation of Jones, raised such a groan at Bernard Varley, he stepped back a little, and said to an officer near him:

"Can you tell me the meaning of all this? Why, in the name of fortune, is the man not hanged?"

"I really don't know," said the officer, dryly—"do you?"

This question was addressed to a turnkey, who had sidled up tolerably close to Varley, and who replied at once:

"I hasn't no sort o' idear."

Then the sheriff stepped up to Varley, and said:

RETRIBUTION AT LAST WAITS ON BERNARD VARLEY.

"It seems, sir, we are not to have a hanging this morning, notwithstanding all our preparations."

"No hanging?"

"No; something has happened which induces the authorities to postpone the execution. I believe there are serious doubts of the guilt of Rowland Percy, and an expectation that some other person may be accused."

Varley's colour first deepened on his cheek as the sheriff spoke, and then it left him altogether.

He turned of an ashy paleness.

"Who—who is suspected?" he managed to ask, after a long pause.

"You must excuse me in the present stage of the matter from making any disclosures," replied the sheriff. "The Mayor of York appears convinced of Rowland Percy's innocence, and, as you see, in deference to his opinion, the young man is respited."

"Respited—respited?"

"Yes, respited. I think he will be saved."

"Well—well, I thank you for your information. Murder should be punished. I cannot understand it, however. Good day, sir—good day. I will risk my passage through the throng. I am going—I am going."

He turned to go into the castle, and thence to some outlet.

His limbs trembled, and his voice was thick and indistinct.

It was clear he scarcely knew what he was saying, such was the confusion of his mind, and the terrible state into which he was thrown by the sudden stoppage of the execution.

Of course, any circumstance that tended to save Percy must be dangerous to him, Varley. And yet what could it be—what could have happened? Where was the evidence of his guilt, except in his own breast, and that of Twitter's? And the latter to criminate him, Varley, must likewise criminate himself. What could it be, then? How could he be suspected? And yet he would leave the castle—he would hurry from York—he would provide against all accidents by a precipitate retreat, and from a distance calculate and ascertain his chances.

His brain was in a perfect whirl from the mob of ideas that came suddenly to his mind; but the first and foremost of all was to get away—to escape from where he was—to fly from a danger that might be terrible and deadly.

With that object, then, he turned, but there stood exactly in his way an athletic man, who never attempted to move.

Then Varley tried to pass round him, but another man impeded his passage.

The perspiration stood upon the murderer's brow in huge drops, and he tried to go to the other side, but there stood a third man to oppose him.

There was no side open but that leading on to the very scaffold, and when he glanced round him with bloodshot and staring eyes, he saw the official personages, who had come to witness the execution, all looking at him, and him only, as if his proceedings formed the principal object of interest there.

Then he could no longer conceal from himself the fact that there was danger and suspicion of him—that, in fact, he was hemmed in and baited—that some awful revelation must have taken place to connect him with the murder, and at the last moment to free his innocent victim from the toils he had spread round him.

For a second or two he stood irresolute.

Then he turned to the man who stopped his passage into the castle, and said:

"You are in my way—allow me to pass."

The officers had their instructions, and this one at once replied:

"We have orders to detain you."

"Detain me—me?"

"Yes," thundered the Governor, advancing. "You are our prisoner, on a charge of murder."

Varley recoiled, as if he had been shot, and the Mayor immediately added:

"Your accomplice, Samuel Twitter, has written a full confession of everything."

The words had scarcely escaped his lips when Varley made a rush to the front of the scaffold, knocking down the evangelical chaplain on his way.

With one spring he alighted on the ground. So sudden was the movement, and so utterly unprepared for it were the police and military, that he burst through them on the instant, and commenced battling his way through the crowd with a desperation that no one could possibly stand against.

"A madman—a madman!" was the cry, and all eagerly afforded him a passage.

"Seize that man," shouted the Governor from the scaffold—"seize him! On your lives, let him not escape."

Two of the dragoons dashed after him, and the cries and shrieks of the mob as the horses trampled on them became terrific.

Still Varley fought on; but he was neared each moment, and, at length, the foremost soldier reached him, and, by a movement of his well-trained horse, turned him in his flight.

In another moment the villain was held by a dozen hands, and disarmed of his self-protectors, which he had again used desperately and freely.

Escorted by the two dragoons, he was led back to the scaffold by some of the mob, and, when they got him there, they threw him on to it with a vengeance that was enough to break every bone in his body.

"For Heaven's sake, come away from this scene!" said Mr. Anderson to Percy. "This way, this way—come into the castle. What an unexpected deliverance is this!"

"My Miranda—my Miranda!" was all Percy said, and still he clasped her to his heart.

He cast one glance at Varley, who had now handcuffs put on him by the officers, and then he accompanied Mr. Anderson from the scaffold, still so utterly bewildered and astonished at what had occurred, that but for the actual presence of his much-loved Miranda he would not have believed in the reality of his escape.

"You are weeping, dearest," he said, in a low voice to her.

"Yes, Rowland, I am weeping," she replied. "Accept my tears as an omen that our trials are over. I am weeping, and I thank God, who has given me tears at last."

Jones, who had acted as fugleman to the mob from the tree in which he had placed himself, was as much astonished, and as much at a loss to account for the extraordinary turn affairs had taken as anyone could possibly be, and, when he saw Rowland leave the scaffold, he almost let go his hold.

"Keep a look out," he cried. "What'll happen next, I wonder? Here's a pretty go—well, I never! Just tell me, some of you, if I'm on my head or my heels?"

Before Mr. Jones could get this query satisfactorily answered, the Governor of the castle stepped forward to the front of the scaffold, and waved his hand to bespeak a hearing from the dense assemblage below.

Curiosity hushed every sound, so that he was heard plainly and distinctly, as he said:

"I am empowered to offer five hundred

pounds for the apprehension and lodgment in York Castle, or any jail in the kingdom, of Samuel Twitter, accused on his own written confession of the murder of Sir George Rankley, of which murder Rowland Percy is now declared by him, Twitter, to be entirely innocent."

Twitter just heard this address as far as his name was mentioned, and then a kind of film came over his eyes, and all his senses for a few moments fled.

Jones was the only person who did anything exceedingly active on this occasion, for, after a very brief injunction indeed of, "Below, there!" to the persons who happened to be exactly beneath him, he dropped from the tree, inflicting no further injury than treading upon two or three persons toes, none of whom happening to be very delicately shod, or blessed with the aristocratic refinement of corns, readily forgave him, being deeply interested in what so popular a character—as he always managed to make himself in all crowds—was about to do.

This he soon showed them; for, from his exalted position, he had been enabled to take a pretty accurate survey of all surrounding objects; and, among others of interest to him, he had not been backward in discerning Samuel Twitter in the van, as he stood completely absorbed in what was taking place on the scaffold.

With a speed much greater than anyone else could have exerted through the mob, because for no one else, probably, would it have made way half so readily, he rushed towards the van, into which he commenced climbing with the greatest deliberation, quite heedless of whether it was agreeable to the owner or not.

"Hilloa!" cried the man, "we are full enough; we don't want you."

"Don't you?" said Jones. "Do you want to get on in the world, old chap? 'Cos, if you do, I'll jist put you forard a little by a oner in the eye as'll send you into the middle o' next week. Now, Sammy, if you please."

"What do you want here?"

"A old friend o' mine. Sammy, my rum un, kim up."

So saying, Jones raked about the bottom of the van till he found Twitter, whom he lugged up by the collar to a sitting posture.

"Don't purtend all for to be dead, Sammy," he added. "You're turned a waluable article, you have. Kim up. Oh, you won't move, won't you? Wery good. Some chaps want such a lot o' persuading afore they'll do another a good turn."

Twitter uttered a low groan.

"That'll do," said Jones. "It's jist in your line, groanin' and roarin' is. Can't yer walk? Really! Jist lend me your whip, old Brutus."

"My whip," cried the van proprietor. "I—I really——"

"Thank yer," said Jones, laying hold of it. "Now, ladies and genelmen, you shall have an out and out view o' the gallows, so as when

any on yer comes to it yer blessed selves you'll know it agin. Kim up my Prussian blue. There's haction! A fine animal you've got if he weren't lame in three legs."

"Hurrah!" shouted the mob, though they had no idea what for; and Jones, putting the horse in motion, commenced slowly moving through the crowd with the van towards the scaffold.

The mob cheered.

The van proprietor swore in an undertone to himself.

The women who were in the van screamed, for they thought Jones was some madman; and Samuel Twitter, who was slowly recovering consciousness, kept up a low groaning all the way, wondering where he was going.

Then an officious constable tried to stop the progress of the van, but Jones assailed him with such a volley of what is commonly called chaff, and the crowd hustled him so, that he was glad to give up the attempt in despair.

It took about five minutes to reach the cordon of police and military surrounding the scaffold, and then Jones cried out; in a stentorian voice:

"Who wants Sammy Twitter?"

"I do," cried the Governor.

"And I," said the sheriff.

"Here he is, then, as large as life, and twice as natural," said Jones, dragging up Twitter by the collar, and showing him to all who were on the scaffold.

Varley's head dropped on his breast, and he uttered a half-scream, as if from that moment he had given up all hope.

The sheriff directed that a passage should be made for the van; and, when it got quite underneath the platform, Samuel Twitter was handed up by Jones into the arms of the officers, amid such a hurrah from the mob as was perfectly deafening.

"Now for it," said Jones. "Clear away."

Immediately an attack was made on the gallows, and those on the scaffold had just time to escape from it when it was scaled by the mob, and in a few minutes torn to pieces, and carried off in triumph.

CHAPTER CLXXX.

THE CONCLUSION.

OUR story is virtually over; for with the discovery of the real murderers of Sir George Rankley ceased the persecution of Rowland and his beautiful Miranda, who, in all perils, in all difficulties, and under the most trying and disastrous circumstances, had clung so nobly to her faith.

Twitter at once acknowledged his confession in the presence of Varley, and throwing himself on his knees, with the most abject tears and entreaties, implored for mercy.

"Spare me," he cried, "spare me! I am not fit to die—indeed, I am not. Besides, consider, but for me the innocent Rowland Percy would have suffered death. Oh, think of that, and spare my wretched life! I will be evidence, too, against Varley, who is, indeed, a most desperate villain, and my tempter to crime. I should never for a moment have thought of such criminality, but for him. Hang him, gentlemen—oh! he richly deserves it—but spare me as evidence against him. I am willing to swear to all my confession. It is strictly true. You will let me be evidence against him, and so you will spare my life? I dare not die—I dare not die!"

He wept, and wrung his hands with such frantic misery as he made this abject appeal for life, that the sheriff, to whom it was principally addressed, turned away in disgust, saying to the Governor:

"Saw you ever such a wretch? For Heaven's sake, tell him we have nothing to do with the matter, and can neither hang nor spare him of our own will."

The Governor was about to say something to Twitter, when Varley raised his voice, and an unholy fire flashed from his deep-set eyes, as he said:

"Hear me. I will spare you all the necessity of listening to the tale of that miserable wretch, who has brought destruction on his own head as well as on mine. If I am to suffer, he shall suffer too. He has confessed his guilt. I, too, confess mine; so shall his evidence be dispensed with, and he be entitled to no merciful consideration on that account. I confess to murdering, along with Samuel Twitter, Sir George Rankley."

"There, that settles the matter," said the sheriff. "Will you put your confession in writing?"

"Yes; but—but—be quick—for——"

A deadly paleness overspread his face, and his limbs trembled.

Then a smile of triumph curled his lips as he added:

"I—I shall cheat the gallows yet."

"He has poisoned himself," said the Governor. "By Heaven, I thought 'twas poison he had, when he asked for leave to take snuff, some time since, and from a small silver box he has he took something, which he placed in his mouth."

"You—you are right," gasped Varley; "I am poisoned, and 'tis now too late for human skill to save me."

Twitter fell back with a howl of despair, while Varley was immediately carried to the prison infirmary by some of the turnkeys.

There he received such prompt and skilful attention, that, to his maddening rage, the poison was shortly withdrawn from his stomach, and partly counteracted in its effects by powerful antidotes, so that by the evening he was free from its effects, although in a dreadful state of bodily exhaustion and mental agony.

*　　*　　*　　*

A special mounted messenger was despatched to London, with an account from the sheriff of the whole affair, to the Secretary of State, in order that Rowland Percy might be released in due form, although no bar was placed to his liberty in the meantime; and that very evening he supped with Mr. Anderson, whose guests were the Mayor of York, the Governor of the castle, the sheriff, and several respectable inhabitants of the city, who all had been strong believers in Rowland's innocence. And Miranda—was not she there, and happy? Yes, so happy, that her eyes, whenever they turned upon Rowland, would fill with tears, and she could scarcely believe herself so blessed.

Before the party separated, a messenger came to the Governor of the prison to say that Varley was nearly raving mad, and that he had confessed that the will of Sir George Rankley, under which he had taken possession of the Grange, was a forgery.

This declaration put an end to all doubt on that subject, although it produced some difficulty to another person, namely, the veracious and talented attorney who had assisted Varley in the concoction of the document.

An officer was sent to that learned gentleman's office, but he had taken the alarm from the events of the morning, and rather than give the authorities the trouble of transporting him, had transported himself.

The last that was heard of him, was to the effect that he had been naturalized in America.

One accident of a sad character happened in the crowd at the execution.

It was to the poor idiot who had so much tormented Varley.

In the rush that took place to the scaffold, he was thrown down, and so seriously hurt, that he expired before morning.

Rowland and Miranda had nobody to consult but themselves about their marriage, and as that happened to be a point upon which they were quite unanimous, the ceremony took place within three days of that dreadful one on which it appeared almost impossible that Rowland Percy could be saved from a dreadful and ignominious death.

There were numbers of persons at the marriage, both ladies and gentlemen.

Mr. Anderson gave away the bride, and the joy of her heart beamed from the lovely countenance of Miranda.

There certainly were some ladies present, who made a resolution among themselves to have no sort of acquaintance with her, because they considered her conduct very improper, such impropriety consisting in giving the responses to the clergyman in a clear, unembarrassed tone, and when the ceremony was over, instead of fainting in the vestry, or crying, she placed her arm in Rowland's, and smiled —actually smiled—when they, the aforesaid ladies, had been ready—ay, and willing, too —to faint clean away for the last twenty years, had anyone even hinted at matrimony to them.

Then, when the signing of names, and all that sort of thing was gone through with in the vestry, the beautiful bride received the congratulations of her friends, in reply to which she said she was very happy indeed.

The party, then, were passing through the church, when a tall figure emerged from a pew, and, coming up to Miranda, said:

"Heaven bless you! May the joy of this day be only equalled by those that are to come. Farewell!"

"Palmer!" exclaimed Miranda and Rowland, both at once; and then the latter added, as he seized the hand of him who had done so much for both of them:

"My friend, I have made the greatest exertions to discover you. Where have you hidden yourself since I have been free myself to search for you? Remember that my house is your home, and that, do what I may, I never can wholly repay the great obligations I am under to you."

"Nor I," said Miranda. "But for you, I should not feel the glow of happiness that irradiates my heart at this moment."

"Thank Heaven!" said Dick Palmer, "you are happy, Miranda Rankley. Let my own fate be what it may, I—I——"

Emotion impeded his utterance, and waving his hand, he would have hurried away, but Rowland Percy detained him, saying:

"No, Palmer, you shall not go—stay with us. Leave not a gloom upon our hearts on your account, on this most auspicious and happy day."

"You forget," whispered Palmer, "I am a highwayman. I am a hunted, persecuted man. I am a convict, and even now my liberty is at stake."

The sheriff at this moment entered the church, and, advancing to Rowland, said:

"Mr. Percy, the messenger from the Secretary of State has just now arrived. Your own free pardon he brings, as well as a free pardon, which I and the Mayor specially requested for Richard Palmer and his companion, Jones, so that they are both free from this moment, and I have only to hope that they will try to lead a different life for the future, convinced as I am that they are men possessed of sterling good qualities, if they will but make a proper use of them."

*   *   *   *

In the meantime, Varley and Twitter remained securely guarded in two of the strongest cells in York Castle.

The officials of the prison—from the Governor downwards—held both villains in the utmost abhorrence, and there was no fear that the prisoners would derive any assistance from them—they were deaf alike to Varley's wild offers of large sums of money, and Twitter's abject entreaties to be given some chance, however slight, of escaping from their fearful situation.

But the more he failed, the more desperate became Varley's desire—if he could not compass his own safety—to obtain the destruction of his foes.

Foremost among these he reckoned his miserable accomplice, fearing that if Twitter threw himself upon the mercy of the court, and made a clean breast of everything, he would escape the hangman's grasp.

Finding, however, that it was impossible to achieve anything by exciting the cupidity of his jailers, Varley's next course was to obtain the best legal assistance that the promise of enormous fees could procure.

From time to time, he had deposited, in various places of security, large sums of ready-money, and upon these he drew with an unsparing hand for the purposes of his defence.

The trial took place at the ensuing Assizes, and excited even greater popular interest than the trial of Rowland Percy, so short a time before.

But the proceedings were brief.

Twitter's confession was so clear and ample, and so completely backed up, not only by a mass of collateral evidence, but also by the fact that the miserable man himself, in the hope of obtaining a commutation of his sentence, pleaded guilty, that the specious pleas and quibbles of Varley's counsel were altogether useless.

The jury, without a moment's hesitation, returned a verdict of guilty against both the prisoners, and the judge sentenced them to death in a manner which showed that, on this occasion at least, he felt no shrinking from the performance of his painful duty.

Late on the succeeding Sunday evening, the people began to mass themselves outside York Castle, and, when the hour of execution arrived, on the following morning, the concourse was enormous.

The appearance of the condemned prisoners upon the scaffold, was the signal for a yell of execration, which seemed to burst from every throat. So terrible was the sound—so menacing and ferocious the aspect of those who were nearest to the scaffold, that some fear was felt that, unless the proceedings were hurried forward as much as possible, the populace would take the law into their own hands.

Even Varley trembled and shrank back as he heard it, and all the blood in his body seemed to rush back to his heart, and stop there.

As for Twitter, he was literally more dead than alive, and, had it been possible for anything to arouse a feeling of compassion for this dastardly villain, his condition at that moment would have done so.

He had literally to be carried to his place beneath the fatal beam, for his limbs absolutely refused to support his weight.

His eyes rolled, while groans and shrieks burst alternately from his pallid, trembling lips.

In this condition he was carried past his companion in iniquity, who, even on the scaffold, and on the very threshold of eternity, felt so unbounded and malignant a hatred towards his accomplice, that, by a sudden effort releasing his right arm from those who held him, Varley struck Twitter a heavy blow in the face.

Again a yell of execration came from the mob, for Varley's action had been plainly seen and perfectly understood.

The officials closed round him, but Varley, after this one outburst, made no further resistance, his head sank forward upon his breast, and he became, to all appearances, unconscious or indifferent about all things.

And so these two villains reached the termination of the path of crime.

* * * *

Our tale is over, and if we have beguiled a weary hour, or awakened some slumbering sympathies, we are, indeed, well repaid.

The aim of the novelist should be to portray nature in all its aspects; but, while he thus holds up the mirror, he should not forget that he wields an instrument powerful for good or for evil, and, in his transcripts from humanity, he should endeavour, as we hope we have done, to elevate virtue and nobleness —to show how the pure, the truthful, and the innocent achieve—even in their sufferings—a greater triumph than can ever be obtained by the turbulence of vice.

Miranda sold the Grange estates. It was not without a pang that she thus severed herself from the place of her birth, and the scenes of her happy childhood; but she found every object so replete with painful associations, that, in accordance with the wishes of her husband, she quitted them for ever.

"The Grange can never more be a happy dwelling-place for us, dear Miranda," urged Rowland, gently; and with a tear and a smile Miranda acquiesced.

With the proceeds of the Grange estates, Rowland Percy bought a delightful little property in the South of Devon, and here, surrounded by smiling, happy children, they lived a life of uneventful peacefulness, strikingly in contrast with the strange and startling scenes which marked one epoch of their existence.

After Miranda's marriage, Dick Palmer rambled about a great deal; he was seeking for a rest and tranquility which he could never find while so many painful emotions filled his breast. A deep, tender, and respectful love for Miranda was his dominant feeling, and although her happiness was to him the dearest thing in all the world, it was long before he could look upon her with equanimity as Percy's wife.

But time, as it always does, brought resignation, if not content, and Palmer ultimately settled down upon a farm some two or three miles only from Rowland Percy's new residence.

Jones took upon himself the office of bailiff, gamekeeper, ranger (and some said poacher), all in one; but he was happy, and, in a little time, became quite celebrated for his kindness of heart and rough good-humour. At the village inn—where he was treated with much deference—he was a prime favourite.

Sometimes Dick Palmer would find him deep sunk in reverie, and at such times, when aroused from it, Jones would exclaim:

"Dicky, my tulip, shall you ever forget that *warmint* Twitter, and t'other *willain*, Bernard Varley? Isn't it like an old out-and-out dream—all on it, Dicky—quite a *wision!*"

And Miranda! How sweetly and beautifully did her old smile come back to her. Need we say that everyone who had performed a friendly act, or even uttered a kindly word to Percy or herself during their long period of bitter trial, had cause to bless her? No, it is needless—our readers are too well acquainted with the noble, tender, devoted, and heroic nature of Miranda, the heiress of Rankley Grange.

THE END.

E. & H. BENNETT, PUBLISHERS, BEDFORD HOUSE, MAIDEN LANE, STRAND, LONDON.